The Valkyrie

Book One of the
Saga of
Edda-Earth

by
Deborah L. Davitt

Copyright © 2014 Deborah L. Davitt
Maps and interior artwork, © 2014 Deborah L. Davitt
Cover art by Elizaveta Gokoeva (http://ladyowl.deviantart.com)

ISBN-10: 0-9860916-3-4
ISBN-13: 978-0-9860916-3-6

For more information on this and other books in this series, please visit
www.edda-earth.com.

Foreword

I have offered this book solely in electronic form before, thinking that I couldn't make print format work. I was wrong, and am delighted to be proven so. I have had to remove the "bind-runes" that marked each point-of-view and their affiliated appendix, but these were only introduced to make the e-book edition more readable.

No book is ever written in a vacuum. Even the lonely hermit writing by the light of a candle in a shack by a chilly pond isn't really alone; that writer has the company of thousands of ghosts. Every book a writer has ever read, whispers over your shoulder as you write. Everything you've ever agreed with in a book you've read . . . or in my case, more loudly, everything I've ever *disagreed with* in a book . . . comes to the fore. And there are, of course, your characters, directing you, once they've become live and kicking voices in your head, who sometimes, quite adamantly, won't do something that plot requires, on the grounds that Plot is stupid, you the Author are stupid, and they know better. (And quite frankly, they're usually right.)

I do not speak Latin, Old Norse, ancient Sumerian, or Hebrew; therefore, I cannot translate the original texts myself. My languages in school were German, Anglo-Saxon, and Russian. Therefore, I have used many short segments of translations that are in the public domain. None are longer than what might be used ethically in an academic treatise — three to six lines, and little more. As I did not wish to break the reader's immersion in a world in which, for example, John Dryden never lived, I couldn't rightly attribute to him a translation of Virgil. Hence my decision to go with public-domain sources as much as possible for such translations. I make no claims to any of the translations throughout these books, and, indeed, hope that people will be inspired enough to go look up the original texts and read them! These are some of the voices whispering over my shoulder as I write, after all.

People I'd like to thank include Nathan Mittlelman, for giving me the push I needed to explore the "Rome-that-never-died" idea that had been knocking at the back of my head for years, and asking the question, "Would they have magic?"; Alexander Thomas, for his extensive assistance with both Latin language and historical questions; Laura Ballegeer, for reading and responding, particularly in regards to First Nations issues, and many others. Especially, I'd like to thank my husband, Jason Davitt, for always lending his engineer's eye, and letting me know when I'd reached the tensile limits of a character's arc.

A Note on Dates

For a full calendar and timeline of important historical divergences, you may refer to the Appendices. All you need to know at the outset, is that all dates in Edda are not BC/BCE (before common era) or AD/CE (common era). They are noted as BAC/AC: Before the ascent of Caesar, and after the ascent of Caesar. All dates are offset by 44 years as a result.

Thus, 1954 AC is 1910 AD.

Part I: The Morning Star

Caesaria Aquilonis in 1954 AC

Chapter I: Beliefs

Casca: Look you on Caesar; see how like a king
He befits himself; no, no backless bench
For him, like a senator with a toga
Trimmed in purple. Nor is the curule seat
Honor enough.

Cassius: Pride rules him now, where once
his passions did. A throne is his harlot,
His mistress, the object of all his lusts.

Cinna: Is Brutus with us? Will he be constant?

Casca: We have his assurance.

Cassius: Hold. Brutus comes.
He will speak to Caesar. Stand ready, all!

Caesar: Brutus, my loyal friend. What do you ask
Of Caesar and his senate? What mercy
Do you seek, for yourself, or for others?

Brutus: Some here today plain for banish'd Cimber.
I seek only justice, mighty Caesar,
And speak only truth; I am no traitor.
He whom I name a friend, I hold for life.
You are set round with enemies, a bull
Baited by mongrels; their teeth at your throat.
Get you hence! Fly, Caesar, or fall here, with me!

_CONSPIRATORS, enraged, attack BRUTUS. BRUTUS falls, dying, to the Senate
floor. CAESAR, surrounded by Legionnaires, falls back._

Caesar: He who bares a blade on the Senate floor
Defiles it, defies the gods. The bootless blood
Of butchered Brutus stains your hands and souls,
And if the gods' curse falls not on you for it,
Then know that mine will.

Legionnaire: Caesar, your orders?

Caesar: Guards, take them all. They have defied both laws
Of men and of the gods; the law will be
No more or less merciful than the gods.

Exeunt omnes except CAESAR.

Caesar, cradling the body of Brutus: You came to me and spoke words of warning,
Unveiled your heart and unburdened yourself
Of the treachery they tried to instill
In you. But you were constant and faithful,
As steady as Polaris and as bright.
Let all who ever hear the name Brutus
Hear in its place, assurance of trust.

> — Seneca the Younger. The Triumph of Julius Caesar. Act IV, Scene ii, ca. 103 Ascensio Caesare.

Martius 5, 1954 AC

"It's plainly evident that the Aten is the one *true* god."

"It's not evident in the slightest. What is the Aten, but one god out of a whole host of half-beast, half-man creatures, propped up by a pharaoh who's been rotting in his sarcophagus for over three thousand years?"

The words, all spoken in Latin, the *lingua franca* of many nations, fell into a sort of void, as the various murmuring voices in the hotel lounge went silent. It was the sort of gap that one experienced on saying something embarrassing, usually while drunk, at a party.

The two men at the bar didn't seem to notice the heads all around them turning and looking, being far too involved in their dispute. One wore a sun disc of Aten, in gold, prominently displayed at his throat, his crisp white dress shirt open to reveal it. He looked vaguely Ptolemaic, with dark hair worked into braids, and dark eyes, outlined in kohl . . . but his olive skin was a little pale, as if he'd not often been out in the light of the sun he worshipped, of late.

The other man had an aquiline nose—sign of Roman descent, most likely—and piercing dark eyes. In spite of the warmth of central heat in the hotel lounge, he wore a short cloak in gray gabardine over his white shirt with its careful lacing, and matching gabardine slacks. The bull's-head brooch that clasped the cloak at his throat clearly showed his affiliation with the Mithraists.

The lounge was dimly lit, with sconces along all the walls glimmering with the light of incandescent bulbs, which flickered now and then, like candle flames. The power from the grid was uncertain, drawn from the ley-lines in the earth, and was evidently unconditioned here, at the outskirts of the metropolitan Ponca area. In that dim amber glow, dozens of businessmen and businesswomen sat around tables, eating their dinners with varying degrees of gusto.

The solo travelers were easy to spot; they sat alone, now eyeing the arguing pair over the edges of newspapers written in Latin, Gallic, or Gothic—the letters were Roman in two out of three, but the Gothic papers used stark, dark runes, instead. The Gauls in the crowd wore crisp white shirts and, if they were of Pictish descent, plaid kilts that bared their knees.

Most of them had tossed their plaids over their chair backs, and a few boasted blue clan tattoos, made visible as they rolled up their sleeves to eat. The handful of Romans in the room, like the Mithraist, tended towards slacks and light gabardine or wool cloaks. There were even a few Nahautl, from far to the south, easily distinguished by their darker skin-tones, more vividly-dyed clothing, and their bold, black tattoos and partially shaved heads. A small group of them seemed to be attending a pharmaceutical company's conference, and had been drinking *mescal* and laughing as they discussed the benefits of this drug over that one, and the stupidity of the Empire's food and drug regulations. A couple even wore long jade earrings or golden earplugs, by personal preference. Formal accoutrements to add to their white shirts and business cloaks striped in scarlet or gold.

The argument at the bar continued now, the Atenist sitting up, clearly offended. "Half-man, half-beast? The true nature of the Aten was revealed to us before your people even learned how to chisel letters, let alone how to smelt bronze. Akhenaten revealed the truth to us. The old representations were *metaphors*. The hawk-headed man and the sun-disc itself were merely symbols. The Aten is the *symbol* of the true Creator, the god above all other gods." He reached out and poked his companion in the shoulder with one finger, breaching the bubble of space between them. "If you're going to dispute with me, you may as well get your facts straight."

The Mithraist looked down at the finger that had poked his shoulder, then glanced up at the ceiling, as if for patience, and set down his glass of Gallic *uisce beatha* . . . what people outside of Gaul and Novo Gaul often slurred into the word whiskey. . . with deliberate care. "Look. I'm not really here for an argument. I just wanted a drink with my dinner before we head back to the conference tomorrow. But now, you're starting to take it a little too personally."

The Egyptian man flipped his hand in mild irritation. "Porphyry, you're the one who brought up Sol Invictus, the Unconquered Sun, and how the Romans have filched your god for their own purposes—" The Atenist was a belligerent drunk, it seemed. At least, one who liked to argue.

Almost everyone in the room was, at this point, staring at the pair at the bar. The sole exception was a couple at the side of the room, who were only regarding the pair out of the corners of their eyes. They sat in a booth, both their backs to the wall, to the left of one of the wide glass windows, and didn't seem to be business travelers. The man had olive skin, and lively, liquid-dark eyes and a neatly-trimmed dark beard. Unlike the other travelers in the room, he wore denim jeans. In spite of the heat of bodies and the warmth of the kitchen, which blasted out at the pair every time the swinging double doors beside their booth opened, the man kept his heavy gray cloak around his shoulders . . . . though loosely enough, that he could reach under it, if he needed to do so. A particularly sharp set of eyes might have noticed the leather straps under the cloak, over his white shirt, which hinted that the man might be carrying a concealed firearm. His hair was long enough that it still tumbled out from under the raised hood of this cloak, and in spite of the mouth-watering aromas of sausage, venison, rouladen, mushroom sauce, and warm bread, he was picking, desultorily at a salad in front of him, delicately flicking items out of it with a fork.

His female companion might have been Cimbric or Frisian. It was certainly possible; the greater metropolitan area of Ponca was situated between the provinces of Nova Germania and Novo Gaul, and in the close vicinity of several smaller petty kingdoms. The woman had tossed her cloak beside her in the booth, revealing a brown leather bodice currently worn without an undershirt. She'd laced it tightly, showing the clean strength of her long arms and pale skin. But like the man beside her, she also wore blue jeans. No earrings, which could be pulled or twisted or torn from her lobes by an assailant. No silver or gold torc at her neck, and no rings, either. While her pale copper hair was long, it was tied back in a single thick braid and knotted at the nape of her neck. The only trace of softness in her was the hair that had pulled loose around her face after a long day of travel. And at the moment, she appeared far more interested in the food in front of her, than in the argument at the bar.

"Shrimp," the man muttered to the woman, in Latin. He had a heavy regional accent that suggested it wasn't his native tongue. "I was pretty specific, wasn't I?" He held up the pink, fleshy item, offering it to her. "You want this? I can't eat it."

"Me? No. They're vile." Her accent was Gothic, and while she was fluent in the language of the Empire, she'd never lose the accent of her home. Now, she gave him a faintly amused glance, the warmth going no further than her cold gray eyes. "I don't envy you your diet, Adam. Was there *nothing* else on the menu?"

He set the shrimp, gingerly, to the side. "Sausage. Pork chops. Pies baked with lard in the crust."

She poked the steak on the plate in front of her with the tip of her knife, and held it up, dripping juices onto the plate. "Bison?"

"I have no idea where the butcher put his hands before he cut that, let alone what he did with his knives, Sigrun."

"There was salmon gravlax, too."

"That's made by burying raw fish in the ground and letting it 'ferment.' That's another word for 'rot.'" He made a face.

"There's usually salt involved. And it's better than lutefisk."

"Do I want to know what that is?"

"Fish cured in lye."

". . . wouldn't that turn it into *soap*?"

"Only if you let it soak too long. Then yes, you could probably use it to clean floors, if you could abide the stench." She cut into her steak once more, and wolfed down a bite. "My point was, you have options. The gravlax would be *allowable*."

"Allowable, yes. Tasty, no. I also don't see *you* eating it, Sig."

"I'm not fond of fish," she returned, with aplomb.

Adam grinned at her. "You are hardly a good representative of the people who built the boats who brought the armies of the Empire to these shores, Sigrun."

She lifted her head, and her lips curled back from her teeth. It was not quite a smile.

Back at the bar, the argument had picked up speed and steam once again. "You stubborn fool, you revile Aten as being half-man, half-beast, but what about your bull-slayer god, eh? I've been to your temples for the Birth of the Unconquered Sun at midwinter. You show him at the altar, naked, with a lion's head on his shoulders, wrapped in a serpent's coils! How is this any different from the early, best-forgotten practices of my ancestors—"

The Mithraist had clearly had enough. He leaned forward, and began to bait the Atenist now. "It's not just your *ancestors* who bowed down before hippos and crocodiles," he pointed out, needlingly. "Everyone else along the banks of the Nile still does. You're a sect, at best. How many worshippers does your god have? Ten, fifteen thousand, at the most?"

"We are working to educate our people! All the other, lesser gods who were below him are dead, slain in the reign of Akhenaten, may he reside forever in glory with his father, the great god himself. . . ."

"That's not what the Ptolemies say, right down through our beloved emperor, Caesarion the ninth. You're not calling the Imperator of Rome a liar, are you?"

That got heads to turn. Various people stirred uncomfortably. This was the sort of conversation that tip-toed right on the very edge of treason. The hooded man in the corner lifted his head, and seemed to mark the pair at the bar out. "Let it go, Adam," the woman advised, quietly.

"Just keeping an eye on it, Sig."

"We are off-duty, and I would prefer to remain so."

Back at the bar, the Atenist seemed to realize he was on treacherous ground at last. "I'm not calling him a liar," he said, walking back from the precipice. "I'm saying that he's *mistaken*. A man can be mistaken, and not be a liar, or dishonored."

"I think that the emperor would be rather fully informed about whether his godly ancestors through his grandmother of honored name, Cleopatra, are alive or dead." Bland words. The Mithraist was *enjoying* himself now, it seemed.

"And an emperor cannot be lied to, eh? Cannot be blinded with falsehoods, just as other, lesser men are? Just as you yourself have been blinded your whole life with lies. Your Mithras is nothing more than Aten in another guise, and you *will not* see it!" Vehemence now, the Atenist almost spitting in his haste to get the words out.

"Not according to the god-born. I've *met* a god-born, a descendant of Mithras. And he'd actually seen the face of our god. Been touched by his very hand. I think I can take his word that my god and your god are not the same." The Mithraist's heavy eyebrows beetled over his aquiline nose.

"The god-born? A bunch of sorcerers and liars who've banded together to hide the *truth* from others. To keep us enslaved to a hundred false gods, and to the 'god-born,' with them." The Atenist had a prepared response for every question or statement, it seemed.

For the first time, the woman's head came up at the table where she and the dark-haired man sat in the corner, her eyes flicking over the increasingly agitated and drunk Atenist. The Mithraist was now clearly stringing the angry man along, giving him enough rope with which to hang himself.

Thunder rumbled in the distance, and the bartender, a huge bear of a Goth with long blond hair in a braid to the center of his back and a heavy reddish beard, leaned over the pair. His Latin was heavily accented as he told them, "I think you cannot handle your honeybeer and *uisce beatha*, yes? I think perhaps I cut you off."

The follower of Aten laughed at the bartender, which showed how drunk he actually was. "We're just having a friendly conversation, aren't we, Porphyry?" He grinned, a white flash of teeth in a dark face. "The worship of Aten predates your Mithras by thousands of years. Why can't you just admit it?"

Thunder rumbled again, outside. The storm seemed to be getting closer. The handful of Gauls and Goths in the room looked up a little uneasily. The wide plains that swept to either side of the river Aeturnus bred savage storms, cyclones that could sweep down unexpectedly, like the finger of an angry god, and carry whole houses up into the sky, shattering them and scattering the pieces over miles. The hooded man in the corner booth gave the window beside him a cautious glance.

The Mithraist scowled. He hadn't liked, quite evidently, being told his god was just another face of someone else's. "Atahuti, you can go to the well of 'we had revelation before your people learned the secret of fire' only so often. A revelation granted later is no less valid or real. In fact, I'd say it's *more* real. Because the god who is light and creation reveals new things to us as we grow in our ability to understand them, and the universe that he created for us. Your Aten is a disc. Me? I know that Mithras isn't the blazing ball of plasma that hangs in space. But I know he *created* it—"

"The disc is a *symbol*. Aten is the Creator behind it all. And thus, we end where we began. You'll trot out the magelings that call themselves god-born again as your proof that your god is different, somehow, than the one true lord of the universe, and we'll go back around the circle once more."

"The god-born are worthy of respect. Every god-touched born is a descendant of Mithras, touched by his divine grace, whether they know it or not—"

White light, followed by a crash of thunder then, shaking the walls. Static electricity hovered in the air, making everyone's skin crawl. For some reason, in the booth in the corner, Adam very gently put a hand on the bare arm of his female companion. "Easy, Sig," he murmured. "You're the one who wanted to stay off-duty."

"They are being . . . extremely offensive."

"I know. But the steak's good, right?" Adam had caught the eyes of the Goth barkeeper move to their booth, and a couple of the more perspicacious customers tossed silver coins down on their tables, and headed for the shelter of their rooms. For her part, Sigrun cut another bite, scowling faintly, and they listened to the debate rage on.

"And still, you won't admit that Aten is the true name of your god. You won't admit that your understanding is precisely the same as mine—that there is a single Creator behind the entire universe—and that your priests have just corrupted his worship for political gain and their own power."

"Atahuti—"

"Oh, it's all right." The Egyptian leaned back in his chair, gesturing expansively. "You, at least, are more advanced in your beliefs than so many others. You at least understand that there is only one true god, even if you mispronounce his name and venerate him falsely. You don't look for a god that sours milk. You don't look for household gods and spirits in every tree in the accursed forest. But you're as stubborn as a follower of the god of Abraham when it comes to admitting the truth." He chuckled. "At least you don't act like they do. They act as if every last one of them was god-born, when in fact, everyone knows they have no god. He's as dead as all the idols that Akhenaten smashed, two thousand years ago. That's why they have no magic, and pray at the altar of natural philosophy, instead."

This time, the flash of white light and the thunder coincided, and the noise was deafening. The grid here was ley-powered, so the lights didn't cut out, but the walls of the hotel actually shook. Car alarms—newfangled and desperately annoying—started to go off in the parking lot outside, whooping and wailing like banshees. Had anyone glanced out the window, they would have seen rain sheeting down horizontally in the dim light of the streetlamps, lashing at the rounded hummocks that were the old-fashioned looking cars common here, the ones with footboards that swept up into the fenders, which beetled over their eye-like headlamps.

No one even glanced at the windows, however. Their attention was drawn, instead, to the pellucid glow now filling the room, streaming from the table in the corner. The woman there still stared down at the surface of the table, at her largely uneaten meal. And under her skin, runes were now clearly discernable, glowing with white light. It stung eyes used to the low, flickering light of the sconces on the walls, and made it painful to look at her. The man beside her pinched the bridge of his nose, sighed, and moved in his seat, loosening his cloak from around himself. Readying himself to back her, if needed. "Sig . . . don't," he muttered, quietly. "Not worth it."

"Yes. It is." Her tone was flat. "They've been asked once to stop. I will ask them again. Politely."

"Fair enough . . . ."

"Oh. . . . *damnú air.*" Someone cursing in a variant of Gallic spoken here in Caesaria Aquilonis.

"*Scheiss.*" A solid Gothic curse, that.

"*Goddescild. Cildes Tiwas.*" God-born. Child of Tyr.

The words were the same in a half-dozen dialects, as everyone in the room did their absolute best to turn *invisible*. The woman finally stood up, locked eyes with the pair at the bar, and then crossed the room to them on light feet. "I cannot help," she said, in her lightly-accented, but perfectly understandable Latin, "but to have overheard your disputation. Perhaps I might be of some small assistance in improving your understanding." Her teeth bared, a lupine grin, and her eyes held a steel-sheen coldness. "First, however, tell me this. Surely such learned men as yourselves must be priests, yes?"

Neither of the men moved. Back at the table, Adam had planted an elbow on the table, and now leaned his head on his fist, watching the encounter with mild amusement in his dark eyes. *Oh, good. At least she's talking with them first. Always the best option. Dialogue first. Doesn't always work . . . but at least if you start with it, you've <u>tried</u>.*

After a moment, the follower of Mithras shook his head, his eyes wide. "Ah . . . no."

"No, but that does not mean I cannot read the holy books of my religion and interpret them for myself," the follower of Aten, informed her, a little more staunchly. "The *god-born* do not have an exclusive hold on the *truth —*"

He's not quite backing down from his assertion that they're charlatans who simply have strong gifts in magic and use the pretense of the gods to hold onto power, but he's at least not calling her a sorcerer to her face. It was actually rather fascinating to watch. Sociology in action; one person had stood up to challenge the man, one person with enough personal gravitas . . . and the entire balance of the room shifted.

"No," the woman murmured, but the word still carried through the complete silence in the restaurant. "We do not. I have, however, been privileged to meet my god. My great-grandsire. I know who I am. I know why I am here. I serve him and I execute his will. I do not think you can say the same." The word *execute* had a slightly portentous sound as it hung in the air, and she tipped her head very slightly to the side. "You should not speak so of the followers of the god of Abraham."

"They say they have but one god, but everyone knows that the Holy of Holies in their Temple is *empty*. They have *no* god —" The follower of Aten's words started off strong, but started to crumble, as he added, defensively, "And yet they act as if every one of them is god-born."

Her not-really-a-smile had vanished at his words, and the sense of *pressure* in the room, as if the barometer were, in fact, pushing up increasing millibars of mercury, had become intense. "That is," the woman told him, biting off the ends of her words, "because it is said that their god considers them all to be his children." She reached out and pushed their plates away on the surface of the bar, with a delicate finger — one suffused with a fretwork of shimmering runes under the skin. "Now," she said, with careful precision, "you are both in violation of the just and wise Edict of Emperor Diocletian II, which says that every citizen of the Empire, and everyone resident in every province and client and subject state of the Empire, may hold to whichever gods they choose, but that none may force their gods upon another. And that all may venerate their gods in whichever way they choose, except for the sacrifice of humans."

The Mithraist swallowed, and asked, tentatively, "Ah . . . in what way are we breaking the law?"

"Your friend here breaks it, in that he is proselytizing. To you, but also, in such a way that everyone else here must *listen*." She stared the Atenist down. "I wished only for a peaceful dinner this evening, and not for *learned discourse*. It is time for you to be silent, or to leave."

The Egyptian stood, looking angry. "You don't have the right to tell me what to do. I'm a citizen of the province of Egypt, and I am not subject to you. You *god-born* are arrogant, and your arrogance will be your undoing. You will not always be able to cow everyone you meet with a show of force. A new day is coming. One in which the power of the so-called gods will be in all our hands, every man and woman will be as a mage, and there will never again be common-born and god-born." He lifted his chin.

The woman looked at him, wearily, and took a slim leather folder out of the leather poke tied to the belt loops of her denim jeans. At the table in the corner, the hooded man tensed a little, but Sigrun opened the folder carefully, showing only one half of the credentials therein. "I am a sanctioned *ælagol*." The word meant, more or less, *law-giver*, but in context, meant she was an adjudicator. Fully empowered to arrest someone, under Imperial law, and turn them over to provincial authorities . . . or within the bounds of Novo Germania or Germania itself, to try, convict, sentence, and even execute people who had broken Germanic provincial law.

The other half of the folder carried her *other* credentials. Which didn't need to be waved around in a crowded *taverna* or lounge. Too many eyes.

"I will give you one more chance. Leave," she told the Atenist. "Sleep off the wine-courage that makes you speak so."

The Mithraist slipped down off the barstool, and started to retreat, holding his hands up. He hadn't, very evidently, wanted to get into this discussion to start with, and had been baiting the Ptolemaic mostly out of irritation all this time. "I apologize, *domina*," he said, politely, using the current preferred Latin term of respect for a lady. "Boredom and a long day. I'll leave now."

She accorded him a slight nod, and he retreated, but the man at the corner table kept the Mithraist in the periphery of his vision. Just in case. He was watching the whole room now, with the blank, defocused gaze of a trained fighter. Seeing everything. Focusing on nothing in particular.

The Atenist, on the other hand, looked past the woman's shoulder. Made eye-contact with the man at the table, and the Egyptian's eyes narrowed, and a smirk crossed his face. Adam stiffened slightly, suddenly wary. He *knew* that look. The Egyptian suddenly smiled, without mirth. "Oh. I *understand*. The barbarian woman likes sucking circumcised c — "

At the table, the hooded man looked up at the ceiling. "Bad move," he muttered. "Very bad move."

Another clap of thunder shook the building. And before the Egyptian could even react, the tall woman caught him by the wrist with her right hand, stepping deftly in behind him and pulling smoothly up between his shoulder blades. There was no effort in her movements, and though the man resisted, her single hand remained rock-steady, forcing him forwards onto the bar with an ungentle thump. "All right," she said, her voice tired. "That's one count of proselytizing without a license to preach, and in a public establishment, at that. One count of disrespect towards an officer of the law. The first is usually a two solidi fine." Two solidi would pay the rent of a one-bedroom apartment in most major cities in the Empire and thus represented a stinging rebuke to someone found guilty of a crime. "The punishment for the second offense is usually determined by the whim of the magistrate in question. By happy chance, I *am* a magistrate." She paused. "Do stop struggling. You have no hope of freeing yourself."

She produced her rarely-used shackles from where they rode at the small of her back, and clicked them into place around the first wrist, casually planted a knee against the Atenist's back, and reached around to seize his other hand. At which point, he managed to turn his head and spit into her glowing face. "God-born *whore*."

The man in the corner uncoiled from the booth at that point, taking two steps closer. "Sig — "

The woman let the Atenist's left hand loose just long enough to shift position, still retaining control of his right. Her own left hand slid up, found the back of his neck, and she slammed his head, face-first, into the counter. Hard.

Everyone in the room winced at the dull thud, and the bowl of almonds beside the man fell off the counter, scattering its contents all over the floor. "I am going to take your current state of blessed silence as an apology," she informed the limp, unconscious body, and finished shackling the man. She then started to lift his head by the hair to evaluate the damage . . . and the hair came away entirely in her hand, leaving her starting, nonplussed, at the wig in her hand, and the shaved pate beneath. And then she recoiled reflexively, flicking the wig away from her with a grimace of distaste.

Muffled titters of anxious laughter ran through the crowd, as the rain outside pounded against the windows. "Taunt a god-born? Fool," Adam heard in Latin from the table to his right, and caught sight of a couple of Gauls raising their tankards in the woman's direction, in salute. He moved over behind his partner, and lifted the man's head now, himself. The nose was shattered. He'd broken enough noses and jawbones in his life to recognize the signs. "And here I thought you were merely going to be *testy* with him."

Sigrun grimaced. "I have logged over eighteen hours in a plane and quite a few more in a crowded motorcar in the past two days. So I might be ill-tempered. But I wasn't going to throw him through a window, if that was your concern." She accepted a rag from the barman, and wiped her face clean, before tossing the dirty rag on the Atenist's back. "That creates *far* too much paperwork."

"And leaves far too much of an impression on people's minds," Adam muttered. He was already quite certain that everyone in the lounge would be talking about this incident when they went home, or headed to their conferences, or even spoke on the telephone with friends later this evening. And they were supposed to be keeping a low profile.

He was thus somewhat relieved when the barkeep and one of the waiters lifted the shackled Atenist and took him outside for the moment, while, in the distance, he could hear the blare of approaching sirens. They resumed their seats in the corner, Sigrun steadfastly ignoring the stares of the other diners as she began picking at her bison steak once more. After a few minutes, the barkeep came over, and settled two mugs of honeybeer on the table in front of them. And when Sigrun reached for her poke to pay, the bear of a man leaned down and murmured to her quietly in some twisty dialect of Gothic.

Whatever he said caused the woman to flush and shake her head. She removed five denarii from her poke, and tried to pay the barkeep, but he lifted his hands away, refusing to take the coins, and walked away, grinning toothily. "What did I miss?" Adam asked her, as he went back to flicking items out of his salad. He'd caught *æðeles ides*, one of the few Gothic phrases he knew — *noble lady* — but nothing more.

"He thanked me for removing an irritating pest, and said that as I had served in place of an exterminator *and* provided the evening's entertainment, that dinner was on the house." Her tone was irritable.

Adam chuckled. "He did not say that."

"The entertainment part, he did not, correct," Sigrun acceded, with a sigh. "He was far too polite to say it."

"But it was on his mind?" he needled.

". . . of course it was." The woman rubbed gently at her eyes.

"I can't take you *anywhere*, can I, Sig?" He offered her a forkful of his salad. "Want a bite?"

"All that I wanted," she muttered, glumly, "was to eat a quiet, peaceful meal without anyone here in Ponca knowing that we are here. A steak on the government's denarii. Then go upstairs to my room, take a bath, and sleep, before going back on duty in the morning. It didn't seem like so much to ask."

"We've got a lot of work to do tomorrow," Adam acknowledged, and then gave her an amused look. "I did tell you not to bother. I deal with idiots like that one all the time. The ones who think we don't have a god, just because there's no idol in the Tabernacle of the Temple. And I'm fully capable of taking care of myself." He quirked a quick grin at her, and took off his heavy cloak, finally having warmed up enough to do so.

The cloak had concealed a lean frame, one well-trained in the defensive arts developed in the mountains of Judea. The leather harness over his shoulders carried an artifact rare in this part of the world: a revolver pistol, tucked at the small of his back. A Velserk .45 caliber, in fact, with six bullets loaded and ready to go. Such weapons were currently almost unknown in Nova Germania and Novo Gaul. While almost every house had a smoothbore musket or a blunderbuss, available for hunting or self-defense, they all only held one round of ammunition, and the best small arms generally available were single-shot, muzzle-loaded pistols called derringers.

Of course, most people in this area of the world also had their bullets enchanted by a local sorcerer or technomancer if they thought they were in danger of being attacked by local gangs, robbers, or just someone with a grudge. There was absolutely nothing magical about the Velserk, however. It was resolutely, and charmlessly, a mechanism of metal.

"I know you are capable of defending yourself. You wouldn't be a lictor if you weren't." Sigrun flapped a hand at him in annoyance, and sawed at her steak again, as, outside, the blue-and-red lights of a *gardia* vehicle appeared on the road, and turned into the hotel's parking lot. "But this is *my land*, or close enough that jurisdiction wouldn't be much of an issue, even without our . . . other credentials. And enforcing the laws of that land, and of the empire, is my business. People like that," she jerked her chin towards the bar, where new people were filtering in slowly to take seats, and the noise of conversation in the room had picked back up again, "are half the problem with the world today. They can't distinguish metaphor from reality. The philosophers of Hellas and Judea and Nippon and Rome have studied fossils in the rock. We know that humanity evolved over time, and that the gods taught us creation stories that we could understand easily, when we were all savages together." She rubbed at her face. "The natural philosophers launched a rocket into space in . . . . when was it? Twenty-nine, thirty?"

"Nineteen twenty-nine. The year I was born."

That got him an odd look, one that seemed to be comprised of mild incredulity, and then she shook her head. "What?" he asked.

"Nothing." Sigrun shook her head again, and shrugged. "We *know* that the sun is a flaming ball of gas. Even our Mithraist acknowledged this. And we *know* that there are gods who are associated with its power. Sol Invictus, Aten, Mithras, Sunna." She gave him a sidelong glance. "No offense intended."

"Sig, I don't approach my monotheism with idiocy. I'm perfectly aware that there are other gods. They're just not *my* god. I don't have a covenant with them. Whoever the rest of you unwashed unbelievers," and here, he gave her a lightning-quick smile, "choose to worship, is between you and your gods."

"This particular unwashed unbeliever *really* wants a bath." Her tone was plaintive. "The plane ride to Marcomanni from Britannia was quite long, and the drive here from Marcomanni was almost equally so. Every muscle I have is stiff."

Adam did his best not to laugh. "I still can't believe that *you're* scared of planes."

"I'm not in *control* on a plane." She sounded nettled. "It's a chariot in the sky. Technomancy. I don't pretend to understand entirely what keeps it in the air."

"One hundred percent natural philosophy, if you're flying Hatasahl or Hellene Air. It's only technomancy if it's Alroma, Qin Air, Air Carthage . . . eh, you know the list."

"You say that as if natural philosophy were any more of a

comfort."

"It's science, Sig. It's all perfectly explicable natural forces, the burning of fuel for combustion engines, lift, force, and thrust. Things my people and the Hellenes have been working with for centuries." He found a tomato at the bottom of his salad and popped it into his mouth, chewing for a moment, before adding, "Ley-power, though . . . that's where I draw the line. Tapping into the earth, into raw creation itself, for power? It makes me uneasy. And the rest, eh. Sorcerers at least train to use their power. Most of their lives, in fact. Discipline their minds. Technomancy . . . putting magic-powered devices in the hands of any idiot with enough money to afford it . . ." He shrugged, uncomfortably. "It makes me uneasy."

She shook her head, frowning faintly. "That's a little parochial, Adam. Ley-power has given people light and power for devices in their homes — without being bound to smelly coal-burning plants — "

"Judea uses nuclear reactors, these days — " He felt compelled to defend his homeland.

"Oh, that is obviously *so* much better." A hint of sarcasm in her tone. "And think of this. Ley-powered devices, like those motorcars out there? Travel used to be something reserved for the wealthy, in the main. People well-enough off to own horses, which required stabling, fodder, land, exercise, and constant care. Ley-taps and ley-power are a miracle of the modern age, and the ley-grid employs thousands of technomancers and ley-mages. Sorcerers . . . the users of *seiðr*, as my people call it . . . have not always been held in high esteem. The Gauls have treated their ley-mages better. And the result is a better standard of living for everyone. It's hard to see the harm in that." She glanced up, as he, too, caught sight of the *gardia* officers looking into the lounge, and speaking in low and earnest tones with the barkeeper.

"That doesn't make it *right*." His voice was low. "But looks as if they're playing our song over there. Well, yours. But I can hum along, and pitch in when I know the words."

That netted him a reluctant chuckle as they stood, pushing away from their meals. "At least they're meeting us indoors. You dislike the cold here."

"I don't think your northern climate is going to give me pneumonia."

"No, but I will get to hear you complain about it every time we're outside for the duration of this trip."

He grinned at her again. "Of course. That's the fun of it."

They stepped out into the hall outside the lounge for the modicum of privacy from the prying eyes of their fellow diners. From the windows out here — windows that Adam stood well back from, out of long habit — he could see more of the modest, eight-story brick building that made up their hotel. There was a chain-link fence around its parking lot, separating the vehicle zone from the complimentary outdoor pool behind the building.

The *gardia* were the enforcers of provincial law throughout the

Empire. They were trained in local laws and ordinances, and also handled the bulk of *everyday* enforcement of Imperial-level laws. If someone committed murder, for example, they could be prosecuted under either provincial or Imperial laws. When someone crossed provincial borders in the execution of a crime, however, the *gardia's* jurisdiction was limited. Such crimes fell into the hands of higher legal organizations.

These *gardia* officers were all Gauls, and wore heavy wool mantles, which they flipped outwards to expose badges on the leather vests underneath. Each badge displayed the horned head of Cernunnos the Hunter, on a star-shaped background. "You want to explain what happened here?" one of them asked, tiredly, getting out a notebook with thin pages of foolscap.

"Unlicensed proselytizing," Adam told the pair, calmly. "The Egyptian was told, by my count, three times, to stop, before he descended to personal insults."

"Hmm. His version of the story . . . now that he's regained consciousness. . ." a sidelong and slightly disapproving look at Sigrun now, "is that your lady friend here used magic on him."

"I wouldn't stoop to using the power of the gods on one such as him." Sigrun's voice was flat. "It would be dishonorable. After he insulted me personally, I did, however, execute justice on him."

"Justice? In your opinion, I take it?" More than a hint of an edge there. These officers had been called out from whatever warm hole they'd tucked themselves for the duration of their shift and now were being asked to deal with something that they'd rather not.

Sigrun's reply was crisp. "I am a sanctioned *ælagol.*"

"You're a god-born of Valhalla. This is *Novo Gaul's* soil. You're claiming jurisdiction?" A note of pure skepticism, and not unwarranted, from one of the two men.

"I think I can safely claim that, yes." Sigrun's tone was calm.

Headshakes from the two men. "We're going to need to see some identification."

Both of them moved slowly, so that the officers could see their motions. Sigrun opened her poke again to display a leather folder containing her identification, handing it over silently . . . and letting both of her badges be seen this time. Adam's id was in a wallet, carried in the rear pocket of his jeans, and he held it open for the officers to examine.

The two officers' expressions changed, tightening into grimaces. "Oh . . . gods damn it . . . you're both with the Praetorian Guard?"

The Praetorian Guard had become, over the centuries, far more than just the bodyguards of the Emperor of Rome. They were the single largest security and intelligence network on the planet, with jurisdiction in any client state or province of the Empire. They had divisions devoted to forgery, illegal magic use, murder, kidnapping, sedition, intelligence, and counterintelligence, and remained the bodyguards of high officials throughout the Empire as well.

Sigrun carried an *ælagol* badge and identification card, which identified her as Sigrun Caetia. God-born, resident of Burgundoi in Nova

Germania, and *ælagol*. Opposite that, she also carried a silver badge engraved with the *fasces,* an Imperial eagle, and the name of the sitting Emperor, Caesarion IX. Her technical title, inscribed on it, was Special Agent to the Regional Praetorian Office of Nova Germania, and the badge also had the word *lictor* engraved beneath that. That gave her two levels of jurisdiction, Imperial and Gothic provincial.

Adam's card informed anyone who cared to read it that he was Adam ben Maor, resident of Jerusalem in the province of Judea. Special Agent to the Regional Praetorian Office of Judea. And a *lictor*, as well. Lictors were the personal bodyguards of high-ranking Roman officials. They added weight and gravitas, and kept the official from being assassinated by random locals. The more powerful and impressive an entourage of lictors, the more weight an official really had, in many ways.

"We are, believe it or not, trying to keep our presence here quiet," Adam said, softly. Local *gardia*, in his experience, had something of a love-hate reaction for Praetorians on their turf. Praetorians were highly trained and professional, but they were also the elite. And where they went, there was usually a solid chance of trouble.

"*Focáil,*" one of the officers swore, handing the badges back. "Sounds like our boy over there had a really bad night then, eh?"

"I was going to let him walk away with a warning, at first," Sigrun replied, shrugging. "He knew I was god-born and an *ælagol* before he made his insults personal. A broken nose is the least he deserves, and now, you will not be put to the trouble of putting him in the stocks and whipping him, as I could have requested."

"You could have just challenged him to a duel, ah . . . *domina.*" The officer wasn't entirely sure how to address her, it was clear, and had opted for the Latin respectful form of address, rather than the Gothic one.

"That, too, would have had him at an unacceptable disadvantage. I do not use the powers of the god-born unfairly." Sleeping atop a glacier would have seemed warm and comfortable, compared to her voice. "However, I should note that once he progressed to personal insults, he did say a few things that warrant further investigation. For example, he suggested that some day soon, the power of the gods would be in the hands of all."

"A revolutionary?" An uneasy glance between the two.

"If one far from home, perhaps." She shrugged, expression distant. "I will put in a call to regional Praetorian headquarters. Hold him on the proselytizing charge and suspicion of sedition for his comments about the ancestry of the Emperor. That should enable you to keep in him the cells for a day or two, until someone can be spared to come and question him, and then perhaps take him off your hands." She exhaled. "May we go now?"

"Ah, can we ask what the two of you are doing in town?" The voice held little hope. These two members of the local *gardia* were out on a nightly beat patrol, after all.

"I'm afraid we can't discuss that, but we're trying to stay out of any jurisdictional disputes." Adam put a smile in his voice, and with that, they could finally go back upstairs. They headed for the brass cage around the elevator, and stepped inside, and Adam shifted uneasily as the ley-powered device jolted into action. Even after two years in India, and a year on this continent, he still didn't entirely trust anything that didn't run on electricity.

As the doors slid shut, he draped his cloak over his shoulders again, just to get it out of his hands. "You know, Sig? If I ever get to drag you to Judea, you're going to *melt* from the heat."

"May all the gods forbid. I've been to the deserts here in *this* hemisphere, for training. The Mojave is an unkind place for those of my blood." She shuddered, and the elevator dinged softly, the doors swinging open to deposit them on the fourth floor.

He walked her to the door of her room, with instinctive courtesy. "Don't envy you having to explain tonight to the propraetor. So much for our low profile." He grimaced. "Not to mention the fact that the other lictors won't be thrilled with all our jobs being made more difficult."

"I'll apologize to our colleagues, and explain everything to Livorus. He'll listen. He's Roman. They appreciate reason, but they also understand when it is necessary to say *this far, but no further.*" Sigrun found the room key in her poke, and unlocked it, giving the room a cautious glance from the hall. "Will you call your home?"

"They're eight hours ahead. If I call now, I'll wake the whole house."

"All right, then. See you in the morning. The Chahiksichahiks await, after all."

Adam turned away, his hood still up over his head. Then paused, and turned back. "You don't think they'd have already sacrificed the girl, do you?"

Sigrun paused in the act of closing the door, and poked her head back out into the dim light of the hall. "She was kidnapped from Marcomanni three days ago. The vehicles used in the kidnapping were spotted along Imperial Highway Eighty several times between there and here. We know she's in the vicinity, and we received a call from within Chahiksichahik territory, telling us both that she's being held there, and why." She shook her head, her expression tight. "It's a five-day ritual, Adam. They used the first day just to transport her from Marcomanni, get over the Aeturnus River, and into their own territory. Then they need to 'purify' her for four days. They *can't* sacrifice her for at least another three days."

He counted off on his fingers. "Today's dies Lunae . . . Martis, Mercurii, Jovis . . . ."

"Yes. Thunresdæg. Wodensdæg, at the earliest, if they somehow started the rituals in the back of their motorcar." Her countenance had taken on a grim cast once more.

He smiled without much mirth. Arguing over the names of the days among the people on their team had become a running joke. He occasionally tossed out the names in Hebrew, just to get a reaction, just as Ehecatl would say them in Nahautl, or Ptah-ases spoke them in Egyptian.

"I'll leave you to call the propraetor's room, then."

"I'll just walk down the hall and tap on the door. I have been with him for five years. He does not stand on much ceremony with me." She shrugged. The fact that she didn't look a day over twenty-two, but she periodically made references that suggested that she was far older than she appeared, was part of what intrigued Adam about his partner. She was a puzzle. And Adam ben Maor enjoyed puzzles.

For now, he chuckled, bade her good night, and headed for his own room. It was next door, and, technically, part of a suite they shared. The Empire didn't spring for sumptuous accommodations for its agents, unfortunately, and every line in an expense report needed justification.

Inside, Adam flicked the switch on the wall, and incandescent bulbs lit up, dulled by translucent, amber-toned Bakelite shields to a dim golden glow. Bland, white walls, with a single black and white print of Gallic knot-work, which hung above the headboard of the wrought-iron bed. A cabinet, with a spherical, ley-powered far-viewer device in it dominated the wall opposite of the bed, so someone could, if they wished, prop themselves up in bed and watch cinema or news until they went to sleep. Beside the far-viewer, a cabinet for clothing, and, between that cabinet and the bathroom area, a locked door into Sigrun's half of the suite. There was a bathing area—quite Roman in style, with tiny blue and white tiles all over the floor, a deep tub, and a shower head jutting out of the tiled wall. An indoor toilet, an amenity for which he was grateful; this area was semi-rural, and there *were* places in the world where Roman hygiene had not pervaded.

Out of habit, Adam turned off the room lights and moved to the room's window to look out warily, checking his surroundings. He was uneasy around almost any window, and the large, broad ones that were common in Novo Gaul and Nova Germania just seemed like security risks to him.

The *gardia* vehicles were just pulling out of the parking lot, the old-fashioned, boxy motorcars spinning their wheel as they rounded the corner, lights no longer flashing. Adam shook his head. *Sigrun has a temper.* His lips quirked under his beard. Sigrun was a *battle-maiden.* What her people called a *valkyrie.* She was the god-touched descendant of Tyr—or Tiwaz, depending on which Goth you happened to be speaking to, on any given day. Of *course* she had a temper. *But she has control, too.*

Before Sigrun, he'd never met another god-born. Judeans had none of their own, and magic had been outlawed in Judea under the rule of Saul, some three thousand years ago. Adam had heard that the statistics outside of Judea for people born with the gift of sorcery in their veins might be as few as one in a thousand. God-born were even rarer than that. He'd managed to pin Sigrun down to some numbers a month or so ago; she'd stated that between Germania, Nova Germania, and the petty kingdoms of northern Europa, like Gotaland, her gods claimed some two hundred and twenty-five million worshippers. And that there were some twenty-two thousand god-born, total, spread among those lands. Except that they didn't make up one out of every ten thousand births. Some of them had lived for centuries. And the lineage did not necessarily pass directly from father to son, or mother to daughter. The odds of meeting a god-born in a given life-time were low. The odds of working with one? Almost impossible.

Adam exhaled as he stared out the window. No danger seemed to be lurking in the night. The streetlights burned steadily, only tiny fluctuations visible from the unconditioned ley-line power they were receiving. Beyond them, he could see the slumbering city of Ponca. The terrain here was so incredibly *flat*, like a table. And even with only the slight elevation of being on the fourth floor, he could see a large swathe of houses around the hotel, many of which still had lights burning in their windows. The skyscrapers at the heart of the town were . . . modest. Hardly worth the name. Just tall office buildings in a city whose economy largely revolved around the grain and cattle industries of the fields that extended pretty much forever on all sides of it.

He was never going to get used to the *scale* of things on this continent. You could fit Asia Minor, Byzantium and all, into one small corner of Nova Germania. Judea, including Samaria and Jerusalem? Would rattle in the panhandle area of Novo Gaul, far to the southeast of here. The Aeturnus might not be as long as the Nile, but a river it took ten or fifteen minutes to cross by car on a wide bridge? Got one's attention.

Adam sighed, and shut the curtains before flicking on a light, feeling out of place. But, he was here to do a job. He went where the Empire told him to go. And in this case, he and Sigrun were supposed to be protecting a propraetor, and hopefully preventing a diplomatic disaster of monumental proportions. Not to mention, the murder of an innocent thirteen-year-old girl.

He tossed his cloak at the desk in the corner of the room before pushing the room's thermostat higher. The radiator under the window creaked a little as more steam poured through the pipes that snaked across the outer wall to its accordion-like metal surface. He took his revolver out of its concealed-carry harness, and tucked it in the nightstand beside the bed. Sat down in the chair by the desk, and took out a scroll and a skullcap from his suitcase, along with a white prayer *tallit*. For a moment, he looked into the depths of his clean laundry and hygiene supplies, and debated the phylacteries. It wasn't like him to hesitate. He didn't normally use them when at prayer, but some Judean sects believed that the phylacteries, and proper attendance on the rituals of his faith, offered a certain amount of additional protection from ill-intended magics and the powers of the god-touched. However, the incident in the restaurant downstairs had affected him more than he'd acknowledged. For the moment, he was self-conscious of his faith, the way he usually *wasn't*.

Then Adam shook his head and tied the talismans on. They weren't going to do him any good in his suitcase. If, in fact, wearing them did any more good than saying the words, and *meaning* them. He read from his scroll, quietly, and fifteen minutes into his devotions, he became aware of a brilliant white light seeping under the locked door to Sigrun's connected room. It sometimes seemed a little unfair. Sigrun had *met* her god. She had absolute assurance of his existence. Adam, on the other hand, only had faith. He'd never met a priest or a rabbi who'd met the god of his fathers, face-to-face. To be honest, he didn't actually *want* to meet the god of Abraham on a personal basis. That was the sort of thing that turned someone into a judge or a prophet, and that was really not a burden he wanted to carry around.

But it would still be nice to have some of the serenity that came with assurance. To be able to speak to one's god, and hear a voice in return. But that was the point of faith — to believe without evidence. He preferred science, evidence, and natural philosophy, by and large, but did his best with faith from day to day. Sigrun, on the other hand, for all that she was god-born, didn't have faith. She didn't need it. She had assurance. Two very different things.

Now, the locked door between their rooms let in various noises from her side; the sound of water splashing as she turned on the bathwater, for instance. The harsh *zzzzz* as the zipper of her overnight bag opened. The rustle of clothing, and at that point, Adam let his scroll roll up, and turned on the far-viewer. He was sure he'd never get used to the fact that the spherical ley-powered devices projected images in three dimensions, when the conventional square tube devices of Judea, which were electrically-powered, produced two-dimensional images.

There were only three channels in this largely rural area. One featured a gladiatorial competition held in Rome last week. Another featured a ritual game of ball played this morning down in Tenochtitlan, with the great stepped pyramids of the city center in the background. And the third was a droning report on the politics of the Senate, and Consul Tacritus' condemnation of the recent fighting between Raccia and the Mongol Khanate, and the Separatist Movement in the Quechan provinces.

The Roman Senate was an interesting institution at this point in history. It was still entirely made up of patricians from old families in Rome proper. Roman citizens had, therefore, representation. Citizenship throughout the empire had certain qualifications, and there were differing levels of it, as well. Merely coming from some city on the Italian peninsula wasn't enough to qualify someone as a full citizen of the empire. A full citizen was born in Rome, and, in this day and age, could be either male or female (an influence, Adam knew, from the Gallic and Gothic tribes that had become so much a part of the Empire). That being said, in antiquity, a requirement for citizenship had been enough income to own and maintain at least one slave for a household. Today, slavery was still legal in much of Europa, Africa, and Caesaria Australis, though not in Germania, Britannia, or Gaul. Here in Caesaria Aquilonis, it had been officially abolished in . . . 1943 AC, he thought. Something like that.

So there were patricians in Rome, represented by the Senate. There were non-noble citizens in Rome, who mostly represented by the Plebian Council and their elected Tribune. And then there were the provinces. People who lived in provinces, such as southern Italia, Sicily, Gaul, Germania, and Australia, had limited, regional self-rule, with Roman-appointed governors to hold the laws of the Empire in place. They were represented on the imperial level through the Plebian Council, to whom they sent elected or appointed delegates on a yearly basis. Subject kingdoms, such as Britannia, Judea, Egypt, and Carthage, had, over centuries of negotiation, won larger degrees of autonomy, but their people were still nominally subjects of Rome. They, too, sent delegates to the large and fractious Plebian Council. Nova Germania and Novo Gaul had been directly settled by Germanic and Gallic tribes under the auspices of Rome; they, like Britannia, had been permitted limited self-rule, and were on the Plebian Council. Tawantinsuyu had negotiated an alliance, and had a Roman governor, but some degree of autonomy, while Nahautl and the Quechan provinces had been conquered, hundreds of years ago, and were under the direct administration of Roman governors to this day, with significantly less self-rule.

Adam was aware of the grumbling all through the Empire, that it was hardly fair for half the world to be under the control of fewer than a hundred old patrician families who happened to have been born inside a tiny region on a small peninsula in Europa. But the truth of the matter was that the Senate only had so much power. The Emperor had more in many respects, and, over the centuries, the Plebian Council had accrued quite a bit. The Senate in its current incarnation existed as an . . . intermediary of sorts . . . between the Emperor and the Plebian Council. They existed to check the power of the tribunes, had the power to rubber-stamp most imperial appointments, and certain positions. . . such as the *aediles* for Rome itself. . . could only be held by a patrician. Outside of Rome proper? Anyone could be an *aedile*, depending on local laws and ordinances. If local law said that the person in charge of distributing tax revenues to public works was open to anyone, and that it was an elected position, that's what it was.

It was an odd, cobbled-together system, one that sat atop centuries of precedents and evolutionary turns, but it allowed regions of the Empire breathing room . . . while everyone still contributed to the whole. There were the core Roman Legions, for example, but every subject nation contributed levies of troops to the Foreign Legions. Judea's Legion levies were sometimes distributed through other Foreign Legion units . . . always a possibility, when doing one's required years of service, as it was considered good for there to be some cross-pollination of cultures between the various legions . . . but the bulk of their levy forces remained in Judea, in the Judean Defense Forces. They had legion ranks, and were considered a part of the Legion, as a whole, but they were typically called the JDF by people within their province.

Rome still had a strong bias for nobility among its officer corps, but nations like Judea and Britannia and Gaul and Germania made merit and education the standard for determining who an officer should be. Adam had been one himself, during his years of service on the Judean border, on Domitanus' Wall—one of only two structures on the planet large enough to be seen from space. It ran from Judea, walling them off from the lands of Assyria and Media, up along the border of Persia and Rome, up through Asia Minor, along the Mongol border, as well. On the northern border, where Rome butted up against Raccia, Rome had decided that it was more cost-effective in the long run to put together a string of forts without walls. They couldn't continue the wall far enough north that the Mongols couldn't just ride through Raccia and swing around to the south and attack Asia Minor . . . so the best option simply became manpower, communications, and even minefields, as technology developed. And enough mages to counter the Mongol shamans, as needed.

So Adam sat and watched the news with a slightly jaundiced eye, shaking his head over the protestors in Xunantunich, all holding signs in Quecha and Latin, demanding an end to a Roman occupation that had already lasted for centuries. "Yes . . . that's going to get results," he told the far-viewer, and turned the device off, preparing to go to bed. As he'd told Sigrun, an hour or two before . . . they'd have a very long day tomorrow.

Martius 5, 1954 AC

Frittigil Chatti huddled in the small lean-to into which she'd been shoved after being removed from the motorcar's trunk, in which she'd spent the last several hours of her trip . . . wherever she was. The thirteen-year-old was colder than she could ever remember being. The shed was made out of branches, and had been covered with canvas and some sod to keep out the wind, but was so low that she couldn't have stood up, even if her hands and feet hadn't been hobbled together by lengths of braided sinew. The tough leather cut into her wrists, and she couldn't tell if her fingers were numb from the cold, or from the loss of circulation.

She'd peeked out, cautiously, an hour ago, to see what she could see, and had found the backside of one of her guards positioned right at the entrance. She knew they had guns. Muskets, but a bullet could move a lot faster than she could. She'd inspected the back and sides of the lean-to, looking for a way that she could dig her way out, but as soon as she'd started scraping at the dirt, the guard had come in, slapped her, and told her that if she tried that again, he'd break her fingers. Fritti had barely comprehended the words, but she'd nodded, earnest with terror, when he'd asked if she now understood her position.

So . . . she couldn't dig her way out. She couldn't slip past the guard. And she was tied at hands and wrists, with a length of cord keeping them knotted together. Fritti had tried to be brave at the start of it all, when the men had gotten out of the motorcar in Marcomanni, and, holding a map, had asked her for directions to a hotel nearby. They'd been strangers, with heavy accents in Latin. They'd been dressed oddly. Everyone she knew wore some leather—vests, jerkins, trousers, whatever—but these men had worn leather skirts wrapped around their waists and had had shaved heads. What hair they had left pomaded with something that smelled like cooking fat into a thick spike at the center of their scalps. She'd assumed they were Nahautl who didn't have the distinctive tattoos, colorful cloaks, or earplugs. Her parents had raised her to be kind to strangers, and helpful to those in need. What possible harm could there be in giving someone directions, when they were lost?

The back of her head still hurt from where one of them had hit her with a short club. All she'd known at the time was a searing white shock of pain, and then darkness . . . followed by awakening someplace dark. Not tied up, but jostling everywhere, with the smell of vulcanized rubber tires and machine oil. The hum of a ley-powered engine.

They'd never told her their names. Never told her why she was their prisoner. Never talked to her beyond telling her to get out of the trunk and to go ahead and relieve her bowels . . . while one of them watched to make sure she didn't run away. She could hear them talking in the front of the car—the shapes of the words were foreign, but she could hear them through the seat, from the trunk. And when they'd arrived here . . . wherever *here* was . . . they'd shoved her into this lean-to. Had women come and dress her as if she were one of them. A shaman had arrived, and mumbled some sort of prayer over here, and then they'd bound her hands and feet, and left her here.

A timid voice at the entrance caught her ear, and she looked up eagerly from where she was curled up in a small ball, shaking from the cold. Then a woman carrying a stone lamp with a single burning wick ducked into the shed, and set a bowl of . . . meat? Some sort of thick stew? . . . on the ground. "Eat," the woman said, briefly. Her accent in Latin was thick, and she didn't look at Fritti, keeping her eyes on the ground, as if shamed . . . or afraid.

"What is it?"

"Bison. Usually, only hunters—only men—can eat this. You are privileged." She turned to leave.

"Please stay. Please tell me why they're doing this to me. I didn't do anything wrong. . . ." Fritti tried not to cry. She was from Marcomanni. She shouldn't weep. But she was thirteen, and very, very far from home. "I didn't do anything. . . ."

The woman still wouldn't look at her. "One of the men dreamed of you. He knew he would know you when he saw you, and he did. So they took you."

Fritti had just scooped a mouthful of stew up, and now, couldn't swallow as her eyes rounded. Her muffled sound of consternation didn't make the woman laugh. "Don't worry. Your virginity won't be threatened, Marcomanni." The woman still looked away. "You will be given to the Morning Star. It is a . . . very great honor. One that has not been given in hundreds of years."

Fritti's stomach clenched on the food, and suddenly, though she didn't understand a word that the woman said, she wasn't hungry anymore. Instead, she was even more afraid.

"Eat it. Do not waste any of it." The woman turned and left, and darkness filled the shed once more. Fritti couldn't see the stew, which tasted as if someone had taken dried, salted meat and let it soften somewhat in warm water with. . . cornmeal mush and maybe squash of some sort. At least it was warm. She finished the food with her clumsy, bound hands, and curled back up again, keeping her hands against her chest to prevent frostbite, and shivered. Wondering what morning would bring.

Martius 6, 1954 AC

Sigrun awoke with a start, just before dawn, and sat up, shedding blankets. She'd left the room's radiator off; a blanket was fine, but more than that, and hotel rooms tended to get stuffy. She stared at the window, and dawn's first gray light, unblinking for a moment, and then stood, digging in her suitcase. Today was Tiwasdaeg . . . Tuesday, as people in Novo Germania tended to slur the word, or dies Martis, by the Roman calendar. Even without the possibility of having to fight a battle today, it was Tyr's day, which meant that she needed to wear her regalia.

She braided her hair, and knotted it neatly at the nape of her neck. Nothing for an enemy to grab, here. No jeans today; brown leather breeches, well-worn and broken in, so that they flexed with her legs easily. One of her usual leather bodices, and a padded tunic over that, to keep her skin from being scratched and chafed by the next layer. . . . which was ring-mail. Fine-gauged steel wire, looped and woven, in a shirt that hung past her hips . . . a solid forty pounds of weight that she bore easily, being used to it. Knee-high boots, flat, with rubber soles with heavy tread, for traction even in the worst of footing, and ankle support. Poleyns and greaves, buckled in place for knee and shin protection, the greaves positioned over the boots. No long, heavy, binding cloak today; she needed to be able to *move*. She rarely felt the cold anyway. But she did need to wear her feathered cloak.

Her last partner in the Praetorians, Cunomorinus Villu, a Gaul from Nimes, southwest of here, along the coast of the Pacifica, had referred to the cloak as her chicken-suit. He'd frequently told her, laughing, that it looked Polynesian, somehow. It was made of white swan feathers, and hung just to her hips. When Sigrun wore this, and carried a spear, it meant that she was on the official business of Tyr. Going about her god's work.

Or, as today, that it happened to be a Tiwasdaeg.

And today, when she might be facing combat? She left her room carrying a light helmet, which had cheek and nose pieces, but left her eyes and lower jaw uncovered. It was solid, high-quality steel. It might not stop a well-aimed round from a Judean sniper rifle, but it would definitely stop a musket ball or an arrow, and offered protection from shrapnel and slashing weapons.

Padding down the hall, she nodded to Ptah-ases, the lictor on duty outside the propraetor's door. The Ptolemaic shaved his head daily, oiled his dark skin for protection, and wore kohl around his eyes, for much the same reason. He was also in remarkably good shape for a man in his mid-forties, lean and agile. At the moment, he gave her a narrow-eyed look, and then allowed himself the faintest curl of a smile, teeth white in his dark face, before running one hand over his perfectly smooth scalp. "You were busy last night, weren't you, valkyrie?"

Gentle needling. Ptah-ases was one of the most skilled sorcerers she'd known in all her years in the Praetorian Guard, and did her the courtesy of not treating her any differently than any other subject of the empire. Sigrun grimaced. "One of your countryman was drunk, and making an ass of himself in public. I apologize for any extra attention this accrues to us. But other than to the local *gardia*, Adam and I didn't identify ourselves as members of the Guard, or lictors." She kept her voice down, and glanced around, making sure that the various travelers leaving their rooms this morning, and the maids serving the various rooms with breakfasts and newspapers on trolleys, weren't listening to her words.

Ptah-ases snorted. "From what I heard, the man had it coming. Most Atenists aren't like that, I hasten to point out." He chuckled. "*I'm* not. I fully acknowledge that my faith was *defunct* until the eighteenth century, when the old writings were recovered. For me, it's a personal choice about worshipping whatever lies beyond the gods of this world—whatever created *them*. I don't even need to give it a name. I don't feel a need to get belligerent about it."

"You also don't generally get drunk when you're out of town, and you also don't exactly have a lot to prove," Sigrun told him, her tone wry.

"Sorcerers at my level should never get drunk, anyway. Remind me to tell you some time what happened at the graduate seminar I attended once at the University of Alexandria, where two of the students decided to partake of some peyote they'd had smuggled in from Caesaria Aquilonis."

Sigrun winced. "Did they decide to slay any invisible dragons?"

"No, but they thought the professor had turned into a bear and when he approached to find out why they were giggling and staring into space, they thought the bear was attacking them." Ptah-ases looked resigned. "They panicked and attacked him, when his defenses were down. They brought one of the chandeliers down on him, and he didn't react quickly enough. There was glass everywhere."

". . . gods. Was he all right?"

"If they'd been alone, he wouldn't have been. Two of us stepped in and restrained them—I had to practically strangle one of them to knock him out—and then called for the doctors. As it was, he almost died of blood loss." Ptah grimaced. "The campus officials took pictures as an object lesson in what not to do."

Sigrun shuddered. Normal humans did quite enough damage, in their minds or out of them. Sorcerers, summoners, ley-mages, and god-born were held to a higher standard. She changed the subject slightly. "The man last night was surprisingly belligerent about his faith, Ptah. I've met other Atenists besides you. This was the first one who tried to say that I didn't *exist*. Or that everything I am is a lie." It still troubled her, a little. She didn't know, some days, what this modern world was coming to, really.

"Believe something strongly enough, and the world might shape itself to your belief," he replied, lightly, and touched her shoulder, gently. "Look. I'm a decorated veteran of the Foreign Legions. I've been a Praetorian for fifteen years. My wife and children are happy back in

Thebes. I find that the people who are loudest in matters of faith? Are using their own as a club. A way of cowing or beating others down. A matter of power. They're bullies, trying to make themselves bigger and more important, than they really are, because no other facet of their life has any real meaning, my friend." Ptah-ases shrugged. "Try thinking of how small and insignificant and petty their lives are, my friend. And rise above them."

Sigrun regarded him, and smiled faintly. "You give good advice, even when it grieves me to hear such things." She nodded at the door. "Is the propraetor available?"

"He's up, he's had his coffee, and he's being shaved. He has dispatches to read, too, so make it brief. I'm going off-duty in an hour and getting some sleep. Assuming I'm allowed to." Another quick, needling smile. "You might have plans for another incident today. Do you? Just so I'm apprised of the schedule."

"You have short-timer's disease in the worst possible way, Ptah."

"By the sun, yes, I do. I cannot *wait* until my replacement shows up and I can finally cycle home. See my wife and children. Bask in the sun. You northerners can *keep* your snow, valkyrie," The Egyptian chuckled, and tapped on the door. "Sir? Caetia to see you," he called through it.

"Let her in," a voice called back, in perfect Latin, free of any regional dialects. The very crispness of the speech indicated that the speaker was a patrician, native to Rome. "It's that, or I continue listening to the two of you chatter in the hall, yes?"

Smile widening slightly, Sigrun stepped through the door, and bowed her head, bringing one fist to her chest in a light salute. "Propraetor. Good morning."

Propraetor Antonius Livorus sat in the bathing area of the hotel room, patiently allowing his personal body-servant to shave him with a straight razor, didn't turn his head, but he did lift a hand to acknowledge her. "A moment," he murmured. The proprietor wasn't a tall man, barely five foot six in height, and built on lean, wiry lines. He was in his late forties; his iron-gray hair was cut short, and barely brushed forward over his high forehead; his face was almost cadaverously thin, and his blue eyes were sharp and piercing behind the sharp prow of his patrician nose. Sigrun towered over him, but felt, as always, slightly awkward and oafish around him; the man held a certain leashed power about him, and she respected his incisive intellect.

The Hellene attendant negotiated the tricky area under the propraetor's nose. It wouldn't do to give the representative of Rome a nick in a visible area today. It would detract from his gravitas, among other things. A propraetor's duties varied, and sometimes greatly; the title meant, literally, 'beside the praetor.' Praetors were elected or appointed from the patrician class, as needed, to fill many roles—some led armies in times of crises. Most, however, were magistrates. A propraetor was a special appointment, only given by the sitting emperor or empress. Livorus' full tile was *propraetor inter cives et peregrinos* . . . or a magistrate empowered to resolve disputes among citizens and foreigners. This could mean between citizens and subjects, or even subjects and the subjects of foreign kingdoms. And being appointed directly by the emperor gave the man a vast degree of latitude and personal power. Livorus in particular had the quiet reputation as the emperor's right hand, and personal trouble-shooter.

The propraetor gestured his attendant away, and wiped at his face. "I will never understand how someone can do this properly themselves," he murmured, gesturing at his face as he turned to study himself in the mirror.

"Personally, I can't fathom allowing anyone that close to my throat with a naked blade, sir." Sigrun watched as the Hellene began to clean the blade and other hygiene equipment.

Livorus chuckled and moved to a chair at the room's single desk. His simple breakfast was only half-eaten; nothing more than toast, fruit, and coffee. "So. Sigrun. Fair morning to you, as well. I trust you had a restful evening?" Faint humor in those pale blue eyes.

"Ah . . . about that, sir? I just wished to apologize once more—" Sigrun didn't shift from foot to foot. She knew precisely on what grounds she'd acted the night before, and was confident that anyone who reported her presence would mostly report, *a valkyrie* or *a god-born was involved in a dispute last night* not *a Praetorian had an Atenist arrested for public drunkenness, proselytizing, and harboring potential revolutionary sentiments.* Still, Livorus could be angry at the potential for jeopardizing a delicate diplomatic situation. And if he was, she'd accept it.

"I've already had the local Praetorian office call in to verify that you are who you said you were." Livorus dismissed it with a wave of his hand. "We've more important things to focus on today, my dear."

Sigrun allowed herself one brief exhalation of relief, and then she focused on the matter at hand. "What time do you want to meet with the Chahiksichahiks, sir?"

"Arrange for it at the ninth hour antemeridian, if you would. It may take several hours of negotiations to allow us onto their lands to *look* for the girl." Livorus' eyes went cold. "And that is if, and only if, their leaders do not know what business their shamans and god-born are about."

"Their shamans and god-born are, generally speaking, among the leaders of their people. I find it hard to believe that their elders wouldn't know precisely what is going on." Sigrun kept her face expressionless, but her stomach twisted. The Chahiksichahiks were treated, under the laws of Rome, as a petty kingdom. They had signed a formal, if limited alliance with Rome, but had a few diplomatic ties. They had their own land, the borders of which they guarded, and which had been, in the main, respected for hundreds of years. The terms of their status as a subject state mainly involved a guarantee that they would not be harassed on religious grounds or for their land, so long as they did not participate in human sacrifice, didn't make war on their neighbors, and so on. They had little in the way of material wealth, being primarily hunter-gatherers, and thus paid almost no taxes—something that chagrinned their neighbors in Novo

Gaul, and even larger, more industrialized regional nations like the Diné or the Iroquois Confederacy.

Kidnapping a young girl and holding her captive with the potential for sacrificing her would certainly break at least two of those treaty clauses. The problem was, the *gardia* in Marcomanni had an informant within the kingdom send them a tip to tell them that the girl had indeed been taken prisoner, with the intent to sacrifice her. They did not know *why* someone would wish to do this, after centuries of peace between the nations of this land. Livorus had even speculated that this could all be a sham. That someone within the tribe had wanted to discredit their king and elders, and that the kidnapping had been staged, to make Rome retaliate. The permutations along that line of thought—that it could be a deliberate provocation to make Rome or Nova Germania overreact, and look bad to the other petty kingdoms—got successively more tangled, the longer they'd tried to think them out.

All in all, it required a delicate touch, and Livorus had been handed the problem. They'd interfaced with the local Praetorian office in Marcomanni, questioned the girl's parents, and moved where the evidence had taken them. . . . but there was still a high degree of uncertainty in the entire situation. They had no understanding of the true motivations involved. Which always made a scenario that much more dangerous.

Livorus nodded to her now, and picked up a dispatch. Printed in the clear on foolscap, the entire surface was covered in neat Roman letters, all equally spaced. No clear words, anywhere. He placed a thin foolscap template over it, blocking out some of the letters on the page, revealing others. The letters that appeared in the windows of the stencil spelled out the *real* message. He'd burn the template once he'd decoded today's messages. One-time stencils, usually bound in a tablet together, were vital to the security of messages sent by the empire. If even one code tablet went missing, all others from the same batch were immediately discarded. "We'll give them the benefit of some doubt, my dear," Livorus told her, neatly transcribing the message to a wax tablet for easier reading. "The Chahiksichahiks have been a fairly peaceful subject state for centuries. They've abided by the laws of Rome for generations. I doubt all of them wish to throw away stability and security for an ancient ritual." He tapped the stylus against his chin. "I doubt a fight will even be required. With luck, all that will be required is showing the *fasces*, and they'll turn the girl over to us."

"Wouldn't that require their leaders to know where she is, sir?" Sigrun's tone was exquisitely dry.

The propraetor glanced up, and blue eyes met gray, just for an instant. "Caught me, my dear. No, I don't actually believe that they're all innocent of knowledge. But I have no doubts that they *wish* to be ignorant of it. And that they'll protest, vigorously, that they had no knowledge of the kidnapping, or of the shamans' intentions towards the girl." Livorus nodded towards the door. "Dismissed. Get some breakfast. It's going to be a very busy day, I fear."

Sigrun made her way back downstairs, nodding to Ptah-ases on her way back out again. Down in the dining area, Adam and the last member of Livorus' entourage were eating breakfast. "Fair morning," Ehecatl Itztli told her, looking up, his dark eyes amused.

The Nahautl man wasn't physically imposing, being built on slim lines, but he moved like a jaguar. Of their group, he and Adam were the closest in skills; he wasn't a mage of any sort, but he knew very well how to kill a magic-user. Like many Nahautl men, he shaved his head on both sides, leaving a long, straight, black line of hair, like a horse's mane. Unlike many younger men, however, he chose not to spike this with egg whites or pomade, letting it hang loose to his shoulders. The scalp itself was tattooed in thick, black images. A serpent and a jaguar were visible there, and, on his arms, bared to the elbow by his rolled sleeves, images of his strange, squat-looking gods. Sigrun knew that across his back he had a feathered serpent, as well, indicating that he'd consecrated himself to Quetzalcoatl in his youth, as well as Tezcatlipoca, the jaguar god of his people. Each marking was intended to protect him; the tattoos served as invisible armor, and had been placed on his skin by skilled Nahautl priests and sorcerers. Several of them even allowed him to turn himself *invisible* . . . without being a sorcerer or ley-mage, himself. Ehecatl grinned at her over his coffee. "I see you're back in the chicken-suit."

Sigrun winced as she sat down, picking up her breakfast menu. "Don't say that," she told him, but without force. "That was Villu's thing."

"I'm carrying it on in his memory." Ehecatl quipped, but an expression of regret shifted over his face briefly. He glanced at Adam. "You're new enough to the team that you probably don't know all the details, but the man you replaced? Cunomorinus Villu. Bravest Gaul I've ever met." He grinned again. "Managed to put up with Sigrun here every day for two years."

Adam chuckled. "She's not so bad." He flagged down a waiter for Sigrun, who sighed and ordered toast, fruit, and tea, herself. "You know, when I joined your detail, everyone told me that Villu had died, but no one ever said how."

Sigrun stared down into her cup, feeling sick to her stomach. "It was in Hellas, of all places," she managed. She didn't like remembering it. Her first partner, a Nubian sorcerer, had rotated out of the detail, in the natural manner of things. Villu had replaced him, and she'd just gotten used to the man when disaster had struck.

"Hellas?" Adam's eyebrows shot up. "They're civilized there. I wouldn't have thought of it as a place that the propraetor would be visiting."

Ehecatl chuckled. "You'd think that, but the man's called *everywhere* on the globe. In this case, a Roman diplomat had been accused of raping and murdering a Hellene girl. The locals were up in arms. Can't blame them. I would have been, too." He shrugged. "We got on-scene, and it turned out that we could definitively prove the diplomat's whereabouts the whole evening. He'd been with his wife and a group of guests for a dinner party. All the servants and slaves and all the guests—even the people who didn't like him—said that he was there. And yet, we had twenty people in a *taverna* ten miles away, insisting that they'd seen him walk out the door with the girl just before midnight."

Adam raised his head, his dark eyes narrowing. "Disguise of some sort?"

"Spirit. A malefic one," Sigrun said, grimly, the word bitten off. "Doppelganger. What the Gauls call a fetch. Usually takes the victim's own face and haunts them. Tells them that they're about to die. Does nasty things to the victim's family and friends. The worse they are, the nastier the things they do." She swallowed a sip of the tea the waiter had just left on the table for her, scalding the back of her throat. She welcomed the pain, obscurely. "My guess was that the doppelganger would have moved on to the diplomat's wife and children next. They . . . like the fear. They like the pain. They relish the betrayal."

Adam frowned. "I thought spirits had to be . . . summoned." He said the last word with distaste. Sigrun wasn't surprised. He'd fought on the Wall for years, and grown up in Judea, a province perennially under threat from attacks by Persian, Chaldean, and Median magi.

"Some do. Some are here in this world, more or less permanently. Some can come here at will." Sigrun shrugged.

"So, was this one summoned?" Adam persisted.

Ehecatl shrugged. "There was a certain amount of evidence that the Roman diplomat had offended a local summoner. We couldn't prove that he'd summoned the fetch and bargained with it to impersonate the diplomat. We could have run back to Athens to find ourselves a different summoner to bind or banish the spirit. . . even bargain with it, for information—"

"I won't bargain with that sort of spirit," Sigrun said, tightly. She'd seen the girl's body in the morgue, and stared now at her toast. Wondering if she'd see another girl's body in a morgue slot by the end of the day.

"Proof would have been optimal," Ehecatl reminded her, and rubbed at his eyes. "Hellene law even has provisions for spirit-testimony—"

That provoked a mild snort from Adam, but he didn't interrupt. "At any rate," the Nahautl man said, wearily, "The locals did have legends about a spirit in a local cave that liked to play tricks. We tracked down where it had its lair. Sigrun and Ptah-ases went to go kill it. But Villu and I stayed behind to protect the diplomat and Livorus."

Sigrun very carefully set her cup down. She'd lost what little appetite she'd had.

Adam winced. "I think I see where this is going. The mob in Hellas was still out for revenge, and didn't believe what you'd found?"

She shook her head slowly, staring down at the wood of the table. "It's not always the monsters that we have to fight," Sigrun said, quietly. "Sometimes, the worst monster of all, is humanity itself." She closed her eyes against the pictures in her mind. The Roman villa, the local consulate, had been filled with shattered tiles, broken furniture, and blood. "Ptah and I heard you over the radio," she added, looking at Ehecatl, her lips tight. Once again, fruitlessly apologizing, "We just couldn't. . . . get there fast enough."

"Villu was a damned fine ley-mage. But we were too far from the local ley-lines for him to do much. One of the reasons he was back on protective detail, and not off in the mountains, helping to kill the fetch." Ehecatl rubbed at his face, his expression bleak. "You get thirty, forty people in a room together, and they're just . . . a mob. They're not people anymore. They're an animal. One mind, many bodies, all howling, and no thought in them but blood. It's a kind of madness. And one I don't wish to see again." He stared out the window into the bright sunlight, his obsidian eyes unreadable. "They broke through the barriers he put up, between the front door and the atrium. Flooded into the house. And they tore Villu apart, for standing between them and the diplomat."

"How'd you escape?" Adam asked. His voice was respectful of the pain and the sacrifice, but calm, too. Sigrun glanced up, assessing him. Her new partner had clearly seen his fair share of battles; she'd read his dossier thoroughly, but she was just getting to know him, really. Just starting to understand what he was made of.

Ehecatl shook his head. "Turned invisible. Got to Livorus, and got him out, and then went back for the diplomat and his wife . . . ." He stared down at the table. "I got the wife out. Her husband . . . no. Then I went back in for Villu. There . . . wasn't a lot left of either him or the diplomat. And that's when Sigrun and Ptah-ases got back. Carrying the remains of the fetch . . . not that there's usually much left of a mostly incorporeal being, but . . . ." Ehecatl spread his hands and grimaced.

". . . this one manifested itself. Enough that it could violate the girl, and kill her. Blood binds." Sigrun grimaced. They all knew that much. "It must have been doing this sort of thing for a very long time, to have been so powerful." She pushed her plate away, aching inside, and put on the mask she'd long ago learned to wear.

"And what did you do with the mob of people?" Adam asked, leaning forward now, steepling his fingers in front of him, resting his elbows on the edge of the table. This, she could see, interested him.

Sigrun sighed. She'd *wanted* to kill every last one of the mother-loving bastards. She was *capable* of having waded knee-deep in their blood. "We arrested them," she muttered, and threw the crust of her toast at her plate. "With extreme prejudice in some cases."

"I seem to remember you begging them to resist." Ehecatl looked at her.

Sigrun closed her eyes. The mob had cut the copper wires that conducted ley-line power into the dwelling. Nothing but blackness, the clatter of broken tiles underfoot, the screams and shouts of enraged people. The only light coming from flashes of storm-born lightning outside, illuminating the narrow rooms and turning people into alabaster statues, caught, as if in stop-motion photography, turning to see what approached them. Eyes, shadowed in their sockets, glimmering as the irises caught pellucid light. Look of open-mouthed horror. Ptah-ases swearing viciously and probably blasphemously in his native tongue, and hurling people up against the walls, where metal sconces, usually used to hold lights, twisted themselves into manacles, wrapping around arms and legs like vines. Smell of blood, ozone in the air as another, even closer thunderbolt slammed down scant feet from the villa. Finding Villu's limp body, the eyes torn out, stabbed multiple times, throat slashed, ears torn from the skull, hanging by sinews, his groin a mass of red. The mob had taken their anger at the *diplomat* . . . the *fetch* . . . out on him. And for no other reason than that he had been there, and had barred their path.

In the here and now, thunder rumbled in the distance, in spite of the clear sky. Sigrun shook herself and looked up. "It was a very bad day," she said, clinically, and put it all to the back of her head. Everything except twin whispers: *If I had been faster, he would not have died . . . .* and . . . *never going to let it happen again. Never.*

Adam nodded slowly. "It sounds it." He paused. "How were they punished?"

"Oh, it was very *Roman*. There were trials. I went back to testify," Ehecatl said. He stared into his coffee cup.

"So did I," Sigrun added.

"And the punishments?" Adam persisted, almost gently.

"Crucifixion for the ring-leaders." Sigrun's words were stark. "I thought about taking pictures for Villu's wife and children, but decided they'd had enough."

"Odd," Ehecatl said. "I *did*. His wife thanked me for sending them."

Sigrun looked up, and met the man's eyes. And nodded, in respect. "She's a strong woman."

Adam, for his part, nodded rather matter-of-factly. "And the others?"

"Hard labor. Twenty years each. I was surprised that the jury was as lenient with them as they were, but the judge stated that they could consider the *convincing* nature of the fetch to be a mitigating circumstance, creating a kind of communal madness. I think they called it the Bacchae defense." Sigrun grimaced. She personally thought that every last one of them should have been executed, but the jury had spoken, and the law was the law.

"The Bacchae defense?" Adam blinked at her. "Like Euripedes?"

"Yes." She shrugged. "The play shows how King Pentheus was torn apart by Bacchae, wild men and women inspired by the spirit of Dionysus. And while the king's own mother tore her son asunder, and while she felt grief and despair for the act, it was the god's doing, not theirs. They were merely the hands of his justice." She grimaced, her lips taut. "The prosecutor argued that there is a difference between divine retribution and the work of a malefic spirit, and that there was no evidence that the fetch had influenced any of them, other than by making itself appear to be someone that they knew." She caught Adam's look. "It seemed an unusually irrational decision by the Hellenes. But all of the attackers were locals." Her lips twisted slightly.

Adam nodded again, and said, quietly, "It's good that you remember him with honor. And with humor." He glanced at Sigrun.

"Chicken-suit, eh?" He smiled slightly, and shifted the subject, slightly. "Me? I wouldn't say that about the cloak. It looks soft. But the *armor*? Impractical! A bullet won't just go right through that . . . it'll tear the rings apart and send them as shrapnel through your body." He lifted his eyebrows. "We have something in Judea now. We call them flak jackets. You should consider them. Unless the armor is just for show?"

Sigrun snorted, appreciating the change of subject, and realizing, suddenly, that Adam was saying more than what the words outwardly meant. *He wants to remind us that he's not Villu?* She thought about it, and corrected herself. *No . . . more that he's not trying to replace him. Asking us to differentiate between them, and not to . . . punish him? Or overprotect him, perhaps?* Internally, she shrugged; he'd been her partner less than three months, and she hadn't gotten a good feel for him yet. She'd watch his back in the field, same as she would any other new, young Guard, until she knew what he was made of.

In response to his actual, spoken words, she raised her eyebrows slightly, and replies, "No. Not just for show. Your flak jackets may take a bullet, but they won't turn a stab or a cut, now will they?"

"The philosophers are working on that, I'm sure," he told her, and nodded to the door. "We should get going, yes?"

Chapter II: Rituals

It is well-known to all that live today, how Gaius Julius Caesar became not just tyrant of Rome, like Sulla before him, but was crowned as the first king since ancient times; he was styled <u>imperator</u>, and accorded most of the power usually reserved for a tribune of the plebeians, for the plebeians did love him. He was, however, in his fifty-fifth year when he was granted this privilege by the Senate. He had spent many of the previous years lobbying for the right to call as his heir any son of his born to any of his many amours, or even to call as many or all of his amours wives as he wished, like a potentate of some distant and barbaric kingdom. This, the Senate would not allow, but when Caesar took power, he chose to disinherit the young relative he had previously favored, Octavianus, and instead formally adopted his natural son by Cleopatra VII Philopator: Ptolemy Caesarion Julius Philopator Philometor, styled by some Caesarion the God-Born.Cleopatra his mother had long called herself the embodiment of Isis, and there is no doubt in any mind that the woman was indeed god-born, divinely touched by the mother-goddess of the Nile; she had a fascination about her that drove men mad, including Caesar. She had already elevated her young son to be her co-ruler, and had begun training the boy to rule before his father came to Egypt to claim him as the rightful heir to the throne of not one, but two powers.

This boy-child was a stripling of only three when Caesar became imperator. Had Caesar died in that year, there is no doubt that young Caesarion would have been killed in the ensuing power struggle. Instead, Gaius Julius Caesar ruled as tyrant and imperator for fifteen years, and lived to see his son win his first victory in Gaul, and parade in triumph through Rome.

Caesar died when Caesarion was only eighteen, and the Senate took immediate steps to prevent the tyranny of Julius Caesar from becoming a monarchy; they met to try to enact laws that would strip Caesarion of any claims to his father's fortune and to re-assert his bastardy. Caesarion had learned politics at Cleopatra's knee, however, and had already bought as many votes in the Senate as money could ensure.

Whereupon, certain members of the Senate, taking a cue from the late conspirators who had attacked Caesar in the Forum, made attempts on the life of Caesarion. He was, however, seemingly proof against poison. Whether it was the measure of the divine blood of Isis and Osiris on his mother's side, or whether he, like Mithridates, dosed himself daily with every known poison in order to build a resistance against them, remains unknown to this day, but it is said that Caesarion drank cheerfully and freely from every cup, and was never the worse for it.

In despair, the conspirators gathered weapons, and moved to attack the young man personally, as he walked to the Senate to be invested with his father's title. And when the assassins gathered around him, Caesarion, a young man in the prime and vigor of his youth, well-trained in military matters by his illustrious father, seized a knife from the hand of one of the conspirators, and struck down his attackers.

This show of prowess reminded the public that Caesarion was actually god-born on both sides of his parentage. Caesar had issued coinage with portraits of his divine ancestors, Venus and Aeneas, and had often sacrificed to Mars. The god of battle had always favored Caesar in his campaigns, and now, the charisma of Venus and the favor of Mars seemed to be passed on to his son. And the plebeians loved him all the more for it.

Ptolemy Julius Caesarion Philopator Philomator was thus invested with the title of Imperator in the year 15 AC, and ruled from that moment until his death in 55 AC. He is chiefly noted for the period of peace and expansion that he brought to the Empire, a period of stability unlike the previous periods of periodic civil strife that had marked the Italian peninsula. He made peace with the Gauls and the Germanic tribes. And in 26 AC, Caesarion, that son of Egypt, traveled personally to Judea, where he met with the leaders of the followers of the god of Abraham.

The legions were in position at the gates of Jerusalem, but the Imperator entered the city not as a conqueror or a king, but in the garb of a Roman legate. He carried with him the fasces, and spoke liberally and generously with the elders of the city. He listened to their grievances with regards to taxes and the presence of the foreign king Herod, and agreed to allow them a greater degree of autonomy and religious freedom . . . so long as they agreed to enforce Roman law in all other ways within their borders. He ejected Herod from the province, and permitted the priests to return to the region to a theocracy . . . again, with the provision that they would honor Roman laws and taxes.

With the legions present, it was clear that the young and charismatic leader could have burned their city and their temple to the ground. That he did not do so was considered a sign of weakness by the fractious Senate, and Caesarion was impelled to show some severity upon his return to Rome . . . .

– *Gaius Suetonius Tranquillus , De vita Caesarum, ca. 103 AC.*

Adam drove their car, an Arma XII, a Hellene import that ran on ley-energy, through the streets of downtown Ponca. It was an old-fashioned model, with huge fenders and an overall bulbous look, which, coupled with its upright front window, made him feel somewhat as if he were driving inside of a shoe. Sigrun sat in the front seat with him, watching out the window, while Ehecatl and Ptah-ases flanked the propraetor in the backseat. The Egyptian was dozing, lightly, trying to cram a night's worth of sleep into a catnap.

Downtown Ponca didn't have the traffic problems of Rome, Novo Trier, Jerusalem, or Edo; it really was a backwater of Novo Gaul. Adam even spotted a few horse-drawn farm wagons . . . . but there were more motorcars on the road than he'd really expected. A couple of Judean imports. Tsunams. Mehymans. They were known as dependable, reliable models, but they couldn't run on ley-energy without an engine replacement, so he didn't see many of those here. Kusabanas, Takas, Aloga, and Epibintores, however . . . all budget models from Nippon and luxury cars from Hellas? Those he saw in plenty.

He took them through Ponca, and out into the open, flat prairie land of the region. Flat as a table, and covered with farms and bison ranges as far as the eye could see. The Gauls had taken the name of their city from the tribe who'd lived here when they'd moved through the area originally, back around 550 AC. Of course, the Gauls had been, at the time, largely tribal, themselves. Sent here at the direction of Rome. *We want your lands north of the Alps and Apennines to be peaceful. Send your excess population across the sea, settle this new land, and don't make trouble for us anymore,* had been Rome's dictate, and the Gauls and Goths had taken this as a kind of blessing. It had allowed them to send their young, restless young warriors, the so-called 'wolf-packs' to where the landless men couldn't actually start wars with the neighbors. Everyone had profited. Other than the natives of Caesaria Aquilonis, arguably. But while the Goths and Gauls had been significantly more technologically advanced than their neighbors, in possession of iron and steel weapons and armor, it had still taken them centuries to shape the provinces as they were known today. To make peace with local spirits, and to find an equilibrium point with the tribes with whom they allied themselves. Adam didn't doubt that the history of the continent was written in blood . . .but that was probably the truth of history everywhere.

The Chahiksichahiks held a region well outside of the city proper, at least forty miles. Adam had taken them west, following the green signs that read *Romana Via LXXX.* Roman highway eighty. If the Romans did nothing else well, it was build roads; the poured-stone pavement was perfectly smooth, neither narrowing nor widening appreciably, and the road arrowed undeviatingly west in a perfectly straight light.

"We've got a turnoff in about a mile," Sigrun warned. He could see how tightly she was gripping the inner handle of the door, in spite of the fact that the car was barely going forty-five miles an hour. She was not an easy passenger. Another facet of her personality that amused him.

"I know," Adam replied mildly, and touched the brakes as they came up on the exit, which was clearly marked with the flags of the petty kingdom of the Chahiksichahiks, and signs that read, in Latin, *Now leaving the province of Novo Gaul. Obey local laws and ordinances.* Adam's lips curled down at that message. *How about Roman laws? Are we obeying those today?*

He didn't entirely *trust* the technomancy of the vehicle, but he did appreciate the fluidity with which the motorcar cornered. Even the uneven transition from concrete to dirt road was smooth, with only a little drift of the rear tires on the unstable dirt surface, in spite of the fact that the vehicle was rear-wheel drive. "Wake up," Ehecatl told Ptah-ases, shifting around in his seat to loosen the obsidian knife he carried in its sheath. The volcanic glass should have been fragile and prone to shatter, but it was, apparently, heavily enchanted. Ptah-ases had tried to explain it to Adam once. Apparently, since glass was largely silica, it could be used to store spells quite effectively. Adam hadn't pretended to understand that.

"I'm awake," Ptah said now, not opening his eyes. "The road is warded. Trigger stone embedded under the surface of the road. They'll know we're coming, no matter how quiet the engine of this vehicle is."

"Our intention is not to sneak into their lands," Livorus said, mildly. "I have no objection to them knowing that they have guests. Let them know that Rome is here. It will make some of the elders begin to think more carefully about recent decisions they may have made."

Wonderful. Adam was alert now, watching the scant trees planted on either side of the dirt road, either as a wind-break or for cover, and he kept both hands on the wheel, ready to spin them out of the way of any incoming fire. "Ptah?" Sigrun said, sharply, her head swiveling to the right. Out of the corner of his eye, Adam caught movement behind the line of scrubby, wind-bowed trees, and swore mentally.

The Egyptian sat up, his dark eyes suddenly intent. "Border guards?"

"A few too many for a regular customs check," Ehecatl noted, shifting in his seat. "I've counted at least six so far."

"Same," Adam replied, succinctly. "I'm only catching sight of a few here and there, mostly back in the long grass, beyond the trees."

Ptah's eyes went vacant for a moment. "Three more," he said. "I think. They're using spirits to mask themselves, and that's really hard for me to detect."

"How many are carrying guns?" Sigrun asked, rolling her shoulders. "I only see two with muskets."

"Agreed," Ehecatl returned, tersely. "Four with bows, that I've seen. Those will be the ones with enchanted arrows, and the like. Possibly poisoned heads.

"Steady," Livorus told them all, and Adam could see in the rearview mirror that the propraetor's expression had yet to change. "The Chahiksichahiks correctly regard this land as their sovereign territory. They feel they have a right to defend it." His tone was placid.

By treaty, the region was treated as a subject kingdom within the borders of the province of Novo Gaul. That the Chahiksichahiks didn't really have kings, so much as *elders*, didn't much matter; the Gothic and Gallic tribes had had dozens of petty 'kings' who'd been little more than tribal elders, themselves, centuries ago, when they and Rome had first met and clashed. The Chahiksichahiks didn't see themselves as a kingdom, as best Adam understood it from the dossiers and other materials he'd read on the region in the last few days; they regarded themselves as a *people*, and nothing more. They'd been primarily agricultural, once, centuries ago, before they'd moved to this land from Nahautl, but had moved to hunting the buffalo herds that crossed their lands. Hunting was a prestige activity; only men could participate, and meat was a privileged food.

The fact that the farmers of Novo Gaul had domesticated bison around twelve hundred years ago, and wanted to protect the herds that they maintained was therefore another source of conflict between the peoples of the region. It was apparently somewhat common for a private herd to be mistaken for a wild one, and stampeded towards pit traps. Whether this was out of genuine error on the part of the hunters or not, was a matter for the local courts and imperial adjudicators.

One of the tribal elders, an outspoken priest, had recently and loudly spoken against farming, and had stated that any agriculture more than the subsistence agriculture practiced by his people was simply a means by which people raped the earth, their mother, and forced her to give them her bounty. Adam didn't follow the logic, but it was a matter of belief, and thus, not his concern.

What *was* his concern were the half-dozen visible hunters who now emerged from the tall prairie grass, all under arms, and moved to block the road. Several did carry muskets . . . old-fashioned, but more than enough to punch through the windows of the Arma . . . and Adam slowed the motorcar to a halt. "We're not getting out, correct?" he asked, tersely. "The vehicle's almost like an embassy. Roman soil.

"I'd prefer to keep metal around us as long as possible," Ptah advised. "I can reinforce the walls and windows. I do better with solid matter already in place, instead of having to force air to change states."

"The approach I take will depend greatly on what tack they take with me," Livorus told them all, with unruffled calm. "I'm willing to give up a certain amount of my dignity, and the dignity of Rome, if it gets the girl back alive, and if it soothes some rather strained relations in the region."

"*Strained*," Sigrun said, and snorted.

Adam didn't even need to ask why. The Marcomanni had a strongly warlike past, just as most of the other Gothic tribes did. That one of their children had been kidnapped, and might yet be sacrificed, if the informant from within the tribe was at all accurate? Might motivate that entire subprovince to take up arms and march. Other cities, like Cimbri might follow suit. Novo Gaul wouldn't appreciate the intrusion, but they'd probably overlook it, in the interests of peaceful relations with their provincial neighbor . . . and probably wouldn't even weep to have the hunters of this small kingdom eliminated. All without even having to dirty their own hands. "If this is a provocation," Adam muttered under his breath, "it's *stupid*." They'd discussed this ad nauseum on the way here. The possibility of this being a set-up was real. "There are fewer than ten thousand Chahiksichahiks. How are they going to stand against the wrath of the Empire?"

"Not just them," Sigrun replied, shrugging, and sat forwards in her seat, one hand on her door, ready to exit the vehicle, if needed. "Maybe they want to inspire all the old tribes to remember who they are. There's been a lot of intermarriage in the last fourteen hundred years. Most of the old tribes are . . . integrated." She frowned, watching the hunters approach the car, their weapons on their shoulders. Her left hand moved down, between the seats, to the spear she'd brought with her, the butt of which rested on the backseat, beside Livorus. "No. Wrong word. *Dissolved*. Like salt in water. You can't look at someone from Marcomanni and tell who has Chalahgawtha blood and who doesn't." She shook her head. "There are only a few of these petty kingdoms that hold to the old ways. Some of them are quite modern within their lands, with cities and industry, and trade between themselves and the Roman provinces. Maybe the Chahiksichahiks want people to . . . remember."

"No way to tell without further information," Livorus said, his tone clipped. "Silence now."

The lead hunter reached the driver's side door, and reached out to tap imperatively on the glass. Adam unrolled the window, and looked up at the man, studying him quickly. A shaved head, except for a single long, black scalp lock, stiffened with some sort of pomade and tied back from his face; a leather jerkin; and skirt-like flaps of leather wrapped around the man's waist, which rode over elaborately cross-tied leather leggings. Various amulets and charms wrapped around the man's neck, and the man carried his musket over his shoulder with an ease that bespoke long familiarity with the weapon. The dark eyes were hard, however, and Adam took that as his measure of the man. *No love of outsiders. Well enough. I've stood guard at a wall between my people and outsiders, myself.*

"State your business," the man said, his Latin accented, but clear.

"We bring the propraetor of Rome," Adam said now, tersely. "He is to meet with your elders. We attempted to make contact this morning, by calling your embassy in Ponca, but no one there answered the telephone." Modern technology was apparently forbidden within the Chahiksichahiks' territory. Those who were sent out to deal with the rest of the world were permitted to use it, but only to placate outsiders. That . . . irritated Adam, but he supposed it was probably the people's choice. *Then again, how many of the people here have an actual voice in what their leaders decide, I wonder? I don't think this is a democracy.* "Please stand aside and allow us to pass."

"No further," the man informed them all. "No motorcars on our land. Shaman says they will bring evil spirits with them."

"We have no summoners with us," Ptah-ases put in, mildly. "We bring no spirits with us."

The man shook his head again, his face set in stern lines.

Adam wasn't sure if the man accepted the words of his shaman at face value, or if this was simply an excuse being given to make the propraetor of Rome *walk* onto their lands. "Sir?" Adam deferred, politely, to Livorus.

"It's their land. We'll play nicely for the moment," Livorus said, and gestured at the window.

Adam rolled it back up again, as Livorus asked now, tightly, "Ptah?"

"I can protect you propraetor, but the rest of us are going to be on our own," the Egyptian replied curtly, picking up a bag and preparing to sling it over his shoulder. Adam could *feel* the tingle of magic being worked as the sorcerer drew in his will, and the air around them rippled, just for an instant. "I could *try* to expand the shield, but I can't guarantee that I'll be able to catch all the musket balls. They move rather quickly."

"Keep your shield focused on the propraetor," Sigrun said. 'The rest of us are paid to be shot at periodically.

Adam snorted and removed the key from the ignition, then opened the door and kept it between his body and the hunters. He kept his movements slow, too, as he saw them lower their weapons into firing position. Behind him, Ptah got out of the car, ahead of Livorus, who was followed out by Ehecatl. Each of the lictors formed a living wall around the Roman man, who wore, on this most formal of occasions, an actual toga, with purple trim. The toga was not often worn outside of the Italian peninsula anymore; it was a drafty and impractical garment for modern life. That being said? Meeting with a head of state *always* called for formal attire.

In his left hand, Livorus held a bundle of sticks. The *fasces*. As much a symbol of Rome as the eagle was. In ancient times, the lictors had carried these for consuls and magistrates. In the modern era, bodyguards needed their hands free for guns and magic . . . . and membership in the Praetorians had been opened to provincials in the past two hundred years. Allowing a non-Roman to carry the *fasces* was considered . . . improper. Thus, the propraetor carried Rome with him, wherever he went. "Sigrun, my dear? At my right, if you would? Adam, lead us out," Livorus murmured, and met the eyes of the hunters squarely. "If you'd be good enough to escort us to your king? I have business with Lesharo today."

The words rather squarely took the armed escort that would surely have been imposed on them anyway . . . and turned them into an honor guard that Livorus had requested—no, even *expected*—as his due. Even using the name of their chief elder had power. It put Livorus on an equal footing with the king of these people, at the very least. Adam kept his smile from reaching further than his eyes, and made sure he could reach his revolver. There were too many guns around him, and now that he was out of the car, he could see signs and symbols etched on the muskets. Gothic runes. *Imported enchantments. Imported technology. So they allow this, but not modern conveniences. Things that would give their people more information, like far-viewers and telephones. Two points just create a line, though, not a pattern.* He wasn't enough of a scholar to tell if the spells on the weapons were potent or not, but a gun was, in the end, a gun. They could all kill perfectly well, magic or no magic.

Their escort took them, by foot, two or three miles further along the dirt road. Adam's senses were on edge, as he strained for any sign that they were about to be attacked, but he kept his face blank, devoid of all expression. He could smell smoke, and, in the distance, he spotted a row of low hills, and his eyebrows rose slightly, as he spotted lean-tos around those hummocks of earth. *That would be the village, then.* Adam could see dozens of small fields around the hills—just-planted corn, perhaps, and what might have been squash vines, but no wheat, that he could see. *That priest's denunciation was not of their own farming, but the farming of the Gauls. The plow as a form of rape. And yet . . . it's another way of controlling their own people, isn't it?* Adam grimaced internally. He was supposed to be as neutral in his observations as he could be. But it was hard to see elderly women scratching out rows in the earth with bone hoes. There was nothing charming about hard labor, no matter how contemporary writers liked to romanticize it.

He was also aware of Gallic and Gothic traditions that called for a 'Great Marriage,' between the land to be plowed in spring, and the people who would work it. It was ritualized, symbolic, and respectful; the Gauls and Goths also had hunting traditions and hunting deities as well. The priest's denunciation thus sounded . . . heavily political. Setting up an antithesis: *we are hunters, and therefore more in touch with the gods and the world than our neighbors, who are farmers.*

From an outsider's perspective, such as his own? It sounded as if someone wanted to re-enact the transition from the Neolithic era to the Bronze Age, all over again. Wanted the hunter-gathering Neolithic tribes to go fight against their farming neighbors, with their bronze swords and armor. That first long awakening into written history had taken centuries of bloodshed in Europa, Asia, and the Fertile Crescent, if scholars and historians who studied such things were to be believed. So why would *anyone* want to re-create that division point? Especially if they happened to be on the inevitably-losing side? Irrational.

That line of analysis led him back to Sigrun's comments over breakfast. It *could* be political. It could be an effort to dance just close enough to the edge of provocation to inspire the other petty kingdoms of this land to unite behind the Chahiksichahiks. Behind history, honor, and tradition. But something just didn't smell right about this to Adam.

Dozens, even hundreds of faces, suspicious and grim, peered at them out of tunnel entrances that led into man-made hills. The Chahiksichahiks were mound-dwellers. They knew the weather of these plains, and built underground lodgings, rather than risk having their possessions, or even their lives, wrenched from them by a cyclone. Adam kept an eye on them all, the spot between his shoulder blades begin to itch as he felt, more than saw, people emerging from their mound-homes, and filling in the road behind them. "Steady," Livorus said, again, in Latin.

They'd just reached the largest of the mounds, and one of their escorts gestured for them to enter through the long, low tunnel. "This is the dwelling of Lesharo. I will go and give word of your arrival," the hunter who'd spoken before told them, his face impassive.

"I give you thanks for your careful escort," Livorus addressed the man directly, and without any irony that Adam could detect. "I will commend you to your king for your courtesy in your treatment of my lictors and myself."

The man didn't change expression, but vanished into the tunnel mouth. *"And now the waiting game commences,"* Ptah-ases commented in Hellene. The language was almost as good as a code on this side of the world. *"They may put off permitting us to enter for as long as courtesy permits, and test our patience so."*

"Unless, of course, the king and the elders truly know nothing of recent events," Ehecatl returned, slowly, and carefully, in the same language. A school-boy's diction.

"They may simply wish to see a propraetor squat in the dirt outside their homes. To prove that they can humble Rome." Sigrun's Hellene was as fluid as water passing over stones.

Livorus again held up a hand for silence. "Ptah? Do you have my chair in your pack?"

"Of course, sir." Ptah-ases unslung the bag he'd carried from the car, and removed its contents, assembling a curule seat, the backless chair reserved for patricians of Rome. He set it up in the road, and asked, "Would you like for me to arrange for some shade, sir?"

"No, the morning sun is pleasant. This interlude provides me a chance to review notes and dossiers. If you'd be so kind?" Livorus held out a hand, and Ptah removed several folders filled with foolscap from the bag as well, handing them to the propraetor as he now sat, perfectly calm and at his ease in the morning sun. Ehecatl and Ptah now turned to face the rear, while Sigrun and Adam remained at attention, facing front. Faces stolid, revealing nothing, the lictors guarded Livorus as the propraetor thumbed through his notes, as at ease as if ensconced in his office. "Do keep in mind," he added, calmly, in Latin, and loudly enough for the Chahiksichahiks around them to hear, clearly, "that discourtesy is often a tactic used to throw negotiators off the game. An attempt to irritate a diplomat into bad decisions and missteps. Be easy, my friends."

From the uncomfortable shifting around them, Adam was somehow certain that Livorus had hit the mark.

After forty minutes, the lead Chahiksichahik hunter re-appeared, stating, impassively, "Lesharo and the elders will receive you now." The wording clearly suggested that Livorus was here as a petitioner.

As they moved forwards towards the earthen mound, however, Adam felt his steps slow, subconscious reluctance shackling his feet. A hand landed on Adam's shoulder from behind, and he tensed. And then Livorus himself, that steadying hand on his lictor's shoulder, pressed him further forwards. Adam eyed the mound, swallowed, and ducked his head to enter the tunnel. It looked a little too much like a tomb for his tastes. And brought back very bad memories. Taking refuge from a Persian attack in one of the forts along Domitanus' Wall, panting as he and five other men ducked into a pillbox-like structure, peering cautiously out of one of the windows. Seeing the bodies of dozens of other Judean soldiers on the ground outside, scattered there by an explosion, or a djinn attack . . . only to find a fist slamming through the barricaded window. Recoiling, firing his pistol at it, but the hand and the arm it was attached to, moved like a whip, reaching around, bending at unnatural angles, blindly groping for and finding the throat of one of his companions. Dragging the man, screaming, into the narrow window, ramming him, head-first, into the iron bars there.

Hands. More hands, all reaching up and gripping, ripping. Tearing at his fellow soldier, tearing at the iron bars set in the ancient stone wall . . . . Confusion, consternation as Adam and his fellows dragged the soldier away . . . which gave one of the *ghul* at the window all the opening it needed to wiggle and worm its way through an aperture far too small for a healthy man to fit through. Bonelessly squirming through, its flesh compressing and even tearing off on the jagged remains of the iron bars that the masses of hands had snapped away . . . and then the *ghul* had stood and attacked the defenders, even as another of its fellows birthed itself through the window. And another. And another.

Malicious *awareness* in the dead eyes, even as Adam had fired his gun at the damned thing, over and over again. Screaming from the other men in his squad as a place of safety suddenly became a nightmare, nothing but arms and hands tearing, teeth ripping in the darkness, suddenly not being able to *shoot*, because every one of the *ghul* had a

Judean soldier in its grasp . . . breaking arms, twisting necks, and still the *ghul* came. Most of them still wearing their Judean uniforms, horribly enough, because a Persian magi saw bodies on the ground as an *opportunity*. Magi and other summoners could cram either elemental or demonic spirits into a body, a host vessel of some sort. Elemental spirits tended to be confused by dead human bodies. They needed direction. Demonic spirits? Self-willed, malevolent, and powerful to begin with? Were incredibly difficult to leash . . . not that most magi cared to leash them, other than to keep them from attacking their own forces.

Adam took a deep breath, reminded himself that he was half a world away from Judea, and strode into the mound, putting the image of *hands* reaching out of the darkness out of his mind.

The heart of the mound was actually spacious enough for about forty or fifty people to live, if they weren't picky about how crowded they were, with a hard-packed earthen floor, and a hole in the roof through which smoke from the fire pit at the center of the mound could escape. It was warm under the earth, sheltered from the cold of Martius outside, and filled, as it was, with living bodies. Small stone lamps burned at the edges of the circular room, where various people were engaged in handiwork of various types, and Adam could smell the press of bodies, and the remains of the morning meal, thick in the air around him.

The tribe's chief, Lesharo, sat with the rest of his advisors around the glowing coals of the banked fire pit. There were a half-dozen men around the fire-pit; to Adam's surprise, most of them looked somewhat younger than he'd expected, none older than forty, besides the man who was obviously their leader. Lesharo had a hawk-like face, and iron-gray hair, but seemed older than Livorus, perhaps in his early sixties.

None of the elders rose to greet them. A silent cue as to how much respect would be given to Rome in this meeting. Adam stepped out of the way, falling to the right, standing beside Sigrun now, even as Ehecatl and Ptah-ases stepped to the left, forming a V-shape around and behind Livorus. Honor-guard and body-guards, at once. Ptah-ases even carefully set the curule chair in place for Livorus on the hard-packed floor. And Livorus sat in it, with his back straight, suddenly far more regal than any king. The chair itself was an unspoken message, really. *I am not here as a petitioner. I am here, sitting at my ease, not standing before you uncomfortable on my feet.* And more: *I am not here alone. I bring Rome with me.*

There was almost a minute's pause. "Why does Rome come to us today?" one of the younger men asked, finally breaking the silence. He didn't look any older than eighteen.

Livorus looked at the young man for a moment, his face expressionless. Then he turned and looked directly at Lesharo. "I am Antonius Valerius Livorus, and I am a propraetor of Rome. I was elevated to that post by the personal hand of Caesarion IX, long may he reign. When you speak to me, you speak to him, and Caesarion *is* Rome. I come today to speak with the king of the Chahiksichahiks, Lesharo, and to treat with him honorably and fairly, as men do."

The chieftain's face shifted slightly, and he flicked his eyes in the direction of the adviser who'd spoken. The younger man cleared his throat, and replied, "Then, Antonius Valerius Livorus, propraetor of Rome . . . know that we will hear your words. Why would you treat with us today?"

Ah. Their king does not wish to speak with Livorus today. A calculated slight. Is it to reinforce his power within the tribe, by staging a deliberate provocation, to the face of the Roman envoy? Adam thought. He hated not understanding the nuances of the people around him.

Livorus sighed. Turned, and looked at Ehecatl. "Itztli? If you would be good enough to speak for me?" Still in the Latin that everyone there clearly spoke. But also, it was clear that if the chieftain wished to play games, Livorus could play them just as well, if not better.

The Nahautl man straightened, a flash of amusement touching his dark eyes. He clearly saw all the delicate maneuvering for what it was. Power, prestige, position. Jockeying for dominance. "As you wish, Propraetor," he said, and turned to face the tribal chieftain directly. "I am Ehecatl Itztli. I bear one of the lesser names of Quetzalcoatl, in his aspect of the gentle and merciful west wind, Ehecatl. I honor all of his faces, even the terrible visage of the vengeful morning star." Adam could see a ripple go through the crowd at those words, though he did not understand why. He hoped Ehecatl was catching the subtexts. "I am a Jaguar warrior among my people, and dedicated myself to the defense of Nahautl and the service of Quetzalcoatl and Tezcatlipoca nineteen years ago." All amusement left his face. "Your people, it is said, once lived far south of here, perhaps among my people, and wandered north, when a great flood came. We are cousins, and I ask that you greet me as such."

"You are a slave of Rome," the young advisor said, and Adam watched the chieftain's eyes flicker to the young man again. Adam was uneasy, and he couldn't put his finger on precisely why. Then, realization hit. *Wait. All the dossiers said that these people revere age and wisdom. If the chieftain is listening to this youngster . . . there's something important about him. But what? Is he a shaman? I can't tell by his clothing . . . .*

Ehecatl's expression tightened faintly, but he exhaled, and tried again. "I am a Praetorian in the service of Rome. But I have also fought in the service of my people for longer than you have been alive, young one." His dark eyes glittered in the low light. "Is respect for age and experience dead among the Chahiksichahiks? I would not have thought it possible. Not among a people so attuned to . . . tradition." His glance swept around the dark interior of the mound-house. Adam thought the words a fairly stinging rebuke, though quietly spoken. Ehecatl turned his attention back to Lesharo, ignoring the young man completely now. "Chieftain and elders, a young woman of Marcomanni was kidnapped four days ago. She was seen being dragged into a vehicle, and that vehicle was spotted several times between here and Marcomanni." He paused, and Adam wondered if his fellow lictor would mention that they'd received a tip, apparently from someone within the Chahiksichahiks' kingdom, stating that the girl had been brought there. He was relieved, however, when Ehecatl went on, mildly, "It is in the interests of Rome, and of everyone in the region, to see if this account can be verified, and to see to the young woman's safe return. Have you seen her, or do you know of her whereabouts?" Ehecatl produced a black-and-white photograph. Adam already knew what it looked like—a young Marcomanni woman, with dark hair for one of her people, laughing as she leaned against her horse.

The various leaders barely glanced at the picture, before shaking their heads in the negative. "No," the young man replied, for the others.

Which was when Sigrun dropped the tip of her spear into the hard-packed earth of the mound floor, and a distant clap of thunder accompanied the gesture. Looking up, Adam could see the round patch of blue sky above rapidly beginning to gray over.

Livorus looked at Ehecatl. "Would you be so good as to introduce my other lictor, who is also present as a representative of Nova Germania today?"

"We know what she is. Woman. Outlander. Goth." The young speaker cut in. Each word served, in a way, to denigrate Sigrun's status. At least, to categorize it, by sinking it, strata by strata, below his own. And in responding directly to Livorus, rather than to Ehecatl, he broke the façade of polite disengagement by the leaders.

Livorus, for his part, didn't deign to look at the young man. Ehecatl smiled without mirth. "Yes, and again, no. You see, Sigrun Caetia is a lictor of Rome —"

"What manner of man requires a woman to guard him?" That was marked with a sneer.

Livorus sighed. Adam was tempted to do so, himself, but kept his eyes on their surroundings, and the movements of the people around them. Checking their body-language. "Ehecatl?" Sigrun said, quietly, and took off her helmet, the rune-born light beginning to shimmer under her skin, as thunder once more shook the earth. Closer, this time. "I'll finish the introductions, if you don't mind."

Wearing that nimbus of light like a cloak, and her spear still in her right hand, point down, grounded on the earth, Sigrun stepped forward. "You were given the opportunity to deal with us fairly, and in Roman fashion. With civility. With words. With reason. I am god-born. Tyr One-Hand is my grandsire. God of justice. God of laws. God of war and of storms. I know when lies are spoken before me, and lies have been spoken here. You have seen this girl. She is of my people, and thus falls under my protection. Now tell me where she is, before the civility of Rome falters further."

Adam gave the elders credit. They flinched, but they didn't give ground. But this time, it was their leader who spoke, directly. "And what would you do, god-born? Fight us?"

"It always amazes me," Ptah-ases commented, once more in Hellene, *"how quickly they stop seeing her as a woman."*

Livorus held up a hand to still his lictors. Sigrun stared at the chief, and replied, calmly, "Dueling with you would be dishonorable, but if you attack me, I am well within my rights to defend myself." Her eyes narrowed. "Where is your shaman? I do not see one here. Is he with the girl, perhaps conducting rituals meant to purify her?"

A flicker of glances, and then, hastily, another lie. This one evident even to Adam. "There is no reason to be alarmed. There was no kidnapping. She wished to marry one of our tribe, and she is considered underage by Gothic law. She feared her family's anger—" This, again, from the young man off to the side.

"If that one opens his mouth again to lie," Livorus said, conversationally, gesturing at the young man, and speaking to Ehecatl, "please tell the king and his elders that I request that they remove his tongue and present it to me as a gift. In reparation for my time . . . and Rome's time . . . that his words waste." Unease in the faces of the elders on the council. Clearly, they didn't think that they could reprimand the young man. Not even the chieftain looked ready to chastise him yet.

Livorus exhaled and abandoned the pretense, looking directly at Lesharo now. "I would have asked for permission to search your lands. To speak with your people directly. You are leaving me very little in the way of choices, King Lesharo." Again, the very careful application of a title that the Chahiksichahiks did not themselves use. But in using it, Livorus was according the man the respect due to a sovereign head of state. And also, at the same time, holding him accountable for all the doings of his people. A delicate thing, that. "You have the reputation of a reasonable and good leader of your people, if one bound to ancient traditions. Do I need to demonstrate the traditions of my people? Would you see the iron fist of Rome? Or can we come to an agreement that allows the girl to walk free?"

Another flicker of a glance between the old chief and the young man, and the chieftain, reluctantly, it seem, opened his mouth to speak. "It is the demand of the gods," he began, lifting his hands and spreading them. "We *must* obey."

"And it is the policy of Rome," Livorus said, grimly, "and has been for over fourteen hundred years, to allow subject nations freedom to worship their own gods, but with one caveat: that there will be no human sacrifices made. That is the sole exception to the Edict of Diocletian." He paused, for a moment, and said, quietly, "Ehecatl? Would you please enlighten these good people as to what happened when the Nahautl rose in rebellion four hundred years ago, and some of your priests wished to go back to making sacrifices of captives taken in border skirmishes with Novo Gaul?"

Ehecatl's expression didn't change. "The regional militia based in Novo Gaul and Nova Germania marched south, with several full Roman legions alongside them. The entire town in which the sacrifices were being performed was razed to the ground, not one stone left standing atop the others. The children and women were taken as slaves back to Rome. Every man was executed, and the priests of Tlaloc and the other gods who had cut the hearts from the sacrifices? They were crucified, along the road leading away from the city."

Adam spoke then; it was out of turn, but he *had* to say it. "There is honor in showing courage," he said, distantly, keeping his hands at his sides. "There's a value in showing your people your courage, your willingness, to slight Rome to keep their traditions alive. My people have walked that path before. But it's the courage of a man approaching a tiger's cage, and turning to tell others, 'Come and see! I defy its claws, and it does nothing!'" He paused. "Is it wisdom to poke the beast with a stick?" That's what it really struck him as. The chieftain might have been convinced to go along with this as a way of uniting other tribes behind him, impressing allies among the other petty kingships of Caesaria Aquilonis . . . who seemed to take turns daring each other to go closer and closer to the caged beast . . . but sooner or later, the tiger *would* lash out with a heavy paw, and then what?

Livorus passed a hand over his brow, wiping away sweat. They were working to redirect the chieftain's mind here. Negotiations were always tense business. And in this case, half the people in this large room were armed. "You can tell your priests and shaman," he said, not unkindly, "what we told the people of Nahautl and Tawantinsuyu and the Quechan provinces, hundreds of years ago. That the gods of Rome are more powerful than their gods."

"I don't see your Roman gods here," the younger advisor replied, sharply, before the chieftain could answer.

"Shiriki! Be silent!"

It was the first time the chieftain had shown any temper at all, but his words didn't stop the younger man from continuing on, his eyes narrow, "I dreamed the dream, Lesharo! I saw the Morning Star, and he told me it was time for the sacrifice. The shaman and I performed the divinations. We listened to the voices of the gods on the wind, and they told us that the *true* sacrifice was needed, not just the ritual one that we perform every year." He turned his head aside and spat, a calculated insult. "I don't see the vaunted gods of Rome. I see only a Goth woman who dares to speak for the feeble gods of her people."

Sigrun's attention had been captured. "Do you challenge me?" she said, quietly. "And which god is yours, that I might know my opponent?" It sounded . . . ritualistic. Formal.

"Shakura, the sun, is *my* grandfather, and I speak for him here." Flash of pride there, as the man lifted his head . . . and the sun suddenly pierced down through the gray haze of clouds overhead. Blinding shafts of light pierced through the mound's smoke opening, as if the sun had suddenly reached its zenith.

"*Harah,*" Adam swore, grimly. *He's god-born. No wonder he can speak so far out of turn. No wonder the elders are deferring to him.*

The man lifted up off the ground, hovering in mid-air, his body suddenly suffused by flame. "Sigrun—" Adam started to move towards her.

"Formal duel," she called back. "I have to answer his challenge. Find the girl!"

And with that, she, too, lifted off the ground, a cold wind racing in through the mound's tunnel and smoke opening, racing around in a circle, coiling tightly, and dousing the drowsing fire in its pit. "Outside!" Lesharo, the chieftain, shouted, and the younger man, Shiriki, laughed and rose up through the smoke vent, into the sky above . . . and Adam flinched and looked away as a golden pillar of fire descended from on high, slamming down into Sigrun's form, showering past her to land on the packed earth floor.

Almost everyone inside screamed and ran for the single tunnel exit; Adam had to drop his shoulder and stand against a tide of humanity, to avoid being trampled, and squinted up at the hole in the roof, tears in his eyes from the searing light that had just shone into the darkness, and dazzling violet afterimages obscuring his vision. He could just make out two tiny figures in the sky overhead.

Livorus, for his part, had stepped in front of the council of elders once more preventing them from joining the exodus for the entrance. He held the *fasces* still in one hand, loosely. "I rather take *that* as an admission of guilt," he said, dryly, sidestepping the rush of fire as neatly as if he were merely out for an evening stroll and wished to avoid a bucket of water being thrown at a yowling cat. "Where's the girl, King Lesharo? No more games, if you would."

The chieftain raised both of his hands, frustration and anger written plainly on his face now. "She's being prepared for the ritual, over a mile from here," he admitted, grimly. "I told them that the yearly symbolic sacrifice to the Morning Star should be enough. They said this would be a spiritual reawakening for our people. Like the Ghost Dance of a century ago, only . . . more true. And *necessary*."

Ehecatl stiff-armed a fleeing person away from Livorus, and snapped out, "Your Morning Star is much like Quetzalcoatl's dark aspect, yes? Somehow, my people still believe in him without sacrifices!"

Livorus made a dismissive gesture. "To be honest, I don't really care right now. Have some of your men take us to where she is, or just point in the general direction." Livorus' eyes were glacial. "But rest assured, we will revisit this subject at another time."

Lesharo grimaced and pointed to the southwest. Livorus snapped his fingers, and he and the lictors broke out of the mound, just as white light split the sky, simultaneous with a clap of thunder, and rain poured down, lashed by wind. Adam stared upwards, seeing a roiling mass of clouds seethe in from the east, misty tendrils reaching out like grasping hands, encircling the pair of aerial duelists . . . and then the clouds tore apart as another beam of fire poured down from the heavens, and the pair, who were almost wrestling in mid-air, vanished as the fire concealed their forms. Ptah-ases cursed in Egyptian. "That . . . is not good."

"She can hold her own," Livorus said, sharply. "The girl's our priority! Move!" The propraetor, pushing fifty years of age, kilted up the heavy hem of his formal toga, and, with the speed of a younger man, began to run through the increasingly slippery mud, in the direction that the chieftain had pointed. He was an ex-legionnaire and still in good trim, but his three lictors rapidly began to outpace him.

Adam glanced to see which of them should hold back and protect the propraetor, and Ehecatl waved him on. "Go! I'm with him!"

Adam took the man at his word, and increased the length of his strides. He easily outpaced Ptah-ases; the sorcerer was in good shape, but he was in his forties, and had spent much of his life locked in study and contemplation, honing and shaping his mental gifts. Adam, on the other hand, was just twenty-five, and had spent the last six years of his life in daily training for just such activities. As such, he was the first over the small hill, rain soaking his body, and another vivid white flash of light throwing the world into stark relief as he looked down into the prairie beyond.

A wooden scaffold had been erected off to the south, about three hundred feet away; three wooden supports, all leaning in on each other, but driven firmly into the earth. He could just make out the squirming, fighting body of a girl there, her arms over her head, tied to the supports of the scaffold. From her jerking, erratic movements, she was probably on her tip-toes, at best.

All too aware of the target he made at the top of the hill, against the sky, Adam dropped to a crouch, drawing his pistol and cocking it as he surveyed the area; there was a group of men there, not far from the scaffold, trying to keep a bonfire lit in spite of the driving rain, and taking torches from it. He wasn't close enough to make out what they were saying, but it surely looked as if an argument was breaking out, from the gesticulations.

Ptah made it up the hill next, breathing hard. "I thought," the Egyptian shouted over the howling wind, wiping at the rain that had made the kohl around his eyes run, "that they were supposed to time the sacrifice with the rising of the morning star on the fifth day."

"This isn't the purification part?" Adam asked, his head jerking up.

"No. That's mostly done in the village, as far as I've read. This? This is where they use the torches for the final purification of her genitals and then touch her with their war clubs . . . and then they all stand back and start shooting arrows at her. The man who dreamed the Morning Star dream gets the honor of the first shot."

Adam pointed upwards. "I think he's a little busy right now."

"They're already moving on ahead of schedule. I don't think they're going to wait on him. Not if appeasing the gods is so very *necessary*." Ptah grimaced.

"There are at least twenty men there. And some young boys, too."

"This is how we teach the young what's important, yes?" Ptah growled it out. "Do you see muskets?"

"Three. No. Four, just the guards. Everyone else has bows."

"Thank the Aten for old-time religion."

The clouds tore asunder again, as another huge burst of light exploded in the sky, like a star going nova. The sphere of light and energy radiated out in all directions, and Adam was simultaneously blinded and deafened as the air tore asunder. The shockwave drove him to the ground . . . and then the abused air, abhorring a vacuum, retreated back the way it had come. For an instant, he thought he'd be pulled off his feet and into the air, following it, and reached back, grabbing Ptah's shoulder to help anchor them. A glance upwards showed him that the explosion had left smoke behind, like the dim and misty images of a nebula taken by a space-based telescope. And also showed him two figures tumbling now, limply, arms and legs wide and uncontrolled, towards the earth. *Harah. Shit, shit, shit.* "Tell me we have a plan, Ptah. Can you catch her?"

"Aten. No. Not until she drops within sixty feet of me, and by then, I think we're going to be up to our necks. All we can do is hope she wakes up on her own." Ptah gestured sharply at the field in front of them. "You take the ones on the left, I take the ones on the right, and we both pray to our respective gods very loudly."

"I think I can manage that part." Adam gritted his teeth. He couldn't help his partner. Not at the moment.

But he could help the girl.

"Cover me. I'll go in first," he said, and Ptah made a gesture with his left hand. Adam could *feel* energy crackling around him, and shuddered a little, before turning and running, crouched low, in a zig-zag pattern for the group of men carrying the muskets and bows. The Praetorians had few rules of engagement, generally speaking. He didn't *have* to give these people fair warning. But Adam's general sense of ethics told him he'd sleep better tonight if he did. They weren't soldiers. They were . . . misled civilians. "Stop!" he shouted, over the wind, as he found a hummock of dirt and rocks to crouch behind, twenty-five yards from where one of the men had just shoved a burning torch against the girl's groin. Purifying her with flames. *God damn it.* He could see the girl's mouth open, but the scream was stolen by the wind. He drew his gun, and thumbed the safety off. "Drop the weapons! Now! On the ground!"

The high priest, who, like most of the others, held a bow with an arrow already on the string, turned. Identifiable mainly by his age—his hair, in its scalp-lock, was pure white—and the elaborate markings on his leathers, the priest looked grim. Stared at him, directly, and at Ptah, coming up from the right. Then up into the sky, where Adam knew, distantly, two figures were *still* tumbling, a measure of how high up they'd been . . . and shouted at the other men around him. Adam didn't speak the language, but he didn't need to, in order to understand as the men put arrows to strings. Half of them aiming at the girl, still, and half of them spinning to aim at him and Ptah.

Adam ducked behind his hummock of ground and felt at least one arrow bounce off the shield of raw energy Ptah had put around him. The winds were, at least, sending half the arrows astray. *One more thing to be grateful for,* he thought, distantly. Found a target. Center of mass. Pulled the trigger, twice. A forty-five caliber bullet did a hell of a lot of damage to a body, and he'd opted for hollow-points today, which made for a much larger exit wound than an entry point. He ducked again, this time as musket balls slammed into the hummock of ground in front of him . . . crackling with energy, the balls were actually white-hot. *Son of a bitch.* He could see the puffs of steam rising in front of him as water trickled into the holes in which they were lodged. *Guess I know how they were enchanted,* he thought, and stayed down for a moment, finding his next target. Watched as two of the men tried to raise their guns and fire on Ptah, only to have the metal of their musket barrels collapse inwards. Seal. They didn't realize it in time, and pulled the flintlock's triggers anyway . . .

. . . and the muskets exploded in their faces. They screamed, dropping the weapons and clawed at their bloody eyes and cheeks, blinded. Adam took that moment to come back up, and fired again, two more bullets, at another man who'd turned to shoot an arrow at the girl. Pure muscle memory; he'd done this a thousand times both in practice and in real battles. His aim was a little high, however, and he caught the man in the back of the head, which resulted in an explosive shower of gore. *Four*, Adam counted. Four bullets down for him, four men total, out of the fight . . . and then he ducked back down again, swearing, as the men began to spread out, looking for cover of their own, firing arrows right at him. At least the other two with muskets weren't able to reload the weapons. Ptah had melted these muzzles down, as well. Unfortunately, the men switched to knives, and started to move in on the sorcerer. Adam risked a quick glance at the scaffold, and swore, again, as he saw that the girl, dangling limply by her wrists, had been pierced by arrows in a half a dozen places.

His stomach twisted. The dossier had been brutally frank about the nature of the ritual. It was a fertility rite, in its most basic sense. It was a re-enactment of how the Morning Star had, supposedly, in the first days of the world, tracked down the Evening Star, and raped her, breaking the 'stone teeth' in her vagina, and from that rape, had begotten on her the first human, a woman. The men of the Chahiksichahiks were, thus, symbolically, the Morning Star. The girl became, ritually, the Evening Star. And they were thus, penetrating her body with arrows consecrated to the Morning Star, raping her metaphorically while sacrificing her. When she was dead, they'd lay her to rest in the ground, after making sure as much of her blood was spilled into the hungry earth as possible. It wasn't all that dissimilar from ritual sacrifices performed in ancient times in Europa and the Fertile Crescent. But the problem was, not only wasn't it allowed . . . it wasn't *needed*. Human sacrifice had been forbidden everywhere that Rome held sway for two thousand years, *and crops still grew.*

Adam tamped down on the rage. Put it back behind his eyes, where it would add to his focus, not detract from it. And leaned out to fire again. *She could still be alive. Just . . . have to get to her.* He aimed and fired, smoothly. Another man died, and he couldn't let the reality of that penetrate through his combat haze.

Sigrun, in the meantime, had had risen up through the mound entrance, following the god-born of Shakura, wind coiling around her . . . only to have an almost liquid mass of fire pour down on her from above. She gritted her teeth against the pain, trying not to scream. The fire around her burned so hot that it instantly consumed all the oxygen around her, and her lungs burned almost as much as her skin as she reflexively burst up and out of the cylinder of flame, tumbling through the air, supported by will and intention, and nothing more. Her feathered cloak was no more than a web of charred net now, and her chain mail and metal helmet were melting in places, scorching her padded undertunic. Sigrun swore and knocked the helmet off and shrugged out of the chain shirt, swooping and spinning in air to dodge any incoming attacks. She let them fall to the ground with her spear, the wooden haft of which was on fire. Her skin was blistered in places, blackened in others, and it *hurt*. Fire always did; there was no escaping that.

She acknowledged the pain, and then grimly put it aside, reaching out with will and god-born powers, tearing at the sky. Clouds pulled back into place across the horizon and she directed the lightning that was the heavenly twin of her usual spear at her opponent.

Natural philosophers still didn't understand how lightning *really* formed. Oh, they knew it was electricity. They'd talk about positive and negative charges in the atmosphere, and the formation of linkages between them, and conductivity . . . but what *caused* it, they really didn't know. Sigrun didn't understand it any better than they did, but she could feel the invisible leader stroke comprised of negative energy descending, and guided it for her target, let it pass through him to the ground . . . and then watched as the *return stroke* of power, from the earth to the cloud, raced back up, with three times the force. Air displaced with physical force, slamming her to the side, and deafening her for a moment, but she'd been braced and ready for it.

The lightning stroke would have killed any normal human, and left a fractal pattern of jagged, angry burns across half his body, but her enemy was as god-born as she was. As such, she arced upwards, and, with him still stunned, slammed a shoulder into him with her full bodyweight and all the inertia of an inbound missile.

Physics was physics, even for the god-born. Two objects could not occupy the same space, and when they met, the object with more mass and inertia tended to win. The man hadn't been able to brace, stunned as he was; as such, she hit him, and they *both* went flying in the direction of her charge. Sigrun scrambled to solidify her advantage in spite of the way her bones creaked at the impact, wrestling with him in the air, reaching for a knife that was in her boot to put it to his throat, only to find his fingers wrapped around her own. She slammed a knee into his groin, the steel *poleyns* over her knee, hot enough to burn unshielded skin, adding to the damage she could do. His fingers slackened as he doubled over, his eyes going vague. Her fingers snapped free, closed on her knife, and stabbed upwards, under a rib and into lung.

Her opponent threw himself backwards, and in clear desperation, still mid-air, spread his arms wide and arched backwards, looking up to the sky. Sigrun's eyes widened as he screamed "Shakura! Grandfather! Aid me! My life for my people!" *Oh, gods. He's sacrificing himself. His blood's already spilled . . . .*

His body exploded into flame, and he curled in on himself, fetal-style, the flames going white, too intense to look at. A piece of the sun, right here, blazing heat scorching out in every direction. Sigrun *flung* herself away, all too aware of the Hellene legend of Icarus. *Look what happened to him, when he flew too close to the sun,* part of her mind remarked distantly, as she dove away, purely ballistic . . . and then the man's body exploded in a fireball. Like a star going nova, the flame went in every direction, and was preceded by a shockwave that hit her like a wall of pure force, sending her tumbling in air. And then the fire hit, scorching her skin, and for an instant, for Sigrun, the world went *away.*

Dim awareness of wind. Cool rain, splashing on skin that was screaming with pain, somewhere at the far reaches of consciousness. Wind, blowing in her face, pressure against her body. Sigrun opened her eyes, and vaguely realized that she was spread-eagle in the air, falling towards the ground below, in the odd, slow-fast, dream-like state of pure freefall. She could see the patchwork of the fields of Novo Gaul to the east, darker greens of small wood stands, lighter greens of new-planted soy, browns where some fields had just been plowed for wheat, the large, wild expanses of open prairie, a herd of buffalo, like a brown wave, in the distance . . . high enough up to see how the horizon curved *away* in both directions, and still falling . . . . *Falling. Wait. Why am I falling? Why do I hurt — oh, the duel, the girl — shit.* Memory returned, with a vengeance. *Where are the other lictors? Where's Livorus?*

She got control back, not daring to touch her own face or skin yet, when even the pressure of air against her flesh made every nerve in her body scream. She pulled herself upright in the air, and looking around frantically, spotted the body of her opponent, still limp and falling, several hundred yards from her. She circled to keep an eye on him, while darting glances at the situation on the ground. She caught a glimpse of Livorus, crouching seemingly alone near the top of a hill. She couldn't see Ehecatl, but she knew the Nahautl man had probably made himself invisible, and was ranging out around Livorus . . . there. Someone had moved in, flanking around Adam and Ptah, and Ehecatl's invisibility field dropped as the man moved in behind the assailant, and the obsidian knife plunged home.

She could see the rest of the situation clearly. Adam and Ptah, exchanging spells and bullets with the locals. A three-timbered scaffold, at the edge of the long field . . . Sigrun's gray eyes focused in on that, with the clarity of a hawk's. She could see the girl's limp form. Could see the long-shafted arrows protruding from her body. A cold and cleansing rage went through her, clearing her mind, and she landed in the middle of the field, ignoring the winds that attended her as they laid into her burned flesh like an icy whip. Just then, the body of the other god-born hit the ground a hundred yards from her, shattering into chunks of charcoal on impact, the blackened bones protruding through the ruined flesh. An eyeblink's moment to think, *He sacrificed himself for this ritual. For his people. That's a degree of fanaticism we've rarely seen in modern times. What is going on here?*

The thoughts were dim and distant, however, and she didn't have time to ponder them. Her spear, haft blackened from god-born fire, snapped to her hand from where it had fallen to the ground, and a half-dozen arrows winged towards her. She slashed at them with a gust of wind, though one managed to graze her left shoulder, and she could feel hot blood pouring from that line of fire, mingling with the raw, dull ache of the burns all along her arms and torso. *Now would be a good time for the others to take advantage of the distraction I'm providing,* she thought, and raised her voice above the howl of the wind. *"Stormum ábéatne,"* she called out her challenge, *"Beoth gethancol, or losian." Storm-beaten ones, be suppliant, or perish.*

At the back of the crowd, a hundred feet away. she could see the wind-lashed high priest, still holding his bow in his hand. Could see his teeth bare, as he set arrow to string as he aimed, not at her, but inexplicably, high into the air. Could feel *power* suddenly, singing in the air, and she half-closed her eyes and shouted to the others, "Another god-born! Their high priest is god-born!" *This was not in the dossier. Assuming I live, I'm going to have a few words with the people in Intelligence who prepared the briefing materials for this mission . . . .*

The shaman let his arrow fly, and Sigrun watched as it turned into a red streak in the air, arcing up, straight overhead . . . and at the zenith of its arc, as it tipped and dropped down, it split apart. Each new dot of light split apart again. And again. Dividing into a rain of fire, each a red-hot falling star that tore at the very air as they screamed towards the earth. Towards all of them.

For a dumbstruck moment, Sigrun had no idea what to do. Part of her screamed that she needed to dive for her new partner, Adam ben Maor, and shield him. Part of her shouted to charge the god-born shaman. Another voice said she needed to fall back and cover Livorus. And she had only seconds to decide. *Ehecatl is with Livorus. The propraetor is protected. Ben Maor is capable, but he's . . . human.* "Ptah!" Sigrun shouted. "Shield yourself!"

She flew across the intervening space, her feet barely skimming the ground, and landed atop Adam, driving the man to the ground, getting her body between him and the incoming meteor storm. Shards of sky-born rock slammed into the ground around them like hail, sending up clods of dirt from tiny impact craters. Splatters of liquid hot dirt, turned into microscopic beads of glass, fanned up, one just beside her face, splattering across her cheek in a feathery fan of pain. And she cried out in agony as one of the white-hot chunks of rock slammed into her back. No larger than a musket ball, she was fairly sure it broke her shoulder blade. *No matter. It's not a mortal wound. I'll heal.* She rolled off of ben Maor and staggered back to her feet, dazed, trying to get her bearings once more. She couldn't move her left arm at all, and her skin felt as if it were cracking off her face and torso.

Ptah was down, the sorcerer crumpled on the ground, hammered by a half-dozen of those meteorite impacts. "Are you all right?" Sigrun asked Adam, trying to focus.

"Fine," he said, rolling up to a crouch. "What about *you*? You took one of those in things in the *back*—"

Doesn't matter. "Don't worry about me. We have to kill the priest. He dies, the rest of them will stand down, I think—"

They both said the last part simultaneously, paused, and then, immediately, they both started talking again. "Can bullets kill him?" Adam asked.

"Yes. Bullets can kill almost anything. He's not a monster. It won't take special metals." She took an unsteady step forward, feeling searing pain in her shoulder ignite at the jolting shock of the step. "Technically, I . . . should be challenging him to a duel." *Except I just fought one, and am in no condition for a second. Not for a day or three.*

"You're in no shape for that right now." Adam's voice was sharp. "The last one beat you half to death. Another one will finish the job."

Not arguing, she pulled, in exhaustion, at the roiling clouds overhead. Felt the negative charge of the precursor strike, and tried, desperately, to aim it properly. She wasn't holding her spear. Not being in contact with a weapon made of metal made this much harder, and her concentration was shot.

Lightning lanced down in between them and the high priest, sending all the other men running for cover. The thunderclap had pure physical force behind it, and Adam, who'd turned his face away from the brilliant white light, turned his head back, took careful aim . . . and fired directly on the high priest, who was already setting another arrow to his string. He'd had time to reload his pistol. Five of the six bullets were discharged, aimed at center mass of the target.

The bullets reached their target before the string could be pulled all the way back, and the shaman fell to the ground, dying. The dull report of the bullets seemed . . . anticlimactic, somehow. Sigrun groaned, and let the storm die. "Get the girl," she told Adam, dully. "I'll be right behind you." She turned and looked back at the hill. Ehecatl and Livorus were picking their way down; Ehecatl had one arm raised across his chest, and she thought she could see blood staining his upper sleeve. His tattoos offered a certain measure of protection, but he was far from invulnerable.

None of them were, really. "Ptah needs help!" she called to Ehecatl, and gestured with her good arm towards the fallen Egyptian, before heading, step by jolting, painful step, off in Adam's wake.

Adam ran forward, gun still in hand, warily keeping an eye on the various men with bows, most of whom were staring at the bodies of their two god-born in total shock. At the scaffold, he holstered the weapon and clamped down, hard, on the horror he felt at the sight there. "I've got you," he told the girl. He wasn't sure if she was alive, let alone conscious, but it was good practice to *talk* to a patient or a victim before putting hands on them. He reached up, trying to find a spot on her bare and bloody body that there wasn't an arrow protruding from, leaned her against his own torso to support her dead weight, and pulled out a knife, flicking out the blade to saw at the rope. When that snapped, she sagged limply against him, and he lowered the girl to the muddy ground, gently, trying to get an inventory for first-aid. He put two fingers against her throat, and was surprised when he felt a faint throb there. Weak, erratic, faint, a heart fluttering out its last beats. She wasn't breathing, though. "No, you don't," he told her, tossing his knife aside. "You're not dying on us. Not today."

The hell of it was, he wasn't even sure where to *start*. If he pulled the arrows, he could do more damage removing them. He wasn't a surgeon. But one of them was in her chest, another in her left arm, a third in her belly, and she had two in a thigh. At least one had clipped the girl's cheek, leaving a slash there, too. The one in the chest would interfere with chest compressions, if he needed to try to do her heart's work for her. *First thing's first*, Adam thought, and checked her airway. No obstructions. He leaned down, and gave her two breaths, and checked her heart again.

Nothing.

"*Perfututum.*" Latin was wonderful for profanity, he found. "*Lehizdayen.* Come on." He moved gingerly into position, and, grimacing, started chest compressions. The girl's body was small, and all too fragile in appearance. He needed to keep the blood circulating to her brain and her heart tissues, with fresh oxygen. And the problematic arrows in her chest and stomach would just have to *wait*.

Compressions, then he slipped back to the side, and put his mouth over hers again, pinching the nose shut, to breathe for her again. Not even paying attention to the others around him at the moment; he couldn't watch his back *and* perform CPR at the same time. He had to trust in the others.

Light touch of a hand on the back of his neck, as he prepared to move back for more compressions. "Her heart beats more strongly," Sigrun told him, kneeling beside him. "You can stop the chest-compressions now."

"What—how do you know?" He was disoriented, thrown out of his focus.

"I know. I can always tell if a wound is mortal. These . . . almost. But not quite." Her rune-marking were glowing again, and even as he watched, he could see the burns and cuts on her arms and face starting to heal. Turning from black-charred ash and blisters into pink, new, healthy skin, as the light within her consumed the wounds. She reached out—slowly, and with evident pain; the wound in her back still hampered her, it seemed. Her fingers closed around the arrow in the girl's chest. "I would pull these myself, but I cannot right now. I need your hands."

Adam stared at her. "You're mad. If I pull the arrows, it'll make it *worse*. I'm not a surgeon."

"No. You're not. But it'll be fine. Better now, than when she wakes up. Less pain for her." Sigrun's smile was wan. "Adam. Please. Trust me." She pointed at the arrows. "Pull them. They can't be in the wounds for what I intend to do."

I have no idea what in god's name she's talking about, but all right. "Fine. I can follow orders." He set his teeth and put a hand on the bare skin. Braced. Tested the angle, gingerly, and then pulled the arrow out. One fluid motion, feeling resistance from the bones and softer tissues as he did. Then he threw the arrow to the side. Blood trickled out—a fairly good sign that Sigrun was right, and that the girl's heart still beat. He moved on to the next, pulling the arrow from her belly—it had lodged in the liver, he thought, as if the shot in the lung wasn't bad enough—and that was when he realized that pellucid light was radiating out around him. His head jerked up, and he saw that Sigrun had put hand on the girl's shoulder, and now sagged forward with a low groan of pain.

"What the *hell?*" Adam demanded, and reached forward. Jerked her hand free of the girl's body . . . and saw *no wound* in the girl's chest. Blood, yes, smeared everywhere. .. .but nothing more than a thin, puckered, white scar. He turned Sigrun by her arm and shoulder towards him . . . and saw, to his horror, blood pouring from a deep wound in her chest, revealed by her leather bodice. "Sigrun—"

"Won't . . . kill me." Her voice was tight, and her face taut with the pain. "Please. You're making this . . . much more difficult. Slower. Just . . . pull the other arrows."

Adam swallowed, hard, and bit down on all his questions and objections. And pulled the rest of the damned arrows, watching, in mild awe, as every one of the girl's wounds healed before his eyes . . . transferred to Sigrun's body. The woman knelt, curled in on herself, white light suffusing her, flinching a little as she took each wound from the girl. Bled for the girl. "You've got to let me put pressure on those," Adam said, feeling completely useless, putting his hands on his partner's shoulders.

"I'll . . . heal." Sigrun slumped forwards.

The girl's eyes flew open, and she stared up at the now-cloudless sky, and then bolted upright, awkwardly crossing her thin arms over her chest. She looked around wildly, and Adam hastily pulled off his cloak, offering it to her, as Livorus moved up behind them. Adam glanced back, and saw that Ehecatl was helping Ptah to sit up, in the distance, and that the various Chahiksichahiks men had all scattered at this point. *Wise decision*, he thought, dryly.

"What . . . what's going . . . I thought I was going to die," the girl whispered, clutching the cloak to her. "I hurt so much, and then there was only darkness. I thought I'd see the faces of the gods when I died."

"You did not die," Sigrun rasped, and Adam could see a flesh-wound in her arm, taken from the girl, healing. The bleeding had stopped, and a puckered scab formed . . . and, as Sigrun evidently concentrated, the scab smoothed. Paled. Turned into a white rune-mark under her skin, blazing with inner light. Another sign of her covenant with her god, her bond with him. Adam watched now as Sigrun hesitantly reached out to put a still-bloody hand on the girl's shoulder, as if she thought the young woman would shy away. "You are safe, little one. I swear that on the name of Tyr One-Hand."

Livorus looked down at the girl now. "Frittigil Chatti?"

A numb nod from the girl. Livorus crouched down and offered her his hand, not taking visible offense as she shrank away, and huddled closer to Sigrun. "I'm Propraetor Antonius Livorus. You're safe now, and we're going to take very good care of you." He stood back up again. "Sigrun, my dear, you're all right?"

"The wounds were deep. But they will heal." Sigrun straightened where she sat, weariness in her face, and all the rune-born light fading from her now entirely.

"Excellent. Is our god-born priest here yet numbered among the living?" Livorus gestured in the direction of the shaman who'd called down the meteorites from the sky.

Sigrun shuddered, and Adam put his hands on her shoulders for a moment, cautiously, being respectful of the still-raw burns. "His wounds are mortal, but he yet lives." Her voice was barely audible.

"Good. I think I would like to ask him, before he passes, why he thought that trying to provoke *war* with the entirety of Nova Germania and Novo Gaul was a wise decision." Livorus stepped away, heading towards where the crumpled body of the shaman lay.

The Roman's sandals squelched through the mud as he picked his way to the fallen priest's body. He stood there for a moment, looking down at the man. The white hair was combed back from the priest's face into the customary scalp lock used in this small kingdom, and he could see splotches of crimson spreading across the leathers covering the man's chest. The dark eyes were glazed, and the man's breathing was rapid and shallow. Livorus tucked up the hem of his toga and crouched down beside the man's body. "Not a good day," he said, quietly. He wasn't sure if the man could hear him, or if he were already past hearing any earthly voice. "I could order a punitive expedition into your lands for what you've done. I could have your entire kingdom put to the sword. I would greatly prefer not to have to do so." He paused. "Give me a reason why I should not. Tell me why your gods demanded this ritual. If, in fact, they did so. Or tell me it was all for your own aggrandizement. Your own power." He put as much persuasion into his voice as he could muster. To convince this dying man to give him *something* he could use.

For a moment, he thought the man was far beyond the reach of any words. Then the head turned slightly, and the glazed eyes looked past him. Through him. "The Morning Star . . ." The words were barely audible. "My grandfather's father . . . ."

"Yes?" Livorus leaned closer, trying to *will* the words out of the man. *Don't lie. Don't die with a lie on your lips. Give me something I can use.*

". . . came to my dreams, too. Told me . . . darkness was coming. That he was weak. Couldn't . . . protect us. Couldn't protect . . . himself. That he needed . . . a sacrifice. He needed our belief. Our faith. The faith of . . . all . . . the people." Blood trickled from the man's lips, caught and channeled by the sere lines that bracketed his mouth. "Darkness is coming, Roman." The eyes closed, then re-opened, vaguely. "Do you know . . . where your gods are?"

"What?" Livorus asked, nonplussed. The question made no sense.

"Doesn't . . . matter. He had . . . his sacrifice. My blood . . . will save . . . my people."

"No! Not yet—damnit." Livorus swore when he realized that the old priest had already passed beyond where his voice could reach. "What does that even *mean*? How am I supposed to keep your people alive if that's the only reason you can give me?" He realized that he was berating a dead man, and sighed, taking a breath to calm himself. Looked down. Saw the blood from the corpse, staining the mud around the body, and exhaled again, forcefully. "If all that was required was someone's blood in the earth, you might have saved us all the trouble and killed yourself, to begin with," Livorus muttered, savagely, standing back up again. "Sacrificed yourself, someone from your own tribe. Not some poor child, whose people dwell seven hundred miles from yours. Who have had little, if anything, to do with yours. Your people are surrounded by Gauls, not by the Goths. None of this makes sense."

Livorus gave the corpse a weary glance. Articulating his arguments out loud usually helped him see patterns, tendencies, and motivations. And he usually did this in the privacy of his own rooms, with no one else around but a family pet, or, at most, one of his lictors. In this case, he suspected that applying rationality wouldn't get him anywhere. But he had to make some kind of sense of it, in order to understand precisely what level of response Rome needed to make here, in reaction to what was a fairly flagrant violation of several treaties they'd made with this small kingdom. *No. I need to know more. I'll question the chieftain, the other elders. Have my lictors talk with the local plebeians . . . damnation. Half of them are too wounded to move, at the moment. I should have had the closest Praetorian office send extra officers . . . but I didn't anticipate a fight. Nor that they would have god-born. And more lictors would have been construed as too much of a threat.*

His mind churned. Three of his formidable lictors were injured, and they'd need at least one of the others to drive them back to Ponca, with the girl. No phone lines here in this small kingdom. No technology of any kind. *There's a radio in the car. We can put in a call to the local barracks. Bring in regional legionnaires. An option, though a heavy-handed one. No, relations before this past year have been acceptable. We'll call the local Praetorian office for backup. Might take a few hours . . . and my people need respite, and medical care. So does the girl.* He nodded to himself. *If Ehecatl has only a broken arm, and if he's willing . . . he can stay here with me and ensure that evidence isn't removed from the scene. He's the best choice anyway, being from Nahautl. He has better cultural understanding than the rest of us. And then new officers can handle the questioning. See who here were willing accomplices . . . some of the men were, certainly . . . and who among them were simply too afraid to stand up to a god-born. Wouldn't be the first time. And if we can . . . find the person who called in the information to the Praetorians in the first place. Though we may never know who it was. Silence might be their only assurance of safety.*

Livorus moved back over to his lictors. Ptah's unconscious form had been dragged to the rest of them, where they could guard him, and Adam was rigging a sling for Ehecatl's left arm using the man's own belt. And as he worked, the Judean man told Sigrun, sharply, "You should lie down. The chest wound isn't all the way healed yet, and I'd put denarii on it that the abdominal wound hasn't closed yet, either."

"Good luck," Ehecatl told the younger man sardonically, as the belt loop tightened into place around his shoulder blade. "Do you really think she's going to listen to you?"

The Marcomanni girl, swathed in ben Maor's cloak, huddled into

Sigrun's side, and rattled at the valkyrie in some dialect of Gothic, rapid-fire. Livorus understood Gothic, and could hack his way through Burgundian, but Cimbric, Trierian, and the half-dozen other dialects that filled the cities of Nova Germania were just sufficiently *different* from each other, that it was not just a matter of a heavy accent. He could pick out words here and there, like *nýdnimung*, which he thought was *rapine* . . . or maybe just *kidnapping*. Forcible seizure, certainly, but nuance was lost on him. Livorus came to a halt near his lictors and the girl, and asked, "What's our status?"

Ehecatl tried to shrug, and then winced, aborting the gesture. Livorus could smell charred flesh, and Livorus could see, through the burned remnants of the man's shirt, that the upper arm was blackened, and the flesh curved inwards, as if a bite had been taken out of the bicep by red-hot teeth. "I'm all right. Ptah's slipping in and out of consciousness. Wounds to upper left thigh and right shoulder, sir. He's stable, for the moment. All the wounds were almost completely cauterized, but I think his femur might be cracked, if not broken entirely. We need to get him to a hospital. And I don't think Sigrun should be healing anyone else today," the Nahautl man replied crisply.

Livorus nodded. "Are you in good enough condition to stay here, Itztli? We're going to call in as many Praetorians as we can, and treat this area as a crime scene. But someone needs to stay here to observe, and ensure that nothing is taken."

Ben Maor's head lifted. "I'm uninjured, sir," he reminded Livorus. "Itztli needs a hospital as badly as the rest of them do."

"Yes, but when you speak, the locals hear 'foreigner,'" Ehecatl reminded Adam, tiredly.

"Shouldn't matter. We're all provincials together."

"It shouldn't matter, but it does." Ehecatl grimaced again. "I'll get through it, *dominus*," he told Livorus, nodding once.

The propraetor nodded, respecting the former Jaguar warrior's strength of will, as always. "Sigrun, my dear, can you walk? Can you help this young lady back to our motorcar?"

"Yes, propraetor. I think so." Sigrun started to get to her feet, the lines of her face tautening as she did.

Ben Maor cut in, sharply, "Sir, she should not be walking, and I do not care what kind of magic was used to repair her wounds. She lost a great deal of blood, as did Frittigil here." The man stood. "I'll go back for the vehicle, and bring it here."

Livorus looked around at the scattered bodies on the field. "They won't thank us for bringing our technology onto their lands." His tone was completely neutral.

"I'll explain it to them." Adam's tone was curt. "They can have *some* of us off their land all the quicker if we bring the car to the wounded. Besides," he added, looking back at the body of the fallen priest, "I think the greatest source of their objections has already been silenced."

Livorus grimaced. The young man was angry, and he understood it. But anger wreaked havoc on diplomacy. That being said? The plan made sense. "Go get the car, then. And use the radio. Get in touch with the local Praetorian office, and get more agents down here. This is now a crime scene."

Adam nodded, stiffly. "Yes, sir. Already planning on it. Have I your leave?"

"Go."

Adam turned and loped off, hearing Livorus speaking with Ehecatl, behind him, about staying behind, though the man was injured. Adam grimaced. *He* should be the one staying behind. He hardly had a scratch, and Ehecatl's arm needed antibiotics and a course of burn treatments. As he ran, he saw dozens of people all watching him in the distance. *Let's hope they haven't found their guns, or decided that bows and arrows would make for a way of quietly changing the whole story here,* he thought, and kept jogging along the path that led to the mound village, slowing to a crisp walk. Ptah's life did depend on speed, but he also couldn't look panicked here. They needed to look in charge, in control. People tended to default to following the orders of those who *looked* like they were in charge. Just human nature, really. But he also didn't want to look threatening, either, which could trigger a very bad response from the people peering out of their mound-houses and lean-tos again.

The same group of hunters who'd escorted them in, approached him now. "The chief wants to speak with you," the leader told him.

"With the greatest of respect to your chief, he will have to speak to the propraetor. I'm not permitted to speak on his behalf." Adam took refuge behind this solid excuse, and met the man's eyes calmly, having to look up a bit to do so. "We're taking the girl back to her family . . ." he saw the man's eyes shift to the side, and the faint shadow of a grimace touch the lips, and thought, *You knew, and you didn't like it . . . but you also didn't do anything about it, did you? How much of it was that the god-born frightened you? How much of it was that it was just easier to go along with their ideas? That . . . I'll never know.*

Adam cleared his throat, aware that he'd paused a little too long, and pushed onwards, "So, yes. We're taking the girl home. And we have injured people who require medical attention. I've been directed to fetch our vehicle to facilitate that. I hope you'll permit that."

Another eye-shift. "The shaman has said that the motorcars are filled with evil spirits, and that allowing them onto our lands would permit the evil to come here."

Adam exhaled. "I think it's fairly clear . . . that the evil spirits were already here. Don't you think?"

The man stepped out of the way. "Go. Bring your machine. And tell your Roman that the chief would speak to him."

"I'm sure the propraetor will be happy to speak with your king . . . once he is sure that his lictors and the girl are comfortable." Adam was proud of that one. He even managed a perfectly polite tone throughout, and moved past the group of hunters, his hand itching for the grips of his revolver, and feeling the center of his back practically tingle. But he didn't turn his head to look back. He was neither Orpheus nor Lot's wife, and he knew that looking back would mean showing weakness here. Something he absolutely couldn't afford.

About fifteen minutes later, he drove the Arma back towards the field, detouring around the mound village and its gardens, bumping and jolting over the rough terrain, and hearing the undercarriage scrape on stones. He stopped, and then he and Ehecatl loaded Ptah into the backseat, though Ehecatl's aid was necessarily one-handed. Once they got Ptah in, Adam re-dressed the Egyptian's wounds, asking, "What hit you?

"Meteorites." Ptah swore, as Sigrun, Frittigil, and Livorus all approached the vehicle now, Sigrun actually leaning on the girl's shoulder, and her body curving inwards, shoulders hunching, then straightening again, with every step. The Egyptian looked up at her as they all gathered around the car, and said, "Heh. Guess their . . . god-born . . . weren't total traditionalists. Son of a *whore*, ben Maor, be careful—"

"I am. You're barely even bleeding. The wounds are perfectly *cauterized*." Adam was rattled. He'd seen plenty of strange wounds in battles with Persia, but nothing like this before. "Best I can do here is to put on real bandages, not pieces of shirt, and make sure they're not quite so tight."

Sigrun leaned against the car, and, clearly, trying to take Ptah's mind off his pain, asked, "What do you mean, they weren't traditionalists? They wanted to perform the oldest sacrifice known to their people. How much more *traditional* can someone be?"

Ptah grimaced as Adam finished tying off another bandage. "A hundred years ago," he said, from between clenched teeth, "I'd be willing to bet . . . by the *disc*, ben Maor, that *hurts* . . . that that arrow trick he did . . . would have been nothing more . . . than lines of light. Energy. Because . . . a hundred years ago . . . all anyone really knew about falling stars . . . is that they were . . . streaks of light." He exhaled. "These weren't."

"They sure looked like full meteorites, though I think we'd need a chemical analysis to find out if they actually dropped from space," Adam confirmed. "Rocks, red-hot from atmospheric friction, and accelerated to near terminal velocity."

"It's lovely to know that the cause of natural philosophy is of benefit to all mankind," Livorus muttered.

"Couldn't catch them," Ptah said, closing his eyes again. "Too fast. Kinetic energy should be just kinetic energy . . . but I just couldn't react in time. And while I could feel . . . nickel-iron in them . . . there wasn't enough to grab. I'm just not as good with *rock* as I am with metal." Ptah grimaced as Adam finished the last bandage. "Some of the young tyro technomancers coming up would roast me for saying that . . . ."

At that moment, Adam became aware of movement at the periphery of his vision, and spun, half-drawing his gun, just as Ehecatl's knife cleared its sheath . . . only to let his hand fall away from the weapon once more. One of the Chahiksichahik women was drawing closer, her hands up, so that they could see she meant no harm. "Yes?" Livorus asked, turning towards her. "Are you here to attend to the body of your priest?"

"That is . . . that is what I told the others. That I would tend his body, and the body of Shiriki. And . . . I will do so." she said, looking at the ground. "But I also . . . ask for the protection of Rome." She glanced up, and then down again, rapidly. Adam thought she might have been beautiful, if not for the lines of a very hard life on her weathered face. "I am the daughter of Kuruk, our shaman." Her little gesture directed their eyes towards the body on the ground nearby, and they all stiffened a little. Her tone was not what Adam would have expected from the daughter of a man whom he'd just killed. A stab of guilt went through him. It didn't matter that a review board would probably rule the kill justified. It was very hard to look at the woman's face, knowing that his was the hand that had ended her father's life.

But there was no hatred in her face or eyes. Just . . . resignation. "I am called Dyani."

Livorus said, very gently, "You were the one who called the Praetorians, weren't you?"

Her only response was a hasty nod, and another sidelong glance at the area around them. Checking for any of her people who might be listening.

"That was very brave of you," Livorus told her, inclining his head. "If I may ask . . . ?"

Strands of her long hair had worked their way free from her braid, and covered her face now. "For as long as I can remember, my father has spoken for the gods. He was the oldest and wisest of the shaman. The other shamans of our people travel the lands. We stayed here, at the holiest of sites, the seat of the chief. Everyone always . . . listened to him. The other elders might have disagreed with him . . . but everyone respected him." She shook her head. "Twenty years ago, there was a young man of the people who thought that there could be a balance between the old ways, and the ways of the outside world. That we could still respect the gods, and the world, and not have to live entirely as our ancestors did." She sighed. "That young man was my brother. My father exiled him, and the youngest children were forbidden to learn Latin shortly thereafter." She turned and looked at her father's body, no anger in her face. Just weariness. "Shiriki was my brother's best friend, but he did not speak for the new ways, or for my brother."

Adam blinked. The god-born of the sun-god had looked no more than eighteen. But Dyani's words suggested that the hot-head had been close to twice his own age. Livorus nodded slowly, absorbing the woman's words, and said, quietly, "And you were given as a wife to this friend of your brother, weren't you, my dear." It wasn't quite a question.

And the woman nodded, rapidly, and Adam could only stare in shock. They'd killed *both* her father and her husband, in one day, and while there was sorrow in her face, there was no vengeance at all. *Either the strongest woman I have ever seen, or the most worn,* he thought, stunned.

"They hated Rome," she said, after a moment. "They hated everything about the world outside our lands. They hated that my brother left our people for the sake of Rome . . . even though I knew that my brother left not because of Rome, but because he wanted a better life for himself. And for everyone around him." She shrugged a little. "Everything continued as it always had," the woman told them, lowering her head again, and even Ptah sat up to listen more carefully now. "Until last year. When the crops failed, and the hunts brought back barely enough food to feed each family. They conferred together, and consulted the omens." She sighed. "Shiriki had the dream weeks ago. The elders argued, and argued, and argued. My father had become convinced over the years that there needed to be a great spiritual awakening among all of the people of this continent. And now he kept saying that the gods needed more power than they had, and that the Morning Star, the best hunter of them all, needed to be made more powerful. That all our people would *die* without this sacrifice. Shiriki believed it, too. He believed the dream."

Livorus glanced over at Sigrun. "My dear, you'd be able to tell the difference between a dream sent by a genuine god and a random emanation through the gates of Morpheus, wouldn't you?"

Sigrun tried to shrug, and winced. "Sir, my gods don't deal in dreams. When Tyr needs my attention, he speaks to me directly, or sends word through the Odinhall." She looked from Frittigil, huddled against her side, to Dyani, in front of them. "He believed what he believed. And he acted based on that belief. Why did you risk stopping them?"

Dyani's dark eyes rose. "For two reasons. First, I believe as my brother once did. That change must come, or our people will surely die. And second . . ." she shook her head, "I cannot believe that the Evening Star enjoys watching young women suffer as she suffered. Every life is already filled with pain. Every life is already a sacrifice to time. We don't need more." Though quietly spoken, barely above a whisper, her sentiments, in the gender-segregated society ruled by elders like her father, would have sounded revolutionary, indeed.

"Come with us, then," Livorus said, nodding. "Their bodies will be . . . retained as evidence, shall we say? And you can come with us to ensure that they will be treated with the proper respect. Once the investigation is done, they can be returned to your people for . . . burning or burial, whichever is your custom."

Dyani huddled in on herself, nodding, and turned away to go towards her father's body. Sigrun patted Fritti on the shoulder, and stood, wearily, sucking in a breath as the broken bones in her shoulder blade grated on each other. And walked after the woman, gritting her teeth as every step now brought fresh pain with it. The adrenaline of combat had long since turned to a chemical ghost in her veins. "I'm sorry to intrude upon your sorrow," Sigrun said, as gently as she could, as the woman turned towards her, startled. "But would you permit me one, very intrusive question? I will respect it, if you choose not to answer."

The woman turned back towards Sigrun, and inclined her head, a faint light of curiosity coming into her weary eyes. "You may ask."

Sigrun hesitated. She had a decent grasp of human nature. "You said that you were given in marriage to Shiriki. And that he was the friend of your brother. Did you ever love him?"

Expressions flickered across the woman's face, fleeting with her thoughts. Mild affront, tiredness, a hint of cynicism, and resignation. "I loved him before I married him, as everything that my people ought to be. Brave, bold, and as bright as the sun itself. He watched my brother exiled, however, and only spoke of him with bitterness afterwards. He did not believe as I did about the future of our people, and I . . . held my tongue." Sigrun could see a faint flash of resentment and anger, deeply sublimated. "I watched him stay ever-young, however, always hot-headed, as I grew older. As my father, though also god-born, grew older." Not resentment this time, but bone-deep weariness. Some god-born aged more or less as humans did. Some, like Sigrun, did not age physically at all. And some remained the emotional and mental equivalent of their physical age for far longer than they should. "He was a good man, in the main. A good enough husband." Another weary shrug. "He was faithful, and he did not beat me. But I would not call what I felt love. More the memory of it. Love's shadow." She looked at Sigrun, and then down at the corpse of her father. "Love dies."

Sigrun felt she should do *something* to help the woman, but she was one-handed at best, at the moment. And though the old priest, Kuruk, and the younger god-born, Shiriki, had done their best to kill her and her companions, it seemed . . . respectful . . . to incline her head for a few moments, and honor them both as warriors in a cause she both understood, and completely opposed. Who wouldn't give their life for their people, after all? But . . . involving the girl? Beyond the pale.

With Dyani to take into protection, and Frittigil to take with them, the motorcar would have been overcrowded even if they didn't need the entire backseat for Ptah, who couldn't walk. Livorus had to change his own plan, and kept his lictors together, until the Praetorians from the closest office arrived, hours later. It was a small number of people, but all were well-armed, and carried medical supplies with them.

With several vehicles and drivers at their disposal, they were finally able to leave the area. Adam took Livorus aside and argued, strongly, that Ehecatl should now be sent to the hospital with the rest of the lictors. Livorus agreed, immediately, and Adam thus took charge of the fresh detail of Praetorians, and Livorus prepared to negotiate with the elders. "Without two god-born present to both force his hand, and guard his back for him, Lesharo may be more . . . amenable to the gentle overtures of diplomacy." He ducked his head down into one of the motorcars, and told Ptah, "You're not to bleed on the upholstery, you understand? That *will* come out of your salary." A quick lift of the eyebrows conveyed the real message.

Ptah chuckled, and then groaned and reached for his shoulder. "I'll . . . do my best." He settled back again. "Be careful, sir."

"You tell me this? Not a scratch on me? Obviously, *I* have not forgotten how to duck. Or perhaps it is merely that you never learned to do so." Livorus turned and looked at Ehecatl. "What are you waiting for?"

Ehecatl thumped a fist to his chest, lightly, around the sling. Then he got into the car, moving Ptah-ases' feet and dropping them, gingerly, back down again. "So . . . you're not going to tenderly cradle my head in your lap?" the Egyptian sorcerer asked, putting on a grin.

"Do I look Hellene to you?" Ehecatl asked, dryly, trying to buckle himself in. "Stop moving around, Ptah. If you kick loose bone marrow into your blood stream and give yourself an embolism, I think Sigrun may ride to the afterlife and beat your ghost with a stick."

Sigrun, sliding into a different car with Frittigil, turned to give them both a diamond-hard stare. Adam snorted, while Ptah-ases actually chuckled at that, then groaned and put a hand to his shoulder. "Don't . . . don't make me laugh."

"It's only funny because it's *true*," the Nahautl man assured him, solemnly. "All right, let's get a move on. I'm rather looking forwards to my pain-killers. At least, once someone with enough clearance to listen to my classified babbling is present to stand guard over me."

"At least you *get* some pain-killers. Sorcerers can't—"

Livorus closed the door on their amicable, though pained bickering, and tapped a hand on the roof, and the driver turned the key in the starter. The engine caught, and purred to life, and then they were off, slowly trundling over the fields once more, followed by a larger truck, into which Dyani and the bodies of her kin had been bundled.

Adam watched them go, and then trailed Livorus with the new Praetorians, back to the mounds of the village. He stood, his face an impassive mask, behind the Roman as he and Lesharo, who'd regained some of his composure in the past hours, began to fence once more with one another. This time, however, Livorus took a decidedly more aggressive negotiating stance. "As I said before, when you speak to me, you speak to Rome," Livorus began, without any further preamble, on re-entering the mound, pitching his voice to be heard across the whole of the enclosed area. There were few people in the mound now. Just the elders, none of the families who usually dwelled here. "What do you have to say to Rome, I wonder?"

Adam watched the leader's nostrils flare, slightly, as the man sank down into a crouch at the fire pit, which was dark and cold now. "I give you my word that I never intended for it to go as far as it did. They spoke of a need to re-awaken our people. To re-awaken all the tribes of this land, and bind us more strongly to our gods. The need to hold to the old ways. It seemed a . . . good message. A worthy one. I agreed with it. Until they brought the girl here. Then, it was too late to stop them. They had too many allies."

The words of kings and leaders are rarely more lasting than those traced in water, Adam thought, cynically. *They say what needs to be said, at the moment it needs saying. Survival is all. But that is, I suppose, their job.*

Livorus' brows rose. "King Lesharo, your people have violated not one, but several treaty agreements with Rome and your neighbors. You are the leader of your people." Livorus held up the *fasces*, which he'd tucked into the folds of his toga at some point, and now gripped once more. "I ask you, what apology you are prepared to make to Rome and the nations around you."

Lesharo raised his head, a world of weariness in his expression. "What apology would Rome accept?"

Livorus regarded him steadily. "In times past," he said, meditatively, "other representatives of Rome would have demanded nothing less than your immediate crucifixion, along with all those responsible."

No reaction in the man's face, besides resignation in the eyes.

Adam wondered what Livorus was thinking. Impossible to tell, really. The propraetor went on now, smoothly, "Times change, but only in so much, King Lesharo. This is what I would have of you. First, a formal apology, on your behalf, to Rome, to her allies, to Frittigil Chatti, her family, and the province of Nova Germania. Second, I require that every single man and woman who was involved in the attack on her be put to death. I will make an exception for the children who were onlookers at the sacrifice site, and those who provided food and comfort to her, or merely guarded her during her captivity. Punishment will be reserved to those who were directly involved in her kidnapping, those who fired on her, and those who fired on us when we were attempting to effect her release from her unlawful captivity. I will require them to be turned over to local authorities for summary execution. However, I will forgo the traditional crucifixions, in deference to local custom. I believe Novo Gaul still employs, on occasion, the wicker cage and the fire, but Nova Germania has adopted the more merciful public beheading, and I'm assured that they do not permit the headsman to drink alcohol before the proceedings."

The elders were stirring, grimaces of anger and resentment on their faces, but also traces of relief, which were wiped away by Livorus' next words. "As for you and your elders . . . " Livorus stared grimly at the leader of this small nation, and let the silence hang there for a moment, before continuing. "I believe those who are chiefly guilty are already dead. I will not require your life, King Lesharo, in repayment for the crimes against this girl and against our nations, but I will require that reparations be paid to the girl and her family directly." He held up his free hand, forestalling any words from the chieftain and advisors. "I know that you have nothing among your people that the family of a Marcomanni girl would find of value. You *barter* with outsiders, and trade goods for your muskets and metal knives. You do not use coin. In times past, I might have required that some of your people be sent as slaves to the girl's family, but Nova Germania and Novo Gaul have outlawed that practice. Instead, I require that *one* child from the family of each man who is executed for having taken part in this conspiracy, be sent to a boarding school in Novo Gaul. Close enough to visit their relatives, but they will be expected to improve their minds, and learn Latin. Roman ways. Roman thoughts. Roman ideas. They will attend for a total of three years, and will learn a useful and productive trade in so doing. What they do with it, at the end of that term, will be up to them." Livorus stared at the king. "You may now thank me for my mercy."

It was heavy-handed, but it could have been far more so.

The other Praetorians now began the work of taking pictures of the crime scene, taking Adam's descriptions of where the various shooters had been standing, and so on. They took the various men of the kingdom into custody. Adam didn't envy them that work, or having to listen to the despairing wails of the men's wives, or having to separate the men who'd willingly (or less willingly) walked out to shoot a thirteen-year-old girl, in the name of their gods, from the families who loved them.

It wasn't, however, thankfully, his job today. He opened the door of the last spare car that the other Praetorians had brought with them for Livorus, closed it behind the man, and got into the driver's side, and started them off for Ponca once more. "Sir?" he asked, after a few miles of silence had passed.

"Yes, ben Maor?"

"You could have marched a garrison in there. You could have had the entire village executed, every man there crucified, and then moved in bulldozers to level the houses and tamp it all back down for the prairie grass to cover again next year." He looked in the rearview mirror; Livorus was, once again, reading reports in the backseat. The man never *stopped* reading them, it seemed.

Livorus looked up from the papers, and took off his reading glasses. "Yes. I could have. And if I had, I'm quite certain that someone back home would have put forward a motion in the Senate to have my name chiseled on a marble plinth somewhere. Tastefully. In letters about this high." He held up his fingers, illustrating. "On the whole, I think that the days in which the Empire *had* to rule by force are mostly behind us. I prefer to use reason, when I can. And in sparing their lives, and seeing to it that some of their children are educated in things other than hunting and gathering, I might have secured Rome a long-term ally, rather than a graveyard. Perhaps the son of the late high priest, if he truly lives in exile, might be found. Might be convinced to return to his people, and help advise them." He shrugged. "Certainly, their leader will owe me, personally, his life. That's a string that can be pulled, in the future, if needed."

Adam kept his eyes on the road. "So that was the reason, then, sir? Practicality?"

"Lives are valuable, Adam ben Maor. It takes eighteen years and more to build a man or a woman worthy of the name. That's an investment that the world cannot afford to squander. And I will not willingly throw them away." Livorus settled his reading glasses back on his nose. "Admittedly, some of the conservatives back home will undoubtedly suggest that I've gone soft, and that Emperor Caesarion should replace me with a younger, more aggressive man. Then again, I'm a political appointee. I don't have to run for office. I can do things that aren't *popular*." A faint, wintery smile. "I find that rather freeing."

Chapter III: Scars

Akhenaten ruled for seventeen years before his death, under mysterious circumstances, between 1336 BAC and 1334 BAC. His reign was turbulent, and marked by many changes to Egyptian culture. In year 5 of his reign, Akhenaten apparently grew discontented with the political power of the priests of Horus, which constrained his ability to rule. He broke with tradition, taking a new name and dedicating himself to the sole worship of the Aten, then depicted as both the sun disc and as a hawk-headed god. For a time, he permitted the worship of other gods to continue.

More radical changes came in year 9 of his reign, in which scholars prior to the eighteenth century AC were only able to ascertain that an unknown event caused the pharaoh to order an end to the worship of all other gods. Records recovered in the tomb of his wife, Nefertiti, however, now suggest that the priests of Horus attempted to assassinate him.

In retaliation, he directed that the images of the gods be destroyed, their statues and relics brought to his palace, their names effaced from all monuments, and that even the plural form of the word 'god' should be stricken from all public writings. Only the stylized sun-disc of the Aten would be permitted to be worshipped, and he, as the divine son of Aten, was the only intermediary through whom prayers to the Creator-God of All could be passed.

Every pharaoh before Akhenaten had insisted that they were in fact, gods, but this was largely a matter of politics. While god-born traits passed through their complex family lineages, they were not present in every child of a given dynasty. Certainly Akhenaten, who, from his highly naturalistic portraits and statues, appeared to be deformed, even disfigured from some genetic condition possibly caused by inbreeding, had never shown such powers, according to all records of the time.

However, after receiving the idols of the various gods, and destroying them in his palace, Akhenaten's behavior became increasingly erratic. He began to dress in public wearing wax breasts, to suggest he held both male and female powers of generativity, and there is widespread scholarly debate as to whether or not he began a sexual relationship with his son Smenkhkare at this time as well. While incest was common and accepted within pharaonic families, it was generally restricted to marriage between siblings.

The truth of the matter will never be known, but what is known, is that Akhenaten moved his family, including his wife, Nefertiti, their six daughters, and his lesser wives, including the mother of his son, later known as Tutankhamen, to his new temple city, named Akhenaten in his own honor. And he began to effect miracles to demonstrate that he was, indeed, the son of Aten.

Nefertiti had been appointed his co-ruler in year 15, under the male name of Neferneferuaten. There is evidence that she attempted to check the worst excesses of his 'reform' movement, and became responsible for much of the day-to-day ruling of the kingdom, taking over control of taxation and other such mundane matters, while her husband continued to serve as the conduit to the divine realm. Much of this information, as well as information on the mysterious death of Akehnaten, comes from three relief panels in Nefertiti's tomb. These hieroglyphic panels are much debated, and are in a remarkable state of preservation. Most of the artwork is in the unusually naturalistic style of the period.

The first panel shows the executions of the priests of Horus, who were fed to the crocodiles of the Nile. It shows the anger of foreign kings, to whom Akhenaten had sent poor gifts, statues of gold plated over wood, but from whom he had demanded richer gifts in return. It shows these kings preparing for war, and shows the workers in the fields, holding out sheaves of grain that have only a few stalks in them. Signs of famine, most scholars agree. The final image on this panel shows officials bowing to Nefertiti, begging her for assistance, but the figure of her husband clearly holds her back.

The central panel is the one in most dispute. It shows the pillared great hall of the palace and Akhenaten seated there, his family around him. It also depicts a huge figure — larger even than the pharaoh, whose divinity was customarily demonstrated by giving him larger size than all other figures in a composition. This figure is the center of the debate. It is armored, but the armor covers the _entirety_ of the body, in a manner highly atypical for the period, and the style of this anomalous armor is not recognizable as Assyrian, Hittite, or Egyptian. Every joint and seam appears to be adorned with highly ornamental hooks and spikes, and the face is concealed except for a slit in the helmet, which reveals eyes, that the artisans used flakes of gold to depict on the tomb wall. The rest of the original pigmentation on this figure is black, not a normal color in which the bronze armor of the period was typically depicted.

Some scholars believe that the figure is meant to be depiction not of an individual, but of divine retribution. Unfortunately, the iconography does not match that of any known god, Egyptian, Sumerian, or other. Scholars who believe that it represents divine retribution refer to the figure as "the god-beast." Those who believe that it represents some sort of creature summoned by sorcerer-priests of the era refer to it as "the Assassin." The more histrionic class of historian refers to this figure as "the godslayer," allying the creature, rightly or wrongly, with the supposed god-slayers that ostensibly wiped out much of the Babylonian, Assyrian, and Hittite pantheons, almost nine hundred years before the events of Akhenaten's reign.

The bottom of this panel shows Nefertiti and the royal children escaping, as the Assassin and Akhenaten confront one another. Magic surrounds Akhenaten's hands, while the creature tears at a one of the massive pillars that supports the roof of the palace. In the next image, the ceiling collapses, and Nefertiti turns to look behind her. The only thing visible under the rubble is a pair of golden, stylized eyes in the darkness beneath the stones.

The third and final panel shows Nefertiti reigning as a regent for Smenkhkare under the name of Neferneferuaten, and then for Tutankhamen, as well. She oversaw restoration of the worship of the other gods, although it was clear that many of those gods were now dead. She was overthrown by the treacherous priest Ay, who, in turn, was supplanted by the common-born general, Horemheb. The pantheon now consisted primarily of Aten, Amun-Ra, Isis, Thoth, Sekhmet, Horus, and Set, along with a handful of minor divinities.

The cult of the Aten died until the eighteenth century AC, when the recovery of the tombs of Akhenaten, Nefertiti, and Tutankhamen led to a revival of the beliefs, and wide-spread rebellion against the Roman emperors who maintained control through their descent from the Ptolemies, and thus, from Isis, Amun-Ra, and Horus.

It is not known by what mechanism Akhenaten 'killed' the gods. It is not *even known if they died by his actions, or by the actions of the Aten. That does not prevent people from referring to the pharaoh – slain, supposedly, by a godslayer! – as a godslayer himself. His name remains an anathema to this day, except to the followers of the Aten, to whom he is a hero. But then, for many, Atenists are also anathema. Only the Edict of Diocletian II has prevented the revived Atenist cult from being wiped out, several times over, in the past several hundred years.*

*– Ra-Apeppi, <u>Ancient Egypt: The Dynasty of Akhenaten the Godslayer,</u>
"Introduction." University of Novo Trier Press, 1956 AC.*

<u>Martius 6, 1954 AC</u>

Sigrun tried not to move at all, feeling the dull aches in her shoulder, chest, and abdomen, as she sat in a chair beside Frittigil's bed, watching the various doctors and nurses poke and prod the girl. The girl's thin hand clutched hers as the physicians took pictures of the healed arrow wounds – little more than thin white scars. Took her blood-pressure. Took blood. They were definitely the *taking* sort, and the various Gauls twitched under Sigrun's watchful eye. "You'll dispose of it once you've tested it?" she asked, pointing at the glass vials of blood.

The nearest nurse, a rangy Gallic woman with golden-brown hair tied in a knot at the nape of her neck, held up gloved hands. "It must be preserved as evidence, *domina*. Hospital policy, and standard procedure. But all tissue and blood samples are kept under secure guard, and labeled only with numbers. Someone would have to know the numerical system, in order to know whose sample was whose."

Sigrun lined the toes of her boots up with the cracks in the tile. "Very well," she said, quietly.

Hospitals bothered her. Part of it was the smell, she knew; the floor polish, the antiseptics, the whiff of effluvia from a cart filled with used bedpans, the aroma of sickness and pain on people's skins. The sounds. The chill, persistent beeping of a heart monitor. The squeak of gurney wheels on the tile floors. And part of it was simply bad memories. She'd never been sick, herself; never had measles, mumps, rubella, chickenpox, the flu, or even the common cold. But her first memories, dim and indistinct, were from the age of three. Sitting at her mother's bedside in the hospital, staring at the tired face. *"Where did all your hair go, Mama? It was so pretty long."*

"It fell out, little valkyrie. The doctors gave me medicines to make the disease go away, but they made my hair fall out, too."

"Those must not be good medicines."

"They're. . . the best. . . we have."

Looking at her mother's face, and feeling <u>shadow</u> over that bright spirit. Knowing that the coldness <u>meant</u> something, was dangerous and scary, and she tried to make it go away. But she couldn't. "Fæder said you were too sick for me to come here. He said I would tire you out."

"You don't tire me, little one. It makes me happy to see you here." A gentle hand on Sigrun's little head, but truthsense twinged. *Mama had never lied*

before. She was happy to see Sigrun, but Sigrun *did* tire her. And the little valkyrie had hushed, in the face of the first lie she'd ever sensed from her mother, and the cold darkness that was . . . somehow inside of her.

"Ragnhildr?" Her father, tall and wide as an oak, came into the room. Took her mama's hand very gently in his big one. "There's one more option. I found a god-born of Eir. She's going to try to help you."

Her mother had nodded against the pillow, her face pinched. And then Sigrun had looked up as the figure, wearing a white cloak and hood, entered the room. Hope had filled her, for a moment. *She can make the shadow and the cold go away. I can't. But she can.*

The woman had pushed back her hood, revealing coppery hair, and put a hand to Ragnhildr's head. White light radiated out from her, but the older god-born had looked down at the younger one, and they'd both *known* that the shadow wouldn't pass. "I can make her more comfortable," the older woman said, quietly. "I can make sure there's no pain."

Ivarr had put his head down on the bed beside his wife's hand, and wept, openly, as her weak, frail hand combed gently at his long hair. And her mother held out her other hand to Sigrun, and had told her, "Be brave, little valkyrie. I love you."

That had been the last time Sigrun had seen her mother, before they'd taken her to her pyre. The only clear memory after that was watching the flames dance around the shrouded shell that was all that remained of Ragnhildr Caetia.

In the here and now, Frittigil sat up in her hospital bed, once the nurses were gone again. "Shouldn't they be looking at you, æðelinga?" the Marcomanni girl asked, her voice thin. "You. . . you're hurt, aren't you? B-because of me?"

Sigrun shrugged the question away, trying not to let the wince at the motion show on her face, and let the memories fade. She didn't dwell on them often, but the hospital was an inescapable reminder. "I heal very quickly," she told the younger woman, quietly. "Given a good meal and a night's rest, I probably won't feel it in the morning. The cuts and punctures have sealed over. The burns are fading. The bone will take a little longer, and the deeper muscle tissues." *In the meantime, it hurts like Hel's seized me with her claws, but you don't need to know that, child.* Her healing did not function as a human's did, entirely. It functioned continuously, but more quickly and effectively when she was able to concentrate on it. And it worked from most life-threatening to least life-threatening. Staunching bleeding was almost always the first order of business for her body, unless breathing was compromised. "They will bring in a woman who will ask you questions, and conduct a physical examination. It will be a little personal. I can leave, if you want, or stay, if you like."

The girl's dark brown hair slid forward over her face, like a veil. "What do you mean, personal?" Her voice edged upwards in pitch.

Sigrun kept her voice gentle. "She will ask you questions about how the men treated you while you were a prisoner. And she will need to use some swabs in your private areas."

"Why?" The girl's voice slid up another half-octave, and Sigrun reached out, once more offering a hand for Frittigil to take, and felt the almost desperate clasp of the girl's fingers.

"Because we need to know if they did anything to you. Well, anything else." Sigrun kept her voice as gentle as she could. She knew she wasn't good at this part of the job.

"They didn't!" Frittigil whispered, shrinking further in on herself.

"I didn't think that they had. But the doctors have to document everything." Sigrun squeezed the girl's hand, lightly. She didn't want to explain it, but the whole point of the Morning Star ceremony was to re-enact, symbolically, the rape of a virgin goddess, and thus the sacrifice of innocence. Raping her would have unfitted her for the sacrifice. But the doctors and the Praetorians needed documentation for the upcoming trials, however summary they might be.

Then the nurse came back in, all gentle, non-threatening questions, and took down the girl's information. And put the rape-kit to use. "Can I go home now?" Frittigil asked, forlornly, once the procedure was over.

Sigrun looked at the doctor. "There's no need to keep her here for observation," the doctor said, shrugging. "Her wounds are completely healed. I would have thought the scars several years old, if I hadn't been told. Your wounds, on the other hand, *domina*—"

"Don't require any assistance," Sigrun told him, hastily. "Don't trouble yourself on my account." She paused. "Frittigil? We've already called your parents—"

"Are they coming here?" The look of pure relief in the girl's eyes caught at Sigrun's heart.

"It's a ten-hour drive," Sigrun reminded the girl, gently. "While they want to see you, and you want to see them, we thought it best if the Praetorians escorted you home tomorrow." *And Livorus thought it might be a good idea to keep this all as quiet as possible. Any reporters following the story of Fritti's disappearance in Marcomanni will just see her returned to her parents, and the matter of a neighboring petty kingdom attempting to revive forbidden practices thanks to what appears to be a small group of extremists... doesn't need to get blown out of proportion. It didn't happen.* "For tonight, as the doctor just said, you can stay here, or you can stay with me, in my hotel room. Or you can have your own room at the hotel, with Praetorian guards. It's up to you." She kept her voice even as she outlined the choices. Giving the girl agency in her own life right now was extremely important.

The girl looked at her, and nodded, frantically. "With you, please. I don't want to stay here alone."

I've become a security object, Sigrun thought. It wasn't necessarily a bad thing, but it would have helped to have had some of the girl's family here from the start, but that once again raised the specter of the news media. Livorus had reasoned that if Fritti really were here, the presence of Frittigil's family and possibly reporters, following along behind the family like vultures, could have heightened tensions, and, if the tip as to her whereabouts had been wrong, they'd have had her family drive seven hundred miles for nothing. "All right. Let's get you some clothing. I'll send my partner to the gift shop for you, if that's all right?"

An hour later, the girl was dressed in a light cotton tunic with the words *Ponca Metropolitan Hospital* on it, with a stylized image of the Gallic god, Grannus below it, healing the sick. A nurse had donated a skirt from her own locker, as well—one so large, that they'd needed to give her a length of rope as a belt. Her outfit was completed by a pair of hospital slippers. She looked a waif, which couldn't be helping her mental state, but it beat a hospital robe.

Sigrun caught the girl watching Adam cautiously as he drove them back to the hotel. "We're going to have to leave the door between our rooms unlocked tonight," Adam told Sigrun, pragmatically. "If I hear something, I don't want to have to break it down to get in there."

Sigrun considered that, and then nodded. "I will probably sleep like the dead tonight," she admitted. "Just as soon as I eat something." Her chest and shoulder still ached, which wasn't a good sign. She'd had to heal a lot of damage today, and her body, while an excellent conduit for Tyr's will, was still mortal. More or less.

Some days, a little less than more.

They ordered room service meals, and Sigrun told Fritti, calmly, "We'll all eat together."

Another rapid glance from Frittigil to Adam. *"Do. . . do we have to?"* the girl asked, in the regional Gothic dialect of Marcomanni. Every major city in Nova Germania had been settled by a different tribe, and over the centuries, there had been linguistic drift. The Gothic dialects spoken on this continent differed from those spoken in Europa, and every city here had a different dialect, as well. The advent of the far-viewer and radio had helped to stabilize the dialects of Nova Germania, at least. They were close enough that someone from one city could usually pick up the other dialects quickly, but they were different enough that, spoken quickly, an ear unaccustomed to a dialect would have picked up nothing more than sounds. Nuances were often completely lost. Most Goths born on the continent defaulted to Gothic, Cimbric—Sigrun's own dialect—or Latin, as a bridge language.

"Géa." Sigrun kept her voice gentle, but firm, as she went on, quietly, in Gothic, *"Adam is a good man. He is my partner. He will not hurt you. You have had a bad experience, yes, but you must learn to see again, as you saw before. Not everyone is a threat. This is why we will eat together."*

Frittigil turned and stared at her. *"You say partner, but you do not say witan."*

Sigrun blinked. Opened her mouth to reply, and realized that she was flushing. Every dialect of Gothic had the same pronouns as most other languages of Europa: *I, thou, he, she, it, we, you, they,* and the formal second-person mode of address: *you.* All branches of Gothic also had another pronoun: *witan.* We two.

Witan was used between two people who were as close as kin, as close as lovers. Between two people who'd fought together, bled together, nearly died together, or between husband and wife. It was never used on any other occasion, and Sigrun had never in her life actually employed this word. *"Ah, no. I did not mean to make you think that."* Sigrun rapidly debated how much honesty would be helpful here. Saying that Adam had only been on the team for three months would not incline the wary girl towards much acceptance. *"Master ben Maor has been a Praetorian for two years. He also performed cardiopulmonary resuscitation on you, when you were wounded."*

"Oh! Oh . . . I'm. . . I'm sorry." Frittigil looked down at her feet, and slid cautiously over to the table to perch, uneasily, at the edge of her chair. *"I didn't mean to sound ungrateful. . . ."*

"I heard my name in there. Do I even want to know?" Adam asked, smiling at them. "My Gothic isn't worth much yet. Gallic, well, I can ask for directions to the local bathhouse, and that's about it." He rolled his eyes. "Nimes-on-the-Pacifica dialect only, at that."

"Nothing. It's not important." Sigrun shook her head. There was no sense embarrassing the girl by revealing Fritti's lack of trust.

Still, the young man's eyebrows rose. "Oh, and now I am *consumed* by my curiosity."

"Then be devoured by it, Adam ben Maor, and may you give it indigestion."

He laughed and took a seat, breaking the bread apart and murmuring something complicated under his breath in his native tongue as he did so, bowing his head, before giving a piece to Frittigil and another piece to Sigrun. Sigrun tucked into her food hungrily. She needed protein, and a lot of it; she'd used a lot of her body's reserves today. Steak, therefore, was on the docket again, along with mashed potatoes and green beans. The potato was a distinctive dish of Caesaria Aquilonis and Caesaria Australis. They'd been unknown in Europa before the colonization of the new world. Unfortunately, the hotel's cutlery turned out to have a very dull knife. In annoyance, Sigrun dug in her luggage for a moment, and found her *cadena*; this was a personal kit in which someone carried their own knife, fork, and spoon. She still carried it with her, mostly as a habit and a courtesy. In Nova Germania, one didn't expect everything to be supplied by a host; it was considered good form for a guest to bring their own utensils.

As for the others, Adam had managed to find an inoffensive chicken dish on the menu, and they'd let Frittigil order whatever she wanted, and she'd picked bison *klopse* in white sauce with mushrooms and mashed potatoes. "Don't eat too fast," Adam warned the girl, genially. "You don't want to be sick."

"They . . . they fed me." Her Latin was a schoolgirl's. She obviously didn't use it in everyday conversation much. "Maize. Squash. Dried meat. Had crackers at hospital."

Meat, because she was to be treated very well before the sacrifice. Privileged foods. Sigrun's lips curled down.

There was a busy silence as they all ate, but they all eventually slowed down, and Adam pushed his plate away first. "So," he said, leaning back and tilting his head. "The regional Praetorians brought your armor to the hotel while you were at the hospital."

Sigrun grimaced. "Yes. I had to take it off. The fire the sun-born one used on me was . . . quite hot. And the metal only trapped the heat."

"It melted in places. The rings are congealed." Adam stood, and obviously noted how Frittigil started back from him as he did, but didn't change his movements. Just headed over to the far-viewer stand, and took a satchel from there, handing it to Sigrun. She opened it, and sighed. He was accurate in his assessment; the rings had run together, beading in places, as they'd melted.

"This will need repairs," she muttered. "Or just will need to be melted down and made new."

He sat back down, raising his eyebrows. "It won't stop a bullet. Obviously, it doesn't stop *fire*."

"It would not have slowed the meteorites hurled by the god-born of the Morning Star, either," she allowed, equitably. "It *does* stop blades and arrows."

"I could order you a very good flak jacket. Would definitely stop bullets." He arched his eyebrows, smiling at her.

"Yes, but as I asked earlier, will it stop knives?" Sigrun shrugged.

"No. But we could put your ring mail on top of that."

"Then I would be slowed by the extra weight. My best defense really is my speed." She looked down at her plate, feeling a wave of tiredness pass over her. "And neither will stop fire."

"An asbestos coat over the top of all of it, then. Like a firefighter." He nodded soberly, and they were both a little startled to hear Frittigil giggle, quietly. "Oh, wait, you'd be slowed even more, then." Adam's tone was pragmatic. "The chain mail is heavy, and does you very little good." He paused, and added, reflectively, "Three months as your partner, and I didn't know you could heal like that. Why wear armor at all?"

Sigrun leaned back in her own chair, watching Frittigil eat, before turning to look at Adam. "Three reasons. First, I wear it when it is Tyr's day. Respect. Second. . . I heal, yes. But it still *hurts*, and I prefer not to endure it if there's no reason. And third. . ." She shrugged. "I can still die, Adam. I'm not a goddess."

Of course, every one of my people knows that gods can die. That they will *die. That Ragnarok, someday, will happen, and that then, the world will be renewed. But it will take the lives of many of the gods. And of course, there are the legends of the godslayers . . . .*

Adam leaned forward. "I'm your *partner*, Sigrun. I need to know things like this. I need to know when I'm *supposed* to be worried, and when I can and should step back. You keep secrets, Sigrun. We all do—it's what we're paid for. But you keep things in that you really should tell people on your *team*." The junior agent was evidently both irritated, and fascinated at the same time. Sigrun had seen the look of interest in many other eyes over the years. She'd gotten used to deflecting it, as it tended to make her feel like a bug on a plate. Though Adam's interest was less threatening, somehow, than some of her previous partners' had been. Now, Adam tapped a finger against the table for emphasis. "So. What does it take to kill you?"

She looked down at her plate. "I am a valkyrie." Sigrun shrugged slightly, only feeling the ache faintly now in her shoulder. "That means, largely, that I will die in battle, Adam. No sickness will claim me. And even in battle, it would probably take an immediately mortal wound. Decapitation, or complete obliteration of the heart. Almost anything else . . . it might take a while. But I'll heal from it." She shrugged, smiling a little wryly. "I just won't enjoy the process." She was very aware of the girl watching them as they spoke in Latin.

"And the way you healed Frittigil here?" Adam sounded . . . almost a little *angry* about that, and Sigrun's eyes snapped up, startled. "Why?" He tapped the side of his fist against the table for a moment, evidently looking for the right words.

"Why what?" she asked, after a moment.

"It's a gift from your god, right?"

She nodded, not understanding where the quiet anger under his words was coming from. "Then why," Adam asked, clearly leashing his temper a bit, "does your god require that *you* take the wound? Why not just heal someone directly?"

Sigrun blinked again. "Ah. . . I see where you're confused. Tyr is not a god of healing. He is a god of *justice*. His gift is . . . tempered. He requires that I understand the suffering of a victim, in order to restore them." She swallowed, and then admitted, more quietly, "Also . . . blood binds. It is a sacrifice. Of sorts." She shrugged. "It's not a mercantile arrangement. But there is a saying: *ex nihilo nihil fit.*" *Nothing comes from nothing.* "You have to give, if you wish to receive."

Adam shook his head and turned away. He wasn't entirely sure why he was so irritated by this, but it seemed deeply unjust for a god to inflict such pain on a loyal follower, and for no other reason than that she wished to help others. But . . . it wasn't his faith. And it wasn't his business. But he knew it irked him to see the slowly-fading wound in Sigrun's upper chest. Still dark red, still livid against her skin. It seemed so completely *unnecessary.*

And yet, on the other hand, an hour outside of town, as they'd been? If she hadn't done precisely what she'd done, the girl would be dead now. Her family would be in mourning in Nova Germania, and any number of outraged people would be trying to come across the border, looking for revenge. "Explain something else to me, then?" he said, leashing his irritation for the moment.

Sigrun's brows rose as she began clearing the plates, and Adam settled in to his nightly routine, cleaning his gun, since he'd fired his revolver today. "What troubles you?"

"It's not so much troubling, as . . . I already knew about the lightning and the wind. And the spear. And the flying." He had the Velserk completely disassembled now, and was working a bore brush with solvent through the empty barrel. "How do you even *train* to fight god-born?" His words weren't entirely born of frustration. He'd dealt with the god-born shaman in his own way, using just his own training. But short of carrying ground-to-air missiles, he wasn't sure what he could possibly do to help when Sigrun was ten thousand feet in the air above him. Even Ptah hadn't had the range to assist.

Sigrun blinked a little at the question. "Like most things. You learn by doing it."

Fritti's head moved back and forth as if she were a spectator at a Nahautl *ollamaliztli* ball game. Adam just looked at Sigrun, patiently, and the woman relented. "I spent four years at the Odinhall undergoing rigorous training against and with other god-born. My instructors were all valkyrie and bear-warriors. There were lessons in understanding the basics of magic and illusion, overseen by a two-hundred-year-old valkyrie, born of Loki, named Reginleif Lanvik." Sigrun's tone was rueful. "None of us could ever quite live up to her expectations, which were very high." She shook her head, her eyes distant. "Basic medical instruction, from valkyrie of Eir and licensed physicians. Combat strategy and tactics from bear-warriors twice my age. And everyone I sparred with, was another god-born. Learning to control our powers, instead of being controlled by them."

Fritti's eyes shone with interest. "Everyone has heard of the training of the god-born at the Odinhall," the girl said excitedly, but still with a hint of shyness. "They say that the first lesson is understanding pain."

Adam grimaced, but Sigrun nodded. "Understanding and accepting, yes." Her eyes flicked to Adam. "I crashed into the sun-born one today, doing close to my top flight speed. I was braced for the impact. He was not. That doesn't mean that the impact did not hurt. If I were anything other than a god-born, I'm sure that my bones would have shattered. You have to accept that sometimes, what you do, will hurt. But if it's worth doing, you do it anyway."

Adam had a feeling that those words weren't directed so much at him, as at Fritti, but he snorted anyway. "I'll accept that, in part, but the *best* combat doctrine is one that does maximum harm to the enemy, and no harm at all to yourself."

Sigrun's smile was very faint. "As I said. . . I heal."

The conversation dropped there, as Sigrun found a seat across the room and settled in with a book. Adam continued to work, Frittigil watched him break apart the gun, wide-eyed. "Why . . . why does it have the round. . . thing?" She frowned, obviously hunting for the right word in Latin.

"The cylinder? So that it can hold six bullets at once."

"Why do you need so many?"

"Because sometimes, I'm fighting more than one bad person at once." He broke the words down simply for her. "Like today."

She put her head down on the table. He'd noticed that she was acting much more comfortable around him, and that was a relief, but he was worried that she'd remember that he was male and freeze up again. He didn't like seeing the beginnings of scars in this young psyche. After a moment, Frittigil asked, not looking up, "Why me?"

Adam passed a brush through the barrel of the gun, which he'd removed entirely from the rest of the mechanism, and looked at her. "What do you mean?" He kept his voice neutral, knowing it was important to let *her* talk things out, at least a little.

"Why did the gods let this happen to me?" Hurt, bafflement, anger. "I was good. I never got into trouble, not like my sisters. I believe in the gods. Why would they abandon me?"

Why do bad things happen to good people? The quintessential question most thinking people came to, sooner or later in life. Adam looked up at Sigrun, who was watching from across the room, over the top of her book. "I don't know what answer Sigrun would give you," Adam told the girl, quietly. "Some people believe that everything happens for a reason. That bad things are a test, a challenge."

Sigrun's very faint snort suggested that she was not an adherent of this particular philosophy. "And you?" Fritti asked, biting her lower lip.

"I think bad things happen to everyone, and that bad people make them happen, most of the time. Even, sometimes, good people, who make mistakes. Have bad judgment. Almost everything that happens to people, is the result of other people. Nothing more." He kept the words in Latin as simple as possible. The girl's grip on the language just wasn't good enough for complexity.

Sigrun leaned her head back against the chair as the girl turned. Fritti's eyes were bright with tears as she asked, "Is he right, *æðelinga?*"

Adam caught the wistful half-smile that crossed Sigrun's face. "I don't know," Sigrun told Frittigil, and he saw the girl's eyes widen. He was surprised, himself. He'd have thought that *certainty* was one of the primary traits of someone who was in the direct service of a god.

"You don't know? But . . . you are god-born!" Frittigil seemed to share his reaction.

"That does not mean I have any more answers than anyone else, little one." Sigrun walked slowly back over to the table. She clearly still ached. "I can tell you what I believe. Maybe you will believe it. Maybe you will find some other answer that you like better." She put a hand on the girl's shoulder, her diction softening. Contractions and light slurs in the clarity of her Latin, but still speaking slowly enough for the girl to understand. "For me, it's. . . simple. Bad things happen, because the gods don't control everything. There's *wyrd*, but there is no fate, no matter what people like my sister may believe."

"You have a sister?" Adam said, mildly. This was the first he'd heard of this, and Sigrun's face shuttered. "Nevermind. What's *wyrd*?" Adam asked. He'd heard the word before, but he really wasn't clear on all the nuances.

Sigrun made a flicking gesture with her free hand. "Some people translate it as fate, but that's not right. It is . . ." She frowned. "We all have a path that we're born to. Part of that is family. Where we start, our condition. But what steps we take along that path are our own. Sometimes we make good decisions, and sometimes, we're just fortunate, and we rise. Sometimes we make bad choices, or our feet slip on a stone. And at the end of the path, the gods reward us for doing right and punish us for doing wrong. But what we do in life . . . that's our responsibility. We have a choice about how we walk that path, and with whom. And our companions' choices along the path . . . shift the path under our feet, just a little. But it's not controlled by the gods. Or there would be no point in existence at all." Sigrun stifled a yawn with her fingertips. "But now . . . it is late. And I'm too tired for philosophy. There's a cot in my room for you, Fritti." She lowered her head to Adam. "Rest well."

"Sleep sound," he returned. "I'll try not to make much noise."

He didn't sleep much, himself; he finished his prayers and his reading, and sat up in a chair, dozing lightly, but mostly standing guard. He didn't think that anyone would really risk coming after the girl again, but a retaliatory strike against the propraetor and his entourage wasn't out of the question. And yes, there were other Praetorians guarding Livorus, and one on this floor of the hotel, watching over them . . . but Adam's sense of responsibility wouldn't let him rest. Livorus had chartered a direct flight from Ponca back to Marcomanni in the morning. There would be time enough to sleep then.

As such, he heard Frittigil muttering in her sleep several times, and, cautiously checked on both of them from the doorway, only venturing in to cover the girl with her blanket, which had slipped loose. And, so long as he was there, anyway, he pulled up the blankets over Sigrun's still form, too, before padding back out of the room on silent feet.

It was thus a shock to hear Frittigil's voice calling frantically for Sigrun, around five antemeridian. Adam lunged out of his chair, drawing his gun, and making it to the connecting door between the rooms in three strides. He flicked on the light and canvassed the room, hurriedly with his eyes, looking for intruders . . . and found none.

Fritti knelt on the floor, covering her face with her hands, as Sigrun, looking just as awake as Adam himself was now, tried to tug the girl's hands back from her face. "What's wrong, little one?" Sigrun asked gently. "Was it a bad dream?"

"*No. No, it was . . . strange.*" Fritti let her hands fall from her face, and managed to switch to Latin. "I saw a star on the western horizon drop down and become a woman. She wore leather clothing, all beaded and beautiful, but she was very sad. And a man of my people walked out of the darkness and joined her, and he told me not to be afraid. To come to them." Fritti was pushing her Latin as far as it would go. "So I walked to them. And I knew the man was Baldur, the shining one. The god loved by all, but hated by Loki, who was killed by the mistletoe, and who was and will be reborn after the end of all things." She raised her face, an expression of awe suffusing her features, and Adam felt his jaw go slack. Fritti's eyes had been dark blue yesterday. It had been in her physical description in the Praetorian files, for god's sake. Right now? The blue had darkened to the blue-purple haze of twilight, and dozens of tiny stars seemed to fill the night sky that surrounded her pupils. *I'm not sure how that should be recorded as on her driver's license, whenever she gets one,* he thought, numbly. *Star-shine blue? Galactic glory? Milky Way magenta?* The humor helped him stabilize his thoughts, somewhat. He was looking at someone who had been marked out by a god.

Sigrun, however, simply nodded. "And what else did they say to you?" Her voice was gentle. "They had a task for you?"

Fritti looked confused. "Not . . . not as such . . . the woman told me she was sorry I had suffered for her sake. That she never had wanted the ritual to be performed on anyone else, and that her people were supposed to bind *themselves* to her, not to use other people for that. And that she didn't want blood. And then she reached out and put her hand on my head, and I felt so much better. . . and she faded away. And Baldur said while the Evening Star had bound me, I was his now, too, because I'd died and come back. Just like he did. Well, like he will, anyway." Fritti looked a little uncertain now. As if she weren't entirely sure how to feel about any of this. "*Æðelinga*, what do they want me to do?"

Adam's mouth finally clicked shut. *I will never get used to how their gods just . . . talk to them directly. Does it make them weaker, to have that guiding hand always at their elbow? Does it make my people stronger to have to make every decision on our own? Who's to say, really?*

Sigrun nodded to herself. She'd *wondered* if the girl would be marked out by someone. While Frittigil was frightened, and clearly scarred by the experiences of the past few days, the girl hadn't been babbling, or a catatonic wreck. There was steel in the girl's heart, and her metal had been proven in a fire that most people would never face in the whole of their lives. Sigrun reached out to put a hand on the girl's arm, lightly, and told her, "You must decide for yourself, young one, what you are to do with your life. Choice is the burden of every god-born of Valhalla. You know of the choice of the valkyrie, yes? Who on the battlefield lives, and who dies?" At Fritti's nod, Sigrun squeezed her arm, gently. "You already had great gifts within you. A good mind, and a strong heart. The gods may have given you other gifts, besides the sign of their favor on your face." At Fritti's confused look, Sigrun reached under her bed, and pulled out her charred spear, so that the girl could see her own reflection in the polished metal. It was the closest thing to a mirror that Sigrun owned, and she didn't look at the reflection on the side facing her, keeping her gaze locked on Fritti's face, instead.

She could feel the muscles in the girl's thin arm go rigid as Fritti flinched back from her own eyes. "Be at peace," Sigrun told her, setting the spear aside. "Baldur is a gentle god, and the Evening Star seems to be a benevolent goddess. Whatever their gifts are, the Odinhall will see to it that you are trained in their use. You will not be a danger to yourself, or to others. That, I can promise you."

She wasn't sure if her words helped at all. Sigrun had been born what she was. There had never been a time when she wasn't god-born, and when it hadn't been impressed upon her that she was different from other people. Not better. Not worse. *Different*, with different expectations. But after a moment's thought, she understood why Fritti had pulled back. "The eyes are different, yes. But they are a lovely mark of favor. One easily covered with the smoked lenses that are so popular these days, if you so wish it. No one more than twenty feet away will even notice them." Sigrun raised her eyebrows, and felt Frittigil relax, incrementally.

"Will . . . will I have to go to the Odinhall?" Fritti asked, her voice thin.

"I do not know. You have been marked by two very different gods. For you to be trained solely at the Odinhall might be an affront to the Evening Star." Sigrun shrugged, and helped Fritti back to her bed, feeling her eyes burn a little with tiredness. "I doubt you will be able to sleep anymore this morning, little one. We can order breakfast, and you may shower first." Sigrun paused. "You will doubtless like to put on some clothing, I am sure."

Fritti looked down at herself, and her sudden expression of embarrassment was acute. Other than in the very coldest climates, most people in the world slept naked, with eiderdowns in winter for warmth. Fritti had apparently not been entirely comfortable with Adam's presence and had, as such, kept on her heavy tunic from the hospital gift shop . . . which still skimmed her upper thighs. Every essential was covered, but she still yanked the hem down and scuttled rapidly for the bathroom, mumbling excuses under her breath.

Sigrun herself hadn't stripped down; she had wanted to be prepared if there were any disruptions during the night . . . though this wasn't quite the sort of interruption she'd expected.

While Fritti was in the shower, Sigrun put in a call to the Odinhall, to confirm what the girl had experienced. Adam looked surprised, and muttered something about the wheels of bureaucracy being the same everywhere. "It's best to make sure that this really was Baldur and the Evening Star, and not a . . . very convincing spirit," Sigrun told him, grateful that the sound of the water covered her voice from the girl.

"It's interesting that you don't take revelation at face value," he told her, his eyebrows arching.

"I could see that there were no lies in her eyes," Sigrun told him, simply. "But that does not mean that someone did not lie to her." At that moment, the line she was on, was taken off hold, and she heard a voice on the other end. "Brandr?"

The voice that came in response was a low bass rumble. *"Waes hael, Sigrun, my old student."* Brandr had been one of the lead instructors in Sigrun's time at the Odinhall. *"I checked upstairs with Dvalin. The Keeper of the Runes says that her name was indeed inscribed in the rolls of the god-touched last night. She is a valkyrie, now . . . of a sort."*

"Am I supposed to make arrangements with her and her family to send her to Burgundoi? I think it would be unwise to tear her away from her family immediately. She needs them, and they will need to hold her tightly to them for a year or two." Sigrun addressed her old mentor with respect.

"Not until she is sixteen. But she will need a pedagogue, a mentor, of some sort, in the meantime. I'm not sure who will be sent, if the family cannot afford the training. And of course, there will be the need for her to be . . . conversant with the beliefs of those who follow the Evening Star, apparently."

Brandr sounded grim. *"Her life just became incredibly political, poor thing."*

"Only as much as she chooses for it to be," Sigrun returned, and heard Brandr's roar of laughter on the other end, before they both said their farewells, and hung up. Catching Adam's glance, though the Judean man had turned away, politely, during the spate of Gothic speech, Sigrun smiled a little. "She's very young," Sigrun said quietly, hearing affection in her own tone, which surprised her. She usually took longer to warm up to people. But Fritti was, after all, young, and easy to like. "But she's strong. She'll be just *fine.*"

Several hours later, they boarded their small chartered plane at the tiny Ponca airfield, along with Livorus and two of the regional Praetorians they'd been assigned, temporarily. Livorus had taken one look at Fritti, raised his eyebrows, and moved to take Sigrun's hand and now held it lightly in both of his. "You're quite well, my dear?"

"Much better this morning, sir. Thank you." Sigrun's spine snapped straight. There was only a trace of excess pink to her skin this morning, as if she'd suffered a bad sunburn a few days ago. No other evidence of the previous day's fight remained visible to the eye.

"Is our young guest's current condition any concern of the Empire's?" Livorus asked.

"Only in that it suggests that my gods and the gods of the Chahiksichahiks may be taking a direct hand in attempting to better relations between their peoples."

"That is, in fact, above my pay-grade. I endeavor to repair relations between nations, but am singularly ill-suited to negotiate with gods. I will leave that to the Emperor and whichever of his sons he intends to make the next high priest of Mars or Jupiter. . ." Livorus glanced off into the mid-distance, and then shrugged. "Young Hadrianus, no doubt. Though it is difficult to imagine the twelve-year-old he is now, in the stately robes of a priest of Mars Pater."

Livorus released Sigrun's hands, allowing her to sit down and buckle herself into place. Adam took the seat beside her, directly behind Livorus, who seated himself beside Fritti, and the two final Praetorians took the row in front of the propraetor. Even though the plane was chartered, it was still remarkably cramped. Adam gave the vehicle and the single steward they'd have for the flight a final careful once-over, and then, as his gaze returned to his own row of seats, was highly amused to note that Sigrun had gripped onto the arms of the chair, and that her knuckles were already white.

They had yet to leave the ground.

"Would it help if I held your hand?" he offered, leaning closer to lower his voice, needling lightly.

A flick of her steel-sheen eyes, and she muttered something under her breath.

"What was that?"

"I said that you may *bite me*, ben Maor."

Adam laughed out loud.

As the plane lifted off, Frittigil, in the seat ahead of them, turned around, her eyes wide with amazement, and chattered excitedly at Sigrun in her native tongue. "What was that?" Adam asked.

"This is *wonderful!*" Frittigil told him. "Is. . . exciting! To be free, like a bird, yes?"

Adam grinned at her, and found that the expression came easily, for all the girl's changed eyes. The young woman probably needed, more than anything, for everyone to act *normally* around her for the next several years. And he determined to do precisely that for the rest of the trip. "I've always liked flying, yes. I wanted to be a pilot, when I was young. Actually. . . I wanted to be an *astronaut.* I wanted to be the first man to walk on the moon."

That, he realized, had gotten Sigrun's attention. She'd turned to look at him, and frowned now. "So why are you not a pilot?" the Cimbric woman asked him.

Adam shrugged. "When I went into the Judean Defense Forces for my required two years, I asked for pilot training, and got special forces instead." He leaned back in his chair, relaxing visibly to help Sigrun calm down as the plane began to bank and rise higher. He could feel the pressure change in his ears already. "Turns out my superiors were right. I was a lot better at fighting on the ground than I ever thought I'd be. I got done with my required two years, and felt I should. . . I don't know, keep protecting my people, so I stayed in for another two. I was in the middle of deciding whether I wanted to go to school for an engineering degree, to try to get into the space program that way, when the Praetorians came calling." He included them both in his wry smile, feeling the plane dip and sway as a wind gust caught them. "I thought about it. And I decided that half the reason I wanted to go into space was the thrill of exploring. Seeing new things. I could do that with the Praetorians. And I could meet new people that way. Hard to meet new people on the moon." He said the last to Frittigil, who laughed shyly, ducking her head down behind the seat.

Of course, the *other* half of him had argued that the stars were their destiny, and that having his name written in them, forever, as an explorer, an achiever, a dreamer, would be a wonderful thing. But he'd reflected on it, and decided that he could do a lot of good in the Praetorians. Could protect people. And he could cheer on the space program from the sidelines, and they'd take his heart to the moon and beyond. Someday. But that part, he didn't mention.

Sigrun volunteered, unexpectedly, "I personally believe that in a galaxy with so many stars, there must be other life out there—oh, Hel's *teeth.*"

That last, as the plane dipped into an area of thermal disturbance, and turbulence began to vibrate through the frame. Sigrun dropped her hands back onto the arms of her chair, looking resolutely straight ahead.

The best part of their job, Adam mused, several hours later, was getting to see things like Frittigil running into her parents' arms. The joyous tears in her mother's eyes, the way her father lifted the girl clean off the ground, holding her tightly. It made up, in part, for the insane hours, the daily danger, and the knowledge that people out there could be targeting Livorus, or them, with bullets, magic, or both. The expressions of dumbstruck awe on their faces, and on the faces of Fritti's sisters, however, as they caught sight of her eyes, made him distinctly uneasy. They didn't drop to their knees in homage, however. Merely touched her face, and kissed her again, chattering rapidly in their native tongue.

He and Sigrun did their best to fade into the background, like good lictors should, as Livorus spoke with Fritti's family. Accepted their wrist-clasps, accepted their tearful thanks, on behalf of Rome, and then withdrew. But both parents advanced on Sigrun, and again, there was a long and twisty-sounding conversation. Adam was struck by the polite respect with which Sigrun's words were heard. *Again, no bended knee. But they're listening to her as if she were a judge. . . all right, technically, she is, I suppose. Ælagol. Whatever.* He caught several words he did recognize — Burgundoi, a city on the Pacifica coast, north of Nimes, where he'd been briefly stationed in Novo Gaul. The Odinhall, where Sigrun had studied, probably a temple or something. And Valhalla, where her gods were said to live.

And then she withdrew, with a slight bow of her head and a smile, and instead of a leader of her people, once more became a graven-faced lictor, adjunct to Livorus, and nothing more. Fritti wouldn't leave it at that, however, and darted forwards, wrapping her arms around Sigrun's waist, and surprise crossed the valkyrie's face. A few more quick words in Gothic, and a few shoulder pats, and then Fritti went back to her family. And as they left, Adam glanced back in time to see Frittigil waving shyly in farewell. And a smile crossed his bearded face, just for a moment, before they headed back aboard their plane. "She needed a little more reassurance that your Odinhall wasn't going to eat her?" he gibed Sigrun, lightly.

"She asked me, if I weren't too busy, if I would mind exchanging letters with her. I told her I was always busy, but never too busy for that. Training a first-generation god-born is very important. And if I can offer her any guidance, I would be proud to do so." Sigrun's tone was calm, as she settled into the plane's seat once more. *At least with these ley-powered contraptions, we don't have to wait for them to refuel. The batteries are just changed out.*

"And now, we must return to work," Livorus told them both as the plane turned and began taxing once more for lift-off.

"I don't believe we ever left off, propraetor," Sigrun told him, tiredly.

Livorus settled his dispatch case on the seat beside him, and leaned across the aisle to speak to them. "We're going to head back to Rome, by way of Novo Trier. We need a bigger plane to cross the Sea of Atlas, and will likely touch down in Londonium before making our way home. I need to make a full report to the Imperator and the Senate on all these doings here in Caesaria Aquilonis. Additionally, Ehecatl will be out of action for about two months. Ptah-ases . . . probably closer to six." He grimaced. "Ptah was already due to cycle off of my detail as it is. We'll pick up permanent replacements for both of them when we get to Rome, I suspect." He gave Adam a wintery smile. "You will no longer be the new conscript. Instead, you will be the seasoned veteran."

Adam shook his head. He didn't like it, but if Ehecatl and Ptah were that badly injured . . . he gave Sigrun a sidelong look. Technically, she could heal them, he supposed. But then again, both men had refused to *let* her. And, given the physical toll that such healing imposed on her, he couldn't see letting her do the same for him, either. She might well say she was fine this morning, but her face still looked drawn and tired under the pink residue of the burns. "It's our loss," Adam muttered. "I didn't have a chance to work with them for long, but they're both damned good at what they do."

"We might get Ehecatl back when he finishes his recovery," Livorus told them, with a faint shrug. "He has no immediate retirement plans. Ptah has been looking forward to seeing more of his wife and children, however. We'll see. In the meantime. . ." he looked directly at Sigrun, "I have a question for you, my valkyrie."

Sigrun turned, her eyebrows rising. Adam had never heard Livorus refer to her by that term before. Always the light 'my dear,' but Livorus never said it in a condescending way, or even a possessive one. The man clearly held Sigrun in respect and affection, but his tone was always . . . detached . . . when he spoke to her. "Yes, sir?"

"Our friend, the late priest of the Morning Star, told me, before he passed, that he'd saved his people. And asked me if I knew where my gods were." Livorus snorted. "What did he mean?"

Sigrun blinked, rapidly. "His blood *was* poured out on the earth. His life given for his people," she replied, clinically. "He could have meant it quite that literally. He saved his people, by . . . becoming their sacrifice. By binding them more tightly to the Morning Star, and giving the god the power of his life." She shook her head. "But to ask if you knew where your gods *were* . . . that doesn't make sense."

"I know *precisely* where my household gods are," Livorus replied, dryly. "On my altar, at home, near the fireplace in the largest receiving room. They're bound to their images, bound to my home, and have been, for centuries. As to the rest of the gods, as far as I know, they're either incorporeally listening to prayers in temples, overseeing the virtues in men's hearts, or, if you're feeling particularly literal—or Hellene—squabbling on Mount Olympus."

Sigrun cleared her throat. Livorus raised his eyebrows. "Yes, my dear?"

"Valhalla exists, *dominus*. To the best of my knowledge, so does Olympus."

"There are at least three mountains by that name, of which I am aware." Livorus' eyebrows remained lifted.

Sigrun shifted, a little uneasily. "There is the physical reality, a mountain in Hellas. And there is the . . . metaphysical reality. That mountain, as best I understand it, contains a gate. An opening." She gestured, clearly uncomfortable, even a little embarrassed. "To the realm where the gods dwell." She shrugged. "I am not an expert, sir. In my time at the Odinhall, my instruction in metaphysics was limited."

Adam shook his head a little. He knew perfectly well that there were other gods. He knew perfectly well that they took physical form—it would be somewhat difficult to have god-born without that prerequisite. Although there *were* all the Hellene legends about golden showers and women being raped by geese and bulls, which . . . which, on reflection, he really hoped were *metaphors*. "You mean, if you blunder into the wrong cave on Mount Olympus, you could wind up in the Hellene's afterlife?" Adam asked now, letting his amused skepticism show.

"I think that if you blunder into the wrong cavern anywhere, and take a bad step, or meet a bear, you'll wind up in *someone's* afterlife," Sigrun returned, with a faint trace of a smile, and then sobered. "I don't know if I'd call it the afterlife. If you went through, and were not caught by a guardian and turned back . . . you'd be in the realm of the gods. And that is not a place meant for mortals."

Adam wanted to be skeptical. . . . but he also knew that there were limits to his understanding of the world. And at the discomfort, yet assurance in her voice, he simply nodded, and Livorus did the same. The propraetor returned to the original subject now, frowning. "I've never much concerned myself with *where* the gods are. It's . . . a ridiculous question." He stared at them both. "But a dying man used his last breath to taunt me with it. Why?"

Sigrun stared at him, and slowly shook her own head. "I have no idea, sir."

Adam lifted his hands. "I don't suppose that the Chahiksichahiks believe in any . . . physical location for their gods? Any mortal bodies or forms?"

Livorus shook his head. "Not to my knowledge. Turning a captive woman into the semblance of the Evening Star is the closest that they come to that. But they don't seem to believe that the Evening Star comes to *inhabit* her during the sacrifice, or any such thing." He exhaled and turned back in his seat, picking up his dispatch case. "Think on it, while we continue in our travels, if you would. I would very much like to have this question answered."

"So would I, *dominus*," Sigrun murmured, "But a great deal of what just happened outside of Ponca . . . we're never going to get all of the details, are we?"

That was, in fact, the *worst* part of this job, Adam had already discovered. They were the trouble-shooters. Livorus was sent in when most other methods of diplomacy had failed, or when there wasn't time to lay much groundwork. They were sent in, with minimal information, and expected to get results. . . and while they had to stand for review on incidents that devolved into violence, and Livorus had to stand before the Imperator and the Senate and give an accounting for his decisions. . . they very often were taken out of the loop, once they'd left an area. It was no longer their concern. It was back in the hands of the diplomats who may or may not have made the mess in the first place.

Livorus sighed a little. "Patience, my dear. No, you aren't members of the diplomatic team, or the investigative team that will be dealing with the whole of this situation for . . . probably a decade or so to come. . . but both of you have unique insights, and keen minds. Any thoughts you have, no matter how odd? Bring them to me." He looked back down at his papers. "And now, if you'd both begin preparing your written reports? I'll need them by the time we get to Londonium. My staff will type them from your written notes once we arrive in Rome."

Chapter IV: Alterations

Electricity, whether alternating current or direct current, is simply not a safe mechanism for the transference of power. The potential for shocks that result in injury or death is simply too great for any ethical person to recommend tamed lightning as a power source. There are multiple methods for generating it, I will agree, and some of these methods are inexpensive, and even, I will grant, inexhaustible, such as wind and solar generation. But other methods, such as burning coal, which should be reserved for warming people's homes? Hardly seem worthwhile. It makes no sense to burn an entire forest, to light a single lamp. That is why I advocate tapping ley-lines. They exist, have been used for centuries already by ley-mages, are safe, inexhaustible, and, best of all, do not generate smoke, soot, and ash when used. A city which uses ley-energies to provide light for its citizens will be clean and wholesome, and everyone in it will breathe easily, as free men ought, rather than being choked by a slave's collar made of grime and disease.

— Thomas Mauritus, founder of modern ley-engineering, 1555 AC, in a speech before the Roman Academy of Natural Philosophy.

The incandescent bulb was developed, I must admit, as a toy for my children. I found that I could hold one in my hand, and cause the filament to smolder dimly with only a little transference of ley-energy. I thought of it as a training device for them, so that they could learn to tap ley-lines, and see evidence of their own success. I never imagined that I held in my hand something that would replace candles and whale-oil lamps. Until, that is, my wife told me to hold the 'jar of light' closer over her work, and thanked me for providing, clear, steady light that did not flicker or change as she sewed. Suddenly, a whole world of possibilities opened before me.

— Thomas Mauritus, inventor of the light bulb, 1570 AC, in a speech before the Academy of the Philosophers, Britannia.

<u>Martius 29, 1954 AC</u>

The phone rang, a jarring, invasive sound like a slightly more harmonious dental drill. Adam sat bolt upright in bed, shedding sheets and blankets, and wondering, just for a moment, where in god's name he was. Dim light filtering in from a window showed him rental furniture, not at all to his taste or comfort, including a Roman-style dining couch and backless, folding stools that filled the pre-furnished apartment he was renting for his stay in Rome. He'd been given the option of staying full-time with Livorus and his family, but had declined, needing a little mental space from the job.

The phone rang again, and Adam stumbled out of bed, taking the two steps required to get to the desk, thumped his shin against the backless chair there, swore, and caught the phone on the third ring. *"Ave?"* he said, out of habit, in Latin.

"*Shalom*," was the reply on the other end, in a familiar voice.

Adam blinked rapidly and changed mental gears. "*Shalom, Imah*," he told his mother. "*It's nice to hear your voice.*"

"*The phone could be picked up from your end, occasionally,*" she told him, lightly. "*How have you been?*"

In the background, he could hear his father's voice being raised, and the voices of his sisters, arguing about something or another. Theirs was a large, noisy family, much prone to squabbling. "*Fine, thank you. And you and Father?*"

"*He's been busy at work, as usual.*" Maor ben Emmet, Adam's father, had worked for the Judean Intelligence Office for over twenty years now. Adam largely regarded his father as a distant, if approving force in his life, and had spent many evenings at home with his brother and sister, trying to solve little cryptographic puzzles his father had set them. Usually just letter replacements, until they were old enough to have learned both Latin and Hebrew . . . at which point their father had started swapping between the two languages for his codes. His older brother had *hated* the game, but Adam had enjoyed it. Then again, he'd been good at it, and Mikayel, two years his senior, had struggled with it. Struggled with seeing patterns, with transposing letters from one alphabet to another, or words from one language written in a different alphabet entirely.

His older brother had had inventive ways of punishing Adam for 'showing off,' back in the day. Whether it had been being able to memorize more Torah verses, or deciphering the code of the week correctly, there'd always been a price, at least until Adam had hit his growth spurt. The price wasn't usually physical—there'd been little hitting tolerated in the house. And he hadn't, generally speaking, lost whatever treat he'd been given for winning. But winning had, invariably, been a reason for Mikayel to run him down, verbally. To tell him that only showoffs had to win every time. That he wasn't any better than Mikayel. And, for a number of years, Adam had believed every word his older brother said. Mikayel was, after all, older. He knew more, by definition. However, higher education and four years in the JDF's special forces, compared to his brother's stint of two years in the corps of engineers? Had taught Adam to respect himself, and his own abilities. Not to flaunt them, but not to denigrate them, either.

"*What did you do for Passover?*" Determined good cheer in his mother's voice.

Adam grimaced, already anticipating his mother's reaction. "*I had to travel over it, actually.*"

"*Not on Yom Tov, I hope?*" The first two and last two days of Passover week were Yom Tov, festival days, and travel on them was forbidden.

Adam sighed and looked up at the ceiling. "*Yes, and on Shabbat, too.*" He'd been called in by Livorus in Britannia on what was, for him, a non-working day, and they'd been on a plane for the New World hours later, landing first in Greenland for fuel, and then in Novo Trier, and then they'd hopped to Marcomanni. They'd arrived so late on die Solis evening—Sunandaeg, whatever—that it had been dies Lunae when they'd finished talking with Fritti's family and local authorities. They'd gotten a few hours' sleep, and then, because no planes had been available, they'd driven seven hundred miles the next day to get to Ponca, arriving in late afternoon. And the worst of it was, they almost hadn't been in time, anyway.

"*Oh, Adam, you know better –* " Disappointment and worry, comingled, and it irritated him.

"*A girl had been kidnapped in Caesaria Aquilonis. We had to cross the Sea of Atlas and get there before she was killed. I think I will be forgiven much more quickly for not observing a high holy day, than for letting a girl die, don't you think?*" Adam heard the irritation in his own voice, exhaled, and tamped down on his temper. His mother didn't deserve it. "*I'm sorry. I don't mean to snap. But no one has ever, in the history of the world, committed crimes on a convenient schedule.*"

"*I know, I just worry for you. Two years in all parts of India, and then I thought another two years in Novo Gaul, but instead, now, you're running all over the world. Britannia, Nova Germania, Rome . . . .* "

I know, he wanted to say, as he stood at his desk. *And it's the chance of a lifetime, and I wouldn't trade it for anything else on earth.* But his mother had already gone on, "*And in between all the running around, I wonder if what's really important isn't getting lost.*"

Adam picked up the phone's base, tugged the cord gently, and walked back over to the bed. If it was going to be *this* conversation . . . again . . . he'd prefer to be lying down for it. "*I like to think that saving lives is somewhat important, Imah.*" He kept his tone gentle, but dryness leaked in, anyway.

"*Oh, of course it is! I don't mean to that your job isn't worthwhile. I just . . . I see your brother, married now for six years, two beautiful children, a lovely wife, a nice home . . . he has roots. He's part of the community.*"

Adam let the words roll past him. He'd heard them before. He'd undoubtedly hear them again. He even quelled the rebellious voice inside that questioned whether being a 'part of the community' in Jerusalem was of any interest to him at all. He didn't speak until his mother added, quickly, "*I just want to make sure that you don't let life pass you by, Adam. You need a wife, a home here in Judea. I took the liberty of talking to a matchmaking service –* "

"No." His voice was firm.

"*There's nothing shameful in using their services! They find people who are perfectly well suited to one another, and whose families can get along –* "

"No, Imah."

"*And how else are you going to meet a nice girl, if you're traipsing all over the world, hmm?*"

Adam cleared his throat. "I do all right." He smothered the grin that quirked his lips, even though his mother couldn't see it; it would show up in his voice if he let it get away from him. "*You really don't need to worry about me, Imah. I'm not planning on settling down any time soon. If and when I do, I'll be sure to tell you, all right? Just, please. Don't waste money on a matchmaker for me. I'm not likely to be home to meet any of the girls any time soon, and I'm surely not going to get married by proxy . . . or leave someone alone at home to stare at the walls, while I'm out traveling the world."*

"You could have a wife travel with you!"

Adam looked up at the ceiling again. Some of the other Praetorians did that, and it might work if they were in a position with, say, an ambassador or at a consulate, where they were going to stay for a couple of years before moving. His current position was challenging and interesting, and ensured that he was rarely in one city for more than a month at a time, other than Rome. Even here, his apartment had a musty, unlived-in smell to it. He opened his mouth to try to explain, but his mother had already swept on. *"What do you mean, you won't be home any time soon? I thought you were going to take leave . . . . "*

Adam did his best to extricate himself from the conversation, finally pleading that he really needed to get ready for work. Once he hung up, he shook his head, and padded to the lavatory, and rubbed at his face; he'd let his beard grow back in, these past six months in Novo Gaul, Britannia, and Nova Germania. And technically, he probably should leave it in place, but Judean Defense Force regulations nattered at the back of his mind: *No facial hair. Facial hair interferes with the seal of a gas mask, and is a haven for lice and fleas, not to mention an admirable handle for an opponent to seize. Officers and enlisted must be clean-shaven while on active duty.* There were a few sticklers here and there who wanted to cite the Book of Jeremiah about the prohibitions on shaving, but almost everyone agreed, these days, that those all had related to mourning traditions that didn't exist in the modern era, and a desire to separate the people of Abraham from the nations around them, such as the Hittites, Elamites, Sumerians, and Egyptians. For anyone who was concerned, there were exemptions offered. In his current job, Adam tended to default to whatever let him blend in more readily with the local population. And in Rome, that meant shaving. A decision he'd put off for a few weeks . . . but now that he'd had the same damned conversation with his mother as he'd had the last several times they'd spoken?

It was definitely time to shave.

As he did so, he considered the past three years, reflectively. India had been . . . interesting. A rigid caste-system, everyone's lives even more controlled than in Judea, but it seemed like half the temples had erotic statuary in them. His Roman protectee, an ambassador, had made a point of sight-seeing and getting outside of the major cities, trying to understand the locals. As such, Adam had actually met a *nagarvadhu*, or a 'bride of the city,' a type of courtesan. The women of her region actually *competed* to become what she was; there was no shame at all in it, and successful ones were taught song, dance, poetry, and commanded sums so large that only princes could afford a night of their company. The position seemed to be equivalent to what a *geisha* truly was, in Nipponese culture. He'd met *devadasi*, as well, women, who, like priestesses of Ishtar in ancient Babylon, gave themselves, not for coin, but to replicate for devotees of their faith, the divine impulse in sexual form. He . . . wasn't quite sure he understood that, but it was emphatically religious, and it was *not* prostitution. That much, he'd been clear on.

So his eyes had been firmly opened in India, so far from home, but where most of the women were tightly controlled by their families, and he hadn't been entirely eager to get involved in someone else's religious rituals, precisely. However, Novo Gaul, and even parts of Nova Germania? Quite a different world, again. The women of both provinces had, historically, more rights than even Roman women. A Roman woman, in the days of the Republic, had been able to divorce . . . *if* her father had arranged for it, and accepted her back into his house. Gothic women? Even thousands of years ago, they'd had the right to divorce, in their own names. And Gallic legends spoke of women like Boadicea, who'd led her men into battle against Rome in Britannia. And the Goths clearly revered the valkyrie. So, their cultures had long had far more freedom for women than cultures like Judea, Persia, or even Hellas.

As a result, the concept of female equality had spread from the Gallic and Gothic regions, particularly in the new world, to the rest of the old one. And in Caesaria Aquilonis? The women tended to be strong-willed and upfront about things. Adam had been taken aback the first couple of times he'd been propositioned by an interested female in Nimes in Novo Gaul. Apparently, with his dark hair, dark eyes, and olive skin, he was interestingly exotic and excitingly foreign. Whatever it was, he wasn't going to complain about it. At all.

Having gotten dressed, he got on with his day. He'd had half of yesterday, and half of today off, as well, so he'd actually gone out the night before, to the baths, which were, for Romans, and for most Roman provincials, the focal point of social and civic life. The baths were always divided between male and female sides. There were gymnasiums for wrestling, sparring, playing ball, and whatever else. Libraries, shops, and restaurants ringed each bathing complex. You could listen to music or a poetry reading while taking a steam, and while some Romans took a day off of work to go to the baths, they generally did a good deal more than simply bathe. They talked with their friends, they ate good food, they shopped.

Adam had, for his part, found a *taverna* and had a couple of glasses of boiled wine from the Isle of the Blessed. One of the waitresses had taken a fountain pen and written her phone number in Sanskrit numerals on the back of the foolscap paper that was his receipt; Adam had chuckled and left a silver denarius and an bronze assarius, the last being her tip. Half a denarius per glass of wine. Rome was . . . expensive to live in. In Judea, the wine would have been half the price. Then again, in Judea, he wouldn't have had to buy imported boiled wine.

Then again, Rome was the city at the heart of the world, or so its residents liked to think. In reality, there were larger cities—Beijing, for one, in distant Qin. There were older cities in the world—Memphis, Thebes, Jerusalem, Babylon . . . the list went on. But Rome was the heart of the Empire, and it throbbed, day and night, as people came to and from it, and traversed its winding streets.

Adam caught a ley-powered streetcar, and watched from his seat as drivers in motorcars and on scooters jockeyed with overburdened trucks in the crowded streets. Seemingly suicidal pedestrians plunged right out onto the roads, surging in packs through traffic that miraculously slowed just in time for them to cross the streets. He made his way from his apartment, which was located in a skyscraper in the area that had once been the Field of Mars, to Livorus' palatial villa on Palatine Hill. Nodding to the guards at the gate, he made his way around to the back entrance, and began his rounds.

There were other lictors assigned to protecting Livorus' home and family, not to mention Livorus' personal guards, but it made Adam feel better to have verified the perimeter. Having wended his way to the top floor of the villa, Adam paused and looked out a window, shaking his head. Up here on the third floor, the windows at least made him less uneasy, and he could appreciate the view.

Livorus' family was old, and distantly related, supposedly, to Marcus Antonius, who'd been a follower of Gaius Julius Caesar in the late days of the Republic. It showed; the family home on Palatine Hill was at the very heart of the city. Off to his left, he could see the Aventine Hill, where foreign kings and queens stayed; it was not considered to be within the 'sacred' soil of Rome, and thus, foreign rulers could be accommodated there. This window also looked down at the marble-sheathed walls of the Circus Maximus . . . and, as he walked around to the back of the house, he had another fine view, this one of the white and gleaming walls of the Colosseum . . . with the relatively new, retractable glass and metal roof that had been Livorus' own pet project, while he'd been *aedile*. Sketches of that retractable roof hung, framed, in various places in the villa. Adam understood that the roof had been quite a divisive project. The Colosseum had been built to accommodate the ever-increasing crowds of Rome, in 114 AC, by Emperor Livianus, the grandson of Caesarion the God-Born. It was, as such, one of the most ancient buildings still standing, and the metal and glass addition had been termed a *desecration* and a *travesty* by its detractors . . . but the more recent addition of swamp-coolers had been less controversial, and had met with universal approbation.

From another window, as Adam paced around the top floor of the sprawling villa, he could see the temple of Jupiter Optimus Maximus Capitolinus. The original had been built twenty-five hundred years ago, give or take; it had burned in 1660 AC after a great fire had swept through Rome, though it had been largely a stone building. The emperor of that period, Julianus III, had rebuilt the temple, larger and grander than before. And, of course, the palace of the emperors crowned the Palatine, with an open plaza before it. That building dated back to Caesarion I; the plaza was a more recent addition, built in 1334 AC.

Most of Rome gleamed bone-white under the afternoon sun, by the deliberate efforts of a hundred generations of public servants. Roofs were red-tiled, but the walls of all public buildings were either faced in white marble or their poured-stone was required to be painted white, to match. Even the skyscrapers that now filled the Field of Mars were largely white, though architects had obviously tried to incorporate as much glass as possible into their designs to get around this restriction.

There was no soot in the air to stain that stark whiteness, and the city was so bright, it almost hurt to look at, reflecting almost as much light back to the naked eye as the winding bends of the Tiber that cut through the maze of buildings. It was beautiful and terrible at once to see so much of the power of Rome expressed in its architecture. The uniformity of ideas, of purpose, of belief, the strength of will to carry them out . . . and the endurance, to continue in their path for over two thousand years.

Now, he headed down the stairs; the inner walls of the stairwell had more windows that faced into the villa's atrium. Those windows, at night, were particularly bad for him; he could picture hands shattering the glass from the other side, and *ghul* crawling through. He put the thought out of his mind, and strode down the last flight of the marble stairs, stopping as Livorus' three children, all under the age of twelve, ran through the lobby with their tutors in tow, their laughter ringing back off the tile floor and frescoed walls. Two of them had their father's curly, dark hair, and the youngest clearly took after their mother, Poppaea, with dark golden hair. That youngest was a boy, no more than four years of age, and, because he was so young, someone—perhaps his mother—had hung a protective charm around his neck, a *fascinus*. Made of metal, it was in the shape of a phallus, and thus, considered lucky, or at least capable of turning away the evil eye.

The first time Adam had seen this, his eyebrows had gone up, and he'd given Sigrun a mildly incredulous look. It wasn't that he was unused to other cultures; he'd spent two years in India as a lictor for the Roman ambassador. And Hindus had lingam and yoni symbols in plenty to represent male and female creative and sexual energies. Those were, however, usually fairly *abstract*.

Sigrun had caught the glance, and chuckled. "Romans do love their phalluses, don't they?"

"I had no idea how much."

She shrugged. "When a conquering general comes home for the traditional triumphal march, they put a phallus underneath the old-fashioned chariot, so that it hangs there, freely. Unless he chooses to parade inside of a tank, instead. In which case, they sling it underneath the main gun."

"So, you mean to say that he really does have the biggest swinging d—"

"Yes." Sigrun had nodded to him, managing to keep her face sober, but she'd gone pink, which interested him. There weren't many things Sigrun blushed at, but this was one of them. "Also, just listen to the word for these luck charms, these amulets. *Fascinus*."

Adam had stared at her for a moment. "Oh . . . *gehenna*. Like the *fasces*?" He'd started to laugh, and had to cover his mouth, turning away so that Livorus' family didn't notice. "You mean to say that whenever a praetor or propraetor carries the *fasces* out to some place to conduct talks . . . he's not just shaking a bundle of *sticks* in their faces, yes?"

Sigrun had put both hands up and over her face, flushed rose by this point, and had laughed uncontrollably for a moment, garnering a few looks from Livorus and the other lictors as unloading of the propraetor's luggage had continued apace. "No, it's definitely a bundle of sticks, and the words aren't *related*," she told him. "It's only symbolically that he's waving all of Rome's collective—"

"Say no more, say no more," Adam had told her, almost gasping for breath at this point. "I . . . never made that connection before. Thank you. I have learned something new today." *Actually, I've learned two things. What you sound like when you actually let go and laugh. It's a good sound, and a good look on you, my friend.*

Back in the here and now, he watched the children trundle by, ignoring their surroundings as if they were . . . completely normal and everyday. And to them, of course, they were. The frescoes on the walls, for example, were probably five or six hundred years old, and done after the style of Pompeii. One of them invoked Flora, the goddess of spring; she was entirely naked as she danced among the flowers of a meadow. The other, set just beside the door, was an image of the god Priapus—the ugly god of boundaries, nature, and lust, who was cursed with a comically oversized penis, a permanent erection . . . and impotence. Adam was not really sure how the three conditions coexisted, but this god was depicted as cheerfully weighing his erection on a scale, opposite a bag of gold . . . and apparently, the penis weighed more, to the glee of the nymphs and satyrs around him.

Adam shook his head. Images in general were more or less frowned on in Judea, although some less conservative communities allowed frescoes and the like, so long as they weren't *worshipped*. There were public bathhouses, in the Roman style. But people in Judea were, by and large, a little more modest about their bodies than Romans were.

"My wife hates the frescoes," a voice said, from off to the right, and Adam turned, surprised, to see Livorus standing in the door to his library, looking up the stairs at him in evident amusement. The Roman, in the comfort of his own home, wore slacks and a long-sleeved shirt, and not a toga. But then, the toga was highly formal clothing, in this day and age. "I believe she would like to paint over them and put up something *abstract* in their place. I have told her, however, that I have found Priapus' capering amusing since I was a child, I rather enjoy Flora; and, as they've both been here longer than I've been alive, I can hardly begrudge them their place in my home. And that if she wishes to spend money supporting 'art for art's sake,' or whatever that movement calls itself . . . that she should spend the money on a new set of paints for our youngest son. The results will be about the same." Livorus smiled, faintly. "Come in, ben Maor. We've got a few dossiers to go over, with regard to my new lictors."

Adam nodded, and followed the man into the library, where Sigrun was already sorting through file folders filled with pictures and typewritten reports. They were the two highest-ranking lictors, of those who would travel permanently with Livorus, and Sigrun had been with the propraetor for almost five years already. Her word would carry a good deal of weight, but they both had a vested interest in choosing people with whom they'd work well, as a team. "I've pulled a few names," she said, looking up . . . and then paused, staring at him. "What happened to your *face?*"

"I shaved. What, I'm not allowed?"

A rapid-fire series of blinks. "I . . . you look different." She shook her head, evidently flustered. "Other than Romans, I am not much accustomed to seeing men past the age of sixteen without a beard. Forgive me."

Adam grinned at her. "So you're saying that I look like a girl, eh?"

"No! I'm . . . not saying anything. At all." Sigrun blew a few strands of pale hair out of her face, in clear exasperation, and slid a pile of folders across the table in his general direction. She shook her head, and suddenly, was all business again. "A pity Zoskales Ezana isn't available."

"Who's he?" Adam asked, taking a seat and opening the first folder.

"My partner, before Villu. A Nubian sorcerer — from the lands south of Egypt — and a very good one." Sigrun looked at Livorus. "However, *someone* recommended him to the Imperator — "

"Guilty as charged," Livorus said, pleasantly, and sat down on the room's single, large couch, turning on the far-viewer, taking a bunch of grapes from a nearby plate. "Forgive me, but there's a floor debate in the Senate that I really must watch. Continue. Ezana is not available." Livorus turned the dial on the far-viewer, negotiating through the twenty or so channels of programming to which Rome had access. A flicker of images. A satyr play, heavily bawdy, down to the fake phalluses worn by the male actors as they chased the females around the stage. *Click.* Something heavily moral and tragic by Seneca. *Click.* A sweating couple, caught in *flagrante delicto*, full penetration. "Twenty channels, and I can never find the one I want, when I want it," Livorus muttered. "And while this *is* someone being fucked in the ass, it's not actually my political opponents. Not quite what I had in mind." *Click.* "Ah. Here we go." He settled back as the picture formed, showing the columns and backless benches of the Forum, and a commentator began to drone out an introduction for this senator or that.

Adam shook his head. Judea had thirty or so channels broadcast for far-viewer reception, and he'd had his mind forcibly expanded in India and in the course of serving Rome . . . but he still couldn't quite believe the things that Rome put on the airwaves for public consumption. No scrambling the signal, no special times of day, nothing. Then again, during the early and late decadent periods, various emperors had decreed that anything that happened in a given script was required to happen, in reality, on stage. The number of tragedies put on by theaters had dropped to nil, overnight. None of the actors wanted to die for their art. They might have the same social status as a gladiator, or a prostitute, but actors didn't usually face *death* in the course of their daily work.

He returned his attention to the dossiers, though it was surprisingly difficult to focus, at least for a moment or two. "Sigrun?" Adam asked, after a moment, and glanced at her. Her face was impassive, and unreadable, for the moment.

"Yes?"

"This one from Britannia . . . Trennus Matrugena."

"What about him?"

Adam rubbed at his face. "He's a *summoner*." For him, that meant one thing: a magus, like one of the Magi.

"It's his secondary profession. He's studied ley-magic for ten years. The summoning is . . . well, it's not a hobby." Sigrun shrugged.

"I should damned well think not." He rubbed at his newly-shaved face again, trying to suppress the images springing from behind his eyelids. "I don't really want someone who wakes up *ghul* on the team."

"He doesn't. Read the file. His teacher in the ley arts was killed by a rogue summoner. He helped track the killer down, killed the man, and then went to the University of Londonium to learn about more of the mystic arts than the local druids could teach him. He's been hunting summoners gone bad ever since."

Adam grimaced. "I'm not convinced that there's such a thing as a *good* summoner, Sig." He folded his hands on the table. "It's a short-cut to power. And they always seem to end up making pacts with creatures from the spirit realm that they *can't* control, and then they get loose, and the rest of us get to clean up the mess. And, usually, the bodies." The last he muttered, half under his breath.

Sigrun looked at him steadily. "I spent two years on the Roman-Persian border, Adam. And another two on the Mongol border. I've seen my fair share of what Chaldean and Persian magi and Mongol shamans can unleash."

Adam squinted at her. This was not the first time he'd had an indication that she was older than she looked. Outwardly, she looked no more than twenty-two, twenty-three at the most. But she'd served with Livorus for five years. And now she claimed four years of experience on the eastern borders of the Empire. "How old *are* you, Sigrun?"

"Old enough to know I don't know everything, and there's an end to it." Sigrun flipped her fountain pen around in her fingers, redirecting it, like the conversation. "Why so resistant, Adam?"

"I don't want to see *ghul* fighting beside me," he replied, shortly. "They tend to pull loose of their summoner and start attacking everything in sight. And if I never see a djinni or an efreeti again, it'll be too soon."

Sigrun's eyes widened. "I remember that in your dossier, when we were evaluating you. You have a commendation in your jacket for single-handedly destroying a djinni. Or at least, banishing it from the mortal realm." She paused. "What happened?" Her voice had shifted. Become gentler.

Adam shrugged. It was not one of his better memories. "The Medes were trying to provoke us, over the edge of Domitanus' Wall. They're the usual cat's-paws of the Persians. They don't want to provoke Rome directly, so . . . . "

"The Shadow War," Sigrun said, nodding in agreement. A war fought conducted by intermediaries, it had been quietly seething between

Persia and Rome for decades, but it was mostly *fought* by Media, Chaldea, and Judea. "I know the politics, Adam. What happened?"

He looked down at the folder, seeing not a picture of a man of Britannia, all tattoos and braided hair, but a sun-blasted section of the desert through which the Wall passed. "The Medes sent a skirmishing party, and managed to sneak over the Wall," he said, quietly. "It's not impenetrable. Nothing is. They got down into one of the small towns about a mile from the wall itself. Set off gas grenades among the civilians. That was bad enough. We had them pinned down, though, in a school—they'd attacked at night, and the battle had gone on for hours, so no children were there, thankfully . . . ." He stared into the mid-distance for a moment. "We kept shouting for them to throw down their weapons and come out. Then my captain said it had gone on long enough, and shouted to them, 'Very well, from this moment forward, no quarter asked or taken.'" He sighed. "And that's when their magus summoned the djinni. It . . . rose up like a light wind from the desert at first, and then there was nothing but stinging sand, everywhere. A plume, like one of the cyclones of your plains, but made of sand and will. And it looked at us, without eyes . . . and moved right for us. The Medes used the distraction to break and run." He shrugged. "How do you shoot wind and sand? How do you kill it?"

He pictured it again, standing there with his Aphek assault rifle in his hands, uselessly firing rounds into the plume, wind tearing at his face as the *thing* approached, two miles high, at least, contracting down to a mere hundred feet, so that they could see its top, see the filmy, ephemeral face that hovered above the vortex, made up of fine sand, ever-shifting, ever-changing, and two mad, golden eyes, staring right at them. Finally *seeing* the eyes hadn't made it any better. He'd aimed for them at first, trying to find some weak spot . . . . but nothing.

They fell back, feet churning over the clay of the roads, trying to find a building unoccupied by civilians in which to take shelter. The djinni tore the roof off the first building, reaching in with limbs made purely of wind and had sucked two men up and into its vortex; they'd risen, screaming, up and through the creature's substance, propelled thought-fast, hundreds of feet into the air, and then allowed to fall. "My captain tried a rocket on it," Adam muttered. "That got its attention. It picked him up . . . specifically him. Towered back up to its full height, touching the sky . . . and then its whole length just went . . . . red."

Sigrun closed her eyes for a moment, in pure empathy, and he appreciated that. The captain, ben Chayyim, had been a friend. And they'd found pieces of his flesh, and his armor, three miles away. "How did you destroy its form?" she asked. "I never saw one *that* powerful. Most of them were . . . dust devils."

Adam grimaced. "Most of them *are* just dust devils. No one had seen one this powerful before. But . . . my captain had had the right idea. Fire consumes air. I knew if we didn't try something, we'd just be picked off, one by one, and then most of the town. I threw a grenade at it, got its attention, and *ran*. Led it to an ammunition dump. Those have nice, lightweight roofs. I think it was playing with me, really. Toying with me. So, I set a few charges inside the building, waited for the damned thing to pull the roof off . . . and then ran, setting off the detonators behind me." Adam swallowed. The force of the blast had mainly been directed *upwards*, right into the face of that howling wind, but there'd been enough explosives in that ammunition dump to level a small city. There'd been just enough side-blast to take him off his feet and send him sailing, and he'd hit the ground, hard, rolled around, and stared up in time to see two pillars, one of roiling fire, and one of sand and air, intertwining as the djinni, belatedly, struggled *not* to draw in everything around it . . . . and then was consumed by what it, itself, had consumed. Adam looked down at the folder again. "It was a very bad day, Sig." By destroying its form here, he'd sent it back to the spirit-realm. But a djinni like that could be summoned again, if not immediately. He hadn't ended the threat.

She reached across the table, and very lightly put her fingers to the back of his hand, and he glanced at her, startled, but didn't draw away. "I understand," she told him, quietly. "But this Matrugena comes very highly recommended by law enforcement in Britannia and northern Gaul. He's spent much of the last several years hunting rogue summoners from a group called *Sangua Foederis*. Blood Pact. I would like to meet the man, at least, before dismissing him from consideration."

"Well, if you're going to be *fair* about it," Adam muttered, grimly, "I suppose I don't have much to say."

Sigrun regarded him, and asked, politely, "Would it help if I held your hand?"

Adam blinked, hearing his own words to her aboard the plane weeks ago tossed back in his face, and laughed.

She quirked her eyebrows and gave him a quick, light grin. "How about this one? Not a summoner, I swear." She slid another folder across the table, and Adam opened it, flipping through the pages quickly.

"A technomancer?" He shrugged. "Sounds the same as Ptah, really."

"Well, a *sorcerer* who happens to know his technomancy, yes." Sigrun fidgeted with the folders in front of her.

"This is Ptah's replacement, and the summoner is Ehecatl's?" Adam flipped through the pages rapidly. "We had parity before, two of us who didn't really do magic worth a damn, and two people who . . . did. More or less." He gave her a sidelong look. "Ehecatl's tattoos really didn't count. Handy, though."

"Lighter weight than armor, certainly. And I've seen an arrow bounce off of him." Sigrun gave him a look. "Want some?"

"Not an option. Markings on the skin are forbidden."

"The list of what rules you follow and which ones you don't is a little idiosyncratic."

"I follow the ones that make sense to me and that are in the scope of reason. Dietary laws exist to keep people from being sick. The markings on the skin rule . . . probably originated to distinguish us from all of our neighbors. Like the beards. I can get behind it, because tattoos are permanent, identifying, and if done incorrectly, can be a health hazard. Plus, if some marking ties me to spirits or gods not my own, that's a real problem." He rubbed a hand over his currently-clean cheek. "That being said? Built-in flak jackets would be useful." Adam tapped on the page ahead of him. "Back on the subject of parity and team balance?"

Sigrun laced her fingers together, propping her elbows on the edge of the table, and rested her chin on her fingers, a characteristic pose. "You and Ehecatl are both very effective at your roles. But I don't actually see a need for a stealth specialist, to be honest, other than in very limited circumstances, and Ehecatl tended to . . . stand out . . . in areas that weren't Caesaria Aquilonis. Remember all the people staring at him in Britannia? And that was even an area of the world where people really appreciate skin markings like his." She shrugged. "Admittedly, people have to *see* him to stare at him, and he's the best there is at not being seen . . . but I think you're better with your weapons of *natural philosophy*. As to the summoner . . . please remember that he's also a ley-mage. We haven't had a ley-mage since Villu died. And they are very useful."

Adam looked back down at the folders again, studying the sorcerer. "Kanmi Eshmunazar? That's a Carthaginian name." He read, further. "Tyre? It's a province of Rome . . . " Tyre was north of Judea, and had been firmly under Roman rule for centuries. Carthage itself, including vast tracts of land ruled previously by the Numidians, was mostly in Africa, with the exceptions of city-states like Tyre, and still paid a token tribute to Rome every year, as a subject kingdom. There was unrest in Tyre; most of the natives of Eastern Carthage still considered themselves Carthaginian, and wished to be re-organized as part of the overall Carthaginian province, rather than being a separate political entity with its own Roman governor. Rome had steadfastly refused this request. "He's got an interesting record. Four years on the Mongol border . . . two years of protective work in Carthage and Byzantium . . . married for six years . . . . "

"That can be either a sign of stability or a source of stress," Sigrun advised, dryly. "Don't use it as a determining factor."

"He's not going to like your summoner any more than I do, if he fought Mongols for four years."

"Since when is Matrugena *my* summoner?"

Adam grinned at her. She reacted rather nicely to teasing. "All right. How do you want to meet these two?"

"Formal interviews won't tell us much besides if they know how to answer questions. I'd rather meet them in the wild." Sigrun raised her eyebrows slightly.

Adam considered it for a moment. There was merit in what she said. "I trust you don't mean 'stage a crisis' or anything like that?" he offered, cautiously.

Sigrun snorted. "No. Just . . . socially. See how they react to crowds, to people around them. How they treat people when they don't know precisely who's observing them. And yes, to the unexpected."

He turned it over in his mind. "We can ask them to meet us at the baths, I suppose."

"Well, *you* can. I'm not allowed on the male side of the complex." Sigrun put her hands on the table. "Once you've introduced yourself, take them to a *taverna* in the vicinity — *Agnellus*, perhaps? I can slip in and watch and listen. They probably won't notice they're being observed. And if they do, it'll speak well for their powers of observation."

Adam grinned suddenly. "Sig."

She blinked. "Yes? Did I miss something?"

"They're going to notice you."

"It's not Tyr's day. I won't be wearing anything that stands out. No armor, no feathered cloak, no spear in my hand. It'll be fine."

Adam's shoulders shook. "Sigrun. You're my height. Not quite six feet tall, but close. You're copper-blond. And while it's not dies Martis —"

"Tiwesdæg —"

"Whatever. You stand out in a crowd. Not quite as badly as Ehecatl, I'll admit, but . . . . "

Sigrun gave him a narrow-eyed stare. "I will be fine."

"Do you want to put denarii on this?"

"I will put money on this: They won't know I'm a lictor in the Praetorian Guards. They won't even know I'm god-born." Sigrun nodded, firmly.

"Half a solidus says they make you before you say one word."

"You're on."

After five postmeridian, everyone in Rome tended to congregate at the *thermae* — the baths. People would bathe for an hour or two, eat dinner, go out for wine, and then go to the theater or whatever their chosen late-night activities were. The baths were ubiquitous, bustling, noisy, and not a place for modesty at all. Adam had been raised in a culture that prized that last quality; for example, in Judea, one did not, when using a urinal, turn to talk to the man next to you, make eye contact, or anything along those lines. In the public baths, people sat around stark naked, in the pools, or taking a steam. The most one *might* have was a towel.

It required certain mental adjustments. Most notably remembering not to hit anyone whose eyes dropped below neck level.

Adam tossed his rolled-up clothing into a public locker and secured it with a combination lock he'd purchased for this purpose. He had about a half an hour to shower in the tepidarium — pre-cleaning was required before using the full baths — and maybe get a few laps in at the swimming pools, out in the frigidarium. Tepidaria typically had a pleasant warmth radiating from the walls and floors, from steam pipes that crisscrossed the area behind the tiles, and had once been used for anointing the body with oils, and cutting the grime away with a strigil, a hook-like tool designed to scrape the skin, but the prevalence of soap in modern society had removed that as a necessity. However, in this room, as in others like it, there were massage tables set up, away from the showers, where people could be rubbed down after coming out of the baths.

Voices rang off the travertine tiles that covered floor and walls in a wash of subtle colors, and he padded through the hygiene area, tossing a few coins into an attendant's bucket to get an unoccupied stall — one without a servant, thank you — to sluice down on his own. Rome, unlike most of the New World, still had slaves, and the bath attendants — all male on this side of the complex — were representatives of this lowest caste of society.

The shower water was lukewarm, deliberately so; it was intended to wake up the bather and prepare them for the rooms that grew warmer, the deeper into the complex one wandered. Adam found the archway that led to the frigidarium, instead, and dove into a pool, once he found an unoccupied lane. He had to admit, this room was aesthetically very pleasing; colonnades of golden stone lined both sides of the long pool, supporting a vaulted ceiling, which was surmounted by an oculus for light . . . and which had been glassed in, at some point in the hundreds of years since this building had first been constructed. And at least, the exercise area wasn't completely packed with chattering people.

After about forty laps, and when the wall clock read fifteen after six, Adam pulled himself out of the pool and wrung his hair dry, padding once more, light-footed, for the arches that led to back to the tepidarium, and then made a right, into the hall that took him into the caldarium's heat. The room was a sauna, and foggy with steam; Adam let his body get used to the heat before bracing himself and stepping down into the water; the entry end was probably around a hundred degrees, and stepped up, the deeper one went, to about a hundred and twenty at the far end. He had no intention of boiling himself, and only a few minutes were really necessary. He stepped back out again, and found a stone bench to sit on for a few minutes.

The trick to finding someone in the crowds — and everyone, eventually, came to the caldarium, even if only for a few minutes — was to look at people without actually seeming to look at them. Adam had a pretty good idea of what his targets looked like. Both were a little older than he was — the summoner from Britannia, only by a year, but the Carthaginian was five years his senior. And it didn't take long to spot them in the crowds, as they arrived promptly at thirty past the hour. Both looked a little out of place in the crowd as they made their way through the chattering groups of Romans and Hellenes.

Adam had to admit, the baths weren't a horrible place to see how someone reacted to being out of their element, and not in their home territory. Both men had been raised in Roman provinces; neither of them could be complete foreigners to the notion of the *thermae*. Of the two, Kanmi Eshmunazar looked slightly more at ease, however. He was surprisingly short — shorter than Adam himself by about four inches. The sorcerer from Tyre had olive skin, short, slightly wavy dark hair, and eyes so black they looked like obsidian that had been worn by water. He found his way to the pool, exchanged polite pleasantries with the people there, and slid into the water like an eel, ducking under the surface of the water, only the top of his head visible, for so long that Adam wondered if he were trying to drown himself. He finally surfaced, and leaned back against the wall, staring up at the ceiling, as if he saw something in the roiling clouds of mist beyond mortal ken.

The other man, Trennus Matrugena, was not at all what Adam had expected from his dossier. For one thing, the man was *huge*. At least six and a half feet in height, he was broad in proportion, like a wrestler or a boxer. The Pict had dark blond hair, dressed back in a half dozen braids, with a neatly trimmed beard, and swirling, geometric knot-work tattoos in blue ink over about sixty percent of his body. Certainly, every square inch of his arms and legs, and a stag's head occupied his back. In spite of general prohibitions against jewelry in the baths, he wore two amulets on long chains around his neck, as well.

Half the people in the baths turned to look at the 'barbarian,' who was, for his part, doing his best not to make eye-contact with anyone at all. He didn't slip gracefully through the crowd . . . mainly because he was looking up at the ceiling . . . and periodically bumped into people, with hurried, profuse apologies and a quick, sheepish smile . . . and then actually slipped at the edge of the pool, stumbling down into the water, recovering his balance at the last second. Adam could see the man shake his head and look back up at the ceiling again, the line of his shoulders clearly stating that he was *not* relaxing in the hot water.

This is our summoner? Adam wanted to ask. *This? He . . . can't possibly be. The labels on the folders were switched. The Carthaginian's the summoner. Except . . . it said* ley-mage *and summoner. Not too many ley-mages from Carthage or Tyre.*

He could see both of them, periodically, looking around. Trying to spot *him*, probably, though when he'd left messages at both of their hotels, he'd only left his name, affiliation, and the meeting location. Adam chuckled to himself. This was really . . . sort of fun, he had to admit it.

Though next time? He'd pick a different location.

He shook his head, stood, and padded over. "Eshmunazar? Matrugena?"

Both heads snapped up, as the two men tried to turn around, caught completely off-guard, with mildly comical glances at each other as they recognized each other's names. "Yes?" Eshmunazar said, cautiously. "Who wants to know?"

"I'm Adam ben Maor. No, no, don't get up. I'll meet you outside the frigidarium, and we can go get a drink and something to eat. Our fourth, Caetia, will be joining us later." Adam was being scrupulously fair about his bet with Sigrun. He wasn't going to use her first name, and he was fairly certain that the men hadn't been informed about the nature of the protective detail for which they were 'interviewing.' That was mostly the purpose of this meeting.

Back out into the tepidarium, chuckling under his breath; both of them had scrambled up out of the water and splashed after his wake. Adam found that a quick plunge into the cool water of the frigidarium's pool at least slowed down the sweating that the heat of the caldarium tended to provoke, and thus, was mandatory before he pulled his clothing back on.

He tended to dress in a way that attracted little attention to himself, wherever he happened to be traveling at the moment; in Nova

Germania and Novo Gaul, that had meant jeans and a laced shirt, with a travel cloak against the cold. Here in Rome, the same clothing applied, but he didn't need the cloak. To his mild surprise, on exiting the baths, Eshmunazar wore a white caftan with tan pants below, with a white skullcap, and Matrugena couldn't have stood out more if he'd tried. He wore a blue-green plaid, wrapped around his waist and flung over one shoulder, with a white shirt and knee-high boots . . . and a pair of scholarly glasses perched on his nose. "I know," Matrugena told him, before Adam could say a word. "I didn't know how long I'd be staying in Rome, so I didn't see much purpose in buying clothes for here." The man's Latin had a light and lilting accent, a tribute to the Celto-Gallic languages spoken in Britannia. "I was so surprised that the Praetorians asked me to join them . . . it's taken a while to sink in as real." He laughed, shaking his head.

Adam's eyebrows had risen at the colorful, checked garment. "I've rarely seen one of those outside of books and magazines." They hadn't been common in Nimes-on-the-Pacifica, for example; that city hadn't been colonized by Picts. But he'd seen one or two in Ponca, now that he thought about it. All on travelers.

The summoner shrugged. "The kilt developed out of the move towards keeping sheep in the lowlands about six hundred years ago. They're warm, can be used as a bedroll when you're out in the wilderness, and the patterns were easy enough for the women in every family to weave inside the home."

"And the fact that you stand out in your forest?" Eshmunazar asked, raising his eyebrows.

"That's actually a good thing when you have a lot of men out hunting deer. I don't particularly *want* a stray arrow or bullet catching me." Matrugena's grin suddenly split his face. "I'm surprised you didn't point out that I'm wearing a dress."

Eshmunazar glanced down at his own caftan, and bared his teeth. "My hypocrisy only goes so far. Besides, Romans have told the rest of the world for millennia that anyone who wears *trousers* is a *barbarian*."

Matrugena shouted with laughter. "It's true, though, isn't it?"

Eshmunazar turned back towards Adam, shrugging now, himself. "As for me, I don't have Matrugena's excuse. I've spent the last few years in Egypt and Byzantium, though, and being redirected to Rome before re-assignment? I didn't think I'd be staying here long. If I am in for a long stay, I'd like to know for certain, so I can start the process of getting an apartment here for my wife and family." The Carthaginian snorted as Adam led them back out into the now-darkened streets, lit by ley-powered lamps, and to a crowded *taverna* with a glowing, florescent sign over the door that depicted a bunch of grapes falling into a glass, and a flock of sheep, alongside the *taverna's* actual name: *Agnellus*.

They could only find seats at the bar in the jam-packed interior, and Adam tossed his unused cloak over a fourth bar-stool to save the seat for Sigrun. "Whether or not you stay in Rome . . . " Adam called through the crowd noise, and then admitted, ". . . well, you won't, much, if Caetia and I decide you're the ones we want working with us."

The Carthaginian grimaced. "Another heavy-travel job? Can you tell us anything about it? Personnel won't tell me a damned thing about the position."

Adam waited till the harried server at the bar got to them, and took their drink orders. Matrugena asked for uisce beatha; Eshmunazar asked for *arak*, and Adam, since he was actually on-duty tonight, asked for coffee. "And menus, including one for our fourth," he added, jerking a thumb at the empty seat beside him.

Once they had the vellum menus in hand, and Adam was sure that the server wasn't paying attention to them, he told them, just over the hum of crowd noise, "It's lictor work. Bodyguard to a propraetor."

Matrugena's head snapped up from his menu, his blue eyes widening behind his glasses. "May the Morrigan have mercy," he said, staring at Adam. "You're jesting with us, yes?"

Adam shook his head, still studying the man cautiously.

"What in the phantom queen's name do you need someone like me for that, now?"

I've been asking that for about five or six hours, Adam thought, but without force. There was something oddly *gentle* about the big man. For all that he looked like a bear, the prototypical northern barbarian, his big hands were careful as he lifted his glass, as if he were afraid he might break it. "Caetia liked what your dossier said about you. Me, I need a little more information. Hence the meeting."

There was a pause, as they ordered their food. Adam sighed over the exceedingly limited options, as usual, but Eshmunazar had no problem ordering a bowl full of fish stew, something that had mussels and eels and . . . god really only knew what else. Matrugena ordered venison, and Adam finally opted for lamb, looking at the seat beside him. *Completely avoiding the meeting isn't going to win the bet, Sigrun*, he told her, mentally. He looked up and around the crowded restaurant, not seeing her at all.

At about this point, a couple of unattached women had spotted the empty seat at the bar, and made their way over. Lovely in a thoroughly Roman way, with curly hair, liquid dark eyes, and low-cut blouses. One of them smiled and asked Adam, "Mind if I take that seat?"

"Ah . . . saving it, actually. For a friend."

"Will he really mind?" She leaned in closer over his shoulder, and Adam stifled a chuckle.

"I'm pretty sure that if my friend doesn't get dinner, I might not live to see the morning," he told her, cheerfully.

The other two women were, for lack of anything better to do as they waited for a table to clear out, chatting up Kanmi and Trennus. Kanmi looked completely relaxed and at ease, turning around from the bar to talk with them, responding with a smile to their light, meaningless flirtation. Trennus, on the other hand, shifted uncomfortably as one of the women put a hand on one massive shoulder. "So, what do you do for a living?" Adam heard one of the women ask Trennus.

Good enough place to start, he thought. Trennus, for his part, had flushed at the attention, but, on being asked what he did, sat up a little straighter, and in his lightly-accented Latin, began to explain, with some enthusiasm, "Actually, I'm a ley-mage and an intercessor. Which is to say, a ley-engineer, but with more background than that." He smiled at the woman, a little uncertainly.

"What does that even mean?" She laughed, throwing her head back. Adam watched it all in the mirrors over the bar, keeping an eye on the crowd behind him the whole time. He thought, from the flush in her face, visible even in the dim light around the bar, that she'd already had a couple of drinks. The woman currently behind him, who was crowding in so close it was actually triggering some of his threat responses, making him uneasy, leaned in again, asking, "So, I haven't been here before. What are you having? Is it any good?"

He turned a little, responding politely, being far more interested in what one of the men he was here to evaluate had to say as Trennus replied, "Well, ley-power is what keeps the lights on in here, yes?"

"Oh, I know *that*. Everyone knows that!" A titter. "It comes out of the ground, doesn't it?"

"Well, yes and no. The ground is just where the most accessible ley-lines are. They can actually be anywhere that there's matter. There are probably ley-lines on the *sun*. Probably really powerful ones, in fact. But standing there to use them is somewhat problematic, don't you think?"

"On the sun?" A blank look of total astonishment. "You're joking."

Trennus started to gesture with his hands, enthusiastically. "Look, it's very simple. You know how the solar system works, right? There's the sun at the center, and the planets are each in their orbit around it. All spaced out around it. And, on an even bigger scale, there's our galaxy. A super-massive black hole at the center, and all the stars, rotating around it, like spokes around the hub of a wheel."

Adam blinked a little at the astrophysics lesson in the middle of a conversation about magic, and then caught the slightly uneasy look on the woman's face as he turned further. Kanmi had an expression of cynical amusement on his face as he, himself, divided his attention between the third woman, and Trennus' reply. "Here we go with the 'so as above, so as below' dogma," he said, with a certain resignation.

"I'm not much inclined towards Hermeticism," Trennus informed him, smiling.

Plutarch had made Hermes Trismegistus famous. He'd been one of the god-born, it was clear, who'd lived somewhere around 1270 or so before the common era. He'd descended from a god-born of Thoth who'd fled Egypt after the excesses of Akhenaten and settled in Mycenae, and had claimed to descend from Hermes, as well. He'd been an influential thinker, but most of his writings had been in Linear B, a script which hadn't been translated until this century. A few of the theurge's writings had been passed on in other languages by his students, and his thoughts on alchemy, astrology, and magic had been stored in the Great Library of Alexandria, where they were still available for all to read. Many thinkers since the man had lived had been influenced by his ideas on divine and demonic spirits—everything he'd written was the basis for Western summoning traditions, at any rate—and he'd also postulated that everything on earth was reflected in the spirit realm. Plato had echoed and extended upon the idea with his notion of the Ideal. That in the mortal realm, there might be dogs, but each of those dogs was just a shadow of the perfect Dog that was, somewhere, in the realm of the Ideal.

Adam didn't know if he bought into any of Trismegistus' teachings, but it was still an influential mode of thought. Now, however, Trennus went on, "It's just a matter of natural philosophy, Kanmi. A matter of what can be proven, and modeled mathematically." Again, the language of science entered the realm of magic, and left Adam staring. "We know what our solar system looks like. We know what the galaxy looks like. And that model is repeated, almost precisely, at the atomic level. There's the nucleus of the atom—not unlike a small star—surrounded by electrons, which orbit it. It's too small to see, naturally, but just because we can't perceive something, doesn't mean it doesn't exist." He'd been gesturing the whole time, illustrating the center of the solar system or atom, sweeping his fingers in circles to show the orbits. "Now, there's the whole issue of quantum strings."

The woman Trennus had been talking to looked a little glassy-eyed. Adam covered his mouth to conceal the smile that insisted on tugging at the corners of his mouth. "Tanit's tits," Eshmunazar swore, crudely, looking up at the ceiling. "We're not really going to get into this, are we?"

"I . . . ah . . . what does any of this have to do with why the lights turn on?" one of the women ventured. Behind her, Adam noticed another woman working her way through the crowd towards the bar. He blinked; he'd never seen hair that long before, at least not unbound. It fell in ripples past her hips, pale gold in the dim *taverna* light, and it caught his attention. Drew his eyes down to her hips and legs; she wore a long skirt of some black, lustrous material, slit up to the thigh, showing knee-high boots. His eyes flicked back up again, catching an impression of a black leather bodice, commonly worn by Gothic and Gallic women, leaving long, slender arms exposed, along with parts of her shoulders and the upper swells of her breasts. He made unexpected eye-contact from across the crowded room, and the woman smiled at him, her face lighting up. Reflexively, Adam smiled back. *Do I know her? No . . . I'd remember someone who looks like that . . . damn.*

He dragged his attention back to the conversation at hand, still trying to keep his eyes on the crowd. Trennus and Kanmi were lightly arguing now, Trennus still trying to explain the very basics of ley-magic to their audience. "Look, the math isn't simple, but in ten dimensions, it works out perfectly. There are strings that connect one point in reality to another point. They always exist in pairs. Pairs resonate with each other. Admittedly, they're not really *strings*. That's just a word. And they can be open or closed when they intersect with each other, but that's beside the point."

"What *is* the point?" Kanmi asked, tiredly. "That these tiny, invisible strings can affect each other, and we can affect those strings. If you pull on one, you pull on the other. If you pull energy from one, it will, eventually, cycle back to the other. Now, this is why it's important that I mentioned that everything in the universe happens both on microscopic and macroscopic levels." Trennus gestured, his face lighting up once more. "If the solar system is a perfect emulation of an atom, just on a larger scale, then what's to say that there isn't a microscopic version of these energy strings that tie the universe together . . . and a macroscopic version?"

"The fact that we can *see* the solar system, and we *can't* see your ley-lines?" Kanmi said, dryly. "They don't exist."

"Then how are the lights burning in this room then, eh? Tell me that, and I'll buy you another glass of that poisonous-smelling white drink."

"All magic derives from the *will* of the person using it, and the redirection of existing natural forces, such as gravity, or energy, expressed as sunlight, chemical reactions, or exothermic energy, like fire." The Carthaginian looked at Trennus, clearly needling him. "When you use your powers, you're just using your will, and you're *visualizing* the power coming up out of the earth or the sky or the water as the method by which your mind has been trained to exert your will, nothing more."

"And the lights?" Trennus said, patiently, pointing at the closest one.

"A manifestation of the collective will of a given population. We know that energy can be stored. I can store my will, and the energies I've redirected from my environment can be stored in batteries as electricity, among other things. And I can use that electrical charge to fuel my own sorcery."

"A normal person doesn't have enough 'will' to lift a feather—"

"But you put enough normal people together, and collectively, they have the will of a god—"

"All right, I'll grant you that. But how is it that a ley-center can output more power than a thousand people put together, when the closest people to it might be a handful of shepherds in the Cotswolds, eh? Explain that to me." Trennus wasn't offended, it was clear; rather, he was grinning widely, clearly enjoying the academic debate.

"Ah . . . I think a table's clearing," one of the women offered, and headed away. Her friend, who'd been the one asking Trennus what he did for a living, followed at her heels.

"See, you scared them off with all this quantum mechanics and math in ten dimensions bullshit," Kanmi told the younger man from Britannia without charity. "I do the math for a living, and I *know better.*"

Adam's newfound friend looked after her companions, and then back at him. "You *sure* you're saving that spot?" she said, lowering her eyelashes. "It doesn't look like your friend's coming."

"It's not like Sig to be this late," Adam admitted, tossing the latter half of the statement towards Kanmi and Trennus, frowning a little, noticing that the woman with the long golden hair had just moved in beside them, off to his right, and was trying to flag down the bartender. He scarcely noticed, as a wave of concern suddenly hit him. *In fact . . . harah.*

She could've gotten in an accident on her way here. She hates driving, and wouldn't fly around all these people in the city, so she could have been walking, and people drive like maniacs around here. And getting hit by a car . . . that doesn't count as a 'battle-wound,' does it? I should call her apartment and see if the doorman saw her leave . . . Adam cleared his throat and started to stand up. "Let me go make a phone call . . . ."

Kanmi continued to heckle Trennus, their conversations overlapping, "What woman is *ever* going to be interested in things like that? You might as well put up a sign that says 'in bonded servitude to books, in perpetuity.'"

"I don't know," the Gothic woman said, lightly, accepting her drink from the bartender, and walking back around to the other side, her elbow brushing Adam's arm as she took the empty seat beside him, moving his cloak out of the way. "I thought it was the closest thing to an understandable explanation of ley-energy that I've ever heard. Far better than my instructors at the Odinhall managed, and you kept me interested in the subject." Her eyes were gray behind the smoky bands of Egyptian kohl that outlined them.

Adam's head snapped towards her, two entirely separate trains of thought colliding in his head, resulting in one singular reality, as Sigrun smiled at him over the edge of a glass of mead. *He hadn't recognized her.* And it took a moment or two to shake off the cognitive dissonance. He was used to thinking of Sigrun as a person, of course—a partner, naturally. Beautiful, without question, but it was the beauty of a sword. If aesthetics were best expressed when form followed function, then a sword was beautiful in its singularity of purpose . . . clean lines that were intended to kill. Ptah-ases and Ehecatl had chuckled about how the people they often dealt with tended to see her as a woman first, and then were rapidly forced to reassess her as a living weapon in the hands of her gods. He had . . . no idea what to do with the fact that he had just gone from seeing her as a weapon, then a woman, and now, suddenly, as *both* at the same time.

Fortunately, there were other distractions. The woman who'd been flirting with him the whole time suddenly looked embarrassed, flustered, even, and withdrew, muttering apologies, following in her friends' wakes. The other two males had both turned to look at Sigrun, and, recovering his composure, Adam said, "Nice of you to join us, Sig."

"I have been here for a while. I believe you owe me half a solidus, ben Maor," Sigrun told him, cheerfully. "I told you they wouldn't notice me. In fact, I do not even believe that *you* noticed me. That should make for another half solidus."

"Oh, I *noticed* you." Adam's tone was rueful. "I just didn't *recognize* you. I didn't even know you owned a skirt."

"I'm in disguise," she returned, with aplomb.

"Is wearing the hair down retaliation for my having shaved today?" He paused. "If it is, I'll risk it more often."

"Oh, nonsense. I can't wear it like this in the field. Just makes for another handle for someone to grab me by." Sigrun raised her glass to the two newcomers. "I think introductions are in order."

Adam looked back at the other two. Trennus stood, immediately, and came over to bow very slightly over Sigrun's hand as he told them, "Gentlemen? Senior lictor, Sigrun Caetia."

"*Waes hael, æðelinga,*" Matrugena told Sigrun, in some dialect of Gothic, and rattled at her for a moment in her own language—as far as Adam could tell, without accent.

Sigrun smiled in delight, and returned the greeting. Adam only picked up about one word in ten from the exchange, and stared at them rather blankly until Kanmi cleared his throat. "And for the rest of us who only speak civilized languages?" the Carthaginian said, quirking his dark eyebrows.

"Sorry," Trennus said, lowering his head sheepishly. "I can't believe you actually liked the explanation. I tend to go on, like a lecturer, once you get me going."

"It was very clear," Sigrun told him, and looked at Adam. "I don't suppose you ordered for me?"

"Didn't know when you were going to get here, and didn't know what you'd want, other than half a cow, still bloody." Adam shook his head. He wasn't sure why he was nettled, but he was, at the moment.

"What a thing to say," Sigrun told him, and flagged down the bartender again.

Kanmi, for his part, leaned past Adam to speak to her directly, "From the way ben Maor kept calling you *Caetia*, I thought we were going to be meeting a man of Rome, not a Goth."

"I'm Cimbric." Sigrun's tone was crisp. The tribal distinctions tended to be lost on anyone who wasn't actually a Goth, themselves.

"Much the same thing." That got the Carthaginian a look. He pushed on, anyway. "Are you married to a Roman, then? Or is your father Roman?"

"Neither. My family's name was once 'Spaar,' or *spear*. Some Roman bureaucrat, when my tribe moved to Caesaria Aquilonis to colonize, decided that our names were too barbaric and unpronounceable to be recorded in the tax annals, and wrote it down as the Latin word for spear, instead." She shrugged. "It's been that way for five hundred years. Not going to change now." She turned and looked at Adam. "We're going to need to find a quieter place to talk after this," she added. "I don't like having to shout to be heard."

Quieter places were actually rather difficult to find; almost every restaurant and *taverna* in Rome was jammed to the seams with people. After they'd eaten, they finally found a public park, illuminated by ley-lights and the moon, and settled on the edge of a splashing fountain, as lovers wandered by, hand-in-hand, through the darkness. "So," Kanmi said, dryly, propping his elbows on his knees and folding his hands together, dark against his white outer robe in the dim light, "what was the purpose of the exercise tonight?"

"To see how the two of you react to different pressures, different unexpected things. It's on a small scale, compared to actual battle. Also, to give us a chance to assess you in a social setting." Sigrun shrugged, and, as she sat at the edge of the fountain, started to braid her hair, catching it all at the back of her neck and bringing it around to her left shoulder to work it. "You wind up spending a *lot* of time together on a normal lictor detail. Hours spent scouting a venue for your protectee. Hours spent in a car or a small apartment, doing surveillance. It helps to get along fairly well with one another.

"And ours isn't really a normal lictor detail," Adam added, quietly. "Propraetor Livorus doesn't just stay in Rome. He goes . . . everywhere."

That made both of their eyes widen. "The Imperator's own troubleshooter," Kanmi muttered. "Damn." He exhaled. "All right. What more do you two want to know about me . . . or us, for that matter?"

"Most of my questions are for Matrugena," Adam admitted, tilting his head back to look up at the stars, tracing constellations with his eyes, ruing, more than a little, the fact that the city lights obscured the Milky Way. He didn't have to be on perfect alert here, and looking up into the heavens always tended to calm him. "For instance, your file says you're a *summoner*, in addition to a ley-mage." Adam's head tipped back down, and he stared at the taller man for a moment, feeling as if his own face were suddenly a mask he wore.

Matrugena dipped a hand in the water of the fountain, looked into the pool in his hand, and then tossed it back in. "Yes. What of it?"

Eshmunazar snorted under his breath. "I suspect ben Maor spent enough time on the Persian border to be as wary of summoners as *I* am." A quick flash of a grin, all edges. "And for me, that's after having gone to the University of Athens and worked with a few. And spent some time at conferences with a few more."

"True enough," Adam admitted, tautly. "I can't say I'm thrilled with the idea of working with a summoner. It's an inevitable and slippery slope into desiring more and more power, Trennus; dealing with spirits is inherently evil." He paused; the man was regarding him steadily. "Isn't it?"

"Knowledge is neither inherently good nor inherently bad," Trennus told him, with a certain sober intensity. "Knowledge is neutral. It's what we *do* with what we know that matters." He shook his head. "Look, I'm very careful about the spirits I summon. I bargain with them cautiously, and for very limited purposes . . . by and large. I mostly learned how to do this so I could *banish* them."

"You *bargain* with them?" Adam asked, incredulously.

Sigrun glanced between the two of them, and to Adam's surprise, intervened, with a smile. "While we're on the topic, why are you even a mage, Trennus? You don't honestly seem the type."

Trennus gave her a grin in response. "What, I don't look like one? Don't the glasses give it away?" He took them off for a moment. "Near-sighted. Can't see a damned thing outside of ten feet without them. If medicine or magic ever comes up with a pill or a spell that fixes vision? Point me to the front of the line." He paused. "Or is it the tribal markings?" He held up his arms, displaying the patterns there.

"Could be the fact that you look like a great hairy bear," Kanmi told him, not changing expressions.

Trennus looked down at himself. "Well, yes. There's that, too. Useful when it comes to wrestling with spirits."

Sigrun snorted. "Our last sorcerer was Egyptian, about five foot six, and bald as an egg. The man he replaced, two years ago? A Nubian close to seven feet tall, and black as coal. He runs marathons as a hobby. There's nothing that says a mage must be small and wheeze heavily when he or she walks up a flight of stairs."

Adam held up a finger. "Back up. What do you mean, *wrestle* with spirits?" He wanted to get back on topic, as quickly as possible. This was his single biggest concern at the moment. Trennus genuinely didn't seem like a bad person. But . . . . summoners had temptations.

Trennus grimaced. "At the risk of sending everyone into a deep slumber, I'll explain as quickly as I can." He paused. "Actually, how much do you actually know about summoning and spirits?"

"Spirits are insubstantial. They come from another realm. Summoners can stick them in the bodies of the dead, or unleash them on the living. There are different types, and some are a good deal more powerful than others." Adam was pretty definite about all of that.

Trennus weighed the empty air on his palms. "Correct in essentials. They do inhabit another dimension. Possibly more than one. They generally don't talk about that, or at least, the good ones and more . . . indifferent ones . . . don't. And you can't take the word of any of the malicious ones for anything. They lie." He shrugged. "They also perceive reality much differently than we do. I take them as . . ." he smiled, a little sheepishly, "Don't laugh . . . I take them as if they're aliens from a distant planet."

Adam's head snapped back slightly, and he stared at Matrugena. This was not at all what he'd expected to hear. And against his will, he found himself *liking* the man, damn it. His own interest in the stars and galaxies and physics, his own love of science fiction tales of aliens and other world . . . all somehow tied together with Matrugena's view of magic. "Go on," he invited, after a moment. "What was this about wrestling, and banishing?"

Trennus shrugged and spread his hands. "You take my alien analogy? Each spirit comes from a different planet, or . . . tribe. What have you. You can make some generalizations . . . elemental spirits will adhere to certain principles. Earth spirits are generally slower and more stable than air spirits. Air spirits tend to be easily distracted. But you also have to understand that each of them is an individual, with a history, and many of them have recollections of previous interactions with humanity. Some of those experiences have been good, some not so good. They have motivations and desires, too." He frowned. "Most of which are fairly difficult for us to understand. But, to simplify, in order to deal with a spirit, you have to make a bargain with them. You never get something for nothing."

"*Ex nihilo nihil fit,*" Sigrun muttered. *Nothing comes from nothing.*

Adam threw her a sharp glance; it was what she'd said when he asked her why her god required her to feel the pain of another's wounds in order to heal them.

"Precisely!" Trennus exclaimed, his face lighting up. "It's wonderful being able to speak with someone who understands what I'm talking about. And it also ties in rather neatly with the principle of conservation of mass, wouldn't you agree?"

Sigrun stared at him, clearly groping at the back of her mind for a memory. "It has been quite some time since my studies in the theory of magic," she admitted.

Kanmi snorted. "I think you had her right up until you brought thermodynamics into it."

Trennus grimaced, rubbing a hand over his jaw. "Well, you understand, don't you?" he appealed to Kanmi, who just chuckled.

"He means that matter cannot be created or destroyed," Adam supplied, dryly, and watched as Kanmi looked at him, clearly surprised. *Sorry to disappoint you, mage, but I did want to be an astronaut when I was younger.* "And neither can energy. Except that if these spirits come from . . . another dimension . . . you're technically adding mass or energy to this dimension, and subtracting it from theirs. I think."

Sigrun shook her head, and tied off the end of her braid. "That is similar to how it was explained to me in my education. But somehow, it sounds more technical when you say it."

Trennus, however, was beaming as if he'd found an apt pupil. "Precisely so. That's why when you bargain with a spirit, you have . . . well, let me start from the beginning. You need to know a spirit's Name. Sometimes, they'll just arrive and *offer* services. Those you tend to want to be wary of, because they'll eventually want more than you're willing to give, but you're already in energy debt, and you don't even realize it. But, because we're all standing on the shoulders of those who went before us, most summoners have a book of Names. Minor names, minor spirits, don't require a lot to bargain with, but they're weak. The stronger the spirit, the more closely they tend to guard their Name, the more they'll ask in return for services, and the more they can do for you." He held out both hands like the balances of a scale, and lifted one, then the other, as if weighing his own words. "Right. So, first option in dealing with spirits. You summon one with its Name. You agree to give them something that they value. Ideally, it's something you don't value. What they value varies." He paused, and went on more quietly, his low voice barely audible over the babble of the fountain beside them. "I have a, er, permanent agreement with a spirit that's dwelled for centuries in the woods around my home in Britannia. I know her Name because she approached me and offered it to me. She wanted to help me deal with the summoner who'd brought all of his . . . very bad spirits . . . to our home."

"This is the *Sangua Foederis* member that was first cited in your file?" Sigrun asked, quickly.

Matrugena nodded rapidly. "I've been helping to hunt down the rest of the organization in Europa for the past few years. He was the first one flushed out in decades." He grimaced, and scratched at his light beard for a moment. "They practice and preserve forbidden rituals."

"I thought you said that there's no such thing as evil knowledge," Adam said, sharply.

"There isn't. But there's no good reason to use someone's Name to wrack them with pain," Trennus returned. "To distort who they are, tear at their spirit. Just as an example."

Adam shrugged a little. "Sounds as if that's mostly a concern of the spirits."

Sigrun coughed into her hand. "Actually . . . humans have Names, too. True ones."

Matrugena's smile lit his face. "Yes, precisely. Not everyone knows their own Name. I don't know my own yet. It takes introspection. Or sometimes, a spirit might read it in your soul, and tell you."

"I find it a little hard to believe that a name has that kind of power," Adam said, skeptically.

"What makes you turn and look faster than the sound of your own name?" Trennus returned. "And a true Name defines you for who you are. It can grow and change with you. But it's a part of you. And knowing it will give someone power over you." He shook his head. "Where was I, anyway?"

"Your wood-spirit," Eshmunazar told him, turning his head to stare off into the shadows.

"Right, yes, thank you. The spirit gave me her Name, and we formed an alliance." Trennus pushed his glasses up. "Now, I'm bound to her, and she's bound to me. Specifically, I carry a token that she can find anywhere in the world, and will come when I call her. She's not a vastly powerful spirit, but she can grow. All spirits can grow and change. Just like humans can. They're just . . . much slower about it. Usually."

Adam was fascinated despite himself. He'd loathed and feared summoners since he could remember, and having been targeted by them innumerable times on the Wall, that loathing and fear had been compounded. But knowledge was the enemy of fear. Still, he remained uneasy. "All right," he said. "So what exactly are you giving . . . her? A tour of the world?"

Trennus chuckled. "Well, yes, that. She's curious. She wants to see more of the world than just the forests near my home. But I also agreed to do two services a year for her. I have to go home and plant oak trees in her forest, and I have to kill her a deer. Not with a gun or magic, but with a bow, my own hand, my own strength." He shrugged. "Giving life, giving a sacrifice, if you really want to put it in those terms. But comparatively minor, because she's a minor Name, for the moment." He exhaled. "Now, some spirits don't want anything, but they respect strength. They'll work with you out of a sense of honor if you can beat them at a contest. That's why I said being physically strong comes in handy."

Adam shook his head. "Now that I would pay to see, I think."

Trennus scooped up another handful of water. "There might not be anything to see. A contest can be about willpower, about physical strength, about courage, about wits . . . I've heard of one that got a summoner to agree to a duel, and then chose *music* as the contest. You'd best know ahead of time what you're agreeing to, or you'll come out on the worse end of the bargain. You invoke them, you bargain with them or fight them, and then you *bind* them. And, in every binding, you, too, are bound. So you'd better be damned careful what you bind." He shrugged. "Like every other promise you make, you put a little of yourself into it. It's just a matter of degree."

"You said *wrestling*," Sigrun asked, glancing between the mage and Adam. "This wasn't much gone over in my training, I'm afraid. Sacrifice and bargaining, yes. Wrestling . . . not as much."

Trennus shrugged. "Yes. Some of them will just . . . incarnate themselves, and you really do have to wrestle them into submission." Trennus exhaled. "And that's a principle means of banishing them. It's much easier if you know their Name, however. A minor spirit can be thrown out of the world by using its Name. A major spirit? You have to be ready to fight them. Bind them with words, with power, your own strength, and put them into something that they can't readily escape. Blood's a last-ditch solution—"

"It's not a solution!" Sigrun said, sharply.

Trennus held up a hand. "It's not my first choice. It's got drawbacks. But I'm being honest here about the solutions available. Once it's bound, you've got to make sure it never gets unbound again. Binding it in this world is risky, but if all you do is banish it, it can just be summoned again." He shrugged. "Everything's a tradeoff. That's why most people don't like dealing with summonings. I've got a natural advantage in summoning, though. I can hook into a ley-line and use its energy to augment my own natural will in dealing with spirits . . . but that's of limited help when they want to wrestle in their incarnate form."

Adam half-snorted. Kanmi looked amused. "I've sat through seminars on the topic," the sorcerer said, looking at the ley-mage, "but I can't say I believe it."

"Is it really so hard to believe?" Trennus said, looking surprised. "History and legend are filled with examples. Heracles had to fight Antaeus, who was much more than just a god-born. He was a spirit, and stronger in connection with the earth, yes? They wrestled and fought until Heracles lifted Antaeus free of the earth. Then he was able to kill the spirit—bind and banish it, out of the mortal form it had taken. And of course, there's the Judean tale of the angelic spirit and Jacob, wrestling all night, a contest of strength." Trennus stopped and gave Adam an apologetic, embarrassed look.

Adam's eyebrows had gone up, nearly into his hair. "That's . . . an interesting interpretation," he said, trying to decide if he were more amused or more offended. His reaction was hanging exactly at the mid-point between the two.

"You should hear the priests of Heracles from Hellas on the subject," Trennus told him, with a sigh. "Of course, to their way of thinking, Heracles was a god-born who had his mortality burned away, and ascended to become a god. So what any summoner has to say on the matter, is irrelevant to them."

"That," Sigrun said succinctly, and without changing expression, "would *hurt*."

Adam turned away to cough into his hand. Trennus and Kanmi blinked a little at the apparent *non sequitur*, and then Trennus nodded and continued with his commentary. "But, to my way of thinking, it's all perfectly analogous. The spirit and your Jacob wrestled, until the spirit saw it couldn't defeat him. The spirit struck him in the leg, making him lame, and marking the start of their bargain—don't eat of the meat of this part of any animal, where I've struck you. More of a symbol than a real energy transfer, but the spirit already knew it couldn't *beat* him. But there needed to be an *exchange*. And then your Jacob demanded a favor in return, and the spirit gave the human a new Name, and a blessing." Trennus raised his hands. "I personally would have asked for slightly more specific terms, but spirits have been growing and developing at least as long as humans, if not longer. They might have been more trusting, so long ago, and less . . . canny . . . about bargains. The same applies to humans. It was a more trusting age, perhaps."

Adam rubbed at his face, amusement winning out. Trennus clearly didn't mean to be offensive at all. He was almost childlike in his enthusiasm and interest, but he also clearly knew more about this topic than Adam ever *wanted* to. "You don't raise *ghul*?" he asked, point-blank.

Trennus' face twisted. "Gods. No. You can ask a spirit to enter a lump of clay shaped like a man—a golem—and you'll get better results. Telling a spirit to enter into a dead human body . . . damages the spirit, more often than not. Indifferent or good ones will start to become malefic . . ."

"That's arguable," Kanmi said, sharply. "It's just as possible that it's not the act of entering the dead that does that. It's just as likely the close affiliation with an evil-minded human—"

"Certainly, but either way, it's clearly evident that an elemental spirit put into a dead human body tends to go mad, and if they kill their summoner, afterwards, they'll just stand there and try to break the body. Poor things. They'll stand there slamming their heads against a wall, trying to release themselves."

Poor things? Adam thought, staring at Trennus. That was not any sort of compassion he'd ever thought to hear.

Trennus had paused. "Though, if you absolutely *have* to, I understand that earth elementals are the least badly affected. I can't imagine any circumstance that would make me do that, though. And of course, malefic spirits are all too eager to get access to a human body."

"It's postulated that they use access to dead bodies as practice for infiltrating living ones. Possession," Kanmi offered.

"It's certainly possible, but there's not a lot of evidence, either way."

Sigrun finally held up her hands in surrender. "I . . . think we've heard enough," she said, and looked at Adam, inquisitively. "At least, I have."

Adam nodded, slowly. "Do you have any other spirits bound to you . . . or should I ask, are you bound to any other spirits?"

Trennus looked down. It was the first time he'd done so in the entire conversation. "I . . . well, yes. One other. She's . . . small. She was very damaged by the summoner she was unwillingly bound to before, I, er, dealt with him. I'm sort of keeping her safe till she heals up." He shrugged.

"It's not a stray kitten," Kanmi said, sharply.

"No, definitely not. But she's injured. And probably will be for a long time. Spirits don't heal easily. I mean, they heal when they return to the Veil, in terms of energy loss. But she had . . . parts of her essence, her being, torn away. It's like having an arm amputated, for us. They don't grow back." Another quick shrug.

Adam nodded slowly, and filed it all away for the time being. He looked at Kanmi now. "We've spent most of tonight grilling Matrugena," he said, dryly. "Hope you don't feel left out."

"Practically a nonentity," Kanmi said, his eyes narrow, but a faint smile playing on the corners of his lips. "I take it you don't have any reservations about me?"

Sigrun shrugged. "More of a concern about how you'll interact with the other people on the team," she said, quietly. "You were born in Tyre?"

"I was a dock-rat, yes. My father served on merchant boats. His father was a fisherman." Kanmi's eyes were still narrow. "What of it?"

"Your file suggests that you've had a few altercations with people who are high-born." Sigrun's voice was neutral.

"Only when they acted as if an accident of birth actually made them better, smarter, and naturally better-looking than me." Kanmi bared his teeth for a moment. "What does it matter? There's no one on this team who's a noble."

Trennus coughed into his hand.

Kanmi turned and gave him a pained look. "Eat shit and die. You're not a noble."

"Well, only so much as being the son of a local king makes me." Trennus looked up, clearly uncomfortable. "I was apprenticed to a ley-mage young, and expected to earn my way, same as all of my people."

Another long, steady look. "I can't hate him," Kanmi announced, after a moment. "It'd be like kicking a puppy."

"Hey!" Trennus looked mildly offended.

"If he's the worst of our *nobility*, then I think I won't have any problems." Kanmi looked at them all, a bit challengingly. "I don't suppose you're next in line for the throne of some petty kingdom, Caetia?"

She shook her head silently, looking mildly amused. "No."

"It's getting late," Adam muttered to Sigrun, looking back up at the stars.

"I know." She sighed. "What do you think?"

Adam rubbed at his jaw for a moment. "I think I can work with them," he agreed, much to his own surprise. "Of course, can they work with you?"

"I'm not nearly as bad as Ptah always made me out to be."

"No, but you're definitely full of surprises." He chuckled at the dark look she sent him.

Sigrun turned to look at the other two. "Final approval is the propraetor's, of course, but, for myself . . . welcome aboard." She regarded them both. "Livorus lives on Palatine Hill. Make your way to his villa at eight antemeridian tomorrow, and we'll see about getting you both to work." She looked at Adam. "Looks like we might be heading back across the Sea of Atlas."

"That problem in Nahautl? Tenochtitlan?"

"Yes."

"Good." Adam nodded.

"You don't like Rome?"

"I like a few more time zones between me and my family." He chuckled under his breath. "Matrugena? Eshmunazar? Nice to meet you. See you in the morning."

"Wait," Kanmi said, his eyes narrowing again. "You know everything about us, from our dossiers. Do we get to ask anything about the two of you?"

"That does seem a fair bargain," Trennus said, looking into the fountain's ley-lit depths.

"That does seem fair," Sigrun allowed, quietly.

Kanmi stared at them for a long moment. "Matrugena and I are both magic-users. What are your specializations?"

Adam snorted. "You want to know how you fit into the big picture?"

"In a word? Yes."

Adam looked at Sigrun. "She kills things. I carry her bags."

Kanmi snorted. "No. Come on. Speak truth."

"I am," Adam protested.

Sigrun gave him a remarkably dirty look. "*Fikkest thu,* Adam ben Maor." She looked at Kanmi. "He handles Judean, Hellene, and Nipponese weapons, and can plant and defuse explosives of all sorts. I believe he has even worked with one of the punch card adding machines."

Kanmi's face actually lit up. "A *calculus?*"

"Yes," Adam acknowledged. "It did a multiplication problem involving a number eight digits long in about a quarter of a minute. But it took up an entire room."

"Oh, then we will have things to talk about, then, my new friend." The sorcerer grinned at him. "But what about the mysterious and redoubtable Caetia?"

She sighed, and relented. "I'm god-born," Sigrun admitted, shrugging it off. "I am a valkyrie, born of the line of Tyr."

Adam could see that the specifics were meaningless to Kanmi, though the man's face tightened slightly at the word *god-born* . . . and a look of narrow-eyed appraisal crossed his face. Trennus' eyes, on the other hand went wide, and he said, "A swan-maiden, then? Like Morrigan's raven-children?"

"More or less. I can summon lightning, so long as I have access to the sky. I fly, I can heal. Lying to me generally is not an option, though people try it anyway." Sigrun again shrugged. "I think, judging by your dossiers, that we'll all fit well together on the team. Everyone will have a place where they excel, and where the others will be weaker. It should work well."

After a few more moments of conversation, Adam glanced over at Sigrun. "May I walk you back to your apartment?"

She gave him a faintly amused glance. "I doubt anyone in Rome will accost me, Adam."

Kanmi shook his head. "I don't think Rome is *that* much more civilized than Tyre, Caetia. A woman walking alone, at night, is a target. Then again . . . " he gave her another appraising glance, "perhaps they would be fools to try."

Sigrun just raised her eyebrows. "They would indeed."

Adam pictured the likely results, and winced. "My way of dealing with them will result in less paperwork than your way. Come on. Let's go." He slid a hand under her elbow, lightly, and then let her set the pace as they walked away from the other two.

"You say that as if I can't control myself," Sigrun told him, once they were out of earshot. "I do have other options besides lightning."

"Yes, but how many of them are non-lethal?"

A pause. "I could just *punch* them. Carefully. Being mindful that their teeth do not grow back."

"Yes, and so can I." He squeezed her elbow lightly. "But, fair or not, just by virtue of me walking with you, it probably won't even come up." Adam paused. "So, no plans on having your mortality burned away, like Heracles?"

Sigrun shuddered, and he could feel it run through her whole body. "Burns hurt worse than any other wound, and Heracles was supposedly burned alive, because he was already dying of slow poison. I can't imagine a pain bad enough to make me consider throwing myself into a pyre, Adam. I don't want to." She glanced up at him; their eyes were almost at the same level, something he rather enjoyed. "And no. No desire at all to shed my mortality and become a god. I am what I am. That's my *wyrd*. I walk my path, and I have good people alongside me. What more is there?"

"There's always a way to improve," Adam told her, as they climbed into a trolley car bound across the nightscape of the city. "If you're not reaching for the stars, what good is life, anyway?"

Sigrun smiled, but it was a rueful look. "It's a good thought, Adam, and I like it . . . but I'm not convinced it really applies to me." She sat back in the seat of the trolley, the street lights outside flicking past, briefly illuminating her face and then casting it into shadows again. "I don't think I'm capable of being anything more than what I am right now."

"*Shtoyut.*" The word was harsh. "Of course you are. You're

human, aren't you?" There weren't many people on the trolley at this hour of night, and none within earshot.

"More or less," Sigrun told him. "Sometimes, a little less, than more."

Part II: The Tears of the Children

Nahautl, 1955 AC

Chapter V: Ripples

Sargon of Akkad was one of the greatest kings of antiquity, and one of the first who composed an official autobiography in a form that was not mere oral poetry. Chiseled in rock, he proclaimed, as best anyone has been able to translate to date, "My mother was a changeling, my father I knew not . . . My changeling mother conceived me, in secret she bore me. She set me in a basket of rushes, sealed with bitumen, and cast me into the river, which rose not over me. The river bore me up and carried me to Akki, the drawer of water, who took me as his son and raised me. Akki appointed me as his gardener. While I was his gardener, Ishtar granted me her love, and for four and fifty years, have I exercised kingship."

Most scholars currently agree that to would seem that Sargon meant that he was conceived and borne by a desert spirit, along the banks of the Euphrates. A changeling could be a djinn, but it is more likely to have been a _lilitu_ spirit of the wastes. These female-seeming spirits embody both death and fertility, and are said to be able to change their appearance on a whim, and can incarnate themselves, adopting flesh with which to tempt mortal men. However, for one of these creatures to bear a child would be highly unusual.

It is impossible to say if this birth was the result of a bargain made in good faith between spirit and mortal, or if it were in some manner forced on the spirit, but the resulting offspring was certainly cast off, and adopted by a king, or a 'drawer of water.' And the offspring was apparently striking enough of a spirit-born to have drawn the attention of the fertility goddess, Ishtar, making him both spirit-born and god-touched at the same time. It is said that he was so beloved of Ishtar, that she even gave to him one child, conceived and borne in secret, named En-he-duanna, later High Priestess of Ishtar. It is therefore no wonder that Sargon of Akkad felled hundreds in battle, toppled teetering Sumer and established the laws and disciplines of Akkad in the place of the old Sumerian ways. With boundless energy and determination, he carved out a place for himself and his dynasty in history.

Sargon's grandson, Naram-Sin, however, held little reverence for the gods, though he himself was named for the moon-god, Sin. Records on cuneiform tablets hint that his god-born aunt, En-he-duanna, warned the young and heedless king not to attack the city of Nippur . . . or at least, if he did, to spare the temples there. There is one tantalizing hint in these tablets that a foreigner had come to Naram-Sin, and told him that the gods had no right to rule over men. That men of such lineage as Naram-Sin could be as gods, themselves, and if he had the power of the gods, why should he not take up what was rightfully his?

Naram-Sin sacked the temple of Enlil in Nippur, and took up the idol there, shattering it on the ground for all to see. This first attack apparently was followed by wide-spread famine and disease in the whole of the lands claimed by Akkad. Naram-Sin attacked more temples, for the grain stored inside of them, and disbursed some to loyal warlords, and kept the greater part for his court's use. Tax records from this time period indicate that many people had difficulty meeting their dues, whether in measures of grain or wine.

Records of this period are rare, and even when found, difficult to translate. In many cases, they are contradictory. Some records suggest that _namtar_-demons —

creatures like the lilitu *that may have birthed Sargon in the desert, unstoppable and invincible — fought at the king's side as he sacked the temples. Some records suggest that the* namtar-*demons were already engaged in a conflict with the gods, which had resulted in the famines . . . and when the king attacked the temples, he fought gods already locked in struggle.*

Thus it is arguable if Naram-Sin, sometimes called "the first godslayer," deserves this epithet. It is unknown if he killed any of the gods of Sumer by his own hand. He may have sacked their temples and destroyed the idols to which they were bound, but whether the gods fell as a result of his actions, or at the hands of the namtar-demons is unclear. Regardless of the proximate cause, many of the gods of Akkad and Sumer were now dead, or at least, dispersed. The compact between the gods and the line of kings was severed by Naram-Sin's pride and vanity. The fields failed to ripen, and within three generations, the mighty empire of Akkad, was no more. Sumer rose to ascendancy once again. A few of the gods had been left alive, such as Ishtar, mother of the Akkadian line. Marduk and Ninutra's worship increased, as hers did; there were no other gods for their people to follow.

By the time of Nabû-kudurri-uṣur (Nebuchadnezzar), ca. 1170–1147 BAC (before the ascent of Caesar), unrest had become widespread once more, as invading Elamites attacked. One record, the Enmeduranki *legend, suggests that the Elamite invasion, led by King Ḫulteludiš-Inšušinak, was a punishment for previous failings of the kings of Sumer and their people:*

"In the reign of a previous king . . . good departed and evil was regular. The lord . . . gave the command, and the gods of the land abandoned it . . . . Evil demons filled the land, the namtar-*demons [Fragment missing] penetrated the temples. The land diminished, its fortunes changed. The wicked Elamite . . . [Fragment missing] His attack was swift. He devastated the habitations, he made them into a ruin, he carried off the gods, he ruined the shrines."*

We take this as evidence to help substantiate an otherwise spotty historical record, which suggests that Ḫulteludiš-Inšušinak attacked Sumer at around this point in time, with or without the assistance of early magi, who may have summoned demons to assist him. He was certainly pre-occupied with destroying the temples, like Naram-Sin before him, and apparently melted down the idols for their precious materials. And Ḫulteludiš-Inšušinak is considered by most chroniclers to be the 'second' godslayer . . . though there were few gods left for him to slay.

That the namtar-*demons reappear, sometimes called* godslayers *in the ancient texts, is intriguing. They appear to be self-willed spirits, not allies of the Elamite king, who was also engaged in destroying temples at the time. They appeared. They slew. They vanished again . . . and after this time, do not appear again in the Sumerian or Babylonian historical record. The few physical descriptions that remain suggest that they varied in height, and were made of flame, stone, ice, air, or metal. A modern student of magic may scoff that these sound like simple elemental spirits . . . which an honest commentator must admit that they might well have been. There were few summoners in those times who were not priests or kings. The ability to beseech the gods or spirits for favors was not a prerequisite for rule, but it helped, much in the way that having technological innovations such as sharper, stronger swords helped these kings overcome their enemies. Someone who could unleash a handful of spirits* could *decimate an army and overthrow a kingdom.*

However, it is clear that these were no simple spirits. They overcame gods, *not just men, and their presence wrought destruction wherever they went. Whatever secret the ancients possessed to summon such fell creatures is lost, and best so. For if they had the power to destroy gods, then they had the power to destroy the whole world.*

—Bailos Aiskhulos, <u>Legends of the Godslayers.</u> *University of Athens Press, 1945 AC.*

Iunius 2, 1954 AC

Trennus?

It was a whisper in his mind. The man's eyes snapped open, instantly, and he rolled up to an elbow in bed, reaching for the two amulets on leather cords around his neck. One of them was warm to the touch. *Yes, Lassair? What's wrong?*

He used the spirit's Name silently, and with infinite care and gentleness. She was a delicate thing, and misusing her Name could damage her further than she already had been. Names were power, as he'd tried to explain to Adam ben Maor months ago. Names—*true* Names, anyway—defined a spirit or a person. By naming something, you circumscribed it. Limited it. In a way, it would be freeing to be without a name. Then, you would be . . . undefined. But you would also lack the power that a Name brought. And if you twisted someone's Name, or re-defined them, you could alter their very reality.

He'd seen the rituals in grimoires he wasn't technically supposed to have. But knowledge shouldn't be blotted out. Efface something, and it had a tendency to be re-discovered, a generation or two later. A page or two from a lost book would re-surface, or some researcher would build along the same paths of thought laid down in perfectly innocent books. No, the only real solution was to ensure that the people who had the knowledge also had the ethics, understanding, and self-control *not* to use it . . . without a damned good reason.

White light poured between his fingers from the amulet, turning his fingers ruddy as the light shone through his flesh and the spirit manifested. Feebly, because Lassair had been under his protection for only a year or so. The amulet was a convenience for her, really—a conduit. It helped her manifest more easily. *Your friends are outside. You asked me to awaken you when they were near.* Her mental voice was as light and sweet as a carillon's notes, carried on the wind.

How close?

She didn't answer in words; for a moment, Trennus felt disoriented as his perceptions stretched. Suddenly, he could see through the walls of the hotel, though not with his physical eyes. And he immediately spotted his fellow lictors—not their physical forms, but their spirits. Shining, silver steel for ben Maor . . . . and a figure comprised of the blue-white light of a levinbolt, sheathed inside a gray storm cloud. Sigrun. *Damn. You should have woken me earlier.* Trennus kept the thought gentle, and stood, kicking the sheets away and grabbing his clothes.

You needed to rest, Lassair told him, calmly. *You were awake all night, guarding the man to whom you are bound for now, and will doubtless be awake again all of tonight. I care for you, as you care for me.*

Spirits had a hard time with names that weren't *Names*. Names that were just pretty sounds were meaningless to them. *Lassair* as a Name, for example, actually meant *flame* in one of the ancestral languages that had given rise to Pictish and Gallic. There were legends, minor ones, admittedly, among his people about a spirit with a similar name . . . *Lasair*. He wasn't sure if she was *that* Lasair, the spirit of flame and growing plants and harvesting crops. There was no difference in the sound of the names, and spelling was just . . . orthography. Idiosyncratic in any language. But that being said, her name *meant* something. He'd tried to tell her what his given names meant. For instance, Trennus meant *strong*, and Matrugena meant *good bear*, amusingly enough. And surprisingly, she'd managed to hold onto that. But it wasn't his *Name*. Trennus wasn't sure he'd ever know what his truename was. It sometimes took years of dedicated study and meditation to learn it . . . but once you did learn it, you could offer it to a spirit for a stronger pact. Of course, doing so was dangerous. It required a great deal of trust.

Trennus shook his maunderings away. "I'm being mothered by a spirit," he muttered out loud, and pulled a shirt on over his head, before looking at his trousers in distaste. In the interests of at least attempting to blend in a little better with Rome's population, and now, with the population of Tenochtitlan, he had traded in his kilt for a pair of slacks in soft-woven cotton, and was doing his best, as the days on duty as Livorus' lictor passed, to get used to the way the damned things felt. They made it difficult to bend his legs and their tendency to ride up . . . everywhere . . . was truly annoying. He was of the opinion that trying to look ordinary was probably a lost cause; he stood a head and a half taller than most residents of Rome and Tenochtitlan, with the exception of other 'barbarians.' Nothing would induce him to cut his hair, worn loose with thin braids to keep it out of his face. And wearing long sleeves in the heat of a Nahautl summer to cover his tribal markings was not the most enjoyable experience of his life. Back home, he'd run through the woods in snow up to his knees with no more on than his boots, socks, kilt, and a wool shirt, maybe with his plaid draped over his shoulders if it happened to be actively snowing. The heat here in the Nahautl capital was . . . enervating. *How close are they now?*

Just outside the building. Stormborn's spirit is always very easy for me to see approaching.

Trennus grinned. Lassair was like a cheat-sheet to life's little mysteries sometimes. She'd immediately whispered to him that Sigrun was god-born, on first meeting the woman. He hadn't been sure that the spirit had the right of it, so he'd still been a little surprised when Caetia had admitted to it . . . but it was a good confirmation that Lassair could pick out strong, powerful human spirits, even if they were bound to gods. While Sigrun had provided a dry, factual overview of her abilities in that meeting, no details had been provided until they'd all gone out in the field together to practice team tactics. Ben Maor had asked Kanmi to illustrate some of his abilities, and the Carthaginian had noted that he could hover off of the ground, by means of manipulating gravity fields around his body, but rated this one of the hardest things he'd ever learned to do.

And then the sorcerer and technomancer had looked up in time to see Sigrun, who'd been three hundred feet away — well out of earshot, in other words — lift off the ground in effortless flight.

Kanmi had dropped back to the ground and sworn under his breath. Fortunately, he'd only been about three feet off of it. "All right. I don't know whether to complain that *that* is not fair, or whether to accuse her of showing off." He shook his head, mild irritation crossing his face. "Seriously, what the *fuck* is she doing guarding a propraetor? Don't the god-born have better things to do, like noting down when sparrows fall and telling people what to do?"

Trennus had caught the expression that had crossed ben Maor's face then — mild annoyance, quickly masked. "To be honest, I don't know why she's chosen to serve Rome. I think she sees it as another way of serving her people, and her god. Past that, I've respected her privacy on that count." His words held a hint of a suggestion there; clearly, he expected them to follow his lead on that matter. But Kanmi wasn't the sort to follow *anyone's* lead, unless it was a matter of a direct order. And even then, the sorcerer tended to like to know *why* an order had been given. Trennus frankly wondered how the man had ever gotten through four years of military service on the border with Mongolia, but there was no denying that Kanmi knew what he was doing, as far as magic went. On the other hand, Kanmi had edges, and reacted oddly to some of the most mundane things. Trennus regarded him as a puzzle.

Back in the here and now, Trennus finished getting dressed, and headed down to the hotel's lobby, feeling Lassair's invisible presence following him. His other spirit, Saraid, was quiescent, for the moment; she usually only appeared when called, or when she sensed danger to him. She mainly appeared as a white hind, but could adopt stag form, as well.

He felt the elevator's sway in the pit of his stomach, and wished he'd taken the stairs. Trennus was always just *happier* when he was in touch with the ground. Finally, the brass diamond mesh of the antique elevator cage opened before him as the lift reached the ground floor, and Trennus stepped out into the lobby, eyes automatically canvassing the area. Like much of the rest of Tenochtitlan, this hotel showed cultural synthesis on almost every level. There were Roman-style pillars all through the large, open room, supporting the ceiling without blocking off eye-lines, but the floors were brown tile, and the walls were plaster over adobe brick, and painted with vivid, almost garish colors, and in a style he'd never seen before coming to this part of the world.

One entire wall was covered with a circle filled with geometric, winding shapes, centered around a mask-like face. He'd been told this was a calendar, but he couldn't read it. The rest of the images in the murals were of . . . people in their daily lives, really. Going to offices, shopping in markets, working in fields, repairing motorcar engines . . . whatever the artist had felt like showing. They were depicted in their native costumes, down to feathered headdresses. That was, he suspected, something of a artist's joke; he'd seen plenty of people working machine shops in coveralls, maybe with jade earrings, or stripped down to loincloths to work in fields, but he'd yet to see anyone wearing feathers on anything but *formal* occasions down here.

He'd been to a couple of temples so far here, and sometimes the local gods and goddesses, like Quetzalcoatl or Coatlicue or . . . a whole host of names that Trennus found completely unpronounceable . . . were depicted in Roman fashion, in three-dimensional, free-standing statues, with the ideal body proportions promulgated by centuries of classical Hellenism, but still with their native garb and accoutrements, including headdresses and earrings. In some temples, he'd seen *Roman* gods depicted in the Nahautl style, with heavy masks, skull-like visages, and claws.

Propraetor Livorus had shaken his head over those. In pure amusement, Trennus thought.

Trennus put his back against one of the brightly-painted walls, standing between two planters filled with jade-green jungle plants, and waited. Half a minute later, ben Maor and Sigrun entered the lobby through the revolving glass door, and immediately spotted him. "You're going to have to tell us how you always know we're coming," Adam told him. The Judean man, Trennus thought, still was uneasy with him; the brown eyes were perpetually wary.

"Oh, I could," Trennus told him, lightly. "But then I'd lose my mystique." He adjusted his glasses on the bridge of his nose as Sigrun chuckled, and noted that ben Maor hadn't smiled. Trennus sighed. "Very well. One of my bound spirits recognizes you two and Kanmi very well by now. She lets me know when you're around." He grinned as ben Maor shifted slightly, clearly uncomfortable. "She even has names for you."

Sigrun looked around, as if the god-born woman expected to see the spirit. Perhaps she could, but Lassair was keeping tucked out of sight. "Do I want to know what she calls us?" ben Maor asked.

"Nothing rude," Trennus told him, lowering his voice. "You're Steelsoul. Sigrun here is Stormborn. Kanmi is Emberstone. The propraetor doesn't have a name yet."

Adam blinked at that, shook his head, and muttered, "I'm not sure whether to be complimented or disturbed."

Trennus chuckled. "Oh, complimented. I'm not sure if these are your Names, or if she's just picked nicknames for you. On the off-chance that she's pulled your truenames? I wouldn't noise them about. Just in case."

"I'll take the same care with the name as I do with blood samples," Sigrun told him, nodding. "It's not wise to give anyone any sort of a hold on you."

Trennus nodded. It was a pleasure working with her and Kanmi; they understood where he was coming from. Adam's lack of understanding of even the basic rules of magic was disconcerting. Most people at least understood the concept of keeping a house-spirit happy.

Leave out some bread and milk once a week, and the spirit would usually do small jobs, like dusting or keeping the drains clean. Having glanced at Sigrun, however, his attention was now held. She wore her usual black leather bodice top, laced comfortably, but for once, there was a black evening dress underneath, with slightly dressier boots than usual. "What's the occasion, *æðelinga?*" He liked calling her *noble lady*. It was a gesture of respect that cost him nothing, made her chuckle, and, for whatever reason, seemed to make Adam twitch a bit.

Sigrun grimaced. "The propraetor's brainstorm. He doesn't want anyone here to know what I am, for as long as we can keep it under wraps. He has a distaste for putting every card he has on the table for all to see that's almost reflexive."

"We've been here for weeks," Trennus felt compelled to point out.

"Tonight is the first night that we're doing something in the public eye." She sighed. "So, the plan tonight is, we need to look like a strong force around Livorus, but at the same time, he wants to distract anyone watching from what our strengths actually are . . . and in between confusing any observers as to what my actual *role* is—" her voice turned even glummer, "he seems to think that I might be able to distract observers from watching the four of you."

"Four of us?" Trennus asked, immediately.

"We're getting Ehecatl Itztli back tonight. Thank god," Adam said. "He's been out on disability for a bit. But the more eyes, the better. Come on. Walk and talk."

Trennus trailed along behind them, out into the nightscape of the city of Tenochtitlan. He wasn't sure about having another team member; they were only just beginning to gel, in terms of their chemistry. "He's Nahautl?"

"Yes, born and raised. He knows the language and the people. He'll be in the propraetor's box to keep Livorus advised of all the things the diplomats here might not have briefed him on." Adam shook his head. Trennus had noticed that while Adam was a skilled negotiator, himself, he had the career military's faint distaste for diplomats.

The local Praetorians had provided them a black Epibintores VII with bullet-proof glass, and it was waiting at curb. A valet had brought it around for them, which meant that they would need to check it for listening devices. Before they climbed in, however, Trennus frowned, and glanced at Sigrun. "You said something about your role?" Trennus asked, and then suddenly got it as he caught ben Maor's grim look.

"Yes. He seems to think almost everyone here will see a pretty young thing on his arm and assume she's his lictor in name only." Adam's voice was curt. "I'm not in favor of this plan, but the propraetor proposes, and we dispose." He gestured towards the door. "Come on. All of us are on tonight."

"All of us?" Trennus muttered, folding himself into the front seat. With his frame, the backseat of any vehicle was simply not an option. He straightened, cautiously, and felt his head brush the ceiling. "That's going to make the dayshift tomorrow nasty."

"Tell me about it," Sigrun muttered, getting into the backseat, directly behind him. "I've been on duty since eight this morning," she added, leaning her head back as ben Maor tipped the valet and slid into the driver's side, taking the wheel.

Trennus glanced at her as the ley-powered engine hummed to life. "What are we doing tonight?"

"The propraetor has been invited to a cultural evening by the local governor and the king," Adam told him, digging out a small electronic device from one pocket, and activating it. It wouldn't help with any passive recording devices, but it would block any radio signals leaving the vehicle. "We need to be a visible presence, apparently. After that, we *might* be heading to the palace."

"It's the first time the *tlatoani* has agreed to see the propraetor," Sigrun agreed, her eyes closed. *Tlatoani* was the local title for the emperor of Nahautl. "I would say it should be interesting, but the chances of them doing any substantive conversing at a cultural evening are . . . limited."

Trennus groaned under his breath. They'd been in Nahautl for three weeks at this point; three weeks spent mostly waiting for various people to agree to see Livorus. "Considering that half the decisions that the local emperor makes have to be endorsed by the regional Roman governor, I'd have thought that the governor would tell him 'meet with the propraetor,' and it would be over and done with."

"*Patience,*" Sigrun counseled, in Bláthach Gallic. The Bláthach Peninsula had been colonized largely by Picts and other Britannian tribes, which meant that the dialect was close enough to his native Pictish for them to use it as a bridge language, though he spoke Gothic very well. She had a very light accent in his tongue, and Trennus found it charming. "*Some of it is genuine scheduling conflicts. Some of it is posturing to show how important and busy each person is. And some of it seems to be that the tlatoani wants nothing to do with Livorus. He has a reputation, after all.*"

"*I'm patient. I'm just wondering if we're ever going to make progress.*" Trennus glanced up as Adam grunted in annoyance and swerved around a truck in the late-night traffic. "Sorry. Latin it is." He grinned at Adam. "I promise, we're not telling secrets."

Trennus had occasionally wondered if he dared ask Sigrun out for a cup of tea. There were no regulations against fraternization. But though Sigrun seemed fond of all the lictors on the team, he couldn't read her reactions, and he thought it entirely likely that he'd have no chance at all. He'd been good with girls back home, just after his apprenticeship had begun. He'd gone to the midsummer fires with a different girl each year, and had enjoyed the festivities enormously . . . and then his mentor had been killed, he'd spent half that year tracking down her killer, and then he'd been off to Londonium. And from that point on, he'd been either in a library, in the field, chasing rogue summoners, training at the gym, or, once a year, out in the forest, killing a deer for Saraid. Somewhere along the way, he'd lost the knack of talking to women properly. Summoners didn't tend to be social creatures. Most of them tended to be reclusive.

And people's reaction to summoners depended greatly on what

region they were from. Traveling summoners tended to get a bit less respect, and a bit more suspicion; they weren't known to the local spirits or people. An intercessor who'd spent his or her whole life in a given city, like Londonium, working to help the humans and spirits there understand each other, formalizing contracts and bindings between them, might have the social rank of a magistrate. If they found that a human had broken a contract with a spirit, and had been trying to force the spirit to continue with their end of the bargain, the summoner could take legal action. The Chaldean and Median Magi, for example, were *revered* by their people; they held the whole of their societies together, inside the Persian Empire. But because the Magi had so much power, people who lived close to their borders, who had no summoners of their own, or few . . . such as Judeans like Adam . . . regarded summoners with outright fear and suspicion.

He risked another glance back at Sigrun, and then turned his attention out the window of the motorcar, studying the darkened cityscape; hundreds of thousands of lights speckled the region. Tenochtitlan was, like Venetia, a city of bridges. Dozens of them crossed Lake Texcoco, from the central island long occupied by the Nahautl, to the banks, which now housed sprawling suburbs, like Tlatelolco. It had been, centuries ago, an independent city-state, but had been absorbed into the greater metropolitan whole. Some of the bridges were ancient, and Roman-built, with the characteristic arched supports that reminded Trennus of aqueducts back in Europa. Others were modern suspension bridges made of webs of steel cable and poured stone. All were lit up at night, lines of light crisscrossing the dark waters of the lake. Ancient canals still cut across the central island, and people still paddled canoes under the poured-stone bridges of the modern city. And night or day, these waterways reflected light back up at the sky.

That mix of modern and ancient was found everywhere in the city center; the old step pyramids dedicated to Quetzalcoatl and the sun were intact, though the *tzompantli*, or skull racks, had not had their displays added to for centuries. And alongside these ancient stone buildings were newer ones. Skyscrapers thirty and forty stories tall, and even a couple of modern pyramids, built, still, in the stepped fashion . . . but in glass and steel. These were illuminated at night, and their light cast the ancient stone ones into stark relief. Most of the buildings were accessible from the second floor, and the first floors were left deliberately empty, to allow for flooding; single-family homes in this region were built on stilts, again, to allow the lake to do what the lake would do.

The only drawback as far as Trennus was concerned, other than the muggy, fiercely hot climate, was the *mosquitoes*. The damned insects were prevalent here, and he hadn't gone a day without two or three bites. They'd all had to have malaria shots before coming to this province for precisely that reason.

Trennus peered around again. "We're not heading for the palace," he noted.

"Not yet," ben Maor agreed. "An *ollamaliztli* competition, first. I've only seen clips of it being played on the far-viewer before. It's supposed to be almost as visceral as anything put on in the Colosseum in Rome. I suppose we'll see."

"By visceral, do you mean we're actually going to be seeing people's viscera tonight?" Trennus asked it almost casually. "I don't like to go to gladiatorial matches that are scheduled to go the distance if I've eaten first." Mortal bouts weren't common in the arenas these days, unless a convicted felon had asked for the chance to fight for his life. But every once in a while, two gladiators decided that they'd insulted each other too many times, and the grudges could only be washed away by blood.

"No idea, but we're all going to be too busy watching the crowd to see anything on the court, I suspect." Ben Maor took an off-ramp, arcing down from the overhead bridge and into the crowded maze of streets that covered the island at the center of the city and the lake. Showing his id, he got them into a parking lot barricaded to the general public, beside an ancient stone building, rebuilt and expanded upon over the centuries, until it had the general appearance of a Roman coliseum on the outside. The exterior arched openings were filled with statues of the local gods, illuminated by spotlights at night. Hundreds of people filed along the walkways beside the huge building, heading in through large glass doors. Trennus, on exiting their car, could hear the roar of the crowd from inside the arena, screaming and cheering, a wall of sound that actually vibrated in the ground and in his sternum.

He half-closed his eyes for a moment, and looked with his inner senses. Sure enough, this arena was positioned *directly* atop a ley-line, and it was in resonance with another one that paralleled it, less than a mile away. That was a lot of energy to tap directly into. Sometimes, a resonant pair was separated by a long distance; they might be a hundred miles apart, for example, and that made for a poor line to tap into. Sometimes, two lines intersected, and if both were open lines, it made for the best and strongest feed of ley-energy possible. "What have you got?" Adam asked.

"They built it in a good place," Trennus commented. "It's not going to subside, sink, or tilt over, like that tower they built a few hundred years ago in Pisa. Even if Popocatépetl over there—" he gestured, vaguely, to the west, towards a volcano usually visible on the horizon, "happens to erupt, the seismic disturbance from that probably won't do much to the building." He stomped one booted foot on the ground. The earth here was soggy and a little apt to slide, but the people here had built, and built smartly, in accordance with the ley-lines and the geology of the region. That pleased him, obscurely.

Adam gestured, and they all headed into the building, showing their identification again at the door. "Kanmi already scouted the venue," Sigrun noted, as they headed up centuries-old stone steps, fighting their way through crowds of people in colorful Nahautl finery, all vertical lines and light cottons, imported from Egypt and southern Novo Gaul. "Livorus wants me next to him, along with Ehecatl."

"Well, you are supposed to be his sweet young thing. I wouldn't let you out of arm's reach, either," Trennus told her, lightly, and then realized what that sounded like, hastily retrenching, "I mean, if I were him.

Not that he is . . . I mean . . . gods."

Sigrun just looked at him, smiled, and put a hand on his shoulder. Even through his long-sleeved shirt, her hands were cool. Trennus winced. "I swear, once upon a time, I knew how to talk to women. I went to the bonfires all the time. It was easier, then." *Before . . . everything.*

Sigrun shook her head. "We're people, nothing more. It's easy. Open your mouth, words come out." She gave him an amused look. "Most of the time, you have no problem talking to me."

"That's because most of the time I don't think of you as a w . . . I mean, I think of you as a colleague, most of the time." Trennus paused. Looked at ben Maor. "You want to throw me a line here?"

Ben Maor's eyebrows hovered close to his hairline. "Would you like some salt for that foot you're currently mouthing?"

Trennus sighed, and flicked his braids back over his shoulders in mild annoyance. "No, no, it's tastier unseasoned."

Sigrun chuckled, and offered, changing the subject, "Kanmi's going to be in the rafters, along with imperial and gubernatorial security. You will be at ground level, mixing with the, well, sorry . . . peasantry." She grimaced. Nahautl society was still highly stratified, more so than even Rome's, and certainly more so than Novo Gaul or Nova Germania's. "Adam's going to be outside the box, keeping an eye on everything behind the scenes. With a gun."

Trennus nodded, all business now. "Anything in particular I should be looking for?"

"Anyone who looks like they're looking up at the box where Livorus and the governor are sitting. While you're at it . . . listen. Mingle. Talk. See if you can pick up anything on the political situation here." Sigrun shrugged, and gave him an apologetic look. "I know. It's difficult to split your attention between information gathering and body-guarding, but this is a pretty good opportunity. We need to make the most of it."

"I don't know if you've noticed it, but I don't exactly look like a local. Kanmi might have a better shot at it than I do."

"Yes, but then we'd have you positioned in the rafters, some two hundred feet above ground," Adam told him, and Trennus grimaced. It wasn't that he was afraid of heights. It had a lot more to do with the fact that it was much easier to pull on ley-lines when he was in contact with the ground. Solid matter was richer in ley-lines; this form of matter was simply denser, and had more strings attached to it, as a result, than the more diffuse states of water and air. There *probably* were ley-lines in space, connecting one star to another, but no ley-mage had yet taken a Judean or Hellene or Nipponese rocket into space to find out.

"You could be in the rafters with a rifle, Kanmi on the ground, and I'd be on guard in the background," Trennus offered, and glanced behind them as another, much shorter man cut through the crowds of people to get to them. There was only a faint trace of a smile in his dark eyes, and the Nahautl man wore a white, sleeveless shirt and trousers, cut loosely and in local festival-day colors — which was to say, brilliant vermillion, with chartreuse lines. His sleeveless shirt showed dozens of black-inked tattoos

. . . and heavy scarring to his upper left arm, which looked rather as if a shark had taken a bite out of it. "Company," Trennus said, tersely.

Sigrun turned, and her face lightened into a smile. "Ehecatl. There you are. Ehe, this is Trennus, your replacement on the team. Unless you want back in permanently. In which case, I will tell Livorus make room on the payroll for *both* of you."

The band of tension that Trennus hadn't even realized had wrapped around his chest broke at her words. They *did* consider him part of the team.

He watched as Adam and the Nahautl man traded wrist-clasps. "Good to see you again. You're looking a lot better than the last time I saw you," Adam noted.

Ehecatl snorted, and held up his left arm so they could all better the twisted mass of scar tissue—a deep channel, in fact—that carved through the side of it. "I'm still working on getting the strength back, but the doctors reattached the ends of the muscles. I'm at about eighty-five percent, they say. With time and work, I might get as much as ninety-five percent back. But I won't know what I *can* do till I've seen proper action."

Sigrun winced. "I could have healed that, old friend. Now that it's healed on its own, I can't help you."

Ehecatl made a rude noise in her direction. "You already had the girl's wounds, and you had to finish healing those yourself. By the time you were done returning her to her family, I was out of surgery and on medical leave. It's not a problem . . . and I think it would be presumptuous of me to expect healing every time I fall down." He gave her a tight grin. "Aside from which, I've seen what it costs. No, no. I'll lick my own wounds."

He turned and offered a wrist-clasp to Trennus as Adam introduced them. He looked up at the Pict, and shook his head. Trennus was a full foot taller than he was. "You're definitely not a stealth model, are you?"

"I've snuck up on deer in my home forest a few times," Trennus told him, smiling ruefully. "Anywhere else, it's not my strong point, no." He shook his head, and glanced at Adam. "All right. I'm on the ground, then."

They'd climbed up to the level of the box seats, and now, he nodded to them all, opened the swinging door in front of him, and headed down into the huge stadium. The swirling cacophony of voices that hit him like a wall, magnified as each voice echoed off the poured-stone steps and floors. As he pushed his way carefully through the crowd as he reached the lowest floor, he eyed the small court, built at ground level. This was an *ollamaliztli* court; the national pastime of Nahautl, which had once been played before major sacrificial events. History stated that once upon a time, the losers had gone on to become sacrificial victims, themselves.

The court itself was the oldest part of the building, and was sunken, with stone walls, and two loops of stone statuary, sticking out of the walls at the narrow ends of the rectangular playing area like a key from a lock, perpendicular to the ground. There were a handful of players warming up on the court; they were barefoot, but wore loincloths, loin-guards, and wicker greaves, as well as a sort of yoke, made from aluminum, strapped to their waists, to enlarge their overall pelvic region. This yoke both protected them, and allowed them to strike the ball harder. The ball itself was made of hard rubber, black, about a foot in diameter, and about six pounds in weight. The players could not use their hands to catch and throw, and kicking the ball directly might actually result in a broken bone in a foot. No, all strikes had to be done with the hips . . . and this was a full-contact sport. Complete with tackling and grabbing. Eye-gouging and choking were the only prohibited tactics. If Team A managed to get the ball to hit the wall at the back of Team B's side of the court, it counted as a point. If either team managed to rebound the heavy ball through the loop of stone on their opponent's side, it was an automatic win. Since the stone ring was eighteen feet above the court level, this very rarely happened.

At court-level, he milled with the people who occupied the cheap seats directly behind the expensive court-side benches, buying a cup of *pulque* — fermented agave nectar, as light and sweet as hard cider — from a vendor to blend in, and held the metal cup lightly in his hand, pretending to drink periodically. A glass wall separated the audience from the players, so that these tin cups couldn't be thrown down on them for a bad performance. *A good thing, too, or else we'd be having human sacrifice here today after all, eh?*

Trennus, that's not very funny.

Lassair? What are you doing?

You can't understand a word these people are saying, Trennus.

Well, no.

How do Stormborn and Steelsoul expect you to ask questions and listen to people's discontent, if you do not speak their language?

. . . I have no idea. I'm just following orders, my lady.

Let me fix that for you.

Trennus' head snapped upwards as a fizzling sound filled his ears. *What are you doing?* He turned, and looked at the pair of Nahuatl in festival-wear beside him, a man and a woman . . . and realized that they were speaking in . . . Pictish. Or at least, he was *hearing* them in his native dialect of Gallic. Their lip movements didn't match the sounds his mind perceived, however.

"What do you think? The players from Tikal have a lot of supporters in the crowd today."

"I think half the city of Tikal decamped and drove up Imperial Highway one hundred just to see this match." The woman's voice sounded grim.

"That's got to tip the odds a little in their favor." Forced lightness in the man's voice.

"I don't see why. The ball court in Tikal is half the size of this one. It's not a regulation court at all . . . they play by Quecha rules down there. They won't be able to chase the ball nearly as well as our men can." She looked around. "Look at them all, wearing the colors of the Quecha flag."

Even though the couple was standing right next to him, they apparently felt perfectly free to voice their opinions, under the shelter of their native language. The man shrugged, pulling on the woman's long, black braid gently. *"They're not all separatists. Just because they speak Quecha, and are Quechan by culture, doesn't mean they're rebels."* He picked up the end of her braid and stroked her cheek with it. *"Doesn't mean that they're the ones who killed your brother."*

"And that doesn't mean I won't cheer loudly if one of our men happens to break the nose of one of these Tikali bastards."

Trennus pulled his mug up to his lips, quickly, as the couple turned to give him an odd look, and then offered them an inane grin, before offering, in Latin, "I hear injuries are very common in this game. Is that true?"

They both gave him a look that fairly shouted, *what a tourist*, and then the man explained, in decent enough Latin—and Trennus could tell these were the man's own words, because his lips matched the shape of his words, *"Immo.* Yes. There is a saying . . . ball players wear armor made of bruises. They suffer concussions. Broken bones, when they are hurled to the ground, or into the stone walls of the court. In the old days, surgeons were kept on hand to cut open bad bruises, to reduce the swelling."

Blood binds, Trennus thought, reflexively, and wondered if people still understood the old sacrificial roots of their favorite pastime. "Sounds like war," he offered, pretending to take another sip of his *pulque.*

The man surprised him by laughing. "It is war! A better type than one fought with spears and swords and guns, yes? I would rather come here, and cheer for my team, and support them with breath and spirit, than see a thousand men die on a battlefield."

The woman next to him turned, frowning. *"Men die on battlefields anyway. The games don't stop that."* Back into words that didn't match the shapes her lips made.

"There hasn't been open warfare in over four hundred years, and I do think that the games help with that."

"Our version of the Romans' bread and circuses? Free rations of maize to the poor and blood-sports to keep us occupied. Oh, I cheer as loudly as the rest, but I know that it's all just shadows—"

Trennus pretended to ignore their conversation, as he studied the crowd and the boxes overhead, instead. Watched for people who happened to be looking up at the boxes, instead of down into the court, where the game was now in play. Watched for people who just sat there, unmoving, rather that leaping up with the rest of the crowd to cheer a heavy hit. He caught a glimpse, out of the corner of an eye, of the black ball slamming directly into one of the player's faces, and the spray of blood that splattered the glass partition . . . followed by a wave of people rising up from their benches to pound their fists against the glass, cheering gleefully. Trennus looked away, scanning the crowds again. He couldn't help but think that this was a very damned *good* substitute for sacrifices. There was a little symbolic blood spilled, and there were at least twenty thousand people in the arena at the moment. Depending on which side someone came down on in the academic dispute he and Kanmi had been having for three months now, this was either something that a spirit could be very pleased at having as a ritual bargain . . . or it could be the collective will of twenty thousand people, amassed and directed at a symbol. Either way, the air was rife with power, potential, and blood-lust . . . tightly channeled and contained. Trennus wondered, fleetingly, if the players were enjoined against having sex the night before the game. It was a common superstition, and if the games were a substitute for battle, the injunctions might be the same. The reasons for ritual celibacy could range from 'don't expend your seed and spirit, because then you won't have enough energy/spirit/fortitude the next day' to 'stay chaste as a sacrifice or demonstration of purity to whichever god you've entrusted yourself.'

It was an interesting train of thought, but not one he could really pursue at the moment. A voice cut in over the announcement system, booming back from the old stone walls, and spoke in Latin, "Ladies and gentlemen, we have a break in play while the Tikal player has his nose set. Please rise and remove your shoes in honor of Achcauhtli, *Tlatoani* of Tenochtitlan and king of kings, and of Governor Marcus Caelestis Dioscuri! *Ave*, Emperor Achcauhtli! *Ave*, Marcus Caelestis Dioscuri!"

In Nahautl culture, everyone was supposed to go barefoot before their emperor. Trennus sighed, hooked off his boots, tied them together by the laces, and hung them from his neck. He'd be damned if he lost them for someone else's customs. And then he went back to sweeping the crowd with his eyes and his other senses, looking for any tell-tale signs of mood or magic. He flicked quick glances up to the royal box, where Propraetor Livorus had already been seated, and saw him rise, along with Sigrun and Ehecatl Itztli and caught a glimpse of the Nahautl emperor—a man dressed in turquoise and violet pinstripe slacks, a solid shirt in the same turquoise, and a rich, shimmering, pinstriped cloak . . . . *Gods, I hope the pinstripe fad dies soon. People are starting to look like zebras in their business suits, these days . . . or, in this case, zebras that mated with parrots.* A crown shaped like an eagle's head shadowed the *tlatoani's* face, blue-green quetzal feathers sweeping back from it. The emperor also wore large golden earplugs and a number of other golden ornaments. He now raised his hand, acknowledging the crowd, who cheered and stomped for him. In the box above, Ehecatl knelt, in spite of his status as a lictor to Livorus, until his sovereign acknowledged him, permitting the man to rise.

The various Nahautl in the crowd wore a mix of modern and traditional clothing; some poorer men still wore loincloths and cloaks, and little more . . . though given the climate here, Trennus could understand *why*. Others wore slacks, with matching, colorful cloaks. The women's skirts tended to be colorful and short, and their blouses were white and distractingly thin.

Tren made his way back through the crowd, stopping to listen every time he thought he saw an argument, or someone who was looking up, at the boxes, instead of at the ball court. And every time, the words fizzled for a moment, and then the two people arguing began to speak in Pictish. *How are you _doing_ this?* he finally asked Lassair.

*They understand their own words. I touch their minds very lightly. And
I relay what they mean to you, as you best understand words. It is a little taxing. I
cannot assist you with every conversation around you. Just the ones you wish to
listen to, intently.* Her voice was gentle.

Trennus swore mentally. *That's a substantial investment of energy,
Lassair. And I didn't ask you to do this. Or bargain for it.*

No. You didn't. I see this as a fulfillment of our general contract.

*Still, it's not fair, and I would prefer to do something of equal value for
you in return, rather than be in any way your debtor.*

*Trennus, when will you understand? You saved my life, my existence.
Everything I do for you, is repayment of that debt.*

Locked in mental debate with the gently-spoken spirit, looking
around for any threats, magical or mundane to the propraetor, barefoot,
and carrying a cup of untasted *pulque*, Trennus didn't see the small
Nahautl woman before he almost ran her down. "Excuse me," he told the
dark-haired woman, immediately, and with some embarrassment. "I'm
sorry. Are you all right?" He steadied her on her feet with a light hand on
her shoulder.

Dark eyes stared up at him, and Trennus looked down, saw how
thin her blouse was, and how short the skirt, flushed, and dragged his eyes
back upwards, even as she said, in Nahautl, which translated into Pictish
in his mind, *"Clumsy oaf! Why don't you look where you're going?"*

"I said, I'm sorry. Are you all right? I didn't break any bones in
your foot, did I?" Trennus looked up and around, scanning the crowd
again.

She switched languages to Latin, "I'm fine, no thanks to you."
Back in Nahautl, she added, as if to herself, *"I try to avoid being trampled
more than once or twice a day."* Her grumbles faded, however, and she
added, suddenly, "Why, you're from Europa, aren't you? You don't look
like you're from Novo Gaul. Are you with the governor's staff?" Suddenly,
she had a hand on his forearm, and Trennus looked down and blinked.

Oh, you think she's pretty? I can leave you alone.

*Oh no you don't, Lassair. Not when you're translating for me. Besides, I
don't think this is a distraction I can afford right now. Morrigan's mercy, it could
even be a <u>deliberate</u> distraction. She keyed in on 'governor's staff.'*

He did his best to extricate himself politely, and found another
conversation to listen in on, watching the box seats carefully. And did his
best to put out of his mind how pretty the young woman he'd almost
trampled had been. *Just concentrate on the work. Nothing but the work.*

The palace of Emperor Achcauhtli was a sprawling complex,
covering almost three hundred acres of land at the heart of Tenochtitlan's
central island, and consisted of dozens of buildings. There was a *zoo* on the
grounds—made open to the public only in the last century—and it had
had salt and freshwater ponds for decorative fish since about the
fourteenth century AC. Now, the complex had decorative fountains in the
Roman style, which were lit up brilliantly at night with ley-power, the

blue-white light extending from each open courtyard to touch the palm and rubber trees and ferns and all the other plantings in the palace gardens. At least two hundred guests milled to and fro in the central courtyard, where the emperor of Nahautl sat on a throne on a raised dais, where a couple of Roman eating couches had been positioned to either side, for the comfort of the governor, Dioscuri, and of Livorus, as well. Everyone was shoeless, naturally, and Sigrun wiggled her bare toes against the cool tile of the courtyard, and just hoped no one dropped one of the glass flutes used for serving Gallic sparkling wine, or a bottle of *pulque*. That would get messy and painful, very quickly.

The Tenochtitlan team had thrashed the Tikali team, quite literally; one of the Tikali players had been carried, unconscious, from the arena, with a skull fracture. Halfway through the match, Livorus had leaned over to her, where she sat beside him, and murmured, "Not quite as gripping as gladiatorial combat, I think."

There *were* arenas here in Nahautl; they were common all through Caesaria Aquilonis, as far north as her home in the city of Cimbri-on-the-Caestus. There were professional gladiators, and death on the sands remained a common means of executing murderers and rapists. Sigrun had shrugged. "At least both teams appear to be equally skilled. It makes for a more gripping match than an exhibition of justice."

"There is that," Livorus had agreed, equitably. "It's also something of a step up from bull and bearbaiting. I've never been much interested in seeing an animal torn apart by a pack of dogs. Never quite seems a fair contest, though the crowd always loves it."

"Am I being suitably decorative, propraetor?" Sigrun had asked, after a moment, arching her eyebrows.

"My dear, you are always suitable, and on this occasion, perfectly decorative." Livorus had taken her hand and given her an amused, almost affectionate look. "Most of our audience below is looking at you, and wondering about the proclivities of a debauched Roman senator, and not paying the least bit of attention to Ehecatl, ben Maor, or any of the other lictors' movements. There are times when I need all of you to look like the fingers in Rome's fist. And sometimes, there is value in being underestimated."\ "Then perhaps it would have been best to have one of the lineage of Loki among your lictors, *dominus*." Sigrun raised her eyebrows at him. "They are, by far, more skilled in illusion and deception than one such as I."

"Do you happen to number any of them among your acquaintance?" he asked, as if making small talk with her.

"One, yes. Reginleif was one of my instructors in the Odinhall."

"Is she available?"

Sigrun's brow crinkled. "She's remained at the Odinhall for the past seventy years or so. Or did you mean socially? I believe that she is married."

"Ah, well. You will have to do your best, my dear, as must we all." Livorus went so far as to kiss her fingers, lightly.

She'd stood to show respect to the emperor and Governor

Dioscuri, and done her best not to raise her eyebrows; the governor had clearly gone a little native in his years here. He still wore a white toga with purple trim on this official occasion . . . but he also wore jade earplugs, and his hair curled almost to his shoulders, far longer than the Roman norm. His Nahautl wife, a woman introduced as Nochtli, trailed along behind him, dressed in native finery.

Now, in the gardens, as Livorus ate from a table situated in front of his couch on the dais, Sigrun was free to circulate and mingle. Not something that she did well, and she knew it. She also didn't speak a word of Nahautl, so she was forced to rely on Latin, Hellene, Gothic, and Gallic. For the moment, however, she stood by the propraetor's couch, listening to the conversation between the emperor, the governor, and Livorus. They'd been put off for weeks by Achcauhtli; Livorus had explained it all as an elaborate political dance, about a week ago. "He wants to look as if he's not at Rome's beck and call," the propraetor had told them in his hotel room, dryly. "He wants to look independent and strong, in front of his people. Hence, holding the personal envoy of the Roman Imperator at arm's length." Livorus had shrugged. "It's often a problem, particularly when time is of the essence, but kings move at their own speed, and our governor here has indicated that he can only motivate the emperor so far."

Now that he had access to both the governor and the emperor at the same time, Livorus wasted no time at all in coming to the reason for their journey to this distant kingdom. "Your majesty," he said, smoothly, taking a bunch of grapes from the table in front of him, "it pains me to bring this up so early in the evening, but I would be remiss if I did not extend the concerns of the Imperator to you. We have heard rumors that there may be human sacrifices being offered in your country once more." Livorus raised a hand to prevent any reply. "I do not level any accusations, of course. You have been a loyal and excellent ally for the fifteen years of your reign, as was your father, before you."

Achcauhtli raised his eyebrows slightly, his eyes like obsidian in the shadows of the garden, and waved his attendants away; they set down their trays and retreated, immediately. The emperor turned and gave the governor, Dioscuri, a dark look, before turning back to Livorus. "It pains us," the emperor replied, using the royal *we*, "to express ignorance of this sad possibility, but nevertheless, we must. If such a thing exists, we suspect strongly that it would be confined to backwards, rustic areas. We have had . . . unrest . . . in the past few years in the largely Quechan southern reaches of our fair lands. We have requested, repeatedly, leave from Rome to put down the guerillas near Tikal who rebel against our reign. This is a matter of self-rule and autonomy, yet Governor Dioscuri and your revered Imperator have both denied us the ability to enforce our own laws and edicts."

Some provinces and subject states had more autonomy than others. Nahautl had fairly strong autonomy in domestic matters, and was permitted to have a standing army of its own, in addition to Legion forces within its borders. However, they were not permitted to use those troops without the direct order of their Roman governor. Sigrun glanced past the emperor towards Dioscuri. The governor glanced up at the night sky in resignation, and leaned further on his elbow towards the center of their conversational grouping. "The reason why I have advised so strongly against using military force, for several years, is simple. If *Rome* chooses to chastise the rebels, we would undoubtedly send the Legions in, with vigor. Tikal and the other cities would run with blood." Dioscuri went on, patiently, "This may incite *more* rebellion, not less, and the Quechan and Tawantinsuyan provinces to the south could rise up, as well. Everything I permit, I must weigh against the overall political situation, both south of here and north of here—"

"We have not asked for the Legions. We have asked to be allowed to mobilize our own army—"

"Allowing you to use your own forces is still an act of Rome," Dioscuri replied, clearly choosing his words carefully.

Sigrun kept her thoughts to herself, but added, mentally, *Or it will look as if Rome is weak, in not putting the cities to the sword, themselves. Of course, he cannot say that to the emperor, to his face, but they all know it.*

"You are leaving us with very few options besides watching part of our empire go up in flames, or *disobedience* to Rome," Achcauhtli said, biting off the ends of his words. "We are still a sovereign nation. We may be a subject state, but within our own borders, the power of the *tlatoani* is supposed to be absolute—by treaty!—but Rome insists on tying my hands." From the royal *we* to the personal voice, in an instant. "And yet, Rome shows no interest in resolving the situation, themselves."

"The entirety of the southern continent could go up in flames. And that *is* Rome's interest in the matter." Dioscuri's voice was surprisingly firm. For as long as Achcauhtli had been on the throne—fifteen years, at least—Dioscuri had been governor. No, longer; he had been an assistant to the previous governor during the reign of Achcauhtli's father.

At that point, Nochtli approached her husband's seat; the Nahautl woman was small but lovely, with a round, sweet face, and wore, this evening, a vividly red dress, with red feathers tangled in her crow-dark hair. She murmured to her husband for a moment, and he nodded, looking over at Livorus. "Propraetor, if you wouldn't mind? My wife would like to introduce your, ah, lictor around the court." Dioscuri gestured. "And these are discussions of policy, I think, best left for fewer ears."

Sigrun noted the pause before the word *lictor*, and sighed internally. Dioscuri really should know better than to assume she was Livorus' mistress, but she was dressed more *decoratively* than usual tonight, and didn't have her spear in hand.

For his part, Livorus merely smiled, thinly. "I trust my lictors with my life, Dioscuri, and have no secrets from them that I can readily think of. But, as you wish. Sigrun, my dear? If you would be so kind?"

Sigrun tapped her fist to her chest, immediately, and bedamned to the fact that she was wearing a dress while saluting him. "As you wish, *dominus*." She turned as Nochtli approached, and lowered her head in respect to the governor's wife. "My lady? What will you?"

Nochtli smiled up at her, tentatively, and in smooth, pure Latin that was almost without accent, told her, "Let me introduce you around. You and the propraetor are . . . close?"

Sigrun wanted to close her eyes in annoyance, but then she'd have missed Ehecatl's amused grin as she passed his position in an embrasure along the courtyard wall. On the one hand, being thought to be Livorus' mistress might seem to give her political power, or at least, influence over him. On the other hand, damn it, she had her dignity. "I have been his lictor for five years. I came to his service in 1949." Her tone was brisk and businesslike. "Before that, I was an *ælagol* among my people for ten years." That much, and no more, she'd give the woman. Just enough to put the governor's wife back on her heels a little.

Nochtli started to laugh as she directed the taller woman through the crowds. "You're pleased to jest with me? You can't be much more than twenty."

Sigrun looked down at her, expressionlessly. "I rarely am pleased to do so, my lady." She looked around the crowded courtyard. "Now, to whom *would you* have me speak?"

Nochtli Dioscuri blinked, rapidly, obviously re-evaluating matters. Then she drew Sigrun to the edge of the courtyard, into the shelter of one of the pillars there. Sigrun threw a glance over her shoulder, looking around, immediately, for her fellow lictors, and caught Adam, Ehecatl, and Trennus' eyes; Adam nodded over his drink, telling her, without words, that he was keeping an eye on her. The knowledge was a relief, almost unaccountably so. She could probably tear any single person here asunder with little more than her bare hands—other than her fellow lictors—but she was still on edge. There was a hint of rain in the air, and a suggestion of electrical currents in the atmosphere, high overhead, but that wasn't it. It was the impression of hidden undercurrents in every conversation around her, and of being deep in social waters with which she was unfamiliar. *Couldn't Livorus just have brought his wife with him on one of these trips? Of course, that would mean a second protective detail . . . and one for the children, or they'd have had to leave the children in Rome . . . and Poppaea is . . . Poppaea. Functionally useless in almost every way. Nevermind.*

"Mistress Caetia? I would like to introduce you to Tlilpotonqui Tototl. High priest of Tlaloc, He Who Makes Things Sprout, for all of Nahautl." Nochtli smiled at the man on the other side of the pillar, who was holding court there with a handful of people, most of whom seemed to be listening to his every word intently. "High priest, this is Sigrun Caetia. One of the propraetor's, ah, attendants."

Tlaloc . . . Tlaloc. Damn it. I'm going to have to ask Ehecatl for more details. She was not as strong on the Nahautl pantheon as she should be. And the perennial 'ah' before the term *lictor* was getting on her nerves. She was, however, on someone else's territory, so Sigrun reined in her temper, not aware of the low rumble of thunder in the distance. She offered her hand for a straight-forward Roman wrist-clasp, and found that the priest simply stared down at the appendage for a moment, before raising his dark eyes to study her face.

The high priest was a short man, around Kanmi's height, but

unlike many of the party-goers, he was fully clad in traditional attire; no hint of Rome, here. In his case, this consisted of a black and red cloak, wrapped around his body, without a shirt, and a fringed and beaded loincloth in the same colors, with a tall, black-feathered headdress, which displayed the fact that his scalp was shaved at the sides. His body held just as many tattoos as Ehecatl or Trennus, but Sigrun had no idea what any of them meant. Again, she was deeply grateful that Ehecatl was on hand. She already had a list of questions for the man almost as long as her arm. The regional Praetorian office had given them thick stacks of dossiers, but at the moment, Sigrun couldn't remember seeing any folders on the high priest of Tlaloc. *I might not remember the name, but I think I'd remember the face, if I'd seen it before. He's distinctive. As if he was carved out of a solid piece of jade, and left to weather for centuries . . . .*

The high priest had been looking up at her while they'd been appraising one another, and Sigrun realized, suddenly, that the electrical potential in the air was much stronger than it had been at any other point in the evening. She glanced up at the clouds before the lighting bolt forked from horizon to horizon, and let her head roll back for a moment, as the first patter of rain fell, striking her on the face. *I think that this one is god-born. He doesn't have the hallmarks of the sorcerer. But he does not introduce himself as such, and nor am I supposed to do so tonight, in defiance of all custom and courtesy.* Sigrun stifled a grimace, and asked, instead, as pleasantly as she could, "Tlaloc is more than just god of rain and crops, as best I recall." As she spoke, the other guests muttered and began to move towards the doors to get in out of the midnight rain. "He is the lord of lightning, lord of the earth in which things grow, and lord, too, of the earth that consumes the dead, is he not?" Her frantic pawing at the hints of memory from her time in the Odinhall had borne some fruit, at least.

The high priest's faintly supercilious stare softened, replaced by a look of interest. "You know something of our ways."

"I am something of a scholar of the ways of other people, though I cannot count myself an expert on any save my own. For example, I read that once, that Tlaloc was offered sacrifices of human hearts in your temples, along with many of your other gods." Sigrun didn't say the words as a challenge. She put neutrality into her voice, as best she could, wondering what the man would say in reply.

A feint, as his eyes flickered to the side. "You're from Nova Germania, yes? Your people once made sacrifices, too."

"Not in over two thousand years, and even then, it was rare." Sigrun shrugged. "Sometimes, a female slave might have volunteered to be buried with her master, after accepting the seed of all of his men." *Of course, while legend says that this was voluntary, and my people regard free will as sacred, I have to wonder how often this was truly the case.* "In some tribes, there were Yule sacrifices every nine years. And of course, there are legends of kings who'd sacrificed their own sons to gain unnaturally long lives." She leaned against the pillar as the rain began to fall more heavily, watching in mild amusement as almost everyone wearing feathers scurried for overhangs to protect their finery. "That being said? If we had a bad king, even two thousand years ago, my people could unseat him from his throne." A notion enshrined in the law, in fact . . and kings had been supplanted, in Nova Germania and Novo Gaul, at least, by elections and democracy. Those Hellene concepts had found fertile soil in the new world.

Her skin crawled a little, as electrical potential built in the air again, and the rain began to pour down harder. Nochtli, the governor's wife, intervened, asking, mildly, "Can we not step under one of the balconies, my friends?" She moved a little further away, trying to draw them with her, her red dress already clinging to her.

"I am quite comfortable, receiving my lord's bounty," Tototl replied, lifting up his hands as the rain splashed down into them. "I wonder that you should speak of supplanting kings, barbarian woman."

"Are we not both barbarians? Do we both not speak Latin as a second or even a third language?" Sigrun's lips quirked at the corners. She'd found a fencing partner, apparently. She glanced at Nochtli, and inclined her head, feeling rain pour in a steady stream down her nose, like a downspout. "My thanks, *domina*, but I, too, am more comfortable under the open sky." She smiled with forced cheer at Nochtli, and then turned and looked back at Tototl. *Two can play this game.* "I spoke of dethroning bad kings among my own people. I spoke not at all of yours, nor of anyone else's."

"Do you not consider the Imperator of Rome to be your king?" Sly, cautious words, implying that she harbored traitorous thoughts.

"I consider him to be the *Imperator*. As your own emperor stands above the petty lords who govern the various cities subject to him, so does the Imperator govern kings." Sigrun paused. "And yet, even the Imperator is subject to the laws of Rome. Admittedly, he makes the laws, but over the centuries, there have been efforts to contain even the absolute power of the Imperator." She smiled again, faintly. "I find your people's history interesting, high priest. I know, for example, that a common man could always rise through the military, or the priesthood. As my friend Ehecatl Itztli has done. He was common-born, and rose to a high rank among the Jaguar warriors before becoming a Praetorian." Sigrun glanced around, trying to find her fellow lictors, and failed. Either Ehecatl had gone invisible, or he, like the others, had had the great good sense to get in out of the rain. "And yet, for all your society's mobility . . . have your people never thought of dethroning a bad king?"

A twitch, just barely visible, under his eyelids, fairly shouted to her that he was concealing something as he replied, "All of our kings descend from the Toltecs. The first-born children of the gods. To do such a thing would be . . . sacrilege." His eyes were hooded.

He's hiding something. But I can't tell what. He hasn't spoken a direct lie yet. "Ah, so your kings are god-born, are they?" Sigrun knew that wasn't quite true. There hadn't been a true god-born on the throne of Nahautl in about four hundred years . . . not since the last time Rome had been forced to march in and chastise the province. "But the title of emperor does not always go from father to son, is that correct?" Sigrun could feel the rain's intensity start to ease a little now, but she was already soaked to the skin. Her dress was clinging to her legs, but at least her leathers would dry well. She wasn't sure about the silk of the damnable skirt.

"No. Sometimes, the *tlatoani*, in times past, has been elected from the imperial family, by the aristocracy. Huitzilíhuitl, our second emperor here in Tenochtitlan, was elected so. The *tlatoani* have always come of the blood of the gods. But they rely on the wisdom of many to rule." His voice was serene, and absolutely unshaken now.

Interesting reaction points he has. "And are you, by chance, of the blood of the gods?" Sigrun asked, and could feel the electrical charge overhead building once again. This time, however, she diverted it. And instead of sending lightning forking from horizon to horizon, she brought it down on a radio tower's antenna she could just see blinking, peacefully, past one of the buildings in the palace complex. She didn't dare bring it down any closer; she wasn't holding anything metal, weapon or otherwise. Touching metal gave her a much finer degree of control over lightning.

As the thunder echoed against the walls of the palace, Tototl drew himself up, studying her, his eyes narrow. Sigrun made a point of looking in the direction of the lightning bolt, as if surprised by it, and then looked back down at him. "I am," the high priest assured her, with dignity, after a moment's pause.

So, you descend from nobility. Doesn't automatically make you god-born . . . but I can feel someone touching the weather, the same way I can. And while it could be someone else, why not a priest of 'He who makes things sprout?' She thought for a moment, and then asked, "So, you could rule as a . . . *tlatoani?*" Sigrun knew she'd mangled the word hopelessly.

The high priest's eyes went wide, and he glanced from side to side, eyeing Nochtli for a moment, as she'd ducked under a nearby balcony, trying to find some kind of shelter from the wet. "I am only a very distant relation. And I am a priest. Only a king may rule."

"Interesting," Sigrun managed a smile she didn't feel. "It's been lovely meeting you, high priest. I wish you and your people fertile fields, and much rain." She looked up at the sky, from which drizzle still fell, adding, "Though perhaps no more today." She nodded to Nochtli. "My lady? Should I return you to your husband now?" She ducked under the cover of the balcony herself now, and reached back to squeeze water out of her braid.

Nochtli Dioscuri gave her a wide-eyed glance. "You should not speak to the high priest so," the governor's wife muttered, sounding upset. "He is a good man. He tries, very hard, to preserve our cultural heritage."

"You know him well, then?" Sigrun asked. *Might as well figure out the undercurrents here. If I can.*

"He's been a friend of my family since I was a child." Nochtli still sounded perturbed.

"You are noble-born, yourself?" Sigrun tried to make her voice as conciliatory as possible as they splashed, barefoot, through the puddles towards the entrance of the palace building into which the rest of the party had gone for refuge from the storm.

"Well, yes. To a degree. My father worked his way into the aristocracy through military service. He was a Jaguar soldier, when he was young." Nochtli shrugged. "He fought in a few border skirmishes with the Quecha, alongside the Legions, long before I was born. He married my mother, who was from an old noble family, and the rest, as they say, is history. The high priest traveled with the army in those days. He was younger then, of course."

"High priest Tototl is god-born, is he not?" Sigrun tried to put dates to the last serious border skirmishes in which the Legions had been mobilized. *Damn it. Again, I need Ehecatl's mind. Nochtli here is . . . thirty-five or so, I think. Her father served against the Quecha and had to work his way through the aristocracy to marry her mother, Jaguar warriors are recruited at fifteen, and undergo several years of rigorous training . . . . Her father is likely in his late sixties to early seventies . . . .*

Nochtli had almost stopped in her tracks, and looked embarrassed, now. "It is said that all of the great noble houses descend from the gods. In ancient times, emperors had commoners who *looked* at them killed, and their feet were not permitted to touch the ground. They had to be carried by slaves, or walked on fine rugs strewn before them on the ground. Some of the highest noble families demanded similar privileges, as time went on. In spite of Rome's . . . discouragement of the practices."

"So you're saying that all the old families are god-born, then?" Sigrun said, pleasantly. *Apparently, our definitions of the term seem to vary a little.*

"Every member of the old families is accorded that respect, yes."

A very neat dodge. You have been the wife of a governor for a while, haven't you, for all that you still fluster around your family's very old friend. "I meant no offense by the question, *domina*. I merely wished to get a feel for the high priest's age. You said that he was much concerned with maintaining your people's cultural traditions and heritage."

"Oh, as to that, he's been involved in such movements for at least fifty years," Nochtli said vaguely, waving the question of Tototl's age away.

They stepped through the old stone doorway, into a wash of golden light and the damp heat of many bodies, and waited as servants came over with towels to help them dry their feet. Sigrun again tried to wring out her braid, and gave it up as a bad job, before trying one more information probe. "So, the high priest still speaks with you regularly, even though you are married to a Roman?"

Nochtli looked appalled. "Of course he does. He's not at all prejudiced. And through my charitable works, we've become even better acquainted now, than when I was young. The people revere him. He brings rain to the crops through Tlaloc's blessings. He's a good man."

Of course he is. He's just hiding something, and I don't know what. It's probably nothing. Diplomats and politicians are paid to hide things. There were dozens of gods in the Nahautl pantheon. Many, if not *most*, of them had been offered human sacrifices in centuries past. She probably shouldn't be suspicious of the man just because he wasn't perfectly forthright with a complete stranger on first meeting. And, in truth, he'd said nothing actually wrong.

Sigrun sighed, and told Nochtli, "Of course he is. My apologies," before turning away . . . to find Adam ben Maor standing directly beside her, and blinked. "I . . . didn't know you were there."

"You were distracted." Adam picked up the damp coil of her braid in gentle fingers, and wrapped a towel around it. "You know, most people have the sense to get in out of the rain. I'd tell you that you're going to catch your death of a cold, but, well, colds are caused by viruses."

". . . and I have never been sick in my life." Sigrun reached back to take the towel and dry her own hair, smiling at Adam faintly, and stepping away from Nochtli Dioscuri.

Adam, for his part, wouldn't let her take the towel. "No, no, this is easier." He added, in a mutter, "And gives us cover to talk for a moment."

In a quieter tone, she asked him, "Please tell me we're making headway."

"Other than the fact that Livorus has been redirected onto the topic of slavery, how it's currently only used for debt in Nahautl, and how the Senate is now debating banning it entirely in the Empire—"

"They've debated *that* every year since 1850 AC. It's not going to be eliminated in the next decade. Reformed further, I can see, but it's too good a punishment sentence for criminals, and keeps them out of prisons." Sigrun shrugged. It had been eliminated in Nova Germania and Novo Gaul when she was about eighteen, but it was such an integral part of Roman culture, that she didn't see it ending any time soon. "Most of the rest of the world still has slaves. My former partner, Zoskales, was a sorcerer from Nubia. He said that of the four million people living in his country, fully half were slaves when he grew up. His mother was one, in fact." Sigrun shrugged. "I don't really like it much, but the world is, what the world is."

Adam finished with the very tail end of her braid. "Don't look at me. Relatives have been known to serve in the houses of their richer family members in Judea, and there used to be slavery for captives of war, but other than imported Roman and Hellene slaves . . . and not many of those . . . it hasn't been much of a factor in centuries." A quick, droll smile. "No one's begetting extra children on their wives' handmaidens anymore." He paused. "Not on purpose, anyway."

She half-turned, squinted, and shook her head. "I don't understand. But I'll pretend, for the moment, that I do."

Adam chuckled at her, and gestured at the throng of still-damp people. "Back to work?"

"Back to work." Sigrun sighed. "I think I'd rather be getting shot at. It's simpler."

"Pretend the words are bullets."

"Very helpful, ben Maor. Very helpful."

"I live to serve."

Kanmi Eshmunazar moved around the interior of the large palace building, dodging servitors with trays, occasionally snagging a snack from one or another. Aristocratic nibbles here seemed to tend towards meat, deep-fried inside of envelopes of flat dough, with cheeses. Tasty, really, but finger food filled the hollow of his belly very slowly indeed. And, being a sorcerer, he tended to need to eat a lot, in order to fuel his sorcery. He knew perfectly well that sorcery was a matter of willpower . . . but when you used your own body as a conduit for will and magic, it *did* use up caloric reserves. Nothing came from nothing, after all.

He wore a dress version of his work clothes—as such, he wore rubber-soled shoes, and a leather vest with dozens of small pockets, occupied by a seemingly random assortment of items. Copper-topped nickel-metal hydride batteries, chosen in spite of their annoyingly high rate of self-discharge. High-energy snacks, such as Nahautl chocolate, wrapped around raisins, tucked into little paper sacks. Circuit boards, chosen for their ability to modulate energy, particularly electricity, with tiny capacitors strung along their length like colored beads. Coils of copper wire, a large magnet, an iron knife, and a silver one, too. *The trappings of the modern shaman,* Kanmi reflected, his lips quirking as he studied the room. He despised the well-dressed guests, mostly on principle, and chuckled under his breath as they twitched uncomfortably in their damp clothing.

He didn't see any threats in the room, which was a sort of art gallery, filled with Roman, Nahautl, and even Qin masterpieces, but that wasn't his only task here tonight. It was difficult to keep his mind on the job, however; he'd scouted the ballgame venue, perched in the rafters for the entirety of the match, and had now been watching this room for hours. His eyes burned, and the best part was, one or two of them tonight, probably him and Trennus, would go from this detail directly to guarding the propraetor first thing in the morning. Kanmi might have four hours to fall on his face and sleep before doing this all over again. *It's a shitty job sometimes, but it pays the bills.*

At that moment, he turned to cover another quadrant of the room, and finally spotted Sigrun coming into the room from outdoors, soaking wet. Ben Maor was with her, and Kanmi couldn't hear their words from a distance, but could see the expressions. Mostly blank, quick exchanges, glances around the room. *About time you made it back in here, god-born,* Kanmi grumped, silently. *The more eyes, the better.*

At that point, one of the party-goers bumped into him, and Kanmi spun, eyes narrowing . . . and then widening again, in surprise. The face was familiar, but in a setting like this, so far from any with which he'd had previous association, he couldn't *place* it. Green eyes—unusual in a Nahautl—dark-tanned skin, dark, long hair, earplugs, markings on the skin, slacks and a white shirt, and an equally white smile splitting the dark-tanned face. "Kanmi Eshmunazar, as I live and breathe!"

It took a moment for the sorcerer from Tyre to find a name that matched the face in memory. "Gratian? Gratian Xicohtencatl?"

"One and the same!" Gratian offered him a hearty wrist-clasp. "By the gods, I didn't expect to see you here. How are you?"

Stunned, Kanmi could only manage a startled smile, before reflecting that he and Gratian had never really been close. "Fine, and I thank you for asking. Gods. I think the last time I saw you was . . . seven years ago? University of Athens?"

"Yes, I graduated a year ahead of you."

The University of Athens was the foremost school for technomancy in the West, and ranked just slightly ahead of the University of Edo, in far-off Nippon. Kanmi had spent four years there, training in sorcery and how it could enhance technology, and be enhanced, itself, by an understanding of natural philosophy. The origins of technomancy were ancient, and went back to before even the Mongols' attempted invasion of the West. Someone bright had put sorcerers beside catapults, and told them to heat the stone loads to red hot. To increase the force with which they were thrown. To control where they landed, by manipulating the airflow around the stones.

As a result, Roman catapults, ballistae, and mangonels had had *pinpoint* precision, and their boulders had landed in enemy formations and shattered into red-hot splinters. Arrows had been enhanced with similar applications of raw will, and sorcerers—the first technomancers—had looked for ways to embed their will in arrows, and, later, in arquebus shot and musket balls. Lightning had been examined and found to be a natural force—a different state of matter and energy than fire and earth and air and water—and accessed as another tool in the technomancer's repertoire. Gravity, magnetism, friction, and even *light* were all tools, as well.

As such, students usually studied physics and chemistry in addition to natural philosophy and sorcery. Kanmi remembered Gratian now; both of them had been equally out of place in Athens, surrounded by Hellenes. Kanmi had learned Hellene in Carthaginian sorcery preparatory schools, but he hadn't been fluent enough to listen to lectures in it with any degree of comprehension until halfway through his first year. Gratian, the son of a Roman woman with a Nahautl minor lord, had been in much the same boat, and had been in charge of a small student group dedicated to bringing together people from different provinces and subject kingdoms and giving them common causes and activities. So that they wouldn't feel quite so alone. Kanmi had always been a bit of a loner, and had viewed most of the parties and social outings as an enormous waste of time. He vaguely remembered something about politics being associated with one of the subgroups, a topic he normally avoided like the plague—another good reason to avoid anyone associated with the group. And of course, in his third year, he'd met Bastet, and gotten married. Even more reason not to be wasting time with a group of over-privileged wealthy brats.

Still, it was pleasant to see a familiar face, and one belonging to someone in a similar line of work. Kanmi put all of the memories to the back of his mind, and merely asked, "So, what are you doing these days, and how did you get an invitation to the *emperor's* personal party?"

Gratian laughed easily. "Oh, I've worked my way up through the local ley-grid company. It's state-run here, of course, but they're always in need of a good technomancer. Started out rebuilding transformers in the field about seven years ago. Now? Vice president of Research and Development, with a close working relationship with Installations and Maintenance." He nodded, radiating pleased self-assurance. "We're installing new taps in the Tikal region right now, in fact. Get those people down there some actual *power*, and they'll see the world in a whole new light."

For all of Kanmi's teasing of Trennus, he knew perfectly well that ley-lines existed. What their actual *source* was, was up for debate, as far as he was concerned, but he didn't quibble now. Arguing over academics with someone who'd gone into business, rather than pure theory, was usually not a winning conversational gambit. *"It works and don't ask why, so long as the money keeps coming in,"* was the usual attitude Kanmi had encountered.

As it was, he did his best not to change expressions as he thought, *Doesn't hurt to have an aristocrat for a father, now, does it?* Out loud, all he said was, neutrally, "Sounds interesting."

Actually, it sounded anything *but*. His hours might be horrible, and the job might take him away from his wife and children for months at a time, but at least it wasn't *middle management*. Sitting at a desk, watching life pass by, measured out by how tall the sheaf of reports in front of him was.

"Oh, it is, it is." Gratian grinned at him, all pleasure. "And it gets me invitations to social events like this one, once in a while. I meet and greet with the high aristocracy, and get them to invest a little more in the common man. Some of them actually take an interest in the little people now and again, or can be motivated to do so."

Oh, Asarte's tits. You are the political type. All right, so I work for a politician, but I don't have to talk about it all damned day. Theoretically everything Gratian was saying accorded with Kanmi's own beliefs; he detested the aristocracy on principle, and inherited wealth on the same basis. On the other hand, he'd rather kiss an electrical socket, full-tongue, than kiss up to an aristocrat to get them to hand out a little of their ancestors' wealth. Kanmi made a general sound of agreement in Gratian's general direction, and added, "Power to the people, eh?"

He'd tossed out the phrase, using it as conversational time-keeper. It let him sound as if he were paying attention, when, in fact, his eyes were mostly on the room around them.

He wasn't so distracted that he missed Gratian's start of surprise. *"Potentia ad populum,"* the man returned, shifting the words into antique Latin, out of the more commonplace modern dialect that they were currently speaking. "The potential and power inherent to the great mass of people, if only they could overcome their own inertia, eh?"

Having no idea where this was going, Kanmi let the current tug him along with it. "I've always been a proponent of the notion that if you gather enough people together, and get them to focus on what they truly desire, you can focus their combined will to do remarkable things." *Admittedly, if you bring together five thousand perfectly normal, untrained people, and get them to all stare at a feather, they might be able to excite the motion of the air molecules around it just enough to stir the barbules of the feather, but I doubt if they could move the damned thing just by wishing . . . .* As it was, he thought his comment little more than a platitude.

"Yes, I remember that about you. Scholarship boy, weren't you?" Gratian was focusing on Kanmi intently now.

"Good memory. Yes, I was." Kanmi glanced around, trying to find a way to redirect the conversation away from himself, and back onto Gratian and the man's odd reactions. "With your family's connections, why didn't you study at the University of Rome, instead of the University of Athens?"

"My choice, really. I wanted to breathe the air of free men," Gratian said, airily. "To imbibe, directly, from the well-spring of democratic thought."

Democracy. Yes, so long as you happen to be male, free-born or freed, and have land or a certain level of income per year. Oh, wait, no, they gave free-born women who met the monetary clauses the vote about thirty years ago, didn't they? Far more likely that you wanted to go there for the night-life. Which Athens has, by the cartload. "And here I'd thought all this time that you were actually there to drink from the well-spring of that terrible pine-resin wine . . . ."

Gratian chuckled. "Well, you did keep your distance at the time." He paused. "So . . . ." After a pause, the other mage asked, "what brings *you* here?"

A shrug. "Four years on the Mongol border, and then the Empire came calling for other services."

"Hmm, well, yes, can't beat a government paycheck, can you? Feeding on the beast, eh?" The words made Kanmi's eyes narrow slightly again. *And you say this, given that you have a job with a state-run power company?*

Out loud, Kanmi replied, noncommittally, "It's steady. My wife doesn't like the long separations."

"Oh, so you're not here in Nahautl on a permanent assignment? What a pity. I could have stood to have another *proper* technomancer around."

"I'll be here as long as the propraetor is, and no longer." Kanmi frowned. He'd missed a conversational current here, somewhere, and he knew it. One moment, a riptide had been pulling him one direction, and then he'd been released.

Gratian's eyebrows arched. "Oh, so you're one of the *lictors* for Propraetor Livorus? My mistake. You *have* come up in the world." A pause. "You say your wife doesn't like the long trips away from home?" He snapped his fingers, smiling as if he'd just remembered something. "Nubian woman, I think?"

"Bastet, yes." Kanmi reached into a pocket in his vest reflexively, and brought out a round watchcase; on the inside, his wedding picture, the only one he ever took with him anywhere. A simple, black and white picture, him in a white caftan, and Bastet in a dark, striped dress. She was half a head taller than he was, arrow-straight and thin, with rich, dark skin that the camera completely failed to do justice to, unfortunately. "Her father *claims* to be descended from a one-eyed archer queen who repelled the Roman legions from Nubia, back in Strabo's time." It was an idle comment. Kanmi wasn't particularly good at small talk. "I've always had my doubts about that, though."

Gratian's face lit up in interest, however, and the riptide was carrying Kanmi along again. "You know, it's a pity that she's not with you. As is, since you're alone here in my country, I simply *must* introduce you to some like-minded people. You won't lack for entertainment while you're here in the capital, I promise you." The Nahautl man's smile grew sly. "Why, I have a standing reservation at one of the best brothels here in Tenochtitlan. When next the propraetor can spare you, do give me a call." He offered Kanmi a card with his name and telephone number on it. Embossed in the upper corner was the image of a black and yellow bumblebee—which matched the clasp of the light business cloak Gratian wore tossed around his shoulders this evening.

Reflexively, Kanmi accepted the thin vellum square, and watched the other man leave. *Now what in Astarte's name was that all about, anyway?*

Chapter VI: Backgrounds

The history of the kingdom of Judea stands as an anomaly. With the Persian Empire and its subject kingdoms to their east, Egypt to the west, Carthage and Byzantium, under the direct rule of Rome, to the north, and the vast, empty deserts of the Sinai Peninsula to the south, they are hemmed in on all sides by either empires, the sea, or an inhospitable wasteland ruled by nomadic tribes. This has resulted in dozens of waves of conquest of the area over the millennia, which should have ensured cultural cross-fertilization . . . and did, to a certain extent. However, the people of this small province cling to their own traditions, culture, and religion. There are groups outside of the major cities who live precisely as their ancestors did, thousands of years ago, tending herds of sheep, cattle, and camels, with only a bare interest in the modern amenities of cities like Jerusalem. But within the major cities, cultural cross-pollination . . . and resistance to that hybridization . . . has created strange new efflorescences.

For example, the region is situated at a crossroads for close to a dozen cultures, all of which use magic in some form or another. Persian Magi and nomadic shaman have hurled spells at the walls of this desert province for centuries. Egypt and its god-born have long trafficked in spells of some form or another. Rome, with its long history of massive engineering projects, has had a historical bias towards natural philosophy and reason, but has a tradition of god-born as well, going back to Aeneas, not to mention Romulus and Remus.

Judea, however, has had a religious prohibition against the use of common magic for almost three thousand years. Magic is variously described, by the denizens of that land, as a 'crutch' or 'a betrayal of the covenant.' They cite King Saul's prohibition of magic, and get along with the products of natural philosophy alone. They have no god-born, or at least, have not had since the days of their prophets and judges. Historically, any of their people who might have been termed 'god-born' by other peoples, are difficult to identify in Judean records, because none of their historical wise men, prophets, judges, or heroes have ever called themselves the son of a god, the way, say, Heracles, Achilles, Hermes Trismegistus, or Asclepius did.

While it is easy to see why they would not wish to risk their god's displeasure by making bargains with the gods of other peoples, or by benefitting from a foreign god-born's powers, it is less easy for an outsider to comprehend why they would not wish to pursue the powers of a sorcerer or a ley-mage. A sorcerer's abilities, to an outsider, look to be wholly the product of his or her own native will. But to many Judeans, a sorcerer takes the power of god into a mortal's hands; they view this, apparently, as arrant presumption. Ley-magic, which is derived directly from the energies of the cosmos itself, and can be tapped by largely mechanical means? They reject utterly, again on the grounds that it is taking the power of god into mortal hands.

It seems likely that over the centuries, the oligarchy of priests that has traditionally governed this largely theocratic province, may not have wanted outside influences to impinge upon their hold on their peoples' minds. The presence of Roman governors, traders, and citizens has at least introduced republican principles into the governmental mix, and into the Judean mind.

With all this being said, the history and geography and philosophy of the region has resulted in a people who are enormously self-reliant, and who have developed unique technological solutions to problems found nowhere else on earth. While Hellas and Nippon both have exceptional academies for natural philosophy, and even currently work with Judea on a number of joint ventures in natural philosophy, including space exploration, both countries split their attentions between magical and scientific methodologies. Judea does not.

For proof of how effective their scientific innovation can be, look no further than the topic of gunpowder. After Leif Dalgaard first circumnavigated the globe in 1000 AC, it took less than a hundred years to open up trade over the seas with Qin, India, and Nippon, thus limiting the value of the old overland Silk Road caravan route . . . and bringing Qin gunpowder to the West. It was largely dismissed as a novelty item by Western philosophers. The first cannons, cast of bronze, _exploded_ in half along their weld seams, and their impact on the battlefield was entirely secondary to what a team of trained sorcerers could accomplish with a massed group of catapults, ballistae, and mangonels. This was proved to Rome's satisfaction in 1264 AC, when the Mongols, after pressing deep into Raccia and overthrowing much of Qin, turned south and west towards Asia Minor, attempting to move into Roman holdings. Construction on Domitanus' Wall was halted as quick-moving Legion units escorted lightweight catapults through the rugged terrain of Asia Minor, and, while protecting their battle-mages with their lives, rained death down on the light, swift horses of the Mongols. The Mongols couldn't move quickly enough to react to the heightened speed and power of these lightweight siege weapons, and, likewise, couldn't counter the longbows of the squads called up from Britannia, whose fletchings were enchanted by the Legion's cadres of sorcerers. Likewise, on the occasions when a Roman legion was forced to march into Fennmark and Gotaland or other such regions to chastise a petty king there, most commanders felt that digging a tunnel under an enemy's walls and setting a gunpowder charge was an unnecessary risk to the men, and cost far too much in terms of time and manpower. Why do any of that, several tribunes argued, when all one really needed was a handful of well-trained and well-fed sorcerers?

The Mongols' attack blunted, they turned back to the east, and swarmed through the Persian empire's subject kingdoms, and eventually, turned back to the west, attempting to break through Domitanus's Wall in Judea. Judea, which had no well-fed, well-trained battle-sorcerers at its disposal, looked an easy mark, in spite of the presence of Roman legions in the province.

However, the Judeans had been studying the gunpowder that tribunes, far and wide, considered 'too dangerous to use as anything but a novelty.' And in 1275 AC, the product of that research was used, as for the first time in recorded history, iron cannons were employed against an enemy. These weapons could be loaded more quickly than Roman catapults and ballistae, and had significantly reduced chances of exploding, compared to the brazen counterparts tested by the Legion.

By 1380 AC, the Judean army had developed the first 'hand-held' cannon, called a _tevtah_, or, in the parlance of the Romanized Gauls who first saw it in use on the Wall, an '_harquebus_.' These match-cord lit weapons couldn't match the longbow's range . . . but they equaled or exceeded the amount of force that an enchanted arrow could muster.

To this day, the Judean Defense Forces do their utmost to counter the attacks of summoners, sorcerers, and Magi largely with weapons derived solely from gunpowder sources. As of 1925 AC, Judea had produced its first 'assault rifle,' capable of firing around five hundred rounds per minute. While some military commentators consider this a game-changing advance, others are more dubious about their practical utility. They cannot, for example, do any substantive damage to a djinni.

Judean military doctrine generally advises against direct confrontation with djinn and efreet, however. They counsel their soldiers to seek the spirits' summoners, and shoot <u>them</u>. By and large, <u>most</u> summoned creatures will return to their home plane once their summoner has been killed. There are, however, always exceptions to every rule.

Judea is the only country on Earth that has a fully electrical power grid, without any ley-line tapping in use. They briefly burned coal and gas to fuel their power plants, and then disregarded fossil fuels as dirty, limited, and not obtainable except by trade. As such, they moved over to solar and wind power early, and, since the splitting of the atom in 1939 AC, have built the world's first nuclear power plants as well.

Their launch of the first rocket into outer space in 1929 AC also helped to spark a space race between them, Hellas, and Nippon; the result of which is the Joint Lunar Base, which is projected to be built at some time in the 1960s, assuming that funding continues at current levels.

— Vorvena Senebelenae, <u>The History of Natural Philosophy in Judea</u>. University of Divodurum Press, 1953 AC.

Iunius 3, 1954 AC

Adam awoke at close to eleven antemeridian, slamming a hand down on the button of his wind-up alarm clock before his eyes even opened. Groaning, he sat up in bed. They had been up very damned late the night before, but he needed to relieve Trennus in about an hour, just to let the Pictish man get a few hours of sleep. They had a meeting scheduled with Livorus at five postmeridian. He rubbed at his eyes, and decided that there was no faster way to wake up than to force his circulation to get moving. As such, he rolled out of bed, stretched, and dropped into military pushups on the cold tile floor of the hotel bedroom, keeping his elbows tucked to his sides. A hundred of those, in under two minutes. Then he pushed a table out of the way and used the scant carpeted area in the small room for a hundred sit-ups, in the same amount of time. *Not enough time for a run. This will have to do.* He padded into the bathing area, which was largely a standard Roman setup, with a standard toilet and a shower, as well as a deep bath. He dug into his luggage for his tin of shampoo powder, got into the shower, and poured the fine-milled powder into his hand before letting the water dissolve it into bubbles between his palms.

A quick scrub of his long hair and his body, and then he wrapped a towel around his waist, and regarded himself in the room's foggy mirror. Five o'clock shadow tended to appear much earlier than evening for him on the best days, and yesterday had been particularly long. He rubbed thoughtfully at his face, before grimacing. Most of the locals were clean-shaven, so he defaulted to that, lathering his face from a bar of shaving soap and scraping his jaws and cheeks clean before getting dressed. *I wonder if I could convince either Trennus or Kanmi to spar with me after the meeting?* he thought, tapping lightly on the connecting door to Sigrun's half of the suite. Trennus had made a point of saying he actually had to *wrestle* with spirits, and the Britannian was a physically imposing specimen. He might be an interesting challenge. *I'm restless. There's been too little to do on this mission. Or maybe I can convince Ehecatl to test how strong his arm is, now that he's back on the team.* He and the Jaguar warrior had had a good arrangement, previously; he'd traded lessons in *bitahevn,* or the Judean Defense Forces' art of personal self-defense, for Ehecatl's lessons in Nahautl knife-fighting, called *tecuani,* or Jaguar style. The knife-fighting had been developed for using big, jungle-cutting knifes, back in the day, and was still used by Jaguar warriors and Nahautl levy forces to this day.

"I'm up," Sigrun called back through the door, and unlatched it from her side. As the door opened, Adam caught a rush of scents; she'd obviously just showered, herself, and her hair was wet and smelled of apples. "The meeting is at five, yes?" Rapid words in Latin.

"Yes. Breakfast? Actually, make that dinner . . . or whatever." Adam stretched a little. "Maybe *you'd* be willing to spar with me a little, first. Trennus is probably dying for sleep, and Eshmunazar won't thank me for waking him." He chuckled a little. "Of course, you'll drub me."

A startled flicker of her gray eyes; he'd never asked before, though he wasn't entirely sure *why* he hadn't. It wasn't that he was foreign to the concept of female soldiers. Women were required to serve a single year in the JDF, mostly in non-combat roles, though, in the last two decades, it had become possible for women to volunteer for combat specializations. In the Roman Legions, proper, women could volunteer for non-combat positions only, currently. In levy forces from Egypt, Carthage, Nahautl, and other such countries, women were not permitted to serve, while in Gothic and Gallic forces, women provided fully half of their levy forces. And he had, from the outset, always seen Sigrun as . . . something of a weapon. A person, too, yes; he'd joked with her and always made an effort to get to know her, which was difficult, really; she said little about herself. Never spoke about her family or any friends outside of the Praetorian Guard. He had the impression, in fact, that the job was her entire life, at the present.

After a moment, Sigrun smiled a little, and said, lightly, "It is possible that you could drub *me,* Adam. My training is in a different style than yours. It would be interesting to match up with you, yes. Good practice. But perhaps not today? Trennus does need relief soon."

"I know . . . I know. I'm just twitching from lack of activity in the past weeks." Adam nodded at the door to the hallway. "Let's relieve Matrugena and let him get some sleep."

The meeting with Livorus at five postmeridian was conducted over a light supper in the propraetor's room, and was *lively* as they all debriefed. Adam hadn't had as much contact with the locals as the rest of them had the previous night, and his eyebrows went up as Sigrun described Tototl: "He didn't specifically *say* that he was god-born, but he is an aristocrat, and in local society, that usually does mean descent from the god-born, doesn't it, Ehe?" She turned and glanced at the Nahautl man. "Other than those who worked up through the ranks themselves, or who had ancestors who did, by virtue of excelling in the military or priesthood." Sigrun's word-choice, as always, was highly precise, her light accent in Latin giving her words an abrupt cast. "I do not think a mere priest of Tlaloc would have had the ability to control weather, as I believe he did last night."

Ehecatl shook his head. "I give a nod to Tlaloc's altar on the festival days, but the last time I visited one of his temples was when my wife was first pregnant." His voice was subdued. "It's considered polite to give thanks for the first-born. But my wife and I were more comfortable going to Centeotl's temple after that."

"Why's that?" Adam asked, raising his eyebrows.

"Centeotl is the god of maize and fertility. Well, currently, he is." Ehecatl grinned, briefly. "The original tribe that worshipped him called him Chicomecōātl, and said he was a young and beautiful maiden."

". . . I thought Tlaloc was your fertility god," Adam said, after a moment.

"He is. He's one of many. You have to understand that Nahautl did not turn into one country overnight. Quetzalcoatl, the feathered serpent, was worshipped by the Olmecs, who ruled this area before my people. He's worshipped under other names in Quecha, too." Ehecatl shrugged. "But as my people spread out, and conquered other tribes, their gods were added to our gods. All are venerated. Some are just . . . faces of each other. Different names for the same god. Some are greater and lesser powers. It's all perfectly clear if you're raised to understand it. I have the impression that outsiders can't keep track of it, though."

"I follow it perfectly well until I'm told that the world's been destroyed four times already," Sigrun replied, smiling faintly.

"You Goths think that the world is going to end next Tuesday," Ehecatl told her, a grin spreading over his face. "How is it a stretch that we think it's already happened? Matter of fact, isn't one of your gods supposed to be dead right now?"

Sigrun looked up at the ceiling. "I blame this on my ancestors," she said, and everyone in the room chuckled. "Baldur is supposed to be killed by Loki, out of jealousy, yes, only to return to life during the great battle at the end of the world. Yes, he is currently alive and much worshipped. Tyr, on binding Fenrir Vánagandr, the greatest of all wolves, was supposed to have his hand bitten off. Fenrir has been bound twice, but Tyr has two hands, and is called Tyr One-Hand, because of what is said will occur when Fenrir is bound for the third and final time. Fenrir will break free, slay Odin, the sun, and the moon. Loki will begin Ragnarok, the end of all things." She paused. "The problem with much of our ancient legends, is that for my ancestors, time was all one piece. To this day, there is no future tense for verbs in Gothic. So the singers of the ancient sagas may have meant that something *would happen* but the tenses suggested to later listeners that it had already happened." She shrugged slightly. "That explains *my* people's confusing legends, Ehecatl. It does not help anyone to understand yours."

Adam winced a little, inwardly. A language that had no future tense suggested bleak things about the outlook of the ancient Gothic tribes. They believed that the world would end. There was no point in worrying about next week.

The rest of the people in the room chuckled again, and Ehecatl relented. "All right. A children's overview, without the nuances of which god came from which tribe. This is how the official priests tell the tale, for the masses." He cleared his throat. "There are two greater gods, whom almost no one worships directly—the Hellenes don't have any temples for Gaia, you see? Just for Demeter. Same idea. These two are Ometecuhtli and Omecihuatl. Now that I've said the names, forget them." Ehecatl flicked his fingers, as if throwing something away. "They had four sons. Tezcatlipoca, Quetzalcoatl, Huitzilopochtli and Xipe Totec. Each of these four gods is a Tezcatlipoca—yes, I know that it's the same name." Ehecatl leveled a finger at Trennus, who'd just opened his mouth to ask a question, clearly. "Deal with it, you foreign barbarians."

"You have been wanting to call me that for some time, have you?" Livorus said, mildly. "Perhaps you have what we called 'short-timer's disease' in the Legion."

"Oh, I didn't mean you, sir. I meant all these other barbarians." Ehecatl nodded, and Kanmi chuckled under his breath. "Tezcatlipoca himself is the Black Tezcatlipoca." He pointed to one of the intricate jaguar tattoos on his arm. "He's the god of night, magic, judgment, deceit, volcanoes, and jaguars. Most outsiders would consider him an evil god."

"Like Loki. But . . . not." Sigrun frowned, and picked up one of the oranges from the bowl at the center of the table in Livorus' suite. "Judgment *and* deceit."

"How can you possibly judge someone for a crime you've never committed?" Ehecatl asked her.

"I do that *all the time*, Ehe, but I accept that it makes sense to you," she surrendered.

"So he's . . . like Shiva," Adam put in, tentatively. This concept had been a struggle for him, in India. "Hindus don't worship Shiva to ask for evil. They try to . . . placate him, as best I understand it."

"Precisely. I venerate Tezcatlipoca. He's a jaguar, and so am I. We both hunt the night. But I also worship the White Tezcatlipoca, Quetzalcoatl. I was named for his aspect as the west wind. He's the lord of mercy . . . but he's also the Morning Star." Adam felt a little chill go through him at the words. "He's vengeance incarnate, when he's in his aspect of Tlahuizcalpantecuhtli." Ehecatl rolled off the syllables without hesitation. "Mind you, this is where Sigrun here is going to laugh a little."

"Because, as best I recall, he had to die to become Tlahuiz . . ." Sigrun flapped a hand, and amended it to, "the Morning Star."

"Correct." Ehecatl nodded.

"So he's alive and dead at the same time, just like Baldur?" Adam said, slowly.

"Pretty much."

"And this *doesn't* make your heads hurt?" Adam asked them both, shaking his own.

Ehecatl chuckled. "Keep in mind, *sacrifice* was the heart of my culture, if you'll pardon the pun. Sometimes the gods even sacrificed each other."

"They got better, I trust," Kanmi put in, deadpan, leaning back in his leather-covered chair.

"Mostly." Ehecatl raised his eyebrows at the Carthaginian. "You don't have a problem with the concepts so far?"

"No. The worship of Baal-Hamon these days is similar to that of Tammuz. We celebrate him being torn to pieces to bring fertility to the fields once a year." Kanmi shrugged. "He seems to get better, too. Move it along. I still haven't heard the name 'Tlaloc' in any of this."

"Huitzilopochtli is the Blue Tezcatlipoca, and he's the patron god of the city of Tenochtitlan. One of our sun gods, too. Xipe Totec is the Red Tezcatlipoca, the flayed god. Supposed to look like a husked ear of corn. He's another fertility god. The priests used to flay captives in his honor, wear their skins for a few weeks, and would dress the statues of the god in the skins, as well." Ehecatl looked around the room, expressionlessly. "I don't apologize for my ancestors. It's not done these days, and there's an end to it."

"*Tlaloc*," Kanmi said, making a gesture with his fingers, as if reeling in a fish on a line.

"I'm getting there. The first time the four younger gods created the world, every time they'd make something, Cipactli, the giant alligator, would eat it. So Tezcatlipoca lured her with his foot, which he lost in her mouth—yes, like your Tyr, Sigrun—and he and Quetzalcoatl had to destroy her so that they could get back to creating the world."

Trennus held up a finger. "I don't mean to make trouble, but if the four gods were the only things in existence, how did an alligator come along and eat anything?"

Ehecatl put his face down in his hands. "You have no idea how much trouble I got into for asking that exact question at a festival for Tezcatlipoca when I was a boy," he said, through his fingers. "I don't know. The priests usually splutter and say she willed herself into existence, or that the four Tezcatlipocas had already made the other gods before they tried to make the earth."

"So why'd they make her, if she was such a troublemaker?" Kanmi put in, his grin edged.

"*Anyway*," Ehecatl went on, blatantly ignoring the Carthaginian, "with her out of the way, they made the world, they made giants, they made animals, but nothing could live without the sun, so Black Tezcatlipoca was chosen to be the first sun . . . except he was the god of night, and was missing half a leg! He was a very poor sun, so Quetzalcoatl knocked him out of the sky, the sky went dark, and Tezcatlipoca ordered his jaguars to eat all the people that they'd created together. And that was the first time the world ended." Ehecatl wagged a finger at Kanmi, who was evidently doing his best not to laugh. "You weren't much good at temple when you were a child, were you?"

"I didn't go," Kanmi replied, promptly. "My family was too poor. Temples eat money, ever noticed that? Also, how many times do I have to ask about Tlaloc here? I might need to start keeping a tally." The Carthaginian's eyes glittered.

"I'm getting to him. Quetzalcoatl was the next sun-god, but he was too merciful, and his new, normal-sized humans became arrogant, and stopped paying attention to the gods. Tezcatlipoca decided to remind them of his power, and turned all the humans into monkeys. Quetzalcoatl had loved these flawed humans. He didn't mind their arrogance. But seeing them turned into animals enraged him, and he destroyed the world with terrible storms. They remade the world, and yes, Tlaloc was the next sun." Ehecatl gave Kanmi an amused glance. "He's the rain god, He Who Makes Things Sprout. But while he was away being the sun, Black Tezcatlipoca stole Tlaloc's wife, the goddess of sex and flowers."

"Not bad for a one-legged fellow," Kanmi allowed. "I assume that he must have started off life as more of a tripod." It was said dead-pan, and with no emphasis on the words.

Adam had been watching Sigrun's face during this portion of the conversation, and the fact that she choked on her tea made him laugh so hard, he almost inhaled his own thick cup of Tawantinsuyan coffee. Trennus put his face down in his hands, his shoulders shaking, and Livorus shook his head in resignation.

"Undoubtedly," Ehecatl told the Carthaginian, nodding regally, but his lips quirked a bit. "At any rate, Tlaloc was angry, and refused to send rain. A drought swept the world, and the humans begged him for rain. He found their voices irritating, so he *did* send rain . . . except it was a rain of fire, and the new earth perished. His new wife, Chalchiuhtlicue, became the next sun. She was a water goddess, and benevolent, but Tezcatlipoca was jealous of how loved she was by the people, and told her that his *judgment* was that she was not really kind, but pretended to be, so that people would love her. She wept blood for fifty-two years, and the people were all drowned. Quetzalcoatl was particularly annoyed by all this, and crept to the underworld, where he found the bones of all the humans. He used his own blood, and brought them back to life, on this, the fifth world, where Huitzilopochtli is the sun now. And because Quetzalcoatl gave of himself to give us life, we're supposed to give back to the gods. That's the origin of the sacrifices, in a nutshell." Ehecatl shrugged. "You may now forget absolutely everything else I've just said."

"To summarize," Kanmi said, baring his teeth, "Don't get on Tezcatlipoca's bad side."

"Pretty much," Ehecatl agreed.

"The refresher on the background information is helpful," Livorus said, putting his fingers together, "particularly for those of us who aren't entirely familiar with your culture. But where does this get us in terms of last night's encounter with the high priest of Tlaloc?"

Ehecatl looked into the mid-distance. "As I said, I'm not much of an authority on the priesthood. But I doubt they'd let someone become high-priest who'd just . . . done a good job when he was a young man. You can rise somewhat, but going from altar attendant to high-priest . . . it's not done, sir. I can ask around, but I'd assume he's very likely god-born."

Sigrun grimaced. "I think so, yes." she agreed. "I was under directive not to reveal myself or make a challenge, but he may have been able to tell . . . in much the same way I had hints, myself." She sent an apologetic glance towards Livorus, who dismissed it with a flick of his fingertips. "It's probably nothing, but the governor's wife mentioned that he's a cultural conservative. This . . . probably unfairly makes me think of Kuruk, the god-born of the Morning Star up by Ponca." She shrugged. "I'll put it out of my mind."

Livorus nodded, clearly filing it all away for the moment. "What else did we encounter last night?" he asked the others.

Trennus shrugged, and recounted several tales of civil unrest, and the locals in Tenochtitlan's deep-seated dislike of the Tikali rebels. "There seems to be deep-seated bitterness," he concluded.

"That is something of an understatement," Ehecatl muttered. "The state-run media don't give the rebels any air-time—it's a deliberate policy, so as not to reward them by passing on their message—but I haven't seen this much anger in my own people in a long time. Something *is* going on down in the jungles."

"There's been a fair bit of blood spilled," Trennus volunteered, to Ehecatl's evident surprise. "Several fatalities, just among the families of last night's people at the ball game."

"They just offered you this information?" Ehecatl said, his eyebrows rising slightly.

"Well, no. I don't think they knew I could understand them." Trennus looked away.

Adam raised a finger. "Ah . . . actually, *I* didn't know you could, either. Your dossier doesn't say you speak Nahautl."

"I don't." Trennus grimaced. "One of my spirits decided to be helpful."

Adam's eyes narrowed, mostly out of reflex. "So we're more or less taking your spirit's word for this?"

"I don't think she'd invent all of this," Trennus replied, a little sharply. "Spirits don't tend to have complex imaginations. That's something they tend to pick up from humans. That, and more complex motivations. They tend to be a little elemental until they've absorbed a lot of human traits." He shrugged. "No offense," he added to what looked like empty air, "but most spirits are actually fairly *uninterested* in humans until summoned and either are forced to do something they don't want to do, or asked to do things that actually interest them, and are rewarded for it." Trennus paused. "Which is going to get me going down a side-path to this conversation that we can't afford right now. Don't mind me."

"You and I can talk about metacognition and the development of human psychology in inhuman subjects later," Kanmi told his fellow mage.

Adam did his best not to twitch. Kanmi didn't appear to intend to be arrogant or condescending; he just assumed, for the most part probably correctly, that such topics wouldn't interest most normal people. And, in truth, Adam *wasn't* all that interested . . . except that anything more he knew about spirits might give him new insights in fighting them. But he couldn't help but feel vaguely insulted that Kanmi didn't think he and Sigrun were intelligent enough to follow along in the conversation. *Something to talk to him about later. Non-confrontationally. He probably doesn't even realize he's isolating Trennus and himself, by his very wording.*

"A little out of scope for this meeting," Livorus agreed, dryly. "Kanmi? What about you?"

The sorcerer from Tyre grimaced and stared out the window of Livorus' suite, peeling an orange with his bare fingers. "Well?" Sigrun prompted, after a moment.

"I had a very odd encounter with a former classmate from the University of Athens. Gifted technomancer. Half-Roman, half-Nahautl, born into a semi-aristocratic family here in Tenochtitlan." Kanmi threw his peels towards the room's garbage pail . . . lightly redirecting them with a gesture in the air when they looked apt to miss. "I never really knew the fellow well, but he was . . . very interested in speaking with me further. The more so when I noted I was a member of the Praetorian Guards."

He recounted the whole conversation, and Adam shook his head. "That sounds like a recruitment effort," Adam offered, after a moment. Kanmi *did* sound like a good candidate for, well, espionage. He didn't talk about his wife often, but he'd mentioned, at least once in Adam's hearing, that she didn't like the long separations that the job brought, though he'd just moved her and the children from Tyre to Rome. She also didn't, apparently, much like Rome. And Kanmi's overall slightly cynical demeanor, and distaste for aristocracy, even for god-born . . . yes, Adam could see why someone would see him as a potential recruit.

"Recruitment into what, is the question?" the older man asked, sounding tired. "I've been to all the usual counter-intelligence briefings. I recognize what it *could* be, but Xicohtencatl wasn't exactly a revolutionary at the university. He was . . . earnest, I suppose. And maybe a little bored, with more money at his disposal than was good for him." Kanmi shrugged. "What could he *possibly* be into?"

"Not sure," Sigrun replied, interlacing her fingers and propping her chin on them, her gray eyes intent. "Could be something as simple as an invitation to join a technical and job-support *collegium*. *Collegia* aren't just about being from a given neighborhood in Rome anymore, or just social clubs." She shrugged. "A lot of people use them for networking, as I understand it."

Kanmi made a face. "It didn't quite feel like that," he admitted.

"Allow yourself to be invited in," Livorus said, his tone austere. "Investigate. If it turns out to be nothing, all we've wasted is a little of your time. If not . . . then you might have stumbled onto something interesting." The propraetor leaned back in his chair, pushing away the remains of his own meal, some sort of roasted quail dish. "Now, for the results of my own conversations last night, both the governor and the emperor have suggested to me, that if any of the rumors we've heard of human sacrifice are true, they're likely to be the result of people who are looking to return to the old ways. And that no one in a major metropolitan center like Tenochtitlan would want to do that. Not where there's abundant ley-power, there's art, culture, poetry, and all the advantages that the mix of Roman, Gallic, Gothic, and Nahautl cultures bring." Livorus sighed. "I did remind them that while familiarity with what's foreign usually *does* make people more open-minded . . . it's just as possible that people who want power for themselves can respond to entrenched power in other's hands, by attacking their origins. And nevermind the advantages and changes that have come with it."

Adam looked to the side. There were groups of zealots in Judea who lived apart from the rest of society, who refused to pay Roman taxes or send their young men to serve on the Wall to become part of the troop levy sent into the foreign legions each year. They didn't send their children to Roman schools, refused to speak Latin, and other such signs of protest. They were tolerated by the communities around them. Mostly because the only alternative was storming their armed compounds and trying to *force* them to re-integrate with the rest of Judean society. Some of them were so retrograde as to not allow women to walk freely, without escorts, in public, as if they were all still members of some tribe of herdsmen in the fifth century BAC. *What would happen,* he wondered, *if their ideas began to become more pervasive in Judean society? If they became the symbol of resistance to Rome? Would that be . . . more or less the same thing as what Livorus sees here?* He didn't like the mental image at all.

Livorus looked around the table. "We don't have much in the way of a starting point, even after three weeks. That said, I've been asked, officially, by Governor Dioscuri, to 'look into' opening dialogue with the rebels near Tikal."

Groans rose from all five lictors' throats. Livorus gave them a spare glance. "Now, now, what's not to like about this? It's only an area of heavy jungle in which armed guerrillas have held the countryside for a decade, periodically harassing the garrisons and the townspeople who don't sympathize with their goal. It's only a region where the guerrillas speak Quechan instead of Nahautl, and almost none of them speak Latin. There's little in the way of a ley-grid down there—Eshmunazar, you'll want to talk with your . . . new friend . . . about where, precisely, the state power company is putting in ley-tapping stations . . . ."

"On it," Kanmi replied, opening a notebook and scribbling something down with a fountain pen.

"Good. You and Matrugena will be looking into that. Several of the ley-stations were attacked in years past. At the moment, the rebels seem to be leaving the newer platforms alone. In examining the stations . . . you might be able to talk with the people building them and guarding them. Find out why the rebels' tactics have changed." Livorus pushed his glasses up his nose, and studied his own notebook, which lay beside his plate. "Sigrun, my dear, you're a natural to go find and talk with the local priests. They're the lifeblood of these small villages. Their temples provide food and clothing for the indigent, and they are where almost every resident, even the rebels, will come, eventually. The village priests see a great deal."

"They are hardly likely to speak to me freely, propraetor. I am not one of *their* god-born." Sigrun objected, looking uncomfortable. "And I do not wish to try to intimidate or bully the locals."

"Which is why our good Itztli will be going with you. Do your very best not to look like a valkyrie, my dear. My advice would be to try to look like you are Itztli's new wife, and wish to understand his culture better—"

It was rare for any of the lictors to interrupt the propraetor, but in this case, Adam's objections were beaten out by Ehecatl's laughter. It fought its way free of the man's throat, and rang back off the walls. Sigrun gave him a resigned look, finally asking, after a few moments, "When you're quite done?"

Ehecatl managed to slow himself to a mere chuckle. "My wife, Coszcatl, would not be delighted with this plan. There is also the small matter of credibility, *dominus*." He grinned. "While I do not deny that Caetia would be a *catch*, she's four inches taller than I am. Who is going to believe that she's my wife?"

"I'm your height," Kanmi said, dryly. "My wife's Caetia's height."

"And do people have difficulty believing that you're married?" Trennus asked, not, apparently, above needling Kanmi.

"Her colleagues think I'm a figment of her imagination." Eshmunazar's tone became even more arid. The man never spoke of his family at all. *Then again*, Adam thought, *none of us do. This is the first time since I've met Ehecatl that he's even mentioned his wife's name.*

"It's not just the height," Ehecatl put in, his grin fading. "It's the fact that I can't picture Caetia here married to *anyone.*"

"Thank you," Sigrun said, tiredly. "I appreciate this compliment."

"We could send her with Matrugena instead. They actually look like a pair. And there's Matrugena's obvious infatuation with her, to make it look the more realistic." Kanmi's retaliation on Trennus was wickedly fast.

Adam held up two fingers. Though Ehecatl had been senior on the detail before he'd come along, Livorus had made it clear that Adam and Sigrun were still in charge of the lictors for the moment. "If I could get a word in edgewise? Esh and Matru, you first met Sig in that *taverna* in Rome, and didn't think twice about who she was, at first." *Any more than I did.* "So long as she doesn't start *glowing* on us, I think she can pass as a . . ." he hesitated over the wording.

"Perfectly normal human being," Sigrun said, looking at the ceiling.

"I wasn't going to put it quite that way."

"And thank *you* for that vote of confidence, Adam. Ehe, I will be sure to hang on your every word as dotingly as I am capable of doing."

Even Livorus smiled faintly at that one. Ehecatl shook his head. "Gods. Ptah should have been here for this. He's going to need pictures the next time I see him, for him to believe this." Ehecatl had known Sigrun long enough to know *precisely* how to tease her.

Adam glanced back at Livorus now. "With four of us off investigating, that's going to make protecting you problematic at best. I'll call the local Praetorian office and get us a little more manpower." At Livorus' expression, he added, "Sir, there *are* guerillas in that region, and you would make a most excellent hostage to trade to Rome for political considerations, or the release of captives in Nahautl prisons."

Livorus sighed. "My reluctance stems from the fact that the local Praetorians are, in fact, largely that: local. I detest having to suggest that anyone's loyalty might be compromised, without proof, and before having even met them, but the possibility exists."

"I'll keep an eye on them," Ehecatl promised.

"And I'll have one of my spirits keep watch, as well," Trennus volunteered. "A normal human won't even notice that she's there."

Kanmi slid a glance Adam's way, as he shifted uneasily in his chair. "I think some of us might be more concerned about the spirit's trustworthiness, than the local Praetorians'."

"I can't deny that it would be useful. I'm concerned about the cost, however," Adam managed, as neutrally as he could. "Matrugena's always been very upfront about every interaction with a spirit having a price."

Kanmi bared his teeth. "Oh, come now, Matrugena seems to be in good health. A little awkward with women, but still interested in them. I don't think this female spirit of his would make you into a *galli*."

Galli were followers of the goddess Cybele, also called *corybants*. The Great Mother, as she was known, had only been incorporated into the worship practices of Rome during the Second Punic War, mostly because a line in the Sibylline Oracles that had been interpreted as indicating that Rome could not win the war without her support. The goddess was eastern in origin, much in the way that Dionysus was not originally a Hellene god, and her rites and propitiations were very much against the grain of standard Roman faith. Orgiastic and hedonistic, as opposed to stoic and restrained . . . and the goddess had had a mortal lover, a shepherd known as Attis. In his exaltation at seeing his lover revealed as a goddess, he had, legend said, castrated himself and flung away his genitalia. He was worshipped in his own right as a minor vegetation god. *Galli* were men who, traditionally, while in a state of religious ecstasy, castrated themselves with special tools. They then dressed as women from that moment on . . . assuming they survived the process, which had been something of a question, in the old, pre-antibiotics days . . . and served in the temples of Cybele as priests and dancers.

Rome had moved very quickly to regulate the cult of Cybele, and had passed laws that forbade any Roman citizen from becoming a eunuch in her service. *Well, Rome does feel rather strongly about the phallus. Come to think of it, I'm fond of my own.*

Adam and Trennus both, therefore, gave Kanmi a dark look for that one. "Now that," Trennus said, "is not a bargain I can imagine making."

Adam looked up as Livorus said, his voice dry, "Well, not that it affects any of us here in this room, but at least these days, the procedure is medically-overseen, and doesn't involve any of them slipping on their own blood on the temple floors. It really should have fallen under the same heading as 'human sacrifice,' but Diocletian II didn't wish to go against the Sibylline Oracles, for fear of what might befall the Empire." He shrugged. "And it gives an outlet and a recognized place in society for those who might not have felt male to begin with."

Adam grimaced, and Trennus again shook his head. "I don't ever want to be in a position where I think that kind of sacrifice is the only way to win," the Pict noted. "But again, we're . . . wandering, I think?" He raised his hands, "I'll ask my forest spirit to do it. She'll enjoy seeing the jungles, anyway."

Livorus nodded, and looked around at all of them. "I realize, it's not even a needle in a haystack. All of the human sacrifice rumors have been coming from the *central* reaches of Nahautl, not from the southern regions. At the moment, our actual overt mission is to open a dialogue with the rebels, and see if we can get them to reconcile with the government of this kingdom. While we're there, we might well be able to find information towards our *real* goal. It's not perfect, but these things rarely are." He sighed. "At least I need not worry about the five of you nearly as much as the men I commanded during the Mongol-Qin Provocation."

Adam's head came up. That had been in 1949, and he hadn't known Livorus had been involved in it. He shot Sigrun a look, and she shook her head, slightly, before murmuring, just loudly enough for him to hear, "Just before I joined his detail. I'll tell you later."

Livorus stood, brushing off his hands. "Get everything you need together, and finish any final business you have here in Tenochtitlan. Speaking of which, I'll need four of you with me tonight. No, not you, Sigrun, my dear." He waved her from the room.

Adam looked at the others, at a loss, as Sigrun, a slightly puzzled expression on her face, left the room. This wasn't status quo behavior from the propraetor. "Sir? We're not bringing Caetia with us where we're going?"

"Gods, no. I cannot think of anything more likely to bring about disaster, in fact." Livorus shook his head, putting his hands behind him, loosely clasped at the small of his back. "As is, I'll be visiting one of the local licensed brothels this evening," Livorus told them all, not changing expression. After a moment, he added, "It's not that I think my senior lictor would necessarily disapprove, you understand. It's the fact that the other patrons of this fine establishment might make the very serious mistake of thinking her *for hire*." He paused, one eyebrow arching. "Imagine it, if you will."

Adam had to close his eyes for a moment. Kanmi guffawed, Trennus flushed, and Ehecatl turned his face away, chuckling slightly.

Adam could, all too clearly, picture some drunk trying to paw Sigrun or trying to draw her into a room . . . which would surely end in bloodshed. Possibly a defenestration. Certainly, paperwork and *attention* being paid.

"There's no man in the universe brave enough," Kanmi muttered, shaking his head as Adam opened his eyes again, and they all headed for the door, getting the propraetor to his car, and Adam obtaining directions, grim-faced, from the doorman at the hotel to a place called the Jade Fan. Ehecatl whistled under his breath at the name. Beyond that, the other lictors didn't react, and neither did Adam. It wasn't as if the ambassador he'd guarded in India hadn't visited the *nagarvadhu*, or bride of the city, on a few occasions, and for more than the pleasure of her conversation and musical talents.

He was fortunate, that in driving, he could concentrate on the roads. Traffic. Making sure that they weren't being followed. The other three, while keeping an eye on the vehicles and pedestrians around them, were, however, free to respond to Livorus.

Trennus, for example, rather hesitantly asked, "Why this particular establishment, sir?"

Livorus looked up from his newspaper in the backseat, and glanced at Trennus. "Is this car clean of listening devices?"

"I checked at noon," Adam replied. "It's been out of our hands for about seven hours at this point, however."

Kanmi reached out, put his hand on the metal crossbar of the window beside him, and Adam felt a tingle of raw electricity through his own hands, and had to fight the urge to let go of the wheel. "Warn me next time," he told Kanmi.

"Next time, you'll know," Kanmi assured him, calmly. "Car should be clear of bugs now."

Livorus pushed his glasses back up his nose, and looked at Trennus. "In answer to your question? Centehua Izel is one of the top attractions at the Jade Fan. A courtesan of renown hears a certain amount of information from her clients, and she *is* on the payroll of the Praetorian Intelligence Office." He raised his eyebrows at them all. "However, when dealing with someone in her position—"

Adam could have sworn he heard Kanmi mutter, " . . . or positions . . ." very quietly, but when he glanced at the older man in the rearview mirror, the Carthaginian hadn't changed expression.

" . . . one must go to her, rather than compromise her." Livorus looked at Kanmi. "Was there something?"

"Not at all, *dominus*," Kanmi said. Adam had learned, rapidly, that Kanmi *only* used honorifics and titles when attempting to deflect attention.

Livorus' eyebrows went up, but Kanmi met his eagle-like stare steadily. "Glad to hear it, Eshmunazar. Else I would have to deny your expense reports when or if you claim entertainment costs this evening."

Kanmi's lips twitched. In the dark of the car, it wasn't possible to see if Trennus flushed, but his voice was a little strangled as he asked, "Ah . . . what, m'lord?"

"It's often covered under meals and incidentals," Livorus replied, calmly. "But you'll have to itemize. The government only covers up to about a half solidus; anything past that, or if the establishment doesn't charge standard rates for services, you'll have to cover on your own."

"A half-solidus?" Kanmi replied, sounding startled. "Surprisingly generous of the personnel department." Two solidi a month might cover the rent for a one-room apartment in a large city. "Of course, depending on how *upscale* the place is, that might only cover a blowjob."

"You might be able to bargain the lady in question down, if you make it worth her while." Livorus' tone was detached. Austere, even. "I can't say that I've ever had a problem with getting a discount." His paper rustled as he folded it up to stow it. "On the left, ben Maor."

"I see it, *dominus.*" Adam spotted the dark green fluorescent sign he'd been looking for, and guided their vehicle in to where the valet attendant awaited them. He was the first out of the car, and moved around to the rear, opening the rear passenger door, allowing him to cover Trennus' exit with his own body, and then Livorus'.

As the door opened, and Trennus emerged, the summoner asked, in a baffled tone of voice, "But . . . forgive me, sir . . . aren't you *married?*"

Livorus, emerging next, actually paused and stared up at his towering Britannian lictor. And sighed. "My dear young man, what has my being married to do with anything?"

Trennus looked back down at the propraetor. "Ah . . . everything, I would have thought . . . sir."

"Ah. We have a romantic amongst us." Livorus began to walk down the cobbled sidewalk, his lictors now all flanking him. "You do realize that the entire lineage of the Imperators of Rome is based on Caesarion the God-Born being the legitimized bastard of Gaius Julius Caesar, yes?" Livorus paused. "Aside from which, it is my considered opinion that in everything in life, there is a balance, and one should strive for moderation. That means, in effect, exercising well, but not overly. Eating well, but not overmuch. Drinking wine, but not to a stupor. And having carnal relations, when the lack thereof might prove a distraction, but not falling into uxoriousness, either." He waited for Trennus to close the vehicle door behind him, and headed for the front door of the establishment, Adam in the lead, and Kanmi bringing up the rear. Still, he could hear every quietly-spoken word. "You, for example, Matrugena, are a prime example of a man whose lack in the area of carnal satisfaction might become a distraction to him. You're easily swayed by a pretty face. A young woman could ask you to do *anything*, and you'd be apt to agree, merely because it means you might get a smile, the touch of a hand, perhaps a kiss out of it. A moment or two's respite from loneliness. This lack is readily remedied at such an establishment as this, and would clear your mind."

Adam gave Matrugena full credit for not snapping back at this assessment. Rather, the Pictish man said, slowly, "And your lady wife does not disagree with this opinion?"

"Why should my wife object to my visiting a brothel while I'm abroad?" Livorus asked, stepping through the door that Adam held open for him. "They are licensed, clean, salubrious places. Better that I should go there, than to the bed of one of her friends, or, the gods forefend, dally with some random woman with a squalling brat in the other room, and lice and vermin upon her person. If I spread my lust with one of her friends, or, worse yet, became attached to one of them, *then* I would cause my wife pain. If I brought disease or vermin into our bedchamber, I would cause her shame. Best for everyone if I make use of the services of a healthy, willing woman, whose name I don't know, and wouldn't remember tomorrow even if I did know it." Livorus turned, and discreetly passed Adam a small silk bag that clinked as the Judean took it. "You will be needing this once we're inside."

Adam slipped the bag into his sleeve, for the moment. He wasn't sure how much of Livorus' attitude was a put-on for any listeners, and how much was his real opinion on the matter. They were definitely here for information, but he didn't doubt that Livorus would be getting his money's worth in other ways.

Outside, there were quite a few people roaming around at night in this area of town. Mostly locals, but a few tourists, it seemed. All well-dressed, they tried to crowd past the lictors, and found them an impenetrable wall of flesh. Inside, the state-licensed bordello was a fairly typical example of a high-end establishment of its kind. It had plushly upholstered furniture, lush jungle greenery in stoneware planters, rounded pillars that stretched up to the high, vaulted ceiling of the lobby . . . and a large sign, written in Nahautl and Latin, with stick figures illustrating most of the options available. With prices beside them. For anyone who happened to be curious about the *particulars* of any given service, there were far-viewers on consoles, tucked in and around the greenery; the orb-shaped devices were the ley-powered variety, which meant that they had fully three-dimensional images, if ones in black and white, and the various heaving, gasping figures depicted therein gave clear demonstrations of the various activities available. There were also various women standing in alcoves in the walls, raised just above the level of the floor. Each was either nude or just barely clad, and they stood in a variety of poses, slowly shifting, or outright dancing in place, to the sound of light music filtering in from a hidden speaker.

Adam took one look at the room, and thought, *God. Where am I supposed to put my eyes? How am I supposed to protect the propraetor if I'm trying not to look at anything, but everything's screaming for attention, all at once?* He took a deep breath, and looked around, trying to treat it like a Hindu temple, instead of what it was: a place of commerce.

It . . . didn't really help. But he did his best to keep his mind on the job at hand.

Behind him, Livorus said, lightly, "Are you quite sure, Matrugena? I'm sure we can arrange for you to be . . . what is that lovely phrase? Ah, yes. *Comped.*"

"That is really quite generous of you, propraetor," Trennus told the other, his voice still strangled. "I'll get by on my own, however."

"Then do not blame me if you develop some sort of nasty

condition, brought on by an imbalance of the humors."

"Sir? You're putting me on. *No one* believes in the balance of the humors anymore."

"You really should take advantage of the offer," Kanmi put in, needling Trennus. "Both you and ben Maor have the worst cases of inner tension, caused by obvious blue balls, that I've ever seen."

Adam looked over his shoulder. "How in god's name," he asked, "did *I* get into this conversation?" *I've been keeping my mouth <u>shut</u>.* "If I wanted a matchmaker, I'd tell my family to go ahead and set something up for me."

Kanmi widened his dark eyes. "Who said anything about a wife? I'm talking about *relaxing* for an hour or so."

"That's quite all right," Trennus said, quickly.

Adam, for his part, just looked at Kanmi. *What is this, another way of marking status? Trying to come over worldly-wise and older than the rest of us? Or is this just your . . . bent sense of humor, Eshmunazar?* "I don't see you or Ehecatl jumping at the offer," he said, after a moment.

Ehecatl spread his hands. "Leave me out of this. I have a wife and three children, and I am *not* a Roman."

Kanmi looked up at the menu of services above the front counter, and at the bored young Nahautl woman, scantily clad, underneath it, waiting to take their order, as if at a diner. "It's a very nice selection. And don't get me wrong . . . it's *tempting.*" He shook his head after a moment. "However, my wife is both Nubian and a physician. She'd turn me into a *galli* surgically, and then I'd *have* to go worship Cybele, because Astarte would no longer have any use for me." He nodded to himself, then grinned at the others, challengingly. "However, the two of you have no such impediments. You're bachelors! You should be living the lives of such! And here, the girls are clean. No diseases. No vermin in their hair, and their breath is probably even sweet." Every word was a needle of some sort.

"I'll pass," Adam replied. "Never needed to pay before. Not starting now." Admittedly, his experience wasn't extensive, but there'd been a couple of women while he was in the JDF, and a few more, since being transferred to Novo Gaul. Enough to know he wasn't exactly desperate for options. The Hindu temple *devadasi* had been interesting to watch, but he hadn't been interested in participating in the rites of an alien goddess.

Livorus smiled faintly, and gestured to Adam. "If you wouldn't mind . . . ?"

Oh, so now I'm a pander as well as a bodyguard. Adam sighed, and moved to the desk, where the bored young attendant suddenly flashed him a much more attentive smile. "Centehua Izel, please."

"Her price for an evening is two aurei."

Adam did his best not to choke. A gold aureus was worth ten golden solidi. A solidus was worth ten silver denarii. A denarius was worth ten bronze assarii. As a lictor, one of the highest-paid soldiers in the Roman Imperium, Adam made four golden aurei a month—enough to rent an nice apartment in a good district of Rome, feed himself, and possibly, if he saved, to buy a house somewhere else, as well . . . but the asking price for this unseen prostitute could pay seven families' rent for a month, if they weren't worried about being a little crowded. Money meant something in Rome; the economy had never deviated from the gold standard. Dropping half a month's pre-tax salary on an evening with a woman seemed . . . moderately ridiculous to him, but he'd seen his ambassadorial charge spend at least the same amount on the 'bride of the city' in India. And without, as far as he'd been able to tell, the prospect of gaining information.

"That's not on the sign . . ." he managed.

"Sweetheart, if you have to ask, you can't *afford* her."

Good thing Livorus handed me the coin before we came in. It's beneath his dignity to handle the pecuniary transactions himself, but I'd be damned if I wrote a draft on my personal bank for this. Adam counted out the coins, and, on looking at the small fortune in gold in his hands, shuddered inwardly. There were at least sixteen fat golden aurei in the purse, and twice as many solidi. That was enough to purchase a rather sumptuous motorcar. *I suppose this means I have the propraetor's trust!*

Centehua Izel herself emerged to greet the propraetor, once enough money to feed a family in modest means for a month had traded hands. She was slim, dark, and lovely, with a single tattoo twining around one ankle, and dressed in a Roman-style draped dress of translucent silk — that, imported from Qin, surely. Her dark eyes had smoldered with interest and intrigue . . . either she was a *phenomenal* actress, or she was genuinely interested in the propraetor . . . and she escorted Livorus to her room, which his lictors had to examine before they could allow him to stay with her, alone. *"Do try to cry out if she decides to knife you,"* Adam told the propraetor, in Hellene.

"I would never do such an unmannerly thing," the courtesan assured him, also in Hellene, which while accented, was still perfectly grammatical. She'd been *educated*, and well, it seemed.

"I'll be able to ensure that nothing untoward occurs," Kanmi told Adam in Latin, his voice completely neutral.

"You're not going to be looking in through the balcony window, are you?" Trennus asked quietly in the corridor, his eyes widening.

"Looking . . . no. I can use a sort of gravitic pulse that functions in much the same way as radar. I get a very clear sense of where everyone inside of about a hundred yards is. Humans tend to be softer than their environment." Kanmi went through the door, first, and checked it, before heading to the tall glass doors that led to the balcony, where he'd be standing watch in the night.

And so, for the next hour or two, Adam stood in a tile-lined hallway outside of a room, the other side of the door guarded by Trennus, with Kanmi outside the balcony window, while Ehecatl went invisible and patrolled the grounds. And Livorus . . . negotiated . . . with Centehua Izel.

Adam watched, expressionlessly, as various other women took men . . . and other women. . . to their various rooms, turning the signs on the outside to read 'occupied,' and then, after an allotted amount of time passed, escorted them back out again. *At least they don't clock in and clock out,* he decided, distantly, and just watched the faces. Memorized them, mostly out of habit. And did his level best to ignore the noises from past the door he guarded. *My job could be worse. It could be a lot worse, in fact.*

When Livorus emerged, his expression and body language were absolutely no different than when he'd passed into the room. Adam, blank-faced, gestured for his charge to follow him, and led the way out, Kanmi and Ehecatl once more bringing up the rear. Back in the car, Kanmi once more electrified the vehicle, shorting out any listening devices — or plain *melting* them — and Adam asked, neutrally, "Did you obtain any information, sir?"

"The name of the rebel leader. Information on him, his interests, and methods of getting in touch with him down in the Tikal region. A good expenditure of time, I think. Chan Imix K'awiil . . . which translates to, apparently, 'Smoke Jaguar.'" Livorus picked up his newspaper, and asked Ehecatl, "Know anything about him?"

"It's a Quechan name. The same as one of their early rulers. Either he wants to ally himself with that ancient king in the popular imagination, or his parents had pretentions to grandeur. Or, he actually could be noble-born." Ehecatl's voice was detached.

Livorus nodded, and began to read, while Kanmi shook his head and looked out at the dark city. Trennus rubbed at the amulets around his neck. And Adam just drove. Trying not to think at *all.*

As they arrived back at the hotel, however, and as Livorus headed up the stairs, under Trennus and Ehecatl's watchful eyes, Adam turned back to the bar to get a drink . . . and Kanmi joined him, at least for a while. The Carthaginian was surprisingly fastidious, asking for an earthen bowl with water, and a glass of arak . . . and then put a fingertip just above the surface of the water and murmured under his breath for a moment. The water *seethed*, suddenly boiling, and steam rose from it. Adam paused, his own glass touching his lips, but not drinking, and continued to watch as Kanmi murmured again, and this time, the water stilled. The steam vanished. And, after a moment, a thin skin of ice formed atop it. The sorcerer tapped on the ice with his fingers till it broke, then added the water to his *arak*, which turned milky-white, immediately.

"Don't trust the water, eh?" Adam said, after a moment.

"No. Do you?"

"I'm drinking wine for a reason."

After sitting, staring into the milky glass for a while, Kanmi finally said, dryly, "Two gold aurei for two hours? Enough money to pay my rent in Rome and feed my family all month without having to touch my wife's salary from the hospital. " He shook his head. "Her pussy must be an independent life form, capable of sitting up and performing tricks."

Adam inhaled at an inopportune moment, and choked on a sip of boiled wine. "That is . . . not really a mental image that I wanted, Eshmunazar."

"But it *is* the one that occurred to me, and now I give it to you.

Free of charge. And I wish you well of it, until you can pass it along to some other poor, unsuspecting person." Kanmi swigged back his drink. "Going to be a gods-be-damned long drive tomorrow. Into the next day, even." He shrugged, and began to stand. "Get some sleep—"

Adam held up a hand. "Before you go? Wanted to talk to you."

Kanmi looked surprised, and sat back down again. "What's on your mind?"

"Team-building, really."

"I thought we did that back in Rome."

"No, we addressed team tactics. There's a difference. We're not really used to working as a proper team yet, and that's partially my fault. I'm not used to working with this much raw magic." Adam smiled, faintly, trying to show he wasn't trying to antagonize Kanmi. "That being said, we're in danger of isolating ourselves from each other."

"Part of that's the hours. We're each pulling a six-hour shift as the official 'on-duty' lictor with one other person awake at the same time—the person who just got *off* shift." Kanmi beckoned the bartender over for another drink. Adam was surprised and pleased that the Carthaginian wasn't fighting him on the issue, or acting insulted. "Having Itztli aboard will help with that, a little. And the additional Praetorians, even if we do wind up having to keep an eye on them, too."

"That's true, but I want to mix up the rotation. And now that we'll have some additional help, we can at least have people off-rotation at the same time, and do more than just fall on our faces and sleep. Maybe we can get some sparring practice in, together. Cards. Anything that works, really." Adam shrugged.

Kanmi gave him a cynical look, and laughed. "You don't think a few card games is going to make us all swear eternal brotherhood, do you?"

Adam snorted. "No. But it's something to do together that we all can manage."

"Could try drinking games when we're all actually off-duty at the same time. No, wait. Caetia probably can't physically get drunk, and Matrugena and I are very high on the list of people who never, ever should lose control of our inhibitions. What does that leave . . . ? Oh, I know. *Floral arrangement.* That'll do nicely." Kanmi's tone was caustic. "Or maybe ceramics. We can all sit around using potter's wheels and create lumpy coffee mugs and call them *art.*"

Adam found himself chuckling. "When you come up with something more useful, let me know. Till then, good night, Eshmunazar." Adam was fairly pleased with how that had gone. He'd managed to suggest to Kanmi that he shouldn't isolate himself, without directly telling Kanmi that he'd been tending to isolate himself and Trennus, and had regained control over the conversation, when Kanmi had been about to dismiss him.

In the morning, as they all prepared to head to the south, packing their motorcars with their luggage and the propraetor's goods and servants, Sigrun asked, cheerfully, "So, did you have a good time at your mysterious errand?"

Adam grimaced. "Can we not talk about that?"

"What's the matter?" Sigrun frowned.

"Nothing's the matter. I just don't want to talk about it." Adam shrugged. It wasn't her fault that they'd all gotten quite a bit more of an eyeful—and an earful—last night than was probably healthy. "How about if you tell me, on the way down to Tikal, what happened with Livorus in the Mongol-Qin Provocation."

She studied him. "No. Not a fair bargain."

"What?" Adam stood up so fast, he clipped his head on the trunk of the car.

"Just ask Trennus. He's all about *bargains*. You tell me about last night, I tell you what little I know about the events in Qin."

Adam debated it for a moment. He'd be driving with her, while Kanmi and Trennus were to be driving with the propraetor and the body servants, and Ehecatl had the vehicle with the additional new Praetorians, to whom Adam had just introduced himself, a few minutes ago. It *would* while away a long drive. "All right, but you first." He slipped into the driver's seat.

Sigrun got into on the passenger's side, closing the door of the ley-powered car behind her. She leaned back in the seat and cleared her throat as Adam started the engine. "So, the Mongol-Qin Provocation. Livorus had been an ambassador in Qin . . . mid-ranking . . . for about a year when it started. I wasn't on his detail yet. I was not assigned to him until he got back from Qin." Scenery started to blur past, as they and the rest of the vehicles in their small convoy got underway, crossing one of the suspension bridges on their way out of Tenochtitlan, light reflecting back from the murky waters of the brackish lake that cradled the heart of the city. "So, you know that various bands of Mongols periodically harass Raccia and Qin. They're poor, they're nomadic, and they cross the borders pretty much indiscriminately. The Khanate doesn't firmly control all of their people . . . or at least, claims not to. Sometimes, they use various tribes as cat's-paws. To see what Qin or Raccia will do, in response to an attack. To test their will." Sigrun sighed. "So, 1949, three minor khans crossed the border into Qin and attacked a ley-line tapping facility on the periphery of their grid. It was just being built, too. They killed the guards, and took the engineers hostage. Half the engineers were Roman, half Qin. Just . . . people doing their jobs." She turned to look out the window. "They sent one of the local villagers with one of the guards' heads back to the closest outpost of the Qin empire with a message. 'We have hostages and we have demands. We want the Qin occupation of this, our traditional land, to come to an end. A withdrawal of your garrisons. And the destruction of all ley-stations in this area, as they are an affront to the earth and the spirits.'"

Adam exhaled. "That . . . couldn't have gone over well." He paused. "The Empire doesn't usually negotiate with hostage-takers. Not unless it's someone very high-ranking." *And then, if the price is a ransom, they might pay it . . . or they might use the negotiations as a stall tactic until they can find where the hostage is, and send in a team to effect a rescue.*

Sigrun nodded, leaning back as they finally left the outskirts of Tenochtitlan; they now had a twenty-hour drive ahead of them. "Generally, Rome doesn't negotiate," she agreed now. "But they were in the middle of Qin. There were no Roman garrisons nearby, other than Roman embassy guards and a few lictors. And if Livorus had mustered out troops and driven from where his consulate was to the Mongol border, he might have offended his Qin hosts. So Livorus gathered his lictors, just his personal bodyguards, and drove out to the border, after telling Qin authorities he meant to try to get his people back . . . theirs too, if he could manage it. They gave him leave to try, but told him that they were mustering their garrisons, and that he had best talk quickly."

"Weren't the Mongols apt to kill their captives if they felt threatened?" Adam asked.

"If they killed them too quickly, they would lose leverage, or at least, lose human shields." Sigrun grimaced. "So there was Livorus, with just himself, the *fasces*, and four lictors, meeting with three minor khans and several hundred of their soldiers. He told me he'd made sure to empty his bladder and bowels before beginning negotiations. He was lucky. They offered him hospitality, and he told them, plain and simple, that his people and theirs had fought before, when the Khanate sent troops into Asia Minor and from there, down into Byzantium and Judea, seven hundred years ago . . . and that the western khans perpetually test the will of Rome along that short border. He told them that he, and Rome, had no interest in the dispute between them and Qin. But that if they forced Rome's hand here, today, that Rome would have no choice but to *become* interested." She shrugged. "They did not want to risk the enmity of their own people, if Rome began attacks to the west. So they released the Roman engineers, most of whom had been beaten and tortured, to Livorus. He bundled them all into the trucks, but he couldn't, no matter how he tried, convince them to release the Qin engineers. He tried telling them it was a gesture of good faith. They saw it as a symbol of weakness. So he drove away, a hero in the eyes of Rome . . . but had to leave seventy men behind." Sigrun sighed. "By the time the Qin garrison got there, the Mongols had decamped, rather than face the Qin army directly. They had destroyed the ley-facility . . . .and they had left all of their prisoners behind. Impaled on pikes."

Adam swerved to avoid a pothole in the poured-stone road, and stayed completely silent for a long moment. "That . . . puts the propraetor in a whole different light," he said, after a moment.

Sigrun nodded. "I respect the man. I really do. I also suspect he still has nightmares about the men he had to leave behind. Qin or no, I think he sees it as a failure on his part." She paused. "All right. I've fulfilled my half of the *bargain*. Speak. Where *did* you all go last night?"

Adam's eyes shifted to the rearview mirror, where he could just see part of one storm-gray eye and the curve of her cheekbone. "Ah, Livorus wanted to go to a brothel."

Sigrun's head snapped towards him. "You're pleased to jest. That was all he had in mind?"

Adam's lips twitched ruefully. He'd noticed that her mode of speaking with the other lictors, and even Livorus himself, tended towards the painfully formal. No contractions, no slurring of words in Latin. However, with him, once in a while, she'd slip into a colloquial form . . . as she just had. Still, she didn't sound entirely shocked. "I swear, it's true."

She shook her head. "Well, it has been a while—not for a year, I think? He doesn't frequent them often." She quirked him a grin. "Ptah-ases used to ask to go with him. His wife never cared. So did Villu. Something about being able to charge it to their expense reports."

Adam did his best not to swerve off the road, and did his best not to laugh out loud. After a moment, cautiously, he asked, "I thought you'd be bothered."

"No, why should I be?" Her voice was almost carefully casual.

"Germania and Gaul don't permit it, I thought." He couldn't quite believe he was having this conversation.

"It's permitted, so long as the facilities are licensed and clean. There just aren't as many brothels per capita in our cities. Largely, I think, because our women are much freer than in other provinces." Sigrun shrugged. "Societies with clean, licensed, and regulated prostitution, in the Roman fashion, have lower incidences of violence against women. It provides an outlet that's safe for all, and a livelihood for women who have . . . limited education and options. And some of the women are actually highly educated. Would I like to see them have more options? Yes. But at least I know that in a legal brothel, the women are there by choice, and haven't been picked up as runaways and forced into a life of slavery, or aren't selling themselves on a street corner." She shrugged again. "There's a difference." She paused, and out of the corner of his eye, he could see her expression shift. "So, how is your expense report looking?"

Adam choked, and then laughed out loud. "I'm not looking to add anything from the Entertainment category, if that's what you're asking." He paused. "A few extra drinks from the bar on getting back to the hotel, but other than that, the accounting department shouldn't be spending any overtime on sorting mine out. Or any of us, really."

"Well, that's . . . surprising, really." Sigrun blinked. "At least, as regards Kanmi. But then, you and Trennus do seem to be good boys."

Adam turned his head just enough to grin at her. "Oh, but that's where you're wrong. So very, very wrong."

Sigrun laughed, a ripple of sound that was surprisingly dark-toned and pleasant. Adam gave her a look, and then added, "So what's with this nice *boys* talk, eh?"

"Trennus seems young, in some ways. Inexperienced, in others."

"He's a year older than I am."

"Yes, but you come across as older." She shrugged a little, and rolled down the window of the car to let the steamy air whip across their faces.

Adam glanced behind them, verifying that no one seemed to be following the convoy at the moment. "I'm going to take that as a compliment."

"It was meant as one." Her tone was unruffled, but she paused and noted, "Yesterday was Frigedæg."

"Dies Veneris, yes."

"And today is Sæternesdæg."

"If you're asking me why I was out after sundown with the propraetor, and why I'm driving today, the answer is 'because Livorus and the rest of the world will not work on my schedule, no matter how nicely I ask him.'" Adam glanced at her. "But if you want to take a turn driving . . . I wouldn't say no."

"When we come to a rest area, of course I will." Sigrun paused. "Your god will not be angry with you?" Her tone was concerned.

"I run my life by the general assumption that my god thinks of his people as grown-ups. There are guidelines for behavior, but by and large, we're expected to make our own choices and deal with the repercussions of them ourselves." He shrugged. "Every faith says that we're the children of the gods. But I personally think that what every parent wants, more than anything else, is to see their children grow up. What's the point of having children if they just *stay* children?"

Sigrun nodded, lifting her eyebrows. "Not a bad philosophy at all." She paused. "But that being said, you could have told Livorus. The propraetor *is* flexible about his lictors' faiths. He's rarely objected to me wearing the chicken-suit, for example." A smile curved the corners of her lips.

"Yes, but if I didn't go last night, he'd have been short a bodyguard."

"I could have gone."

Adam's head turned completely towards her, just for a moment, even as he continued driving. "You could have gone?"

"Yes, of course."

"To a *brothel*?"

"I don't see why I couldn't have managed." She sounded embarrassed and annoyed at once.

Adam whooped with laughter, and absolutely couldn't *stop* for the next half mile. Every time he almost managed to catch his breath, Sigrun would ask "What?" and he was off again on another jag of laughter. There was no possible way in which he could tell her, in words, what a *bad* idea this was, so, after a few moments, he took a hand off the wheel, and very lightly tugged on her braid. "You know, on the whole, I think my god would think it a much better thing that I do my job, and you know . . . prevent bloodshed."

"I don't think I'd *kill* anyone, Adam. I *can* control myself." She sounded vexed.

"Trust me. There would have been blood."

"Adam, I'd be standing there in armor, holding a weapon. I don't think anyone could possibly be confused as to my purpose there." Vexed, bordering on waspish. Also, *confused*.

"You underestimate the power of the male imagination." Adam had both hands on the wheel again. "Also, in case you haven't noticed, you're more than reasonably attractive. The women there could accuse you of trying to steal their livelihood."

Sigrun twisted in her seat, and the look of incredulity on her face made him laugh all the harder.

And with that, there was little more conversation, for the next hour or so, as the green-brown marshes became the jade-green haze of the jungle, and their wheels ate the miles.

Iunius 6, 1954 AC

Twenty hours of driving, with a stop overnight in a substandard traveler's hotel, brought them to the Tikali region at sundown on Sunnandæg night.

Monandæg morning, Sigrun rose at dawn, as did all her fellow core-team lictors. Adam had talked them all into at least an hour of sparring before breakfast each morning that they could fit it into the schedule, and Sigrun had to chuckle at Kanmi's skeptical expression as he stood, leaning against a wall beside Ehecatl outside the hotel. They were in a small, sunken courtyard usually used as a ball-court, currently partially flooded at one end from overnight rains.

Adam and Trennus had already gotten started. Trennus had height and weight on Adam, and, when he pulled off his shirt to compensate for the muggy, thick air, looked surprisingly muscular and fit. He was good, but he didn't have Adam's level of speed or training. There had been a time in the Empire when every boxing match in an arena only ended when one man died. Generally speaking, that had been phased out; likewise, not every gladiatorial fight in the arena ended in a death, either. Nevertheless, there was a large segment of the population that *enjoyed* gladiatorial fighting and bare-knuckle, no-holds-barred fighting, and could watch it in person or on their far-viewers. Many enthusiasts participated in fighting *collegia*, as well. And because of the wide reach of the Empire, literally hundreds of fighting styles had been imported from dozens of cultures.

Praetorians, in order to be able to do their jobs, needed to be able to counter whatever they happened to encounter. Adam's style was *bitahevn*, the JDF's system of self-defense, which derived from various western and eastern martial art systems, and had been developed over centuries as Roman and Judean traders had explored Asia and Indonesia. There were elements of something called *muay thai* in it, along with boxing, grappling, and wrestling. He'd picked up Nahautl knife-forms from Ehecatl, and after two years in India, had learned something he called *mushti-yuddha*, which was a hard-strikes school that employed kicking, punching, and elbows. He was all about speed and power and not *being* where his opponent thought he'd be.

Trennus, laughing, admitted, "I'm not much good at the dodging around part. I generally just try to close and grapple."

"Dodging is a very good thing to learn when knives are involved," Ehecatl called.

"Typically, when I've used weapons, they've been swords, three-and-a-half feet long. They're for taking the legs off horses . . . and people." Trennus used his reach to his advantage, and closed on Adam again. "And again, typically, when fighting someone else carrying one, we try to get the swords off-line, close, and grapple."

"You can't always rely on brute strength, Tren. Sooner or later, you *will* find someone bigger and stronger."

"Already have. I have older brothers, you know." He got his arms around Adam's waist and started to throw the shorter man to the ground . . . only to have Adam's hands, thought-fast, slap lightly against his ears, simulating a move that would have damaged his eardrums, or at least stunned him and forced him to release his grip.

They went back and forth a few times, and then they broke apart, beckoning Kanmi and Ehecatl in; Trennus moved to work with Ehecatl, while Adam beckoned to Kanmi. The Carthaginian shook his head, but went along with the exercise. "I'll agree that a strong body helps make a strong mind," he said, shortly, "but I'm no good at this. Never will be. But I'll be your punching bag, if it makes you all feel better."

"Not really the point. The point is, we can all learn things from each other. I can't learn how to *do* magic, I suspect, but I can learn *about* it. You might not learn how to field-strip a gun or rig a detonator from me, but you might learn something about the process." Adam shrugged, and walked Kanmi through how to throw someone, from the shoulder, two or three different methods.

"I'll admit that I wish I'd known how to do this when I was a child, back before I knew I was a sorcerer," Kanmi said, after a while, and gave Trennus a bright, tight smile. "You're not the only one with older brothers."

Sigrun had mostly sat atop the high wall of the ball court, looking down, until Adam looked up and asked, "You joining us, or what?"

"And miss watching my own private arena matches? I thought I might lounge up here like an Imperatrix and call someone to bring me grapes."

That made them all guffaw. Sigrun slid off the wall and dropped the full eighteen feet to the ground, not even thinking about it. Her boots squelched in the water, and a half-dozen mosquitoes immediately buzzed around her, sensing a new source of food. "The footing here is miserable."

"Talk to management about it." Adam told her.

"I might, at that." She shrugged. "Who do you want me working with?"

"Each in turn. Kanmi first."

She could, simply by virtue of what she was, and how she'd been trained, see the shifts in body language before Kanmi even moved. Caught and redirected his strikes, letting his energy, his inertia, flow past her, before simulating a throw, to avoid actually dumping him in the puddles and stone of the ball-court. He was faster than Trennus, and a little stronger than she'd expected, which made it a bit more fun. Sigrun nodded to him as they stepped apart. "You've worked for a living at some point, Kanmi. Would it spoil your mystique if I asked what you did before magic called you?"

He snorted, and massaged a wrist where she'd demonstrated a throw's set-up with a little too much vigor. "Everyone in my family, or almost, is a fisherman. My father was a guard on a merchant ship on the Mediterranean, but my grandfather was a fisherman. Still is. He used to take me and my brothers out on the boats when we were younger." His eyes shifted to the side, his face closed. "But I haven't hauled in a net since I was twelve."

Sigrun filed the fact away. His determined dislike of anyone he thought to be high-born, or who thought themselves, for that reason, better than he was, matched up with a desperately poor background. His dossier had hinted at some of that, but it had been vague on particulars.

Trennus, on the other hand, was very fit indeed. "A lifetime of hunting deer and tramping through the hills behind my father and brothers. Twenty miles in a day was a light day during hunting season," he admitted, chuckling under his breath. A petty king in Britannia in this day and age was very often an administrator and a trained lawyer, among other things, but Trennus' father had played as hard as he worked, and usually donated half of the game that he hunted to the poor . . . or it fed his own family in their large stone house. As such, the tall man was physically powerful, and Sigrun made a point of not allowing him to get her into a hold . . . until Kanmi laughed and said, "What happens when someone his size actually does get ahold of you, Caetia?"

Sigrun shrugged. "Grab me from behind," she told Trennus, who flushed a little, but did as he was told . . . and she dropped to a crouch, shoving her hips back to create space, stepped a little to her right, and dropped her hand down to groin-level. "And then I grab and I twist," Sigrun said, lightly. "Nature's great equalizer."

"And that is when I drop my hands and clutch myself, and stagger away mewling," Trennus said, laughing.

"There's also the fact that you could pick him up and throw him with one hand," Ehecatl put in.

Sigrun grimaced. "It doesn't pay to advertise, Ehe."

Kanmi shook his head. "It's all good in theory. But I can add force to any punch I take with magic. I can throw someone harder with magic, than I can with my hands."

Sigrun glanced over at Adam, who had an oddly patient look on his face. "Of course you can," Adam said. "It's just that there are times when you're not going to advertise that you're a sorcerer. Or someone, somewhere, somehow, will figure out a way to cut you off from magic." Adam looked at Kanmi, who was already opening his mouth. "Don't," ben Maor said, quickly. "I'll listen to you both on the *source of magic* discussion . . . again . . . some other time. But that's not what I really want to talk about right now."

"Let me put it this way. Punch me," Sigrun told Kanmi.

"What?"

"Just punch me. Hard as you can."

Kanmi squinted at her. "This sounds like a set-up."

"That would be because it is. Hit me, Kanmi. Show me what you're made of. Throw in some magic. I won't mind if it lands."

"This could be fun," Ehecatl said, finding a stone bench to sit on.

"It's the *if it lands* part that's making me suspicious." Kanmi frowned at her, and then punched, a hook aimed for her face, and she could *feel* energy behind it, even as her hand shot up . . . and she just *caught* his fist against her palm, and closed her fingers. Held it. Didn't redirect the inertia into a throw.

Kanmi looked up at her, his hand held, not in a bone-crushing grip, but still very much immobilized. Oddly, there was no affront in his face. Interest, but unlike many men she'd met in her life, no wounded ego at all. "So what you're saying is, this is completely a waste of time for you?"

"*No.*" Sigrun gave him a look. "I mean that Adam is correct. This is a useful exercise for all of us. Cross-training promotes flexibility. And gives us all a better understanding of many different opponents. None of you were trained in the Odinhall in Burgundoi. I was, for four years. All of the things I can do, were taught there, or I picked up on the Mongolian border, or up in the countries of far northern Europa, or from my fellow lictors. But I am what I am, and I can't change it. I can barely even *hide* it. The rest of you are not so crippled in that. You can all choose to be . . . what you are not. You can be more than what you are today, or choose to appear to be less" Sigrun released Kanmi's hand. "You are . . . extraordinarily fortunate. All of you." She nodded to Adam. "I'm going to go eat, if you don't mind." Unconsciously, her phrasing softened, relaxed. Inasmuch as she was aware of it, she used the informal tone in order to demonstrate that Adam was her co-leader on the detail, to reinforce his status for the other, newer lictors.

"What, the rest of them don't get a shot at you?" Trennus asked, picking up his shirt to pull it on, covering his various tribal tattoos, and the amulets he wore once more.

"Some other time, maybe," Sigrun murmured.

"I'm holding you to that," Adam called after her, lightly, and she raised a hand in acknowledgement, before heading up the stairs out of the ball court and back to the hotel.

The practice, the team-building, as Adam called it, had taken an hour. And now, they needed to get to work. They were divided into teams today. Trennus and Kanmi were to visit a local ley-energy platform, newly built; Adam and Livorus were heading into the city center to speak with the regional nobles and the leader of the local Roman garrisons. And Sigrun and Ehecatl were assigned to speak with the local religious leaders. "That is, actually, exactly how our contact in Tenochtitlan said to contact the leader of the rebels. To get in touch with the temple of Chaac, which is engaged in a serious rivalry with the regional temple of Tlaloc. Similar gods, different names." Livorus raised his eyebrows. "When you enter that temple, and engage one of the priests in conversation, mention that you've heard the names of some of the ancient rulers of Quecha. Eighteen Rabbit. Head on Earth. Smoke Jaguar." Livorus held up a hand. "Please, try not to laugh. What would *your* names render as, if translated, pray?"

"Battle-rune," Sigrun replied promptly. "And the last name means *spear.*" Her lips quirked. "Battle-Rune Spear, as opposed to Eighteen *Rabbit?*"

"Windserpent Obsidian Knife," Ehecatl put in, grinning. "One of the lesser names of Quetzalcoatl. It has a little more dignity than Head on Earth, yes."

"Man, son of Light," Adam replied, looking up at the ceiling. "I'm really not making that up."

" . . . er, *strong,*" Trennus said, after a moment. "From the family of the good bear." He fidgeted at the table. "I think that *does* beat Head on Earth."

Kanmi shook his head. "Don't ask me to participate in the party game here. I'm named for some dead king of Carthage or another. I'm sure it's something embarrassing like 'he eats babies for breakfast.'" He looked around the table. "So, where's this ley-facility located?"

Chapter VII: Investigations

Welcome to Hellas, the land of Socrates, Aristotle, Plato, Euripides, Aeschylus, and Sophocles! Enjoy our white sand beaches and a culture of hospitality that goes back to Homeric times. Book a tour of the Parthenon or journey to fabled Delphi to delve into the mysteries of your future in a private consultation with a Pythian sibyl. See the Colossus of Rhodes (rebuilt in 76 AC, on the site of the original), or experience the bounty of the Ephesian Artemis with her hundreds of breasts. Debate philosophy on the campus of the University of Athens in the morning, take in a play or listen to a poetry reading in the afternoon, feast on lamb and fish and drink good wine in the evening, and know that, in the morning, whatever happens in Hellas, stays in Hellas.

— The Hellene Board of Tourism, 1951 AC

There is a lively debate as to what allows the Pythias of Delphi to access their powers here, as no other place in the world. Some attribute the best prophecies of antiquity to ethylene vapors which once rose from the rocks of the caves. These were, however, cut off after a series of earthquakes in 645 AC. There were no god-born of Apollo in residence at the temple as it was being rebuilt.

The priests and priestesses, in order to maintain their livelihoods, and their connection to their god, turned to a variety of psychotropic compounds, some imported from India, or as far away as Caesaria Aquilonis and Caesaria Australis. It worked; the Oracle at Delphi was saved, and continues to dispense good, if cryptic advice to this day.

In truth, god-born Pythias do not require any such chemical intervention; their gift of prophecy travels with them, no matter where in the world they might be. But remarkably, that gift comes to its fullest potential only here, in sacred Delphi — in the total absence of the ethylene vapors that once were the region's hallmarks. Truly, Apollo must smile on this place as no other.

Some travelers to Delphi have complained of headaches, migraines, nausea, and vivid hallucinations regarding events in the future or the past. All tap water in the region is checked routinely by Imperial specialists, and rates highly for its potability. Air quality in the region is also monitored, and is usually considered better than that of Rome or Athens. Travelers with pre-existing medical conditions such as heart disease, high blood pressure, and pulmonary diseases such as tuberculosis are, however, advised to exercise caution when exploring the area around the temple by foot, as they should in any mountainous region.

Travelers are also warned not to accept offers of prophecy from any person outside of the Temple grounds; there are fakes, charlatans, and addicts all through the countryside who will invent prophecy and mutter incomprehensible words for a few small coins. These are beggars, and should not be trusted. Only accept real, one-hundred-percent verifiable prophecies given by a genuine Pythia.

— The Delphic Board of Tourism, 1953 AC

Travelers are advised that organic and chemical compounds legal in Hellas are not necessarily legal elsewhere in the Empire, and any illegal substances found in your suitcases will be confiscated, and you will be subjected to a fine of no less than two aurei for the attempted importation of such drugs without a pharmaceutical license, doctor's prescription, or writ of religious dispensation.

Travelers are further advised that many social diseases are common in Hellas, and to exercise caution and sobriety in their excursions in this land. Condoms are available for free in all hostelries, courtesy of the Imperial Council of Physicians.

— The Imperial Department of Travel, 1954 AC

The rumors of the prevalence of social diseases in Hellas are greatly exaggerated! Our brothels are subjected to the same rigorous licensing standards as any other portion of the Empire, and our incidence of disease in the rest of the population is below five point eight percent.

— The Hellene Anti-Defamation League

Iunius 6, 1954 AC

"Agent Caetia?" The words were in Latin, and caught Sigrun's ear as she passed by the front desk with Adam as they headed for the front door.

"Yes?"

"There's a call for you. Long-distance, from Hellas. Will you accept it?"

Sigrun winced. There was only one person who'd be calling her from Hellas. "Is there a private place I can take the call?" she asked, shifting her shoulders uncomfortably.

"Of course—you can use the manager's office."

Sigrun stepped into the tile-walled office, dodging around a rubber tree in a pot—people around here seemed to be intensely fond of bringing jungle plants indoors, for some reason—and picked up the black phone on its cradle on the desk, studying the flashing lights at the base, below the rotating dial. She pressed the red light to transfer the call. "*Waes hael,*" she said, after a moment. No Latin *ave*. She knew who this was.

"Sigrun!"

Her little sister had *always* greeted her in exactly this way, a cry of pure joy. For a moment, Sigrun was lost in a flash of memory.

. . . walking to the front door of her father's house in Cimbri, built in the oldest part of town, close to the edge of Lake Caestus. Slipping in, late at night, the dining room the first room visible in the old-fashioned home . . . only to see a swirl of long, tawny hair and a child's nightgown, and to be hit somewhere around waist-level by a projectile comprised mainly of skinny arms reaching around her in a hug. "Sigrun!" Sophia exclaimed, looking up at her. "Oh, I'm so happy you're home. I had such bad dreams about you."

"Little one, what are you doing up? It's after midnight."

"I dreamed you were coming home. Mother and Father said it wouldn't be for a week, but I woke up and knew you'd be here." Sophia regarded her with wide green eyes, the color of a dark wine bottle. "I had such _bad_ dreams about you the past month, Sigrun."

Sigrun ruffled the dark gold hair lightly. "I was very safe in the northern kingdoms. This wasn't even as dangerous as when I was on the Mongol border, when you were six. Just guarding a bunch of diplomats and passing around platters of food." Sigrun knelt down, dropping her spear and her duffle bag on the floor, and not caring if the weapon scratched her step-mother's precious hardwood floor. "I brought you a gift. A nesting doll, from Raccia. Let me get it out of my bag." She was aware, peripherally, of Ivarr and Medea entering the dining room, both of them in night robes; she'd really meant to slip in _quietly_, and not disturb them. To pass, like a ghost in the night, if at all possible.

"That's not what I dreamed about, sister." Sophia's ten-year-old inflections were still piping, but held more stubborn will than there had been the last time Sigrun had seen her sister. "I _saw_ you. You walked a dark road, heading east, always east, and the sky was like blood behind you, as the fires of a dying god consumed the world. Ashes fell from that sky like snow, settling on your hair, which was matted and soaked with blood, hanging down around your face like a medusa's snakes." Sophia's voice was dreamy, and her eyes had gone unfocused. "You had a raven on one shoulder, one eye clear and amber, the other white as milk, and it held a silver key in its beak. You had a spear in your hand, that glowed like a levinbolt, and carried a child under your heart, but the father is both alive and dead, and you had been both married to him and never truly wed, and he'd been young enough to be your son and old enough to be your grandfather when the child blossomed in your womb." Sophia's eyes widened for a moment, and she added, still, in that same, dreamy voice, "This is how the world ends, sister. In fire, and not in flood. And you'll be there to watch it die."

Sigrun released her hold on the girl and just _stared_ at her for a long moment, as their father bellowed, "Sophia! I told you not to repeat that nonsense!"

Sigrun held up a hand, for the first time in her life, to stay her father's words. "Father, stop."

Ivarr didn't listen. He took a step forward, and caught Sophia's shoulder in his big hand. "That is no way in which to talk to your sister, Sophia. You should be _ashamed_ of yourself—"

"I should cane her hands for this. For telling _lies_." Medea's tone was venomous, and that got Sigrun's attention, her head coming up with a snap.

"Stop it." This time, Sigrun had let the rune-born light appear on her skin as she stood up, but she addressed only her father, putting herself between the girl and her parents. "Father, there are no lies in her eyes. I would see them. She's not inventing this. This is what she has _seen_." She looked past her father's shocked face towards Medea, once her pedagogue, and now her step-mother, and gave the woman a cool look. "It appears that the blood of the gods flows on both sides in this family. However, Father, I would recommend that you find Sophia a teacher other than your wife. As her previous student, I would not give her my recommendation as an instructor for god-born children."

A flare of temper, a narrowing of Medea's green eyes; the Hellene woman was half a foot shorter than Sigrun, and had dark, wavy hair. Sigrun met that stare with her own. *"I'll not allow you to cane her for speaking the truth,"* Sigrun told Medea, grimly, *"the way you caned my hands weekly if I couldn't speak my lessons word-perfect on the first try."*

Her father's head had spun towards her. Sigrun had never mentioned it. There had been no way to *prove* it, at the time. The cane marks healed within a half hour of being administered, and, in those years, even public schools had permitted caning as a disciplinary method for stubborn, willful students. But when Sigrun had been old enough to leave home, she'd done so with a joyful heart . . . until she'd learned that her father had *freed* Medea, whose family had sold her into slavery to pay their debts . . . and had subsequently asked her to marry him. When she'd learned that Medea was pregnant, all Sigrun had been able to hope was that the woman would treat her own flesh and blood better than she'd treated Sigrun herself.

It had been a long night after that point, but Sigrun had never forgotten the words of prophecy Sophia had spoken. For the first few years, they'd haunted her thoughts on the nights in which she couldn't sleep. As they continued to show absolutely no sign of coming true, she was able to distance herself, mentally, from the vividness of the words.

Unfortunately, there was only really one place in the world for a god-born of Apollo with the gift of prophecy, and that was Delphi. Where Sophia had gone at the age of eighteen. And Sigrun felt, somehow, as if she'd lost her beloved little sister eleven years ago, because of it.

"Sigrun? Are you there?" Quick, light words, in their native Cimbric. Faint slur in the speech, dreamy, detached tone. Light sound of muffled, female laughter in the background. Rustling and shifting, too, unmasked by the static in the connection. Sigrun did a little mental math; Delphi was eight hours ahead of Tikal. It was nine antemeridian here, and thus . . . five postmeridian there. *I suppose I should be grateful she can still talk,* she thought, grimly.

"Yes, Sophia," Sigrun replied, tiredly, sitting down on the edge of the desk, feeling as if the entire world suddenly had come to rest on her shoulders. *"I'm here."*

"I had a dream about you," the drowsy, muzzy voice on the line breathed into her ear, and the hairs on the back of Sigrun's neck prickled. *"You're walking into a trap, sister. I can see it . . . ."*

"Sophia," Sigrun managed, her throat tight, feeling as if she were holding onto a thin piece of cord a thousand miles long . . . and that she was trying to reel that fish in with her bare hands. *"Sophia, sister . . . there is no fate. Only wyrd."* She'd tried to tell her sister this, so very often, but between the training at Delphi, and the visions . . . Sophia didn't listen. Or at least, didn't hear. The two were much the same.

"Beware the black bird, Sigrun . . . ."

Sigrun leaned her head back against the wall, still cradling the phone. *"That's a little vague, Sophia. You don't mean the one on my shoulder at the end of the world, do you?"* Sophia's visions had been appallingly clear and precise when she was a child, but on going to Delphi, and being subjected to the training and the drugs . . . it was as if her inner eye had clouded.

Then again, maybe she takes the drugs just to <u>dull</u> the inner eye. Maybe she can't stand to see so clearly, and wants nothing more than mortal sight. I could understand that . . . if only she made sense when she talks now . . . .

"Don't be silly . . ." Sophia giggled on the other end of the line, echoed by more female laughter in the distance. Then she sucked in her breath in a gasp, and told Sigrun alertly, and more rapidly, "*The black bird at the end of time is a <u>raven</u>. This one is the size of a man, and he'll tear the heart out of you, if he has a chance, and feed it to his god. He wants his god to be powerful, so that he can share in that power, but there's another creature there . . . a bumblebee. And he wants to bleed the god out on the ground so that everyone can lap up the blood, like dogs.*" Sophia laughed, a dazed sound, and then gasped again. "*Ah . . . have to go, Sigrun. Talk later, all right?*"

Sigrun hung up the phone without saying good-bye. It wouldn't have done any good even if she had. And then she sat there for a long moment, rubbing the tears out of her eyes.

Those wouldn't do any good, either.

When she'd calmed down enough, she considered her sister's *prophecy*, such as it was, as dispassionately as she could. On the face of it, it made no sense at all. Then again *prophecy* never did. It was all mind-games, really. Something someone would either cause to come into being, like poor damned Oedipus . . . or wouldn't understand until it was too late, anyway. *What does this tell me that I didn't know ten minutes ago?* Sigrun wondered, and then sighed. *Not a <u>damned thing</u>. Should I tell Adam? Livorus? Any of them?*

No. They'll just start second-guessing everything, too. Let them be free of the gods-be-damned <u>gift</u> of <u>fikken</u> prophecy.

She stood and made sure her face was dry and set in composed lines before stepping out of the manager's office. She caught ben Maor's concerned look at her from past the reception desk. "Everything all right?" he asked.

"Just family." She shrugged.

"Everyone okay at home?"

No. Sigrun swallowed, and replied, briskly, "Everyone's exactly the same as they always are. Nothing to worry about."

Nothing to worry about at all.

"Let's get going then," Adam told her, his eyes narrowing slightly. Clearly, he didn't believe her, but wasn't going to push. "You have priests to interview with Ehecatl, and I have contacts to make with the propraetor."

Kanmi had followed Livorus' orders the night before, and had called Gratian Xicohtencatl. The Nahautl technomancer had been startled to hear from Kanmi—it had showed in his voice. "Can I convince you to come to my house this evening for a little get-together?" Xicohtencatl had asked. "Just a few friends from work and some of the technomage societies here in the province . . . ."

"Unfortunately, I'm about halfway to Tikal," Kanmi had said, putting joviality in his voice that he hadn't felt.

"Tikal?"

"That's life in the retinue of the great and powerful. Close your eyes in one city, open them again in a completely different one." The irony in his tone hadn't been hard to fake at all. "I thought you'd said you were opening new ley-platforms down here. Isn't that sort of risky, given the political atmosphere down here? Don't your engineers and workers get attacked by the locals?"

"Kanmi, this is exactly what I've been talking about," Xicohtencatl's voice had become unctuous at that point. "I'm making sure to provide jobs for the locals, as well as for the highly-skilled engineers being sent down there. There's job training, so that the people of the region can maintain the platforms, once they're finished being built. Not only are we bringing power to the people, but we're empowering them."

Kanmi had filed the surely well-worn catchphrases to the back of his head "You sound like you've been practicing that speech for the next time you get in front of your emperor's council of advisors."

"If I thought they'd listen, I'd tell them that, certainly. That speech is meant more for investors."

"I thought your power company was state-run." Kanmi pulled the loose thread, not pouncing, but trying to sound tired and a little bored. Both of which were true, so again, it wasn't hard to fake.

"Oh, it is. But there are other kinds of investment. We're talking *people capital*, Eshmunazar, my friend. If you can get people to buy into an idea, there is almost nothing that you can't do."

It could have been perfectly innocuous. It was a boardroom sort of platitude. Except there was something almost coy in the way Xicohtencatl said it. Kanmi let it pass, however. In many realms of life, it didn't pay to appear to be too eager. Not in love, not when buying a motorcar, and certainly not in espionage. "So, as I said, I'm heading to Tikal, and carrying the propraetor's baggage," he said, downplaying his own position as carefully.

"Oh, come now, surely a lictor does more than that?"

Ah. You did check into what I do for a living. All I said before was that I was on Livorus' staff. That could mean anything from getting him coffee, taking dictation, looking good in a dress, or being a lictor . . . depending on the propraetor in question, of course. "You'd be surprised how dull the job can really be," Kanmi said, putting ennui in his tone. "The travel really starts to get to you after a while." He yawned, deliberately. "So. If I'm going to Tikal, is there anything actually *interesting* in the area, for whatever few off-hours I get?"

"Are you looking for entertainment, or for something that might intrigue the fine mind I remember from university?"

"I wouldn't say no to entertainment, but you were telling me that your new stations down there are unconventional? I don't know that much about ley-power, but I appreciate good technomancy."

"I could probably get you a guided tour of one of our facilities, if you'd like . . . ." The words sidled out. As if they weren't bait at all. "And perhaps an introduction to some of our better on-site engineers?"

"I don't know if I'm going to have the time," Kanmi demurred, then offered, "but if I happen to have a free hour or two, I might take you up on that."

The main purpose of the phone call done, Kanmi allowed Xicohtencatl to guide the rest of their conversation. His job now was to *listen*, and try to find keywords and phrases that prompted reactions. Hiding his motivations — and how closely he actually listened to people, and how fast he found their patterns — was nothing new. This was just slightly more important than ascertaining that ben Maor worried that the rest of the squad took him seriously as a senior lictor, poking Trennus solidly in his insecurity with women, or delicately seeing just how close to the line of insubordination Livorus would allow him to get. Those were all for his own amusement. This? This was real.

That had been two nights ago. Today, in an open-topped vehicle with a high undercarriage and roller bars, Kanmi and Trennus bumped and jostled over the ill-kept jungle roads with a couple of locals as guides. Kanmi mopped at his face, and muttered to Trennus, "To think I've traveled around the world only to find a climate even worse than Tyre or Carthage."

"I'll take your word for it. Gods, what I wouldn't do for a cold breeze from home right now." Trennus was flushed from the heat, and Kanmi thought the Britannian, fair-skinned as he was, would probably burn right through his cotton shirt. While it might be amusing to watch the high-born, naïve young man turn beet red in the sun, and eventually peel, on the balance, Kanmi thought that heatstroke would probably be a bad idea. Certainly, it would mean that he'd have to do twice the work at the ley-platform, and Trennus would be lying about, being fanned and handed cool drinks. Kanmi looked up at the sun, and considered things for a moment. *A ten degree gradual decline in ambient temperature, and . . . if I can manage it . . . reflection of ultraviolet spectrum light . . . no, absorption. I can use the energy later. Or even now.*

He exhaled, and began the mental work of setting up a thin barrier in the air directly around them; soap-bubble fine, it was invisible to the naked eye, but stopped the wind from rushing into their faces . . . while still allowing air to circulate, out the bottom of the vehicle. Trennus gave him a dubious look. "Not a notable improvement," the man said, mopping at his face again. "I'd prefer a warm breeze to no breeze at all."

"Wait for it," Kanmi told him, and completed the overhead dome. *Now, if I do this right . . . I can use one incantation to power the other.* He concentrated, hard, and the dome darkened, faintly, becoming like smoked glass. Their driver swerved, nearly ramming into a boulder in their path, and stopped, staring wild-eyed around them. "It's not an attack," Kanmi told him, irritably. "Just keep driving."

The shield itself was made of air and hovered right with them; the darkness was from dirt and dust from the road that he worked into it, and also a component of pure *will*. It both created a barrier for the UV, and absorbed it. The solar energy, Kanmi wove into his second incantation, his lips moving silently. The words weren't really necessary. It was all a framework in his mind, and the words were just a conduit, a way of creating and understanding that fretwork of energy. The new incantation, powered, began to draw energy out of the air around them . . . cooling it.

And because he actually now had an energy surplus in the form of heat, and all the batteries in his pockets and equipment bag were fully charged, Kanmi let the heat bleed out behind them, in a wavering mirage that made the jungle ripple like an image in a pond.

End result: A pocket of space ten degrees cooler than ambient, UV protection, one unnerved driver, two uneasy guides, and two much more comfortable lictors. All things considered, Kanmi was pleased.

"All right," Trennus admitted, bracing himself as they hit yet another kidney-rattling hole in the road, "that's a *handy* talent there."

"Just a derivation of a few other things I can do." Kanmi shrugged. "This is the less combat-oriented, and thus, more *interesting* application. A little more subtle."

It took three hours of slowly grinding through the jungle, but eventually, they reached the ley station. Kanmi lowered his smoked-glass lenses from in front of his eyes, and stared as they finally breached the barrier of trees that had separated them from it.

Ley-facilities were generally called towers because they were usually about six stories tall, and had spires that often reached up at least twice that height into the sky, and also because the oldest ones were usually built of stone. In Novo Gaul, where the technology had been pioneered, centuries ago, they had usually built alongside, or as a part of the local castle or defensive structures. Ley-power had helped turn mills to crush grain without having to rely on wind or water, and had provided novelty lights to the rich and powerful, at first. The base of every tower still housed large, loosely-wrapped transformer coils that worked on resonant principles. Metal rods were driven down into the bedrock to anchor the foundation, and to tap the local ley-line itself, whenever possible. Typically, such facilities were connected to the rest of the grid they serviced by long strings of insulated copper wire strung out on tall poles.

This ley-tower was strikingly different than most other large modern tapping facilities. From its two-story, squat base, it had a metal mast fixed atop the roof — tall, well over a hundred feet in height — which was braced all along its length, with non-conductive cable, linked to various points on the roof. At the very top of the mast, there was a sphere, which looked to be made of copper plate, molded over some sort of framework and riveted in place. And there was not a single line leading away from the facility.

"What," Kanmi said, with great precision, standing up in the back of the vehicle, "the *fuck* . . . is that?"

"This is the ley-tapping facility," one of the guides spoke up in poor Latin, turning to look over his shoulder at Kanmi. "Is new type, yes? More efficient this way. No wires!"

Kanmi's eyes narrowed as he looked around more carefully. The earth was raw here, from where the trees had been hand-logged. Most of them were, in fact, still in a pile off to the east, waiting for a truck to carry them back out of the jungle . . . or to just rot there, and be consumed by insects from within. He studied the guards—most of them were Nahautl, from the clothing and tattoos, although a few might have been local Quecha—and most carried muskets. By the standards of the region, they were heavily armed, but while they looked alert and ready, they didn't look to be on edge. *"Matrugena, please tell me you speak Hellene."*

"Of course I do. I went to university." Trennus' lilting, rolling accent carried over even into Hellene.

"Praise the gods. You're the ley-mage. Anything else unusual here that I'm not seeing?" Kanmi was now thoroughly twitchy.

Trennus stood, his head popping through the bubble Kanmi had been maintaining, swore, shielding his light-colored eyes, and then squinted as he looked around. And then frowned, and ducked back down into the vehicle to address their guides, "Who did the surveying for this site?"

"Ah . . . don't know, *dominus.* Can take you to site manager, yes?"

They bumped and thumped over the broken ground to a shack built alongside the facility, where they were introduced to the building site manager, a Nahautl man with the improbable last name of Momoztli. Kanmi and Trennus had agreed in advance not to flash their Praetorian badges unless absolutely necessary, and Kanmi took pains to drop Gratian Xicohtencatl's name before they started asking questions.

The site manager tugged at his jade earplugs, rubbed at his nose, and answered, "Yes, it's an experimental new form of ley-platform. Gratian Xicohtencatl developed it, along with the rest of the R&D department at Nahautl Ley and Power. We're already drawing more power than the last two facilities we tried to build, combined. In the six hundred and sixty-seven megawex range, actually." Clear pride in the man's tone, and Kanmi just stared at him for a long moment.

A *wex,* named for Aelfrid Wex, one of the inventors of the steam engine, was a unit of measurement used for both electrical current and ley-energy. It allowed people to demonstrate comparable amounts of energy in both systems, and was commonly defined as one *jaso* a second . . . minus any losses due to energy conversion or transfers.

"I'd like to see the survey reports," Trennus asked, politely, but firmly, and once the manager produced the charts, the Britannian unrolled them on a long table, and began studying them, pushing his glasses up his nose periodically.

Kanmi gave Trennus a none-so-patient look. *"Talk to me, Matrugena."* Back into Hellene, for limited security.

"None of this makes sense," Trennus muttered. *"I think someone made a terrible error in the placement of this facility."*

"They're building it in the wrong spot? Someone's 'investors' are going to be pissed."

Trennus disregarded Kanmi's joke in his agitation and switched to

Latin to include the facility manager in the conversation. "The two previous plants were over here," he jabbed a finger at the map, indicating a location to the east in the jungle, "is that correct?"

"Yes. Both were attacked by rebels and destroyed."

"How?" Kanmi asked, bluntly. "You've got very well-armed guards here in your security forces. Or is that a more recent development?"

Momoztli tugged at his ears, nervously. "First platform, I didn't work on. I'm told it was less well-guarded; this was ten years ago, before the guerillas became quite as prevalent. It was burned to the ground, overnight. Pure arson, just . . . alcohol poured on the floor and a lit match." The Nahautl man shrugged, and leaned back in his chair, his back resting against a metal cabinet filled with circuit boards designed for monitoring the flow of ley-energies. Along one wall was a bank of analog meters and dials, their needles all vibrating slightly. "I did work the second site. We hadn't even finished *building* it when the rebels came, five years ago. Shot ten of our security men, tied all of us engineers up, and set the building on fire." His expression, for all his relaxed pose, was taut. "I was just as glad to hear we weren't going to build on the same damned ground again."

"What's the rebels' problem with the ley-platforms?" Kanmi asked, eying Trennus as the man continued to mutter under his breath in indecipherable Gallic, flipping through the maps in what looked like total agitation.

"The platforms are part of the Nahautl empire," Momoztli said, putting his feet up on the table, forcing Trennus to move around him. "You know, and I know, that ley-power comes from Rome. The rebels don't even care about Rome, except that the garrisons get out and try to chase them down periodically for disturbing the peace. They just don't want any part of Nahautl down here. Nevermind that they've lived under the rule of the *tlatoani* for what . . . eh . . . five hundred, six hundred years now?" The man sounded disgusted. "You can't *reason* with people like that."

Kanmi grimaced. Part of him understood the perspective. His people had been under Rome's boot for nineteen hundred years, give or take a decade or so. And Carthage, destroyed in the Punic Wars and rebuilt by Rome, still gave a token tribute in silver, every year, to its conquerors. "I serve Rome, and I do so willingly and loyally, but sometimes I wonder what the world would be like without Roman armies all across the world, Roman ideas in our minds, Roman words in our mouth, Roman coins in our pockets." He shrugged, tossing it out there, just to see if any of the other men in the shack would, later, perhaps approach him for sounding as if he were open to other ideas. "That being said, sometimes all the reasons people give for doing things are really just excuses." He looked at Trennus. "You're going to be a while with that, aren't you?"

"Yes. Probably. I'm also going to want to get outside and walk the ground." Trennus sounded preoccupied.

Kanmi sighed, and looked at Momoztli. "How about if you take me on a tour of the inside of the facility? I'm going to want to use my own meters, and get a look at how you have this whole thing set up." He managed a grin. "I went to school with Xicohtencatl. University of Athens. I'm not out to steal his patents. I just want to be able to ask him a few intelligent questions when we get back to Tenochtitlan."

For the next two hours, Kanmi clambered all up and down and through the low building, taking measurements at various stations, and jotting them down in a small foolscap notebook with a fountain pen. The problem was, every time he plugged his meter in, he got numbers that didn't make sense to him. This plant was putting out enough energy to power a mid-sized city. The Tholberg coils in the lower levels were huge, and churning with power, behind their shielding, and he drew a rough sketch of the facility in his notebook, frowning slightly. Again, he'd visited a number of these facilities in his career, and he'd never seen this many Tholberg coils in one place before. They were the brainstorm of Niels Tholberg, an eccentric Gothic inventor who'd lived at the same time as Thomas Mauritus, and who'd engaged in a vigorous, overseas debate with the inventor from Novo Gaul, about . . . everything, really. The nature of ley-power, the nature of electricity, methods of transmitting both, methods of transforming each into useable current.

Finally, he stepped out of the swelteringly hot building, and back out into the equally sticky, humid, jungle air, and slapped a mosquito away from his arm, without thinking. He caught one of the guards by the arm, and asked, "Matrugena? The Pict? Where did he go?"

"That way, Master Eshmunazar."

Kanmi trotted off, and found Trennus, his braided hair soaked with sweat, and mud up to his knees, near the edge of the forest, where there was a tall fence, intended to keep out intruders. There were a couple of guards nearby, probably to keep Matrugena from being targeted by any rebels who might be out in the jungle. Kanmi lifted his head and scanned the trees, all too aware of the fact that, five feet back of the fence line, the greenery became an impenetrable wall. He sighed, and gave in to his own paranoia, allowing a gravitic wave to pulse out from him . . . sliding out through the area around him in a sphere. Bouncing back off of trees and rocks and the weapons of the guards with hard *pings*, and from their softer bodies with a quieter sensation as it reflected back to him. It was his own personal version of radar, and Kanmi exhaled when he'd determined that there was no one within about fifty yards of them besides the guards. *"What have you got?"* he asked, again, in Hellene.

Trennus lifted his head; he'd burned, sure enough, pink circles surrounding his eyes and a stripe of red down his nose. *"I have no idea what this facility is running on,"* he said, cutting a glance at the guards. *"but it's not ley-power. They're also being somewhat careful not to let me near the west side of the property. I can feel something buried in the earth there, but I can't get a good read on it."*

"What do you mean, it's not ley?" Kanmi had his own confusing readings from his multimeter, but he wanted to hear this directly from a ley specialist.

Trennus folded his arms across his chest. *"I mean, their original location, four miles east of here, was right atop a ley-line that was in* perfect *resonance with a line directly above it, in the air. It's a rare formation, but perfectly viable. This design, with the low building and the odd mast? I could see it working in that location."* He shrugged. *"There isn't a ley-line here to* tap, *Eshmunazar. The closest is that original one they built on, four miles from here. Close enough that I can work with it, but so far away, that a ley-tap positioned here shouldn't work. And I don't care how experimental it is."* He looked up at the facility's tower, and shook his head. *"To top it off? It doesn't* feel *like ley-power to me. I can't bend this or shape this."*

"I know what you mean. I'd say it feels like electricity, except my multimeter doesn't even register *it on the electrical settings."* Kanmi grimaced. *"It detects as magical force, but yes, it doesn't* feel *like ley-power. Or even sorcery."*

"If I had to put my finger on it, I'd say it feels like a major spirit, working with Veil energies. Except I've never felt anything this powerful before." Trennus shook his head, sweat trickling down his cheeks and into his light beard. He frowned. *"See if you can convince them to let you around to the western side. Can you use that gravitic pulse of yours like ground-penetrating radar?"*

"Not with any degree of definition. I can tell you if something is buried there that's a contiguous mass that's denser or less dense than its surroundings."

"Please do. I have a really bad feeling about this place. My spirits are . . . agitated here."

Kanmi nodded, and went back to the main facility. A short conversation with Momoztli convinced the manager to walk him around the property, personally, as Kanmi took pictures of the walls and the mast. And, on the western wall, he unleashed another gravitic pulse, expecting to find something *denser* than its surroundings. Something mechanical.

As it happened, he found something less dense, in places. As soft, in places, as the bodies of the guards around him, with a harder interior. Again, similar to the guards. Also, about the same size as a man.

Kanmi kept his face still, and chatted lightly with Momoztli for another half-hour about the structure of the mast, the composition of the copper sphere atop it—"Oh, it's just an iron latticework, with copper sheeting over it, no, there's nothing else inside of it, besides cables,"—and then got back into their vehicle to start their long trip back to Tikal proper. Kanmi re-established the protective bubble over the open top of the motorcar, and leaned back in his seat, every jolt and bump hitting his already-abused spine like a prizefighter. And didn't say anything, even in Hellene, on the way back, just sorted through his notes, and kept an eye on their guards . . . guides. Just in case.

They were dropped off back at their hotel, and Trennus, pulling at the shirt he'd completely sweated through, commented, in the lobby, dryly, "I'm going to drink half my own bodyweight in water—"

"Don't. Beer's safer here."

"They don't boil it?"

"I wouldn't trust it, this far south of Tenochtitlan." He snickered. "I boil it myself, just to make sure. Beer, or let me boil the water for you, if you can't manage it yourself."

"Eh. Fire, heat, thermodynamics . . . not a specialty." Trennus grimaced.

"Clean up, we'll brief the propraetor, and we'll get fluids in you. No sense dying of heatstroke here."

"I wonder if the gift-shop . . . such as it is . . . has some sort of ointment for the burns."

"You need to start carrying an umbrella. Or buy suncream."

"I never remember that the stuff *exists*. It only came on the market a few years ago."

"Buy some, you albino polar bear. That, and a pair of smoked-glass lenses will help you in the more southerly latitudes." They got into the elevator, and watched the brass mesh cage doors close. Kanmi leaned against the back wall with a muffled groan.

"*Can we talk yet?*" Tight words in Hellene.

"*No. Wait till we're in the propraetor's room, and we've cleared for devices.*"

"*Bad?*"

"*Could be worse.*"

They cleaned up—one didn't go before the propraetor sweaty, muddy, and otherwise filthy—and then met again, a half hour later, outside of Livorus' room, nodding to Ehecatl, who had guard duty that afternoon. Livorus looked up as they entered, one hand poised above his usual stack of reports and ciphers. "Yes, gentlemen? You have something to report?"

Kanmi closed the door behind them, and sent out an electrical impulse, a quick spike that would damage any delicate listening equipment, and then, lips moving silently, pulled another barrier of air over himself, Livorus, and Trennus. This one was a little different. It still allowed air itself to move through the barrier, so they wouldn't suffocate inside of it . . . but he consciously deadened the movement of sound through it, outside of a few feet. This would, hopefully, defeat any non-electronic snooping devices. "We can talk now," he reported, his voice tight. "We have some interesting information, yes." He looked at Trennus. "But in answer to your foremost question, Matrugena? The reason why your spirits were disturbed at the facility was that there was a body buried under the western foundation. About the size of a man. I couldn't tell the level of decomposition, but there's still soft tissue remaining." He grimaced. "Gods. I can't tell if it was a murder victim, an accidental death that was covered up, or an actual sacrifice, but that facility was built on blood."

"That tallies with my spirits' reactions," Trennus said, taking a seat as Livorus gestured each of them to a chair. "And more. That facility is *not* a ley-energy platform. It's nowhere near any ley-lines, not in the ground or in the air. It's built on solid ground, at least, but my bound spirits say it's fouled by what's in the earth." He grimaced. "They recognize the area as . . . bound." Trennus paused, exhaling. "The concepts are a little difficult to convey, but, they recognize the land itself as the territory of some other spirit, and it's . . . demarcated by some sort of a bargain."

"One bound in blood?" Kanmi asked, sharply.

"Possibly." Trennus grimaced again, tugging at one of his braids in mild agitation. "Manifesting there would put them in danger of the *attention* of that other spirit, so they wouldn't do more than whisper in my ear while we were there. I'll ask a few more questions, see if I can get some more answers, but I can tell you this much, already: the amount of energy being produced by that platform isn't possible just as the result of a blood-bound bargain between someone and a spirit."

Livorus looked ready to speak, but Kanmi cleared his throat. "Ah . . . Matrugena . . . I have an answer for that," the sorcerer said, after a moment, and pulled out his sketchbook, and flipped to the pages on which he'd drawn the Tholberg coils, over a dozen of them, large enough to stretch from floor to ceiling in the two-story building. "I don't think this platform actually produces anything. I think it's a *receiving* station."

"Well, that's all a ley-platform really is. It receives energy from the ley currents, and transmits them onwards. And I know I said that the structure looked like it would be better for pulling from an air-based line, but, there aren't any there, and as I said, the energy doesn't *feel* like ley . . ." Trennus trailed off, as Kanmi lifted a finger at him. "What?"

"It's not ley. We know that. Stop thinking in those terms." Kanmi tapped a finger against the diagrams in his notebook. Hastily sketched as they were, he thought he'd understood the purpose. "Transformers can work in both directions, right? You can both step up energy—electricity, for example—for transmission over wires, and step it back down again, for use locally. If it's in the wrong modality, it'll burn out whatever appliance you're trying to power with it on the far end, so you *have* to step it down." He looked at the transformers he'd sketched. "All of these, I think, are designed to step power *down*, Matrugena. They're taking power from somewhere . . . the *sky*, for all I know . . . and bringing it down into a form that local equipment can use."

Livorus and Trennus both stared at him. "But there are no wires," Trennus objected. "They'd still need to transmit the power elsewhere, to where it would be needed, and that's what they *said* . . . ." He paused, his mind clearly working. "I'm really rusty on this," he admitted, "but Tholberg had some crazy notion of *storing* electricity and loosed ley-energy in the ionosphere, correct?"

"Because that couldn't *possibly* lead to the degradation of the ozone layer or anything like that, and everyone would wind up needing a personal lightning rod on their roof, which doesn't present *safety* issues at all. Not to mention that you'd be expending more energy lofting power up there than you'd ever get back down again," Kanmi said, waving a hand irritably. "But yes, say that wherever they're currently storing . . . whatever this energy is . . . it's a latent charge. This facility draws it down, and then will distribute it . . . gods, for all I know, they plan to *arc* it to similar, smaller facilities all through the area." He rubbed at his face. "That would be a . . . gods-be-damned big lightshow, if it were electricity. But it's not. It's magic, and I don't know what they're using to collect and condense the energy. Or what they're *planning* on using, anyway. I don't see a lot of ley-power in this area, as is. What little there is, gets wired in from north of here, and we're on the very edge of the grid. Hospitals and the governor's house get priority."

Livorus could have ensconced himself and his lictors in the palatial luxury of the governor's house. It said something about the man that he hadn't, and that, more than anything, Kanmi . . . respected. As much as he could respect a patrician, anyway.

Now, the Carthaginian gestured around the hotel room, formulating his thoughts. The elevator in the lobby was a counterweight system, with low power usage; the lamps in this room were all oil ones. Kerosene, in the main; it was distilled from coal-bearing rock. No air conditioning. Little in the way of refrigeration, beyond ice boxes, which was making him leery of eating anything involving meat at meals. Of the *very* few things that were powered . . . phones were, at least minimally, but those could have power transmitted along their existing lines and infrastructure, along with their signal. He shook his head. "They obviously haven't moved into the infrastructure-building phase. Whatever *that* might entail."

"If they used a sacrifice at the site of the initial receiver," Trennus said, his voice suddenly faintly nauseous, ". . . *if* the station is a receiver, as you say, and *if* that body was a sacrifice by the builders, and not . . . a blood-binding by a random unethical summoner . . . then wouldn't they also have to perform similar sacrifices at each additional reception site?"

Livorus stared at them both. "This is all purely speculative, at the moment," he noted, quietly. "You're ranging very far afield, with little evidence."

Kanmi nodded, immediately. It was hard *not* to let his mind go leaping, to find the next most logical step in the chain. But the propraetor was correct. They didn't even know for certain who the body in the grave was yet, or how he or she had died.

"Our first step is to get the *Roman gardia* down here, not the locals," Livorus went on. "And we'll exhume the body as soon as they arrive. But we'll need to do this quietly, I think. Else we'll arrive there and find . . . nothing, I suspect." The propraetor leaned back in his chair, and regarded Kanmi steadily. "Give your dear friend Gratian Xicohtencatl another call . . . hmm. *After* we've gotten the Roman *gardia* down here. The closest available would be in . . . Copan, I think." He stood, and pulled a map from a drawer in the room, unrolling it across the table, ducking back into the silencing field. "Yes. Some three hundred miles south of here. That would have them here inside of a day, rather than taking two days to drive down from Tenochtitlan." Livorus tapped his fingertips together. "That will do. Maintain your sound-proofing, if you would, Eshmunazar, though it will do little good if our phone line here is tapped." He picked up the phone, regarded the buttons at the base, under the rotary dial, which lit up, minimally. He awarded Kanmi an inscrutable look before toggling one of them and asking the front desk to put a call through to the regional switchboard . . . which, in turn, connected him to the *gardia* in Copan.

Kanmi and Trennus stepped out of the room after the phone call had been completed, and Ehecatl, who'd been guarding the door, asked, "So, anything I need to know?"

Kanmi studied the Nahautl lictor for a long moment. "Not for right now," he said, cutting a quick glance at Trennus. He didn't know the man. Didn't know what his loyalties in the region were. Caetia obviously trusted Itztli—it showed in how the valkyrie's face softened a little around him, as it rarely did around Kanmi himself, as yet. But he wasn't sure if he could trust the valkyrie's assessment of the man. Not yet. "Things could get a little interesting in the next day or so, though."

"Interesting? That's usually code for 'don't expect to see your wife and children for a few weeks." Ehecatl raised his eyebrows.

In spite of himself, Kanmi *wanted* to like the man. They were almost the same age, and had many of the same concerns. He hadn't seen his own family in close to a month, himself. "Don't tell anyone you've decrypted the cipher," Kanmi told him, grimacing. "They'll change the codebook on us."

Over dinner in the bar, Kanmi watched in amusement as Trennus did his best not to stare too much at the lovely waitress who brought them their drinks. She wore a traditional Quechan outfit . . . which was to say, she had a colorfully-striped cloth around her hips that served as a very thin skirt . . . and she wore a necklace of turquoise beads that draped down to her tanned, rather pert breasts, the dark rose nipples completely visible, as she wore nothing else. Trennus was doing his level best to look anywhere but at the woman at the moment, a task rendered more difficult by the fact that he was seated, and she kept bending over to ask him questions in lightly-accented Latin. She clearly thought Trennus was *fascinating*, and leaned in over his shoulder to ask him about Britannia as she placed their bowls of water for them. Asked him about the tribal tattoos on his forearms, so different than Nahautl markings, as she handed them their menus.

And then she made the fatal error of asking him what he did for a living, and Trennus, who'd been replying with a little discomfort to begin with, now launched into an enthusiastic and altogether *relieved*-sounding monologue about ley-lines and their traditional uses in Gaul and Pictish Britannia. At which point, the Quechan waitress backed off, hastily, and all but fled towards the kitchen. "Is it *really* that hard to talk to women, Matrugena?" Kanmi asked him, shaking his head. "Find something of *common* interest. Don't just drone on about your personal hobbyhorse." Kanmi couldn't resist the urge to needle the younger man. Trennus was simply so even-keeled, it seemed possible that he'd never react to any taunt, beyond a faint flush. He leaned back now, and put on a professorial tone, raising a finger. "Think of women . . . as spirits. You're the summoner here, after all. The first step, is you get her Name. Then you find out what motivates her. You bargain with her in terms of what that motivation is. And then you get what you want. Simple, yes?" Kanmi arched his brows, wondering if this would finally piece Trennus' equanimity.

All the ley-mage did, infuriating enough, was laugh, sheepishly. "I don't think it quite works like that. Besides, I'm not really looking to *bind* one."

"Oh, but it's far more fun that way." Kanmi smothered his grin behind his glass and a bland tone.

"Wait, what?" Trennus' face, already sunburned, flushed redder.

"I am, after all, a married man." Kanmi nodded, virtuously, and watched the flush spread. "Ah, there's hope for you yet. A dirty mind does lurk behind that façade of innocence."

Trennus coughed. "No . . . I mean, that's not . . ." He looked up at the ceiling. "Gods. I just want to know what to talk *about*. I don't actually care about theater actors, the chariot or motorcar races at the local circus, or any of that."

"Get her talking about herself. That's usually anyone's favorite topic." Kanmi shrugged. "Everyone in existence is an egotist. Figure out what a given woman's interested in, and adopt her concerns. Just don't talk about magic to a non-mage. You'll confuse them and make them feel inferior and angry. It just never goes well." He went out of his way not to talk about his work with his own wife. She knew he was a technomancer. She knew he was a Praetorian. Past that, his work didn't come in the front door. There were *reasons* why there were so many *collegia* for magic practitioners. Magic that hadn't been state-sanctioned or controlled by the priests, centuries ago, had gotten sorcerers and summoners persecuted, until they'd banded together, and managed to convince society to give them the respect due to all professionals—such as doctors and magistrates—and equal rights under the law. Of course, enforcing the law on magic-users was a very, very different thing . . . .

"Or," Sigrun said, from behind Kanmi, dryly, and Eshmunazar sat up, hastily, "you could just wait until you find someone who already shares your interests. There's meeting someone halfway, I'll grant you, but giving up who you are, or pretending to be someone you're not, is never the route of wisdom."

Kanmi grinned up at her. "I've gotten where I am in life precisely by pretending to be who I'm not," he informed her, feeling the *arak* expand warmly through his belly.

Sigrun gave him a tired, but amused look. "That explains why there is always at least one lie in your eyes, Kanmi. Of course, I know that usually, the lies are unimportant ones, and, as often as not, involve the fact that you care far more about everything than you care to let on."

How much do you see with those fucking god-born eyes of yours, anyway? Kanmi felt his own narrow, just for a moment, and then he covered it again. "Unfair advantages aside, Caetia, you and ben Maor should join us. I trust your day's gone better than ours has?"

The pair sat down, both looking freshly showered. "Can you arrange a little privacy?" ben Maor asked, easing his way into the booth.

"After you've both ordered, sure. Will somewhat stand out if the waitress has to sit in your lap to hear you." Kanmi bared his teeth at the younger man. Ben Maor seemed to have more trigger points than

Matrugena did. Matrugena would blush or stammer, but never seemed to get angry. Ben Maor, on the other hand, could be pushed. Could be provoked, but not easily. And of course, Sigrun was quick to irritation, and slow to forgiveness. It was just *interesting* seeing what made each of them react, like putting chemicals in a solvent, and seeing what boiled over in a laboratory beaker.

The Quechan waitress made her way back over to offer menus and drinks, and Kanmi found it enormously amusing to watch ben Maor's eyes track down, and then jerk back up again. "I keep reminding myself," the man noted, as the waitress walked away again, "that I'm not in Judea anymore, and that local customs can be very different."

"Yes, but at least the scenery is pleasant, isn't it?" Kanmi offered, blandly.

That got both Trennus and ben Maor to glance, sidelong, at Caetia. Who, for her part, lifted her eyes and looked directly at Kanmi for a long moment. And then she offered, unsmiling, "I find the jungles lovely, but the ground here is too flat."

"I was actually commenting on the delightful ranges of hills hereabouts," Kanmi told her, blandly.

Sigrun straightened, completely, her spine set like a sword-blade, and her shoulders came back. The gray eyes held, for a moment, no more warmth than a winter storm, and she tipped her head to the side, like a bird, and there was total silence for a long moment. And then she lowered her head back to the menu, and offered, calmly, "It says that the guinea pig was slaughtered today. That should be fresh, Adam."

Ben Maor flipped through his own menu hastily. "It also says, if I'm reading this right, that the fish is raw, but has been 'cooked' in acidic fruit juices." He paused, and then read, "Includes clams, shrimp, and snails."

"So. A salad for you, then?" Sigrun's tone actually held a hint of a tease.

"I'm still looking." His tone was resigned, however. "*Salpicón* . . . Beef, something called adobo, mint, radishes, peppers . . . avocados, tomatoes . . . ."

"I'll try that," Sigrun said, immediately.

"It is, I hasten to point out, a salad." Ben Maor grinned at her suddenly. "I'll admit that meat is involved here, but it *is* a salad."

"Could it be anything else?" Her tone was droll.

"No refrigeration," Kanmi warned, keeping his voice low. "How good *is* god-born digestion, anyway?"

Her faint smile faded. "Oh, spoiled meat won't kill me. It will just make me wish that it would," she admitted, with a sigh, and held up her earthenware cup of water. "Just as the tap water might not be . . . entirely up to Imperial standards."

That actually made Kanmi snort, ruefully. *Points for honesty, at least.* He encircled the table in the field that deadened sound waves in the air, and then flash-boiled the water for them, before removing the energy once more, making the water chill, as he allowed the heat to disperse back into the ambient air. "All right," he said, looking at them again. "What did you all find?"

"Not as much as you did apparently," ben Maor told him. "Livorus and I spent all day in talks with the regional governor."

Sigrun shrugged. "Ehecatl and I made contact with some of the local priests. Even the priests of Chaac have heard of our friend Tototl," she added, between bites. "Also, they do not like him."

"There's a surprise," Kanmi muttered, leaning over his own bowl of spicy vegetable stew.

"Why not?" Trennus asked.

Ben Maor smiled without humor, his dark eyes serious. "The governor had a few things to say about that, actually. Tototl seems to be pushing something he calls pan-Caesarianism. That all the peoples native to the new world should band together, revive their old customs and religious practices. Sounds *just* like the god-born of the Morning Star, doesn't it?"

"Ehecatl was somewhat annoyed by that," Sigrun put in.

"Yes, but that's not exactly new in *any* subject kingdom," Kanmi noted. "I've heard the same line repeated in any number of taverns and street markets in Carthage."

"Yes, but this is slightly different, in that he wants to unite all of the disparate petty kingdoms of both Aquilonis and Australis under one roof," Sigrun replied, her tone grim. "And naturally, he wants that roof to be his own. Nahautl." She picked at her salad with her fork. "Tawantinsuyu has their mountain gods, completely separate from any other religion in the new world. The Quecha have their own gods. Some of their gods overlap with Nahautl's, but just as many don't, and they wouldn't care to be forced into worshipping Nahautl gods, or in Nahautl fashion. And of course, the kingdoms in the north don't follow the same gods at all. Tototl is tip-toeing *just* along the line of the Edict of Diocletian. He's not advocating for conversion so much as . . . integration. But only for the indigenous provinces and kingdoms." She sighed. "It's not so much religion, I think, as politics."

"Throw out Rome," Trennus said, tiredly. "Of course, once you throw out Rome, you have to have someone else be in charge, and why *not* the Nahautl?" The young Britannian looked sober. "He seemed to have the ear of the emperor up in Tenochtitlan. Do you think the emperor endorses this?"

Sigrun shook her head. "Above my pay grade," she replied. "No way to know at the moment, either." She sighed and stretched. Kanmi's eyes went, appreciatively, to the full press of her breasts against the laces of her scoop-necked bodice; she'd been unable to wear a shirt today, thanks to the heat, but hadn't been out much in direct sunlight, the way Trennus had been; as such, she was only lightly pink in some places. The fact that the bodice was also cut short, to allow her freedom of movement in combat, meant that her taut midriff was also exposed above the line of her jeans. It wasn't hard to notice that ben Maor's head actually tipped towards her for a moment as she stretched, rolled her shoulders, dipped her head to loosen the long muscles of her neck . . . or that Adam's gaze lingered on her for longer than he'd focused on the scantily-clad waitress.

"And now that I've eaten, the propraetor wants me to head right back out again and . . . keep watch over your ley-tower that isn't a ley-tower to make sure no one does any digging tonight." Sigrun sighed and finished her stretch.

Trennus' head snapped up. "You're going to drive three hours through the jungle? There are no lights. The road was barely a road during the day, let alone at night." His voice was concerned. "Take one of us with you, at least. Me, anyway. I . . . literally can't get lost." The younger man chuckled, ruefully. "I always know which way magnetic north is, and I can orient myself by the local ley-lines."

Sigrun chuckled. "Actually, Trennus, I was going to, you know . . . ." She pointed upwards. "Fly. It's faster than driving, and they won't notice me, the way they would notice a car arriving."

Trennus flushed again. Kanmi saw a delightful opportunity here, and jumped on it. "Oh. I *see*. Caetia, you absolutely should take Matrugena with you. Just sweep our lad here up in your arms and fly off with him. It'll be *romantic*, and he clearly is smitten with you, as it is." Kanmi fought down the grin as Trennus' mouth dropped open in complete horror. "It could even work out. I've never seen two people more in need of getting laid in my life."

The fact that the temperature dropped ten degrees at the table, Kanmi registered as a local loss of energy in the air, and made him laugh almost as hard as the cold stare he received from Sigrun. Trennus put a fist to his forehead and rubbed there for a moment, his massive shoulders quaking, in between what sounded like an impassioned apology to Sigrun in her native language, to which she returned a few words in the same tongue. Impenetrable as a secret code, and Kanmi could read the irritation growing in ben Maor.

Back in Latin, now, Trennus said, "You'll be three hours away by car. You'll be out of range of the handheld radios."

"Can't be helped." Sigrun didn't look happy about it. Neither did ben Maor, for that matter.

Trennus looked to the side then, as if someone whispered in his ear, and his eyebrows rose. "Ah . . . can you, ah, see spirits, Sigrun?"

"I can see the one hovering beside you at the moment. It's just barely there, isn't it?"

"She's . . . weaker than she should be, yes. What the summoner who last bound her did with her . . . damaged her." Trennus' hands opened and closed back into fists. "She's more than a little scared of going back there, but she says she can go with you, and if you need help, she can travel back to me faster than you can, and let us know that you need help. I'd send the stronger one with you, but my forest friend is keeping watch on Livorus, while watching the other Praetorians for us."

"Any help you send, will still take three hours to get there," Sigrun replied, pragmatically.

"Better than no help at all," ben Maor said, sharply, and with more than his usual force. "I'm not much of one for employing spirits, but this sounds like a better option than no communications at all."

Sigrun raised her hands in surrender. "All right. You convinced me."

Trennus nodded and pulled out his notebook, writing something down on a scrap of foolscap with a fountain pen in Gothic runes, pushing it across the table to Sigrun, and removing one of the amulets he wore around his neck, holding it out to her. She mouthed the word there, and hesitated before accepting the amulet. "I thought this was how your spirits could locate you."

"This one can locate me with or without the amulet. The amulet's a conduit for her, though."

Sigrun pulled the leather cord over her neck, and Kanmi offered, brightly, "See? Now he's even giving you *gifts*."

The god-born woman awarded Kanmi a glacial stare and tossed two silver coins on the table to cover her meal. "Thank you, Trennus. I appreciate the help. Let us hope that I will not need it." She stood, which forced ben Maor to stand to let her out of the booth, and headed for the door.

Kanmi released the sound dampening field to call after her, "You're only proving my point, you know!"

At that point, Matrugena excused himself, too, and Kanmi was left with ben Maor, who leaned his elbows on the table, steepled his fingers, and said, dryly, "You know, I asked you to be more of a team player."

"And expressing a sense of humor *isn't* going to make me more a part of the team? Lighten up, ben Maor."

"Sense of humor is one thing. Embarrassing people is something else."

"That was *light* compared to the kind of jokes they'd see in the Legion, foreign levies or otherwise, and you know it." Kanmi snickered. "If Trennus had a locker, I'd be pinning pictures of naked women to it by now. That boy needs to relax in the worst way."

"I'll agree with that, but don't make Sig a part of the joke."

Kanmi's eyebrows went up. "I think she can take care of herself."

"Exactly the problem. You push her too hard, and you're going to find out what your own teeth taste like." Ben Maor gave him an amused look.

"What is life without risk? But, out of pure respect to you, noble leader, I'll take it under advisement." Kanmi finished his water, bared his teeth in Adam's direction, and headed for bed, himself.

Iunius 7-9, 1954 AC

When she flew, Sigrun instinctively kept a bubble of controlled wind around her, to shield her eyes and face from the tremendous airflow that gusted around her when she hit her top speed. She'd always been able to control wind—localized gusts that let her slap away arrows, for example. She had no real way to measure her top speed, however, besides counting mile markers on an Imperial highway and trying to judge it against a pocket watch, but she suspected that she could do better than three hundred miles an hour if she really needed to *push*.

A spirit flew alongside her this time, however. Its name was, according to the piece of paper Trennus had handed Sigrun, *Lassair*. And the creature made Sigrun slightly uneasy. It was a wisp of air and fire, the dull red glow of a banked coal at the bottom, stretching up into gossamer-fine white tendrils at the top . . . but sometimes, it distorted and assumed a faintly humanoid shape, like a ghostly woman. All white, with what looked to be blood-red eyes . . . and then it vanished again, back into that barely-perceptible shimmer. It floated along beside her as she flew, keeping pace easily. "Can you understand me when I speak?" Sigrun asked it, in Cimbric, more or less to test it.

Yes. Words are thought. I understand the thought, not the words. The words were cool flame inside her mind, and Sigrun frowned, understanding that this had been, once, an elemental spirit of fire. There was a warmth to Lassair's presence that was more than merely destructive, however; it was life-giving. But weak. Very, very weak.

"May I know the nature of the bargain between you and Trennus?" Sigrun asked, cautiously.

One of the stipulations of the contract is that we cannot speak of it, except if it would cause either of us damage to remain silent, or unless someone has already ascertained the nature of it.

Sigrun grimaced. *That doesn't sound precisely promising.*

I assure you, Stormborn, that I will not allow any harm to come to him. I am bound to him, and he to me. He saved me. I will, someday, return the favor.

"Do you hear everything that everyone thinks?" Sigrun's discomfort was only increasing.

No. You are bound to a god. You wear the amulet, and thus, I can hear you quite clearly at the moment. Trennus, I can hear, always. Steelsoul and Emberstone, sometimes, if I focus. Emberstone is not bound to anyone. Serpentshadow is not bound. Steelsoul is bound, but not . . . tightly. Those with quiet voices, gray souls . . . are much harder. I can make their words evident to Trennus if I work to do so. The spirit's use of Trennus' human name was evidently deliberate.

Sigrun breathed a little easier after that. The spirit was, for the moment, fairly limited in what it . . . no, *she*; it was definitely a she . . . could do.

After that, she spent the bulk of the night perched high and uncomfortably in a jungle tree, overlooking the ley-platform's compound, with a good view of the western wall. Half that night, she spent slapping away mosquitoes, moths, spiders, ants, confused tree-frogs, and the occasional startled bat, while Lassair hovered in air beside her. The area made her skin *crawl*, and Lassair shared her unease. *This is a bad place*, Lassair whispered to her, as the stars crept in their course overhead.

"Yes. It is. There is *power* here, power without *direction*, without . . . *intention* . . . but there's also a sense of . . . will?" Sigrun shuddered. She'd seen the results of an experimental psychotherapy process once, called lobotomization. Somehow, this energy felt like the blank, soulless stare of one of the patients who'd been given this treatment. But with an undercurrent of darkness. *Is this the trap my sister spoke of? Am I about to be tricked or captured? No. There is no fate. There is only wyrd and the choices along the road. The choices of others shape that road, but we have the ability to decide our own fates. If only, sometimes, in choosing how and when and where and with whom we will die. I cannot let her affect my thinking or my decisions.*

As dawn broke, Sigrun's eyes burned with exhaustion, but she still spotted a group of men tromping over to the western wall, with shovels. "Lassair? It's time for you to go get Trennus and the others. I think I can divert these good people for three hours or so."

I do not need to leave you. Trennus can hear my voice from here. I will assist you, however I may. Lassair flickered uncertainly. *I do not know how, though.*

"Just . . . watch my back." Sigrun slid off her tree branch. "And have Trennus go to my room and get my regalia, would you? It's dawn on a Tiwesdæg, and I feel underdressed." She hovered in the air, still concealed among the branches of the trees, some eighty feet above the ground. From her angle, she could see through the branches as the workers began to dig.

Her spear hadn't left her hands all night, and its weight was a comfort now. *All right. You have all very considerately built the region's biggest lightning rod for me, and it's even grounded. Let's see if it can handle electricity as well as whatever it was designed to conduct. If nothing else, I might be able to melt down the transformers, if they're not rated for the load.*

Sigrun looked up at the sky, which had already begun to cloud over, throughout the night, and felt the first cool spatters of rain against her face, smiling as if she'd just received a lover's kiss. The winds began to howl, tearing at the branches around her, and flocks of birds rose, panicked, into the air, as Sigrun reached up for the clouds with her will . . . .and brought the lightning down.

The thunder was ear-shattering, and followed so close on the heels of the flash of brilliant white light, that they were almost indistinguishable. The men on the ground shouted in consternation, looking up at the sky in clear panic, as blue-white arcs of electricity ran down the frame of the conductive mast. But they didn't stop; they kept digging. *Need a little more convincing?*

She brought it down again, and again, and the third time, the copper sphere atop the mast actually fractured in half. Random electrical arcs sparked out, starting spot fires in the jungle and around the entire compound, and the men finally dropped their shovels and ran for cover, shouting to each other. "I don't suppose," Sigrun called above the banshee wail of the storm that was starting to roll in, "that you can understand what they're saying?" She couldn't summon rain, or anything other than very localized winds. That it *was* raining, in addition to the lightning she was generating overhead was strictly a coincidence.

I . . . think they are afraid that their god punishes them?

"Oh, this should be interesting."

It was a long three hours. Sigrun knew that the storm would slow the others down in reaching her, but her only other alternative was landing in the compound and standing atop the supposed grave site and fighting all comers, on her own. She could *do* that . . . but the problem was, she'd probably wind up killing all of them. Not to mention, wind up taking a few musket or pistol balls along the way, and bullets *hurt*. *Not an optimal solution, as Livorus would likely say. It leaves us with no one alive to answer questions.*

So she used lightning and belief to her own advantage, and every time the men looked apt to come back out and start digging again, she brought the lightning back down again.

But it was with a surge of relief that she spotted the line of motorcars approaching the gates, all covered with special tarps against the rain. "Are those our people?"

Yes. Trennus is with them. Joy in the spirit's voice, and relief, which surprised Sigrun mightily. She watched as the various guards tried to deny the vehicles access . . . and smiled a little, tightly, as the Roman *gardia* exited their motorcars and showed their identification badges. She swooped down for a landing, just off the side of the road, in the dense trees, and pushed her way through the vines onto the muddy track, one more figure lost in the confusion, and made her way to the propraetor's car. A hand opened the door from the inside, and, soaked to the skin but not shivering, Sigrun slipped inside. "Baal's *teeth*," Kanmi swore at her, and handed her a towel, "did you try to drown yourself?"

"Yes. Slowly. One drop at a time." Sigrun began to dry off. "Did you bring my regalia?"

Trennus, in the front seat, hoisted a bag over the center console back to her. Sigrun grabbed it eagerly, and pulled out at *least* the feathered cloak. The armor and everything else, Tyr could forgive her for, but the cloak was important. "I've always meant to ask," Adam asked, quietly, "why it's *swan* feathers?"

Sigrun fastened it at her throat. "*Valkyrie* means *chooser of the dead*. But our oldest name was *swan-maiden*." She shrugged. "It is said that in order to take the skies, we once changed shapes into swans or ravens." She took the amulet from around her neck, and handed it back to Trennus, with a word of quick thanks.

"Like the raven-maidens who attend on the Morrigan," Trennus said, his eyes unfocused for a moment.

"Yes. Once, long ago, your people and mine were probably one."

Kanmi, in the meantime, had fallen against the side of the car with silent laughter. "A *swan*," he finally gasped out. "The bird that waddles around on land and honks and hisses."

Sigrun gave Kanmi a resigned look. "Yes," she replied. "Precisely so."

"You're a goose-maiden." Kanmi gasped out again, still laughing.

"On the whole, I think I preferred the chicken-suit joke," she murmured, looking up at the tarp that served as a ceiling, and the vehicle bumped forward through the gates.

The next several hours were very busy. The civilian guards, hired to protect the site, had been busy putting out spot fires throughout the whole complex, and half the Tholberg coils inside had been melted to slag. Enough remained, however, for Kanmi to get good, solid, black and white pictures of the apparatuses. Sigrun was able to confirm for the *gardia* that no one in the uniforms of the security force had been among those doing the digging; this limited the amount of questioning and processing required.

The guards were therefore told to put up their weapons and go to their barracks while the gardia were on site, and all of the engineers, and the site manager, were shackled to pieces of equipment inside the main building for safekeeping and questioning. Even so, the Praetorians and Roman *gardia* were very busy indeed, as they tried to ascertain if people had known was down there, what they'd been told they were digging for (a leaking water pipe had been the tale, apparently), and who had given the order to start digging.

It turned out that the site manager, Momoztli, had given the order, and thus, he received the most intensive questioning, under the direction of Livorus himself. All he would say was that he'd received a phone call from Gratian Xicohtencatl overnight, telling him not to worry the workers, but that there was a possibility that there might have been a ground shift that would have opened a fissure filled with ethylene gas under the facility, from a cavern deep below the earth. That if the gas wasn't vented, they'd run the risk of the facility eventually exploding.

Sigrun looked over at Trennus and Kanmi for that one. She already could see the lie in Momoztli's eyes, and Trennus, actually, was the one who snorted. "There's no cavern below this site on any of the geological survey maps," he said, with surprising sharpness. "It's all limestone around here, so there's a chance of bubbles in the terrain, I'll grant you . . . ." Trennus half-closed his eyes, and, after a minute, added, "I just don't *feel* any."

Livorus looked at the site manager, who was now sweating, and flicked a glance at the two *gardia* members in the room with them. "I'm going to leave you with these two upstanding gentlemen," the propraetor said, austerely. "And when I return, I hope that you will have reconsidered your intransigence."

In the next two hours, the *gardia* did, in fact, recover a body from the west side foundations; it showed about six months of decomposition, which suggested it had been placed here at exactly the same time that construction had begun. That was enough to haul in everyone who'd worked at the site at least six months ago for a stint in the local cells.

Momoztli looked pale when he saw the corpse for the first time, and began to babble, incessantly, that he hadn't *known* what was down there. Livorus gave Sigrun a glance, and took her out of the room, into a small controls area, with the others. Most of the panels had suffered scorching damage, which Kanmi was muttering about in annoyance, as it made his job of ascertaining what the devices had been meant to do, that much harder.

"Truth?" Livorus asked her, as the other's heads came up.

She rocked a hand back and forth. "I suspect he didn't know what was down there until he received the phone call this morning," Sigrun murmured. "There's fear in his eyes, sir. Fear and lies." She shrugged. "He knows what the penalty for murder is. He doesn't wish to face either the gallows or a gladiator. He should be well-motivated to speak the truth now, but still, he fears."

"Then we'll need to pull in Gratian Xicohtencatl for questioning as well, as soon as possible. Kanmi, belay that phone call to him."

"Haven't even had a chance to think about getting to a telephone, sir. There's too much equipment here that I really need a trained ley-engineer to understand. Matrugena's good, but he's a ley-*mage*. This is all . . . wiring and conductivity and machinery." Kanmi sounded harried.

Livorus sighed. "Too much to do, and not enough bodies to do it. We'll need to establish that this was actually *murder* first, and not just a work accident and cover-up, however."

"Which will give Xicohtencatl all the more time to flee, if he's going to." Sigrun rubbed at her eyes, irritably.

Livorus patted her upper arm, lightly, with a thin, dry hand. "I'll have the gardia in Tenochtitlan begin surveillance." He snorted. "Of course, it seems that our communications with the gardia in Copan were also compromised, as these people here began digging about two hours after I ordered the Copan *gardia* to come here. Something about which I intend to have a conversation with the regional governors."

By the end of the day, they hauled fifty men and one corpse back to Tikal, something that had the locals all hanging out of their balcony windows to stare, and which clearly agitated the Nahautl gardia. Not only were Imperial *gardia* being employed inside a local jurisdiction, but the local governor was being overridden by a propraetor. Toes were, in fact, being stepped on, with great abandon.

Two days later, however, the medical examiner had her report. She was a lovely Nahautl woman in her mid-fifties, with iron-gray hair tied back from her face, jade earplugs, and a white doctor's robe over her colorful blouse and skirt. "I'm glad you could all be here for the autopsy results," she told them as they entered the chill morgue room; it was located in the hospital, and, as such, had some of the only stable ley-power in the region, though Sigrun could see the incandescent bulbs wavering up and down as they burned. "If I hadn't seen it for myself, I wouldn't have believed it, and I want as many witnesses as possible to corroborate my report." She sounded uneasy.

"Dr. Yolotli, please. Just speak the truth, as you understand it." Livorus, in spite of the smells in the autopsy room, could have been at a society function, complete with sparkling Gallic wine and canapés.

The medical examiner sighed, and put several X-rays up on a board, turning the backlights on with quick flicks of the switches . . . and then pulled back the cover from the body. Everyone in the room had seen death before. Sigrun knew that Adam had fought *ghul*. Trennus' dossier said that he had, as well. Neither of them flinched. Ehecatl and Kanmi had both seen active combat, but neither had often seen advanced decomposition, apparently. Kanmi turned his head away, grimacing for a moment, and then swallowed and looked back.

There shouldn't have been a lot left; it was a wet climate here, and though the body had been buried eight feet below the earth, out of range of scavengers, decomposition, heat, humidity, and insets should have had their toll. There was, however, a *surprising* amount of skin and flesh left, tight-wrapped to the bones, as if the body had, against all logic or probability, been *mummified*, and had turned a dark mahogany color. "How?" Livorus sounded intrigued. "The body should be nothing more than bones, if it has truly been there for six months, in this climate."

"That's our first mystery, but it's at least explicable," the medical examiner replied. "In ancient times, in Britannia and other northern countries, human sacrifices were thrown into peat bogs there." She glanced at Trennus, who held up his hands in a *don't look at me* fashion. "The water of these bogs is sufficiently acidic as to prevent decomposition, and the skin was tanned in the process, like leather, becoming a seal against further decomposition. The water runoff from our swamps is slightly acidic as well, and I suspect that whatever energies may have been leaking from the ley-plant may have facilitated the process." Dr. Yolotli lifted a file folder, and handed them a sheaf of pictures. "This first, the full body image, was this body when we first brought it in. Please note the lack of any damage to the torso, the lack of incisions, cuts, anything of that nature." She pointed to various salient points on the body as she spoke. "Our subject is a male, approximately age twenty-eight, of Nahautl or Quechan ancestry — though I tend to believe Nahautl, from the extensive tattooing and earplugs."

Ehecatl nodded, grimly, looking at the body. "He was a Jaguar warrior," he said, suddenly. "He has the jaguar tattoos on his legs, the paws and claws on the undersides of his feet, as I do. This was an elite soldier."

Dr. Yolotli looked up, alertly. "He certainly was in good physical health at the time of death. His teeth were in excellent condition . . . but his dental impressions are not, however, on file, at least, not locally. I had taken this to mean that he belonged to a tribe that clings to the old ways, out in the hills."

Ehecatl shook his head, firmly. "No one but Jaguar warriors receive *these* tattoos. The ones on the soles of our feet, in particular, aren't often seen. Anyone who tries to wear them, without *being* one . . . has to deal with offended Jaguar warriors who might take exception to having *our* markings worn by an outsider." His expression was taut, and he bent slightly to pull up his trouser leg, and shucked a shoe, in order to show identical markings there. "You can ask for a records search on dental impressions from the Jaguars' main facility in Tenochtitlan. Should narrow the search for you."

Pulling dental matches was not an overnight process, even in highly urban areas like Rome. The paper descriptions and X-rays weren't kept in some singular document repository, and each dentist's office was responsible for cooperating with law enforcement requests in their own time. This still generally required a local law enforcement office to put out a request to neighboring jurisdictions, transmit the description of the dental work, and age and sex of the body to be identified, and wait for hundreds of people to go through thousands of files. Such a search could be sped up if there were known missing persons . . . and an elite solider who'd gone absent without leave would surely be one of those. This would speed the paper chase, as would Livorus' weight. They couldn't expect much more than this, however; it had, after all, only been two days since the body had been found.

"Go on," Livorus said, putting the pictures back down again. "What's the cause of death?"

"There is no damage to the skull," Dr. Yolotli said, with precision. "No signs of blunt-force trauma to incapacitate this person. There are ligature marks at wrist and ankles, indicating that he was a prisoner at some point." She held up a hand to stay the questions on everyone's lips. "Remember, that there were *no incisions* on the body when it was brought in. I took an X-ray of the chest cavity," she pointed up at the screen, "and noted that there was something missing." She paused. "His heart."

Sigrun's head snapped up. The X-ray was a mass of shadows to her; she couldn't read it. "I then proceeded to make the usual Y-shaped incision," Dr. Yolotli went on, "and, indeed, there is no heart in this body. It was removed, by some method that left no visible marks on the sternum, the ribs, or the surrounding tissue. The blood vessels around the heart do not look to have been cut, either. If anything, the tissue is striated, and deformed. As if the heart were *pulled out*, still beating, through the surrounding tissue." Dr. Yolotli shook her head, clearly rattled. "This should not be possible, by any method."

A chill uncoiled across Sigrun's shoulders, and in spite of herself, for one of the few times in her life, she actually shivered. Livorus sighed. "Magic, then."

"Magic," the medical examiner agreed. "And murder."

"When the two are found together in this part of the world, a third word is usually involved," Livorus murmured. "Sacrifice."

"I cannot speak to that, *dominus*. His head was not removed for display on a skull-rack—"

"Well, that *would* be rather obvious," Kanmi muttered, under his breath.

"—which was traditional throughout the region for sacrificial victims, particularly ones taken in battle. And if he truly was a Jaguar warrior . . . being taken in battle is the only way he would likely have been made prisoner." The doctor wrung her hands a bit. "Which means they could have kept him long enough for the wounds to heal, or—"

"Or someone dosed his *pulque* with poppy-juice," Ehecatl muttered. "Wouldn't be the first time someone was rolled in a taverna that way." His expression was dark. "But if he *was* sacrificed . . . . he was the highest sacrifice that could be offered. A strong warrior, in the prime of his life."

"And if it was done to somehow derive the energy at the platform site," Trennus said, suddenly switching to Hellene, *"that suggests that we may have broken whatever bargain that the performer of the sacrifice wanted to make. That means that another death might be owed. And more victims, suitable strong warriors, will need to be found."*

Adam grimaced. "Is there any way of telling *who* did this, or what?" he asked, in Latin, addressing the doctor, directly.

She shook her head rapidly. "I don't even know where to start," she admitted, frankly. "This is not my area of expertise."

"Preserve the body," Livorus told her, briskly. "I think we have enough here to bring in both Xicohtencatl for questioning . . . and high priest Tototl as a. . . hmm. Consultant. We'll let that be the official reason, for the moment, anyway." He waved a little. "Let us make it so, shall we?"

Iunius 10, 1954

There was a knock at the connecting door between Adam's room and Sigrun's, just before dawn on dies Veneris . . . Frigedæg. Adam struggled upright in the sheets, reaching for his gun on the nightstand, until he realized what the noise actually was. "Yes?" he called across the room.

"Adam," Sigrun's voice was apologetic, "Sorry to wake you, but Livorus just got the call. The Jaguar warriors got back to the medical examiner late last night with a possible match. Quauhtli Citlali, a young forward *optio*, apparently, or whatever the local equivalent rank is. Went missing seven months ago while on leave down here with family."

Harah. "By family, do you mean—"

"Wife and two children, yes. Ehecatl's close to cutting open his hand and swearing blood vengeance. And I don't blame him." Her voice held a grim note. "Get dressed. There's more."

"It's not even five antemeridian yet. What else could there be?" Adam started dressing anyway.

"Local *gardia*—all Nahautl, of course—up in Tenochtitlan can't find Xicohtencatl and Tototl. Get dressed, I can't shout all of this through a door."

Adam grinned, and prevented himself from telling her she could open the door from her side any time she wanted, and in any state of dress she preferred. She probably wouldn't be terribly amused, and this wasn't really the time for jokes.

The meeting in the propraetor's room found most of them grainy-eyed and nursing cups of local coffee. Livorus himself looked, as usual, well-rested and calm. Adam had no idea how he did it. "Let's go through what we know, thus far," the propraetor said. "We know that the various civil authorities cannot seem to find either Gratian Xicohtencatl or Tlilpotonqui Tototl."

"I'm not surprised about them not being able to find Tototl,"

Kanmi muttered. "He's probably god-born. There are people who'll protect god-born just on that basis, let alone the political power he has." The Carthaginian rotated a rectangular piece of paper in his fingers, rapidly. "Xicohtencatl, though . . . I wouldn't have thought he *could* hide worth a damn."

Ehecatl's lips pulled from his teeth for a moment. "What do you remember about his skills?" he asked the sorcerer.

Kanmi snorted. "He's a traditionalist, when it comes to his actual sorcery. Which is to say he's an elementalist. He didn't take the courses that I did, in physics, in thermodynamics, any of it. As far as raw sorcery goes, he's fine with there being four or five elements, as if we've learned nothing about the way the universe works since Aristotle walked the earth. A hundred or more elements in the periodic table are just too confusing for the traditional mindset. Traditionalists don't care why things work, just that they do." He held up a hand when Ehecatl opened his mouth to reiterate the question, and went on, "That being said? He's damned good at the elemental specialties, particularly fire, as best I recall. It's a typical specialization for someone who expects to go into military work. I never really sparred with him, but I'd expect rapidly-expanding bursts of flame that he can land anywhere he wants, with very good accuracy—"

"By rapidly-expanding, do you actually mean *explosive*?" Adam asked, quickly. "Like a grenade?"

"Yes. Almost exactly. Problem is, to create a rapidly expanding exothermic event once reaching a target area, you need to start with something that has explosive potential—a thimbleful of black powder, in a cloth bag works nicely—and then you can just expand the yield of the explosion . . . or you have to pull all the ambient energy in the environment together and . . . it's tedious and the yield you get is more just . . . a wash of fire than anything really damaging." Kanmi grimaced. "Now, typically, this isn't all they can do. And he's also a technomancer. Which means he *should* be carrying batteries, like I do, for stored energy. He might do things as disparate as a stream of fire arrows, or . . . engulf someone, head to toe, in a pillar of flame. Depending on his skill, power, and resources, he might be able to get that fire up to about seven hundred degrees. Enough heat to melt lead, at least." Kanmi sighed. "The good news is . . . ."

"There is good news in this?" Sigrun asked, raising her eyebrows. Adam could see a shudder go through her, where she leaned against a wall, her arms crossed. He remembered that she had mentioned that fire hurt more than any other kind of wound, and was the slowest wound to heal.

Kanmi grimaced. "Somewhat. He's going to be powerful, but his training has . . . limitations. I've been trained in . . . concepts. Physics. Whatever he can do, I can *undo*, just by re-directing the energy." He rubbed at his face. "It's . . . very difficult to put in layman's terms."

"You're more powerful than he is." Ehecatl shrugged.

"No. Not more powerful. More *flexible*. I'm not limited to a half-dozen things I've rehearsed a thousand times. I understand the systems that make the universe work, and I use them." Kanmi sighed. "It's easier to show than to tell, but we don't have time for this right now." He looked over at Trennus. "Suffice to say, Matrugena and I both have resources that a traditionally-oriented sorcerer lacks. But Xicohtencatl is a technomage, as well." He flipped the card around in his fingers again.

"What *is* that?" Sigrun asked, pointing.

"This? His business card, if you can believe it. I tried calling the number this morning. No answer. Not exactly a surprise."

"Your spirits couldn't track him using it, could they?" Sigrun asked Trennus.

Both mages' eyes widened. "No," Trennus said, "but that's a very good idea. In this case, it's just not personal enough of a belonging."

Sigrun held out her hand. "May I see it?"

"Be my guest." Kanmi held it out to her, indifferently. Adam moved to look at it over her shoulder, and shook his head. Red-embossed lettering on a white background of cardstock, with a black and yellow bumblebee perched in the corner.

"Why a bee?" Adam asked.

"I think his house name means 'angry bumblebee,' or some damned thing. He wears a bee-shaped clasp for his cloak, too." Kanmi shrugged.

For some reason, Sigrun's hand was shaking as she passed the card back to Kanmi. "So," she said, rubbing at her eyes, "we have no way to know where they are right now. But we have every indication that they are both guilty of *something*. Innocent people rarely hide." She tapped the side of her fist against the wall in frustration. "And no leads here."

"We do have other things yet to attend to," Livorus reminded them all. "Dealing with the local rebels, which was Governor Dioscuri and Emperor Achcauhtli's direct request to me. These two can't hide forever. Sooner or later, they'll be sniffed out. For now? Everyone, dismissed."

The various lictors turned to file out, and, in the hall, Adam caught Sigrun's elbow, lightly. "What's wrong?"

"What do you mean?"

"Something about that card is bothering you."

Sigrun shook her head. "It's . . . nothing." Under her breath, and angrily, she muttered, "There is no fate. There is only *wyrd*."

Adam stared at her. "All right. If you feel like talking about it . . . you know where I am, right?"

That got him a surprised smile, which actually lit up her face and eyes. "Always."

Chapter VIII: Secrets

In the modern Empire, there are three forms of subject state: two of them are provinces, and the third is the so-called 'subject kingdom.' Almost every subject state that exists today has moved back and forth from one status to another. Let us examine these terms for greater clarity.

The first type of province is directly governed by Rome. Local government barely exists. Gaul, Britannia, sections of Germania, Hellas, Byzantium, Carthage, and other regions have been provinces; Gaul remains one. Carthage was turned into a province at the end of the Second Punic War, when their line of kings was severed. Egypt, for all that it was a kingdom, where the rule of the pharaohs extended back for thousands of years, was first a subject kingdom, and then a province, a status it retains to this day. The entire continent of Australia, for example, is currently a Roman province.

Some provinces attain a degree of autonomy and self-rule. They retain a Roman governor, who helps regulate all imperial-level matters, such as imperial taxes, the levying of troops, and diplomacy with neighboring nations, but can govern themselves internally more or less as they wish. Novo Gaul and Nova Germania went through periods in which they had local tribal leaders for their various cities-kings, not to put too fine a point on it-but also had town hall meetings, or, in Gothic parlance, "Things." This led both provinces to adopt direct democracy for city and regional governance. Judea, by way of comparison, was a theocracy, run by its priest caste, when it was first taken in hand by Herod. When the Judeans rebelled, and refused him as a king, Caesarion the God-Born allowed them a degree of autonomy, and permitted their theocracy to be reinstated . . . so long as they obeyed the laws of Rome, and their appointed Roman governor. The priests chafed, and there were periodic minor insurrections for about three hundred years, but by and large, it has been a stable province since. Judea has, over the centuries, taken on more of a republican form of government, adopted from Roman norms. The landed elites, such as priests and rabbis, and professionals like teachers and engineers, form a senatorial class; the remainder of the population comprises their plebiscite. They have some interest in democracy; they maintain that every citizen, male and female alike, must serve in their army, for example, and they permit women to volunteer for front-line positions. To call this nation a 'subject kingdom' is clearly laughable.

The term subject kingdom is a product of a different era, and a term that has not been altered to subject nation or subject state in the nomenclature of the Empire partially because reprinting 750,000 different government documents, laws, and periodicals that include the term would be prohibitively expensive. That another generic term has not entered popular parlance is possibly the result of laziness of thought on the part of most speakers of Latin, but the term also reflects a genuine historical confusion as to what these regions actually are. For again, many of them have changed their status over time.

In simple terms, a subject nation may be one of two things: The first is an ally, which pays tribute and homage to Rome, but retains the right to govern itself. They engage in diplomacy with all nations on their own terms, set their own taxes, and negotiate tariffs independently. Examples of this form of subject nation include the Iroquois Confederacy and the Comanche Alliance in Caesaria Aquilonis.

The second type of subject nation is closer to provincial status. They retain local authority like an autonomous province, but also have much more active Roman governors. By and large, they are considered to be more 'distant' from Rome, and their citizens tend to have fewer rights as Romans. They are typically strong nations who were brought under the governance of Rome by the sword or by treaty.

The distinction between 'subject nation' and 'province' is often highly politicized, and a matter of perspective. A Carthaginian nationalist will likely refer to his native region as a 'subject nation,' implying that his people are not a part of Rome, and that they are subjugated under the rule of Rome. In terms of how Rome's laws describe Carthage, including its holdings in Tyre, each region is considered a province of the Empire, with Roman governors in each of the various cities and regions. Carthage has never won the self-rule of provinces like Judea or Britannia . . . . but Carthaginians, as provincials, have more rights and protections under law than relative newcomers to the Empire, such as the Quechan provinces.

As a counter-example, consider Britannia. It was once a province, but has petitioned for, and been given, autonomous provincial status. They retain a Roman governor to represent the whole island, and remain a part of the Empire, but while they have dozens of petty kings, they have no 'high king' or 'emperor' of their own. These petty kings assemble once a year for a Congress; laws are then passed and judges and magistrates are appointed for the next year. Cases that have proven insoluble for local magistrates are presented before a high court, which holds power for one month a year. This is not so much monarchy, as a sort of feudalism, though Britannia, like Novo Gaul and Nova Germania, has outlawed the custom of thralldom.

Regions like Nahautl, Quecha, and Tawantinsuyu face similar problems of terminology. All three are ruled by Roman governors. Tawantinsuyu came into the Empire purely by treaty, and thus has a status between that of a province and an allied subject nation. Nahautl began paying tribute some six hundred years ago, and moved from a tribute-paying ally to formal subject kingdom, to its current status, which is closer to that of a province. Quecha was repeatedly chastised by Rome for its bellicose behavior towards its neighbor, Tawantinsuyu, and was annexed by force three hundred years ago. All three have been invested in heavily by Rome, with the extension of ley-power and other such technology, and their citizens are accorded Roman rights-and protections.

We would like to propose the formulation of an alternate term: affiliated nation. This would be used to describe nations that hover between the status of subject nations and provinces, and would remove the confusion which dogs the issue in all scholarly journals and governmental publications. This might have the added benefit of improving relations between Rome and these affiliated nations, since they would no longer be forced into an unduly subordinate role, and would not be trapped in some lingering shadow of times past.

-Erastus Collonus, "Sociolinguistic Problems in World Politics," in *The Roman Journal of Political Science*, vol. LXXVI, Spring, 1953, pp. 57-58, University of Lorium Press.

Iunius 11, 1954 AC

The engine's roar was a dull and constant drone. The smell of its exhaust was foul, and tore at the lining of Adam's throat. No sight; the canvas bag over his head let him breathe, but even peering down at himself or the floor wasn't an option, unlike a mere blindfold. His hands were tied behind him, with rope, and every bounce and jostle over the rutted, uneven road threw him into Sigrun, with not much hope of holding his balance. "Sorry," he muttered, for the twelfth time, as his shoulders slammed into hers.

He knew they were in the back of a kerosene-powered truck, one that had a raised bed, slab-like sides, and a canvas tarp thrown over the top to keep the sun and the rain out. He'd seen that much before their captors had pulled the bag down over his head. He'd even recognized the type of vehicle . . . it was a hundred years and more out of date. Kerosene-fueled motorcars were kept in *museums* in Judea; he found it almost difficult to believe that the damned thing ran.

"At least the others will be able to track us by the sound, right?" he told her, above the sound of the engine, trying to keep their spirits up.

"If not that, then by the smell," she agreed, her voice tight.

He tried to edge his head closer to hers, risking—and receiving—a direct clash as his forehead slammed into her temple as they hit another bump in the road. Adam swore under his breath, and finally got close enough to ask, more or less in her ear, through the bags that covered their heads, "*Can you get free of your ropes?*" This, in Hellene. He didn't trust his incredibly poor Gothic for passing messages in the back of the truck.

"*Yes. Not a problem. But we should wait and we see before we make any sudden moves, yes?*"

"*Agreed.*"

"*They took your weapon, correct?*" Sigrun's choice of words was very careful.

"*They found the pistol at my back, yes.*" He didn't know if their captors spoke Hellene, and he wasn't about to volunteer that they'd missed the smaller revolver in an ankle holster.

"*Ah. Understood.*"

Impossible to tell how much time had passed as they bounced and jostled, sweated and seethed. Adam pulled at his wrists, trying to work some sort of slack into the sisal, but knew, grimly, all he was managing at the moment was to rub his wrists raw. Like the ligature marks on the tea-dark skin of the half-mummified man they'd pulled out of the earth under the ley-power station.

A mantra began to beat in the back of his mind. Trennus, commenting on how, if this were a sacrifice, they'd disturbed the terms of the contract, and whoever had struck that bargain would be looking for an appropriate sacrifice to set the balance right again. *This was a bad idea,* Adam thought, and began to work at his wrists again. He'd be damned if he were going to have his heart torn out of his body, or die this far away from home.

They'd gotten a message the previous afternoon from the priest of Chaac that Sigrun and Ehecatl had spoken to a few days ago—the one who was supposed to be a contact for the leader of the local rebels, the mysterious 'Smoke Jaguar.' The priest had asked for Ehecatl and Sigrun to meet him the next day—dies Saturni—not at his temple, but at the city's *tiyanquiztli,* or marketplace, after local curfew. "Because this doesn't sound like a trap at all," Adam had commented, sardonically.

"Of course it is," Livorus had told them. "It may well be the only way to get in touch with the rebels, however. We must go to them on their terms, so that they feel safe. But we will arrange to ensure that we can turn the situation around on them." He'd smiled faintly, as he looked up from his usual pile of documents. "They won't know what you are, my dear."

"Hopefully not, sir," Sigrun agreed, grimacing. "We'll need an extraction plan, as well. I'd be happier if Eshmunazar and Matrugena were with us."

That, however, hadn't been an option. Livorus had sent Kanmi and Trennus, hours before, back north to Tenochtitlan, to help the *gardia* up there go through Gratian Xicohtencatl's house.

"None of you can remain unseen the way I can. I'm better for a backup, and, if needed, extraction team," Ehecatl had told her, thoughtfully. "I'll make myself invisible and shadow you. I'll stay in radio contact with the other Praetorians, so if and when your radios are taken, we'll still have a line of contact."

"She can't go alone," Adam objected.

"Of course not. You would be her escort."

"Won't the fact that the newlywed Sigrun suddenly has a different male escort be suspicious?" Livorus asked, raising his eyebrows.

"We, ah, didn't go with that particular story, *dominus,*" Ehecatl admitted, chuckling faintly. "No matter how doting Sigrun tried to look, we both kept winding up laughing. We went with how she and her *actual* new husband were friends of mine, and were here looking into the possibility of moving her husband's business here. Lower wages. And apparently, Sigrun was a scholar of other cultures, and wanted the grand tour while her husband was engaged in business meetings . . I thought that she and Trennus could pull off the newlywed act fairly well, but in his absence . . ." Ehecatl shrugged and looked at Adam. "Congratulations. I'm sure you two will be very happy together."

Adam kept his lips in as straight a line as he could manage. Sigrun sighed. "Very well. We'll say that Ehecatl couldn't make it to this meeting, and that my dear husband did not wish for me to be out wandering a strange city alone, after dark, should it become an issue."

They'd arrived at the marketplace around midnight—fully on dies Saturni—and Adam had been glad that Ehecatl was close by, hidden by his shroud of invisibility. This was the defining mark of a Jaguar warrior; they specialized in stealth tactics from their earliest training at age fifteen in the *calmecacs*, or houses of lineage, where young nobles or exceptionally gifted commoners were educated. Only at graduation, at the age of eighteen, were they given the tattoos that allowed them to turn truly invisible . . . and then they entered the elite ranks of their nation's military forces.

Even knowing that Ehecatl was around somewhere, Adam hadn't dared to look for the man as a priest of Chaac had materialized from behind a closed shop . . . followed by eight or nine other figures, all male, and wearing little more than what jungle workers might—heavy boots and loincloths, their faces swathed in light scarves. And all of them armed with jungle knives, at the very least.

"And who is this?" The priest had challenged Sigrun, but he'd been staring at Adam.

"My beloved, Adam ben Maor," Sigrun answered, her accent thickening slightly over the lie. "Our friend could not be here tonight. You may say anything to him that you would say to me. I have no secrets from him."

"Your *friend* wore the tattoos of a Jaguar warrior," the priest had muttered. "You and he both gave a . . . certain passphrase to me the other day," he'd gone on, staring at Adam still. "I don't know if we can trust you or not, but that's not for me to decide. Smoke Jaguar . . . will see you now." The priest's teeth had bared briefly in a humorless smile, his words a parody of the receptionist at a doctor's office.

And then the various men had moved in around them. Had relieved Adam of the gun at the small of his back, and had taken Sigrun's knife and spear from her. The latter was a potentially wasted effort on their part, Adam knew. Sigrun spent time with every new spear—even if all she was replacing was a broken haft. She carved runes into the wood to match the ones on her skin, and rubbed her own blood into the wood. The weapon was therefore blood-bound to her, and she could call it to her hand whenever she needed it. She'd told him that the weapon couldn't be locked inside of anything, and there couldn't be walls in between her and it, but even so, calling Sigrun 'disarmed' because she wasn't carrying a weapon was mildly ridiculous. She was a weapon, made incarnate.

None of it made him feel any better about surrendering his gun, or allowing himself to be bound, hooded, and shoved into the back of a truck by people whose faces were hidden, and dragged somewhere so deep into the jungles that they could wander for weeks on foot without finding a way out. *Well, all right, Sigrun can fly, but I suspect she'd get rather tired of carrying my carcass around, wouldn't she? Of course, I could also look at it this way: they actually care that we can identify them. That might mean that they don't actually plan to kill us.* Adam shifted again, pulling at the ropes . . . .

. . . and the truck finally slowed to a lurching halt, sending him slamming into Sigrun's form again. "Sorry."

"It will heal."

Squeak of the rear gate being lowered. Shaking as feet trod the bed of the truck. Rough hands on his elbows, hoisting him up, and then they walked him to the back of the truck. "Sig?"

"I'm with you."

Stumbling, fumbling, pushed and prodded along, feeling the pre-dawn coolness on his body. The footing changed, from gravel to something smoother . . . slabs of stone, perhaps. Sound of a door opening, being propelled inside. "There's a stool here," one of their captors told him. "Sit."

Adam did what he was told, his stomach churning. He didn't handle being helpless well, and at the moment, there was nothing he could do. They could, if they wanted to, take one of their jungle blades, of either obsidian or of steel, and cut his head off, and he'd never even see it coming. Every part of him rebelled at that thought; every part of him resisted the notion of being at the mercy of someone else's will. He'd go out fighting, if he could.

It made him feel indefinably better, however, as their captors pushed Sigrun to a stool beside him; he could feel the cool rush of air from the movement, the press of her knee against his.

Rustling, and then, finally, a voice spoke, in heavily-accented Latin, "So. What would you have Smoke Jaguar hear?"

Sigrun shifted slightly, but remained silent. Livorus had directed Adam to do the talking when they met with Smoke Jaguar, if at all possible. The propraetor did not wish anyone to know that he had a god-born in his entourage. Sigrun was the weighted die in their cup, and Livorus wanted her to remain so. Thus, Adam spoke up. "Let me ask that question a different way. What would Smoke Jaguar have the propraetor of Rome hear?" he asked, trying to sound as calm and relaxed as possible, as sweat trickled down the hollow of his back. "We are his ears. What you say, will be carried to him."

"Ahh, so my information from Tenochtitlan was indeed correct. You are not looking to move a business concern here, but actually are the lictors of a Roman dignitary. Such honesty is . . . refreshing . . . from Rome." There was mordant irony in the voice, as the man went on, "How unusual, to have a propraetor interested in hearing our grievances and our demands. Always before, Rome has said that to hear us . . . would give us weight."

"Times change," Adam replied, evenly. "In truth, however, we were not sent here, initially, to deal with Smoke Jaguar. That is the concern of the Nahautl emperor, and Governor Dioscuri, and they have asked us to deal with the rebels while we are here."

"Deal with? Does this mean to make a bargain? Or do you mean to kill us all?" The voice was lightly amused.

"The propraetor has a great deal of autonomy in his decisions," Adam said, quietly. "He is the Imperator's eyes, ears, and hands, just as we are his. By and large, Livorus is a good man, who prefers to err on the side of leniency. But that does not mean he lacks ruthlessness, when it is needed."

"That is not an answer." Scrape of metal on stone, repetitious and steady. The sound of a knife being sharpened.

Adam, under the bag that covered his face, grimaced.

Psychological tactics in interrogations worked most effectively when the subject didn't understand how they were being employed, and to what ends. But even knowing what was being done, and why, didn't entirely eliminate the fear reactions. "I'll be clearer, then. The propraetor hasn't yet decided what to do about the so-called rebels in this area. What message you send him, through us, will probably make that decision much easier for him, however." Not a threat. Just clear, plain, simple words in good Latin.

"Interesting." The knife scraping stopped. "For what reason *were* you sent here, if not to deal with Smoke Jaguar?"

"We seek information on rumors of a return to human sacrifices in the region. And we intend to put a stop to it, if it's true." Adam's words were blunt, now. "We found at least one body under the ley-power station. This is . . . not usual. And we understand that Smoke Jaguar and his people have, in times past, attacked ley-facilities, but have left this one undamaged. Does Smoke Jaguar stand with the people who left a sacrificed human under the foundations of the power-station?"

Mutters in Quecha. He couldn't tell what they were saying, but the tone was clear: consternation, and not a little fear. A few short, sharp words from what sounded to be the leader . . . and then the bags were pulled from their heads. Adam blinked, rapidly, in the sudden light streaming in through an open doorway to his right, and looked around quickly, to get a feel for his surroundings. The building had walls made of corrugated tin, and what looked to be a roof thatched from jungle leaves, and a dirt floor. A highly temporary structure, in other words, one that could be abandoned without loss . . . and the ground would soak up blood, too, if the prisoners needed to be killed here. Adam tried to keep that last thought out of his face and eyes as he looked up and met the eyes of their captor.

Smoke Jaguar, or Chan Imix K'awiil, was of about average height for a Quechan man, or just about five foot two . . . significantly shorter than Adam himself, who was an inch less than six feet in height. The man also apparently came from Quechan nobility of some sort; unlike the waitress in the restaurant at the hotel, his teeth were filed to vicious points. Adam didn't really want to think about how much that must have hurt, and how prone to cavities teeth like that had to be. The man's hair was dark, and worn long, tied back from his long face, and his dark eyes were cold. His skin was covered in a mass of tattoos, as well, all probably with meanings that the Judean man did not comprehend. But he wore jeans, in place of a loincloth, in spite of the heat, and solid jungle boots, though his chest was bare . . . and at the moment, he was flipping a long steel jungle knife in one hand, catching it by its hilt. "Easier to judge a man's heart, if you can see his eyes," the leader of the Quechan rebels said, looking right at Adam. "I swear on the bones of my ancestors, and by all the gods, I did not know about the sacrifice till you spoke of it."

Adam met the man's eyes, and then looked, sidelong, at Sigrun. Her uncanny talent for knowing truth was very helpful in situations like this. She nodded, curtly, once. *All right. Progress.* "I am glad to know that,

Chan Imix K'awiil," Adam said, carefully, hoping he didn't mangle the name.

"What else would Rome know? What else would Rome understand?"

"You have attacked previous ley-facilities, as I said, but not this one. Why attack them before? Why not attack this one, now?"

Smoke Jaguar flipped his knife around in his hands. "The ley-lines are a fetter," he said, after a moment. "A shackle. A way the Nahautl seek to bind us. Make us dependent on them. My people don't wish to be bound. We wish to be free. Free to join with the rest of Quecha . . . to the south. To be one with our people again."

Adam remembered, all too well, Ehecatl's cynical reaction to the briefing on the rebels' supposed goals. *"Yes, and I guarantee, that ten years after they join the Quechan Provinces, and have been the most affluent part of a crushingly a poor nation for the whole of that time, they'll be begging to come back to Nahautl and be the poorest in a rich nation. No one ever wants what they have in front of them. All the words about how they speak Quechan, they're ethnically Quechan . . . sound like so much horseshit to me."*

He didn't quote the Nahautl man to Smoke Jaguar now. Simply nodded, and asked again, "So why *not* attack this one? Was it simply inconveniently located?"

The Quechan man grimaced and spat, displaying those pointed teeth again. "A year ago, a priest of the Nahautl came to the south, and a Roman pigfucker with a Nahautl last name. The priest went to all of the temples here. Temples who had supported us in our struggle, you understand? And he stirred them up. Tried to tell them that Chaac was the same as Tlaloc, and that they should all be worshipping the way they do in Nahautl. Because they were the same god. The priests laughed him out, but some of the people . . . they listened. Because he was *god-born*. They listened, and they followed." Smoke Jaguar spat again. "The world would be a better place without any god-born, I think. And I think the Roman pigfucker agreed with me on that."

Sigrun stirred, but didn't speak. Adam didn't dare look at her. "Go on," Adam invited, quietly.

"I didn't like the god-born priest. Didn't like a Nahautl man coming in with Nahautl beliefs. He wanted us to worship the gods in the oldest ways. I don't like Rome . . . but I have three children. A son. Two daughters." Smoke Jaguar flipped the knife around in his hand again. "In the old days, a daughter could be sold for seven hundred cacao beans as a future sacrifice. Because the priests said that without sacrifice, the sun would be destroyed. Rome came. Sacrifices stopped. The sun is still here." He flipped the knife around in his hand, one more time, and then leaned down to stab it into the earth. "Whether you call him Chaac or Tlaloc . . . the heart wasn't enough for him. Them. Whatever. He demanded the sweetest sacrifices. He demanded tears of the victims before they were taken to the altar. Parents tore out the fingernails of their own children to force them to weep, so that the tears could be collected in a bowl for the gods to drink." He'd been staring at the knife embedded in the ground, but now raised his eyes and met Adam's gaze, squarely. "I don't know if the gods required it, or if it was how the priests and the god-born held power, but why would I ever want to go back to that?"

Adam nodded slowly. He didn't need to look at Sigrun to see the sincerity in the man's eyes. "What does this have to do with the ley-facility being left untouched?" he asked.

"That was by agreement with the other one. The Roman pigfucker." Smoke Jaguar spat again. "I don't like him much either, but he's a sorcerer. He's in an alliance of convenience, I think, with the priest. It won't last long." The man's filed teeth bared in a cold grin. "Their goals are too different, and I can see the hate in both their eyes. The pigfucker wants to fight Rome. Get rid of the governor. He thinks he can use the priest to that aim, and then . . . rule Nahautl. Keep the king as a puppet." Smoke Jaguar shrugged. "Priest thinks the same thing. I don't care about them, except that the sorcerer swore that he'd free Tikal. Let us join with Quecha, when he throws out Rome." Another shrug. "I don't think it'll happen. But confusion to the Nahautl is good. He asked for us to step up our attacks, to be distracting, so that when the 'revolution comes' to the north, all eyes will be on the south, and the legions will not be positioned to resist." Smoke Jaguar exhaled. "A dream over mescal fumes, perhaps. But not attacking their facility, in exchange for access to his information sources? Increasing the number of our attacks, while remaining cautious, in exchange for supplies? That was a bargain worth making." He shook his head. "If he and the priest *did* plant a sacrificed man under that ley-station, and if they return to this area? I will send you their heads, *myself.*"

Interesting. He's loyal to his culture, his people, but he's not a reactionary. The two usually go hand in hand. He might be pragmatic enough that Livorus can actually negotiate with him. Adam leaned forward, in spite of his bound hands. "Look . . . I'm Judean. My people struggled against Rome, centuries ago. We won self-rule, not by force of arms, but by . . . bargaining. Diplomacy. It took a long time, but my people are largely *free* today." He met the Quechan's man's eyes. "But I understand what it means to wish to be free of another country. Of another's power."

Smoke Jaguar nodded after a moment, and Adam knew he'd made a connection there, inside the man's head. That could make all the difference. The Quechan man now saw him as at least *similar* to himself. And that could be built on. He exhaled. "The priest is named Tototl, correct? And the sorcerer is named Xicohtencatl?"

Smoke Jaguar looked up, clearly surprised. "You knew already?"

"Not this," Adam said. "Tell us *everything* about the two of them. Everything you know. I will bring your words to the propraetor. And if you agree to refrain from violence for a term of six months, as a show of good faith, I think that Livorus would agree to arbitrate discussions about some measures of local autonomy. You might not get everything you want. Not at first. It's slower this way. But as you just told me . . . we don't have to go back to the old ways of doing things. We don't have to sacrifice the blood of our people, to achieve what we want. Not in this. Not here. Not today."

He was almost shaking with the effort to convince the man. And he was actually surprised when Smoke Jaguar began to converse with him, quietly, and at much greater length, about what he'd learned about the two conspirators, over the course of the months he'd been reluctantly affiliated with them.

For her part, Sigrun remained silent, except, near the end, when she leaned in closer and whispered to Adam, "Secondary locations?"

Adam blinked, and then realized, *Good point.* "My companion asks a good question. Do you know of any fallback locations to which they might have fled?"

Smoke Jaguar shook his head, and looked off into the mid-distance for a moment. "Teotihuacán," he said, suddenly.

Adam blinked. That name hadn't been included in any of the briefing materials he'd looked at. "Ah . . . what?" he asked.

"It's an abandoned city," Sigrun supplied, quietly. "It fell over five hundred years before Tenochtitlan was built by the Nahautl. It was thought to be a place of myth, until the ruins were relocated about twenty years ago by a group that was interesting in mining opportunities north of Tenochtitlan." She shrugged. "Archaeologists have been excavating the whole place since then. Multilevel apartment homes. Huge pyramid temples."

The Quechan man turned and stared at Sigrun, openly. It was the most she'd said all at once. "How do you know all of that?" Adam asked. "That wasn't in the mission briefing . . . ."

Sigrun flushed. "I . . . ah . . . like to read about history and archaeology," she admitted. She caught the look Adam was giving her, and muttered, under her breath, "You read about astronomy all the time."

Smoke Jaguar shook his head, and dismissed the sideline. "Teotihuacán was once a great city. A trading partner of Tikal for many years, until it was abandoned. The priest, Tototl . . . said that the Pyramid of the Sun was the holiest place in Caesaria Aquilonis. That it was over a cave, from which all mankind had been birthed. *Chicomoztoc.* And he said that this was Tlaloc's most sacred temple."

Sigrun paused, her eyes flicking from side to side, as if she were reading a book inside her mind. "From what I remember, no one knows for certain to which god the Pyramid of the Sun was dedicated. Even the Temple of the Moon is in dispute . . . there are images of a spider goddess there, but . . . ." She shrugged.

"All I know is what they told me. If they were to go anywhere, it would be there, I think. They sometimes talked about the power that lay hidden under it, in the cave of life and death." Smoke Jaguar shrugged. "I'm no priest. But I know Chaac's sacred places are caves, *cenotes.* Places from which life can be born . . . and into which we pass, when it is our time to go into the earth. Life, death, life."

Sigrun exhaled, and looked at Adam, nodding. "It does make sense."

Their hands were untied, and Adam had to rub at his hands, cautiously, to allow blood-flow to return, and Smoke Jaguar, no fool, had his priest of Chaac draw up a document, written on two pieces of foolscap from Adam's notebook, that stated what Adam had agreed to do—to speak to Livorus about arbitrating some measures of regional autonomy, in exchange for the rebels' vow to use peaceful methods of resistance for at least the next six months. Adam signed both, making sure that all the words were written in ink, and took his copy, folding it and putting it in his pocket, for lack of anything better to do with it. It didn't look or feel like an important historical document, but he supposed it might become one. In time. If it didn't become an infamous one, if everyone on all sides broke their words, instead.

They were fed, loaded back into the truck—this time, with their arms unbound, but still with the bags over their heads—and the rebels began the long drive back out of the jungles. Just being able to use his hands in the truck made it much more comfortable, and easier to keep from slamming into Sigrun. No words, the whole way back, though Adam was dying to know if Ehecatl had managed to stick with them the whole way to the rebel compound, or not. Even using Hellene for that query might be too much of a risk.

And thus, at sundown on dies Saturnis, they were pushed out of the truck. Their weapons were dropped at their feet, with the warning, in Latin, "No tricks. We have guns trained on you right now . . . ." and then the rebels left them there, at the side of a road outside of Tikal. Adam found his feet, pulling the bag off his head in time to see the vehicle, disappear back down the road, and into the jungle once more, a cloud of noxious vapors trailing behind it. He bent to scoop up his pistol as Sigrun retrieved her spear.

"Think Ehecatl made it with us?" Adam asked as they began to trudge towards the town, using the massive temple of Tikal as a landmark. The road wasn't an Imperial highway by any stretch of the imagination, but at least it was poured stone, unlike the mud track in the jungle that they'd just traversed, twice.

"Of course I did." The Nahautl man's voice came from directly to Adam's left, and the Judean's head rocked back, his eyes widening. "I'm not going to drop my invisibility until we're back in town, and I have a chance to make it look like I was there the whole time." Ehecatl snorted. "I was on the side of the truck with you, both times. But the guards kept looking in, so I couldn't really tell you I was there, eh?"

"So, you know where their camp is?" Sigrun asked.

"I know where their camp is *today*," the Nahautl man returned. "These rebels pick up and move around a lot. This was probably a temporary meeting spot, nothing more. They've been a pain in the ass for over ten years down here. And their leader hasn't stayed alive by being an idiot."

Adam cleared his throat. "So, you listened to the whole conversation?"

"Best I could, yes. Believe me when I tell you, if I thought they'd been party to the sacrifice, I would have stayed behind to kill his men, regardless of your word, ben Maor." Ehecatl's voice, coming out of empty air, was grim. "He sounded genuine about that much, at least."

"And the agreement itself?" Adam asked, wiping sweat off his face.

"We'll see. I doubt the *tlatoani* would be much pleased to have these lands defect to Quecha, but as for me, I could care less. Let them go. Watch and see how many of their people migrate north to Tenochtitlan, and see how quickly Smoke Jaguar and others like him rule an empty land."

"The problem will be convincing your emperor that Rome has a right to give away his lands," Sigrun muttered. "But, that's not what any of us are paid to worry about."

They made a full report to Livorus in his rooms, and the propraetor listened, his blue eyes distant, and reviewed the paper Adam had signed. "I'll have to coordinate with the Foreign Office back home, to a certain extent. Lifelong bureaucrats with a nuanced view of a region thanks to long study of a country and its customs tend to take it somewhat amiss when a political appointee comes into a situation and rearranges all the place-settings and cutlery." Livorus' tone was exquisitely dry. "Suffice to say, this won't be an issue that we'll be able to resolve in a week or two's time. And our investigation must go on. Now, as to that . . . Teotihuacán?" Livorus pulled out a map and traced their route with a finger. "Another two days of driving, at the least," he murmured. "Even if we were to leave tonight . . . and we must inform Eshmunazar and Matrugena along the way. Hmm. They'll be best served by going through Xicohtencatl and Tototl's residences, while they await our arrival. Perhaps they'll find corroborating evidence." Livorus looked around. "While I'm not exceptionally fond of the notion of spending the next six months here in Nahautl arbitrating talks between rebels and the local government . . . exceptional work on the diplomatic front today, ben Maor. Thank you." He paused. "Let us hope Smoke Jaguar has not given us a false lead and a wasted chase, eh?"

Adam accepted the praise, but shifted uneasily. They *were* banking a lot on the word of a rebel. Sigrun's truth sense was one thing, but it only told her when the person *knew* what they were saying was a lie. It didn't help at all if the person in question were ignorant or misinformed.

As they headed for the suite of rooms that they'd been allocated to clean up and at least get a night's sleep after a very long, hot, sweaty day . . . and Adam frankly thought he might pass blood in his urine tonight from his bruised kidneys after the rough ride in the truck . . . he paused outside the door of his room. "Archaeology?"

"It's interesting. It shows us how civilizations were born, and how they died. It shows us how they transformed. It shows us that some gods died off with their people. And, going even further back, it shows us how we came to *be*." Sigrun paused, unlocking her own door, and leaned on the frame. Hanks of her hair had worked their way free over the course of the day, and hung in sticky, sweat-stiff strands around her face. "I liked reading about how they found the remains of *Homo habilis* last year, and how the natural philosophers are arguing about how they fit into the history of mankind."

Adam just stared at her for a long moment, his lips twitching. "And this doesn't bother you at all?"

She stared at him blankly. "I don't understand the question."

"You're god-born. You talk about gods and civilizations dying and don't even bat an eyelash. You mention the remains of humans that predate creation myths. And it doesn't bother you?"

Sigrun half-laughed, half-snorted. "I would have to be pretty stupid not to comprehend that the gods gave us reason with the understanding that we would *use* it. And that the history of humanity is a long, upwards struggle towards reason, and that as we have learned, the old metaphors that the gods used to teach us when we were young, have been altered, and they have given us new ones to help us understand our new discoveries." Her smile faded. "But as for the rest? Yes. Everything dies. Every single one of my people knows this, Adam. It will all end in fire. In Ragnarok. Some people see it as a literal battle between good and evil. Some people think now it's a metaphor for the sun's rapid expansion into a red giant, consuming all life on Earth. Either way . . . everything ends."

"You have the most depressing point of view in the *world*, Sigrun."

"That doesn't make it any less true, Adam." A faint smile. "As I said a few days ago, my native language doesn't even have a future tense. Consider what that means about the point of view of my ancestors, and how surprised they would be, to realize that we're all still here."

With that, she walked into her room, and closed the door behind her.

Iunius 11-13, 1954 AC

Trennus and Kanmi had, on reaching the midway point of their trek back north, stopped, found a hotel, and called back to the hotel in Tikal to check in with Livorus . . . only to hear that Sigrun and Adam, with Ehecatl, were going into what was almost certainly a trap. "Fuck," Kanmi swore, hanging up the phone in the public booth in the lobby, and had pounded the side of his fist against the glass wall of the booth for a moment, even as Trennus, on the other side, raised both hands, palms up, and mouthed, *"What?"* at him.

Kanmi had opened the door of the booth, and muttered, "Upstairs."

"Bad?" Trennus' eyes widened slightly.

"Could be worse. I'm not sure how, but it could be." The part that was annoying him more than anything else, was that if they'd known about the meeting just a few hours before, they could have been there to back the other half of the lictor team up. Instead . . . they might not even know the outcome tomorrow night, when they reached Tenochtitlan and had access to a phone line again.

He explained the mess as best he could to Trennus, who paced back and forth in one of their adjoining rooms, his braids bouncing as he shook his head. "I should have left one of my amulets with Sigrun," Trennus muttered. "We'd have been able to keep in touch that way—"

"Or we could have actually gotten a vehicle from the local Praetorians that actually had a two-way radio—"

"It's AM band at best, limited range, and hardly secure." Trennus flipped a hand at Kanmi irritably. "Unless we're all willing to sit there and use one-time pads and spell out messages, assuming they caught us while we were still in range . . . gods." He rubbed his face.

"We can't do anything about it," Kanmi told the younger man, pragmatically. "Best we can do is get some sleep and do our jobs in the morning."

Kanmi, for his part, couldn't take his own advice. He swore, somewhere around two antemeridian, and got out of bed to go stare out the window into the darkness for a while, one hand flat against the glass. It was the same old feeling of being helpless and knowing that someone was in trouble, all over again. He peeled his hand away from the glass and looked at the skin there; it was clean and unscarred, not blackened and bleeding, as he somehow thought it ought to have been.

And when he finally did sleep, he was plagued by the damned dreams. They'd haunted him since he was twelve, and had stood in the harbor at Tyre, knowing that his father's ship was due to come in, but that there was a storm. Thunder, lightning, high winds, waves surging in twenty-foot swells. Most captains had actually left the marina, or had had their ships pulled up on shore; no one wanted to risk their livelihoods, letting the ships slam into the old stone quays.

Standing on the shore, watching to see if their father's boat would enter the harbor, the three boys huddled in oilskin cloaks against the cold rain. Kanmi was the youngest; his two older brothers were both apprentices on fishing boats, and had looked at this tempest-tossed day as a welcome respite from leaving the house at dawn. Hanno shoved Kanmi, five years his junior, towards the foaming, filthy water just below their feet. "You're scared of the water, aren't you, baby?"

In his sleep, Kanmi grimaced, fighting the dream. Half the time, it ended as it had when he'd been six; his brothers holding his head down under the water till he nearly drowned. Hearing the sound of their laughter, distorted through the brown, stinking harbor water.

This time, however, the dream flickered, and he again saw the ship coming into the harbor; the captain was desperate to get his goods ashore, and was taking risks, thinking that his large cargo vessel could handle the waves. *Wind howling. The ship hitting another boat that had capsized earlier in the day . . . .no, that's not how it happened . . . his older brothers ducking his head under the water . . . stop it, or I will kill you, you shits, I know how to defend myself now . . . .*

Standing at the edge of the water, seeing the ship hit by a massive wave, and breaking in half. Jumping down into the water himself, putting his hands, instinctively, against the stone pillars that supported the quay, and getting driven into the rock by the pounding waves. Reaching out with mind and will and feeling the motion of the waves, the energy in them, each one a curve, what he knew now to call a sine wave . . . and flattened the curve. Took the energy from the waves into himself, almost bursting with it, needing to put it somewhere else. Energy and matter couldn't be created. Couldn't be destroyed. They could only change states.

So he gave the water's energy to the rock, with himself as a conduit, and the harbor turned as flat and glossy as a mirror, and he'd <u>screamed</u> as he pulled his hands back from the red-hot rock, blackened and bleeding as his brothers reached down to pull him back up, "What are you doing, baby, no one told you to jump in — oh, gods, what happened to his hands?" Steam coming up from the water below the quay as the waves took the molten rock and <u>shattered</u> it, sending jagged splinters of stone everywhere . . . but the people on the boat were safe, his <u>father</u> was safe . . . . And so long as his father was around, his brothers wouldn't try to drown him again.

He awoke, sweating, as he usually did from that dream. His brothers hadn't actually associated his actions with the bay settling down. They'd hauled him home, cursing under their breaths, unable to account for his burns to his mother, and because Hanno and Tabnit *had*, on several occasions in his younger years, held his head down under the sea's waters, they'd been afraid she'd blame them for the burns. A trip to the hospital later, the news broadcasts over the radio calling the calming of the waves the act of an unknown sorcerer who had undoubtedly saved the lives of the entire crew of the *Ninutra Star* . . . and the young doctor in the ER had made the connection, on seeing that Kanmi's clothing was soaked in salt water, and hearing his brothers babble about the stone shattering beside the quay.

His brothers had been sullen, angry, and not a little jealous when he'd been sent to the local academy of sorcerers for testing . . . and had passed, with flying colors. All they knew, all day, every day, was the backbreaking labor of pulling in nets. *Must be nice, never having to lift a finger again, huh, baby? Spoiled brat.* They didn't understand how dangerous sorcery was, but his teachers drilled it into his head. He could have killed himself. Most first-time sorcerers, untrained, *did*. He'd found somewhere else for the energy to go. Most people didn't realize that, and burned themselves alive.

That had been rather sobering. But he'd happily escaped the resentment at home to go live in a world of magic and science. His parents couldn't afford the fees at any of the schools, so he'd *had* to excel, if he didn't want to wind up a hedge-wizard or a sea-caller, out on the damned boats, trying to calm the waves or lure the fish to the nets, day after day. The Academy of Tyre had taken him in because they couldn't, in conscience, *not* train a sorcerer with his level of aptitude. The Preparatory School of Carthage? Full scholarship, and thankfully, hundreds of miles away from his family. The University of Athens . . . again, full scholarship. His brother's resentment, for all that they had both had wives and children by that point, hadn't dwindled. They were convinced he'd never do a day's honest work in his life.

Kanmi looked at the clock. Five antemeridian. Less than three hours' of sleep, but he knew he wasn't going to be getting any more. It all tied together in a sick knot, because Caetia and ben Maor were in danger, when he should be saving their hides right now. And of course, he and Trennus were heading to investigate Xicohtencatl, whom he'd met at the university, and it all just . . . congealed in his head.

His brothers had always bullied him for being younger and weaker, and Kanmi had hated them, every minute of his life. He believed, powerfully, that those who happened to be stronger than others didn't have a right to dominate the weaker. And there were all kinds of strengths that let small groups of people control others. Physical power. Being stronger or taller or better trained with a weapon. Political power, derived from noble birth. Financial power, derived from, usually, noble backgrounds, or, sometimes, an ancestor who'd had a genius for technology or business. Religious power, derived from an effort to convince people to think as a group . . . which was just really a type of political power. Magical power, derived from training and talent. And, of course, the god-born themselves, whose mere *existence* was inherently unfair. They were born with power that most others had to work to achieve. Many of them held political or religious authority on top of their existing, inborn powers, and, to Kanmi's way of thinking, most of them tended to be *bullies*. People out to hold down the little people, the masses. To hold their heads under the water until they cried and begged just to be allowed to live in peace.

That Caetia didn't, in general, flaunt her powers, didn't make her any less of a god-born. That Matrugena didn't, most days, act like the son of a king, didn't make him any less of a naïve, noble-born child—and a physically large and imposing sort, though he didn't carry himself like the giant he actually was, a foot taller than Kanmi himself. Ben Maor was neither god-born nor a noble, and thus, the least offensive of his companions to Kanmi's more democratic leanings. And yet . . . Baal take it . . . . he actually liked all of them. Respected them, even. But that didn't mean he'd *ever* give them a free pass.

The drive the following day had largely been a silent one, and they'd had to meet with the Tenochtitlan *gardia*. Jurisdiction was jurisdiction, and it didn't pay to step on other people's toes unnecessarily. "I don't know what you'll think you'll find," a Nahautl detective in red slacks, a white, sleeveless shirt, and a formal, colorful cape told them at the door of Xicohtencatl's large, familial manor. "We turned this place inside out."

"Fresh eyes," Matrugena told the Nahautl man, smiling and pushing his glasses back up his nose. And then they'd gotten to *work*. Kanmi had half-closed his eyes and pushed out his other senses, looking for places in the house where energy patterns were distorted, uneven. Where charges of energy had been left, residual traces of magic and will.

"Getting anything?" Matrugena asked, poking his head into the study after an hour's search. "I'm gathering that he left in a hurry. Half the clothes in the bedroom were dumped on the floor."

"Yes. He left a half-dozen charged batteries here, in his desk. That's like a man taking his pistol, but forgetting his bullets. Either he was in a hurry, or wherever he's going, he expects to find more." Kanmi pushed a chair with leather cushions out of the way, and studied the area under it; a rug protected the floor from the chair, but there was something off here. Patterns in the floor indicating . . . material had been altered, and recently. "Help me move the desk."

Matrugena obliged, sliding it out of the way, as Kanmi pulled up the rug and stared at the tile underneath. "Does this look odd to you?"

"The mortar's a different color," Matrugena replied, immediately. "Either he put in different grout in a repair job, or . . . ."

"He shifted its composition back to mud, and reset it too fast," Kanmi finished. "Huh. Didn't think he could manage that trick." He gave Trennus a look. "You mind? I'm less effective with solids. Not as much practice."

"Sure." Trennus' eyes defocused, and Kanmi could feel a rush of power, as the mortar in the area promptly altered state; for *him*, this trick would have required heating the molecules and forcing ambient fluid in the air in between the solid portions of the matrix that comprised the mortar. For Trennus, it was an entirely different operation; ley-energy excited the material and shattered it all into a fine powder, allowing them to tip up the tiles, carefully. "Well, what do we have here?" Kanmi muttered, and they lifted the rolled-up sheets of paper to the desk, spreading each out and studying them. "This . . . this is a design schematic for those altered Tholberg coils we saw down in Tikal," he told Trennus, after a moment.

"This one's a ley-line map of the area north of Tenochtitlan. Revolving largely around a region called . . . Teotihuacán." Trennus mangled the pronunciation, shook his head, and went on. "It's noted as a ruined city. Gods. Whoever built this place originally . . . really knew what they were doing."

"How's that?"

"It's located directly atop where two lines intersect, and are in resonance. Geologically, fairly stable . . ." Trennus leafed through a few other charts that were tucked in with this one. "Huh. That's unusual."

"What?"

"There's a large, natural cavern underneath this pyramid. Typically, you don't build heavy architecture over the top of open spaces in the earth . . . this one is even, technically, what they call a *cenote* around here, or was, when it was built." Trennus pointed out a note on the map. "It was considered a road into the underworld, like all *cenotes*. They're supposed to replicate the birth passage. You know, long tunnel, water—"

"Yes, thank you, I was there for the birth of both of my sons. There's usually quite a bit of blood and screaming involved, too. Would you like more details?"

Trennus blinked, rapidly, and shuddered. "Ah, no. That's quite all right." He recovered. "Usually, being positioned over a natural spring and cavern like this would be . . . stupid . . . but the ley formations in the area make it actually very stable. Also doesn't hurt that the pyramid's built like a damned mountain." He paused. "At any rate, it's set up right atop two major ley-lines that both intersect each other and are in resonance with each other. That's . . . actually rather rare. A *lot* of potential energy to be tapped there."

They flipped through the papers some more, and then Kanmi swore out loud. "Well, I think we've figured out where they were transmitting power *from*, that was reaching the station in Tikal." He gestured to a series of schematics, that showed Tholberg coils below the pyramid, and a series of wires leading to a large, proposed mast similar in design to the one they'd seen much further to the south.

"No," Trennus said, immediately. "It's a rare formation, certainly, and very powerful, but there's no way they'd be getting enough power out of it to send it that far south, not without losses. And as *you* keep reminding *me*, the power we were detecting at the Tikal facility wasn't ley."

Kanmi exhaled. Matrugena was, annoyingly, correct. "Well, perhaps we should drive up there and check the site out."

They were preparing to call Livorus' hotel in Tikal that night to get permission to do precisely that, when the phone in Kanmi's room rang on its own. On answering, Kanmi's eyes widened as ben Maor's voice came over the line, and a wash of relief passed through him—relief he quickly masked. "So, you're alive. And here I thought your head would be decorating a pike down there."

"My skull isn't much of a prize. Though, truthfully, I was more worried about my heart."

"Eh, one leads to the other."

"True enough." The lightly-accented, elegant Latin paused, then picked up again, "We got a line on a possible location for our bumblebee and our other lost soul."

"So did we. Temple of the Sun, Teotihuacán." Kanmi was delighted at the pause that this garnered on the other end of the line.

"Glad to have some confirmation."

"Should we go scout it out?"

A pause, as ben Maor conferred with Livorus and the others, so far to the south. "Negative. We're actually a day behind you. We'll be there . . . sometime very damned late tomorrow night. The propraetor says to continue to look busy. Don't tell the local *gardia* what you found—"

"We took it out without letting them see it. Locked it all in a hotel safe in Matrugena's room that I, well . . . welded shut. Chain of evidence, if we're concerned with it, should be intact." Kanmi paused. "Look busy, eh? We can do that. We'll check into the priest's house in the morning. Then . . . northwards?"

"As soon as we get there and can roust out enough local *gardia* support . . . damn. Actually, Ehecatl's saying something about that right now . . . . *Eagle warriors*? Why . . . oh." Ben Maor paused. "Fair enough. Eagle and Jaguar warriors come from all over the Nahautl Empire, he says. Less chance of them being bought than local *gardia* in Tenochtitlan."

"Fair enough," Kanmi agreed, grimly. "I don't want to go in there without being fairly confident in the people who have my back."

Iunius 14, 1954 AC

The window outside the propraetor's room was dark, and through it, they could all see the lights from Tenochtitlan's skyscrapers and bridges, not to mention the spotlights atop its pyramids. It was barely four antemeridian, and Sigrun's eyes were grainy.

Livorus looked around the room. "Are you quite certain you wish to do this now?" he asked his various lictors. "Would it not be better to wait a day, when you're all well-rested?" He turned and glanced at Sigrun.

"I napped in the car when Ehecatl took a turn driving," Adam said, and turned to look at Sigrun. "Sig?"

She shook her head. "I am as rested as I am likely to be." Her expression was hard. "Propraetor, if this is their main location, then it's wise to go to them as quickly as possible—if they're even there—before they either conduct another sacrifice, or have a chance to disassemble whatever machinery they have there . . . or simply destroy all evidence and go deeper into hiding." She bit her lower lip. "We should go, and as quickly as possible." The combination of the machinery and the sacrifices was bothering *all* of them. It simply didn't make sense.

She'd taken the time to observe Tiwesdæg; she'd pulled on her chainmail shirt, helmet, and feathered cloak once more. And, naturally, given the humid climate, Sigrun was now sweating heavily. "Bullet-proof flak jackets," Adam reminded her, his voice silky with temptation, and his eyebrows arched playfully.

"It would still be warm. And bulky."

Livorus was to stay behind, guarded by the various new Praetorians; Sigrun was a little uneasy about that. This was her detail, hers and Adam's, and she didn't know these men and women particularly well. She hadn't read their dossiers, hadn't gotten to measure the steel in their souls. But they couldn't leave any of their main people behind, and Ehecatl in particular wanted in on this venture. Xicohtencatl and Tototl were responsible for the death of a Jaguar warrior. A brother, if one he'd never met. The Nahautl man's expression was made of stone as they drove north. A truck, following them closely, held five men from the local barracks of the Eagle warriors. Where Jaguar warriors relied on stealth, Eagle warriors were among the best stand-up fighters in the Nahautl Empire. They carried traditional enchanted obsidian knives, like Ehecatl did, but also single-shot derringers, spears, and smoothbore muskets. Sigrun didn't know if any of that would be useful, but even numbers could be very useful, just on a psychological level.

The dirt road to the archaeological site was poorly marked, and there were no lights alongside the rutted track; Teotihuacán was not exactly a tourist attraction, not with the ancient pyramids and bright lights of Tenochtitlan just thirty miles away. "Lights off," Adam commented over the short-range radio to the truck behind them. "Tire noise can't be helped, but let's not announce ourselves." *At least these are ley-powered vehicles,* he thought. *Not as good as electric, but much quieter than that damned kerosene-powered combustion engine on that truck down in Tikal.* "Only problem is, now

I can't see a damn thing," Adam muttered.

"I can see in the dark," Ehecatl muttered. Heads turned. "*Jaguar* warrior, remember? We have certain sorceries we don't share with outsiders. Let me drive, ben Maor."

"One of my spirits can let me see in the dark, too," Trennus volunteered, sounding apologetic. "Doesn't help the rest of you, though."

"Have you ever tried having her help other people?" Sigrun asked.

"It won't hurt to ask, I suppose." Trennus pulled one of his amulets out, and murmured very softly for a moment. Adam could just barely hear the word *Saraid* . . . and then slammed on the brakes as, impossibly, a glowing white hind walked out into the road ahead of them.

The truck behind them almost slammed into their rear, and Adam swore under his breath, and moved out of his seat, trading places with Ehecatl, muttering, "A little *warning* next time, Matrugena —"

"She's nervous." Trennus hesitated. "Do you object to letting her touch your mind, ben Maor? Or should I leave you out of this, assuming it works?"

Adam gritted his teeth. "I want to say no, but it would be really stupid to refuse," he managed, after a moment, as Ehecatl restarted the motorcar.

The spirit delicately leaped up onto the hood as the car moved ahead, and for a moment, all Adam could see were the prancing, dancing legs of a *deer* . . . and then the doe's head slid through the roof, and huge, wide, faintly luminescent eyes stared directly into his. *Oh, my lord. This is really not what I signed up for . . . .*

. . . and then the darkness around him simply peeled back. It wasn't as if it were daylight, no. But he could see everything now in monochrome. Shades of gray. His companion's faces appeared crafted of marble. The road was a path of silver; the trees, sculptures in steel and alabaster. His heart raced as if he'd just sprinted a mile, however, and he released an explosive breath, grateful that he'd moved to the center of the seat to let Ehecatl drive. He might have bent the steering wheel in his moment of acute panic.

"Very nice," Kanmi muttered, under his breath. "Better than using a gravitic pulse as radar. That, I have to ping out constantly, and no one else can understand it."

Sigrun, to Adam's surprise, reached over and actually put a hand on his forearm. "Not so bad, is it?"

"Not bad at all," he agreed, tightly, and edged the car forward at a better clip, but tension still fairly sang in the air. "What did you have to promise for it, Matrugena?"

"Your first-born," Trennus replied, his tone mild.

Adam froze, just for a moment. "What?"

Kanmi barked with laughter. Trennus ran a hand through his braids, laughing sheepishly. "Oh, come *on*. I can't promise anything on anyone else's behalf. It's an energy or experience exchange. In this case, I have to burn some sugar for her later, or eat raw honey on her behalf." Trennus shrugged. "It's a minor task for a minor service, nothing more."

After a moment, Adam changed the subject, deliberately, "Is it just me," he said, "or is this road going *straight* northeast?"

"About fifteen degrees east of truth north," Trennus supplied.

Everyone looked at him. "I told you, I really can't get lost," the Britannian noted, sounding embarrassed. "I read up on the site before we came here. The local archaeologists want to make it out to be the same angle as the sun's in summer, to account for planting, or orienting the entire city towards a mountain not even visible from here . . . . it couldn't possibly be that the buildings are aligned with the ley-lines here." His tone became dry. "Gauls and Picts were not the only ones to notice their existence and make use of them, after all."

That got a brief laugh from everyone in the vehicle, and then they were actually approaching the site, itself, visible in spirit-vision as silvery shapes that blocked the sky and the stars, all stepped terraces and sloping ramps. "That one," Kanmi muttered, pointing, and Adam could see it was the largest pyramid present . . . and had had a sixty-foot-tall steel mast, like the one they'd seen at the 'ley-station' in Tikal, added atop it.

"I wonder why none of the archaeologists have objected to the site's use." That, from Trennus.

"Do you really think that any of the ones who objected are still alive?" Kanmi's voice was cynical, as always.

Adam pulled the car to a halt, and they all stepped out. "Underground, eh?" he asked, trying not to let his unhappiness with that show. Underground made him think of *ghul*. "I expect it's a tomb, too?"

"Probably in part," Sigrun agreed, softly. "I'm not happy with this either, Adam. Underground, I'm cut off from the sky. But with luck, they might not be down there right now. We might be able to investigate at our leisure."

"Yes. But when have we ever been that lucky before?"

Ehecatl looked around at them all, and said, quietly, "I'll scout ahead. Eagle warriors?" He looked past the lictors to the five Nahautl soldiers accompanying them. "Follow behind the others. Watch our backs." He shimmered into invisibility, and Adam could barely hear the scrape of his soft-soled boots at the Jaguar warrior slipped off ahead of them, into the gray-tinged night.

It took a few minutes for Ehecatl to find the access tunnel's entry point; he padded back to the rest of them and whispered, "Guards. Three of them. This will need to be quick, and quiet."

"I'll go with you," Adam murmured in response, and glanced at the others. Quick, Sigrun could do. Quiet, not so much. But quiet was a specialty of his from his days in the JDF. "Matrugena?"

They closed on the guards, each of whom was armed with a derringer and a knife, and Ehecatl circled around behind the right-most, just as Adam circled around behind his own target. He timed his steps carefully, reached out, and snaked his arms around the man's shoulders and throat. Caught his chin with his right hand, and lifting up and around, using his left hand on the man's shoulder as a counter, snapped his neck, and then followed the body to the ground, easing the man down. He kept one hand over the mouth, as he did, just in case there was enough consciousness left to cry out, and looked up in time to see Ehecatl emerge from invisibility behind his own man, one hand clamped over the target's mouth, the edge of his obsidian blade flaring briefly to life with some sort of magic, and then the knife slashed the carotid artery, blood spurting everywhere.

Then he heard a surprised yelp from the third guard, and spun, ready to help Trennus, only to see something that made his stomach turn. Trennus was holding the man down on the ground, pinned, and pushing him *into the earth*, which was roiling and bubbling viscously as it swallowed him. Trennus was entombing the man at the same time as he was drowning him, and the crouching Britannian's face was contorted in a grimace as he held down his struggling victim, feeding him deeper into the mud pit that had spawned at his feet. When all that was left were the feet sticking up, Trennus stood, took a step back and gestured, sharply . . . and the ground stopped bubbling, and the intolerable sucking sound ceased, as well. "I really don't like doing that," Trennus muttered. "We should also be cautious about spilling blood here, Ehecatl. Killing of any sort can generate a power exchange that spirits will tap, but blood? Blood *binds*. And we don't know entirely what we're dealing with, not yet, anyway."

Ehecatl looked at where the guard's feet still stuck out of the ground. Swallowed. And replied, "Whatever you say."

They signaled the others to come forwards now, and headed down into the tunnel that the guards had surrounded. It had been cut into the earth, centuries ago, widening an existing natural tube, and faced with huge limestone blocks, to stabilize the walls and ceiling. Adam swallowed, and took a couple of deep breaths before heading underground, following in Ehecatl's silent, invisible wake.

After about eighty feet, Adam signaled a halt, and peered, cautiously, out of the tunnel and into a large, natural-looking cavern. Gray spirit-vision wavered, for the area beyond was lit by an uncanny, flickering blue-white light. There were five tangled stalagmite mounds that reached up to the ceiling to grip the fingers of their dripping stalactite mates; the largest, in the center of the chamber, was only comprised of stalactites, reaching down like icicles to touch the surface of an irregularly-shaped pool. However, every wall in the cavern had been smoothed, and statues of various improbable creatures . . . probably Nahautl gods, or their predecessors . . . stood guard around the periphery of the chamber

In between the statues on the western side of the room, and dispersed evenly on either side of what looked like a low stone altar, were a dozen Tholberg coils, humming with power. Blue-white light coruscated up and down them, looking oddly *liquid*, but being fed by arcs of raw . . . lightning? . . . emanating from a huge figure behind the altar. For a moment, Adam thought it was another statue . . . until it moved, slightly, where it stood.

Half again as tall as the average human, the creature wore an elaborate headdress and armor made largely of what looked to be *bones*. It had huge, goggling, empty eye-pits, each the size of a human hand, an open, gaping mouth with fangs. Distantly, Adam realized that he could hear the Nahautl guards behind him, praying, fervently, in their native tongue.

Oh. We're . . . so completely fucked. Adam backed up a step, running directly into Trennus as he did so, and then stopping dead.

A human voice rose above the hum of the machinery in the cavern. A chant, in Nahautl, that Adam couldn't understand. "What's he saying?" Kanmi hissed.

I'll help. The words were a soft, feminine whisper in his mind, and Adam recoiled, instinctively, trying to fight the intrusion . . . and then his eyes widened as the words spoken in Nahautl, he suddenly understood as Hebrew. *"Tlaloc! Lord of lightning, lord of water! You who make things sprout, hear our prayers! We have given you sustenance, you who have been starved of sacrifices for countless generations. We have given you the tears of children and the hearts of men to invigorate and strengthen you. And now, your servants are in danger—"*

You have taken as much as you have given. The voice was silent, and also needed no translation. Adam swore and put his hands to his head against the searing pain there. **You have given blood and flesh and tears, and you have taken my power unto you. As agreed. But now, the place of sacrifice to the south has fallen to the hands of the unsanctified. I grow weak. You bleed me like parasites . . . and so must blood feed me.**

Sigrun managed to whisper, "I can see Tototl. He's to the right of the altar. The arcs of power are going right to the Tholberg coils and missing him—"

"It's following the path of least resistance," Kanmi muttered, just barely audible above the crackling and hum of power in the cavern. "From the . . . *god* . . . to the Tholberg coils, through the air. It's powerful enough to break down the air itself—I can smell the ionization already. Then it passes from the coils . . . hmm. I can see a copper bar in the ceiling. They've drilled down through the pyramid itself to present a conductive element for the power to transmit up to the mast on the roof. They're not tapping the ley-lines for power here. They're using them for *stability.*" The sorcerer's voice was dazed.

"A load-bank," Trennus agreed, softly. "Like putting copper bars in a bath of saltwater to discharge electricity into. Gods. I don't even know what that would *do.*" The summoner stared at the room, his face bewildered. "Is he *bound* here? Is the god actually a *prisoner?*"

"Is that even *possible?*" Sigrun hissed.

"Maybe it's a willing compact."

Adam let the whispers fly past him. "Anyone have a visual on Xicohtencatl?" he asked, tersely. The magic part of the situation, he couldn't do anything about. He *could* do something about the people in the equation.

"I do," Ehecatl's whisper drifted out of the dimness. "He's on the other side of the stalactites. In the water. I'm going to move up and take him." There was terror in the Nahautl's voice, but determination, also.

"No, *don't*, he'll see you—" Sigrun hissed, but Ehecatl, invisible, had already slipped away.

Even as Ehecatl moved, however, the huge figure behind the altar stirred. Seemed to sniff the air. *Intruders. The unsanctified have entered my temple. Give me their blood, child of my line, and I will overlook your folly and your transgressions. Feed me their hearts and their tears, and I will feed you freely, in turn.*

"Oh, Baal, Astarte, and Tanis. This was not in my contract," Kanmi said, in a sinking tone, as the high priest, Tototl turned from the altar, peering towards the darkness of the tunnel . . . and Xicohtencatl, who'd been in the water, suddenly rose up to walk on its surface, as if he were a bug skating on the fluid's surface tension.

"You think we have any chance at diplomacy?" Adam asked Sigrun, feeling an odd surge of light-heartedness.

"I don't give us any chance at all." Sigrun said, flatly. "And running would be entirely useless. But you may certainly try your diplomacy!" She ducked back against the wall of the tunnel, as did Kanmi, Trennus, and Ehecatl, as blue-white arc of light slammed into the rock wall to their right. Mere lightning wouldn't have hurt her, but who knew what *else* was in that spark of energy?

Adam cleared his throat, feeling numb. *What in god's name am I supposed to say? Release the god and come out with your hands up?* "We're here for Xicohtencatl and Tototl, for crimes against the Imperium," he called. *Specifics can damned well wait.* "We're not here for a fight. This can be resolved peacefully." *Right. Sure it can.*

I will not permit you to take this priest of my line, or my bound servant. The voice was completely dismissive of Adam, but the god's eyes focused now, not on him, but on Sigrun, to Adam's side. *A child of the northern gods, here? They dare send one of their servants into our lands? They have grown arrogant.* The god paused. *Arise, ahuizotl. Arise, and defend your master.*

The ground to either side of the altar began to twist and distort, in much the same way Trennus had made the earth boil into mud outside, and small, twisted, bulging figures slightly smaller than wolves began to emerge from those brown pools. Whatever they were, they were sickeningly smooth, as if glistening birth-sacs encased them.

"I was born to fight lost battles." If a voice could be described as ashen, Sigrun's was. She raised her face, and white rune-wrought light emerged from her skin, turning her eyes into unreadable dark pools. "And today's as good a day to die as any other. I couldn't ask for better company."

"All things considered, I'd like to pass on the dying part," Kanmi retorted, and then he started incanting, rapidly.

And that was pretty much when all hell broke loose. Adam's .45 was already in his hand, and he and Sigrun both ran to the right, heading for the cover of the stalagmite mound to the north. Kanmi and Trennus both darted to the south, to a different stalagmite, and the Eagle warriors, clearly uncertain, stepped forward in the tunnel, hesitating. "Either move up, or clear the area!" Sigrun called to them. "We're not asking to fight one of your gods. You're being asked to *free* him!" Another blue-white arc of energy broke loose from one of the Tholberg coils and slammed into the rock beside her . . . possibly directed by the god, or by Xicohtencatl, she couldn't be sure which. Splinters of superheated rock flew through the air, and Sigrun dove to the ground, shielding her face with her left arm.

"We're sure of that?' Adam asked, as his fingers closed on her arm, pilling her further into cover behind the stalagmite mound.

"At the moment, the god looks like a captive to me. Figure it out later!"

Then Adam ducked out around her, trying to get a shot on Tototl or Xicohtencatl. He fired on the sorcerer, who was closer, and swore as he saw light flare in front of the man's form, and heard the bullet ricochet off the rock behind him. "He's got some sort of a shield in front of him, facing this direction. I'm going to need to a better angle."

"Ehecatl's going after him, too," Sigrun noted, tersely, having caught a tiny flicker of movement that betrayed the Jaguar warrior's position. "Try not to hit him. We only just got him back on the roster." *Damn it. Those creatures birthing themselves from the ground are almost free, and I can't call any lightning without access to the sky . . . .*

"He's *invisible*. He gets in my line of fire, I'm not going to have any choice about hitting him." Adam leaned out and tried another shot . . . and swore as the sorcerer caught sight of him, turned, and a whip of pure fire appeared in his hand, uncoiling and lashing directly for Adam. He barely ducked back in time. The lash hit the stalagmite mound in front of them, and the rock mound that sheltered them turned *molten*. Sigrun grabbed Adam and swung him, redirecting his movement, so that they both circled now, around to the north side of the mound. "I thought he was supposed to be *limited* in power," Adam muttered under his breath. *I'm taking this out of Eshmunazar's hide. Assuming any of us live.* "Think you can get to him, Sig?"

"Yes," Sigrun said, her voice grim. "Can you cover me?"

"Can distract him, sure." Adam leaned out, and opened fire again. This time, the sorcerer had to turn and spin his shield of force around to defend himself . . . and that was when Ehecatl tried to go into the water to attack the hovering sorcerer. All it took was one foot in contact with the water, and the Nahautl man *screamed*, his invisibility collapsing around his form, his body arcing and spasming.

Without even thinking, Sigrun leaped out from behind the stalagmites and flew forward, barely hearing Adam's shout of "Sig! No!" behind her.

She caught Ehecatl under the arms and pain shot through her. Lightning, for her, was little more than a lover's caress, or at least, what she imagined one would be like. An effervescent sensation against the skin and along the nerves, making her body sing, and then gone again. Sigrun got her arms securely under Ehecatl's, and launched herself to the cover of a different stalagmite mound, this one closer to the altar, and dropped Ehecatl, whose body was still *twitching*, in its shelter. She crouched protectively over Ehecatl and called her spear back to her hands, from where she'd dropped it beside Adam. "Come on, Ehe, you've had worse," she told the Nahautl warrior. "Get up. We need you."

In the meantime, Adam had gotten a clear look at the monstrosities being birthed from the cave floor. *He Who Makes Things Sprout, my ass,* was his only clear thought as the creatures burst from their glistening birth-sacs, snout-first, lips pulling back from curving white teeth. Dog-faced, four-limbed, with black, sleek flesh that looked as smooth as a frog's. At the end of each limb, a clawed, monkey-like paw, and, sprouting from their hindquarters, a long, prehensile tail, coiling into loops . . . with another hand at its tip. And most disturbing of all? Their eyes were completely human.

His mind rebelled against what he was seeing, and he flinched for a moment as the creatures opened their mouths to howl and gibber at the ceiling. Hunt-calls.

"*Ahuizotl!*" one of the Eagle warriors shouted, in dismay, and the five of them unlimbered their muskets and began to open fire on the creatures.

In the meantime, on the other side of the pool, Kanmi and Trennus were looking directly at another pack of the same creatures. "I have no idea what those are," Kanmi shouted. "Can you banish them?"

"They were summoned by a *god*. I'll try, but I might only be able to slow them down."

"Do that—oh, *shit!*" Kanmi ducked as the magma-like whip being controlled by Xicohtencatl sizzled through the air over his head, searing a line through the stalagmite mount behind which he and Trennus were taking shelter. "I'm on Xicohtencatl. Do what you can about the dog . . . things. Then start breaking the Tholberg coils."

"Are you *crazy?*"

"I really hope not. I think that's how they're redirecting the . . ." *Gods, help me, I don't even want to say this is possible, "god's* energy." *I have to assume he's allowing them to do so.*

"That could also blow us somewhere into next week. All right, all right, I'm on it." Trennus sounded rattled.

Kanmi sucked in a breath, heard another series of shots, and watched as one of the demon-dogs fell to the ground, bleeding *black* out on the earth. There were enormous amounts of energy in the air right now, but most of it was emanating from a god, and he had no idea what would happen if he tried to use it or reshape it to his own ends. *Probably blow my damn head off,* he thought, grimly. *So I'll just work with what Xicohtencatl gives me.*

He stepped out from behind the stalagmite mound, planting the rubber soles of his shoes firmly on the ground, and reached into his pockets. Cupped his hands around the batteries he found there, and pulled up a shield around himself—just in time, as Gratian attacked him with that lash of fire. The barrier gave Kanmi enough time to see the lash of fire for what it was: a portion of the stalactite curtain behind Xicohtencatl, liquefied with raw magic, and turned into a blade of searing heat. Still physical, however. Not just a pure energy release, as flame was. *I can work with that*, Kanmi thought, just barely smiling . . . . and pulled all the energy out of the liquefied stone, setting up the construct in his mind and muttering under his breath. The suddenly-cooled stone, flung like a spear, slammed into the far wall of the cave, where it shattered. Kanmi was left with far too much energy on his hands, so he redirected it as soon as it came to him, backwards against the flow of the stone, recoiling into Xicohtencatl's flesh in a wave of flame and heat. "Buzz a little louder, bumblebee," Kanmi taunted. "You're going to have to do better than that."

Trennus felt chips of stone cutting into the flesh of his upper arm and face as the spear of stone shattered against the wall, but he was focused on the monkey-dogs that were heading straight for Kanmi, as if they knew the smell of magic, and hungered for it. He reached down into the earth, seeking out the ley-lines and their resonant force, and tapped it. As he did, he reached a hand up as if snatching a ball out of the air and snapped his fingers closed around empty air.

In response, the limestone of the cave floor boiled up like skeletal fingers and closed around one of three remaining dogs like a cage. It howled and reared up to tug on the bars with its monkey-like hands, scrabbling with its long claws . . . and then the other two were on him. One of them was bleeding black from a musket ball that had been fired into its side. Tren caught the first one that launched itself at his throat, taking it out of the air, spinning, and slamming it to the ground on its back. His hands *tingled* at the touch of the creature's slimy skin, but he put it to the back of his mind.

Then the second creature, the wounded one, darted behind him and sank its fangs into the tendons at the back of his knee, tearing at it as if the beast were a wolf in truth. Trennus shouted and staggered, feeling blood already coursing down the back of his leg, hot and wet, and managed to turn. Focused. And pulled the stone of the cavern directly up, in one smooth spike, skewering the creature through belly and spine. A distorted, hellish whimper, a mix of human, dog, and monkey harmonics, and then the light went out of the all-too-human eyes.

The bleeding from the back of his wounded leg was problem number one. He needed to get that under control. Trennus yanked off his shirt and tied it around his knee, trying to slow down the blood, at least. Problem number two was . . . worse. His hands were tingling far more now. His mouth was dry, and his vision skewed. "Poison!" he shouted. "The dogs' skins! They're poisoned somehow!" *Trust me to find these things out the hard way* .... Trennus shook his head and tried to focus. It wasn't unlike all the bad parts of being drunk—the room spun, the floor tipped from side to side, or at least appeared to do so, as his equilibrium gave out completely. Trennus dropped to his knees, swearing, and tried to focus his mind. *Have to take out the Tholberg coils* .... *Lassair? Saraid?*

I'm . . . *here.* Lassair's voice was terrified, little more than a whisper. *This is a very bad place, Trennus. He can see me. I'm trying to stay as small as I can.*

I am here, as well. Saraid's soft voice was no less frightened.

Can you help me? He didn't have time to bargain specifically.

I . . . *might be able to stop the bleeding.* Lassair ventured.

No, clear the poison first, if you can.

Trennus, if you die, I die with you. Bleeding first. Then the poison. But . . . *I'm going to need to* . . . Lassair's sense shuddered. *I'm going to need to be inside your body to fix it.*

There was little that terrified the gentle spirit more. The summoner who had bound her before Trennus had released her, had used her, in so many foul ways. He'd bound her into dead bodies, so that they would move, like a *ghul* . . . and then had fucked the rotting corpses, requiring her to move the body convincingly for him. Forced her to dwell inside of a mortal shell that had no functioning nerve pathways, no spark of life. And in between performances like this, the summoner had also compelled Lassair to give of her own energies to heal his body. Keep him young and healthy. He'd robbed her of her energies, never any return, just compulsion by will and by Name. No bargains. Just . . . theft and rapine.

Trennus had, quite deliberately, never thought of the man's Name since he'd killed him. Then again, when he'd been done with the man, he hadn't had a Name anymore. There were reasons why he felt compelled to protect and nurture Lassair, and show her that not all humans were vile. And there were reasons, too, why Lassair panicked at the mere thought of being contained in a mortal body.

Just do what you can to clear my head. This will all be over soon, either way.

No! Saraid's sharp cry was echoed by Lassair, and they both manifested at the same moment. Lassair flared into white life beside him, and, terror in every part of her being, slipped into Trennus' body. He felt her like a flame, all through him, and part of him fought her, with all his considerable mental strength. *Please, I can't fight you and my own fear at the same time. Please, relax. Let me help you* ....

Saraid stood before him, in her ephemeral stag form, attacking the monkey-dogs with her antlers as they advanced on him. She didn't have enough substance to throw them, but with every blow, the creatures cringed away from her pale glory, hissing and screeching in pain. In that moment of reprieve, Trennus leaned against the rock, and stared ahead of him. He was supposed to be doing something right now. Something important. But his mind was going gray and vague, and the world around him .... blurred. *Trennus! Hold on! You go, we both go!*

Sigrun, for her part, had pulled Ehecatl more or less upright as his body stopped spasming. "You all right?" She could feel the power of the god radiating everywhere in the cave, and it was making her sick to her stomach. The closer she got to him, the worse the nausea became.

The Nahautl man rolled the rest of the way to his feet, and staggered, leaning against the wall where she'd taken cover. "Give . . . give me a minute . . . ."

"Don't have one—on your feet!" And that was when the black, slime-sided dogs closed on them. A couple of musket balls from the Eagle warriors slammed into the head of the closest, killing it, but then three others were on her, and she didn't have time for anything else. She caught one in midair as it launched itself at her with a monkey-like spring from its hind legs, and jabbed it in the belly with her spear, stepping through. She let its inertia and seventy pounds of squirming, dying flesh pass her, reversing the spear's direction to allow the beast to slide off the blade and onto the ground behind her, and then scythed the blade back to slice the muzzle off the next incoming dog. The horrible part, as it opened its ruined maw to howl in agony, was that human tears bloomed in its eyes.

No time to think, no time to reflect, because in that moment, the third one launched itself through the air and landed on her right arm, staggering her for a moment. Four sets of claws scrabbled for purchase, jabbing through her chain shirt, but unable to rend. White fangs tore into the side of her throat, and as she worked a hand up to try to tear it off of her, the creature loosed its grip with its rear claws and did a *handstand* of sorts. Its spine undulated, and it brought its rump down over her head, allowing its prehensile tail to come into play, wrapping around her bleeding throat like a noose, constricting tightly just above where its fangs were buried. The freakish hand at the end of the tail worked its way up now, reaching for her eyes with its savage claws.

Adam watching from cover, stared at the creature for a dumbfounded instant, and then shouted. "Hold still, Sig!" over the noise of battle. Disregarding Xicohtencatl for the moment—the sorcerer seemed heavily occupied by the mage-duel between himself and Kanmi, anyway— he aimed very carefully with his .45. He was all too aware of the fact that Sigrun had told him there were two absolutely sure ways to kill her. Removal of the head and a wound that obliterated her heart. He considered a .45 hollow point to be just as valid a way of decapitating someone as a sword-blade, when all was said and done. As such, he held his breath as he aimed, and did a little silent, but very fervent praying as he squeezed the trigger.

The monkey-dog . . . whatever it was . . . exploded in a shower of black gore, and Sigrun tore its tail from around her throat, gasping for air. But, to Adam's disgust, four more of the creatures had just finished being birthed from the ground. Two of them charged Ehecatl—the Nahautl man fired his one-shot derringer directly at the creature. It was a fire-enchanted bullet, and his aim was true, but it didn't matter; the creature staggered, but slipped around behind him, tearing at his hamstrings, while the other caught at his throat, pulling him to the ground. A tumble of arms and legs, and Adam couldn't risk firing into that scrum . . . and then there was a yelp of inhuman pain as Ehecatl rolled atop the beast, and sank his obsidian knife deeply into its chest. "The damned things definitely have poisoned skins!" Ehecatl shouted. "Feels like touching a poison dart frog!"

Harah. Adam fired at the fourth creature as the one under Ehecatl died — and missed. He was peripherally aware that Sigrun was laying waste to two more of the creatures with her spear once more . . . .but the last creature leaped on Ehecatl, and the Jaguar warrior and the beast rolled across the floor, panting and struggling, the human's efforts already weakening from the effects of the poison in his body, and the creature's inhuman contortions bringing them closer and closer to the altar now . . . .

On the other side of the room, Kanmi did indeed have Xicohtencatl's full attention. "It doesn't have to be this way," Gratian called to the Carthaginian mage. "I know you, Kanmi. I know how you think. And right now, you're *fighting for the wrong side.* This is a revolution. This is how it starts . . . we throw out Rome. We give the country back to its people. And then we go about liberating the rest of the damned world."

Oh, you have got to be kidding me, Kanmi thought, distantly, his mind reaching out to his surroundings, looking for the faintest wrong twitch in the energy patterns and currents around him. "You mean to tell me," he said, maintaining his shielding in front of him, "that this is all for the benefit of the common man? What exactly do you know about the common man, patrician?"

Kanmi was dimly aware of more of the dog creatures running through the area, birthing themselves from mud pools closer to the tunnel entrance, and attacking the Eagle warriors there. One of them killed one of the dogs with a knife to its throat, and then threw the obsidian blade directly at the sorcerer; Gratian's shield of power, invisible when not under attack, caught the blade, stealing all the kinetic energy from it, and letting the stone knife fall into the water at his feet. *That's a powerful shield, but it's static. He has to shift it, can only face it a one direction at a time . . . he really never has learned flexibility, has he?*

He felt the twitch of power, and was ready as Xicohtencatl pulled in energy, and the ground under Kanmi's feet began to superheat, the rubber soles of his shoes melting. Kanmi hissed and took the energy out of the rock again, this time sending it into the pool under Gratian's feet. *I wonder what will happen if you get too much energy in that water. I can see copper wires running from the Tholberg coils . . . you're mediating the god's energy through them, and running it into the pool, so it's . . . less direct. So you can tap it, use it, but not have to be a god-born to do so. A technical transubstantiation, in place of a religious one. But you've got a finite capacity for energy, Gratian. We all do. And I don't think you're nearly as good at finding different places for energy to go as I am.*

As it was, the superheated pool boiled, instantly turning into a blast of steam that hit and cooked the other mage from below. Gratian screamed, and Kanmi's awareness of the whole battle situation widened for a moment, as he heard shots being fired, and screams from the other side of the pool. "You think you know what the common man wants?" Kanmi gritted out between his teeth. "The common man wants food on his table, a wife, a couple of kids, and not to have to worry about any of them being hurt or killed or sacrificed to a god. The common man wants to be *left the fuck alone.*"

Gratian hissed and sent a spray of a hundred tiny droplets of fire at him; too many to count, too many to react to in time. Kanmi tore energy out of the air in front of him, and the air itself solidified into a slab. He couldn't keep the nitrogen-oxygen mix solid for long, and he needed something else to do with the energy, which he was pouring into the batteries in his hands, feeling even these high-capacity cells heat up. *Don't explode, don't explode, I don't want acid burns all over me or metal embedded in my hands . . . .* The fireseeds slammed into his barrier, which was only an inch thick, and already subliming away, not even making it back into liquid form before dissipating as cold gas back into the atmosphere . . . but the barrier stopped the projectiles. And then Kanmi pulled the energy back out of the batteries, grunted with the effort, and *threw* the solid wall of frozen air at Xicohtencatl.

Nitrogen, oxygen, and even carbon dioxide chilled to the point of solidifying are cold enough to do tissue damage on contact with human skin, and Xicohtencatl was clearly not expecting a defensive shield to be turned into a projectile. His shield was tuned, currently, to absorbing kinetic energy from small objects — knives, bullets, and spears — not to repelling two hundred pounds of frozen death. Kanmi couldn't see the man's face, thanks to the size of his projectile, but he could imagine Gratian's eyes widening in surprise as it slammed into him, at about twenty miles an hour, and then fell down, like a door without supports, driving him down into the boiling water below. "Hail and farewell, you son of a bitch," Kanmi told the sorcerer, who was trapped below a sheet of rapidly-dissipating ice, and suspended in boiling, electrified water. Gratian might be good. But even the best sorcerer tended to be only capable of defending against one or two things at a time. And pain was a magnificent distraction and deterrent to sorcery. *Not to mention, he hasn't gotten to the point yet where he doesn't need to incant to cast. Kind of hard to incant when you're trying not to inhale the water.* "Have a nice trip across the Styx, assuming you believe in it." He glanced back, and blinked. There was a phantom stag hovering in the air between him and Trennus, and Trennus' entire body was limned with white and red flames. Kanmi reached for the heat of the flames, trying to keep them from burning Trennus to death . . . and found absolutely no heat. No energy that he could grab. *Oh, gods, those are his bound spirits . . . .*

Trennus' eyes snapped into focus, warmth drifting all through him. *Is that better?* Lassair asked him, a little frantically.

Oh . . . gods yes. Actually, that feels . . . really good. He staggered upright, and glanced around; Kanmi was slamming a white wall of something at the sorcerer in the pool, gunshots on the other side of the room, Eagle warriors fighting with the damned monkey-dogs, screaming and trying to pull them off of each other, and then turning and tearing at empty air with their hands and knives. Two of them were actually setting on each other, and Trennus swore and hastily pulled the stone of the floor up around each of them to protect them from each other. *Gods, thank you. I could have turned on Kanmi or someone else if you hadn't pulled the poison out of my body.*

It seemed to be similar to the toxin of poison dart frogs in some ways, but more hallucinogenic than paralytic, Lassair offered, hesitantly, slipping back out of his body and diminishing in size to a handful of wispy flame once more, hovering in the air beside him. *What will you do now?*

What Kanmi suggested. We've got to stop them from bleeding power from the god and using it. Trennus looked at the closest Tholberg coil and grimaced. It was undoubtedly secured by a long metal bolt, deep into the earth. He could, fairly easily, cause an earthquake here, but that would bring the pyramid down on their heads. No, his best bet, really, was to overload each Tholberg coil in turn. Of course, that was going to release a great deal of energy. Trennus set his teeth, reached down into the ground, and pulled on the resonating energy of the intersecting lines once more, feeding as much of it as he could at once, into the closest coil.

The coil, not designed for *this* much energy, promptly began to melt; the housing, subject to too much heat and stress, cracked down the center and exploded outwards; and the insulation in the housing promptly went up in sullen red flames. *One down,* Trennus thought, and focused on the next, all too aware of the Eagle warriors behind him, fighting and dying. "Esh, *help* them! I've got the coils!"

"One thing at a time . . . ." Kanmi growled in return.

The fight had, thus far, only lasted two agonizingly long minutes, as best Sigrun was aware on the other side of the room, as she killed another monkey-dog and ran forward, trying to stop the one that had Ehecatl by the throat. She speared it through the body, and then Tototl, who'd been uninvolved in the fight thus far, was in front of her. The god-born of Tlaloc was somehow covered in glistening obsidian, as if the earth itself had flowed up and over his body to protect him from her. The face was an expressionless mask, no features visible at all besides the eyes, which were large openings that mimicked Tlaloc's own cavernous and empty eye-pits.

Without a word, Tototl backhanded Sigrun away, the heavy, rock-covered fist sending the god-born of Tyr flying backwards into the stalagmite mound behind her. The second impact, from behind, was enough to daze Sigrun for a moment, and when she opened her eyes again, she saw that Tototl had picked Ehecatl up bodily, and thrown him onto the altar. A string of words in incomprehensible Nahautl, raising one of his hands towards his god, keeping the other massively heavy hand down on Ehecatl's throat, preventing the struggling captive from rising . . . . and then he plunged his free hand down, all glistening obsidian, into Ehecatl's chest. From her angle, she could clearly see that he was somehow wrist-deep in her friend's lung cavity, without so much as a drop of blood being spilled, and Ehecatl writhed in agony as that hand closed on his heart.

Adam, splitting his attention and his ammunition between targets, saw that Gratian was down, and fired twice more at the various monkey-dogs bursting out of the earth near him, and then spun, seeing Sigrun go flying. He lashed out with a foot to keep another dog at bay, kicking hard enough to fracture its jaw and send it whimpering away. With a little space cleared, Adam had a chance to see that Tototl had Ehecatl down on the altar. *Ya ben shel zona.* He aimed for center of mass, directly at the rock-encased body, between the shoulder blades, and with his last round before needing to reload the .45, fired.

Obsidian is, structurally and chemically, really only volcanic glass. The hollow-point bullet *shattered* the rear armor, and the impact drove Tototl forward over the altar, knocking him over, and forcing him to pull his hand out of Ehecatl's body to break his fall.

Sigrun shouted something wordless and launched herself, her feet not even touching the ground as she slammed into the high priest, sending them both tumbling. She didn't have access to the sky, so she had no lightning to call. Her spear was useless. All she had was the strength of her body, the training of her mind, and the knowledge that it *would heal.* She and Tototl wrestled, a tangle of arms and legs, until Sigrun came up on top and began throwing punches directly at the god-born's masked face. It didn't matter that she was punching rock. It didn't matter that her fingers were bleeding. *It will heal.* A mantra in her mind. *Hit him again.* It didn't matter that the skin was peeling back, and the bones were exposed. *It will heal. Break through the stone. Get down to the flesh itself.* Her knuckles fractured. *It will heal. Ehecatl might not. Electrocuted, poisoned, bitten, and then a hand trying to tear out his heart. Ehecatl, who's as faithful to his gods as any man of Nahautl could be, dying at the behest of these people? No.* Another punch. *Get down to his face and _end_ this.*

Another concussive blast, another Tholberg coil exploded. "Stop!" Adam shouted across the pool to Kanmi and Trennus. "I think the coils are what are keeping Tlaloc tied here! You break those, and he'll be free!"

One of the two remaining Eagle warriors, from his cage of rock, called, sounding dazed and utterly confused, partially from the poison of the monkey-dogs, and partially from circumstances, "Isn't . . . isn't the goal . . . freeing him?"

"They've been siphoning off his power, and Xicohtencatl was using it to fight us!" Kanmi shouted back, and enveloped another monkey-dog that had been trying to worm its way into the rock cage with an Eagle warrior with his mind. He incanted, concentrating all of the ambient heat around him, condensing it, and setting the beast on fire.

Adam switched to his backup .38, kept firing at various dogs, and shouted back, "Yes. And I don't really see him around here right now. I do see a pretty angry god, though! Get the Eagle warriors out of here, and help Sig! Ignore the coils!"

Trennus stopped in the middle of popping the sixth Tholberg coil, and looked across the pool at Adam. *Sigrun first.* Trennus started forward, eying the rock-like armor of the high priest and determining how best to *shuck* it from him, when Tototl managed to heave and roll with Sigrun again, this time propelling them towards the pool. Tangle of arms and legs, and the high priest forced Sigrun's head back into the water. She snarled and resisted, keeping her mouth and nose clear, but the pool's water began to roil and *rise*, like the fingers of a hand, or like the limbs of an octopus wrapping forward over her face in long, clear strands *Oh, the Morrigan take you.* Trennus directed a ley current right at the rocky surface of Tototl's armor, riddled with cracks as it was. The blow shattered the chest, arms, and mask of the armor. The high priest flinched back, looking down at his exposed belly, chest, and arms, and Sigrun managed to work a leg free to kick him away from her, sitting up, a shroud of water still around her head. "Esh!" Trennus shouted. "Get that off her, before she drowns!"

Kanmi, on the other side of the room, where the two remaining living Eagle warriors were still caged in rock, and where he'd been fighting to keep the monkey-dogs from getting to them, looked up, and muttered, "Oh, *shit.*"

Sigrun, for her part, was starting to panic. She couldn't breathe, her fingers went right through the water like . . . water . . . and no amount of telling herself that death by drowning wasn't a battle wound convinced her heart, lungs, or nervous system that they weren't about to die. Through the wavering mask , she watched as Ehecatl, holding one hand to his chest in obvious pain, slid off the altar, an obsidian knife in his free hand. He stepped behind the retreating high priest . . . and slammed the knife through the man's back, where Adam's bullet had already shattered the armor. She could see the point of the knife emerge through the man's chest, directly through the sternum. As the priest's body went limp, the water around her head released itself to gravity's grip, sheeting down to the ground once more. Sigrun gasped for air, and sat there, shuddering, still feeling the power of the god *vibrating* through the air. "Eh . . . Ehe . . . " she croaked, trying to get to her feet, and reaching for her old friend's hand. Whether to help him to stay standing, as he rocked on his feet, or to ask him to help her up, she really couldn't have said, at the moment.

Behind the altar, Tlaloc's empty eye-pits stared down at the body of his fallen high priest. And just for a moment, the fanged mouth smiled. ***Blood spilled, and flesh given. A beating heart stilled, at my altar, and by*** *my sanctified blade. The rich and powerful blood of the gods, spilled for me.*

Oh, *Hel's cold heart,* Sigrun thought, and managed to find her feet at last. "Fall back," she called. Her voice was a raven's hoarse cry. "Fall back, get out of here!" She called her spear to her hand, but knew it was useless. She couldn't fight a god. No one could.

"Matrugena, drop the cages, let's get these men out of here!" Kanmi shouted, and Trennus spun. Saw the two Eagle warriors he'd imprisoned to keep them away from each other's throats, and let the stone that imprisoned them drop back into the ground. "Go, go, go," Kanmi urged, shoving the disoriented, mildly poisoned men towards the tunnel exit. He turned, however, in dread, feeling a *shift* in the energies in the room. "Come on," the Carthaginian told the others, his voice thick. "Run, damn you!"

"No point," Ehecatl said, quietly. "He's a *god.*"

"He's *bound,*" Trennus said, tightly. "Somehow. For the moment, anyway. We'll leave. Quietly. Peacefully. We're not the ones who bound you." The Britannian raised his voice, but his tone was still . . . deeply respectful.

No. But you have also slain my servant. The death's head smile somehow seemed to widen.

"Didn't he just seem pretty happy about his servant being killed for his sake?" Kanmi muttered, backing towards the door. "You're grateful, you want revenge, make up your mind . . . ."

Trennus let the words pass him by, as Lassair and Saraid both demanifested now, and passed into his body, huddling inside of him. Sheltering there, and trying to shelter him. It felt . . . odd. *Gods respect bargains. Just like spirits. History's full of examples of that. Adam tried negotiating when we first came in, but he's not . . . an intercessor. A trained bargainer with spirits. Worst that can happen is that I get my fool ass killed.* "He wasn't a faithful servant, though, now was he?" Trennus tried, hobbling slowly towards the door. Lassair had stopped the bleeding, and he could stand on the leg, just by locking the knee, but he couldn't flex it at all; the tendons were just too damaged. He was sweating as he tried to find the right words that would reach a god. Logic and reason didn't always work on spirits; their motivations were sometimes just too different from a human's . . . and he had no idea if the usual things that worked on spirits would work on a *god* . . . but he had to try. The others might be able to get free, if this succeeded. And you wrestled with spirits in the flesh, in the mind, and with words. *I even already know this one's Name. Not that I'd dare use it.* "He bound you, bound you in blood. He offered sacrifices to feed you, but he and the other, they took as much as they gave. You said it yourself. A faithful servant gives more, out of love, doesn't he? Out of devotion?" He paused. "And these two, they didn't give out of devotion.

They gave out of a desire for power. That's not the way it's meant to be, is it?"

For just an instant, he thought he'd gotten *through*. That he'd dared to bargain in words, and had prevailed with reason and with sense.

And then the god spoke again, in a voice that howled with madness, *They were mine. I will have recompense. And they have left me . . . a way out.*

The lictors had clustered now, in a tight little defensive perimeter around the tunnel, the two Eagle warriors having already cleared the area. Ehecatl was still breathing in short, harsh pants, clutching at his chest with his left hand. "Better to go out in battle," the Nahautl man said, in between breaths, "than to die of a damned *heart attack*. Cleaner. More honor."

Adam reloaded his .45, his fingers deft and sure, and nodded to Ehecatl. "Least you got the bastard." Adam turned and looked up at Matrugena. "You tried," he told Trennus, calmly, distantly. He'd never expected to count a summoner a *friend*, let alone be likely to die beside one. "It was nice working with you."

"Nice knowing you, too." Trennus put a hand against the tunnel wall for balance.

"Will you two save the noble farewells?" Kanmi snapped. "I'm trying to feel what he's doing . . . oh, Baal's teeth."

To the sorcerer's senses, it was all too clear. The god's energies pulsed through the remaining Tholberg coils, and, following the path of least resistance, tracked along the copper wires strung from the machines to the pool of still-steaming, but now much cooler water. The energies poured into the water . . . and into the empty, hollow shell of Gratian Xicohtencatl's body.

Kanmi's eyes flicked across the room and stared at the hulking avatar of Tlaloc bound behind its altar by machines and magic. "How does a god get an avatar?" he asked, sharply. "Do they *make* them, or can they use human bodies?"

Sigrun stirred. "Both have been known to happen," she replied, her tone uneasy. "Eshmunazar, this is probably not the time for theoretical quandaries."

Kanmi swore internally. Just as a spirit could be forced into the dead body of a human to make a *ghul* rise in the hands of a clumsy human summoner, now, the god's very essence was transferring from the avatar bound at the far end of the cavern into a new vessel. If Tlaloc were *free,* he wouldn't need to do this; he'd just use his existing form. If Tlaloc were free, he could also just hop instantly to the new body, Kanmi was fairly sure. But if they could catch him midway through the transfer . . . they might be able to damage him. Dissipate him. Send him back to whatever misty realm gods occupied when they were not on earth, watching sparrows fall.

Kanmi looked around, wild-eyed. "Destroy the coils," he told Trennus.

"But Adam just said *not* to—"

"They're how he's transferring!"

"And if we unbind him, we're going to have a really angry god in the same room with us!"

"And if we don't disrupt the transfer, we're going to have him incarnate twenty feet from us anyway! *And* in a dead body, at that . . . if that drives a *spirit* crazy, it might well do the same to a god, for all we know!"

Trennus stared at Kanmi. "On three. I've got the three on the right."

"I've got the three on the left. One . . . ."

" . . . two . . . ."

"Three," they both said together, closed their eyes, and overloaded the six remaining coils. It didn't take much; the machinery was on the verge of melting into slag, anyway, overloaded by the raw energy coming off of the god. The cases shattered into red-hot fragments, sizzling across the large cave, a few dropping into the pool with a hiss of steam. Kanmi could feel raw power in the room, some of it dispersing, like ambient cosmic radiation, into a mere crackle of force . . . and the rest *coalescing.* "Shit," he whispered. "Didn't work."

And at the center of the pool, a head rose from the water. Barely visible, it was black against leaden silver, for there was little light left in the cavern now, beyond the dull red, smoke-obscured glow of the burning insulation from the various machine's casings. "Back up," Adam told them all, breaking and tossing a flare into the cavern, just so they could see what was coming for them.

In the flickering white light of the flare, they could all see the figure of a man once more begin to rise out of the depths, until he stood on the surface of the water. But Gratian Xicohtencatl was no more. His skin and flesh had been cooked in the boiling water, and had split away, showing the red muscle tissue beneath. His eye-sockets were blank and empty. And his face had a rictus grin, displaying teeth that were rapidly elongating into fangs. "Xipe Totec," Ehecatl said, in a tone of horror. "He looks like Red Tezcatlipoca, the Flayed God. The priests used to flay men every year, and dress his statues with the discarded skin, or wear the skins, themselves, in place of robes, for spring fertility rites. They are *not* the same god, but he wears the face of the Flayed One!"

*I am **free**. You could not stop me. The old body, I discard like the husk that it is. Your pale Roman gods will not stop me now. I am free and I will feast on the blood and the tears and the flesh of my sacrifices again, and my people will be strong once more!*

Slowly, Sigrun stepped out in front of the rest of them, trepidation seething in the pit of her stomach. This was certain death. Then again, a valkyrie was born for precisely this purpose: to fight lost battles, to save those who could be healed, to carry home the slain, or to be slain themselves. "Now would be a good time for you all to retreat."

"No," Adam said, shortly. "We all stand together."

"You don't understand. I . . . have to challenge him. I do not even have the sky down here. I'm . . . little more than a normal human without the sky. I'm sorry. Just *go.*" The last was a whisper, and she didn't even know to whom she was apologizing. Sigrun turned her gaze back towards the god, and set her spear in her hands, walking forward. Her voice shook as she lifted her chin and spoke. "I do not say well-met, Tlaloc. The gods of Rome made a covenant with you and yours, centuries ago, when they and theirs forbade the offering of human sacrifices. That covenant has bound you. The world has moved on since you last tasted of your people's sacrifice. And they are stronger without those sacrifices, today, than they ever were before. Parasite god, feeding on the bowels of your people, on their tears and their sorrows. What know you of loyalty? Only the whip, the scourge, and the sorrow of a people enslaved to your will."

This was precisely the *opposite* of what Trennus had been trying to do, and he closed his eyes for a moment, quelling the impulse to swear. This wasn't diplomacy. This was a challenge issued, a gauntlet thrown down. ***Foolish child. The blood of gods may run through your veins, but it will make your tears all the sweeter, and your heart fairer meat for my hunger.***

"Come and take them, then," Sigrun said, her throat tight, damning her friends in her heart for not *running*. For not taking the chance she was giving her life to give to them.

The corpse raised its hand, and lightning shot out of fingertips that showed bone through the flesh, striking Sigrun, and slamming her back into the wall with its force. She struggled back upright, gritting her teeth, and hissed back, "Lightning is my god's gift to me, parasite. Feeder on filth and the lives of your own people." She lifted her spear, just as Tlaloc unleashed another barrage of blue-white light at her, and actually *caught* the electricity this time, on the blade of the spear. She could smell the air ionizing around them as the lightning, redirected, arced back towards the god. But Tlaloc probably had no upper limitation to the amount of heaven's fire he could absorb.

"You will have to have to find another trick," Sigrun told him, defiance in her words, but not in her voice. She knew there was no way to win. The only choice here was in how she was going to die. The lightning wouldn't kill her, but she had no illusions that the god wasn't capable of *improvising.*

In the meantime, Adam's head had swung around, staring up at the ceiling, his mind whirling at something approaching the speed of light. "She needs *sky.* Matrugena . . . can you open a damned hole to the open air down here?" He flinched back as a blue-white spark arced off of Sigrun's body and spidered, briefly, to the floor, close to his foot, leaving a scorch mark before it died.

Trennus' head swung up. "Gods . . . I don't know. I could bring the whole damned building down on us. The material *has* to go somewhere! I can't just make it disappear!" Matter and energy could not be created or destroyed. They could only change states. That was a fundamental law in the universe, and it was a matter of debate among natural philosophers if even *gods* could break that rule.

He swore quietly under his breath and reached into the earth again for the bright and searing lines of power he could see, roiling beneath the surface, and pulled on them. Poured their power up into the roof above them, but at an angle, so that he'd be cutting through what felt like twenty feet of dirt and rock and then boring through the actual stones of the pyramid. Not straight up through two hundred feet of rock to its pinnacle, but a far shorter distance: out one of its stepped sides. The best he could do was turn the stone to dust or mud, which poured down from the opening that he positioned at the far end of the cavern, to lessen the chances of the ceiling falling on all their heads. *All right*, he thought, pouring more power into it. *Sigrun needs sky? We'll give her sky.*

Unfortunately, Tlaloc had apparently just realized that the lightning bolts that usually worked so effectively on mortals were completely useless against the valkyrie. The electrical storm ceased, and the blue-white light that had filled the cavern died with it. "Got anything better?" Sigrun taunted, trying to keep the god's attention squarely fixed on her.

"Lord of water and rain," Ehecatl muttered beside Adam, sinking down to his haunches and holding his chest. Even in the dim light from the dying flare in the cavern ahead of them, the man's face looked gray. "He who makes things sprout. Lord of the passages to the underworld. Fertility. Life out of death."

Thus, it wasn't a complete surprise when the waters of the pool under the god's feet rose up like a giant hand attached to a long, sinuous, transparent hand, and seized Sigrun in a giant's grip, shoving a thumb over her head . . . and her head simply popped into the water that made up the thumb. For the second time in a half hour, Sigrun was in danger of drowning on dry land, and just as when the high priest had tried to kill her before, it was useless to try to fight. Her spear cut through the water of the hand, and the water resealed itself, without a wound, in the wake of her attack. And the hand inexorably dragged her towards the cenote.

Sigrun dug in her heels and fought, trying to fly away. Her lungs already burned from the smoke in the air, and she knew she wasn't going to be able to hold out as long this time before her body forced her to suck in another breath.

Watching from the tunnel, and feeling, yet again, helpless, Adam asked, "Eshmunazar?"

"Working on it," Kanmi muttered. "If I superheat it and dissipate it as steam, that would *work* but it'll *parboil* her, and I don't think she's going to thank me for it."

"Kanmi! She doesn't have time for *theory!*" Adam's voice was a crack this time.

Theory was the last thing on Kanmi's mind. He was struggling to keep at bay the memory of his brothers holding his head down under the waters of Tyre's harbor. Helplessness and fear.

He shoved the memories aside, and snapped his fingers. "Surface tension. Got it." He dug through his pockets until he found what looked like nothing more extraordinary than a tin of shampoo powder, opened it, and flung the entire contents towards the hand of water. It was, in effect, nothing more than a construct, a golem, this one formed of water and godly will, rather crafted of clay and animated with a hapless earth elemental to provide its motive force.

He hadn't been joking the other day when he'd mentioned that *starting* a chemical or physical process was much, much harder than *continuing* it. The soap contained amphiphilic compounds—surfactants, specifically, which would break the surface tension of water by interacting with the fluid at the molecular level. The powder flew out, propelled by Kanmi's will, hit the surface of the water, and then Kanmi incanted, framing the spell that would increase the rate at which the surfactants dissolved the bonds between the water molecules at the surface of the giant construct. Kanmi gritted his teeth, and powered every bit of his will into his power matrix . . . . and the water fell to the ground in a wave, bubbling a little from the shampoo. "Yes!" Kanmi shouted, as Sigrun staggered on the very edge of the cenote. "I will *not* fear death by water. Not today, not tomorrow, not *ever*."

The empty eye-pits of the god turned towards him, and Tlaloc moved the ruined lips into a ghastly smile. And that was when the same living lash of fire that had been in Gratian's hand appeared in the god's. Except that the god wasn't using the rock behind him as a source of the material and just supplying energy to superheat and manipulate the substance; this was the air itself, transmuted to plasma. *Oh, shit,* Kanmi thought, and dove out of the way. The words of his spells tumbled out as he pulled up every shield he had, from kinetic absorption to the shell of frozen nitrogen . . . and then that shell, which had turned the world, briefly, to darkness . . . lit up blazingly white as the stream of plasma hit it.

Kanmi didn't have time to swear. He frantically stole energy from the plasma. Redirected it. "Little help here!" Kanmi shouted after a moment, sweat beading on his face as he held his hands out in front of him, a barrier of pure force protecting them, raw starfire being sent right back at the god, just the way Sigrun redirected the electrical storm, moments before. He had just enough time to think, to wonder, *This is a water god. He should have very specific attributes. Very specific abilities. All the tales of the gods say that they are jealous, and when one steals the thunderbolts from the other's pockets, they hunt him down and punish him. How is he doing this . . . could he have learned it from Gratian's mind? Can gods, like man, evolve? Or is it just that he once was a sun-god, and remembers the tune, and some of the words?*

That was just distant chatter at the back of his mind, however. He couldn't really pursue that line of thought, however; he was far too busy trying to keep from being incinerated, and it wasn't a fight he could win, as evidenced by the rising pain in his hands and forearms as the heat he was struggling to redirect began to intensify, and the very air around him began to overheat as well. "Seriously. Could use some help *right now*! But don't let me rush you!" Kanmi shouted.

Trennus, for his part, caught the surge of powdered stone pouring into the cavern from the tunnel he was boring up to the sky, and pulled it in a cloud across the cavern, swirling it around Tlaloc like a flock of starlings at sunset. It was about a ton of material, all told, and the ley-mage knew he couldn't *possibly* have done this, except for where he was standing, right now. Atop two full, gloriously resonant ley-lines. He clapped his hands together, like a child forming a snowball . . . . and the dust congealed, becoming a boulder, with the god trapped inside, like an insect in amber. "Instant fossil," Trennus muttered, and let the stone go, falling into the cenote. "This *would* bind a spirit, if I carved its Name into the stone . . . this might only slow him down, though. Come on. Let's get out of here before he breaks free," he told the others, starting to back away. His tunnel through the ceiling was complete; Sigrun had a clear view of the sky from the very depths of the earth. *Though hopefully, that won't matter. And hopefully, several generations of archaeologists don't curse us any more than they'll curse Tototl and Xicohtencatl for driving a lightning rod through the whole damned structure.*

Trennus hadn't gotten more than three steps when the water *exploded* upwards, shards of stone carried with it, lancing into the ceiling above. ***You dare? You dare to think that you can bind me, like some petty spirit?*** It was a roar in all their minds as the god, emerged from the water, glowing dusky red now. ***Die!***

Fire enveloped Trennus, and he dropped to the floor, rolling and trying to beat the flames out. Adam threw his cloak over the Britannian, trying to muffle the flames, but to no avail . . . and that was when Sigrun, with a clear view of the sky, slammed into the god at her full flying speed, sending them both flying to the far side of the cave, into the soft mound of sand and stone dust that Trennus' efforts had created. The god, distracted by this impertinent new target, released the fire on Trennus, and backhanded Sigrun halfway across the room. Wind kicked up, suddenly, swirling the dust in the room like a djinni's tail, and Adam swore as lightning came down, pulled through that small opening in the roof with lethal accuracy, slamming into the god's avatar. "If it doesn't work on you, it probably won't work on him!" Kanmi shouted over the howling of the wind that was one of Sigrun's primary defenses, shielding his eyes against the dirt.

A blur of light through the wind and the debris, and then the wind *died* and Adam could hear Sigrun's scream, as she, like Trennus before her, was engulfed in flame. ***You will be a fitting sacrifice to me. The blood of the other gods will run. I have foreseen it, in my exile and in my weakness. They will all die, and only a handful will remain, and I will rule!***

Adam took one panicked look at Sigrun, as Trennus, only lightly scorched, but bloody and barely able to walk on his bad leg, tried to get to his feet. "Kanmi!"

"Trying." The sorcerer's voice was strained, even as Sigrun screamed again, in agony. "I don't have a lot left."

Adam stared at the god in a mortal shell, with the closest thing to hatred he'd felt all day. Everything till now had merely been a mad scramble for survival. Now, this . . . creature . . . spirit . . . god . . . was torturing Sigrun, and for what? Pettiness, because its toys had been broken? Toys that had actually captured and enslaved it . . . Well, if they really had. The nuances weren't important right now. Understanding the situation wasn't important right now. Right now, the only thing that mattered was survival.

He raised his gun, useless gesture that it was, and fired at the god across the cavern from him. No effect, of course; the bullet bounced off a shield of raw will that surrounded it . . . but Tlaloc's head swiveled towards him, as if *surprised*, and for one instant, the flames around Sigrun died.

In that moment, Adam's mind raced. *He didn't sense it coming. No magic. No will. No power. How much of him actually transferred from body to body?* he wondered. *How much of him actually dispersed, when Kanmi and Trennus destroyed the coils? Is he strong enough, powerful enough, omniscient enough, to see this before I even make the attempt? Or is there, as Sigrun keeps telling me, no fate . . . . just wyrd?*

"Sig! Bring him back to the pool! Then come to us!" Adam commanded as he remembered, with perfect clarity, killing a djinni, dispersing its essence, with little more than modern explosives and a little guile. *Maybe all I did was send that djinn back to the Veil, like Trennus has said. Maybe that's all I can do now. Don't have explosives this time. But I think something a little bigger than a bullet, that he can't see coming, might do the trick.*

Sigrun, the god's fire once more wreathing her body, did as Adam bade, and forced her body into the air. Flew to the center of the pool, and dropped into its cooling waters, dousing the flames . . . but the water was its own torment on the burned and ravaged flesh, and she heaved herself back out onto the shore . . . just as Tlaloc moved to the center of the pool to renew his flames on her body. ***Beg***, the god told her. ***Weep for me. Give me your tears.***

"*Fikkest thu,*" Sigrun rasped out. She wouldn't weep. She wouldn't beg. She was a battle-maiden of Tyr, and she did not fear death.

The fires exploded out towards her from the god's hands once more, and Sigrun closed her eyes.

"Don't help," Adam told Trennus and Kanmi. "Not this time. He can't feel this coming." He raised his newly reloaded .45, and aimed. This time, not at Tlaloc in Xicohtencatl's body, but at the stalactite curtain above the god's mortal form. One shot. Two. Three. Tlaloc never even looked up as the vicious stone teeth fell from the ceiling, and impaled the broken and battered body of Xicohtencatl's body, driving him down into the waters. The fires surrounding Sigrun's body flickered, and went out.

For a moment, absolutely nothing happened, as the body began to sink into the dark waters of the *cenote*. Adam wasn't honestly sure that the god wasn't just going to start crawling up out of the water again, like a damned *ghul*, so he kept his gun in his hand . . . and then he saw green light coming up out of the water, making the whole pool glow like a jewel. *Harah. Have to get Sigrun out of there.* He holstered the gun and ran forward as the light began to contract, intensifying as it did so. He bent down, and scooped up her body, not caring, for the moment, if he damaged her burned skin any further. They needed to get out of here.

The light contracted down to a single, white-red point, too dazzling to look at, like the sun at high noon. He threw Sigrun over his shoulder in a fireman's carry and ran, shouting to the others, "Go! Go, damn it, *run!*" He could see Matrugena's pained hobble, Ehecatl's bent-shouldered shuffle, and knew, grimly, *We're not going to make it.*

He'd barely reached the mouth of the tunnel when the power behind him *exploded* outwards, like a star gone nova. The shockwave hit them all, and they were *thrown* up the tunnel. Adam landed on Sigrun's legs and was unable to stop her upper body from unfolding gracelessly back to slam her head on the stone floor. The ceiling overhead gave an ominous rumble, and dirt and stones as large as a child's fist hailed down on them. Adam rolled back to his feet and hauled Sigrun back over his shoulder. "Come on, come on! On your feet!"

He later had no real recollection of how they all got to the surface. Trennus always swore that Adam had grabbed him by the elbow and *hauled* him up the rest of the way, but Adam only remembered running and rocks and the grinding sound of the tunnel collapsing behind them. Only remembered his heart trying to pound its way out of his chest and thoughts that amounted to a mantra, *One more step, just one more step, one more step, just one more step* . . . and then, out into the blessed gray light of dawn. "Don't stop!" Kanmi, bringing up the rear, and holding Ehecatl's arm over his shoulder as he helped the man out, shouted up to Adam. "Keep going! If the cavern underneath collapses —"

The whole thing's going to go. Adam kept running. He wanted to be *nowhere* near the monumental structure, in case blocks of stone the size of a man decided to roll their direction.

At five hundred feet, they stopped, and Adam let go of the grip he had on Trennus' arm, surprised, as the taller man slumped to the ground. Adam eased Sigrun's limp form to the ground as well, and then winced as stone ground on stone, an audible wail of protest, as the ancient structure began to collapse, from the inside out, the center of the pyramid dropping first, like a cake taken from the oven too soon. "Oh . . . gods. People are going to be . . . very angry with us." Trennus managed, panting a little.

It was inane, but inanity was really all any of them had left. Ehecatl slumped in the long grass, his face gray, and Kanmi stared down at him. "Ah . . . I think his heart's damaged," the sorcerer told Adam in a low mutter. "I don't know what to *do* for him. I'm certified in first aid, but this is beyond my skill level."

"Let him lie back. Prop his feet up on something, cover him with a cloak —" Adam looked up from where he was trying to find Sigrun's pulse in her throat, without damaging her skin any further. Unlike the fight against the god-born in Ponca, months ago, this time, there wasn't a single part of her that *wasn't* burned. Her skin was a mass of weeping red blisters and black, paper-like curls that threatened to turn into ash at the slightest touch. The water of the cenote couldn't have done her any favors, either. Adam's eyes focused on Kanmi's hands, held mutely in front of him, and he realized that Sigrun wasn't the only one who'd been burned; Kanmi's hands showed red, second-degree burns completely covering the palms, with blisters all up his wrists and forearms. "Damn it. Sorry. Get Tren . . . . " Adam's words faltered, realizing that Trennus had been lucky to get this far, on a leg that had been bleeding heavily, and might have tendon damage. "Give me a minute to get her . . . comfortable . . . and then I'll do what I can for the rest of you."

Adam finally found Sigrun's pulse. It was thready and weak, but there. But as he watched, the rune-fire markings shone, dimly, through the blackened skin. *It won't kill me,* she'd said at dinner the other night, at the prospect of foul water or rotten food. *It'll just make me _wish_ it would.* "Come on," he told her, and put a hand, very lightly, on what was left of her hair—a fragile, brittle mass that had congealed together in places, and shattered at his touch. "Fight it. You're really good at fighting, Sig. What's one more battle?"

Wearily, he stood, and walked over to the car, where the two Eagle warriors who'd survived the battle had taken refuge. Both of them were bloody and covered in vicious claw-marks from the monkey-dogs . . . and both had knife wounds, from where they'd turned on each other, as well. They'd managed to bandage each other up, however, and looked as weary and heart-sore as the rest of them did. They had, after all, lost three of their comrades today . . . and seen one of their gods made *captive* to humans. *If he actually was a captive.* Adam's head spun, and he put the thoughts aside. *Focus on the task at hand.* "Gentlemen. Whatever's left in the first aid kits, grab it, and some blankets. The others are . . . not doing so well."

The first eyed him, cautiously. "What happened down there? We didn't see anything after we were ordered to retreat." He grimaced. "Eagle warriors are never supposed to retreat. In the old days, we'd be going home now to be executed by our own men."

"These aren't the old days," Adam said, crisply. "And I thank god for that." He meant it, too. Sincerely. "I'm not entirely sure what happened down there, to be honest." Truth, that. He didn't even know if the god could . . . re-manifest, or if he'd killed it, somehow, against all expectations. "The first thing I need you to do is to carry Ehecatl Itztli to the truck you used to get down here. He's going to need to be transported flat, with his feet elevated."

He brought the medical kit back over to the others, and laid a thermal blanket over Sigrun, before he started to, loosely, wrap Kanmi's hands in gauze. "I'm surprised you're not burned worse," he told Trennus, still feeling a little dazed.

"Lassair," Trennus said in incomprehensible explanation, clearly still dazed.

Adam stared at him blankly. "One of my spirits," Trennus said. "That's . . . shit. That's, well, her name." He rubbed at his face. "Don't noise it about. She was still overlapping me, partially, from having stopped the bleeding in my leg." Trennus pointed down. "She's fire, in a way. Not a fire *elemental*, but . . . gods. I can't really define her. Part of what makes dealing with her a challenge. She, ah . . . I think she took most of the flame for me. Frankly, I think she *ate* it."

"You said her Name," Kanmi said, and staring down at his white-swathed hands. "That's against the rules, summoner."

"She trusts all of you enough to tell you all your true-names. Seems . . . only fair . . . you should know hers, too." Trennus started to heave himself to his feet.

"She stopped the bleeding?" Adam said, finally focusing in on what had been said. "Can she help Sigrun?" He gestured towards the god-born woman, feeling, for about the fiftieth time that night, helpless.

Trennus shook his head. "I don't know. She's not answering me at the moment. I think . . . that what happened down there . . . scared her almost to death."

Adam's teeth hurt for a moment. "Sig's life could depend on this flighty, frightened spirit, and she's just . . . scuttled off to hide?"

Trennus grimaced. "Adam, she's a spirit, and she just watched a god *die*." Trennus glanced around to make sure none of the Nahautl men were in earshot. "Personally, I'd like to find a hole and hide in it myself."

And that was when the enormity of it actually hit Adam for the first time. Gods weren't supposed to die. Although, clearly, they did. But usually they were killed by *other gods*. The Titans gelding Uranus and leaving the creator to die, only to be replaced by their own children in the continuous power-struggle that was the Hellene pantheon. Baal dying and being torn apart every year, to allow the world to bloom, dying and being resurrected to allow the human race to endure. Osiris being murdered in the Egyptian legends, Loki murdering Baldur, in the Gothic ones. Although the Gothic legends were such a muddle of past and present and future that Adam didn't claim to understand them. Baldur *had* been murdered and *would* be resurrected at the end of the world, except he was also a currently worshipped and manifest deity.

It gave him a headache to try to figure it out, so he didn't even try. Adam focused on the here and now. "Are we sure he's actually . . . dead?"

"I don't think both of my attendant spirits would have *fled* like this if he were just . . . I don't know . . ." Trennus waved vaguely.

"Down with a deific migraine," Kanmi proposed, expressionlessly. "Hung over on too much nectar."

Both of them turned and *stared* at the technomancer. "What?" Kanmi said, slumping where he sat. "I don't think there's such a thing as the sniffles of the gods."

Adam really wished he could smile. Instead, he sighed and pulled back the thermal blanket to check on Sigrun. Her burns looked, perceptibly, a little better. "All right. She's healing. Let's get her to the car, and from there, to a hospital." He couldn't deal with the concept of having killed something that was supposed to be immortal. Ineffable. His mind insisted on making it smaller. So he scooped Sigrun back up onto his shoulder, and the three men headed for their vehicle. Trennus stiffly got into the backseat, and Adam settled Sigrun down along the rear bench, with her feet elevated in Trennus' lap.

"This is probably not the time to be giving her a foot massage," Kanmi warned Trennus, hauling himself into the passenger's side at the front of the car. The sorcerer's humor was fairly clearly a defense mechanism. One he employed relentlessly.

Trennus muttered something that sounded suspiciously like "*Póg mo thóin,*" which happened to be about the only Gallic Adam knew. *Kiss my ass.*

He snorted and got the car started, then told Kanmi, "Get on the radio while I drive. Fill Livorus in, and . . . gods. Get us directions to the hospital. Though . . . Sigrun could be conscious by the time we get there. Get . . . the *gardia* out here." He rubbed at his face, and got the wheels back up onto the main access road, trying not to bump and jostle all his injured passengers, and watching the truck with Ehecatl and the Eagle warriors starting to follow them.

Kanmi nodded, and reached for the radio's microphone with cautious, bandaged fingers. Then he paused, and said, "Ben Maor?"

"Yes?" Adam concentrated on getting them back to the poured-stone highway.

"What in the gods' names do I even *tell* Livorus? Do I tell him, over an open radio channel, that we just *killed a god?*"

"Gods, no, don't put it that way," Trennus said, immediately, his tone horrified. "And when it comes down to it . . . we're not the only ones responsible. I don't think we *could* be."

"All right, what's your explanation, then, *summoner?*" Kanmi challenged.

"I think he was weakened already, from the lack of sacrifices and the lack of . . . fear, I suppose, in him, from the Nahautl. So Tototl and Xicohtencatl were feeding him with sacrifices, yes, but just enough to perpetuate him . . . and they were weakening him at the same time by sending his energies all over the countryside. I suspect their goal would have been an . . . equilibrium state. Exactly as much energy out as in, and, well, never feeding him so much that he could release himself." Trennus found a chip of stone in one of his braids and picked it out. "We . . . and by *we,* I mean ben Maor . . . just finished the job."

"So, how does it feel to be a godslayer?" Kanmi looked at Adam, his eyes narrow.

Adam glanced up, into the rearview mirror, and then back down again, feeling lost. "Not my god."

"No, but someone's. You're going to be up there with fucking *Akhenaten* on everyone's most-hated list, if this gets out." Kanmi leaned back in his chair as they headed back towards Tenochtitlan.

"Yeah. It . . . doesn't seem like something I want to list on a resume." Adam stared blankly at the road, still . . . unable to assimilate it.

None of it seemed quite real. "Would that go under employment history or under useful skills?"

"Hey." Kanmi shook his head. "It might come as a shock from *me* of all people, but this is not the time for jokes." He stared at Adam. "What do I say to Livorus?"

Adam looked up, after a moment. "Tell him . . . there shouldn't be any more sacrifices in Nahautl. And when we can actually talk to him in person . . . then *he* gets to decide, what, if anything, *anyone* gets told." Adam swallowed. The high probability of being turned into a scapegoat in this situation had just occurred to him, and he didn't like the thought . . . but Livorus was Roman, and practical to his core. *It would just be easier to tell the truth, or part of it, and hang me out for the mobs to tear apart, than to engage in any kind of a cover-up, wouldn't it?*

And then one more, deeply disquieting thought that twisted his stomach ran through his mind: *What did Tlaloc mean when he said all the other gods would die, anyway?*

Chapter IX: Reverberations

Emmer grain has been used in Rome since the early days of the Republic. It was the original lifeblood of Rome, making up the daily porridge or puls that everyone, from the plebes to the patricians ate, though patricians added wholesome eggs and meats to their porridge. Round, flat loaves of emmer bread were distributed from public bakeries in the early days of the Empire, and these are still granted to paupers to this day. Wheat bread has, however, become more common, as it is more easily cultivated in a wide variety of areas all over the world, including in the central plains of Caesaria Aquilonis.

Cuisine in Rome has gone through periods of simplicity and hedonism, by turns. It is fair to say that in ancient times, there is little that a wealthy Roman citizen could not acquire for his table. Dormice and snails were bred locally and eaten as snacks; live fish were transported from the sea to ensure that their flesh would not spoil before reaching a Roman table. Spices, and in particular a condiment called garum (fermented — not to say spoiled — fish sauce), were commonly in use.

Over the centuries of contact and trade with Qin and Nippon, Roman cuisine, already cosmopolitan and innovative, became more international. Noodles were introduced in about 1100 AC, from Qin, and Roman ambassadors sent to Nippon were introduced to what was known in the area as 'sour fish' or 'fermented fish,' and what is now called, more commonly, 'sushi.' Several Roman ambassadors considered eating the fish raw to be almost as uncivilized as the old custom, in Rome, of watching a fish die at the table, to demonstrate its freshness to the guests . . . and certainly as barbaric as the Gallic and Gothic custom of drinking milk, which was considered by most Romans as to be only suitable to the manufacture of cheese.

In ancient times, Romans generally drank wine or vinegar, watered, or with a neutral-flavored spirit added to increase the alcohol content; beer was considered almost as barbarous as milk, and was certainly an indication that someone must be from a distant province, such as Gaul, Germania, Britannia, Judea, or Egypt.

Today in Rome, you cannot walk twenty feet in the Field of Mars area, without encountering a Nipponese sushi restaurant, a traditional Nubian cookery, a Gothic taverna selling wheat beer or honeybeer . . . or a fusion restaurant, such as Somnium. Somnium is the invention of chef-owner Leonides Stavros, who follows the philosophies of the ancient Epicureans. He believes that experience is everything, and his dishes are designed to provide a new experience to whomever happens to walk through his doors. If you've ever had a desire to try stir-fried dormouse tossed with chicory, fenugreek, and a light dash of wasabi, served over emmer noodles, this is the place for you! For more traditional Roman banquets, such as boiled flamingo with honey, garum, and coriander, consider Adamas, in the Palatine Hill district.

— A Tourist's Guide to Rome. Mannius Raptis, Ludivicus Press, Rome, 1954 AC.

Iunius 14, 1954 AC

If there was a constant in the universe, besides the speed of light and the effect of gravity on space-time, Adam ben Maor rather thought it might be the quality of hospital food. He was perfectly healthy, and there was no way in which he could possibly eat what was on the covered tray in Sigrun's room. He'd uncovered it to take a peek, and grimaced. Cold quinoa puls, with a cold poached egg on top of that. A ceramic mug of water, and a glass container of gelatin. "I'm going to sneak out in an hour and go get you something *real* to eat," he told her sleeping form. "I have no idea what that will consist of in Tenochtitlan, however. Maybe one of those corn flatbread things filled with meat and peppers, and to *gehenna* with whatever your doctors say."

Sigrun's eyes didn't open. She'd proven to be an intractably stubborn patient. On recovering consciousness in the car, and being told they were going to a hospital, she'd actually panicked—marking the first time Adam had ever seen her do so—and categorically refused. "No. No hospitals. Will recover. Hospitals are where people go to die." Trennus had had to hold her feet still—gently, because her body was still fighting to recover from the burns—and Adam had assured her, over and over, that they really needed her to go, that they *all* needed to go . . . they were just going together as a team, staying together, and they couldn't let her go off alone, could they?

Crazy as it had sounded, it had worked, and she'd subsided, losing consciousness again. As often as she'd told him she could only die of a battle-wound, her fear of hospitals didn't seem quite rational. But what fear was ever really the product of the forebrain? His fear of going into tight underground spaces and his dislike of standing near windows weren't really rational either, were they?

On reaching the hospital, Ehecatl had been moved, immediately, to a cardiac unit. Kanmi and Trennus had been sent to the ER, Trennus for some surgery to the back of his knee, Kanmi to have his burns looked at . . . and the various hospital staff had gone into an absolute tizzy on seeing Sigrun's condition, and moved her to the intensive care burn ward. They'd been set to give her morphine and to begin debriding her skin to remove portions of the third-degree damaged areas, but her eyes had snapped open and she'd caught the doctor's wrist in an iron grip, holding the morphine needle away from her. "No. No drugs. No morphine."

Adam had moved in, and told the doctors, carefully, "She's god-born. She heals very quickly, given a chance. You probably won't need to debride her. Just . . . I don't know. Give her fluids and antibiotics, and let her body fight on its own."

"And where precisely did you get your medical degree?" The doctor's tone had been sharp, but Sigrun would *not* let go of his wrist, and Adam had been frankly afraid that if any of the other orderlies moved in, she'd snap them all like so much kindling.

"I don't have a medical degree, but I've seen how she heals. These wounds were inflicted less than two hours ago. Look at them. Look at her skin, and the rune-marks you can see there. And trust me. She's going to be both the best and the worst patient you've ever had." Adam had taken a step closer to the bed, and gently worked his fingers around and under Sigrun's, respectful of the damaged skin "Sig? Let him give you a shot for the pain. It's got to be driving you out of your mind right now."

The gray eyes, the only *normal* spot in a face covered in red and black weals, and crawling with rune-marks that were fading in and out of existence, focused on his. "No drugs," Sigrun told him, in a vehement croak. "Do not . . . .*work* on me." The words were taut, and broken down into short, rasped phrases. Between smoke and actual heat damage, not to mention the monkey-dog that had almost strangled her, her vocal cords were in bad shape. "Five. Ten minutes. At most. And then I need them again." Desperation in her eyes. "Don't want to need them. Don't want to be addicted."

Adam winced and put a hand on what remained of her hair, and watched her flinch at the pain before he quickly lifted his hand again. "If you let them give you the shot, you might be able to sleep," he told her. "And if you sleep, the pain will still be away, and your body will get to heal. Let them give you the shot."

"Just one. Promise me."

"Just one. And an IV. We'll talk again when they've seen how fast you heal, all right?"

She'd released the doctor's hand at that point, and Adam had been able to see her fingerprints emblazoned on the doctor's wrist in livid red.

That had been about two hours ago. The morphine had taken effect, and he'd seen the tautness go out of her body as she stopped *fighting* the pain. She'd relaxed into a gentle sleep, instead, after the IV had been set up. The doctors had insisted that Adam wear a surgical gown, slippers, mask, hat, and gloves inside the room as he sat there, patiently, but after the first hour, he'd known it wasn't going to be needed for long. Where her skin had been black, it was now red. Where the skin had been red and weeping with blisters, it was now the vivid pink of a bad sunburn. The old and damaged hair had broken away from her scalp in spiky, melted shards, which he'd brushed away from her pillow, and he was both startled, and yet not surprised at *all* to see that new growth was already starting to come in, a pale gold stubble that he thought had already grown to the length of the tip of his forefinger.

Thirty minutes ago, the doctor had come in to stare at her for a moment, and then ordered her an invalid's meal and left, shaking his head. "She can have it if her throat can manage it when she wakes up," the doctor had instructed Adam.

Adam turned the uncomfortable bedside chair towards the table, pushing the inedible meal out of the way. He unscrewed the cap from a fountain pen to start to write notes for his report for Livorus. How do I even begin this? he thought.

"There you are," a cultured patrician voice said from the door behind him, as if the mere act of writing the propraetor's name had invoked the man.

Adam turned and started to stand; Livorus waved at him and murmured, "No, none of that." He stepped in, lifting a mask over his weathered face, his blue eyes alert over it. "Well, now, ben Maor," Livorus said, softly. "Your god must be fond of you, indeed. Not a scratch on you."

"Not for lack of trying, sir." Adam sat back down again, feeling tremendously uneasy.

Livorus looked down at Sigrun. "I expect her to be out of here by nightfall," he noted quietly. "Though it might take the hair a trifle longer to grow back to its old length." The propraetor actually lifted her hand, cautiously, in his own gloved one, delicately avoiding all the blisters there. "You're going to be just fine, my dear," he told her motionless form, gently. "You can't leave me alone with all these children. Whoever will I have to talk to?"

Adam blinked, not knowing what to make of those words at all. Livorus sighed, set her hand cautiously back down on the bed, and turned to meet his eyes. "So, I understand that you've defaced a local monument today, among other serious transgressions. What do you have to say for yourself?"

Just as Adam opened his mouth to reply . . . though he had no idea what to say in response . . . the phone beside Sigrun's bed rang, a long, loud trill like a damned jungle bird, and he fumbled for the receiver, trying to still the ringing before it woke her. "*Ave?*" he said, quietly into the mouthpiece, looking up at Livorus, trying to convey with his expression that he was about to get rid of whoever it was and go back to replying to the propraetor's questions with due respect.

"*Adam?*" A soft female voice almost breathed his name into his ear, and he didn't recognize the voice at all. No one he knew would know to call this hospital, this hospital room.

"Who is this?" he asked, sitting upright, going on alert. There were no windows in the burn unit. There couldn't be; dust was forbidden in here, as was direct sunlight.

"*Oh, Adam, it's so good to finally hear your voice,*" the woman told him, her own tones drowsy and languorous. "*I've seen such things about you. You've been a godslayer since before you were born, did you know? You've done it before. You'll do it again.*" Light Gothic accent. Young. Probably not more than twenty-five. Twenty-six at the most. From her inflections, either drugged, or mostly air between her ears.

Adam stood, holding the phone in one hand, the receiver in the other, and pulled on the wires to get to the door, looking down one side of the hall, and then the other. *Who knows?* he thought, frantically. *Who in god's name did Kanmi and Tren talk to besides Livorus? There was no one else there besides Ehecatl and the two Eagle warriors . . . and the warriors saw nothing, and Ehecatl wouldn't talk . . . .* "I don't know what you're talking about," he said, evenly. "Who are you?"

"*Me? Oh, I'm sorry, where are my manners? I'm Sophia. Sigrun's never mentioned me, has she?*" For a moment, bright irritation in the voice, and clarity. Focus. And then back to the dreaming tone. "*Poor old Akhenaten never had a chance. Not that he was much of a god, hmm?*" She giggled a little. "*The ones in Babylon-that-was, though? They at least put up a fight, didn't they, godslayer?*" She paused. "*Oh, but of course you don't remember. They're not your memories yet.*"

Whoever this is, she's insane, Adam thought, *but somehow has today's news right on tap.* "All right, Sophia," *If that's actually your name . . . .* "I'll play along. What else do you see?"

"Lots of things." It was a teasing purr now. *"I know that like your Moses, you'll die before you see the Promised Land, but you'll finally be yourself again after your demise."*

Adam stopped moving. This wasn't what he'd expected to hear. *"You'll be a stepfather to your own daughter, and your wife will be your widow ere you meet her again. I see a dark shadow standing over and around you, made of order and the law, though it is an assassin of kings. And its name is your name, and your name is its name. Adam. Adam, Adam, Adam, son of light."*

His fingers slipped on the body of the phone, though he had a death grip on the receiver. "Who in god's name *are* you?" he gritted out from between his teeth, distantly aware of the phone hitting the ground at his feet, and jangling as it bounced on its curly cord.

"I told you, I'm Sophia! Oh, do put Livorus on. Sigrun won't let me tell him not to shake hands with the man who hates his roof. He'll boil the blood in his veins if he does. Oh, and is Kanmi there? I want to tell him I'm so sorry about his wife." Rattling on now, like an errant gossip. *"And Trennus, that dog. I want to tell him to watch out for himself. Lassair started out as a fertility goddess, did you know?"*

At that point, Sigrun opened her eyes. The old dead skin on her face was sloughing back in places, revealing fresh pink underneath, but her expression was alert. "Who is it?" she asked. Her voice was better now, no more a harsh raven's croak. "You look like you've seen a spirit."

"Someone named Sophia."

"Oh . . . gods." She held out her hand for the phone, imperatively. Adam handed it to her, numbly, and sat down on the edge of the chair once more. He watched her eyes narrow as she said, "Sophia? *Waes hael."*

Sigrun closed her eyes as she heard her sister's voice, speaking in Latin. *"I'm glad you're awake, Sigrun. I tried to time my call for when your eyes would be opening after the morphine, but I was a little early. I warned you about the trap, and you fell right into it."* A sigh.

Sophia's sleepy tones got on Sigrun's last nerve, and she replied, in Cimbric, "No. The trap wasn't a trap. We were taken prisoner, but released. You were wrong."

"That wasn't the trap I was talking about," Sophia scoffed lightly, and in Latin. *"You're still in the real trap, sister. Besides, you know I was right. I'm always right."*

"You have not been right about the black bird on my shoulder or the end of the world *yet*." Sigrun shifted to Latin, conforming to her sister's speech mostly out of habit.

"Not yet. That's still a real vision, though. But you did find the bumblebee and the black bird."

Irked, Sigrun replied, "You are such a child, Sophia. Yes, there was a 'bumblebee.' You were right about that. But there was no 'black bird the size of a man.'"

Livorus coughed into his hand, and Sigrun looked up, startled, covering the mouthpiece with her hand. "My lord?"

"Tototl's given and family names," the propraetor said, quietly. "They, ah, actually mean 'black-feathered,' and 'bird,' respectively. I don't know how this is relevant, or who this person *is* . . . . "

Sigrun felt as if she'd bitten into a rotten tomato. She had interested eyes on all sides; Livorus and Adam were fascinated observers at the moment. "It's my sister, *dominus*."

"The god-born of Apollo? The Pythia?" Livorus had, after all, read her entire dossier five years ago. None of the others had.

"She's seen true since she was ten years old, sir, but she sees far too much, too far ahead, and never anything useful." Sigrun grimaced. "She told me to beware of a trap and to look for a bumblebee and a black bird several days ago."

"And you didn't tell *us*?" Livorus asked, raising his eyebrows.

"If I had, we would have gone down every wrong path imaginable." Sigrun heard Sophia asking, on the phone, *is that Livorus? I want to talk to him! It's important!* "Sir, do you actually want to hear what she prophesies about you? I strongly recommend against it. It brings nothing but trouble."

"So far, she seems more accurate than the gentlemen who perform the weather auguries on the far-viewer. Somehow, every time I want to go to the seaside, they say it will be sunny, and it promptly rains." Livorus held out his hand for the phone.

Sigrun handed it over, and watched as Livorus' face drained of color. After several moments, the propraetor said, merely, "Thank you, my dear. It's very kind of you to try." And then he handed the phone back to Sigrun, who took it, reluctantly.

"See, that wasn't so hard," her sister told her dreamily. *"It won't do any good, of course, but at least I've told him."*

"The seer who told Caesar to beware the ides of Martius changed his so-called fate," Sigrun pointed out, tartly. "Nothing is set in stone. If you'd just *realize* it . . . ." She trailed off. Nothing was set in stone, not even her sister's behavior. She *had* to try again. If only for her own sanity. Of course, she knew the answer already from her sister's voice. She didn't even need to ask the question. "You've taken the drugs again." Her tone was flat. "You abuse your gift, Sophia."

"You're angry with me. You're disappointed in me." The words were rote.

Sigrun lay back against the pillows, the pain in her heart worse than any pain of the body. "Yes, I'm angry with you. Yes. I'm disappointed in you." *And I've said this so many times, and without any effect at all. Gods, why did they have to send her to Delphi?* One more time. One more try. She had . . . just enough ability to care to try one more time. Today. "You know, if someone drinks every single night, there are problems in their life that they are not addressing. What does it say about you, that every time I hear from you, you are on a vision drug?"

Sophia didn't answer the question. She just repeated herself.

"You're angry with me. And you'll be angry with me for a very long time. You'll even be angry with me after I die. You're too good at being angry, sister. Someday, you'll be so angry at yourself, that you'll cut yourself in half." Sophia's voice was drowsy. *"You'll hate yourself for living, you'll hate yourself for feeling, and you'll be angry at the whole world for being what it will be, but you'll be one of only a handful of people who can save what's left of it. So you're just going to have to love the world, Sigrun. And that'll be one of the hardest things you'll ever have to do."*

Sigrun closed her eyes. "Sophia. I've had enough for one day. So I will tell this to you in good, plain Latin so that you may understand it clearly: Leave my friends and colleagues alone. They are not to be bothered with what you see. And for the last time, there is no fate. There is only *wyrd.*" Her free hand clenched and unclenched in the blankets. "Goodbye, sister. Please be well."

She hung up the phone, and stayed silent for a long moment, controlling her breathing. Controlling the tears. Finally, she opened her eyes, and looked at the two men in the room with her. Livorus and Adam both looked . . . deeply uneasy. "Forgive me, both of you," she muttered. "She has this effect on people. I try not to inflict her on anyone who knows me." Her eyes slid towards Adam. "I'm sorry you had to deal with her."

"I'd forgotten that you *had* a sister. I think you've only mentioned her once," Adam admitted.

"I don't talk about her." *Ever. If I can help it.* Sigrun's eyes started to drift closed again. Now that the pain was a little further away, as her body was working through its recovery process, she was tired again. She was also, unfortunately, ravenously hungry. They'd explained it to her in the Odinhall; her metabolism sped up when she needed to regenerate damage, whether inflicted on her, or taken from another person. From nothing, nothing. She needed to *eat,* no matter how tired she was. "I don't suppose," Sigrun said, cracking her eyes open again, "that there is any chance at all of me getting some food, is there?"

Solemnly, Adam picked up the tray from beside the bed, and for a moment, Sigrun allowed herself to hope. When he lifted the lid and showed her the contents, however, she let her lips quirk a little, in spite of the pain that even a trace of facial expression brought. "Adam ben Maor, if you wanted to kill me, you should have just left me to die in the temple. This? This is the stuff of which vengeance is made."

"No, this is the stuff of which *puls* is made. But I take it you want something *real* to eat?"

"Would kill for it."

"Well, we'll see what I can go scrounge, eh?"

Livorus looked down at her, and once more took her hand in his own gloved one as he stood. "We should let you rest, my dear. This is, by far, the worst injury I've ever seen you sustain." Concern behind the cool mask of pragmatism that Livorus always wore. After five years in his service, however, Sigrun hardly needed the eyes of Tyr to see through it.

"There's a saying among my people," she managed, settling back down among the pillows as carefully as she could. Even the faintest shift of position brought the sheets into contact with patches of skin that hadn't previously been touched, and hadn't quite healed yet. "That which does not kill us, makes us stronger."

Livorus' lips quirked. "I'd expect nothing less out of a barbaric northern philosopher. Depressing, but aptly Stoic." He pressed her hand with exquisite gentleness. "I would prefer not to see how strong you are capable of becoming."

"That may not be something I have a choice in, sir." Sigrun managed a faint smile for them both, and raised a hand as the door closed behind them. Her stomach growled at her, and she hissed in annoyance. The body required feeding, in order to maintain the healing that it was engaged in, and it did not care that what she'd been left by the hospital staff was unpalatable. All her body knew was that it smelled sustenance. So she pulled her tray to her, wincing as every movement made too-tight skin tug and crack . . . and ate. As fast as she could, her hands shaking in her need, and tried not to taste any of it as it went down.

When she had finished eating, she cautiously pulled at some of the dead and itching skin, wanting nothing more, at the moment, than a handful of *sand* to scour herself with . . . and *stared* at the number of new rune-marks seething under her skin. *Scars. Prettier ones than the average mortal is left with, but scars, nonetheless. How many of them will I have after this? And how much stronger will I need to become, if I've even a* hope *of turning aside these futures that my sister believes are foreordained?* Sigrun leaned back, and for the first time since awakening, the actual weight of what had happened in the last day hit her, and she began to shiver, uncontrollably— she, who never felt the cold. *Oh, gods. Oh,* gods. *I have to contact the Odinhall. I saw humans using technology to mediate the power of a god. No, it's worse. Much worse. I helped* kill a god. *The gods cannot make war on each other . . . . I may have just started a war between the gods themselves.*

Her stomach clenched, and she had to take deep breaths to keep herself from throwing up everything that she'd just eaten. *I think I might be lucky to survive the next week. And my death might even be* just, *from the perspective of my grandsire, Tyr.* She swallowed hard, and tried very hard not to consider the possibility that she might be executed as a criminal against the gods themselves. It might not *matter* that Tlaloc had been deranged. That he and his mortal attendants had resumed the custom of human sacrifice. That, having stopped the technomage and the god-born, she and the other lictors had largely been trying to save their own lives from that moment forwards. That wasn't the point. The point was . . . they'd *won.*

No one expected humans to win against a god. It wasn't supposed to be possible.

She closed her eyes and rocked, feeling the weight of the meal in her stomach like a stone. *Tlaloc was weak,* Sigrun reasoned. *His power was diminished. Loss of the belief and fear of his followers, on whom he'd preyed. The machinations of Tototl and Gratian Xicohtencatl. Their siphoning his power off for . . . the gods only know how many other power supply stations like the one we found in Tikal. There might have been dozens. Something to look into . . . they wanted a system of dependency that they controlled, perhaps? They wanted people relying not on ley, which is inexpensive, abundant, and inexhaustible, but on a power that they controlled, could give and take away at a whim . . . except they wouldn't have controlled it. Not in the end. Unless they controlled a god. What pride . . . .*

She realized, suddenly, that she was finding rationalizations, and that the rationalizations didn't matter. Nothing she did or thought right now was going to make a difference when it came time to face her gods in the Odinhall and account for her actions.

Sleep, however, beckoned, and she couldn't fight it. Her body had the food that had been the sole reason she'd awakened, and now it needed time to digest and use that sustenance to rebuild. Her last thoughts were a confused amalgam of *we really didn't mean to* and *at least if I'm executed next week for deicide, I can't possibly be around for the end of the world, right? Sophia will have to admit to being wrong . . . .*

Outside in the corridor, Livorus beckoned Adam out of the room, and the younger man followed, trepidation suddenly sucking at the pit of his stomach. "Let us allow her to rest, shall we?" Livorus murmured as he closed the door behind them. "Let us walk, ben Maor. We have much to discuss."

Adam winced, and followed. He hadn't had a chance to write up his notes, let alone find an unused typewriter with a decent ribbon somewhere in this hospital . . . . *If I could even find one with Latin characters.* He suddenly pictured a typewriter entirely configured for Nahautl ideograms and syllabic symbols. *So, this pictogram of a corpse wrapped for burial, next to the glyph representing a hollow-eyed god . . . yes, that takes care of page one, in its entirety . . .* He put a hand over his face and rubbed, briefly but fiercely, at his eyes. He was obviously punch-drunk if he was finding *that* amusing. "Sir? Can I ask what Eshmunazar and Matrugena have already told you?"

Livorus raised a hand to stop him as they got into an elevator with a half-dozen orderlies and nurses, all of whom looked tired and harassed. "A moment. The top floor, if you would, ben Maor."

Adam pushed the button for the highest floor of the seven-story structure, and watched the brass cage doors slide closed. Trepidation continued to build as they slowly ascended, and finally, exited. Livorus didn't even speak then, but rather found them a set of stairs that led out onto a roof. Adam followed, feeling the sticky heat of a Tenochtitlan afternoon hit him like a wool blanket soaked in hot bathwater, and eyed the railing around the edge of the roof. "Ah, sir? For the record, I'm not actually Roman. I can't be ordered to fall on my sword for the honor of the Empire." It wasn't entirely a joke. Adam closed his hands and put them behind his back. If someone wanted him to be a scapegoat, they'd damned well have to kill him.

"Noted, ben Maor." Livorus' tone, as always, was austere. "I think the various reactions I have seen so far today have both been fascinating and instructive, as well. Do you mind explaining to me, in your own words, what transpired overnight?"

Ah. He's looking for discrepancies between everyone's accounts. Adam exhaled, and marshaled his thoughts. It was surprisingly difficult; he was still relatively numb, and his mind was hazy. "We went to the Pyramid of the Sun, having received information, as you know, sir, that it was a potential hiding place, a fallback point, for the two individuals who were of interest to us as potential adherents of a religious revival movement oriented towards human sacrifice." He was almost composing in his head as he spoke, putting the words together as he would on a page. Formal diction, careful phrasing. "On arrival, it became clear that this was not just a fallback position, but the central location from which they were working to replace Roman and local sovereignty," *that sounds so much better, somehow, than 'effect a coup using the rendered power of a god,'* he thought, and went on, cautiously. "They had entered into a power-sharing arrangement both with themselves and an indigenous, ah . . . entity." *Because we can't say a god in a formal report. It will detract from our credibility when some bureaucrat in Rome reads it and promptly decides that we're all absolutely insane.* Adam looked up at the pale blue sky, and shook his head. "We were observed, and after I attempted to engage the conspirators in a diplomatic exchange, they attacked. Xicohtencatl, as far as I could tell, was trying to convince Eshmunazar to switch sides . . . without effect, I might add." In retrospect, Adam felt ashamed of his concerns about Kanmi's loyalties. No matter what hold Xicohtencatl thought he had on the Carthaginian's psyche, his words had pretty much bounced off Eshmunazar. "We managed to get Tototl and Xicohtencatl down, at which point, the, er . . . ."

"Indigenous entity," Livorus said, without changing expressions as he leaned against an air vent and used his walking stick to poke at a pigeon nest atop a chimney nearby.

"Yes . . . the *entity* moved its . . . consciousness . . . to Xicohtencatl's body. I'd like to point out that Matrugena actually tried to, well talk it down." It sounded absolutely futile, and a little stupid, but Adam felt it important to show that no one had really lost their head. That multiple avenues had been explored.

"At what point was the decision made to go for a kill on the . . . ah . . . indigenous *entity*?"

"Caetia indicated that she would attempt to engage it in a duel to allow us all to retreat. I told her that we would stand together as a team. The . . . entity . . . would just have hunted us down. And I did not feel that there was any way in which we conceivably could outrun him, sir. Not once he had . . . unbound himself." Adam cleared his throat.

Livorus' eyebrows rose. "Yes, the chances of outrunning the . . . *entity* . . . in a motorcar . . . do seem to be slim. And it is an open question if finding a Roman temple of, say, Jupiter, would have proved any sanctuary." Adam felt the knot constricting his chest start to ease, only to tighten again as Livorus murmured, "For the record, however, could you explain to me precisely how the creature died?"

And now I find out if Livorus really is as loyal to us, as he always seems to be. *Because I'm going to tell the truth here. God help me.* "Ah, it was something of a team effort, sir." Adam chose his words carefully. "Itztli was out of the fight. He couldn't do anything to the entity, and he was having cardiac problems. Matrugena and Eshmunazar had helped establish that the creature could sense incoming magical power. It was fixed on Caetia, apparently considering her the biggest threat. It wasn't, however, reacting to bullets until *after* I fired. So Caetia pulled it back, the other two kept it distracted, and I brought part of the ceiling down and impaled its head." Adam grimaced. "Wouldn't have worked if it weren't so weakened by . . . all of the surrounding circumstances. I don't think it could *escape*, sir. Not till we provided it with a body that it could reach . . . through the machines. It found a loophole, essentially."

There was a moment of absolute silence. "So, this is the sort of thing that happens once in a lifetime." Livorus' tone was bland, as if killing *entities* was a commonplace occurrence.

If what that complete madwoman said on the telephone not twenty minutes ago has any bearing on reality at all . . . I certainly hope *so.* Out loud, all Adam said was, "I can't imagine it happening again, sir." After a moment, he dared to ask, "Propraetor? What are your intentions with regard to . . . informing local authorities about the . . . ah . . ."

"Disposition of their *entity*?" Livorus exhaled, and stared out over the glistening expanse of Lake Texcoco, all the silvery bridges and skyscrapers that made up modern Tenochtitlan. From the roof of this hospital, they could even see the central island, with the palace and the temples. "I am unaware of any process by which the rest of their gods might lodge a formal protest with the gods of Rome, ben Maor."

Adam managed to choke the laugh back into a snort. He might be punchy, but this really didn't seem the time to chuckle. Livorus eyed him for a moment. "I cannot control what the gods do, or do not do. I can only control what *I* do."

Adam waited for it. Livorus moved at his own pace, and asking again, would only suggest to the propraetor that Adam had little patience. After a moment or two, Livorus went on, his tone meditative. "There is a tale, ben Maor, that when the Mongols invaded Raccia, and the northern portions of the Empire in Asia Minor, that they sacked a city up there, and the twelfth, sixteenth, and twenty-seventh legions caught them still in the ruins. The Mongols refused to come out, and there were still inhabitants alive. Some were those who had actually opened the gates of the city from within, in the partial hope of making the sack of the city less grievous for themselves and their neighbors . . . some were citizens who were still offering resistance." The propraetor paused. "It is said that a somewhat overzealous legate gave the order to attack everyone in the city. No quarter given or taken. Kill them all, and let the gods sort out who was innocent and who was guilty." He paused, and gestured at the glistening, modern city spread before them, in all its sunlit glory. "I propose a variant on this long-established route to victory. I propose to say as little as possible about the fate of their . . . *entity* . . . and allow the priests and the people of this good land to sort it out for themselves."

Adam blinked. This was not what he'd expected to hear. "Sir?"

Livorus shrugged. "My dear boy, there's no good face to be put upon a tale such as this. If we admit that Rome had anything to do with the death of the . . . creature in question . . . we ignite fires of rebellion everywhere in Nahautl, even among people who *despise* the old ways. There's quietly avoiding embarrassing past behavior, and there's desecrating cultural identity. Many people here still feel strongly about their warrior ancestry. They're as proud of that as any Roman is of twins who may or may not have suckled at the teats of a bitch wolf in a cave. Can you imagine the rioting we would have all across the entire Italian peninsula if someone attempted to ban the Lupercalia?" Livorus shook his head. "No. We stay quiet as long as possible and watch to see how *they* spin it. I would put a golden aureus on it, that the priests will simply continue venerating the absent . . . entity . . . and simply never even mention to the general population that he's gone. Certainly, that is what the Egyptians did for centuries after the reign of Akhenaten." He paused. "And in the end, it is the right of the individual to determine what they believe. And if a god simply stops answering prayers? What difference will it make to most of the people here?"

Adam shivered a little at the second mention of the name Akhenaten in a half hour, and tried very hard not to think about the issue any further. "Thank you, sir."

"It is the proper course, as I will inform the Imperator." Livorus gave him an austere glance. "Dismissed, ben Maor. And thank you."

Adam did his best to put all of it out of his head. To concentrate just on whatever task was at hand. Getting Sigrun real food. Checking in on Trennus, post-surgery. Checking in on Ehecatl and Kanmi. Livorus was with him for the Ehecatl visit, and the Nahautl man was still a little ashen. "They're calling it a cardiac strain," he told them, quietly, from his hospital bed. "Not quite a heart attack. But there's been some damage." His dark eyes studied Livorus. "That's the second time this year. I think it might be time for me to consider retiring."

"You're only thirty-five. You're young," Livorus said, quietly. "Many good years left in you."

"Yes, but after what I saw yesterday . . . ." Ehecatl stared off into the mid-distance. "I saw monsters with the eyes of humans," he finally said. "I don't know whether they were human souls, twisted into those foul forms, or . . . what. But I saw them die. And I saw something greater than them die, too. I . . . it's made me reconsider some of my priorities, propraetor. I'd like to be able to see my sons grow up. I'd like to spend more time with my wife. And no matter if I'm on your detail or not, the Praetorians and even the Jaguar warriors will keep someone like me busy." He leaned back. "I'll be submitting my letters of resignation as soon as they let me out of here. But it was an honor serving you, *dominus*." He looked at Adam, squarely. "And it was an honor working with you, too, ben Maor." He extended his arm for a wrist-clasp, in spite of the IV tubes hanging from it, and Adam wove his hand through them to return the gesture, carefully. He was grateful, too; there was no sense from Ehecatl that the man *blamed* him for the death of one of his people's gods. Many people would have. Ehecatl did not.

In another room of the hospital, Trennus opened his eyes, emerging from a haze of anesthesia. He reached, immediately, for the cords that usually hung from his neck; he had a clear recollection of arguing with a nurse in Latin about how jewelry wasn't permitted in a surgical area, and him telling her, with a good deal more force than he usually employed in any conversation, *For the sake of all the gods, you're operating on my leg. How can something around my neck and under a drape possibly contaminate my <u>knee</u>?*

For a blind instant, he thought they'd confiscated his amulets in spite of all his protests, and he inhaled, preparing to shout for a nurse . . . and then his fingers found what they'd groped for, and Trennus exhaled. *Saraid? Lassair? Are you there?*

I hear. Those were Saraid's quiet, reserved tones, and Trennus smiled faintly.

You didn't leave.

No. Though I hid. There was much . . . disturbance. Saraid still sounded terrified. *There were tears in the Veil itself, from the energies loosed. Vortexes, from this side, and from the other, currents crossing. I held to the amulet you carry as to a lodestone.*

Summoners were taught that there was a wall, or barrier, between the dimension in which the Earth and the rest of the physical universe existed, and the dimension in which the spirits typically abided. The dimension of the spirits was known simply the Veil, and summoners could part the barrier into the Veil for short periods. *Tearing* it did not sound like a good thing. Trennus shuddered. *Is it repairing itself? Will spirits continue to cross?*

I . . . do not know. Saraid's voice was a whisper. *Things that come through from our side of the Veil . . . son of my woods, not everything from our side is good or kindly. And if they are brought through unbound, without a bargain or a strong will to hold them in check . . . .*

I know. Trennus' stomach roiled. The monkey-dog creatures had been . . . spirits. He was fairly sure of that. Spirits that had been given a form that somehow suited them, but their eyes had been almost human. And, of course, Tlaloc himself . . . . Trennus' mind rebelled. *Lassair? Please, hear me.*

Of course I hear you. The fragile fire-spirit's voice was a thread of sound in his mind. *I never left. I cannot leave. We are bound, you and I.*

Trennus' head actually rocked back in relief. *Gods aren't supposed to die, not any more than we are . . .* Lassair told him, manifesting as a wan ball of pale light near his head . . . *but it's possible. We all come from beyond the Veil. If I can face dissolution, so, too, can they.* Stark terror in her voice. *I crawled deep inside your heart, Trennus. But the god's power pursued me even there. I was still . . . open. I had been taking the fire onto myself, away from your skin. And when he . . . <u>died</u> . . .* her tone was horrified . . . *I felt him come into* *me.*

Trennus sat bolt upright in the bed. *"What?"* he said, out loud, in his native Pictish. "He's not—you're not—are you all right?"

Outside his door, he could see a nurse stop and stare in at him, and he turned away, flushing a little. *Yes, stare at the crazy man.* Trennus shook his head rapidly. He was all too well aware of the ways in which Lassair had been violated by a human. She'd just described something that sounded uncannily like being violated by a god. *Lassair . . . .*

He wasn't . . . him. *He wasn't himself. It was just . . . power. I didn't want you to be damaged by it. So I swallowed it.* She sounded agitated. *Trennus . . . there's too much of him and too little of me. I don't know what to do with this. I think it might consume me.* Raw, mortal terror of unbeing. Of her own awareness being snuffed out and *replaced.*

Trennus shook his head, vehemently, against the pillows. *No. Take more of me, my strength. Balance yourself.*

Trennus, the bargain was for only a little piece of you. Enough to keep me alive till I recovered—

Take from me!

If I take, I have to give. The ephemeral ball of light wobbled closer to him, and actually sank down into his chest. Trennus was rather glad that most humans couldn't see this. Sigrun was, in fact, the first non-summoner he'd ever met who *could.* Lassair had liked that. *Stormborn makes me feel more real,* she'd confided. *It's nice to be* seen *by someone besides you.*

Now, he could feel her inside his chest cavity, though she was surely not physical at all. Just a radiant warmth, tugging very gently at what made him, him. What a sorcerer like Kanmi would surely call his will, or what a philosopher would call his soul. *Take what you need,* Trennus told Lassair, as he had, just around a year ago. *Feed from me, and live. I won't let something so beautiful die.*

They left you damaged, she whispered. *The tendons are connected again. The muscles, too. But left untended, you might not walk again. May I fix what has been broken?*

If . . . you wish . . . don't exhaust yourself, though . . . .

Energy does not appear to be a real problem at the moment. Control of it . . . that is a very real problem. Perhaps if I pour some of it into healing you, it will help. Lassair sounded uncertain.

Trennus wasn't really sure if experimenting with a dead god's energies was precisely the course of wisdom, but soul-binding Lassair to keep her alive had probably not been wise, either. But he'd done it, anyway. *Beautiful one,* he told the wisp of energy inside of his heart now, *just be . . . gods, be careful, that burns . . . .* His fists clenched in the bed sheets as golden fire poured through all of him. It was concentrated in his knee, of course, but there was backflow. It hurt and it felt good at the same time, and he thought, dizzily, for a moment, that she'd given him too much, and he was going to die in the hospital bed, become nothing more than a smoking corpse in the middle of the sheets, and part of his mind noted, *Probably the best place for it, all things considered . . . .*

. . . and then she eased the flow a little, and Trennus opened his eyes. Pulled back the blankets, and pulled up his knee to examine it. "No pain," he said, out loud. "No numbness from the anesthetic anymore, either." He stretched it, grinned in pure relief, and told her, happily, "I'll be able to *run* on this, won't I? Run, hunt deer with my brothers, and wrestle? *Thank* you."

I think so, yes. She didn't even sound tired, just a little uncertain . . . but her pleasure at his happiness and gratitude wafted out of her as she emerged from his chest once more. This time, however, the little wisp expanded. Wavered into almost the form of an incandescently bright human female, all indistinct curves, and eyes like banked coals. Wisps and tendrils of gauzy light, all around her, tossed by an unfelt breeze, as she hovered, supine, above the bed, just for a moment . . . and then back to the little ball of light. *I feel better already, too.*

She was, technically, feeding on him. He absolutely intended to release her before he died. As soon as she was fully healthy once more. He counted it a very fair bargain, because, from his perspective, he wasn't particularly *using* his soul. Life-force. Will. Whatever. She needed it more than he did, and she gave far more than he thought his share was worth. Trennus swung his legs over the edge of the bed and tested his weight on the repaired leg. It buckled, but only a little bit. Between the doctor's natural philosophy and her magic, he was well-mended, indeed. *I think we make each other better, Lassair. Bargain made is bargain met, and all that.* He looked around. "I don't suppose either of you saw where they took my clothes?"

Forgive me. I did not take notice. Saraid stuck an antlered head in through a wall. Most spirits didn't quite understand bodies, let alone clothing for bodies. Bodies were just clothing for the human spirit, in their opinion.

Trennus just laughed, and held his gown closed behind him and walked out, barefoot, into the hall. "Can I get my clothing back?" he called to a nurse, who just stared at him, wild-eyed, and started shouting at him in Nahautl. Which Lassair politely translated for him, of course.

Ah, gods, my life is getting stranger every day. But it's hard not to feel really good right now.

In another room, Kanmi had had his hands swathed in gauze, and had been handed a pain pill, which he had regarded with a longing gaze, before sighing and telling the nurse, "All right. It's not a good idea for a sorcerer to take anything narcotic. Ever. Got aspirin?" His tone had been annoyed, and he didn't care who heard it.

The nurse had called the doctor, and the doctor had tried to order him to take the medication, on the grounds that pain would impede his recovery, and Kanmi had, solely for illustrative purposes, picked the doctor up off the ground with his mind, not moving from his perch on the bed. "Do you really want me seeing pink elephants?"

"I assure you, it's non-hallucinogenic!"

"Just give me some damned aspirin, all right?"

They gave him the aspirin, and cleared away, telling him he could check out after they finished giving him a full IV of antibiotics, and after he picked up his prescription for creams, specialized burn ointments, and more oral antibiotics . . . and that he should probably see his primary care physician in four or five days, or sooner if his condition worsened. *I got off easy. Not as easy as ben Maor, who escaped injury by virtue of being underestimated . . . but easier than Matrugena or Caetia did.*

He was moodily trying not to pick at his bandages and reminding himself that increasing the rate of flow from the IV would probably do something nasty to his veins, when the phone rang. His dark brows rose, and he picked up the receiver, awkwardly, between two flattened palms. "*Ave?*"

"*Kanmi! Oh, thank the gods. I've been trying to get in touch with you for hours. The Praetorians finally patched me through three switchboards to your hotel, wherever you are.*" It was his wife Bastet's voice, speaking Latin, as she usually did when they were together; even after eight years in Tyre, from med school until this past year, when he'd been able to move her and the children to Rome, she still didn't speak his native Carthaginian. Latin, not a problem; everyone at the hospital spoke Latin. And she was the only doctor they had who spoke Egyptian and Nubian, which meant that she got stuck with translation duty every now and again . . . but he'd always privately wondered why in Baal's name she still didn't speak more than twelve words of his language. For his lack of facility in *her* language, he had the excuse of not having actually lived in Nubia . . . but he'd picked up a toddler's vocabulary from their children, at least.

"What's wrong?" Kanmi asked, immediately, however, putting all the usual irritations and strains of working so far away from his wife to the back of his head. "Are the boys all right?"

They'd waited until Bastet was done with medical school, and had intended to wait till she was done with residency, too, before having children. Himilico, their eldest, had been a bit of an accident, and had resulted in them needing to rely on Kanmi's mother in Tyre for childcare, because Kanmi himself had been off doing Praetorian work and Bastet had been in her apprentice years at the hospital, sometimes away from home for twenty-four to forty-eight hour stretches. Bodeshmun, or Bodi, was only three, and had been a bit more deliberately planned . . . .and now, between their two paychecks, they actually had enough money to afford a good pedagogue for the two boys, a Hellene woman who'd had impeccable references. "*Himi had a bad fall,*" Bastet told him, quietly. "*Yesterday. He was playing with the neighbor's children, and you know how the apartments here in Rome are . . . all the metal fire escapes?*"

Kanmi closed his eyes and swore. He could picture it all too clearly. His family lived on the fifth floor. "Bastet . . . oh, *gods*, is he all right?"

"*He caught his arm in one of the drop-down ladders. It could have been a lot worse.*" She sounded ragged. "*I was at the hospital when the pedagogue brought them both here. His left forearm's broken, both bones, and he was terrified, of course . . . but gods, what a little legionnaire. And Bodi wanted to give him his*" *favorite stuffed marmot for the overnight stay at the hospital yesterday."* Bastet's voice had been proud, but now started to hold an edge. *"I couldn't find you! You weren't at the hotel where you said you'd be! I had to call the regional Praetorian headquarters, and they transferred my call to you, once I convinced them that I was who I said I was. Were you out drinking or whoring or something?"* A hint of bitterness there.

Kanmi was already seething with guilt. He knew it was irrational. Even if he'd been there, in Rome, he'd likely have been at work. But if he'd *happened* to have been home, if he'd *happened* to have seen it happen, he could have stopped the boy's fall from the fire escape . . . or at least, he'd have been more attentive than the pedagogue clearly had been. Of course, it was damned easy to second-guess when you were over three thousand miles from home. But the accusation of being out *carousing* was particularly irksome, especially since he rarely had more than one or two drinks in an entire week. He couldn't have more than that, for the same reason as he couldn't have a narcotic painkiller. He was an extremely powerful sorcerer.

On the other hand, she was clearly upset, and felt guilty because she hadn't been there, and she was taking it out on him because he wasn't there, and because he was the only available target. Understanding it didn't make it any easier. And since they'd been married for nine years, he'd heard it all before. Repeatedly.

Familiarity didn't make it easier, either. But at least it let him keep his voice even, rather than yelling back at her, as he once might have. "No, Bastet," Kanmi managed, biting off the ends of his words, "I'm actually in the hospital at the moment, myself."

There was a clear pause. And then, remorse and shame in her voice, *"Oh, gods. I didn't know! Kanmi, are you all right?"*

"Burns. Second-degree. Most of the surfaces of both hands. I look like a mummy, and it hurts like a bitch, but I'll be all right. I just can't pick anything up for a week or two." Kanmi's voice was clipped, but he was trying to soften it. "Let me talk to the boys . . . no. Wait. What time is it there?" It was past five postmeridian here, add eight hours . . . . "When can I call back, and what hospital are you at? The one you work at?"

"Asclepius Northwestern, yes. Kanmi — I'm so sorry — "

"I know. Me too."

Yes, you're always sorry. And I'm always sorry. And I know damned well that I'm going to come home, and we're going to wait for the boys to be in bed, and we're going to have the same argument we've had a hundred times before. Four years on the Mongol border, and then I was supposed to be home and underfoot all the time, working for the sorcerer's preparatory school in Tyre or at a university, or something. But when the Praetorians think you're good enough, and they come calling, you don't say no. Two years of diplomatic work, where I was just a few hundred miles away . . . that wasn't so bad. And it was better than me being in Mongolia. But now, not knowing where Livorus is going to be from week to week . . . Kanmi sighed. He knew his wife hated it. He understood why. He wasn't particularly fond of being away from her for long periods, either; her gleaming dark eyes, the brilliant white of her smile when she laughed, the soft darkness of her arms, had been all he dreamed about when he was away for years. Though lately, it was getting harder to picture her face. And when they were together, he'd never given a damn that she was four inches taller than he was, and had always ignored the stares they got when they walked around, hand-in-hand, in public.

What he could not understand was why she didn't grasp that his job was important. He wasn't a doctor, the way she was. But he could save lives. Admittedly, he was better at ending them. But it was what he could do, and he was very, very good at it.

And they'd argue and hash it out, and they'd continue sailing along for another couple of months . . . maybe even another half a year, and then they'd have the *exact same argument* again. Only next time, it would be louder and more vehement and take longer to patch up. That was the worst part, really. Knowing that absolutely nothing would change, unless he gave up doing what he was better at than about ninety-nine point nine percent of the rest of the world. Unless he asked for reassignment from a damned prestigious position, one that was *allowing* them to have a pedagogue for the boys and live in Rome, not in fish-stinking Tyre. Because she was never going to change her mind. In truth, being more or less a single mother with an absentee husband wasn't what she'd signed up for. She'd signed up for romance, for being swept off her feet, and the promise that she'd never have to go home to Nubia again.

The pause in their conversation had gone on a little long. She had evidently been waiting for him to apologize more, or explain himself further. *"The boys would like to hear from you, I think."* Her voice limped out onto the phone line, at the same moment he told her, *"But this long-distance call is expensive. Let me call you back when it's ten or so your time, all right?"*

And then they hung up, and Kanmi said every bad word he'd learned on the docks, growing up in Tyre. It was an international port. The list was extensive, colorful, and above all else . . . heartfelt. He'd get it out here, in the room. That way, when he saw his coworkers again, all they'd see was the cynical smile.

Iunius 15-20, 1954 AC

The next two days passed in a blur for the four lictors. They were all put on administrative leave, because their actions at Teotihuacán had resulted in the deaths of three Eagle warriors and two civilian casualties as well; such things required review. Even if their actions were currently so highly classified that their review board was apt to consist of the Imperator and the commander of the Praetorians and no one else . . . their actions still required examination. Which meant that they were effectively stood down. Ehecatl had submitted his resignation, as he'd said he would, but he'd be going to Rome to stand for review, the same as the rest of them. And to sign any number of non-disclosure documents, more than likely.

Livorus, with a certain resignation in his tone, told them, "I'll need another full lictor team while you're undergoing review. I fully expect to be here in Nahautl for the next six months, working out at least a preliminary set of power-transfer arrangements between Emperor Achcauhtli, Governor Dioscuri, the governor of Tikal, and the Quechan rebels."

"Are we sure that Achcauhtli didn't have something to do with all of this?" Kanmi asked, dourly, as he sat at the table in Livorus' palatial hotel suite in Tenochtitlan, very slowly peeling an apple with a small knife. The process with his bandaged hands looked so laborious that Adam finally sighed and took both the fruit and the knife away, cutting it for Kanmi as if the Carthaginian were a child.

Livorus raised his eyebrows at Kanmi. "That will doubtless take countless man-hours over the next year or so to determine, Eshmunazar. The records obtained at Tototl and Xicohtencatl's estates . . . though I certainly doubt if *all* have been, or ever will be recovered . . . have yet to turn up more than that each man yearned to make himself the overlord of Nahautl, and to control Emperor Achcauhtli as a figurehead. Each, naturally, after having displaced the other as the main leader." He sighed. "No one ever quite seems to grasp that triumvirates in government are usually unstable, historically speaking, and even partnerships of only two, inevitably fail as one partner turns on the other. Every time there is a revolution, anywhere, the result is almost inevitably a dictatorship, run by a single man — or woman, I suppose — " he gave Sigrun a quick, almost sly smile, and she raised her eyebrows at him, "with the short-lived revolution of the Gracchi brothers being the only counterexample that I can easily bring to mind. And look what happened to them."

The Gracchi brothers, who'd lived a century before Julius Caesar, had attempted to institute Hellene-style democratic principles in the old Roman Republic . . . and had both grossly overestimated the will of the plebeians and severely *under*estimated the amount of corruption already inherent to the old Republic. One of the brothers, with three hundred of his followers, had been clubbed to death after attempting to extend the rights of Romans to non-Roman Italians. The other had been killed, along with three *thousand* of his followers, shortly thereafter, mostly because Roman plebeians had jealously wanted to retain their rights and privileges without extending them to people outside of the sacred hills of Rome itself.

Livorus sighed. "At any rate, what little we do know about their motivations . . . and *little* describes the case aptly . . . suggests that Xicohtencatl truly did wish to toss Rome out, but felt that the best way to do so would be to first, provide services that Rome could not — power, for example — and second, to gain power over Achcauhtli and the common people. By religion, if by no other way. His writings seem to indicate that the notion of actually *controlling* the . . . ah, entity in question . . ." he glanced around, indicating he did not trust their environs completely, "did not occur to him until quite late. Classic example of overreaching and hubris, I believe. Tragic, really. It would make for quite a play, if the entire series of events weren't classified." He paused. "Tototl's motivations appear to have been as outlined by Smoke Jaguar. His writings indicate a preoccupation with uniting the native peoples of the new world against their Roman 'oppressors.' And to do so, he wished to re-ignite in them the fires of the traditional forms of worship." Livorus paused. "One wonders what, precisely, he would have done when he encountered native populations who did not happen to worship or acknowledge his god." He paused. "Other than preparing them as sacrifices, of course."

All five lictors stirred around the table, uncomfortably. "I do not wish to imagine that further," Sigrun acknowledged, quietly. "Bloody internal warfare, I am certain."

"More than likely," Ehecatl agreed, tiredly.

Livorus sighed. "I expect that the Praetorians and local *gardia* will spend the next six months to a year sorting out who else was involved. Who in Xicohtencatl's 'research and development' teams knew precisely what they were dealing with, for example. Such a large endeavor can't have been the work of two men, working alone."

Kanmi stirred. "The *gardia* sent me some typewritten copies and photographs of documents that they found at Xicohtencatl's office. Pamphlets from a few political groups he was involved in—can't say I'd want to be a member today, eh?—and the newsletter from a technomancer's *collegia* called 'The Source Initiative." He shrugged. "I'm reading through it all now, but I'm not finding anything really subversive. Other than a few people proposing that becoming too dependent on ley-energy might stifle creativity and innovation, or something like that. Nothing really world-shattering, though."

"Keep digging," Livorus told him, firmly. "Few people are really creative enough to come up with any thoughts on their own. We *all* absorb ideas from those around us. What we read. What we watch on the far-viewer. Some people have a greater ability to analyze, synthesize, and extrapolate from sources than others, but most people merely know how to repeat what they've been told. Our two conspirators might even have been the *leaders* of their little intended coup . . . but they didn't draw the idea out of the ether, either."

"What are your intentions with the Quechan rebels near Tikal, sir?" Sigrun asked, bringing their meeting back on track.

"I do not wish to reward bad behavior, but if it's a choice between wiping out the entire population of a region, with the potential to ignite two other provinces into rebellion, and this . . . we'll try some limited regional autonomy." Livorus gave Adam a chill glance. "With the understanding that if they take what they're given out of a spirit of benevolence, and continue to agitate, steal, kidnap, and murder, that all autonomy will be revoked, martial law will be imposed, and the legions *will* march in, to include airstrikes on anything that so much as looks like a rebel base. Women and children will not, under those circumstances, be spared." Livorus exhaled. "War's a dirty business . . . but Rome has never shied from it."

"I'm just sorry we can't be down there with you until the review has been conducted," Adam replied, and he meant it. He'd more or less gotten his propraetor into this mess. It was his job to protect the man through the whole process, and what was he getting instead? Downtime. Probably a return to Rome in the next week to give personal testimony in front of someone . . . very high-ranking. Nothing to look forward to, really.

Livorus shook his head. "If it weren't for the diplomatic business I find myself ensnared in, I would be there with you. As it is, I expect to conduct several high-security phone calls from the governor's palace and will probably face a few closed-door meetings of the Senate when I do return home." He shrugged. "So long as the Imperator is reasonably well-pleased, I will probably not be censured." The propraetor spread his hands. "I believe your travel arrangements are for the twentieth, yes?"

Sigrun coughed into her hand. "Ah, about that, my lord?"

Adam turned to regard her in the plushly-appointed hotel room that Livorus and his various servants currently occupied. She looked far better than she had two days ago. No more suppurating mass of weeping blisters and peeling skin. The last traces, really, were a lingering pink burn over most of her body, as if she'd been in the sun too long, and the fact that her waist-length braid was gone. Her hair had still grown back in at a far accelerated rate from human norm, but the strands of fair hair that waved all around her face, like soft down, were no more than three inches in length.

"Yes?" Livorus asked, arching an eyebrow.

"I've been summoned to the Odinhall. That, for me, regrettably takes precedence." Her expression tightened. "The Praetorians do not generally recognize any other authority as superseding their own, but . . . this is not a matter of an earthly organization." Sigrun was evidently selecting her words with care. "If I do not go to the Odinhall, it is not a matter of being stripped of citizenship, land, titles, or anything so petty. Disobedience to the gods is a capital offense for one such as I am."

Livorus' eyes widened slightly. "You received word last night?" He frowned. "Usually, I'm informed when my main lictors receive urgent phone calls." He glanced at Kanmi for a moment, his expression unreadable; Adam wasn't sure what that was about, but resolved to ask as soon as the meeting was over.

"This morning. The Odinhall, ah . . . doesn't particularly need to place telephone calls or send telegrams, *dominus*." Sigrun rubbed at her forehead. "I was summoned. I must go. And I would be . . . greatly indebted, sir, if you could explain matters to the Praetorians, and tell them that I will gladly stand on their carpet to be caned at their leisure, assuming I can do so. I may not be permitted to return to the service of Rome after I have . . . finished accounting for my actions." Adam could see the line of muscles in her throat move as she swallowed.

"Of course," Livorus replied, immediately. "I'll speak to the commander of the Guard myself."

"Would it do any good," Adam asked, surprising himself, "if we were to come with you? If we offered testimony?"

Sigrun actually chuckled, a single, rueful snort, and shook her head. "I rather doubt it. I, ah . . . don't think you would be allowed to speak before the, ah, tribunal." She was clearly edging around something. "They would not consider it to be your business."

Adam shook his head. "All right, back up a moment here. You

could be barred from further service with Rome, the Praetorians, or with this team." He leaned back in his chair, frowning and scrubbing at his freshly-shaved chin with his knuckles. "I'd say that any of those three *make* it our business, Sigrun. You're an integral part of this team. If they're going to take you away from us, I think we've got a right to say something about that." He looked at Kanmi, Trennus, and Ehecatl. "You?"

Kanmi snorted. "I say that if the rest of us have to go hang by our balls from meat hooks in the Praetorian main office, she should *not* get out of that particular joy." He bared his teeth at Sigrun. "Though I think the command staff will find it challenging finding a place to sink a meat hook on you, Caetia."

Trennus closed his eyes and chuckled, visibly fighting off the image. "If pushed to translate that out of the original Eshmunazar," the Britannian said, dryly, "I think that means 'if we're all going to hang, we may as well hang together, as separately. Which I agree with. If . . . somewhat less colorfully."

"I'm in," Ehecatl said, simply. "I'm probably already in as much trouble with my own gods as a human *can* be, and live. Going to the Odinhall can't get me any further into hot water, can it?"

Adam gave him a look, not wanting to think about the kind of trouble the gods of Nahautl could make for Ehecatl. They might not kill him, outright, but they could take a long and subtle vengeance on him. *Look at the book of Job, for the kinds of misery that can be inflicted on a human by a god,* he thought. *Every child dying, the death of your wife, boils and plagues and poverty . . . and that is my god, who was testing Job's faith. Of course, the book of Job tells us that God gave Job as many children again, as he lost, but that doesn't erase the sorrow endured for the death of each beloved child, does it?*

Sigrun shook her head, but Adam could see from the growing softness in her gray eyes that she was genuinely touched. "I appreciate it . . . but I do not think your words would be heard. You should all report directly to Praetorian headquarters. You are . . . you're all already in enough trouble. Don't . . ." She paused, and Adam could hear the shift in her speech into a less formal mode. "Don't make it worse for yourselves, on my account."

"Yes, well, stuff that," Kanmi informed her. "I want you at the damned hearings for the Praetorians. If you're there, we all stand a much better chance of getting out of this with our hides intact. And me? I *like* my job. It pays the rent and ensures my children get a good education. It also covers their medical bills." He looked up at the ceiling, and grimaced. "No. I'm going there, and if I have to yell from outside the door at whoever your commanders are that we didn't do anything wrong deliberately . . . I will."

Sigrun's lips twitched, and she slowly put her head down on the table and just *laughed*, uncontrollably, for almost a minute. After the first fifteen seconds, the various men were looking at each other uneasily. "Ah . . . did we miss something?" Adam asked.

"Yes, but . . . you won't understand." Sigrun's shoulders were shaking. "You won't understand till we get there. Come along, you daft fools." She glanced at Livorus. "With your leave, of course. And once we've arranged for other Praetorians to take our spots."

Livorus waved. "You're all on administrative leave," he said, shrugging. "Rome is sending new lictors to relieve the local Praetorians who joined the team. Go. Go, so that you *can* return to us, my dear."

"Thank you, sir." Sigrun glanced at the rest of them. "All right, gentlemen. Let's go get our plane tickets."

Trennus winced as he stood. "Couldn't we just take a train?" he asked, plaintively.

"I don't like it any more than you do, Trennus," Sigrun told him, equitably, and with a degree more familiarity than she'd previously spoken to any of them. There was even a smile there, if an uneasy one, as she looked up at the tall Britannian. *We who are about to die,* Adam thought, his lips quirking faintly, *may say thou to one another,* apparently.

The planes out of Tenochtitlan were ley-powered and quite modern, as befit a jewel in the crown of the modern Empire. Adam was thus amused to watch both Trennus and Sigrun *jitter* the entire long flight from the Nahuatl city to Burgundoi. The city was close to four hundred miles north of the palm trees and sunny skies of Nimes-on-the-Pacifica, the Gallic city to which Adam had been assigned for a while after his stint in India . . . and over two thousand miles northwest of Tenochtitlan. "At least we don't have to transfer planes," Adam told them both cheerfully.

Trennus opened his eyes just long enough to give him a dirty look. "You're a *ley-mage,*" Kanmi told Trennus, with a faintly malicious grin. "How can you possibly be nervous about this?"

"Because ley-lines are scarcer in the air than on the ground, and no one's yet worked out a passive system for recharging ley-batteries while an engine is drawing from them. In other words, if the batteries fail, the whole plane crashes, and there's *nothing I can do about it,*" Trennus shot back, in the sharpest tones Adam had ever heard him use. "I like staying on the ground. It's . . . much safer there."

Ehecatl quietly rolled his eyes, and leafed through an in-flight magazine's foolscap pages. Kanmi leaned back, grinning to himself, and obviously taking mental notes for later use.

Since Nimes and Burgundoi were along the same western stretch of coast on the western shores of Caesaria Aquilonis, Adam had expected . . . something of the same environment. Palm trees. Warm breezes. Getting off the plane on the tarmac, he was surprised to see how gray the sky was here, and how *chill* the wind, especially after the damp heat of Tenochtitlan. He shivered a little, and pulled his cloak a little tighter; suddenly, it was hard to believe it was Iunius.

The city itself, spread out around and encircling a shallow bay, had skyscrapers that were akin to those he'd seen in Novo Trier; there was something just fundamentally different about Gothic architecture than Roman buildings. The buildings, tall and narrow, raced up to the sky, but instead of the clean austerity of Roman pillars and arches, which might have had a naked god or a cluster of grapes for decoration . . . most of these buildings had *gargoyles.* Some of the buildings were surmounted by hundreds of the beasts, and just looking at them, less than a week after having fought the monkey-dog *ahuizotl*, made Adam feel distinctly uneasy. He half-expected to see the creatures take off like a cloud of bats and careen through the twilight sky.

He was driving, as usual, and was actually rather startled to realize that their rental vehicle was a solid Judean import—electric engine and all. "The power grid here—it's electric?" he asked Sigrun, startled.

"It's a mix. Both ley and electrical power plants are here, and it depends on which neighborhood you're in, what type of outlets you're going to have." Sigrun leaned back in the passenger seat, her eyes blank as she stared out the window. "Some of the older buildings suffered damage in the Great Earthquake four years ago, in 1950. The regional ley-mages didn't even feel it coming . . . but they were able to stabilize most of the large buildings, including the bridges. And the Odinhall survived it. The gods would not permit it to fall." She looked around at the city, and Adam spotted scaffolding on a number of buildings that were under construction . . . or reconstruction, as the case might well be.

For all of Adam's unease with the damned gargoyles, he thought Burgundoi might possibly be one of the most beautiful cities he'd ever seen. They had to cross the bay on an enormous suspension bridge, which Sigrun told them was called the Ceasterhild Brycgian, or the Citygate Bridge, from the airport, which was on the mainland, to get to the center of the city, which stood on a peninsula on the other side of that dark blue bay. He could have lived without the crazy street grid, however; the city was old, having been built sometime in the 1200s AC, and all of the buildings were perched atop rolling hills.

Sigrun had been giving him low-voice directions of left, right, left at the next stoplight for a while, and finally, told him, "It's ahead, on the right."

Adam looked around the crowded downtown street; there were people packing all the sidewalks, and there were skyscrapers on all sides, interspersed with a few parking garages. "Where?" he asked, baffled. He was looking for a low, wooden building. Or a taller one, with a palisade. A castle, perhaps, like the ones developed in the new world during the early wars between the Gothic and Gallic tribes, against the Comanche Alliance and the Lakota Nation. Something that shouted *Goth* to his senses.

Sigrun pointed, and Adam set a foot on the brakes as he looked up.

The Odinhall was not built in wood, but in steel and poured-stone. It was, by far, the tallest building in Burgundoi, surmounted by a roughly triangular spire, and with two 'wings' of poured stone jutting out from its sides . . . and those wings housed literally thousands of animal statues and gargoyles. It was a sleek and fundamentally modern building that took Adam thoroughly by surprise. "We can leave the car over there," Sigrun said, pointing at a five-story parking garage. "They'll take the Praetorian identification and comp us."

On walking in the front lobby, Adam began to feel more and more out of his element. The walls were all wood-paneled, and the floors seemed to be oak, and highly polished . . . but the reception area held images of the caduceus and of a winged woman holding a chalice . . . Eir, the goddess or valkyrie associated with healing, his memory tossed up after a moment's frantic thought. "Ah, Sig? This is a hospital?" Adam asked, feeling lost as the five of them cut their way through the crowds of thoroughly Gothic people. He hadn't seen this much blond hair in one place since the Novo Trier airport, on their way back to Rome after the whole Ponca disaster.

"Yes. The bottom ten floors are." Sigrun tabbed one of the elevator buttons, and waited patiently . . . even as some of the people around them started to notice, and react to them. Adam, Ehecatl, and Kanmi got overt stares; olive skin, dark hair, and dark eyes were, as any number of women in Nimes had pointed out to Adam, intriguingly exotic in Gallic and Gothic regions. A couple of people addressed Trennus in Gallic, with friendly smiles and wrist-clasps. And Sigrun . . . well, it was the Novo Trier airport all over again. She wasn't wearing her regalia, holding her spear, or channeling any godly power; the white runes were nowhere in evidence on her face. But this wasn't Ponca, with its mix of Gallic, Gothic, and indigenous citizens. This was the Odinhall, and everyone there knew a valkyrie when they saw one. Smiling women came over and asked her soft questions in Gothic or Cimbric or whatever, and held out their babies for Sigrun to lean down and kiss. Brought their toddlers and adolescents over, so that Sigrun could crouch down, and give them lightly admonitory words or blessings or . . . *something* . . . in their native tongue. What looked to be lawyers and magistrates, in gray tweed slacks and cloaks, came over as well, holding their briefcases, to shake her hand, meet her eyes, and ask for what looked to be the same thing.

Adam was highly uncomfortable. They were treating her like a celebrity, in a sense, but someone who was far more accessible than a king or a queen or a philosopher. It wasn't adulation, and Sigrun didn't treat it as if it were her due. This was just . . . part of her job. And for the first time, Adam understood why she tended to say that a god-born of Tyr's first and last task was *duty*.

"We're going to need to change elevators on the thirtieth floor," Sigrun told them all as they got in, and an attendant nodded to her, and pushed the button for the highest floor that this elevator could access. "This one only serves the public floors—the hospital, the temples, the administrative offices for each. That includes investment offices for tithes and how those funds get distributed to the truly indigent." She shrugged. "After that, there are apartments for the physicians, the living quarters for the highest-ranking priests and priestesses, and after that, floors dedicated for the training of priests, priestesses, magistrates, and god-born. A university, I suppose you might call it. There are dormitories. Entire floors dedicated to practicing the art of combat. And above all of those is my destination."

"This is a small city," Ehecatl said, his voice quiet. The Nahautl man looked a little uneasy, and had his back to one of the elevator's walls.

"On a busy day, there are seventy thousand people in the

building," Sigrun agreed.

"That's the size of a city," Trennus agreed, looking just as uneasy as Ehecatl, but probably for different reasons. They were now three hundred feet above the ground, after all.

The elevator came to a halt, and they disembarked, following Sigrun as they wended through narrow halls to a different elevator—this one, with a guard post, with a glass window overlooking the lobby. The guard booth was occupied by two huge men. One had light brown hair, which fell in a braid to between his shoulder blades, and the other was as blond as Sigrun, and wore his hair loose to his shoulders. Both wore their beards short-cropped. However, when they stood and emerged from the guard room, Adam blinked and stared up at them. Both were over seven feet tall, towering over even Trennus . . . and broad in proportion. "Sigrun. *Waes hael.* You are expected." The darker-haired one leaned down and engulfed the woman in a hug, lifting her clear off the ground, and rattled something indecipherable at her in Gothic.

"Brandr, put me down, please." That, in Latin, so clearly for the benefit of her fellow lictors. "Yes, these are my teammates. Adam ben Maor, Kanmi Eshmunazar, Trennus Matrugena, Ehecatl Itztli . . . this is Brandr Ilfetu. He is a bear-warrior. Of Thor's line. And one of those who trained me here."

Adam blinked, and reassessed. The man didn't look a day older than Sigrun, but his face was scarred—no rune-marks to conceal the scars. His blue eyes were steady, however, and he was bluff and hearty as he engulfed each of their hands in what could only be described as a paw, clapping each of them on the shoulder with brother-and-equal vigor. Trennus and Adam both swayed a little at the enthusiasm, Ehecatl endured it expressionlessly, and Kanmi was bowled over entirely. "Nice to meet you," Kanmi said, picking himself up from the floor, his eyes narrow. "Excuse me while I get a stepstool so I can give you the kiss of friendship in exchange."

Brandr chuckled. "These men are all right, Sigrun. All have good hands, hearts, and eyes."

"I knew that already," Sigrun murmured. "They want to go up with me."

"They do?" Brandr's eyes widened. "Well . . . I don't expect that they'll be allowed into the highest floors, but I don't see any reason why they can't see the training areas, at least." His teeth flashed white behind his beard. "We have a large class this year, Sigrun. Right around when your sister was born, back in . . . what was it, twenty-nine, thirty? . . . we went from four to seven god-born children a year, to more than thirty a year. It's much more fun training that many of them at once, than it was training one valkyrie and three bear-warriors for four years." Brandr looked over. "Don't you agree, Erikir?"

"More fun for the students, than when we went through," the blonder man agreed, smiling at Sigrun. "I don't think they go to bed aching nearly as badly as we did."

"Eh, you all *healed*, didn't you?" Brandr laughed. "All right. Up you go."

Adam did a little mental math as they got into the new elevator. "So, your sister's my age?" he said, mildly. That was both a relief, and slightly disconcerting. Sigrun looked to be more or less his own age. He'd known she was older than he was, but not by how much. If she had a living younger sister, that put her more or less . . . well, it made her younger than he'd thought. *How old is she? She can't be in her eighties if her sister is my age. I mean, yes, technically, a man can father a child in his eighties, but I'm not thinking that it's going to happen if her father's a hundred years old . . . unless her father is also god-born . . . .* Adam rubbed at his face. There were questions he was not *about* to ask, out of respect for Sigrun's privacy, but the question of how old she actually was, was starting to drive him slightly mad.

"Wait. Caetia, you have a sister?" Kanmi said, looking over, sharply. "New information. Is she young? Is she presentable? Can we marry her off to Matrugena here so that the poor lad can get over his clear infatuation with you?"

Trennus made a rude gesture at Kanmi, lifting a hand to tuck his thumb between his index and middle fingers. "I thank you for your interest in my love life, or lack thereof, but I don't need a matchmaker."

Sigrun gave Kanmi a dark look. "I don't talk about her."

"No. You certainly have not." Kanmi grinned. "Details, details."

And of course, Kanmi asks the things the rest of us won't, because for him, words are weapons. Information is a weapon. "This, from the man who didn't tell us that his oldest son had fallen and broken an arm a week ago," Adam said, looking up at the ceiling. "I had to hear it from Livorus. Stow it, Kanmi. Everyone's got things they don't want to talk about. I don't mention my family much, either."

"You see, I didn't realize you had one, ben Maor. I thought you were just a summoner's construct. Someone in a darkened room says your Name, and you appear in a flash of light and a swirl of iron duty."

Ehecatl and Trennus both laughed at that, and Adam gave Kanmi a look, before laughing himself, if reluctantly. It was really the only way to deal with the sorcerer. If you reacted in any other way, he'd lead you into a maze made entirely of edged words, and you'd cut yourself open trying to fight your way out.

This elevator deposited them on what was, apparently, a training floor, and they passed an enclosure with a one-way window that allowed them to look in on groups of young people being trained in hand-to-hand, spear, and sword combat. Half were men, half were women; the men were all around the same size as Brandr, and they were all cross-training with one another. And they all seemed to be going at full strength and full contact, though with wooden training weapons, thankfully. Adam winced as one of the young men was thrown into a wall and bounced off. The young man regained his feet, shook his head, and started to foam at the mouth, before charging back at the trainer who'd thrown him, tackling the older, more scarred bear-warrior. "Battle-madness," Sigrun noted, clinically. "Male god-born are known for it, among my people. Part of their training here consists of learning how to restrain it. It's not always an advantage to lose your mind in battle." She gave them all a sidelong smile. "Just think what this team would be like, with a god-born of Thor on it, rather than me."

Adam grimaced. Sigrun's tactics tended to be straight-forward and direct, and she met force with force, words with words, but she never lost her head. The night in Ponca when the Atenist had insulted her was the closest he'd ever seen her come to losing her temper . . . and even then, her response had been highly measured. He wasn't sure he could work with a bear-warrior, especially one prone to uncontrolled rages. That seemed as if it could hinder a team as much as help.

As they watched, the instructors managed to pin the huge young man, and simply held him to the floor; the fact that it took three other massive bear-warriors to do so was perhaps the most frightening part. Then they simply rode out the rage, while the other students continued to work around them. "You trained with three bear-warriors? For four years?" Trennus said, staring as one of the men on the other side of the glass picked up and threw one of the women, who barely managed to turn the attack into a roll in time.

"Some things never change," Sigrun replied, gesturing at the four men around her with a little quirk of her lips.

Trennus snorted a little, and passed a hand over his braids. "I was just about to say . . . no wonder you have so many, ah . . . ." he hesitated uncertainly.

"Scars?" Sigrun shrugged. "As they say, whatever fails to kill you, makes you stronger." She put a hand on the window, and stared through at the practice room for a moment. "I had a good deal of practice in becoming strong here, yes." She shrugged again and turned away, leading them onwards.

One more elevator, and now they were on the sixty-fifth floor. The elevator opened into a space that was completely open, pristinely white, and seemed to stretch for miles in every direction, as if there were no internal walls, and they had exited the elevator into an entirely different plane of existence. It was lit, from above, as if there were a small sun inside the building.

Adam shielded his eyes, blinking rapidly, and could not make himself step forward, at first. "It's all right," Sigrun told them all, her voice gentle. "You can step out. You probably won't be permitted beyond here, though." She moved out ahead of them, and then took each of their hands, in turn, as they all winced at the brightness of the light, and set foot on a reassuringly real and solid floor. Adam peered down, and saw, faintly, tile lines under his feet. That, too, was somewhat reassuring. They hadn't actually taken a wrong turn and wound up in *Valhalla*, at least.

When he looked up again, however, the white, limitless space had vanished, and he hovered somewhere in a galaxy completely filled with stars. He was part of the darkness outside the Milky Way, watching the limitless points of light burn in front of him. And then he began to fall forwards, into and through it, seeing clouds of nebular gas whip past his face. Planets, thousands of them, each with their own moons, atmospheres, mountains, volcanoes . . . some with rings, like Saturn's, some gas giants so close to their suns that lines of fire poured between them and their star. "Everyone sees the room differently," Sigrun's voice told them all. "It's a little overwhelming the first time. Come on. Take normal steps. You'll find your path."

How? How am I supposed to walk when I'm . . . ahh. All right, I'm not so much stepping, as . . . directing myself in space . . . Adam squinted. He could see the others now, all drifting with him through the starfield. Trennus was looking around with every evidence of delight. Kanmi's expression was speculative, and Ehecatl had dropped to a crouch, and now stared around himself with mild suspicion. Sigrun didn't walk here, Adam noticed, so much as she . . . hovered.

There was a shape in the distance, in the next globular cluster of stars, which, as Sigrun lead them towards it, resolved into a desk. Behind that desk, bathed in the light of a half-dozen newborn and furious stars, was a man half Adam's height, scratching carefully at a large book with a goose-quill pen. His face was wizened by age, and his long white hair and beard caught periodically on the pen, making him stop and mutter irritably. "Dvalin," Sigrun whispered, her tone deeply respectful, then spoke in quick, sharp Cimbric.

Yes, yes. You're expected. The words seemed to be in absent-minded Latin, but the lips behind the beard didn't move, and the glowing blue gaze that the creature raised from the papers in front of him were anything *but* thoughtless. Adam felt the others all shift a little, and he was finally starting to understand why Sigrun had laughed when they'd insisted on accompanying her.

She wasn't facing review from any earthly authority for having participated in the death of a god. She was facing her own *gods*.

Adam turned and looked at Trennus and Kanmi. "Having waited and gone to Praetorian headquarters," Kanmi muttered, "is starting to sound like a wonderful idea that I should have pursued."

"At least," Adam murmured, softly, "it'll be over with quickly if they decide to drop us out a window for our temerity."

Trennus, for his part, was looking around with an abstracted expression, smiling a little, as if he could see things that the others couldn't. "It's beautiful here," he finally said.

"Beautiful, but dangerous," Ehecatl told them, still watching his surroundings. "You have to be careful in a place like this. You never know what's really behind the next tangle of vines."

What do they all see? Adam wondered, for an instant.

Sigrun. Daughter. Come to me. It is time.

Adam's head rocked back, and he stared as a figure appeared beside the desk. The voice was neither harsh, nor severe; but merely calm, as was the face of the man now standing there. He was even taller than the bear-warriors downstairs, with flaxen hair, still bound back in the same style of braid. But where the others downstairs lumbered, this man bore himself as lightly as a candle flame. As if his feet did not quite touch the floor. Adam didn't quite dare to meet the eyes, and never could quite quite remember what the face looked like, afterwards, but he had an impression of storm-touched steel. Electric blue.

And the god . . . for a god it was . . . was no more locked in the past than the rest of the Odinhall. For while he carried a spear in one hand that held all the fires of a levinbolt, he wore no armor or furs, but a simple pair of gray leather pants, a white shirt, and a gray cloak . . . but with a golden brooch and buckles. And while he leaned on that glowing spear in one hand, the other hand had what surely looked like a modern wristwatch on it, if one crafted of soft, pure gold.

This was not Tlaloc, a god that had been damaged by the fading belief of his followers even before he had been bargained with and bound, his powered siphoned off to provide power for people's . . . .washing machines and motorcars and whatever else ley-power was normally used for. This was Tyr, Adam understood, suddenly. The Gothic god of justice, duty, honor, and loyalty. A god rich with the belief of *millions* behind him.

**Your friends love you much, daughter of my line,** Tyr said, unexpectedly, _**that they would come so far for you. Would dare so much. Know, humans, that though you are none of mine, I honor you for your loyalty. And I say to you that it has not been given in vain. Though you may not go to your valkyrie's trial, understand that I know what is in your hearts . . . and your testimony will be weighed, as if you had spoken it, in truth.**_

Part III: Wounds

Eurasia in 1955 AC.

Middle East in 1955 AC.

Chapter X: Preparations

The history of what is now the Persian Empire is a tangled and contentious one, in which Rome, Hellas, Judea, and Egypt have all played their parts. Sumerian Ur was supplanted by Akkadian Babylon . . . and Babylon was conquered, repeatedly, by various tribes. The Elamites, the Assyrians, and the Chaldeans all contended with the native Babylonians for rule, but in the main, these were tribes whose gods had been slain in or around 1100 BAC. A few gods remained, of course, but the loss of entire pantheons had a keen effect on the people of the area.

The Chaldeans, who, during their short-lived hold on Babylon, ruled as far west as Tyre, Megiddo, and Jerusalem, achieved dominance by allying with another kingdom, the Medes. By the time of Nebuchadnezzar II, the Chaldeans had a firm grip on the region, and they did it almost entirely by virtue of their magi.* The Chaldeans had almost no god-born; few, if any, had been born in the region since the godslayings. They had, as a result, developed different methods of accomplishing the same results: the Magi. The Chaldean Magi were astronomers, natural philosophers, alchemists, sorcerers, and summoners. Nebuchadnezzar II himself was a notable magus, and, it is said, designed the Hanging Gardens himself. He was also noted for having prophetic dreams about the fall of his empire. Prophecy is usually the hallmark of the god-born, but in this case, it is widely presumed that Nebuchadnezzar's attendant spirits brought him these intimations, which were interpreted by one of his Israelite servants, a man named Daniel.

After the fall of the Chaldean Empire, the Chaldeans were subsumed into the general population of Babylon, but remained particularly noted as sorcerers and summoners. Their magi became an entire caste of sorcerers, summoners, and philosophers who served the later rulers of the region, in particular the Achaemenid Persian kings, such as Darius, Cyrus, and Xerxes. This is the origin of the scholastic organization and intertwined family lineages known today as the Magi.

Now, the Achaemenid kings were followers of Zoroaster, and while Hellenic writers, and even Roman authors, such as Pliny, misunderstanding the region and its history, called Zoroaster the first inventor of magic, modern scholarship indicates that this is definitely not the case. All archaeological evidence indicates that much of the magic that was not tied specifically to a god – sorcery, in essence – was largely an invention of the Chaldeans. Ley-magic was independently discovered in the lands of the Gauls. And summoning has been used in almost every culture, since before each civilization developed writing; it is clearly attested in the legends of Sargon of Akkad, for example.

No, Zoroaster was almost without question a god-born; however, followers of his philosophy do not believe that their creator god, Ahura Mazda, manifests in any material way on Earth. They believe that he is all that is good, and no evil originates with him, and that he has servant spirits and lesser gods that do his bidding and interact with mankind. This is, in many ways, similar to the modern beliefs of Atenists, reflecting a contemporary feeling that there must be a larger, greater, more mysterious force of creation behind the gods that we know here on earth.

The Achaemenid Persian kings swept westward, conquering and holding much of what we call Persia to this day; the Chaldeans, Sumerians, Assyrians,

Akkadians, and Medes all became subject kingdoms under their boot. They found the subtleties of sorcery and summoning as the Chaldeans understood them to be highly useful and effective, and employed the Magi heavily in battle. They required spirits to rampage through enemy lines, and ordered the summoners to bind spirits into the bodies of their most trusted men. Ten thousand men were so bound: the honor guard of the Achaemenid kings. They had, before this point, been called the Anûšiya, or companions of the king. Once the Chaldeans bound spirits to each man, however, they were called the Anauša, or the Immortals, for the Hellenes who fought them swore that they could not be killed. An arrow or a spear or a sword, alone, was not enough. Unless the body was beheaded, or the heart cleft in twain, the Immortal in question simply pulled the offending weapon from his body and went on fighting. That the fabled band of three hundred Spartans under the command of Leonides held off the Immortals for as long as they did is a testament to the carefully-chosen strategic location of Thermopylae, as well as to the skill of the Spartan warriors. Still, there was only one way in which such a lopsided battle could end: with the massacre of the Spartan soldiers.

Herodotus writes, however, that the Magi warned Xerxes that the spirits were growing restive, and demanding better bargains, refusing to keep the bodies of the men alive in this fashion. Such heavy magics require vast amounts of energy, and the strain on the minds and bodies of the Immortals themselves must have been fearsome. (See Chapter 15: The Modern Immortals, for details on how the Magi eventually overcame these technomantic problems.)

The Achaemenid forces met the disparate city-states of Hellas, and clashed in repeated battles that shaped the very course of world history. Some Hellene city-states paid the Persians tribute for generations, and others remained unconquered. This period of cross-cultural fertilization is, most sources agree, the origin of Hellenic sorcery, as the natural philosophers of Hellas examined and systematized Chaldean-origin mysticism.

This lasted, of course, until Alexander of Macedon amassed his armies and pushed eastward, defeating the Persians under Darius III, the last Achaemenid king. According to classical sources, Darius retreated repeatedly, and Bessus, a satrap and relative of Darius', slew his own king and assumed command of the scattered remnants of the Persian forces, in a last, futile effort to save his people from Alexander's armies. Alexander captured, tortured, and executed Bessus. Another of Darius III's generals, in an effort to appease Alexander, gave the Macedonian emperor Bagoas, the eunuch who had been Darius' favored catamite. Alexander apparently received the gift with great favor, and bestowed upon Bagoas the title of Beloved.

While Alexander was the single greatest commander of military forces in human history, there is considerable debate in the scholarly realm as to whether or not he was god-born. There was extensive propaganda that surrounded his birth – his mother claimed to have dreamed that her womb was struck by lightning, for example, while she was carrying him. And he later claimed descent from Heracles and Perseus – Heracles, who ascended to godhood, and Perseus, who remained a god-born until his own death. No great powers are, however, attributed to Alexander. Rivers did not still themselves at his approach. The heavens did not split themselves asunder with lightning at his command. And he died at the age of thirty-two, either of poison or disease . . . two things to which most god-born seem largely immune. In the end, his amazing success as a general is not diminished, but made the greater by his mortality.

Alexander's tragic and youthful death left his generals to carve up his empire, and gave rise to the Seleucid kings of Persia, who all claimed descent from Seleucus I Nicator, and their lands, at the height of their power in 300 BAC, reached as far west as Asia Minor, parts of Syria, and parts of what is, today, modern Judea. The Seleucids, descendants of Alexander's generals, promoted a Hellenistic culture, but sorcery remained common in their empire – far more so than in Hellas. Indeed, many of the Seleucid kings were competent sorcerers and summoners in their own right. They fought vigorously with sister kingdoms, such as the Ptolemaic Pharaohs, some of whom had god-born might from intermarriage with the Egyptian line of kings . . . but in the era of Antiochus IV, in 216 BAC, the Seleucids drove the Egyptians back into Alexandria itself.

This brought Proconsul Gaius Popillius Laenas into the fight, in an effort to negotiate an end to the conflict that threatened Rome's grain supply in Egypt. It is said that when the Proconsul met with Antiochus, the king held out his hand in friendship, and the Proconsul, rather than accepting it, placed into his hand tablets that held Rome's demands. When the king replied that he would read them at his leisure and consult with his court about them, the Proconsul drew a circle around the king's feet and demanded an answer.

The king accepted the demands of Rome, and retreated, never to attack Egypt again. Scholars of the mystic arts will clearly recognize what the Proconsul did; he drew a binding circle around the king, and <u>cut him off from his attendant spirits.</u> He may even have threatened to remove their binding links and cut Antiochus off permanently from the spirit realm. Remarkably, Gaius Popillius Laenas is noted in the Senatorial records of the era as that rarest of things at the time: a patrician who understood summoning. Also, Antiochus clearly saw the prudence in avoiding further conflict with Rome. Instead, he preoccupied himself with attempting to Hellenize Judea, and requiring the Judeans to worship Hellene gods. These heavy-handed practices resulted in the Maccabean Revolt. Today in Judea, the rededication of the Temple after the revolt is still celebrated as Hanukkah. By 187 BAC, Judea had fully established its independence from Persia.

The following centuries were marked by instability, civil war, attacks by the Parthian king Mithridates, and the establishment of Roman client states in the region. Pompey, in particular, attempted to create stable governance in the region, and finally did away with the Seleucid line. Armenia and Judea were permitted to continue under their existing kings, but Pompey established Syria as a Roman province, including coastal areas as far distant as Tyre.

Persia itself, further east, fell under the control of Parthians like Mithradates, and they remained the staunch enemies of Rome, not permitting any further expansion to the east. They now rejected the Hellenistic culture that had been imposed on them for a hundred and fifty years or more, and returned to their cultural roots, embracing sorcery, summoning, and their own brand of natural philosophy. And they promulgated Zoroaster's teachings more powerfully than at any time since the Achaemenid kings, and reinvented themselves as the true spiritual successors to ancient Babylon.

This is the cultural legacy that we see in the Persian Empire today, and it informs all of their actions, to include the so-called 'Shadow War' between the Empire and Rome, which is played out, ceaselessly, in Judea, Syria, Tyre, and Asia Minor.

* _Note_: _Magi_ is a slippery term. _Magus_ is the singular, and used for both men and women. It can be used as a title of respect, as well. _Magi_ is both the plural of _magus_, and the name of a noted organization of sorcerers and summoners. You may denote 'Persian magicians,' plural, generically, as magi. When referring to the organized group of magic-users, many of whom have intermarried and pass their powers along generational lines, however, use the term _the Magi_. If someone within the Persian Empire is a magus, and dares to call himself or herself one of the Magi, and has not been initiated properly to this assemblage, they would best be advised to make out a final will and testament.

– Citlali Xipil. _Babylon: A Historical Survey_. University of Tenochtitlan Press, 1945 AC, pp. 10-12.

<u>Februarius 25, 1955 AC</u>

The news report on the far-viewer continued to natter in the background of the apartment in Rome as Kanmi passed his two sons their bowls of _injere fit-fit_, which was shredded sourdough bread from dinner the night before, cooked lightly in clarified butter and various spices, each with a pool of 'barbaric' yogurt in the middle (Romans still had the oddest dietary prejudices when it came to milk products, Kanmi had long since decided). He then handed them each a larger piece of bread with which to spoon the food into their mouths. "Come on," he chided them, impatiently. "You need something on your stomachs before your pedagogue sits you down for lessons all morning." Privately, he wasn't actually quite sure what the pedagogue, Alala Koikinos, could really teach Bodi, who'd just turned four, but Himi was set to start school in fall, and Kanmi was emphatic about wanting to make sure his elder son was proficient in Latin and Hellene before he began. He wasn't expecting Himi to be able to read in both languages immediately, but his goal was ensuring that Himi wouldn't face the same problems he, himself had had when he'd first gone to school in Athens, with only a textbook knowledge of Hellene. Both of his sons had been raised in Tyre, so they actually did understand and speak modern Carthaginian . . . but Kanmi had been making a point of speaking Latin and Hellene whenever he was home over the past two months, and jokingly using Nahautl words for things to force the boys to 'correct' him. It became more of a game that way, and he'd quickly noticed that they _retained_ whatever they giggled at. "Bodi, don't pick at it, just _eat_ it."

"I don't like it," Bodi pouted. Kanmi always tended to see more of their mother in the two boys than himself; their skin tone was somewhere between Bastet's coffee brown and his own lighter olive, and they had her liquid dark eyes . . . but their hair was closer to his shade of brown, and had more of the wavy consistency of his, as well—something Bastet muttered gratitude for every time she worked a comb through the boys' hair. She kept her own hair cut severely close to her skull, for practicality's sake. She did work in a hospital, after all.

"You had it yesterday and liked it fine then. Eat."

"I think he means he'd rather have a Roman breakfast, like when we stayed at the neighbors' last week. *Puls* with eggs and nuts." Himi piped up, tentatively.

"Yes! I like *puls*." Bodi was definite on that matter.

"Sorry. Don't have any. Eat." Kanmi took the double-chambered vacuum coffee brewer off the stove, now that one side had finally finished decanting into the other, and poured himself a cup. Bastet hated the damned thing—she insisted that coffee was a *ceremony*—but Kanmi did not really have an hour in which to prepare coffee every morning. He dumped sugar and cream into the cup and stirred rapidly before taking a hasty sip. *Barbaric cream*, he thought, with amusement. *Romans think milk is only suited for making cheeses, and if Bastet caught me putting milk in her coffee, I think she might actually cut my fingers off. I can't win either way, but by the gods, it tastes so much better this way.*

The boys reluctantly sat still and ate, while Kanmi, finally freed from riding herd on them for a minute or two, turned up the volume on the far-viewer. It was a technomancy-based unit, and as such, was a perfect sphere of glass, populated with tiny, black-and-white, three-dimensional figures. "In other news today," the anchor, a perfectly made-up Roman female with softly waving dark hair, intoned, "the Senate has moved into week two of its investigation of Marcus Caelestis Dioscuri, former governor of Nahautl, and his wife, Nochtli. The governor was recalled three months ago, to make an account of how members of his household, to include his wife, were involved with the late high priest of Tlaloc, Tlilpotonqui Tototl, who allegedly was part of an attempted coup against the sitting emperor of the Nahautl, Achcauhtli." The anchor paused. "Governor Dioscuri has seemed wholly calm in the face of the questioning, in spite of detractors who have speculated that he may have 'gone native.'" A quick flash of Dioscuri, wearing his senatorial toga as he entered the closed session of the Senate . . . and the camera lingered on the gold earplugs he wore, just for a moment. "It is widely expected that the former governor will be acquitted of any personal wrong-doing, and his hearings are only scheduled to proceed for two more days. After they end, however, the Senate will be questioning his Nahautl wife as to the particulars of her acquaintanceship with the deceased high priest. Nochtli Dioscuri has gone on record only as saying that the late priest and alleged conspirator was 'an old family friend.'" The anchor's voice swooped a little on the quoted words.

Sucks to be them, Kanmi thought, not without sympathy, but mostly, he was dispassionate about it. The part of him that *delighted* in seeing someone high-born, wealthy, or powerful find their downfall was partially silenced by the realization that the governor had been, for years, tempering Achcauhtli's more aggressive tendencies, and that without a strong hand to check him, the Emperor of the Nahautl might take matters into his own hands in dealing with the Quechan rebels . . . regardless of the limited self-rule accords that Livorus had just finished brokering for the

Tikali region. That was a major factor. Dioscuri mightn't have known what his wife was getting into, with her fundraisers for what were, in the main, charities . . . and it really was an open question if the wife had realized anything herself. It could have been perfectly innocent. By the time the Senate's questioning was done, and the media had had its say, she could look like a victim, and have actually have been a co-conspirator . . . or she might be painted to look like the downfall of the Roman empire, and have honestly been tarred merely by association. *It's a hell of a world we live in,* Kanmi thought, glancing at his sons. *I have to trust we got as much information out of Nahautl as possible, and that the lawyers and magistrates will make sense of it all. The system isn't perfect . . . but it's all we _have_. If we could just keep the media out of it . . . though they say they exist to keep the politicians honest . . . hah!*

The news report started up again. "In other news out of Nahautl, Iuhicatl Matatl is the seventeenth member of the state-run ley-power company to have pled guilty to conspiracy to commit ritual murder. This is in regards to the third power plant so far found with a murder victim buried under its foundation. Authorities have tied these ritual sacrifices to Tlilpotonqui Tototl and half-Roman noble Gratian Xicohtencatl, who both allegedly were involved in the aforementioned coup attempt. The sacrifices were, authorities claim, part of an effort to revitalize Nahautl religious practices that have been dormant for five hundred years, and to capitalize on that religious enthusiasm to promote Nahautl self-identity." The anchor paused, looking at the camera. "Matatl, who had been charged as a co-conspirator, swore under oath that his participation in the plot solely involved helping to design the new ley-facility, and helping dig the grave for victim number three, Xoco Tepin. He further swore that he did not participate in the sacrifice, and that he did not know how she had met her end, because there were no marks on the body indicating foul play. He swore that he was told there had been an accident, and that the body needed to be hidden to avoid publicity, and that he feared for his job if he did not comply." The news anchor paused. "Xoco Tepin was twenty-two years old, and had just finished her nursing degree when she went missing from the campus of the University of Tenochtitlan early last year. As a result of the plea-bargain, Matatl has had his sentence of death by crucifixion for participating in human sacrifice commuted to a lifetime of slavery. Tepin's parents, who have been on hand for the executions of all those involved in their daughter's death, expressed satisfaction with this trial's outcome."

I should think so. The two men who picked her up by way of a campus personals ad, posing as a nice young man looking for a virgin wife to placate his conservative, traditional family, and then dosed her with chloroform and dragged her off into the wilds for Tototl to tear her heart out while it was still beating, so Tlaloc could drink her blood and her tears . . . those two, I went to their executions, myself. This poor slob probably didn't know a damned thing about what was going on. He was just an architect who happened to be on hand when they were all out of people with shovels. Still, he had to have known _some_ kind of power was being pulled down, and that it wasn't ley. He probably thought, poor idiot, that it was electricity or magnetism, or some damned thing. Kanmi drank the rest of his coffee, and had just managed to put it in the sink as Bastet exploded out of the bathing area at a high rate of speed. He could smell sweet oil on her skin as she leaned down to give him a quick kiss; she was wearing a skirt and a lab coat today. "Going to be late tonight," she informed him, quickly, her mind clearly already at work. "Double shift. I'll be home . . . probably around four antemeridian."

Before Kanmi could even reply, she'd opened the door to the hall, and the pedagogue was outlined in the frame, one hand raised to knock. "Come in, come in," Bastet urged the Hellene woman. "I'm going to be late. I'm so sorry. I'll talk with you about Himi's mathematics tomorrow!"

The door closed behind Bastet, and Kanmi shook his head. *And to think she complains about my not being here.* He looked at the tutor, and said, "Actually, I'll talk with you about his math now. I have time before work. My wife forgets when I'm here, I think." He turned the far-viewer off, with a click, and managed a thin smile for the woman. Bastet had insisted on giving the pedagogue a second chance after Himi's accident. Kanmi, for his part, hadn't agreed, but he'd been stuck in Nahautl for six damned months, so he couldn't really intervene. Every time he looked at the surgical scar on Himi's left arm, from where the doctors had had to implant brackets and rods to allow the bones to grow back together properly, however, he *seethed.* And he didn't care if the pedagogue knew it. In fact, he rather hoped she did.

In another part of Rome, in a gymnasium run by the Praetorian Guards, Trennus and Adam had met before breakfast for their daily sparring practice. Most wrestling matches, in traditional Roman-Hellenic schools, were still done in the nude. *Bitahevn,* the quintessentially Judean martial art, however, had been derived from a number of Asian martial art traditions and the old sword and spear techniques that had been used in Judea for centuries. Thanks to the Asian influences and Judean modesty laws, practitioners wore *gi* tops and pants, while remaining barefoot. Adam and Trennus were, therefore, the only two clothed men in the entire gym. Female Praetorians were required to wear clothing on the wrestling mats, regardless of what art they were practicing; until twenty years ago, women in the Praetorians had had entirely separate practice facilities, until it was correctly pointed out that they *needed* to practice against men, since they were far more likely to wind up fighting men on the job.

Over the past several months, Adam had been greatly pleased by having Trennus as a sparring partner. Once the Britannian had loosened up a bit and lost his shyness and inhibitions, particularly at sparring where an audience could see them, Adam had gotten a measure of his real skill. The Britannian had half a foot of height on him, and about fifty pounds of weight, but Trennus didn't rely on that, or his raw strength; he was skilled on the ground, and simply *getting* him there was a challenge for Adam. What Adam lacked in inches and pounds, however, he made up for in speed, agility, experience, and native talent. Working against a larger opponent was always a good challenge. And teaching was the best way to learn and reinforce what he knew, anyway.

Adam ducked under a punch that he was damned glad hadn't connected, turned, slammed his hip into Trennus', and, with light hands on Tren's elbow and shoulder, propelled the larger man to the ground, before dropping to straddle and throw elbows and punches. Trennus got his elbows up, deflected the blows, and, as Adam got in, trying for a choke, actually managed to roll over, slamming a forearm down across Adam's throat . . . making him swear mentally. Once Trennus wound up in the mount, it was an uphill battle to unseat him and get back to at least even ground. Trennus grinned at him good-naturedly as Adam twisted to get the constriction off his windpipe, snaked a hand up, and demonstrated a thumb to Tren's eye to get him to pull back . . . which took at least fifty pounds off of Adam's chest. More than enough to work with. Adam pulled his body sideways, and fifteen brutal seconds later, was back on top . . . but this time in the guard, having his ribs compressed by Tren's legs. Not optimal, but an improvement. Fifteen seconds after that, he finally got Tren in a choke that worked, and Trennus tapped on the mat, signaling submission. Adam got back to his feet, having sweated nearly through his *gi* top over the past forty-five minutes, and grinned, offering Trennus a hand up. "Good one. You're making me *work* for every inch lately."

"Sort of the point, isn't it?" Trennus accepted the hand up, and wiped at his face. The long braids he wore would make an excellent handhold for an opponent, as Adam had pointed out midway through their first month together on the job; Trennus had grinned and acknowledged the fact, but added that he'd bind someone with magic before he'd consider cutting his hair.

They'd been practicing together every morning for the past two months, and for the six months in Nahautl, it'd been at least every other morning, as duty permitted. The other Praetorians here in the Roman gym were used to seeing them at this point, and Adam was aware that a couple of Romans had taken to 'keeping score' for them on a blackboard in the corner. If money was trading hands as a result, he was carefully remaining oblivious to the fact. And sparring had long since gone beyond 'job readiness' and simply become a way in which the two men routinely spent time together. As a result, they'd become very good friends. Adam would never have thought to have said that of a summoner before the past year, but it was true.

It was the chorus of whistles from between teeth that got his attention as he and Trennus were both mopping at their faces with towels. Adam looked up, and saw Sigrun walking placidly into the workout area, ignoring the various men who were breaking from clinches all around to react to her presence. Adam had seen a few of the men respond to other female guards entering the room a bit more crudely—invitations to come over and *polish their swords*, for instance. This was a whole different level from Kanmi's button-pushing. Kanmi pushed *everyone's* buttons—Adam's, Tren's, and Sigrun's—and in as many different ways as possible. He didn't single Sigrun out on the basis of her being female.

The reaction here in the gymnasium was another thing entirely. On the one hand, he understood it; the Praetorians were, after all, a largely male organization, and a quintessentially Roman one, at that. They liked establishing territorial boundaries when there was an intruder present, and they categorized a woman as an intruder in this space. And Adam himself was used to a certain amount of gender segregation from his childhood in Judea. On the other hand, the point behind gender differentiation in Judea was to show respect for one another . . . or so he'd been raised to believe, anyway. He'd started to question that first in India, and then in Novo Gaul and other places. But that didn't matter. What did matter, was that the lack of respect *here* grated on him. Women had been in the Praetorians for the protection of the empresses, consuls' wives, and diplomats' wives for generations. They were held to close to the same physical standards as the men, and the fact that they endured hazing just to be allowed to do their jobs . . . irked him. Most of them seemed to pretend to ignore their own gender just to get through the day. Which might be, now that he thought about it, what Sigrun herself did.

Of course, every man in the room knew *precisely* what Sigrun Caetia was. And knew that she could probably break any man there with her bare hands. Which was why it stopped at wolf-whistles for her, with perhaps a random, *"Hey, valkyrie!"* from someone in the safe anonymity of the far side of the room. She ignored the teasing without any visible facial reaction, not even glancing at the various men as she padded, light-footed, over to Adam and Trennus, and looked up at them. Her hair had grown back fairly rapidly after the burning she'd suffered in Nahautl, falling to her shoulders now, though it was tied back in a neat tail at the moment. "Here to spar?" Adam asked, as if nothing had happened at all.

"No. Livorus called. We all need to report in this morning. He has a new assignment, and we're all slated to go with him." Sigrun shrugged. "Sorry to catch you both before breakfast."

"Not a problem." Adam jerked a thumb in the direction of the locker room and bathing area. "We're going to need to clean up first."

"I can wait here." Sigrun's tone was indifferent. "Perhaps I will work on my spear forms."

Adam could hear someone behind him mutter the blatantly obvious, *"She could handle my spear any time . . . ."*

Before he could turn and glare, however, Sigrun had turned her head incrementally, and looked *down*, in contravention of most male conventions. "No," she said, without changing expression. "I'm trained in long spear and half-spear, Forsetti. You do not even qualify as a *dart*."

The chorus of cheerful jeering that ensued—all at Forsetti's expense—carried Adam and Trennus out of the room.

Forty-five minutes later, the four lictors were standing in Livorus' library, hands behind their backs as they awaited the propraetor himself. Adam's eyes swept over the shelves and shelves of leather-bound books, the old-fashioned scroll rack behind the desk, the sand table near the window that overlooked the atrium . . . there were maps on the sand table, all rolled neatly, save one, which looked like a close-up view of Asia

Minor, the Caspian Sea, the Caucus Mountains, Judea, and the Persian border, and, at the extreme left and bottom, Egypt. His eyebrows rose, and he said to the others, quietly, "Eshmunazar? I have a feeling either you or I are going to be in for a homecoming of sorts."

Kanmi looked away from his absent study of one of the books on a shelf, and followed the direction of Adam's stare. After a moment, the sorcerer's shoulders slumped. "Better you than me," he said. "I've no desire on earth to see Tyre again."

Adam chuckled, but he knew that trying to get Kanmi to say anything more on the topic was a lost cause. It was ironic, really; the sorcerer was usually the quickest of any of them to volunteer an opinion on something, so long as it was acerbic, querulous, or amused, but trying to get him to say so much as a word about his family or his upbringing . . . . There was a wall in Kanmi on those topics, and in close to a year of service together, Adam had never seen that wall breached. Not even after they'd killed a weakened god, or met a fully empowered one. *You'd think that experiences like those would bring people together,* Adam thought, his lips quirking up.

Seeing Tyr in the Odinhall had been a baffling and powerful experience, and one that had brought up all his previous thoughts on the topic of faith and certainty. In his estimation, there were only a few basic types of people in the world, when it came to matters of faith. There were people who were deeply insecure in what they themselves believed, and therefore had to shout to the world what they believed was the best. They joined a faith not because it was what they truly believed, but because it was the best club or gang to belong to. They wore its colors, ate of its bread and drank of its wine, and were absolutely determined to convince everyone else around them of the rightness of their particular path. Not out of charity, not out of faith, not out of devotion, not out of conviction . . . but because *they* would feel better and superior if they convinced others to join. Because it meant that they were right, the others had been wrong, and that validated their choices. The Atenist, on that long-gone stormy night in Ponca, had been a perfect example of that type: insecure, loud-mouthed, and obnoxious. This wasn't faith, and it couldn't be called certainty, either. Adam had no time for them.

Then there were people who had been brought up in a faith, and followed it for the same reason that they held whatever their political beliefs were: it was what their parents had done, said, and believed. Trying to discuss either politics or religion with that type was a lost cause, because no thought had ever been invested in either; whatever they had been told over the dinner table when they were six, was what they would believe when they were sixty, because they had never, in all the decades in between, ever met anyone or heard anything that challenged their worldview, or made them stop and reflect. This wasn't really either faith or certainty, either. This was habit.

There were people out there who had inner faith, who didn't need to flaunt it or browbeat others with it; they had a serene, inner confidence to them that Adam frankly envied, a balance to their demeanor that spoke volumes about their character.

There were people who had *certainty*, but no faith, and those were dangerous, dangerous people. They were *certain* that they knew what the gods wanted, certain about the rightness of their path. *Certain* people were like Tototl, and they could take horrific advantage of the insecure, could fill the insecure's hollow, echoing emptiness with their own certainty . . . but they didn't actually have faith. Just a lust for power, and a construct in the mind that allowed them to grasp at it.

There were people like Adam himself, who'd been raised in a faith, but had learned to question it, to make decisions, learned to evaluate the traditions of his family and create his own understanding. He didn't have the secure *certainty* of someone who believed exactly what everyone else around him believed, of following rules and traditions that had been handed down for generations, but he was content that his god understood his heart, his motivations, and his principles, and that he was doing the best he could with a world that had moved on, somewhat, since mankind had been first inclined to smelt bronze into swords.

And there were people like Sigrun. The god-born, who had absolute certainty in the existence of their gods, but who, perhaps deliberately on the gods' part, seemed to have no more answers than any other mortal in some respects. Who seemed to have fewer choices than other humans, though more power.

Seeing the face of her god hadn't shaken Adam's faith in his own, but it *had* raised more questions in him than he'd had before. Why did some gods, like Tyr, appear to move and change as humanity, for lack of a better term, evolved? Why did some gods, like Tlaloc, remain buried in the past? Was it a matter of who worshipped them? *Did the belief of humanity shape its gods?*

That last one . . . kept him up at night, if he let himself think about it too much. Gods were supposed to be . . . gods. Unchangeable. Immutable. But if that were true, if the gods weren't able to comprehend that in the course of six or ten or twenty thousand years that humanity itself had changed, or would change—or if the gods hadn't, in fact, *planned for that*—then the world was really in trouble, wasn't it?

And all that in addition to the monumental issue gnawing at the back of his head . . . the pure fact that he'd seen a god die. Actually, it had died at *his hands.* All right, there had been a lot of other people involved, but he'd struck the final blow, and they were . . . ninety-nine percent sure that the god was dead. All the way dead.

That was another issue that kept him awake at night.

He'd endured the yearly call from his mother and father after Yom Kippur; he'd explained, once again, that last year, he'd been in Delhi, and this year, he'd been in Tenochtitlan. There was a notable lack of any Judean temples or synagogues in each area; most Judeans were homebodies, really. There were a few enclaves of engineers and natural philosophers who'd settled in Hellas or Nippon or even Qin, maybe a handful here and there in the bigger cities in Novo Gaul and Nova Germania . . . but he couldn't just walk down a street, find the right door, and participate in the day of atonement.

And, truthfully, what was he going to reflect on this year during the season of self-examination and contemplation, beyond what haunted him almost every night anyway? *I killed a god this year. Oh, it was a foreign and idolatrous one, so that makes it <u>better</u>, somehow? That I've somehow gone against the natural order of things? All right, so he wasn't a very <u>good</u> god, and his people are probably better off without him? I'm . . . somehow not comforted by any of this. Because some things shouldn't be possible, and history's shown that whenever gods have died—be they Egyptian or Babylonian or whatever else— something <u>worse</u> has almost always taken their place. Though what could possibly be worse than Tlaloc is beyond me.* Adam had shuddered at the thought. *Well, there's always people. People could take his place. <u>Certain</u> people, driven into <u>uncertainty</u>. There's a combination I don't want to see.*

The metaphysical issues were classified. The physical reality of countries outside of Judea was almost impossible to explain to his mother, though his father had merely told him, "I understand. You're doing good work in places in the world where there are few others of our people."

"I don't see why you can't take a few days leave and come *home*," his mother had groused, when she'd been put back on the line.

Adam had put them off as politely as he could, and realized that, given any choice in the matter, he wouldn't be taking leave in Judea for the next ten years. . . . and done his best to lose himself in the work. So he would be too damned tired to *think* at night, when he headed back to an empty hotel room or an equally empty apartment, and had no companionship but the incessant drone of his thoughts, all of which told him that Sigrun and Trennus and Kanmi were right. Nothing came from nothing. And that there was always a cost. He'd killed a god.

And there was probably going to be a price.

At that moment, Livorus entered the library, and four spines straightened just a hint more. The Roman waved at them all, gesturing towards the low-backed chairs in front of his desk. "Good morning. Thank you all for arriving so promptly." He stepped behind his desk, and put on his glasses to peer down at the papers on it, blue eyes intent. "We've had a good two months of relative calm. I hope you've enjoyed them."

Adam shrugged, and felt the others reacting in much the same way, scuffing shoes over the tiled floor. Livorus chuckled. "You are all far too much like finely bred-chariot horses. You're only happy when you're about to race in the Circus Maximus. Well, consider your chariot harnessed behind you. The Imperator called me to dine with him last night. This information does not leave this room—no need to look around. We've already been swept for bugs this morning." Livorus leaned back in his high-backed leather chair, and looked at them all steadily. "You're all aware of the Shadow War."

The Shadow War had been going on for decades between the Roman and Persian Empires, conducted largely in the smaller border states and provinces between the two larger empires. It was a game of tit-for-tat. Assyria, for example, was a prime area for incursions by either side, for the area had been bisected by Domitanus' Wall, which ran northeasterly through their lands to the Caspian Sea; the Caspian itself was part of the line of demarcation, and had been built primarily to hold the Mongols out of Asia Minor. Every port city along the Caspian was heavily fortified, in case either the Persians or the Mongols tried to make a landing on the western shore . . . and then the Wall picked up again slightly to the north of the sea, before petering out again near the Raccian border.

Armenia, which was claimed as a non-province subject nation by Rome, was another area frequently targeted by agents on both sides of the Shadow War. The city-states of Damascus and Tyre—Old Carthage and Western Assyria, in short—were also frequent targets for provocative attacks, as were areas of Judea itself. Adam had spent most of his time in the Judean Defense Forces stationed along the section of the Wall that ran from the Gulf of Persia northwest, paralleling the flow of the Euphrates. "You might say I have some small awareness of the conflict, sir," he said, not changing his expression at all.

Kanmi grimaced. "I'd expected to be sent to the West Assyrian front for my four years. Just as glad I was sent to the Mongol border, instead." His expression was stony. "A Chaldean Magi was sent to Tyre on a retaliatory strike for . . . some damned thing I don't even remember . . . when I was sixteen or so. He summoned earth elementals that rampaged through entire port area. Destroyed docks, broke several levies. Killed a fair number of people when their houses flooded."

Trennus looked up for that. "Huh. Odd choice."

Everyone looked at him for a moment. Their summoner flushed. "I'm just saying, it's a port city. I'd have summoned water elementals and made use of the ocean that's right there, making them that much stronger. I can only assume he didn't know any water elementals by Name."

"Do me a favor and don't introduce them to any," Kanmi said, shortly. "They rousted out my entire school to go hunt the damned things down. The teachers considered it an excellent practical lesson, and we were all sent out with a full sorcerer . . . but all we could really do was disperse the forms they'd incarnated into, unfortunately."

"That'll temporarily banish them, yes." Trennus shrugged.

"JDF protocol usually suggests killing the summoner." Adam shifted. "No offense, Tren."

The Pict gave him a quick smile, lifting his hands lightly. "None taken. Of course, you don't necessarily need to have a summoner present for certain types of summonings." He shrugged again. "You know the old legends of a djinni being kept in a lamp?"

Adam did his level best not to picture, yet again, the djinn towering a mile above the small border town near the wall, and the destruction it had caused. "I'm aware of them, yes," he managed, tightly. Sigrun, to his surprise, reached out and put a hand on his shoulder, and he felt himself relax at that light contact.

"You can bind a spirit into almost anything if you're strong enough. I personally like something as unbreakable and immovable as possible . . . ."

". . . like turning a great deal of sand into rock around something large and unfriendly?" Kanmi's expression didn't change, as he gently reminded them all of what Trennus had tried, over half a year ago, on a god.

". . . yes," Trennus replied, after an uncertain moment. "Precisely like that. Gem-stones, for instance."

"The Magi are the ones who pioneered that form of sorcery," Kanmi offered, immediately. "They came up with storing spells inside of crystalline matrixes. Probably as an off-shoot of storing djinn in rings and bottles. And once you store energy and a pattern inside a stone, it's just a hop and a skip to modern technomancy." He paused. "All right, it's a hop and a skip that took eight hundred years, but you get the point."

Trennus nodded, enthusiastically. Adam raised a finger. "What does this get us?" he asked, raising his eyebrows.

"Just that there might not always be a summoner nearby to kill," Trennus replied. "You can confine a spirit into gems, bottles, metal containers, even common rocks, if they're prepared the right way. Once you've bound them, you can put them somewhere for safekeeping, if you don't want them getting loose again." Trennus shifted. "Salt water, by preference. It's close to blood in terms of its chemistry, and it's . . . something of a buffer element. I won't bore you with the specifics, but it *works.*" The big man slid his glasses further up his nose. "Now imagine, if you would, binding a spirit into something that's fragile, deliberately. A medallion, for example. A jar. A glass bottle. And then having someone transport it and break it where a very angry malevolent spirit can do the most harm."

Adam winced. He'd heard of the tactic being used, but since the person transporting the object would probably be the first thing that the demonic spirit would turn on, it wasn't used frequently. At least, not by people who knew what they were carrying. "They've occasionally distributed bottles along the Wall," Adam said, tightly. "Ones filled with alcohol and rags. They set fire to the rags and throw them at soldiers there. And once in a while . . . some bright summoner fills the bottles with other things, too. It's the sort of trick you don't get to pull on your own people more than once . . . unless you get them to volunteer for it." He grimaced again. What enraged spirits could do to a human being, if they were powerful enough to incarnate, wasn't pretty. *Just think about those monkey-dog things under the Pyramid of the Sun . . . or rather, I should probably try not to. Their eyes were too damned human.* He cleared his throat, and tried again. "Which is to say, yes, I'm aware of . . . some of that. And you never really know what you're going to get, along the Wall."

Livorus had been listening to the byplay patiently, and now looked around his study. "The latest round of hostilities really got its start back in nineteen-thirty or so," he said. "East Assyria began to agitate for re-unification with West Assyria, and demanded the return of lands historically held by their ethnic group in Armenia. West Assyria declined to be reunited on the wrong side of the Wall; while they made it clear that they would greatly appreciate being able to communicate with families on the other side with more ease, they didn't actually wish to become a part of the greater Persian Empire once again. The subject nation of Armenia also declined to have Persia directly on their doorstep. Again." Livorus sighed. "East Assyria began to send magi against the wall, as well as staging attacks along border towns. This was very likely in response to pressure from within Persepolis to act as a cat's-paw. It all probably started because Rome had just formalized a new set of trade agreements with India, on Persia's eastern border. It . . . escalated." Livorus looked away, his expression distant. "Sometimes, it seems as if the West-East Assyria issue raises its head every single time Rome does something that Persia does not like. As it was, at the time, there were attacks as far west as Damascus, Megiddo, and Tyre."

"I barely remember this," Kanmi admitted. "We had to evacuate my primary school when a series of fire elementals were unleashed in the neighborhood, however." He frowned. "I was about six."

Livorus shrugged, faintly. "I'd just rotated off of the northern borders, trying to keep the Raccia-Mongol conflict from spreading south. My entire legion was, perforce, moved to West Assyria and planted more or less atop the Wall for the remainder of my years of service. I was ordered to cross the border no less than three times in that time span for retaliatory strikes." He rubbed at his nose. "It is never a comfortable sensation, to be leading the mission that might turn the 'shadow' war into a real one. And of course, there was the whole Gazaca incident, in which dozens of Persian magi slipped across the border and set up shop, hidden among the civilian population of that border city." He sighed. "Concealed by sympathizers, and by those too frightened to tell them *no*, they conducted assaults all through Western Assyria."

Sigrun suddenly spoke up. "You led the strike on Gazaca? I remember reading about it in the newspapers when I was at the Odinhall." Her expression was intrigued. "As I recall, the commander at the time was noted for having spared the civilian population, permitting the local soldiers to surrender after confiscating their arms . . . and for having decorated the walls of the local bazaar with the bodies of the summoners who'd been involved in the disturbances." She looked at him calmly. "That was you, sir? I hadn't made the connection."

"It was a number of years ago, my dear, and we were hardly acquainted at the time." Livorus smiled faintly, but it didn't reach his eyes. "I was actually criticized at the time for having been too kindly on the local population, but I was trying not to start an *actual* war. The second strike on Gazaca was led by a different young tribune, a year later, after more provocations. It involved air strikes, and it killed about one third of the city's civilian population. People who were *citizens of a Roman province*. The provocations halted at that point, and it was hailed as a *success*." Livorus looked out the window into his atrium. "History will be the ultimate judge, I suspect, of who was right, and who was wrong there, but in my opinion, there's almost no way to win in the area around the Wall." He paused, and added, with another faint smile, "However, you do console me, my dear. At least you of all my lictors can remember all that transpired during that unfortunate period of my life, before I resigned my commission and turned to politics, instead."

Adam blinked. He'd known Livorus had served, but not the precise theaters. All of this was extraordinary new information. And it again, hinted that Sigrun was far older than the other lictors, but as usual, he couldn't quite determine by how much. "I didn't know, sir," he admitted, with genuine interest. "Then again . . . ."

Livorus awarded him a faint smile. "You were, quite literally, a babe in arms at the time, ben Maor. You were born in what, twenty-nine?"

"Yes, sir." Adam and Trennus were the closest in age of the main lictors; Trennus was not quite a full year his elder.

"I said that it was almost impossible to find a victory in that part of the world." Livorus looked around at them all. "I've been offered an opportunity to try to make right what I think was an appalling error of judgment by the young tribune who succeeded me in my command twenty-five years ago. But to do it will require . . . a certain amount of careful negotiating to avoid it becoming worse. And, best of all, it might not even be a genuine opportunity, but a trap, instead." He raised his eyebrows at them all. "Interested yet?"

All of them leaned forward. "What is it?" Kanmi asked, quietly.

"The principality of Chaldea has made several furtive offers through intermediaries in the last year. And they've been joined by Media in the past month, in asking to meet with a Roman diplomat empowered to negotiate directly on behalf of the Imperator . . . asking to be taken into the Roman Empire as subject states." Livorus' lips quirked. "Now, what do you say to that?"

Every mouth dropped open. Sigrun was the first to recover, however. "That would be an almost certain cause for war by the Persians," she said , immediately. "Media, Chaldea, and East Assyria are their border states, their buffer against Rome. If they lost Media, they would be cut off from the Caspian. If they lost Chaldea . . . ." Sigrun looked dumfounded for a moment, and groped for words.

"They'd lose the single largest group of magic users they have," Trennus supplied, unexpectedly. "The Chaldean and Median Magi are not the *only* summoners in the empire, but historically, they were among the first, and they're still considered the best."

Adam, for his part, had a very good mental map of the region, and was already shaking his head. "No," he said, bluntly. "Persia's never going to allow this. If they lose Media and Chaldea, East Assyria becomes the tip of a very thin peninsula, and Babylon itself becomes a border state, precariously perched on the Euphrates." He shook his head again. "Even if it *is* a legitimate offer . . . sir . . . even *discussing* it with the Median and Chaldean representatives is . . . probably not a good idea." Belatedly, Adam cut off his words. He didn't actually have a *say* in this. His job was to protect Livorus, nothing more. On the other hand, if he didn't mention how insanely bad an idea this was, he wouldn't *be* protecting the propraetor.

"At the very least, it'll be an invitation to get the representatives of the two nations and their leaders mysteriously killed," Kanmi said, gloomily, filling the silence as Adam met Livorus' eyes, wincing internally at having so far overstepped his bounds. "Not to mention you, too, Propraetor." The unexpected addition of Livorus' title underscored Kanmi's words.

Livorus looked at them each in turn. "I am aware, believe me, of the potential repercussions. As is the Imperator. He is, however, of the opinion that we cannot afford *not* to pursue this opportunity, as it would mark the first possibility of genuine dialogue in an intransigent area in over twenty-five years. And for me, personally, it represents the chance to redress past errors." He paused. "Additionally, there is one thing that we have in our favor. Persia has long stated that the issue of West and East Assyria is one of human rights. That the world as a whole should stand back and allow the two halves to re-unite . . . under the auspices of the Persian Empire, naturally . . . out of recognition of the principle of self-determination. Rome could throw that argument back into Persia's teeth, and declare that if Media and Chaldea have determined that they no longer wish to be subject to Persia, then the Persian Empire must recognize their rights." Livorus' smile was wintery. "No. I don't expect it to *work*. But it is something that might be strutted out upon the world's stage for a time."

"You spoke of errors, sir." Sigrun paused. "Those mistakes were not necessarily yours. Both you and the other tribune were under order from the General Staff."

"That does not remove from me either responsibility or culpability," Livorus returned, quietly, but with force. "So yes. I will be traveling to Judea as soon as the travel and security arrangements can be made. This will undoubtedly take a month or two, as even the Chaldean and Median intermediaries will need to make similar arrangements . . . and all of us will doubtless need to been seen as traveling there for other, more *sanctioned* reasons. Some manner of cover will be required."

Adam reached up and scrubbed, furiously, at his face for a moment. "There's a meeting of the International Space Commission in Maius or Iunius this year, in Jerusalem," he offered. "It rotates every year between Hellas, Judea, and Nippon. You could attend that, as an interested observer from Rome."

Livorus' lips quirked. "My dear boy. If I were to bring you to such an event, we would lose a lictor among the various panels, and possibly to the mercantile booths." He paused. "That being said, it is not a bad notion. And yes, it *is* a matter that Rome should take a more active interest in, I am aware. Merely funding Hellas' program is, perhaps, not enough." He gestured. "Formulate other notions. The less this looks like a high-stakes negotiation team, the better."

"In that case," Sigrun murmured, tipping her head to the side, her eyes narrow and considering, "should you not consider taking your wife and children with you, sir?"

Livorus gave her a pained glance. "Judea is not precisely the province that my lady wife so often asks to sojourn in."

"The provinces cannot, sir, all be Hellas."

Livorus snorted faintly. "I am not over-fond of the notion of taking my family into what could be the line of fire. They would require full protective details of their own." He clasped his hands in front of him on the desk for a moment and regarded them, clearly revolving variables in his head. "On the other hand, it would surely make our business in Judea look more of a . . . family outing . . . than a high-level diplomatic mission." He raised his eyes. "I will be certain, however, to mention to Poppaea that this was *your* notion, my dear."

"By all means," Sigrun agreed, her tone equitable. "I will be happy to take the blame on your behalf, sir."

Adam remembered the first time he'd heard Livorus' wife's name . . . Poppaea Sabina. He'd asked Livorus at the time, "Wasn't that the name of one of the early empresses?"

"Actually, it was the name of both a mother and a daughter who both happened to become empresses, by marriage." Livorus had looked mildly amused. "We are long since past the day when a woman was solely named by her father or husband's cognomen, with perhaps a 'first' or 'second' or 'elder' or 'younger,' involved. What antique *charm* we may have lost by adapting the old system of *praenomen, nomen,* and *cognomen,* I believe we have more than made up for in specificity. I cannot imagine walking into my house and calling out 'Antonia Valeria Livorus!' and having both my wife and daughter reply 'Yes?' I much prefer calling for Poppaea and Aquila, rather than shouting, 'you, who belong to Antonius Valerius of the house of Livorus!'"

Livorus' expression had been mildly amused at the time, and was again, now. "Speak truthfully," he told Sigrun. "You will be *most* relieved to have my wife along for this venture, will you not? So that you will not have to resort to any various impostures?"

Sigrun started to reply, then just *smiled* at Livorus, merrily. "Yes, *dominus,*" she told him, after a moment. "Just as you say."

Livorus chuckled. "I leave this all in your capable hands. Interface with my secretary and the rest of my staff. Make this happen." He gestured towards the door, and his lictors, as one, stood, brought their fists to their hearts in respect, and inclined their heads, before leaving.

Outside, Adam shook his head, as they stood on the small landing overlooking the lobby of Livorus' palatial home, with its very Roman frescoes on the walls. Priapus and Flora. "No small task," Adam said, quietly. "I think we've a better chance of getting the moon base operational in the next ten years than of seeing the Persian border quiet and at peace in my lifetime."

Kanmi snorted, faintly. "Doesn't feel like a step down, does it?"

Adam looked over, startled, at the sorcerer from Tyre. "What do you mean?"

"Last Iunius, we were dealing with human sacrifice, and, well, *gods,* not to put too fine a point on it." Kanmi shrugged. "Now . . . we're back to political shit."

Trennus snorted under his breath. Sigrun turned and gave Kanmi a direct look. "We spent most of the last eight months chasing down members of a political conspiracy to overthrow the Nahautl government and end Rome's influence in the region. Human sacrifice or not, it was all 'political shit,' just as you say." She grimaced, however. "Just on a different scale."

Kanmi moved over and rested his hand on the balcony's rail, looking back over his shoulder at the rest of them, every line in his body taut and almost angry. "Yes, and every time I've tried to follow the propraetor's original orders to investigate further into the background of the whole conspiracy—and by that, I mean more than just the people *used* by our angry bumblebee and our black bird—I've been stonewalled." He slapped one hand on the rail, in mild agitation. "I've spent eight months trying to find out more about the whole 'Source Initiative' and whether it's more than just a professional networking group. Every time I request Praetorian assistance with it, I'm told that it's been assigned to someone else, and that I'm not to pursue it." He grimaced. "Are the rest of you encountering the same problem?"

Sigrun shifted a little, and Adam caught the look of discomfort on her face. "Sig?" he prompted, quietly.

She shrugged a little. "It has bothered me," she admitted, reluctantly, "that when I reported the dying words of the god-born of the Morning Star . . . the question of 'do you know where your gods are . . . ?' and when I reported that humans had harnessed a god as a technological power-source . . . the response was that they asked a different valkyrie to look into the matter." She looked at the floor for a moment. "Admittedly, the god in question was weakened, and the humans in question were powerful, but why cut me out of the investigation entirely?"

"You aren't receiving any copies of their results?" Adam asked, surprised. Admittedly, Sigrun hadn't brought the topic up in Nahautl, any more than Kanmi had, but since they'd all been extremely busy, Adam hadn't given much thought to what they might be finding. Or not finding, rather.

"It's been put on a need-to-know basis, and apparently, I do not need to know." Sigrun frowned. "I'm acquainted with the valkyrie they assigned. Reginleif was one of my instructors at the Odinhall. She is of Loki's line. If there is deception and trickery, she will find it. I just . . . don't know why they would keep me out." She glanced at Kanmi. "It's not just you. But, in truth . . . this is not a step down. Everything we do to protect the propraetor is of equal value."

Kanmi grimaced. "I know. That's what I think whenever my wife complains about my job. It's just an easier lie to tell myself when there's a grain of truth in there, somewhere." He glanced at Trennus and Adam. "And the two of you?"

Trennus shrugged. "I wasn't really involved in any of the investigations directly . . ." He glanced down, and to the side, and then shook his head. "But this is what I've been the most concerned about." He looked up, and met each of their eyes in turn. "My various spirits insist that Tlaloc is *dead*. That being said, I think that one or both of them . . . caught a piece of him. A portion of his power, at any rate. One of them has been fighting to retain her personal identity in spite of it for the past eight months. We know, from physics, that energy, like matter, cannot be created or destroyed." He looked around at all of them, his expression as taut as Adam had ever seen it. "What happened to all that unbound energy? Perhaps the identity behind it was destroyed, but the *power* was not. It could not be." He shrugged. "We saw the kinds of creatures he summoned. The *ahuizotl* . . . I've made a little headway in studying them, at least. They were independent spirits, capable of incarnating on their own. They're well-attested in Nahautl mythology. A spirit has to be fairly powerful to create a physical form on this side of the Veil." He exhaled. "What I'm getting at is . . . I haven't been blocked from researching the issue, but I haven't made any headway on it, either."

Sigrun had looked up as he was speaking, and her eyes had narrowed. Now she said, sharply. "Trennus?"

The Britannian's eyes widened slightly, almost comically. "Yes?" His tone was apprehensive.

"When you say that one or both of your spirits *caught* some of the god's power . . . was one of them the one who was injured to begin with?" Adam understood why Sigrun was being so very careful not to use the spirit's name; Trennus was chary with true-names.

Trennus' eyes flicked to the side, and he nodded, once. Silently.

Sigrun exhaled. "Would you care to estimate how much more powerful she is today than the last time I saw her? I noticed that she's been . . . staying out of sight. I thought that she'd been *further* damaged in that battle." She paused. "Would she have enough power to incarnate, now?"

Their summoner looked away, this time up, as if listening to someone or something, and then, finally, reluctantly, held out a hand, high in the air. "Lassair?" he said, quietly. "If you wouldn't mind?"

Sigrun's sharply indrawn breath made Adam's head turn. Her gray eyes had widened in shock, and in watching her, he actually missed the precise moment that Lassair willed herself into existence; there was merely a brilliant light now shining in his peripheral vision, and apricot-gold suddenly washed over Sigrun's face. His head snapped around, and his mouth dropped open.

Perched on Trennus' wrist was a bird made entirely of flame, or so it appeared. It was the size of a hawk, but with incredibly long tail feathers, much like a peacock's. The body itself was white-hot and too searingly bright to look at directly; ethereal wisps of white and apricot fire billowed out from the body as a whole, like veils, or a halo. The tail and flight feathers were pure gold flame, with wisps of red around the very outer edges, each with markings, again, like the eyes of a peacock, which burned blue-violet. The bird's eyes gleamed the cherry red of a forge. "Gods," Kanmi muttered. "That's the *Phoenix*. Not *a* phoenix. *The* Phoenix."

"She's been experimenting with different forms," Trennus commented, looking at her with a hint of fondness in his expression. "This is one of her favorites, I think."

Surprisingly, the fierce-eyed creature tucked her head, hopped onto Trennus' shoulder, and hid her face and beak in the Britannian's braided hair. Perhaps more surprisingly, it didn't burn.

"She's beautiful," Adam said, staring. He . . . wouldn't have thought that could be said of a spirit, but there it was.

"It is good to see you looking so well," Sigrun added, directly to Lassair, smiling slightly. There was delight, and a little awe, really, in her face. "You were smaller, and much hurt when I first met you. It is a rare pleasure to see someone heal."

And heal without your having to pay for it in your own blood and pain, Adam thought, glancing at Sigrun.

At Sigrun's words, the firebird lifted her head, and suddenly launched herself, fluttering over to land on the valkyrie's shoulder for a moment. To Adam's shock, he heard the creature's words in his mind, as he had, once before, when she had intruded gently upon his mind to translate words spoken under the Pyramid of the Sun for them all. *Well met, fair-sister. Your heart is far kinder than you allow others to see.* The bird ran her viciously hooked beak through Sigrun's hair, pulling a tendril or two loose, before sweeping her face along the valkyrie's cheek, as gently as a dove. *You should let others see your heart more often, Stormborn. It is a good one.*

"Yes . . . well . . . let's not noise that about, hmm?" Sigrun actually chuckled, and watched, still a little wide-eyed as the creature flew back over to Trennus . . . and then disappeared again.

"Oh ho, so Matrugena's attendant spirit likes you, eh?" Kanmi's tone was sly.

Trennus flushed, visibly, and told Kanmi, a little irritably, "Knock it off, Esh."

Adam wasn't entirely sure why he was irritated, as well, but also couldn't help but notice that Livorus' children, who'd just trooped in from outside with their tutors in tow, had been staring up at them all in abject fascination. "We're putting on a show here," he murmured, and cleared his throat. Trennus looked abashed, and Kanmi made a shooing gesture at the children, who scattered, laughing. "Back on topic?" Adam told them all, crossing his arms over his chest. "I agree with you all. We *are* being kept out of these issues. We're being told to focus on our job—protecting Livorus. And I agree with that, too." He paused. "But anything we can do to look into these issues . . . so long as it doesn't conflict with the main job . . . I'm all for it." He moved over to stand next to Kanmi, looking down into the lobby. "Though I suppose there's little enough I can do to help answer any of the questions."

Kanmi shook his head. "Keep your ears open. Someone could inadvertently say something to you that they wouldn't think is meaningful to . . . well . . . ." he paused, and actually awarded Adam a faintly apologetic smile.

"A completely nobody like me?" Adam grinned.

"I was going to say a completely *normal* person such as yourself." Kanmi bared his teeth.

"I'll keep it in mind."

Martius and Aprilis both flew by in a whirl of preparations for the trip. Separate protective details were needed for Poppaea, Marcus, Aquila, and Amantius, the whole of the Livorus family, as well as for the tutors and servants that would be accompanying them on the trip. Kanmi found, to his annoyance, that once his wife, Bastet, heard the few details he was able to offer about the upcoming trip—to include the fact that the propraetor's family was coming along for it—nothing would persuade her that this wasn't a golden opportunity for a family vacation. "You do realize that I will be *working?*" he told his wife, acerbically. "This isn't a pleasure trip for me. You won't see me any more than you do when I'm working twelve on, twelve off on Livorus' detail here in Rome."

"This barely qualifies as an official trip," Bastet told him, folding her arms across her chest. "The propraetor's bringing his family. Why can't you?"

Kanmi looked up at the ceiling, and took deep breaths to keep himself from snapping at her. *Because it's a sham*, was something he couldn't tell her. He couldn't break security and tell her that the whole appearance of the trip was a deliberate façade. The best he could do was try to present every single disadvantage to her proposed plan that he could. "It's Judea, Bastet. The climate is just as miserable there as it is in Tyre."

"Well, we're all used to it. Hot and miserable. The boys have been a little homesick for Tyre—don't scoff, I know how you feel about the city, but to them, it's home . . . ."

"Yes, but this is Judea we're talking about. They don't even have a ley-grid there. It's all electrical power and the gods-only-know what else. The only public baths in the whole of Jerusalem are in the Nipponese and Roman neighborhoods. It'll be primitive at best."

"You *are* aware that where I grew up in Nubia, my family did not have indoor plumbing?" Bastet's dark eyes narrowed. "I think I can manage the privations of Judea."

Kanmi thought, desperately. "We'll be so close to Tyre, we'll practically offend my mother and father if we don't bring the boys there."

"I can tolerate your brothers and sisters-in-law for a day or so, if you can. I actually like your mother, you know."

"Why are you so determined to go?" Kanmi finally asked, in pure desperation. He didn't want his family there. It would be one more thing for him to worry about, one more potential distraction.

"Why are you so determined to keep us away?" Bastet's eyes narrowed further, and her full lips turned down. "Kanmi . . . husband . . . I cannot remember the last time we took any sort of a trip together. Before the children were born, I was busy with medical school and after Himi was born, there was my formal apprenticeship in the hospital . . . now that they're actually old enough to travel, and before Himi starts school officially . . . this is the best time that we'll ever have to do something together as a family."

Yes, but I spend so much time traveling, that the last thing I want to do is more of it. I want to come home, spend my time with you and the boys peacefully, and . . . did you have to choose this trip? Nahautl would have been better. At least once we got past the explosions and the potential for being arrested for defacing a monument and maybe deicide. Kanmi exhaled. "I will ask the propraetor. If he says no, then we must abide by his decision."

Unfortunately, Livorus noted that having more family along, and not less, might reinforce the perception that this was a trip revolving around pleasure and good-will between Rome and Judea, rather than high-stakes diplomacy, espionage, and the like. "Bring them along, but we'll assign the same lictor team that looks after my children to yours," Livorus told Kanmi. "We'll send them on the same museum trips. Your wife will appreciate it, mine will be puzzled by it, and both families will be well-protected."

A band around Kanmi's chest eased. "Thank you, *dominus*," he told Livorus, quietly. It was the first time he could remember saying the word *dominus* and meaning it.

Chapter XI: Cross-Purposes

It is a common mistake made by many scholars of sociology and anthropology, to assume that any culture, past or present, is or was monolithic. One cannot judge the entirety of ancient Babylon by the recorded deeds of her kings; fortunately, many cuneiform tablets remain that show us tantalizing details about the lives of ordinary citizens. We might not know the price of a cup of beer, but we have recipes for how it was made. We might not know how a merchant transacted business, but we know how much he paid in taxes. We might not know what the average person thought about crime, but we know which crimes were prevalent, because we know which crimes had laws enacted to punish them. But to say we know precisely how different segments of their society thought about or felt about anything, beyond what their recorded history and legends have passed down to us . . . is a dangerous set of assumptions to make.

Likewise, in today's world, no country or culture is an edifice made out of one singular piece of stone. Think of culture, rather, as something that grows, like the slow accretion of a stalagmite mound upon the floor of a cave. Drop by drop, the water from above deposits minerals in one place. The ceiling of the cavern may shift through natural causes, changing the flow of water, and thus, the shape of the mound itself will alter, in turn. The shape we see today may echo what an observer might have seen a century ago, but the color of the sediment may have changed, as adulterations from some other layer of minerals may have been introduced . . . just as influences from other cultures may adulterate a given society.

To see this concept in action, let us examine the culture of modern-day Judea. It is not monolithic. They have records of their history and culture that date back to the Bronze Age, in much the way that Egypt, Persia, and Hellas do. That Bronze-to-Iron-Age culture is the underlying shape of their stalagmite mound. The ceiling shifted and adulterations entered the mix of the water coursing over the stone — Roman governors attempted to enforce Hellenistic values and beliefs, two thousand years ago, without great success, while Antiochus IV made the same effort to enforce Persian beliefs and customs, with the self-same lack of success.

Cultural change is rarely successful when it is forced upon a subject population. The wise edicts of Caesarion I and Diocletian II allowed Judea to maintain its own cultural heritage without feeling threatened by the outside world . . . but trade, commerce, and the exchange of knowledge did a better job of Hellenizing the region than swords ever could.

As such, there are populations within Judea who hold to the underlying shape of their culture and embrace its most ancient forms and formulas. There are portions of the population that are Hellenized, and embrace Roman culture and learning, and have syncretized their own traditions with those of Rome to form unique thoughts, ideas, and a distinctive culture of their own. There are portions of the population, that due to proximity to Little Roma, Little Hellas, and Little Nippon, the areas of Jerusalem dedicated to foreigners, have grown to embrace foreign ways. There are segments of the population that fall along all portions of a continuum between both extremes of cultural openness and cultural conservatism.

And the same can be said of <u>every other culture</u> on Earth. To ask 'what does a

Hellene think of spending tax money on spaceflight?' or 'What's the Judean position on the expansion of the ley-grid?' or 'What does a resident of Germania think about maintaining Domitanus' Wall?" is to ask a question that cannot be answered.

— Janna Magnusson, <u>An Introduction to Contemporary Sociology</u>, pp. 17-18.
University of Divodurum Press, 1953 AC.

<u>Maius 5, 1955 AC</u>

Adam rubbed at his face as he cradled the phone against his shoulder, and peered out the window of his apartment in Rome. His words were a quick, dry rattle in Hebrew. *"Yes, I'll be getting in sometime tomorrow. No, I can't be more specific than that, Imah."* A pause. *"Security. Of course I trust you and my father, but then I also have to trust whoever you trust."* Another pause. *"No. Please. Look, I'll come to the house, but please don't make a big deal out of this. It's not a vacation. I'm there to work."*

On the other end of the line, his mother replied, pointedly, *"Adam, you haven't been home in over three years. It is important to me. You've missed so much. Your brother just had another son. Rivkah's just graduated from college. Chani's finished her required year of service, and just started college, herself. And you've missed so many holidays."*

"Imah, please. Don't invite the entire neighborhood. I won't have time to be there."

"No, of course not the entire neighborhood." Adam interpreted her faintly guilty tone as *no, just half of it,* and he closed his eyes in annoyance. His mother swept on hurriedly, *"And of course, we would love to meet your co-workers. We've heard . . . well, not much about them, but it would be wonderful to meet the people with whom you spend so much time."*

Adam put his forehead against the window frame, and rapped it there, once, solidly. *"I can't make any promises,"* he said, after a moment. *"I will ask them. They will, however, be working, too."* It wasn't that he didn't want to picture any of his coworkers meeting his family, he found. It was that he *couldn't.* The worlds were entirely separate in his mind.

He managed to hang up on his mother politely enough, exhaled, and got his wits back together. He was due at the firing range in a half hour. About four weeks ago, as they worked to get things together for the Judea trip, Sigrun had asked them, as they stood watch together at Livorus' house, "So . . . firearms in Judea. They're somewhat different than the muskets and blunderbusses I am accustomed to seeing, yes?"

"Quite a bit more advanced, yes. You're not going to see any enchanted bullets or cold iron-wrapped-in-silver loads, or whatever it was that Ehecatl was using—"

"He used iron wrapped in tin, actually. Counter-spelling agent, in many cases. But go on."

Adam had shaken his head. "No derringers. No muskets. Rifles— much better accuracy over longer distances. They're a perfect weapon for an assassin . . . a high-powered rifle can take someone's head at a mile out, in the hands of a marksman. No single-shot weapons, either. Everything's at least a revolver, and I was trained on an assault rifle that is automatic for use on the Wall . . . . "

"The automatics are belt-fed, yes?"

"Clip or belt, yes. The top rate of fire is over five hundred bullets a minute, but only in short bursts. Damned things overheat."

Sigrun winced. "I'm glad no one's really adopted them elsewhere. Imagining a belt of enchanted bullets is uncomfortable. But I suppose it's only a matter of time before Rome's enemies copy the design and adapt it for magic." She sighed, and added, "It might be useful for me to understand how these weapons are used. I could even see carrying one for use inside of buildings, when lightning is impossible to summon, or would cause too much property damage or risk to other lives. Would you mind giving me a few lessons?"

Adam had grinned. She'd come to sparring practice more infrequently than Trennus, but far more often than Kanmi. Trennus had yet to qualify on a pistol, though Kanmi, surprisingly to Adam, was an excellent marksman, but only with an incredibly old-fashioned two-barreled derringer. If Sigrun opted to learn to use an actual revolver, Adam thought he might be able to get their two magic-users to at least consider it more seriously, as well. Of course . . . they all had other options, as he usually had to remind himself. "Sure," he'd told her. "Not a problem at all. Considering your hand and wrist-strength, I don't think I'll even need to start you on a .38 or anything like that. You can just start with my .45. That way, we won't even need to scrounge for ammunition or anything."

Sigrun had given him a politely blank look. "And the numbers mean . . . ?"

Adam had opened his mouth to reply, and then paused and squinted. "You're putting me on, aren't you?" *She's got to understand calibers, doesn't she?*

Her lips had twitched, faintly. "Perhaps a little."

At the firing range the next day, he'd insisted that she put on ear protection. Sigrun had given him a direct look. "You do realize that when I'm working, there tends to be a lot of thunder?' she'd told him, raising her voice to ensure he could hear her through his own ear coverings.

"Yes. I've noticed that. Still, you probably want to be able to hear when you're ninety, right?" He paused. "You're not ninety already, are you?"

Sigrun's eyes narrowed. "No."

"Just checking. You refuse to tell anyone when you were born, and there are all these hints and intimations that you're actually an antiquity, so I have to ask these things just to make sure." He'd paused. "You'd make it easier on yourself if you'd just admit to how old you actually are. I don't understand the secrecy."

Sigrun shrugged. "There is a valkyrie who is over two thousand years old, Adam." She met his eyes squarely, letting him see that she wasn't joking. "Eir. She is considered a minor goddess of my people now, and has god-born of her own. Of her line, of her power. She's *worshipped.*

And she's also . . . ." Sigrun sighed. "A product of her times, as I understand it. She has no interest in current medical science, for all that she *is* healing. I . . . have no ambitions of that nature." A quick, rueful smile in his direction. "My age is irrelevant, except that knowing the exact moment of someone's birth is almost as good a handle on their identity as knowing their truename, or having a vial of their blood. Have all three, and you've *got* them. Ask Trennus sometime about it. His year of birth was in his dossier, but not the date, if you'll recall."

Adam had blinked. That was more information than he'd actually expected to receive. "All right. I'll bite. Why *does* blood bind?"

Sigrun looked up at him steadily. "People used to believe it was because it represented the life-force energy of the creature it came from. And, to a certain extent, in sacrifice, that's still true. A priest sacrifices a heifer or a lamb on an altar, or Trennus hunts down a deer in the forests of Britannia for his bargain with his wood-spirit. And then the spirit or the god consumes the life energy, certainly. But blood truly binds because it identifies who we are."

"DNA?" Adam guessed.

"Precisely." She paused. "There's more to it. Trennus or Kanmi could explain it better, but you remember how Trennus said that salt water was a good buffer for spirits because it's chemically similar to blood? The salt is part of it. Water is a purifying element, and that's a part of blood. Salt is a symbol of purity, but it also helps conduct electricity and even magical power. I'm not a scholar of such things . . . but it all interrelates."

Adam had shaken his head. "All way beyond me. But I'll file it all at the back of my head, in case I ever need it." He'd smiled and proceeded to break down his gun to show her the component parts. How they went together again. What did what. How to load it. "Finger outside the trigger-guard until you're ready to fire," he cautioned, out of habit. He'd trained too many people for the words not to cue up by rote.

And since then, once a week, they'd met at the firing range, and he'd adjusted her two-handed stance with light, impersonal hands. Tried not to notice the fact that whatever shampoo powder she used seemed to be apple-scented. Given her suggestions on improving her aim, how to look at the target and the aiming blade on the pistol with both eyes open, and the like. It wasn't a surprise that she was a natural shot. But it *was* a surprise how much she seemed to enjoy it and the process of improving her skill. And he enjoyed it, too. She wasn't particularly talkative, confining herself solely to the topic at hand, but there was companionability even in the silence. And they took to getting coffee after each hour at the range, too.

Today was no different than the rest of their practice sessions, though Sigrun noted that she had to leave early. "I need books for the trip," she admitted, when pressed. "Long hours with nothing to do and probably being cooped up in between shifts means I'll need to occupy my mind somehow." She shrugged.

They were in one of Rome's many cafés at the moment, watching people ebb and flow around them. Adam had mulled over their previous conversations, and now commented diffidently, "So . . . valkyrie can live to be two *thousand* years old?" He sipped his coffee.

Sigrun made a face at him over her tea. "Yes. Well, in theory." She sighed. "Nothing but a mortal battle-wound, Adam. And whatever doesn't kill me, makes me stronger." She glanced around, cautiously, and pulled her cloak over her shoulders for a moment, to shield her form from any curious passers-by . . . and channeled some of the divine energies within her. Adam's eyes widened slightly.

He'd never made an exact count, precisely, but . . . "There are more rune-marks on you than a year ago."

"Ninety percent of my body had third-degree burns, Adam. It would have killed a normal human. My scars might be prettier . . . but they're also more useful, in a way. I think they've strengthened my skin." She shrugged. "We respond. We adapt. We're human that way." She smiled ruefully. "If nothing else, we learn how to duck faster."

"I should hope so. You don't always have to answer force with force."

A quick smile over the top of her cup. "It's the only way I know, Adam."

He considered her for a moment, then asked, cautiously, "So, on another topic . . . you hearing *anything* from the Odinhall and the investigation?"

She shook her head. "No. And I am not asking anything directly. Not while I have a choice in the matter." Sigrun wrapped both hands around her cup, as if even she were chilled. "I have met Tyr twice in my life. The second time was to be questioned to see if the events in Nahautl were some sort of presage of Ragnarok. I could cheerfully live to be a thousand if I could be assured never to have that kind of conversation again."

"Ragnarok?" Adam repeated, numbly. "They thought that . . . it could be a sign of the end of the world?"

"They thought that it was possible."

"So . . . was it?"

Sigrun shook her head, and set her teacup down. "That's the thing, Adam. No matter what people like my sister believe . . . there really is no *fate*. Even the gods weren't sure if what transpired in Nahautl was a presage . . . or a coincidence. Think on *that*." Her gray eyes were clear, and filled with conviction. "Then again, my sister has been telling me since she was ten years old that I would live just long enough to see the world end."

That chilled Adam. He'd seen how uncannily accurate some of Sophia's prophecies were, but like all prophecies, they seemed to be understandable only in retrospect. And given that, he didn't like the sound of *anything* Sophia had told him about himself, ten months ago. "Do you believe her?" he asked, quietly, stirring his coffee with a spoon.

Sigrun stared down into her cup for a moment. "Considering how long valkyrie can live? Adam ben Maor, you have my word on it that I do not lose sleep over Sophia's prophecies regarding me." She grimaced. "All right, the first month or so, I did. And once in a great while, when I can see it in my own mind as clearly as if she painted it there, on the backs of my eyelids. But there *is* no fate. My destiny is my own. And I will not permit her to control my *wyrd* with words. I will wrestle with it, and if need be, die for it. But every choice along the road will be my own."

Adam smiled. He had to admit, that wasn't a bad philosophy. She looked across the table, and changed the subject. Entirely. "So, I have almost finished packing," she informed him, calmly. "I have even purchased extra suncream for Trennus as well as for myself, in case he should forget. I did not enjoy the sunburns I received in Nahautl, and I don't wish to repeat them."

His lips quirked. "You're afraid of sunburns."

Sigrun gave him a look. "They hurt."

"You had third-degree burns over ninety percent of your body."

"Sunburn is not a battle wound." She shifted around in her seat, looking away. "Also, direct sunlight has been more . . . uncomfortable since the burns, than it was before."

Adam blinked, and immediately regretted having teased her. "I'm sorry. I didn't realize."

"I didn't make an issue of it. I will wear my suncream and live with it." She paused and looked up again. "What else should I be aware of?"

"There are modesty laws, but they only really apply to Judeans." He took in her blank look, and gave her a half-smile. "Some of it depends from community to community, or even individual to individual. It largely ties in to how each person happens to interpret our holy writings. For example, in the smaller farming communities, men aren't allowed to shave or trim their beards, and their hair must be cut in specific ways." He shrugged. "Depending on how conservative a family is, a woman might be expected to wear sleeves no shorter than her elbows, skirts no shorter than the knee . . . pants are prohibited, and married women need to cover their hair, lest they provoke the lust of men other than their husband."

He caught the dubious glance she shot him. "Hair provokes lust?"

"Depending on the authority." He gave her a lopsided grin. "One of the thinkers I particularly like commented once that modesty laws should be a common-sense thing. If it's common for a woman's fingers to be seen, then her left pinky isn't going to inspire lust. Likewise, if everyone around her typically walks around with their hair exposed, it's not . . . well . . . ."

"An *illicit* thrill."

"I have it on good authority that centuries ago, the mere sight of an exposed female ankle was enough to make a good man slather at the mouth." Adam's lips quirked up. "They were a little hard up for things to get interested in at the time, I think."

"The human imagination can turn *anything* into a fetish. All the more quickly if it's something forbidden," Sigrun returned, dryly. "Do all these modesty laws only apply to women?"

"Oh, no, men need to cover their heads as well, but that's nothing to do with marriage." Adam shrugged, and thought about what other pitfalls someone who wasn't a native might run into. "Ah. Don't be surprised if some men refuse to clasp wrists with you.'

Her eyebrows shot up. "You're pleased to jest with me?"

"No, I'm really not joking. It's an extension of the modesty ideals. It's supposed to be a way of demonstrating respect for women, and acknowledging that any touch could inspire lust in the man offering it."

Sigrun stared at him. "That must make military service alongside women extremely difficult for them."

"Oh, if it's a matter of life and death, people are allowed to touch people of the opposite sex." Adam pointed out quickly.

"You've never seemed to have a problem clasping my wrist or sparring with me, or whatever else." Sigrun was clearly trying to phrase it delicately. She came from a culture that was almost entirely alien to these notions. And while Rome might have deeply patriarchal roots, they didn't extend in all the same directions as ancient Judean thinking had. He didn't even want to get into the times of the month at which a woman was considered *unclean* and couldn't be touched by even her own husband, and no one in her family could sit where she'd sat. He had a distinct feeling that telling Sigrun that a woman could ever be considered unclean would either offend her to the core, or make her laugh in total abandon. Sigrun hesitated, and added, just as carefully. "In fact, you made a point of putting a hand on Fritti's shoulder, back in Ponca. Just to comfort a frightened girl."

Adam shrugged. "I'm pretty Romanized in most respects. Most everyone you'll meet in Jerusalem is, honestly. There could be one or two sticklers for the old ways that you might encounter. I'm just trying to give you an idea of some of the reactions you might get." His eyes flicked down to the leather bodice she generally wore; in Nahuatl, she'd switched to a cloth one, to deal with the heat, and she hadn't been able to wear a shirt underneath for four out of the six months of their stay. "I know you're likely to find Judea uncomfortably warm, even in spring, Sig. I, personally, have *no* problem with the fact that you'll wear a bodice without a shirt underneath." Adam did his best to keep his grin at bay and out of his voice. He *really* didn't have a problem with the generous curves her outfits typically displayed. And of course, there was the pure fact that Sigrun's clothing was simply . . . commonplace to Nova Germania. Nothing out of the ordinary, really, and she wasn't actually displaying herself, so much as wearing what was comfortable and allowed her to fight effectively. "There might be someone out there who'd tell you to cover up, though."

"Because my hair or my body might inspire them to lust." Sigrun's tone was exquisitely dry. Clearly, she thought the chances of that were low, just as she had when he'd walked her home any number of evenings here in Rome. Then again, her ability to protect herself was well beyond that of a normal woman. "They could try not looking. Exerting a modicum of self-control. Or, if that is beyond them, they could cut out their own eyes, like Oedipus."

"Drastic."

"But it would certainly prevent them from seeing anything that would incite them." Sigrun toasted him with her cup. "I have no problem with dressing in a different fashion if I were to enter your temples or tabernacles. That's respect. But in a public street? This is still the Empire, even if it's an autonomous region." Her eyes glittered for a moment. "They will simply have to ignore the barbarian bitch."

His head came up. "Don't," Adam told her, gently. "Don't call yourself that, and don't borrow trouble before it happens."

Sigrun exhaled. "You're right," she admitted, after a moment. She smiled faintly. "I think that, right there, sums up why Livorus is considering you for overall command of his lictor detail." She raised her eyes, still smiling. "You're the most balanced of any of us. And you're wise."

Adam's eyes widened. "I wasn't aware he was considering that." He coughed into his hand. "Wise for my age, eh?"

"Wisdom isn't always measured in years. Though having a number of them at one's disposal does help." Sigrun shrugged. "I am far wiser now, than when I was younger." She changed the subject. "Need I be concerned about mosquitoes?"

"Nowhere near as bad as Tenochtitlan," he replied, immediately, and reached into his shirt pocket for a small leather case he'd brought with him. He'd considered giving these to her on the plane tomorrow, but now seemed as good a time as any. "The tropical sun was a little hard on your eyes in Nahautl, as I recall." He slid the case across the table to her. "I think these will fit you."

Sigrun looked startled, and opened the case on its hinges, peering cautiously down into the box as if she expected it to explode in her face. "Oh!" She sounded startled. "Smoked lenses. Like the ones you and Kanmi wear." She looked up, smiling. "I've never worn glasses before."

"Should cut down on glare for you. Try them on."

She perched them on her nose, grimaced, and fiddled with the earpieces, frowning in discomfort until he took them back from her hands, and adjusted them to fit her better. "There. How's that?"

"Much better." She turned her head this way and that, looking around the café. "You're right; the light bouncing off the windows is much less bright this way."

He couldn't help but notice that she hadn't so much as picked up a spoon to check what the glasses looked like on her. The windows were all on the far side of the café; she couldn't possibly see her reflection in them. "You don't want to check to see if they look all right?"

"I could see enough reflected in your eyes. Besides, your expression didn't change, and you didn't suggest that I could exchange them." Sigrun paused, and asked, awkwardly, "How much do I owe you for them?"

Adam shook his head, suddenly mildly irritated. "Nothing."

"I'm sorry. You're trying to ensure my effectiveness in the field." She paused, and added, quickly, "You could very likely put them on your expense report and be reimbursed—"

"Damn it, Sigrun. Do you have to make *everything* this hard?" He put down his cup with more force than he'd intended, and the handle snapped off in his hand. He stared down at it for a moment, before gingerly putting it on the table, beside the cup. He'd meant the lenses as a friendly gesture. Or something like that. He wasn't actually sure at the moment *what* he'd meant by them, except that at the moment, her backpedalling was like a slap in the face. After a deep breath, Adam managed to level his tone. "They're a *gift*."

Her eyes were wide, and she hesitantly reached across the table, offering her hand. "I'm sorry," Sigrun repeated. "I didn't mean to offend you. They're a lovely gift, and I will wear them with gratitude."

After a moment of staring down at the cloth over the table, and the crumbs of the flat emmer bread they'd torn up and eaten with cheese, Adam looked up again. "Sorry. Overreacted there."

Sigrun shook her head quickly, but Adam forestalled her before she could say anything more. "Let's change the subject?" he offered, with a hint of a smile.

Clear gratitude in her eyes, shining for just an instant. "Ah . . . yes. Actually, as I said earlier, I should go to the bookstore before they close." Another hesitation. She didn't want, evidently, to leave them on this awkward, uncomfortable moment. "I don't suppose you'd care to join me?"

"I'd like nothing better." He couldn't help but chuckle at the surprise in her eyes. In close to a year and a half on the job together, this was certainly the longest they'd spent together off-duty, and the longest that they'd conversed about things that weren't work. Adam was pleasantly surprised by the quality of the bookstores; they had wonderful tomes with full-color plates on the planets so far explored by automated probes. He showed her the black and white photographs of Saturn's rings in one of the books that he bought, and eyed the stack under her own arm. Three different alphabets—Gothic, Latin, and Hellene, and that was just at first glance. "Archaeology, history, art, natural philosophy . . . . I think you may need some for the other arm, just for ballasting purposes," he informed her, lightly. "May I at least walk you home?"

The walk was pleasant. He'd never before been invited in to her apartment, but tonight, he had a sense that she wanted to apologize to him, in a way, for her earlier misunderstanding about the smoked lenses. "My home is in no way comfortable," Sigrun told him, "but if you'd like to come up for a while . . . ?" She trailed off, looking away.

Again, he had the strangest sensation that she had no idea what to do or say. It was out of his experience in dealing with Gothic or Gallic women, most of whom were fairly forthright. He didn't have the sensation that she was being coy, either. *Coy* and *Sigrun* could not coexist in the same sentence. "I'd like that," he told her, lightly, and put a hand, very lightly, on her shoulder, where her spring-weight cloak was tossed back and out of her way, suddenly very aware of the sensation of her skin under his fingers. *This does not mean in any way that she's interested in you*, his higher cognitive powers warned him. *This is Sigrun. She's . . . god-born. She doesn't even seem to look at people the same way as others do.* The lower functions of mind and body, however, were suddenly much more alert. *Stop it, you idiot.*

Looking around her tiny apartment, he was struck immediately by two things. First, she had not been joking when she called it uncomfortable. She had a single armchair in her living area, upholstered in leather, a footstool in front of it, and a small table with a lamp on it — ley-powered, like most everything else in Rome . . . and nothing else in the way of furniture, besides groaning bookshelves. No far-viewer. A radio, with an old-fashioned player for cylinders of music — mostly harp, violin, and pianoforte pieces, from a quick glance along the shelves of recordings. All either Gallic or Gothic in origin. "You make Spartans look like hedonists," he called to her, looking around as she made her way to the kitchen to find a second chair.

The only life and color in that small living area came from the pictures on the walls. Water-colored lithographs and photographs, framed, of the various places she'd been, apparently. There was a new one, leaning against the wall, as yet unhung, of Tenochtitlan, with its pyramids, skyscrapers, lake, and bridges. Another of Burgundoi, the Odinhall, and the bridge across the deep waters of the bay. A picture of what, by its inscription, was Cimbri-on-the-Caestus, her home town. Two or three of cities in northern Europa and Raccia. One of Rome itself. Another of the city of Delphi, including the temple of Apollo there.

There was a fireplace tucked in the corner, which looked largely unused. On the mantelpiece, a handful of black-and-white photographs. One was of a Cimbric man, standing beside a seated woman with pale hair, who looked strikingly similar to Sigrun, but without the steel in her eyes. The woman wore a smile as she held a child in her lap. Beside that, another picture, which captured the same man, older now, beside Sigrun, who looked no different in that image than she did today. Her father wrapped an arm around her shoulders, and a young girl, no more than nine or ten, stood in front of them. While her father and sister smiled, Sigrun was expressionless, and the image had been sliced with a sharp knife at some part; her father's left arm, and whoever had been beside him, had been edited away. Other than that . . . no other pictures, though an album sat on the table beside the chair. "Mind if I look?" Adam asked, as Sigrun dragged a wooden chair back in from the kitchen.

She shrugged, and perched on the edge, gesturing for him to take the more comfortable armchair. "By all means. Can I get you anything? I discarded everything that could go bad in my absence, so there's not much."

"No, thank you."

"Tea, at least, I can manage. Give me a minute to put the kettle on."

Adam sat down, and leafed through the pictures. A handful from Sigrun's childhood, apparently. He was tempted to look for dates on the backs of her infant pictures, but decided that she might take that amiss. Judging from the clothing, however, it had at least been in this century, which made him sigh in relief. There was a single picture of her mother, looking frail, ill, and hairless in a hospital gown, holding her daughter. Then an image of a Gothic funeral pyre, and those gathered to light it, including the toddler who'd been Sigrun. A series of images of her and her father, usually with a stern-faced female pedagogue with dark hair in the picture, and a very old-fashioned slave collar around her throat. Then, surprisingly, a picture of the father and the pedagogue, minus the slave collar and with a wreath of orange blossoms on her hair. Their hands were tied together in the image with a white ribbon, and the pictured was accompanied by a yellowing card marked in heavy, elegant Gothic runes, which Adam couldn't read. Presumably it was a wedding announcement. There were a few other pictures from their wedding . . . something to do with breaking cakes and a fire, and an exchange of rings. Sigrun herself was nowhere in the wedding pictures.

A few images of the younger girl—presumably Sophia. A few snapshots labeled as *The Raccian Border*, the *Caspian Sea* or *the Northern Lights*. Images of Livorus with Ptah-ases, Ehecatl, and a Nubian and a Gaul that Adam didn't recognize . . . but could guess at the identities. And a few more, from the past year or two. At the back of the album, he found newspaper accounts, in Latin and Gothic, about cases she'd settled as an *ælagol*, incidents they'd settled as lictors. A cursory glance at the dates told him she had, indeed, spent ten years as an *ælagol*.

And for all of that, the album felt . . . oddly empty. Adam pointed at one of the pictures as Sigrun came back into the room with tea. "Your sister? Sophia?"

"When she was young, yes. There's one near the back of her when she went to Delphi, her first day officiating as a Pythia. She sent me a copy. She's in her regalia." Sigrun's tone was colorless.

Ten or so pictures of Sophia when she was a child, and <u>one</u>, now that she's grown. No pictures of your father since he married . . . except the one highly-edited family portrait on the mantel. Almost no pictures at all of you, yourself. Oh, there's information on where you've gone and what you've done . . . but you're not in the picture. Adam found it fascinating, what you could learn about a person from what they chose to display in their homes. Everything had meaning, and you could connect a coherent narrative out of it. Especially in a home like this, which was clearly never intended to be seen by anyone else. Nothing here was for show or for display. He'd be willing to bet that if he were to open the door in the wall to the north, which clearly led to her bedchamber, that there wouldn't be a double bed in there at all. *I'd be surprised if there's more than a <u>couch</u>.* Adam cleared his throat. "Do you get a picture from each place you go?" he asked, gesturing to the walls.

"Yes. If I'm there for more than a day or two, I try." She shrugged and looked around. "I'm sorry. It's no more than what I need, and it's really more of storage shed than a home. I have a storage place in Burgundoi for the things I inherited from my mother, but that I haven't wanted to transport overseas." Another faint shrug.

Adam set the album down. He wasn't sure what to make of the signals he was getting here. Generally speaking, being asked into the home of a single Gothic or Gallic woman was an invitation to explore the way to the bedchamber. On the other hand, he wasn't getting any of that sensation from Sigrun. It was hard to deny the evidence that suggested he might be the only person she'd invited into this sparsely furnished apartment since she'd rented it. The fact that she sat across the living room, a full five feet away, in that uncomfortable chair, only reinforced his perception that there were no signals here. And yet . . . . Adam smiled slightly, stood, and gestured for her to take the comfortable chair . . . which she adamantly refused, at first, until several rounds of insistence and counter-insistence persuaded her to move . . . and he promptly sat down on the floor beside her. "See? Perfectly comfortable," he told her, and stretched his legs out, picking up one of the books she'd just purchased for their trip, and watching, out of the corner of his eyes, how wide her own had gone. *Like a startled maiden*, Adam thought, highly amused, and flipped through the book. "*Ancient Egypt: The Dynasty of Akhenaten the Godslayer*," he read out loud. "Sounds like a page-turner."

He found a set of plates, images taken from the tomb walls of Nefertiti, and stopped to stare at them for a moment. The golden eyes staring out of the pit gave him a sense of creeping horror, for some reason. "Apparently, she got a good look at the godslayer in question."

"The Assassin," Sigrun said, quietly, leaning forward to look over his shoulder at the book. "Those eyes give me chills. They really do. Like they're looking at me." She actually did shudder. "Nefertiti and her children were lucky to escape."

"From the way the creature's pointing in the panel before the entire palace collapsed on it . . . " Adam said, dryly, "the various respected archaeologists seem to think it told her to leave." He looked up at her. "Next you'll be saying that a godslayer can't be a good man, by definition." Internally, he grimaced.

Her hand actually fell to his shoulder. "I might have said that before last year," Sigrun agreed, quietly. "There is, however, new evidence on the topic to consider. And I pride myself on being a good *ælagol*."

Adam chuckled, and was startled, some two hours later, at how quickly the time had flown by. They'd done nothing but talk, mostly about the interests that the various books they'd purchased had expressed, and he hadn't realized just how hungry he was for just that. Talk. Companionship. Something that wasn't work. She wasn't ignorant about what was in outer space, but she hadn't cultivated much of an interest before this . . . but asked good questions as he once more flipped open a book to show her the moons of Jupiter, or the dormant volcano complexes of Mars.

Finally, she reminded him, at close to midnight, with something that sounded like regret, "We have an early morning flight."

"So we do," Adam had agreed, and levered himself to his feet. They'd had nothing to drink but tea since coming to her apartment. And as she opened the door to let him out, he'd leaned forward, just for a moment, wondering if he should kiss her cheek, but reading startlement in her eyes, he quickly changed the gesture into another, finding a hair caught in the shoulder of her bodice, and freeing it for her. "Good night,

Sigrun."

While Sigrun's apartment was in the Esquiline Hill area, and had been picked, surely, for being in an out-of-the-way neighborhood, equidistant between the ancient, terraced gardens of Maecenas and the local nymphaeum, a rotunda dedicated to the nymphs, Trennus had chosen an apartment complex in the Quirinal Hill area, near the baths built by Flavian II, predecessor of Diocletian II. The apartments were within walking distance of several libraries, restaurants, and shops, so Trennus never had to do more than perhaps take a trolley to them. But unlike Sigrun's apartment, it had also been selected for the resonant ley-line directly under the complex. Where Sigrun's apartment had a door onto a balcony for easy access to the sky, Trennus' apartment was situated on the ground floor, with access to the complex's small kitchen garden.

Anyone who happened to visit both apartments—as Adam had— might have been struck between the similarities, as well as by the differences. Like Sigrun's home, the shelves of Trennus' apartment were lined with books, and there was, as in her apartment, a notable lack of a far-viewer. His shelves were, however, also lined with pictures of his large and boisterous family. He had no less than four older brothers, all of whom were married and who had produced children, resulting in visitors, like Adam, being treated to a barrage of Celto-Roman names that they'd surely not remember in the morning. There wasn't the slightest trace of dust on those shelves, but the icebox was empty even of ice; Trennus didn't cook for himself, though he'd have been happy to cook for a guest . . . if he'd had any.

And, of course, the landlord of the building would surely not refund Trennus' security deposit when he moved out, because the summoner had scored a binding circle into the wooden boards that made up the floor of his living area, which he'd stained dark with a variety of herbal concoctions over the last year. Most of the time, he kept a couch and a low table positioned over them, but at the moment, Trennus had moved the couch into a corner, leaning up against one of the few bare spots on the walls, and stacked the low table atop the one in his kitchen, for free access to his binding circle. He sat at the center of the circle now, reading Names quietly from a grimoire. As each spirit answered, Trennus bargained silently with it in turn. Most took no more than a sentence or two; either they were interested, or they weren't. He had a feeling he might need to have a handful of helpers available for the Judea trip, and he'd actually made a few more alliances with spirits during his time in Nahautl than he'd expected . . . but many spirits were bound to local areas. Few were as unbound, in that sense, as Lassair was. Even Saraid, though powerful, became less so, the further from Britannia they traveled.

Lassair had convinced him to move a mirror from the bathing chamber out here, and, while he worked, she was manifesting and de-manifesting. He could just see it out of the corner of his eye. He was, privately, amazed at the changes in her in the last ten months or so. Before, she'd wavered, barely more capable of form than a jellyfish, really, sometimes flickering into a vaguely feminine shape before dissipating back into tendrils of red-tinged white energy. Always beautiful . . . but hardly even *there*. Now, however, the phoenix was one of her favorite shapes, certainly, but it was hardly the only one she'd mastered. *This one could be very useful, don't you think?*

He glanced up, and saw that the phoenix shape had given way to the dainty form of a hind, the body ivory and apricot, the dainty hooves wreathed in flames. "I think Saraid may object to you stealing her favorite form. And how would that be useful?"

You could ride on my back for a quick escape.

"Lassair, I would break that poor creature's back." He made several banishing gestures, poured another cup of wine and sifted sugar into it, before setting the mix on fire; it was all done in a metal cup for a damned good reason. "Etain," Trennus said, reading from his grimoire, and using his *will* to pull the attention of the spirit in question.

A dazzling spark of light, like the sun, appeared before him. *You speak my Name, and offer my favorite sacrifice. What will you with me?* A hint of intrigue in the spirit's thoughts. *Do you still wish information on the remnants of Tlaloc?*

"Do you have any to offer?"

I could find some —

She's fibbing, Trennus. Make her go away. She doesn't have anything, or she'd be asking for something of value now. Lassair's form shifted, and became a sleek and deadly pard, made entirely of glowing amber flame, with her ever-present ruby eyes.

"Unless you've got something more specific, all I'm interested in is your promise to help when I go to the lands of the god of Abraham."

There? Why would I ever want to go there? It would take more than sugar and wine to entice me to go to that place There are no profitable alliances to be made in that land, nor anything of real interest..

"Then begone, spirit." Trennus winced and cupped his hand over the flames, putting them out, and Etain vanished with them. "I'm going through this list at a frightening rate," he admitted, glumly, and turned the page with a finger not covered in soot.

Yes, but do you like this shape?

Trennus looked up, and evaluated the pard. "Dangerous," he told her. "Very dangerous. You'd tear right through an enemy with those claws. But you'd be a target, too. People are very frightened of big cats, and rightly so. You might be better off sticking with the phoenix."

How about a griffon? She shifted. *They have the claws, and the wings. And I could carry you through the air.*

"You know how I feel about flying. No, thank you."

He was just about to speak the next name, when there was a knock at the door. "Master Matrugena?" an older woman's voice seeped through from the door.

It was Sappronia, his landlady. "Gods," Trennus muttered, in annoyance, and then called through the door, "Mistress Sappronia, if you're having problems with your *lares* again, I must remind you that they are *your* household gods. You have to leave them their cup of wine and their bread, or they *will* view your contract as null and void. That's why the drains are always in such bad order!"

Well, either that, or it could be because Latronicus on the third floor pours his cooking oil into them every day, Lassair pointed out, pragmatically.

I'm sure that doesn't help them, no.

"Master Matrugena, I really must speak with you, and I'd prefer not to shout through the door!"

Trennus looked down. He was sitting cross-legged, had four open grimoires in front of him, along with a silver knife, two bottles of wine, a sack of sugar, a pot of honey, and a small glass jar of lamb's blood scattered inside of his work area, and had *just* put out a fire in a metal goblet filled with alcohol. The potential for catastrophe if he stood up now was high. "In a minute!" he shouted back at the door.

I'll get it, Lassair told him, cheerfully, and incarnated completely. As a fire-wreathed gryphon, all golden fur, and savage, foot-long eagle beak.

"No! Lassair, not like that!" Trennus slid his books to safety at the perimeter of the circle, and stood, gingerly, brushing off his kilt and sending sugar and salt falling to the floor as he did. *You'll scare her to death, and that's not really the way to get out of this month's rent.*

Oh, then maybe I should look like this, then? Lassair's form blurred. Shifted. Pulled inwards, moving towards the white hue that was her baseline, spirit-only state . . . and then assumed the amorphous shape of a human woman. Red glow at her bare feet, as if she stood on coals. Curving figure, lithe waist, and a lot more *details* than the last time she'd tried human form. For one, there were apricot-gold flames that formed nipples this time, and more flames that curled shyly between her long, slender legs. Trennus blinked and jerked his eyes up, and saw that her hair still billowed out around her, as if caught in a storm, white, but tinged with amber-gold . . . and the eyes were still the ruby glow of banked coals. But there were no features. No lips, no nose.

Gods, Lassair, no, you're still in spirit form, you can't even open the door — Trennus wasn't entirely thinking straight at the moment; this was the first thing that happened to pop to mind.

Oh, that. Human form's a little complex. I'm never quite sure what all the bits are supposed to be. Lassair shifted, and, for a moment, became *male*. *For example, I'm really not sure what to make of this. I don't really like this shape. Though, to be honest, being both at the same time doesn't feel all that uncomfortable.* She shifted again, amorphous and immaterial, the curves of hips and breasts becoming pronounced again, but the male and female aspects becoming conjoined at the legs. Like a statue of Aphroditus in a temple, a union of opposites. *Which do you like, Trennus?*

"Ah, the first one," Trennus managed, averting his eyes hastily and picking up at least the bottle of wine before he managed to kick it over. He ensured that he'd banished everything in the vicinity that he'd been working with, stepped out of the circle, and opened the door before

Sappronia could knock on it again. "Mistress Sappronia, I've told you before, I will not bargain for you with your *lares* if you won't adhere to your side of your bargain with them. You might be the owner of this place, but they aren't really *tenants.*"

He looked down at his landlady, who was staring up at him, and belatedly, Trennus realized he'd answered the door wearing no shirt, just his kilt, barefoot, holding a bottle of wine in one hand . . . and, as he watched her eyes track behind him, Trennus inwardly prayed, *Please, please, please let it be the phoenix that she's seeing.*

"I, ah, apologize," Sappronia told him, her voice strangled. "I didn't mean to intrude. I just wanted to ask about the next month's rent, since you said you'd be out of town."

"I left the next two months' worth with your daughter this afternoon. I have a receipt written in her handwriting for it, too. Check with her." Trennus didn't *dare* turn around just yet. Just kept his voice nonchalant. "If that's all?"

"Ah . . . yes." Sappronia actually leaned to the right to keep peering into the door as he closed it in her face. *Oh, gods, this does not bode well.*

Trennus turned around, eyes on the floor, braced himself, and looked up. Lassair wasn't ephemeral at the moment. Not at all. She'd incarnated, just for an instant, and there were veils of diaphanous golden gauze drifting over her body, revealing and concealing at once, showing the clean line of long, slender legs. Even through the gauzy covering, her skin had that sun-touched honey overtone that had entered her spiritual form of late, adding luster to the base ivory tone. His eyes moved up, cautiously; curving hips, narrow, taut waist, breasts that strained at the cloth, pink crests still visible underneath . . . feathers made of flame, the long peacock-like flare of them, white to white-gold, blue-violet eyes, all along the backs of her arms, and extending along sweeping, glorious wings that emerged from her back . . . . white hair, shot through with glitters of gold here and there . . . red-dyed lips, a pert nose, high cheekbones . . . and ruby-red eyes, fringed with long lashes. *Is the face better this way?*

The bottle slipped out of his numb fingers at that point. "What?" It hit the wood floor with a thump, not breaking, but red wine pouring out over the floor like a libation before a goddess.

Lassair lifted a hand, and studied the bird-like talons that glittered at the ends of her fingers. *Are the features better this way? Or should I keep working on them?* She dissipated back into incorporeality again, but retained the *form,* the sweet smile still playing on her lips. *Is it better this way . . . or this way? More like Stormborn, perhaps?* A slightly sterner cast to the features, her overall body elongating slightly, taking on a slightly more athletic build. *Or . . . different in some other way?* The features shifted again, taking on a sweeter, more winsome cast, as her eyelids slid down, almost shyly, a glitter of gold appearing briefly in the irises.

"I . . . think I'm . . . going to sit down now," Trennus decided, after a moment, letting his shoulders hit the wall, and sliding down. He'd been concentrating, intently, on work, and had just had several shocks in a row, the last of which had been a direct hit on his libido.

No, no, you'll get the wine all over your kilt, and then you'll have to change out of it. Lassair's form collapsed inwards, becoming the amorphous ball of light and shadow that she usually manifested as, all flickering flame and tendrils of energy.

What . . . wine . . . oh. Trennus looked down, just in time to realize why his feet were wet, swore, and padded on just his toes for the lavatory, where he grabbed several towels and brought them back out. All things considered, he was rather grateful for the distraction.

Were the clothes sufficient? I understand that humans are uncomfortable with their corporeal nature. Which is odd, considering that you're mostly corporeal all the time. She bobbed along beside him, like a firefly for a moment, right at the level of his elbow.

Trennus did his level best to suppress any number of images that promptly *leaped* into his mind. She had somewhere in the neighborhood of eighty percent of his soul in her keeping at the moment. It wasn't as if she couldn't *hear* him, but there were definitely things he tried, very hard, to keep suppressed when he could feel her presence. Her previous summoner had used her in horrific fashion, and she really didn't need to hear or feel human male urges, as far as Trennus was concerned. It could panic her, and he didn't want to cause her any discomfort.

Red eyes appeared in the swirl of white light, appearing to study him. *The one who bound me before is dead. I know that. You killed him. And more.*

Trennus winced. Her previous summoner . . . the man had been a Gaul. He'd had a name, and a Name. Trennus wouldn't even think the name, and the Name itself . . . he'd dealt with that. The kinds of things that the summoner in question had done, the ways in which he'd bound his spirits and compelled them, had outraged all of the local spirits. His actions had resulted in strings of possessed villagers being forced to do things, and awakening, appalled, with fragmentary memories of killing their own families while a shadowy figure watched and applauded. Stealing money from banks, and handing it over to a faceless person, before having their throats cut. There had been just enough survivors to put together a pattern, and the pattern had led Trennus to a vineyard, bought within the past five years, but with the fruit left on the vines to rot, the trees withering in the ground as the spirits of the earth and nature all around fled in revolt against what was being done there. So he'd made his way in, masking his path with ley-energy . . . and had watched and listened to the bound spirits. One of them had dared to tell him the true Name of the summoner . . . and Trennus had found the man in the pressing shed, raping the decaying, dead body of a former worker. A body with a spirit bound inside of it. Forcing energies out of her as he did, draining her. Binding her essence into him, to promote his own long life. Lassair.

He'd been able to *see* her, bound inside the decaying corpse. Just a flicker of flame. Barely there. He'd seen the knots of compulsion that bound her to the summoner, and he'd tossed her just a whisper of thought: *What's your Name? I'll protect it. I'll protect you.*

Just a shimmer of thought had conveyed her Name to him, and he'd *used* it, used it to divide her from the summoner, stolen her as she manifested in the palm of his hand like a dying ember . . . and even as the corpse dropped, limply, to the floor, and the other summoner had looked up, confused, his pants down around his ankles, snarling . . . Trennus had whispered the man's true Name, and begun the words of a spell no one was supposed to know.

He'd found it in the belongings of the *Sangua Foederis* summoner who'd murdered Senecita Tancorix, the ley-mage who'd been his teacher. Saraid had taken the grimoires and hidden them, entrusting him with them. He'd concealed this knowledge from everyone, including all the summoners who'd taught him in Londonium. It was, fortunately, a completely useless spell . . . unless you happened to know your target's Name.

But with that? You could unName them. Write them right out of reality. Oh, people would remember the person. They'd still have been born, all the things that they'd done would stay done. Time didn't unravel itself, just for a Name. But that person no longer *existed.* What Akhenaten had wanted to do to the gods of old, by effacing their names from the monuments, Trennus had done in a moment of cold, plain rage. He'd unmade a man, and he'd seen, just for an instant, the total panic in the man's eyes. This wasn't death. This was oblivion. Mind, body, and soul, erased.

He'd never tell anyone what he'd done. There was no one who'd think it other than an inherently evil act. Maybe the gods themselves would judge it so, but if they had, none of them had informed him of that fact, as yet. Truthfully, it would probably have been cleaner to put a bullet into him. But Trennus hadn't had a gun. He'd just had words and power and knowledge. And, as he'd told Adam ben Maor a year ago . . . knowledge itself was neither good nor bad. It was the ends to which it was put that made it so. Looking at Lassair now, Trennus could not believe for an instant that he'd acted wrongly.

And that dying flicker of flame had had so much of her life removed, so much of her essence . . . her Name had been all she could remember of herself. There had been no past for her, beyond what her summoner had demanded of her. No self left, beyond that, either. And Trennus had refused to let her die, to drop into oblivion with the man he'd unNamed . . . so he'd bound her, himself. More to the point, he'd bound *himself* to her. Ceded her fifty percent of his soul, on the spot, just to keep darkness from claiming her. And that, too, he couldn't think of as a bad thing at all. All those thoughts, at once, raced through his mind, and just the act of remembering let him calm down. "Lassair," Trennus told her, gently, tossing one sodden towel at his sink, and beginning to mop up the rest of the wine with a second, "The human form was lovely. Truly. And I thank you for startling away the landlady for at least the rest of the night. But . . . ."

You didn't like it? Wistfulness in her tone.

Trennus looked up at the ceiling. *Gods.* "No, I liked it. I'm just not likely to think straight around you if you manifest like that. Nor would any other man." He turned and gave her a rueful look. "It's a corporeal thing, really. Sometimes, our bodies think for us. You manifest like that, and it's not my mind or spirit that's doing the bulk of my thinking. I . . . well. You probably don't understand."

Bodies are definitely strange, confusing things, she told him, after a moment. *Still . . . there's something familiar here. Like a memory. Every time I incarnate, it feels a little closer. This last time, the closest of all.* Confusion, and intrigue now. *I would like to remember more. From . . . before.*

Trennus looked up at the ceiling. "All right," he told her, in a tone of resignation. "I foresee weeks of wearing a blindfold and cold showers ahead of me."

These are strange rituals. What do you hope to accomplish with them?

"Preservation of my sanity, Lassair. Preservation of my sanity."

Maius 6, 1955 AC

Hatasahl Flight 149 left Rome for Jerusalem on time. Adam found the sound of the ventilation system to be quite soothing, and the roar of the jet turbines exhilarating. Jets were among the few Judean-built vehicles that actually used an internal combustion engine, as opposed to electrical battery systems, and they used chemical propellants, unlike almost every other modern vehicle. "Ley-powered planes are quieter," Kanmi complained, cheerfully from where he sat, one row up, with his family. He'd turned around to look back at Adam, and shook a finger at his fellow lictor, as if the noise ratio around them was the Judean's fault.

In close to a year of working with the Carthaginian, not one of his fellow lictors had, until today, met either the mysterious Bastet or Kanmi's two children; Adam hadn't known what to expect of Kanmi's wife, though he'd known she was Nubian and tall. He was startled to realize that Bastet stood a good four inches taller than her sorcerer husband. Likewise, he'd known from the single wedding picture that Kanmi carried with him, that she hadn't been subjected to the Nubian custom of lip-plating, which involved piercing a woman's lower lip and stretching it around a series of increasingly wider diameter discs. It was considered a mark of beauty among some of the more southern and rural tribes, but apparently, Bastet had been raised in one of the larger cities. She also definitely did not have the self-effacing demeanor of the few Nubian women Adam had met, here and there, in Jerusalem over the years. She'd been sent to the University of Athens by her father, and had definitely taken on a more Hellenized and modern manner. Adam's eyebrows shot up now as he overheard her telling Kanmi, in a tone of annoyance, "I really don't see why we couldn't have taken an Aloma flight. The propraetor is *Roman.* I don't know how I'm going to get any reading done with all this incessant engine noise. I have at least three journal articles I need to get through."

"You were the one who said you wanted a vacation," Kanmi said, turning back to her, his voice absolutely neutral. There was none of the needling tone he usually employed on his fellow lictors. "Perhaps you could put the journal articles to the side for the moment." He then leaned forward and made sure his younger son was buckled in correctly.

Adam knew that Kanmi was agitated at the moment, but there were no signs of it in his voice or face. The sorcerer had caught him before they'd boarded, pulling him aside to reiterate, "I'm not enthusiastic about having my family along for this."

"We'll keep them out of trouble. Chances are, there won't *be* any." Theoretically, no one besides them, Livorus, and the *Imperator* knew what this trip was about.

Theoretically.

Of course, there were all the couriers who'd taken messages to Chaldean and Median contacts and the Chaldeans and the Medians themselves . . . . Adam grimaced. "All right, I realize that we don't have a good track record on staying out of trouble. But . . . the other lictors, the ones in charge of Poppaea and Livorus' children? They're *good*. They'll take care of them."

"I know. I just feel a need to express, once again, how completely fucked this entire notion is. And I couldn't convince her *not* to come." Kanmi's face had been an expressionless mask, but his tone had been as furious as Adam had ever heard it. And then he'd exhaled, and put it to the side. "Once they're in a safe location, however, you can count on me, ben Maor."

"Why does everyone keep telling *me* these things? I'm actually not in charge."

"Livorus said you were. Effective this morning. He said he'd run it by Caetia to make sure she wasn't offended to be outranked by someone technically junior to her on the team." Kanmi shrugged. "Makes sense to me. Short-term, this assignment, you know the area better than anyone. Long-term . . . " Kanmi's eyes narrowed. "Well, we'll see."

Adam looked up at the ceiling. "Well, that would have been nice to know."

"You know the propraetor. He does things in his own time, and in his own way. I'm sure he'll tell you that you're in charge sooner or later." Kanmi's tone had held needles, as had the quick flash of his grin.

Kanmi had introduced each of the other lictors to his family. Himi, age six, and Bodi, age four, had stared up at Trennus, in particular, *squeaked*, and had hidden behind their mother for a moment, peering out, wide-eyed. Adam figured that he understood why; the Britannian stood a foot taller than their father, and his sleeves were rolled up, displaying both blue-ink knot-work tattoos and the fact that Trennus actually carried a fair amount of muscle mass. Finally, Himi had edged out, as Trennus dropped down to a crouch to talk to them, his eyes kind behind his glasses, and, after a moment, had asked, in good Latin, "Why do you wear a dress?"

Kanmi had *shouted* with laughter, and Trennus had looked up at the ceiling. "That's my boy," Kanmi had chortled . . . just as Bastet had frowned, her expression irritated. "Don't encourage him," she'd chided. "Himilico, that's *rude*."

"No, it's all right, and nothing I haven't heard from men five times his age." Trennus offered Himi a wrist to clasp. "It's not a dress. It's a kilt. Long and storied tradition. This pattern can only be worn by someone in my family. Anyone else who wears it, well, they get their heads knocked in. Or they get laughed at. One of the two."

Bastet, for her part, on being introduced to her husband's coworkers, had no idea what to do with them. She'd never entirely understood how he'd gotten pulled into the Praetorians in the first place; his degree in technomancy at the University of Athens had been in an engineering specialty. She'd assumed he'd be taking a job with some engineering firm, possibly with the ley-grid, or, at most, that he'd have gone back to school to get his doctorate, so he could teach. Instead, he'd been drawn in as a levy to the legions, and from there, he'd been pulled into the Praetorians. She'd assumed it was for his technical acumen. She knew he was brilliant, in that regard, but everything he'd ever talked to her about, back in their school days, had been practical applications of magic to technology. Sending power through capacitors and vacuum tubes and wires to modulate it. The potential for *calculi* to speed up the mathematics needed for military enchantments. Things like that. The fact that he'd been tapped for a protective detail? She'd chalked it up to the fact that they needed someone to check if the telephones had been tapped and to ensure that the lights stayed on.

The huge Pict was clearly a *barbarian*. Nevermind that his wrist-clasp was as gentle as if he held a baby chick in the palm of his hand; he was clearly one generation removed from frothing at the mouth and charging into battle, painted blue and naked. The long braids, the tattoos, the hairy arms, throat, and light beard, not to mention the 'kilt'? Since living outside of Nubia, she'd adopted many Roman and Hellene ideas. To dress as something other than Roman was to *be* a barbarian. And she'd done her best to be Roman in her demeanor and dress.

The Judean man was at least a known factor. Many Judeans came to Tyre on business; their capital city was only thirty or forty miles from the provincial border, after all. This one, for all that Kanmi introduced him as the leader of the detail, looked younger than her husband, and that didn't make sense at all . . . except that, well, Kanmi was an engineer, and this one, clearly, was a solider. Probably intelligent enough, but still, soldiers were knuckle-draggers. Everyone knew that.

And the final introduction was to some Gothic tribeswoman, who wore, for some unknown reason, a cloak made of white feathers that came down to her waist, over the top of a leather bodice and black jeans. Cold eyes, cold face, cold hair, all washed-out and diluted-looking, like the third round of coffee poured from the same beans. *Baraka*, the third pot was called. Bastet had given her husband a quick, cautious glance, trying to discern if he liked this ice-pick as the Gothic woman had given her a quick, impersonal wrist-clasp. Bastet's eyes had narrowed when she'd caught amusement in Kanmi's glance at Sigrun. He *did* like the woman, but the female seemed to have about as much personality as the spear she carried in one hand. And with that, a shock of relief, in Bastet's mind. *Oh. She's a tribade.*

And with each of them neatly categorized in her mind, Bastet had dismissed them all. Two barbarians and one Judean, none of them particularly intelligent. They were the workhorses of the protective detail, the ones who were in charge of throwing themselves in front of any bullets or arrows destined for the propraetor, and her Kanmi was their technician, the one who made sure that their radios and devices worked.

It wasn't that Kanmi had never talked to Bastet about his job. And it wasn't that she didn't think her husband was good at what he did. It was all a question of very selective hearing and memory, and how she'd isolated and segregated information in her head, as a way of dealing with it. She didn't have to worry about Kanmi if he wasn't in danger, and clearly, a technical specialist in charge of radios and electronics wasn't going to be in much danger. He even carried a slide-rule in one of his pockets! And if she didn't have to worry about him, she was free to be irritated with him for not being around as much as she'd like him to be. And clearly, since all he was, was a high-priced technician, *her* job was the more important one. She saved lives at the hospital. And the sooner he stopped playing around, and got real job, one that let him *stay* home, without all these separations, the better it would be for her and the children. But instead, he was being stubborn about it.

So, she put on an uncomfortable smile and made nice until it was time to board the flight. This was the first time she'd ever been on a pleasure-trip in her life. Her father had allowed her to have more of an education than other women in Nubia tended to receive, on the assumption that she would return home and live a dedicated life of service to her people; she'd expected to do nothing more, until she met Kanmi, and, in marrying him in defiance of her father's wishes, had quickly changed her citizenship to Carthaginian. And then medical school, apprenticeship in the hospital, two children . . . yes, the whole *vacation* idea was a new one. And she intended to make the most of it.

The flight from Rome to Jerusalem wasn't actually all that long. Fourteen hundred miles, in a more or less straight line, made for four hours or so in the air, all told. Adam passed the time watching the others in first class, particularly Trennus and Sigrun, who each had convulsive grips on the arms of their chairs. He finally leaned to his left, across the aisle, to where they sat side-by-side in the seats across the aisle from Adam, and told them both, "You do realize that the safety lecture on entry is just standard procedure, right?"

"Don't help me," Trennus said, not opening his eyes. "Please. Just don't try to help me."

Adam smothered a chuckle.

Eventually, they came in for a landing, and Adam looked out the window, smiling faintly to himself at the sight of the red and blue tile roofs below, glorious splotches of color that stood out against the mostly white walls of the clustered buildings, visible as their plane banked and started its runway approach. He could just pick out some of the ancient walls, designed and built for the city's defense. Sigrun surprised him by calling around Trennus, "It looks so crowded!"

"A lot of the buildings and roads have been there, more or less in their current configuration, for over two thousand years," Adam called back across. "It's hard to widen a road when the buildings can't be torn down or moved because they're historic. So people tend to build between or on top of existing buildings. The city's expanded a bit in the last two hundred years, though." He looked back out the window, picking out, easily, the Second Temple on the eastern side of town. Most buildings in the Old Town area weren't allowed to be taller than the Temple. All of the skyscrapers and office buildings, as a result, were on the extreme western end of the city, past even Zikron Yosef. It made for interesting traffic patterns. He was fairly sure there weren't too many other cities in the world in which people *left* the city for the suburbs during the workday, and turned around and went the other direction at nightfall.

On landing, and with the cabin doors opening, he got his first taste of the air of home in three years. A whiff of jet fuel made him cough, but the *smell* was the same. A little more humidity in the air than outsiders tended to expect, but just the taste of the dust at the back of his tongue informed him, at the brainstem level, that he was home. And truth be told, he wasn't sure how he felt about that.

Adam stretched and got back to business, making sure everyone's handheld radios were on the same channel. "Eshmunazar, the propraetor's baggage, please," he called over. This was actually fairly important. They had to ensure that no outsiders handled Livorus' baggage. Less of a chance of being bugged, that way. His family's luggage was the province of *their* lictors, thankfully. As he stood, he adjusted his gun in its holster; no concealed-carry for him, today. He had a flak jacket on beneath his shirt, and a light gray, short cloak to cover his torso. He really wished he'd been able to get Sigrun a gun, or convince her to purchase a flak jacket of her own. He glanced back, and ensured that yes, she and Trennus were bringing up the rear, while Livorus had offered his arm, without changing his expression at all, to Poppaea, his wife.

Adam had been told that theirs was an arranged marriage. It showed.

Adam led the way down the extended stairs of the plane, his body always directly just in front of Livorus', and slightly to the left, trying to block any shots that might be aimed for the propraetor's heart. At the base of the ramp, there were regional Praetorians, and a variety of reporters, with credentials pinned to their lightweight cloaks as they hefted their far-viewer cameras and still photography boxes with their large flashes perched on top. "Propraetor! What brings you to Judea?"

"A goodwill tour," Livorus replied, with a faint, wintery smile.

"I've been reliably informed that the state of natural philosophy in Roman schools could be improved, and my hope is that in coming here, I can boost awareness of that fact . . . and perhaps encourage a generation of young people to consider working in the aerospace industry that has been pioneered by Hellas, Nippon, and Judea." He waved a hand lightly. "Other than that, I would like to regard this trip as a holiday of sorts, and ask that the media in general respect the privacy of my wife and family for the duration."

Yes. Because that's going to happen. The news media hadn't had *time* to catch wind of where they were or what they were doing in Ponca. But after the sensationalistic details about the human sacrifices in Nahautl had gotten into the newspapers and far-viewer reports, Adam had gotten a crash course in media relations. They hadn't been able to keep the press *away* from Livorus for the six months they'd been in Caesaria Aquilonis. And where the propraetor went was still, apparently, big news. *And if this mission is, in any way, a success . . . or, god forbid, a public failure . . . this is only going to get worse.* Adam kept his face set in stony lines, and led the way past the press line, to the waiting vehicles. All good, solid Judean motorcars, he was relieved to note. All electrical engines. He opened the door, and got Livorus inside, watching the entire area, feeling acutely exposed. *Need to arrange for a covered exit from planes and vehicles in the future,* he decided. *Out on the tarmac, away from the buildings, was a local security decision, and I . . . just don't like it.* He slid in after Tren and Sigrun, as Kanmi came up at the rear with the luggage, and slipped into the car now, himself, and their small motorcade began to move out.

Passing the front of the airport, Sigrun pointed out a group of protestors with wooden placards. All of the writing on the signs was in Hebrew; as such, Adam was the only person besides their driver who could read it, and he snorted. "What is that about?" Sigrun asked. "Anything to do with our arrival?"

"No," Adam replied. "They're a fringe cult. Zealots. They find a public venue once or twice a year to inform the rest of us that the end of the world is nigh, and that we all need to repent."

Sigrun gave him a quizzical look. "Ragnarok?"

"Something like that."

"How long have they held this belief?"

"Since the last Roman occupation, about two thousand years ago." Adam shrugged. "They change the date on the end of the world every few years. For the most part, they don't bother anyone, other than making traffic a nightmare every once in a while, so no one bothers them."

"Odd." She shrugged, and the subject dropped.

However, they'd barely pulled onto Roman Highway VIII when the driver's radio crackled. The words, coming over the radio in rapid Hebrew, made Adam's head swivel, and the driver swerved. Adam swore under his breath, and shifted in his seat until he could get a good look to the north; the airport was south of the city, proper, and they were heading east along Highway VIII . . . yes. There it was. *"Dominus?"* Adam's voice was tight. "We have a small problem."

Livorus looked up from the dispatch that he was reading. "Oh?"

"If you look to your left," Adam pointed, "you'll see what is clearly a large efreet in the center of Old Town. It was apparently summoned in the lobby of your hotel, sir."

Every head now ducked and rotated, as all the passengers stared out the darkened windows of the vehicle in consternation. Sure enough, a dark funnel cloud, lined with *fire*, was streaming out of a four-story building, extending up to the heavens like the finger of an angry god. "There is no way we can go there," Adam said, shortly. "Emergency crews are undoubtedly already responding. Counter-summoning measures need to go into effect."

"Were the other, ah, people we intended to meet here, scheduled to take rooms at the same hostelry?" Livorus asked, mildly, looking out the window with interest.

"Not to my knowledge, sir. There's little way to call them and ask to see if their accommodations have suffered a similar problem." *Not without drawing attention to them, as well.* Adam's tone remained tight, and his mind raced. "We're going to need an alternative place to put you, for the moment, sir, until we can find someplace properly secure—" Two *gardia* cars tore past their motorcade, heading for an off-ramp that would take them into the city center. Smoke was already billowing out of the hotel, visible in black belches rising to the sky alongside the pillar of darkness and fire that was the efreet, and Adam winced. Djinn were bad enough. Efreeti were *worse*, by far.

"Do you have someplace in mind?" Livorus asked. "You're local, ben Maor. You're also my lead lictor, in this case. Use your best judgment, but you are absolutely correct. We do need someplace to stay, under the radar, as it were, and somewhere we can set up a command post and see what, precisely, is going on here." He tapped a finger against the top of his dispatch case in his lap. "I'm not in favor of sending the children and the other half of the motorcade to a second location. Not yet. Not until we know more."

Adam nodded, considering several alternatives rapidly. There were hotels in the western districts, but those might well be where the Chaldean and Median deputations had set up, and he didn't want to draw any fire their direction . . . *if* this happened to be directed at Livorus, instead of being a random attack, which was certainly possible. It would be an amazing coincidence, but coincidences *did* exist in a universe without fate.

He needed a place to take his protectee. There were *gardia* stations, but the local *gardia* was going to have its hands full with emergency response right now, and trying to make sure there weren't any other attacks. There was only one place here that he knew well enough to cover every entrance and exit. He just didn't want to use it. It thus took him thirty seconds of trying to find any other alternative before he turned and looked at the driver. "Take us off highway eight. Take Imperial Highway twelve north, to *Mishkenot Sha'ananim.*" *Peaceful Habitation*, the neighborhood was named, and he hoped it lived up that reputation today.

He tabbed his radio, and informed the rest of the motorcade of the change in plans, as well.

"Where in Baal's name are we going?" Kanmi demanded, sharply.

"A house I know. I'm . . . aware that the residents are home today, too." Adam looked up at the sky for a moment, and decided that the universe must have a sense of humor.

All of the lictors were on high alert at this point, shifting positions in the car to ensure that Sigrun had the seat to Livorus' left, her body blocking his from the window. Adam stayed to Livorus' right, while Kanmi and Trennus, for the moment, stayed alongside Poppaea, Livorus' wife. Two of her bodyguards were at the very rear of the large vehicle, and were facing the hindmost window. The young Roman matron glanced around at them all, fear in her face and eyes. "The children won't be informed as to what's going on, correct?" she asked, her voice wavering. "It would just frighten them."

"Hopefully, it'll just be an unexpected stop," Adam told her, quickly. "A little detour into a residential neighborhood for a bit."

They got off the highway, and Kanmi muttered, in aggravation, "You've got to be kidding me. Not one of the street signs off the highway is in Latin. I can't tell which *direction* I'm facing."

"Northeast," Trennus told him, not changing expression.

"More or less, yes," Adam said. "There are three enclaves of, well, foreigners in the city. Mevi'eat Roma, Mevi'eat Nippon, and Mevi'eat Hellas. Little Rome, Little Nippon, and Little Hellas. The Roman area's northeast of where we're going. The Nipponese section is way off to the southwest, close to the university district, and the Hellene district is right next to it. We'll be able to pull help from the consulate in Mevi'eat Roma or the governor's house in Old Town if we need it, that much faster, for being closer by . . . but we shouldn't be in an area we'd be expected to go. Under the radar, but close to aid." He shrugged. "Best I can do, till we get more information."

"This will be fine," Livorus told him, as the motorcade barreled through an intersection, ignoring the red lights and the irate horns of the other drivers, the squeal of wheels as a large box truck slammed its brakes to avoid hitting the large, boxy lead car. The drivers were now in escape mode: *don't stop, don't slow down. Keep moving. If you've stopped, you're vulnerable.* "Turn left up here ahead," Adam told his driver. "Tell the lead car we're going down Sh'drah Ben Affan."

The neighborhood had a crenellated wall around it, and gates that closed at night. "Limited access points," Livorus noted, approvingly.

"It was built during a nervous period in history," Adam noted. "Incursions over the Wall were more common two hundred years ago." He paused. "When we reach our destination, there should be a secure phone line available for your use, sir."

He could feel everyone's eyes on him, just for a moment. Livorus blinked. "Ah. Your father's in Judean Intelligence, as I recall?"

"Yes, sir." Maor ben Emmet, Adam's father, was a senior director in the Judean Intelligence Office. Adam had never mentioned that fact to his fellow lictors, though, since Sigrun had likely read his dossier before he joined the team, she probably had already known . . . though she might not have remembered.

"That will do, and nicely," Livorus acknowledged, and the whole car swayed again as they spun around a corner. Adam was now relaying turn-by-turn directions to the driver of the lead car by radio, and pedestrians were scattering out of the way, turning to stare at the line of black cars as they passed. *Inconspicuous. We're doing a fine job of that today.*

"Cobbles?" Kanmi suddenly asked, his voice acid. "Really? Cobbles?"

"It's an old city," Adam replied, feeling mildly defensive. "The roadwork crews can only upgrade so much, so quickly."

The streets weren't just cobbled. They were narrow, and twisting. with the old stone houses jammed in tightly against each other, all piled up on a hillside, with narrow alleys in between. For all that, it was a lovely old neighborhood, with tall trees and flowers in most of the yards. "Here we are," Adam said, pointing. "That one."

There were already cars parked in front of the house—few that he recognized, though the low-slung Mehyman family car might have belonged to his brother, Mikayel. Adam exhaled. *I was very specific,* he thought, grimly. *I told them not to make a big deal and not to invite the entire neighborhood. That I didn't want to see anyone outside of my immediate family.* But there was no real reason why people would have gathered at his parents' house in the middle of the afternoon on a dies Martis . . . Tiwesdæg, whatever . . . except that he'd said he'd try to drop by in the evening.

His irritation would have to wait, and everyone extraneous was simply going to have to leave, and it didn't matter if that strained his parents' hospitality or not. Adam had the door of the car open before it had even finished moving, and could see the front door of the house opening as well. His nerves were on edge, his first responsibility was to the safety of the propraetor, and *he didn't recognize* the man coming out of the house. His first thought was, simply, *Harah. It's a trap. Whoever set up the efreet at the hotel researched Livorus' lictors and found my parents . . . .* The thoughts were a lazy second compared to the speed with which his body reacted, drawing his revolver and aiming it, even as he rapped out in Hebrew, *"Halt! Hands in the air!"*

Whoever the man was, he stopped where he was, wide-eyed, and raised his hands, just as two women, one with her hair tucked back under a snood, and the other younger, with her hair worn loose, emerged from the front door as well, and froze in place, eyes showing white. *"Back up,"* Adam said. He didn't have time for this. *"Where is the family of Maor ben Emmet?"*

"Right here, son," his father's voice came from the door, relatively calm and soothing. Maor appeared in the opening, his hands up, and he stared at the entire motorcade, just for a moment. *"You can put the gun down."*

"Not till I've checked the house." Adam lowered the pistol

slightly, but was so far into work mode, he didn't even realize he'd switched back into Latin. "Once the residence is cleared, we're going to need to make use of it, sir. Praetorian business. Also, we need access to your secure phone-lines."

At about this point, the entire *rest* of his family boiled out of the house. His mother, Abigayil, half-shrieked on seeing him with a gun in his hands; his brother, Mikayel, actually muttered something that sounded suspiciously like, *he's showing off again* to his wife, and Adam's two younger sisters, Rivkah and Chani, had both opened upstairs windows to peer out. *Leave it to my family to have to do all of this on the front steps. They couldn't possibly have stayed inside.*

Still, no time to deal with it. Adam turned his head, very slightly, as Kanmi, Trennus, and Sigrun each emerged from their respective doors of the car. "Caetia? Eyes in the sky, please. Get a couple of the other lictors up on rooftops on the roofs of the other houses so we have lines of sight all the way around the neighborhood."

"Lot of civilians around here," she muttered, pushing her smoked lenses back up her nose.

"All too aware." Adam flicked a glance at Kanmi. "Eshmunazar, you're clearing the house with me. Can you do anything to secure the various doors and windows?"

"Not without effectively welding the doors into their frames. Which I can do, metal or not, but we do that, and we cut off our own escape routes." Kanmi's words were quick and terse.

"Matrugena, what are we talking about in terms of ley potential around here? Can you protect the propraetor without backup?"

Trennus grimaced. "The good news is, your local ley-power is completely untapped. The bad news is, the closest resonating line is about two miles back to the south. And it's a powerful one."

Adam was momentarily confused. "That doesn't sound like a bad thing."

"It's under your main temple, ben Maor. I think your god and your priests might be mildly offended if I use that." Trennus shrugged. "I can still use ambient ley. Worst comes to worst, I can draw a binding circle and do a general summoning, see what in the area answers."

"Bad idea," Kanmi said, succinctly. "You don't know what you'll get."

"Why is it bad?" Adam asked, quickly.

"It's the mystical equivalent of him raising his kilt and waving the *fasces* around." Kanmi and Trennus had *both* picked up that phrase from Adam and Sigrun.

"I wouldn't say *that*," Trennus put in, quickly.

"You could attract malefic spirits just as easily as any other," Kanmi retorted. "Leave that for a last resort, is my advice."

Livorus, who clearly could hear every word from inside the car, asked, mildly, "Waving the *fasces* around?" He paused. "I've never quite heard it expressed quite this way before. Please. Elucidate."

There was a pause as the lictors all scrambled hastily to find something—anything, really—to say in response, besides, from Kanmi's expression, *Shit, he wasn't supposed to hear that* . . . . and then Adam simply moved them on. "Worry about that later, Matru. Step one, clear the area. Step two, secure the propraetor. Step three . . . everything else."

They got to work. Adam and Kanmi cleared the house, moving past Adam's agitated family, Kanmi pausing just long enough to toss a smile at Adam's young nephews as they clustered around Mikayel's feet. They checked the house over, and then they started hustling people inside. Adam pointed at his father's study, which was located in an inner room, without windows, and with only one door. "In there, sir. Defensible, and has the phone lines."

Livorus, in the meantime, as calmly as if he were at a gala somewhere, had introduced himself to Adam's parents, bowing his head very slightly over Abigayil's hand, and giving Maor a very correct nod. "I'm grateful for your hospitality, and I apologize for requiring it of you. If I might prevail upon you, ah, ben Emmet, to arrange a call to the local Praetorian headquarters . . . ?" Livorus had already removed his cloak, handed it to Abigayil, and was rolling up the sleeves his shirt now, briskly. He rarely showed his arms, save when he wore a toga, but the house was warm, and everyone was tense and sweating.

Adam had long since stopped actively noticing it, but his father's startled glance at Livorus' left arm caught his own attention. Maor ben Emmet blinked, and said, in a surprised tone, "You were *branded* in the Legion, Propraetor?"

Officers were almost never branded. The custom had originated with common soldiers who were committed to twenty-year terms in the Legions. This had been the case even before the brief, ill-considered period of fifty years in which one particularly dim-witted Emperor had tried to ban all Legionnaires from being married—but he'd also banned homosexual behavior at the same time, as being too Spartan and Hellene for proper Roman men. All of this, on the theory that his men should take all of their sexual energies and put them into their fighting. (This set of edicts had resulted in booming business for brothels, the emergence of a tradition of camp followers, and disorderly conduct directed at native women in any number of subject kingdoms, before the emperor's order was rescinded by his own grandson, who'd re-instituted the old customs of Caesar's era. To whit, legionnaires could and should be married for the stability it brought to their lives, and that honorable service would be rewarded with a small parcel of land upon retirement. Later refinements to the codes had allowed for stable liaisons of a period greater than seven years with people of either gender to be considered the same as marriage.)

And, of course, *officers* had always been exempt from the provisions on marriage. Officers were nobles. Patricians. They were meant to stand above the common soldier, not alongside. There were rules and regulations—strict ones, at that—to prevent fraternization. Livorus had only served for a little over ten years, but he'd taken the symbol of a *lifer* . . . the Eagle of Rome, which was branded into their very flesh.

"Ah, yes. My men asked me to accept it shortly after the Gazaca debacle. The rank and file wanted to give me a crown of grass, but that would have required that I save the entire legion by my own hands, and all I had really done was prevent the loss of civilian lives." Livorus sighed. "They had heard that I'd been asked to retire. They came to the command tent . . . about twenty representatives, led by my *primus pilus* centurion. And told me that they knew I'd never *really* quit fighting, even if the damned politicians at home took my command from me. And they asked me to take the symbol of a lifer. Just like they wore." Livorus shrugged. "How could I possibly say *no*?" He pointed at the door to the study. "But, we have rather more urgent concerns than the distant past at the moment. If you wouldn't mind?"

Adam turned back away, and got back to coordinating with the people setting up outside. They'd pulled the cars to the side of the house to try to look a little less conspicuous, Kanmi's family, Poppaea, Livorus' children, and their various servants and pedagogues had been herded to the large family room Adam remembered so well from childhood. Kanmi's wife had managed to hiss, "What's *going on?*" at her husband, but Kanmi had held up a hand in an *I'll get back to you* fashion, and gotten on with securing doors and windows, warding the metal frames of each with an incipient electrical charge and telling everyone *not* to touch them. "You become the closed circuit on these, and it will not tickle," he warned. "Keep the children, in particular, away. What hurts an adult might kill one of them, and I won't be held responsible for that."

Elah, Adam's sister-in-law, had protectively pulled her children closer to her at his words, her eyes wide.

Trennus, for his part, had moved the dining room table out of his way, and set up a summoner's binding circle, drawn in chalk, on the tile there, which had made several members of Adam's family skitter away uncertainly. "*We've got someone working dark magic in our house?*" Mikayel called, indignantly, from the dining room, before stalking back into the living room to pull up a chair. "*Where does this end?*"

"Not dark magic," Adam said, in a preoccupied tone. "*Matrugena's the best summoner I've ever seen. And there's not an evil bone in his entire body.*"

He put to the back of his mind that both his sisters, Rivkah and Chani, were peering in the door of the living room in avid curiosity at Trennus. This went into the category of *things I do not have time to deal with* for the moment. After several minutes of preparation, Trennus said only one word out loud: "Saraid."

A pure white stag promptly manifested in the middle of the dining room, which made Rivkah and Chani *squeal*. "Go scout, please. See if there are any disturbances among the spirits local to us. No more than a mile, if you wouldn't mind," Trennus told the spirit . . . which lowered its regal head, and leaped cleanly through the wall to the left, through into the living room, darting through the bodies of those in there, who all shouted in alarm . . . and plunged through the outer wall, disappearing into the neighborhood.

"*Adam, a word, please,*" his mother finally demanded, as Sigrun came back in through the front door, finally taking her dark glasses off, the snowy white of her swan cloak still over her shoulders in spite of the heat that was causing her face to perspire slightly. It was the only part of her regalia she was wearing today. He watched as Sigrun put her shoulders to a wall and rubbed gently at the back of her neck with both hands, exhaling for what was probably the first time in the last hour, *"What is going on?"* his mother pressed. *"It's not that it's not lovely to see you and your . . . friends . . . and coworkers . . . but a little warning would have been nice. And why are you moving them in here?"*

"It's been quite a show," Mikayel agreed, dourly, from his seat near the window into the atrium. The house was built along the lines of a Roman villa, like many others in the neighborhood. *"Nothing like seeing the big man in charge."*

Adam shot his older brother a look. He didn't have time to deal with any of this. So he took his mother's hand and gave it a quick squeeze. *"Imah, I'm sorry,"* he told her. *"Someone summoned an efreet into the propraetor's hotel. We should be out from underfoot as soon as we've confirmed that there's a second hotel we can go to, and can secure it."* He glanced around. *"In the meantime, I can introduce you to my coworkers, if you like."* He switched to Latin. *"Imah, this is Sigrun Caetia. She's been on Livorus' lictor detail the longest. Sigrun, this is my mother, Abigayil—"*

Sigrun immediately crossed to offer Abigayil a wrist-clasp. Adam watched as his mother's green eyes widened comically for a moment as she looked up at Sigrun, and tentatively accepted the gesture, which Sigrun tended to administer with hail-fellow-well-met vigor, regardless of the recipient. "It is a pleasure to meet you," Sigrun told Abigayil in Latin, managing a faint smile. "You have a lovely home. Our apologies for disarranging it and intruding upon your time."

Adam choked his laugh into a cough, and then added, "While I'm at it, I might as well introduce you to the rest of the family. Sig, this is my brother, Mikayel—" Even as he spoke the words, Adam remembered, belatedly, that his brother had adopted much more conservative ways since marrying Elah; her family was actually quite orthodox in most respects. And he'd gotten deeply involved in their entire social circle over the years, which had altered his views and behaviors.

As such, as Sigrun extended her hand for a wrist-clasp, Mikayel just looked down at the offered appendage, and then back up again at the valkyrie, nodding once. "Nice to meet you," was all Mikayel said, in Latin, and Sigrun let her hand drop, her incipient smile faded, and she shot Adam a sidelong glance.

God. I do not have time for this, was his sole thought as he sighed and was about to move on to introduce Sigrun to his sisters, who still hadn't *left* the dining room area. They were apparently fascinated with watching summoning magic being worked, so Adam decided to skip them for the moment. "My father's in the study, I can introduce him later. That over there is Elah, Mikayel's wife . . . and, ah . . . I have absolutely no idea who you all are," he told the other people crammed into the living room with the propraetor's family, Kanmi's family, and everyone else, "but I'd guess you're neighbors." Adam gave them a slightly apologetic smile, and stayed in Latin to add, "Sorry about earlier. I don't make a habit of introducing myself with a gun in my hands."

His mother actually draped a hand over her eyes for a moment. *"Ah . . . well. We've only just recently been introduced, ourselves,"* she said, awkwardly. *"This is Avishai ben Ilan, his wife Menuha, and their daughter, Nahal."*

Adam nodded at each, briefly, noting in passing that Nahal, the daughter, wore her dark, slightly wavy hair uncovered, and didn't seem to have a wedding ring on any of her fingers. A distant voice at the back of his mind remarked that she was pretty enough—dark eyes, honey-touched olive skin, a heart-shaped face and a pert nose. All of that, however, was lost as suspicion rushed back into his mind. Sudden, inexplicable acquaintanceships, and he was trusting these people around Livorus and all the other protectees? *"What do you mean, you've only recently met?"* he asked, frowning.

"Oh, this is unbelievable," Mikayel groused. *"It's bad enough that I dragged my entire family over here in the middle of the week for your* shidduch *and to meet the prospective bride, but now I have to watch the whole 'look at me' show, too."*

That hit Adam from two different directions at once. He had never really gotten along *well* with his older brother; even as children, doing their schoolwork, memorizing Torah verses, or untangling one of their father's cryptographic exercises, Adam had always been a little bit better than Mikayel, and no matter that his brother was several years his elder. The one time he'd come home on leave from Praetorian work in India, Mikayel had told him bluntly that joining the Guard was just another way in which Adam was *showing off*, somehow. Just like being invited into JDF Special Forces had been, somehow, showing off, as well. Adam had bitten his tongue, and in the spirit of family harmony, walked away, not knowing how to explain to his older brother that their parents' love was not a zero-sum game, that none of their affection for Mikayel was diminished by Adam's accomplishments . . . or that all *he* ever heard about from their mother was how wonderful Mikayel was. How exceptional his life, his wife, his family all were, how *happy* Mikayel was, and why couldn't Adam be just a bit more like his brother?

That was one layer of the irritation searing through him; and that it was the third such comment since walking through the door just made it kerosene atop kindling. The actual match to the fire was the word *shidduch*. Formal matchmaking. His mother had hired a *shadchan*, a professional matchmaker, who'd studied him and his family, and neatly slotted him next to a woman and *her* family, and then his mother had invited them all over to get to know them, to see if the two families might get along . . . and had intended to drop the entire thing in his lap. *Look, see? We found you a wife. Do you like her?*

This, in spite of the fact that he'd told her, repeatedly, *not* to do exactly this. Adam's teeth hurt from clamping them together, and he was dimly aware that there had been at least fifteen seconds of total silence around him. He caught Sigrun looking back and forth in confusion between him and his family. The whole conversation had been in Hebrew, which, of course, Sigrun didn't speak.

"*Imah*," Adam said, very quietly, and still from between clenched teeth. He didn't *dare* speak any louder. If he did, he was going to start shouting, and from there, it would get progressively uglier. "*I am unsure what part of no you did not understand the first three times I told you not, under any circumstances, to engage a matchmaker for me. That I would not, ever, consider an arranged marriage. That I can and will find someone for myself, when I'm ready and I choose to do so.*" In spite of every effort, his voice rose anyway. "*Your friends and their daughter should leave now. I have nothing to say to any of them, and I trust we will not meet again.*" He saw the man's face set in grim lines, and the wife and daughter's expression crumble in humiliation, and he briefly regretted his intemperate words were, but he was too *angry* at the moment to rein it in.

"*You can't tell our mother whom to invite into her own house —* "

"*At the moment, yes I can!*" That actually was a shout. "*I could have had them sent away in the first ten minutes, but didn't, out of nothing more than courtesy and a desire not to embarrass my parents any further. Apparently, no one here has any concern along those lines for me!*"

Dimly, Adam was aware, as his brother stood up to shout at him again, and his mother hastily stepped in between her two sons, that Trennus had moved out of the dining area, eyes afire, literally, as his spirits showed him what they perceived in the distance. Trennus' words were a faint buzz for him, in Latin. "We have a problem," but he was talking to *Sigrun*, though his eyes were on Adam and his family. "I need a minute here."

And then Mikayel was back in Adam's face again. "*Just who do you think you are, little brother? You don't have the right to raise your voice in this house —* "

Sigrun's voice, rising in mild amusement. "Trennus, I'm listening to people shouting in a language I do not speak. Is it a big problem or a small problem? I do not know if we can handle any more big problems today."

"*Who do I think I am?*" Adam dropped from a shout back into a cold, clipped, utterly controlled tone. "*I think I am a Praetorian Guard. I think I am the chief lictor to a propraetor, whose life is in my hands. And I think I don't need any further useless distractions.*"

Trennus again. "My forest-spirit spotted something as she was scouting. It's big, it's heading our way, and she and my other spirit don't recognize it. Neither do I." The summoner pulled Sigrun out of the room, to a window at the front of the house; Adam could just see them out of the corner of his eye through the long hallway, but the situation seemed to be handled, and he still had his older brother approximately two inches from his face.

"*Useless distractions? What, we're worthless to you now, big man? We only have value when you need us for something, huh?*"

The radio at Adam's belt crackled. "*We've got something overhead. Not a plane. Moving like a large bird. Can't get a good read on it.*" That was the voice of one of the Roman lictors they'd placed on rooftop duty.

"*Mikayel, please. Just stop. This is my fault,*" their mother interjected, but that was just more fuel to the fire for Mikayel.

"*No, it's not your fault. It's his fault. He thinks he's better than us. He thinks he's better than everyone —*"

"*Back off. Sit down. Now.*" This was the command tone Adam had learned as an officer in special forces. Pure steel.

Mikayel actually stepped back, and Adam was still staring at him when a hand tapped his shoulder from behind. "What?" he asked in Latin, but didn't turn away.

"Adam, I don't know what the problem here is, but if it's not life-threatening, it needs to end now. We need your mind in the fight," Sigrun informed him, tightly.

Adam's head snapped around, and his brain re-aligned. "What have we got?"

"That," Trennus said, pointing at the front windows. "Whatever it is, it's big, it's flying, and I think it's circling the house right now."

"Powerful," Kanmi added, coming in from the direction of the atrium. "I've been trying to get a read on it. It's not a construct, it's not human, and power's coming off of it in waves."

Adam moved cautiously to a window. "We're talking a summoned creature, then?" *Not a god, right? Just a perfectly ordinary spirit of some sort?*

"I think so," Trennus admitted, as something overhead briefly blotted out the sun. "L . . . the phoenix says it smells *old* to her."

It does. The words slipped into everyone's mind. *It smells of dust and tomb air. Whatever this is, has not walked the earth in millennia.*

"That's . . . comforting." Adam looked down in time to see a massive winged shadow pass over the neighborhood street outside, over the bicycles of the neighborhood children, dropped on their sides at the bottom of gravel drives, when the children had, in the last hour, come home from school to houses probably filled with worried parents peering out their windows at this house. "So we're talking a very powerful summoner, to have pulled this thing up out of time's abyss?"

"Someone with access to old materials, like one of the Magi, possibly. Or, as I've told you before . . . it could have been bound into a storage matrix," Trennus returned, crisply. "All you'd need to do is put an object like that somewhere where someone *else* shattered it . . . atop a partially opened door, like a bucket of water in a stage comedy, would do, if nothing else."

"I'm laughing already," Kanmi said. All four of them watched as the shadow passed by again, this time clearly larger and lower.

"Sig? You think you can use lightning on it, or match it in the air?" Adam asked.

She shrugged, and Adam was, vaguely, aware that half his family was peering in the door, watching and listening. "Won't know till I get a better look, Adam. Besides, I'm not supposed to do that sort of thing in other gods' territory. It's considered rude." Still, the light outside started to dim a little, as if clouds were starting to form. A rarity, that. Rain was almost nonexistent in the region during the summer.

"That didn't stop you in Ponca." Adam's mind was detached, distant, as he stooped and picked up the locked carrying case he'd taken from the car. Unlatched it, and started assembling the assault rifle he'd not actually had to use since leaving the Wall. His hands remembered their jobs well enough, however.

"The god-born there directly challenged me. That's different." Sigrun's voice was empty.

"How about Tenochtitlan?" Kanmi offered, as the shadow passed by again. This time, Adam could hear the wing-beats even through the glass of the windows, as the entire house had gone quiet. The shadow was fainter this time, as the sky faded to gray.

"The high priest drew on power in front of me. Again, a direct challenge."

"He was waving his *fasces* in your face, and you kicked him in it, eh?" Kanmi, again.

"Pretty much."

"You all do have an unhealthy interest in the *fasces* today," Livorus told them, from the door behind them.

None of them turned. "Is there anything I can do?" the propraetor offered.

"It's much harder banishing something without knowing its Name," Trennus said, simply.

"Introduce yourself?" Kanmi offered, without humor.

"Get in touch with the local Praetorians, sir," Trennus glanced back over his shoulder at Livorus. "If this thing was summoned . . . it'll have left residue where it came through the Veil. If it was imprisoned, and the prison was broken, there will be shards. Remnants. Clues. Even a partial Name might let me bind it."

"I can do that." Livorus moved back down the hall, his heels clicking against the wood flooring briskly.

How in god's name did it know we were here? Is this random, or is this targeted? Adam thought, as he snapped the clip of bullets into place in his rifle now. "Everyone needs to get back," he ordered. "Basement. Father's study. A bathing chamber—one without any windows."

There was a pause in the wake of his words, and then the creature they'd only seen the shadow of, till now, landed atop the house across the street . . . and the tile roof there buckled under its weight, causing the creature to lift back off again, and this time land on the chimney, for better support.

Adam's eyes widened. It was a giant, bipedal figure, easily three times his own height, but it bore only a peripheral resemblance to a human. Instead of a mouth, it had mandibles, like a spider, which twitched and moved constantly. Its eyes were large, and eagle-like, as were its massive wings, which, now mantled, still must have spanned at least twenty feet. Dark brown, glossy feathers covered most of its body, and he could see that its hands, which had two thick fingers and a thumb each, had viciously curving talons on them. It shifted atop the chimney, and Adam hissed as he caught sight of an up-turned tail, which looked like a scorpion's, down to the barbed tip. To make matters worse, the creature wore armor, a massive breastplate that looked like . . . tortoiseshell, set with turquoise. "Old-fashioned," Adam said, his voice distant.

"Probably hasn't been out in the fresh air since the Bronze Age." Trennus' voice was just as calm as Adam's.

"Yes," Kanmi said, slowly crackling his knuckles. "We should probably demonstrate why armor isn't much use anymore. Armor is just an opportunity." He smiled, very faintly.

"Don't get cocky," Adam warned. "Sig?"

"Yes?" Deadly calm in her voice now.

"Be rude."

"You're sure? I wouldn't want to offend everyone here."

"I'm sure. Be very, very rude."

"I can do that." Sigrun reached out and opened the window before Kanmi could stop her; electricity visibly arced from the metal frame to her hands, even as the rune-markings under her skin began to glow. "That *tickles*, Kanmi," she informed him.

"Oh, you say that now, with my wife in the next room? When I have to let that one slip by, unanswered? Unfair, valkyrie. Unfair." Even the light humor of the words was a shell now, disguising the fact that they'd all gone into a blank sort of combat fugue. Adam, Kanmi, and Trennus moved to the various other windows in the room, Kanmi unwarding them . . . . and Sigrun held up a hand, calling her spear to her. It shimmered into existence in her hand, and she said, exhaling, "*Nos morituri te salutamus.*"

Sigrun, in truth, loved flying. She'd learned to do it at around the same time as she'd learned to walk, and she couldn't remember a time when she couldn't do it. On the other hand, the only times she ever got to fly were purely for utilitarian purposes. Getting a message to someone more quickly. Surveillance. And, of course, combat. So there was always a rush of joy when she took to the air, followed by grim focus on the task at hand, and today was no exception. She slipped out the window, felt the initial jolt as gravity reached for her . . . and then she simply declined its invitation, spinning away as she felt her ever-present attendant winds burst into life around her, a swirling, living cloak that caressed her skin. Her spear firmly in hand, she heard the creature's bellow of challenge, and she brought the lightning down in a jagged bolt, aiming for its head. Tingle of incipient charge became reality, and the thunder that echoed to life was shattering, rattling every window in the neighborhood. She glanced around, assessing the tactical situation.

In a word? Bad. Houses filled with civilians. Trees. Streetlights — though metal was her friend. Cars in driveways, alleys, and along the edges of the road. Running behind both rows of houses, phone and power lines strung from poles.

The creature raised its head, clearly staggered by the bolt, but it was only very lightly scorched. The mandibles parted again, and that shearing sound, like metal being torn, once again echoed back from the walls around them. Over the radio tucked at her waist, Sigrun could hear Adam's voice, ordering the other lictors who'd been tasked with protecting Poppaea and the children to move to clear the houses of the neighborhood. "Get those people out of here while Caetia has the thing distracted!" Adam snapped.

I can't guarantee how distracted I'm going to keep it, Sigrun thought, and ascended through the air another thirty feet, so that she hovered above the creature, but out of its reach, above the midpoint of the cobbled street, as the first splatters of rain began to fall. "Lightning minimally effective," she called into her radio. "Try something else." She hit the creature again with another bolt of lightning, and heard, for the first time ever outside the range where they'd practiced in Rome, the rapid-fire *bam-bam-bam-bam-bam* of an assault rifle, as Adam entered the fight.

From her angle, she could clearly see the bullets striking the creature, and black blood oozing down its sides as it howled in pain "You're hitting it," Sigrun told Adam over the radio, cautiously hopeful . . . and then the creature leaped off the chimney on which it had perched, like an oversized gargoyle . . . and, keeping its feet together, plunged through the roof, disappearing through the shattering tile as if into quicksand. *Shit.* "Negative target. It's in the house." *Where there are people. Shit, shit, shit.* "Going in after it."

"Bad idea," Kanmi said over the radio, just as Trennus said, "Pull it back out again. Get it on the *ground,* where I can do something to it."

"I'll do my best," Sigrun replied, tucked the radio back on her belt, and dove into the house in the wake of the creature, debris and broken tile hitting her in the face as she flew. This was a *bad* idea, and she knew it, but there wasn't really much she could do about it. There were humans inside. And none of them were apt to heal nearly as well as she could.

She threw one arm up in front of her face to protect her eyes. Floorboard, wallboard, jagged pieces of two-by-fours that made up the under-flooring, all stuck out like jagged talons, scraping her arms and sides as she plunged, headfirst, through the attic, second floor—cold rush of water from a damaged pipe pouring out at her. And then landing on the first floor, feet barely touching down on the tile. *Where is it, where is the damned thing . . . ?*

And then *impact* against her side, throwing her back across a room.

It was a glancing blow, fortunately, and she managed to spin around in the air, landing with her feet *on* the far wall, perpendicular to the ground, knees tucked in a crouch. She looked up, and caught sight of the massive creature. Its wings had surely been what just hit her—they'd unfurled to half their flight length and slapped her aside. The ceiling was twelve feet high, the creature easily another six feet taller than that . . . and it was thus hunched over, snarling, in the middle of a kitchen, its head and shoulders jammed against the swaying, half-fallen kitchen lights. The residents were screaming and running away, scrambling for the front door, even as the creature tore a tall appliance free of the kitchen wall with one hand. *Icebox*, Sigrun thought, reflexively. *No, they're called <u>refrigerators</u> here, heavier—*

The icebox sailed across the house at her, and Sigrun reflexively leaped out of the way, rolling to a halt by a window and coming up, slightly dazed, as the appliance slammed through the wall where she'd just been, punching a hole through it to the outside. She looked at the gap in the wall, swallowed, and thought distantly, *All right, I'm keeping it distracted . . . what's step two? Right. Get it outside again. Probably need to get it angry. Lightning has minimal effect. Let's try cold steel.*

The thoughts flickered, feeling like molasses poured on ice in winter, slow compared to the speed with which her body was already moving. She dove over the top of what had surely been a living room sofa moments ago, and was now mere kindling, and then vaulted back up again, turned, and threw her spear. A longspear like this was not meant for aerodynamic flight or pinpoint accuracy. She therefore aimed at center of mass, and hissed a little as she saw her throw rise too far up, threatening the creature's head, instead.

To her astonishment, the creature moved erratically, and the spear's head sheared into one of the aquiline eyes, and lodging in what might have been the nasal cavity, at about a forty-five degree angle. It gave a cry like tearing metal, and then *charged* her.

Sigrun leaped for the exit that the creature had so considerately made for her in the wall of the living room, bursting back out into open air seconds before the enormous creature tore through wallboard and a stone façade behind her, reaching up with a single huge paw and latching onto her foot. Massive claws tore through her boot, plunging into the flesh of her left ankle and calf. Even if they hadn't penetrated, the crushing force was enough to make bone grind on bone as she choked back a scream, and, caught, she fell forwards, her flight momentum now caught in her ankles, knees, and hips. Spikes of pain jabbed through them, as the joints all threatened to dislocate, and tendons and ligaments protested their treatment.

Shit. Shit, shit, shit. Sigrun regained control of her body and flipped down, calling her spear back to her hand. Leg still held, she tucked in and down, bending in half, and slashed up at the beast's hand with all her considerable strength . . . She felt the steel make contact and tear through resisting flesh and bone, *just* as the creature's scorpion tail arched and flicked up over its own head and stabbed the air *exactly* where her heart had been, moments before.

She felt the air movement over her back as the tail stabbed forward and recoiled, and looked up between her own knees in time to see one droplet of poison weep from its tip, and fall down onto her face, stinging like distilled hatred . . . and then she threw herself backwards again, still in flight, arching and plunging through the air. And promptly ran into the wall of another house with a bone-jarring thump. She could feel the clawed hand that still gripped her ankle with inhuman strength, but it had been torn free of its attendant forearm at least, and the creature, now crouching in the side yard between the two houses, raised its arm to stare at the black-bleeding stump of its wrist, and howled once more.

Inside the ben Emmet household, pandemonium. The single lictor who'd stayed back to guard Poppaea and the rest of the Livorus family was a Nahautl woman. As such, she held a single-shot derringer in one hand, and a knife and a twin of the first derringer rode at her belt as she crouched by the doorway, constantly looking from the room's single window, to the hall, and back again. "Stay back," she told everyone else in the living room. Poppaea's children did not huddle close to their mother; rather, all three of them clustered near one of their pedagogues, a motherly-looking Hellene woman in her forties. Himi and Bodi Eshmunazar, on the other hand, were both trying to scramble into Bastet's lap at the same time, and Mikayel ben Maor and his wife were trying to keep their own children calm. The rest of the ben Emmet family was there, as well, other than the head of house, who was locked in the study with the propraetor.

The entire house shook with another clap of thunder, and the assault rifle, down the hall, began to churn out rounds again, *bam-bam-bam-bam-bam*. The children screamed and covered their ears, and most of the adults winced at the noise, as well. Mikayel edged closer to the door, evidently trying to get a glimpse of what was going on. "They're going to get us all killed. What's going on?" he demanded of the Nahautl guard.

The lictor snorted. "Do you even know who these people *are*?" she shouted, over the sound of another tearing crash. "Livorus only picks the best. Half his lictors have been poached by the Imperator, but he's gone on record as saying he won't *let* Caesarion take any of these four, unless *they* request to be taken. I don't know about the politics, but that says a gods-be-damned *mouthful* to me. Now sit down, shut up, and let me do my job." She turned her back on Mikayel, and crouched once more beside the door, derringer in hand.

In the study, Maor ben Emmet and the propraetor stood near the desk, as Adam's father set up a secure call to the local Praetorian office and to the local *gardia* . . . and stood back, his arms folded across his chest and his eyebrows raised slightly, as Livorus waded into the mess. "Yes. This is Propraetor Antonius Valerius Livorus. So far today, my intended lodgings have been compromised, and my detail is currently under attack by what appears to be a very large demon." The propraetor's voice was completely calm. "No, I will not wait on hold. You will put your superior on the line so that I can provide my recognition codes to someone capable of *recognizing* them. And you will do so now."

A three-second pause, and then the propraetor did, indeed, exchange several recognition codes, before going on, grimly, "Yes. About the large demonic creature currently wreaking havoc in one of your residential neighborhoods . . . . You've had calls to your emergency lines about that? What an extraordinary thing. Yes. It's quite real. Listen to me, very carefully. You might wish to write this down." Livorus paused. "Someone had to have summoned it. If they summoned it, there will be an energy trail, leading directly *here*. Back-trail it, find the source, find the binding circle used to summon it on the ground, and get someone there with a working knowledge of counter-summoning and do something about it." His expression remained completely unruffled as the entire house shook, and the sound of the assault rifle spitting out ammunition started up again. "If it was not summoned, but rather *released* from some form of imprisonment, you will again need to back-trail it to its source. Look for its point of origin. Wherever it first emerged, there will be *something* that does not fit. A piece of ancient pottery, an ancient, broken lamp, a medallion with a shattered gem. There will be writing on this item. In a city this large, and with such a noted university, there will be, I trust, someone capable of *reading* this writing. Put the two things together. I need to know what this creature is, and, if possible, its Name. Yes. I'll hold." Livorus put a hand over the mouthpiece of the phone, and looked at ben Emmet wearily. "Bureaucrats. I find holding their hands as they work through a simple thought-process extraordinarily trying at times, don't you?"

On the desk in front of them, the various lictors' voices came through on the radio that they'd handed to Livorus, all speaking Latin for clarity among the joint forces represented here. Maor recognized his son's voice in and among the others, and watched as Livorus began to tap the side of his fist against the wood of the desk, lightly, but in evident fury, as the battle raged on.

"*Callisuni, Duros, repeat, get off the roofs, you can't do any good up there. Get to the ground and start moving civilians out of the area!*" That was Adam.

"*Caetia's pulled the creature out of the opposite house. Out of range. Caetia, get it back to the street. I need it within sixty feet for anything I can do.*" That, from the Carthaginian.

"*No shot for me, either,*" Adam noted. "*Caetia, fall back, and give me status.*"

"*Moving. Lightning largely ineffective. Mostly irritates it. Cold iron seems to work. Keep shooting.*" The Cimbri woman's voice was strained.

"*What in the Morrigan's name is attached to your leg?*" That, from the big Pict, sounding rattled.

"*Its claws. I cut its hand off above the wrist, but it's . . . persistent.*" A pause. "*I'm at street center. Here it comes.*" No terror. No fear. Just . . . plain, flat, numb words.

Livorus hit the desk again, harder, one hand still over the mouthpiece of his phone, and began to curse, a quiet, steady, heart-felt string of invective. "I don't suppose," he said, after running out of breath, "that I could trouble you to look in my luggage for my old legion sword? I never actually go anywhere without it. I just haven't had to use it in a number of years."

Ben Emmet stared at the man for a long moment. "You're not

going to go out there." It wasn't quite a question.

"No. Battles are best fought by the young, and if I went out there, I would be in the way . . . or, quite likely, the beast's target. Still, just holding it in my hand would be a comfort right now." Livorus paused, and uncovered the mouthpiece. "Yes, I'm still holding."

Adam swore internally as Sigrun pulled back, landing in the middle of the road. Making herself bait. She was actually leaning, heavily, on her spear, her left foot raised off the ground, with, as Trennus had pointed out, a huge paw still attached. From his vantage point, he'd seen the neighbors from across the street run out their front door seconds before the refrigerator had come out the wall of the house and into the right side-yard, where it had slammed into the neighboring house and burst open, sending fruit, vegetables, and covered ceramic dishes everywhere. He could see Callisuni and Duros, dropping down from their perches, Callisuni across the street, trying to get people to move out of their houses and *away* from the area, but terrifyingly close to the enormous creature as it stomped after Sigrun. The space between the houses was simply too cramped to allow it to unfurl its wings and take flight. *Thank god.* Duros, off to Adam's right, was on this side of the street. "I've got a shot on the creature," Adam said, his voice calm. "Taking it." He wasn't sure what good it was doing, but Sigrun said that cold iron was at least having an effect on the creature, and he needed to give her all the help he could. The rifle recoiled into his shoulder, and he could see the creature rock back for a moment . . . but then it just kept moving forward, steps increasing in speed. It was so heavy that every single tread actually shook the ground, and wingspan or no, Adam couldn't fathom how the beast could fly. *Magic. Always magic.* He adjusted, and fired another series of rounds in a tight cluster, aiming for the armored chest, wanting to test just how strong what looked like *tortoiseshell* really could be. "Armor's holding," he reported, after looking through his scope. "Probably enchanted. Target head and limbs, if you're using a gun." He followed his own advice, lifting his gun slightly, and firing again, this time right for the creature's head . . . and it reeled back, throwing an arm in front of its face. *Got your attention, did I?*

The creature stormed forward another couple of steps, to where the neighbors' Tsunam Mark 7 was parked in their gravel driveway, and actually stomped a foot on the car's trunk, and *tipped* it back, dropping into a crouch behind it. Adam fired another burst of rounds at the creature behind its improvised shield, and said into the radio, tightly, "Target is adapting to modern conditions. Callisuni, it's too damned close to you. Get the civilians out of there, and run."

"*Civilians are away. I have a shot on it from behind. I've got a fireball round in this derringer. Taking it.*" The Gaul's voice was very calm.

"No, damn it, don't, let it stay on Caetia!"

The Gaul took his single shot from the neighbors' front porch, and the round lit up like a falling star as it shot towards the demon . . . and then the creature screamed, stood, holding the car in its one good hand . . . and threw the vehicle, like an Olympic athlete hurling a hammer, right at the Gallic lictor. Adam shouted something incoherent, and opened fire again, even as lightning came down once more . . . but the car was already in flight, and slammed, full-force, into Callisuni, taking out the lictor and the porch's support pillars, too. The civilians, who were running away, heard the noise, turned to look . . . and stood, as if rooted in place with terror, as the beast lifted its head to howl once more.

"Couldn't you stop it?" Adam shouted in Kanmi's direction.

"No. Too far." There was anger and anguish mixed in Kanmi's tone, but tightly, even rigidly suppressed at the moment. "It's like trying to knit with two needles at the ends of sixty-foot ropes. I need it in range." The sorcerer opened his window, and started to duck out through it, and Adam reached out a hand and jerked him back.

"Stay here. Caetia, pull that damned thing back. I'm going after the civilians. Duros, keep the ones on this side of the street *moving*. Don't let them look back."

"I'm going down, too," Trennus said, tightly. "I've got to start prepping a circle. Might be able to slow it down, or bind it, even if I can't banish the damned thing."

Adam opened the weapons case at his feet and pulled out several grenades on a strap, tossing them over his shoulder. He wasn't sure he wanted to get close enough to use the damned things, given what had just happened to Callisuni, but it paid to be prepared. Then he opened his second-story window and dropped down onto the slanting roof of the first story, and then slid and slipped his way to the edge, before sliding his weapon on its strap, to his back and dropping down. He hung by his fingertips from the edge of the roof for a moment, before dropping and landing in a crouch. Trennus dropped beside him, seconds later, and they both took cover behind a parked car, for a moment. Adam offered Trennus his .45, and Trennus held up his hands, palms out, refusing. "I have no idea how to use that thing. I'll hit Sigrun with it."

"Can you distract it?"

"Not without tapping that ley-line."

"Do it." Adam popped up from behind the trunk of the car, and took a couple of shots at the creature, which was already moving away from the house and towards Sigrun, who remained, invitingly, at the middle of the street, shouting challenges at it in Cimbric and pulling down lightning on its head . . . usually without any noticeable effect, beyond light singeing. His eyes widened slightly as it kicked over a light post, the metal bending with a shriek . . . and then stooped to pick it up. "Caetia, get out of there."

"It's not close enough yet," she returned, over the radio. "Esh and Matru need it closer? I'm *bringing* it closer."

"Sig, it's going to eat you alive. Move!" Adam fired several more times, in rapid, controlled bursts, but couldn't *stop* the creature as it lifted the light pole in one hand; the pole itself wasn't all that much taller than it was, itself . . . took a step forward . . . and lightning sizzled down into the *pole* this time.

That hurt it. The metal conducted the electricity that much more effectively than a direct hit, and more of it, apparently. The beast howled in agony. "Good one, Sig!" Adam shouted . . . and then the beast unlocked from its paralysis and swung the blisteringly hot pole in a wide arc, right at Sigrun herself. *Oh, harah . . . .*

Sigrun registered the impact, but reality went away for her, for a moment or three. She never remembered sailing through the air like a ragdoll hit by a club. She never even remembered slamming, back-first, into the fire hydrant across the street. All she remembered, was opening her eyes, and seeing clouds above. Rain pouring down at the same time as seeing water geyser upwards in a white line and stream back down again, spraying her face and body. And *then* the pain hit, and her vision skewed as her body tried to pull her back down into oblivion once more. She panted, shallowly, as pain stabbed in from all directions; her left ribs were a mass of agony, surely broken; her spine and right ribs, almost as bad. Sigrun reached out her right hand, and called her spear back to her. Leaned her head against the hydrant, which was still pouring fluid up into the sky, like a waterfall crazily in reverse. For a moment, it was hard to understand what was up, and what was down. Then the hulking creature moved into her field of vision, its huge wings lifting. Blocking her view of everything else. Lifting the lamppost once more.

Sigrun concentrated, hard, on trying to *heal* . . . and on timing the moment at which she'd need to fly. If she even *could.*

Over the radio, inside the study, as Livorus stood, still on hold, clear, sharp words rattled out in between crackles of static. *"Caetia's down."* The Carthaginian's voice, that.

"Is she dead?" That, from the Pict.

"She's moving." Adam, voice hard. Maor ben Emmet raised his head. There was cold, clear professionalism in that voice, but also a note he'd never heard in his son's tones before.

"Fucker hit her pretty hard. Had to have thrown her thirty, forty feet, right into that hydrant. Anyone else would be dead right now." The Carthaginian again.

Livorus, for his part, hit the desk with the side of his fist so hard, that everything on it jumped. But his voice stayed absolutely calm as he spoke into the mouthpiece. "Yes. I'm still holding. Tell your people to get a move on. I've got one dead and one injured so far here. No. Don't send emergency response vehicles till I give the word that it's clear. Unless you have several dozen people with assault rifles to protect your paramedics, I cannot guarantee their safety. Is that clear?"

Back outside, Adam snapped into his radio, "I trust that's close enough for you now?" and ran for Sigrun, dropping down by her to fire on the creature again. *Have to keep it off her, and stop it from pursuing any of the civilians down this east side of the street. Not that it seems interested in them for the moment.*

"Oh yes," Kanmi said, from the window of the house, his tone fiercely delighted. "And people have finally given me things to work with. Even better."

Until this moment, the only forces at work in this battle had been a few spatters of rain, some lightning—handy, but the beast seemed to largely ignore it—kinetic force, from the creature's punches and throws—inertia, and gravity. All useful, in their way, but they'd all been at the periphery of Kanmi's current range. Now, however, there was a metal pole right in the center of his reach, and it was hot from the direct lightning strike, though, again, the incarnated spirit seemed to be ignoring the heat. There was water exploding upwards from the geyser, as well as all the rain. Everything—*everything*—was a possibility for Kanmi. So long as he had a starting point. And at the moment, he had that, *and* his fellow lictors were providing distractions for him. So he slipped out his own window and dropped down over the edge, briefly reducing the effect of gravity on his mass . . . probably the hardest skill he'd ever learned . . . and ran for the cover of a nearby tree. "All right, you lumbering antiquity," he told the creature, quietly. "Let's see what you can do."

He held up a hand, palm out, and then twisted it around with a decisive snap, setting up the construct in his head. Sorcerers always started with words and gestures. At his level, the words or the gesture could be dropped, and he was looking forward to, eventually, being good enough to do without *either* . . . but that might take a very long time. The more powerful the effect you wanted to produce, the more *assistance* was needed, with words or gestures, batteries, circuits, and whatnot. This? This was a simple effect, relatively speaking. There was already heat in the metal of the pole as the creature swung it back to slam it once more at Sigrun. All he needed to do was increase the heat, and *bend*. There was already an incipient curve in the metal as it whipped around towards the Cimbric woman . . . Kanmi encouraged the flex and the heat. Hastened it. And wrapped what was now red-hot metal around the demon in a glowing red coil.

The creature had been stepping forward, and, caught by surprise, stumbled. Screamed in pain. Kanmi grinned and pulled all the heat out of the metal, leaving just enough to ensure it wouldn't turn instantly brittle, and sent it, with a minor loss, directly into the creature's tortoiseshell armor. *It might resist cold iron and bullets fairly well, but let's see if it burns, shall we?*

Trennus, in the meantime, had realized that he needed to get the damned thing away from Sigrun, and Adam, who'd moved to stand over her, gun in hand. He moved west, out of cover, and looked around for somewhere to draw his binding circle. *You have got to be kidding me. Stone, gravel, cobbles, more stone. And water everywhere. Can't use chalk. Blood will wash away. What a wonderful location. I really don't want this thing smudging a line and breaking free.* He pointed down at the cobbled street, tugged on ley energies in the vicinity, and cut the stone with raw power, tracing the outer line of his circle, tying it at the end with a figure-eight knot, symbolizing infinity. The inner markings formed almost as quickly, but he was, deliberately, leaving the very center of the wide, twenty-foot diameter circle empty, for the moment. "Try to pull him my way," Trennus said into the radio. "Esh?"

"*You're going to try to wrestle with this thing?*" Adam's voice cut in. "*Matru, you might not have noticed, but it's <u>bigger</u> than you are.*"

"Size isn't all that relevant in this."

"*Keep telling yourself that,*" Kanmi cut in.

"Can you turn it towards me?"

"*Sorry. All I've got is damaging stuff to work with at the moment, not herding. Have your spirits lift their skirts. It's an apotropaic gesture. Better yet, lift your own, Pict.*"

"You're so *helpful.*" Kanmi was, technically, correct. The reason why Livorus' youngest son wore a *fascinus* was, in essence, to turn away bad spirits. Just as technically, when a statue of Aphroditus lifted her skirts to show her comingled genitals, it was an echo of rituals in which menstruating women had once gone out into the fields, lifting their skirts to, in theory, drive off evil spirits. The underlying concept was, more or less, that sexuality, fertility, generativity were powerful forces, even in human hands, and could be wielded against spirits. And when a woman bled, she was at the height of her spiritual power . . . or at least, was in tune with the forces of the waning moon, of darkness, and could, theoretically, tame malefic spirits, or turn them away. It was all *very* old magic, magic so old it wasn't really magic any more . . . but Trennus was aware of it all, and aware, too, that in this part of the world, as with the nomadic tribes who called themselves Romany, when a woman bled, she was considered impure, and dangerous, that she wasn't to touch or to be touched, until she was clean once more. What was powerful and useful in one region, was dangerous and to be avoided in another, and it generally meant that the cultural divide was sometimes a cultural cliff.

That was all at the back of Trennus' mind, but none of it was any real *use* at the moment. He crouched in his binding circle, his hair wet and in tangles over his back, and whispered, "Lassair?"

Yes?

Get his attention, please.

That sounds like a very bad idea.

I've had better. Pull him here, into the circle.

Give me a moment. He's . . . very angry at Stormborn.

Adam stared up at the advancing creature, leaned down, and grabbed Sigrun, sliding an arm under one armpit and hooking around so that his wrist locked under the other, hauling her back, while trying to still aim and fire, using her shoulder as a prop for the gun. Sigrun actually yelped and told him "Don't pull me, don't pull me!" White light *poured* out of her, making her unbearably bright to look at.

"Have to get you to cover—" Adam hauled on her, and pulled her into the side-yard of his parents' house, where all the various vehicles of the motorcade had been parked, and, getting her behind one of them, rose up to fire again, just as the massive creature struggled, surged, and shattered the metal bonds that Kanmi had wrapped around it, and clawed the armor it wore off of its body. There was a horrible smell of burning flesh in the air, and it threw the armor aside, where it hit a tree . . . and the tree went up in flames, instantly.

For all of that, it was looking right at Adam at the moment, one eye missing, one hand missing, burns and scorch marks and bullet holes, and still, horribly, alive. *No armor. Let's see if your chest is any more vulnerable than your head.* Adam raised his gun and went to full automatic on the rifle, continuous stream of fire, even as the creature picked up one of the cars at the foot of the drive. used it as a shield . . . and then it stepped forward, ponderously. Bowed, almost comically, tucking its head . . . and the stinger lashed out, slamming through the glass windows of the car, and Adam threw himself backwards, the barbed tip missing his heart by scant inches.

Kanmi, for his part, grimaced and looked at the geyser of water behind the creature. He could *probably* render it into hydrogen and oxygen, and there was more than enough ambient heat for him to focus to light the hydrogen . . . but he wouldn't be able to control or contain the explosion. It could hit ben Maor and Caetia, or level half the houses on the block. *No good.*

"Back it up, ben Maor," he called into the radio. "Just keep firing. I'll increase the force of the bullets' impacts."

"*It's got a car, Esh.*"

"Yes, it does. I'll take care of that."

"*You better.*" Fear in ben Maor's voice, and for a damned good reason.

Kanmi was close enough this time. Twenty feet, not over sixty. As the beast hurled the car directly at Adam and Sigrun, Kanmi *caught* it. Robbed it of all its inertia, making it drop to the ground, and redirected just the raw force back at the creature, concentrating it into a small square area of its body, like a punch. Kanmi slapped his own knuckles into his opposite palm, and watched in satisfaction as the blow snapped the creature's mandibles.

———

Inside, Livorus told the person on the other end of the phone line, "Slow down. Spell it phonetically. *Iota. Sigma. Tau.*" He wrote each letter down on a scrap of foolscap, with great care.

———

Outside, Sigrun staggered back to her feet. Adam, seeing the damaged mandibles, gaping wide, had safed his rifle and let it dangle on its strap, reaching now, instead, for the grenades he'd been carrying. "Esh? Fire in the hole. Improve my aim?"

"I can only work with what I'm given, ben Maor. Throw."

Adam pulled the pin and threw. He'd always had very good aim with these, and he ducked, spun, and pulled Sigrun back down with him, as he saw the grenade land in the gaping, screaming, broken maw. The explosive force made the car lurch into their spines, and sent shattered glass flying everywhere, cutting open the back of his neck. Adam cautiously turned to peer around the car once more.

It still loomed there like a figure out of nightmare. The entire bottom of its skull was a smoking ruin. It had no mandibles, and only one eye and one hand left, and it *still stood*, in defiance of every rational thought. "My god," Adam said. "What do we have to do to *kill* this thing?"

"We probably can't kill it," Trennus said, over the radio. *"We need to* bind *it."*

Livorus padded out into the body of the house, stepping over broken china knickknacks knocked from shelves, nodded to the lictor who was keeping everyone safely back in the living room . . . and stuck his head out one of the front windows. "Matrugena!" he bellowed, in a stentorian tone that could have been heard across a parade ground. "It is something called a *pazuzu*. It was considered a demigod or a demon of the night winds. Its realms were filth, poison, and disease. Its Name is *Istafa'n.*"

The creature's head turned. It looked directly at Livorus, and its real target in sight, and its *Name* on Livorus' lips, it dropped everything to charge for the house, mindless and enraged.

Two things happened at once. A living pillar of fire leaped up under its feet as Lassair exploded to life, catching and tangling the beast . . . and Sigrun, healed enough to move, at least a bit, took to the air and hit the creature like a living bullet, catching it around its ravaged head and neck and hauling it to the ground with a resounding impact. "Could use . . . a little . . . help here . . ." Sigrun managed. Wounded or not, it still outweighed her by over two thousand pounds, and it reached up with its one remaining clawed hand and latched onto her arm, squeezing. "Little help!" Sigrun repeated, and managed to get to her feet, hauling back.

Trennus, make the ground lift! Lassair's thought cut through everyone's minds, and Trennus, still crouched in his binding circle, like a spider in a web, grinned. Ley-energies rippled out, and the street itself undulated like a cat arching its back, forming a hill. A wet, slick slope, with water pouring down both sides, and Sigrun yanked at the behemoth that had clamped down on her arm, and was trying to rake the flesh from her bones, struggling to pull it down the hill. *Emberstone, help her!*

"On it," Kanmi muttered, and, gritting his teeth, decreased local friction under the creature's body. Decreased gravity's effect on its mass. He didn't have any *force* to work with at the moment, besides Sigrun's, so he increased that, as best he could, and shouted, "Fly, Caetia, you have more force to work with that way!"

"I do that, and I'm going to lose an arm, Esh!"

"Just do it! We all know you heal quickly."

Sigrun swore, and threw herself into flight. She could feel additional energies boosting her own, and realized what Kanmi was doing, even as she hauled the creature across the lines of Trennus' binding circle. Blood was pouring down her arm freely, and it was not unlike riding an agitated bull as the creature heaved and struggled and fought. "Is just its Name going to be enough?" she shouted, even as Trennus moved in, wrapping his arms around the other side of the creature, forcing its head down to the ground.

Dimly, she realized that the Pict's hands were bloody, and had just enough time to wonder *why*, before the ground underfoot shifted from stone to mud. "No," Trennus called back. "Need it in the mud, Sigrun. Earth binding."

She didn't question it. Just did, exhaustedly, what she could do, and the two of them, working together, heaved and fought and forced the creature's head down into the mud. Her blood poured freely down her right arm, to the ground, mingling with the earth and the water there . . . which, under Trennus' command, rippled and flowed up and along the massive body. "This is working better than I thought," Trennus gritted out, and then the mud *froze.* Solidified. He raised his bloody hands, both of them clearly slashed open, and brought them together in a resounding slap . . . .and said one word. "*Istafa'n.*"

What was now a statue of the creature began to contract. Compress. Heat rose from it as Trennus continued to mutter, and runes began to incise themselves across the surface. Words of warning in a dozen languages, and the creature's Name, over and over. *Istafa'n. Pazuzu. Demon of filth. Dangerous and bound.*

Sigrun stood there swaying, staring at the statue, then at the ground, at her own blood, and then at Trennus again. "Trennus . . . ."

"Yes?" He looked up from his work as the rain began to abate, and Kanmi and Adam began to, warily, walk towards them. Kanmi went so far as to prod the statue at the center of the binding circle, as if looking for cracks.

"You blood-bound it."

"Had to. I could bind it to the circle with its Name. But I didn't have a prepared object. I had to create the prison with ley, and I needed enough power to bind it to the prison." Trennus looked down at his bleeding hands, just as Lassair, in her phoenix form, landed on his damp shoulder with a sizzling hiss.

"Trennus . . ." Sigrun wanted to shout, but she was just too damned tired and still in too much pain. Her leg hurt, badly enough that now that the adrenaline flow was reduced, she couldn't stand on it. Her arm ached. Her ribs stabbed her every time she breathed. Her spine held a dull, grating agony. *But at least none of these are burns. Burns aren't a clean kind of pain at all.* "I bled on the ground, too. My blood was in that binding." She wearily called her spear back over to her, so that she'd have something to lean on, like a staff, and got the weight off her leg.

His head jerked up, and he swore. Viciously. "Oh, gods. Sigrun, I'm *sorry*."

Adam raised a hand as the four of them turned inward, forming a circle. "For those of us who *didn't* apprentice in magic? Pretend I know nothing on the subject, and explain. Use small words." He held his fingers up, about an inch apart.

Trennus opened and closed his bleeding hands. "Blood binds. What you bind, you're bound *to*. It's a rope that goes both ways." He shook his head. "Someone *could* break the statue. That would unseal it, and the creature would come after whichever of us happened to be closest. Failing that . . . our descendants. It would smell our kin, from over hundreds of miles. It would *know* them."

"DNA," Adam said, his voice empty.

"Yes. Admittedly, whoever performed the binding has priority." Trennus rubbed his face. "If we're alive when it happens, it'll come for us, not our kin."

But you are mortal, Trennus. Stormborn is not, at least, not quite. Her life is likely to be very long, indeed, and you believe you have made of her a target, for all of it? Lassair's tone was concerned.

"I'll be very careful crossing the street." Trennus grimaced. "And we'll sink this thing in salt water. Deepest part of the Mediterranean we can find. That way, even if, gods forbid, some ship drops an anchor and breaks the statue . . . the salt water will be a buffer. It won't wake up. It won't come looking for us." He reached out, and actually, very carefully, put his arms around Sigrun. "I promise, I *will* not let this bounce back on you." He grimaced again, his eyes wretched. "I wondered where the extra energy was coming from."

Adam shifted, irritation plain in his expression. "You'd better *not* let it bounce back on her. Accidents happen, and I know it, but for *god's sake*, Trennus . . . ."

"I know. I'll make it right." Trennus looked at Sigrun and Adam. "I never make bargains I don't intend to keep. You know that."

Sigrun nodded, and Kanmi, looking around as the rain finally died to a light mist, said, dryly . . . and very quietly, "I think we took out an . . . *entity* with less trouble than this, last year."

The god was greatly weakened. This ancient . . . demigod . . . was not. He had been captive for over three thousand years, nursing his hate. Lassair's tone was definite as she peered at them all from her avian eyes. *The strength of his hate was far more powerful than anything I could muster. He had memories that I could touch, however, as you bound him. Memories of an army. Bronze spears, tearing at his flesh. Bronze-tipped arrows. A summoner of great power, a prepared vessel, a pot made of common clay, but his <u>Name</u> upon it, in letters baked in fire and prepared in blood.*

They spilled his blood on the sand, and he took three dozen of their lives that day, but they had another spirit with them. One the likes of which I have never seen. The spirit of air and poison could not see it, not with Veil senses. Lassair's voice was terrified. *A spirit whose name was inscribed on a cuneiform* *tablet, bound there in blood, just as they sought to bind the <u>pazuzu</u>. They gave the tablet to their greatest warrior and told him that he might have to be their sacrifice. And when he fell at the spirit's hands, and lay there, broken and bleeding, he took the tablet out from under his armor, with bleeding hands, and he spoke the word written there . . . and the spirit came.* Her voice held horror. *Its name was not a Name. It was <u>Gevah</u>.*

"Mountain," Adam translated, feeling odd. It was a common enough word in Hebrew.

It rose up from the clay and the blood around the fallen warrior's body. The body was repaired, but the essence of the human . . . the <u>pazuzu</u> could not see his spirit in Veil sight, as if he were utterly bound to some god. The body rose up again, this time twice the height of a mortal man, and made of stone, the bones of the earth. His fists had become boulders. Lassair paused. *And so they fought, until the <u>pazuzu</u> was beaten . . . and Gevah himself lay dying on the ground. The priests took the blood and lives already spilled that day, and bound the beast with their sacrifice. His last sight in this world gave him satisfaction . . . the creature of stone was crumbling into dust. Perhaps the <u>pazuzu</u> slew this other spirit, in truth. I do not know. Then the <u>pazuzu</u> only knew darkness and hatred for an eternity, until he <u>awoke</u> and smelled blood. Not the blood of those who had bound him. That has grown faint over the centuries. But blood, human blood, from a . . . a body-covering . . . that had been used to shroud his prison. And smelling it, he hungered, and in hunger, he hunted. He understood that the price of his release was to kill this man. The one to whom you are bound, Trennus.*

"Livorus," Trennus muttered, and shrugged off his shirt, disturbing the phoenix on his shoulder as he did, so he'd have something with which to bind his bleeding hands . . . and then they all turned. Looked at the wreckage around them.

"Callisuni?" Adam asked, wincing and pointing across the street at the neighboring house's front porch.

Sigrun leaned on her spear and shook her head. "It was almost instant," she said.

"You're sure?" Adam asked.

"I can always tell when a wound's mortal. I don't think he had time to feel it when the car hit him." The words limped out, empty consolation that they were.

"All right. Let's get you inside. Get your leg and Tren's hands looked at. And then figure out what we do next."

Chapter XII: Subversions

The history of modern aviation begins with hot air balloons, which were first used as signaling devices in Qin between 264 and 324 AC. While this innovation was known in the West after the circumnavigation of the globe by Leif Dalgaard in 1000 AC made the opening of ocean-based trade routes to Qin and Nippon possible, it wasn't until 1607 AC that the first tethered hot air balloon flight was displayed at an exhibition at the Imperial Palace in Rome . . . almost sixty years after the locomotive was first demonstrated. The first untethered manned hot air balloon flight occurred, again, in Rome, in 1645, piloted by a pair of Gauls, the Locinna brothers.

These balloons were initially seen as novelty items that allowed the common man the gift of flight enjoyed by birds, sorcerers, and some god-born. Early sorcerers and many priests actually opposed them. Documents written in the period suggested that sorcerers believed that the skies would soon be as crowded as a market square, and that this could not be allowed for a mere fancy. Priests of the period stated that flight was a gift from the gods, and should not be placed in mundane hands.

Practical applications were slow to be seen. Hot air balloons were large, visible, and at the mercy of the winds. Using them for surveillance over Domitanus' Wall was primarily a Judean innovation, as they had no summoners who could call spirits for surveillance flights or god-born who could engage in aerial reconnaissance. The balloons were used, once or twice, for high-level aerial bombing attempts. They were, however, far too visible and slow-moving to be truly effective. Persia's cannons could tear them from the sky, negating the need for expensive bargains between Persian magi and their djinn.

The first manned, fixed-wing flight occurred in 1825 AC, just outside of Novo Trier, and was conducted by Ursus and Wystan Abered, two brothers from a large ship-building family. Their goal was to out-compete other companies that moved goods and people over the northern Sea of Atlas. To do so, they decided to try to build ships of the air. After several notable failures with hot air balloons, they addressed most of their efforts to fixed-wing, heavier-than-air craft. The result was the first biplane.

Adoption was swift for cargo and passenger use, but it took seeing airplanes used for bombing runs during the 1855 Caspian Crisis for the rest of the world to see the military utility of airplanes. Judean bombers lifted off from airfields outside of Judea and traveled into Mongol territory, bombing seaports held by the Khanate there, and returning to Judea on a single tank of chemical fuel. Persia objected to their airspace being violated, naturally. However, their slow-moving ground-based artillery was ineffectual against the speedy bombers, leaving Persia to voice its objections solely with djinni and efreeti. Thus, after that notable success, the Roman Empire began building its own fixed-wing aircraft.

By way of comparison, the helicopter is a peculiarly Judean invention, the first wide-production model being developed in Judea in 1875 AC. It has, however, been heavily adopted for use in the forested wilds of Raccia and Nova Germania, especially for the evacuation of injured people to medical facilities and dealing with wildfires. Judean Defense Forces use helicopters as troop transports and mobile weapon platforms, as well.

The ornithopter, however, was developed in the Persian Empire in 1895 AC as an alternative means of air travel, and has been broadly adopted and adapted by India, Qin, Mongolia, and parts of the Quechan and Tawantinsuyan regions of the Roman Empire. In Persia and Mongolia, the ornithopters are powered by compelled, enslaved spirits; in Qin and other areas, ley-powered engines are used to give the beating wings their motive force. The ornithopter had superior mobility compared to most fixed-wing aircraft . . . until the development of the jet turbine in 1915 AC. This innovation, the product of a Hellene-Judean engineering team, once more raised the stakes in the continuing technomagical race . . . .

— Wulfric Atargiet, A Brief History of Manned Flight, pp. 12-13. Carlfugol Press, Cimbri-on-the-Caestus, Nova Germania, 1934 AC.

Maius 6, 1955 AC

In the distance, sirens began to wail, echoing back off of houses as the *gardia* cars began to approach from the highway. "Duros?" Adam called into the radio.

"Copy, ben Maor. Civilians are secure, I'm coming back up to check on Callisuni."

"You can check, but Caetia says he's gone."

"Damnit. Well, she'd know, wouldn't she?" The Hellene's words were bleak. *"Coming back to the house, then."*

Adam got Sigrun's left arm over his shoulder, all too aware of the muffled grunt of pain as he did so. "You, ah, need to do anything for Callisuni?" he asked, tentatively. Valkyrie did mean, technically, *chooser of the slain.*

She shook her head, limping forward with his assistance. "He was a Gaul, and the wound was instantly mortal. Even if he were a Goth, Jute, or Frisian, the best I could do now is to bear witness." She sighed. "As we all will."

Adam helped her toward the house, aware that behind every intact window in the neighborhood, curtains were twitching as people *watched.* "You always know when it's a mortal wound?"

"I always know when someone's going to *die,*" she corrected, hissing under her breath as he helped her up the steps. The demon's claws were still *embedded* in her ankle, the hand itself still wrapped around her calf, though the muscles had gone limp now. "Disease, poison, wound. Doesn't matter. I know when there's no hope left."

"That sounds . . . appalling." Adam opened the front door, nodded to Livorus, who stood just inside the hall, and was waving them each in.

A firm wrist-clasp from the propraetor, and a clap on the shoulder. "Damned good work," Livorus murmured. "Shame about Callisuni."

"He died bravely," Adam said. "Unnecessarily, but bravely. I told him not to take the shot, and he did it anyway." That one was going to keep him up nights, he knew.

"I'll note the former, but not the latter, in my letter to his family," Livorus said, and lightly lifted Sigrun's chin with his knuckles. "You're all right, my dear?"

"I'll be fine," she replied, sounding weary. "I heal from the most life-threatening wound to the least. Though the bones are knitting far more quickly than I'd have thought. The cartilage around them, though . . . ?" She paused. "I feel as if someone hit me with a lamppost."

"Someone *did* hit you with a lamppost," Kanmi noted from behind them, as Adam helped her into the dining room, looked at the binding circle on the floor, sighed, and lifted her onto the table, which had been pushed up against the wall. The few place settings toppled out of the way as he settled her into place.

"Oh, yes, that's right," Sigrun said, leaning back with a muffled groan. "Mystery solved."

Interested eyes peered around the frames of the two doors that led into the dining room, one on each side of the room. Peripheral awareness of all the faces: his family, the propraetor's family, Kanmi's family, guests . . . sirens in the distance, getting louder . . . mutters in Hebrew and Latin. His mother, bolting for the emergency medical kit in the bathroom, and coming back with it. "I'm a trauma nurse, let me through . . . ." His brother's soft comment, in Latin, "Perhaps she shouldn't be in combat, if she's this bad at it . . . ."

"No, good lady, give me the kit," Livorus told Abigayil, instantly, taking it from her hands. "We're all quite well here, I suspect."

Trennus trudged into the room last, scraps of his shirt tied around his hands for the moment, soaking wet and wearing little besides a kilt and boots. He moved into the dining room, pressing past Adam's two younger sisters. "We're going to need to burn the claw," he said, as Lassair's phoenix-shape leaped off his shoulder and fluttered to land on the table beside Sigrun. "Not a souvenir any of us want to keep. Sigrun, I'll get you some dry clothes while I'm digging for mine, all right?"

"Let me fix your hands first," Sigrun said, reaching for Tren's wrists. There was a single bloody streak on her left cheek, and the open wounds on her arm had scabbed over already. White rune-light began to pour out of her, and the wound on her arm went from raw, livid weals of red to thinner, pinker lines. She managed to raise her eyebrows, humor shining through the pain. "I don't want your blood all over my clothes."

"You worry about *you* right now." Trennus told her firmly. "The phoenix can take care of these little bumps and bruises, if I ask her nicely." He patted her shoulder with one bandaged hand, winced, and left the room, pushing past the crowd at the doors once more.

Sigrun muffled a curse as Adam lifted her foot in gentle hands and began to tug, gently at the claws of the demon's paw. "I think it's embedded in the bone, Adam. The skin and muscle just healed around it." She latched onto the edge of the table and swore, viciously, in her native language. "Much the reason why when I have been shot before, I have had the ball extracted before the healing can begin. Gods . . . please, don't pull." That, from between clenched teeth. "You're going to have to cut the skin open."

Adam shook his head. Unlike every other wound he'd ever seen her take, this one was red, inflamed, and swollen. "Looks like an infection," he told Livorus, who'd just moved over to look, kit in hand, while Abigayil hovered nearby, uncertainly, *staring* at them all.

"Poison, I think, is more likely. That is what that demon reigned over, apparently. Disease, poison, filth." Livorus opened the kit, and extracted a scalpel. "You generally aren't subject to poisons or disease, are you, my dear?"

"No, sir. This . . . is probably magic. Extract the claw, and everything should heal well."

Livorus held up the scalpel, fresh from its package, and asked, calmly, "Do you want something for the pain, my dear?"

Adam already knew what the answer was going to be, and simply unbuckled his belt, handing her the leather strap. "No," Sigrun replied, leaning her head back against the wall and looking up at the ceiling. "No blood of the poppy for me. It takes too much to do any good, and it dissipates too rapidly." She looked back down, and gave Livorus a pained smile. "As a side effect, I have never been drunk, either."

"No great loss, my dear. I find that the more someone has had to drink, the less interesting they become. Anyone who has to shield themselves from the harsh light of reality with a comforting haze of alcohol is a coward." Livorus knelt, and said, "Matrugena?"

"Here, sir." Trennus pushed his way back into the room, pulling a fresh shirt over his wet hair, his kilt still dripping all over the floor. He tossed Sigrun's bag down beside the table.

"Your hands are well enough to hold our valkyrie down?"

Trennus looked at his hands, grimaced, and beckoned to Lassair, who hopped over, landing on his forearm, and stroked her head along his palms. "Should be, sir. My, ah, spirit here . . . she fixed my knee in Nahautl pretty well, and these were just surface cuts." The phoenix fluttered up now, landing on the room's chandelier, and preened, her golden light outshining the electric candles there, even as the fixture rocked precipitously.

I can assist with Stormborn's healing, if she will accept my aid, as well . . . . but I think that once the claw has been removed, that her flesh will heal as it always has. Lassair's rich mental voice spilled like honey through Adam's mind, and he watched half his family *flinch* at it.

"Thank you, sister," Sigrun replied, giving the spirit the same title that Lassair had used for her, months ago, in Rome. "I trust I will not need any further assistance."

"Can we have a little space?" Livorus asked, calmly. "Matrugena, hold her legs. Ben Maor, keep her down on the table, if you can. Sigrun, my dear, please do not actually damage the rest of my lictors. I know you're perfectly capable of doing so. Eshmunazar . . . clear the room for us, if you would, please?"

"My pleasure," Kanmi said, quickly, from near where his wife stood, staring at him, as his sons clung to his legs. "You heard the propraetor, everyone. No one needs to watch surgery unless they're an apprentice doctor . . . ."

"I *am* a doctor," Bastet said, trying to push her way into the room. "I'm not going to stand by, and watch someone *butchered* at the hands of an amateur."

"Rest assured, dear lady, I have extensive experience with battlefield wounds." Livorus tone was dry. "Sigrun, my dear? Your choice. My hands, or hers."

"Yours, sir." Absolute trust in her voice. "Wouldn't be the first time."

"Those arrows in the lands of the midnight sun *were* somewhat annoying for you." Livorus' tone was bland.

"They healed. Just do it, sir. Get it over with."

"It's your funeral," Bastet said, folding her arms across her chest and scowling. "Or rather, your amputation."

"Out, please, everyone. Now." Livorus' tone brooked no further arguments.

Adam settled the belt between Sigrun's teeth, gave her an encouraging nod, and let her hold onto his wrists, while holding hers in his. Trennus knelt down and locked his massive arms around Sigrun's legs. "Sorry about this," Trennus told her, setting his head down on the table beside her knee, and looking away.

Her entire body arched when Livorus made the first cut, and Adam could smell the foulness of the pus coming from the wound. Could hear the drip of fluids and blood as they poured out on the floor of his parents' dining room. "Necrotizing poison," Livorus assessed. "Like some snake bites. I'm down to where the claw pieced the bone . . . and I think my scalpel is already dull." His tone was dry. "Your skin requires a hacksaw, my dear. Eshmunazar! Your assistance, please!"

Kanmi came back into the room, pushing past his irritated wife, trying to leave his children at the door. "Keep the skin and muscle pulled back," he said, his voice detached. "Sigrun, try not to heal too fast on us here. I can barely see anything. Also, don't move."

The muffled sound from the back of Sigrun's throat carried the imprint of syllables, though none were readily distinguishable. "That didn't even require translation," Kanmi noted. "I don't see a way around this. It's going to have to be burned out."

Sigrun's body when slack for a moment, and then tensed again, like a bow being strung, as Kanmi set to work. The foul stench of burning hair . . . or in this case, claw and bone . . . rose chokingly . . . and then Kanmi reported, "That's the first claw tip."

"Work anything that remains out of her bone. Don't want any of that remaining behind," Trennus warned.

"Tell me something I don't already know, Matrugena," Kanmi returned, acerbically. "I think I've got it. Next side . . . *dominus*, go ahead and make the cut . . . ."

Fifteen agonizingly slow minutes later, they were done, and Livorus lightly bandaged the ankle. "Just to keep the blood off the floor, my dear. I know you'll likely heal up inside of the next hour." He patted her leg. "Nice work, Eshmunazar. Very steady."

"Not my first time cutting something out of someone's bones. First time where the patient wouldn't take pain medication, though." Kanmi replied tersely.

Trennus sat up, releasing Sigrun's legs, and patted her knee lightly, as he helped her sit up. "Doesn't do any good, Esh," Sigrun told him, quietly. "It's not a question of bravery. The medicine lasts all of five minutes, and then I need another dose. And then another. And I *won't* go down that road."

"You, me, and Trennus. The happy trio who can't, shouldn't, or won't take our medicine." Kanmi shook his head as Sigrun flexed her foot, experimentally, and Adam could see that red and blue lights were flashing in the darkened hall outside the dining room, coming in from outside. The *gardia* had finally arrived.

Trennus gave Sigrun one last, apologetic pat on the knee, even as she reached out and gripped her friend's big shoulder. "It's all right," she told him. "Needed to be done." A faint smile. "Even the binding outside . . . needed doing." She focused in on him, now that the sickening pain was down to a dull, aching throb, and told him, "Thank you, Tren, for not letting me kick anyone." Sigrun hardly ever used nicknames or shortenings of people's names. To do so . . . let them in, and she hardly ever let anyone in. But she'd called Kanmi *Esh*, and Trennus *Tren*, and had done so reflexively . . . and for a moment she had to let herself feel it. A sense of belonging.

Trennus flashed her a quick smile, his eyes lighting up behind his glasses as he stood, and Sigrun could see *both* of Adam's sisters—she had yet to get names for half of these people, and it was irking her—eying the tall Pict, and falling back into the hallway to giggle to each other behind their hands. Sigrun understood precisely why; the man was built like his family's namesake, a bear . . . but in spite of it, there was an essential gentleness and grace about him that showed in how he moved, how he'd hold someone's hand on being introduced to them. And, additionally, he had the added bonus of being exceedingly foreign, bordering on exotic. Sigrun herself couldn't help but notice all of it, but there was also something fundamentally innocent and *young* about Trennus, that made her categorize him differently than Adam or Kanmi. *The innocent, the idealist, and the cynic who's had his ideals betrayed,* she thought, muzzily, and looked out one of the doors at Livorus, who had just reached his wife and children, and had bowed, very correctly, over Poppaea's hand. *I suppose that makes Livorus the pragmatist. And that makes me . . . nothing, really. An observer of the human condition.* She picked up her sodden swan cloak and tossed it over a chair to dry. Checked her spear, noting that the hand-forged steel blade looked corroded from the demon's blood, and set it aside, before digging for more dry clothing. Trennus had only brought her fresh jeans. He hadn't apparently wanted to go through her shirts and bodices. The least she could do for Adam's family was to not smell of wet leather and blood. Or, for that matter . . . she ran her hands down the backside of her jeans, and sighed again. *Yes, the cobblestones tore this pair to shreds. I probably shouldn't be walking around their home with my arse showing. It lacks a certain respect.*

Pandemonium. A dozen conversations going on at once. Kanmi, back out in the hall and dealing with his wife and sons. "Kanmi, I'm a *doctor*. I really want to take a look at that leg. None of you had *any* business doing surgery in a non-sterile room. None of you are qualified—"

Kanmi paused in the hall, and gave his wife a look. But it was a gentle one, or at least, as gentle as he could make it. He was usually extremely careful to leave work at work, and home at home, and he really didn't like the two parts of his life mixing in this way. He never talked about work at home, if he could avoid it, and *having* to explain his work reality to her . . . didn't feel right. "Bastet . . . I've pulled enough musket balls and arrows in my day, and cauterized the wounds, to know a fair bit about field medicine. And believe me when I tell you, Caetia's going to be fine. She's *god-born*. I've seen her pull out of far worse." He turned away and shouted down the hall to Trennus, "Will any fire do for that demon claw? Or does it need to be *special*, burning blue with salt in it or something?"

"Fire should be fire," Trennus called back, once more digging in the suitcases and packs that lined the hallway.

"You finally changing your skirt?"

"I thought I might put on something drier, yes, now that I don't have to hold Sigrun down."

"Don't see how you can stand that thing, anyway. One good gust of wind from Caetia at the wrong moment, and suddenly, the whole world has confirmation of what you Picts don't wear beneath it." Kanmi caught the sudden wide-eyed looks of Adam's two sisters, as they ducked into yet another doorway, and looked up at the ceiling. *Oh, that's precious. The good news is, Adam won't have to kill Trennus for touching either of them. I'm not sure he'd know what to do with either—or <u>both</u>—if they sat themselves down in his damned lap.*

Trennus, for his part, looked back across the hallway and actually bantered in return, "You're just jealous, Eshmunazar. I had my fill of chafing in Nahuatl, thank you. If I don't have to be inconspicuous, I'm damned well not going to deal with trousers if I don't have to. I'll wear something in a hot climate that allows for *airflow*." A bright smile. "Which is probably why the traditional clothing of Tyre is a long and flowing robe, is it not?"

"Caftan, yes, but I still wear pants underneath." Kanmi grinned right back at him. It was far more fun when people started issuing retaliatory fire. "Say, if L . . . your spirit could fix your knee back in Tenochtitlan and your hands just now, couldn't she have fixed the *chafing* issues?"

Trennus flushed. "I wouldn't ask her to do that."

Kanmi grinned more widely. "You do have a tendency to miss the best opportunities, Matrugena."

"Stow it."

"Besides, it wasn't chafing that was the real problem in Nahautl," Kanmi went on, relentlessly. "It was the mosquitoes. I heard this high-pitched scream one night, looked up, and there one went. Size of an owl. Had a mouse impaled on the end of its proboscis. Mouse's little legs were wiggling, like this." He held up a hand in front of his nose in demonstration. "Mosquito was so big, it had *landing lights* on the bottoms of its wings." He looked down at his sons. "No joke."

Bodi looked at him suspiciously. "You're teasing us, Daddy." Himi, being older, actually got the joke, and just *laughed.*

"You two are all right?" Kanmi asked, crouching down beside them for a moment. "All the noises were pretty loud."

"It was a *little* scary," Bodi was willing to admit.

"Bodi's a baby. I wasn't scared." Himi folded his arms over his chest with a worldly air.

"Well, then it was your job to make sure he wasn't scared, wasn't it, Himi?" Kanmi pointed out, reasonably. "Just because you're older and bigger doesn't mean you're better than he is. It just means you have more *work.* Both of you, let's get you out from under everyone's feet. I think there's a kitchen around here. Move."

The two boys skittered off ahead of him, and Kanmi regarded Bastet warily. There was an edge in his wife's expression that suggested she hadn't liked being put off, and that she had questions that went beyond the fact that he had a pretty good grip on emergency medicine. Actually, his grasp on that was probably better than hers; she worked in a hospital, certainly, but she was a general practitioner. He'd seen a lot more wounds and outraged bodies, he was certain, than she had. He reflected, quickly, on what had gone on outside, and decided that, fortunately, as sorcerous combat went, what he'd done had largely been invisible. *All right, other than wrapping a red-hot lamppost around the creature. And lighting up its armor. She probably didn't see that, and she* <u>couldn't</u> *see any of the other things I did.*

"Kanmi," Bastet asked, her eyes narrow as the boys ran towards the kitchen, ducking and dodging around the dozens of other people in the house, "I have a few questions . . . ."

Kanmi wasn't sure if he should be relieved or not as ben Maor popped out of the dining room, interrupting them. "Esh," Adam said, looking down and putting a hand on his shoulder. "Really good work out there, as usual." He shook his head.

"I work with what people give me." Kanmi flicked a glance at Bastet and added, neutrally, "The grenade right in its mouth was all you, ben Maor."

"Sure it was." Adam's tone was dry. "Keeping it off of Sig, forcing it out of its armor . . . that was you. Still surprised you didn't really light it up —"

"Only fuel I had was the hydrogen in the water —"

"Yes, *no.* That would have been a bad idea. That's a little combustible." Adam grinned. "That's one of the primary propellants for rockets, actually. I like the houses around here where they are." He jerked a thumb at the front door. "I think I need to get out there and coordinate with the local Praetorians. Quick question before I go do my job. I could see that the bullets were doing the trick, but very slowly. This might not be the only such creature we see here, at the rate we're going. You think you can enchant my rifle clips or pistol bullets, or something?"

"It'll be bullet by bullet, unless I enchant the actual rifle itself. Either way, I'm going to need the specifications on your weapon. I add too much heat or friction to each bullet coming out the barrel, and you can say goodbye to it as it melts to slag in your hand."

"Let's take a look at that tonight. If we have to, we can run tests."

"What's our next step, boss?" Kanmi didn't actually mean the words ironically. But every question from him was a poke. It was a matter of honor. Or habit. Or both, really.

"Getting Livorus the f—" Adam glanced at Bastet, and cut off the word. " —out of here, if we can. We need a different location. Problem is—"

"They tracked him here once. I'd be willing to bet, from what Matrugena's spirit said—"

"Yes, blood, I got that much. Damned if I know where they got it from—"

"Same place I would. Laundry services. You think the people who work in the laundry get paid worth a damn, ben Maor?"

Adam grimaced. "Fair point. But the last time he was *here* was twenty-five years ago. Someone kept it *that* long?"

"You know as well as I do how long hate lingers in this part of the world. I can picture someone grabbing the blood-soaked uniform when he was just a trib and holding on." Kanmi's head lifted, and his eyes narrowed.

"Think you can track it?"

"Hard. Records from that long ago will exist, but gods only know how accurate they'll be as to who was in the *laundry* at the time."

"Might not have been them. Could've been his personal servants." Adam gave him a direct look. "Keep thinking. We're going to want to dig on this. This probably won't be the only attack on him."

"Baal's teeth, there could be attacks on . . . " Kanmi glanced at Bastet, and changed his wording, ". . . other people. Right now, in fact."

"Yes. That's what I'm going to be asking about. Among other things. Keep them all safe, Esh. Sig's more hurt than she's letting on."

"Usually the case." Kanmi pulled his lips back from his teeth briefly. "Don't worry. There's nothing the four of us can't handle. And right now . . . I've got this."

"About time you recognized that." Adam's grin was infectious, "Anything I can do for you before I get back to work?"

He considered it for a moment. "I think I'd kill for something to eat right now."

"We've got a side of raw demon out there that we could get

Matrugena to unstone for you."

"No, that's all right. Though I have to say, with it propped up on that hummock of dirt like that, arse up . . . it looks like it's just waiting for a god to come down and fuck it in the ass." Kanmi considered that. "Though that would have to be a pretty desperate god." Another pause. "Maybe a Hellene one. There's apparently nothing they won't screw."

Adam snorted at that one, before he moved out of range, heading for the front door, where Livorus, surprisingly, corralled him, and pulled him to the side, talking quietly and urgently. Kanmi was surprised as Bastet walked away without further questions or comments, her dark eyes narrow. But he knew he was going to have to handle this before the end of the trip.

He wasn't looking forward to it.

By nine postmeridian, there were still red and blue flashing lights outside in the street, though it had grown dark. Thanks to the condition of the road outside—most notably, the two large cranes that had been moved in to try to lift a giant, three-thousand-pound statue gently onto a flatbed truck—it was evident that no one was leaving the neighborhood tonight. Adam had tried talking to the regional Praetorian commander about getting a helicopter in to take Livorus, his family, and perhaps Sigrun and Trennus with them, but the truth of the matter was, landing a helicopter in this neighborhood was out of the question. The streets were too narrow, the houses too close together, and none of them had roofs that could hold a chopper. Adam glanced out the window, and saw that the various neighbors were all still milling around, and watched the local newspapers and far-viewer reporters, who had shown up to get pictures of *everything* . . . though, at the moment, the *gardia* and Praetorians were stonewalling the reporters. This was a random attack by an unleashed and ancient demon, just a raw terror event. No, no one in particular had been targeted. This was a quiet neighborhood, where no one of any account happened to live.

Adam felt that he should be out there and dealing with this, except that Livorus had told him, explicitly, not to go back outside once the media had arrived. The regional Praetorian commander could come in to coordinate. None of the lictors were to go out. *If they see you out there, they'll have confirmation of my location. Let's not give anyone that.*

So instead, he was dealing with his *family*. Something he'd really prefer not to be doing.

His parents moved around, trying to make sure all of their new guests were comfortable and fed. Hospitality was an obligation. Even if all that was left in the pantry was a can of chickpeas, food needed to be offered. So, challah bread. Leftover cholent from dies Saturni. They'd already set out a number of dishes for their guests, and in expectation that Adam would be home for dinner, so there were little pots of hummus and pita bread, and his mother hastily turned on the stove to hard-boil eggs and warm up lentil soup and any other leftovers she could find in the freezer. And she'd even scrounged up *hamantash* for all the children;

Livorus' brood thanked her politely in Latin; Kanmi's blurted thanks in Carthaginian; and Mikayel's expressed gratitude in Hebrew, which left a delighted smile on his mother's face for about ten minutes.

Adam tried to scarf down food while dealing with the various *gardia* and Praetorians coming in the door, and their questions and concerns. And pressed, in turn, for information on what was actually going on all over the city. He'd been told that *someone* had taken a shot at a high-ranking Chaldean woman who happened to be in the city today—Erida Lelayn. Which was the name of the Chaldean negotiator that they were supposed to be meeting with Livorus tomorrow, along with a Median negotiator named Kashir Maranata. Lady Lelayn was in the city, ostensibly, to look for a high-ranking Roman husband, to improve relations between the Empires in that fashion. "Is she alive?" Adam had asked, tightly.

"Yes. Was taken to the hospital for a minor graze to her arm. Her bodyguard is swearing vengeance, throwing his weight around, and generally being a pain in the ass to the local *gardia*."

"Any other attacks?"

"We had *ghul* rise near another hotel. It's been a busy damned day."

"You're telling me." Adam had rubbed at his face. "I need a secure location for the propraetor. I'd really like it before morning."

"We can move him to the governor's house."

"Nice and secure, but everyone in creation will see him go there." Adam exhaled. "All right. Best we can do for now. How soon can we have the road cleared?"

"If your *ley-mage* gets out there and flattens the road back down, maybe two, three antemeridian."

"Done." Adam had turned around and almost walked right into his mother . . . and sighed as she noted, gently, but insistently, *"Adam, please. I know you're busy, but you can take a break, can't you?"*

"Not really, Imah, but thank you for feeding us all—" Adam really wanted to duck what he could feel coming.

"That's hospitality. And you are not listening to me, young man," she said as they walked back into the living room area, where Livorus and a few of the others were camped out. Adam couldn't help but notice that his father was staying *well* out of this conversation, and had, in fact, set up a chessboard—a game that was also called *shah*. Livorus disliked the game, but was giving Maor a run for his money at the moment, with Kanmi watching the proceedings from the chair beside them . . . while carefully incising each bullet Adam had given him with symbols and mystical energies. His brother, Mikayel, was in the room, slouched in a chair at the far end of the room, watching a far-viewer. An electric model, it was monolithic, square, and housed in a wooden cabinet. Sigrun and Trennus were both reading near the atrium window, dividing their attention between the chess game, the books in their hands . . . and looking up, occasionally, when the words in Hebrew grew too heated. As they were, now.

Adam's mother put her hands on her hips, and looked up at him, and demanded, *"Would you at least talk to Nahal and her family? They've gotten to see a lot about you today. They're impressed, in spite of your temper earlier — "*

Adam's lips compressed to a thin line. He didn't want to think about anyone watching him do his damned job. *"I'm not here to impress them, Imah,"* he said, curtly. *"And we'll be out of your hair by about two, three at the most, I think."*

"Adam, please, talk to her. I think she'd make you a wonderful wife, and you need that stability, that structure — "

"You don't seem to understand," Adam said, for what felt like the fifth time, with as much patience as he could muster. *"I talked with her for a half an hour earlier, while you were cooking. That told me everything I really needed to know about her."*

"Nahal's a sweet girl, Adam. Why won't you give her a chance?" His mother was upset.

"You know, I have really had it to here with all the Hebrew," Trennus muttered, raising a hand above his head and waving, vaguely.

"Now you know how I feel about all the Gallic you and Sig speak," Adam shot back, without turning.

"A sentence or two once a week is one thing. This has been nonstop, and all of it has been arguing," Trennus retorted. There was a fizzing sensation in Adam's head, which seemed vaguely familiar, but he was, unfortunately, heavily distracted at the moment.

"What can you possibly say about the girl, that's not just complaining to be complaining?" Mikayel asked. *"She seems sweet."*

"Have you ever noticed, that when the only word someone can come up with to describe a woman is sweet, it's actually code for vapid?" Adam returned, holding onto his temper. *"She's my age, almost twenty-six, and acts no older than sixteen. She has a four-year degree in art history, and you know what she's done with it?"* He paused. *"Nothing. She could be a graphics designer for an advertising firm, she could be teaching art in a school, or she could be a museum docent. She is, instead, a shop clerk who sells lingerie. And, from what little I can decipher between the giggles, she gets a discount there, so half of her paycheck goes back to her employer every week. The other half of her paycheck appears to be dedicated to making stained-glass sun-catchers based on Nipponese themes. Oh, and apparently, she's a Nipponophile, or would like to be. Though she doesn't, apparently, speak the language. Or any language besides Hebrew and a smattering of Latin."* The fact that the girl had chattered about dressing up like a geisha and going to parties with her friends, who all dressed the same way, had set Adam's teeth on edge. He suspected that she knew very, very little about what a geisha actually *was*. She just liked the image. He, on the other hand, had at least visited Nippon, while on leave from his Praetorian work in India. He knew *precisely* what a geisha was, and he didn't romanticize it any more than he romanticized the 'brides of the city,' in India.

Mikayel folded his arms across his chest, and stared at Adam. *"You're honestly complaining because our mother found you a girl good-enough looking to work in a lingerie store?"*

"No," Adam replied. Objectively speaking, Nahal was decent looking. Dark hair, dark eyes, clean skin, generous figure. The problem wasn't her appearance. *"She's pretty enough, I suppose. Doesn't really matter, though. What I'm saying, is this: Her family somehow deferred her year's required service in the JDF. Then her parents paid for her to go to college, and they've all treated it as a finishing school instead of an education. She's gotten a college education, but instead of finding a profession, she's still a* <u>shop-clerk</u> *at twenty-six. She clearly has no imagination. No aspiration. No determination. That's a person who's going to be a shop-clerk for the rest of her life."* Adam paused. The words were stark, and he knew it was probably unfair on such a short acquaintance, but this was the truth as he saw it. *"I'm saying that I'm sure she was sweet when she was sixteen and she's sweet now, and she'll be just as sweet when she's thirty-six, forty-six, and fifty-six, and that she's going to die a very* <u>sweet</u> *old lady . . . who will never have had an interesting thought in her life. And she'll have filled her days with a variety of completely useless hobbies involving making decorative items that no one actually wants, instead of doing or making anything that actually matters."* Adam exhaled. *"So, yes. She's pretty. She's insipid. She's vapid. And anyone who thinks I could spend more than ten minutes around her without putting a bullet in my own brain obviously has never met me in their life."* He gave his mother a direct look with those words. *"Imah, you like her because she's . . . easy. She'd never tell you no, she'd give you grandchildren, and I'd be bored out of my skull for the rest of my natural life. No. No more* <u>shidduchim</u>*, you understand me?"*

"You really do think you're better than everyone around you, don't you?" Mikayel snapped, as their mother winced. *"It's not as if you have a degree in anything besides killing, yourself."*

Adam glared at his brother, and for an instant, all he could visualize was hitting his brother hard enough to loosen teeth. Adam had been poised to go back to school for an engineering degree in the hope of working in the space program when the Praetorians had called. He didn't have a formal education yet, no, but he spent a solid chunk of every week reading everything he could on space, astronomy, jet propulsion, rocket propulsion, physics, and chemistry. His hands trembled with the need to control his anger. *"You know what? You're right. I don't have a degree. And you're right about this, too. I do think I'm better than someone who will, clearly, never be anything more than she is today. Never grow. But consider this."* He met his brother's eyes. *"The only reason you're currently in possession of your teeth is because you're family. Consider* <u>that</u> *before opening your mouth again."*

As he took a breath to calm down, the exhalation hung as mist in the air in front of him, and he blinked, startled. The room was *cold*, and Adam suddenly realized that Kanmi and Trennus were on their feet, looking at Mikayel, eyes steady, expressions . . . blank. Sigrun wasn't bothering with blank. She'd gone to actively hostile, but hadn't risen—not yet, anyway. Livorus had raised his head, and his eyebrows were elevated, as well.

"Oh, gods," Trennus muttered, in the mellifluous notes of his native Gallic . . . which resounded, in Adam's ears, in Hebrew. *Lassair's translating. Harah. This can really only get worse, can't it?* "They're actually trying to set him up with an arranged marriage? How archaic."

"Not to mention, demeaning to both the man and the woman," Sigrun added. The words were in her native Gothic, the sound of them a lash in the room . . . but they were translated as well. "Last I checked, Adam was freeborn, not a slave."

"Now, now," Livorus murmured. "My own marriage was arranged. And I've three wonderful children as a result of it." His glance towards the other room, where Poppaea and his children were resting, spoke volumes, however, and every one of his lictors' faces went stony. Unreadable.

They were all aware that Livorus and Poppaea had separate bedrooms, and exceedingly separate lives. They were cognizant that the propraetor and his wife only ate dinner together once a week, with their children, on dies Solis, if he happened to be in Rome. They understood that Livorus didn't speak to Poppaea about political matters. And while he'd talk to any of his lictors about current law-making efforts with perfect cordiality, it was to Sigrun that he tended to unburden his mind about sociopolitical and historical issues. And they all knew perfectly well that when they were abroad, Livorus had no qualms about visiting licensed brothels. "My dear wife frequently spends whole weeks at a time at a spa near Pompeii," Livorus noted now. "She's become quite the sponsor of aspiring artists, and throws a wonderful dinner party, when required. She has nothing to complain about, and neither do I. What more could someone ask from an arranged marriage?"

Adam realized that a year ago, he'd have taken those words at face value. Now, however, he heard the dryness, the irony, in the propraetor's tones, and winced, internally. Livorus knew precisely what his marriage lacked. Love. Passion. True companionship. Livorus was conveying, indirectly, approbation and approval to Adam. *Stay your course.*

His own father, at this point, raised his head from the chessboard, and turned to look at Abigayil. *"Leave the boy alone,"* Maor told his wife. *"He'll get around to it in his own good time, and right now, you're practically driving him towards a vow of eternal bachelorhood. Let it go."*

Adam appreciated the intervention on his father's part, and was mildly surprised by the fact that Trennus and Kanmi both stayed on their feet, watching Mikayel as his brother shrugged, his expression alternating between insult and annoyance, and finally retreated, leaving the room. Only then did Trennus and Kanmi sit back down again. His mother only wilted in on herself, turning to face his father, saying, *"I didn't mean it like that!"*

"Abigayil," Maor said, gently, in Latin, "I think we've aired enough of the family's dirty laundry for one night, don't you?"

Lassair, on Trennus' shoulder, gave a birdlike trill, the first actual vocalization from the spirit that Adam had ever heard, and he shot her a dark look. "Yes, and thank you for that, featherpate." He wasn't going to call her by her name, not in front of his family. He wasn't entirely thrilled at having his home life seen in this light.

Trennus reached up and put two fingers to Lassair's beak . . . and the bird mock-nipped at his thumb. "I'd apologize for her sense of humor," Trennus noted, smiling, "except that until recently, I hadn't realized that she had one."

All things grow, Trennus. All things strive. Those that are worth knowing, at any rate. The phoenix's voice was surprisingly saucy.

"It's . . . all right." Adam grimaced. "I'm sorry, everyone. I never let personal matters get in the way of the job. You know that." His eyes were locked on his fellow lictors.

To his surprise, Kanmi was the one who spoke up, calmly, "It's all right, ben Maor. We all have to be so deep in the propraetor's life, that it's . . . better, and certainly more convenient, if we leave ours at the door when we come to work in the morning. I've done the same thing with every job I've ever had." His smile was faint, and didn't quite reach his eyes. "When we get the propraetor's family to a hotel, I've got a couple of stories for you, if you want to hear them. Maybe over some *arak*." He shrugged, bowed his head to the others, and withdrew from the room. The chill lessened as Trennus and Sigrun withdrew in Kanmi's wake, each of them lightly resting a hand on Adam's shoulder as they left the room.

Trennus, for his part, started packing up his belongings. The house had felt warm and welcoming at first, though the constant arguing had certainly put him on his guard. He was used to a certain amount of boisterous yelling from his own family. Five brothers and two strong-willed parents had made for a loud home; he'd been shocked at how quiet his ley-mage master's house had been when he'd moved in with old Senecita. Not to mention, how much easier it had been to read and concentrate without the constant distractions. Now, however, the warmth had been replaced by pure awkwardness. As such, he started sweeping grimoires into his bags with practiced gestures, making sure that each volume was locked shut with its leather bands snapped closed. Tossed his silver knife and his steel combat one in, as well; he'd had to clean the steel one after cutting open his hands earlier . . . and looked around for the rest of his things.

Much to his surprise, Adam's two sisters were hovering near, and the older of the two shyly handed him his kilt—they'd put it in the dryer for him, apparently. "Ah, thank you," Trennus told them, testing the fabric. *Good enough. Shouldn't damage the books.* He tossed it in, as well.

"You're really a summoner?" the younger one asked, her eyes wide. She'd taken some time, in the past couple of hours, to go put some Egyptian kohl around her eyes, and had reddened her lips with Hellene lip-gloss. Even her cheeks were a little pinker now. Trennus thought it a rather odd reaction to the disaster zone outside, but he thought she might be afraid to be caught on camera by the news crews without having primped a little first. "I'm Chani, by the way. No one's settled down to give any proper introductions at all." She dimpled up at him.

The older sister cleared her throat. "And I'm Rivkah. Please excuse my sister's forwardness." She tipped her head to the side. "But . . . yes. I never thought I'd meet a summoner who was . . . one of the good guys." Her Latin was excellent, while her sister's was more heavily accented.

Trennus grinned, not offended at all. "You wouldn't believe how often I've heard that from Adam." He tightened the strings on his bag and tied them off, carefully. "As I keep telling him, knowledge is neither good nor bad. It's the ends to which it's turned that make it so."

Chani regarded him, smiling a little. "So, because you're a good summoner, you don't deal with demons. Like that one out there." She pointed vaguely towards the front of the house. "You don't deal with *gehenna* and the fallen angels."

Trennus blinked, and sighed. "Look, I'm the first to admit, I don't know much about your religion, but the first thing to understand about summoning is that it . . ." he looked up at the ceiling, "both does and doesn't have anything to do with religion at all. All spirits come from the same place, the same realm. The Veil, as we're taught to call it. Beneficent, malefic, elemental, or disinterested. All the same place. Some of them started off bad, some of them started off good, and some of them . . . *we've made* malefic or beneficent, over the centuries. Because they're . . . reactive to the people who summon them. We shape them, and they shape us. All bargains go both ways." He saw Chani's eyes go vague, but Rivkah's stayed sharp and focused.

"So you're saying that demons don't come from *gehenna*?" Rivkah asked him, straight-forwardly enough. "That's not what we're taught."

Trennus held up his hands, palms out. "I'm not here to tell you what to believe, or what not to believe. I'm just saying that every spirit I've ever spoken with has told me the same thing. They all come from the same realm. That creature out there comes from the same exact realm as my bound spirits. Your religion's, ah, demons . . . might come from some other place." He tactfully stepped around the topic. "Most people use the term *demons* to mean a malefic spirit, of any sort. It's a fuzzy term."

Rivkah advanced a couple of steps into the room, drawing Chani in her wake. "So . . . you mostly work with good spirits then?" she asked, hopefully. "Angels, I suppose?"

Trennus winced internally. This was the problem with dealing with people who had a limited frame of reference in these matters. Behind the two girls, he could see Kanmi in the hallway. Leaning against a wall and *laughing*, silently. "Again, I don't know much about your angels," Trennus replied, mendaciously. "But by and large, I bargain with beneficent and elemental spirits. Malefic ones, I wrestle with, bind, and try to push back out into the Veil."

Two sets of blinks, and Chani asked, putting a hand on his arm, very lightly, "You *wrestle* with demons, then?"

Trennus looked down at her hand, a little uncertainly, but neither pulled away, nor reciprocated. These were Adam's *sisters*, and it was probably just a friendly gesture. "I try to avoid it, if it's not absolutely necessary. And most of the time, it's a question of will, not physical strength. Though, yes, I've had to fight them physically before today." His eyes widened a little more as Chani got just a little closer now, but there was still about a foot of space between them. It wasn't *improper.*

"Are all the markings on your skin for your, ah, angels, then?" Little flicks of her eyes under the kohled lids.

Trennus pulled his arm back now. Being touched by a woman felt . . . damned nice. Probably a little too nice, to be honest. "Ah, no. They're all to do with my family and my tribe in Britannia. The bears on the forearms are for my clan. The serpents on the wrists mean I apprenticed with a ley-mage. They're for wisdom. My father wears them with wings — as dragons, really — to show, well, his rank." He avoided the word *king* like a plague. "The others were done at various points. When I became an adult. The stag on my back is part of my bargain with one of my spirits, but that's not always the case. She's also the spirit of our forest, so other people wear her image, too." He shrugged.

"So, what does bargaining mean?" That from Rivkah, a little more pragmatically.

"Usually, it boils down to an exchange of services or energies. Little sacrifices, little tasks. The more limited the bargain, the more limited the task: give an offering of something of value to you and the spirit that has energy in it. Some spirits like libations of wine. Some like sugar. Some prefer the burning of sweet-scented oils. Burning is often favored because they can draw the energy directly into themselves."

"Burning oils?" Chani asked, blankly. "Like olive or sesame oils in the Temple?"

Oh, gods, she's ahead of the curve and doesn't even realize what she just said. "Almost exactly," Trennus replied, plastering a smile on his face. "The bigger the bargain, the bigger the service you need to perform. One of my spirits asks me to go home to Britannia once a year to hunt and kill a deer in her forest, so that she can partake of its blood and its life, and so that I stay bound to her forest, even though we travel all over the world."

Slow nods. This was a familiar concept. "Like sacrificing a ram or a heifer," Rivkah supplied. "That's why dealing with spirits is frowned upon. It's a perversion of sacrifices made to god."

I wouldn't say that, Lassair told them, as the phoenix leaped off the lamp on which she'd been perching, and landed on Trennus' shoulder. *I would call it a matter of scale. The gods are the sharks and whales, the leviathans that swim in our sea. But every creature of the Veil is a fish.*

"You don't exactly look like a fish," Chani said, taking a step backwards, though Rivkah stayed precisely where she was, lifting her chin a little defiantly.

I could look like a fish if I chose, but I was speaking metaphorically. I cannot tell you what the other side of the Veil is like. Your minds do not understand a world without dimensionality, physicality, and time. If I put an image in your minds of that place, your senses would scream at you and try to render it comprehensible, but no two people would generate the same understanding. It is impossible. Lassair's tone was calm, but there was a hint of challenge there, too, and Trennus didn't understand why. Now she added, *You seem uncomfortable with my phoenix form. I am fond of it, but here.*

Let me try another.

Don't forget the clothing! This isn't the baths in Rome.

Of course I won't forget. Her thoughts were for him alone, he knew, as he felt arms encircle his waist from behind, and glanced down, a little apprehensively, to see a light ridge of flaming feathers extending up from the forearms . . . and a head worm its way under his right arm. Red hair this time, almost as dark-toned as a ruby. *You see? Neither fish nor fowl nor beast. I am who I am, and nothing more.*

Rivkah had pulled her hand away from Trennus' arm as if burned when Lassair assumed her harpy-like humanoid form. Trennus cleared his throat. "Ah, so . . . welcome to Magic and Theology 101," he said, wincing. "The biggest and most powerful spirits ask for sacrifices that are less tangible. More abstract. They ask for . . . mental effort from large groups of people. Adherence to certain principles. Codes of behavior. Routine, even daily sacrifices—not eating certain foods, for example, to bind the group together, and to the spirit."

Rivkah's eyes widened. "That sounds like they think they're gods." She sounded absolutely horrified by that thought.

Behind them, Kanmi actually *choked* on his laughter. "Stop that," Trennus told Kanmi. "They're getting it in ten minutes, rather than spread out over the course of an entire semester."

"Oh, I'm aware. I'm aware that usually, they'd have been handed an entire reading list to plow through, and the smartest students would notice that every single religion has sacrifices to make, and ninety-nine percent of those sacrifices are exactly the same things that spirits request in their bargains with summoners. These two are getting a passing grade, though the existential horror in first-year sorcery students is always . . . oddly fun to watch." Kanmi grinned from the hallway, just as Lassair tightened her arms around Trennus further. "The correct answer for your term paper, ladies, is 'gods dwell beyond the Veil. Therefore, they are a type of spirit. Everyone can and will disagree on how long they've existed, and whether or not they created the physical world, but you can't argue with the fact that humans deal with gods in precisely the same terms as they deal with spirits.'"

"Well, *pagan* gods can be spirits," Chani said, uncertainly, her head whipping back and forth between Kanmi and Trennus. "Not ours."

Kanmi nodded, smiling faintly. "I'm sure that's true," he told her, cheerfully, just as Trennus grimaced and made a *stop now* gesture behind the girls' backs. "I wouldn't think more about it, if I were you." He looked at Trennus, and raised his eyebrows at Lassair, who immediately resumed her phoenix form, flapped to Tren's shoulder, and tucked her head under her wing. "Ben Maor passed the word. We can finally get out of here. You packed?"

"Have been." *Oh, gods, just get me out of here before I get in any more trouble.*

"Then let's proceed to the getting the fuck out of here part."

With the reporters having been cleared to the far end of the street, and with the several overturned cars and the very large demonic statue finally hauled out of the way, they were able to get their motorcade back up and rolling. The red and blue flashing lights of the *gardia* vehicles moved off first, trying to draw the media away, and Adam watched as Poppaea's lictors, red-eyed at the loss of one of their own, moved Livorus' and Kanmi's children out to the cars. The youngest ones didn't wake up as they were buckled into their seats.

Sigrun wasn't even limping as she and the others formed up around Livorus himself, and got him back to his vehicle. "Onwards," Livorus told them. Even his voice was deathly tired at this point.

The regional governor's mansion was ancient. It had been built during the last Roman occupation, and had been maintained as a center of governance for about five hundred years; now, it served primarily as an embassy, and the position of governor of Judea was largely an in-name-only title. The building, still, had been updated frequently over the centuries. It had both electrical generators and ley-taps internal to it, one as a backup for the other—a rarity in this region. The palace had its own well, to avoid dependence on the local water supply . . . and it had Roman legionnaires and Praetorians from all across the Empire to guard it. This was as secure as they could get. It just smacked of *forting up*, and the whole point of this expedition was to look as if they weren't here for any important reason at all.

Once their vehicles got through the gates, Adam got a good look at the JDF troops with assault rifles patrolling the outside perimeter, and could feel the crackle of heavy enchantments in the air inside, not to mention the grim faces and tight professionalism of the legionnaires who formed up around the vehicles in their camouflage uniforms. He exhaled deeply for the first time in what felt like hours. "Thank all the gods," Trennus muttered, as they got everyone into the building itself.

Adam gave him a droll look. "I couldn't help but overhear your little dissertation earlier. You still believe in gods, even though they're effectively spirits?" He'd decided not to say a *word* to Trennus about his sisters. Tren had acted perfectly properly with both.

Trennus blinked, rapidly, and shook his head, as if rattling his brain back into place. "Yes. They exist. No one actually knows how old they actually are. They might well predate humanity. And I've done my fair share of bargaining with them." He grinned, briefly, but without humor, a bleak look settling into his eyes. "No, Adam. I believe in them. Any sane man would, in this world. Whether they're the most powerful spirits there are, or the genuine creators of humanity . . . they're here. And so are we."

With all of their protectees safely in their beds, Adam knew he should be seeking his own. Every time he closed his eyes, however, he saw the events of the last day behind his closed lids. The efreet reaching up to the sky, the fires and smoke emerging from the hotel in its wake. The *pazuzu* landing opposite his childhood home, atop a roof that had belonged, years ago, to a family that had had three children . . . all around his age. Aharon, Ayelet, and Daniel. He'd been trying not to think, all night, if their parents still owned that house. Not to let himself imagine that they had been the ones running out the front door, while Sigrun had been distracting the huge creature that had crashed through their ceiling. He'd seen people. A few children. Probably too old to be the offspring of his old playmates, but . . . he could have asked his parents if the ben Keshet family still lived there. He hadn't. He didn't want to know, not today. Tomorrow . . . maybe. But not today.

His mind ground on relentlessly, showing him Sigrun landing against the hydrant with bone-shattering force. The *pazuzu*'s tail lancing through the car's windshields and almost touching his sternum. Kevlar armor or not, he didn't think he'd have survived that.

Usually, he was much better at calming his mind and sleeping, no matter what happened to be going on. But there were too damned many unknowns, at the moment. The Chaldean emissary had been shot. *Ghul* were being raised in the streets. All the things that Jerusalem was supposed to be clear of. All the things for which the Wall existed to protect the rest of Judea. And, of course, the constant background irritant that was his family. Adam swore under his breath, stood, pulled on his clothes, and went for a walk.

He found Kanmi pacing around on one of the balconies, much to his surprise. "Shouldn't you be asleep?" Adam asked.

"Shouldn't you?"

"Yes, but you have a wife here . . . ." Adam trailed off, at the cynical flick of Kanmi's eyes.

The sorcerer shrugged. "Part of me can't sleep, for thinking of what could have happened to them. I think I'd get past it and go to sleep, but Bastet wants to know, all of a sudden, about my entire career, and she's apparently pissed at me. I'm not entirely sure why. It's not like I've ever *hidden* what I am." He shrugged again, and stared down into the darkness. "Get this. She's angry that I didn't tell her I had a field medic certification." Kanmi raised his hands. "She's a doctor, yes, but it's not like this would have made for dinnertime conversation. 'I had to amputate two legs and set three broken arms in the past six months on the Mongol border. How was your day?'" The sorcerer's voice was acerbic.

"Sounds like that's just standing in for everything else she's mad about." Adam shrugged himself now. He was no expert, but sometimes, people said they were angry about irrational things when the things they were really angry about were too big to be easily summed up.

"Oh, probably." Kanmi exhaled. "I told her not to come on this trip. I told her . . . at least once a day, sometimes twice, that this was a bad idea. I couldn't tell her *why* it was a bad idea. So now, I suppose, it's my fault that she's here, the children are here, and I apparently didn't tell her it could be *dangerous*." He shrugged, and pointed at the eastern horizon. "Sun's starting to come up."

"So it is." Adam stared at the thin line of gold there, and there was silence for a long moment.

"You've got an . . . interesting family, ben Maor."

"Tell me about it. There are reasons I haven't been to Judea in three years. I spent last Passover in Rome, at a tiny synagogue in the Judean district in the Field of Mars." Adam shrugged.

"You seem to get better holidays than Carthaginians do. I should convert. All we get is the spring equinox rituals. Which the priests of Baal-Hamon actually stole from the story of Tammuz's torture and dismemberment and subsequent resurrection every spring, so that the crops will grow."

"That's something of a common theme in most religions in this part of the world."

"I know. Egypt has Osiris being torn apart and resurrected. We have Baal-Hamon as Tammuz. Every year, my children get to make little gods out of bread, tear them apart, dip them in red grape juice to symbolize his blood, and eat the god to be one with him." Kanmi made a face. "I sometimes think the northern tribes have it a little better. At least they're just rolling eggs around in the grass to symbolize the return of the sun. It seems a little less . . . on the nose . . . with the whole sacrifice and blood thing."

Adam snorted a little. "Well, nothing from nothing, like you all keep telling me."

"Oh yes." Kanmi paused. "And I definitely prefer it to the bad old days. I wouldn't have Himi if it were two thousand years ago."

"Sacrifices to Baal and Moloch."

"Yes. First-born sons were preferred." Kanmi grimaced. "See, you say you're Judean in public, and people might give you a look for being the stubborn sods who won't use magic . . . but I say 'Carthaginian' or 'Punic,' and people look at me, and I can see them thinking 'baby-killer.' On the whole . . . conversion does sound pleasant some days. Pretty much why the boys, now that I have them in Rome . . . to Tartarus with Baal. They can go to Jupiter's temple with the rest of the city." He paused again. "Family."

"Yeah."

Silence. After another minute or two, Kanmi ventured, putting his hands on the cold stone of the balcony rail, "If it's any comfort, your family is infinitely preferable to mine. At least you and your brother still are capable of speaking to one another. My brothers kept trying to drown me when I was younger."

"I'm sure it felt that way. My brother used to joke about putting me in the well in a sack—"

Kanmi snorted. "No, I meant that literally. They'd take me to the pier and hold my head down under the water and laugh while I struggled. That stopped right around the time we all discovered I could do *this*." He invoked fire around his hands, just for a moment, and afterimages danced in front of Adam's eyes even after he dismissed the flames. "Of course, they still don't think I'm doing a job that a *man* should do. For them, a man's job is a full day of hard, backbreaking, physical labor. And when they get off work, they go to a taverna, drink to ease the pain in their muscles, and then go home to their wives, reeking of fish, sweat, and beer.

I feel sorry for my sisters-in-law, to be honest." He paused, as Adam stared at him. Kanmi hadn't revealed this much about himself or his past in the whole of the last year. "And you know, the thing is . . . even if I *could* tell them some of the things I've done in this job of ours?" Kanmi turned and looked at Adam. "You know . . . *entities,* and things that would make their eyes bulge out of their very skulls? I wouldn't do it."

"Why not?" Adam was making rapid mental re-adjustments.

"Because even if I did, it's not as if they're ever going to admit, 'Yes, you're better than we are.' And me telling them . . . would be like asking for their approval. Their approbation. In the end? Just plain *fuck them.* I don't care enough about them to want to include them in anything I've done since leaving home." Kanmi looked back down into the darkness. "Your family's better than that. Your brother may not know who the fuck you are, but I think you can educate him. And he might respect you, once he understands that you're a different person than he thought he knew. Your mother . . . eh. Mothers are mothers. They never really know who their sons are." Kanmi's tone held weariness and cynicism.

"And who am I, then?" Adam asked, dryly, "that they *don't* know me, Esh?"

"You've been out into the darkness, beyond the fence line of reality, where most humans stay inside those bounds all their lives. You've wrestled with demons, with Matrugena. You've seen the forces that make up the universe bend at a man's whim, with me. You've fought gods, with Caetia. You're not the boy your brother remembers." Kanmi straightened up, and looked at him, levelly. "Find a way to show your brother who you are, short of killing him, is my advice. Me? I don't have any halfway measures. That's why it's best I don't spend any time with my brothers." A cynical grin. "Get some sleep . . . boss."

Maius 7, 1955

Sigrun emerged from the bath complex on the grounds of the governor's mansion at just past eight postmeridian. While some ancient buildings had had hot water piped to every room, this one, while palatial, even by Roman standards, only had indoor plumbing set up for the lavatories themselves, and small sinks. All other hygiene needs were dealt with in the baths. As for the baths themselves, she thought that the art on the walls inside — definitely from the Latter Decadent Period — was a bit of a reaction to the local culture. Even the women's side of the baths had frescoes depicting various figures, male and female, female and female, male and male, and groups of three and more, in sexual configurations that seemed highly athletic, and, in some cases, judging by the incorporation of non-human mythological creatures like harpies and centaurs . . . probably somewhat painful, as well. Sigrun had shaken her head over those, and washed up as quickly as possible, escaping back to the main house. She'd been told that the building had originally been the site of the Palace of Herod, which had been torn down, all but the outer walls, and rebuilt as a gesture of goodwill after the meeting of Caesarion I with local authorities. That it had been built even grander on the inside hadn't mattered much at all; the point was, it was no longer *Herod's* Palace.

Inside, everything was a whirlwind of activity. "What's the news?" Sigrun asked, slipping into a small conference room, where Livorus and her fellow lictors were already assembled, staring at a map of Jerusalem.

"There you are. Good. We were just about to get started." Adam tossed her a quick smile. "All right. This is our current location. Governor's palace, here, northwest side of Old Town." He tapped on the map. "Here, still in the Upper City, to the west of the aqueduct, is the site of the efreet attack yesterday. The Grand Hotel Eytan." Adam tapped the map again, to the southeast of their current location. "Here, at the Pool of Bethesda, is where the *gardia* found a large smashed urn, wrapped in the uniform shirt of a tribune, with old bloodstains on it. The urn had been tossed off of one of the surrounding buildings. They suspect from a window of the Hotel Chaya. They're looking into who had rooms reserved all along that side of the building, but that's going to be slow going. It's outside of Old Town, so it's ten stories tall." Adam exhaled, sharply, and steepled his hands in front of him, clearly looking for self-control. "The falling urn also killed a passer-by on impact."

"That would've woken the *pazuzu* up even more than the blood on the shirt," Trennus muttered, leaning back in one of the rolling chairs around the conference table. "The blood on the shirt just gave it a target. The fresh blood . . . sacrifice." Their Britannian summoner grimaced uncomfortably as the rest of them looked at him.

"Still, it takes a certain amount of *luck* to hit someone several floors down," Livorus murmured.

"Not luck at all if you've got the right sorcery on your side," Kanmi said, flatly.

"Or a spirit. If someone's loosing a demon that was bound three thousand years ago, that speaks of . . . very deep knowledge in the ancient secrets. And you don't want to take the chance of going up against a demon like that without several powerful bound spirits of your own," Trennus said, his tone just as flat as Kanmi's.

"So," Sigrun said, quietly, "what we're suggesting here is that the person responsible had probably planned this out ahead of time, as a contingency. In case the efreet didn't kill Livorus. Or as a distraction, to cover his or her retreat. You suggested Magi involvement last night, Trennus."

"It's the answer that's easy to leap to in this part of the world," Trennus admitted. "The *pazuzu* is a Mesopotamian spirit. It was clearly housed *somewhere* for three thousand years. Which isn't to say that its prison couldn't have been taken as spoils of war by say, Alexander the Great and bounced from tribute collection to tribute collection for centuries. It could have found its way to the collection of a private individual who had no idea what it was. There's no way to know without doing some extensive provenance work and back-tracing."

"Or finding the person who dropped it to the ground and asking him or her some pressing questions," Kanmi's expression was hard.

"We'll keep an open mind," Livorus said, firmly, adding much more quietly, "There are people right here in Judea who wouldn't welcome Chaldea or Media into the Empire." Livorus paused. "Too much blood on *both* sides of the Wall."

Adam nodded, and moved them onwards. "The local *gardia* think that the efreet was loosed early. It was apparently bound inside a glass bottle that broke inside of a piece of baggage being handled by a bellhop in the lobby. The only survivor from the lobby was a maid who managed to duck into a stairwell for cover. The rest, the *gardia* and the Praetorians are piecing together from reconstructing what's left of the burned-out lobby, and security camera footage."

"I always forget that you have that available down here," Livorus murmured. "I must admire its utility in the current situation, though I rather abhor the thought of a society where it might become prevalent."

"I wish cameras weren't needed, myself, sir," Adam returned, evenly, "but I can foresee a day when Rome will adopt them, as well. It would cut down on crime."

"A discussion for another time, I think." Livorus waved it away. "If the goal at the hotel was truly assassination, the choice of method was ostentatious, with far too much potential for collateral damage and too many chances at missing the correct target. Our would-be 'assassin' left a bag to be collected here at the Hotel Eytan. Hastened away, either by foot or by ground vehicle, to the Hotel Chaya and . . . waited about an hour. He or she then loosed a much worse creature on the world and . . . then what?"

"Unknown," Adam replied. "Here's where it gets interesting. In terms of the timeline? The Chaldean representative was *shot at*, with a Judean-style rifle, over here at the outskirts of Little Nippon, well outside of Old Town, to the southwest. That occurred about at the same time we were fighting the *pazuzu*. *Simultaneous* with that, the Median emissary's hotel, up in the Hellene district, about five miles north of the Chaldean attack, was surrounded by *ghul*, raised from a local ossuary." He rubbed at his eyes. "Three summoning attacks, and one attack with a Judean weapon. All in the same day. Some of them with overlapping times."

"It's certainly possible that some Judean group does not in particular care for Erida Lelayn," Livorus noted, dryly. "She's the niece of the current satrap of Chaldea, Adadnirari the second. She's related by blood to about five or six of the most important of the Magi, and is Chaldean nobility in her own right, as well as being a noted Magus, herself."

Adam looked down. "There are groups," he admitted, "who wouldn't weep to see a Chaldean noble killed. But for the attack to occur at the exact same moment as a *ghul* attack on the Median emissary . . ." Adam leafed through his notes quickly. "Kashir Maranata? And at the same time as an attack on you, sir?"

"It does strain the limits of probability," Kanmi noted.

"So, treat as a possible coincidence," Sigrun said, quietly, "but also look for connections." She flicked the wet tail of her hair off of her shoulder, and added, "I hate to point it out, but if the Chaldean emissary comes from a family heavily involved in the Magi, her people would likely be perfectly capable of raising precisely what we've seen so far. An ancient demon, a powerful efreet, and apparently a swarm of *ghul*."

"Precisely so," Livorus replied. "However, we'll need to speak with the woman in question personally in any event to get negotiations started. You can tell me then if there are lies in her eyes, my dear."

"*Dominus*, if she's a politician, the problem will not be determining if she's lying or not." Sigrun's lips quirked up at the corners.

"The problem will be ascertaining what she's lying about at that exact moment?" Livorus returned her very faint smile. "Indeed, my dear. Indeed."

By afternoon, they were out in Judea's late spring heat, canvassing the convention center at which the air and space exposition was to be held. Jets and rocket boosters were being displayed in the parking lot, which caused a headache for people who might have wanted to use the area for their vehicles, but the outdoor venue at least allowed thousands of people to get close to the technology and see it first-hand. A Persian-built high-altitude ornithopter was actually on display was well; Sigrun had never seen one up close, and she eyed its bronze-toned wings, which were in an upswept storage position as it sat on the poured stone, with interest. "They say they're better at low-velocity aerobatics than a jet," Adam murmured in her ear as they passed, trying to fit in with the crowd for the moment. That was . . . somewhat problematic for her. Adam was wearing a small skullcap; between that, and his local-boy looks, he didn't get so much as a second glance from the people around them. Sigrun, on the other hand, did. She was used to it, however. In Nova Germania and Novo Gaul, European Germania and Gaul, and northern Europa, she received stares because the people there knew a valkyrie when they saw one. Most other places, she got the stares for being overtly foreign-looking. About the only place she hadn't been stared at, in her life, had been Raccia. It had been *refreshing*.

Adam nudged her in the ribs as they moved past. "These ornithopters always make me think of pteranodons, the way the wings pull up for storage." He paused, and asked lightly, "Think it can outduel you?"

"It's a large plane," she replied, clinically. "It might be faster than I am . . . though I doubt it . . . but it can't *turn* faster than I can. It does, however, carry those rotating barrel guns under each wing. Those . . . could prove uncomfortable." She slid her smoked lenses down her nose, and commented, wryly, "No, it's the *jets* that frighten me, Adam. They're much faster than I am, and the air-intake on their engines could prove very problematic for me. I could be sucked in." She considered it for a moment. "My best option in dealing with any of them, other than lightning, would be to disrupt the air currents around them." A shrug. "Also, the missiles that they carry? If they start carrying radar systems that can lock onto me?

Very much a problem."

"You say that so calmly, it makes my blood run cold." Adam caught her elbow, and deftly directed her through a side-entrance into the convention center, proper, as they both flashed their identification at the guards there. "I really did want to be a pilot, you know, and picturing someone sitting outside my canopy window, waving, and proceeding to flip my plane end-for-end by altering the airflow over the wings? Bad image. Even if it's you."

"I cannot for the life of me picture you as a pilot, Adam," Sigrun told him, taking off her glasses and letting her eyes adjust to the dimmer light inside the cavernous interior of the convention hall. Over a hundred kiosks had been set up, displaying different manufacturers' wares, and she could smell rubber, metal, and the odd tang of plastics, a foreign and not wholly pleasant smell for her. Six long rows of back-to-back booths, occupying the poured-stone floor, and no less than fifteen total swinging metal doors leading into the actual floor-space. Most of them were already locked and blocked off by security, herding people in through one set of doors and out through the opposite side, but fire codes meant that someone could open any of these doors from the inside . . . and someone with the right knowledge might be able to do so without setting off the alarm. On the north and south sides of the wide, open floor, the exits led to various smaller conference rooms . . . one of which they were planning to use to pull in each of the representatives for the meeting. Subtly. "You know, Adam? This is a perfectly horrible position to put Livorus in. There are so many variables, my head spins."

"I regretted suggesting it the instant we started looking into the actual arrangements," Adam agreed. "Unfortunately, this was the only large public event during the time period to which everyone agreed." He covered his mouth and muttered the words quietly, to avoid anyone reading his lips, and they got to work, checking entrances and exits. The route they'd take Livorus through the convention hall, which would, thankfully, be cleared, one row at a time for their party's passage, by convention hall security. They'd have plenty of *gardia* patrolling as well . . . and JDF forces had been brought in to add to the manpower, as discreetly as they could arrange it. They were only visiting specific booths, the owners of which had passed background checks. Still, there were a *lot* of bodies in the convention hall at the moment, pushing and jostling. Probably about three thousand total, at the moment. Too damned many, and packed in like herring in a tin. Dizzying array of different cultures, too. Judean men and women in skullcaps and *tichel*, wearing a variety of business suits. Some of the men with long beards, and others, like Adam, clean-shaven, or nearly so. Hellene men and women, in business-wear as well, though a few women—booth attendants, meant to draw the eye— wore *peplos*, in shimmering white folds. A handful of Nipponese at booths, showing off finely-made control systems, with huge banks of switches and circuits that looked somehow magical to Sigrun.

They managed to slip by an endcap table, and Adam played the tourist for a moment, pointing up at a display that read *The World of*

Tomorrow, Today in Latin, Hellene, Hebrew, and Nipponese. "Loke, Hidde, and Mertin Space Systems," he read. "Gothic startup, I think? Look at *that*. They want to put a station at the Libration point between Earth and the moon . . . and use that as the way-station to the moon. That's Phase One. Phase Two . . . build an actual underground colony on Luna." He used the Hellene term for the moon; the Hebrew word was *L'banah*.

"Everything is underground?" Sigrun asked, dodging another body, and staring at the plans.

"Yes. For protection from radiation. Also, it's easier to pressurize something that already has several tons of dirt and rock atop it, than to have to build a dome or something." Adam just stood there for a moment, his dark eyes gleaming and a smile wreathing his face. "And as to why . . . ? Much easier to build ships for space, *in* space. That way, you don't have to make them capable of atmospheric exit and re-entry. You can use them to go fetch asteroids, use them for raw materials. Build ships that can get us to *Mars*." He pointed at another board. "That's Phase . . . Five, I think, if I'm reading this correctly."

"You think humans should go to Mars?" Sigrun looked across at him, and let her eyebrows arch.

"Yes. Absolutely. Everything we've learned as a species has come from *striving*. The *side-benefit* of learning to do one thing, is we learn so much more about other things along the way. We've learned a lot about medicine from learning how to make war more efficiently. Not really the best way to learn something, right? I'd like to see what we can learn from doing something really worthwhile. By exploring. By building a whole new world." Adam paused, and looked at her, sidelong. "And . . . you were just seeing if you could get me to go off on a rant, weren't you?"

"I find it amusing. Also, interesting. I like to learn new things, too." She pointed at the underground colony pictures. "I don't see you living underground, Adam. Not without being in a cold sweat for the rest of your life."

He made a face at her. "Maybe we won't have *ghul* on the moon."

"I think humans will drag their problems with them, no matter where they go."

"Careful. You sound like Kanmi."

"No, he's the cynic. I'm just an observer of human nature." Sigrun pointed to their left. "Conference room's that way."

As they got ready to go on full duty, Adam, in the conference room, tossed each of the other lictors a flexible vest made of very heavy material. "Put these on," he told them. "These won't stop a rifle bullet, but they should stop most revolvers." He looked up at the ceiling. "Assuming no one's invested in tungsten-core bullets. At the least, it'll slow the bullets down a bit." He took off his cloak and pulled on his own vest.

The other three looked at the vests, and looked at Adam. Kanmi shook his head slightly. "You have any idea what I'd do to someone wearing one of these, ben Maor?"

"Roast them alive, probably."

"That, or tighten all the filaments so that it constricts them and renders them unable to move or breathe." Kanmi grimaced. "We're going to be seeing Chaldeans and Medians, ben Maor. We're talking about the original sorcerers. I'm not worrying about bullets. I'm worried about fire. I'm worried about being drowned where I stand, in open air. I'm worried about one of them knowing how to turn the poured stone under our feet to dust and sinking us in it, like Matrugena here can do."

"And I know that someone took a shot at the Chaldean emissary with a high-powered rifle today," Adam returned, evenly. "There've been experiments with ceramic inserts for these vests for rifles, but nothing successful so far. This is the best I can do to keep us all alive." He looked around, and added, looking into the mid-distance, "Though, to be honest, I don't think the attack on the Chaldean woman was actually meant to kill her."

Sigrun's eyebrows rose. "Why not?"

"The *gardia* finished checking the scene. Only one bullet appears to have been fired. And it missed. Personally, I was trained to double-tap. Either this is someone who doesn't know what they're doing, they were interrupted, or they deliberately didn't take a second shot." Adam shrugged. "Wear them. You, too, Sig."

"You three can at least wear shirts over them," Sigrun muttered, and began struggling with the fastenings. "It's going to be obvious that I'm wearing this, Adam."

"Let it be obvious. You're on a protective detail in Judea. Everyone knows we have guns here." Adam helped her get the vest over her head, and cinched it up for her. "There. How's that feel?"

"Like a turtle's shell."

"I've seen you wear thirty pounds of chain mail before. This is less than ten."

"Yes, but chain mail *moves*. This does not." Sigrun grimaced. "Let's go meet the propraetor's car, shall we?"

And thus, ten minutes later, Adam had doffed his skullcap once more to become a faceless protector around the propraetor; all four of the main lictors were on duty, and Sigrun could *feel* the energies both Kanmi and Trennus were maintaining around Livorus' form, though neither man showed any visible strain as they walked. But because the two mages had their attentions occupied in this manner, it was up to Sigrun and Adam to watch the crowd and the booths that much more carefully. Each row was cleared out by security, but that didn't mean someone couldn't hide in this booth or that. And while there were lictors around Poppaea and the children, it was still up to *them* to protect Livorus.

And then their steps happened to take them down a row of booths already cleared for another visiting dignitary's deputation. "Everyone smile," Livorus said, doing so, faintly, himself. "Let us prepare for *diplomacy*."

"Lie and pass the teacups, yes, *dominus*," Kanmi muttered.

Livorus paused in his steps, and beckoned his lictors closer. "Keep in mind," he murmured to them all quietly, "From the perspective of the

Persian Empire, and its various subject nations, Rome has largely . . . how *have* you all taken to putting it? Ah yes. Brandished the *fasces* in their faces since the days of Antiochus IV. Nevermind that those were Hellene emperors in Persian clothing; they still see two thousand years of being told *no*." Livorus' smile was faint. "You know, and I know, that what we largely did was tell them *no*, they couldn't try to take Egypt over, and no, they couldn't have Judea or Tyre or Asia Minor, either. As I recall my history, the Lydians cheered the Legions in the streets when they arrived." Livorus looked around at them all. "You're all members of the . . . forgive me . . . subject states that Rome built as a protective ring around the heart of the Empire. The Chaldeans and the Medians are very much in the same position as each and every one of you."

"Understood," Adam returned, his tone even. "Somewhat hard to keep track of, sir, when one lives next door, and not actually among the Seven Hills of Rome."

———————————

The Chaldean deputation practically *seethed* with enchantments. Sigrun had rarely sensed this much magic in one place, at one time before. The Chaldean emissary, herself, Erida Lelayn, was known to be an absolute firepower of a magus, which was unusual; while women with sorcerous powers were trained as magi, few attained her level of power . . . though her family was very highly placed among the Magi. Through the bodyguards flanking her, Sigrun could see the woman's dark, curling hair, dressed in elaborate ringlets, under an elaborate headdress of multiple layers of silk scarves. Her eyes gleamed like basalt pebbles, marked out with kohl, and kohl had been used, again, to trace symbols on her forehead, cheeks, and chin—informing anyone who looked at her that she was of the Magi. Her clothing was made of rich, heavy silks, an over-robe of dusty red brocade above a black underdress, with heavy gold embroidery everywhere, and she had a half-dozen small pokes dangling from her belt, and wore a small fortune in jewelry that was all probably heavily enchanted. In spite of it all, she had a round, surprisingly sweet face that, to Sigrun's eyes, actually wavered slightly from spirit energies around her. Invisible to most mortals, a python twined around her throat and shoulders like a stole, lividly green, and radiating power; a second snake, this one a cobra, twined around her right wrist like a bracelet, radiating red fire as it raised its head to hiss. A hawk, apparently made of moonbeams, landed on her shoulder, and another layer of translucent light pulled up around the young woman's form. "Three spirits on her," Sigrun murmured. Her eyes shifted to the rest of the guards, and she tensed, slightly. The man to Erida's right carried the kind of sword one really wished would be left in the history books—about three feet in length, with a vicious sickle curve. He also carried a bow, strung, over his shoulder, and a quiver at his waist. *Not god-born, though. I think.*

"Three spirits manifesting," Trennus corrected, softly. "I'm sensing about a dozen others, between her and the bodyguards."

"I don't see a damned thing," Adam muttered.

At which point Lassair manifested, physically, landing on Trennus' shoulder and shrilling a single note that pierced the air.

The Chaldeans, as one, looked at the firebird, and their eyes widened slightly as Lassair settled down to preen lightly at Trennus' braids, even as he tried to shoo her, gently, away. "Propraetor Antonius Livorus? I've heard so much about you. What an unexpected pleasure," Erida finally said, with a sweet smile that didn't reach her eyes, as she stepped forward through her flanking bodyguards, offering, not a hand to be clasped, but putting both hands together at her heart to bow, minimally. Sigrun caught a glimpse of a bandage under Erida's brocade sleeve, mostly concealed. *All right. She hasn't healed completely from the attack, no matter how composed her face is right now.*

Livorus didn't bow. He did, however, nod, briefly in response. "Lady Erida, I presume? I have not had the pleasure of making your acquaintance before." He gestured Poppaea closer. "My lady wife, Poppaea. Our children." He gestured again, and the children lined up, wide-eyed, but drilled in formal manners since the day they were born. "May I enquire as to what brings you to an air and space exposition?"

The words were a set piece, light and inane. Erida replied, airily, "Personally, I wanted to see how, precisely, the Hellenes and the Judeans were spending their money. There are those among my people who believe that they are building weapons platforms in space, with which to rain down death on Persia."

Livorus looked around. "And do you believe that, Lady Erida?"

"My mind is open, and therefore, unclouded. I am here to see what I may see."

"Then perhaps you might join my small party. We might make less trouble for security in that fashion."

"You display a surprising amount of solicitude for your underlings, Propraetor." There was a brief hint of ice in her eyes, but she accepted Livorus' left arm, while Poppaea remained on his right. There was a brief exchange of stares between the two sets of bodyguards . . . and then they all fell in, moving to encircle their various protectees, as they made their way through the convention hall, and to the side room, where the Median emissary was already waiting for them. Kashir Maranata was in his mid-forties, and stocky. Not fat; muscled, rather, and his dossier suggested that the man, who was a relative of the current satrap of Media, Daiukku, spent much of his free time working out with his bodyguards. His dossier also indicated that he currently had two wives, neither of whom were along with him on this trip, though his chief bodyguard, strikingly, was another female magus. Sigrun evaluated, fast. Maranata wore a saffron-colored over-robe, an inner one of white linen, and a matching, rounded cap. Heavy gold rings . . . and no spirits directly perched on him, though he, like Erida, had heavy magical shielding around him, as well. *Well, this could be worse,* Sigrun told herself as twelve bodyguards and three negotiators moved into the conference room that they'd inspected no more than twenty minutes ago, and had been under guard all time since. "Poppaea, my dear," Livorus told his wife, lightly.

"I'm sure you would prefer to continue to examine the exhibits with the children and your lictors. This is about to become dreadfully tedious."

Poppaea shrugged, her expression already bored. "Yes. Of course, my dear husband." She gathered the children and her guards, and left, and the door dogged shut behind them all.

Sigrun untucked the watch she kept chained to her belt and usually snugged inside the newfangled hip pocket of her jeans. Snapping the case open told her that it was well after five postmeridian. *They're going to need something to eat during this meeting. We checked catering, we have food-tasters on hand in the kitchens . . . but this is convention-hall food. The tasters might not be able to tell the difference between that and genuine poison . . . .*

"Thank you all for joining me today." Livorus told the other emissaries, and settled his elbows lightly on the table as he sat. "I trust you have not been unduly discommoded in your travels?"

"Other than a minor incident, doubtless with Judean agitators yesterday?" Erida murmured in reply. "Not at all."

Livorus noted, lightly, his eyes sharp, "Apparently, someone imported some sort of Persian relic that caused a traffic entanglement that caused me a few delays."

"Yes, I did hear something about that," Erida replied, coolly. "I troubled my staff to do a little research about this relic. Quite interesting. Apparently, a number of antiquities were stolen from the Persepolis Museum last month. A very large clay urn, as well as about three dozen of what were categorized as 'spirit bottles.' Half of them were categorized in the museum's file card system as djinn containers. The others were all older, and categorized as *alu*." She folded her hands together neatly. "No one seems to know where they might have gotten to."

"A puzzle," Livorus agreed, tightly. "Forgive my ignorance, but *alu*?" He glanced at Trennus. "Matrugena?"

Trennus shook his head. "I'm not familiar, myself, sir."

Erida shrugged, tilting her head to the side slightly. "They are very ancient. Every last one of them, that we are aware of, was caged centuries ago, and their bottles laid to rest in a variety of tombs. We rather used to treat the tombs of our kings as . . . ordnance disposal sites, I'm afraid. We would send powerful spirits to rest with them, to protect them. Forever. At least until the archaeologists came along and dug everything back up again. Now, we haven't precisely *opened* any of these bottles, but contemporaneous writings on cuneiform tablets left in the tombs describe tall, gaunt creatures with the heads of hyenas and eyes that glow green in the darkness. They are spirits of the night, apparently. They hunt in packs, following a female pack-leader, just as hyenas themselves do. And there is nowhere they cannot reach in the dark. They supposedly become wisps of smoke in the darkness, passing through the cracks under doors. Nothing can bar them in their hunt besides light. Their laughter terrifies, and their bite is death."

Sigrun stirred uneasily. "Perhaps at some point in the future," she said, very quietly, and to Livorus, not to anyone else at the table, "these two kingdoms should consider locking such items in secure ordnance facilities? Or ensuring that the creatures within should be banished permanently, rather than . . . stored?" Her tone was as neutral as she could make it, but after dealing with the *pazuzu* last night, she was in no mood to hear about anyone's cultural treasures or cultural history. These were *weapons*. Living, self-motivated weapons that could be turned against a single target, or unleashed in a public area to slaughter civilians. She'd seen a fair number of summonings on the Mongol border, but the *pazuzu* had been devastatingly powerful, if primitive in its methods.

"A point to add to any future discussions. Thank you, my dear." Livorus' voice was just as quiet as Sigrun's had been, but she knew that the other negotiators had likely missed little.

"For myself, only *ghul* rising in the streets around my hotel. Most disagreeable," the Median emissary noted, letting the by-play pass him by, rather than making an issue of Sigrun's words. "Even if this were a warning, I would still push on with these talks, Propraetor Livorus. May we begin?"

Livorus raised his eyebrows slightly. "Straight to business." This was unusual for a Median, Sigrun knew. They tended to like a few hours or even days of getting to know the *feel* of someone, before getting to business. Even haggling in a market might take place over several cups of coffee.

Maranata looked around. "Can we arrange a little privacy?"

Livorus gestured to Kanmi. "Eshmunazar? If you would be so kind?"

Kanmi lowered his head and murmured for a moment, and a ripple of energy pushed out through the room. This was a larger version of the sound-deadening field than he'd used in the past; the edge of the field stopped the energy of sound waves from transmitting through the air past a certain point . . . and, just for verification purposes, Kanmi said, "Radios off, please," and sent out an electromagnetic pulse, as well. One sure to disrupt any listening equipment that their guests might have brought in, since the room had been secured by the lictors and the *gardia*, though it shouldn't affect the radios that everyone carried, so long as they were currently turned off. As the lictors' were. "You can turn your personal radios back on now," Kanmi added, and Sigrun clicked the switch on the one at her waist.

There were a few murmurs from the various sorcerers in the retinue of the Chaldean and Median emissaries, and Lady Erida's fine brows rose, slightly; Sigrun took that as an indication that Kanmi had just surprised them. When the sorcerer from Tyre raised his head, his expression was blank, but there was a sardonic twinkle in his eyes that suggested that Kanmi was enjoying himself.

Sigrun glanced at Livorus for permission, and then stood, planting herself by the door, so that she could listen to the conversation inside the bubble with one ear . . . and listen for trouble outside the door with the other. That was one of the unfortunate side-effects of Kanmi's ability; it worked both ways. "There," Livorus said now. "Much better. You were saying, Lord Maranata?"

"Yes." The Median ambassador toyed with the gold chain of office that swung across his chest. "Well, it's hardly a secret that over the past five years, I've pushed Satrap Daiukku to pursue trade policies that would allow us better access to Roman markets. It's also hardly a secret that the Mongol Khanate is putting pressure on our northern border again."

"And you cannot turn to Persia for assistance?" Livorus commented, his tone neutral.

"Emperor Tiridates, tenth of that name . . . is aging and ill. His mind wanders. The court physicians say it is no more than the natural effects of aging, but given the wide number and variety of favorites the Emperor enjoyed in his youth, one must wonder if it is a more social ailment than mere dementia." Maranata's voice was as dry as sand. "He has twelve sons, Propraetor. The Empress herself is barren. His twelve sons are thus spread out between three official queens and five concubines. He has not named an heir, and the Persians have never allowed the throne to fall to merely the eldest, except if he happened to be born of the legitimate Empress."

"You expect infighting, then?" Livorus said, calmly.

"Propraetor, I expect nothing less than *civil war* inside the next three years. Satrap Daiukku agrees with my assessment. And we believe that it is time to remove our people and our country from the reach of that incipient conflict." The envoy toyed with his chains again. "We wish to retain our ports along the southern Caspian Sea. History tells us that every time the Empire has had one of these dynastic spasms, neighboring nations attempt to scavenge from the Empire's middens. Better to be absorbed by Rome, than eaten alive by the Mongols or overrun by Raccia, yes? And in exchange for that, we're quite willing to give you levies of troops. Minor tribute."

"Magi?" Livorus said, almost idly.

"In limited numbers, yes." Maranata's voice was cautious. "We would have to negotiate how many. We would prefer to keep the majority for self-defense."

Livorus glanced at Erida. "And you, Lady Erida. What is your government's position at the moment?" Chaldea was a thin strip of a nation, located almost entirely along the eastern side of the Wall.

She folded her hands neatly in front of her. "We have a very similar proposition for you, propraetor. However, our concern is that we could suffer repercussions for withdrawing from the Empire. Our citizens currently serving in Persia, proper, could be prevented from returning home. Our country could become a battlefield." Her expression was neutral. "We would require certain provisions for our protection. Of course, as subject kingdoms, Rome would be required to protect us, yes?"

Livorus smiled faintly. "Yes, we would be required, in the spirit of reciprocity, to defend you. Which would put Rome in direct conflict with Persia for the first time in over a century. You would have to give us something of equal worth to that risk. For example, we already have ports on the Caspian Sea. What can you offer, above and beyond your magi, to make the risk of open hostility all that much more palatable to Rome?" He tapped his fingers together. "With that being said, of course, as subject kingdoms, you would be required to cease and desist in any hostilities across the Wall, against Asia Minor, the Eastern Carthaginian provinces, and Judea."

Dark glances exchanged between the two other envoys. "And here it is, we were told that you, Propraetor Livorus, would be interested in undoing some of the wrongs of the past, and not merely interested in the monetary and political gains of the Empire," Maranata said, dryly.

"Oh, but I am. But I will not commit Rome to a struggle that is largely for the convenience of outsiders, without ensuring that Rome sees something from the bargain." Livorus smiled thinly. "Come now. Let us bargain in trust and in fairness with one another. You are, many of you, summoners. Surely, you must have some experience with the concept."

Sigrun watched the table, keeping one ear on the conversation, and one ear on the hustle and bustle of the conference hall outside, as the three envoys began to get past the 'good faith' generalities, and start negotiating in terms of hard facts. Livorus wanted conditions that protected all sides, and told the others, with brutal frankness, "I fully expect that, should your civil war not materialize, you will not be looking to Rome, but continuing to look to Persia."

"If the emperor died tomorrow, there *would* be civil war. The longer he lives, the longer his various sons have time to make alliances, solidify power bases, and attempt to kill one another," Erida acknowledged, with equal, and breathtaking honesty. She slid a glance towards her chief bodyguard, and added, "I don't suppose that Rome would be interested in speeding Persia's slide into civil war?"

They're lovers, Sigrun thought, instantly. She could read the glances, the body-language, but there was something . . . off about it. *She loves her bodyguard. Trusts him, implicitly. And he made that suggestion to her before they entered the room. Why?* Her eyes flicked to the body-guard, the one who carried the sword and the bow, and caught the hard look in his eyes, the way his body actually faced away from his lover, not turned towards her, though his eyes didn't leave her face. *That's not actually a guarding position. He's not watching the room. He's watching her, to . . . make sure she says it? . . . and his body-language says disaffection, not intimacy. What does that even mean?* Sigrun watched as the man slid a hand under the table, and kept her eyes open, even as she said, silently, *Lassair?*

Yes?

Please ask Trennus to watch Erida's chief bodyguard. Something's amiss with him.

Yes. We know. He doesn't look right to me. I . . . can't focus on him. One moment he's there, one moment, he . . . looks like the woman. Distress in Lassair's silent voice. *We think it's some form of a misdirection enchantment, one designed to draw pursuers to him, instead of her.*

What would be involved in that?

Blood. Hers. Menstrual, by preference. A charm would work better, if she bled directly into a vial, but even rags soaked in her blood would do.

. . . All right. More than I needed to know. Tell the others?

I will pass the information to them, yes.

Out loud, Livorus was responding to Erida, "No, I think not. It is not in the Empire's interest to deliberately destabilize Persia. To do so would be to strengthen the Mongolian Khanate and the Qin Empire." His blue eyes were level as he added, calmly, "Beyond the mere practicalities, there is also that old-fashioned notion of Roman honor. I may not be much for the days of the old republic, but there are principles from that era which I do admire."

Erida actually smiled, faintly. "I rather thought you might say that, propraetor. But you will admit that it was necessary for us to know if you were a man of principle or not."

"Oh, I am thoroughly unprincipled, when the occasion demands it. This does not." Livorus turned a page in his notebook, and began writing once again.

Outside, in the convention center lobby, people continued to file through the single set of opened double doors. It was *hot* today, miserably so, even by Judean standards, though it was early Maius. Everyone agreed that the unseasonable torrential rains of yesterday had contributed to the mugginess that now left everyone in line with a severe case of lassitude . . . but that meant that vendors were doing a brisk business pouring cold beer and honey mead into paper cups, and handing over paper cones filled with shaved ice to people in the lobby. Past the double doors, guards stood by the turnstile attendants, who were tearing tickets and letting people through the mechanical arms that barred their way through the doors.

It was hot, boring, dull work. And the members of the JDF had no idea why military backup had been requested, above and beyond the military police on hand to make sure that no one did anything untoward to the aircraft on exhibit in the parking lot. "Would be better if we could stand inside with the booths," one of the young soldiers commented, wiping his face and adjusting his rifle on its strap around his neck. "At least there's air conditioning inside."

"And there are pretty girls in skin-tight silvery spacesuits inside to look at? Mind on your work." The young soldier's lieutenant glanced up at a man that the attendants had stopped at the entrance. He saw olive skin, dark hair, neatly cut, and a couple days' growth of beard, and light khaki shirt and jeans. The young man also had a paper sack in his hand, wrapped around a bottle, the neck of which barely protruded from the paper.

"I'm sorry, sir. No outside food or drink inside the main exhibition hall. There's a recycling bin over there for glass," the attendant told the man helpfully.

"Sorry," the man replied, in good Latin, smiling. "Let me just finish drinking this, and I'll toss it." He turned away towards the recycling bin, tilting the bottle back to his lips, and then slid it into the receptacle with enough care to ensure that it didn't shatter inside. He walked back over, bought a map of the booths, and wandered inside with the rest of the crowd.

The young lieutenant relaxed back against the doorframe. He'd just come on-shift at two postmeridian, and he had a good five hours of his shift left ahead of him. He'd wondered at the man who'd just walked in . . . it seemed early in the day to be drinking hard liquor, but it could have been one of those fancy new individual beers in a glass bottle. There certainly hadn't been much smell of liquor as the man had passed. But, it was warm, and in the end, the man hadn't been a problem. He'd done what he'd been asked to do, and left the prohibited item outside.

Back in the conference room, after three hours, and several trays of dormice on sticks, hardboiled eggs, pickles, and a variety of other foods had been moved to the room to remain almost entirely uneaten by the envoys themselves, it was well after eight antemeridian, and dark outside. The convention center would remain open for at least another hour, and Sigrun was slightly restless. The more so, as details began to be hammered out. Entering the Roman empire brought with it attendant problems and privileges. The fact that Babylon itself would be now so close to the edge of Roman territory, being adjacent to Chaldea, was a problem. Agreeing to allow Roman garrisons inside their territories was another, and deciding what percentages of foreign levies, such as the Judean air force, could be admitted inside their border would largely have to be handled at another time.

It was boring, tedious work to partake of, and to listen to. Thus, Sigrun wasn't particularly surprised when the various bodyguards all began to stand up and move around, in turn, trying to stay awake. Alert. On guard. Eventually, Erida's chief bodyguard stood, himself, and moved back from the table. Found a comfortable place along the wall, just halfway through the sound-dampening field, just as Sigrun herself still stood against the wall by the door. He was directly behind his protectee, and still watching her, and the room, warily. Sigrun wasn't entirely sure why she was uneasy with him, but it all boiled down to what she called her truth-sense. It was partially a godly power, true, but it wasn't entirely magical. She was simply very much in tune with facial expression. Body language. What she called the lie in someone's eyes was really a matter of both. And this man was lying, to his protectee, at least, and it put Sigrun on edge.

So she was only partially distracted when one of the other bodyguards dropped a wineglass with a loud shattering sound, and she caught, out of the corner of her eye, the lead bodyguard's hand dropping to his pocket. "Hey!" Kanmi blurted, his head snapping up. "Someone just transmitted a radio frequency signal—" his head swiveled towards the lead Chaldean bodyguard. "You son of a *bitch!*"

Magic. Magic happening faster than even god-born senses allowed her to see. Kanmi was rarely an attacker. He followed principles akin to those of martial arts in his magical practice; he used other people's powers, other people's attacks, against them. This was one of the rare exceptions, and Sigrun felt the wave of raw force as it slammed into the Chaldean man, pinning him to the wall . . . but she could see some sort of an energy shield in place over the man, like a shell, keeping Kanmi's attack at bay. "What's going on?" Erida demanded, raising her own hands into position to incant, and energy flaring to life around her. "What's the meaning of this?"

Kanmi struggled to hold the Chaldean bodyguard in place. Chaldeans had been, as he'd reminded the others just hours ago, the first organized magic-users in recorded history. That didn't mean they were the best. But it meant that their entire culture was *steeped* in lore. Every child born in Chaldea grew up hoping he or she was a magus. It was a ticket out of poverty and privation, and every child was tested for the gift of magic when they were eight years of age. The Magi were their heroes. The closest thing to god-born that the Chaldeans *had* were sorcerers and summoners. And it felt, very much, as if this bodyguard were both. The wave of force that Kanmi had slammed the man with had been pulled from the batteries in his pockets; he had nothing ambient here to work with, besides cold, clear, air-conditioned atmosphere, and the warmth of human bodies.

Starting from *nothing* was the very hardest thing a sorcerer could do, nothing more than will and their own body. *Come on,* Kanmi thought, trying to hold the man pinned, one hand out in front of him as if he'd slapped the bodyguard to the wall like a fly. *Try something. Give me something to work with. Or just stand down. Make my life easy for once.* But it was like trying to nail butter to the wall. Everything he did, there were . . . shields around the bodyguard, and they weren't made of sorcery, but of spirit-energy. "Matru!" Kanmi snapped out, too busy to bother with the full name. "Get ready to banish—"

The man against the wall raised his head, and a single drop of blood trickled from the corner of his mouth, testimony to how hard Kanmi had hit him. A rippling wave of *words* in Chaldean, and Kanmi could feel the energy coming at him, and tried to parry it, but it wasn't force. Wasn't heat. It was like trying to parry *fog. Ah, shit. He's an elementalist, and he's not specialized in fire. He's water.*

The spell hit his body, and Kanmi felt his veins bulge, could see them rippling in his forearms as his blood pressure suddenly *spiked.* Pain. Searing pain, as the water in his body began to *migrate,* forcing its way out of his veins, leaving red blood cells like jelly, abandoned in its wake. *Ah, shit, shit, shit,* Kanmi thought, struggling with it, trying to get a *grip* on the enchantment. *It's all going to pour out on the floor . . . .*

. . . and then, instead, he realized that he couldn't *breathe.* His breath was coming in short, quick pants from terror already, but he couldn't get the breath down any further than his trachea. His son, Himi, was asthmatic. He knew the panicked look in his son's eyes when he suffered an attack, and knew it was reflected in his own now, as the water from his body rose up in his throat, and Kanmi dropped to the ground, coughing and choking, trying to expel his own body's fluids that threatened to drown him. *Drowned on dry land. I said it hours ago. Fuck you, Chaldean. You die.* The thoughts were muzzy, however. Kanmi knew all too well that if the attack weren't stopped, he'd die inside of a minute. Not enough liquid blood to pump through his heart. The turgid flow was already causing his heart to spasm. Even if the spell stopped right *now* . . . Kanmi's thoughts were distant, but frighteningly clear. Even if he resisted, the sticky globules of blood clotting in his body could turn into pulmonary embolisms. Could become a stroke.

He needed to reverse this. He *could* reverse this. He knew he could push the water back into his veins and ease his own blood-flow. He just couldn't. The knowledge of *how* was there, but drowning creates a reflexive panic. The body itself takes over. Fights to live, when it's the mind that will save someone. *Someone kill this son of a bitch. Someone save my life.*

Sigrun had already fallen in beside Adam and Trennus, guarding Livorus; Adam had pulled a pistol . . . and she could feel the backwash of energy moving across the room, like a whip uncoiling from a practiced hand. The Chaldean bodyguard had one fist raised, and was muttering under his breath, rapidly. He was a Magus, and his incantations were just as fast as Kanmi's. Eshmunazar tried to catch it, but it wasn't force, it wasn't heat, it wasn't energy . . . it was . . . pressure, and it was *subtle*. Kanmi swayed on his feet, and began to gasp and choke, and he began to cough up red-tinged, frothy water from deep inside his lungs. Sigrun's eyes widened.

He's drowning in his own fluids, Lassair hissed from Trennus' shoulder. *The water in his blood is passing into his lungs. The blood is left to congeal and curdle in his veins. Stop the dark summoner!*

"Call off your bodyguard and I'll call off my lictor," Livorus told Erida, but before anyone could so much as *move*, the lights in the building went out, followed by screams, clearly audible as Kanmi's sound-dampening field dropped. Even emergency lightning systems were down, and Sigrun's skin crawled. She could still see energy fields and spirits, but not the people that the fields surrounded, or the spirits attended upon. She had less than a second to register that, and then she heard a groan and a thump from Kanmi's direction. Split-second to make a choice. The source of the spell, or her drowning friend?

Shouting, "Stay with Livorus!" at Adam, Sigrun launched herself for where she could still see the energy field of the bodyguard . . . only to be caught, in turn by *something* that materialized between her and her target, blocking her view. She slammed into it full speed, unable to stop herself in time, and felt whatever it was lurch a little at the impact . . . and then she looked up and met green-glowing eyes in the darkness, three feet over her own head. Could smell something wild and unkempt, like wet dog fur, and foul breath passed over her cheek as clawed hands dug into her upper arms. *Light,* Sigrun thought, and channeled power through her body, illuminating herself from within. *Light, light, light!*

From the middle of her self-enkindled blaze, Sigrun looked up into the huge maw of what looked like nothing so much as a hyena, mouth open and slavering down at her . . . but it was a hyena that looked something like a man, as well. Rail-thin body, sparse fur, dark and barely dappled with lighter speckles . . . clawed hands, tearing into her skin . . . and green-glowing eyes. The creature bared its teeth at her and howled with laughter, a mad, wild sound that chilled Sigrun into her soul.

Chaos. Madness, as several of the bodyguards in the room turned to run, bursting through one of the other doors and out into the darkened hallway. The lead Chaldean bodyguard leaped from the wall to his envoy, and snaked an arm around Erida's waist, settling a knife at her throat. Trennus, shouting at the bodyguards fleeing the scene, "No! Stay in the light! Stay in the light!" even as he tried to stand in front of Livorus, and Kanmi, on the ground, continued to heave out his life's fluids from his lungs.

Lassair flared into brilliance, and Sigrun knocked the *alu*-demon's hands away from her arms, even as Adam's hand dropped into place beside her, holding a revolver . . . and fired, point-blank, on the demon. Sigrun spun away from the sound, flinching instinctively, but the demon had already leaped backwards and out into the darkness of the hall, crashing through the closed door, leaving nothing more than trails of smoke . . . and leaving them in a room with the Chaldean envoy, who now had a knife pressed to her throat by her own bodyguard, while screams and cries of mortal terror and mad laughter echoed from the convention hall outside.

Chapter XIII: Invictus

The history of humanity is also the history of disease. The history of war is the history of wounds and their treatment. Consider how different history might have been, if the virulently infectious 'black plague' of 1304 AC had been transmitted slowly by travel along the Silk Road, rather than being contained, to both the infected humans and the rats that carried the fleas, which were constrained for weeks at a time on the cargo ships that moved between Asia and Europa. As it was, in many cases, the plagued ships were lost with all hands as the sailors, fevered and delirious, were unable to tend to tillers and sails, wandered lost for miles over the ocean, or arrived on shore with all hands aboard dead.

As it was, a few port areas suffered from the disease, and might have spread the illness further inland, but the Empire, which had an excellent understanding of hygiene and possessed good communications, rapidly quarantined the areas and burned the bodies and belongings of the dead, limiting the effects of the bubonic and pneumonic plagues. All told, only two million people died of both diseases in Europa between 1304 and 1308 AC. If infection rates in Europa had been similar to those reported in Qin and India, where the disease first spread, casualty estimates for Europa might have escalated to as many as 75 to 100 million people dead inside of two to four years. The constraints of sea travel and the rapid response of informed city officials in the ports of the Empire prevented a catastrophe unlike any that Europa has ever known.

Smallpox, however, remained the scourge of mankind for centuries. In 1505 AC, a Qin physician named Wan Quan was the first to publish a study on the potential for inoculating people against the disease. His methods were crude, by modern standards . . . but he was a giant in the medical field that sadly, too few people know about today. He took the skin lesions of people infected with smallpox, and reduced these scabs to a fine powder, which he then blew up the noses of healthy individuals. The small number of weakened viruses remaining in the scabs induced a milder version of smallpox in the healthy test subjects . . . and provided their immune systems with the necessary antibodies for the disease.

Wan Quan's methodology was published and translated over the next hundred years, and transmitted into the West, where Eadward Gann, a Britannian, published in 1575 AC his notes on cowpox, and how infection with this disease seemed to confer immunity to smallpox. From these two avenues of research came a smallpox vaccine for the general population in 1585 AC.

Bacteria were directly observed that same year in independent laboratories in Judea and Hellas, as microscopes were developed that were capable of sufficient magnification. This led directly to the development of germ theory. The Romans and Hellenes, already notably fastidious in their bathing practices, had already introduced soap to the public baths, above and beyond the olive oil and strigium used in antiquity; their populations were notably healthier than other areas of the world. This kind of evidence led to improvements in hospital hygiene and battlefield medical practices, both of which have saved countless lives over the years.

On the topic of battlefield medicine, surgery has lagged in many areas, compared to the rest of common medical practice. Surgery required the development of anatomical knowledge, which was systematized in Hellas; however, Judean religious practices made autopsies and the use of cadavers problematic. Judean physicians, however, have had no problem using the knowledge garnered by Hellene doctors and applying it for the betterment of living patients. Surgical practices, however, required the development of better anesthesia and hygiene. Hellene physicians used diethyl ether to anesthetize chickens as early as 1531 AC. And poppy juice had been used as a sedative for centuries, but it was not distilled into morphine until 1697 AC, when it was used in field hospitals. By 1701 AC, ether and chloroform had been refined to allow for amputations and internal surgery, but patients continued to die due to infection.

Packing wounds with moldy bread had been a folk remedy since the time of Alexander the Great, but determining specifically which mold spores produced the antibacterial effect did not occur until 1756 AC, when Dr. Alexander Argyris discovered penicillin. It was first used in field hospitals during the War of the Caspian Sea (1753-1763 AC). As a result, less than twenty years later, in 1771 AC, the first Caesarian procedure was conducted, in which mother and child lived.

Birth-control methods have existed for almost as long as humanity itself. Ancient courtesans used vinegar-soaked sponges, and some ancient Egyptian women reportedly used vaginal plugs made from baked crocodile dung. The sheepskin condom, however, with all its ease of use and utility in preventing the transmission of disease, was developed in Hellas in 1215 AC. Initially, this contraceptive was intended to cut down on the number of women petitioning various governments for the support of children born out of wedlock to legionnaires and sailors, which represented a drain on the public coffers. It was immediately noted that the number of soldiers afflicted with social diseases declined, and because the sheepskins were undeniably effective, Imperial officials made these items freely available to the poor and indigent, so that they might have another option besides leaving their newborns exposed to die outside the outskirts of major cities. The condom became a stable of bawdy comedies from the 1300s to the 1400s AC, and a frequent trope with which a cuckolded husband in a play might discover his shame . . . but the stock figure of the deluded old husband was usually convinced by his cunning young bride that this was merely her thimble, or some other common object.

Hormonal birth control, in contrast, was pioneered in Nova Germania, as part of the women's rights movement, and the birth control pill became available commercially in about 1885 AC.

Today, most medical technology is developed largely in three countries: Judea, which has no god-born or magical recourses, Hellas, which has the tradition of Asclepius, and Nippon. Rome is the direct beneficiary of advances made by these three countries, and has some of the finest hospitals in the world. More distant regions of the Empire are dogged by a lack of trained doctors, a distaste for preventative or internal surgery, and a reliance on magic to create cures that natural philosophy can also purvey. Where magic and natural philosophy work in tandem, as in Hellas, medicine is at its best, though arguably, Judean surgical practices are among the finest on earth. It was they who developed the heart-lung bypass machine, which is vital for most cardiac surgery today, and are pioneering treatments for cancer, including the use of chemotherapy and radiation.

— Despina Pachis, <u>An Introduction to Modern Medicine</u>, p. 7. University of Athens

Press, Athens, Hellas, 1945 AC.

Maius 7, 1955 AC

Only seconds had passed. Adam's eyes watered in the brilliant light of Sigrun's rune-marks, and he kept his revolver trained on the bodyguard-turned-captor, who still had a knife to Erida's throat. "No shot," he muttered, quietly. The man had pulled back so that his face and body were mostly behind his human shield.

"Stay back, or she dies," the man warned. "No magic," he added, shifting just enough to address the other Chaldean bodyguards.

"*Abgar, you're insane. The Satrap will execute you —*" Adam understood *just* enough Persian to catch the gist.

"*The Emperor will reward me for doing my job, as I have done these fifteen years. Keeping an eye on rebels and fools. If you're wise, you'll drink poison now, before either of my lovely spirits takes you tonight . . . or the emperor's torture master uses you to instruct his apprentices in the fine art of extracting information.*" Abgar's voice was cold. Back in Latin: "Everyone, *back*. Or I slit her throat here and now."

"She's dead anyway," Sigrun said, her voice cold. "She might be your lover, but you already plan to kill her. With a Judean weapon. Just like the rifle yesterday was meant to look. Adam, for the sake of all the gods, don't —"

Right. Don't shoot, or if I do, for the lord's sake, don't miss. He wondered, in passing, how Sig *knew* some of that, but he *trusted* his partner. Trusted her ability to see truth in people's faces and eyes. And as he caught the man's eyes sliding towards the captive, away from them, just for a second, Adam knew it was true. Sigrun's words had hit a nerve, and Adam wanted to take the shot while the man was distracted . . . but no. Too damned close to the captive's face.

The man snarled and dragged the Chaldean envoy back towards the darkened hallway. "Follow, then. Let your friend die on the floor. Let her die on my knife." And then he was through the doorway, leaving behind a stunned tableaux: The stunned Chaldean and Median bodyguards — those who hadn't run as terror coiled through them from the mad laughter of the *alu*-demon — stared after him, as did Maranata, the Median envoy.

Then everyone moved at once. Trennus dropped to his knees and straightened Kanmi's body on the floor. "Got to get the water out so you can breath," he told the Carthaginian, sharply, pressing down just below the centerline of Kanmi's back. "Get a full breath when you can." Fluids gushed out of Kanmi's mouth as if he were a grotesque statue in a fountain, and Lassair fluttered down from Trennus' shoulder to land beside Kanmi, the phoenix resting her head against the mage's face. Adam could see the focus in Kanmi's eyes start to waver, even as Trennus said, sharply, "No, you don't. You don't die, Esh. Not today."

At the same time, Livorus turned and pointed at the door. "Go!" he told Adam and Sigrun. "If the Chaldean envoy dies, the whole treaty could be off the table. Keep her alive."

"What about you, sir?" Adam replied, sharply. His job was keeping the *propraetor* alive.

"I'll stay here with the Median envoy and his bodyguards. Gesture of good will. Matrugena will assist you when he's able. Go!"

Adam pulled his radio free of his belt, and tabbed it on as they headed for the door, cutting through the cross-chatter of frantic voices on it. "This is ben Maor. We have a Chaldean dignitary who's been taken hostage by one of her own retinue. He is armed and dangerous, and is a known sorcerer and summoner. Apprehend if possible, shoot to kill, if necessary. What's our status?"

"*Demons, multiple contacts, multiple locations —* "

"*Civilians all stampeding for the exits, can't get a shot on the demons —* "

"*One minute they're there, the next they're gone —* "

"*Can't see the damned things, other than a flash of the eyes —* "

"*Ben Adir, where are you?*"

"*Ben Erez is down, I just saw one of those things come out of nowhere, just a puff of smoke, and then claws and teeth —* "

Adam pushed the button to squelch everyone for a moment, and transmitted into the ensuing silence, "Get someone to the utility rooms and get the damned lights back on. The demons pull back from light, and may *have* to stay solid if they're not in the dark. Use flashlights if you have to. Battery-powered lanterns. Anything you can. If the utility room's not the answer for the overhead lights, find a generator, or trace back and see if the power lines have been cut. Move!"

Then he grabbed a flashlight from atop a cabinet, holding it in his left hand, still gripping his pistol in his right, spinning to clear the darkened hallway, while Sigrun pivoted left to clear her side. Very faint glow from the emergency overhead panels near the end of the hall. Just enough illumination to chart a course in the dark; the light from Sigrun's rune-marks was far brighter. "Clear," she said. "I think." Her voice was tight. "Adam, I can't *see* these creatures the way I can usually see the non-manifested spirits . . . they're just not visible at the moment."

"Understood. I can't see *any* of this, so you're ahead of me. Which way did they go?" Adam swept his flashlight from side to side, and caught the faintest ripple of *something* ahead of them. Training said *don't fire at what you can't identify* and instinct said *shoot, shoot now,* and training and instinct fought for control of his trigger finger. Instinct won. He pulled the trigger, twice, and he heard something *howl* and pull back into the door of another conference room. *Three shots,* he counted, mentally. *Three left. These were the silver-plated bullets, the ones Kanmi said he'd 'borrowed' some of my mother's silver forks to make for me. Let's hope I don't waste many more of these.* He couldn't let him think about Kanmi coughing out his life on the conference room floor. Not now. "That way?" He pointed right.

"Closest exit door is left, leading to the loading docks. Abgar's just as vulnerable in the dark as the rest of us."

"Do you really think he's vulnerable to them? Maybe he has a bargain with them."

"We know these are *alu* from Lelayn's description. We know their bottles were stolen from a museum. I doubt he knows their Names."

"We have only her say-so for that. This could be a set-up." Quick, sharp words as they cleared their surroundings.

"Suspicious, aren't you?" Sigrun paused. "No, I think they were released from their containers when he sent the signal. Las . . . she said Abgar was masked as Erida, though some sort of binding enchantment that makes them look the same, to spirits. So no. He's vulnerable. Tied up with a hostage."

"Till he kills her," Adam replied, his throat tight. *Damn it. Damn it all. How did they even get the alu in here?*

"He can't, I think. Not yet. Not till he's clear of the spirits he's loosed. She's his double. He's her double. It's like a scent-breaker thrown down along a trail."

They edged down the hall. "We're leaving enemies behind us." His shoulders were up against hers as he watched behind them, and she watched ahead of them, her inner light and his flashlight all that was keeping the demons at bay.

"I know. Can't be helped."

"Do they need to be solid to attack?" Adam asked, holding the revolver steady.

"Yes. At least, I think so. Spirits can possess humans. Demanifested, they can pass through humans, they can shield humans, and they can interact, but only with our minds. They have to be solid to attack us physically. That doesn't mean, however, that just because we can't see them, that they're insubstantial. They could just be invisible, the way Ehecatl could turn himself."

"Really wish I'd gotten you a revolver before we came here, Sig."

"Me, too. I feel defanged indoors." He glanced back over his shoulder and saw her kick the exit door open, and then shifted his gaze back to the hallway. Another ripple, just outside the fragile beam of his flashlight, and Adam fired, twice—*one bullet left, need to reload*—and saw a demon ripple into reality just in front of the door to the conference room in which the others were holding fast. It howled, smoke wisping out of its chest where he'd landed his shots.

"Silver works!" he shouted to the others . . . and an arrow slammed into the creature's arm from inside the room, this one alight with some sort of fire. *Phosphorus-tipped,* part of his mind noted. *They picked that up from JDF's bullets. Surprised none of them are carrying derringers . . . .*

But it was a distant set of thoughts as he fired once more, crouched, tucking the flashlight between his arm and body, and then flipped the revolver open, reloading smoothly, even as he heard cries and commotion from down the new hall, past the doorway. "We've got this, go!" came a voice from inside the conference room. *Trennus.*

Adam spun, giving his back to the foe, though his shoulder-blades itched, and looked down the hallway with Sigrun, quick, wincing peeks, as he heard the chatter of automatic gunfire and . . . snarling, grunting, cries of pain. Animalistic, savage, and unearthly, all at once. He snapped back as he *felt*, more than saw, something pass by his face. Another quick peek, and all he could see were vague shapes moving in the darkness at the end of the hall. Chatter of gunfire, a cry of pain—barely audible over the screams and cries coming from the main hall itself. Quick glance to the left, flicking his flashlight beam that direction, while Sigrun's pale radiance continued to fill the air around them. Bodies seemed to *coalesce* in the light. Snarling hyena-creatures locked in combat with the Chaldean bodyguards who'd fled out the other door of the conference room in a blind panic. And at the sides of the Chaldeans, fantastical beasts, like a gryphon with a foot-long beak and the body of a lion, rearing up on its hind legs to struggle with one of the hyena-beasts, black blood splattering everywhere. Adam's head jerked back the other direction. "Loading dock area's blocked, don't think they could've gone that way—"

"There's a JDF soldier at the other end of the hall," Sigrun replied, quickly. "He's under attack by an *alu*. That's where the machine gun fire is coming from." Her eyes were dark pits in the center of all the radiant lines and swirls on her face. "I can *get* to it, Adam. I can take it off him."

"And what?"

"Turn it around to face you, and you can shoot it."

And then you're going to get two in the back from a panicked guard who thinks you're spirit, Adam thought, grimly. He swore mentally and pulled her back into the shelter of the door again as another chatter of bullets rattled off. *I want to help the soldier. I need to. But the envoy's first priority. Harah. Well, no one ever promised me easy choices, did they?* "Someone get those lights back on again," Adam snapped into the radio, and took another cautious peek. *All right. They didn't go all the way to the south end of the hall. They can't get into the service area doors without going past our guy to the south—*another *wince* as he heard the unmistakable crunch of bone over the screams and cries from the convention hall itself. "He couldn't go north, he couldn't go south, that means he took her out into the convention hall." *Least optimal solution for him, but he can work his way through the crowds, if the demons leave him alone, right?* "Go."

"Adam, the soldier—"

"Is paid to take risks, just like us." Adam fumbled in the pockets of his protective vest, and came up with what he was looking for: a stick flare, which he snapped in half with the brilliant white flare of phosphorus, and threw down the hall towards the man fighting with the *alu* demon. *Give you a little help,* he thought, at the creature's form coalesced in a swirl of darkness amongst the light, and it turned its head to snarl, and he saw green eyes glaring at him. Marking him out.

In the conference room, Trennus had squeezed most of the water from Kanmi's lungs, understanding all too well that the red-tinged fluids flooding out on the short nap of the brown carpet were his friend's life. "Come on, Kanmi, *breathe*," Tren muttered, and heard the sharp report of two shots from the hall. *Lassair!*

His heart is damaged. The blood is as thick as mud inside of it. It strains to beat, flails itself. His mind requires air as well.

Help him!

I will not let Emberstone die, no. The phoenix's light vanished as Lassair slipped into Kanmi's body, and Trennus looked up, in between heartbeats, to see an *alu* demon outlined in the door. *Saraid!*

The white stag burst into existence between Trennus and the creature and lowered its huge rack of antlers, leaf-green light streaming from its eyes. Saraid was incorporeal at the moment, but her light was just enough to hold the *alu* at bay for a moment. Just long enough.

Kanmi opened his eyes and took his a shuddering breath. His mind was fuzzy and distant. Not enough oxygen to the brain. He turned his head and felt damp roughness against his cheek. *Seawater. I'm on the beach under the pier again. Hanno and Tabnit pushed the game too far this time. Mother's going to be so sad. Father's going to beat them both with a strap and then turn them over to the gardia. They must be panicking.* Distant. So very distant. *So this is what dying feels like.* Still, he couldn't quite believe it. There was a warmth in his chest to combat the unpleasantly familiar tightness there, and the *panic* was fading. His vision skewed, and his chest *hurt*, but now, he could fight. Just the way he always had.

Not wet sand. Wet *carpet*. Salt tang, still, but not *seawater*. Kanmi's eyes focused. His fingers scrabbled weakly against the rug, and he choked out the first word of a spell. *Return. Enter. Renew. Pass through.* He set up the construct in his mind and pictured water molecules burrowing through his body. First, what remained in his lungs. That was the easy part. Passing through the semi-permeable membranes of his cells, through the alveoli and into the tiny capillaries in his lungs. Fast. Probably too fast, just as it had all been drained into his lung cavity too quickly. It burned like fire, but his heart began to beat more regularly. His mind began to clear, and that gave him enough impetus to try to sit up.

"Stay down!" Trennus shoved him back to the floor. "You're in no condition to fight."

I am fighting, you great big lummox of a summoner, Kanmi thought, without animus, and redirected his mental construct. Oriented it at the water on the floor, and directed the water and salt to *return*. His kidneys would pay for this later, filtering out any impurities. He *couldn't* pull anything into himself large enough to impact a vein, fortunately. He swore viciously as the semi-permeable cell membranes of his skin, usually designed to keep things *out*, were forced to accept water back *in*. His own body's fluids or no, his body wasn't designed to do this, and it protested. Every nerve screamed. *I am not a fucking amoeba, and someone is going to pay for this.*

He forced his way back up, and blinked as he felt the warmth depart his chest. Kanmi couldn't usually see demanifested spirits, not the way Trennus and Sigrun could, but just for an instant, he caught a flicker of flame. *Thanks, Lassair.*

We could not let you go, Emberstone. Protect the one who binds you!

"Go! We've got this!" Trennus shouted into the hall as an arrow from one of the Median bodyguards behind him sliced into the *alu*'s arm. He stood slowly enough to ensure that the archers behind him wouldn't shoot him in the back, and stared up at the green eyes that were all he could see of the *alu* demon in the darkness of the hall, outside the reach of Saraid's pale radiance. Trennus' stomach tightened. The *alu*, individually, were far less powerful than the *pazuzu* had been. *I can do this.*

He'd been explaining the rules, such as they were, for binding and summoning to Adam for close to a year now. A few could pass the Veil either direction, of their own free will, but the vast majority *had* to be summoned. Once they were here, there were three main methods of dealing with them: killing their physical form, which might only banish the spirit, unless it was another spirit who did the killing. And then there were the options of binding and banishing. Banish a spirit, and they were shoved back into their own realm once more. Binding kept them here in this realm, but caged. Banishing required more effort than binding, and a banished spirit, if it couldn't just re-enter the world of its own accord, could be re-summoned . . . unless the summoner who banished them found some means of making that banishment permanent.

A summoner could use a piece of his life-force . . . or soul . . . to seal the Veil behind a spirit. That would keep them contained beyond the Veil for two, maybe three times the life of the summoner, much in the way blood-binding a spirit into an object held that spirit in place for the life of the summoner. Spirits banished impermanently could be re-summoned almost immediately, though they'd be dazed and weakened. And here was the part that was art, and not natural philosophy: Every spirit was different. Some were weak, some were strong, and you could only generalize so much. Trennus could bind or banish a weak combative spirit without its Name, generally by wrestling it into submission, either mentally or physically. A spirit of medium strength, he needed more leverage—its Name, a full circle, blood, or something like that. It was the same principle as grappling an opponent physically; the more points of contact you had, the easier they were to control.

The *pazuzu* had been very powerful. Even with its Name, Trennus hadn't had enough *holds* to banish it. Even binding it had been tricky. No prepared container. So he'd used blood-binding and an improvised container. These creatures . . . less powerful. But still dangerous. *Let's see what you've got*, he thought, and said, "Light!"

Lassair, once more out of Kanmi's body, flared into brilliance, and the *alu* in the doorway hissed, one paw pressed to the arrow in its opposing arm, and moved away . . . which was when Trennus attacked, reaching down into the earth for the ambient ley-energies all around him, adding to his own strength and speed. His left hand shot out and seized the creature's right wrist, as it was turning—the wounded arm was soaked in black blood, and slippery—and began to pull down and into the room at the same time. The hyena-like head turned, reflexively, discolored yellow teeth flashing in Lassair's pure light, and Trennus barely got his right hand in position in time, open-palm strike to the base of the creature's jaw knocking the head up and *away* . . . and then he locked his elbow, struggling to keep the fangs from turning, the mouth from biting off his hand, or tearing out his throat. Second by second, shifting his grip, jabbing for the green-glowing eyes, causing the monster to flinch away, which gave him *time*. Time to lash out with one foot, ley-energies coursing through him, and kick the creature's knee, dislocating it if not shattering the bone, and then twisting, pivoting, driving it to the ground.

Raging, writhing, bucking thing comprised of fur, teeth, claws, rage, and will. Like fighting a man with knives clutched in both hands, except there was a *hyena* head in the mix. Everything a deadly weapon. Trennus followed the creature to the ground, recoiling, trying to get in the rear mount behind it, even as it spun on the ground, reaching under itself with its left arm, turning, twisting, latching onto his left bicep with one clawed hand, huge fingers curling in and behind to cut into his triceps, boring in, tearing, drawing blood. *Fine, you want blood, you've got blood.* He jerked free, controlled that paw with one of his own, and got his other arm locked under the maw, along the throat. The beast had just enough speed and strength to twist its body once more, and lashed out with its left paw now, and caught Trennus' left leg, just behind the knee—*gods, what is it with my knees?*—driving through skin and tearing at muscle and tendons. Trennus swore, wrenched his leg back, got his *other* arm locked in place, and dropped his full bodyweight on the *alu*. Not enough, not with a creature this size . . . but he reached down into the earth for ley-energy, and *became* earth. Added to his own relative mass, allowing himself to be the stone that bore down on the creature. *"Not going anywhere,"* he told it, in his native Pictish.

Then he lifted his head and snapped at the others in the room, "Need a container. *Now*."

A Chaldean bodyguard who clearly *wasn't* a summoner looked around wildly and came up with a waxed paper cup, holding it up, only to be chastised vigorously by one of the others as they continued to scramble through the room's items. "This," Livorus said, quickly, opening an ice bucket brought by the catering people. No sparkling wine, naturally. This was a *convention hall*, and they hadn't wanted to draw attention by arranging anything fancy. And with Livorus there, no one had dared to offer *beer*; beer was unRoman. Uncivilized. Barbaric. Instead, there were individual bottles of *wine coolers* in the ice-bucket, each with its own cork. Trennus had thought these newfangled individual bottles terribly wasted on something so fundamentally undrinkable.

The propraetor worked the cork, which was oversized at the top, to allow for easy opening—no corkscrew needed—and removed it, with a faint pop, before pouring the out on the floor, almost like a libation. "I trust this will do, Matrugena?"

"It'll . . . be . . . fine . . ." Trennus grunted, still holding the creature down. "So long . . . as no one . . . turns off the damned lights . . . ." He had a bad vision of him holding the creature pinned, Lassair's light fading, and it turning into a wisp of smoke in his arms, just to rematerialize *behind* and atop him, its teeth crunching down on the back of his neck and shattering the spine and brainstem in one shot. "Someone . . . draw a damned circle . . . ."

One of the other summoners grabbed a marker from a dry-erase board and hurried over, tracing the binding circle on the rug—having to go over in some places, several times, to make sure the lines were true. "Bottle," Trennus snapped out, and Livorus rolled it to the middle of the circle, and the *alu* bucked and writhed, trying to get to it, trying to *crack* it. Trennus growled and forced it *back*. "No, you don't." He turned his head, verified that the circle was finished, and began the second phase of the battle, the mental one. Forcing the *alu* out of its physical form, with pure willpower. Forcing it to dematerialize, constrained by the circle itself. It dissipated under him like morning fog, and Trennus' body slumped to the ground, but he'd been ready for that. He could still *see* it, a distant and wavering form, misty and immaterial . . . and he paused. *I could try to banish it . . . no. Don't have enough other spirits to leverage for help, and I'm not using a piece of my life-energy to seal it past the Veil permanently.* Trennus raised his head, and looked around the room. The other summoners all had a spirit or two coiling around them, protecting them. "I can banish, if you help. Or we re-bind."

The Chaldeans and Medians exchanged uneasy glances. "Bind," they chorused in agreement.

"Keep in mind, any one of you tries to claim that this is a *cultural artifact*, and tries to take it back?" Trennus gritted out, "I'll note that it's in a *wine cooler bottle* and break it over your heads." He brought his hands together and started the ritual of binding. It was simple enough. It named the creature being bound by Name, if known, by type, if known, and then set up constraints. *In perpetuity until the container or its seal are broken.*

The insubstantial creature howled, a sound only audible within the minds of the people in the room, and Trennus forced it into the green glass bottle, reached out his hand imperatively, and Livorus slapped the cork into his palm, and Trennus tried to cram it back in the hole . . . . "Won't fit," he muttered, struggling.

"Got it. Move your hands," Kanmi muttered from where he was kneeling on the floor. Trennus pulled his hands away from the top quickly, just trying to keep the cork across the top of the bottle, which was actually wiggling and writhing in his hands, as the demon inside fought to be free, the outside of the glass turning cold and frosty as the *alu* stole energy from the air, trying to render the glass more brittle. Easier to break.

The top of the bottle glowed red-hot, and deformed in on itself like a drop of sap hardening in the air. The demon, sealed so, was *bound*. Trennus eyed the bottle as he set it, carefully, on the floor. "Bartolo and Iacobus," he read from the label. "Spirit, be known that your Name is . . . apparently Watermelon and Elderberry, from this day hence." He was giddy, his arm and knee hurt, and the gods only knew how many more of these *alu* were out there. Out there, in the dark, where Sigrun and Adam had gone. "Esh, stay with Livorus. I'm going after Caetia and ben Maor." Trennus made it back to his feet, and told Lassair, in his mind, *Think you can stop the bleeding?*

I can try, but providing light from within you might prove problematic.

Do your best, please. Then yes, light.

"I'm coming with you—" Kanmi started to get to his feet, and then sank right back to his knees.

"Stay down," Trennus told him. "Livorus needs *someone* here. Close the door and get some *light* going in here." He reached down and gave Kanmi a wrist-clasp. "Stay safe."

"Stay *alive*," Kanmi told him. "Take a bottle or two with you for the road."

"Yesterday, I'd have said I'd only drink one of these if my life depended on it." Trennus grabbed a couple of bottles anyway. "Apparently, it does."

In the convention hall itself, pandemonium. Earlier in the day, there had been eight or nine thousand people working through the booths in a slow ooze, jostling like red blood cells in tight capillaries. Now, there were about a thousand people left, mainly booth workers, vendors, and a few latecomers. They'd heard a series of light snaps, like a popgun going off, or the rattle of a string of firecrackers. That had gotten a few heads to turn inside the hall, but no one had panicked. No one had run. Just the mild curiosity of a herd of cattle, detecting something unusual, like a scent on the wind.

Then the lights had gone out, leaving the reddish glow of emergency backups, which were DC-powered, and only by the exits. A few yelps of surprise, followed by desultory jeering. Again, no real panic. The thrum of a surprise, alarm. Footsteps, hesitant in the pitch black. Reaching out blindly, brushing into cloth, skin, people around them. Fumbling for a flashlight, or just standing still in a booth, trying not to blunder into anyone else. *They'll have the lights back on in a minute. Maybe someone forgot to pay the bill?*

Then, sneaking suspicions rose. *That popping sound a moment ago sounded like gunfire. Maybe there's a lunatic with a gun? No, don't hear the gardia or the JDF firing back . . . .*

. . . and then, the first scream from outside, in the lobby. The first sound of real gunfire, as an automatic rifle went off, full-bore. The doors at the front of the hall slammed open—only the darkness of a starry sky visible through the windows of the front lobby and rotunda, and a few glimmers from the lights from the parking lot and the cityscape beyond. The shapes silhouetted in the doorframes were black against black, with staring, mad, green-glowing eyes. And then they all heard the laughter. Mad, fey laughter, echoing everywhere, bouncing off the walls.

The first sound of gunfire had been enough to incite panic, and the laughter simply added to it, as people ran, every direction, at once. Some, at the back of the hall, tried to run towards the only exits that they knew weren't blocked, the ones at the front of the hall. The places where the emergency lights glimmered faintly. The people at the front of the hall, turned to get *away* from the noises, from the dark shapes that appeared like predators around a waterhole . . . and the two masses of bodies collided in the aisles. Unable to see, unable to dodge. Headlong impacts. Cries of pain as nose met forehead, as limbs tangled and individuals dropped to the ground . . . just to be trampled by the people behind them. Screams of pain from the people on the ground, panic from the tangles of limbs above them, feeling flesh give and yield under their feet. One or two people kept their heads, shouting, *Everyone stay where you are, we're trampling people!* Dizzy glances back over shoulders, fighting to move forward, bodies all around, seeing eyes in the darkness. Behind. Beside. Being herded.

Unable to move left or right, booths and bodies blocking the way. And then one of the sets of eyes vanished to the right, and there was a whisper of sensation through the air, fine as the rustle of silk . . . and then the eyes reappeared, to the left. Sickening sensation of *absence* as suddenly, the body to the left, the one that had hemmed and pressed in, was *yanked* away. There was a hole in the crowd. A place to go. A vacuum. Instinct screamed in the brainstem, *Don't go that way!* And then *pushed* that way by the pressure of bodies to the right. By the bodies behind. Struggling . . . and then the mad laughter started again, and the crush got tighter. Harder to breathe. Sheep being herded. Fish being forced to school.

Voices rose in howls of anger and outrage, an inhuman chorus . . . and then more holes at the edge of the crowd as people were torn away. Terrified screams. Hot splash of *something* against a face, and trying to get *away*, trying to get to the *center*, where it was *safe* . . . .

Adam kicked open the next door, and they stepped into the convention hall itself. Sigrun's rune-marks, too bright to look at directly up close, provided a wan bubble of light barely ten feet across, which seemed fragile and insignificant as Adam looked up at the catwalks seventy feet above, and spotted a pair of gleaming green eyes looking down at them. He fired, directly at one of them, making the eyes vanish, as the creature found a different patch of shadow to hide in. "Sigrun," he told her, dropping the muzzle of the gun back down, and eyeing the wrecked booths and the squirming mass of humanity down the long corridor ahead of them, "have I ever mentioned that that light of yours makes it very difficult to sneak up on someone?"

"Periodically, yes." Sigrun crouched, using the corner of a booth for cover. "I have apologized."

"I take it all back. I *love* your light. Make more of it."

"Believe me when I say that I am *trying*."

Adam looked around, trying to assess which way Abgar could have gone with the Chaldean envoy. Forwards, through the scrum . . . no. "Left, Sig! Down past the end caps, it's the only clear path!" *And that way he can try to get to one of the side doors, through one of the emergency doors into the south lobby, and then, out.*

He just hoped he'd guessed correctly, as they moved south. Screaming people, grabbing for Sigrun's arms, for her light, panicking, as if they were drowning, and she was their only hope of life. Sigrun slamming them away with the haft of her spear, and two *alu* materializing, just outside of the range of her light. Adam caught the ripple, the gleam of the eyes, aimed both flashlight and pistol, and fired the instant the pale yellow light forced the demon to appear, fully visible. He had a fraction of a second to make it count, and the silver-plated bullets caught the creature in the chest. It threw itself backwards, and its companion vanished in a wisp of smoke. *Two bullets. Four to go . . . .*

. . . and then the creature was *behind* him, claws raking through the back of his bullet-proof vest. Adam spun, and his gun was slapped from his hand, flying to the ground. He slammed a foot into a wiry gray torso with all his strength, and pulled his combat utility knife, hoping that steel would have *some* effect on the damned things . . . *Steel's still cold iron, after all . . . .* The beast came in at him, and Adam spun right, pure reflex and muscle memory, sweeping his hand up and backhanding the knife directly into the beast's throat. . . where it *snapped,* but was embedded. The creature stood there for a moment, swaying uncertainly, its paws reaching up for its throat, almost curiously . . . and then Sigrun was there, a blur of speed, her spear whirling in her hands as she slashed downwards across its torso, keeping the blade away from Adam himself. "Need it down!" Sigrun shouted, and Adam complied, kicking one of its legs back, while shoving it forward, even as Sigrun pivoted . . . and brought the blade of her spear down across the back of its neck like an executioner's axe, caught for live far-viewer feed.

The body fell to the floor, and black smoke wisped up from it . . . but the body failed to dematerialize. "What's that mean?" Adam snapped, diving for his gun, shoving a civilian out of the way to do so. "Banished? Dead? What's death to a spirit, anyway?"

"Kill the body, and they'll take a while to reform. Might need to be re-summoned. If anyone even still knows their Name. Depends on the creature. Binding and banishing are more effective. Just killing the body . . . they can come back from that sometimes. But not always." Sigrun tossed the information back at him, already turning to look for another target.

Adam checked his gun, and looked at the civilians. He couldn't just leave them there. And there was no safe way out for them. Damning himself for an idiot, he handed the closest one his flashlight. "They avoid light. It won't hurt them, but they prefer to attack with an advantage. Keep together. Keep the light moving. All I can do for the moment." Then he followed in Sigrun's footsteps, feeling . . . naked and unarmed without his light.

Lassair hovered over Trennus' head, emitting a steady golden radiance that kept the *alu* at bay. Off to the left, Chaldean summoners, still fighting two *alu* with raw magic, and the power of their own manifested spirits. To the south, his right, he caught sight of two JDF soldiers fighting with one of the demons at the end of the long hall he was in, trying to keep the creature near a single, lonely flare on the floor. Trennus swore and tugged on the ley-energies in the ground. He was trying not to tap the lines directly, out of respect for local beliefs, but that resolve was being tested at the moment. *Going to need more light,* he told Lassair. *Sorry.*

Oh, don't worry. Light, I can give you. The phoenix blazed into pure glory overhead, and the entire corridor was bathed in her radiance. The *alu* spun and howled, and tried to run for a doorway, back into darkness. "No, you don't," Trennus muttered, and snapped his empty right hand closed on the air itself, and the poured-stone floor liquefied and snapped upwards like fingers, echoing his movement, trapping the spirit in place. "Keep it in the light and kill it!" he shouted to the two soldiers, both of whom were bleeding . . . and both of whom just nodded in his direction before unleashing their assault rifles on the caged creature, which was trapped as much by the flare's light as by the stone.

Trennus could hear its screams and howls, and answering howls of rage from its fellows . . . and spun back around as two more creatures abandoned the summoners they were fighting at the north end of the hall, trying to come to the aid of their pack-mate. One hit him, hard, dropping him to the ground . . . and the bottles in his left hand slipped and shattered on the ground, spraying his face with syrupy-smelling liquor and glass shards even as he hit the ground himself.

In a daze, Trennus reached out with ley-energies. He wasn't fighting for his life right now. He had just enough concentration to reach out and shape the poured-stone floor . . . and the arcs and curves of a binding circle sliced through the surface, stopping the demons in their tracks. Trennus rolled out of the circle, his ears ringing from the *rat-tat-tat-tata-tata-tat* of the assault rifle rounds, each burst of noise echoing back off the walls, the screams of the dying, caged *alu,* the howls of fury from the two trapped in the circle.

The Chaldean bodyguards that had been in the hall, fighting desperately with the *alu,* dashed up now, and Trennus rolled to his feet. "Find bottles back in the conference room. Bind or banish, I don't care which, but don't let them back out again." And then he ducked out into the main convention hall, and spotted Sigrun's pale radiance to the south. Could hear the screams and the panic and the mad laughter of the demons, and swore again as Lassair swooped in after him. "We've got to give these people more light. They don't stand a chance without it . . . ."

Not a problem. Lassair rose, soaring towards the ceiling of the convention center like a comet, the long plumes of her tail radiating fire out behind her in long streamers. For an instant, Trennus felt alone and exposed in the dark . . . and then the phoenix became a *sun,* pouring out flame and light at ceiling height, brightening the convention center to an almost noon-day glare.

Every *alu* in the vicinity was forced into visibility, and they snarled in frustration, before tipping back their heads and giving out that soul-chilling laughter once more. *Stay there, out of reach!* Trennus told Lassair, and glanced around. Adam and Sigrun had vanished, deeper into the heart of the crowd and the booths, and there were *alu* simply rampaging now, seizing screaming people from the crowd and *throwing* them. *Where are Sigrun and Adam?*

South of you. Hurry. They have found the one who wears his lover's blood as a mask. Lassair paused, and tried to convey some of the confusion that the various spirits were having to Trennus. Erida's 'pattern,' for lack of a better term, was all over Abgar. Her DNA, reinforced and invigorated with magic. And *his* pattern, somehow, was in her, making them two-in-one, one person, two bodies—*Oh. His DNA is _in_ her. They had carnal relations recently. And they amplified it with magic. It's probably somewhat common. In that way, they present a doubled image to most minor spirits.*

Probably as recently as this morning, Lassair confirmed, her tone intrigued. *The pattern is strong. He has bound her energies with her emotions, but the bond is almost unraveled now.*

Trennus always knew which direction he was facing. It had to do with the ley formations in the earth, currents of power, and, probably, magnetism. Back in the hallway, he'd been facing east; currently, he faced west. So he spun to his left and *ran,* ducking around panicking civilians, and shouted at them as he passed, "Stay out of the booths! Stay out of the *shadows!"*

Sigrun and Adam had swung down one of the long rows of booths just as Lassair went off like a star going nova overhead. "I think I love that spirit," Adam muttered, and Sigrun nodded, fervently, as radiant golden light filled the entire area. The civilians in the knot of people ahead of them all looked upwards, cheered for a moment, and then the *alu* were back, and Adam fired on one that was in range, sending it hopping over the wall of a booth for cover on the other side.

Then Sigrun spotted their quarry, as the crowds parted a little, and she could see Abgar forcing Erida through a gap in the bodies, knife still at the woman's throat. "There!" Sigrun shouted, and again, richly rued the fact that she was cut off from the damned sky.

Adam shook his head, and called in return. "No clean shot. Too many people." In truth, the crowd looked like nothing so much as a mass of worms erupting from the ground after a rainstorm.

"Then it's on me."

"Are you fast enough?"

"I don't know. Stay in the light!" Sigrun leaped into the air herself now, kicking free of the entangling arms and legs around her. So hard not to see the humans around her as *obstacles*. Impediments. She knew they weren't, but the grasping hands and bodies had pulled up battle reflexes to which she didn't dare yield. Sigrun hovered for a moment, watching as her prey worked his way through the crowds, and at least two *alu* gave him and Erida a quizzical glance, before working in tandem to isolate a woman from the crowd, chasing her away from the rest. One lurched in front of her, driving her to the side, dividing her from her companions, who reacted by trying to reach out and grab the *alu* . . . and then another *alu*, in the shelter of one of the booths and its shadows, reached out and seized the woman by the hair, and then leaped to the top of the dividing wall between two booths, which trembled under the creature's weight.

Sigrun, midair, swore and threw her spear, which lanced out and caught the creature between its shoulder blades and thus, right through its heart from behind. It teetered atop the wall, its grip on the woman's hair slackening, and the captive dropped to the ground on one side, even as the *alu* toppled the other direction. Sigrun called her spear back, and looked around for her main target. She'd lost him in the crowd once more. *Hel's frozen heart. Where is he?* She canvassed the crowd, and spotted them again. *Damn. They're right by the exit.* "Adam!" Sigrun shouted. "West! Run!"

And then she dove, herself, with as much speed as she could muster. A body at rest needed a certain amount of time to accelerate. She knew that her top speed was somewhere in excess of three hundred miles an hour, but she needed time and space to get up to that maximum. She had neither here . . . but she could still move at a good clip, and sailed through the doors into the darkened main lobby, wind rushing through her hair and her rune-marks ablaze with light.

"Stay *back!*" Abgar warned, knife still pressed to Erida's throat. No blood yet, though . . . and Sigrun thought she understood *why*. Too much of Erida's blood, before he was ready, would ruin his mask. Sigrun could still see his bound spirit twining around him, like a python. Could see one of Erida's bound spirits, the hawk-like one, trying to land on Abgar's spirit, clawing, harassing.

Sigrun landed on the ground, hearing the howl of *alu*. The screams of people all around her, here in the darkness past where Lassair's light reached, and the *rat-tat-tat-tat* of machine gun fire echoing back off the bare walls and floors. But her eyes were locked on the couple in front of her, and she was straining, too, for the sound of footsteps behind her, lost in the din though Adam's movement would surely be. She circled, cautiously, to the right. Forcing Abgar to turn with her, keeping Erida between the two of them. "There's no way you can get out of this one," she told him, stalling for time. "Too many of the envoys and their bodyguards saw what you did. No story you set up, here and now, will mean anything."

"None of you will live to tell any other tale." Abgar's tone held supreme confidence, and Sigrun's eyes flicked up in time to see his python-like serpent swing its head around and *engulf* Erida's hawk in massive jaws. Erida stiffened, and her body convulsed, as if in agony.

Spirits can kill spirits, just as gods can kill gods. Diamond cuts diamond, after all. Sigrun's thoughts were distant, dispassionate even. She met the woman's eyes as they opened once more, and Sigrun apologized, formally, "Forgive me, envoy." A very slight inclination of her head, at odds with the chaos all around her . . . and Sigrun let her light *die*. Used the cover of the darkness to leap forward, and strike, not at Abgar, who was still solidly shielded behind his hostage . . . but at Erida herself, feeling the blade of her spear slash into the other woman's leg as Sigrun dove, rolled, and came up *behind* the pair, letting her light flare back to life as she once more channeled Tyr's might.

Abgar whirled with her once more, but this time, Erida's blood was on the ground, and Sigrun *smiled* at Abgar. "I think the spirits can smell the difference between her and you now." *They should be able to tell fresh blood from the masking blood you're wearing. Now you're not one entity in two bodies, but two individuals. Of course, the wounded one is more of a target . . .* "They'll tear you to shreds, Abgar. They might tear her apart, too, but it won't be a Judean bullet in her heart or in her head, now will it?" *Come on. Lose your temper. Let her go and attack* me.

Back in the conference hall, Adam forced his way through the crowd, peripherally aware that Trennus had fought his way to his side. Lassair's light was keeping the damned creatures visible . . . but all of the *alu* had retreated into the lobby, out of reach of her light. "Have her stay here. Keep the civilians safe," Adam shouted up at the big Pict.

"Understood. Sigrun went out that way?"

"Following Abgar."

"Then I guess we're following her!"

They shouldered through the crowd, Adam spotting Sigrun's pale radiance and getting through the door into the lobby first. Smell of blood, of panic, of gunpowder. She had the summoner and his captive at bay, and Adam could see, dimly, in the faint light coming in from the parking lot, a couple of JDF soldiers advancing on the lobby from the north, weapons at the ready. Unmistakable outline of the assault rifles in their hands, even seen in silhouette. "Stay back!" Adam shouted. The *last* thing any of them needed was for someone with a load of panic firing on the wrong target right now. He had Abgar dead to rights, but it was dark, and even as he started to squeeze the trigger, the Chaldean bodyguard spun, presenting Erida as a target. Adam couldn't stop his fingers, but the muscles of his arms twitched, and he managed to fire the shot wide, up into the window behind the pair, instead. "Matrugena, you got anything?"

"I can try to banish his spirits, take a little of his armor off him," Trennus answered. "Can't use ley on him. She's too close. He'll take her with him."

"Do what you can!" Adam moved north, separating from the Britannian, trying to force Abgar to spin again. Get him to present his back to Sigrun and her lethal spear.

Abgar snarled, and dragged Erida further back, into the rotunda that was the main entrance of the building. Gaining cover, he actually spun her around, kissed her full on the mouth, and shoved her away, into the center of the lobby, and shouted, in Persian, "*Spirits! I offer you her blood! Come take it!*"

Harah. He saw his plan wasn't going to work. He's improvising. Adam's thoughts were distant and he tried to close the gap, running forward to Erida's side, to protect the envoy. And that was when absolutely everything happened at once.

Erida, free, staggered, and bleeding, hissed, and Trennus, for his part, could feel the shape of the spell she'd been holding readied, waiting for the moment that she was free to use words or gestures to release it. As Abgar was a water elementalist, Erida was an air elementalist. "Sigrun!" Trennus shouted, even as the valkyrie blurred forwards. "Don't get near

Abgar! Don't!"

The air around Abgar rushed *away* from him in all directions, with an audible clap of thunder, and a barely-visible bubble, more of a line of demarcation than anything else, shimmered in a sphere around him. Hardened air. Resisting the pressure outside, as Erida had created a *vacuum* inside. Explosive decompression on Earth was no more pleasant than it was in space. Trennus had enough time to see all the capillaries in Abgar's eyes explode, and then blood poured down his face. In a panic, the man turned and tried to run, but the sphere of emptiness was centered on *him.* If he held his breath, the very air inside his lungs would expand outwards, causing his lungs to shred from the inside. And if he exhaled, there would be no air. He'd be unconscious in seconds, dead in minutes, though his spirit-serpent coiled around his body, trying to sustain him. Abgar pounded a fist against the surface of the bubble even as Sigrun, diverted by Tren's warning, skidded off to the side, spinning to stare at the man as he raised a hand and obviously *tried* to incant . . . but with no better luck than Kanmi had had, earlier. *His spirit might be able to sustain him,* Trennus thought, remotely. *Have to make sure he's done here.* He reached out for ley-energies once more, bringing the poured-stone that underlay the tile floor up in a spike, spearing through Abgar's body from below like a stalagmite.

But even as Trennus' attention was locked on the traitorous bodyguard, Adam's was caught as two more *alu* appeared, just to the north of him, materializing like smoke between him and the JDF soldiers. Their eyes were intent on Erida, who was wounded, blooded. Smelled like prey, and who had been *offered* to them, like a savory dish, or a sacrifice. *Not today,* Adam thought, and pushed the envoy behind him. "If you've any magic to do, do it now!" he told her, and fired on the *alu,* just as behind them, the JDF soldiers, seeing the enemies that they'd been fighting for the past horrific twenty minutes, opened fire, themselves. Full automatic on their rifles.

And in the darkness, the *alu* demons bared their teeth, and *vanished* into smoke once more, and the fire from the automatic weapons struck Adam ben Maor solidly in the chest. His bulletproof vest took the first couple of rounds, but the next six punched their way through.

Pain. Searing pain. He looked down at his chest numbly as his gun fell from his hand, and he dropped to his knees, looking back up again, and catching a single pair of green-glowing eyes looking down on him from the darkness. The last coherent thought he had was *This isn't the way it's supposed to happen . . . .*

Fifteen feet away, Sigrun could only watch, stunned, as the bullets fired by his own people passed through the smoke of the insubstantial *alu*-demons, taking Adam to the ground. She leaped forward in a rush of wind, dropping her spear to the ground beside him, dropping to her knees and rolling him over to yank the vest open. *No. No, no, no, no.* The material had taken a couple of the bullets, certainly, but it wasn't designed to stop more than the bullets of a revolver. Blood—his white undershirt was a mass of it, and it was spurting from at least one center-of-mass wound, spraying her face. And Sigrun *knew*, with the same uncanny certainty that she'd *known* it, decades ago, when her mother had been in the hospital, that Adam ben Maor was about to die. It was a sense that all valkyrie had: they knew when a wound was mortal. It related to their earliest name: *chooser of the dead.* Later generations had embellished on this, and suggested that valkyries selected the worthiest of the fallen to pass to Valhalla. A comfort for a grieving widow, perhaps, in a culture that believed that death in battle was the highest honor that existed. A culture in which suicide was permissible, and not at all shameful—a culture in which death could redeem someone's honor, much as it could in Roman and Nipponese culture.

In truth, the valkyrie had chosen who was worthiest to *live*. They had *healed* on ancient battlefields, and sent the strongest and best back out into the fight. Valkyrie of Eir—the valkyrie, who had, like Heracles, left behind her mortality to become a goddess in her own right—could heal directly. Could even heal some diseases. Some valkyrie, like those sealed to Loki, couldn't heal at all. But every one of them *knew* when the moment of death was at hand. And they all knew that they had choices to make in that moment.

Sigrun knew that these wounds were mortal . . . for Adam. *But maybe not for me.* She had seconds to decide. She was still mostly blocked from the sky, and what was invisible and immaterial, she couldn't fight. She was useless in this battle. But Adam . . . Adam was not. And outside of this battle . . . god-born were servants of the gods, and of humanity. So many people wasted their lives in tedium and monotony, and were so limited in scope, intelligence, and capability, that they might as well never have left the caves. But there were some who dared to dream. To reach for the stars. Adam was one such. And he meant far, far more to her than she'd ever wanted to admit. Admitting that she valued something was a sure path towards losing it. Her childhood and young adulthood had taught her that lesson.

One second. Two. Feeling the heart *spasm* on the bullet that had nicked the aorta. Sigrun lifted her head and snapped at the Chaldean woman behind her, "Can you pull the bullets? Do you or your spirits have the magic to do it?"

Trennus then, at her side. "If she doesn't, I do—oh, gods." He sounded horrified and shaken, however, as he finally got a look at the wound. "Sigrun, no. There's nothing we can do. Taking the bullets out will just—"

Sigrun raised her head and used the voice she *never* used on mortals. It was the voice of the law, the voice of Tyr, and it clanged back from the walls with echoes of iron and steel. "Pull the bullets now, Matrugena." She spared a glance for the Chaldean envoy. "You. Defend us. They will return shortly."

She could see Trennus' head snap back in the illumination from her own skin, and, wide-eyed, the Pict obeyed, kneeling and holding his hand over Adam's body, so that the bullets snapped up and into his hand, as if drawn by magnetic force. As each one emerged, Adam's body twitched and convulsed, and Sigrun could feel his life falter under her hand. "No, not today," she told him, and put her hand on his chest now, feeling the heart *twist* under her palm. "Get on your feet, Adam ben Maor. There is work yet to be done."

And then she took the wounds. All of them, all at once, because doing them one at a time wouldn't save him, and the pain of it might erode her will to go on. The bullet that had slammed into his right shoulder, the least grievous. The two in the right lung. The one to the belly. And the two to the sternum, including the one that had perforated the heart.

Sigrun curled in on herself, feeling the balance of mortality sway and shift. *I have chosen*, she thought, distantly. *I have chosen who will live, and who will die. I have chosen the worthy to live on.* His tissues knitted. Hers frayed. God-born blood poured out of her chest, and Sigrun slipped to the ground, feeling . . . pain and peace, at the same time. A little regret. And a curious sense of amused sorrow. *What will my sister say . . . to see all her futures . . . unwrought?*

And then her light went out.

Trennus, watching, but unable to *stop* her, and not knowing what would happen if he tried to knock her away before the transference was complete—he could well end up with *two* incapacitated friends on his hands, rather than just one—also had his hands full. Sigrun's light died, leaving them all in darkness, and Trennus snapped out, *Saraid!*

I come!

The stag once more materialized, a faint, dim golden glow around it. Scarcely more than a candle's worth with which to wish away the dark. Trennus reached down with a numb, shell-shocked hand, and hauled Adam upright, even as the man began to cough, wrackingly, forcing curdled blood out of his chest. "Get up, ben Maor, there's still more of them!"

Adam sat up in a daze, not even knowing where he *was*. It hurt to breathe, and when he coughed, he could taste blood, thick and metallic-tasting, in his mouth, and he spat. "How—"

"Sig's down. I need you on your feet." Trennus had stepped into command, and a good thing, too, for all Adam could do for an instant was stare down at Sigrun's crumpled body. Trennus took off his shirt and wadded it up, pressing it against the wound in Sigrun's chest, trying to slow the arterial bleeding. The only thing that could possibly be keeping her alive at this moment was the healing of the god-born. "Damn it, Adam! Use the time she's giving us!"

That got his attention, and Adam fumbled for his backup gun in his holster at his ankle, and looked for a target, even as Trennus demanded of Erida, the Chaldean envoy, "Have anything we can use?"

"Light is not my specialty," she admitted, tightly. "One spirit provides a shield against bullets. The second protects me from poison. My third was meant to protect me against magical attacks, and to attack other spirits, but it's *gone*." Her voice was tight.

"Know any other Names?"

"A few. My sorcery is all air-based. It will not affect these spirits much, if at all."

"Start invoking. I'll provide the circle." Adam saw lines slash themselves into existence through the tile floor.

"Won't the lines of the tile interfere?" the Chaldean asked, her tone neutral.

"Not as wide as I'm making the circle's own line," Trennus replied, curtly.

"Protective or binding?"

"Binding. They can get in, but they can't get back out."

"Excellent." Adam glanced up just long enough to see the woman biting on her own fingers hard enough to draw blood, and then bringing her hand in a hard, downwards arc. "Akh," she whispered. "*Akh*. Come and feed. I give you your preferred sustenance, and all I ask is *light*. Drive these creatures to us. *AKH!*"

"Spirit's not answering," Trennus told Adam, tightly. "Either the bargain's not enough, or it thinks the *alu* are too much to deal with."

Adam looked down at Sigrun's body. She was dying, dying of wounds she'd taken from *him*. They needed to *end* this, so they could get her some proper medical attention. "The firebird?" Adam asked Trennus, his thoughts racing. "She helped heal you before. And she's *light*."

"I can call her, but if I do, we're putting every last one of the civilians in there, back in the dark," Trennus said, grimly.

Harah. Adam stared down the hall. The two JDF soldiers at the far end of the hall, having stopped and stared in horror for a moment at having subjected someone to friendly fire, were under attack again. He could just barely make out the shapes that half-formed from billows of smoke, forcing them to turn to defend themselves, only to vanish, as another *alu* appeared directly behind them. Pack tactics. Like wolves who'd learned magic. "What in god's name do I do, Tren?" he asked, as Erida started another invocation.

"We need them back here, or dead. Both, preferably. Killing them right here in the circle would be best, but . . . ."

Adam didn't dare fire his pistol. The JDF soldiers didn't deserve the return fire. Instead, he handed it to Trennus, who took it gingerly, as if he'd never held such a thing before in his life. "Fingers outside the trigger guard unless you mean to shoot." He leaned over, ran a bloody hand over Sigrun's hair, and felt one ragged breath warm his wrist. Then he picked up her spear, swallowed, and stepped out of the circle. "Hey!" he shouted. "You want blood? I've got plenty here for you!"

The *alu* turned, laughing, but the mad sound had no effect on

Adam. He should have been dead already. He was living on borrowed time, time Sigrun had given him, and he had to make that gift count. He had to save her life, the way she'd saved his. His sole focus was on the green eyes as they rushed towards him in a swirl of smoke, and he reacted *before* the demons materialized behind him, turning and slashing with the spear. It felt *odd* to use a weapon so primitive, but oddly satisfying as he slashed through a body that was invisible to his eyes . . . but was clearly there. Resistant. Tangible. A beast howled, and Adam spun again, working the spear in a figure-eight pattern, high and low, covering the maximum area possible, catching and nicking the creatures over and over as they tried to circle him. Tried to rush in and out of reality. Sometimes all he caught was smoke. Sometimes, the spear came away from a slash wet with black blood. He let pure combat instinct take over, keeping his eyes wide and unfocused, reacting on rhythm, feeling, motion. Let his subconscious tell him when a strike was coming, and drove the spear through an invisible throat . . . and then turned and administered a vicious side-kick to the crumbling body to direct it back towards the circle where Trennus and Erida awaited.

"Got him!" Trennus shouted, leaving Sigrun long enough to reach over the edge of the circle and yank the *alu* into the circle, where he looked around wildly for a container, spotted a vending cart nearby that hadn't been overturned, and forced the floor to rise and ripple, bringing the cart to him. He grabbed the first container he saw . . . . an untapped metal barrel filled with beer . . . and started the words of the binding, hissing them out as he crammed the demon's essence into the container. The sides turned frosty as the energy exchange took effect . . . and then Trennus dropped back down to a crouch, once more trying to keep pressure on the wound in Sigrun's chest. His shirt was soaked red already. *Going to need to get Lassair in here . . . but can't until the civilians are safe . . . .*

Adam ducked under another swipe of claws—catching them across his forehead, for his pains, but avoiding decapitation—and barely noticed it through the gray haze of adrenaline when Erida shouted out one last name. "Illa'zhi! Light of the dead!" . . . . but the blaze of fire that went up caught his eye, and the *alu* around him all howled, morphing back into full visibility and solidity as an *efreet* appeared in the middle of the summoners' circle. A swirl of black smoke and living flame, twisting in on itself in a vortex.

Adam stared, just for an instant. *Oh, lord. Please, not this. Sure, it's light, but they're malefic.* "What did you trade?" Adam shouted, slamming the butt of the spear into another *alu* muzzle.

"A year of my life!" she shouted back. "Less, if we let it feed on them. Worth the trade." Her dark eyes were like chips of black glass in her smooth face.

Adam rolled out of the cringing circle of *alu*. "I wish it nothing more than a hearty meal!" he declared. "Good appetite!" *Please. God. Don't let it burn the building down.*

And then the efreet closed on the *alu*, and there was nothing more than screams and the smell of burning hair and flesh. Tendrils of fire lashed out of the whirlwind, scorching the tiles of the floor and charring the ceiling above, but Adam no longer cared. He limped back over to the others, realizing, belatedly, that he'd taken a handful of rakes and claws, and that he was, once again, bleeding. It didn't matter. He dropped Sigrun's spear, and dropped to his knees, checking her vitals with a bloody hand to her throat. Her heart was beating, but just barely. Terribly erratic, in fact, lurching in fits and starts under his fingers, and her breathing was shallow. *The burns under the Pyramid of the Sun were bad enough,* he thought, numbly. *She didn't have to take these. She chose them. What am I going to do if she _dies_ because of me?* He didn't dare move her, not yet. Just cradled her limp hand in his, and looked up at the blaze of fire that was a damned *efreet*, one of his worst nightmares, that was burning their enemies alive . . . and felt nothing. Not fear, nor wonder. Just numbness.

After a moment, he managed to remember why they were even here, and reached for the radio at his belt. "This is ben Maor," he identified himself. "The efreet in the lobby is a friendly." The words tasted odd in his mouth. "Lobby is secure. Start getting the civilians out into the parking lot. We're going to need emergency medical teams. Repeat, get all the civilians out through the *front lobby*. And . . . "he paused, drawing a blank, and then found the words again, "get every person out there to turn on their car, particularly the headlights. Let's get as much light out there as possible." *We don't know if any of them are left alive.* He stared into space for a moment, and then changed to the Praetorians-only channel. "Eshmunazar?"

"I copy," Kanmi's voice came back, tight and clipped. "You want us to come to you?"

"Yes. Front lobby. Chaldean dignitary is secure from her . . . ah . . ." Adam's mind went blank again, as he stared down at Sigrun's face.

"Assassination attempt?" Kanmi offered, into the silence.

"Yes," Adam said, his tone limp. "That." A curl of blackened ceiling plaster fell past his cheek, and he knelt. Picked Sigrun up— carefully, very, very carefully, not even trying for a fireman's carry this time—and carried her to the door. *I can't let her be trampled by the people trying to escape.* "Come to the main entrance. We'll be outside, and can get you to the vehicles."

About a minute later, someone in the JDF managed to get the building's emergency generator back online, and at least a few light panels over exits came back on. Adam looked at Erida. "Could you ask your . . . friend . . ." he indicated the towering pillar of fire and wind, which had spawned *eyes* to look down on them, "to go into the rest of the center and provide light? *Not* damaging the people inside, and *not* burning the building down?" It . . . paid to be specific with efreeti, from all the legends.

Erida looked up at the vast creature. Adam could *hear* the words of the reply in his head, and this was not Lassair's voice, which held the gentle, welcoming warmth of a hearthside seat in winter. This was a voice that roared inside of his mind, spoke of hunger and desire and consumption, with hisses and crackles. *You summoned me to save your life, and instead, provided me a feast. I was in danger of almost owing you service, instead of you owing me life. I will do this . . . though it is a pity that the god-born woman is not fit to meet me in battle at the moment. It would be interesting to match strengths with her.*

"You can keep right on being curious about that," Adam gritted out.

The efreet *laughed* at him, and swirled into the main hall, where, yet again, people inside shrieked in terror . . . but it rose up and became a smaller, compacter whirlwind, its destruction contained. If only for the moment.

This freed Lassair to swoop in from the main hall, and she landed on Sigrun's chest, pecking away Trennus' shirt from the valkyrie's body . . . and then chirruped at Trennus and Adam. *I can slow the bleeding. The wounds are very deep, but she fights. My sister never stops fighting.* Rueful admiration in the spirit's voice. *The day she does, the day her heart breaks, the world will be a colder and darker place for it.*

The next four to eight hours saw nothing but pandemonium at the convention center. Red and blue lights, flashing across the parking lot. High-powered search lights, attached to portable kerosene-powered generators, lighting the night as if it were day. Ambulances screaming away, carrying the civilian and military wounded. Fire trucks spewing chemical retardant foam at the roof of the convention center.

Adam, Trennus, and Kanmi kept a firm eye on Livorus, Trennus and Kanmi getting him to the vehicles before the pair escorted him back to the governor's mansion. The Chaldean envoy, Erida, wound up going with the Median one, Maranata, to the Median consulate . . . in spite of the Persian ambassador showing up on scene and demanding that they should all return with him to the safety of *his* embassy. Adam overheard part of that conversation as he was helping the paramedics load Sigrun into an ambulance, and watching the first-response workers haul the bodies of the other injured people from the convention hall. They'd set up a triage area, but the paramedics had taken one look at Sigrun's wounds and moved her to the head of the line. *She wouldn't want that,* a voice said at the back of Adam's mind. Sigrun had steadily maintained that the other lictors should be given medical attention before her, because of her ability to heal. *To gehenna with that, though. She's got a wound in her heart. The only reason she's still alive is her damned god-born healing.* Adam could see the shock in the paramedics' faces as they assessed her wounds. *Even they know she should be dead.*

They closed the doors on her, and Adam was left, for the moment, to turn and look around the controlled chaos in the parking lot. The news media had arrived, and were putting up mobile broadcast antennae off to the side. He could see JDF personnel walking around with heavy weaponry, on guard. Dozens of *gardia* officers, putting up crime-scene tape, taking pictures, interviewing the survivors, most of whom had had blankets tossed over their shoulders. A paramedic waved Adam over to try to put bandages on his various claw marks, and offered him at least a change of shirt, boggling at the bullet holes and blood on his existing one. *"How . . . ?"* the woman began, in Hebrew.

"One of my companions is a healer," Adam replied, tersely, accepting the fresh shirt, which had the hospital's crest on the left side, which he recognized as the one at which his mother worked as a trauma nurse. *Please don't let her be on duty tonight. "I'm barely bleeding. I'll be fine."* He limped towards where the last of their motorcade's vehicles was parked, and flashed his badge at a *gardia* officer who tried to stop him from leaving.

This gave the news media just enough time to spot him, and move in. *"Agent ben Maor? Lictor, over here. Can you give us any sort of a statement?"* Voices, flashes from photography, right in his face.

He had just enough time to wonder how the hell they recognized him, and scrambled to assemble his thoughts. *"We're not releasing any official statements tonight, as far as I know,"* he began, in Hebrew, keeping his face stone-straight. *"Information is still being developed by local law enforcement."* That was code for *we haven't decided what we're going to say.* He paused. *"And it would be premature to say anything at this time."*

"Adi bat Eran, Jerusalem Daily News. Lictor, was Propraetor Livorus inside the facility at the time of the attack? His family was observed leaving several hours ago."

Adam cursed mentally. He hadn't been told what to say, and didn't want to confirm anything before Livorus had decided if he'd officially been present or not. *"I'm not at liberty to discuss the propraetor's movements."*

"Hayyim ben Itamar, the Gethsemane Gazette." Adam had always found it amusing that this particular local newspaper had named itself after an upscale park, but there it was. *"What were you doing here, if the propraetor was not at this location?"*

"I have a lifelong interest in all things aerospace," Adam replied, blankly. *"I took the opportunity tonight to examine the proposed moon base exhibitions."*

Hands waved frantically. "Hesperus Catsullus, with the International News Bureau, Jerusalem branch." That, in Latin, caught Adam's ear. "Lictor, the propraetor was photographed leaving the scene an hour ago in his motorcade. As were several high-ranking Persian dignitaries, in separate vehicles. Were they here to meet with one another?"

Damn it. "As I just said, I'm not at liberty to discuss the propraetor's itinerary. As to the Persian dignitaries, I'm not on the distribution list for their schedules." It was snide, but Adam was *tired.*

"Adi bat Eran again. Lictor, my station's viewers would like to know . . . one of the other lictors, the Britannian, wears his native garb while on duty. The, ah, kilt, I think it's called." The woman licked her lips nervously as Adam turned and looked at her. *"We've had a number of people call in to ask, in the last day, why you don't wear the skullcap. They ask if you're ashamed to be Judean."*

Adam just stared at her, as all the cameras flashed again. *"In the midst of this crime scene,"* he said, after a long pause, *"I think that was an incredibly trivial thing to ask, Madam bat Eran."* He held up a hand to forestall her. *"No. I'm not ashamed to be Judean. But I also don't choose to advertise it, when it makes me stand out from the other lictors. I also don't chose to wear it in daily life, again because it makes me stand out in every other country within the Empire. I choose not to be observant, Madam bat Eran, because it allows me to defend the rights of people who chose to be so. I'll go to my grave defending people's right to observe the rites of our faith as much or as little as they choose. But anyone who accuses me of being ashamed of what I am, just because I do not behave in precisely the same way in which they do? Should strongly reconsider their opinions."* The words were bitten out. This was his entire argument with his brother, all over again, years of it, and he was having it with his entire country instead of with Mikayel. Adam nodded curtly to the reporters. *"I have nothing more to say. Good evening."*

He sat behind the wheel of the car for a moment, not knowing what the hell to do or where to go, and then, wearily, tabbed the radio embedded in the console. "Ben Maor here," he said into the receiver. "What's the propraetor's status?"

A familiar voice came over the speakers, one of the lictors from Poppaea's detail. *"He's back at the governor's mansion, and we've got twice the number of guards on the place that we had before. Matrugena's at the hospital. So's Eshmunazar, for observation. From the looks of you on the far-seer just now? So should you be."*

". . . oh. Oh, lord. That was *live?*" Adam turned inside the car and stared back at the parking lot.

"Yes. And judging from the reactions of the JDF guards around here when you started into Hebrew, you really need sleep, ben Maor. If it's any consolation, a couple of them seem to want to clasp your wrist and buy you a beer."

"Right . . ." Adam stared off into the distance. ". . . All right. I'm going to the hospital now."

The nighttime streets were still surprisingly busy. Little Roma and Little Nippon did thriving business when Old Town had shut down for the evening, as did the Hellene district. But the main hospital was in Old Town, so Adam wended his way through the narrow, cobbled streets, found the newish parking garage beside the ancient hospital building, and limped his way to one of the doors. The drive had given his muscles plenty of time to stiffen up, and they screamed, unrelentingly, as he made his way to the ER entrance.

Inside, he allowed a doctor who *wasn't* occupied with treating some of the victims from the convention center to clean, suture, and bandage his various claw marks. And asking about Sigrun and the others and waving his badge got him a report. Trennus had been admitted for observation. Kanmi was in a bed on the third floor, being dosed with saline and blood thinners. Sigrun was in surgery, and the doctors needed to talk with him and Trennus about her. In fact, a doctor in green surgical scrubs appeared at his left elbow in his treatment cubical as the nurse was finishing the last of his leg wounds. "Agent ben Maor? Agent Matrugena said you'd known Agent Caetia longer. I need to ask you a few questions about her treatment." Most surgeons in Judea were either clean-shaven, or had very minimal beards, for hygiene purposes. A mask could only do so much, after all. This doctor was no exception, having only a slight goatee, and short hair, easily kept under a surgical cap.

Adam nodded and straightened up. "What's her condition?"

"We're . . . not really certain." The surgeon sounded uncomfortable. "We've never actually operated on a go . . . a, er, spirit-touched person before." He ran a hand over his hair in mild agitation. "We opened the chest cavity to work, immediately, on the heart itself. This was . . . actually extremely difficult, as her skin resisted the scalpels. We were forced to use rotating saws that we'd normally use to cut through bone, in fact." The surgeon looked at Adam. "Forgive me. I don't usually explain such details to those who know the patient well, but you have to understand that this is . . . a highly exceptional case. We noted that she was . . . healing rapidly and that her body was resisting being *open*, in fact. However, because her heart was having such difficulty beating—it was damaging itself with every beat, essentially . . . we have attempted to hook her up to a heart bypass machine to allow us to stop her heart from beating, so we can repair the damage to the aorta." He sounded bewildered. "Inserting the *cannulae* into her veins to allow her blood to be circulated without her heart was almost impossible. And the heart . . . even though it was damaging itself with each beat, now that it's no longer moving, her regenerative abilities seem to be knitting the organ together as quickly as we can suture it. There's a paper in this, I think, if she'll allow us to publish it."

Adam stared at him, feeling nauseous. He didn't want to picture Sigrun splayed open on a table like one of the autopsies he'd attended in the Praetorians. "I don't think this is really the time to be talking about *journal articles*." At his tone, the doctor looked abashed, and held up his hands in apology. "What do you need to know?"

The doctor shook his head, rapidly. "Is this . . . normal?"

"She recovered from second- and third-degree burns over about eighty percent of her body last year. I'm not sure what 'normal' is for a valkyrie, but I suspect her healing abilities are among the most powerful of her kind." Adam winced as the nurse beside tied off the last suture on his arm. "Once you're sure that the heart is healing, and you've removed the . . . tubes that connect her to the heart-lung machine—"

"The *cannulae*, yes . . . ."

"You might be able to close her up and let her healing take over." Adam raised his hands, indicating his general ignorance.

"Do you know what her blood-type is? We've been trying to match her, and a Hellene doctor on staff says she's type 'AK negative.' Which we're not familiar with, unfortunately." The surgeon raised his own hands now. "He's telling us that standard procedure on . . . a spirit-touched . . . is to provide type O-negative human blood and not worry about cross-matching."

Adam blinked, and had to think back to the hospital in Nahautl. "That's what they did for her in Tenochtitlan, yes. The extra antigen group makes it impossible for her to donate to a normal human, but universal donor blood is still universal. She can accept it. And I know her type is rare, even for a god-born. They're, what, five percent of the world's population, and I think her blood type is carried by five percent of the god-born population."

The surgeon just stared at him for a moment. "Does she have any allergies to medication?"

"No, but she'll be a pain in your ass when she wakes up . . ." Adam refused to say *if she wakes up*, ". . . on the topic of pain medication. She'll refuse to take it." Adam forced a smile. "I'd recommend clubbing her over the head and giving her the medication anyway. In fact, I volunteer to help." *God damn it, Sig. Why in god's name did you do this? It should be me on that table, spread open like a Roman priest is about to try for haruspication. Not that they'd find much of a future in my entrails.*

"I . . . see." The surgeon hesitated. "Also, I wanted to ask about the nature of her wounds. They look like bullet wounds, but there were no bullets *in* the wounds."

Adam grimaced, and opened the neck of the hospital gown he'd been given. "That would be because she took them from me, doctor." He pulled the fabric out of the way, showing the white, clean lines in exactly the places where the bullets had penetrated his skin. "You'll note that the scars are all in the same precise places as the wounds are on her?"

The doctor opened and closed his mouth. "I . . . ah. Thank you, Agent ben Maor. That's all the questions I had."

That was, naturally, the moment that his mother, as a senior ER nurse, put her head around the corner, and got a good look at the healed scars that hadn't been there the day before. The sutured claw marks on both arms, one leg, and his right ribs. Her green eyes, under her nursing cap, went wide, and she paled before her professional mien returned. Adam pulled the annoying patient gown back into place and nodded to her as she said, "Ah, I took the liberty of getting you some clothing from the gift-shop, Agent ben Maor."

"Thank you," Adam replied, accepting the paper bag from her. "Pretty much everything I wore earlier is a total loss." His slacks had been blood-soaked and slashed through in multiple locations. His shirt had been stiff with blood, and had had multiple bullet holes through it. His shoes might be salvageable, once they were rinsed. He looked around, but the surgeon had already retreated. "How soon can I see the rest of my team?" he asked Abigayil instead.

"Ah . . . Eshmunazar's upstairs, resting. I think the Britannian is with him. You won't be permitted to see the Goth woman until she's in post-op," his mother told him.

"Any chance I can use the shower facilities before I put the clothes on?" he asked, and brought the tail of his hair around in explanation. The entire lower third was glued together by dried blood, and the vast majority of the rest of his body was in similar condition. They'd had to clean around each of his wounds to suture them, but there was no getting around the fact that he reeked of blood and smoke and, god help him, hyena sweat.

"Ah . . . I think we can make an exception for you, Agent," his mother told him. He could see her hands shaking, but was impressed by how steady her voice was as she ushered him through the halls. He had a feeling she'd unleash a torrent of questions on him as soon as she had him alone, but she surprised him again by just reaching up and hugging him very tightly at first. "I'm so very glad you're all right," she told him.

Then the questions had started. Was he all right, what had happened, couldn't he at least consider a job that didn't involve him being cut to ribbons by demons? Had that really been an *efreet* that the news media had captured on camera? Shouldn't he talk to a priest or a rabbi to see if his soul was in danger from having accepted magical assistance derived from a heathen god?

Adam did his best not to snap. He could hear the stress, love, and fear in her voice, but it was hard not to deal with her the way he'd dealt with the reporters. He made his escape into the showers, and emerged, having kept his bandages dry and feeling quite a bit more human. He checked on Kanmi and Trennus. Kanmi's room was ablaze with Lassair's light, as she perched on Trennus' shoulder. And Trennus sat beside Kanmi's bed in a folding chair, reading a book, glancing up as Adam entered the room. "He's asleep. Probably best for him."

Adam glanced around. "His wife's not here yet?"

"Showed up an hour ago and demanded to see his chart." Trennus' voice was quiet, but the Pict's lips curled down at the corners, an unexpected expression from him. Trennus hardly ever frowned. "His doctor and she wound up each throwing their weight around a bit. When she got the answers she wanted, she had a few words with Kanmi, and then left. Said he was in stable condition and they could talk about him quitting the Praetorians when he got out of the hospital."

Adam's eyebrows rose. The *last* thing he wanted was to lose a member of his team, and he honestly couldn't imagine working with a sorcerer who wasn't Kanmi at this point. The man was versatile and powerful, and they'd just started being able to respect each other. "I don't want to break in a new team-member," he commented, blankly. "He wants out?"

"He told her there was nothing to talk about, and that he was keeping his job as long as the Praetorians wanted him." Trennus' lips quirked. "I'd always been told that Nubian women were self-effacing. Bastet's . . . anything but." His smile widened. "Not that there's anything wrong with that. Pictish women are spitfires."

There was an unspoken *but* at the end of the sentence, and Adam shared it. *Strong-willed is one thing. But likely to impede Kanmi's ability to function? Will a marriage divided over his job become a problem for the rest of us?* Adam was, however, far too tired to deal with any of that right now. He changed the subject, squinting at Trennus. *No bandages.* "You're looking fit."

"Lassair took care of my cuts." Trennus raised his eyebrows at Adam.

"If it costs a year of someone's life to get emergency assistance in battle, what in god's name *are* you paying to have her fix your wounds and . . ." Adam looked at Lassair for a moment, "provide light to read by?"

Trennus' lips quirked up. "Oh, she does a bit more than that."

"And my question remains."

"Bad manners to discuss the terms of a bargain."

Adam found a chair and slumped into it. "I can't go see Sig till she's out of surgery. So ignore my bad manners and talk to me."

Trennus shook his head and set his lips. It was Lassair who answered, *I offer my aid freely, Steelsoul. Godslayer.* The phoenix's head tilted, allowing her to look at him with one ruby eye, and then the other. *Trennus saved my life. My existence depends on his. It is . . . mutually very beneficial for me to aid him.* She tipped her head again. *I could heal your injuries, if you wished. No bargains are needed, between some people. There is . . . giving freely. Without expectation of return. This is something that Trennus has taught me.*

Adam stared at the firebird. "I . . . ah." His stomach churned for a moment. "I think I'll wear my wounds for now. I . . . don't . . . . Once was enough today." *Sig already paid for one set of wounds. Don't need Lassair paying for another set. Besides, my mother would have it that my soul's in enough peril already as is.*

Your soul is in no danger from me, Godslayer. When Lassair spoke their names, they sounded as if the words had weight and substance. When Lassair said the word *Godslayer*, it had a different sound to it than when Sophia had used the term, almost a year ago. And the spirit had caught more of Adam's thoughts than he'd intended. *I only heal whom I love, and I have grown to love each of you. Your souls are fair to look on. Even though each of you believes them blemished. I healed Stormborn earlier, or tried to. Emberstone, I could only repair his heart. There was too much water in him for me to easily deal with, otherwise. I am not good with water.*

Adam shook his head. "I might take you up on it tomorrow. But . . . not today. I . . . thank you, though." He shook his head, staring at the bland tile floor, and then told Trennus, "Lassair seems to be a bit more powerful than the rest of the spirits we saw today. Other than the efreet, maybe." A whisper of memory came back to him then. Sigrun's deranged-sounding sister, Sophia, on the phone from Hellas. Telling him that Lassair had once been a *fertility goddess.* The firebird certainly didn't *look* like one.

"The deranged idiot's soul-bound her," Kanmi said, opening his eyes, proving that he hadn't been sleeping, or at least, hadn't been for a while. "That's *dangerous*, Trennus. Human souls are the coin that malefic spirits traffic in. She's not a lost puppy." Kanmi looked at Lassair, his eyelids heavy. "No offense."

None taken, Emberstone. I have not tried puppy-form yet. Do you think it would suit me? Lassair's tone was unruffled.

Adam's head had snapped up. "Ah . . . soul-bound?" he asked, apprehensively.

Trennus was giving Kanmi a very dark look. "She's not malefic. She was *damaged* when I found her. She was down to a tiny spark. I didn't have enough personal power, didn't know the Names of any spirits that might help. All I had to give her was *me*. So I did." He gave Adam and Kanmi a defiant look. "Lady Lelayn bargained for a year of her life. Soul, life-energy, whatever. I gave Lassair here part of my life. My soul. Whatever you want to call it. It binds her to me, and me to her. Kill me, you kill her. Kill her, you kill me. Fortunately, she's . . . pretty difficult to kill, unless you're another spirit."

Adam's mouth had dropped open. This sounded like a deal with a demon out of folklore. He sat silently, absorbing that for almost a full minute. "And what do you get out of this?" he finally asked. "Eternal life?"

Trennus winced. "No. Gods, no. Her last summoner had ahold of her Name and was forcing every last bit of energy out of her to prolong his own life. He'd been doing that for . . . seventy-five, eighty years. He'd done it to other spirits before her. Along with other things." His face had turned to granite, and Lassair had tucked her head into his hair, mantling her wings as well.

"So what the fuck did you bargain for?" Kanmi rasped.

"Nothing." Trennus cleared his throat. "I didn't ask for anything in return."

Kanmi dropped his head back to his pillow with a look of stunned disbelief. "You are the most complete idiot I've ever met," he told Trennus. "Case studies will be written about you for summoning courses. Each one will be entitled, 'How *not* to do it.' You handed over part of your soul and *didn't* limit the bargain in any way?"

He said I could stay with him, and when I had healed enough, I could help him in his work. And when I had recovered completely, I could leave, without any further entanglements. That is how I came to learn of giving freely, and without expectation of return. In doing so . . . it seems that you often do receive more, in the end, than you gave. It is an interesting system.

Kanmi sighed, and pulled his pillow up and across his face. "Ben Maor? Shoot me. Shoot me now," he said, in a muffled tone from behind it. "I'll make it easy. The pillow will muffle the sound."

Adam half-snorted, and stood back up, still eying Lassair and Trennus cautiously. "Since we all owe Lassair our lives . . . and quite a few people in the convention center do as well . . . it seems like a bargain that's working out pretty well," he said, slowly. "I'd have preferred to have *known* about it before now. But I guess you'd tell me it wasn't my business."

Trennus flushed. Kanmi pulled the pillow away and said, changing the subject completely, "So, that Chaldean magus? Having heard what she did to Abgar . . . and if she weren't, you know, *nobility* . . ." Kanmi's tone was mocking, "I think I'd throw over Bastet and ask her to marry me. My age, my type, and all that magical power." He looked up at the ceiling. "Eh. Best I can do is ask if she'd let me study her tomes."

Adam left the room to the sound of Trennus and Kanmi laughing, though Kanmi's laughter had a rusty, pained sound to it, which would surely persist until his lungs had recovered completely.

It was late, and Sigrun wasn't out of surgery yet. Adam headed back to the governor's mansion, checked in with Livorus, and raided Sigrun's room, grabbing her suitcase for her—which held all the books she'd purchased to kill time with here in Judea—as well as a clean change of his *own* clothing. Then, for lack of anything better to do, he went back to the hospital. By the time he got there, it was nearly dawn on Maius eighth, and Sigrun had finally been moved to a room. Adam was allowed to sit there in a folding chair, much in the way Trennus was sitting with Kanmi, and he stared down at her pale face and the fall of loose hair over the white pillowcase, his hands clenching and unclenching. She was breathing on her own, at least. No intubation.

So he sat there, listening to the heart monitors, and, with a look over his shoulder at the door, muttered a few, quiet prayers to his own god, for her health. With the blank realization that he *valued* her. Valued her company. Wanted to talk with her more. Wanted to make her laugh. Finally, he simply couldn't hold off sleep any longer. He faded out.

The sound of the door opening snapped his eyes open, and Adam found he was reflexively, reaching for a gun. His subconscious was still in combat mode, expecting a threat from any direction, and he'd half-risen from his chair before he was fully conscious . . . and then blinked as he met his sister Rivkah's eyes. *"What are you doing here?"* Adam asked, surprised.

"I work *here. You'd know that if you kept up with family news at all."* Rivkah stuck her tongue out at him, saucily. Adam relaxed, giving her a quick hug, before sitting back down, as his brain finally started to function again. *That's right. Nursing degree. Following in Imah's footsteps.*

"You're not actually a full nurse yet, though, right?" Adam asked, trying to fill the silence as Rivkah carefully took notes down on the levels in the saline IV and the numbers on the monitors.

"No. Just a nursing assistant. Till I finish school." Rivkah shrugged. *"It's a job. It's good experience."*

"Imah found the position for you, didn't she?"

A dour glance. *"I* am *capable of making decisions on my own, brother."* A faint flicker of guilt crossed her face, however, and then she added, scrupulously, *"Although, yes, she did mention that there was a job opening. She wants to keep track of me, I think."* She filled a paper cup with water from a pitcher, and set it on the stand beside Sigrun's unresponsive form. *"You have the* oddest *coworkers, Adam."*

He raised his eyebrows. *"You and Chani seemed rather interested in Trennus."*

Rivkah flushed. *"He's very different from what I thought a summoner would be like. And he's much different from all the . . . very nice young men . . . that the matchmaker Imah hired has dutifully brought to the house for me to meet."*

"Oh, lord. So I'm not the only one."

"Oh, no. Doesn't help that Chani's been sneaking out at night covered in Hellene paint. Makes it so Imah and Aba don't feel like they can trust her, but I think all she's doing is sitting around in a café with friends." Rivkah shrugged again. *"Imah is on a grand quest to see us all settled and happy. Aba is . . . Aba."* Their father had been a distant figure for them, growing up. That had apparently not changed since Adam had left the house. Rivkah looked down at Sigrun, and pointed at the stack of books Adam had placed on the nightstand, for when the valkyrie awoke. *"You know, I wouldn't have thought she even knew how to read."*

Adam's head snapped up, and he fought down a hot flare of temper. *"I don't see why you'd think that,"* he told his sister. *"Half our time on the job is spent reading case files written in Latin."*

Rivkah waved her hands quickly. *"Calm down, Adam. You have to admit, it's an odd picture. She carries a* <u>spear</u>*, and the first time I saw her, she was wearing a leather bodice and a cloak made of feathers. How much more primitive can you get?"* His sister made a face, and Adam grimaced. Sigrun had *asked* him about the modesty issues here in Judea, but she was, when all was said and done, a lictor in the employ of the Praetorian Guard. She had as much right to wear her deerskin bodices as Trennus had to wear his kilt, or Adam had, for that matter, to wear his skullcap. Or not. *"The next thing we all know, all four of you are outside fighting that . . . creature . . . and then you all came back inside, covered in blood, half the neighborhood wrecked, and she sat down and read a book."* She paused. *"Once the bleeding stopped, anyway."*

"You know, if you talked to her, you'd realize how educated she is."

"There hasn't really been a chance."

"You found enough opportunities to pester Matrugena."

Rivkah flushed and sat down next to him. Adam gave her a patient stare. *"People have enough stupid ideas about* <u>Judeans</u>*,"* he told her, bluntly. *"The last thing we need to do is have stupid ideas about other people. I know for a fact that she speaks and reads three or four dialects of Gothic. She speaks Gallic well enough that she and Matrugena chat together. She speaks and reads Latin. What were your marks in Latin again, Rivkah?"*

"Oh, I speak it well enough. I just didn't like reading all those boring old plays and poems." Rivkah's tone was airy.

Adam picked up the first book in the stack and handed it to Rivkah. It proved to be the art history book on the tomb of Isis that he remembered Sigrun purchasing before they left Rome. This was written in Latin. The second book was the collected plays of Sophocles — in the original Attic Hellene, with footnotes in modern Hellene.

"She reads this, too?" Rivkah sounded startled. Hellene and Hebrew were the twin languages of science and philosophy, after all. Most truly educated people in the Empire spoke Hellene. It was a sign of being cultured.

"Her sister's a Pythia at Delphi." Adam hadn't really looked at the books as he'd dragged them out of the suitcase. The last one in the stack had Hellene lettering on the cover, but the title wasn't what he'd expected. *The Pentateuch.* The Hellene name for the Torah. Inside, the pages had

columns of Hebrew facing columns of Hellene translations.

Just then, Sigrun awakened. "Sig. About time you woke up." Relief surged through him as she looked around, her gray eyes clearly dazed. "How do you feel?"

". . . like a gutted fish."

Sigrun closed her eyes again, and Adam leaned forward, catching her hand in his. *Come on. Stay awake. Be the pain in everyone's ass that you know so well how to be.* "Close enough," he told her, squeezing her fingers. "That was your own bright idea, I might add."

The eyes opened again. ". . . whatever doesn't kill you . . . ." Barely audible.

"Makes you stronger. I really don't want to hear that one again. For someone who *hates* hospitals, you certainly spend a lot of time in them." Adam realized he was gripping her fingers too tightly, speaking too sharply. Rivkah, at his side, was already stirring in protest, and put one hand lightly, on his left forearm to stop him. "God *damn* it, Sig, what were you *thinking*? I didn't ask you to take the wounds for me." He didn't care if his sister heard the words.

The steel-sheen eyes widened. Palest gray at the center, dark rings around the outside of the iris. Oddly dark lashes, considering how light her hair was, brushing against her cheeks for a moment as she closed her eyes, and then managed to open them again. Sigrun licked her lips, and told him, ". . . better me . . . than you. My job. To decide."

"To decide who lives and who dies?"

". . . yes. *Valkyrie.*" She swallowed, and Rivkah hastily stood and offered her a tiny sip of water with which to wet her mouth, with a caution not to swallow any of it. "We . . . always know. When people will die."

Adam seethed. They'd covered this before. "So what?"

"So . . . we know . . . when we can do . . . something. Can make a choice. My mother, when I was three?" Sigrun paused, her eyes sliding shut again. "I knew then. Knew it was mortal. Cancer. Eating her away from the inside. Couldn't help her." Sigrun swallowed, hard. "*Could* help you. Battle-wound." She opened her eyes again.

Adam leaned forward, and so she couldn't look away from him, his face within a few inches of hers. "Those wounds were *mortal*, Sig. I don't want you taking a mortal wound for me again. You hear me? I want your *word* on that."

". . . mortal . . . for you." She closed her eyes. "Not for me."

"God *damn* it, Sigrun. You listen to me. You could have died. You nearly *did* die. Do you have a death-wish or something?"

". . . highest honor . . . is to die in battle." Her eyes opened, met his. "Don't wish to die. But my life is . . . service. Tool in the hands of the gods. A weapon." She closed her eyes again, but she didn't stop speaking. "A god-born . . . can never be more than what we are. What we're born to be. Humans can. Can be more than what they are. Reach for the stars. And you burn the brightest of all, Adam. Couldn't let that spark go out. If I died . . . acceptable price." Sigrun turned her head away and clearly suppressed a cough, with an agonized expression slipping over her face.

"No, it's *not.*" Adam wanted to shake her for making it sound rational. Reasonable. "It's not acceptable, Sig, because I'll never accept it. You don't die for me. You understand that? Not for me." His fingers were clenched on her hand, and it took Rivkah putting a hand on his shoulder for him to realize his sister was even still in the room.

"Adam? She only just woke up." Rivkah's eyes were wide. "She's already talked more than I thought someone *could* after . . . ." A helpless gesture at Sigrun's body, shrouded by the sheets.

Adam loosened his fingers. There was plenty of time to talk to Sigrun about all of this, now that he was . . . ninety-nine percent sure she was going to live. "You're right," he told his sister, and then looked back at Sigrun. He shifted to grip her hand with his left, while he raised his right to trace a strand of hair back from her face, with a gentle fingertip. "Sorry, Sig."

"Don't . . . understand . . . why you're angry . . ." Sigrun managed.

Adam swore, all too aware of his sister's eyes on them. Sigrun was doped up on pain medication, at least as much as she *could* be. She was hurt, and in no shape for him to make any sort of explanation. He wasn't even sure he *could* explain it, except that she'd come to matter to him. Deeply. Instead, he shifted the subject. Raised the Hellene copy of the Torah, and asked her, quietly, "You're reading the first five books of my faith?"

Sigrun clearly tried to shrug, but it involved too many core body muscles, and instead winced in pain. "When in Rome . . . ? It seemed . . . a good idea to understand more of the people . . . who live here."

Adam gave Rivkah a pointed look. *Here's your chance. Talk to her.* Rivkah hesitated, and then said, "Translations are always uncertain. Much of the original meaning gets lost."

Sigrun looked up and focused, uncertainly, on Rivkah's face. "Yes. And Hellene . . . is not . . . my first language."

"I could teach you to read it in Hebrew," Adam said, suddenly, as inspiration went off in his mind. "You're not going *anywhere* for a few days, Sigrun. Would occupy the time." *And I have got to keep you in bed. I know you. You're going to try to stand up by tonight. Tomorrow at the latest. And that might actually tear you back apart.*

Sigrun grimaced. "Hellene . . . Latin . . . Gothic. Three alphabets. Hard enough." She looked up at the ceiling, and managed to sound cranky. "Your letters are all different. They run the wrong direction." A pause. "It would be as painful for you as it would be for me." She closed her eyes again. "My pedagogue despaired of me." Another pause. "She considered me a very slow and stupid child, because I was so slow to learn Latin and Hellene."

Adam's head snapped up. "She *called* you that?" It was hard to fathom.

"Yes. Many times. When I was receiving my canings for not having known my lessons." Sigrun opened her eyes again. "Kanmi's children . . . their pedagogue seems a kinder sort."

"How old were you?" Rivkah asked, her dark eyes wide. Adam

could see empathy blossoming in his sister, and mild outrage. They'd been taught Latin and Hellene at home by their father, and there had been cryptographic puzzles and Torah verses to memorize, but they'd never been *caned* for not remembering a lesson.

"She had my care since I was four. Lessons began when I was six." Sigrun's voice was distant. "She said that . . . that it might be my birthright to be a battle-maiden, but that if I couldn't understand more than swords and spears . . . then I was a waste of her time."

"Couldn't you have gone to a public school?" Rivkah demanded.

"Begged to go. Couldn't. God-born have to be . . . educated differently. So we understand our powers are . . . to serve others. Not to rule them." Sigrun closed her eyes.

"I hope your father sent the pedagogue packing," Rivkah said, after a moment. Adam was rubbing his thumb lightly over the back of Sigrun's hand. He was learning more about her in a few minutes than he'd managed to uncover in the past eighteen months, and he wasn't about to argue with the results.

"She was a Hellene slave. Before slavery was abolished in Nova Germania." Sigrun didn't open her eyes, and her tone was weary. "When she was done teaching me, my father freed her. And then they married. I don't ask . . . what passed between them . . . before that." A faint, wintery smile. "I hate that woman. But she did give me a younger sister. Sophia."

Adam blinked in belated realization. *Oh, god. So her teacher also had god-born blood, somewhere along the line. Not expressed . . . more like a recessive gene. Sophia's god-born, too. She raised both of you. But she favored her own flesh and blood, I expect?*

Rivkah finally excused herself. "I should tell the doctors she's awake. I should have done that five minutes ago, actually." She scuttled out, but left looking more thoughtful than she'd arrived.

Adam watched her go, then returned his attention to the book he'd perched on the edge of the bed. "The offer stands. I'll teach you, if you're interested."

Sigrun actually managed a smile. "I wouldn't . . . want to put you through the pain, Adam. I'm not a good scholar."

"Sig, you can speak and read at least four languages in three different alphabets. I would call that *exceptional* by most standards." Adam's temper flared, and he knew that if he ever happened to meet Sigrun's stepmother, he'd be hard-pressed to keep from throttling the woman. "You can learn whatever you want to learn."

"Perhaps. But it's not what I am for."

"What you're *for*?" For an instant, his temper burned brighter. He could, in part, understand why his sister had made the mistake she had, of assuming Sigrun was . . . uneducated. Barbaric. Savage. It was, largely, the only identity that Sigrun allowed outsiders to see. It just drove him *insane* when she accepted the limitations of that role, when she was, and could be, so much *more*. "Sig. You said that humans can be more than what they are. You're god-born, but you're still *human*. Don't settle. *Strive*."

"You're . . . angry again."

"You're damned right I am. You're more than a tool. You're more than a weapon. And, god *damn* it, you're important to me." He leaned forward, and, this time not caring about the morphine or anything else, kissed her, looking down into her widened eyes to see the acceptance and the confusion there. He would have pulled back to tell her, *you can beat the shit out of me for this later*, but her hand crept up. Locked in his hair with frail strength. Adam closed his eyes and kissed her again, feeling her lips part a little under his with a sigh.

It was the sound of the door handle rattling once again that made him finally pull back and return to merely stroking her hair. The doctors and nurses came into the room in a wave, all questions and tests and bustling curiosity, most of which Sigrun bore with patience. They kept trying to hint to Adam that he should leave . . . . but Adam wasn't about to move at that point. Even when they wanted to evaluate the condition of the incisions, the most he did was turn to the side to spare her modesty. A spate of exclamations in Hebrew, *"My god. The ones in the abdomen are gone already. There's nothing there!" "The long incision into the chest cavity remains, but . . . I can't believe the rate of healing. We're going to have to watch this, to ensure that the sutures don't grow into the scar . . . ." "What scar? I don't even see one where the shoulder wound was . . . am I even looking at the correct shoulder?"*

Adam did his best to conceal his smile. And when they all left, Adam turned back to Sigrun, who'd been elevated in the bed, and was regarding him now, wide-eyed. Picked up the book, and pulled a fountain pen out of a nearby drawer, and began to write the letters of the Hebrew alphabet for her on the inside cover. "Alef. Bet. Gimmel. Dalet. Pretty similar to the Carthaginians . . . their Phoenician ancestors gave everyone else alpha and beta and so on. And the languages are related, of course." He gave her a quick look. "I'll trade you for lessons in Cimbric."

"You don't have vowels."

"You don't have a *future tense*. I have no idea how you manage to say that you will be going to the store next week."

"Next week, I go. I am going next week. Easy." Sigrun leaned her head back against the pillows. "We might not have a future tense, but we do have extra pronouns."

He finished the lettering on the inner cover. "What other pronouns can there possibly be?" In most Western languages, there was I, you-formal, thou-informal, he, she, it, we, you/thou plural, and they.

"*Witan.* We two. Used between . . . brother warriors. Lovers. Husband and wives. We two, against the world." Her voice faltered a little.

Adam looked at her, steadily. He already knew that the reserve and the stoicism and the ice were methods of keeping the world at bay. Ways of keeping from being hurt. He took her hand in his again, and told her, simply, "Teach me how to say that." But he leaned in, and brushed a kiss over her lips again, before she could reply, stealing the words.

Chapter XIV: Relations

There are those who claim to know where the human soul goes after death. Valhalla for the dead slain in battle, Hel for the common folk. Hades or the Elysian Fields. Eternity spent inside your own mummy, until the body is resurrected at the end of all things. Those from the distant reaches of Hindustan and Qin believe in reincarnation, instead. With that in mind, I have yet to see or speak to a human soul that had left its body after death. There are those who claim to have done so. I prefer to avoid the subject. Astrology is far more certain an art than necromancy.

What I know, and can prove, is this: There are beings other than humans in this world. They come from their own world, which is divided from this one by a curtain of energy. These spirits vary in power and disposition, even as humans themselves do. Some are attendants on the gods. Some are freeborn, for lack of a better designation. Some are well-inclined towards humans, some are malefic, and some are utterly indifferent to us and our realm.

They live outside of our space and time, but may enter it. Early philosophers, such as Boethius, claimed that being outside of time would allow a being – such as a god – to see the whole of time, and thus, know the predestinate future. Some spirits claim to know the whole of time, but they are hardly any better guide to the future than astrology.

Spirits who enter this world generally do so, at first, without bodies. Spirits may either possess a human body or may be impelled to provide motive force to a ghul, to use the Persian term, or a golem. More powerful spirits may manifest bodies around themselves, and these bodies are often subject to rules, according to their individual type. From whence these rules derive remains, at this time, a mystery to us. But there are more types of spirits in heaven and earth, than we can dream.

You may bargain with a spirit. You may bind it. You may banish it. Your chance of doing any of these things is greatly improved by the use of levers. Archimedes once wrote that if he had a lever long enough, and positioned in the correct spot, he could move the Earth. This is true of spirits as well. What are the levers that will add to your ability to bind or control a spirit?

- *Binding rituals. These include words and binding circles drawn on the ground. No one, at the present time, understands why symbols can disrupt a spirit, but it may have to do with energy resonance patterns.*
- *A containment object. Pottery, glass, stone, metal objects. Things that will endure. Wood is too impermanent. These objects are used for binding, and not for banishing.*
- *The spirit's true Name. Names define and shape a being. A Name gives you control. Naturally, most spirits and most humans guard their true Names tightly.*
- *Knowing your own Name. If you know your own Name, this gives you power. Certainty. Control of yourself. Be extremely wary of offering your Name in bargain. Because then, the spirit can control you.*

- <u>Assistance of other spirits</u>. *If you are unable to subdue a spirit on your own, a spirit involved in an on-going pact with you, or one specifically allied with you for this purpose, can be of some aid.*
- <u>Blood-binding</u>. *Most spirits relish blood as a sacrifice; it represents a measurable iota of a human's life-energy. It connects the summoner to the working of the magic. Some localities, laughably, frown on this practice.*
- <u>Animal sacrifice</u>. *Chickens, goats, sheep, cows have been commonly sacrificed to the gods for millennia. Again, this is a measurable flow of life-energy that can empower your wreaking, and can be used to empower a spirit, as well. This is, however, frowned upon, even more so than blood-binding.*
- <u>Human sacrifice.</u> *This practice is forbidden in all places touched by Rome. It is still practiced, supposedly, and much in secret, by Mongolian shaman and Chaldean Magi. It has been described as undeniably effective, as the full life-energy, or soul, of the human involved, is a rich source of power.*
- <u>Soul-binding.</u> *This practice is highly controversial. Giving a portion of one's soul to a spirit links the practitioner to the spirit, permanently, or until the bargain is resolved. There is danger in the practice, if the spirit so bound is malefic. Turning over the whole of one's soul will surely result in the same outcome as revealing one's Name to an unscrupulous spirit or person: enslavement. The rewards, however, are unparalleled, as I can attest to from personal experience.*

If the spirit has manifested physically, and presents a clear and present danger to you, then you must deal with both the body and the spirit. You may kill the body, certainly. Spirits that are relieved of their corporeal form become disorganized, and are forced into the Veil. Most require being re-summoned to return to the mortal realm. Some few, however, are powerful enough to freely transit the Veil of their own accord. These make for powerful enemies.

Thus, killing the corporeal body is normally just a first step. Killing the body, and binding the spirit before it flees to the Veil is certainly an option, and requires the use of a containment object, preferably one previously prepared specifically for this particular spirit. Killing the body and banishing the spirit requires more power from the practitioner than binding does. Banishing may also only last until the spirit regains the power to return, or is summoned once more.

If the practitioner is unable to kill the body, as is certainly possible with very powerful spirits, then one must consider binding body and spirit alike. Trapping the body in a cave, inside a stone-cut tomb, under a landslide, inside of a vast metal shell of some sort . . . all plausible. And then bind that spirit <u>to that location</u>. This may result in the container being breached by future generations, however, so should be only used as a last resort.

A spirit cannot be banished from its own body. A spirit in possession of a human body, a <u>ghul</u>, or a <u>golem,</u> can be dismissed from this locus through standard banishment practices. A spirit's manifested body cannot be banished.

– Dr. Johann Georg Faust, <u>Summa Animae</u>, 1469 AC.

Historical note: Dr. J.G. Faust, *a Gothic academic, alchemist, astrologer, and noted practitioner of summoning, died of what has been called an 'alchemical explosion' in 1496 AC in the city of Staufen im Breisgau, near the Black Forest in southern Germania. Speculation has been rampant for centuries that this explosion was, in fact, no accident, but the result of a bargain gone wrong with an attendant spirit. The question for all serious students of the Art remains, to this day, a very pertinent one: If one agrees to soul-binding with a spirit, if one exchanges Names with a spirit . . . how does one* <u>know</u> *that the spirit is beneficent? It is well known that malefic spirits lie. And that they are much practiced in appearing to be good and true, when they are, in fact, the very opposite.*

— Maccus Prasto, <u>The History of Summoning</u>, *p. 187, University of Novo Trier Press, Novo Trier, 1936 AC.*

Maius 8, 1955 AC

Trennus Matrugena had gone back to the governor's mansion around two antemeridian, once he was sure that Kanmi was resting comfortably, and that Sigrun had gotten out of surgery successfully. He'd checked in on her, and patted her motionless foot through the sheets, wishing that he could stay . . . but Adam was already ensconced there, waiting for Sigrun to awaken, and there was only one chair, and Adam didn't look as if he planned to be turned out of it. Thus, he'd wished his tired friend farewell before taking a taxi across Old Town to the Palace, himself. Lassair had, with a certain tact, de-manifested for that. He was getting enough stares for being a Pict in Judea, braided, tattooed, and wearing a blood-stained kilt, without adding a live phoenix on his shoulder.

He'd used a *lot* of mental and physical energy over the course of the day. Being a conduit for ley-energy took a toll out of someone, and he'd wrestled, mentally and physically, with demons, been wounded, healed, *and* conducted ley, and stood two stints on first-aid duty. Exhausted in mind, body, and soul, Trennus stumbled into the room he'd been sharing with Adam. Slammed his shins into the edge of one of the beds, swore, and debated dropping onto the bed, still clothed and covered in sweat and blood. *No. Don't want to wake up like this.* But walking all the way over to the bathing buildings inside the complex that made up the governor's residence seemed hardly worthwhile, either.

He compromised. He washed up as best he could in the lavatory sink, threw his clothing over the back of a chair, and lay down on the bed, pulling up just the sheet. He didn't care if they did have this fancy new *air conditioning* down here. As far as he was concerned, Maius meant highs in the fifties during the day, and just above freezing at night, not this constant, faintly humid seventy-five to eighty degrees. He wrapped his fingers around his amulets, and hazily thought, *Lassair . . . thank you, fire-heart. You saved so many lives today. Saraid . . . you did, too. Thank you.*

That is what we are meant to do, is it not? He wasn't actually sure which of them said that.

Ideally, yes. But his thoughts were vague, and very shortly after that, he knew absolutely nothing more.

Dreams finally filtered in. Wonderful, disturbing, beautiful dreams. *Standing in the middle of a bonfire, looking out at the humans dancing around it. They were casting flowers on the blaze, making the smoke rise sweetly. Liquid warmth, like heated honey, all around. So many minds, so much joy, as they cast their sorrows and woes into the fire with the blossoms. They wore leathers, beautifully made. Jewelry made of silver and pieces of amber. It could have been last Midsummer's Eve in the highlands, but it wasn't. He looked up from the heart of the fire, and the stars were wrong. They weren't in their familiar patterns. And he wasn't himself. He had another name, as he watched the humans move away from the fire. Leaving, hand in hand, and going out among the fields. Sharing joy with one another against the cold ground. Reaching out of the fire with hands made of flame, trying to reach them. Trying to share in the joy, trying to return some of what they'd given . . . becoming one with them all, in the darkness. Becoming the men, becoming the women. Taking and being taken, little gasps and sighs in the night. Wondering amazement in his thoughts. They, too, are made of fire. They kindle it in one another. Blazes now, smoldering coals later. New fires, spread from sparks. We are all fire together. And there is joy here. I never want to leave again.*

Hazy consciousness. Recognition that something was . . . different. Warmth. Softness, right up against him. Trennus moved an arm and pulled the softness and warmth closer. Inhaled a scent like . . . rose petals and cinnamon and smoke. It was oddly familiar, so he didn't really think much more of it. Just rubbed his face against soft hair. Found a neck buried under the long tresses and, mostly because he was still dimly thinking about the couples in the dark fields, finding fire together . . . he started to nibble his way down that neck. Found shoulder. Heard a little gasp of pleasure, and pulled his bedmate closer to him. *Best dream ever*, Trennus concluded, rocking his hips a little, involuntarily against her tailbone.

There was a slight pause as his brain, which wasn't working on all cylinders, caught up with his body, which *was*. *Oh, Morrigan.* Trennus' eyes opened in horror. *Please don't let this be one of Adam's sisters. He'd kill me, and I'd let him.*

The room was dimly lit; it had no windows, being in one of the oldest parts of the old palace. He pulled his head and arm back gingerly, and realized that the dim amber light that filled the room was actually coming from her skin. "L . . . Lassair?" Trennus managed. His brain absolutely refused to engage.

Lassair turned over in bed, rolling to her other side, and light radiated, faintly, from her skin. Her form had shifted again. A honey tint kissed her ivory skin. Her hair, always white before, was now garnet red, and it fell in loose waves around her face, with burning phoenix feathers tangled here and there. Her eyes still held the smolder of burning coals, but instead of pupils, there was a blue-violet flare at the heart of each. Trennus tried to meet her gaze, and had to look away, which took his gaze lower. Perfect, rounded curves of breast and hip, the length of her legs as she shifted a little closer. *What's the matter? Why did you stop?* She pouted as Trennus dragged his eyes back up again. *Don't you like me like this? Did I get the form right this time?*

"I . . . ah. . . what?" Trennus managed. He dug down deep for reserves of willpower he wasn't even aware he had, and edged a little further away in the sheets. Lassair in this form was unbelievably beautiful. As if precisely designed and calibrated to drive him completely insane. "Ah . . . yes. You . . . got it right." He swallowed. It was killing him *not* to reach out and run a hand along her arm, down her flank, to her hips, just to see what her skin *felt* like. "What are you doing?"

Lassair smiled at him, and pushed playfully at one of his shoulders, and Trennus let her shift him to his back. *What does it look like I'm doing, silly?* She shifted, and with the fluidity of a cat, was suddenly sitting atop him, straddling him. *I'm seducing you.*

Trennus swallowed. Hard. She felt . . . amazing on him. Every single cell in his body was currently *screaming* at him to stop being a *fool* and not look a gift horse in the damned mouth. He reached out, caught her hips in his hands, and tried to sit up. "Lassair . . . I said I'd take care of you. I . . . don't . . . I . . . you. . ." A horrible flash of what he'd seen when he'd first found her shot across his mind, and he forced it away.

Lassair's expression turned sad, but she slipped her hands along the sides of his face, cradling his jaw, and kissed him. Trennus saw *fire* behind his closed eyelids for a moment, and dimly realized that his hands had shifted, arms snaking around her to hold her tightly. *What passed before was horrible, yes. But you're not. You're wonderful. I love you. And if you're taking care of me, perhaps I should take care of you, too.*

Lassair . . . don't want to take advantage of you. We have a contract. Technically, you're bound to me. You're not a slave. Not a . . . . It was getting increasingly hard to think. Her lips tasted as good as she smelled, and it had been a very damned long time since he'd been with a woman.

. . . Trennus, technically, eighty percent of your soul currently belongs to me. That technically makes you my servant, doesn't it? Lassair's tone was a little playful as she picked up one of his braids and bit the end . . . and then found his collarbone. Neck. And, damn it, rocked her hips against his, sweetly and subtly.

Trennus met the fire's-heart eyes so close to his own. *Well, when you put it that way . . . .*

Stop objecting and love me, Trennus. Flamesower. Trennus' breath caught. He'd never known his Name, and it sounded . . . good . . . but not quite right, somehow. Still, she had eighty percent of his soul in her keeping. It shouldn't have been a surprise that she knew it, or at least part of it. But she used it so sweetly, so softly, when she could have compelled him with it, made him helpless . . . . *You do love me, don't you, Trennus?*

Of course I do. How could I possibly not? He'd just . . . never thought about her in these terms. Rather, he'd never *allowed* himself to do so. Her history with her last summoner was so very bad. And she'd been so fragile and damaged, just a flicker in the palm of his hand when she'd come to him . . . .

That was then. I've grown since then, Trennus. I thought taking human form back in Rome would get your attention, but I must have gotten something wrong . . . .

The female form was beautiful. I just . . . I thought you were playing.

I always play, Trennus. But I also love you. Let me show you how much.

Thoughts flickering like a candle's flame, each to each. They hadn't stopped kissing all this time. Play of tongues, again, like flames melding each other. Her overall heat increasing, fever-hot, reminding him, all over again, that Lassair *was* fire. Pleasant in a hearth. Deadly uncontrolled. Trennus started to roll her to her back, and then stopped. He could feel just a trace of hesitation in her body, and pulled back. *How about,* he offered, lying back, *if you take what you want from your poor servant?*

His reward was in seeing her face light up, from within. Almost bashful, demure, a flicker of joy and coy amusement at the same time. Devastating combination. *That could be arranged . . . .* Warmth of her hands, positioning him. And then the little smile as she sank down, and caught her lip between her teeth, and then all Trennus knew was that he was passing through the heart of a *star*. White-hot flame all around him, encompassing him, but not burning him. Bliss and physical delight, yes, when he caught glimpses of the things their bodies were doing, but he knew she was playing with his *soul* now, too. Caressing it, as if it were a harp-string between their bodies and minds, connecting them to one another, just as their flesh was connected. *Oh, gods, I didn't realize I was already in you all this time . . . .* Watching her face as she reached her own peak, delight and happiness in her face, and fire wreathing her body . . . *going to be hard to explain the scorched sheets . . .* and then rolling her to her back at last. Taking and giving at once. And then passing back through the heart of the star once more. Far, far more than mere physical gratification.

Trennus finally managed to pull away, by a few inches, and settled them on their sides once more. Pulled her back into his chest and stomach once more, and ran his fingers through her hair. "Lassair . . . ."

Mmm. Contentment in her tone, like the crackle of low-burning logs.

"You might be a little addictive, Lassair. I'm probably not going to leave you alone. Fair warning." Trennus found the back of her neck to kiss again.

I don't want to be left alone. I want you. You saved me. You take care of me. Now, it's my turn to save and care for you. Free exchange, Flamesower. No bargains. Just giving and receiving. She caught his hand and kissed the palm, and Trennus groaned a little as she nipped and bit the tips of his fingers, too. He was reacting, and he shouldn't have been able to, not for at least a good twenty minutes or more. *Must be the long dry spell,* he thought, hazily, and slid a hand along her flank again.

A little pause, and Lassair admitted, *I was remembering things, Trennus. Things from . . . before.*

"Before?" Trennus blinked. "Not the —"

No. Not the vile one. Before him. Things I had forgotten. Who I was, I think? What I was?

"The dream I had before I awoke . . . ."

Yes. That was one of my memories. But it was a very long time ago. Your people were different then. And I think I was . . . on the continent of Europa. Perhaps Gaul. Not so far north as your home. Lassair's voice was intrigued. *I want to remember more, Trennus.*

"Hmm. I don't know how to help, but if I can, I will." He had to admit to a certain fascinated curiosity, himself. Spirits were ageless. If not killed, eternal. Technically, they were genderless, as well. They were essences, not organic life forms. It was probably fruitless to love one . . . and Trennus was aware that he both loved Lassair, and was now starting to fall *in* love with her, as well. In the face of that, none of the rest of it seemed to matter much.

The memories are stronger now, than they were before. Perhaps I merely need to do things that I once did? And that will serve as a reminder? Lassair rolled over and began to kiss him, a little more seriously.

Trennus reciprocated, and with interest . . . and then got a look at the clock. Horrible little windup noisemaker that it was, its hands had both just touched the twelve. "Morrigan!" Trennus swore. "It's noon already? I need to get up." His mind scattered into duty rosters and how he must have missed a shift . . . and then realized that Livorus had, in light of the fact that two of his main lictors were in the hospital, and the other two had been wounded, as well, stood them down for the time being. He had the *day off.*

Would you like to spend it here, in bed? Lassair offered, her tone hopeful.

Trennus tried to access his brain. ". . . I should say no. I should say we need to go to the hospital."

Stormborn is awake. She and Steelsoul Godslayer are both well. Emberstone remains at the hospital. He is with the one who binds him. Lassair's tone hardened. *They are arguing.*

"So, you're saying that there's nothing that I can or should be doing, besides staying in bed beside one of the most beautiful women I've ever seen?" Trennus considered that for a moment, and then lay back down to wrap her up in his arms again. *Bargain made, bargain sealed.* He gave her a hopeful look, however. *I don't suppose you want to go to the baths, do you?*

That . . . is a terrifying amount of water. Her tone held trepidation.

Water shouldn't affect you in that form, should it?

I . . . am not sure.

Respecting the fear in her mental voice, Trennus let it go, lightly. *Think you might be able to sneak into the male side? One of the steam rooms, maybe?* He grinned at her as she turned towards him.

Ohhh. Yes. I think I could manage this.

I might begin to have a reputation for an unhealthy fixation on my phoenix, however.

Then I will not manifest until you are in the steam room and alone.

Trennus chuckled at her pragmatic tone. Suddenly, his entire *world* was brighter. And he couldn't think it was anything but a *good* thing to have his soul owned by this beautiful, glorious, powerful being, his Name known to her, as hers was known to him.

Kanmi Eshmunazar got dressed in the clothing his wife had brought to the hospital for him, and, carrying the bag she'd brought them in, and a dispatch case, hesitated. He *should* check out and go back to the governor's residence. See his wife and the boys. *But she's spoiling for a fight. And I don't want to argue just now. It can wait. Besides, Caetia's been in heavy surgery. Should look in on her.* As such, he made his way to the post-op ward, where he'd been told Caetia was recovering. He tapped on the right door, got a "Come in!" from ben Maor, and stuck his head in.

"You're looking a lot better than I thought you would," Kanmi told the valkyrie, concealing his relief. She looked wan and he could see bruises mottling most of her upper chest, where her patient gown sagged down a little . . . but she looked remarkably healthy, given her condition yesterday. *And ben Maor, too. Considering that he should be dead.* "Heard they actually used the chest spreaders on you." His own voice was a laryngitic rasp, and his chest still ached.

Caetia blinked at him. "So I have been told," she replied, tiredly. "It is . . . not comfortable."

"Guess who's refusing to take her pain meds?" ben Maor said, in a dry tone, jerking a thumb at the valkyrie. "Nevermind that pain inhibits recovery."

The two of them exchanged a long look, and Kanmi blinked as he realized that ben Maor was actually holding Caetia's hand. *Oh, ho. The wind sits in that quarter, does it?* There were no regulations against romantic relationships in the Praetorians, or even in the Legion, really, so long as two people were of equivalent rank. Rome wasn't ancient Sparta, admittedly; the Spartans had recommended and even encouraged their soldiers to form liaisons with one another, on the theory that a man will fight harder to save his lover than anyone else. That being said, as female soldiers had entered the Roman army, over time, a similar philosophy had been espoused, particularly because marriage was seen as a virtue in a solider. Around the time of the Industrial Revolution, there had been muttering from the general staff about ways in which to make every soldier as interchangeable as the machined parts of the average artillery piece, and that in order to make everyone the same, everyone would have to be made equal. Nepotism would have to be eliminated . . . and that had been laughed right out of the room, given that there *was* no inherent equality in the legions. The sons of patricians (women weren't admitted into the Roman Legion proper; only in levy forces.) all began their careers as officers. God-born, sorcerers, technomancers, and ley-mages, given their previous high degrees of training, expertise, and raw power, also tended to start their career as officers. Officers had privileges that ordinary soldiers did not. It had always been that way. And an enlisted soldier *could* rise from the ranks, after showing sufficient merit.

Kanmi was all for the rights of man. To his way of thinking, society was like a footrace. Everyone who wanted to participate, should be allowed to line up at the start. But he had no time for the people who, once admitted to the race, stood around complaining that they had the lane that was in the direct sunlight, that it wasn't *fair* that the people to the left and the right had been practicing since childhood, that they didn't have the right running shoes on, and that someone *owed* them new shoes. He didn't have time for people who'd spend their entire time at the race complaining, rather than participating. Practicing. Improving. And if you started with a disadvantage, and *won*? Why, the greater share of glory was yours.

As for the people who showed up at the track, and wouldn't even run, but still complained that the race was unfair, and would have impacted them, if they could have been bothered to compete? Kanmi thought *those* people should be put in the stocks and pelted with vegetables, for making a public nuisance of themselves.

So he had no problem with ben Maor making time with Caetia. Technically, ben Maor had been appointed head of the lictors protecting Livorus for the Judea trip. The position might even stick, but Kanmi wouldn't have a problem with it. Caetia was far more experienced, but she hated talking with reporters and coordinating with other forces. Ben Maor's position as head of the lictors, and her subordinate position *could* be argued to represent a conflict of interest . . . except that Caetia was *god-born*. She was always going to be the first of them sent into the line of fire, and would never tolerate being 'protected.' She had probably twenty years of experience on all of them, and had clearly turned down promotion to head of the detail. Probably several times.

There wasn't much probability of her receiving preferential treatment, in other words. Except maybe having her watch schedule aligned so that she and ben Maor got to sleep at the same time. Assuming, of course, that this whole thing managed to get past the handholding stage. Kanmi suppressed a smile. He couldn't help but think that getting Caetia in the sack, beautiful though the valkyrie was, would be about as much fun as humping a snow-bank. Sure, you might be able to burrow a hole, but sooner or later, frostbite was going to set in, and things might *freeze off.*

But, Baal take it, not my business. He wants to risk his cock falling off from the cold, that's ben Maor's look-out. Kanmi moved into the room, set down his bags, and perched on one of the uncomfortable chairs. Tried to find something to say. Something companionable, that would give Caetia something else to think about besides the pain.

"Someone from the Praetorians dropped off a nice thick set of files for me this morning," he finally rasped, nudging the dispatch case with a toe. "Things I've been requesting access to for months." He flicked a glance at Adam. "Someone, somewhere, broke a logjam. If it was you, thank you."

"I did try a little diplomacy with the people over in Archives."

"I'll send you to do all my talking from now on. I have data on the Source Initiative. The membership lists, at least. I can start going through those. See if any of the names cross-match to known troublemakers of any sort. Any criminal records. It's only two, three thousand names, tops. Can't possibly take me more than a few years in my spare time." Kanmi nodded, and ben Maor chuckled ruefully.

Another knock at the door, and this time, Matrugena walked in, looking clean and refreshed and disgustingly relaxed, with Lassair once more perched on his shoulder. *There's someone who didn't spend the night in a damned hospital*, Kanmi thought, grimacing. "You should teach her to be a parrot," Kanmi told the Pict. "She'll stand out much less that way."

"I think she stands out, no matter what form she takes," Matrugena said, smiling broadly. "And you're beautiful in every one of them," he added fondly, turning his head to regard the bird.

Why, thank you. Lassair preened at her feathers.

Kanmi didn't know what to make of that, so he shrugged and pulled another chair across the room with a beckoning finger, and situated it for Matrugena.

"You get anything else in the dispatch case?" Ben Maor gestured at the bags, which Kanmi had placed on the floor beside his chair.

"Thaumometric readings from the Pyramid of the Sun over the past few years," Kanmi replied, leaning back in his chair. "My initial measurements, and those that people have took before and after the event. Magic and its residue are measurable. We measure ley and electricity in wex. We measure sorcery and even spirit energies in thaums. I didn't have the right tools with me in Nahuatl at the ley-plants at first, but it *can* be done." He paused. "There are some anomalies with the readings the various researchers have been getting from the ruins. Fascinating stuff, really."

Ben Maor looked dubious. Matrugena, however, sat up. "Anomalies? What do you mean?"

"There's about half as much power residue in the rocks and the ground as there should be."

Caetia tried to clear her throat. "You . . . really think . . . that you can *measure a god?*" Her tone was incredulous, as she labored to get the words out.

"I can measure the energy output of the *sun*. Not directly, but by observation, inference, and experimentation. Measuring a god shouldn't be that much different." Kanmi gave her a droll look. "I'm not planning on attempting to find out Tyr's vital statistics or favorite color, if that's your concern. I value my health."

Caetia's eyes widened, and she laughed and coughed at the same time, and then curled inwards on herself, even as ben Maor gave her a steadying hand.

Trennus shook his head. "We know that the, ah, entity," he tossed a cautious glance at the door behind them, which was closed, "was weakened, Esh. That might account for the number differences."

"Not really. Magic decays at a known rate, and becomes ambient in the environment. As a result, starting with what's in the rocks, we can extrapolate backwards to determine how much was unleashed a year ago.

The problem is, I was *also* present and can give a fairly good estimate of how much energy that the *entity*—" a quick, mocking smile, "was tossing around. It's less accurate, because it's not an objective, measured assessment . . . but even allowing for my overestimating his power because I was being slapped around like a ragdoll? My numbers still don't match up with the readings being taken at the site today." Kanmi glanced over his shoulder at the door, and then warded the room against eavesdropping. "Right. Our playmate was a *weakened* entity, but a very old one. He was generating enough power in thaums to power a mid-sized 'ley-energy' plant over eight hundred miles away. That was around six hundred and sixty-seven megawex of ley/electrical. Which is close to seven million thaums."

"Meaningless numbers to most people," Trennus told him. "For reference, Adam, a thaum is enough power to lift one ounce of matter at normal Earth gravity. In terms of wex, what Kanmi's talking about at the plant was enough power to light up a decent-sized city."

Kanmi nodded, rapidly. "And that was just the *first plant* he happened to be powering, continuously. There were at least four others, here and there throughout the whole of Nahautl. That's thirty-five million thaums of constant output, or enough to power five mid-size cities *and* he was throwing us around like a child's toys at the same time." Kanmi paused. "Conservative estimate, thus, he had roughly forty to forty-five million thaums to liberate at the moment of his death. The amount of residue in the rock should indicate at least that much. Instead, there's twenty-two million thaums calculated at the time of origin. Enough that it really should have cooked us more than it did. It's a wonder none of us have developed fucking *cancer*, in fact."

"Oh, how comforting. Something else to keep me awake at night," Adam muttered.

Kanmi lifted his hands, palms up. "So, at least *half* of his power . . . went somewhere else." He leaned back, and started talking with more interest and enthusiasm, forgetting the raspy quality of his own voice. "We know that magic follows some principles similar to magnetism and electricity. It can be stored, as we know. It's attracted to similar fields, so it can accrete. After that fight, every battery I had was no good anymore. They'd been overloaded." Kanmi gestured. "Question becomes, where did the rest of our *entity* go?"

Caetia had, midway through Kanmi's words, had leaned her head back against her pillows, her eyes drifting shut, but the monitors continued to ping steadily, announcing that her heartbeat remained even. Now, Matrugena turned his head and looked at Lassair; the phoenix huddled a little in on herself. *I caught <u>some</u> of his power*, the spirit admitted, her tone uneasy. *I did not intend it. And it was almost too much to control. But I do not think I caught <u>all</u> of it. Even the part that . . . suffused me . . . was almost too much.*

Matrugena reached up and stroked a finger along the bird's neck. "As for me . . . not it," the Pict told the others, forthrightly. "It hit like a shockwave. I couldn't do anything except try to shield . . . and Lassair and Saraid, my other spirit, did most of that for me." He paused. "Though Saraid seems less affected."

Kanmi nodded. "I know I didn't catch it. I'm a sorcerer. I might have more will than the average person. But I'm still just human." He looked at Adam. "You noticed any unusual powers?"

"If I concentrate very hard, in the mornings, I can put my pants on one leg at a time," ben Maor returned, dryly. "For the rest? Pretty normal. I think my sense of smell might be a little better, but that could be my imagination." He shrugged. "I've been doing my absolute best not to think about that entire incident."

Kanmi looked at Caetia, who was apparently dozing now. In his mind, there had only been two places where the power of the god could have gone . . . into Trennus' spirits . . . or into a *god-born*. A vessel already supremely prepared to receive godly energies. "Caetia?" he asked, quietly. If she were really asleep, he didn't want to wake her.

"I feel no different," she finally replied, her eyes still closed, and her tone faintly irritable. "I am what I am, Esh. Nothing more. Nothing less."

He didn't know if he believed her or not.

Kanmi's thoughts churned onwards. *If Lassair and Caetia both took a quarter of the total energies released . . . that's somewhere in the vicinity of eleven million thaums _each_. Well, explains why Lassair's suddenly able to manifest in physical forms, like that bird. Caetia . . . the gods only know. She seems about the same. Cold, abrupt. Maybe it just . . . washed through her and transmitted to her god. Maybe she's like a lightning rod like in that way? Possible, I suppose.*

He shook his head. It was a problem to consider at the back of his head. One of the puzzles that he'd revolve in his mind before going to sleep at night. Kanmi glanced up at the room's clock, debated leaving . . . and decided, again, he didn't want to fight with Bastet. Not yet, anyway. There were so many things he hadn't had a chance to puzzle out with his fellow lictors in the past few days. They'd had so little time to talk, between preparing to come here, and all the alarums and events of the past two days. "Speaking of Nahautl . . . .when I was trapped in my room here," Kanmi said, after several minutes of silence, as Caetia appeared to doze off completely, "until they brought me these dispatches, all I had to do was watch the far-viewer. You catch any of the news stories from there?" he asked, his lips curling back.

Matrugena looked amused. "Ah, no. I didn't even get out of bed till noon, actually."

"At least for you, that was a choice," Kanmi muttered. "Anyway, the thing that got me was seeing, in the background of the stories . . . all those priests of Tlaloc. Just carrying on as if nothing even happened?"

"Yes, but what are they going to do?" Matrugena asked. "Announce to everyone that . . . well . . ." A quick glance at the doorway, in spite of Kanmi's privacy spell.

"That would probably incite mass panic and hysteria," ben Maor noted, dryly.

"Maybe they should trust in people to be intelligent and adult. Maybe they should tell the truth. That's what priests are *supposed* to do, aren't they?" Kanmi stared down at the tile floor.

"Do you really think people would *be* intelligent and adult, and not start rioting, looting, and killing?" Matrugena, quick and incisive . . . and surprisingly cynical.

"Best case scenario is that people would accept it as truth and not riot. But it's far more likely that they'd rise up and say that the priests were lying." Ben Maor's voice was glum.

"Oh, I think there'd be plenty of that, if it wasn't handled *right*. Godslayer." Kanmi let out an explosive breath.

Adam actually winced. "All in all, I'd prefer if they didn't mention any of *that* until after I'm dead, buried . . . and buried someplace where no one can find the corpse, at that." He paused. "Usually, you're our cynic, Esh. You're the one who usually points out the dark side of human nature. For the moment, I think they're . . . trying to protect people from each other. Us. Their citizens."

"I think that this is one case where the people themselves should be trusted. Allowed to decide." Kanmi's cynicism usually buried his latent ideals, but they were stubbornly trying to assert themselves today.

Trennus cleared his throat. "I don't like to think what people would do with the information that . . . entities can die."

"They already know that, Matrugena. They know about Babylon and Sumer and Egypt." Kanmi flipped a hand.

"Yes, but they know about things that happened three *thousand* years ago, not last year. And they know that about . . . actual real godslayers. Spirits and demons that strode the earth like giants. Like the nephilim mentioned in old Judean legends." Ben Maor shrugged. "It's abstract. This . . . this is pretty concrete. And it's going to scare the living shit out of some people."

"And for others, it'll just become . . . an opportunity." Kanmi grimaced. "I know. You're right. But . . . I can't think that the priests are remaining silent to protect people. You, me, us, or the people of Nahautl. I think it has to do with power, and control. Just like the priests in Egypt who kept right on carrying on after Akhenaten wiped out half their gods. Makes you think, doesn't it?"

"About what?" Ben Maor looked puzzled.

"Well, if I were you, Adam ben Maor, godslayer . . . I'd honestly have to wonder if your god's still around or not." Kanmi waved a hand. "I know. It's nothing people don't say all the time about Judeans anyway."

"Having second thoughts on converting?" Ben Maor's lips twitched.

"I have no problem worshipping a dead god if everyone knows and agrees that he's dead." Kanmi nodded. "Might be more peaceful that way. I mean, everyone knew Osiris was dead even before Akhenaten came along. Set tore him to shreds and Isis had to bandage him back together, minus one important part, so the rest of the gods had to get together and create the world's first strap-on for him so she could bear him Horus posthumously . . . ."

Matrugena had to turn away and choke down on his laughter, and ben Maor actually snorted a bit. "Made of gold, no less," Kanmi went on, relentlessly. "The Egyptian gods make the Hellene ones look *tame*." He paused. "Oh, and it's yet another instance of the mate of a fertility goddess dying horribly and being brought back from death. Don't get me started on that."

"And you have no problem commenting on them, do you?" Trennus said, managing to get his face straightened out again.

"I'm theoretically subject to Baal-Hamon. A dead god is going to have to scoop himself up out of his sarcophagus and move pretty fast to smite me with lightning before Baal-Hamon whacks him over the head for poaching."

Adam shook his head. "We're getting into depths of philosophy that are way over my pay-grade." He paused. "But . . . as to your question . . . . whatever it was . . . ."

"How can you possibly know if your priests are doing *exactly* what the priests of Tlaloc are doing, or not?" Kanmi arched his eyebrows.

"I can't know it, Kanmi." Adam shrugged. "That's . . . the whole question of faith, isn't it?"

Kanmi exhaled. "At least you're honest about it. The priests in Nahautl . . . . They're not. And it makes me *furious*. How can you even start to make the world a better place if it's all built on a foundation of lies and half-truths?"

Adam looked at him soberly. "I don't know. Like I said . . . way over my pay-grade." He lifted his free hand; the other one still held Sigrun's. "We start with the little things, I guess. Little truths. Because people can't handle the big ones. Not all at once."

The door swung open, without a knock, and all three men shot to their feet. Adam saw both Kanmi and Trennus raise their hands as if to start casting, and his own hand had moved to the small of his back. Everyone on the hospital staff knocked. It was a rule.

The woman who entered now smiled at them, her green eyes wide and glassy. She was shorter than Sigrun by half a foot. Her dark blond hair was long, and dressed in ringlets that fell from the back of her neck, and she wore a translucent white silk *peplos* . . . a traditional Hellene garment that consisted of a single sheet of material, folded to drape across her breasts and fastened at the shoulders with fistula . . . but it left her right ribs, hip, and thigh bare, and the silk itself left . . . remarkably little to the imagination. She also wore thick gold bracelets and an intricate golden necklace, all in the form of serpents. Adam found a safe spot somewhere around her shoulder for his eyes to rest, and wondered just how many people in the hospital had suffered small aneurysms as she'd walked past them. "Ah, I think you may have the wrong room," he said.

"Oh, don't be silly, Godslayer," she purred, looking up at him. Way up. Past his head, in fact. Her focus seemed to be somewhere in the vicinity of the ceiling. "I'm precisely where I'm supposed to be, at precisely the right moment." She frowned as she let the door slip shut behind her. "Though I have to say . . . I thought you'd be taller."

Oh. God. This would be Sophia Caetia. Sigrun's mad sister. And the day was off to such a good start, too. He blinked for a moment as he realized that the two women, for all their differences in height and general coloration . . . could have been thought, by an outsider, to be the same exact age. Neither looked a day older than twenty-two, twenty-three at the most. Adam cleared his throat. "Ah, Sophia? I'm down here."

"That is the first time a man has ever said that to a woman in the history of the world," Kanmi muttered. "You know this person, ben Maor?"

"Oh, of course he knows me, Archmage. We just haven't met before." Sophia nodded to Kanmi. "I did so want to see all of the Four in the same place, at least once, with my own eyes, and not just the eyes of the future and the past." Her voice was dreamy. "The Godslayer, the Binder, the Archmage, and the Ascendant. And the four will become six and then seven, as the Heart of Fire and the Wolf Queen and the Truthsayer reveal themselves. And all of you will need to be united, before the second darkness comes." Sophia looked at her sleeping sister, and without raising her voice, said, "Wake *up*, Sigrun!"

The words carried uncanny force. Sigrun's gray eyes snapped open, and she looked around in a daze. Sophia sank down on the edge of the bed, and told her sister, cheerfully, but still with that dazed air, "Oh, good. There you are. I travelled all this way to see you now that you're finally sorting things out in your own life, so I could tell you some of the things I've seen."

Adam looked up at Trennus and Kanmi; Kanmi met his eyes and touched fingers held in a circle to his temple: *She has a hole in her head, eh?*

"No, Archmage, I'm not crazy," Sophia's voice was patient, and she didn't even turn to look at Kanmi, who stood completely behind her. "I just see *everything*. Everything that was. Everything that is. Everything that will be." She took Sigrun's hand in her own, but still addressed Kanmi, now finally turning slightly towards him. "I did tell you already that I was sorry about your wife, didn't I? But don't worry. The next woman in your life will be your equal, and she'll hold the sun itself in her flesh before the end of all things. She'll be worth coming back from the dead for, I swear it." Sophia's dreamy smile never faltered.

Kanmi's mouth fell open, and he stared at Sophia, before his jaw clicked shut, and he darted half-angry, half-confused glances around the room at the rest of them. As if daring them to say a *word*.

Sigrun tried to lever herself up, and then stopped, wincing in pain. Adam, without letting her see him do it, clicked on the button that would distribute a metered dose of morphine into her blood, and then helped her sit up. "Leave them alone, Sophia," Sigrun managed. "They don't deserve having their private lives meddled with by you."

"They won't have private lives," Sophia said, and sighed. "But at least they'll live."

Adam froze in place and just *stared* at the woman for a moment. *I've known her for five minutes, and I already feel like I'm going mad from just proximity. What is it like to be* related *to her?*

Sigrun rolled her head back on the pillows. "You've taken the seers' drugs again, haven't you?" she asked, her tone resigned. "Perhaps you should come back when you can speak sensibly. When you haven't taken *anything.*"

"Oh, no. No peyote or mushrooms today. But poppy-juice, yes, to slow things down. It soothes my mind. Makes it so I don't see the end of everything all the time. So that the world of now isn't so real, and so fragile, and I don't feel the vividness of death waiting for me after every eyeblink."

Adam could see agony in Sigrun's face for an instant. Worse than the pain of her body. Her voice was very gentle as she tried to reach her sister with logic, "Sophia, if you know *precisely* how the world will end . . . how can you be afraid of death with every heartbeat?"

"Because I know that I will end, too. And before the world does. But only by weeks." Sophia waggled a finger at her sister. "But you'll meet us all again, Sigrun. Everyone that you love, on that black road. And you'll need to protect us and love us and teach us. And that'll be hard for you, because you'll be so angry. You're *really good* at being angry. Why, you're angry even now!"

Sigrun lifted her eyes. Met Adam's, then Tren's, then Kanmi's. And then looked at the door. Adam took that unspoken message, and leaned down. Kissed the backs of her cold fingers. "I'll leave you two to talk." *God. And I thought everyone seeing* my *family was embarrassing.*

"Yes, yes, this," Sophia said, cheerfully. "We never *talk*, Sigrun. And I don't want to wait to die for us to get around to it."

"You're sick, Sophia," Sigrun told her sister, bluntly, as the men all filtered out of the room. Adam could hear the tears in her voice. "It's mortal, and the disease is made of despair."

"I know that."

"You'll die of it."

"I know that, too. Oh, I do think your Godslayer is wonderful to look at. But I really thought his eyes would be golden. So confusing."

Out in the hall, Kanmi shook his head. "I don't think I'd ever have thought that the god-born had drug addiction and madness in their families . . . but I suppose it makes sense. There are enough mad gods, so why *not* mad god-born?" He swung his dispatch case back and forth. "Poor gods-be-damned Caetia," he added, quietly. "I'd hate to come to work with that hanging over my head every day." He nodded to Adam and Trennus, and took off. He had a wife who was waiting for him, undoubtedly ready for a fight, and two sons to hug. Bastet hadn't brought Himi and Bodi to the hospital, on the grounds that they didn't need to see him hooked up to tubes. Kanmi thought that was pure shit, and hadn't minded telling her so. He'd had no visible injuries, not like the others. *No, the truth is, she's angry at me about something, and maybe it's still the fact that I haven't told her every detail of my job.*

So he got back to the governor's mansion, and hugged his sons. Had dinner with his family. And while he wanted nothing more than to settle in with the contents of his dispatch case, he asked Bastet if she were ready to talk. Talking led to arguing, and arguing led to fighting. "This is not like me having married a soldier or a *gardia* officer," Bastet said at one point, almost in tears. "Women who do that, know what they're getting into. When I married you, we were still at the university. You were going to get a job in . . . ley-engineering or at a university, teaching sorcery. The military was going to be a *temporary* thing, so you could work it into . . . I don't know. Consulting. Something." She brushed the tears out of her eyes. "I don't see why you couldn't quit this horrible, dangerous job and . . . do something *safe*. You could teach. You always said you wanted to teach."

Kanmi had found a seat on a backless bench across the room, and had been watching her pace back and forth. Bastet couldn't hold still when she was angry or agitated. Never had been able to, really. "That was until I figured out that I hate teaching," he replied, quietly. "Took that mentoring job my last year at school, remember? All those thankless, entitled brats going to school on their parents' money, who think that they should be able to drink and party their way through each semester, and won't put a bit of work in? Who came to me expecting me to turn their grade around for them? Some people are *too stupid* for education, Bastet. It's wasted on them. I know perfectly well that education is a wonderful thing. That it can uplift people from the gutter. But they have to *want* to be uplifted, and they have to want to work at it. You get out of an education *precisely* what you put into it. And I have no time in my life for people who won't do the damned work." He held up a hand before she could say anything. "That's only part of it, Bastet. Let me finish."

He looked out the window, and exhaled, trying to make sure he was as calm as possible. "There isn't an engineering firm in the world who would take me, Bastet. Not with what I can do. *Maybe* as a security consultant. I have entirely the wrong skill-set. My resume, at present, says 'tactical application of forces and physics to achieve maximum bodily harm to opposition forces and to prevent same to friendlies.'" He looked at his wife, grimly. "Which is to say, I kill, Bastet. I'm very good at it. I don't do it unnecessarily. I do it to save lives. And periodically, I get to amputate limbs or, like today, fall on my damned face till someone else picks me up again. That's the job. I'm *good* at it. Probably in the top two percent in the world. Livorus doesn't pick *slouches* for his lictors." A muscle worked in his jaw for a moment. "We have a good life, Bastet. We can afford a good apartment in Rome. We can afford a pedagogue for the boys. We have insurance. We have all these things because of my job."

Bastet covered her face with her hands for a long moment, and, distantly, Kanmi looked at the clean, smooth lines of her fingers. The way her skin turned just a little lighter on the palms. He'd always loved nibbling along that line of demarcation. Just one of the many ways she was beautiful to him. But the cold certainty that churned in his gut said, *Caetia's mad sister was wrong. This is how the world ends. My world, anyway.*

Bastet looked up. "We have all these things because of *my* job, too." Her tone was defiant. "And it's not good for the boys, that you're so often away. So . . . get that security job with a ley-engineering firm. Do something like *that.*"

Kanmi sighed. She'd just shifted the whole basis of the argument. It was easy to see, when you were completely dispassionate. Before this, it had been danger to him. Now it was, *it's bad for the boys.* A guilt tactic. "I would be away from home just as much, going from one ley-plant facility to another. There would be no difference for the boys." He paused. "And, let me point out, that you are away from home *just as much* as I am. You work forty-hour shifts at the hospital sometimes, come home, sleep, and when you wake up, it's the middle of the night, and the boys are in bed. They see their pedagogue more than they see you. So do not you *dare* try to tell me that I am a *delinquent* father." He met her eyes. "My job is just as important as yours." He didn't want to say it out loud, but, to his way of thinking, his job was *more* important than hers. There were, literally, millions of doctors in the world, and every one of them thought him or herself a little god. There were about three hundred and twenty thousand Praetorians in the world . . . or about .03 percent of the billion people in the Roman Empire. Of all of them, only twenty thousand were lictors — the rest handled Imperial-level jurisdictional issues that local *gardia* couldn't, pursued counterfeiting, espionage, and counterintelligence tasks, and so on. Of those twenty thousand lictors, only about fifteen hundred were sorcerers. Kanmi was in a highly elite group. And serving Livorus was as high as he could currently go, without the headaches of being a bodyguard to the emperor, himself.

He looked up and met Bastet's eyes. "Let me put it to you this way. I will quit my job for the sake of our sons the instant that you quit yours, and then we can decide what in Baal's name we'll live on, besides begging in the streets." Kanmi paused. "Or, we can both realize, here and now, that the argument is *stupid.*"

Bastet flopped down onto a chair across the room from him. She was keeping ten feet of space between them at all times. "So, if you won't quit the Praetorians . . . get a desk job with them. You look through reports all the time anyway."

"Bastet . . . I'm thirty. This is just the *start* of my career. Sorcerers aren't like most soldiers. When the knees give out at forty, when arthritis sets in at fifty . . . other soldiers retire. A sorcerer just gets *better.* And we only get better through experience." Kanmi felt his eyes narrow. "You want me to sit at a desk? You want me to be a paper-pusher? No. I can't do that. That's not who I am." *Not right now, anyway. Give me thirty years or so.*

"You won't even *compromise.*" Her voice scaled upwards into a wail. "What kind of marriage is this, that you won't compromise at all?"

Not a very Roman one, because if it were, this wouldn't even be a discussion, Kanmi thought, but didn't say out loud. *If I were Roman, you'd have been told that this is life, and that you can either deal with it, or get a divorce, and give up your children.* He set his hands down on his knees, and said, with care and precision, "I won't compromise who and what I am, no." He looked at her steadily. "I love you. I love the boys. I'm not going anywhere. But this is who I am." His stomach twisted. All the things he shouldn't *have* to say. That should have been obvious to her for years. "Take it or leave it."

Bastet just stared at him for a long moment, tears in her eyes. And then she left the room without another word.

Gods, Kanmi thought, closing his eyes and tilting his head back. *This could have gone better.*

Maius 9, 1955 AC

Adam tapped on the door of the propraetor's temporary office in the governor's mansion. He was just about to go on-shift again, and wanted a few moments to speak with Livorus before officially starting work.

"Enter!" Livorus called through the door.

Adam moved in, nodding to Kanmi, who stood behind Livorus' desk, looking out one of the high, small windows in the ancient fortress' outer walls. Real glass in the old arrow slits, oscillating fans instead of air conditioning—the building was far too old to be retrofitted for that, unfortunately; the walls made of thick stone—and antique furniture that dated back to the rococo excesses of the Latter Decadent Period, certainly. Livorus looked up from the desk, the legs of which had been fashioned into depictions of Eros, and the sides of which had been carved into acanthus leaves and scrolls. "Ah, ben Maor. What can I do for you?"

"A moment of your time, sir, if I may?"

"You may have two moments, but not three. I really cannot spare a third." Livorus set his pen down. "I trust our valkyrie will be returning to duty soon?"

"The doctors say she'll be allowed to stand today if her current rate of healing continues, and they'll release her when she can walk from one end of the room to the other without the heart monitors setting off alarms." Adam shook his head. Even after knowing her for close to two years now . . . the rate at which Sigrun healed was uncanny. *If it'd been me, assuming I lived, I'd be in the hospital for weeks yet.*

"Good," Livorus murmured, and looked back down at the dispatches. "Then we can return some of my wife's lictors to her shortly, and we can be about our business here."

Adam nodded. He didn't quite know how to broach the topic, so he avoided it, for the moment. "The Chaldean envoy, sir? She's recovered?"

"Yes, Lady Erida is in seclusion at the Median consulate. Both she and Lord Maranata are being pleaded with by the Persian ambassador to come out and meet with him." Livorus' smile was thin. "They've told him to come inside and speak with them on their own turf. During our scheduled meeting this afternoon, I must offer Lady Erida my official *condolences* on the loss of one of her brave bodyguards during the . . . unfortunate attempt on her life." Livorus' tone held mordant irony. "They have a subsequent meeting with the Persian ambassador scheduled for two postmeridian. I would give much to listen in on that conversation. Especially since supposition now is that the late, unlamented Abgar was Persian Intelligence, and had infiltrated the home of Lady Erida's father almost ten, fifteen years ago. Worked himself close to the family. Professed his attentions to her, and then attempted to murder her."

Adam grimaced. "I don't actually see how Persia would profit from this."

"Do you not?" Livorus' eyebrows rose. "Suppose that Abgar, in the course of events, discovered that Lady Erida—a high-ranking member of the Magi—intended not just to defect, herself, but intended to take her entire country with her. That, in fact, many of her fellow nobles and Magi supported her and the Satrap in this intention. Killing her might be a solid method of *warning* people against rebellion, but it might only stiffen their resolve. Make of this pretty young woman a martyr. Now, if it looked as if *Rome*, or at least its cat's-paw, Judea, lured the rebels here, only to kill them?" Livorus' brows arched. "If they made it appear that Rome and Judea could not be trusted, could never be trusted, and were *clumsy* in their attempt to frame Persia for her death . . . the more confusion the better, really. Enough to make people argue and debate and point fingers. To sow suspicions everywhere, and keep Chaldea, Media, and the Magi paralyzed with indecision and fear for another twenty or thirty years, not knowing whom to trust? The status quo, even if it is abhorrent, is at least *known*, my young friend. To put your trust in an uncertain future is a leap of faith. And most people do not have the courage to make it. It is a very good thing that Eshmunazar actually was deadening sound—including radio waves—leaving the area. And was able to register when our would-be assassin transmitted his signal. It forced Abgar into improvisation, instead of following the neat steps of a plan."

Kanmi looked out the window, and put in, his voice distant. "My guess is, once the attacks began, he'd have tried to move Erida away from everyone else, telling her that he thought that this was all a double-cross. She might well have believed him. And once he had her away from the scene, he could have killed her at his leisure, probably using a Judean-made gun, and left the body for the *alu* at the scene. He could have even shot himself with the same gun, for authenticity. Whether or not he'd have actually killed himself to sell the story . . . depends on how strong his motives were." The sorcerer's expression never wavered.

Adam grimaced. Put that way . . . it sounded plausible. "I assume the local Praetorians are looking for Abgar's accomplices? The ones who planted the *alu*-bottles with their small detonators, and cut the power to the convention center."

Livorus nodded. "Naturally. But this is not your concern, ben Maor."

Like the investigation into the conspirators in Nahautl, and the diplomatic issues regarding the Ponca incident, Adam would not be involved in the process. He'd have to testify, probably at length, but the matter would be firmly out of his hands. And he found that this time, it made him twitch. Almost as badly as it seemed to chafe at Kanmi to have the investigation into the technomancers in Nahautl out of his reach. *This is my home,* he thought, and the notion surprised him. He'd run *away* from Judea for so long, and now, the thought of people meddling in *his* territory reminded him . . . abruptly . . . that it *was* his home. "Locals could have been bought," Adam pointed out, hating the words in his mouth. "Counterintel and Judean Intelligence—"

"Will do what needs doing," Livorus told him, firmly. He picked up a sheet of foolscap, and said, meditatively, changing the subject away from the investigations, "Yes, this afternoon's conversation between the Median and Chaldean envoys and their Persian masters will be an intriguing discussion, filled with plausible denials on all sides. They will profess that they were merely here on their appointed errands. Lady Erida may suggest that Rome does not know that her bodyguard was involved in the attack—after all, we're putting out, for public dissemination, that he died saving her life—and the Persian ambassador will exclaim that Abgar surely only acted out of jealousy at the thought of Erida marrying some Roman noble . . . ." Livorus waved a hand in mild irritation. "Stories will be invented for public consumption, and the Persian ambassador will try to convey that his government knows, or suspects, why they were truly here. And they will either be cowed . . . or not."

Adam grimaced. "I hate to think that everything we did two days ago was wasted," he said, quietly. "So many damned lives lost for nothing."

"That is what I will attempt to make plain to both envoys when I speak with them," Livorus said, simply. "That their die has already been cast. It was cast before they arrived here. And to retreat from action now will simply result in deeper enslavement by the empire from which they wish their people to be free." He paused. "And even if they are cowed, and do retreat? Abgar had accomplices. He must have, as you have pointed out. He was in Chaldea when the efreet bottle, the *pazuzu* jar and the *alu* bottles were stolen in Persepolis, a month ago. Possibly that 'theft' was arranged by Persian Intelligence itself. But he needed accomplices *here* to place them. Your father, I know, is already deeply involved in trying to find if there is a Persian network here that Abgar accessed or if he merely paid or blackmailed Judeans into doing small, apparently trivial services." Livorus awarded Adam a faint smile. He'd just told Adam *far* more than his lead lictor had anticipated hearing today. "Something *will* come of all this. This, I can promise."

Adam nodded, and shifted a little uneasily on his feet. Livorus' gaze remained on him, a faintly amused expression on the Roman's face. "I could not help but notice that your family was interviewed for the local far-viewer news channels. 'Local boy makes good,' is always a favorite staple of the newsroom."

A quick, taut nod. "I apologize, sir. I didn't like that they focused on me, and not on the team." *And if I'd moved faster in the parking lot, they'd never have known that we were there . . . no. They saw Livorus leaving with Tren and the rest of the motorcade. Lost cause.* After Sophia had left last night, Sigrun hadn't wanted to discuss her sister, so he'd flipped on the square, monolithic far-viewer in her room . . . and immediately, a news report featuring him had turned up. He'd winced through the whole thing. His mother had been caught and interviewed at the hospital, and had noted, *"Of course we're proud of him. We always knew he was gifted. I just wish he could spend more time at home."* His father, caught coming back from work, had had a proud gleam in his eyes as he'd said, *"Adam has always excelled at whatever he's put his mind to, and now, he does his duty, and does it well."* Chani had giggled through her interview and had mentioned how *interesting* his coworkers were, and Rivkah had admitted, *"He's changed. A lot. Become a little more . . . I don't know. Thoughtful. Quiet."* Mikayel, caught outside of his own house on the other side of town, had grimaced. *"Yes. We're all very proud, I'm sure."* And then he'd turned away, telling the reporters, *Get off my property.*

Adam had reached forward to change the channel, but Sigrun hadn't let him. "There are worse things, Adam," she'd told him, squeezing his fingers, "than having a loving family that cares about you." The words had been less labored than earlier in the day, but she'd still clearly been tired. "Some of them are still learning to see you for who you are now, and not the person you were as a child. That's . . . an ongoing process, I think. A lifelong one. But your family loves you enough to try. You should cherish that."

He'd flicked a strand of hair out of her face. "You say that as if it's a little foreign to you, Sig." He paused, and shifted the rails of the bed down so he could slide, very carefully, an arm under the small of her back. He didn't dare sit on the bed or put an arm around her. She was still far too injured for that. "Of course, having now spoken with your sister twice . . . I think I see why it would be." He regarded her steadily, and kept his voice gentle. "She's crazy, isn't she?"

A tear coursed down her face. "Yes. She has good days and bad days. Today was a good day."

That alone spoke volumes. "And your father? He does nothing about this? Your step-mother?"

Sigrun exhaled. "It's complicated. My father loves me, and I love him. But he looks at me, and I think . . . he sees my mother. It hurts him." Clear, simple words. "Now that my sister is grown, however, I will have nothing to do with his wife." She paused to catch her breath. "There are well-meaning people . . . who would tell me that I should forgive her. Tolerate her, to preserve my relationship with my father, and to give him joy in his declining years. No." A pause as Sigrun clearly struggled for words. "Medea raised me with a cane in one hand to ensure that I understood the duties and responsibilities of the god-born. Her own daughter? No one knew she was god-born. Not for ten years. She was raised human. Allowed to go to school. Treated as . . . every other child is, or should be. Nothing amiss with that, but she was . . . made much of."

Sigrun swallowed. "Dressed as a princess for the harvest festivals, every year. Every conceivable toy or doll she wanted, was showered on her. Some of that was natural. My father was older. Had more money than when I was young. He had the time to dote on her. And no shadow of sorrow over his relationship with her."

Adam poured her a cup of water, and helped her sip it. "She was raised in a loving house, then?"

"Yes. Very. When she was ten, the visions came, and she wasn't ready for them. No one can be, really, but she wasn't strong. And they came *early*. When visions come, it is usually . . . young adulthood. When identity is fully formed." Sigrun swallowed. "Medea threatened to cane her for speaking of her dreams at first, but when she was convinced that they were real . . . by me . . ." and that was guilt in Sigrun's voice, plain and clear, "Medea *encouraged* Sophia to find every manner of new experience. To expand her horizons without restraint. It . . . might have been a good idea for someone older. Someone with a more secure grasp on who they *are*. There are days when I do not know if there is anything of my sister *left* besides the visions, and the ten-year-old mind trapped behind them." She shook her head. "Oh, she's an adult. She has lovers in plenty. Whoever she feels she should be with, at that moment. Whoever vision tells her to, I suppose, or whoever's arms can hold the visions at bay for a while. I . . . don't blame her that." Sigrun looked up at the ceiling. "But I hold her mother personally accountable for *much* that is warped and askew in my sister. Even if I were a forgiving person, I would not forgive that, because it is *ongoing*."

"And where is your *father* in this?" Adam asked again. "How can he look at his own daughter and not . . . intervene?"

Her shoulders slumped. "To be honest . . . I do not know. I think some of it may be genuine lack of knowledge of what's amiss in her life. Sophia is . . . good at concealing the depth of her problems. Some of it may be a desire for domestic tranquility. He doesn't want to fight with his wife, day after day, and never know victory, only continuous defeat. And about a child who is dedicated to foreign gods . . . what can he say? He can hardly count himself an expert, I suppose."

"So what do you intend to do about it all?"

She managed to move her shoulders "Remain in touch with my father. Continue to fight the demons in Sophia. Care for my father in his old age. Bury him when it's time. And, very likely, do the same for my sister, in her turn." Sigrun reached up and actually touched his face, every movement clearly causing her pain. "You see, Adam? Your family . . . not so bad. They're good people. Your mother has a kind heart. Though I would like to break your brother's jaw."

Back in the here and now, Livorus gave Adam a spare glance. "It is perhaps for the best that if the news media fixated on anyone, that they did so on you. They haven't turned their eyes towards investigating what I was doing there that night. They have not examined the records of any of the other lictors. Best not to have the whole team's capabilities exposed at once, I think." He paused. "If you'd take a bit of advice from one who has seen a bit of the world?"

"If you're about to tell me that I should appreciate my family for who they are, Sigrun has already told me so, sir."

Livorus' lips quirked. "Sage advice, but no. On the contrary, I had the opportunity to observe your family at length." Livorus paused. "You have a story, in your faith, I believe, about Cain and Abel? And Cain was the elder brother, who hated the younger, for that he was favored?"

Adam blinked. "Ah . . . yes?"

"Your brother is an envious man. And I will tell you why. Because nature has favored you with intelligence as well as with physical gifts."

Adam stared at the propraetor, whom he respected more than almost anyone else in the world, other than his own father, and shook his head. "He's not Cain. He's not going to kill me."

"No. But he will continue to cut in a thousand little ways, until you make an end of it."

"Eshmunazar said almost the same thing." Adam glanced at Kanmi.

"I certainly did." Kanmi's expression didn't change.

"Eshmunazar has been much in the world." Livorus leaned back. "Your brother envies you, because you have breadth and depth and scope, my boy. He's intelligent enough, in his narrow way. He has found his appointed row, and plods along it like an ox. If you'd take my advice? Surround yourself with people who are of your own intelligence, or better. Enrich yourself with them. If you spend your time with those who are too far below you, well, they might well be good-hearted people. You may even enjoy yourself. But inevitably, you will come to realize how limited they are. You will reduce and limit yourself to their level, or else risk being considered a snob. You risk becoming embittered, and you yourself will never be challenged, stimulated, or able to grow." Livorus clapped his hands lightly. "And by that same token, those around you, who are that limited in scope? Will envy and despise you and seek to tear at you with words and deeds, because they know they cannot match you. That, my dear boy, is your brother's problem."

A quick shake of his head. "What can I do about that, sir, beyond avoiding him?" *I would have thought being on the other side of the world was far enough.*

"Don't tolerate it. Even by so much as a word. The next time he sinks a dagger in your side, return the blow three-fold." Livorus shrugged, and picked up a paper from in front of him. "Was there anything else?"

Adam blinked. "Ah . . . yes." He braced himself, and glanced at Kanmi, wishing that the other man was *anywhere* else for this, but asking Esh to leave, lowering the propraetor's protections for a personal matter? Inappropriate. "I wished to ask your permission, sir, to, ah, court Agent Caetia." It was a matter of manners and propriety to ask; Sigrun wasn't Livorus' daughter, but anything that involved the team of lictors, was, perforce, Livorus' business.

He had to give Eshmunazar credit. The technomancer didn't laugh. Didn't even change expressions. Livorus lifted his head, his eyebrows rising. For an instant, Adam almost thought he'd surprised the man. Then he read the amusement there. "And if I were to say no, ben Maor? Would *informal* courtship then ensue?"

"No, sir. I would begin the necessary process of removing myself from your personal guard."

Livorus nodded, placidly. "Well, we cannot be having with that. I am quite satisfied with everyone's job performance. So, by all means . . . court. Woo. But know this."

Adam blinked and looked up in surprise as the propraetor grinned at him ferally, and went on, "Had I not been wed to my *dear* Poppaea six years ago, when Sigrun first came to my guard? You would not have stood a *chance*, ben Maor. I would have swept her off her feet."

Adam knew perfectly well that the propraetor was, in some senses, jesting . . . but there was a hint of wistfulness in his tone, as well. Divorce among Romans was accepted . . . but Poppaea's family was powerful in political circles. Livorus couldn't divorce her, not without offending them. "I'll keep that in mind, sir."

"Do. Now, as to the rest of my schedule for the day, the morning is all correspondence, I'm afraid. There is the meeting with the Chaldean and Median envoys, as I mentioned. The governor is insisting on a dreadful formal banquet at six . . . ."

Maius 23, 1955 AC

A busy two weeks had ensued. With Sigrun back on her feet, they continued to make the trip look like a mindless photo-op tour. Sigrun, for her part, did her best to shoulder her share of the load as quickly as possible, so as not to leave them on a three-part shift any longer.

There had been changes, even in the few days she'd been in the hospital, chafing to be released. Trennus carried with him a sense of radiant happiness and surprised joy that clung to his skin like the smell of smoke. Of which there was always a faint hint around him now, like incense. Sigrun did not know what to make of this.

Kanmi, in contrast, had sunk into himself in a more grim and cynical mood than ever. Every off-duty hour found him in a break room, going through his lists of names. Often, Himi and Bodi were with him, drawing on the backs of the papers; just as often, Bastet took the boys off to tour the main attractions of Jerusalem. They weren't permitted in the Temple, but they could take pictures outside, for example. Sigrun didn't, again, know what to say to her friend. Black depression swirled around him as clearly as effervescent joy followed Trennus around.

And then there was Adam, and Sigrun was hard-pressed to keep from smiling, herself, whenever she thought of him. Nothing at all, while on duty, of course. They were both too rigidly trained for that. But every time they went off-shift, Adam had politely asked her to do things with him. Go for a walk in the Garden of Gethsemane, or tour the ruins of the Antonia Fortress, which dated from the time of Herod. Pass through Old

Town, with all the tiny shops and stalls, and eat dinner at this restaurant or that, which happened to overlook the aqueducts or the Pool of Bethesda. These proved to be lovely, if brief respites from the workday . . . workdays that included providing testimony to Imperial and Judean Intelligence about the events at the convention center.

To their surprise, they actually got some information out of JI and their fellow Praetorians. Two of the people involved, at least, had been workers for the local utility company, and they were caught trying to flee the province. A handful of others, the ones who had been tasked with planting the containment bottles, which had had blasting caps taped to them, connected to wireless transceivers . . . most of them were dead inside the convention center. One of the men, who had been heavily mauled, survived to make a confession. He was Judean, himself, and had been turned by a Persian agent two years before. Debt and alcohol, apparently, had been the handles used to control him. But it had seemed such a small thing. A bottle, which had felt empty. Put in a recycling bin, and it might *crack*, considering how small the blasting cap was. Surely, nothing bad could come of that. And what was that small task, in the face of having another debt canceled?

Sigrun also noticed that the staff at the governor's continuously mentioned the unseasonably mild weather, which included daily gentle rains that the locals seemed to find highly unusual. Two gardeners eating lunch in the staff kitchen one day, spent the entire hour exclaiming over the fall-only flowers that were sprouting buds, as well as early spring flowers, which had already dropped their seeds, coming back into bloom. *It isn't natural*, they complained, *but we've had photographers come by to take pictures for magazines three times already*. She wondered if it was attributable to the unseasonal rains, or if Lassair had something to do with it; she occasionally saw the phoenix perched on branches in the gardens.

For her part, there were other novelties than the weather and out-of-season blooms. Sigrun wasn't quite used to putting out her hand to have it *clasped*. And while she and Adam couldn't precisely walk hand-in-hand in public—they both were all too aware of the need to stay alert—whenever they happened to have the chance to eat lunch together, Adam did tend to twine his fingers with hers. And she could feel her eyes widen and a flush touch her face every time, as if she were a foolish schoolgirl.

And very close to the end of their visit there, Adam took her back over to his parents' house, this time as a guest, instead of as an emergency stopover for themselves and their protectee. "I think stopping there on business was less nerve-wracking," Sigrun told him, shifting in her seat in the motorcar. The neighborhood was still a mess, and she winced at the sight. At least two houses had sustained substantial structural damage, and were cordoned off with crime-scene tape. The fire hydrant was still capped, and the cobbles were missing in patches. Various neighbors had definitely seen them pull up, and Sigrun could see curtains twitching at windows all around the block. *Oh, gods*, she thought, in resignation. *This cannot possibly go well.*

Inside, at the dinner table, with Adam's parents and sisters present around a table filled with braided bread and roasted chicken and other wonderful-smelling things, Sigrun sat silently at first, trying to figure out how to fit in. The others were, considerately, using Latin, and she was trying to use the fewer than fifty words of Hebrew she'd learned in two weeks' time. More to fill the exceedingly uncomfortable silence than anything else, Sigrun offered, tentatively, "Have the insurance people been out yet to make estimates on the neighbors' houses?"

Adam's lips twitched, slightly. "I don't know if any of them carried insurance that had provisions for acts of god."

Sigrun looked at him over her cup of tea. "Not a god. Malefic spirit. Totally different category."

Abigayil's head swung back and forth between them as they spoke. Adam raised his eyebrows. "You're not actually laughing. Let me guess. In Nova Germania, insurance actually *does* carry provisions for acts of gods, doesn't it?

Sigrun chuffed under her breath. "No one will give payment if you take out insurance against lightning and then, in the next week, call Thor a sissy and bare your arse to the sky while standing on your roof during a thunderstorm, if that is your meaning."

Maor ben Emmet carefully covered his mouth with a napkin and turned his head aside to laugh. "But if a house is struck by lightning?" he offered.

"It's investigated. If it can be proved that a god-born or, yes, a god did it, and it was unjust, then payment must be made." Sigrun had no idea why Maor started laughing again. "Justice isn't just for humans," she said, after a moment. "Justice isn't *justice* if it only applies to some, and not all. And if god-born can be held to account, then the gods need to account for themselves, even if only to each other." Sigrun glanced up at the ceiling. "Or so Tyr and Odin teach. A jury of peers. It's harder for humans to judge the gods."

Adam chuckled. "And how often is a *god* found guilty after being called to account?"

"Loki? Quite often. Thor, occasionally. It takes a while for such cases to work through the Odinhall, admittedly. Sometimes as long as fifteen or twenty years. But we do *try* to see that justice is done." Sigrun met Adam's eyes. "My people were always allowed to unseat kings, even in antiquity. Challenge them. Why should we not stand up before our gods, and ask them why something has come to pass? We might not receive an answer. But we're taught to be strong in mind and body, and show respect . . . and respect will be given to us, in turn." She hesitated, and glanced sidelong at the rest of the table. She'd forgotten that this wasn't one of her usual forthright conversations with Adam on the topic.

Chani's eyes had gone as wide as the dinner plates. Adam, on the other hand, had propped his chin on a fist to lean on the table and now grinned. "That's a perspective we haven't heard much," Maor admitted, and adjusted the subject, deftly. "No, the insurance estimators haven't been out yet. They need for the criminal investigation to be finished, so our neighbors are at hotels, for the time being. I'm sure we'll be hearing about how long they were kept from their homes when they return." His tone was amused.

Sigrun winced, and resumed her silence. There were few topics on she could really contribute; it took all the way until dessert, when the topic of the impending vote to ban slavery throughout the Empire came up. The vote usually came before the Senate every other year, and Sigrun had once told Adam she didn't expect to see it pass in her lifetime. "No, no, change is coming," Abigayil insisted. "You children all don't remember it, but the year Adam was born, when Nova Germania and Novo Gaul both outlawed slavery, everyone thought that emancipation was going to sweep the globe. The Judean government got ahead of it, and signed an emancipation proclamation, making it illegal to buy new slaves, and freeing all current ones. The movement stalled out, but it's *going* to happen."

Sigrun grimaced. "I, ah, actually remember it fairly well," she said, carefully. "My father had freed my pedagogue the year before to marry her, and my sister was born the year the laws were passed, abolishing serfdom and slavery, even debt-slavery. The problem is, debt-slavery at least served a purpose. It forced people to repay their debtors in some fashion, though I don't approve of people selling their children to pay their debts. It should only ever have been imposed on those who *incurred* the debts. The major problem, as debated in the Senate that same year, is what to do about slavery as a penalty for criminal action. As a result of not being able to impose labor as a penalty for non-violent crimes, we've had to build more and more prisons in Novo Germania. The only other alternative is fining someone, which more or less amounts to a minor tax to a rich criminal, and license to do as they please." Sigrun raised her hands, palms up. "I'm not defending the system, but I've watched the results ripple through our legal system for the past twenty-six years, and as an *ælagol* for ten of those years, I've had to deal with the repercussions. I don't see the Romans embracing any change to the current system if they don't see a way to deal with those ramifications within the Italian Peninsula itself. They won't *tolerate* lawlessness and social disorder. Nova Germania . . . we have a little more space. Social disruption, well, we take it a little more in stride. We have banishment as another option, still." Sigrun realized she'd been talking for a while, and shut her mouth with a click.

Abigayil looked as if she'd bitten into a lemon. Maor, on the other hand, sat up, looking interested. "What do you think about stripping someone of some of their rights of citizenship as an option for the Roman legal system?" he asked.

Sigrun suddenly realized that Rivkah and Chani were staring at her as if she'd grown an additional head. "It would be a possible punishment," she told Maor meeting his eyes steadily, "but even early patricians were usually banished from the city of Rome, proper, rather than having their rights revoked." She folded her hands in front of her. "It's not entirely without precedent, but it would be difficult, I think, for people to see some of the potential revocations of privilege as really punitive. How many people actually run for plebian offices? How many people in the more democratically-minded provinces actually vote in elections? Inability to own land or a house, for life, means very little to someone who lives in an apartment." She looked around the table, and apologized, "Forgive me. The law, in any form, is one of my particular interests." She didn't precisely squirm; she was far too used to appearing coolly reserved in public. But she'd wanted to make a better impression this time, than the blood-soaked barbarian of the last visit. And it didn't appear that she was.

Maor smiled. "Don't apologize," Adam's father told her. "We can continue the conversation after dinner, however, at more length."

Sigrun pretended not to hear Abigayil, Rivkah, and Chani hissing questions at Adam as she went into the living area with Maor. Most of them revolving around *how old is she, anyway?* And before they left for the evening, she did take pains to go into the kitchen, where Abigayil was preparing the next day's loaves, and asked if she could help. "Do you know anything about baking?" Abigayil asked, cautiously.

"My father's wife made it part of my lessons when I was a child. However, I only know how to make Hellene breads. *Plexouda. Pitas.*" Sigrun washed her hands at the sink, and, under Abigayil's direction, began to knead the dough for her.

"Your father's wife? The one he freed?"

"Yes."

"Sounds as if it's a happy memory." Abigayil's tone was tentative.

Sigrun didn't answer at first. Learning to cook and bake had been under the category of domestic education, just as Latin, Hellene, Gallic, and other variants of Gothic had been under the category of being lettered, and chemistry, biology and mathematics had been under the umbrella of natural philosophy. After a long pause, she managed one truth that she thought Abigayil would accept. "I liked the feel of the flour under my fingers. It's soft. I liked the smell of the bread baking. It always made me feel as if my mother were still with me. I can just barely remember her baking at night, just like this. And I'd help then, too."

No need to tell Abigayil that she'd 'helped' by hovering off the ground, so that her little fingers and head had been above the counter's height. Sigrun looked up. "Now, let it rise again? Or is it time to divide and braid the loaves?"

"Let it rise again. Everything needs time to be its best." Abigayil reached out and swept a speck of flour off Sigrun's shoulder. "You were very young when your mother died?"

"Three. Old enough to remember her, at least a little."

"Then you know she really is still with you. At least . . . right here." Abigayil poked a flour-covered finger at Sigrun's heart, and then chuckled when she left a smear on the bodice. "Here, let me get a towel."

Outside, in the car again, Sigrun commented, leaning her head back against the seat, "Your parents are good people. And your mother has a kind heart."

Adam nodded, and gave her a side-long look in the mirror. "What?" Sigrun asked.

"So . . . I'm the same age as your sister, hmm?"

". . . yes? I thought you already knew that."

"Well, confirmation never hurts. Do I get any other hints tonight?"

"No."

"Damnation."

After two weeks in Jerusalem's enervating heat, Sigrun was relieved to climb back on a plane to return to Rome. She wasn't entirely sure if, back in a familiar environment, Adam would change his behavior towards her, so it was another relief when, he invited her out for dinner once more, once they were both off-shift. And this time, when she invited him back to her apartment, it was with her heart beating in her throat as if she were about to fight an opponent who outmatched her overpoweringly. But this was Adam, and he was, first and foremost, her friend. Her partner. One of the people she really did trust most in the world. And, technically, she could probably kill him if she needed to, except that she really didn't want to damage him. So it was perfectly *absurd* to be . . . nervous. *Call a fig a fig, Sigrun Caetia. You're <u>scared</u>. You're scared because this matters, and you're . . . vulnerable.*

So Sigrun let Adam into her chilly apartment, turned on the light by the door, and went to go turn up the thermostat for him, so that the steam from the building's thermal plant, in the basement, would ease into the radiator by the window and warm the room . . . only to find her hand caught as she tried to slip past him, and Adam pulled her back up against him, and, with a quick look into her eyes for permission, kissed her, reaching back with one hand to lock the door behind them. "I thought," Adam told her, smiling a little as he raised his head, "that I should get that part out of the way. You look . . ." his dark eyes were a little amused, and a little tentative, "a little nervous, Sig. Don't you trust me?"

"Of course I do," Sigrun returned, immediately, and leaned up slightly to wrap her arms around his neck, feeling the faint scratch of his light woolen cloak, and offered him a return kiss. She didn't really know what to do or to say, so she just let him guide the way. Tangled her fingers in his hair, surprisingly soft under her wondering fingertips. Felt the scratch of incipient beard against her lips and cheeks. Heard him groan a little and felt the vibration of the sound under her sternum as he pushed her, gently, up against the nearby wall in the entryway. Felt one hand tangle in her hair, as the other ran up and down the length of her spine.

"Don't . . . don't have to rush." The words were a whisper against her ear. "We can go slowly, Sig. Really don't want to mess this up." He pulled back, and in the faintly yellow light from the overhead bulb, his face was very serious. Very intent. "What do you want, Sig?"

She closed her eyes, and swallowed. "To be normal," she told him. "To be human, with you."

"Normal's boring and over-rated." He ran the backs of his fingers over her cheek, and down her throat. "But human . . . I've got nothing but that. I can do that."

"And I can pretend." Sigrun's throat was tight, as if they were saying a lot more than the words actually meant.

"No pretending. We'll meet halfway. I promise."

They made it to the hallway, and somewhere in the tangle of arms and increasingly urgent kisses, Sigrun managed to direct them, a little hazily, through the living area and to her bedroom, not stopping at the couch, as it seemed as if Adam wanted to do. *He's trying not to pressure me,* she thought, dimly. But waiting, she felt, would make things worse, not better. *Rip the bandage off. Probably best not to say that to him directly. He might take it amiss.*

It wasn't as if Sigrun were entirely ignorant of the *mechanics*. She'd grown up in a world where Rome ruled. There were explicit images of . . . configurations . . . in every public bathhouse. There were explicitly erotic scenes on most far-viewer channels. A couple of literally-minded emperors, during the Early and Latter Decadent Periods, had decreed that if it happened in the script, it had to happen on the stage, so live sex on stage had been common, and the tragedies of Sophocles and Aeschylus, by popular demand amongst the actors, had been retired from many theater's repertoires. No one wanted to die on stage for the demands of *realism*. So while Sigrun was definitely aware of the mechanics, she had never actually applied them.

She let herself look at him as he pulled his clothing off. Enjoyed the play of muscles in his frame. He was solidly-built, but not over-muscled; he didn't spend all day at the gymnasium building empty muscles with weights; his waist continued in an almost straight line from his chest, while the abdomen, itself, was perfectly flat; his arms weren't merely strong in the biceps, but his forearms and wrists were, as well. She'd already discovered that even though she was almost his height, and a tall, strong woman, her fingertips didn't touch each other when she tried to wrap them around his wrists. It was a little thing that pleased her, obscurely, to know. "Ah . . . I think you might be forgetting something?" Sigrun asked, pointing down. "As I understand the process, the pants will need to be removed, too."

"Later. Right now, you're acting like all the progress we made in the hallway was lost." Adam looked down at her bed. "You really do have a twin-sized mattress, don't you?"

Sigrun blinked. She'd never really expected anyone else to see the inside of her bed chamber, and she'd had this bed frame since she'd first become an *ælagol*. It was thus . . . seventeen years old, if she had to put a number to it. "Is that a problem?"

"No, no." Adam put his head down on Sigrun's shoulder, and reminded himself to be patient. The mere fact that she had a twin bed, hardly more than a barrack's bunk, told him she didn't expect many visitors in here. *Slowly. Patiently.* Kisses, nips, little bites. Anything that would make her gasp. Moan. Relax. And when he felt her muscles ease, turn to water in his hands again, Adam leaned her back against the sheets, and got to work on her clothing. He wanted to make sure she wanted this, and every hesitance gave him pause. He wasn't entirely sure why she seemed nervous. She was an undisclosed number of years his senior, but her reactions suggested to him bad prior experiences. Possibly even abuse, though considering how strong she was, it would have had to have been when she was a child . . . *No. She'd have told me. Had to have been a really bad relationship. So . . . patience.*

Unlacing her bodice. She hadn't bothered with her undershirt tonight, and he was just as glad as her breasts were now available to his hands and lips. She was hypersensitive to touch, flinching a little at any sensation at the tips, so he withdrew, and contented himself, for the moment, with the rest of her. Kissed his way down to her belly, teased her with beard scratch along her waist and flanks, making her laugh. "Didn't know you were *ticklish,*" he told her. "Going to have to file that away for future reference."

Getting her jeans open, unlacing them — she liked the style that laced at the sides, too, letting the wearer control the waist and hip size, completely — Adam had, for the first time, the feeling that this was really going to happen. The feeling of reality, of being in the moment, and that this wasn't some sort of particularly vivid erotic dream. He grinned up at her, and gave her his mouth . . . something he'd learned to do from a Gallic woman whose name no longer mattered. Felt her hands tangle in his hair. Felt her feet brace against his shoulders, as if to shove him away . . . and then she relaxed. Gave in. *Surrendered.* And he thought there were probably emperors who couldn't possibly be more pleased with the conquest of a nation, than he was to have this woman actually surrender to anything. But most especially, to him. The rune-marks on her skin glowed, and began to outshine the dim light of her bedside lamp, and glowed all the more fervently, the higher he brought her, the more he *wrought* her, with lips and fingers and tongue. And then she arched and held there, blazing like a star, and Adam grinned to himself, and kissed the inside of her thigh. *Absolutely no way you can fake it, is there?* He noted, distantly, that rain was falling, drumming against the window and the roof overhead, a steady, gentle sound, as if the clouds were intent on cleansing the whole world.

He let her relax for a moment, and then slid a finger home, testing his welcome, and bit the inside of her thigh, feeling, again, the spasm of reaction in her muscles. As if she hadn't quite expected something. "You ready?" he asked, quietly.

"As I'm going to be, I think." Her voice was a little higher pitched than usual. "That was . . . really *nice* . . . just so you know." Her tone was dazed.

Adam grinned, pure male satisfaction, and moved on top of her, kissing her lips again, eagerly. Feeding there. "Mmm. You're . . . . .you're not on birth-control, are you?"

Sigrun blinked up at him. "I . . . no. Damnit. I'm sorry."

"Don't worry. I brought something." He fumbled in the pocket of his shirt, for a moment, and came up with a condom. Slipped it on, catching Sigrun's wide-eyed stare out of the corner of his eye. He wasn't sure if he should be complimented, or if he should laugh. "I'm not quite

Priapus."

"Thank the gods, no."

Lips and tongues and getting her, once more, to relax under him. Cradling her head in his hands as he edged himself into place. And then, knowing how wet she was, and how open she should be, Adam slid himself in. One smooth thrust . . . and felt her entire body spasm under his, and a low, choked cry of pain. His head snapped up, but he was *very* sure he hadn't rammed into bone or anything else like that; he'd have felt it. "I'm sorry, I didn't mean to—"

"It's all right. It's supposed to happen, right?"

Adam pushed himself up on his elbows, as suddenly, all of her behavior clicked into place in his mind. "Sig . . . why didn't you *tell* me?" He was torn between a desire to curse, and a sensation of awe, joy, and a little trepidation. To have *this* much trust extended to him? To be her first? *I really better make this good.* "I'd have been gentler."

"I . . . didn't know how to tell you." Sigrun bit her lower lip.

"How can you possibly be a virgin? Was every man in the Legion blind and castrated while you were serving?" Adam bit the side of her neck lightly, and added, "Don't answer that. I'll be gentle. And I'll make sure it's better, all right?"

Slowly now. Had to be. The distraction had definitely detracted from his own general excitement. They worked together. Built the fires back up again. And then took each other back over the edge again.

A little while later, listening to the rain fall outside, Adam stroked a hand down Sigrun's flank, and thought, *I am possibly the luckiest son of a bitch alive today.* "Sig?"

"Hmm?"

"I have to ask . . . ."

"It just never came up, all right?" Her tone was a little defensive.

Adam hid a smile; he was lying behind her, one arm draped around her, and kissed her shoulder now, for good measure. "Not what I was going to ask."

"Oh." Sigrun flushed, and he realized, all over again, that when she got *really* embarrassed, the rune-marks glimmered faintly. As if in response to a threat. "Then what?"

"Is *that* going to grow back, too?" Another light little bite. "I don't like the thought of hurting you every time I want to do this."

"Battle-wounds heal. *That* is not a battle-wound." Her tone was prim.

"Any number of poets will tell you that love is a battlefield." His tone was solemn. "And, you know, battle-*maiden* . . . ."

She twisted around slightly, giving him a mock-glare. "Any number of valkyrie have had lovers. Most of them rode to battle together. Had children together. Some of them even threw themselves into their lovers' pyres, rather than live without them." Sigrun raised her eyebrows, and gave him a defiant look. "The term is a name, not a requirement." She nodded. "As to the rest . . . .are you suggesting that we should perform experiments? See if it has, indeed, already grown back?"

Adam grinned. "Oh, definitely. I am a great enthusiast for natural philosophy, as you know. And an experiment needs to be shown to have replicable results. So we'll have to perform it over . . . and over . . . and over . . ." Each *over* was punctuated with a kiss, which finally made her break down laughing. Adam leaned back. "You're blushing again." He found a rune-mark. "One. Two. Three. Four." His finger traced down her throat, and he started kissing each one, instead, voice muffled as he continued, "Five. Six. If I count them all, are they like tree rings? Will that tell me your age?"

"Certainly, if you divide by a completely arbitrary number. I have more scars than years."

"Oh, good to know. That limits the total possible."

"Does it matter to you, that you should know?" Her tone was apprehensive.

Adam considered it. "No. You are who you are. And the years don't really matter. So long as we're not talking centuries, which, given that your father is alive . . . is unlikely."

He turned her over, and realized she was deliberately channeling energy. Letting him count and target each rune-mark. There was a fretwork of lace-like knot-work down the center of her chest, along the sternum, and he realized, as he was kissing along it, that this was, undoubtedly, where they'd cut her open to use the rib spreaders. The thought made his stomach twist, but he pushed it aside. And here, just beside the heart . . . . "This one's different."

Sigrun looked down, and squinted. "Inguz," she identified it.

They'd been working through each other's languages for only two weeks now. He recognized it in general, but . . . . "Why is it different from all the rest?"

"It means . . . completion. Endings. New beginnings. If you draw a chain of them together, they even look like the helix of DNA," Sigrun offered, and her lashes fell over her eyes. "In this case, it means it sealed an almost mortal wound."

Adam looked down at her, and told her, simply, "Never again."

"Never going to promise that, Adam." Steel-sheen eyes raised to his own told him it was true, too.

He kissed her to stop the argument before it began.

The next morning, he was rather delighted to wake up in her apartment, however stiff his back was from her tiny bed. "Next time, my place," he told her, firmly. "My bed is *much* more comfortable."

She flushed a little, and laughed. "I'll go start some tea. I don't think I have a single thing with which to break our fast, before work, though."

"We'll stop somewhere and find a pastry or two." He kissed her forehead, and watched her slip out of bed . . . taking all the sheets with her. The fact that she was modest in front of him amused him enormously, and he couldn't resist watching her get dressed.

However, as *he* was attempting to get ready for work, he noted yet another minor anomaly in her apartment. "Sig?"

"Yes?"

"How exactly am I supposed to shave when you don't have a mirror in the bathroom?" He walked back out, barefoot, and face covered in soap, and looked around her bedroom. Sure enough, the dresser had surely once *had* a mirror. The glass had been replaced by cork, with which she posted notes to herself in foolscap.

Sigrun padded back into the bedroom, stepped into the bathroom, and dug around in the top drawer, finding him a small hand mirror. "Here. This should work."

He shook his head, and before she could leave, caught her with an arm around her waist. "Sig. Tell the truth now. Remember when we met Kanmi and Tren in that *taverna*, and you bet me that I wouldn't recognize you?"

"Yes?" Her eyebrows rose.

"How'd you put on the kohl and the paint?"

"I was at a public bath. There are stores there that sell cosmetics. How do you think they convince people to buy their wares? I had one of the women at the counter put the paints on my face, and bought something for her troubles."

"I want my half-solidus back."

Sigrun grinned up at him. "No. You lost it. You did not know me when you saw me."

Yes. Then. But now, I do. And I think I always will.

Interlude I: Unions

1955-1960 AC

Februarius 30, 1956 AC

1955 had fleeted by, as if propelled by wings. At least three more trips to various locations to meet with Chaldean and Median envoys — always different people, so as to throw off detection. As a result, Livorus noted that he constantly felt as if he were starting the negotiations from scratch every time he met with someone new. Jerusalem was followed by Alexandria, which was followed by Tyre. At the start of 1956, the next agreed-upon meeting place was Byzantium. Eight months of negotiations had created a set of treaties — secret ones, necessarily — that would only go into effect if the Persian emperor, Tiridates X, died without naming a successor.

And in Februarius of 1956 AC, he did precisely that, and the Persian Empire collapsed into civil war. Chaldea and Media immediately declared their independence of Persia, and openly requested admission to the Roman Empire as subject nations.

One particularly ambitious Persian general, Jamshid Artaphernes, trying to preserve the boundaries of the empire for *whomever* succeeded . . . and perhaps with an eye on the throne for himself, which hadn't fallen into the hands of someone outside of the Imperial line in over a thousand years . . . took steps to mobilize the Persian army and to attempt to retrieve the seceding regions. Adam and Sigrun watched far-viewer footage of Persian ornithopters moving in on the city of Rhagae, one of the major Median towns near the southern end of the Caspian Sea that had been included in the treaty with Rome. "They're setting up for bombing runs," Adam told Sigrun as he rubbed the back of her neck, his fingers moving lightly under her hair. "They just locked their wings into glide position . . . ah, *harah*. Here they come." The footage was in color, surprisingly enough for a Roman far-viewer station. They'd undoubtedly taken the footage from a Judean source and re-formatted it for use on a ley-conveyed transmitter. Color and two dimensions translated to an orb-shaped far-viewer designed for three dimensions and black and white resulted in grainy, blurry footage. It was still hard to watch.

Adam winced as he watched the ornithopters on the far-viewer perform their last banking maneuver, and then come right back at the camera's position, bomb bay doors opening in their bellies. He knew his reaction was irrational. This had all happened sometime yesterday, according to the reports. Knowing that didn't help. Every muscle in his body tensed as he watched the payloads drop, and the first explosion rocked the camera . . . and a fireball rent a Median building, possibly a barracks from the look of it. The camera tipped to its side from the force of the explosion . . . and out of the center of the fireball, a pillar of flame emerged, with enormous ruby eyes that looked vaguely like Lassair's. Only this spirit stood two stories tall, and was roughly man-shaped. "Like a golem made of flame," Adam muttered. "I think they're using the chemical reaction of the explosives to feed the damned things."

"What a bargain," Sigrun agreed, grimacing and leaning forward to study the images more carefully.

The reporters on the Roman station stayed remarkably silent through the footage. Only as a half-dozen fire-elementals began to rage through the marketplace, and people ran in every direction, overturning their own stalls and trampling one another, did the commentators speak. *"This was the scene in Rhagae at just past two postmeridian yesterday. We have unconfirmed reports of over five hundred people killed. Median magi are on scene, and have apparently bound the elementals unleashed on their city, while local emergency response teams have worked around the clock to put out the fires and dig through the rubble, looking for survivors."*

"The question on many people's minds right now, is this: What is Rome going to do about this atrocity? More on that, after these commercials."

Sigrun leaned back against the back of the couch in his apartment. "Gods, Adam. I am . . . not entirely certain that we've spent the last eight months doing the right thing, encouraging them to secede. I saw children running out of one of those buildings. It was a school."

Adam's stomach tightened. Missed bombing runs *happened*. No one in their right mind wanted to hit a civilian target. Codes of warfare had changed a bit since the earlier Imperial period, after all. But for all he knew, the Persian general could have ordered the school as a target, deliberately, to break the Medians' will. "I hope it was an accident," he said, quietly. "It's horrible to have to live with, but I'd much rather that, than that it was intentional."

Sigrun turned and looked at him. "That sounded like the voice of experience."

"It is, and it isn't. I was a pretty young *optio* at the time, but . . . my unit was setting mines just over the Persian side of the Wall. It's in disputed territory, but they're supposed to keep people and vehicles back from the Wall itself." Adam realized that his fingers had stopped moving in Sigrun's hair, and had to will them back into motion. "I spotted a vehicle, an old, broken-down, kerosene-powered truck, coming our way. Loaded down with people. Couldn't tell at that range if they were soldiers, farmers, refugees, what. And they were heading, at full clip, right for the area we'd just mined."

"Oh, Hel's frozen heart," Sigrun murmured, her expression horrified. "This story cannot end well."

"It doesn't." Adam grimaced. "We waved them off, fired a warning shot, everything. I had a sniper rifle with me. My centurion ordered me to try to shoot the driver. Better one man, than the whole truck full of them getting killed, if they hit the mines, if they turned out to be refugees, trying to defect, right?" He rubbed his free hand over his eyes for a moment. "So, I looked through my scope. Got a good look at everyone.

The driver wore a uniform. Everyone else wore civilian clothing. I told my captain, he confirmed his order to kill the driver, and I shot him. Truck came to a halt just outside the mined area, and the people aboard were all screaming and acting panicked, and then they shoved his body over, took over the wheel, and got out of there."

Sigrun frowned. "That doesn't end as badly as I expected it to," she admitted.

"Oh, well, the bad part was two days later, when the tribune of the entire southeastern zone ordered my centurion and me to appear before him. And showed us what was being broadcast on Persian far-viewer stations. According to *them*, the soldier had been a deserter who'd forced a bunch of civilians to come with him, under threat to their families, and intended to sell military secrets to Rome and Judea in exchange for sanctuary, but was shot by the Judean military. Thus the fate of all defectors and deserters is death." Adam paused. "Oh, and they had footage of the whole incident. Minus us trying to wave them away. Though they *did* have shots of us digging the mines in place. It was interestingly edited film."

"That doesn't even make sense." Sigrun leaned into him. "Can't people tell the truth from a lie when they hear it?"

"Propaganda doesn't have to make sense. It just has to instill fear. But *I* get to wonder, every so often, for the rest of my life, if they all really *were* trying to defect, or if they were just trying to get close enough to the Wall for an attack. I'll never know if I shot a desperate man or an enemy that day. And while I don't wish that feeling on the Persian pilot who dropped the bomb on that school . . . I'd much rather that, than know it was deliberate. Know what I mean?" Adam nuzzled his face into her hair. He hadn't entirely been joking to Kanmi, months ago, about having noticed an improvement in his sense of smell since the Tlaloc incident. It made him rather hyper-fastidious about cleaning his apartment anymore — which wasn't necessarily a bad thing — and it made the smell of clean skin and hair and Sigrun's core scent absolutely intoxicating to him. "Mmm. You used a different brand of shampoo today. Apple is your usual, but this is . . . ." He inhaled again. "Cherry blossom. That Nipponese stuff my parents sent you for Hanukah." His parents were adapting to Sigrun's presence in his life, if slowly.

"I think you are, perhaps, turning into a wolf," Sigrun told him, laughing, and Adam snuffled more audibly against the back of her neck and mock-growled. He *didn't* tell her, because he didn't want to worry her, that he could tell that she'd showered two hours before coming over to see him, by how much dampness smell was left in her hair. That he could tell she'd had lamb kebabs with garlic, cumin, and cinnamon for lunch. The smell was still on her skin, shower or no. *As unintended side-effects go, I really can't complain. So what if it makes me clean the lavatory daily? It beats being dead.*

He'd even seen a doctor in Judea, quietly, for a CAT scan of his brain. The technology was in its infancy, but no tumors or anything else had been detected. They'd crammed a scope up his nasal passages, too. He just, apparently, had had enough of a shock to his system, that his brain was treating smell as a more important sense. The doctor had likened it to someone who'd been blinded, suddenly having to focus on the remaining senses.

The minimal advertisements, mostly for brands of olive-oil based soap, a new Hellene variety of motorcar, and a brand-new Qin restaurant that had opened in the Field of Mars area came to an end, and the news broadcast resumed. *"Rome's response to the attack on the new subject nation of Media began today with twenty-five thousand troops being moved into the area, and a retaliatory strike being launched against Persepolis itself,"* the anchor informed them, as footage of Roman armored personnel vehicles rolling through gates in the Wall showed on the screen . . . followed by images of Judean jets being scrambled from airfields in the Sinai. *"The Judean Air Force launched a series of bombing attacks directly on the seat of the Persian government today. However, the government of Persia is, de facto, in the hands of Tiridates X's second son, Mithridates, self-styled seventh of that name, but he is being pressed on the west by his elder half-brother, Antiochus, self-styled twelfth of that name, and to the east by Pharnaces, his younger brother by one of Tiridates' concubines. It is hoped that they will not unite in common cause against Rome as the result of this direct retaliation."*

The footage of the Judean fighter jets and bombers did Adam's heart good to see. They were capable of flying so high in the atmosphere, that the Persian ornithopters simply couldn't *reach* them; the wing design and propulsion systems of most ornithopters gave them a flight ceiling comparable to that of a helicopter. Specially designed, extremely lightweight ornithopters could be used in high mountain reaches, but they weren't combat-rated, by any stretch of the imagination. The jet fighters were present solely to escort the bombers . . . and the bombers had bomb-bay door cameras, some of which caught the city below erupting into flame. No elementals. No djinn. Just raw, chemically-powered explosions. Somehow, this seemed a little cleaner to Adam. Not by much, but a little. "Hard to tell what altitude they're at," Sigrun noted.

"I know. They're flying high enough that not even a god-born should be able to get into the sky with them. Most people can't breathe at that altitude without special gear." Adam poked her lightly in the ribs. "And even *you* need to be able to see a target to hit it with lightning."

"And the Persians don't have a lot of god-born. They're Zoroastrian, in the main, besides a few in Babylon who still follow Marduk." Sigrun stared at the screen for a moment, and then reached to turn it off. "Enough depressing news for the time being, I think. This is going to take years, I think." She grimaced.

"If the Persians have been saying for decades that West and East Assyria should have the right of self-determination, and that they should be allowed to exit Rome's domains if they want to be one single country, then logically, they can't oppose Chaldea and Media for choosing to use their own right of self-determination and leaving," Adam told her, in a tone of pure reason.

"Since when does logic have anything to do with governance?'

Sigrun asked him, dryly, and they got up to work on cooking dinner together.

––––––––––––––

Martius 5, 1956 AC

"So, you do realize," Adam told Sigrun that morning, as she pulled her swan cloak over her shoulders to get ready for work, "that we've spent the night at each other's places . . . pretty much every single day that we've been in Rome, yes?"

Sigrun thought about that. "Which day did we miss?"

"Probably none, but I'm allowing for faulty memory." Adam's dark eyes lit up with his smile. "I'm thinking that one or the other of our leases is probably coming up for renewal soon. And it would certainly be less expensive to live in *one* place, rather than in two." He gestured around his small apartment. Sigrun liked it, but found it heartlessly plain. He did have the larger bed, but very little other furniture. A couch, a far-viewer, a kitchen table and two chairs, and vast expanses of plain white walls unadorned by absolutely anything. After the first few visits, Sigrun had, pointedly, bought him a small lemon tree in a pot and put it in his balcony window, so at least the place smelled redolently of citrus most of the time, and there was something *alive* in the confines of the apartment. Adam hadn't minded, and usually sniffed appreciatively every time he walked in the front door with her.

He had a shelf full of books on space and rocketry, however. He'd even started taking correspondence courses with the University of Jerusalem, starting in Ianuarius. Their schedule didn't really permit him to attend full-time classes, so he was doing the reading, writing essays, and completing the tests before sending them back by mail, for grading, while they sent him another packet of work in exchange. It looked painfully dull to Sigrun, but Adam seemed to be enjoying himself as he worked through his first courses in physics and chemistry. "The good news is," he'd told her, shrugging, "no junk courses. No 'you need to be well-rounded, so take something totally at random from art history." He'd given her a kiss. "Besides. Every night I sit up reading with you, there's a better than average chance I'll get a graduate seminar in archaeology or something anyway."

Sigrun had snorted a little at the thought, and looked over his shoulder at the physics textbook. Most of it had been written in numbers. Roman numerals and Hellene numerals were still extensively used in common writing, and both systems had added the convention of a zero, but an Indian numerical system had actually been adapted for most advanced mathematics, on the grounds that it was more economical and easier to write in. It also made adding machines, or calculators, much easier to build, apparently. Adam had actually purchased one for this course, in addition to a slide-rule, but the bulky contraption was used, primarily, to check his work. "Looks like magic spells to me," she admitted.

"Kanmi looked over my shoulder last week and said that *this* equation right here," Adam pointed at it, "was the basis for his ability to warp gravity, very slightly, around himself, so he doesn't take too many bad falls. So it *is* magic. But it's also science." Adam made a face. "And Kanmi does this in his *head*. I'll admit . . . I'm envious."

"Inaccurately, he says," Sigrun reminded him. "He does a lot of rounding in combat, and it makes his spells nowhere near as efficient or accurate as they could be, if he had them all worked out ahead of time." She'd kissed the back of Adam's neck. "I'll hush so you can concentrate."

Two months later, he was still grinding away at the work patiently, almost every night. She didn't mind. She liked it quiet, and going out every night would have been pointless. Curling up with a cylinder of music turning in the machine providing a little background noise as she, too, read, made for a perfect ending to what was usually a long and stressful day.

Looking around his apartment now, however, Sigrun raised her eyebrows. "You're suggesting that we should move in together?" She was secure enough in the relationship now to tease, "Why, this is so sudden!"

"Actually, I was thinking of a little more than that," Adam told her, picking up her hand to kiss the backs of her fingers. "I was thinking we should get married."

Sigrun was surprised enough that she couldn't even answer for a half a minute. She started to answer, realized that she couldn't even shape words, and then just smiled at him, reaching out to wrap her arms around him, before pulling back with as a worried frown creased her brow. "Are you even *allowed* to marry me?" she asked.

Adam looked up at the ceiling. "Yes. Well, technically, there are a few impediments. Officially, women are highly discouraged from marrying outside of the people. Men have a little more leeway in that area." He grimaced. "Just as technically, when we get married, the wife is supposed to convert." He coughed a little as Sigrun pulled a little further back and gave him a look. "I didn't say I expected you to do so. I'm not sure there's anything we could do that would break more rules."

Sigrun tipped her head to the side. "Like killing an *entity*?"

"It's not a hobby! And it's not likely to happen again." Adam gave her a look in return. "So, yes, there might be a few issues. Children, too, might be an issue. They're supposed to be raised in the faith."

Sigrun blinked. She'd been wandering around in a happy daze in her off-hours, and hadn't given much thought to the future. Adam, apparently, *had. Then again, he often comments on the fact that there's no future tense in Gothic.* "Children . . . ." Sigrun shook her head, wide-eyed.

"You don't want any?"

"Oh, I *do*. It's just . . . I never really thought they would be possible for me." Sigrun grimaced. "Between my sister prophesying . . . well . . . end of the world stuff that doesn't matter . . ." she looked at the ceiling, "and well, never really finding a man whom I loved until now—"

"I heard that. You said it." Adam picked her up in his arms and kissed her. "God knows, it's taken you long enough."

That's because I say things without saying them. Sigrun returned the kiss, and then pulled away. "I don't have any objection to them being raised in your faith, if they're not god-born. If they are . . . they're subject to Tyr. The same as I am."

"Sounds fair to me." He gave her another kiss. "And now that that's settled . . . I love you, too, by the way . . . we should get to work." He tugged at her cloak. "You going to talk to Tyr about letting you wear a flak jacket with the feathers?"

"It remains on my list of things about which to ask him when I next receive an audience," she returned. "I hesitate to schedule those without good reason." She opened the door. "Shall we?"

Aprilis 3, 1956 AC

Sigrun sat in the tiny kitchen of her apartment, going through the stack of mail that had been shoved through the slot in her front door over the course of the past week, while Adam paced around behind her, the cradle of her phone in one hand, the receiver in the other, and an exasperated look on his face. She was picking up Hebrew at a fairly good rate, because they alternated evenings speaking exclusively in each other's native language, but his tone was annoyed, and he was speaking at a very rapid clip. This, and the word *Imah*, meant that he was speaking with his mother. Probably about the wedding.

She did her best not to listen, and picked up a letter postmarked in thick Gothic letters, from Marcomanni in Caesaria Aquilonis. Tearing it open, she produced two closely-written sheets in runes that curved a good deal more than was normal, suggesting a young female hand had penned them.

> *Waes hael, Sigrun Caetia, god-born of Tyr, law-giver of Nova Germania and lictor of the Praetorian Guard.*
>
> *I hope this letter finds you well. It has been two months since I received your last letter, and I wish to apologize for not responding more promptly. I have been very busy, though that is not an excuse for ignoring the duty that is courtesy.*

Sigrun's lips quirked. Frittigil had quite evidently been schooled in manners and forms in the last two years.

Behind her, she heard Adam, in Hebrew, rap out, sharply, "*Imah, I am not putting her through any more of this. I can't find a rabbi who will marry us. There are plenty who would cheerfully perform the ceremony if Sigrun were just a normal Goth or Frisian or what-have-you. They find out who she is, and they all get the same look on their faces. The one that says 'This was not covered in my training and doesn't appear anywhere in the manual.' We contacted one in Burgundoi who's used to interfaith marriages, and even he said he'd have to consult with the priests, and that if he didn't consult, any ceremony could be technically invalid. So we're going with Gothic ceremony with Roman civil paperwork, and there's an end to it."* A **pause.** *"Besides, I don't need a <u>ketubah</u> on my wall to know I'm married to her."*

Sigrun sent Adam a look of relief. A *ketubah* was a necessary document in a Judean marriage. It was typically read out loud at the wedding ceremony, and, in theory, if it were lost or destroyed, the couple couldn't live together until a new one had been fabricated. It represented a contract between the couple, and had provisions for who brought what to the marriage. That was all fine by Sigrun. The fact that it traditionally called for a paragraph specifying whether or not the bride had come to the marriage a virgin was, to her, private information that no one besides them really needed to know. *You came to <u>me</u> a virgin,* Adam had told her, grinning. *Yes, but I do not believe there's a way to put that in the writing, and have it remain no one's business but our own,* she'd replied, squirming slightly. *We can leave that paragraph out?* he'd replied. *And if we do, that's an admission in and of itself, is it not?* A quick, amused glance from him. *Damned if you do, damned if you don't, I take it?*

He'd explained that the *ketubah* had been, back in the day, a truly radical document that had ensured a woman's rights in a marriage. It was submitted to the Sanhedrin, or High Court, but the wife kept it, and it defined both parties' rights and responsibilities in a marriage. Sigrun had listened, and while she'd been willing to do a double ceremony, one for each faith, she had certain constraints on her, too. Gothic *godi*, or priests, had no problems with mixed marriages. They were polytheistic. They knew perfectly well there were other gods that other people might honor, and it was perfectly commonplace for a mixed Roman-and-Gothic couple to be married twice, once in a temple of Juno, and once in a temple of Freya. In her case, however, she didn't really answer to the *godi*. She answered to Tyr.

Behind her, on the phone, Adam was trying to explain some of that, diplomatically. *"Goths do things differently. It's called a <u>hand-fasting</u>."* Another pause. *"Technically, it means we agree to marriage for a year, and if we don't separate after that, we stay married. In the old days, however, it took getting the hand-fasted woman pregnant to make it a full marriage."* A pause, and then a tone of irritation: *"Yes, it's a <u>real</u> marriage, Imah."*

Sigrun returned her attention to the letter. Frittigil Chatti was fifteen years old now, and a far stronger person than she'd been a scant two years ago.

> *As you know, I have not been permitted to return to public school, though I have renewed my petition to at least be permitted to stand with my classmates when it is time for their graduation. They all still have at least one more year to go, except for those on track for university education; they have two more years beyond that. Nevertheless, they are my friends, and I wish to stand with them, if I may.*

> *The Odinhall has replaced last year's tutor, who was a priestess*

of Eir. I liked her. She taught me basic medicine as well as languages, history, and mathematics. My new tutor is Radulfr. He's interesting, I have to admit. He is a bear-warrior, and I did not understand at first what on earth he could teach me. While I understand that I must learn to be strong, I did not see myself engaging in combat training. He pushes me, constantly. Why, he's even taught me about magic – seiðr, rather. And he told me that I needed to face my fears. He drove me out to visit the Evening Star's people, telling me that she has marked me just as much as Baldur did, and that it is my responsibility to learn more of her people. He was right – even though I hated to admit it – and I had been neglecting this duty. Radulfr told me that facing my fear would make me stronger. He was probably right about that, too.

I am not quite strong enough in my mind to return to Ponca. Not yet. But I have asked permission to enter the kingdoms that belong to other peoples of the region, and to learn something of their ways, even as some of their children were required to attend Roman schools. I would like it very much if some form of an exchange program were instituted between the Roman-style schools and the peoples of the various small nations around us. I watch the news of the war on the far-viewer at night, and it seems to me that we should <u>all</u> know one another better than we do. And if any good can come out of what happened to me, it would make it somehow worthwhile.

Sigrun nodded over the letter. "Brave child," she murmured over the sheets of paper. "You have a good heart, Fritti. Better than mine."

Behind her, Adam paced back and forth. *"Explain to my brother, then, that it is not his wedding, but mine. Explain to him that if my children happen to be <u>god-born</u>, I will not be raising them in the Judean fashion, and if he objects, then <u>he</u> can explain it to Tyr One-hand."* A pause. *"I realize that Burgundoi is very far away. But the other options were worse . . . well, far northern Europa, for one."* He paused, and switched to Latin, covering the mouthpiece with one hand. "She wants to know why we're not doing this in Cimbri-on-the-Caestus, where you grew up. How do I explain this?"

"Tell her that we have a choice between two places. The Odinhall is in Burgundoi and Áhkká is north of Gotaland. Áhkká is technically closer to Judea, but far, far colder than Burgundoi. They wouldn't like the waist-deep snow at midsummer that they'd experience there." Áhkká was the mountain under which the entrance to Valhalla had been built, in the misty morning of the world. Sigrun could not enter those halls, not while she lived, at any rate. No human or god-born was permitted within. But they could stand outside, on the snowy slopes. Look up at the sky, still alight even at midnight during the summer months, and say their vows. It was an option, at any rate.

"Not very helpful, Sig."

"Sorry, Adam." Sigrun flipped through the letter. "Tell her that the only *entity* empowered to perform my marriage ceremony makes his home in those two places?" Sigrun gave him a droll look. He wasn't the only one with certain constraints on him, little though his mother seemed to believe this.

"Even less help, *neshama*." The word meant *soul*, and Adam tended to use it interchangeably with *mami*, a light term of endearment. Either one made Sigrun smile. He sighed and uncovered the telephone's mouthpiece once more. *"Because the ceremony has to be done either at the threshold of Valhalla or inside the Odinhall. Yes, you'd be permitted in there. It's a public building. Most of it, anyway. That's why we're opting for Burgundoi. See, if we could find a willing rabbi, the Judean ceremony would be held not far from the Odinhall. But we can't, so it won't."*

Sigrun flapped the letter at him to get his attention. "Should we invite Fritti and her family? She's god-touched now, and it would be very nice to see how well she's doing."

Adam gave her a harried wave of assent. Sigrun chuckled and started writing her reply, even as he continued, behind her, to deal with his family. *"If that's how he feels, then he doesn't have to be there. Or acknowledge her as my wife. Or, for that matter, acknowledge me as his brother. I'm tired of these conversations. His life is not my life, and he can go to—don't cry, Imah."*

Sigrun looked up from her reply to Fritti as Adam finally sighed and hung up the phone. "This is going to be a wonderful occasion," she told him, solemnly. "My sister, should she attend, will be speaking in tongues and giving prophecies. She might even bring some of Delphi's serpents with her, since it's a special occasion. Your brother will take one look at her and have a fit of apoplexy. Your mother will collapse in tears. My father's wife will stand back and complain about everything, from the food to how I am dressed. Even the presence of Tyr himself will not cause her to smile. My father will be very pleased, but, on seeing my sister, his wife, and me, all at once, may decide to drink all the honeybeer of his wedding gift to us, himself. Your father will wonder at your sanity. Kanmi will crack jokes and juggle honey-cakes without using his hands. Trennus will take notes. Ehecatl and his family will be edging politely towards the exit, trying not to be rude about it, and Livorus will not even lift his eyes from his dispatches for the bulk of the ceremony." She nodded, soberly. "We should run away together, Adam. I have heard that they perform lovely weddings in Tahiti."

"Tyr would be upset with you." Adam was, in spite of his irritation, starting to smile, reluctantly, at her worst-case scenario.

"He would, I think, understand."

Trennus' only question, when they announced their wedding, was "May I bring a guest?"

Kanmi had *snorted* at this. "The mystery woman you've been courting? I thought she was a myth. Certainly, there's been no evidence of her besides the permanent and rather annoying smile on your face."

Trennus' lips quirked up, and Lassair, in her firebird form on his shoulder, turned to regard Kanmi with ruby eyes. Kanmi folded his arms over his chest and lifted his chin at the manifested spirit. "Besides, how does the average woman react to the constant companion? Do you put a sheet over her perch?"

Sigrun had watched the Britannian's lips twitch again. "Not as such," Trennus replied, mildly.

For her part, Sigrun had watched Lassair closely, since the spirit had admitted to having absorbed some of Tlaloc's energies. The changes in form that Lassair managed to pull off were apparently absolute, and were completely manifested; there also didn't seem to be limits, so long as there was always some tinge of an otherworldly nature. Fire, or fiery coloration. Lassair couldn't *hide* what she was, but when she was a tigress, she was a *tigress*, albeit an incredibly intelligent and apparently tame one. When she was a phoenix, she was a firebird. It was a far cry from the amorphous and rather timid ball of energy she'd been in Nahautl.

Kanmi shook his head dourly and turned back to her and Adam. "I take it this is all being done somewhat quietly, so that no one insane out there tries to kidnap one of you to use as leverage on the other?" He shrugged. "Personally, I'd almost pity any fool who tried."

Sigrun nodded. "Yes. It will not be publicized. It will be noted in Praetorian records, but that is the extent of it."

"Not even changing your last name?"

"Even the men of my family take their name from my god-touched ancestor, Solveig. Her first-born took her name. As did my father, and as did I. It's a matter of honor. Judean custom says that I would be named for my father. Which would be what, bat Ivarr?" Sigrun made a face. "So, will you and Bastet and the boys be in attendance?"

"I'll bring the boys. They need to see more of the world, and Burgundoi will open their eyes a bit." Kanmi shrugged. "Bastet said she couldn't get away from the hospital." His expression told Sigrun that Kanmi didn't believe it himself, and was merely repeating a social lie.

Adam managed a smile to cover the awkwardness. "She'll miss a show, then. I'm personally expecting fireworks of some sort."

———

Trennus headed back to his apartment that night, smiling to himself, Lassair having de-manifested. *Are you quite certain about this?* Lassair asked him, silently, as he let himself in the front door. *There will be at least one god in attendance, if I understand Stormborn's thoughts. He will see me. He will know what I am.* She manifested in a swirl of light, and Trennus wrapped his arms around her. Other than having killed a stag for Saraid this year in Britannia, he had scarcely heard from the spirit of the Caledonian Forest. It was as if the forest spirit were making herself scarce. Giving the two of them room to explore the boundaries of their new relationship.

"Is that going to be a problem? Will a god take offense at a spirit?" Trennus looked down at her, and smiled a little. "I'm a little behind on my otherworldly etiquette."

I do not know. I wish I could remember more from . . . before. The memories are so fragmentary. The earliest here in the world is that moment in the fire, when I realized I did not wish to return beyond the Veil. That I wished to stay in this world, with all it offers in the way of experiences, forever. When I realized what people were. Not mere moving bags of water and carbon, ruled by instincts and impulses as animals are . . . . but . . . kindred spirits. Lassair ran a hand down Trennus' face. *When I realized that they were alive, too. Differently than we are, but aware. And capable of so much feeling.*

Trennus leaned down and kissed her. "It'll come back," he told her. "We'll keep trying as many different things as possible, until the memories are all jarred loose. And then you'll know who you are, completely."

What if I don't like who I am? What if you don't like who I am?

"Not possible. Because then you wouldn't be *you.*" Trennus flicked a twist of curling, fire-red hair out of her garnet eyes, and asked, suddenly, "You know what? Can you *eat* in that form? They'll be serving food at this wedding. You'll fit in a little better if you can eat with everyone else."

Lassair's eyes rounded, and she put a hand to her abdomen, and then lifted it to her mouth. *I . . . . do not know.*

"I'll cook something for you. What sounds good? Can you drink in that form?"

That would involve . . . . liquids. Her tone was slightly apprehensive.

"Yes, but I haven't met a fire elemental yet who didn't like wine or uisce beatha." Trennus pulled her along to the kitchen, not bothering to turn on the overhead lamps; the feathers curling through her hair and the light radiating from her skin was usually enough to find his way. "Let's see . . . damn. I've got to stop living like a bachelor if I'm going to be feeding you." He grinned at her, as Lassair stared at him as if he'd lost his mind. "We have half a cooked chicken, a loaf of bread, some cheese that hasn't gone moldy yet, some apples that have seen better days, and a bottle of red wine. What do you want to try first?"

. . . bread. I think. Her tone was apprehensive as he broke off a corner of the loaf which had evidently been in the icebox for a little too long; it was the approximate consistency of a brick. "I think I could build something with this," Trennus assessed. "Or possibly use it as a weapon." He considered it for a moment.

Lassair tentatively nibbled on the crust he'd handed her, and made a face. There was a distinct burning odor in the kitchen, and his smoke detector went off overhead, wailing loudly. Trennus reached up absently, twisted it loose, and removed the batteries, silencing it. This had become almost habitual with Lassair in residence. He honestly didn't know why he bothered to keep the batteries *in,* anymore. These days, when one of the alarms started going off, they neighbors would pound on the ceiling overhead. He had no idea what they thought he was doing in here, and tried not to meet their eyes on his way in and out of the front door.

"Best I do something else with this bread. Hold on." He managed to cube it with a knife after some effort, and he melted the cheese and the wine together, stirring once in a while as he cut up the apples, too. Then he stood in the kitchen, and dipped the bread chunks in the cheese and wine sauce, feeding Lassair with his fingers, chuckling under his breath at the look of stunned amazement on her face. "This doesn't seem familiar?" he finally said, as she licked at his fingers, trying to get a last taste of the food. He chuckled at the sensation. In eight months, he hadn't quite gotten over the effect she had on him. And didn't really *want* to, either.

No. But I like it.

"No one's ever fed you before?"

Only . . . things thrown into my fires . . . . Lassair concentrated. *Honeycakes, I think. Flowers. Grain and . . . blood. Yes. There was blood. But it was from the entrails of the animals, the sinews and whatever else they didn't want to eat themselves.* Astonishment in her voice as she looked up. *I didn't remember that before!*

"Did you like eating?"

Yes. It is . . . what humans do. And now I understand why. The body requires it, but it is also pleasurable. She looked around. *Though we could have sat down.*

"Yes, but then we'd have had to get back up to go back to the stove with every bite."

I could have kept the food warm at the table.

"I was feeding you. Seems impolite to expect you to provide services during that." He wrapped an arm around her. "All right, next question. Now that we know you can eat with that mouth . . . can you speak with it, too?"

I speak perfectly well without using my lips.

"I know, dear one, but I want to hear your voice. And again, if we're to go out in public together, it'll frighten people less if you can speak to them in words that don't just echo in their minds."

Yes, but mere words leave the possibility of being misunderstood. Words are slippery. Words are false. This? This is truth. She leaned up on her tiptoes and kissed him, and Trennus blinked, rapidly, and picked her up to put her on the kitchen counter. When Lassair kissed like *that*, it completely clouded his judgment. After a moment, however, Trennus pulled away, put his head on her shoulder, and asked, his voice muffled, "Change form, please."

Why, dear one? I thought this was your favorite.

It is, but I can't think *at the moment, and there was something else I wanted to ask you.* Trennus exhaled, partially in frustration, and partially in relief as she shifted, becoming . . . a housecat. With a literally fiery orange coat and gleaming red eyes. "Off of the counter," he told her.

You just put me here, silly.

"I know, but now you're a cat."

She licked a paw at him, and rubbed her whiskers with it. *What did you want to ask me?*

"With Sigrun and Adam getting married, it's sort of been on my mind. I'm due to hunt in Britannia for Saraid again, soon . . . ."

Yes? What does one have to do with the other?

"Maybe this *would* be easier with you in human form. I feel an absolute idiot asking this of a *cat* who's grooming herself at me."

Lassair shifted back. She'd taken care, previously, to wear clothing not entirely dissimilar from Sigrun's normal attire—a bodice, a shirt, and jeans, or at least, their semblance. This time, she was back in her favorite diaphanous, sari-like garment of golden silk. "You're trying to kill me," Trennus told her, with no conviction at all in his voice.

Of course not. You just _fed_ me. Her tone was content. *What was your question?*

"How would you feel about being introduced to my family while we're in Britannia anyway?"

She went very still. *I . . . don't know. I don't mind Stormborn and Steelsoul Godslayer and Emberstone knowing my Name. But not your whole family, I think.*

"Oh, gods. I . . . hadn't even thought that far ahead. I just meant . . ." Trennus winced. "I meant, introduced to them as the woman I . . . well, love. Share my life with."

Share a soul with.

"They probably don't need to know that part. They won't understand."

Are you really sure they'll understand about a spirit, at all? There are any number of very bad stories about spirits who steal away men's souls, mostly having to do with sex. Suddenly, of her own accord, she resumed her firebird form. A sure sign she wanted to have this conversation without his mind being clouded. She wanted to be *fair* to him . . . and that amused and touched Trennus in equal measures.

"There are any number of bad stories about summoners who bind demons and spirits as slaves for the sex, too," he pointed out. "I'm not likely to look any better to them."

Then perhaps it's just better if they don't know.

"I don't really want to hide you forever, dear one. I'm not ashamed. Just . . . it's not entirely everyone's business, any more than it's anyone's business that Livorus finally found himself a pleasant and discreet mistress, or that Kanmi and Bastet plainly aren't getting along."

They haven't slept together in a year. Lassair's tone was matter-of-fact.

"All right, I didn't need to know that. How in the gods' names did you know?" Trennus shook his head rapidly.

He is angry and frustrated, and I just know.

Trennus shook his head again. That was definitely more intimate information than he had *ever* wanted to know about Kanmi. "Anyway, all of that is . . . well, part of the reason I keep asking you to take your favored form when we go over to Sigrun and Adam's apartment."

I know. I haven't yet. She hesitated. *It took them long enough to stop looking at me as if I meant to eat you to ash and cinders after they realized that we were soul-bound, you and I. Stormborn suspects, though.*

"She does? Why am I not surprised?"

She is wise. And older than she appears. I do not call her sister without intention or understanding of who and what she is. Lassair's tone was gentle. *I will meet your family, if you wish it, Trennus. But we had best choose another name for me, by which I will be known to them.*

"Hmm . . . Asha, perhaps? I think it means *hope* in Sanskrit."

Asha will do nicely. The firebird cocked her head at him.

"We should probably talk about the other issue, too," Tren told her, grimacing, and sat down at the kitchen table. He didn't really want to address this, but if they didn't hash it out now, he'd just be in for this conversation again later. Probably in Britannia. "We're bound to each other."

Yes, but there is neither master nor servant between us. We know each other's Names. You have given me much of yourself. You could not even compel me now, if you wished to do so. I give to you freely, of my own accord, and do not make of you a slave or a pet, any more than you do me. The firebird sounded nettled. *Humans overcomplicate things that are very simple.*

"Yes, but that's because there's not as much room for nuance in the language. They'll hear 'bound spirit' and think *slave.* Which you're not." Trennus looked at her, and met those cabochon eyes. "I think I should unbind you."

I do not think you have the power to do so. Lassair cocked her head to the side, and fanned out her wings and tail, as if inviting him to admire her magnificence. *If you unbind me, even if I permitted you to do so, you would be giving up what you have given me. I would be loosed, with eighty percent of your soul . . . or I would have to return it to you.* Her tone was sad. *And I do not think I have ever felt more __real__ than with your spirit indwelling. I would miss it. Terribly. And I do not know how much of Tlaloc's power I have . . . truly assimilated.*

"I free you," Trennus whispered, making a little tossing gesture. "Keep it. It was freely given."

And I do __not__ free you, Flamesower. Her tone was firm as she resumed her human form. *You are __mine__. Humans who do not comprehend what is between us have a very limited understanding, and are not worth your time. We serve each other, because we make each other happy. We give to one another. I see words in your mind. Demeaned? Should __I__ not be the one to tell you if I feel lessened by holding your soul within me? I do not. I feel . . . empowered.* She slipped *through* the table and suddenly sat on his lap, straddling him and Trennus looked up as she started to kiss along his neck. He wrapped his arms around her and hoped, distantly, that there wasn't a price-tag on this kind of happiness, but if there were? He was fairly sure he was ready to pay it.

Caesarius 31-32, 1956 AC

The Roman calendar had been regularized, centuries ago, to having three hundred and sixty-five days in a year, and an additional day inserted every four years. Caesarion the God-Born had looked at the incredible disarray that the old calendar had been in, shaken his head, and consulted with natural philosophers until it was *fixed*. As such, every month in the year but three had thirty days in it. Iulius, being named for Julius Caesar, had thirty-two. So did Caesarius, re-named for Caesarion by his son from Sextilis, previously the sixth month in the calendar. December, previously the tenth month, retained that somewhat illogical name, given that it was now the twelfth month in the calendar . . . but was given thirty-one days each year, and it received a thirty-second every four years, which was treated as an extension of the new year's holidays. Overall, it made for a fairly logical calendar with few questions in it, but it did make the longest and hottest days of summer seem to drag a bit every year.

The weather in Burgundoi, however, on the last days of Caesarius was a mild sixty-seven degrees, thanks to the sea breezes wafting in from the Pacifica Ocean. Adam had been surprised at how many of his former colleagues in the JDF had responded to what had been a slightly short-notice wedding announcement. He'd started off as an *optio*, effectively a second-in-command under a lower-ranked centurion, and had resigned from the Judean levy forces as a ranked centurion, but not as a first-file centurion. He'd commanded up to forty men near the end, but the only way *up* in the JDF would have been to take on command of larger and larger units. Truthfully, now that he was in the Praetorians, and working on Livorus' staff, he probably did coordinate with eighty people a day, but there just seemed to be less paperwork, somehow. And what politics there was in this job, was largely Livorus' concern, and not Adam's.

But as a result of that former life in the JDF, Adam knew a newly-appointed *primus pilus* centurion—his old commander, in fact, Tamir ben Simcha. He also numbered among his acquaintance a handful of other people who'd been on the Wall with him, who'd scraped graffiti right into the rocks, just like hundreds of others before them. Tal ben Tovia and Oved ben Niv had both flown all the way from Judea for the ceremony. *"Mostly out of curiosity,"* Tamir admitted, dryly. *"You've been in and out of Judea a few times and on the news a few more times than that. Was beginning to think you'd forgotten those of us still stuck on the Wall."*

"Oh, never that," Adam replied, accepting the wrist-clasp in the airport's hustle and bustle. Ben Simcha hadn't changed, other than to add more salt and pepper to his short hair—he'd always affected a short, Roman-style cut, mostly to conceal the fact that he was balding. Ben Simcha had been the commander who'd reviewed him after the djinn attack, and who'd ordered him to fire on the approaching truck filled with 'deserters.' And he'd also been the one who'd told the tribune that it had *been* his order, and that he stood by the order. Adam trusted the man, implicitly.

Tal was a farmer's son, and Oved was a diplomat's. Tal was lanky and taciturn, but had an uncanny eye for terrain and where there were hiding places. Oved spoke three dialects of Persian fluently, and had a bright smile that put people at their ease. They'd been good teammates, and good friends . . . and had looked just as curious as Tamir, as Adam met them at the gate to their flight area. *"I've never even been out of Judea before,"* Tal admitted. *"Ten feet into Persia doesn't count, right?"* He did all but stick his head out the window of their motorcar as they drove across the city. *"It's so green here. I don't even know where to look first. It's like my eyes have been starved of this color all my life. There's too much of it."*

Adam had chuckled over that, and just raised his eyebrows when they fired questions at him in the vehicle. Had he already had an *ufruf,* the blessing on the groom conducted at a synagogue a week before the actual wedding? Adam had, with a certain amount of discomfort, allowed his parents to arrange that, since they'd flown up to Rome a week before the actual wedding to do these sorts of things for him. Neither he nor Sigrun had wanted to take an entire week off before the ceremony to handle wedding details in Burgundoi. Even the traditional week of not seeing one another before the wedding? They'd laughed it off. They lived together and worked together. Traditional separation would be impossible, even if they'd wanted to go through with it.

But in little things, they tried to accommodate his mother's scruples. For instance, both Gothic and Judean rites required a betrothal ceremony to be conducted ahead of the wedding itself, though the Gothic ceremony consisted solely of taking one another's hands in the presence of witnesses, and promising to marry each other. They'd done *that* at the Roman synagogue, with Sigrun looking a little apprehensively around her, clearly trying not to let even a single rune-mark show. The wedding was supposed to be about them, and about joy, and it had all somehow gotten messy and complicated, with Abigayil insisting that he needed to do as many things as possible that would preserve his *Judean identity.* On the grounds that "When you look back on this in twenty or fifty years, you won't have given up who you are, and won't regret it."

Adam wondered, yet again, if his mother even knew who he was.

Out loud in the car, he only replied, *"Yes, my parents arranged for it in Rome. And before you ask, yes, there's a mikvah here in Burgundoi."* A mikvah was a ritual bath for purification, with the water drawn from non-stagnant sources. Rainwater was acceptable, so long as it was gravity-fed from the roof, for example. A lake or a stream, yes. Water from a tap, in spite of Roman hygiene practices? No.

Trennus had gotten a rather amused look on his face when Adam had explained this. "The wild water of a place, not tamed, then?"

"You're going to tell me that this is fairly common in magic?"

"Well . . . yes?" Trennus had hunched his shoulders, looking sheepish. "There are even legends that an evil spirit can't cross running water." Trennus had considered that. "I wouldn't want to bet my life on that, though. But large quantities of salt water, I'd risk."

Adam had looked at his best friend for a moment, not smiling. One of the things he genuinely liked about Tren, and Kanmi, too, was the fact that they said what was on their mind. Tren would step gently, but he'd still say it. He waited for a moment, and then let Tren off the hook. "I'm actually aware. I've been to India. I've seen people bathing in the Ganges to purify their souls." Adam had shrugged, and the conversation had mostly ended there, with Tren's look of relief at knowing he hadn't offended Adam.

Tamir admitted, *"I'm surprised they have a synagogue here."*

"It's a fairly cosmopolitan city. I think there's at least one temple for every *faith here."*

That being said, it was clearly a Gothic city, as evinced as he drove them past the towering skyscrapers with the gargoyles rampaging up and down their sides. Adam had finally given in and asked Trennus if any of the statues had bound spirits attached to them. Trennus had nodded, wide-eyed, and told him, *All of them.*

"You have a shoshbin *lined up?"* Oven asked now, staring up at the gargoyles on the closest building. The *shoshbin* was the best man, who took care of any wedding expenses on the day of, looked after the rings, made sure the groom didn't arrive hung-over, and generally was a servant for the day. Adam could have asked any of these three, but he hadn't seen any of them in five years.

"Yes. Good friend of mine. Trennus Matrugena. Try not to stare when you meet him. He's a Pict, and they're . . . colorful. Also, he's a summoner, but definitely one of the good guys." Adam had pulled in at the hotel at that point, ignoring the wide-eyed looks he was getting, all around.

His former colleagues gaped at Trennus as the Britannian strode across the lobby and offered a wrist-clasp. Adam had gotten used to the height, the braids, the tattoos, the glasses, the kilt, and . . . yes . . . the phoenix on his shoulder. Damned few Britannians of any tribe got assigned to the Wall, not every Britannian was a Pict, and . . . not every Pict was Tren. So it was indeed a shock for his old friends. "Nice to meet you," Tren told them. "We'll have to exchange embarrassing stories about Adam later. All right, you'll have to tell *me* some. He's too well-behaved around all of us for me to have any."

"We might have to invent a few," Tamir said, gruffly, and then looked at Adam. "So, do we get to meet the bride, as well?"

Adam grinned. He'd already spotted Sigrun across the lobby, giving him space and time. Also, he'd long since realized that she was inherently oddly shy. Growing up completely isolated from other human beings, other than her father and her pedagogue, and then being trained in the Odinhall with bear-warriors, no other females around, and then being dropped directly into the legions . . . had left marks. She had enormous empathy, and *understood* people, but her ability to deal with them was extremely limited. Adam, on the other hand, had grown up in a large and very vocal family. He had few inhibitions in groups, and made friends readily.

As such, he beckoned her over now, and introduced her . . . and was pleased by how she lit up a little when the others all accepted her wrist-clasp with brother-and-equal grips. "You're the last guests to arrive, other than my family," Sigrun told the men. "They'll all be getting in late tonight." Her tone turned a little grim.

"That doesn't sound promising," Tamir told her.

"I would rather wrestle with one of Trennus' spirits than deal with my family." Sigrun managed a smile to make it sound less bad. "It's a morning ceremony, everyone. And while Adam has decided to fast today, apparently everyone else is free to eat. So there's a table reserved over in the restaurant for everyone in the party."

"I'll be there," Adam said. "It's just that I'll be drinking water and wishing I weren't."

Sigrun chuckled and stepped away to deal with something at the front desk. As she did, Tamir put a hand on Adam's shoulder. "All right. Truth now, son. Exactly which demon did you sign away your soul to, to get her?"

Trennus coughed into his hand. Adam's eyes flicked towards his friend, and he choked down his own laugh. "None. I swear." He raised his right hand.

Livorus was staying at a separate hotel, guarded by different lictors for the occasion, and thus, couldn't make it to the dinner. But at this little gathering, in a private room in the restaurant, Ehecatl was there, with his wife, Coszcatl, who was truly lovely in a thoroughly Nahautl way. She bubbled over with enthusiasm at meeting the other lictors at last, and actually gave Sigrun a hug, which made the valkyrie blink. "Our eldest couldn't make it," Ehecatl told the others, shrugging. "Mazatl just finished his first two years at a *calmecac*. He's received his Jaguar tattoos. But these are my younger two children." He introduced a twelve-year-old boy and an eight-year-old girl, both wide-eyed at their surroundings, and a little shy.

"Carrying on the family tradition, I take it?" Kanmi asked, bringing his sons the to table.

Ehecatl grinned, clearly fiercely proud of Mazatl. "Perhaps he, too, will be recruited by the Praetorians someday."

"Not soon, I hope," Coszcatl said, her tone fervent. "I was used to worrying about you. I could put it to the back of my mind. But worrying about Mazatl . . . ."

"Ah, so you care more about our first-born than about me." Ehecatl's elaborate sigh of chagrin fooled no one, especially not his wife, who just laughed at him.

"No, no. It's just that it's too soon. He was wearing swaddling not two years ago, I swear."

Their amicable teasing was in stark contrast to Bastet's complete absence. Kanmi had brought his sons, as promised. The two boys had met his co-workers in Judea, of course, but that had been months ago, and Bodi had complained about bad dreams about a monster trying to get into the house more than once since then. Kanmi had dealt with that by making his son a little wooden sword and telling him to keep it under his pillow. "Most monsters in Rome are very small monsters. It's rowan wood. Very magical," he'd told his son, straight-faced. "If a monster gets in the room? Call for me or your pedagogue or your mother, and whack the monster with the sword. Should take care of that. But be careful it's not one of the house-spirits. They won't like that."

It'd worked. Bodi had gone right back to sleeping like a rock through the whole night. Bastet had told Kanmi that she didn't think it was entirely appropriate to give their son something that looked like a weapon, and Kanmi had told her, "It's a security object. Everyone needs something to believe in. At his age, it's easier to believe in something tangible that gives him control of his life, at least a little bit. And it's working, isn't it?"

She hadn't had much to say in response, besides a comment that it was a *weapon* and that this could lead him to whacking other little children with it, in emulation of what he saw on the gladiatorial fights on the far-viewer. Kanmi's response had been to enroll both of his sons in an after-school gladiatorial training program intended for children. Discipline, self-control, self-defense, and respect for others. He thought they could use those qualities.

Here and now, the boys were wide-eyed at meeting their father's co-workers again. Bodi clearly idolized Trennus. "You wrestle with the monsters, right?"

Trennus laughed. "Only when I have to."

"Can I learn how?"

"Maybe. But if you've any amount of your father's talents, you might be a very good sorcerer someday, instead."

"At the rate things are going, he'll be a magus," Kanmi grumbled. "And then the world will *end*."

The seat beside Trennus was conspicuously empty. Kanmi cleared his throat and gestured at it. "So, have you been stood up?"

"No, I just have been waiting for the right moment to introduce her. I didn't expect so many people that she doesn't know well here tonight."

Kanmi frowned. "You're starting to sound like Caetia's sister. That made no sense at all. We've never *met* the mystery woman."

This was attracting Adam and Sigrun's attention at the head of the table. Trennus sighed, and stood. "I'll go get her."

"This should be good," Kanmi said with a grin, as he helped Himi cut up his food beside him. "Hey, ben Maor, you think we should lay money on Matrugena here coming back in with an *invisible* woman? Or going outside and coming back in, claiming that she's left for the airport?"

Adam's lips twitched. "I think she exists, whoever she is. I'm just wondering if she's another summoner, or something."

Trennus heard the words behind him, shook his head, and stepped out into the main room, Lassair still balanced on his shoulder. He needed to find someplace where no one was going to see her shift her form. *Are you sure, flame-heart?* he asked her, silently. *I can put up with the teasing until there are fewer strangers around.*

It's a little frightening, showing them my face, when they've gotten used to the other forms, Lassair admitted. *But if I wait till tomorrow, it will just be harder, won't it?*

Probably, dear one. Trennus found the lavatory area, and gestured to the doors. *There you go. No. That's the men's room. The other one . . . there you go. Try not to frighten anyone.*

I know how to do this, Trennus. Lassair's tone was mildly agitated. Not at his light words, he knew, but because of the overall situation.

Trennus waited. No screaming, no sounds of dropped items. This was good. After a moment or two, Lassair opened the door and slipped back out again. *Entirely too much water in there,* she told him as he offered her his arm, and she slipped her hand through to rest on his inner elbow.

"You look beautiful," he told her, sincerely. She did, too. There was almost no way in which she could really tone down what she was, though he'd definitely noticed that she often played with her proportions. Some days, she was slender and athletic, and some days, voluptuous, depending on her mood. At the moment, she was somewhere in between, and her red eyes still held that spark of blue-violet light at their centers, and her hair was a dark garnet . . . with the inevitable phoenix feather tangled in with it. The dress she'd created for herself had a Gothic-style brocade bodice and a rich velvet skirt that entirely matched her hair, and she'd managed to tamp down the light that tended to radiate from her skin. *You've been practicing.*

I'm so very nervous, I don't think I could glow if I tried.

Trennus watched any number of heads turn as they walked back across the lobby. *Careful. Don't scorch the floor.*

I'm trying not to. I really am.

I know. And I know you're scared. But it's all right. They know you already. You've healed Kanmi. You've healed Sigrun. The Morrigan knows, you've helped Adam out a few times, too. Trennus opened the door, and ushered her into the private dining room.

He watched a dozen or so heads lift along the table. Mouths opened, and absolute silence fell. After a moment, Kanmi cleared his throat, and looked down at his two young sons. "Bodi? Himi? Put your fingers in your ears."

"But why, Daddy?"

"Fingers. Ears. Now."

Both of the boys, their dark eyes wide, did precisely that. Kanmi looked up at Trennus, and said, in a tone of utter and amused resignation, "You son of a *bitch*. You've been holding out on all of us." He tugged at his sons' hands. "You can listen now." Kanmi looked back at Trennus again. "And to think I thought she was *imaginary*."

Adam was a little wild-eyed, but Sigrun, Tren noticed, looked surprised, but not overly so. In fact, the valkyrie stood and walked over to offer a wrist-clasp to Lassair . . . who reached out and hugged her, instead. *Is there any reason why we should stand on formality, sister?*

"Ah . . . I cannot think of any," Sigrun admitted, and looked up from Lassair to Trennus, an expression of worry in those clear gray eyes. Easy enough to read, after spending so much time together. *"You're quite certain about this?"* Sigrun asked, in Gallic, in the informal mode used between friends. *"There are those who would say that you have cut yourself off from humanity enough, with your studies."*

I can still understand you, Stormborn.

"*Yes, I am aware of that, but this conversation need not to be for every ear at the table.*"

Trennus reached down and gave Sigrun a hug, himself. She was a very dear friend, and he loved her, in a way. "*Quite certain. And since Lassair is interested in every aspect of being human, I think she might actually engage me more with humanity than otherwise.*" Trennus gave Sigrun a rueful smile. "*She informs me that she wants to go watch a circle dance.*"

No. I have watched them before, from the heart of a fire. I wish to participate. Be a celebrant. Lassair paused. *Will you permit me to celebrate your union with Steelsoul tomorrow, Stormborn?*

"Of course. I cannot imagine not having you there . . . in some form or another. Though if you're there, I think that your other spirit should be, too. She's part of the team, after all." Sigrun *smiled* at that, an expression that was like the sun coming up. "Adam?"

Adam finally stood and came over. Took Lassair's hand in his own, and looked down at the fingers. "I've been wondering why you constantly smell like wood smoke of late," he admitted to Trennus, quietly. "I thought perhaps you had a terribly blocked-up chimney. One overgrown with roses."

"No, but the balcony of my apartment has managed to attract every flowering vine you can imagine. There's morning glory and honeysuckle trailing over the whole thing. I wouldn't be surprised at all if the damned things *did* get into the chimney at some point. I can't explain it, and L . . . Asha here," Trennus smiled, and avoided her name at the last moment, "says they're too pretty to pull away."

They are. They're green and they live and they're beautiful.

"Who am I to disagree?" Trennus smiled, held the chair for Lassair to be seated.

––––––––

The next morning, Caesarius 32, 1956, the entire wedding party and all the guests arrived at the Odinhall. The first unpleasant surprise had actually come at some time after midnight local time, when Sigrun's parents' flight had gotten in from Cimbri. Adam and Sigrun had been just finishing their late dinner with their guests in the restaurant and had entered the lobby of the hotel to go upstairs just as Ivarr and Medea had arrived. Sigrun's jaw had dropped open slightly as the bellhop had had to assist with the revolving metal and glass door at the front, and a Hellene-looking woman with brown, curling hair and green eyes had emerged . . . pushing a wheelchair weighted down by a tall Cimbric man in his late sixties. His hair had surely once been flaxen, but was pure white now, and braided back from a long, rectangular face. The man also had a massive cast wrapped around his right leg, from the hip to the knee, and a grim expression lightened only slightly when he spotted Sigrun.

"*Fæder!*" Sigrun had exclaimed, immediately, and raced forward to drop to her knees beside the chair. It was the first time Adam had ever seen hints in her as to what she might have been like as a child as she caught at Ivarr's arm and rattled at him in Cimbric for a moment, gesturing towards his injured leg.

She even went so far as to reach out a hand, the runes on her skin starting to glow, but her father caught her hand, and told her, firmly, *"No."*

"But I can heal you — "

"No." The spate of Cimbric that had followed was too swift for Adam to follow the twists and turns of the language. It wasn't as harsh-sounding as his native Hebrew, but it was damnably twisty in places, with consonants he was more accustomed to out of Hellene. *Th,* for example, which could be pronounced two different ways, apparently, and could be written with two completely different symbols.

After a moment, Adam approached and put a hand on Sigrun's shoulder. "I only caught some of that," he murmured, in Latin. "Your father won't let you heal him?"

"The wound isn't fresh," Ivarr said, in perfectly good Latin, offering his hand to Adam for a wrist-clasp. "Sigrun couldn't heal it even if I permitted her to try. I took a bad step on the stairs last week." A flash of grim humor. "Ten minutes after hanging up the telephone with Sophia, and her telling me to watch where I placed my feet, else I'd find myself someplace low looking somewhere high. They had to operate and put metal in my hip and thighbone. It will heal."

A flare of temper in Sigrun's eyes, and a twitch at the corner of her lips. Adam knew the signs, but to any outsider, her face would have been blank. Ivarr patted her elbow, lightly. "I'm sorry I won't be able to give you away tomorrow, Sigrun. But I'll be there to watch." Ivarr lifted his head and gave his wife a look.

"We need to get checked in. It was a very long flight, and your father is tired. Travelling so far with such an injury, less than a week after surgery to repair his femur and hip? Has taken much out of him." Medea's words were precise, and clearly delineated exactly how much trouble it had been to make their way here for this occasion. It was all in the tone, somehow. "Let us pass, and he can speak with you again tomorrow, once he's had some rest."

Adam felt every muscle in Sigrun's body tense. "Of course," Sigrun replied, looking at her father, reserve entering her face and voice now. "I regret having kept you. You are, of course, tired." She bowed her head slightly, and moved away from the wheelchair. "If I had known of your injury, I would have told you to stay in Cimbri and rest."

A flash of pain in Ivarr's face, as he half-turned in the chair to look at his daughter, but his wife had already begun pushing him towards the check-in desk. Adam slid his hand to the small of Sigrun's back as she turned away. "He didn't mean to dismiss you. And your step-mother *is* concerned for his health."

"I am aware of both of those things," Sigrun replied. The pure formality of her language spoke volumes to Adam, as did the tautness in the muscles under his fingertips. She was *angry,* but pulling it inwards, as she almost always did. "It does not matter. We should retire, ourselves."

In their room upstairs, he watched her pace back and forth for a while, before offering, quietly, "We can get someone else to give you away, if he can't stand up. Livorus, maybe?"

"Yes. That would be more than acceptable." Sigrun finally sat beside him on the couch and let him rub at her neck a bit. "Medea is Medea. Nothing will ever change her. She did not like me as a child, and she resented being forced to care for me. My father is my father. Proud of me, but stubborn. And then there's Sophia." She bit off each word as she spoke. "Why did it not occur to her to say, plainly, 'do not go back downstairs tonight, Father.'"

Adam *wanted* to say *because then it's not fun for her*, but that wasn't entirely fair. Sophia was *mad*. And her madness wasn't malicious. It just *was*. "Because if she actually said anything that anyone understood, then the future wouldn't happen the way she sees it, and she'd have to admit that the future can be changed, and she can't let anything threaten her reality," he offered, at last, and Sigrun gave him a single, horrified glance for the insight. "Come here, *neshama*," he told her, gently. "We'll fix it all in the morning. Come to bed."

The next morning, Adam had to assure his parents and sisters several times that they were allowed to be on the floor that they were now entering. Sigrun, before turning them over to their bear-warrior escorts outside the elevator, turned and looked around at the various people assembled. "This area of the building will . . . be different," she warned. "Different for each of you. Adam, Trennus, and Kanmi have all been here before. But each person sees it with their own eyes, as I understand it."

Kanmi raised a finger. "I remember it looking a lot bigger on the inside than the outside of the building would permit. I'd love to know why."

Sigrun looked off into space for a moment. "I will certainly use the wrong words. I have to translate this from my native tongue into Latin, and the concepts are not congenial to either language." She paused. "When I asked him once, Tyr answered, thus: This entire room is a construct, taking a piece of the extradimensional aentropic space that exists in three dimensions as humans understand them, with a few others humans are not aware of, but lacks the defining dimension of time. This is colloquially known as the Veil. The room creates a . . . translation matrix . . . which permits direct physical interface between the four-dimensional space known as the mortal realm, and the . . . transdimensional space that is the realm of the gods." Sigrun paused. "I have only the faintest of glimmerings as to what any of that actually means."

Trennus and Kanmi had both snapped upright, however. They looked at each other in excitement, and started firing questions at Sigrun, who raised her hands, and replied, "No, I know no more, and like enough should not have said so much. But Tyr teaches that if someone is wise enough to ask a question, then perhaps they are ready for an answer." She shrugged and looked around. "I will come up by a different elevator and get changed upstairs." She smiled at Adam. "You have what you're wearing?" As always, the formality of her speech softened for him.

He hefted his bag and smiled at her. *My mother is about to have a stroke.* "Yes. And Trennus has the ring. At least, he had better."

"Then I'll let you go." Sigrun leaned up and kissed him, and waved as they all got onto the elevator for the final ascent.

The first thing that Adam heard, as the doors opened again, was a gasp from Himi and Bodi. "It's the Elysian Fields!" Himi said in a tone of awe, and Adam wondered what the child saw.

Just as last time, Adam at first saw blackness, and then he looked out into the heart of space and time. He saw stars in every color, shining cold and steady in the far distance. The haze of nebular gases. The swirl of distant galaxies. Then the distance in the perspective began to decrease, and he saw . . . planets. Moons. Ones familiar from his many books on the subject, but different. Huge. Vast. And still, beyond them, the swirl of billions of stars that made up the single galaxy in which they made their home. As Saturn's bulk moved off to his left, Adam could only think, *We are so small. We are so very small, not even grains of sand in all this vastness. But somehow . . . we still matter.* He had to blink away tears of awe, and looked over to see blank terror in his mother's face. "It's all right," Adam told both his parents, and put an arm around his mother's shoulders. "*I hesitate to ask what you see . . . .*"

"*Light,*" Maor said, his voice oddly gentle. "*Light, everywhere.*"

"*If I walk out there . . . I'll fall,*" Abigayil said, her voice trembling.

"*Mother, what are you talking about?*" Rivkah said, in a tone of awe. "*It's Eden. Or as close as I'll ever see. It's the most beautiful garden I've ever seen. Flowers and fruit and fountains.*"

"*It's not a garden, silly. It's the ocean,*" Chani said, dreamily. "*A cliff looking down on the beach, and nothing but blue waves for miles in every direction.*"

Adam worked on getting the rest of the guests to step out of the elevator. Ehecatl was doing the same, coaxing his wife and children along. Most of them seemed to see something along similar lines, though no two were *precisely* the same. But all perceived aching wonder and limitless beauty. Lassair shook her head when Adam asked what she saw. *You would not understand, Steelsoul. The Veil has no time. No duration, really, not as you experience it. We are not beings of the same dimensionality as humans and all that is in your world. But this is also not the Veil that I know. This is . . . ordered. Constructed. I see . . . lines, contracting down to points. Vortexes. Bricks and blocks and rules to help humans understand this place.* She sounded uneasy, as well.

Sophia, helping to push Ivarr's chair, stopped and stared, her face suddenly strangely at peace. Her father reached up and touched her hand where it rested on the back of the chair. "What do you see, daughter?"

Sophia smiled. "Nothing, Father. I see nothing, and it is everything I ever wanted it to be."

Livorus studied the area, a faintly contemplative look on his face. "I don't suppose," he asked Adam, "that they would allow me to linger and read any of the books?" The Roman sighed. "Or drink any of the wine, either. All imaginary, I fear."

Adam glanced back at Kanmi and Trennus. "Do I even want to know?"

"I see black again," Kanmi asserted. "White lines through it, like chalk on a board, except when I look at the lines, they're made of numbers. Energy in patterns, and *described*. It really is a construct . . . ." he looked around, "and they're numbers I could sit here and stare at for hours. They're *beautiful*. And I'm not sure I could ever understand them." He gave Adam a faint shrug. "Everyone sees their own version of nirvana, eh? I see the perfection of reason and the underlying mathematics of the universe. My sons see what they've been told they'll see." Just for an instant, Kanmi looked sad. "I actually hope it's *not* an illusion. I rather like mine."

Adam swallowed. That was rather more truth than Kanmi ever let anyone see. "Tren?"

The Pict shook his head. "Like last time. It's like I can see through into the Veil. There are spirits all around us. Hundreds of them. All bright and shining and ephemeral, and there's nothing but light all around them."

Adam nodded, slowly. "It's a good bet that when it comes time to take the wedding pictures," he said, "none of this will show up on the film."

"I'd be terrified if it did," Kanmi returned. "Besides, whose version would be there? In objective reality? We're probably going to see a plain white background on those images."

The three lictors now needed to step off to the side, where the dwarf they'd seen here last time, Dvalin, took charge of them. The dwarf, scarcely more than four feet in height, turned and scowled back at the rest of the people in the vast chamber, his feet, to Adam's perspective, leaving tiny impressions as space dust flew away under them. *No pictures!* the dwarf snapped. *Not until the ceremony, anyway.* He scowled up at Adam. *There's nothing here except you mortals that your film can actually capture. I do not understand humans. Why can they not simply sit back and experience a wonder? Why do they want to capture and quantify it? I guarantee, at some point in your future, you people will have cameras grafted to your hands or foreheads, and rather than looking at the world and experiencing it, you will reflexively take pictures of it.* Dvalin made a gesture with his hands, as if parting a curtain, and reality unfolded in front of them all. A small room appeared. *Here. Change your clothing. Leave your belongings on the shelves. And don't touch anything.*

Kanmi, in the small, cluttered room, which had shelves filled with . . . drinking horns and weapons and eating utensils and a dozen different types of devices, including, Adam thought, an astrolabe, narrowed his eyes at the dwarf's back, and reached out and poked a shelf with one finger.

I did mean that, Kanmi Eshmunazar. Fingers to yourself, else I will cut them off and use them as pens. The dwarf didn't even turn around, just closed the . . . door? Yes, on this side of reality, it *was* a door . . . behind him.

Adam just shook his head. "This is one of those occasions where I'm just going to follow other people's lead," he told Trennus and Kanmi. "I'm so far out of my element, I might as well not be in the same universe anymore."

"Technically, you're *not*, if this is a construct for accessing the Veil," Kanmi told him, sardonically, as they all unlaced their bags.

Adam had decided, after hearing from Sigrun what her wedding outfit was likely to be, that if he was going to break most of the rules, he might as well break *all* of them. As such, he'd brought with him the full formal uniform of an officer in the Praetorian Guard. In the JDF, as a member of a foreign levy to the legions, Adam's dress uniform had consisted of a black hat with a red Roman Eagle and a Star of David counterpoised beside each other, and a red cockade to remind people of the old helmet crests, matched with khaki-colored pants and tunic and a black cloak, all of stiff gabardine.

The Praetorians themselves rarely wore uniforms anymore. Bodyguards generally needed to fade into the background, except on formal occasions. Livorus generally required them to look like the many fingers in Rome's fist, not like a cadre of Roman elites.

But when the Praetorians needed a full dress uniform, which served to remind people of the might and splendor of the ancient Empire that they served . . . the only acceptable choice was *armor*. The uniform started with an long, sleeveless tunic of undyed wool, to protect the body from the armor itself, and to provide a limited amount of modesty. The ancient Romans had found the breeches worn by the Gauls and Germanic tribes to be *unmanly* on first encountering those other civilizations.

Since Adam had had previous military service, and wasn't a mage, that meant the *lorica segmentata* for him, a steel cuirass of plates welded together, with shoulder protection that allowed for arm movement, but that didn't protect the vital underarm area, which Adam *twitched* at having exposed. There were veins there, and access to the chest cavity, and while he knew, rationally, that he wasn't going to be lifting his arms much—nor wearing this armor for long—it seemed so singularly *useless*. Then again, this armor had been designed for when men fought in phalanxes and marched in columns and lines to do battle.

In his previous military experience, Adam had earned the right to wear *phalera*. Typically, these discs indicating awards for honor, courage, or good conduct, were worn attached to a leather harness worn over the top of the rest of the armor. He had four, total, two in gold for exceptional service, and two silver ones. One of the gold ones had been for the djinn incident, in fact. He had to cinch down the harness tightly to avoid clattering.

His personal armor also included *manicas*—overlapping metal pieces that provided sleeve-like protection to the outsides of his arms—greaves, which protected his shins, and a balteus which held his ceremonial gladius and secured his *pteruges*, the heavy leather strips meant to protect his upper legs.

While Trennus and Kanmi now wore similar outfits, they didn't bother with the *manicas* or the greaves. They both needed to stay mobile. "Comfortable?" Trennus asked, handing Adam his helmet.

Adam shook his head. "No, but comfort really isn't the point." He pulled the helmet on. For an officer, the crest ran transverse, from ear to ear, rather from nose to nape, but it still had a faceguard . . . and because armor hadn't entirely frozen in time in 150 AC, and he *was* an officer, the faceguard could be pulled down, like a visor, concealing his mouth and cheeks, and had a fine, stiff mesh over the eyes, to protect the wearer's sight. "Between the fact that I clank when I walk, and I've got drafts where there really shouldn't be, this isn't feeling like the best idea I've ever had." He shook his head. "How do you *stand* the kilt?"

"I'm used to it. Helpful in summer. I'll admit it gets a bit nippy when you're trying to walk through waist-deep snow." Trennus' grin got him dirty looks from both Kanmi and Adam.

Adam grumbled and adjusted one more strap. "Ridiculous, inefficient armor. If you're going to trap yourself in a shell like this, it should cover *everything* and not limit mobility."

"They relied on the shield a lot more than anything else." Kanmi pointed out. "We have everything? Tren. Ring."

"You ask one more time, and I'm pretending I've forgotten it somewhere." Trennus arched his eyebrows and grinned.

Adam opened the door back onto the panorama that was the entire *universe*, and, just for a moment, wondered what it would be like to be . . . a disembodied consciousness, roaming forever in that vastness. Always with more places to explore and discover. Always voyaging. It stirred him, but it also seemed an incredibly lonely thought.

Someone, likely Dvalin, had set up *chairs* in the middle of the cosmos for everyone, and the dwarf now impatiently beckoned Adam and the others forward and positioned them up at the front, where Sophia already stood, staring around the room in total contentment. "Stand here. Don't move around. And don't *slouch*, either." Adam stole a glance at his parents, to see how they were doing; his mother hadn't even *reacted* to the Praetorian uniform and the lack of a *tallit*. *Good. This means she's in so much shock right now she can't possibly get any worse.*

A single horn sounded in the distance, and when Adam looked up, Tyr One-hand himself had appeared to his right, and Adam had to control the urge to jump. Tyr wasn't dressed in a suit and a fine cloak today. No, today he wore armor of ancient, worn steel, and a black cloak that looked like the night sky around them. Adam could have sworn that there were stars trapped in the fabric. Real, burning, multicolored galaxies, just . . . distant ones.

A worm at the back of Adam's mind reminded him, again, that *his* had been the hand that had ended Tlaloc, and this was a god, too. Though if Tyr objected to Adam's presence in his valkyrie's life, there had been no evidence as yet.

Tyr now lifted his right hand and spoke. *Be welcome. And be at peace. Today is a day of great happiness, though sorrow always follows joy. Remain on your feet, I pray you. This is how one shows respect. By standing upright and tall, and by showing one's heart and hands.* In the audience, Ivarr struggled to stand before one of his gods, though Medea was clearly trying to push him back down into his chair.

Tyr's levinbolt eyes canvassed the crowd, and stopped on Lassair, and the faint, ephemeral form of the hind beside her, that was Trennus' other bound spirit. Adam could feel Trennus tensing beside him . . . and then something seemed to pass between the god and the spirits, and Tyr actually inclined his head in respect.

The god gestured, and the horn sounded again, and at the back of the hall, a door opened. Light streamed into the universe, as if a floodgate had been opened, and two figures entered. One was Livorus, dressed in his Senatorial toga, and looking oddly prosaic as his sandaled feet caused meteors and comets to skitter out of his path. The other was, of course, Sigrun. Today, she'd chosen to show what she was: a battle-maiden of Valhalla. As such, she hovered above the starry floor, not disturbing the universe an iota. She wore a cloak of white swan feathers that actually trailed the ground behind her, and was pulled up over her head like a cowl, though her copper-tinged hair hung free under it. And she wore armor. Not her old chainmail, but a shining cuirass, bracers, and greaves over her tall boots. Light poured from her rune-marks, and she looked ethereal as she hovered beside Livorus, one hand on his elbow, the other hand gripping, not flowers, but a spear. Adam could suddenly envision her hovering over some ancient battlefield, the last sight some fallen soldier would ever see.

Livorus, as calmly as if he were at some political function, took her hand from his arm and handed her over, gently, so that Adam could clasp her fingers. Sigrun allowed her feet to touch down, and Adam reached forward with his free hand, pushing the hood back from her face, to reveal a band of flowers woven through her loose hair.

For her part, Sigrun remembered, later, only a handful of things about the moments leading up to the wedding. For her, the hall was, as it always had been: a vast and limitless sky, with clouds scudding here and there. No ground below. Just light pouring down from above, and endless canyon walls of thunderstorms intermixed with warm, uplifting thermals. A paradise for birds, or anyone else who loved to fly. She heard Livorus cautioning Adam, softly, "Treat her right, or you'll answer to me," and Adam's quiet reply of, "I'll always try, sir."

And then, just for a moment, Tyr's eyes filled her entire world. *You are sure, daughter?*

Yes.

You will know sorrow. I will not conceal this from you. You will watch him die, slowly, day by day, as he ages, and you do not.

I do not doubt, that when he dies, I will follow him not long after.

The future is unclear, and the road of wyrd ahead is troubled. Take joy while you can, daughter, and receive my blessing with it.

Then, vows. Simple ones. To cherish one another, to treat one another with respect and courtesy, to protect and defend one another, and to live together as long love should live. As Tyr bound their hands with a silver cord, Adam leaned in to kiss her, and Sigrun saw, through her closed eyelids, the flash of a camera. *Dvalin is going to fuss . . . .*

The formal pictures were all taken downstairs, at the reception. Adam sheepishly taking off his helmet and leaning his head against hers for the picture that she knew she'd be carrying in a locket or a watchcase for the rest of her life. Trennus and Lassair were caught with them in another. All four lictors, Livorus, Kanmi's children, and Lassair in another. Ehecatl and his family joining for another work-related image after that. Then one of Sigrun and her family, her sister beside her, staring off into the distance at something invisible to everyone else, some fancy inside her own mind. "So, sister," Sigrun challenged her directly, before dinner was served in the main reception hall. "So much for your prophecies. I am married, and you said I would never be wed." Sigrun was happy, and she wanted to use this moment. She could batter down the visions that locked Sophia away from the real world. "You've said since you were ten years old, that you saw me, never married, but beloved of a man who was both young enough to be my son and old enough to be my grandfather at the same time . . . carrying a child under my heart, a spear in my hand, and a raven on my shoulder, with death in my eyes and the world in flames behind me." Another faint smile. "I'm married now, Sophia."

"Ask his family how married you are," Sophia replied, dreamily. "Ask them in a month, or a year, when time has dulled the wonder. Ask his mother. Ask his brother. Ask the rest of his people."

"You hang a lot on *interpretation*, Sophia. I defy your iron-clad, predestinate fate. There is only *wyrd*." Sigrun leaned in over Sophia's shoulder, trying to shake her certainty. Just enough so that Sophia might let *doubt* into her life. She'd be healthier for it.

"You walk the path that you were always going to walk, and with the people you were always going to walk it with." Sophia reached up and patted Sigrun's cheek lightly.

"But my choices on that path are my own. It is my decision how to meet every turn in that path." Sigrun bared her teeth in a smile. "According to Kanmi over there, there is a new theory called quantum physics. It holds that everything that can happen, *does* happen. And that for every choice we make, the universe shatters, and a new one is formed."

"You make the choices that, in *this* universe, you were always going to make, Sigrun. Because you couldn't be you, and not make those choices." The dreamy tone never wavered. "Everything is happening exactly as I have seen it happen, Sigrun. Oh, and duck."

Sigrun blinked, looked up, and flinched as a tall waiter walked by, balancing a tray full of drinks. She dodged, but one cup fell anyway, and splashed white wine all over her swan cloak and the front of her armor, even dampening the white shirt that peeked out under the cuirass. "I'm terribly sorry," the waiter told her, and caught up a towel out of seemingly nowhere to dab at her cloak. "I thought I had it, and then I didn't. Can you ever forgive me?" He kept dabbing ineffectually at her, and Sigrun felt oddly cold. She rarely felt extremes of temperature besides the heat, but for some reason, the chill of the wine seeped right into her.

"It is of no moment," she told the waiter, staring at his face.

Nondescript. He could have been Burgundian, or Frisian. Pale hair, watery blue eyes, and a fussy demeanor. "Please, do not trouble yourself any further."

The waiter took his tray and fled, babbling profuse apologies as he backed away. Adam reached Sigrun's side moments later, directing a hard stare after the man. "Are you all right?"

"Perfectly, yes." Sigrun shook her head. "A good thing I did not wear silken finery today, yes?"

She turned to look at Sophia, to make a joke about the ineffectiveness of a prophecy that couldn't be issued in time to be avoided . . . and was stunned to see tears in her sister's eyes, just before Sophia excused herself from the reception.

Shaking off the chill, Sigrun ensured that she and Adam spoke with every guest before they departed. Quite a number of her teachers from over her years in the Odinhall at least dropped by to give her their well-wishes. After the fourth or fifth batch of bear-warriors gripped his wrist firmly, Adam was puzzled. He couldn't understand the look of sympathy, even sorrow in their eyes, each time they did so, or gave Sigrun an embrace. And as Erikir clasped his wrist, Adam overheard Brandr telling Sigrun, embracing her, *"We'll be here when you need us."*

"What's that supposed to mean?" Sigrun asked her old mentor, smiling a little.

"Just what I said. We're all here for you. Just know that." Brandr turned, clasped Adam's wrist, and then left with Erikir and a few other god-born, leaving Adam to furrow his brow in confusion. There had been no blame or accusation in the man's eyes. Just sorrow.

Adam cleared his throat. "Ah, I wasn't expecting so many god-born to drop by," he said, to cover the awkward moment.

Sigrun looked down. "It's not often that a valkyrie weds," she admitted. "There aren't many of us."

At that point, Frittigil and her family circled around to speak with them. "Thank you so much for allowing me to attend," Fritti said, shyly offering each of them a hug. Sigrun could see in Adam's face how deeply moved he was that the girl actually embraced him, when, the last time he'd seen her, two years ago, she'd cringed away from even a light hand's touch.

"I'm just glad you're here," Adam told her, patting her back a little before she let go. "You're blooming."

Fritti was, too. She was god-touched of Baldur and the Evening Star, and it showed. No scars anymore, and no rune-marks on her skin. Just health and roses in her cheeks, and her eyes still sparkled, quite literally, like stars. Straight-backed and shouldered now, no more fear in her as she chattered at them both, eagerly about how she thought that her job might be to become a bridge of sorts between Nova Germania and all the smaller kingdoms that shared the continent with them and Novo Gaul. "You know, I thought I saw the bear-warrior who's been mentoring me this year, but when I turned to look for him, he was gone." Fritti danced a little in place. "I didn't think he was going to be here today." She flushed a little. "He's taught me so much, Sigrun."

"Unfold a little of this man's wisdom to me," Sigrun told her, humoring the girl.

"He told me that god-born haven't been born in such numbers as are being born today, for over a thousand years, and that it means that a great war must be coming, and that we all must be ready. And that I was to remember that none of the gods truly wishes Ragnarok to happen. There is no victory, in Ragnarok, he said. Only destruction."

Sigrun blinked. That was a highly unusual statement. "What did you say his name was? I might have seen him here already."

"Radulfr Ecgwine."

Her mind raced. The name meant, *wise-counsel wolf* and *blade-friend.* And something about the name pinged at Sigrun's senses. "I don't know anyone by that name," Sigrun murmured. There were somewhere around twenty-five thousand god-born of Valhalla, all told, spread out between two continents. It was a very small community, smaller than that of the Praetorian Guard. "You're certain that the Odinhall sent him?"

Fritti's eyes had gone wide. "Oh yes," she said, and her parents both nodded, emphatically. "He healed, just as you do, whenever I actually managed to mark him in practice. I never saw him rage, though."

"You would not," Sigrun replied, automatically. "They're trained not to do so, except at great need." She looked around. "You say you thought you saw him?"

"Yes. He was over seven feet tall. They, well . . ." Fritti blushed. Crimson. Clearly, the girl had a bit of a crush on her mentor. "They stand out. But when I looked again, he was gone, as I said."

Adam took Sigrun's elbow in his hand. "A puzzle for another time?" he suggested. "Can anything really go wrong here?"

Yes. Much. But I will not think on it for now. Today is our wedding day, after all.

Ianuarius 11, 1957 AC

Trennus tossed his bags into the back of Adam's car at the airport, and flung his cloak in, with it. "I think I'm actually getting used to the mild winters down here."

Adam snorted. "Where's your lady?"

"She de-manifested for the flight, as usual. Saves money on plane fares." Trennus looked around. *Lassair?*

I'll re-manifest once you're in the car. People tend to stare when I appear out of nowhere.

People stare at you no matter what. His thought was fond. *That's what you get for being noticeable.*

Adam, naturally, had missed the by-play. "It has nothing to do with the possibility that you might break her fingers on takeoff?"

"Hah. No, I try to behave in a more manly fashion when she's around. I keep the gibbering terror to a minimum."

"Trennus . . . I don't know how to break it to you, but she's always around. She's a *spirit.*"

Trennus grinned at him and ducked into the car, hunkering down so his head wouldn't hit the roof. The compact Hellene vehicle that the Praetorians had allocated Adam really didn't suit Trennus' frame. "How's the pilot training going, anyway?"

"Eh, slowly. I can only do it on weekends, so I don't even have two hundred hours in yet. Sig refuses to get into the plane with me and the instructor. It's just a little two-prop trainer, so she follows us around, and my instructor, on seeing her, does a lot of very fervent praying to Apollo, Mercury, Jupiter . . . anyone who might be listening, apparently." Adam got in the driver's seat. "How was Londonium? And your family?"

Trennus scratched vigorously at his hair . . . and felt soft hands come in from behind to rub at his shoulders a little as Lassair manifested in the back seat. "Londonium, wonderful. Good to see a lot of old colleagues again. My family . . ." Trennus chuckled ruefully.

"Didn't go so well?"

"Went out hunting with my father and brothers. Got Saraid her deer for the year. It was good." Trennus grimaced. "Then I told them that I had to tell them something important, and introduce them to someone very dear to me."

Adam pulled out into traffic, and headed for downtown Rome. "And?"

"They thought I was going to tell them I was seeing a Hellene man, apparently." Trennus had just about punched one of his brothers — Riacus, the second-eldest — for that particular comment. "I'm not entirely sure what gave them that impression. I took a number of girls to the midsummer fires when I was younger." He was still annoyed about that.

"Probably a little of Kanmi's problem with his brothers. They don't see him hauling in nets and lines, therefore, he's not a man. You work with books and live in a world of spirits. Therefore . . . ." Adam shrugged. "So, once they met Lassair, that was straightened out?"

Not as well as you might think. I made a point of looking very female for them so that they would understand a little better. Lassair sounded disappointed. *The word succubus was used.*

Adam almost swerved into oncoming traffic as he began to laugh. "It's not really funny," Trennus said, tapping his knuckles against the glass of the window in annoyance. "Even worse was my *eldest* brother — that's Vindiorix, if you don't remember — asking if it wasn't just advanced masturbation, and if I mightn't consider shagging a sheep, since it was clearly less shameful than *selling my soul* for sex." Trennus set his teeth a little at the recollection. His large and very noisy family put Adam's to shame, as far as he was concerned. His eldest brother was ten years his elder, thirty-eight now, pushing thirty-nine, and Vindiorix had three children. The eldest of whom, a son, was just about to turn seventeen. Between Vindorix's wife and three children, Riacus' wife and three children, Catuarus and his wife and their *four* children, and Cor and his wife's three children, it had put at least twenty-three people in the great hall of his father's manor, seated at three different tables, and that was *before* counting the guards and the servants trying to bring in the next course for the banquet in honor of Sol Invictus. Trennus' mother, Marina, was Roman, and a Mithraist by conviction, while the rest of her family paid homage to the Gallic gods. It made the winter solstice holidays last a little longer.

Adam swerved again. "Should I be pulling over?" he asked, mildly. "You have any confessions you'd like to make, like, oh, beating your various brothers into a fine paste?"

"It did take the three other ones to pull me off of Vindiorix," Trennus admitted. "Admittedly, after I gave him two black eyes, loosened his teeth, and slammed a knee into his stomach three or four times, he did admit that he *might* have been over the line." He paused, and went on, resignedly, "And in the meantime, Cor's wife was grabbing her youngest—he's all of three—off the floor and getting the others to the doorway, because we'd just rolled into the damned table, and Vin's oldest son was evidently trying to figure out if he should get into the fight, and Catu was telling him to stay the *fuck* out of it . . . gods. What a mess." He gave Adam a look. "Your family in Judea seems nice and peaceful. What I wouldn't give for a couple of *sisters*."

Adam chuckled. "I'm sure your parents were saying much the same thing."

Trennus looked up at the roof of the motorcar. "My father did suggest that I might not want to settle arguments with the heir to the kingdom in quite that way again. Then again, the family guardsmen were all standing around making bets. They knew better than to get into the middle of a fight between brothers."

"You Picts don't treat your kings with the same kind of reverence as Rome treats emperors."

"Gods, no. You don't get to be king unless you've earned it. And all the nobles get a vote in which member of the king's line rules next. If you'd be king, you'd best be stronger and smarter than everyone else, or at least be able to talk them around to your way of thinking. Vin just forgot I learned how to fight from the same master-at-arms who taught the rest of them . . . and I've learned a few nasty tricks since then." Tren suddenly grinned, tightly. "Used a few of the things you've shown me. He hadn't seen those before."

"So, no charges pending . . . ?" Adam asked.

"No. Vin apologized and ate pottage for a week. Riacus made a couple more comments, but the others fell into line once Vin did. Then it was just working it out with Mother and Father that yes, I'm quite serious, no, don't expect any grandchildren, and so on." Trennus hesitated. His father had said something else. Something he hadn't yet shared with Lassair.

"Son, you saw the white hind when you were a child, didn't you?"

"I did. I thought none of you believed me."

"Your brothers thought you were making it up. The fact that you became a ley-mage and a summoner long ago suggested to me that you probably <u>did</u> see

her." His father had settled back behind his desk, studying Trennus calmly. *"Seeing the spirit of our woods is supposed to mark you out for greatness. Are you really sure that you're doing what you're meant to be doing?"*

"I'm happy as a Praetorian. And the hind wasn't the only spirit I saw, you know. I could always see the house-spirits and all the others. I just didn't realize that not everyone could."

His father had shaken his head. *"That's not what I meant, son. Are you sure about the path that you're on? The choices you're making, and the people with whom you're choosing to share your life?"*

If his father had a specific meaning in mind, Trennus couldn't see it. *"If I were going astray,"* he finally said, *"the spirit of the forest would tell me, I think."*

And there the subject had been left, for the time being.

In the here and now, Tren spotted Adam's sidelong glance, but didn't know what to make of it . . . and forgot about it, and the conversation with his father, as Lassair offered, *I thought that if I got involved, it would largely make matters worse, but I do have to admit to telling Riacus that his youngest son's paternity might be in question.* Lassair's tone was annoyed. Trennus winced. It had been *wicked*, but Lassair wouldn't have involved Riacus' wife if it hadn't been *true*. There had been . . . quite a bit of familial arguing about that.

Trennus leaned back against the headrest, trying to put Britannia out of his head. "So, what's new, here?"

"A great deal, as of today. You missed it, being in the air." Adam grimaced. "You know how Antiochus XII and Pharnaces had banded together for common cause against their brother, Mithridates?"

"I caught that that one opportunistic general . . . Jamshid-something . . . threw his weight behind Antiochus last week, yes." Trennus could keep up with the names of famous Chaldean and Median Magi and *arcessitors*, but modern politicians and generals gave him fits.

"Artaphernes," Adam supplied. "It's a marriage of convenience. Antiochus was winning, and Artaphernes wants to back a winner. Mithridates was older, but he'd angered most of his father's generals in the last year." Adam turned off the main highway, and into the side-streets. "Antiochus paraded his brother in chains through the streets of Persepolis yesterday. He'll be tried for, get this, high treason, probably in the next month. And today . . . ."

Trennus shook his head, staring at the nighttime lights of Rome. "I'm not going to like hearing this, am I?"

"I didn't. Antiochus entered talks with the Mongolian Khanate aimed at ending their long-standing border disputes and securing an alliance with them against Rome." Adam pulled into the parking lot of Trennus' apartment complex. "Livorus says the Khanate will want to be sure Antiochus has legitimacy — or at least, a firm grip on power — before they'll agree to anything. That gives us . . . six, maybe nine months before we revisit the War of the Caspian Sea and the Caspian Crisis and everything else."

"We're due. It's been almost exactly a hundred years since the last war in that area." Trennus' voice was glum. The Caspian Crisis had lasted from 1855 until 1860, and the War of the Caspian Sea had lasted from 1753 until 1763. Each had been a nasty four-way battle in which alliances had rapidly shifted as every side looked for advantages. "I take it we're leaving for Kiev in the morning?"

"Good call. Yes, yes we are. Them and a couple of the smaller northern kingdoms of Europa and Slavic nations." Adam unlocked the doors. "Welcome back, Tren, Lassair."

"Never a dull moment," Trennus said, and got his bags out of the back. "Good thing I already packed for snow, eh?"

At least it will be a new place, Lassair said, slipping out after him. *Though I do not look forward to the snow at all.* She slipped a hand into his arm. *Do you think there is any way in which I could help the one to whom you are bound?*

"I'm not sure. Do you want me to talk to Livorus about it?"

Perhaps. I feel that I should be doing more, somehow.

"Hmm. Something to think about. What do you *want* to be doing?"

I do not know. Making people healthier. Happier. There is a young man in this building, for example, who would make an excellent mate for a young woman who often walks by.

"You . . . want to play matchmaker?" Trennus got inside the front door, and headed up the stairs, his bags over his shoulder, and trying not to laugh. "For people to whom you've never spoken?"

Oh, I have spoken to them. Once in a while. But they have very similar souls. They resonate at the same frequency. Lassair tipped her head to the side as Trennus unlocked the front door and dismissed the spirits he'd set to watching over the apartment in their absence. *Some people have truly beautiful souls. Like you, Emberstone, Godslayer, and Stormborn. I love each of you. I want to see each of you* happy. *Most other people are . . . various shades of gray. They do not stand out. They do not have strong voices. But these two? They both shine pale green. They would be good for each other.* Lassair nodded. *Unfortunately, that will simply have to wait until we return.*

Trennus reached back, and took her hand to lead her into the cold and musty apartment. "I'm having trouble reconciling the idea of global politics and matchmaking," he told her, smiling.

In the old days, and even today, in some places, the two are very much aligned, Lassair reminded him, with a pert smile. *I just want to see people happy. In every way I can manage it.*

It's a good goal. A noble one. But impossible. Trennus closed the door behind her, and wrapped his arms around Lassair.

Never set your sights on anything lower than the sky, she told him, chidingly, and snuggled into him. *You need to sleep, Flamesower. You never sleep when we travel through the sky in the metal machines.*

Tomorrow might be the exception.

October 11, 1957 AC

The Persians and the Mongols formalized their border agreements and their mutual defense pact on October 11. Rome and Raccia had formalized a mutual defense pact two days previously. Kanmi couldn't actually count how many flights he'd taken in the past ten months, but he'd guess the number stood at over forty. Livorus and his lictors had spent at least half of every month outside of Rome proper, the propraetor being the Imperator's clear choice as a diplomatic envoy. The size of Livorus' entourage of lictors had been doubled, in the wake of significant threats against the propraetor; he was gaining a reputation, inside and outside of Rome, as Caesarion IX's right hand. The erstwhile governor of Nahautl, Dioscuri, had gone before the Senate to denounce Livorus as the *cause* of the tensions between Rome and Persia. The man was attempting to rebuild his credibility after having lost the governorship, mainly on imputations that his wife had been involved with the high priest Tototl's schemes. There had been no proof of this, and Livorus had never made any accusations against either Dioscuri or his wife, but the propraetor had never spoken in their defense, either. That explained some of the bad feelings.

Kanmi, for his own part, had spent whatever time he'd had in the past nine months when not on duty, absorbed in two major projects. First, he'd established and maintained contact with Lady Erida Lelayn, the Chaldean envoy they'd encountered in Judea. Their correspondence had begun in a fairly formal vein, with Kanmi requesting permission to study Chaldean mysteries. Erida had not been able to secure him passage into Chaldea at the time, and Kanmi couldn't take a leave of absence to enroll in one of the Magi academies . . . but the lady had, very generously, begun sending him books and scrolls, for which Kanmi, in exchange, sent books on technomancy. It was a scholarly and engaging relationship conducted exclusively by letter, and Kanmi enjoyed it, immensely. He was learning to understand the 'traditional' schools of sorcery better, and in so doing, he was learning how to counter them.

The other major project that took up his time was his continuing research into the Source Initiative. Kanmi remained convinced that Gratian Xicohtencatl's contacts with this professional group of sorcerers, ley-mages, and technomancers had had some kind of connection to his work in Nahautl. But tracing the backgrounds of every member of the group was time-consuming, and required extensive correspondence with *gardia* offices in most of the subject nations and provinces of the Empire, and even several nations abroad. Kanmi now had correspondence coming in from Qin, Nippon, Hellas, Egypt, and Chaldea and Media, almost daily, most of which he kept in his desk. Locked, and warded against intrusion.

At the moment, however, he was engaged in a far less agreeable activity. Himi and Bodi were at home, with their pedagogue, and Kanmi and Bastet were sitting in the office of Ankha, a priestess of Isis. Kanmi would have preferred to have gone to a priestess of Tanit, the Carthaginian maiden goddess of fertility, or even a priestess of matronly Juno. But he had been taking pains to compromise with Bastet, and she'd chosen to have their meetings at the temple of Isis, part of the faith shared by Egypt and Nubia.

The office had hieroglyphics and two-dimensional drawings painted on every wall, and a rather sad and light-deprived potted palm drooped in one corner. Kanmi sat, straight-backed on one end of the small, padded bench, while Bastet, her back stiff, perched at the other, and the priestess rested, cross-legged, on a footstool in front of them. "It's good to see you again, Kanmi," the priestess said, smiling. Her eyes were dark, and kohl-lined, and she wore a wig, neatly braided, but ever-so-slightly askew. Kanmi *itched* to point that out, but kept his mouth shut. "You've missed our last three sessions, but Bastet and I have had some very good conversations. Today, I think it's your turn to talk."

Kanmi shrugged and examined his fingernails. "I don't really have anything to discuss," he said. This wasn't entirely true. It was just that he'd already made the decisions he needed to make, and while informing Bastet of them was probably good manners, it wasn't something he would consider a discussion. But perhaps it would be easier with an outsider present. It might at least keep things civil.

"Oh, come now, that's not good," Ankha told him, shaking her head. "Don't think I haven't noticed that every time we all manage to sit down to talk, you nod your head and listen, but don't contribute much. This is as much your time as Bastet's. You're paying for my time, as well. And I can't very well advise one of you, and not *both* of you."

Kanmi raised his eyes, and met the priestess', steadfastly. "This entire set of meetings *is* a waste of time and coin," he said, calmly. He didn't shout. Didn't snap.

"And what makes you say that? You don't think counseling is an effective means of fixing what's gone wrong in a relationship?"

Kanmi shrugged. "Oh, I have no doubt that it can be. But counseling and advice are only effective when the people involved tell you what the problem really is. But every time I sit here and listen, I hear nothing but lies."

Bastet bristled. "In what fashion have I lied?" she demanded. "Name me an untruth that I've spoken!"

Kanmi sighed. "All right. A misrepresentation, then, if not a lie." He studied his nails again. "Bastet has said, over and over again, that the biggest problem in our marriage is my job. However, other than the first year of our marriage, in which we were both still in school? I've held this job, or others, exactly like it. Actually, the first four years, I was on the Mongolian border, in the heart of the disputed territory north of the Caspian Sea, and only came home intermittently on leave once or twice a year. Thus, I'm actually home *more* now, than I was at the time." Kanmi raised his head, but didn't look at Bastet. "The problem isn't my job. The problem is, Bastet woke up one morning and realized she didn't like who I was."

The priestess opened her mouth to respond, and Bastet spluttered, "That's not true, Kanmi!"

"No? All this came to a head in Judea when you suddenly realized that I'm not a tech, but a bodyguard, sorcerer, investigator, and more." Kanmi still didn't look at Bastet. It hurt too much. He focused on the priestess instead, and went on in that self-same, cool, clinical manner, "Working on the issue of my job won't make the other issue go away. My changing my job won't change who I am, other than to make me angry at having to give up something I'm damned good at, and where people are relying on me to be there."

"I need you to be there, too!" Bastet snapped out.

Kanmi looked at the priestess. "You said this was my time to talk. Is it?"

"It is, actually. Bastet, could you hold those questions until later? I promise, you'll have a chance to respond." The priestess' tone was unruffled, but Kanmi could read her eyes. She wasn't quite sure what to say to him. He'd deviated from the script. He was a little too self-aware for typical counseling techniques to work on him. He'd already asked himself all the questions she could throw at him. And already found the answers, unpalatable though they were.

Kanmi nodded to her, however, in thanks. It did help to have her there to prevent his thoughts from being derailed. "There are only a few ways out of the current situation that I can see. I can change who I am to please her, except that *never* works. Changing who you are destroys the balance of power, and inevitably destroys your own self-respect, let alone the respect that should exist between both people." He looked into the mid-distance. "She can change her *opinion* of me, which she's manifestly done before. Or, we can separate." He looked at Bastet directly for the first time. "In any event, it would be helpful if she'd stop wasting everyone's time and our money by actually discussing the real issue, instead of the imaginary one. The job has nothing to do with it."

"The job has everything to do with it! You're not *here* for us. You're not here for the boys, and it's bad for them."

Kanmi sighed. "Ground we've already covered, Bastet. You have forty-hour shifts at the hospital. You come home in the middle of the night, go to sleep, and you might see Himi for five minutes before the pedagogue takes him to school."

"I will not apologize for my job—"

"Then why should I?" Kanmi's riposte was fast, and the closest he'd come to raising his voice the entire time.

Bastet's mouth snapped shut, and she looked at Ankha in mute appeal. The priestess, however, simply raised her eyebrows and straightened her curling wig with a fingertip. "That is a fair question," she acknowledged. "Do you have an answer for it, Bastet?"

Kanmi watched his wife fume. Clearly, this was not going as she'd expected. The priestess was supposed to be her ally and supporter, present to browbeat Kanmi into going along with her. Ankha, however, was doing her job as an arbiter fairly well. "I save lives in my job," Bastet finally grumbled.

"You know what? So do I," Kanmi replied, still in that same calm tone. "Again, ground we've gone over before. The biggest difference between you and me, Bastet, is that you're using the children to try to blackmail me into doing what you want, whereas I have always accepted you for who you are. But I'm not going to go along with you on this, and I don't give in to blackmail and hostage-taking." His eyes narrowed.

"That's a little dramatic," Ankha warned.

"Perhaps, but it's only a matter of degree," Kanmi said, folding his arms over his chest.

The priestess nodded, and turned to Bastet. "Do you have anything you'd like to add? I know you've told me, but you may not have told your husband, that you worry for him every time he leaves. That you'd prefer it if he took a *safer* job." Ankha raised her eyebrows. "Does it help, Kanmi, to know that some of this is born out of love for you?"

Kanmi shrugged. If it was born out of love, it didn't *feel* like it. He'd always liked being married. He hadn't felt 'shackled' by it, as so many men he'd served with had complained about in his younger days. He had little use for men who went out drinking with friends, rather than going home at the end of their day's work. He'd have a drink when on the road, certainly, but when he was home . . . he was home. No matter that, of late, it felt like thorns had sprouted from every surface in the house, and every thorn was fashioned of Bastet's anger. He tried to express some of this, and knew he'd failed when Bastet snapped out, "Even when you're here, you're not really *here*."

"I play with the boys every night that I'm home. I help *cook*, which is a good deal more than my own father ever did." Kanmi realized how annoyed he was solely by the fact that he was involuntarily doing his deep-breathing exercises, the ones he used to clear his mind for spell-casting in combat. "I'm not entirely sure how much more *here* I can be.'

"Yes, and every night, after the boys are in bed, you go to your desk and you write letters or study your tomes, or whatever else." Bastet folded her own arms now, mimicking Kanmi's own posture. "Would you like to tell me who *Erida* is?"

She said it in a tone that suggested she fully expected, and would be vindicated, by a guilty reaction on his part. Kanmi, for his part, simply looked at her steadily for a moment. "I was wondering when you were going to bring that up. You see, my correspondence is largely classified. As such, my desk is locked. And warded. Anyone who opens it, say, with a hairpin? Sets off an alarm. When you opened it last week to go through my papers, I had to have the entire damned place dusted for fingerprints, and when the people at the office determined that the only prints in the place were yours, mine, the boys', and the pedagogue's, and the pedagogue had had the day off, and you'd been home that day . . ." Kanmi spread his hands, "I had to talk several Praetorians out of bringing you up on charges of tampering with classified materials, which carries the potential penalty of forced servitude, in Rome." Slavery still existed in many forms, inside of Rome and out of it. It kept the prison-population down.

The priestess raised a hand to her face, and gently rubbed at the inner corners of her eyes, pinching the bridge of her nose. "And the name Erida?" she prompted, even as Bastet glared at Kanmi, her chin lifted.

"Lady Erida Lelayn is a Chaldean noblewoman and a noted member of the Magi. If Bastet had read much of the letters, she would surely have noticed that we talk about magic almost exclusively."

"She said she was wounded to the quick, her heart was sore, and that she still ached for the touch of a loving hand in the night," Bastet snapped out.

Kanmi laughed. He couldn't help it. Bastet had made her disinterest in carnal relations clear for over eighteen months now. For her to be *jealous* was amusing, but he knew this wasn't it. It was wounded pride . . . and a search for leverage. For a way in which he was in the wrong, unequivocally. "Yes. You see, she had to kill her last lover. It's put her off relationships, but she sometimes finds it useful to talk to someone whom she knows wouldn't willingly reveal her words to anyone else. Someone who's trustworthy." Kanmi stared Bastet down, and she looked away, clearly confused and torn. He looked back at the priestess of Isis now. "So, at the present time, I have a wife whom I cannot trust with classified documents in the house." His letters to Erida weren't *classified*, as such, but everything on the Source Initiative *was*, and a good deal of what Erida talked about, in regards to her former lover, Abgar, was decidedly . . . sensitive. "She refuses to admit that the real issue is that she simply doesn't love me anymore, but thinks that reshaping me, like a potter molds clay, will make the difference. It won't, and I won't be reshaped. So yes. These sessions are a waste of everyone's time. But I thank you for yours, priestess." He looked at Bastet. It *hurt*, because he could still see the girl she'd been when he'd married her. "Bastet, I've put a lot of thought into this over the past months. We got married in Hellas because . . . we were both foreigners there. Both out of place, and lonely, and something about it *worked*. But I'm not who I was then, and neither are you. I took out a lease on a different apartment this morning." He paused. "Tomorrow, I'll hire a new pedagogue for the boys, they'll come to stay with me, and I'll remove my name from your apartment's lease."

Each word was hard to say, as if he were nailing down the lid of a sarcophagus, and he watched Bastet's eyes go wide in shock and horror. "No! You can't take the boys away!"

"I think you'll find that that is not true," Kanmi told her, as gently as he could. "This is Rome. Roman law is quite specific. The father has primary custody rights to all offspring in divorces and separations. They do not acknowledge that the mother has any more natural bond with the children than the father does. This is our primary residence, and I will be pursuing divorce proceedings here."

Bastet was now, clearly, back on her heels. "But they're *my* children."

"And they're mine, too. But you're the one trying to use them as leverage." Kanmi kept his eyes locked on the pathetic potted palm in the corner of the room, and did his best not to set it on fire with his rage. Deep, even breaths. Spreading calm to every part of his body.

"They'll be better off with me. With you, they'll just be with a pedagogue all the time, while you're off jaunting around the world!"

"That will be for the divorce lawyers and the judge to argue, but I believe we have covered, extensively, that their situation will not noticeably change." Kanmi's eyes were narrow. "But that being said? A pedagogue can travel. You can't. If it comes right down to it? I can have them travel *with* me and ensure their education along the way. They might not get a Roman public school education, but they'll see the world, and a good pedagogue will ensure that they don't miss a single lesson." Kanmi's eyes glittered. "You see, you've given me a lot of time to think about this situation, and come to decisions. And I realized that the conclusions were all inevitable, and that waiting longer to make the decisions was worse than simply taking steps."

He stood, and bowed his head to the priestess of Isis. "I'm going to head back to the apartment now. Thank you for the use of your office while we discussed these matters. I'll pack up my books and clothing tonight, and have the boys moved out by noon."

"No!" Bastet's voice was a wail, and the pain there almost made his will break. Almost. "Please, Kanmi, husband, *no*. Don't take my whole life away at once."

At the door, Kanmi turned and looked back at her, his face bleak. "And what have you been trying to do to me?" he asked her, bluntly. "You wanted to make me choose. The job, or the boys and you. I've chosen. The job and the boys. But not you."

Roman courts required a couple to be separated for a year before divorce could be filed, in cases that did not involve adultery or infertility. As such, Kanmi spent the next year, as war in the east heated up, traveling, more often than not, with his sons and a new pedagogue in tow. He'd deliberately picked an older woman, in her sixties, to quell any suspicions on anyone's part that adultery was going on . . . and he hadn't quite trusted the other pedagogue. She had, after all, allowed Himi to get hurt. And because Bastet had hired her, Kanmi reckoned that the woman's loyalty would be to his wife, not the boys.

Bastet pleaded, through the courts, for visitation rights to her sons, and Kanmi acceded. He didn't see a way out of this situation that didn't end in divorce, but he wasn't going to be cruel; he wanted his sons to be able to see their mother, whom they loved, as often as possible. He even agreed to continue to meet with her and the priestess of Isis, but he truly did not see how the differences could be reconciled. Bastet was apologetic in those meetings, pleaded that she could change . . . and Kanmi inevitably, was the one who shook his head. "And in a year, we'll be back in the same position again," he told her, simply. "The answer isn't for one or the other of us to change. We've already changed. No one ever changes *back*. That's regression, not progression."

However, when Bastet packed the boys up and tried to flee to Egypt, a month shy of their court date, in September of 1958, all bets for Kanmi were off. He pulled every string the Praetorians had, and Bastet and the boys were caught in Sicily, boarding a ship for Egypt, one that had smuggling connections. "And what did you *think* was going to happen?" Kanmi asked her, grimly, when the *gardia* had her in an interrogation room. "Did you think that the smugglers would help you disappear in Egypt under new names? Or did you think that, perhaps, the boys might be sold as slaves? That *you* might be sold as one, too?"

Bastet gave him a searingly angry glance. "I had to do something. They are my *sons*."

Magic crackled in the air around Kanmi, just for a moment, and he stared at his wife, and realized in that moment, that he had no idea who she was anymore. She'd been someone he'd loved, mostly out of reflex, for years. And there had been lingering sentiment. Sympathy. Unwillingness to give her pain, that had kept him from separating from her, for the many months of counseling and arguing and discussing. And now . . . he no longer cared. Oh, he cared for who she *had* been. He probably always would. He cared that his sons loved her. But for whom she was now? Not a whit.

It was *freeing.* "I allowed you extensive visitation rights," Kanmi said, quietly. "I was going to continue to do precisely that in the divorce settlement. Now, however, all such considerations are off the table. Not to mention the fact that kidnapping is a serious crime. I'm also a Praetorian. That gives it a little more weight. I doubt you'll be sentenced to slavery. You're a doctor, and the courts give that kind of education a certain amount of consideration. But banishment? Oh, that's certainly an option." He stared at her for a long moment, shaking his head. "You're supposed to be smarter than this. You obviously thought it all out. You had an escape plan. Not a good one, but still, you had it all planned. Sink yourself in Egypt, where there are thousands of Nubians, but you wouldn't be back in Nubia itself, and wouldn't have to deal with your family."

He shook his head, and the sick feeling at the pit of his stomach came back. Again, not for what was now, but for what once had been. "Bastet . . . I gave you a way out of that life. I ensured you'd never have to go back to Nubia. My mother cared for Himi and Bodi when you were in your apprenticeship years. My family might not have been perfect, but my mother's help is what let you become a doctor. How did I lose your love?"

Tears fell from her eyes, leaving shining trails along the perfection of her dark skin, but she shook her head, and didn't answer.

Kanmi walked out of the room, closing the door behind him, and exchanged a blank look with the *gardia* officer on the other side. *Maybe, months ago, I shouldn't have ripped the bandage off all at once in the office of the priestess of Isis. Maybe I should have been more gradual. Except, we'd been at this for . . . what, eighteen, nineteen months? Did I create this problem, by my own actions? By some lack of action? Except, what could I have done differently? Should I just have rolled over and let her have her way in everything? And yet, what's to say that, if I let her have custody of the boys to begin with, she wouldn't have done exactly this, anyway? She clearly believes that there's something . . . fundamentally wrong with me.* And that was the part Kanmi didn't understand at all.

Once he'd collected himself, Kanmi went, in turn, to collect his sons, who were confused and frightened, and wanted to know why their mother had promised them a trip to see the Pyramids, why they'd been taken away from their pedagogue and their routine, why the *gardia* had swooped down on them at the docks in Sicily, why they were at the *gardia* station, and what was going to happen to Mama now. *I don't have any good answers*, Kanmi thought, numbly, and just held the boys, tightly. *How do I explain betrayal this deep to children so young?*

And so, on October 24, 1958, Kanmi was handed his divorce decree by a magistrate. He acquired sole custody of his children under Roman law. He was thirty-four, and the single father of two boys, in a job that required extensive travel and was fairly dangerous . . . but that he was not about to give up on.

Part IV: Fire in the Heavens

Caesaria Australis, 1960 AC.

Chapter XV: Seiches

Longboats allowed the first Gothic tribes to cross the Sea of Atlas in 500 AC. They made landfall in the vicinity of what we now term Novo Trier and the Iroquois Confederacy, but the longboats, or _skei_, were impractical for transporting the large numbers of people and supplies that would be required for colonization. And colonization was what Rome had in mind for Caesaria Aquilonis from the first moment the continent was discovered. Here was what looked, at first blush, to be a largely uninhabited wilderness, seemingly as desolate and cold as Germania itself. What better place to send the obstreperous northern tribes, while retaining the fertile land north of the Alps for the use of Rome and her more congenial Gothic and Gallic neighbors?

The Goths, Cimbrics, Frisians, and Burgundians, not to mention the various Gallic tribes who were subjected this wide-scale forced migration took their exile, if not with enthusiasm, at least with resignation. Their _skei_ had originally been designed as vessels of war and for trading missions along coasts and along rivers. The ancestors of these ships had carried the Rus into the area of Kiev, and had allowed any number of Goths to make war on other Goths. The shipwrights kept the oars for emergencies, but added a protective upper deck for the safety and comfort of their women, children, and livestock, as well as a second mast and larger sails, allowing them to run _into_ the wind for the first time in history.

The two-masted _skei_ became the method of choice for crossing the Sea of Atlas for generations, and permitted wide-scale colonization of Caesaria Aquilonis. This was the type of vessel commanded by Leif Dalgaard when he circumnavigated the globe for the first time in 1000 AC, with three other small support vessels in tow. He could not have done so without the advanced maritime technology represented by the twin-mast _skei_.

By 1100 AC, twin-mast _skei_ were a familiar sight in the waters off of Edo, Hong Kong, Shanghai, and Macau, as Gallic, Roman, and Gothic traders all plied the waves, purchasing silks, spices, and exotic foods such as noodles to bring home to the Empire, which was hungry for such riches. In return, the traders brought the exceptional ores and armaments of the West, including Damascus steel, and, in time, books began to pass back and forth along the waves as well.

This period was a turbulent one for Nippon, in which the Kamakura shogunate usurped power from the _kami_-born emperors. Regents from the Fujiwara clan attempted to maintain control, stability, and legitimacy, with some success, during the period of time now referred to as the Heian era. During this period, the Mongols invaded and occupied large portions of Qin and Korea, and the Khanate even attempted to invade Nippon itself.

The _sennin_ (Latin: "immortal" or "transcendent" ones; the term in Nipponese is used to denote sorcerers, ley-mages, summoners, and god-born alike, without regard for specificity) of both Nippon and Korea went so far as to spawn a destructive typhoon in an effort to destroy the Mongol's invasion fleet in 1230 AC. Over 40,000 people were killed at sea in a single day as a result of this magic-spawned storm. The Mongols who survived the storm were subsequently slaughtered when they came ashore by the _bushi_.

Over time, the Fujiwara regents became so inextricably entwined with the

Imperial house through intermarriage that one could not reliably be told from the other. They appreciated and understood the benefits of trade with Rome, and their government has maintained that trade relationship without stint for over nine hundred years.

Today, Nippon seems to represent a land of fascinating contradictions for outsiders. They have a rich tapestry of gods, called kami, all their own, but some segments of their population have embraced the Indian tradition of Buddhism, as well as Taoism, imported from Qin. Roman, Gothic, and Gallic gods have shrines here, but these are largely restricted to dock-area neighborhoods. Edo itself has a small, but thriving Foreigner's Quarter – again, situated near the port. There is a strong tradition of kami-born magic in the Imperial and various shogun families and their schools of sorcery and summoning rival the best of what Hellas, Chaldea, and Persia can offer. But unlike many other nations, they have embraced technology, as well. The University of Edo is one of the foremost schools for engineering and technomancy in the world, rivaling the universities of both Athens and Jerusalem.

– Valentinus Crespus Heronus, The History of Nippon, "Introduction." pp. 8-10.
University of Rome Press, 1949 AC.

<u>Aprilis 7, 1960 AC</u>

Lutetia Parisiorum, or the "Swampy city of the Parisii tribe," straddled the Sequana river in northern Gaul. If a boat followed that river north along its navigable length, it would reach the Channel of Britannia. The area had been occupied by a city since the second century after Caesar's ascension, and much of the downtown area still followed the original Roman street grid. Petty kings of the western Carnutes, the foreign Belgae, and the nearby Senones – who called the river the *Seine*, after a slurred pronunciation of their own tribal name – had periodically risen and fallen under the oversight of Roman governors, and the names of the regions around the city still more or less reflected the old patchwork of tribal affiliations. But the province itself had been a contiguous and united domestic unit of the Roman Empire for over fourteen hundred years.

The bulk of the city's important buildings were on the Left Bank of the Sequana . . . the ancient amphitheater and arena were lit up in preparation for twilight, as games and a play were both underway. A little further from the river, the palace of the governor and the palace of the local kings still bustled as clerks left work for the day, heading home. The University of Lutetia Parisiorum stood somewhat downriver of both, all of its buildings lit up brightly, as the school never slept. The oldest building on the campus had been erected in the eleventh century as a shrine to Apollo, Ogmios, and the Dadga . . . all deities of learning and wisdom. It had been followed by a small shrine to Ceridwyn and Hecate, the goddesses of witchcraft and otherworldly knowledge. As such, the University had always leaned towards arcane knowledge, and had, since 1700 AC, sponsored a yearly conference on ley-magic, ley-engineering, sorcery, technomancy, and summoning. An entire building was cleared out for a week to allow professors, industry experts, and consultants who belonged to a variety of professional groups to mingle, listen to lectures, and attend panels.

Minori Sasaki loved the Lutetia Conference on Magicology, and had attended every year since she'd been a student at the university. Unfortunately for her, she was attaining a reputation among the other attendees as an eccentric. In a crowded and overheated lecture hall, the small woman carefully removed her poster-board graphs from her portfolio and began to set them up on tripods in front of the chalkboards. She could feel dozens of people around her all jostling to clasp wrists and chatter. After twelve years in Gaul, she spoke Gallic fluently, and had already learned Latin and Qin at home in Hokkaido before even leaving for the Imperial Palace in Kyoto. She'd added Hellene during her university education, and a good thing, too—most of her coworkers at Eleutherian Industries were either Gallic or Hellene, and it helped to be able to keep up with them as they chattered.

As such, the stream of syllables behind her rapidly resolved themselves into spiteful clarity.

"Oh, it's Sasaki again? What is this, the third year in row she's going to suggest that overuse of ley-energy is causing . . . what is it, weather-pattern changes?"

"No, ground fault shifts and earthquakes. She's an alarmist."

"I'd say it's womanish hysteria, except her last paper was co-authored by Belator Camulorix. He's pretty senior in the department to be staking his reputation on hysteria." That was someone with a Hellene accent, speaking in Gallic.

"I'd be careful how you throw around the phrase 'womanish hysteria' around here. This is <u>Gaul</u>." There was a Roman accent to that Gallic. Little too much roll on the *r*'s.

Minori didn't turn around, but she pursed her lips a little in annoyance. She'd been studying technomancy for twelve years—since coming to Gaul in 1948, in fact—and it would be nice to have her theories accepted on their own merits, but at least the gap between men and women in the professions was much smaller in Gaul than it was back home. Back in Hokkaido, given her status? She couldn't have *had* a profession. She would have been, by now, either married off to one of her father's political allies, or bound as some samurai's concubine . . . except that when she was twelve, she'd manifested a powerful gift for sorcery. No one in her father's household had known what to do with her, so he had taken her to the Imperial court and had her trained there. Which had left her a sorceress by the age of eighteen, with a gift for engineering and mathematics . . . and no place to *use* it. Because, by an accident of fortune, Minori Sasaki had been born the daughter of a powerful samurai and his official concubine. Becoming involved in trade or a profession would have been inappropriate to her family name.

She finished putting up her charts on the wobbling metal stands, and stepped up beside the podium, her eyes on the ground and her hands clasped in front of her as she waited for her introduction. The skies outside were dark and leaden, so she could see her own reflection in the plate glass windows off to her right. She corrected herself, unconsciously, straightening her back a little, holding her shoulders with better poise and grace. She was small, compared to the various Gauls and Goths in the room, but only a little below the average height of the Roman women scattered through the audience . . . and Minori wore heeled boots to make up the difference on days like these. Her glossy black hair was knotted in a bun at the nape of her neck, and while she wore a kimono-like wrapped jacket over her Gallic-style skirt, both were dove-gray, and thoroughly professional.

The emeritus professor in charge of the panel spoke now in Latin. "Please join us in welcoming Dr Minori Sasaki. Dr. Sasaki received her doctorate from this very university four years ago, and has been working with Eleutherian Industries ever since. Her paper today will discuss the Great Earthquake of Burgundoi in 1950—just ten short years ago. Aftershocks from that massive quake were felt as far away as Edo, and at least one tsunami was spawned as a result of it. Dr. Sasaki, what is your contention?"

"That the quake was not a natural occurrence, but rather the effect of ley-line tampering in Nahautl, possibly caused by industrial use."

Skeptical murmurs from all around. Minori ignored the rustles and the whispers, and began showing her various charts, some of which were maps, and some of which were graphs. She drew equations from memory on the chalkboard at the front of the lecture hall. "This is a record of seismic activity in Nahautl prior to the Great Earthquake," she said, tapping her first graph. "Please note that the lines of the graphed activity precisely mirror the expansion of the ley power-grid into southern Nahautl, and the tapping of several new ley-lines. Every time a new facility was built, there were noticeable temblors that resonated throughout southern Caesaria Aquilonis. In 1950, there was a sudden and very noticeable jump in the fault lines here—measured as a six-inch shift!" Minori pointed on a map to an area north of Tenochtitlan, "and you will also note on the map of the ley-lines that this same area is heavily resonant with ley-energy."

"Isn't that where the Pyramid of the Sun collapsed five years ago?" a voice called out. Gothic accent of some sort, harshening the Latin words.

Minori turned around and looked up into the rows of seats spreading up from the low stage on which she stood at the front of the lecture hall. "It is, yes," she confirmed.

"If I may interrupt with one more question? Wasn't that collapse linked to ley-line disruption of some sort? Why didn't this trigger another massive earthquake?"

The details released at the time had been sketchy, and Minori hadn't been able to obtain much information at all about the incident since it had occurred. The most she'd gotten was that an experimental ley-tap had been positioned in the ruins to take advantage of where the ancients had situated their city—atop an unusual and highly resonant ley-formation. "The amount of energy dispersed, all at once, *did* cause local seismic disturbances, resulting in the destruction of the pyramid." She paused, organizing her thoughts. "The previous intermittent energy discharges in the area can be categorized into two types. Some were sharp spikes, such as the one that I believe caused the major earthquake in Burgundoi, resonating up through the fault lines all along the continent . . . and some were gradual discharges, permeating the environment and re-entering the ley-system." She paused. "Imagining the ley-system as an aquifer is actually a helpful analogy in this case. If the aquifer is saturated, the water *must* go someplace, and it will find the path of least resistance. This will result in uplifts and subsidences at other places in the system, many of which can be very far removed from the original flood-point. And flooding will destabilize the ground around the system." Minori's lips tightened. This was the weakest area in her hypothesis, and she knew it. Energy and water were not entirely analogous. "Now, the energy discharge in 1955 qualifies as a 'spike' and I honestly cannot tell you why a spike in this area resulted in an earthquake so far away the first time, but not the second. I have a few hypotheses. First, the continuous discharge of low-levels of energy may have shifted the system as a whole, as too much water in an aquifer shifts the stone around it, carving new channels, or changing the flow patterns of old ones."

That provoked muttering. Everyone knew that ley-lines moved over time, but it was a very gradual process that took place over thousands of years. Current thinking suggested that this was due to the Earth and Sol drifting through the galaxy, causing cosmic strings to shift, as their position relative to other stars changed. It was difficult to imagine that humans, as small as they were, could have an effect on a system this much larger than they were, themselves. "Another possibility is that in the course of the experimentation at the site, someone developed a buffering process that insulated some of the energy discharge. However, since the entirety of the experiment is still subject to a criminal investigation, no information on the methods and processes used is currently available for my study." Her tone held cool irony. She didn't appreciate the information being withheld by the state prosecutors. *It's as if something absorbed the energy,* she thought, grimly. *But I can't prove that. I would have to dig under the pyramid's ruins to see if the state-run energy company managed to put some sort of safeguards in place . . . and to imagine that I'd get permission to dig there? Folly.*

Another hand shot up. "All right." This voice had a Britannian accent of some variety. Minori's head swung up, and she found the face that matched the voice. Male, long, dark blond hair, braided, and a light beard. Between all the hair and the spectacles, it was hard to see his face, but the man was smiling. It had taken her most of her first four years here to learn all the different ways in which a Gaul or a Goth or a Roman could smile. They could smile to laugh, smile to say they were sorry, smile to lie, smile in contempt, smile in joy. Smile, smile, smile, and at first, she'd thought they were like grinning demon masks, always baring teeth. This smile seemed to be kind enough. As if the man didn't wish to say what he was about to say. "Without details on the ley-line tapping experiment at

Teotihuacán, isn't all of this supposition? You're trying to draw a cause and effect relationship through circumstantial evidence. Here are all the things that we think are the effects; therefore, this over here must be the cause. How do you determine which seismic shifts are natural, as opposed to those that you believe stem from ley-grid activity? Where do you get the data on the 1950 energy spike from, or do you derive it, backwards, from the fact that there was an earthquake over a thousand miles away?"

Minori bit the inside of her lips in vexation. She'd wanted to get all the way through all of her math first. All the detailed charts that *showed*, plain as day, that wherever the ley company had expanded, earthquakes had followed. Volcanic eruptions. "Those are excellent questions, that I *will* cover in this presentation, ah . . . professor . . ." She trailed off uncertainly.

"Oh, I'm not a professor, Doctor Sasaki. My apologies. Trennus Matrugena. University of Londonium. Ley-mage and *arcessitor.*" *Arcessitor* was the formal Latin word for summoner, and Minori could see a number of people on the benches around the Britannian edge away now, subtly. This let her see the blue and green kilt, and the fact that his white shirt was rolled up to his elbows to show tattoos along both forearms. Masses of them, all interworked in blue-green ink, to form a harmonious whole. Not unlike *irezumi,* but she doubted that his markings offered the protections that a properly-worked *irezumi* provided. She knew that Nahautl tattoos could render skin like steel, or allow a man to turn himself invisible, but an *irezumi* artist could render the wearer of such a tattoo immune to flame. Immune to cold. Immune to the venom of a snake's bite, or poison in a cup.

Minori cleared her throat. "I traveled to Nahautl myself last year to conduct thaumometric analyses of the rocks around the Teotihuacán site. I couldn't get into the crime area, but my fifth chart is an analysis of the decay of energy in the region . . . and the sixth chart shows what archaeologists charted in the area in 1948 and 1953, when they were conducting ley-surveys of the ruins to determine why the buildings were constructed where they were." She raised her eyebrows. *See? I do my work.* "Their findings were independent of mine, and show that the ambient power levels increased in the region after 1950 . . . and my own information shows an enormous increase in the background energy of the area after 1955." Trying to get her presentation back on track, she slapped a hand against the next poster-board. "The pattern is clear. The seismic events have the Teotihuacán area as the epicenter of the activity, or the smaller, newer ley-taps in southern Nahautl." She took that map down, showing the next map, this one of Caesaria Australis. "And here, in Tawantinsuyu, where the ley-grid has been slowly expanding for the last eight years? We see a similar increase in the number and intensity of earthquakes and volcanic eruptions. Numbers do not lie."

"Numbers can be made to lie. People are inventive that way." The voice had an unfamiliar accent, and Minori's eyes snapped to the right of the Britannian, and she finally took note of the much shorter man beside him, who sort of . . . faded into the background among all the exotic-looking Goths and Gauls in the room. Short-cropped hair, olive skin. Dark eyes, narrowed. No hint of a smile at all. "People lie all the damned time."

Minori's temper flared—the temper that her mother had always told her, would have made her a better son, than a daughter. She felt as if the man were accusing *her* of being a liar. "Yes. They do. But find the lie in my numbers. Show me where they are wrong, and I will look for more data to repair them. I do not have an agenda. My company has no financial stake in the western hemisphere at this time, Professor . . . ?" Again, the pause.

"Oh, I'm not a professor, either, *Doctor*. Kanmi Eshmunazar. University of Athens. Sorcery and technomancy." His words were sharp and clear, and the emphasis on her title was . . . sarcastic? He was suggesting that she *hadn't earned her degree?* "And let's face it. Everyone in this room has an agenda. Some academic axe to grind. Some industrial machine to feed."

Various of the audience members shifted and laughed a little, but it was an uneasy sound. Minori stood there, fuming internally, but not letting it show on her face. She was far too well-trained for that. "I am not one of them."

"And your company isn't interested in providing alternative energy sources?" the man asked, dryly. "And you're not making your name, staking out some obscure academic ground to make it your own?"

"My company provides ley-energy facilities, first and foremost. Most of my managers have suggested that in taking this position, I might actually decrease the chances of our receiving contracts to build such facilities in Caesaria Aquilonis or Caesaria Australis," Minori said, lifting her chin and making herself meet the man's eyes. "I am, in fact, quite certain I have been denied a raise in the last year *because* I persist in asking questions." She was shaking, and her stomach roiled with nausea. Minori *hated* confrontation of any kind, but she'd at least been trained for combat. Confrontation in the social arena was so much worse. "Now, unless you have specific questions to go with your *ad hominem* attacks, Master Eshmunazar . . . ?"

"Oh, if it's a *specific* question that you want," he said, his eyes sharp, "here's one for you. If the energy spikes you're discussing are derived from the ley-system itself, how on earth can *more* be getting put back into the system than originally came from it?" He paused, and then went on relentlessly, "Systems always have *losses*, even ley-taps, *Doctor*. Where is your extra energy coming from?"

Minori took a deep breath to keep her mind clear, as murmurs rose from the audience. "I am not sure," she said, as calmly and evenly as she could, when the man had just more or less kicked directly at the central point of her working thesis, and made the whole structure wobble. "I am not even sure that there *is* extra energy entering the system, or if the energy liberated from the system is changed in amplitude or resonance and then re-enters the system in . . . wrong places. No one has ever, to my knowledge, studied what happens when we *add* energy to the ley-system. Only what happens when we *take* from it. In the end, it doesn't matter if I come up with all the answers, Master Eshmunazar. My only agenda is the truth. And my numbers speak only the truths that I have been able to find so far. I invite anyone with superior information to add to the growing picture. That is, after all, what science is for. To point out areas where we have questions, and to search for answers. I fully acknowledge that the questions I have been asking may not have been the right ones." Minori lifted her chin. "But at least I'm *asking* them."

She stepped back from the podium, feeling numb. She'd been laughed at—politely, of course—in writing over the past few years. Her numbers had been scoured and savaged through several courses of peer-reviews. She'd had colleagues in this very lecture hall question the correlations she'd found . . . but she'd never been called a *liar* before.

An hour later, Minori was more than ready to go home for the night, make herself a cup of tea, and try to forget about this horrible day. However, Belator Camulorix stopped her on her way out of the hall. The aging Gallic professor had white hair, and a noticeable tremor in his hands as he used his cane to navigate through the crowds; stoop-shouldered, he would have been taller than she, had he been able to stand fully upright. Now, however, he met her eyes at level. *"You handled the interruptions well,"* he told her, his Belgae-inflected Gallic gentle.

"I have never heard of either the Britannian or the other one before." Minori was still *seething*. *"I haven't read any papers by them. What were they even doing here?"*

Dr. Camulorix put one shaking hand on her forearm. *"They were here because I invited them."*

Minori stopped in the crowded hallway and stared at her colleague. On the one hand, science *was* self-correcting, and the questions had exposed weaknesses in her arguments that needed to be addressed. On the other hand, she'd just been savaged in public by two strangers, and knowing that Camulorix had invited them felt like personal betrayal. So she remained silent for a long moment, but her expression probably spoke volumes.

"Now, now, I didn't expect young Eshmunazar to jump up and down on you like that. I've heard a good deal about him from some of my colleagues at the University of Athens, however. And he and young Matrugena are precisely the people we need to talk to about some of our little problems of late." He tugged gently at her arm, guiding her out of the main hall, and towards the darkened corridor where his office was. *"They're going to meet with us in my office shortly."* Camulorix dug in his poke, which swung from his belt, came up with his keys, opened the door, and turned on the light.

Chaos. Every book had been torn from the bookcases, the shelves themselves ripped from the walls. Most of the books had been rent in half, along the spines, pages loose and flying freely in the wind and light rain gusting in from the open window. Camulorix stood in the doorway and swayed for a moment, and Minori slipped a hand under his elbow, discreetly, trying to keep him from falling. *"Oh, gods,'* Camulorix murmured, and hooked his cane over his opposite wrist to cover his eyes for a moment. *"My books. My notes. Minori, please, look in the file drawer, and make sure that they didn't destroy my notes."*

"Wait," a voice said behind them, sharply, and Minori spun. On edge already, she raised a hand to set up a spell out of pure reflex, the patterns and structures of it instantly leaping into her mind in lines of white light.

Behind them, the Britannian loomed like a giant, and the smaller man, at his side, flicked his fingers . . . and Minori could feel an energy charge seethe in the air. No, not quite that. *He's a counterspeller*, she realized. *He's ready to pull the energy from anything I give him.* She closed her fingers in a tight ball, crushing the shape of the construct in her mind. "Don't touch anything yet," the Britannian finished, and peered into the office. "Esh, got a camera?"

"No. Too bulky to fit in my pockets," the shorter man replied, acerbically. "Have one of your spirits draw you a *picture*. Sniff around for scent." He looked at the professor. "When was the last time you were here in your office, Doctor?"

"Earlier this evening. Before the panel began . . . ah . . . five postmeridian." Camulorix mopped at his forehead now with the sleeve of his shirt. "Yes, I'd just come back from an early dinner with a colleague. Dr. Sasaki met me here, and we walked over to the lecture hall at . . . fifteen after five." He paused. "Please, can we not at least close the window?"

Minori nodded. She didn't like the way in which the shorter man was looking at her. "Was Dr. Sasaki with you the entire time? She didn't leave your sight until you entered the lecture hall?"

"No, not at all."

"Do you mean to ask," Minori said, slowly, her temper starting to heat up once more, "if I had time to run back down the hall and destroy my colleague's office, before running back down to the lecture hall to begin my presentation without being out of breath?"

"I've learned the hard way not to take anything for granted," the man told her, his eyes still narrow. "Matru, I'm going to take a walk around the back. I might not see anything with all this rain, but we might get lucky. The asshole in question might have left incriminating footprints in deep mud and a neon sign that reads 'I went this way, and here's my name and address.'" He disappeared down the hall, his rubber-soled shoes making no sound on the floor.

Minori stared now as the Britannian held out a hand and whispered to empty air, and a little wisp of mist rose from his hand. "Go close the window, please," he told the coil of fog . . . and it fought its way to the fall wall, struggling against the wind. Grew darker. Denser. Wrapped itself around the handle . . . and slammed it shut, before returning to coil lazily around his hand and wrist. Just for an instant, she thought she saw blue eyes in the middle of the mist, as he gave it a small piece of candy for its pains. "You really are a summoner, then?" she asked, turning her head to watch the vapor creature . . . surely a water elemental of some sort . . . dart off down the hall with its prize.

"Yes. Among other things." He stepped lightly into the room, and a piece of paper and a pen rose from the debris on the floor. Minori watched, her eyes widening, as the pen began to move and skate on the foolscap. Drawing. Sketching. She'd met summoners before, but not one who appeared to have multiple different spirits at his heels. The big man now turned and frowned. "I'm going to need a little light. There's something on the wall here." He held up his hand again . . . and this time a phoenix appeared on his outstretched hand, radiating brilliant light in every direction from its peacock-like tail of flame.

It is really far too wet for me to manifest.

"The window is shut now."

That doesn't matter. It almost feels as if Stormborn were in the vicinity.

"She and Adam are in Judea."

I know. It's been two weeks. I miss them.

"They deserve their first holiday in years. Not that fixing up the house they bought is likely to be very relaxing." The Britannian crooked a finger. The paper and pen floated over obligingly, and he pointed to something on the wall. "Get this, too, please," he told whatever invisible hand held the pen.

Minori craned around the corner, and instantly wished that she hadn't. She hadn't caught the *smell* before. Blood. There was writing on the wall, in blood, in Latin. The letters were crooked, and in all capitals, as if the writer had forgotten the invention of the miniscule case, and read, clearly, **SI TACUISSES, PHILOSOPHUS MANISSES.** *If you had stayed silent, we would have thought you a philosopher* . . . or, less literally, *in silence, there is wisdom.*

Minori's eyes widened. "Is it . . . is it . . . ?"

"Human?" The Britannian cocked his head to the side. "The spirits say not. Probably cow. Whoever did this, dropped a pot of it behind that shelf. It got all over the books—" He looked up as Camulorix swayed again. "I'm sorry, professor. Let's get you somewhere that you can sit down." The Britannian deftly climbed back out of the debris now, and helped Camulorix back down the hall and found him a seat on a low bench there. "Now, I know this isn't the first threat," he said, kindly. "But could you detail the others for me, please?"

Minori shot confused glances back and forth between them. "Professor? You . . . you invited them here because of the threats?" She didn't know what to think at this point. The two were a summoner and apparently some sort of technomancer, but she could throw a rock out a window and hit four or five people of that description on the campus right now.

"Yes, but you were on *my* radar already, Doctor Sasaki." She whirled, and this time, her hand dropped to the sash that belted her wrap-around jacket to her body. She'd successfully lied to people before and told them that the *kaiken* knife tucked there was a nail file, and they'd believed her, much to her shock. From the hard gaze that this Eshmunazar man was giving her, she didn't think *he'd* believe it. "I'd like to ask you a few questions. Let's back up a little. First of all, how long have you been a member of the Source Initiative?"

Minori blinked. "What has that to do with the threats?" she asked.

It was about the last question she would have expected. "And . . . I'm sorry. Forgive me. *Who* are you two again?" She didn't want to say *no* to them. It would be rude. But twelve years in Gaul had left marks on her manners, and she'd learned to be . . . uncomfortably forthright with people when needed.

The shorter man reached into one of his dozens of pockets, and produced a leather wallet. Flicked it open, showing a silver badge there, with the *fasces* and the eagle on it. "Kanmi Eshmunazar. Praetorian Guard. Carthaginian branch, lictor to Propraetor Antonius Livorus. Now, please, answer the question. How long have you been a member of the Source Initiative?"

"A . . . about four years?" Minori had to stop and think about that. "They're a professional organization. They publish an academic journal about energy production to which I subscribe, and they have a conference once a year in Novo Gaul. It's good for networking . . . and why am I even justifying this?" she asked herself, out loud, in disbelief. "It's not a crime to belong to an organization."

"No. It's not." His gaze was as hard and blank as the marble tiles underfoot. "About when did the threats start, Doctor?"

Behind her, she could hear Camulorix answering similar questions, though more gently posed by the Britannian. "Last year," Minori said, slowly. "Right after the last conference, actually. That's when I presented my first set of results linking earthquakes and the ley-grid in Nahautl. Just the local earthquakes. I hadn't been able to show results elsewhere in the globe, yet."

"And the fact that there are no ley-interrelated earthquakes elsewhere on earth?" Eshmunazar asked her, sharply, and, off-balance, Minori blinked. "You haven't looked at the entire Ring of Fire. Ley-power is just as common as electricity in Nippon. Why haven't there been ley-interrelated earthquakes and eruptions *there*?"

"I don't *know*. I *have* looked at the data. But all of the ley-stations in Nippon are over a century old!" Minori finally snapped back at him, tired of defending herself from what felt like accusations from a dozen directions at once. She pointed a finger at him. "Do you know what seiches are?" She swept on, seeing his blank look. "They're the waves that occur in an enclosed body of water, such as . . . a frigidarium pool, or a mountain lake, in response to seismic activity in the earth. I see seiches. I see them *everywhere*. They must originate from somewhere, and my job is to find their point of origin and stop them before they get worse." Minori realized, suddenly, that she'd raised her voice, and she flushed, ducking her head for a moment, regaining her calm.

"Oddly enough," the Britannian said, from behind her, "that sounds more or less like *our* job description, some days."

The other man hadn't let her off the hook yet. "So why do all the old-world stations, the ones that already exist in Novo Gaul, *not* cause the earthquakes? Your data is *flawed*, Doctor—"

He opened his mouth to continue, but Minori cut him off, heatedly, "My supposition has been that the new technology that resulted in the collapse of the Pyramid of the Sun is responsible. *That* is why it's not affecting older installations. . . . " She stopped. Blinked. Rapidly reassessed information from entirely disparate sets in her head. *He asked where the extra energy was coming from* . . . "Gods," she murmured. "There *was* something different about the ones in Nahautl. I remember reading about human sacrifices being buried on the sites . . . but that can't be it. That wouldn't change the *technology*."

She raised her eyes. Eshmunazar gave her a coldly considering look. "No," he said, after a moment. "Murder victims being buried there shouldn't change the technology at all."

Wait, why did he just shift my words? Minori opened her mouth to ask him a question, only to be trampled on by another question from him, instead. "Can you explain to me, Doctor, why it is that in my research on you and your connection with the Source Initiative, it appears that you *don't exist* before 1948?"

Minori froze in place, blinking rapidly. This was a hit from a completely different direction, yet again. *Verbal jujitsu,* she thought. *He works me to lean in one direction, and then another, and then another. Destabilizing the base.* "I don't know what you're referring to," she replied, carefully. Knowing what he was doing helped her to keep her voice steady. "Obviously, I existed before 1948. I'm hardly a twelve-year-old. My passport reads Minori Sasaki, born, Hokkaido, Nippon, 1930 — "

"I'm aware of the lovely work of fiction that is your passport, yes." The man's eyes narrowed once more. "I actually do *my* research, Doctor. I'm *thorough*. Minori Sasaki did not exist before 1948. Your school records are another lovely work of fiction, considering the fact that the various teachers and classmates that I've contacted have no recollection of anyone by that name." Minori's mouth had gone dry as he revealed how carefully he'd been scrutinizing her past. "The school administrators insist that your name is in the rolls, but not one of your supposed classmates remembers you. What you liked to eat. Who you were friends with. If your parents were strict. Which boy wanted to get a look under your robes."

Minori realized that she'd backed up against the wall, and she had her hands up in a prime spellcasting posture, and that the man hadn't so much as *moved*. He hadn't taken a step towards her, but his words loomed. "I cannot account for what other people do and do not remember," she managed. "I was quiet."

"Yes, sorcerers who can cast without spoken incantations, and default solely to gestures are so often quiet and unnoticeable," he said, his eyes glittering in the low light of the hall. "That's military-grade training, at the very least. I can do it myself. I can feel the structure you're already readying in your mind. And I can counter it before you trip it."

"Stop this!" Camulorix said, from where he sat on the couch, his tone frail. "I called on you to *help* us, not for you to attack my colleague — "

"I cannot possibly help your colleague if she won't tell us the truth," the Praetorian said, coolly. "Stop lying. Tell me who you *are,* and how you're involved in all of this."

Minori's hands shook. "I swear to you," she told him, breathlessly, "that the only falsehood I have spoken is my name. And that was changed *for* me, to protect my family when I left Nippon."

An arrested look in his eyes. "To protect your family from what?" he asked, his tone harsh, but his expression more open.

She looked down. "From shame," Minori said, tiredly. "From the shame of having a daughter so . . . inappropriate." There was more to it than that, but it seemed unlikely that they'd understand it, and it wasn't their business. Her past had nothing to do with current events. "My father was . . . generous . . . to permit me to study sorcery at all, but when it seemed possible that I could tear the house down by accident, there was, perhaps, little choice in the matter." She studied the floor, the seams between the tiles. "And when my skills proved to be much more suitable for war and engineering than making flowers and crops grow, he was, again, generous in permitting me to leave Nippon and come here, instead of marrying me off, binding me as someone's concubine, or requiring me to become a shrine-maiden. He is . . . progressive, in that respect. He loves me, in his way." She swallowed. It was intolerable to have to speak of this, but if she didn't tell the truth, the whole of it, then this questioning would just go on and on. Minori raised her eyes. "He did the best he could for me. And now I do the same for him, by not bringing shame to his name."

"And that's all?" Eshmunazar's voice was skeptical. "Is there anyone out there who knows your real name? Anyone who might be trying to go after you on those grounds?"

"I tell you, *no*. All of the threats have revolved around the research that Professor Camulorix and I have been conducting, and I will not be frightened off of it!" Minori shook with the fury she was trying to repress.

"Esh," the Britannian said, gently.

"What?"

"She wasn't in the Initiative in 1955. It's probably a coincidence."

She speaks only the truth as she knows it, Emberstone. Again, silent words in Minori's mind, as the phoenix perched on the Britannian's shoulder chirruped. Her eyes darted back and forth as the two men exchanged glances.

"All right," Eshmunazar said, at last. "Gather up every last bit of your research. You keep anything at your apartment?"

Minori blinked. "What? You're going to make me *burn* it or something?" Inwardly, her heart constricted. Rome was an empire, just as her homeland was. Things like this happened when those in power found scientific research threatening for some reason or another.

"No." The single bald word startled her. "I want to see every single idea you've had in the last year. Every piece of data you've collected. I can correlate it against mine."

What? she thought, stunned, as he looked around. "Your office is at the Eleutherian Industries complex outside of town, right? I'll drop by there and grab everything *else* you have, once we've gotten you to a safe place. Both of you."

"My research is at my house," Camulorix said, shakily. "My wife passed away two years ago, but I have children. Grandchildren."

Another exchange of glances. "Might be a good time for them to take an extended holiday," the Britannian said, mildly. "We'll grab your address book, and you can call them, sir."

This was all going much too fast for Minori's liking. "It's very *kind* of you . . . " she managed, though it was definitely pushing truthfulness to call Eshmunazar's demeanor *kind*, "but the most this is, is industry sabotage. People whose work we're calling into question. *Maybe* someone whose patent is being used in the new facilities — and I'd love to get my hands on the schematics for those — whose work is damaging the environment."

"And coin *isn't* enough reason for someone to kill?" Eshmunazar pointed out, catching her arm and propelling her along. "Even if we were all living in a dream world where money won't buy you a shallow grave, there are bigger things at stake." He looked around. "We've got a vehicle out back. Tren, get the professor's stuff packed up, I'll get them to the car."

Minori resisted in irritation, yanking her arm out of his grip. "I would very much like to know why you think there's 'more at stake,' she told him. "Why should I share my research with you? You saw most of it at the conference, anyway — "

"Because we can guarantee that it wasn't ley-energy that caused the earthquakes," Matrugena said, behind them, already digging through the books and papers in the office. "The energy might have leaped along existing ley-lines, and I won't argue that. But the source itself wasn't ley."

Absolute certainty in that voice, and Minori raged against it. Certainty was a thing of *belief*, not natural philosophy. "And you can prove that?" she challenged them both.

"Yes. Because we were *there* when the Pyramid of the Sun collapsed," Eshmunazar replied, his tone stark. "Matrugena here is a ley-mage. And that wasn't ley. Come on. Car. Now."

Two hours later, Kanmi cleared their hotel suite of any unwanted intruders largely by sending a gravitic pulse through the outside wall, and keeping one hand on the cinderblocks as he 'listened' for echoes. "One of these days," he muttered, "I am going to design a spell that lets me feel body heat a quarter mile away, so I don't have to stand right outside the damned door to do this." *Of course, then the opposition would just send golems in after me. Still, in a world where there are automatic weapons and arrows that can pierce through walls? A couple of panels of plaster-covered wood are damned little comfort, sometimes.* That was, of course, one of the reasons why they'd picked *this* hotel. It had sturdier construction than most, being an older building. And a ground-floor suite was available, so Trennus felt less separated from the earth.

Inside, Kanmi gestured for their guests to take the couch; both were soaked to the skin from the heavy downpour outside. "Get the windows," Trennus told him, lugging in the first two heavy boxes of books and papers from the car.

"Already on it." Kanmi started setting up wards over the glass.

Reinforcing its structure with energy weaves. He'd been working on this with Adam for the past two years. Bulletproof glass was on the market—a lovely Judean innovation, that—but it deteriorated in sunlight. *Bombproof* glass was something else entirely, and Kanmi's lips and hands both had to move for this spell, thanks to the intricacy as he latticed layer after layer of energy and matter together into a laminate. The latticework would disperse energy from an incoming blast or bullet into the cinderblock walls, and the laminate would hold the actual materials in place, as if they were embedded in an additional physical matrix. He'd taken to doing this on the windows of Livorus' motorcar every time the man left his manor. It might not be totally effective against spells, but . . . every little bit helped. The walls, however, were Tren's department.

Kanmi ducked outside for an armful of books and a box of papers, while Trennus, in the room, pulled ley-energy up through the floor, pouring it through the walls. Shifting them from cinderblock structure and melting them into each other. Reinforcing them with each other's substance. There were no more dividing lines of weak mortar, but one contiguous whole. "Home improvements," Trennus muttered now, wringing out his wet hair. "Never my favorite hobby."

"You wind up buying that house that ben Maor and Caetia are suggesting, and that's going to become your job, not a hobby," Kanmi warned. "Last boxes are still outside. Don't see anyone out there watching us, but that doesn't mean anything."

"Yes. I'll grab us some extra eyes when I get back in, and you can ward the door with an alarm."

Ten minutes later, they were doing precisely that, Kanmi enchanting a ringing squeal that should go off when anyone other than the four of them tried to open the door. "What about room service?" Minori asked, her expression still faintly on edge.

Kanmi held up a *Do not disturb* sign and slipped it over the knob before he closed the door, locked it, and slid the chain home. "Matru?"

"Calling us a few extra eyes."

At which point, Lassair appeared next to him, shifting out of phoenix form to coalesce into her full human body. Kanmi caught the way Minori's eyes widened, her lips parted, and the sigh she gave, and his lips quirked. Lassair had that effect on men and women alike. She was simply *so* stunning at this point, that the mind had a tendency to wander, no matter *what* your personal sexual preference happened to be. He had a personal theory that the spirit could probably give a three-day-dead corpse an erection by dancing atop its grave.

It made traveling with her and Matrugena highly annoying. Five years into their . . . exceedingly unconventional relationship . . . they were clearly still going at it like newlyweds who thought they'd just invented sex. This resulted in Kanmi periodically throwing a shoe at the connecting wall between their suite rooms, inevitably followed by hasty apologies and *giggling* from the other side. What made it even worse was that Lassair tended to kiss anyone she liked. With gusto usually, right on the lips. Which meant that Adam, Kanmi, and even Sigrun had been recipients, at some point or another. Kanmi still rather wished he'd had a camera on hand for the first occasion on which Caetia had been on the receiving end. For both the during and the after shot.

With Lassair present and manifested, the room instantly warmed, and the cold dampness in everyone's clothing began to steam up into the air. Trennus grabbed a grease pencil from his luggage and sketched a summoning circle on the floor, and began calling spirits to serve as eyes and ears in exchange for a little wine and sugar.

Kanmi, aware of their guests' eyes on him, cleared the table in front of him largely by shoving a forearm along its length, dropping the telephone and local directory off the edge, and barely catching the lamp in time to keep its bulb from shattering. He set it beside the sphere of the ley-powered far-viewer, and began digging through the boxes himself now, looking for Minori's papers. "You're going to get them all out of order," she said, after a moment, stood, and came over to sort through them with him.

"There's an order to this?" Kanmi said, raising his eyebrows.

"You grabbed everything in my office and shoved it into boxes at random. How did you know how to pick the locks, anyway? I would have thought you'd just . . . ." She waved, vaguely.

"What, melt the lock mechanisms into slag? Messy. Noticeable. Also means it's harder to lock them behind us if we need to."

"There are more subtle methods than that. But subtlety is not what you are about, are you?" Her tone held asperity.

Kanmi raised his eyes, and pushed back, just as hard. "And how would you know about lock-picking, *Doctor*? Does this have to do with your *shameful* past?"

He knew he'd hit a nerve by the way she pulled in a breath to calm herself, and looked down, her fists closing. *We can play this game all day, my dear doctor.* Instead of pursuing the matter, however, Kanmi unrolled a map and stared down at it. "Your earthquake data. Good. I wanted a closer look at this than I got in the lecture hall, anyway." He swore, mostly at himself. "I didn't even *think* of the earthquakes. That sets the timeline back to 1950. Baal's *teeth*, that man worked fast." Gratian had only been back in Nahautl for seven years in 1955. Which meant that, if Minori's data *did* tally . . . their first experiments on first empowering and then stripping power from a god had started only two years after Gratian had returned home. "Problem is, you don't start experiments like this on the best test subject you have," Kanmi muttered to himself. "You use something smaller. A rat. Who was your rat?" *Maybe this wasn't the first time someone did this. Maybe there were smaller-scale efforts. Maybe with spirits? Or maybe, Astarte protect us from fools, Tlaloc was the laboratory rat.* He rubbed at his eyes.

"You realize that you make absolutely no sense whatsoever?" Minori told him, frankly. "How can I correlate my data with yours if you don't make sense?"

"You can't. You don't need to know my data. We're going to put you both someplace *safe*, and take care of this." Kanmi stared at the charts.

Minori grabbed his sleeve at that point. "I've spent three years of my life on this. If you're using my data, then you owe me *something* in return. If the power wasn't coming from the ley-grid, then what's causing it?"

Kanmi stared down at her hand on his arm, and felt every muscle in his body tighten. He looked back up and met her eyes from only inches away. "I can't actually tell you," he said, quietly. "It's been classified so highly, I was *there*, and I'm not even supposed to know." He suddenly saw her, not as a potential suspect, but as a researcher who'd spent her life in a search almost as fervent as his own for the truth, and seeing her that way was dangerous. She could still be in on the Source Initiative's plans, whatever they were. If it even was an organized conspiracy.

Life would make so much more *sense* if everything really was a matter of conspiracies. You could then just go after the networks and unravel them. Real life was messier. People got ideas from each other. But they might operate totally separately from each other, other than that first transmitted idea, like a virus or a germ, taking seed in their consciousness. Sometimes there *were* conspiracies. Sometimes, it was just an idea on the wind. "If I could, I'd tell you," he finally told her. "Information *should* be freely shared between mages and scientists."

"Yes," she told him, her eyes dark and luminous. "It should. What could be so bad that you can't disseminate it?"

Kanmi didn't answer. Just unfurled the map again, and began working his way through it. Firing questions at her about the fault lines in Caesaria Australis that were lighting up currently. "I've spent five years trying to track these assholes down by tracing their memberships. Their connections. Their communications," he finally said, and stared down at the mountains around Cuzco and Machu Picchu. "And now I might finally *catch* the fuckers . . . by tracking their latest gods-be-damned *experiment* and its . . . waste products."

Minori actually glared at him. "I'm so happy for you," she informed him. "No, really, I'm delighted that my data has enabled you to complete *your* research. And here I thought that you were *thorough*."

Kanmi's head jerked up. "You have a mouth on you," he said, after a moment. "Good. I like seeing the real person instead of a yet another fucking lie."

She looked as if he'd slapped her, and Kanmi regretted the words, but there was no way to take them back. And he supposed it didn't matter if he did or not. Tomorrow, they'd get her on a plane for . . . gods. Nippon, maybe. "Where's a good safe place to send you?" he asked, briskly. "Can we send you back to Hokkaido?"

"No!" It was a yelp. "I can't go back. I have to stay in Europa or the new world." She didn't huddle in on herself, but her eyes were haunted.

Kanmi gave Trennus a look, and got a shrug in return. "All right, we'll talk it over with the propraetor. We can work something out."

A look of confusion. "And a *propraetor* is involved in this . . . ?"

"Look, you've just stumbled into one of my long-term projects.

And I'm one of his lictors."

"And he's sufficiently interested in the *hobbies* of one of his lictors—who's researching something so classified that even the gods themselves don't have clearance—that he's going to be willing to throw his weight behind an effort to hide us." Minori stood up straight. "I won't be *disappeared*, you understand me? I will *fight*. Is this some kind of a cover-up? What kind of energy was it? Is it . . ." she paused, as if she were about to utter something horrific, "*nuclear*? Are we talking about something with the potential to end the world?"

Kanmi just stared at her for a long moment. He didn't know whether to laugh or to pound his head against the desk. She'd jumped completely the wrong way. "No," he told her, after a moment. "I have it on good authority that the world isn't going to end till a valkyrie of my acquaintance gets pregnant, and considering the rate at which she and her husband are going, I think we've got time on that."

Oh, that was unkind, *Emberstone.* Lassair's tone held reproof.

Yes, but it's true, though. Kanmi's lips twitched. Sigrun's sister had been *chatty* at the ben Maor/Caetia wedding. Kanmi had told her, emphatically, that he didn't want to know about his own future in regards to the end of the world, and her airy reply had chilled him. *Oh, don't worry. You'll be dead for fourteen years before it happens. But your next wife will be worth coming back from the dead for, I promise!* He'd grimaced and closed his mind to the topic. He'd been up to his ears in Bastet's anger and inexplicable disappointment in him at that point.

Now he shook the thoughts away. "What I'm trying to say, Dr. Sasaki . . . is no, it's not nuclear, and I don't *think* it's the end of the world." *At least, apparently, not yet.*

In the meantime, Trennus had been using the room's phone to allow Camulorix to call his various children and grandchildren and get them to agree to leave their homes on a few unplanned vacations. All of this was difficult to explain to people, without using the words *Look, your grandfather's stumbled onto one group's efforts to turn a god into a battery. Other people want that kept quiet. People who might be trying to* replicate *those efforts. We think it's possible that they'd kill to keep themselves hidden.*

Several phone calls later, Camulorix was upset because he couldn't reach his youngest daughter—a woman in her late forties or early fifties, apparently. "I seem to recall her daughter is pregnant." The professor frowned over his contact book. "If everyone's in as much danger as you think . . . ."

"We'll put in a call to the local *gardia* and see if they can confirm her location," Trennus said, soothingly, and finally got the old man to lie down on one of the couches, before tossing a blanket lightly at Minori. "Make yourselves comfortable. We're apparently getting directions from Rome in the morning. The propraetor's on a plane somewhere right now."

Somewhere was actually *Raccia*, Kanmi knew. Qin had, in the past month, abandoned neutrality in favor of attacking Mongol lands in the east. With the Mongols pinned down in the west, fighting Rome along the Caspian, it was a perfect time for Qin to expand its territory . . . something that made Raccia very, very nervous. The politics of it all made Kanmi's head hurt, but there was no way around it. They lived in the world in which they lived. And he figured that it could be much worse than it already was.

Having so many wards and guards, Kanmi and Trennus had opted to only stand partial watches. And around two antemeridian, when Trennus was in the bathroom, Professor Camulorix apparently got up and left the hotel room, opening the door, which was keyed to his hand, and walked out without an alarm sounding. Trennus discovered that fact about ten minutes later, and woke everyone in the suite up with his swearing. "No," Kanmi told him, sharply, as the big Pict started for the door. "We're not going to all run out there after him. Contact the local *gardia* and let them do their jobs. Security only works if everyone stays *inside* of it." He rubbed at his face.

"I can send spirits out—"

"You have anything of *his* that they can key on? Hair? Blood? Clothing?"

Trennus dropped down to examine the couch. "No hairs that I can detect. Damnit. Maybe his books?"

"Are they *personal* enough?" That was a big question with spirit tracking.

"Maybe. The words written in his own hand . . . perhaps." Trennus sounded dubious, however. "Worth a try."

None of them got any sleep after that. Trennus' various water and air spirits wafted out, and came back with little to report. One of them said only, *Dark place. No light. No life . . .* and Kanmi watched Dr. Sasaki's face crumple at the words. "Can't you do something?" she demanded.

"Like what?" he shot back. "Run out into the dark, no idea which way he went—"

"Probably to his daughter's house—"

"Right, so we're going to leave you here unprotected, or split our forces, or haul you and all of your notes with us." Kanmi shook his head. "No. We forted up. We stay in the fort till dawn."

The Lutetian *gardia* got back to them at six postmeridian, when Camulorix's daughter called them to report that when she'd gotten back to her house, it had clearly been broken into. Shattered front windows, opened front door . . . and her father in a crumpled heap on the floor.

No blood, the *gardia* reported, but an odd, rancid odor, as of burned flesh. No burns on the body, at least, not visible ones. A full autopsy would be conducted, because Camulorix's keys were in his pockets. And there was little physical evidence at the scene, besides the body itself. Kanmi shook his head, and thanked the lieutenant on the other end of the line. "Send the crime scene pictures to the Praetorians for forwarding to us," he said. "And the autopsy report. No, we don't need to see the body personally. Thank you." He slammed the phone down on the hook, and stared off into the distance for a moment, trying to control the rage. They'd taken such *pains* to ensure the old man's safety, and in a fit of stubbornness, he'd just . . . gone off on his own. "Camulorix was . . . a fairly competent ley-mage, wasn't he?" he asked.

"Yes," Trennus replied, immediately. "He was fairly well-known even in Britannia."

"So whoever jumped him either surprised him, completely, or overwhelmed his defenses."

Trennus grimaced. "He spent his entire life training other ley-mages and working on engineering designs. If you don't train for combat magic . . . ."

". . . you play how you practice, yes." Kanmi rubbed at his jaw again, hearing the stubble grate against his fingers, and regarded his fellow lictor. "We're getting on a plane for Rome, and taking her with us." He nodded in Minori's direction. He was startled to see that she'd turned her face away to dab at her eyes. "I think it's pretty clear that we've been watched."

Trennus grimaced. "L . . . Asha's usually pretty good at sensing when people watch us." A sidelong glance at Lassair, who'd been, apparently, asleep in her manifested form, and snuggled up in bed when the old man had slipped out.

They could be employing spirits of their own. It would be simple to pick up items by which someone might be tracked, ahead of time. A bloody bandage, for example. Humans are careless with their blood, nails, and hair in these days. Lassair sounded glum. *I might not be able to see such spirits, if they are quiet and skilled.*

"Do I have any choice about going to Rome?" Minori asked, quietly, and wiped at her face again with a handkerchief.

"Not really. We have to keep you where we can keep an eye on you. And don't, for the sake of all the gods, go walking out a warded front door."

Aprilis 7-8, 1955 AC

It was very late on dies Saturni, or very early on dies Solis. As such, most of Jerusalem was still closed down for Shabbat observances. Adam and Sigrun had, after some debating over their finances, purchased a house together. It had been a bit of an embarrassment to him to realize that she was financially much better off than he was, largely because she'd been employed for an undisclosed number of years longer than he had been, and she had no noticeable expenses at all. But they'd opted to buy the house across the street from his parents. It had been badly damaged in the *pazuzu* attack, and the owners simply wanted *out*. They'd collected their insurance and left the house to the bank . . . and the bank hadn't wanted to rebuild it.

Technically, it was a historic structure, but all the interior damage had allowed Adam and Sigrun to buy it at a very low cost, and they'd subsequently gutted it. As such, their infrequent leaves were not so much vacations, as . . . projects. This time, for example, Adam had run wiring through all the interior walls, so they'd have modern electricity without exposed cables. The air conditioning was functional, something Sigrun appreciated very much in the summer months . . . but they didn't have wallboard hung yet *anywhere,* and the entire interior smelled of sawdust. It wasn't terribly habitable yet, but when they left this time, they were going to have some contractors come in during their absence to do some work. Get a proper Roman-style bath in the master bathroom, with a sunken tub. A mother-in-law suite with a small kitchen of its own was one of Adam's long-term goals. He wanted to be able to offer his parents a place to live when they were too old to get along on their own. Mikayel would probably make the same offer, but Adam had a feeling his parents would be more comfortable in this house, than in his brother's.

The house had been designed in an era when large, multigenerational families had often lived together. As such, it had about a half dozen bedrooms, and the upstairs area echoed hollowly. Adam had just passed his thirtieth birthday, and was giving a certain amount of thought to the future. He and Sigrun had discussed children, on and off, and just this past week, she'd mentioned the ramifications of all her sister's prophecies about her. "I honestly don't know if I can *have* children. Telling me I won't have children until the world ends could be her . . . *polite* way of telling me that I'm barren." Sigrun had grimaced.

Adam had long since decided *never* to mention the words that still echoed, periodically, in his own mind: *you'll be a stepfather to your own daughter, and your wife will be your widow ere you meet her again.* Prophecy was damnable. The words could mean that he might, at some point in time, be missing in action for long enough to be declared dead, for example. The word *wife* could mean someone other than Sigrun. He could, theoretically, screw around, and get someone besides Sig pregnant—an utterly laughable concept, considering that she was, other than Lassair, the single most beautiful woman he'd ever met—and wind up adopting his own child . . . but then Sig would probably *geld* him. But none of that was ever going to happen. Not without him being some other person than Adam ben Maor. "Sig," he'd told her, gently, "when we're ready, and when you're tired of chasing Livorus all over the world, we can worry about it then. I'm not going to be concerned about anything your sister says. It's just asking to go insane." He'd kissed her forehead, lightly. "And I say that, having puzzled over some of her remarks to me over the years. I *like* puzzles, damnit. But I'm missing far too many of the pieces to make sense of hers."

Sig had snorted. "The ones your father comes over and sticks on the refrigerator *are* a little fairer." These usually involved 'simple' substitution ciphers . . . say, the words were all Hellene, but had been written in Hebrew characters, to disguise them from a casual eye. Or, when Maor was feeling particularly clever, they were Latin words, spelled without vowels, written in Hellene characters. *Anything to keep the brain active,* Maor usually told them.

After a moment of silence, Sigrun had added, "I've been on birth control since the wedding, which means I haven't bled at all. Usually, there's at least a little, I'm told . . . ." Physicians, since the invention of the hormone-based pill, had advised women to take it year-round, avoiding all menstrual cycles entirely. In a world where blood was an important component of some spells, and menstrual blood was particularly effective, and either could be used to track the person to whom it belonged, or bind a person to a spirit, this was just plain *common sense.*

"I'm fine with that. Technically, I'm not supposed to touch you if you're . . . well . . ." Adam had just grinned as Sigrun shook a fist at him. He wasn't about to say the word *niddah.* Unclean. "Hey, we both get to have much more fun this way."

Sigrun had sighed. "I know. It's just . . ." She made a face, and finally admitted, "I wonder if the medication might have done something wrong to me. I am not entirely human, after all."

Adam had pulled her close. "You know, there are pretty good doctors here. And if they can't figure out god-born physiology, we can talk to someone in Hellas, Nova Germania, or Egypt when the time comes. In the meantime . . . let's not borrow trouble, eh?"

And so, that night, they were sleeping in the atrium courtyard, under the stars, in a hammock strung between two trees. Sigrun didn't mind the Aprilis chill, and Adam wrapped himself around her, and kept a blanket or two over them as they swung back and forth.

Adam rolled to his back now, and stared up at the stars. The moon was just creeping up over the edge of the roof, casting down pale light, and, reminded, Adam shook Sigrun's shoulder lightly. "Wake up, *neshama.*"

"Hmm?"

"Need you to turn on the far-viewer. The moon landing should be happening right about now."

Sigrun sat up, shedding blankets, and gave him an amused look. "Tell the truth, Adam ben Maor. If I weren't here, you'd turn it on yourself, wouldn't you?"

Adam grinned. "Probably. But you're here, and thus, I don't have to debate between my principles and my desires."

"You want me to turn on any *lights* while I'm up?" she asked, tartly, sliding off the hammock and making it rock from side to side. Her bare skin was very pale in the moonlight, and the runes were invisible, for the moment. "The stove, perhaps?"

"Did we buy a stove when I wasn't looking?" The kitchen had been in the worst shape of the entire house. Other than the wall that the *pazuzu* had thrown a refrigerator through, trying to hit Sigrun. And the roof, of course.

"Yes, *we* did. It arrives tomorrow." Sigrun looked back over her shoulder. "Well?"

Adam sat up to regard her. "If I get up, do I miss the whole 'watch you walk around naked' part?"

Sigrun took two steps back to the hammock, and flipped the blankets up over his head. While he was recovering—and laughing—Sigrun padded off, and he saw a light flick on in what would, eventually, be a living room again, and heard a muffled curse. "Please don't tell me you stepped on a nail," he called, finally slipping out of the hammock, himself, and padding in after her.

"No. It'd heal, anyway."

"I don't like seeing you injured, regardless of how fast you heal." Adam pointed at the far-viewer. "Please?"

"That's better," Sigrun told him, approvingly, and turned the knob, causing the unit to hum and flicker to life. She rotated another dial, found the correct channel . . . and stood there, bathed in the pale light of the far-viewer, as Adam sank to his haunches to watch. "It doesn't get old for you, does it?"

"No. It really doesn't." Adam drank it in, watching as the astronauts began unloading gear from the landing module. Everything so light, it was effortless to lift and carry a huge piece of drilling gear. "I would give just about anything to be able to stand where they are. Just once. *Mare Tranquillitatis*. Look up and see *Earth* overhead." He smiled a little, feeling her hand come down on his shoulder to rub for a moment. "God, Sig. Just look at what we little mortals can *do*. We've got a little station at the Libration point for docking and redirection . . . and now we're going to start taking core samples. Finding a place with bedrock. And then we're going to *build*." He looked up at her, the edges of her face made luminous by the far-viewer's light. "That's what we're for. We're here to build."

For some reason or another, that made her drop down beside him, cup his face in light, almost wondering fingers, and kiss him as if she never intended to come up for air. Adam laughed after a moment, and they more or less crashed to the hard floor, and curled up to watch the rest of the video. Bland, almost casual tones of the astronauts, all speaking to each other in Latin. The *lingua franca* of the joint space mission, since there were Hellene and Nipponese astronauts in the program, too, after all.

About ten minutes after the programming faded to grayscale bars, and he and Sigrun had gone back to their hammock, the phone rang. "I expect you wish for me to get that, too?" she said, after a moment, her voice muffled.

"No. Phone can wait till morning." He kissed her throat. "We're on *leave*."

The phone rang again, shrilling out across the open walls of the atrium.

"Whoever they are—" another kiss, "they seem insistent."

"They can *wait*."

The phone rang again, and Adam, annoyed, rolled over. "All right." He gave her a grin. "You want to get that?"

"You put on orthodoxy *solely* to see how I react, do you not?"

"Most of the time . . . yes." Adam ducked as, this time, a pillow was tossed at his head, and shed the blankets again to follow her, once more, back into the house.

All laughter faded from her face, however, as she answered the line. "Caetia here. Yes, I'm aware of Eshmunazar and Matrugena's location." A pause. "Yes. We can be on a plane in the morning."

Adam sighed. *So much for being on leave.* "At least this time, I got the wiring done," he said, in a tone of resignation as she hung up. "What's the problem?"

"Main dispatch informs me that Kanmi called in, and requested that we return to Rome. No details, besides that he *also* asked for safe houses for two technomancers." Sigrun yawned a little. "So much for sleep."

Adam shook his head. "May as well start packing, yes. He'd better have a damned good reason for us to be called in, though."

Aprilis 8-10, 1960 AC

Guilt. Seething, dark masses of it, coiling up around her like smoke, or mist, roiling over the landscape like waves. Emotions could obscure and dim physical reality. The sky was darker. The confines of the airport, smaller, dingier, the humans within it all glistening, liquid eyes and smooth faces, the enfleshed spirits within them glimmering, some faintly, some brightly. Physical reality and spiritual reality commingled.

Why did I sleep? Flamesower asked that all the other spirits watch and guard, but they only thought to look to the outside. For invaders. They did not know that it was important that the old one left. They are . . . limited creatures. I should not have slept. I should have remained awake, and if I had, the scholar would yet be alive. I would not have let him leave, not without telling Flamesower or Emberstone.

But it felt so good to lie beside Flamesower. This body has needs, and sleep is one of them. It feels wonderful to listen to his breathing. The rush of blood through his veins. To feel the texture of his skin, the way the muscles all fit together so cunningly. The warmth of energy radiating out of him, like a distant star. The flicker of his spirit, buried so deeply inside of him. And to allow my awareness to sink into this body, and experience dreams. They're like visiting the Veil, without having to stay there. But as I dreamed, the scholar's spirit was cut from his body. And human souls are so precious. They only get to experience reality once, and for such a short period, but they experience it so richly, so deeply. They interface with time. And now, one is lost, and it is my fault.

Lassair's steps felt heavy, and her body was tired. Oddly so. She felt . . . disconnected from it . . . in a way that she usually did not, when she had manifested in a human form. *Something is different. Something has changed.* As she waited in line behind Trennus in the airport, patiently — always patiently, because time had no meaning for her, time was infinite, and she was apart from it — Lassair ran her awareness through her corporeal form like a sieve, looking for the source of that difference.

The hormonal flow had altered, she realized. Different types were rising in the bloodstream. She considered manually altering the balance, because it could influence her mood — bodies were *odd* in that way; she should be completely disparate from her physical shell, but she wasn't — and then she ran her attention elsewhere, and found the *source* of the changed hormonal flow. The uterine lining had thickened, appropriate to this time of the month. She'd been maintaining human form more and more in the past year. She'd gotten used to the rhythm and the flow of it, but she'd rarely allowed herself the luxury of staying in the form for a full twenty-four hours. Sleeping in Trennus' arms.

But last night . . . something had *changed*. Lassair realized that her hand had moved, of its own accord, to her belly, and she stood in the middle of the crowded airport, suddenly and completely *happy*.

She could sense the spirits enfleshed around her responding to her joy, as her fires rose, and enkindled their own. Dull sparks became brighter. Bright embers became blazes. Colors, suddenly, everywhere, blues and greens and reds and violets, all illuminating the flesh that enshelled them, lighting them up from within like paper lanterns. Emberstone's dull red blaze, coal in the fire that he was. The spark that was the newcomer woman, sky-blue over sea-blue, directing her attention back at Lassair now.

Lassair let her head drop back on her neck and simply *luxuriated* in the response around her. Felt the soul-cord that bound her to Flamesower pulse with his concern. The cord itself, his soul, was the same dappled green and brown as the glow that lit up his enshrouding physical body from within . . . but wisps of orange flame coruscated back and forth along that link between them. *Lassair? What is it?*

Nothing's wrong. Something is . . . wonderful. Lassair opened her body's eyes, and felt her face smile, even as she realized that light was starting to radiate out of her, though she tried to control it. It tended to make humans stare. *We exchanged energies and said each other's Names and we made something together.* She showed him, in a flash. Let him see the ball of cells dividing and dividing once more. *You are a progenitor. Does this please you as much as it pleases me? I did not know I could create.* Delight. Pure delight, from her, and *shock,* resonating down the link between them.

"You're *pregnant?*" Trennus said, out loud, and just loudly enough that everyone around them, caught by a sudden bubble of silence and wonder, turned and *stared* at him. A few whistles even broke through the crowd, some laughter. Trennus appeared largely oblivious to all of that, however.

Emberstone turned around in line, fully, to stare at them. "What?" The man blinked, his entire essence tightening like a fist. "Let me repeat that. *What?*"

Yes. I am. I should have realized. I usually can tell with humans the moment the male's essence enters the female's, and they become one. I can only assume that I was distracted when it occurred. Lassair's tone was teasing. *Perhaps it happened when the body slept. I will need to learn to divide my attention between dreams and reality, if I can.*

"But . . . wait. I . . . *how?*" Trennus sounded dazed. His mind wasn't keeping up with his emotional reactions, which Lassair interpreted as surprise, incredulity, confusion, joy, and a little fear.

The usual way, dear one. We completed all the required behaviors. Would you like to review them?

"But you've never been pregnant before!" Trennus clearly was having trouble wrapping his head around this thought. For five years, he'd completely discounted the concept of offspring.

Lassair paused. Her memory of . . . times before . . . was hazy still. *Not that I can remember. I think . . . perhaps because I didn't de-manifest . . . oh.* Horror. *If I de-manifest now . . . will it go away with my body?* She blinked, rapidly. *I can't risk that. I will require a plane ticket.*

Emberstone put a hand over his face, as if that could conceal his incredulity and exasperation, and said, under his breath, "You have got to be fucking kidding me. You knocked up a *spirit*, Tren? World's most agile swimmers, is all I'm saying." He shook his head. "Better you than me, though. Come on. Move. We're holding up the line and attracting stares." He nudged the woman with the sky-and-indigo spirit, who was still staring at them both, ahead in the line now.

Tren, clearly still staggered, wrapped an arm around Lassair's body, every gesture tentative right now, as if he thought he could damage her, in some way. *You're really sure?*

Yes. Look! The cells just divided again. Oh, it's so cute.

. . . yes, but a ball of cells isn't really . . . I mean . . . most people don't even announce till the third month, because so much can go wrong . . . Trennus' mind spun, and she could feel it, a hundred disjointed thoughts at once. *It . . . nothing's wrong with it, is there?*

Hmm? Oh, no. I'm reading its life-pattern now. It's a little different than I would have thought it would be. Possibly because this body is manufactured, and I based its life-pattern on an amalgam of females I have encountered that I admire for strength or beauty. Stormborn's life-pattern comprises some of it. The summoner in the place of darkness, where the alu hunted? Some of her. It changes, day to day. And some of it . . . I chained the helix together in patterns I thought pretty, like beads on a string, and lit it from within with my own fire. The child is not quite human, no. But it is wondrous, nonetheless.

Oh . . . gods. Shock reverberated off him, like a plucked string. *But . . . it's healthy?*

Absolutely. Oh, and it'll be a girl. That, as a total aside. *Do you think she'll look like me when she grows up?*

Trennus stopped in mid-stride, thus almost falling. *Oh, do calm down. You have at least nine months to get used to the idea. Though I might be able to adjust that.* Lassair caught his arm to stabilize him, and smiled radiantly at the woman behind the counter. *Hello. I need a ticket.*

The woman's jaw dropped, and shock, surprise, and desire radiated out of her. "I . . . do you have a driver's license?"

No.

"Do you have a passport?" Helpless flailing now.

No.

Emberstone put a hand over his eyes for a moment. Trennus cleared his throat and replied, "She, ah, doesn't need one. She's traveling with us. Same as Dr. Sasaki here. Praetorian business." He produced a flattened piece of metal with sigils on it—sigils that the mortals perceived as binding, though they were meaningless to Lassair—and the woman behind the counter stared at it for a long moment.

"I'll at least need her name for the passenger manifest."

I'm not telling you my Name. We've only just met.

Lassair was, in truth, mostly teasing Trennus at this point. Her mortal beloved cleared his throat and said, "Asha. Asha, ah, Matrugena."

Oh, I get one of your Names!

Well . . . we're sort of married, right? Rapid-fire calculation at the back of his head. *Soul-bonded. Close enough. And . . . apparently having a child. That was what was required to formalize a marriage in some cultures, back in the day. It didn't count till someone got knocked up . . . .*

Well, then I suppose we're married, then. Lassair nodded peaceably at the woman behind the counter. *This is my consort. I am travelling with him. Please provide me a ticket.*

The woman reached numbly down under the counter and ripped a ticket free, and began filling it out, by hand, recording the information in a series of ledgers. After a few moments, she handed it to Lassair, mumbling, "Have a nice flight."

Oh, thank you. This is my first time flying. Well, in one of your metal cages.

Emberstone and the newcomer woman preceded them onto the plane. Lassair was aware of the woman's fascination with her, but a great deal of it seemed to be the interest of a scientist with an intriguing case study. She kept trying to ask Emberstone questions, but he seemed intent on not answering. Lassair debated, briefly, telling the woman that one-way bargains never worked, and that if she wanted information from Emberstone, she should give some in return . . . but mortals liked to decide things for themselves. Advice, sometimes, they'd accept, but telling them what to do? Seemed wrong. Besides . . . they'd probably just go and do the opposite, anyway. Telling them that their spirits resonated with each other's, like a plucked string stirring the echo of the same note from another instrument in the same room would probably do no good, either.

It was like the old scholar, in a way. Lassair still felt guilty that his spark had gone out . . . but they'd told him not to leave the room. But he had, anyway, and while she could have been awake to stop him, her body had been . . . busy, apparently. *And humans have to be free to choose, or . . . they wouldn't be humans, would they?* It was something to consider, at any rate.

Aboard the plane, Lassair settled into the chair beside Trennus, and beamed at him. He looked sufficiently distracted, that as the plane rose from the ground, that he didn't almost even react to the fact that they were now in the air, and not at all on the ground. He still held her hand, however, his fingers locking down a little more tightly every time they hit a little turbulence. But he just stared into space as the drinks cart came by, and Lassair eagerly accepted a small paper sack filled with dried cranberries, almonds, and tiny pieces of Nahautl chocolate, bitter and sweet at once, closing her eyes in appreciation of the flavors. Energy flow. *I may have to eat more often,* she realized, suddenly. *My body might be sustainable by pure energy normally, but the infant may need more nutrients.*

. . . Yes. Probably calcium. Proteins.

You're not happy about this?

. . . I'm confused and I don't know how I even feel, he admitted. *On the one hand, it's . . . clearly happened before in human history.* His mind raced for a moment. *Sargon of Akkad,* he thought, reaching back into his mind for distant history lessons. *His mother was a . . . lilitu of the deserts, I think? One of the type of spirit normally associated with darkness, sex, and the drawing of blood and life?*

Humans always want to make us sound evil. Lassair squeezed his hand, and poured more of the snack into her mouth. She was *ravenous,* suddenly. *All spirits require energy exchanges. I remember people used to give me animal blood in the fires, but I didn't really like that. I liked it when they exchanged their life-essences much better. I remember that much.*

Yes, but . . . the lilitu are supposed to be malevolent.

They'll retaliate if they're injured. They like fertility, as I do. In the ground, in humans, in animals. But everything has a price.

Sex and blood. Death and fertility.

Always.

Not you. I don't see a lot of death in you.

No one's really provoked me in years, and I couldn't retaliate against . . . him. A wash of coldness, and her inner fires flickered. *He knew my Name. Someone . . . someone must have given it to him. I don't know who. But if I ever find out?* Lassair looked up at Trennus, her eyes wide. *I don't think I'll wait for you to unName him or her. I'm strong enough now that I think I would end that person, myself. And I would probably enjoy it.* She looked around. *Do you suppose they might give me another bag of those delicious — oh, thank you!* That, as Trennus absently handed her his own, untouched snack. *It's a good thing I realized early. What if I hadn't eaten for a week or two . . . no. you always make sure you feed me when I manifest.* Lassair carefully ate another almond. Different types of energies had different textures for her, different sensations as she absorbed them. These equated, roughly, to sight, smell, and sound. But none of them had *flavor.* Taste was so decadently organic. *What's on the other hand?*

What do you mean?

You said 'on the one hand, it's happened before.' What's on the other hand?

She could read confusion in him. Distress and happiness, at the same time. He'd ruled out the notion of a family, on choosing to associate himself with her as he had. He'd wanted children, but he could accept a life without them. But the suddenness . . . humans, for all that they inhabited time, seemed to need a great deal of it to grapple with new thoughts and change. Now, Trennus reached over, and put his arm lightly over her shoulders, and nuzzled his face into her hair. "I suppose I'm going to need to look for a house after all. That apartment isn't going to be nearly big enough for two of us and a baby." Amusement, and still a little unease. Not quite fear, but . . . something akin to it.

"Can I ask the two of you to pay some attention to work matters?" Emberstone asked, turning around from the row ahead of them, where he sat beside the sky-and-indigo woman.

"Yes," Trennus replied, but didn't lift his arm from Lassair's shoulders. "Absolutely. Please."

The flight from Lutetia to Rome was relatively short, only about four hours, and Minori had found herself between the Carthaginian technomancer and the window for the entirety of it. She'd tried to ask him a few questions, worded cautiously, about the spirit currently manifesting as an incredibly beautiful human woman seated behind them, only to be brushed off with a "That's between them," or a "Why don't you ask *her* that?"

Truthfully, Minori didn't quite *dare*. Asha—if that was her actual Name—was so beautiful that she took Minori's breath away, and she was clearly a *kami*. *Kami* were to be treated with the utmost respect. Even though the conversation earlier had filled her with raging curiosity.

They were met at the airport by two other Praetorians, one Hellene, and one Nahautl, who cut through the crowd to reach them. Wrist-clasps were followed by an extended conversation, held mostly above the level of her head, on the topic of what to do with her. Minori was more than a little irked to be discussed as if she were baggage, but listened quietly for the moment as the new Praetorians offered to take her to a safe-house apparently usually reserved for spies and informants. Eshmunazar actually shook his head at that. "No. She's not leaving our sight till we've seen the propraetor and gotten her some long-term protection arranged."

Minori looked up, tempted to ask if she had any say in these arrangements, but realized, before opening her mouth, that really, she'd just look childish and sound stupid if she said the words. No, she didn't have a say in this. She'd *somehow* stumbled into something much bigger than she'd thought in her research, and either these two *lictors* were trying to silence her . . . or trying to protect her. She thought it was more likely the latter, but she was watching them, very carefully indeed. Making sure her defenses were up, not just from unexpected outside attacks, but readied against them, as well. She'd had plenty of time in that silent flight to observe that Eshmunazar hadn't actually been reading the book in front of him, but had been watching the passengers around them. Standing guard, while Matrugena and the spirit had . . . worked out their odd life issues. And then Matrugena had taken over for a while, allowing Eshmunazar to close his eyes for the second half of the flight.

"I could take her back to my place," Matrugena offered.

Minori's eyes widened, and she flicked a glance at Asha, and then quickly away again. She wasn't quite sure what she'd do if she found herself alone with the spirit. Probably embarrass herself, utterly. Possibly by babbling in an undignified manner.

"You two need alone time at the moment," Eshmunazar replied, his expression tight. "Believe me, I remember the days well." There was a harsh note there that Minori didn't understand. "Doctor? You're with me. Don't worry about your reputation. We'll have *chaperones*."

Quietly seething at his tone, and surrounded by him and the two new Praetorians, Minori had settled into the car for a trip through Rome—staring, a little wide-eyed, like a tourist, at all the marble-facaded buildings, gleaming and white, until she settled a mask of neutrality back on her face. They wound up at a tall apartment building and headed upstairs, with one of the Praetorians staying down in the lobby, and the other stopping off on the same floor as them, but staying in the small elevator and stairwell access lobby. "I'll start walking the building," the Hellene man said, and moved off as Eshmunazar pulled her down a long, narrow hall, lined with doors, while hauling the small cart packed with boxes of books and notes behind them with his mind. *He's keeping one hand free,* she realized, distantly. *Even here, he's on edge. What did my research uncover that is this bad?*

Minori wasn't sure what she was expecting. The Carthaginian hadn't said two words to her the entire trip, and now unlocked the door in silence, before calling in, "I'm home!"

She certainly hadn't expected two boys to explode out of nowhere, shouting "Father!" and then slam into the technomancer at full speed, babbling in a mix of Latin and some other language she couldn't identify. An actual smile from Eshmunazar as he crouched down to speak with his sons, and return their hugs. It completely changed his face. An older woman—steel gray hair and a set of lenses perched on her nose—appeared and reached out to take some of their bags. "Master Eshmunazar, it's good to have you back so soon," the . . . housekeeper? . . . said, smiling. "The boys have done well with their lessons. And there are letters on your desk. One post-marked Numidia."

His face closed down again. "I'll read those later. Himi! Bodi! We have a guest. Show me your manners and greet her." He turned back and said, with polite distance, "Doctor Minori Sasaki, these are Himilico and Bodeshmun. My sons. Their pedagogue, Bellatrix Mellinari. Everyone, this is Doctor Sasaki. She'll be staying with us until we can get her a safe place to live. Hopefully, no longer than tomorrow. Bellatrix, you can leave. I'll make up the guest bed. No need for you to strain your back."

"Thank you, sir. It's been a long day, I don't mind saying." The pedagogue gathered her things, and headed out the door, as the two boys stared at Minori in unabashed interest. They had darker skin than their father, and lively brown eyes, but they mostly had his facial features, and dark, wavy hair.

"Are you a doctor like our mother?" the older one asked, looking over his shoulder for where his father was, and adding the last in a hushed tone, as Minori stood, a little awkwardly, in the small dining area, and Eshmunazar threw sheets on a couch that folded out into a bed in the living room.

"Ah . . . no. I study engineering and sorcery." Minori relaxed a little. "When will your mother be home?"

She regretted the words instantly. The boys' faces crumpled up. "Never," Himi told her, softly.

"Oh," Minori whispered. "Oh, forgive me." It would be the height of discourtesy to mention the dead, so she couldn't ask if the woman had died recently.

Bodi, the younger one, pulled himself up on a chair at the dining table, where lessons and books were still laid out neatly. "Our mama was bad," he told her, solemnly. "She tried to steal us."

"Mother wasn't *bad*," Himi corrected, immediately. "I still miss her. I want to see her. I think she tried to call when Father was away, but Mistress Mellinari hung up the phone on her. That's rude, isn't it?"

"She's not supposed to call here. She might try to steal us again." Bodi sounded distressed.

"You don't love Mother anymore—" Accusation.

"I don't want to be stolen and go where the monsters are!"

"Baby."

"Stop it right now," Eshmunazar told them, sharply, from the doorway. "Your mother isn't a bad person. She made a few bad choices, that's all. Bodi, there are monsters everywhere, but I'll teach you how to fight them. Himi? What have I told you about calling your brother a baby? You're supposed to help teach him and protect him, not run him down. Both of you, pick up your books. It's dinner time."

Minori again, wasn't sure what to expect. Eshmunazar actually cooked—something she'd rarely seen a man do before—though it was a cold collection of ground grains, tomatoes, herbs, mint, onion and garlic. Light, but flavorful. Afterwards, he pointed her to the small living room, noting, "The windows are warded, but don't sit in front of them. We might be on the fifteenth floor, but that doesn't mean someone can't see you. You can watch the far-viewer, or take your pick of the books on the shelves." And then he went about getting the two boys settled in for the evening. Cleared the dishes, and started digging in the boxes they'd brought from Gaul, setting all the maps back out again.

"If you're going to use my work, I would *like* to participate," Minori finally said, from the doorway . . . and then they were back precisely where they'd been the night before. Arguing mathematics at each other with increasing volume, and Minori finally rapping out, "That's all very well and good, but where do you get *your* first set of numbers for the estimated energy release at the Pyramid of the Sun? It doesn't tally with what I measured at the scene at all." His face went shuttered. "Oh, yes. You were *there*. The numbers you're giving would have *killed* anyone exposed to it—"

"It almost did."

Minori stared at him. "Look, these numbers are so inflated that only a *god* or . . . or a *kami* could have done this, if we're not talking about a nuclear reactor exploding or a ley-line resonating out of control."

No reply. He just kept tracing the lines on the map of Caesaria Australis. Minori's stomach twisted. "I said, only a god or a *kami* . . . ?"

"I heard you. I just didn't choose to respond to your supposition." His tone was an answer, in and of itself. He *could* have pooh-poohed, he could have denigrated her intelligence for even suggesting the idea. But he didn't. He didn't even look up.

Minori found a chair to sit down on, her legs suddenly a little unsteady. "A *god* did this?" she whispered.

"I can't talk about it." He circled several points in western Tawantinsuyu. "The pattern isn't quite the same," he muttered. "But *just* close enough."

"Please," Minori said, quietly. "Please. Let me *help*."

Eshmunazar looked up at her, and for the first time, she saw the fear in his eyes. "You *are* helping," he told her, simply. "But I have to make sure you're safe, too, Doctor."

The next morning, she found all of her books and notes neatly packed up, and found herself bustled out of the apartment before the boys were even awake, and brought across town to a palatial home on Palatine Hill. The center of the world, as far as Rome was concerned. Minori's eyes widened at the opulent furnishings and the . . . unusual paintings on the walls. She would have thought the scenes best kept for a book of *shunga* wood-prints, but Romans were *odd* in so many respects.

And that was where she met the rest of the lictors for the first time, and Propraetor Livorus, as well. She was introduced to another olive-skinned man, with dark brown, lively eyes, and with brown hair tied back from his face in a long tail. His hands were light as he actually bowed very slightly, clasping one of her hands in both of his own. A modified version of the Roman wrist-clasp and the Nipponese bow, and the delicacy of his touch suggested to her that he'd trained in martial arts fairly extensively. Someone who worked in those arts tended to understand that a light touch, used to redirect, could be more effective than a savage blow . . . and didn't need to crush someone's hands to assert strength. "Adam ben Maor," he introduced himself, politely. "This is my wife, Sigrun Caetia."

Adam ben Maor expressed a type of male beauty—clean, compactly built, strong, but graceful, just as Trennus, looming to his left, expressed a different type of male beauty. Bulkier, and more . . . unrefined. Asha had an opulent kind of feminine beauty. Rich curves, a sweet face, and radiance, from within. The woman being introduced as ben Maor's wife was also beautiful, but it was the beauty of a perfectly crafted katana. Minori realized that she'd slowed her own movements, just a little. Was keeping her hands visible, and at her sides.

The woman by ben Maor's side was clearly a Goth of some variety or another, though whether from Germania, Gotaland, Belgae, or Nova Germania, Minori couldn't have said. Coppery blond hair, in a braid to the waist, and nearly as tall as her husband. Gray eyes the color of fine steel, or a winter morning. Beautiful, but cold as frost, in marked contrast to Asha's luxurious warmth. She didn't bow, but did incline her head politely as she offered a wrist-clasp, and Minori could feel strength in those fingers. Like her husband, Sigrun Caetia didn't crush with her touch. But Minori could feel electricity in her grasp. *Kami-touched*, she thought, her eyes widening. *Three sennin, each with great power and skill, and of course, the soldier, too.*

"Ah, Doctor Sasaki," a voice said from behind her, and Minori's head snapped around as a Roman man entered the study. His hair was iron gray, and his eyes, behind simple, rounded lenses, were blue. She would have had to have been almost oblivious to politics as a whole not to have recognized Propraetor Livorus from the far-viewer news broadcasts. "My apologies. A phone call from a colleague in the Senate on the matter of the Qin intervention in Mongol lands delayed me." He gestured for everyone to be seated. "Eshmunazar? The floor is yours."

"I'm not certain I can speak plainly with the doctor in the room." Eshmunazar shook his head, and once again, Minori was infuriated.

"I will sign and swear anything that you wish me to sign and swear," she told him. "I do not know anything about the Source Initiative beyond that they have a very good journal—"

She speaks truth—

"I see no lies in her eyes, Eshmunazar."

The words from the spirit and the *kami*-touched woman overlapped, warmth from one, cold, hard assurance from the other. Eshmunazar straightened. "We're giving her clearance on this based on Caetia and Asha's gut instincts?"

"And yours as well," Livorus gestured. "Your report on her knowledge and data sources was fairly comprehensive. I also have one piece of information that you are lacking, Eshmunazar. Doctor Sasaki's original family name. Ijiun. A samurai clan of considerable power."

Minori's head jerked up, and her lips parted, just for an instant. The propraetor continued, quietly, "I took the liberty of having some of our diplomats shake a few bushes, if not the *fasces*." He pinned the lictors with his stare, and while not one of them changed expressions, Asha suddenly bubbled with silent amusement in a golden wave of good cheer. "Our good doctor was educated at the Imperial Court of Nippon in Kyoto from the age of twelve until the age of eighteen, before being permitted to leave the country and live independently of her family. Somewhat unusual, but her talents are significant. You understand the concept of discretion very well, doctor. And you will be signing an oath before you leave here, which will bind your tongue as much as it binds any of my lictors."

Minori's throat had closed down in fright at the revelation of her original name, and the grimace that crossed Eshmunazar's face had been just as dark as all his other expressions so far at the mention of her family background. She wasn't entirely sure why.

Kanmi had to give the good doctor credit. She went pale as he gave her the bare bones of the events of five years ago, and her eyes widened until the whites showed all the way around as he described the Tholberg coils designed to tap energy from a god—a god that had, in some way that none of them had been able to determine, even after five years of studying and debating their recollections, been *bound* to that place, in some fashion. "Our best guess," Trennus put in, his tone academic, "remains that Tlaloc was *persuaded* to go to the Pyramid, because it was one of his oldest places of power. That the so-called Pyramid of the Sun should have been named after the *cenote* it was built over, the 'passage to the underworld,' in the Nahautl faith. As I was just, ah, reminded yesterday, Tlaloc was a prime example of the linked power of life-and-death. A union of opposites. Out of death, life. Out of blood, fertility. Nothing from nothing." Trennus looked over at Kanmi. "Once he was there, I think they said all of his greater and lesser Names, invoking him. Defining him. And once he bargained with them to be sacrificed to again, they limited him with that bargain."

Sigrun raised a hand at that point, looking uncomfortable. "I am not certain that we can talk about *gods* in the same way that you talk about spirits, Trennus."

Trennus shot Kanmi a quick, rueful glance, and Kanmi glanced up at the ceiling. "You've said yourself that the top human-accessible floor in the Odinhall is a . . . conduit for physical interaction with the Veil," Kanmi reminded Sigrun. "If that's the case, the gods come from the Veil. Same as spirits. I think we can use some of the same terminology to discuss how humans interact with both gods and spirits."

"I knew, somehow, that that was going to come back someday and bite me," Sigrun muttered, rubbing a hand over her face.

"And the fact that so many gods place prohibitions on speaking their Names?" Trennus said, gently. "Speaking someone's true Name gets their attention. Some of the old epithets for death gods were used to ensure that the person speaking them didn't catch their attention, and die, for example. In Germania, long ago, it was common not to call a bear a *bear*, but . . . ."

"Honeypaws," Sigrun supplied, not looking up. "So as not to invite the bear's attention. Back when a bear could easily kill several of the men of a village, or a child who wandered off from a home. Yes. I understand . . . and by all means, continue. I will simply pretend I am listening to a highly theoretical conversation with no application to the real world *at all.*"

Trennus looked around. "So . . . they *theoretically* bound him to that place. They bound him to the machines, which we never got much of a chance to analyze, but I'd be willing to bet there were other things inside of them besides coils of wire . . . and they got him to agree to give his power to the machines and to Tototl and Xicohtencatl, as his disciples." Trennus raised his hands, suggesting that he didn't know if the word was entirely accurate. "I don't have anything to back this theory up, but I've been thinking about it for a few years. Tlaloc was weakened by the loss of faith in him, yes, but he was still . . . far too powerful to be *forced*. And he may have thought, I suppose, that once he gained enough power once more, once enough sacrifices had been made . . . that he could change the terms of the bargain."

That is not uncommon for . . . maleficent spirits, Lassair agreed, her tone uneasy.

"I'm with Sig on the whole 'speculating about the motives of an entity,' thing," Adam said, rubbing a freshly-shaved chin. "But, that being said . . . what do you think that Dr. Sasaki's research shows us?"

"Her research tallies, with every known sacrifice that connected

Tlaloc to a given 'ley-platform' in Nahautl." Kanmi's words were blunt. "The Great Earthquake of 1950, in Burgundoi? If her evidence is correct, that might have been the result of their initial binding of Tlaloc under the Pyramid of the Sun."

Adam looked *ill*. "Then we can all be grateful that we didn't set off a much worse one when the, ah, entity *died*."

"I've been saying for years that *something* absorbed part of the hit," Kanmi said, dryly.

I've admitted to some of that. But I did not take it all. Lassair shifted a little as everyone's eyes found her. *I do not know where the rest of it went. Perhaps the machines?*

"The Tholberg coils were melted into slag. Matrugena and I had made very damned sure of that." Kanmi looked around. "There's something far more disturbing in her data, though." He unfurled a map of all the seismic activity in the western hemisphere, and pointed at the southern continent. "Much more than previously seen, historically speaking. Production of ley-facilities *has* picked up there in the past eight years . . . but we know that ley doesn't cause these kinds of seismic events. But thanks to Dr. Sasaki . . . now we know what *does*."

Silence in the room, and Kanmi watched Dr. Sasaki's eyes flicker from one to another of them. Much to his surprise, she raised a finger, as if asking permission to speak, and when Livorus nodded to her, she said, simply, "I would very much like to be permitted to go to Tawantinsuyu to help with the investigations."

Trennus was already shaking his head. "You're a civilian. We couldn't possibly put you at risk in an official Praetorian operation."

"Technically," Kanmi put in, very dryly, "there have been no *official* investigations on our part. This is just my *hobby*."

Silence, again. Livorus looked around the room. "All four of you were told to stay away from the topic, but I've allowed a certain amount of latitude in continuing to investigate, because I rather thought that the decision to keep you away was . . . ill-advised. And your results have borne out my thoughts on the matter." He reached out and touched the map, reading over the results. "Eshmunazar, you believe that Dr. Sasaki's numbers require further, on-site investigations?"

"Yes, sir."

Livorus set a finger to his lips, a characteristic gesture, and looked off into space for a few moments. "Unfortunately, with Qin entering the field of war at the moment, I simply cannot jaunt off to Tawantinsuyu without good reason." He considered it a moment longer. "Ben Maor?"

"Yes, sir?"

"How confident are you in my secondary tier of lictors, the ones who've been attending me while you and Sigrun were away, and while Eshmunazar and Matrugena were in Gaul?"

Adam sat up, his eyes intent. "Very, sir. Of them all, I trust Horatius Lepidus with command, if the four of us were made unavailable, if that's what you're about to ask."

Livorus nodded. "Yes. Precisely. I will have to discuss this matter with the Imperator, but I think it is possible that you four could be sent as a, hmm. Advance team, I think. Preparing the way for a state visit. Just because there is war in the east, does not mean that we should not look to cement our relations with all our far-flung provinces and subject nations. And under that guise, you should be easily able to use Rome's keys to unlock many doors."

Kanmi snorted a little under his breath. "And why would we four be *allowed* to go, sir? We've been told, repeatedly, to stay out of this."

"Because I shall ask it of the Emperor," Livorus replied, his eyes steady. "And because you have given us *results*, whereas the rest of the Praetorians have given us precisely nothing in five years of investigations. Oh, a great number of technomancers have had their backgrounds investigated and many of them have been questioned, and a few even jailed for sedition, but little else has come of it."

Kanmi caught how Minori's spine had straightened at Livorus' calm words, even as the propraetor turned and studied her. "Eshmunazar," he said then.

"Yes?" Kanmi very rarely added a *sir* to any statement.

"Would Dr. Sasaki add, in any way, to your ability to find the people behind this? She *is* a bona fide member of the Source Initiative, for example. And her findings have put her life in danger." Livorus studied Sasaki calmly. "Would she not be admirable bait? That is, if you were willing to put yourself at such risk, doctor?"

Sasaki's eyes widened, and she said, quickly, and before Kanmi could reply, "Of course. How could I not, with such matters at stake? Thousands of people died in the Burgundoi earthquake, because these people bled off power from the . . . entity . . ." she'd picked up on the self-conscious wording immediately, "and what they didn't transmit through the air, passed through the ley-grid and the ground *anyway*." She twisted her hands together for a moment.

Kanmi ground his teeth for a moment. "It's an idea," he said, tightly. "I don't think it's a good one, but it is a notion. You're one more person that we have to protect."

"I *do* have combat training," she said, quickly, raising her chin.

"And when was the last time it was used in the field?" Kanmi countered, harshly. "There's theory, and there's reality, and a vast gulf between the two."

Sasaki's whole face tightened. "Never," she admitted. "But I can also be more than bait. I am a fully qualified ley-engineer and sorcerer. I might be able to get into facilities that your people cannot, under their guise of preparing for a state visit."

"There remains," Sigrun noted, quietly, "the small problem of interfacing between both halves of the expedition. Dr. Sasaki could become very isolated from us, and that would be neither tenable nor conscionable."

Part of the reason Kanmi, to this day, had a desire to needle Sigrun was her unremittingly formal way of speaking in front of strangers.

Around just the core team, the valkyrie's speech relaxed. But when she said what he was *thinking*, just in that . . . irritating fashion . . . it made it hard not to disagree with her just for the sake of poking at her. Thus, he grimaced in mild irritation, and said, "Caetia's right." A dour glare at the valkyrie, who just lifted her eyebrows at him in return. "If we *do* bring the good doctor with us, which I think is a bad idea, she can't be isolated from us."

Livorus nodded, his expression faintly amused. "Did you intend to bring your sons with you?" he asked, seemingly tangentially.

"No," Kanmi returned, immediately. "Too dangerous."

"You've taken them to Judea, northern Europa, Raccia, and *Chaldea* in the last two years," Trennus pointed out, amiably.

"Yes. All places where the worst that could happen was that a random djinni might break free and rampage, a bomb could go off, or someone might have a gun. Tawantinsuyu? They used to perform child sacrifices to their gods, and we could be talking about another *entity* being either fed, unleashed, or drained. I can protect them from spirits, lions, tigers, and bears. Earthquakes and acts of entities are outside my areas of expertise."

Livorus nodded, still appearing faintly amused. "Your common sense, as always, is unstinting, Eshmunazar. And in which case, since I assume that Matrugena is bringing his beloved, then the answer becomes plain."

Kanmi just stared for a moment at the propraetor, uncomprehending. Until he heard ben Maor stifle a chuckle. *Then* understanding hit, and Kanmi said, firmly, and without preamble, "No."

Livorus raised his eyebrows. "No?"

"No, *sir*." Kanmi put his hands on the table, suddenly infuriatingly aware of the fact that Lassair's amusement was bubbling forth again. "I am not going to *fawn* on the good doctor." He had to admit, the woman was beautiful, in her way, and certainly intelligent, and shared most of his fields of expertise. But all those factors would make the pretense that much more intolerable.

Sasaki, for her part, sat bolt upright in her chair, shaking her head in what certainly looked like distaste. "Surely, there must be another way?" she suggested, tentatively.

"It . . . could work," Trennus said, his eyes narrowing. "We could put it out that you'd been writing to one another for a while. Like your long-term correspondence with Lady Erida."

Kanmi sent Trennus a black glance. Erida had just gotten married a few months ago, and they continued to write to one another in spite of that. It was a very solid collegial relationship, and nothing more. "And then, what? I took it into my head to surprise her at the conference, we slipped off with her and the professor, and just *happened* to ward the hotel room to Tartarus and back?"

"Details." Adam said, flicking a hand. "Can be worked out. Gives us an additional set of eyes, someone who *hasn't* seen everything we've seen before, might not fall into the same mental patterns as the rest of us, and another mage. I'll want to see what you can do, Dr. Sasaki, and see if you can at least fire a gun, but we'll probably have a few weeks before we leave. These things never get arranged overnight. It's a good working story, Esh. It lets us protect her, too. I'm not crazy about bringing a civilian in . . . but by drawing the Source Initiative's attention, or by using her access to the facilities, we might get somewhere with this."

Kanmi folded his arms across his chest, and thought, rapidly. His world suddenly felt like one of Dr. Sasaki's seiches. All the water in it was rippling, and with no visible source of the disturbance. He didn't see any way out, so his best bet was to accede as gracefully as possible, and wring concessions out of *everyone*. Trennus wasn't the only person around the table who knew how to bargain, after all. "All right," he said. "But this is against my better judgment. Dr. Sasaki? We say *jump* and you don't ask questions. Not even *how high*, you understand?"

Adam snorted. "Esh? Coming from *you*, that might be the funniest thing I've ever heard."

Chapter XVI: Lines

Overview

Tawantinsuyu, or the "Land of the Four Quarters," was an established empire when Rome and its Gallic and Gothic allies pushed forward with the exploration of the western hemisphere. The empire, at the time, spanned mainly the western coast of Caesaria Australis, and reached up into what the indigenous peoples of the region called the _Anti_ mountains. . . sometimes corrupted into "_Andes_" by Gothic and Gallic tongues today. Regional kingdoms rose and fell for hundreds of years before the empire based at Cuzco came into existence in or around 1090 AC, and began, around 1360 AC, to expand, both by peaceful means and conquest, taking over other tribes, first in the region of Cuzco, and then further and further from their power base.

The empire was organized into four main governing regions — hence the name of the whole — and the chief ruler of the empire, or the Sapa Inca, decreed that the smaller kingdoms now ruled by his people could retain their traditional religious beliefs, but that they must also acknowledge, as supreme, the gods of Cuzco, including Inti, the sun god. This use of a formal state religion to bind the empire together, along with the general toleration of other gods, has been compared to Rome's own policies.

Religion

The cults of Inti, Supay, and other state gods, as well as the hundreds, if not thousands, of mountain gods and nature spirits worshipped by the residents of Tawantinsuyu, were frequently venerated with human sacrifice. Children were drawn from villages across the empire, and brought to Cuzco. Some of the girls were groomed as wives for the Sapa Inca, and others were returned to their families. But many were fed the diet of nobles for a year, and then taken high into the mountains, and sacrificed there, to appease the god of this mountain, that volcano, the sun, the death god. . . the list was extensive. This was done, at least in part, sociologists believe, to maintain order and a sense of community within the empire. Everyone participated. Everyone's child might be so 'honored.' Everyone shared in the honor, and in the loss.

Culture

In 1475 AC, the first ships from Novo Gaul and Nova Germania crept down along the coasts, past Nahautl, searching for the lands described by their southern neighbors as either impassable mountains, high deserts, and dense jungles. . . but with whom the Nahautl had trade relations, nevertheless. They found Tawantinsuyu, an empire of over twelve million people, where the nobles bound the heads of their children from birth to change the shape of their skulls into a more fashionable cone. Where gold and silver were worked, and where art and culture flourished, but where they had not developed the intricate writing system of their Nahautl and Quecha neighbors. The locals had, however, developed methods of mathematical calculation, such as the _quipu_, which was a series of knotted cords that served as a kind of abacus.

The Plague Years

Trade sprang up, but as the Romans, Gauls, and Goths set up small outposts, diseases promulgated. Tragically, smallpox spread between 1580 and 1590, but Roman hygiene practices limited the severity of the outbreak. As a result of the illness sweeping the empire, Rome stepped in to assist the local nobility and helped the army keep the peace during the plague period. Temples to Hygeia and Asclepius became centers for the treatment of the disease, and when the outbreak passed, these temples became centers for the teaching of medicine.

The University of Cuzco had its origin here, and remains the foremost center for the learning of medical practices in Caesaria Australis to this day. Tours of the plague cemeteries and old plague hospitals are available daily; _call ahead for times and availability._

When the plague had burned itself out, the Sapa Inca of the era, Tupac Huayna, agreed to an alliance with Rome, the better to keep his northern and eastern borders intact. To that end, Tawantinsuyu became a subject kingdom under Roman protection, and paid taxes in order to retain Roman troops and fortifications along their borders. The traditional requirement that Roman gods be venerated alongside those of Cuzco was imposed, as was the equally traditional requirement that human sacrifices be ended.

There are those who accuse Rome of having taken advantage of Tawantinsuyu during a time of crisis and preying upon the Land of the Four Quarters like a vulture or a hyena. There is some validity to this perspective, but Rome did not deliberately set out to infect the indigenous population, and provided palliative care for the sick and the dying. The Empire helped maintain order, but has imposed little of its culture on Tawantinsuyu in the ensuing centuries. The result is a land that has remained little changed, culturally, from the fifteenth century until today. While there are Roman, Gothic, and Gallic temples here and there in Cuzco, these gods are worshipped alongside the native gods, and have not displaced them — precisely in the same way in which Roman and Hellene gods are worshipped in Nahautl, alongside native gods today.

Society Today

The current Sapa Inca — Emperor Sayri Cusi — is the supreme leader of his people, and the Roman governor has little real influence on affairs within Tawantinsuyu; his role is closer to that of an ambassador, or a praetor tasked with dealing with foreign affairs.

Because of the deliberately 'hands-off' policy of Rome towards Tawantinsuyu, technological adoption has taken place almost entirely at the whim of whichever Sapa Inca happens to be in power at any given time. Some areas of the country have ley-grids. Others have electrical grids, powered by geothermal power plants, courtesy of the abundant volcanism in the region. Travelers are advised to bring a full set of adapters for portable devices such as hair dryers and transistor radios, as the power system available in Cuzco or Machu Picchu may differ from one street to the next, and outside of the large cities, this is even more the case. Some areas have no power grid at all, as local nobles have opted to maintain a traditional lifestyle on their lands. Serfdom *still exists in the outlying areas, and travelers are warned against 'rescuing' serfs, as this can lead to prosecution, fines, and even imprisonment.*

Places to Go

The summer palace of the emperors remains located in Machu Picchu, a charming and beautiful city located high in the Anti mountains. Travelers are advised that the altitude may prove debilitating to those unused to it. Take care not to exercise too vigorously at first, and drink plenty of water.

The Lines of Nazca are a cultural artifact, and are periodically added to by the various indigenous shamans. They are visible from the sky, and ornithopter tours are offered daily. No trip to Tawantinsuyu is complete, without seeing this wonder of the western world.

— A Traveler's Guide to Tawantinsuyu. Ymbfaran Press, Novo Trier, Nova Germania, 1951 AC.

Maius 7, 1960 AC

It took the better part of three weeks to set up the travel authorizations and their cover story; the wheels of every bureaucracy tend to grind slowly, and state visits, as they'd learned over the course of their work with Livorus, did not simply happen overnight. Even their trips, which were, ostensibly, the scut-work for such a visit, couldn't be arranged quickly.

Trennus and Lassair had started to cultivate the habit of visiting Adam and Sigrun once a week for dinner. This was part of Lassair's effort to understand and engage with humans, and participate in things of the body more fully. On this particular *dies Lunae*, it was Adam's turn to cook, and as such, it was *shakshuka* tonight, quick and easy, just eggs poached in tomato sauce with mild chili peppers and a dash of spices. He had never actually seen Lassair eat as much as the spirit had been in the past several weeks. . . or seen her maintain the same body for so long.

He considered Lassair for a moment as Sigrun was clearing the dishes. He'd gotten to an equilibrium point with the concept of spirits, in general; Lassair had saved his life, and every other member of the team's. And she and Trennus, to all outwards appearances, seemed to make each other very happy. Adam was just . . . heavily disquieted, when he allowed himself to think about it, by the notion that well over half of Trennus' soul technically belonged to Lassair at the moment. Trennus seemed to regard this as life-energy, but for Adam, the soul was a very different thing. It was, for him, immortal, something that would persist beyond the death of the body. Something *separate* from the mind and the body. Making choices that could affect that was incredibly dangerous, and Adam couldn't conceive of doing the same. . . except, perhaps, for a damned good reason. Then again, Trennus seemed to think he had a reason. And watching Lassair bloom and become a *person*, instead of a shadow of flame, over the past few years. . . Adam had to consider that Trennus might be right.

At the moment, the spirit leaned against Trennus' shoulder at the table, and had just sent a thought after Sigrun into the kitchen, *Flamesower told me last week that I should not necessarily heal people when I find them injured. Do you agree, Stormborn?*

"That would be a matter of perspective. I do not heal everyone I meet," Sigrun replied, coming back in from the kitchen and standing in the doorway, tilting her head slightly. "For one thing, it *hurts* when I do it. For another, my gods teach self-reliance, whenever possible. If you always fix things for other people, they will come to rely on it, and will not help themselves. It weakens them. That is a reason why my gods do not offer many answers, I think. To force my people to learn, for themselves." Adam had long noticed that even though Sigrun spoke of her people, she rarely included herself among them. *Learn for themselves, not learn for ourselves.* He'd asked her about it, once, and she'd looked away with a shrug. *I am a tool in the hands of the gods, Adam. You know that.*

I do not wish to weaken people, but I do wish to help them. Lassair shook her head, red hair bouncing loosely around her face.

"I'm mostly concerned about the energy loss. You can't just heal and heal and heal, and not receive anything in return. That's how you were almost destroyed originally." Trennus' voice was a little tense.

Sigrun headed back into the kitchen, calling over her shoulder, "I have had people *decline* healing before. They didn't wish to become indebted to me, I think."

I would not demand payment. The energy given would not substantially lessen me, and they would give back gratitude, which would help sustain me.

"Gratitude," Adam said, "doesn't last long, and I wouldn't consider it a filling dish. Though, speaking of which, Lassair? I know you like food, but I've never seen you eat like this before."

Lassair's radiant happiness flooded through the room, and Adam had to take a moment to cough and shake it off. Lassair's emotional broadcasts could be downright dizzying. Trennus shifted a little, stretching his long legs under the table, and looked a little embarrassed. "Ah, we've. . . I mean, I've been meaning to talk to you both about that," he said. "Kanmi already knows, since he was there when Lassair, well, realized."

Adam squinted at Trennus. "Realized what?"

That I am with child.

In the kitchen, Sigrun dropped something, with a shattering sound. Adam blinked, "I. . . what?"

We are going to have a child. I did not know that this was possible for me, but I am very glad that it is. Lassair found a morsel on her plate that she'd missed before, picked it up with her fingers, and ate it. *I do not know how much food I should eat to sustain the child. Thus, I let the body tell me how much and when. This seems to be working.*

Adam looked at her, and then at Trennus. He was not *about* to ask how this was possible. Trennus, for his part, cleared his throat. "That's why she's been staying manifested. We're not going to let it impede the work, but I might have to call on Saraid for assistance that I don't normally ask of her. . . or even strike bargains with other spirits." He shifted a little, looking marginally uncomfortable. "For example, that fire absorption Lassair did, back in Nahautl. . . or even, really, healing people, since she has to go inside of them to do it. . . many of these abilities require her to demanifest."

And I am not sure what will happen to the child if I cause this body not to exist, Lassair said, lifting her hands. *I do not know if I can reconstruct the baby as I do the body. Every time I reform the body, it is different, in some way or another.*

It was true. Lassair was as malleable as flame. Her eyes were usually the only feature that stayed the same, from one form to the next. "Ah. . . so that's why you needed the passport. And the travel arrangements." Adam rubbed at his eyes. Getting her papers together had been a bureaucratic nightmare. She didn't have a place of birth, an age, parents, any of it. He'd asked Tren why the man was suddenly bothering with it all after so many years of Lassair blithely de-manifesting for the long plane flights, but a phone call had come in before Tren had been able to reply, and they'd both been distracted. Now, Adam understood.

He sighed, stood, and went to go help Sigrun pick up what remained of a ceramic tureen, though she shooed him away with a mutter of, "If I cut myself, it hardly matters, Adam." It reminded him, vividly, of the time he'd caught her, in this very kitchen, hovering three feet off the ground in order to reach the highest shelves in the cabinets. She'd looked as ashamed as a child caught with a hand in the cookie jar, using her god-born abilities for something *other* than combat. He'd laughed and hugged her. . . and asked her if she'd ever gone flying just for the pleasure of it. It was something as natural to her as breathing, he knew; she'd learned how to fly around the same time as she'd learned how to *walk.* But the blank expression on her face had clearly indicated to him that she had no idea what he was talking about. The whole conversation had, in fact, inspired him to take his flight lessons. He'd always wanted to be a pilot, and he was, for god's sake, married to someone who could fly as if the earth's gravity didn't trammel her at all. He'd watched her slowly relax, and stop looking around to see who might notice her unsanctioned *fun.*

But this time, there was something else in her face. A pinch to the lips, hastily masked. Adam caught her hands, and looked down into her eyes for a moment. "You all right, *neshama?*"

Sigrun made a face. "Just fine." She leaned past him to look into the dining area of their small apartment. "You're going to need a house, you two."

Lassair stood and came to the door of the kitchen, sliding her arms around Sigrun's waist as Adam moved out of range for a moment. Sigrun pulled slightly away from Lassair; where the flame-spirit was very much a toucher, Sigrun was very much *not.* Adam couldn't hear what the spirit said to Sigrun, but he could see the pinched look leave Sigrun's face. Silent communion between the two, so unalike in so many ways, yet similar in others. God-born and spirit. Neither was quite mortal, and both were in love with mortal men. Lassair had innocence, counterpoised against a strong hedonistic streak, and Sigrun had world-weariness and distance, counterpoised against a shy sort of delight when someone let her in. As if she hadn't realized that there were doors in all the walls she kept around herself.

Trennus moved to the kitchen now, as he followed up on Sigrun's comment, moments before. "I know we need a house. I'd love to buy something up in Tarvodubron, near my parents' villa, on the edges of the Caledonian Forest. But the north end of Britannia makes for a long trip to anywhere."

"The house next door to ours in Judea is still up for sale," Adam noted. "Not as long of a plane flight. And we're not all going to be on Livorus' detail forever. Sooner or later, we'll all have to move on. . . but I think we'd kind of like to keep track of you two." He slipped his arm around Sigrun's waist. He knew he could speak for her in this. Tren had become his best friend over the years, and he knew she cared deeply for the Pictish man. Enough to tolerate Lassair calling her *sister*, anyway, and occasionally to return the term.

"Yes, but then we'd be living in *Judea*." Trennus grimaced. "I'd prefer Novo Gaul. Except then I'm back to long plane flights."

"Plenty of time to decide," Adam said, thumping his fist against Tren's shoulder. "Besides, I think Judea's climate is changing. Every time we go there now, it rains. People comment on it." He met Trennus' eyes for a moment. He didn't need to say it out loud. Trennus' gaze tracked over to Sigrun and Lassair, who were still conversing silently. And he nodded, once.

But the only response the summoner returned out loud was, "It's not the climate, Adam—not entirely, anyway. It's your people's truly irritating dislike of magic and spirits." Tren grinned at him. "It would be hard to be who I am, and live in a place like that!"

Maius 8, 1960 AC

Dr. Minori Sasaki had been shuffled from apartment to apartment between the various lictors for the past three weeks, so that no one of them had had to look after her for a long stretch. Kanmi had detected resignation in her expression, and she'd muttered in range of his hearing, that she felt like a package. *Pretty much what you are, at the moment,* he'd thought, but had taken her to the firing range at the main Praetorian building in Rome, so that her skills could be evaluated.

Much to Kanmi's surprise, she turned out to be an excellent shot with a derringer. Ben Maor, predictably, had set her to practicing with a very small, Judean-made pistol, manufactured by Hevim. It held six rounds of .25 ammunition—comparatively, tiny, but Dr. Sasaki might be able to slip the small weapon into an inner pocket and have it overlooked. Even more surprisingly, the doctor started attempting to enchant the bullets herself. It was fairly clear that she hadn't done this outside of a classroom exercise before, however, but Kanmi merely watched as she carefully did her math and began layering enchantments onto each bullet.

The only way to learn this skill was to practice it. He was, however, intrigued by the fact that she actually rigged each bullet to displace the air *ahead* of it. Essentially, a vacuum opened ahead of the bullet's path, displacing air to either side. The trick should add to accuracy, and prevent bullet spin and muzzle velocity from being lost. He'd have saved this enhancement for a sniper rifle, himself, but it was an interesting concept. She also layered in an enchantment that would reduce the ambient temperature of any matter that the bullet impacted with by almost exactly a hundred degrees. The enchantment was set up to remove the energy from the air, tissue, solid matter, and use it to fuel the enchantment itself, recursively. Efficient, it only required the initial energy of the bullet firing, itself, to begin the spell process.

"If you're trying to induce hypothermia as a merciful way of dealing with people shooting at you," Kanmi told her, after listening to her incant, carefully, over each bullet, "I wouldn't bother. If they're shooting at you, they want you dead. Kill them back and kill them faster."

"That's not my intention. I'm setting the diameter at about a three-inch radius. Even if I only clip someone, the cold will kill tissue, almost instantly, and there will be a moment of shock to the body." Sasaki shrugged.

"I don't agree that it's the most effective enhancement you could use, but it's your life, doctor." Kanmi forbore to mention that he might wind up relying on her to watch his back. *Astarte. What a notion.*

He sat against the wall and watched as the others tested her physical skills in the Praetorian gym. To her credit, Sasaki had taken one wide-eyed look around at the naked wrestlers around them, and gone completely stone-faced. Hadn't looked, hadn't reacted to the various cat-calls, any more than Sigrun did. And Lassair. . . Kanmi had never seen the spirit manifest in the gym before, and Trennus was, laughingly, trying to show her a few trips and chokes. . . but gently, setting her down each time on the mats with great care. The cat-calls Sigrun usually got, and that Minori had received, had faded into a kind of awed silence as the other Praetorians got a look at Trennus' 'wife.' Followed by muttered blasphemies in a half-dozen languages. And all the spirit had done in response was look over, wave cheerfully, and ask, *Oh, are we supposed to be naked here? I can disrobe. I wouldn't wish to go against local customs.* Nothing but blithe cheer in her voice, and she'd immediately started unlacing her bodice, only to have Trennus catch her wrists.

If one wasn't used to Lassair, she tended to get a reaction. Kanmi had needed a cold shower two years ago, when she had, in a moment of glee, wrapped her arms around his neck and kissed him for the first time. Right in front of Trennus, too. He'd apologized to Trennus, and the Pict had shaken his head in bemused fashion. *It's all right. She loves all of us, and she doesn't make a distinction between friendship and sensual love. It's all the same to her. But she knows that I do, so that's probably the reason you haven't woken up with her in bed with you, Esh.*

Baal's teeth, tell her I said no in advance, because I don't think I'd be able to say no if she did that. Kanmi had fought down the panic reaction. He definitely didn't want to do that to Trennus. Matrugena was a colleague he trusted with his life, but a *friend*, too, and you just didn't betray people like that. *How in the name of all the gods do you deal with this so calmly?*

Trennus had snorted. *Because I know her. I understand her. She's not human, but it's . . . really not that hard to comprehend. She loves you, and wants to see you happy. Be glad she hasn't tried to match-make for you. Yet. She says you're still too angry to inflict you on any woman.*

In the gym, Kanmi had snickered under his breath as the room had cleared *rapidly* as various male Praetorians headed, in varying states of embarrassment or amusement, to the showers. He then turned his attention back to the mat area where Sasaki and the others were, watching closely. Ben Maor had been practicing martial arts for about seventeen years, and he and Matrugena were both skilled at their respective arts, but Sasaki had obviously also trained, and for quite some time. The doctor was surprisingly fast, light on her feet, and whatever discipline she was using, she knew enough of its principles to use her lower center of gravity effectively. She knew how to get in on a larger opponent. . . but this was all on the sparring mats. She freely admitted never having had to use it in a real-life situation. "What about him?" she asked ben Maor, looking over at Kanmi.

"I'm just an observer, most days," Kanmi replied, shrugging. "If someone manages to get close enough to me to hit me, I'm doing something terribly wrong."

Ben Maor had turned back towards him, and Kanmi held up a hand, seeing the Judean man already starting to draw breath to argue. "Yes, I know. Someone who's fast on their feet can stop someone from drawing a concealed weapon. A gun can be fired before someone can get in to stop it. . . depending on how fast someone's muscle memory lets them be. . . and either someone can shoot me or hit me before I can incant one word. I *know*." He practiced with the others, if irregularly. Even Caetia was taller than he was, and he knew perfectly well that the valkyrie was probably stronger than either Matrugena or Ben Maor. Sparring practice wasn't fun for Kanmi. The most utility he'd gotten out of it had been convincing the other three to let him practice incanting under combat situations. So that he could bring some of his defenses to mind now, even if someone had just hit him in the face, or had him pinned.

The younger man just grinned at him. "Come on. For once, we actually have even numbers, Kanmi. Get on the mats."

Kanmi sighed, and obeyed. And was, promptly, shown just how fast Sasaki actually was, as she easily got in on him and hip-threw him to the ground. She looked *startled*, and began to apologize. "You weren't ready—"

"Oh, no. I was as ready as I was going to get." Kanmi was stronger than she was, but she was much faster, and actually knew what she was doing. He could, more or less, muscle his way out of a couple of the holds she put him in. . . so she wound up compressing his smallest, weakest fingers in a brutally painful lock she said came out of a system called *chin na*. "Now *that*," Kanmi told her, as she walked him forward to the mats, holding nothing more than a couple of his fingers, which screamed in pain, "I want to learn."

"You still need to be able to get in and behind someone to use it effectively," Ben Maor warned.

"Yes, but most of what you and Matru want to teach me is useless for someone my size, fighting someone your sizes," Kanmi pointed out, acerbically. "I need a stepladder to get to Matru's shoulder, let alone his neck. Even you are an uphill battle for me, ben Maor. I can't always pick my fights, but I have to work with what the gods saw fit to give me. Which wasn't much."

So he asked the doctor to show him some of the joint locks, and even ben Maor seemed to be learning something new here. Sasaki looked a little sheepish, even embarrassed, to be teaching, but pleased, too. Kanmi wound up being the demonstration dummy for most of this, as he was short enough for her to be able to effect the throws and movements more easily. So he put his head down on the mats and grimaced a little, periodically. It only seemed fair. He'd gotten his licks in on her research — in public, no less — so letting her grind bone on bone for a while seemed fair. "Are we even?" he asked at the end of the session, and got a puzzled look in return.

Before they left the gym, Caetia walked through spear-against-sword drills with the woman. Kanmi found he enjoyed watching them, but he doubted the utility of kendo sword forms in modern combat, and said as much. "No one's going to let you wander around with a big damned sword."

"No. . . but I have also trained with knives. The sword is more for. . . enjoyment. And in case I should ever need to defend my family's honor in some fashion. Technically, I could also imbue its edge with heat, so that I could shear more easily through an enemy's weapon or armor, and cauterize on the way through flesh." Sasaki shrugged.

Caetia's eyes had gone wide, and she'd tugged at the woman's sleeve with a certain enthusiasm at that point. "Esh, you've been holding out on me for *years*," the valkyrie accused.

"I thought the spear was largely ceremonial. I didn't think you'd *want* me tampering with it," he told her, in mild annoyance.

"No. I want every advantage in combat that I can *get*, as long as the event is not a formal duel. Even a temporary advantage might save lives." Sigrun actually smiled at him. "Tamper at will."

The time passed quickly. One week, Sasaki had been with him, one week with Matrugena and Lassair, and one week with ben Maor and Caetia. . . and then she was back on his doorstep, ready to go to Tawantinsuyu. The boys, for whatever reason, seemed to like her. They enjoyed her stories about growing up in Nippon, and her descriptions, once they cajoled them out of her, of growing up in a *samurai court*. As the daughter of a recognized concubine, Sasaki apparently had full legitimacy as a sort of 'lower-ranked' daughter. She would have gone to some form of a finishing school, and would have been married off, or bound as some lord's concubine, if she hadn't been what she was. "So you didn't go to school? You had a pedagogue, like we do?" Bodi asked the night before they were to leave, in fascination.

"I had instructors. All of my brothers and sisters did, as well. We were taught to write poetry. We learned Qin and Latin. I was the despair of my mother because I did not paint well, and would rather ramble through the countryside than stay at my watercolors." Sasaki shrugged. "One of my teachers thought I was a terrible day-dreamer. Always looking out the window, or reading the wrong book. I liked the ones on clockwork mechanisms, for example. Everything put together neatly. Everything *works*, and there are reasons why it works. My teacher caught me reading one of those books one day, instead of my assignment in poetry, and since it was the third time I'd disobeyed, he threw the book in the fire. I remember telling him that that would make my father angry. It was an old book, in Latin, and very valuable. And then I made the fire go out. I took all the air away from it, so it just died, all at once, and I reached into the coals and took the book out. I didn't even think it was very important, at the time. I thought I was saving his job, and that he would be grateful. Once he finished being angry." Sasaki raised her hands. "Everyone was agitated. They thought I could have burned the house down, or hurt myself. And they all wanted to know why I hadn't told them I could do that." A little shrug. "The problem was, I didn't understand what they were talking about. I'd *always* been able to do little things, here and there. Getting a book I wanted down from a high shelf? Using a gust of air to move a ball more accurately in a game? I thought everyone could do that." A faint sigh. "I was wrong."

It couldn't have been more different of Kanmi's breakthrough moment with his own powers, which had been violent, painful, and the result of pain and fear . . . and probably his own subconscious realization that without his father to keep his brothers in line, he might not *live*. He found he rather envied her that peaceful passage, and his lips twisted. *Even in matters like these, the noble-born seem to get it easy*, he thought. It was irrational to blame her for her elevated birth, but he found that he did. At least a little. Bastet's family had claimed descent from a one-eyed Nubian queen who'd held a Roman legion at bay with her archers, a thousand years ago. Her father was still highly-ranked among the country's nobles. Kanmi grimaced the instant he realized he'd thought about his ex-wife, and put it out of his head. Made himself think about something else, and his mind jumped to Erida, instead. His joking words to his fellow lictors of five years ago. . . . *having heard what she did to Abgar. . . and if she weren't, you know, nobility. . . I think I'd throw over Bastet and ask her to marry me. My age, my type, and all that magical power. Eh. Best I can do is ask if she'd let me study her tomes.* Kanmi grimaced, and looked at the ceiling, and did his best to focus solely on the present.

"So what happened then?" Bodi asked, scooting forward on the couch to get a little closer.

Another little shrug from Sasaki. "My father took me to court. Had me tested. I was instructed by the Court *sennin* for six years. For better or for worse, every talent I seem to have, seems best suited for direct combat.

. . and we do not permit women in our armed forces. My interests and intelligence allow me do well in mathematics and engineering." Minori gave the two boys a sidelong glance, and clearly skipped over some of the issues. "My father allowed me to come to the west, get my various degrees, and to remain here. It's better this way."

"Bed," Kanmi told the boys. "No, no arguments. We'll say good-bye in the morning." He took a little extra time getting them settled in, however.

Bodi, in particular, was upset that his father was leaving on a long trip, and for once, without them. He'd wanted to see Tawantinsuyu, especially the lines at Nazca, and Kanmi just shook his head when Himi, older and a little more astute, leaned over the edge of the higher bunk bed that was his own perch, and asked, "Father? Is it going to be dangerous there for you?"

"My job is always dangerous," Kanmi told the boys, honestly. "But I try to make it less so. Get some sleep."

Danger he could handle. It was more that he didn't know which direction some of the danger could be coming from. Outsiders, the Source Initiative, fine. But there were other possible sources, and Kanmi didn't like the paranoia in which he was currently living. He'd been amazed that Livorus had gotten Imperator Caesarion to agree to this whole mess. But the truth of the matter was, none of the rest of the Praetorian investigators had gotten anywhere with the matter in five years. And yet. . . . Kanmi suspected that Livorus and the Imperator had discussed the possibility that the Praetorian Guard itself might be compromised, somehow. Because it was a bad thought that had occurred to Kanmi himself. There were over three hundred thousand Praetorians. All trained bodyguards and investigators. Three hundred thousand people, all of whom were held to high standards in regards to ethics and trust. *Someone* should have found more information on this topic than Kanmi and his friends had, in their spare time. *Someone may be getting paid to turn a blind eye to something. Which isn't, actually, my responsibility. That's all Internal Affairs.*

But it made him wonder, grimly, how many of his fellow *Praetorians* could currently be trusted. It wasn't a good feeling. Add to that the fact that while Livorus, Caetia, Lassair had all spoken for Dr. Sasaki, *he* wasn't sure what he thought of the woman. . . it made for a fine stew inside of his mind as Kanmi paced back out to the living room, where Sasaki was getting ready for bed, making up the couch herself this time.

Kanmi poured himself his single permitted drink, measuring the *arak* carefully, and added water to it, watching the chemical reaction turn the drink white. "So," he said, after a long moment. He wasn't quite prepared to retreat into his own bedroom, no matter that she was clearly hinting that she was ready for privacy. "You're noble-born. You're pretty. You're educated. Why didn't your father marry you off?"

Sasaki stared at him. "Because most men do not like for their wives to be more powerful than they are. My talents are considered . . . unfeminine. Unattractive." She folded herself down to the floor, tucking her legs to the side, neatly. He'd noticed she tended to prefer to sit that way, over taking a seat on any of the furniture.

Kanmi snorted, and took a sip of his drink. "Fools, then. Baal's teeth, you'd be considered a *catch* in Chaldea. Took Lady Erida's family eight years to find a man they considered proper for her. Nice noble family, with Magi connections, though he apparently doesn't have a whit of power himself." He shrugged. "Well, that, and she was busy boning her bodyguard, so her reluctance to accept any of her suitors might have related to that, too." *Look how well that turned out.* He tipped his head back, finishing his drink, and turned to put the glass in the sink.

There was a faintly shocked pause, and then Sasaki ventured, "Lady Erida? The Chaldean Magus the others have mentioned?" Sasaki's tone was diffident. "Were you close to her?"

Kanmi reviewed his own words. "I wasn't the bodyguard, if that's what you're asking," he noted, evenly. This brought back bad memories of Bastet's unfounded accusations. "I admire her mind, and we still write regularly. Her new husband isn't as intelligent as she is, so I hope, for her sake, she isn't bored with him too quickly. When people are in unbalanced relationships, they get bored, and they don't even realize it's happening until they're looking for outside stimulation."

"I wouldn't have said *boredom* was the issue for a non-*sennin* husband. Frustration and wounded pride, I can certainly see, however."

"You think men have insufferable egos, and can't cope with a woman more powerful than they are?" It was on the tip of Kanmi's tongue to hold up Caetia and ben Maor as a counterexample, but while Adam didn't seem threatened by Sigrun's power, the valkyrie also more or less *allowed* ben Maor to wear the pants in that relationship. It wasn't a question of deferring to him, though. Caetia had obviously declined positional authority as head of the detail, probably more than once. It just seemed that the valkyrie was comfortable precisely as she was. Except that, long-term. . . Kanmi had seen the way the other god-born had watched the pair at their wedding in the Odinhall. They'd covered their expressions of pity with smiles. It wasn't that they thought Sigrun was slumming, so much as setting herself up for an enormous fall. . . .

Sasaki's eyes had narrowed. "I said nothing of the kind."

"You suggested that the problem would solely derive from the male side."

"Male or female, the equation has to balance out."

Kanmi's eyebrows shot up. "On that, we actually agree." He looked around, and realized he'd already put his glass away for the night. *Damn.* "At least we common-born can divorce with relative ease. For the nobility, marriage is usually political. But no one should ever marry someone fifty IQ points lower than themselves. The less intelligent half of the pair, male or female, will inevitably feel intimidated, and they will, eventually, lash out. Either by denigrating intelligence or education as a whole, or by trying to control the other's behavior. . . because they know they're *lacking* in something that the other half needs. And the other half will, eventually, go looking for what they need." He shrugged. *In Erida's case, she'll probably present her husband with a child or two, and then quietly start taking both birth control and lovers more to her liking.* "So, yes. The equation needs to balance.

"What or who made you such a terrible, cynical person?" Sasaki's voice was oddly sad from where she sat on the floor, looking up at him.

Kanmi blinked, taken aback. "Just the world. I am a student of human nature, *doctor.*" He shrugged. "I don't see this ending well, but Erida sounds content enough in her letters currently. And I'm trying to be better at not telling people when they're heading towards an inevitable train-wreck composed mostly of their own bad decisions."

A spluttering choke from Minori, and he shook his head and went on, briskly, leaving the rest of the conversation behind. "Erida's talents are somewhat akin to yours. Very. . . traditional. But she's at least willing to think off the smoothly-worn road of everyone who's gone before her."

Minori sat up, if possible, even straighter. "What is wrong with *traditional?*"

"Oh, nothing, except that it can be predictable. Use water to wear down earth and put out fire. Use fire to destroy air. Use earth to shield against fire. Except I can shatter earth with proper excitation of its molecular structure, heating and chilling in rapid oscillations." Kanmi shrugged.

"Your lady Erida did not agree any more than I do, I suppose? Traditional methods can be very effective!"

"She is not my lady," Kanmi said, patiently. "No. She didn't. Her bodyguard *did* succeed, using very traditional methods, in pulling almost all the water from my blood into my lungs and damned near drowning me. . . before he took her hostage and tried to kill her." He watched as Minori's eyes suddenly went huge, and her mouth fell open. Again, she was clearly a great theorist, but she'd never applied any of her talents in real combat. "Matrugena forced the water out of my lungs, but what was left in my veins was approximately the consistency of wet poured-stone," he went on, clinically. He was ninety-percent sure that the boys were asleep in their room by now. But he kept his voice soft, just in case. "L. . . Asha kept my heart beating, and I used some *non-traditional* methods to pull the water back into my veins, which let my blood un-congeal."

Her voice was horrified. "That must have been. . . very painful."

"It was." Kanmi shrugged. The fact that his heart had tried to go into cardiac arrest was one of the worst parts of the memory. "That being said? Erida killed her bodyguard herself. Neatest application of traditional air magic I've ever seen. She pinned him in a bubble of vacuum, like the little vortex you make ahead of your bullets, depressurized him, and suffocated him. I think that was only appropriate, don't you?"

Sasaki licked her lips. "Why are you telling me this?" she asked, quietly.

"You asked about traditional versus non-traditional. Also, I need you to know that this isn't a game." Kanmi studied her for a moment.

"I am aware of that! Dr. Camulorix died because of all of this!"

"Just keep that in mind at all times." Kanmi's lips pulled down into a grim line. "I'll be doing my best to keep you safe, and you are, from what I've seen so far, pretty good at protecting yourself. Just keep your head if anything goes wrong."

"And what about you?" she asked, suddenly. "Who keeps *you* safe?"

"I do that, too." Kanmi shrugged. "At least till the others arrive. It's worked so far." He glanced back towards the bedrooms, suddenly aware of a shuffling noise, which he identified as Bodi and Himi listening at their door, and sighed. *Astarte, don't let them have heard the bit about the blood-sludge.* A ghost of a smile managed to sneak onto his face, as he let his voice grow in volume. "I've got too much work to do with these two boys to even consider letting myself get killed. And if their tails are not back in their beds by the time I reach their door, they will be standing to eat their dinner tomorrow." Which prompted scrambling behind the door. Kanmi shook his head. *Speaking of predictable. . . .*

"You did not test my abilities," Minori said, just as Kanmi turned to walk down the hall.

Caught, he turned back towards her, raising his eyebrows. "Excuse me?"

"The others. . . they tested me with pistols and self-defense. You did not test me with sorcery. I would know why not." She hadn't moved. Still sat, almost primly, on the floor.

Kanmi shrugged. He didn't really know. "If everything goes right, you won't need to use your abilities at all."

"You do not generally strike me as such an optimist, Master Eshmunazar."

"I'm not, Dr. Sasaki." He sighed. "I saw and felt the constructs you built to use on me and Matrugena when we first met. They were solid. You'll be fine if you can get past the first ten seconds of any violent event." *That's when you really know if someone can handle themselves. When they're surprised and bullets and magic are flying all over the place.*

"But you did not wish to. . . ah, *spar*. . . with sorcery?"

"There's nothing I can teach you in three weeks. No way in which I can really prepare you. 'Live-fire' is for guns and bombs. Sorcery, we can pull our punches all day long, but nothing *teaches* you to stay calm and do the math in your head and weave the power when your life is in danger. You can either do it, or you're dead." Kanmi's words were brutal, and he knew it. "Military-grade sorcerers are in short supply because only half of us who have the power for it *and* are dumb enough to try it, survive our first contact with the enemy." He gestured towards the couch. "We all need some sleep. Good night, Dr. Sasaki."

Maius 10, 1960 AC

A direct flight from Rome to Cuzco wasn't available; there was, however, a flight from Rome to Tenochtitlan, on a conventional, fixed-wing aircraft. . . followed by a connecting flight via ornithopter to Cuzco. Kanmi and Trennus were sent over first, each with a *lover* in tow, with tickets paid for, punctiliously, out of their own pockets. Kanmi rolled his eyes at the necessity of paying Sasaki's way, but every detail needed to be right for this, and he *thought* he'd be reimbursed for this later. At least, he'd better be. Or he and the Finance Office were going to be having some very serious discussions.

Watching Trennus' expression from across the aisle as the ornithopter began to ascend, however, made up for his own ill-temper. Matrugena didn't like flying on his best day, and an ornithopter did not have a smooth flight on takeoff, like a fixed-wing craft. This one launched itself like a bird, gaining speed down the runway in the same way as a conventional aircraft, but also by beating its wings with powerful down-strokes. . . each of which made the fuselage lurch up in the air, and then fall back down again, briefly, before the next down-stroke.

As a result, Trennus had closed his eyes, and was clearly trying not to lose what they'd eaten for lunch on the last flight, while Lassair stroked his shoulder consolingly. "We'll level out once the pilot finds a thermal," Kanmi offered, not keeping the amusement out of his voice at all. "They'll extend the additional wing-flaps for the glide portion, and then it'll be one or two wing-beats every ten or fifteen minutes. You won't notice a difference at altitude." He paused. "Personally, I'm not a summoner, but even I wonder what they offer the spirits that power these things in bargain. . . plus, there's the fact that the pilots can't really fly by wire. They have to be paying attention every moment, adapting to every air current. . . ."

"This one's ley-powered," Trennus returned, his lips stiff.

You are not helping, Emberstone.

I really wasn't trying to, Lassair.

Unkind.

That's me, darling, that's me. Kanmi plastered a bright smile on his face as the flight attendants came by with the cart, mostly to hide the grimace, and took Sasaki's hand in his own. "What would you like, *dear?*" he asked her, trying to keep the needles out of his voice. The disguise wasn't her idea. It probably wasn't fair to take his irritation at the whole scheme out on her. Of course, considering the fact that she *jumped* whenever he touched her, he didn't think that the disguise was going to be convincing at all.

"Ah. . . fruit juice, please," she requested, politely. The stewards had mango juice, milk, wine, water, and *pulque* for this flight. Kanmi reviewed his options, grimaced, and opted for water, which he superheated, and then chilled in its ceramic cup, even as he handed Minori's juice to her. The cups would be collected in about fifteen minutes by the stewards, and the bobbling flight of the ornithopter ensured that those few who accepted anything to drink, had to clutch their cups tightly, and not risk putting them on tray tables. Sasaki promptly flinched again as their fingers brushed on the surface of the cup.

Just who are we trying to fool? he thought, glumly, and got out a book to study, though the constant motion of the ornithopter's wings made reading nauseating . . . but it let him look occupied, while he glanced at the rest of the passengers. *The Source Initiative, and anyone else who happens to be threatened enough by her studies. Whoever it is, they were worried enough to kill for their agenda after seeing Praetorians contact her and the professor. So it's fair to say that we can expect another attack, at some point. The 'disguise' at least gives us reason to have a Praetorian with her at all times. Damn it, we could have put her in with Tren, if Lassair wasn't knocked up all of a sudden. Would have looked more convincing, I think.* His mind was wandering, and he pulled it back on track.

Minori finally fell asleep; the flight was close to three thousand miles, and ornithopters simply couldn't move at the speed of a jet. Thus, they were in the air for almost ten hours. Plenty of time for even Trennus to fall asleep. Kanmi didn't. He stayed awake, reading, and trying to ignore the fact that Sasaki's head had fallen against his shoulder. *She's going to have a very stiff neck when she wakes up,* he decided. *Also, a first-class case of embarrassment, but if I move her, that's not going to fit well with the whole lover image, now is it?*

About two hours from Cuzco, they actually passed over the Nazca region, and their pilot obligingly pointed out the salient features on the ground for them. Kanmi nudged Minori awake and jerked a thumb at the window as she lurched both awake and away at the same time. "You're closer to the window, and you have the camera. . . *dear.* Mind taking a couple of pictures for the boys?"

The light of battle entered her eyes right then. "Of course I wouldn't mind. . . *dear.* You know I adore your sons." Her voice softened for the second half of her assertion, and Minori dug out the camera from the bag under the seat, and started taking pictures, as best she could. "On your right, you can see the Nazca river," the pilot intoned. "Passengers on the right side of the ornithopter can see the spiral tail of the monkey figure, while passengers on the left can see, in the distance, the humming bird figure. Each figure is scraped into the desert pavement of the valley. Some are only geometric figures, others are long lines stretching across the whole of the valley. The monkey, humming bird, condor, vulture, iguana, spider, tree, dancing man, and other figures are ancient. Sociologists and archaeologists from Rome have traveled here to study how they have been built and continue to be used. The valley is unusually rich in ley-lines, and many of the patterns in the ground follow the directions of the ley-lines themselves. Suppositions made by Roman scholars have ranged from the lines being ritual paths walked by worshipers hoping to invoke rain, to crazy theories about attracting the attention of *aliens.*" Good-natured scorn in the pilot's voice. "In truth, as you can see on the right side of the ornithopter. . . the local shamans have been adding to this desert art for centuries. These symbols have always represented the most important spirits, or *huacas,* known to the local people, previous to the establishment of the state religion of Tawantinsuyu, and as you can see, other spirits and gods have been added over the centuries. You can see the sun-mask of Inti ahead, the death-masks of Supay and Vichama. The moon, symbol of Mamaquilla, the goddess most strongly associated with Artemis and Diana, regionally."

Kanmi looked across the aisle at Trennus. Their long-standing debate over the origin of magical power was surely in for another round. Were the paths worn in the ground because the ley-lines were already there, was the power of people's will and concerted belief what drew power there, did the power come from the gods, or did people *give* power to the gods, through the power of their will? Matrugena met the stare, and shrugged. "Idols," he muttered, quietly.

"Foci," Kanmi muttered back across the aisle at him, and jumped now, himself, as Minori put a hand on his shoulder and then slapped the camera into his palm with a smack. "Thank you, dear," Kanmi told her, and put on another smile he didn't feel.

On finally disembarking and getting to stretch their legs for a bit, they eventually found their hotel. Cuzco, itself, was, like Tenochtitlan to the north, an amalgam of modern and ancient cityscapes. The massive stone fortress of Sacsayhuamán remained the seat of the Sapa Inca; it actually, according to Kanmi's reading, predated the Inca kings by hundreds of years, but had been taken over by them as their tribe had come to dominate the region. Built of massive stone blocks, and ranging over three terraces, the original walls were so tightly fitted, even without mortar, that a piece of foolscap couldn't slide between them. A wide plaza dominated the interior of the fortress, though there were modern lights all along the outside.

Kanmi, on looking at it as they drove by in their taxi, couldn't help but picture a time when, a thousand years ago, almost the entirety of a civilization had huddled inside those walls, waiting to be born. "Hard to believe the walls don't topple over in earthquakes," was, however, what he said to the others. "This area's very geologically active, isn't it?"

Matrugena looked around vacantly for a moment. "Yes," he confirmed, and tapped one foot on the floor of the car, rather happily, Kanmi thought. "Lots of fault lines. Lots of volcanism. These are younger mountains. Lots of plate tectonics. . . and the ley-lines in the area are about all that are keeping the area even vaguely stable, I think. I. . ." he stole a look at their driver, and cut himself off, glancing down at the floor for a moment. Kanmi didn't need to be a mind-reader to understand what Trennus had been about to say. *Between the plethora of ley-lines and the geological instability, this place is a ley-mage's* playground. *Good. He's weakened with Lassair stuck in physical form. A little extra power is not a bad thing here.*

The rest of the city had similar monolithic architecture—many of the ancient buildings were formed of stones taller than a man, and sloped subtly inwards—with modern amenities inside. Kanmi's senses *crawled* as they passed from one neighborhood to another, and the insulated copper wires swinging from one pole to the next changed, from corner to corner, from ley to electricity and back again. He had to rub a hand over the back of his neck to make the hairs there settle down. "This place is going to drive me crazy," he muttered, as they passed a modern skyscraper that loomed over a stone structure that clearly dated from the Plague period. He glanced to his right, and realized that Minori was largely unaffected. *Damn. Chalk one up for the traditionalists. I guess if you don't* use *an energy type all the time, you're not sensitized to it.* And while Kanmi didn't use ley at all, Trennus *did*, and Kanmi was constantly around Matrugena.

They were south of the equator, so the seasons were reversed from what Kanmi thought of as normal, but winter here wasn't actually the wettest season; the city received most of its rain during December, at the height of its summer. At the moment, the skies were gray, and little flecks of hail spat down at their vehicle periodically. Their driver turned around to tell them, cheerfully, in Quecha-inflected Latin, "You get lots of snow elsewhere, yes? We don't, here in Cuzco. First snow I ever *seen*, four years ago! Priests said Mamaquilla was laughing, that's why it happened. Rain, yes. Hail, yes. Freezing rain, yes. Never white, soft flakes. Was pretty, but it didn't last. Got a cousin further south. Says their mountains get snow, white-capped all year around. Glaciers, I think the word is. You should go see them. Tours are supposed to be nice."

Trennus, one arm around Lassair, chuckled and chatted with the driver, telling him about the amount of snow usually seen in Tarvodubron, the current seat of the Pictish kingdom in Britannia. Kanmi shuddered at the description, and Minori smiled and entered into the conversation. The two of them actually seemed to take *pride* in the viciously cold temperatures of their homelands, and the waist-deep snow both had occasionally seen. "All right, you win," Trennus told Minori after a while, grinning. "Your island is worse than mine."

"I like winning. I'm not, however, sure that I should enjoy *this* victory." Minori chuckled

Kanmi was startled by the laughter. It changed Minori's entire face, but he had nothing to contribute here. The current temperature was more than cold enough for his tastes. He shook his head, incanting under his breath to increase the warmth available to his feet and hands. Lassair, at least, seemed to agree with him. *You don't need to waste energy doing that, Emberstone*, she told him, with a little mental chuckle. *Here. Allow me.*

Warmth radiated from her, making the backseat of the taxi surprisingly toasty for the rest of the trip. "You're handy to have around," Kanmi told the elemental as they arrived at the hotel.

They were over eleven thousand feet above sea level here, the air was thin enough to tear at Kanmi's lungs, and it was dry enough that it felt as if his lips were starting to crack already. *Wonderful. A higher, colder version of Judea.* Kanmi got the room keys and made a point of wrapping an arm around Minori's waist and smiling down at her. "Apparently, we got a room with a view, on the ground floor, just opposite Matru and Asha. They're on the inside of the hall. We got the outside. Their loss, our gain, *honey*." A room with a window on the ground floor was, to Kanmi's mind, inherently insecure. Swapping rooms wasn't an option, it had become clear as he'd conversed with the people at the front desk. Local culture was pretty ingrained that where you were told to go, you went. Making more of a fuss would stand out, so he'd ward the door and windows, heavily.

He'd felt her jump as his arm had fallen around her waist, but he'd already decided how they could play this out. They'd be the feuding couple, the one on the verge of breakup. The one no one in their sane minds wanted to be around, let alone *listen* to. It would be realistic, and would account for the fact that she jumped every time he touched her. He just needed to talk to her about it in the room, once he'd done all his usual counter-surveillance measures.

Their room, as it turned out, had tile on floors and walls alike, and *echoed*, almost painfully, as the door slammed open. Kanmi grimaced. *We're going to be sleeping inside of a bath complex, for the sake of the gods.* He tipped the bellhop, waited for the man to leave, and closed the door behind them, warding it out of habit, and then reaching out with electrical energies to disable any recording devices in the room. It wasn't likely that there'd be any. . . but habits were habits.

He was thus, highly surprised when Minori turned on him and hissed under her breath, "What are you *doing?*"

Kanmi blinked. "Checking for listening devices—"

"I'm sorry, but that's not what I meant. I meant, why are you *acting* like this?" Minori threw up her hands. "If this is how you treated your wife, I think I understand why she left you!"

Kanmi felt his face turn into stone. Watched Minori's eyes suddenly go wide. He caught a glimpse of his expression in a mirror across the room, and realized that his eyes were completely blank. Dead. Minori closed her own eyes, and began to apologize, "Forgive me. I didn't mean that—"

"Forget it." Kanmi picked up the luggage and moved it into the room. Dropped hers by the bed, and moved his own over to the window. Looked out of it, shook his head at the bright sunlight and various spiky, odd-looking trees around what appeared to be a swimming pool, part of a Roman-style bathing complex behind the hotel, and began to incant over the glass, pressing his hands to it.

"I really am sorry, Master Eshmunazar."

"You should probably forget my family name for the time being, doctor." His voice was toneless as he closed down the curtains. "My given name is Kanmi."

"Yes. I am aware." She didn't actually *say* it, however. "I . . . we were given a role to act, and you are making it very difficult to . . . to . . ."

He didn't turn around. Simply dug a blanket out of one of the dresser drawers, and started setting up the couch. He hadn't slept on the ornithopter flight, he was tired, and didn't particularly want to deal with her at the moment. "To what?" he finally asked. "Act as if we're what we're not?" *Caetia always said I had lies in my eyes. Trouble is, this isn't my lie. This is someone else's and it's a damned fool one.* "Tell you what. You stop jumping every time I put a hand on you, and I'll try to at least make the smiles look more genuine."

"I will try." She sounded painfully confused. "Where I was raised. . . it's not considered proper even for a married couple to touch one another in public in this fashion."

"We could just pretend to *hate* each other. Be in the process of a breakup." *Wouldn't even be a stretch, now would it?* Kanmi took his shoes off, belatedly noticing that Minori had done the same at the door of the room.

He lay down on the couch now, closing his eyes.

"And then why would you go *everywhere* with me?" Her tone was exasperated.

"Because I am a *masochist.*"

A sound, somewhere between a laugh and a growl, made him open his eyes. She now stood only two feet away, much to his surprise, and pointed down at the couch. "And the maids? When they come to change the room? Won't they notice that you are not, ah. . ." She flushed, and glanced at the bed.

"Look, I'm not noble enough to sacrifice my back *every* night of this trip. We'll trade off who gets the bed."

Another sound of total frustration. "That is. . . it's. . . ." She spluttered to a halt. "Why are you making this so difficult? This will not look right. It will occasion commentary."

Kanmi relented enough to say, "In my experience, doctor . . . *Minori* . . . no one will even bat an eye if they think you've banished me from the bed." He closed his eyes again. The closest thing he'd had to a relationship in the past five years had been a trip, every other month or so, to a brothel that Livorus had recommended. Clean, quiet, upscale, discreet, and some of the girls there actually were hedge wizards. They knew just enough to be able to use magic in some very stimulating fashions. . . though Kanmi had made a point of *not* developing a regular girl there. Just whoever was available, and he didn't ask names. He didn't want to develop any illusory feelings. "Unless, of course, you're asking me to join you, doctor." He didn't open his eyes. "Personally, I wouldn't trust me, if I were you. Shit. *I* don't trust me, and I'm *not* you." *And I'm not noble enough to share a bed with someone who looks like you and not get stupid ideas around three antemeridian. Distance is better. Distance is safer.*

There was a pause. "What *did* pass between you and your wife?" Minori finally asked. Her voice was suddenly very sad. "What made you like this? What are you *fighting* with?"

"Oh, it's not her. I was a bitter and nasty person before her. Ask anyone. As to what went on in my marriage. . . ." Kanmi considered telling her it was none of her business, and reconsidered, slightly. "There's nothing in my life I haven't had to fight for." Simple, bald words. "I've fought for my life, my education, my wife, my career, and my children. I lost the battle with my wife. I don't know what mistake, or what *series* of mistakes lost me that fight." He opened his eyes and looked at Minori. "Most people don't like fighting. They'll go along to get along. They'll bend their necks for some noble's noose. Not me." His voice was tired now. "That explain it?"

Minori hesitated, and finally nodded, slowly. "I will try not to jump when you touch me," she said, simply. "If you try to look less dyspeptic. I will smile if you smile. But it would be much easier to act as I am supposed to act, if you behaved as if you were interested in me. In that way." Her tone was confused, and a little forlorn. "If it helps, you could pretend that your sons are here. You are much gentler when they are around."

Kanmi bit back his first three replies, all variations on *mind your own business*, exhaled, and nodded against his pillow. "Let me sleep for an hour," he told her, consciously gentling his tone. "Keep the door locked. And then I will escort you to dinner. First thing in the morning. . . ley-facilities. Matru and Asha get to scout the cultural centers. That all right with you?"

"Dinner would be more than acceptable," she assured him, but Kanmi was already drifting asleep, secure in the knowledge that he'd warded doors and windows, and cleared the room of electronic surveillance.

<u>Maius 11-17, 1960 AC</u>

Minori couldn't complain entirely about Eshmunazar's behavior after that. He was punctiliously polite in every regard. Held a chair for her to sit in at every meal. He took her advice on behaving as if his sons were present, and his manner became, if not gentle, then at least not actively harsh. But there was no warmth in his eyes, except when they happened to be discussing sorcery. Then he opened up and become enthusiastic. Fortunately, this was a topic on which Minori could converse readily. There were very few others that they *could* discuss in public. The on-going mission was out, naturally. The Source Initiative couldn't be spoken of, either. And while Minori had been trained carefully to follow other people's conversational leads, and to adopt their interests as if they were her own, Eshmunazar didn't have any of the interests on which she'd been trained to speak. He didn't read poetry. His opinion on art was that he should be able to recognize what was depicted. She didn't watch gladiatorial competitions on the far-viewer, though he did, and neither of them watched any of the long-running comedies based on the works of Plautus that were currently popular. That left sorcery and technomancy as the only possible topics for them. Their quiet-voiced conversations on sorcery were, actually, the best parts of each day, as they traveled from site to site through the steep and often slick, mountain roads. He'd seen a fair bit of combat, both on the Mongol border, and as a Praetorian, and therefore had the practical experience that she lacked.

She had, however, come to three separate, but interrelated conclusions about the man, based on her observations of him. First was that while Eshmunazar tended to shrug off attempts to get him onto the mats for martial arts training, and only participated if it were required. . . the man treated every conversation as if he were in a fight for his life. His guard was up, perpetually, he obviously kept score in his head, and he constantly jabbed and feinted to draw reactions. He judged people's reflexes, wits, and style based on their reactions. Catalogued their weaknesses and got ready to *strike* in return, if it became necessary. The fact that he got along with Matrugena was a testament, Minori thought, to the Britannian's patience and tolerance.

Second, and connected to both that and Kanmi's own assessment that everything he'd ever wanted in life, he'd had to fight for, was Minori's realization that he, like the other lictors, considered himself more a weapon than a person. At least, when he was at work. At home, around his boys, he was free to be a person again. But as they started visiting ley-facilities, with her telling the facility managers that she'd taken a sabbatical to pursue research for her next book, she watched how he observed everyone around them. He never focused for long, because he saw the whole room, and everyone in it, all at once, and was ready to react to all of it, the instant anything became a threat. And she began to see him as a weapon, as well. A finely-made sword, honed and worn from constant use.

An off-hand comment that his wife hadn't really grasped what he did for a living—*she thought I was a technician*—led her to a third conclusion. His wife would have preferred him to be a tool, instead of a weapon. Or at least, the mysterious woman hadn't been able to reconcile the person at home, with the weapon at work, or the danger of the work, or . . . something along those lines. While every word Minori heard on the subject—and there weren't many—came from Eshmunazar's own mouth, she was left an inescapable conclusion: when Eshmunazar looked at her, he didn't see *her*. He saw someone else. His wife. A faceless noblewoman. A job. She'd pointed this out to him, in their room, as she took the couch the second night. "It would possibly be easier to maintain the disguise if you tried to look at me more as if I were a person," she pointed out, cautiously. "And not a task or an object."

He blinked. "And here I thought I had been perfectly polite. Almost *noble* in my manners."

"It's not your manners, but your demeanor. You continue to act as if I were a stranger." She spread her hands. "If I were watching us on a stage, even at a kabuki festival, my suspension of disbelief would be broken. I think we need to try for actual warmth instead of polite toleration."

"Doctor. . . *Minori*. . . I rarely put an arm around a complete stranger and kiss their hair. Which I did at dinner. Twice. I counted."

Minori had pulled the blankets over her head. "Look," she said, after a minute's silence, staring up at the wool. "Anyone watching will look at Matrugena and Asha, and then look at us, and . . . they're just not going to believe it." It was true, too. Matrugena and his spirit-wife were never further than arm's length from one another.

"All right. I'll grant you that." Eshmunazar's voice was reluctant. "What do you want me to do to fix it?"

Minori, still buried under her blankets on the couch, heard him rustling around, getting ready for bed, himself. She looked upwards, seeing nothing but darkness, courtesy of the thick alpaca wool between her and the ceiling, and swallowed. Asha had caught her at dinner, and had made a pragmatic, if cryptic suggestion. *You and Emberstone resonate the same way, except that he is angry right now. If you and he matched resonances, you would be in harmony. Everyone would see and hear it.* That had seemed. . . fairly clear. Even rational, and the spirit had smiled the whole time, comfortingly.

"We could have relations," Minori offered, her voice muffled. "That would take care of the issue."

There was a slight choking sound from elsewhere in the room. She didn't dare pull the blankets down to see his expression, however. "What a charming offer," Eshmunazar finally replied, when he was done coughing. "I'll pass, but thank you."

Minori blinked. She hadn't expected that response. She pulled her blanket down from over her head, but didn't quite look in his direction. "I didn't think that the notion would make you *laugh*." Her cheeks burned. This was *humiliating*. She was not particularly forward, and even making the offer had cost her something.

"Hah. No. It's not that. It's the 'here, come have your way with me and I'll pretend I'm somewhere else, and *that'll* convince people that we're intimate, because sex equals intimacy' equation you've got there that's funny. You need to check your math, doctor. I've been in enough brothels to know that you've misplaced a one in the tens column."

Minori choked and sat up, and holding the blankets up to her neck. The bed creaked as he settled in, and his voice was sharp as he continued, "You keep asking who made me the way *I* am? I could ask you the same thing. Who fucked your head over so badly, that you think that an offer like that is going to get a man to come running? Who in Baal's name made you think that cringing under the blankets and offering to do the deed is going to excite someone?"

His voice was tired, but there was a reluctant edge of sympathy there. And Minori shrank back from it. "It doesn't matter," she told him, her voice dull, and rolled over on the couch. A moment later, she rolled back over again, and snapped out, "I only offered because Asha suggested it."

"Oh, that makes it so much better. You *really* don't want to. . . wait. *Asha* suggested this?" Absolute ire in his tone as Eshmunazar sat up now, himself, and Minori found somewhere else to look, even in the dark. "What did she say? Exactly?"

"Something about having similar resonances and matching them, so everyone else would see it and hear it." The words emerged reluctantly from her lips. It had made perfect sense when Asha had spoken with her. But then, Asha was so beautiful it was hard to *think* around her.

"Oh, gods *damn* it. Matrugena and I are going to have a *talk*. He said she wasn't going to . . ." A pause as Kanmi found the light, switched it on, and told her, his voice suddenly much gentler, "I don't think she meant it quite that way, doctor. Asha doesn't see a lot of distinctions between different types of love," Minori caught motion out of the corner of her eye, as if he were rubbing at his face, "And if she sees someone hurting, her first instinct is to join with them to make them feel better. It's how she *heals*. She . . . de-corporealizes and gets inside someone's body and fixes it. If we were all spirits, she'd. . . probably just join essences with someone to say *hello*."

Minori felt foolish, suddenly. The warmth radiating from Asha had been . . . heavily compelling. Her own mouth had been dry, and she would probably have said yes to *anything* at that moment in time. "So . . . she didn't mean. . . ?"

"No, she probably actually *did* mean 'have relations,' as you put it so charmingly. But she probably. . . gods. Please keep in mind, that this is *Asha* talking. . . " Kanmi's voice was strangled. "so she probably meant 'you two would be wonderful together if you'd get along better, and yes, you should bind and bargain with each other and exchange life-essences like little furry bunnies.'" He actually mimicked the inflections of the spirit's cheerful mental voice, raising the pitch of his own in mockery. And Minori raised her hands to her face and just *laughed*, helplessly, for a long moment. "Now," Kanmi said, in a tone of resignation, "I have to go across the hall and kill my best friend. Excuse me while I find a pair of pants."

"No, no, no! Then he'll know —"

"As if he doesn't already."

"Oh, *gods*."

"Precisely my point."

The subsequent days had gone much better. Kanmi's body language had been much more relaxed, among other things, which had let *her* relax. Surprising, all the things that the subconscious controlled; when he held himself like a clenched fist, ready to strike, she pulled away from him, and so did other people. Minori could see the change in how people reacted to them as they entered the various ley facilities. They each received hand-clasps, but they weren't getting the uneasy glances of the day before, as people had tried to sort out, even at the instinctive level, what body language was telling them. As such, they started getting answers.

Unfortunately, they weren't the answers that they wanted or needed. "Oh, no. This facility was built in 1950," one site supervisor told her, tugging at an earlobe filled with a Nahautl-style earplug. This particular facility was thirteen thousand feet up a mountainside, and the wind shrieked and howled past the windows of the supervisor's office. "Absolutely, you can take a look around. You'll find we're properly up to code. We can't bury the cables here, because of how rugged the terrain is, so everything has to be transmitted by wires on poles, down the mountainside."

"Can I take a look at your ley-surveys?" Minori asked.

"Sure. We're not in the best location, but we couldn't go higher on the mountain. The peak is considered a holy site. Sacrifices used to be offered there to the *huaca* of the mountain itself." The Tawantinsuyu man in front of them shrugged a little. Like a lot of his workers, he wore coveralls inside the facility, and they all had heavy cloaks of fur and alpaca wool ready to go if they needed to step outside. "We'd get better efficiency up there, but no one wants to disturb someplace that was sanctified, even if it was a long time ago."

Minori exchanged a quick glance with Kanmi. She'd have thought that if this facility were involved at all, that they'd have planted it as close to the old sacrifice site as possible. "If you think you'll be all right alone here, Min," Kanmi said, putting a hand to the small of her back, and rubbing a little through her gray coveralls, "I think I might like to have a look at your Tholberg coils, Master Anyas. I'm really quite fascinated by some of the newer designs."

"Oh, we don't use Tholberg coils here. Straight transformers, I'm afraid."

"Is that so? I'd love to see them anyway."

Nothing here tallies with what he saw in Nahautl. Except. . . this facility has been at the epicenter of at least three minor earthquakes in the last year. So have four of the other sites we're going to look at. Minori stared at the charts, and after taking notes for a moment, realized that she had a camera for a damned good reason, and Kanmi had gotten the manager out of the office so she could use it. So she took pictures of every document she could get her hands on in the next twenty minutes . . . going so far as to open various desk drawers and retrieve hidden files and photograph them, too. Kanmi had offered to teach her how to pick locks, as he'd done in Lutetia at her place of work. . . and Minori had demonstrated, instead, with a slightly embarrassed duck of her head, her ability to shift air pressure inside a lock, briefly solidifying it to press on all the tumblers correctly, and then twist the construct with her mind. It took a high degree of concentration, but she could do it. "Can you do it under pressure?" he'd asked. "Knowing someone could walk in at any moment?"

"I. . . have," she admitted, with a flush. "It has the advantage of not leaving marks, and no fingerprints."

"I am sold on this idea. And would be damned interested in learning more." His eyes had narrowed. "Why do *you* know how to do this?"

"Why do you know how to pick locks?" she countered.

"Because my brothers and I were wharf-rats, and their idea of looking after me for an afternoon, when they didn't feel like trying to drown me, usually involved finding a closed store or a locked house, and finding a way inside. They had me pick the locks because I was too young for prison. Most I'd have gotten was a public caning. They'd have gotten the galleys." The galleys didn't mean being chained to a bench to row a Roman ship, these days. It did, however, mean slave labor for a term of years in the Roman Legion or Navy. Never rising in rank, and usually put to work digging latrines or cleaning bilges. The worst jobs were saved for the worst offenders. Kanmi had shrugged. "They'd take alcohol. Maybe a little coin. They couldn't fence anything fancy." He'd given her a look. "Your turn."

Minori had swallowed. "The Emperor had one Empress and over a dozen official concubines when I lived at the court," she said, quietly, and looked at the ground. "All were expected to be virtuous women. No immodest or improper behavior."

"Because that always works out well. Bored people find ways to amuse themselves."

"Yes." Minori said nothing more.

"And were you bored, Minori?"

"Very," she admitted. "Getting out of the official quarters at first, was like a game. Just as it had been at home, when I didn't want to sit down to write a boring poem that my tutor had assigned me. It got much more serious, later on. When someone else learned what I could do." She shook her head. "I don't want to talk about it."

"As you wish," he'd told her, which had taken her by surprise, and he'd let the subject drop.

So, here and now, she stole information, and did it quickly and well, tucking files back into the desk drawer with gloved fingers, grateful that the weather let her wear these without question. And did the same at the next two facilities that they canvassed over the course of the day.

That night, Kanmi developed the film in their room, with the lights turned off, and the door locked to ensure that the delicate process wasn't interrupted. Minori wrinkled her nose at the smell. "Did you find anything outside the buildings?" she asked.

"No. No disturbed earth. No fresh graves. No bodies that I could detect. That being said. . . my multimeter, every time I plugged it in? Was detecting a mix of energies. Ley and Veil energies, at all of the sites." Kanmi sounded exasperated. "Something *is* going on here, Minori."

It was a measure of progress, Minori thought, that he'd actually used her given name in private, and without the mocking emphasis it normally carried. A timer went off, and he removed a print from its final chemical bath, and moved each picture from tub to tub, after hanging the newest finished sheet up to dry. It was a slow and boring process, and when he was finished, they sat down to pore over all of the maps, charts, and diagrams at greater length.

It was late when there was a tap at the door, in the pre-arranged code that the lictors used to announce themselves to each other. Kanmi opened it to admit Trennus and Asha, both of whom looked exhausted. "We have news," Trennus told them, immediately. "It's not good."

Trennus and Lassair had had been 'scouting locations' for Livorus' proposed trip, and had been, therefore, taking in various cultural sites. Evaluating them, supposedly, for security purposes, because no official state visit was ever complete without some random cultural exchange. This had allowed the pair to visit a number of temples, and today, they'd been scheduled to visit the Nazca valley. "What's the problem?" Kanmi asked, closing the door behind them, and re-warding it. "You only just *now* got back?"

"No, got in an hour ago, but thought you'd still be developing pictures. Besides, we really needed to eat." Trennus carefully moved the blankets and pillows out of the way, and sat down on the couch, wondering how Kanmi's back could *take* sleeping on the damned thing. It felt stiff.

I am remarkably tired, Lassair admitted. *I have been practicing letting my body sleep while I remain awake, however. It is difficult, but possible. Do you think that I might be able to close the body's eyes while the rest of you continue to do what you are bound to do?*

"Sleep," Trennus told her, kissing her forehead. "I'll tell them what we saw today."

Kanmi closed the doors, and re-warded them. "What did you find?"

Trennus closed his eyes, and attempted to order his thoughts. His head was spinning. "We left for Nazca around. . . nine antemeridian," he began, slowly. "We did the ornithopter tour, and you know, we were a lot lower to the ground this time, than when we flew over on the way here. Lassair. . . shit. I'm sorry." He hadn't *meant* to say her name in front of Minori, but he was getting used to having the woman around.

I have no objections to her knowing my Name. I do not think Truthsayer will attempt to bind me with it. Lassair's tone was sleepy, and she'd kicked off her shoes, put her feet in Trennus' lap, and lay back with her head propped up on the arm of the couch. Tren gave her a sharp look. He'd never heard Minori Named before, and caught the look of shock on both Kanmi's face, and the woman's own. However, what he had to say was too important to wait on, so he shook his head, and continued, "Lassair started to feel very uncomfortable in the air over the various markings. You might remember that our original flight plan on the way in actually didn't cross any of the major figures, but just the lines that trace the ley conduits?" Trennus opened and closed his hands a few times. "So, when we landed, we asked to do a ground tour." He leaned back against the couch, and gently rubbed Lassair's feet. "First thing I noticed is that the ley-lines under that valley? Every last one of them is in resonance. And I can't explain why, because it shouldn't be possible. . . but I think that resonance has been artificially induced."

Kanmi and Minori's eyes widened. "That's *not* possible," Minori objected, immediately. "Ley-lines are the macro equivalent of superstrings. We can manipulate their energies, but we can't—"

"Add to them? Change their frequencies? Change which strings are in resonance with other strings?" Trennus replied, sharply. "I'm a ley-mage. I know what I can do with a line, and what I can't do, and I would love to see a map if the lines tomorrow that shows me, yes, this is a natural occurrence that somehow was left out of every textbook I've ever studied, and it's always been this way. I doubt that, however. I doubt it very strongly." He exhaled. "It gets *worse*."

"It gets worse than the ley-lines in a geologically unstable area being altered and possibly supercharged?" Kanmi said, linking his fingers behind his head. "Do tell."

Trennus looked up at the ceiling, and searched for the words. *The lines,* Lassair said, suddenly, for him, *They are binding circles. Huge ones. I brushed the edge of the moon's crescent with my foot, and was trapped. I managed to retain human form. I have worked, very hard, at appearing mostly human. At most, god-touched, like Stormborn. I was trapped.* The body's eyes, as her body slept, didn't open, but the spirit's voice was anguished. *And I was not the only spirit bound to that sigil. There was another inside there. She was vast and old and powerful, and she raged at being caught there. She told me her Name was Mamaquilla. Mother of moon and sea, mother of the gods of this land.* Lassair's voice was terrified.

Kanmi lunged to his feet, and started pacing around the room, stepping deftly over the pictures strewn in neat piles all over the floor. "How'd you get her *out*?" he demanded, turning and staring at Trennus.

"I almost *didn't*. I had half a dozen people shouting at me that she'd defaced a cultural artifact by walking on it, and I caught sight of an old woman, near the back. . . very formal clothing, all high-quality alpaca cloth and good jewelry. Just *watching*." Trennus grimaced. "I didn't want to say that Lassair was *stuck* in their gods-be-damned spirit trap, so I reached for the ley-energies in the ground. Gods." He shuddered a little. He didn't want to say it, but having *that* much energy at his disposal? Flooding through him, responsive to every whim? It had been *intoxicating*, and he'd briefly entertained the notion of grabbing Lassair and finding a piece of ground out of sight of everyone and taking her with all the power in the valley flooding through his veins. In a *sober* state, he could see why that might not be a good idea. Lassair tended to see sex as an exchange of energies, and the sheets on his bed were almost inevitably scorched here and there as a result. He might not *survive* the process if he *participated* while linked into a power line like that.

At the time, prudence hadn't been what had stopped him. Having to deal with the damned trap and the onlookers had. "I broke the edge of the line," Trennus said, shrugging. It had only required a whisper of power, really. "Carefully. Just. . . smoothed it out while they were all shouting. Lassair stepped out, and I put the line back where it was."

The other one came out of the binding with me. She fled. She said she had been bound there for most of two cycles of this world around the sun. That the humans had begged one of her god-born to invoke her at this the new crescent idol, built in her honor on the valley floor. . . and when she arrived, she was <u>bound</u> to that representation. Sealed into the lines. . . not just by the sigil, but with all of her Names and with the ley-energy of the valley. Lassair sounded frantic. *They said she was powerful enough to <u>keep</u>. What that meant, she did not know. Then she called me sister, and fled.*

Trennus rubbed at his face again. "So, once we got them to stop arguing and stop yelling at her for having *defaced* the site, we got moving again. Had to go through the whole tour, with them watching her like a hawk. And I ran a few tests at every one of the lines that we came to. Sar. . . my other bound spirit? She wouldn't manifest. She almost wouldn't come to me at all." That had deeply disturbed him. He'd seen Saraid for the first time when he was six years old. He'd entered into a first binding arrangement with her just after Senecita's death, when he was eighteen. She'd been . . . extremely quiet, even quiescent, for the past five years. They were still bound. But something was wrong, and he wasn't sure what. "I guess she saw what had happened to Lassair." Trennus exhaled. "She wouldn't manifest. But she said that she'd shield me. So, I reached into every circle. . . *very* carefully, and with Sa. . . my other spirit overlapping me. That gave me a buffer in case the symbols were. . . occupied."

"Were they?" Minori asked, her voice very quiet.

"Gods, yes. They were. A couple of them were so powerful, Saraid was terrified. I . . . didn't catch many Names." Trennus' hands were shaking now, and he didn't even realize he'd said Saraid's Name for a moment, then swore under his breath. *Saraid won't thank me for that. But Lassair calls Minori Truthsayer. Which . . . sounds familiar, for some reason, but . . . at the moment, none of that matters.* "Kanmi. . . they've bound dozens of powerful spirits. Ones at least on par with that efreet Erida summoned back in Judea. And at least one *god.* Maybe more. I. . . think they're actually being deliberately bled into the ley-lines." Trennus rubbed at his face. "There are a couple of buildings there that we couldn't get into, including a tower near the center of the valley, next to the tourist station. There might be equipment in there."

There was a moment of silence. Even though they all had the information from the Nahautl incident of five years ago at their disposal, this was on an entirely different scale.

"So that's what's. . . empowering the ley-lines." Minori considered it for a moment. "I don't understand *why.* Even if they decided to go regularize their existing patchwork electrical and ley grid entirely onto ley. . . there's more than enough energy in a properly designed ley-system to run a country. Why *bother* to do this?"

"We're missing pieces," Kanmi said, and picked up the photographs that he and Minori had been poring over before the other pair had arrived. "It's . . . gods. Four antemeridian in Rome. We're calling this in, but we need to give it a few hours. I'll make sure we're not listened in on, on this end, anyway." He gave Trennus a piercing look. "Do you think they knew that Lassair's a spirit?"

Trennus thumped his fist against the arm of the couch. "I don't know. They might think she's god-born, or possessed. There aren't too many spirits who wander around manifested in human form, and pregnant."

"Steady. She's a month along. They're not going to know from just looking at her." Kanmi's voice was bracing. "Objectively, how much danger do you really think she's in?"

Trennus rubbed at his face again. He'd been working on raw nerves for hours now. Lassair had gone from being, in the old days, a creature who'd been acutely vulnerable, to being almost untouchable, other than by another spirit. Vulnerability from her was an uncomfortable return to the old days, and he hadn't thought she'd be a target on this mission. Not really. Not till today. So he was grateful when Kanmi stepped in; *his* brain was clearly functioning just fine.

Trennus knew that Lassair had caught a portion of Tlaloc's energies. She'd been to the Odinhall and *hadn't* been chased off like an errant pest. Then again, Saraid had been permitted to stay, too. *Perhaps the gods of Valhalla are just very polite to their god-borns' guests.*

Lassair could manifest fully, *stay* manifested for weeks on end, and could change forms as freely as Trennus could change clothes. Saraid, by way of comparison, had never given any indications of these abilities. These were all signs that Lassair's power had grown, and enormously. "She could make a fine target for whatever they're doing," Trennus admitted, opening his eyes again, "if they knew her Name. Without that, they can trap her, certainly, but they can't force her to do much of anything." He glanced at Lassair. "Right?"

They can make the attempt, but everything requires leverage, as well you know. Names, or something that I value. Even in her sleep, Lassair's lips turned downwards.

"Well, let's definitely keep your Name under wraps." Kanmi's glance to the side encompassed Minori. "Lassair, you know, generally speaking, the. . . disposition of someone approaching you, yes? If they're hostile or deceptive or not?"

Yes. But not if they are using masks. Carrying imbued vials of other people's blood, for example. Or if they have a bound spirit encompassing their bodies, as when Saraid or I spread ourselves through Flamesower. Lassair didn't sound happy about that. *I could de-manifest. But I don't know what that would do to the child. I have never done this before.*

"In that case, any time we're in the rooms, we set up wards, and if you hear someone at the door, you change form. Turn yourself into a mouse and hide under the nightstand." Kanmi's voice was forthright. "I don't care if they say they're *housekeeping,* you get out of sight."

Won't that harm the child?

"At the moment, it's a ball of cells, and a mouse is a mammal, and one close enough to human to be used for most drug testing. If you were further along, the child would be too big for the mouse, and you'd split yourself in half trying, but fortunately, you just barely qualify as pregnant in most people's books." Kanmi's abrasive tone, once more, was bracing.

Trennus snorted under his breath, as the *sense* in the words got his brain working again. Took some of the fear away. "What in the gods' names would we do without you, Esh?"

"Run around in circles looking for your heads, probably. *Someone* around here has got to have the common sense to tell you that they're tucked up your asses." Kanmi's words were uncharitable, but he grinned at Trennus now. All edges. "All right. We've got three hours till anyone in Rome will be awake. We need to . . . shit. We need to find out how long they've been *adding* to the Lines. That'll give us a timeline, I think, as to when this started. The Lines themselves have been here for about a thousand years."

"They probably *were* originally places to venerate the gods, and large spirit-traps for troublesome, malevolent spirits," Trennus supplied. "The locals call 'demons' the *supay,* which is also the name of their god of death. The ruler of *Uku Pacha.* The *supay* are the spirits of the 'world within,' or the 'land of the dead.' We got the full lecture two days ago when we were looking at the local mines and manufacturing buildings. The locals believe that they live in caves, hence why they didn't do much mining till Rome made contact with them."

"Demons?" Kanmi asked, picking one word out of the flow and raising his eyebrows.

Trennus rocked a hand back and forth. "You know how I feel about that term. In this case, they're death-and-fertility types. Like the *lilitu* of the Mesopotamian area, only not wind and desert spirits. I think the local shamans and summoners would only have bound the worst of them, ones that had gone fully malevolent. The type that might possess an unwilling human as a vessel and use them." Trennus exhaled. "The type that can't be bargained with, because they won't honor any contract. When you deal with something like that. . ." he shook his head again. "There *has* to be a balance between the death and the fertility. Something for something. If all they are is death, and nothing *springs* from the bargain. . . well. Those you bind or banish. And the locals didn't *have* metal jars back in the day, and their oldest pottery vessels all seem to have been open-mouthed, so you couldn't seal them except with maybe wax. They also didn't have writing back in the day, so binding with a Name was probably difficult. The Lines were probably their original solution for sealing away the bad ones." He paused again. "Still the newer symbols. . . seem to be *very* recent. The earth still feels raw where they've been cut."

"Can you tell *how* recently?" Kanmi's voice was intent.

Trennus considered that. He was very in touch with earth and soil. He had to be, in his profession. "Considering the strata and weathering. . . the oldest might be eight to ten years. The newest, no more than two."

"So. . . the oldest was built right around when Gratian and Tototl got started up in Nahautl."

"Possibly. Don't get set on the idea of a global conspiracy, Esh."

"I'm not married to the idea that the two are linked," Kanmi replied, dryly. "I just see potential connections." He paused. "We can confirm that through the locals in the morning. For now, let's look through the rest of the data we collected. There's got to be *some* way in which this is hooked into the ley-grid. They were using Tholberg coils up in Nahautl. This. . . doesn't seem to be the same method. But there has to be something."

It took almost all of those three hours. And it was Minori who found it. "Look," she said, with muted excitement, at close to one in the morning. "Here, this picture of the maps from the third facility we visited. You said that there was a tower in the Nazca valley, Master Matrugena?"

"Trennus," he corrected, absently. "Yes, right at the center."

"This map shows similar structures in a ring, dotted through the mountains around here." Minori's tone was clinical.

"We're over five hundred miles from Nazca. Half our day was spent flying back and forth," Trennus pointed out, tiredly.

"Yes. . . but look at the map of the whole of Tawantinsuyu," Minori said, and grabbed one. Started marking each tower location on it. "Here, outside of Cuzco, the first location Kanmi and I visited. Next. . . northwest of here. Machu Picchu. Northwest of that. . . Ayacucho." She pointed at the translation of the Latin letters that formed the Quecha word. "Spirit-corners. It's a *kami* place, I think?"

Lassair didn't open her eyes. *The men who spoke to us the day before yesterday spoke of that city, yes. Many ancient temples. Some habitations outside of the buildings of the town, said to be very, very old.*

"Twelve thousand years or so," Tren supplied. "Caves, in the main. And most people in the region think of caves as being the home of the *Uku Pacha*. So. . . yes. Possibly."

Minori nodded, and traced a curve between each of the points, lightly, with a compass. . . and swept around to another mark on the map. "Ica," she said. "Land of the Sun, it says. Home of the Paracas, and apparently an area especially sacred to their sun-god. Inti."

She paused and drew neat lines from Nazca to each of the points so far. "Each of these," she noted, quietly, "was the epicenter of a major earthquake in the last ten years. Here, Coropuna? Major earthquake centered here, four years ago. It's a volcano to the southeast of Nazca."

"You're missing a point," Kanmi noted, looking over her shoulder. "If you're showing us a circle, there's not much to the southeast."

"Sicuani," she said, shrugging. "No tower built there yet, according to the map from the file, but one is planned. No earthquakes. . . . yet. But no tower built yet, either. It's not an important religious center, but . . . agricultural. I think. I need *books*." Her tone was impatient.

Silence in the room for a moment, as they all considered the implications. Minori picked up the threads of her thoughts. "So. . . towers. Like spokes on a wheel," she said. "Some of them aren't completed, and some haven't been built yet. But they have Nazca in between, as the hub. Most of them are *near* the ley-stations, but not on the same land. There was one near each of the stations we visited, in fact. And there *are* metal spikes driven down into the bedrock, anchoring the foundations, in each. Copper, in fact. Precisely what you'd use for a ley-platform. . . but they aren't ley-facilities."

"Spokes on a wheel," Trennus said, quietly, and swore. "*Damnú air*. They might be building a binding circle *outside* the Lines, as well. No way to tell for certain, though. It'd be huge, though."

Kanmi looked over Minori's shoulder, reached out, and traced a finger out into the sea. "It's more of an oval, Trennus," he said. "Even if we include Sicuani, it's not really a very regular shape. . . and obviously, no towers out in the sea."

"There could be off-shore platforms," Minori pointed out, immediately. "There *are* ley-lines in the water itself, and in the land deep under the sea."

"Yes," Trennus said, his voice distant, "but I don't think they'd actually need to do that." That got everyone to look at him again. "*Part* of this is using what's in the Lines to. . . make the ley-lines resonate. And part of this is using the ley-energies already in existence to . . . contain, constrain, what's caught in the Lines. It's a self-feeding system, but they have to have enough energy on the outside to maintain the . . . the cage." Trennus grimaced. "The Lines aren't that far from the ocean. For a damned good reason. Salt water. Natural barrier. Many spirits get. . . massively confused in salt water." *Chemically, it's so akin to human blood, and there's so much out there that's alive.* . . . "So they actually save energy by not having to make a complete circle. Part of the circle, the boundary, is already drawn for them, by nature and geography."

"There's more, I think," Minori said, quietly. "Each of these towers is located. . . hmm. Not far from what looks like old holy sites. Some are still in use, like this one, here. The Oracle of *Maucallacta*. It's perched fairly high up on Coropuna."

"The volcano?" Kanmi said, in a grim tone, and Minori nodded. "There's a ley-station there?"

"About two miles from the shrine, which is . . . I can't read this. It's too small."

Trennus looked at the tiny letters on the map. "An *ushnu*. It's a three-stepped platform on which they offer libations to the gods. Liquid sacrifices, like maize liquor." *Like I offer wine and sugar, if that's the spirit's favored bargain.*

"Blood?" Kanmi asked, quickly.

Trennus grimaced. "Not at an *ushnu*, according to what I heard on my tour. But they did comment that human sacrifices used to be offered at the tops of particularly holy mountains. The priests would take the chosen victims, often children, feed them rich foods, and lead them up to the top of the mountain, doped up on liquor or coca so that they wouldn't feel the cold, and either bash in their skulls with a stone club, or leave them there till hypothermia and the high altitude killed them. A volcano. . ." he shrugged. "Historically, people tend to want to propitiate them."

Kanmi rubbed at his face. "Spirits don't really control *plate tectonics*. I would think that people would know that today."

Trennus sighed. "Doesn't mean that there *isn't* a spirit associated with the mountain. Could even be a malevolent one, who saw a chance to take energy from the sacrifices without having to meet its end of the bargain. But. . . kind of getting far afield." He looked at Minori with renewed respect. "So, each tower's being built close to the ley-stations, and to these holy sites?"

She nodded, slowly, and looked at Kanmi. "Would you like to bet that the reason why you didn't sense any disturbed earth, or bodies under the ground. . . ."

"Is that we were looking in the wrong place?" Kanmi's entire body looked like a taut-pulled string. "No bet, Minori. I don't bet on sure things. Gods, I am so *stupid*." He sounded furious, and Tren winced, internally. Kanmi's anger could turn anywhere, and at the moment, it was all directed inwards. Kanmi *hated* missing things. Hated missing the links in a pattern. "We were *right there*. If we'd spread out the search a little further, we could have *found* this—"

"You want us to have wandered through unfamiliar and extremely uneven terrain, in bad weather, in the hopes of finding something that we didn't know was there?" Minori countered. Trennus blinked. The woman's voice was gentle, but the mind behind it was *sharp*. "Kanmi, we didn't have enough data to put the pattern together until just now."

"Doesn't matter. Still should have seen it." Kanmi's agitation was clear. "We'd have put this together a day or so ago—"

"And what? We'd have seen towers, yes. We wouldn't know why they were in a rough circle spread out through the mountains—"

"We'd have seen the one in the center and known Nazca was the key—"

"Please stop. We're all tired. We need to find out what else we need to . . . find out." Minori raised her hands, expressing her own confusion as to what that included. "Make a list. And report in to Rome, correct?"

Trennus was surprised when Kanmi actually stopped, mid-rant. Kanmi usually was not good about that. He tended to need to go on, whether under his breath, to himself, or out loud, to someone else, until the fuel that stoked the fire was consumed. A deep breath, and Kanmi nodded. "All right. Top of the list, when *new* Lines started being built—for certain. What the official story behind that is. Next item, which of these towers was built first. After that, getting access. . . somehow. . . to verify if there are any bodies there, any technology. . . ."

Chapter XVII: Tephra

November 23, 144 AC lives in the popular imagination as the date on which Pompeii died. This is, and is not, true. Pompeii and Herculaneum were destroyed, but still exist; other cities were built a few miles from the ancient site, and it took their name in testament to the original cities.

Pompeii was founded in the sixth or seventh century before the ascension of Caesar. The history of the region is as turbulent as its geology. The city was captured by the Hellenes, Etruscans, and the Samnites before being adopted into the Roman Republic and remaining loyal during the Second Punic War. The people of Pompeii took up arms, like most of the Campania region, during the Social Wars, that brutal period in which Rome's Italian allies fought for the right to be called Roman citizens. Pompeii was one of the cities defeated by Sulla . . . who would, eventually, march twice on Rome himself, carrying arms within the sacred boundaries of the city, and who would become Rome's dictator, enacting numerous reforms, before retiring to a private life outside of Rome.

Earthquakes were common throughout Campania, and it must be noted that the ancients, while fascinated by natural philosophy, did not understand what caused the tremors. Seneca, for example, theorized that the great earthquake of 106 AC was caused by <u>air currents</u> under the earth. Seneca's suggestion that one set of earthquakes might be interrelated with other quakes was perceived as radical at the time, but he never considered volcanism as a possible cause. He reproved landowners from moving away from the city during the quakes, suggesting that the only proper attitude was stoicism: Death is all around us, and we are more likely to die of disease, than in an earthquake.

That the first <u>major</u> earthquake occurred on a day on which two sacrifices were to be held was considered a portent, and auguries and divinations were consulted. Oracles tend to be much sharper and clearer regarding the near future, than the distant one. Most modern philosophers attribute this to the nature of the quantum universe, and assert that the fewer decisions possible in between two points in time, the easier it is for an oracle to make a true prophecy.

All of the auguries were in agreement: Pompeii would die in fire. None of them, however, could agree as to when, or as the result of <u>what</u>. Some foresaw battle — not an uncommon occurrence during the days of the Republic, but during the early Empire . . . hardly an issue. Others suggested that another earthquake might cause the oil lamps to cause another disastrous fire, as had occurred in 106 AC. Only one, the Pythia of Delphi, suggested that the mountain would erupt. Her words were mysterious: "And the bodies will remain buried, and they will weep ashes, and be a monument to doubt."

Many people left as a result of the bad auguries. But many landowners did, indeed, doubt the Pythia's words. They felt that disaster could be averted by making the right decisions, by placating the gods. A new temple of Isis, an Egyptian goddess quite popular in the region, was built and consecrated. Games and sacrifices were offered. A new bathing complex was built. The people of Pompeii were clearly there to stay. And so they did, until November 23, 144 AC, when Vesuvius erupted. The cities of Pompeii and Herculaneum had some time in which to evacuate; Pliny the Elder, the admiral in charge of the region, died, attempting to effect the evacuation of hundreds of survivors. Still, fully <u>half</u> the population of the city died. Estimates run as high as ten thousand lives lost – an estimate comparable to the death tolls in battle from that era.

When the Pythia, as the only augury to have successfully foretold exactly how the region would be destroyed, was approached again, about rebuilding Pompeii and Herculaneum, she calmly told the Roman emissary, "The mountain will now sleep until the world ends."

Rome took that augury, and rebuilt both cities in the shadows of Vesuvius. The eruption did encourage a great development in natural philosophy, and caused people to question why the gods had <u>warned</u> of the eruption, but had not prevented it. The only explanation offered by Stoic philosophers was this: that the eruption may have been <u>necessary</u> to release tensions and gases in the earth. And modern natural philosophy has born that supposition out.

– Aetius Fulvius. <u>The Natural Philosophy of Plate Tectonics</u>, p. 129, University of Neapolis Press, 1959 AC.

<u>Maius 17-18, 1960 AC</u>

Adam was mildly surprised that evening, when Sigrun turned on the far-viewer in their apartment in Rome. It was a ley-powered model, and, as such, a rounded orb of glass atop a stand. She clicked the dial through the stations—Rome had dozens—and then curled up on their couch, a mug of tea in her hands. "Somehow I don't think you're in the mood for *The Menaechmi Return*," Adam said, standing behind her. The modern take on the Plautus original was a long-running comedy series, which relied heavily on the plot device of twin brothers, perpetually mistaken for one another, for its humor. This usually involved their wives and lovers not being able to tell one of them from the other, so one brother usually had to keep someone occupied, whilst the other was off trying to swindle a merchant, or something. There was a parasite character—a poor cousin—who fawned on them, and usually attempted to bad-mouth one to the other in an effort to gain access to their bank accounts. Sig had *opinions* about comedies and dramas that relied on everyone in the story being stupid in order to work.

"Definitely not," Sigrun replied, quietly. "Execution."

Adam blinked. Neither of them usually specifically tuned in to watch executions, or even gladiatorial fights that were conducted with condemned prisoners. He settled in on the couch beside her, and put a hand comfortably around the nape of her neck. "What's the occasion?"

"Murderer from Nova Germania. Considered himself a *hunter*, if you can believe it. Drove from town to town, finding women to rape and kill. Fifty-two known victims over fifteen years, they say. He made his way back to Europa five years ago, and continued his hunting in Rome." Sigrun's neck muscles felt like iron under Adam's fingers, her body singing with tension.

"Got caught, did he?"

"Oh yes. They had him on the evidence here, and that would have been enough to condemn him . . . but then he started to confess to more and more. Bragging, if you like." Her eyes were cold and distant on the screen, which showed the main arena of Rome, with a timestamp that indicated that the film had been taken earlier today. "He confessed to all fifty-two, and ten more here in Europa. He kept trophies. Locks of hair. Blood-smears. He could use them, I suppose, to confuse a spirit hunting for him, but mainly, they say, he kept them for . . . enjoyment."

Adam's stomach turned. "So . . . drawing out the bowels and dragging the body with four horses?"

"No. The magistrates noted in their decision," Sigrun let her head loll back on her neck for a moment, "that Rome has had a law on the books for over two thousand years that states that if a wife is raped, her husband has the right to rape the male who did it in return. They also stated that this law hasn't been enforced in a few centuries, and that lining up . . . sixty-two injured fathers and husbands and lovers could take a while, and that there would be health risks to the men, unless they used a stick, instead . . . ."

" . . . Can I say that I'm glad that isn't what's being shown on the far-viewer right now? Not that it wouldn't be just, but I'm not sure I'd particularly want to watch."

"Certainly. The magistrates opted for poetic justice instead. They said that since the man thought of himself as a hunter, he should be hunted in turn." Sigrun pointed at the screen, where a prisoner wearing nothing more than a loincloth, was shoved into the arena. No manacles. No chains. Just him. And, unnervingly, silence from the crowd. No roar of approval. Nothing.

The charges were read out. The condemned was given a chance to request mercy. The magistrate present looked out at the crowd, and received no acclamation. Everyone present was there to see this man die. The cameras panned out . . . and the lions emerged from their dens in the pits, racing up the stairs into the arena proper. Six of them, all females. *Poetic justice, indeed.*

Adam rubbed Sigrun's neck, and they watched the lions stalk the man. The beasts had been kept *hungry*, and the cheers that the crowd suddenly gave forth agitated the beasts. The murderer kept turning and twisting, trying to keep them in front of him . . . but the eldest female, a wily hunter with a few scars here and there on her legs, moved in from behind and bore him to the ground, applying her teeth to crush his throat. His face was almost completely covered by the beast's great mouth . . . and her sister lions moved in to tear at his struggling belly. Entrails. Blood. Adam could imagine the smell of the shit in the bowels. The crowd roared its approval. *Blood and sacrifice, but in this case . . . I think a just one.*

It was over in minutes, and the lions, to prevent them from acquiring too much of a taste for human flesh, were called away by their trainers and given fresh venison, instead. In very small letters at the bottom of the screen, words appeared: *No animals were harmed in the course of this execution.* "I can't help but notice that during regular gladiatorial games, they don't run that statement," Adam said, dryly, and reached over to turn off the far-viewer. He leaned over and gave her a kiss. "He offended you, didn't he?"

"To my very soul, yes."

"You didn't work any of the cases?"

"No. I verified that, first thing. I can grasp the heat of the moment, an instant of bad judgment, sorely repented. But making of other's lives into toys? Playthings? No." She made a disgusted sound at the back of her throat. "In addition . . . I could see it in him. Guilt, but no remorse, if you understand. He felt none of it, though he was absolutely culpable of the crimes. The law allows mercy, if there is remorse, and recompense can be made. But I could see in him the stain."

"Can you see the soul, Sigrun?" Adam had never quite been willing to ask her that before. He was a little afraid of what he might hear, to be honest.

She shook her head, and he felt a band loosen around his heart. "No. I know that Lassair can, though. She says you shine like a blade, Adam."

"Blood washes off, eh?"

She leaned against him in the dimness of the living room. "Eventually. It might not feel like it, some days, but it does."

"You always know when someone's guilty, though?"

"Yes. Guilty of *something*. It shows in them. That man . . . I don't think he actually had a soul." She shrugged a little.

"It must be nice to be . . . that *certain*." His tone was wistful.

She shook her head against his shoulder. "It is a guide, Adam. Nothing more. Once, when I was in Nova Germania, a man confessed to murder. The blood type at the scene matched his. A man leaving the scene matched his description. An eye-witness identified him out of a lineup. It seemed open and shut, and the little town where he was imprisoned called on me to judge and execute him." Sigrun turned her head to look up at Adam. "But it was a lie, Adam."

"Wait. The evidence was—"

"The same blood *type*. A man who looked enough like him to be mistaken in the dark by an eye witness who was frightened and confused. The man had a son, Adam. The son killed a man in a fight over his wife, and his father, not wishing to see his son executed, swore to the authorities that he'd done the deed." She shrugged. "I told him that I respected his desire to protect his family. His *son*. But that the lies helped no one. Including his son. Who might have been given only a term in prison or hard labor, or even acquitted, if it could be shown that the other man was the first to attack with a blade." She shook her head again. "That was an uphill battle. I had to persuade them both to tell the truth, and show how the evidence all fit. It is not always as *easy* as the valkyrie appearing and rendering judgment." A faint, wintery smile. "However, when someone is guilty, and they resist arrest? There are advantages to being a law-giver."

"Esh and Tren's first report is due tomorrow," Adam said, idly. "I wonder what they've found so far."

"Knowing them? Probably either a manure pile or diamonds.

Possibly both in the same place."

"So, we'll probably be off to Caesaria Australis shortly."

"Good thing I didn't really unpack from Judea."

"Re-pack, *neshama*. It's winter there. Also, pack suncream. Cuzco receives the most ultraviolet of any city on earth."

"You are a treasure trove of strange scientific facts, Adam ben Maor."

"I have been *researching* the city for three weeks." His turn to be dry. "Besides, I know why you've turned down the idea of going to the beach every time we shake loose a little time for vacation. You don't like sunburns."

"No. They *hurt*." Sigrun's voice turned tart.

He pulled her closer. "You've been shot by arrows, shot by musket balls, burned half to death, and stabbed with poisoned stingers, and that's just since I've *known* you . . and you don't like *sunburns?*" Adam didn't like the litany of wounds . . . but her objection to sunburns was like her objection to flying in a 'metal death-trap': Highly amusing to him.

"They hurt, and they do not heal as well as you might suppose. It is not as if I were in a battle with the sun." She paused. "This time."

"Tell me the truth. You wouldn't know what to *do* with yourself if we sat on a beach, would you?"

Another pause. "Likely not." She slanted a glance up at him. "Nor would you."

"Oh, yes, I would." She held his gaze for a moment, and he gave up and laughed. "You got me. I'm not good at just sitting and doing nothing, I guess."

"It's all right." Her tone was gentle. "That's because we're building something, Adam. We're building our life together. What do *normal* people even do on vacations?"

". . . I don't know. Other than sit on beaches?"

"Besides that, yes."

"I'm thinking. Ah . . ." He paused. He was really having a problem coming up with activities. "Go swimming in the sea. With those new compressed air tanks?"

"I have no interest in drowning myself for pleasure. But I enjoy your aerobatics lessons on weekends." Her lips quirked a little. He could just see it out of the corner of his eye.

"So do I." Adam grinned at her. "It fulfills a childhood fantasy, and it serves a purpose. I'm checked out on fixed-wings and small ornithopters now. If we ever need to go somewhere quietly . . . I can get a team in. "

"So practical," Sigrun chided. "You were the one telling me that I have no concept of how to relax. So, tell me, what else do people do?"

Adam sighed. He was running out of ideas. "I honestly don't know. Wear costumes at . . . what's the autumnal equinox celebration in Gaul again?"

"Samhain. That custom originated to keep the bad spirits at bay. Masks. Like blood can mask you from a spirit, or salt water."

"Yes, but these days, people seem to want to wear costumes a lot more. Like that one girl my mother wanted me to marry. The one who ran around dressing like a geisha. Wonder what Minori would have thought of that. I should ask her, just to watch her wince." Adam gave Sigrun a sidelong glance. "So . . . do you ever just want to be someone else?"

Sigrun's her gray eyes warmed a little. "I used to wish that. All the time. But, when I'm with you, I am the person I want to be. A human. Costumes are for children. For people who are still . . . experimenting with their identity, who aren't sure who they are, or who they want to be." She kissed the palm of his hand, lightly. "I did not dare to dream, until I met you, that I could ever be anything other than a weapon in the hands of the gods. You let me be more, Adam. You share your humanity with me. I don't need a costume, and I don't need to pretend. Together, we just *are*."

He cleared his throat. "Yes . . . we are."

It was one of the most powerful declarations she'd ever given him, and he didn't know what to say in return. He shared the emotions. Felt them deeply. But Roman civilization had never much prized romantic love. Distrusted it, on many levels. Latin had a word for immoderate, unbalancing love-for-a-wife: *uxorious*. The Gauls, yes, had many a tale of passion and darkness. Drustan and Eselt, for example, was a tale out of the oral tradition of storytelling in Gaul. It told of a young princess, Eselt, who had been promised to a king, but fell in love with the king's nephew and became his lover, in spite of being forced to marry the aging king. The cycle of stories about them, about passion and the conflict between desire and duty, was deeply ingrained in Gallic culture. And in Judea, the endearment *neshama*, or *soul*, reflected the belief that in marriage, two people's souls were joined. That they truly became soul-mates, in a sense. Adam couldn't quite put it into words right now, but in his eyes, she was his other half. That even if she didn't realize it, she brought light into his life. It had been a pretty bare existence before she'd come along. She brought both a sense of certainty with her, and a sense of wonder about things he took for granted. She adored his parents, and gave forthright advice to his sisters. He just hoped he was conveying some of it by the way he was holding her, the pressure of fingers on skin. That he hadn't known he was poor until she'd made him wealthy with nothing more than herself.

Quiet evenings like these, he cherished. Because he knew they wouldn't last. And this one passed all too quickly. The phone rang at six antemeridian, and Adam answered it, still half asleep. "*Ave.*"

"Ben Maor? Eshmunazar. Have I got a story for you." Kanmi's tone spoke volumes. Ire and agitation and tension sang in it, and Adam sat up in bed, reaching for the light . . . and for the foolscap notebook and fountain pen on the nightstand. *They've got something.* "My end of the line's secure. You've been swept for bugs lately?"

"Yes. We should be clear. Go ahead, Esh."

"All right." A pause, while Kanmi clearly collected his thoughts. "We've found and released, more or less by accident, one bound entity," Kanmi began, irony mordant in his voice. "Matrugena suggests that there may be a dozen spirits bounds and possibly even another entity bound in the same location."

Adam's brain shut down for a moment. "By *entity* you mean . . . ."

"Yes."

"Bound *how?*" He still had trouble accepting that raw technology and magic had managed to contain Tlaloc, but the god had been weakened by loss of belief, loss of sacrifice, and had been in an avatar at the time. Apparently, these things *mattered*.

"Lines on the ground. Ley-lines in the earth. Matrugena's alternating between being impressed at the spell-work and mad enough to chew through an iron bar at the moment."

"You say you released one? Isn't that a little . . . unilateral?" They'd been specifically directed not to be hasty or arbitrary.

"Asha got her toes stuck in the same trap with it. Hold on and let me tell this from the beginning. It won't make much *more* sense, but it'll make some."

By the end of the conversation, Sigrun was already up, dressed, and packing, and Adam was staring into space. "Esh, that doesn't make *sense*. Up in Nahautl, it was being done to avoid *using* the ley-lines, as much as possible, anyway. It was supposed to be 'home-grown' power, that didn't rely on foreign-trained ley-mages —"

"I know. *We* know. We're missing pieces, and we're working at the end of a very long fishing line here."

"All right. I'll see what I can do to help with that. Don't do anything else *unilateral* till we get there."

"Oh, and when you get here, we can be as unilateral as we want?" Kanmi's tone was acerbic.

Adam suppressed a grin. "Not saying that, but let me run it up the chain and see what we're even permitted to do," he replied. "Fortunately, in this case? It's a really short chain."

It was, too. At the moment, on this topic, Adam reported to Livorus, and Livorus reported directly to Imperator Caesarion. The propraetor and the emperor weren't taking many chances with letting information get out of their hands at the moment, largely because they'd seen so little result from the rest of the Praetorians. Adam wasn't sure that was entirely fair to the rest of the Guard, and knew there'd eventually be hell to pay for the fact that the Imperator was skirting the entire chain of command. He was a lictor, and the ranking head of Livorus' detail, but he was hardly the commander of the Praetorians. Not by a *long* stretch. The current commander wasn't going to enjoy having been circumvented.

On the other hand, an issue like this was hardly for public consumption.

As Adam helped Sigrun pack, he asked, quietly, "Five years ago, you had to report in on all this to the Odinhall. They took it out of your hands after the whole . . . entity business . . . and gave it to someone else. Who was that, again?"

Sigrun began to lace up the sides of her suitcase. "Reginleif. She's a god-born of Loki. One of my instructors at the Odinhall."

Adam frowned. "Did I meet her at the wedding?"

"No. She wasn't there. I assumed she had much work to do, because of what we'd stirred up."

"And in the past five years, have they told you anything about her investigations?"

Her movements were jerky now. "No. Not a word." Her voice was taut, and he thought he knew why; she thought this meant that they didn't *trust* her.

Adam reached out. Put a hand on her forearm. "Do you need to call them? Inform them of what's going on?"

Sigrun grimaced. It was decidedly odd to see indecision on her face. Usually, she knew what course of action she'd take, within seconds of being presented with a choice. "If I do," she said, slowly, "there is a fair chance that they will forbid me to go with you. Which will put me in direct conflict between the orders of Rome, and the orders of the Odinhall. And that would pit my loyalty to *you* and Livorus and the others against my loyalty to the gods." She turned, and faced him, her head tilting to the side a little, her gray eyes dark, for the moment, in the dim light coming in from the hallway. "I think, perhaps, that there is little information I can give them until I've seen and assessed the situation for myself."

"That sounds . . . very fair," Adam told her, and grinned to himself. *Either I'm having an effect on her, by telling her she can use her discernment, just like every other human, or Kanmi's rubbing off on her. That was sneakier than I anticipated.*

Within four hours of that, they'd met with Livorus, and then they'd had an emergency meeting with Livorus *and* the Imperator. This was conducted in the imperial palace itself, after having their identification checked . . . and at least one of the Praetorians on duty, a tall, almost cadaverously thin Nubian . . . came over to give Sigrun a wrist-clasp. "Zoskales Ezana," she said, smiling slightly. "It's been a while."

The Nubian smiled, a white flash of teeth. "I regret that I missed the wedding. The emperor had received several new and fairly credible assassination threats. My services were needed here, in Rome." The sorcerer, Sigrun's first partner in the Praetorians, traded wrist-clasps with Adam, and saluted Livorus, tapping his fist to his heart with emphasis. "Propraetor. It is an honor to see you once more."

Then he escorted them into a small study, walls lined with bookshelves and scroll racks, and a single, recessed window that overlooked a pleasant formal garden. A line of phones stood along the antique wood desk . . . and the man sitting behind that desk had a face familiar from any handful of coins that someone happened to spill out on a counter, anywhere in the empire.

Adam had never met Caesarion before, and he was startled to realize that the emperor of Rome and all her holdings was only about six years his senior. Caesarion had taken the throne in 1948, which meant that the pressures of ruling approximately half the globe—and nearly a billion people, in total—had already weighed on him for twelve years. But Caesarion was also god-born, so his hair remained dark, without traces of gray, and his brown eyes, behind that patrician nose, were piercing as he accepted Adam's salute. He even offered a wrist-clasp, surprisingly, a gesture of extreme generosity. For Sigrun, the Imperator had a charming smile. "A pleasure to meet you. I understand that you are more recently derived of godly blood, than I am?" A delicate question, that. Adam wasn't sure what the courtesies were, here, or what entirely what it meant to be more *recently* descended from a god.

"*Dominus*." Sigrun lowered her head in respect. "I am told that my father's mother's mother, Solveig, was very fair indeed, and just, and wise. That she was a law-giver in 1840 or so, when Tyr listened to her judgments and gave to her some of his power. Their daughter, my grandmother, Saga, was born mortal, however." Sigrun's tone was detached. "Solveig was not a warrior from birth, but she felt it was her duty to fight in the Caspian Crisis, and she died there, in 1860. Her daughter was my grandmother; her son, Ivarr, my father. Though I may call Tyr my grandfather, I am descended from but one god, *dominus*, and you are descended from many."

A ghostly flicker of amusement crossed Caesarion's face. "You are fair-spoken," he congratulated her. "I see now why my father's old advisor has kept you to himself. Would you not prefer to come and work for me?"

A flash of unease across Sigrun's face, there, then gone. "Rome has my loyalty and my allegiance, Imperator. But I feel a personal bond to the propraetor, which I do not give lightly. I would prefer to remain in his service for the duration of my time in the Guard."

"Well enough," Caesarion replied, and looked at Adam now, piercingly. Adam wondered what was behind those eyes, and imagined, for a moment, the wheels of a jewel-pointed watch, all churning and spinning. "So your richly talented lictors found the tail end of another, similar plot, and decided to pull on it, Livorus? If I were to turn this over to the rest of the Guard, they would undoubtedly begin to wonder if any of your lictors have some involvement in a massive global conspiracy against the state and the gods."

Adam stiffened. It wasn't an insult. The tone was matter-of-fact. And then the Imperator waved it away. "I don't believe it. I've met you both, now. But that is almost certainly what someone will, at some point, choose to believe, and attempt to prove."

"You've learned much, *dominus*," Livorus murmured.

"All at your knee, friend of my father." Caesarion's tone shifted slightly. "Livorus, my friend . . . I'm sending you with them. It will be a pleasant change for you, I think, to be away from Raccia, Chaldea, and involved in affairs other than that of the infernal Caspian region." He glanced up. "To expedite matters, I will empower both of your senior lictors temporarily as special envoys. This will give them ambassadorial rank, privileges, and protections. Try not to abuse the power I have given you." That last was directed at both Sigrun and Adam. He scribbled on two pieces of paper, signing each of the letters that named both of them *diplomats*. Adam's lips twitched a little as he held the parchment between his fingertips; he'd been called many things in his life. *Diplomat* wasn't one of them. *It could be worse. He could have handed one of these to Kanmi.*

He looked up as the Imperator went on. "I would be obliged if you might remind the Emperor of the Inca of the treaty provisions between his empire and mine. To whit, that human sacrifice is forbidden in all of Rome's holdings, of which his empire is a part, as a subject nation and ally." Caesarion's expression didn't change, but his tone inflected slightly on the word *ally*, and Adam could hear the irony there. "If he will not hear your words, you are authorized to meet with the governor and enact any measures you deem necessary to *make* him hear, up to and including martial law. What they do with their own gods is, by law and necessity, their own affair. There is nothing technically *illegal* about binding an . . . *entity*." Caesarion's mouth pursed slightly, as if he'd bitten into a sour fruit. "However, if what they are doing threatens the safety and well-being of the subject nations around them, who *also* look to Rome for protection, then it does become the business of Rome. Investigate before you confront. And now . . ." he flicked his fingers at them, and turned back to the stack of papers on his desk.

Four hours after *that*, they were on a trans-oceanic flight, one of them on either side of Livorus, and two additional lictors from his overall squad with them, as backup. *At least one thing can be said of this job,* Adam thought to himself. *You definitely get to see the world.* They'd be in the air for at least twenty hours; between the flight to Tenochtitlan, and the ornithopter flight to Cuzco, and any transfers or delays, they were going to be out of contact for almost twenty-four full hours. *Hold it together,* he thought, at Kanmi and Trennus. *We're getting there as fast as we can.* The pair could call in local *gardia*, using their Praetorian rank, but god only knew the loyalties of the local *gardia*. And there was no way of knowing, at the moment, who was behind *any* of this.

<u>Maius 19, 1960 AC</u>

Kanmi had recommended, that for safety's sake, they all stay in the same room. "Matrugena, you and Lassair can have the bed. Dr. Sasaki? You've got the couch. I'll take the floor. Won't be the first time. Also, I'll take first watch."

Trennus hadn't actually raised any objections to that, and neither had Lassair; Trennus was clearly worried about his spirit-wife, and Lassair had no concept of *privacy* that Kanmi could detect. For his part, the floor was fine. At least on the floor, he was less likely to catch the scent of Minori's skin on the sheets and absently think, *Smells nice,* before he woke up all the way.

Minori, for her part, however, objected, at least a little. "Part of what protects us here," she pointed out, raising her fine brows, "is the appearance of normalcy. The lie. The cover. If we suddenly all take to sleeping in the same room, it will attract attention, certainly."

"Only if the hotel staff takes up opening locked doors in the middle of the night to check on our location." Kanmi's tone was sharp. "In which case, we're *perfututum*." *Totally fucked out.*

Her lips thinned. "Part of the briefing *I* was given was on the importance of living the cover. Something that you in particular have had some minor difficulties doing, Master Eshmunazar. Already, you've returned to referring to me as Doctor Sasaki."

Kanmi looked at the ceiling for patience. She was right, in a sense. In undercover work, it was absolutely vital to *believe* your cover story, and try to maintain it even when you thought you couldn't be seen or heard. On the other hand, he desperately *needed* to maintain mental space, and having Tren and Lassair in the same room? Created even more space. Even if the room suddenly felt half its previous size. "Minori," he said, catching Lassair's fascinated glance out of the corner of his eye, "I'll work on that. In the meantime? Everyone needs to stay as safe as possible. We'll move Tren and Lassair here after they've visibly gone into their room every night. I'm not really good with light yet, though it's something I'm studying, so I can't make them invisible, but Lassair can disguise herself—"

"Invisibility is very difficult," Minori said, frowning. "I could arrange *darkness*—"

"Yes, but—"

"Hold on," Tren told them, dryly. "Don't get bogged down in the details. Once we wake *up* in the morning, are we going everywhere together, too?"

Kanmi exchanged a long look with Matrugena. "Exactly my plan."

The argument had gone on for a while after that, but Kanmi had won it. And had lain on the hard, cold tile floor, barely padded by a blanket, and reminded his body that it was hardly the first time he'd slept on the ground. About a half hour before he was due to call ben Maor, Minori draped an extra blanket over him. "Thanks, but I don't need it," Kanmi murmured.

"It is quite warm in the room, for me. You are from a milder climate." Minori's words were just as soft as his. "You slept on the ground often, when you were on the Mongolian border?"

Kanmi shrugged, and sat up to arrange the blankets *under* him. It wasn't the air temperature that was getting to him; it was the cold in the tile, sucking the life out of him. "There. Elsewhere. My parents had a two-room apartment for six people when I was a child. My brothers and I slept on the floor of my parents' room. The three of us had one mattress. I usually got knocked off in the middle of the night. My grandfather slept out in the family room, because he'd be up before dawn to go to his fishing boat. My father, when he was home, slept in the bedroom, but if he had to leave on his ship in the morning, he slept on a cot by the kitchen stove. It was crowded."

She'd stopped moving, and Kanmi tilted his head to look at her. "What?" he asked. "Surprised that my family was that poor? That I wore clothes my brothers had worn, before me, mended three times over before I got a chance to grow into them? That the building was rat-infested, and I could hear them rustling through the walls every night, squeaking and chittering? That sometimes, my brothers and I would be bitten by the rats, in the night?"

She shuddered. "And your sons?"

Kanmi shrugged. Turned away. "When they were born, my parents didn't have the care of three boys and a grandfather. They also had my paycheck, and Bastet's. Better apartment. Better food. Better clothes. No *rats*."

Minori dropped to her knees beside his pallet, bending surprisingly close to his ear. "So when you had a chance to go to school, on scholarship, you did the very best you could."

He closed his eyes. Sleep was finally beckoning, but it was too damned late for it. "Yes. At school . . . I shared a room, but I had a *bed*. Three meals a day. Books. Clothes that weren't rags. It was paradise. I'd have done *anything* to stay. Well . . . almost." Some of the older boys had thought they could use that in him. Had tried to tell the twelve-year-old wharf rat that if he *didn't* do what they wanted of him, that they'd go to the pedagogues and that they'd ensure he'd be thrown out. Kanmi had had a slightly better understanding of the world than they had, however, and enough experience fighting dirty on the docks to know precisely where to grab, twist, and pull. As he'd told Adam ben Maor many times, he had no chance against a larger opponent in a straight fight. His only chance, really, lay in dirty tactics, followed by sorcery.

And his gift for sorcery had also been enormous, and he'd been motivated to learn. *Quickly.* A group of four or five upperclassmen had urinated blood for a week. And when the pedagogues had asked what had happened, how one apprentice student had first, managed to beat five upper-tier students, and second, *why* he'd felt the need to do so . . . the truth had come out, and all five had been expelled, summarily.

"Is that why you hate me? Because I wasn't born into those circumstances?" She sounded distressed.

Kanmi opened his eyes, surprised, and rolled over. "I don't hate you, doc—Minori. I hate the nobility. I hate the wealthy. The *haves*, who were *born* to it, and haven't worked a day in their lives. The ones who couldn't hold anything more challenging than a job operating a cash register, but still have more money than they can count. Them? Yes. I hate them. People like Livorus . . . no. I don't hate him. I *respect* him. He works, Minori. He works every day, like a dog."

"But you don't respect me, do you?" Again, the quiet tone. Not quite reproachful, nor really angry. Just . . . matter of fact.

"I don't *know* you." Kanmi shrugged. It wasn't quite true. He'd been rapidly *getting* to know her. At least as much as she let him know. He therefore knew she had twelve brothers and sisters, all of them half-siblings, ranging in age from twelve years her senior to fifteen years her junior. He knew that her face softened whenever she was around his sons. That she found Lassair almost overwhelmingly beautiful. That she had a gift for sorcery probably equal to his own, but largely untested. That she enjoyed food, savoring every bite. That she, like the rest of them, hadn't entirely known what to do with Tawantinsuyan cuisine. *Ben Maor is going to get here and between the <u>cuy</u> — guinea pigs — cooked with a hot stone shoved in their abdominal cavities, the mayfly larva flour loaves, the alpaca jerky, and* *everything else, he's going to settle for potatoes. Probably just potatoes, for the duration of his stay.* Kanmi's thoughts had wandered, just for an instant, and as a result, he smiled faintly as he reached out, and took her hand in his. "For a noble-born, you don't actually seem that bad," he told her.

"How magnanimous of you," she told him, a prickle in her voice, which made him laugh, though he choked it down, in deference to Lassair and Trennus, who were trying to sleep.

The morning of Maius 19, Kanmi and the others were preparing to leave the hotel to start checking into the *tower* locations, when the attendant at the front desk beckoned Trennus and him over. "You have messages," the man behind the desk noted, and handed each of them a slip of paper.

Kanmi read his rapidly. Excellent Latin, neat, educated hand. "Micos Cornelius," he muttered. "That's a patrician *gens*, if ever I heard one. Could be related to *Sulla*, for the gods' sakes." *But, more likely, one of the governor's family members. He's definitely a Cornelii.*

The note was brief, and to the point. *It is my understanding that you are a technomancer, Agent Eshmunazar, and a sorcerer of some repute. I believe we may claim mutual acquaintance with several mages, including Lady Erida Lelayn. It would please me to make your acquaintance, and the acquaintance of your fellow travelers. You may find me at my home in the Court of the Golden Sun today, postmeridian.* — MC

Typical patrician, expecting people to dance attendance, Kanmi thought, and shoved the note in his pocket. "What have you got? Dinner invitation, too?"

Tren's face had turned stony. "Not quite," he said, and handed the note to Kanmi, glancing around the room lobby. "Is the person who left this, still here?" he asked the attendant.

"She said she would stay outside the main doors. She looked to be very highly ranked. I did not dare say anything to her." The attendant's eyes widened.

Kanmi's eyes skimmed over the paper. The lettering was good, but the writer was unused to penning Latin, evidently. *I had to find you, and your goddess. You were not hard to track. You should be careful. Bad things have happened here in Cuzco of late. My lady and I owe you gratitude, priest. And, grateful though we are, we must ask of you more aid.*

The Carthaginian lifted his head and scanned the lobby, catching Minori's eye from across the room and nodding to her; she and Lassair crossed from the stairwell, joining them. "We're popular," Kanmi said, derisively, as they stepped away. "Matru, you know who this is?"

Tren covered his mouth with his hand, as if coughing, and muttered, into his hand, "God-born, probably," before pulling Lassair's hand through the crook of his left arm.

Yes, Lassair told them all. *The one who watched us at the place of lines is outside the door. She wears no masks. She does not conceal herself, or her intentions, but she is afraid.* The spirit tipped her head, looking towards the rotating glass door.

Kanmi pulled up defensive constructs in his mind, and felt Minori doing the same thing; hers were a little different than his, but rock-solid spell-craft, nonetheless. Mouthing the words under his breath, he extended his personal constructs out to cover her, and the corners of his mouth quirked up, faintly, as he felt her shift, and extend her barriers out to cover him.

Outside, there was a single Tawantinsuyan woman, sitting on the edge of a planter in front of the hotel, watching the passers-by with wide eyes. The local empire was made up of literally hundreds of smaller tribes and ethnic groups whose differences were, unfortunately, rather lost on Kanmi; he did think that most of the women here were among the most beautiful he'd ever seen, with dark brown eyes and straight black hair that they usually wore braided. But the higher-ranked castes still occasionally bound the heads of their children, contorting the skulls into conical shapes as a mark of distinction. Modern medicine suggested that this could result in a variety of ailments and potentially even reduced cognitive development, but common sense had never stopped anyone in history from body-modification in the pursuit of beauty.

This woman was in her sixties, or at least, appeared to be. Her hair was silver, and her face was lined by years spent in the sun; her jowls sagged, and her body, under her loose, colorfully striped clothing, was matronly. But Kanmi received a sense of power from her, nonetheless. A sense of moving tides, of gravity, water. And rather than having the haunting dark brown eyes that were the hallmark of so many Tawantinsuyu beauties, her eyes were inhuman. The schlera were the black of the night sky, and the irises, seemingly without pupils, were a luminous white. *God-born*, Kanmi thought. *An <u>old</u> one, too. Damn. Well, they don't all live forever.*

The woman stood, and offered her hands to Trennus. "I am Cocohuay," she said, quietly. "High priestess of Mamaquilla, and in her line of descent." The woman's voice was surprisingly soft, and soothing, for all the baleful stare of those strange eyes. She turned, and actually half-bowed to Lassair, in clear respect. "My goddess' voice has been lost to me for almost two years, since the Emperor sought to honor her with a place among the Lines. I had thought her angered. Distracted. Something. The priests and men who cut the crescent into the earth, asked me to come and consecrate the image. To sprinkle the earth of Nazca with water from the sea, once a month, to honor the goddess at the full moon. And in two years, nothing. Until yesterday, when she screamed in my mind that she was *released*." She again bowed her head to Lassair. "I have you two, to thank for this. I do not know your name, goddess, and I only know the name of your priest from having asked the workers at the Lines . . . but I would honor you both."

Kanmi stole a look at Matrugena's face. He rather wished he had a camera. The expression there was a priceless mix of embarrassment, discomfort, and determination. "I am *not* a priest," he said, rapidly. "Asha? You want to explain matters?"

I am not a goddess, Lassair said, her mental tones uneasy. *I do not ask for honor or reverence.* She had actually stepped a little behind Trennus, and was peeking out around his shoulder, almost as she would have, years ago, ducked her phoenix head into his long hair. *How did you find us?*

Cocohuay pointed to the planter on which she'd been seated, which, Kanmi suddenly realized, was filled with budding flowers . . . in spite of the flecks of frozen rain spitting down from the sky. "It was not hard to find you. I asked the workers for the name of the one who attends on you, as I said. They gave what information they had, and I traveled here. After that, I needed only to follow spring and warmth. I read signs. As others may."

Trennus cleared his throat, in clear discomfort. "Your note said you wished to ask us for help?"

"Yes. But we should not speak here. Not for long. Too many eyes watch here."

Yes, Lassair confirmed, after a moment. *We are watched, even now, by eyes that have been bound to be here.*

Human? Kanmi thought, shaping the word distinctly.

Yes. No spirits. This city is . . . quiet. There are almost no house-spirits, unlike Rome. No mountain-dwellers or woods-dwellers, as there should be. Lassair bit her lower lip. *The one who watches us is bored.*

Where? Show me.

Lassair did, and Kanmi winced as his vision distorted. Showed him the winding, stone-cobbled street, the gray shapes that were the majority of the people in the cityscape. Kanmi's mind reeled; the spirit had rarely joined her mind to his, and he disliked it, intensely. No one had faces. It was a street full of dolls, or mannequins. On a third-floor balcony across the street and to his right, a brighter speck. Eyes actually visible in the gray, smooth, otherwise featureless face. Eyes that were focused on them, a coil of attention strung between them like a line.

Curious, Kanmi turned his attention to the others standing with him, and sucked in his breath in awe. Trennus was, in the spirit's eyes, vastly tall, seemingly ten feet in height, brown and green bands running along the length of his frame. His face was clear and distinct, and his eyes were still blue, and a cord of . . . himself . . . had pulled out of his side, and coiled over to Lassair, who was all fire in this version of reality. Her flames seethed back along that cord, a two-way binding between the pair. The god-born woman in front of them was barely substantial, a shaft of pale moonlight trapped in flesh. And Minori . . . Minori was the sky over the sea on a sunny day. Pale blue above meeting indigo below, endless and eternal, and Kanmi couldn't stop *looking* at her for at least half a minute. Then he shook his head, hard, wondered what the hell Lassair saw when she looked at him — *probably nothing at all, idiot* — and noted, "Yes. I see him. Let's get out of sight."

"I know his face from somewhere," Minori muttered. "I want to say a conference, maybe? Maybe the one in Lutetia a month ago?"

Kanmi looked back, trying to make it look casual. The problem was, he couldn't place the face at all, though he appeared to be a Tawantinsuyu native. "There's a coffee place around the corner," he muttered. "Let's go in there."

All food production in Tawantinsuyu was technically state-controlled. Every animal hunted, every potato produced, was slaughtered or farmed by peasants under the control of their local lords, and then moved to state-held warehouses. Peasants had once been more or less slaves, bound to their lords and unable to leave their lands. The lords were supposed to provide the peasants with food, water, shelter, and tools enough to do their jobs. It was a damned odd system, in Kanmi's opinion, and it meant that commercial enterprises, such as inns and restaurants and taverns, had all originated from nobles just low enough in social status who'd seen a market in catering to the needs of foreigners, centuries ago . . . and had branched out to serving locals once the economy had adopted the solidus and non-slave peasants had been required, under Imperial law, to be paid for their labor.

Thus, the local cafes were all vaguely cosmopolitan in feel. They offered local foods as well as foreign ones, served locally-grown coffee and, for locals, *coca* leaves to chew. Kanmi couldn't quite wrap his head around walking around with a wad of leaves shoved in his mouth, or spitting the residue out onto the ground, so he was just as happy to stick with coffee. It wasn't presented Nubian-style, but that was fine. In his opinion, when he wanted a cup, it was nice that it didn't take an hour to prepare. Minori accepted a cup, made a face, and muttered, "No one offers tea on this side of the world, I see."

The god-born woman leaned across the table now, as Trennus asked her, quietly, "So what do you need our help for, precisely?"

"Your lady," a glance at Lassair, "is correct. Our land has been going *silent* in the past eight years. Fewer and fewer voices whisper on the winds. I go to the high places, the holy shrines, and I feel *no presences* there. There is a sickness in this land. I have tried to speak to others here about it . . . and I have been met with walls of silence." She shook her head. "I go to young priests, whose mothers I helped to birth them? They say, *no, no, nothing is wrong. You misunderstand. We hear the gods. They are with us.* But I see lies all around me. They show me new temples being built at ancient holy sites. Tell me one is reserved for Mamaquilla . . . but I must keep coming to the Lines, every month." She shrugged. "It is a long trip, for these old bones, but I go." She paused, as the waiter brought a second round of coffee around, and Kanmi ensured that sound was deadened around their table once the waiter left again. "My goddess told me, last night, as I looked up to the moon . . . that every month, when I came to the Lines? Those who had imprisoned her there, bade her *take my body* for her own. Told her that if she assumed me, as an avatar, subsumed me to her will, they would take her, in me, to a far place. Where she would dwell in comfort, not incorporeal, as the Lines prevent her from fully manifesting. That she would give of herself, and offerings would be brought to her." Cocohuay shuddered. "That it would be, as it had been in the old days. My goddess *refused*. She said that she would not sacrifice me, her beloved granddaughter, for a false freedom." A tear trickled down that worn cheek. "They told her that if she accepted, and went to dwell in the temple that they had built for her, she would continue to exist. And if she didn't . .

. that they would sacrifice *her*."

Kanmi froze. "That's not possible," Minori said, her voice horrified. "*Kami* cannot . . . well, they can die . . . but a human cannot sacrifice them . . . ." Her eyes flicked to Kanmi's face.

Trennus sounded dazed. "A mortal *can* kill a god. Under the right circumstances. History tells us that, though no one truly *knows* how Akhenaten did it. Any records were obliterated millennia ago."

More than history, Kanmi thought, grimly. *Tlaloc died at <u>Adam ben Maor's</u> hands. Well, all of ours, but his, more than the rest of us.* "But *sacrifice*," Minori whispered. "That suggests that there is some . . . being . . . to whom the sacrifice would be made."

"The word," Kanmi replied, with a bitterly bright smile, "is *entity*, Minori. *Entity*."

Cocohuay raised an age-spotted hand, which trembled visibly. "Yes. I know, it sounds . . . impossible. But I know what Mamaquilla spoke to me in the silences of my soul. And I heard fear in the voice of a goddess. Some things are too horrible to be permitted." She exhaled, shudderingly. "She told me that almost all the gods are silent. She went to where they dwelled, and they are *gone*. Some few spirits are left. The demons that dwell in caves rustle in excitement. They believe they are coming to power, soon. Handfuls of the others who have fled, responded to her voice. Told her that the gods are all bound. Helpless." She twisted her hands. "You must help free them. Please. I beg of you. You have the power. You are not from here. You are not subject to our laws. To *him*." She glanced around rapidly, her face crinkling in distress.

"To whom?" Kanmi pounced on the word, immediately.

She leaned further forward, covering her wrinkled lips with her fingers. "To the Sapa Inca. The emperor. Sayri Cusi has held power for fifteen years. Everyone had hope when he took the throne." She cleared her throat. "His brother, the original heir, had died before his time. Sayri Cusi was young. Not a god-born, in a family full of them. He had studied summoning and sorcery in Rome. He told us all that he wanted to make the Land of the Four Quarters bloom. To bring in natural philosophy and technology and new jobs. But all of that requires money, or at least . . . something to trade." She sighed. "And for seven years, little changed, other than that the emperor closeted himself with sorcerers and summoners and ley-mages. Some Roman, some native."

"And then?" Trennus prompted.

"They began the public works projects. Building the new temples in the mountains. Building the new Lines. To re-awaken the people's pride in their heritage, they said." Cocohuay grimaced, half-closing her gleaming eyes. "Foolishness. I have lived for two hundred years. I have seen the reigns of *eight* Sapa Incas. In the main, they have tried to preserve the old ways. The economy, in the control of the nobles, the way each person is born to a role." She shrugged. "None of his predecessors thought that *pride* was necessary. Only that people should do as they were told, contribute to the whole, and live quiet, peaceful lives. Pride is for the Nahautl and the Quecha, and their warlike, blustering gods." She sighed. "But while it was unthinkable to speak against his predecessors, because they were the hand of Inti, the sun, on earth . . . every one of them god-born . . . the people *have* murmured about Sayri Cusi and his changes. He *has* permitted peasants to leave the lands of the nobles to whom they have always owed loyalty. That is a good thing. But then they come to cities like Cuzco, in search of a bright new future."

"And there are no jobs for them," Kanmi said, his tone cynical.

"Yes," Cocohuay replied, tiredly. "Except for the public works projects. The building of the towers. The new ley-facilities. There's power to areas that have never had it before, it's true . . . but no one has seen the country bloom." The lines around her eyes crinkled as the lids lowered. "My goddess tells me that she senses power being drawn from the Lines, to each of the towers. And the towers send some of the energy *back*. The power is such that . . . it can only be the work of a god, or gods, she says." The god-born woman closed her luminous eyes for a moment, and then opened them again to look at Trennus. "She asks that you open the Lines. Release those prisoned within, as she was imprisoned. That will, she believes, sever power to the towers."

"Wait," Minori objected. "We don't even know what those towers are *for*. What disrupting the power leading to them could do." She glanced nervously at Trennus, Kanmi, and Lassair.

"We *have* been cautioned against unilateral action," Kanmi said, ben Maor's words ringing in his head.

"And," Trennus added, quietly, "the entire area isn't precisely geologically stable. We weren't sure if the power from the *towers* was going to contain what's in the Lines, or if the power from the Lines area was being used to power the towers, but either way, it's all being funneled through highly resonant ley-lines in the earth. If I go in there tripping everything without studying it carefully . . . the results could be catastrophic."

And yet, if there are spirits captived there — ones who have done nothing against humans — then we must do <u>something</u> *for them,* Lassair objected.

"Last I checked, there were no laws on the books that talked about equal rights for spirits," Kanmi muttered, and caught Trennus' irate stare. "Hey! *You* want to talk to the Senate and the Imperator about legislation for denizens of the *Veil*, go right ahead. In the meantime, I'm going to worry about *this* world." He exhaled. "I don't like the idea of sapients being trapped and used like slaves, no. Even the empire is . . . slowly . . . moving towards abolishing *human* slavery. I'm just saying, we have no idea what we're getting into here, so let's not go running till the others get here, all right?"

"*You* actually want to wait for orders, Esh?" Trennus' voice was amused, but held irritation, too. "You picked a gods-be-damned odd time to start playing by the rules."

"You're the one who said that jumping in and releasing spirits could set off *earthquakes*," Kanmi snapped back. "Yes, I want someone else to give me that order *before* I do anything that could kill ten thousand people."

Trennus grimaced. "There is that. It's just . . ." He balled up a fist and smacked it into his opposing palm. "It goes against the grain."

They made arrangements to meet with Cocohuay again once Livorus and the other lictors had arrived; she was *frantic* for them to take action, here and now, but they were steadfast in their reasons for holding off. "There is also," Minori murmured, "the question of what might happen to her in the meantime." She gave the god-born woman a concerned look. "Does the Sapa Inca have many watchers?"

A tight, unhappy nod from the older woman. "Yes. The more unrest there has been, the more *gardia* he has created, from those who were once peasants."

Kanmi grimaced. On the one hand, he *liked* the social turmoil. He liked the notion that people who'd been downtrodden for generations were getting away from the dirt, if that's what they wanted to do. On the other hand . . . it just seemed that there were new ways of holding people down being created. *Always fear. Always checks and constraints, always the people at the top, be they nobles or the wealthy or the god-born . . .* he exhaled. And yet, here he was. Working with a god-born on his team, and assisting, apparently, this god-born woman, too. "Do you have a safe place to stay?" he asked, reluctantly. They were probably going to *need* her. To provide sworn testimony to Livorus, and to interface with her goddess and . . .the gods only knew what else. She couldn't do any of that from inside a prison cell.

"I have been looking after myself for longer than you, your parents, and your grandparents have lived," Cocohuay informed him, with a hint of hauteur. "I will contact you. Do not look for me. You will not find me. My goddess will hide me."

Sure she will, Kanmi thought, cynically. *She's done a great job of protecting herself so far. All your gods have.*

They headed back to their hotel, and Minori caught his elbow at the front doors. "Same man as before?" Kanmi asked, lowering his head down to her ear, as if to whisper secrets. "The one who looks like a local?"

"Yes. I . . . really think he was at the conference in Lutetia. I think he was one of those in the hall when you and Master Matrugena asked your questions." Her voice was a taut whisper. "Why is he *here*, and watching us?"

"Excellent question." Kanmi's mind raced. *Someone was in Lutetia. Someone did kill the professor. Coincidence, maybe, but . . . .* "Best to give him something to see, then. I apologize in advance, doctor."

"Wha—?" She didn't have time to get the whole word out as he caught her face in his hands and kissed her. It had definitely been a while since he'd actually kissed a woman; the soft feel of lips under his was fairly distracting. Kanmi had mostly hoped she didn't flinch or try to slap him; he was very much aware that Nipponese culture frowned on public displays of affection like this. She did stiffen for a moment, and internally, he winced and prepared to shift in case she reflexively tried to knee him in the groin or anything else unpleasant . . . and then, miraculously, she relaxed. Her lips opened under his, and Kanmi reminded himself, firmly, that it was part of the damned *disguise*, kept the kiss light, and asked, silently, *Lassair?*

Shouldn't you be giving that kiss the attention it deserves? Her tone was arch, from where she and Trennus were already inside the hotel. Kanmi was horribly certain she was speaking to both of them at the same time.

Stow it. Is the man still watching? This, as Minori's hands crept up around his neck and she began to kiss him back, hesitantly. She tasted . . . entirely too good. *Baal's teeth, I'm not good at this undercover shit.* Kanmi's rather dazed thought overlapped with Lassair's reply: *Yes.*

He dragged his mental processes back upwards, and pulled his lips away from Minori's, settling his face against her neck, so he could look behind her, up to where the man on the balcony had been, hours before. *Can you detect any intentions? Any changes in him?*

. . . I can sense that he watches. But his sense shifts. Alters. Blurs. Lassair's voice became more concerned. *He may be using blood to hide himself. It's not a spirit-mask. Then I'd either sense nothing at all, if the spirit was very skilled, or . . . just the spirit itself.*

"Well, that's not exactly against the law," Kanmi muttered.

"But it is suspicious," Minori replied, softly. He could feel the hitch in her breath, attributed it to fear, and moved them both indoors, reinforcing the heavy shielding he held over their bodies. Feeling her powers weave into his, two seamless layers of barriers. It had been a strain to hold them up for so long, and he'd need to eat like a horse at lunch and dinner, but he didn't want to take any more risks.

"Once you're in the room with Tren and Asha," Kanmi told her, quietly, moving for the stairs, "I'll go across the street and see if I can't find our friend and have a little conversation with him."

"Alone? That's unwise. Take Trennus with you. Please."

"That'll leave you and Asha alone—"

"We'll guard each other. You won't be gone that long. And you're not the only one who wants answers." This, just outside the door of the room.

Kanmi, nodded, opened it, and stepped inside. Once they'd closed it behind them, he put his hands behind his back and noted, clinically, "Get it over with."

Minori blinked up at him. "Get what over with?"

"Slap me, if you're going to."

"Why would I do that?" Her blank stare seemed genuine, and then she flushed. "Oh. Because of . . . oh. No. You were . . . improving the disguise. As I requested you to do." She moved away, flushing more brightly, and Kanmi looked after her, a little puzzled.

"So . . . we're all right then?" he asked, tentatively.

A quick, embarrassed-looking nod. He stared at her averted head for a moment, shrugged, and replied, "All right then. Thank you for not taking it amiss. I'll grab Tren and go find this asshole now. And don't forget, we have *dinner* with the son of the regional governor tonight." He rolled his eyes, grateful that she didn't seem inclined to put him on the rack with questions or concerns or the desire to talk about the incident, so he took that as a sign of favor straight from the gods themselves, and went to get Trennus, as promised.

Unfortunately, when they came back out again, the man watching them had vanished, beyond even Lassair's ability to detect. Something that made them all very uneasy, indeed.

That evening, the four of them made their way into the noble's district of town. The city's highly stratified culture might have made it more difficult to know how to dress or what to expect, but, fortunately, Micos Cornelius was the son of a Roman patrician, although he'd been raised locally. "My father served here during the tenure of the last Sapa Inca as well," Micos informed them as he ushered them into his *triclinium*, which had frescoes in the Roman style that depicted centaurs carrying away screaming human women.

Now there's an inducement to appetite, Kanmi thought, and blanked his expression before glancing around again. He sighed internally. He'd never quite gotten adept at eating Roman-style, lying down and raised on one elbow. *At least the Romans don't send their women away during the meal, as the ancient Hellenes who started this whole fashion used to,* he thought, but it was Trennus who asked, politely, "Forgive me, but surely there aren't enough couches. Will the ladies be joining us? Why, I don't even see a couch for your wife."

Oh, shit. Good call, Tren. We don't want to be separated from Minori and Lassair. Not after today . . . .

A flicker of expression crossed Micos' face. "My wife Pitahaya is, unfortunately, at a medical facility to the south. Her condition doesn't really allow her to enjoy company much, these days, I'm afraid." He gestured at the three couches currently set up, and added, lightly, "I'm old-fashioned. The couches in my house are wide enough to accommodate three people each, and I see no reason to have the ladies leave us. Nor, I think, would you be thanking me if I had invited you all to dine with me, only to chase the loveliest members of our company away at once!"

Kanmi took the time afforded by Micos' extravagant mannerisms to school his face once more as he escorted Minori to the couch that they would, apparently, be sharing as they ate. Two diners on one couch permitted one to choose between lying behind one another, spooned up, as new lovers generally chose to eat, or a head-to-toe configuration, generally favored by strangers, or those long enough married to appreciate the ability to converse with company without having to look over someone else's *head* the entire time. He'd never gotten the hang of three people reclining on a single couch, and Livorus had never required his guests at the villa to triple up.

Still, given their cover, there was only *one* way in which he could eat with Minori. Thus, moments later, he found himself curled up behind her, his noses inches from her hair, his hips inches from her rounded backside, and doing his level best to ignore both facts. *I am obviously being punished for something,* Kanmi thought, tiredly, and focused his mind as entirely on the conversation flowing around him as he could. "I really must apologize for the lack of truly Roman delicacies," Cornelius told them as servants brought in the first course, which appeared to be *cuy*, or roasted guinea pigs. "I'd offer dormice, but even with modern refrigeration, I find I just don't trust them unless they're brought live from the Italian Peninsula and killed and dressed here."

Kanmi reached over Minori and pulled a tiny leg from a carcass, before rubbing it gently against her lower lip as if to entice her to eating straight from his fingers. *Don't stiffen up, don't flinch,* was his mental mantra, and he was relieved as she accepted the morsel, stripping some of the flesh from the bones with her teeth. "You'll find that my friend Matrugena here is a Pict. That means that he truly will eat anything, except perhaps insects." Through the general laughter, Kanmi tried to probe for a little information. "So you've lived here your entire life?"

"Yes, besides the eight years I spent in Rome at university. Studying sorcery and summoning," Cornelius gestured. "And here I have four guests who bring all my favorite interests under my roof at once." He smiled, but his eyes seemed to be lingering on Lassair at the moment. "Of course, I've diversified my studies over time. I've had to, as the Sapa Inca has turned to me for advice on this matter or that."

"And what has he asked you for advice on?" Trennus asked, slipping an arm around Lassair to break off more *cuy*, and fed her, as well. The spirit's eyes half-closed in appreciation of the food.

"Farming, and ways to improve crop yields, so that we can get our serfs off the traditional *suka kollus* farming methods. They can make use of incredibly marginal ground, but they're exceedingly labor-intensive. Once we have a sustainable agricultural base that doesn't require backbreaking labor by fifty percent of the population, we can put those people to work doing other things. We can free them." Cornelius' voice was earnest.

And what methods have you looked into, to improve the crop yields? Lassair asked, genuine interest in her voice, but the spirit looked uneasy about something. A whisper crawled through Kanmi's mind, in Lassair's silent voice . . . *he is masked. He wears a lock of his wife's hair, her life-essence amplified with magic. I cannot see him, not clearly. I cannot see his spirit.*

Kanmi considered that, rapidly. Vials of blood and lockets (literally, cases intended for carrying locks of hair) were not uncommon among the nobility for their masking qualities. A governor's son would be an excellent target for extremists, and there *was* unrest in Tawantinsuyu. He glanced around, and saw the shadows of bodyguards on the balcony, outside the room's single window. It all made sense, certainly.

Out loud, Cornelius was explaining now, "Largely, to be honest, weather control, my dear." His eyes lingered on Lassair, as many a man's did. "I've been fascinated by the bumper crops being harvested in places like Rome and Judea of late, which local scientists are attributing to truly amazing weather patterns. Periodic storms that have yielded more rainfall in Judea in each of the past five or six years, than any of the past hundred on record. Similar patterns in the Italian Peninsula. It's enough to get people there talking about microclimate change." He smiled, but it didn't reach his eyes.

Five years would also be the amount of time that Lassair's been living with Trennus in Rome. And given the fact that every time Caetia frowns, I hear thunder in the distance . . . eh, could be coincidence. "See what I know?" Kanmi tried to force a chuckle. "I didn't even know it had been a good growing cycle. I only notice if the price of chickpeas goes up at the market." The servants had just brought in another course, this time a soft, white local cheese. Kanmi reached for a bite, but Minori beat him to it, and leaned back to offer it to him, turning to whisper against his ear, "I'm lactose intolerant."

Of course, I'd know *that if we actually were an item.* Kanmi took the morsel of food out of Min's fingers, and redirected his attention to their host. He went on, quickly, "Weather control seems as if it would be a huge energy cost, as opposed to better fertilizer and tilling methods. Plus, if you make it rain more here, it'll result in desertification elsewhere, won't it?" *And with no way to be sure of where it would occur.* Intent focus on the work and the words. Anything that let him not think about the smell of the good doctor's skin and hair.

Micos shrugged. "Then that would be the problem of the people who lived there, would it not?"

The conversation was like that all night. It staggered to strange topics several times. Over wine, Cornelius admitted that his wife had Paredes' disease, a congenital shaking illness that caused the muscles to spasm, and eventually caused paralysis and degeneration of the entire nervous system, including, eventually, the brain. He didn't disclose how long she'd had it, or how far advanced it was, but admitted that he'd exhausted all that modern medical science had to offer, and that the gods and priests weren't much help, either. His voice was tinged with bitterness as he added, "I've been researching alternative treatments for some time."

Alternative treatments usually quack and fly south in winter. They were on the dessert course by now, and Kanmi was doing his best to feed Minori and himself sorbet, while ignoring the fact that his left arm, pinned under him for this exceedingly long dinner, was a mass of painful pins and needles. Not to mention the fact that every time Minori moved, she brought her backside right up against him. He tried to take his mind off it, by pushing Cornelius a little on the subject of the Sapa Inca, and the man modestly admitted to having become a more prominent member of the emperor's inner circle than his own father, the provincial governor. "My father looks to the past, I'm afraid. Sayri Cusi looks to the future. As do I." Again, his eyes lingered on Lassair.

Trennus, locking an arm around his spirit-wife, tried a few questions, himself. "What do you think of this recent spate of earthquakes in the region?" and "are you in favor of terminating the electric grid that exists here in Nahautl in favor of ley-power?" but Micos wouldn't be drawn into many side tracks. He kept bringing the subject back to fertility in the land, fertility in the people, and fertility in the *minds* of the people. A period of rebirth was needed, he thought, for his people to take their true place on the world's stage. And by *his people,* the middle-aged Roman clearly meant the people among whom he'd lived since birth — those of

Tawantinsuyu.

As they left for the evening, none of them noticed that behind them, the various potted plants in front of Cornelius' elegant villa were currently in full bloom, in spite of the persistent chill in the air.

Kanmi shook his head as they got into their car. "Well, that was probably something of a waste of time," he admitted to the rest of them. "He might have Sayri Cusi's ear and some surprisingly radical sentiments for a Roman patrician, but . . ." He grimaced. "He does have a surprising number of bodyguards, though."

"To hear him tell it, Sayri Cusi doesn't blow his nose without asking him if it's a good idea," Trennus replied from where he was driving their motorcar, with surprising dourness. "If he's half as important as he thinks he is, maybe the bodyguards, the wards on his home, and the masking techniques to hide his spirit are justified."

You didn't like him, Lassair said, a saucy sort of smile on her face.

"I'm used to men and women staring at you, Asha." Trennus shrugged, keeping his hands on the wheel and his eyes on the road. "That doesn't bother me. His wasn't the usual kind of staring. He was . . . evaluating."

Back at their hotel, Kanmi took the longest, coldest shower he could remember taking in years, and leaned against the tile the whole time, trying to figure out if he'd be able to tell the good doctor *no* tonight, if she again told him that they needed to make their cover seem more real. And when he stumbled back out into the main room, the fact that she was already asleep on the couch was both a relief and disappointment at the same time. *Mind on the mission,* he told himself, and prepared to stare at the ceiling for a few hours. *Caetia and ben Maor should be here soon enough.*

Maius 20-21, 1960 AC

After twenty-four hours of travel, the last ten hours of which had been in an ornithopter ride so rocky that even Adam had looked a little strained, and Livorus' famous composure had been tested, Sigrun wasn't entirely sure if it was the ground that was moving, or if the fluid in her inner ears was still sloshing around. In either case, she had to concentrate to move properly. She slid on her smoked lenses as she preceded Livorus down the ornithopter's stairs to the ground, warily watching their surroundings. Dark clouds loured over the city of Cuzco, and Sigrun's mood matched them as they spat down speckles of frozen rain.

They'd called the ground team at the hotel from the Tenochtitlan airport, just to make sure nothing had truly changed. Tren had sounded agitated, and promised details when they got in. When they arrived at the hotel, and Livorus was set up in the best suite on the top floor, the four main lictors, along with Minori and Lassair, met there to debrief. Lassair threw her arms around first Sigrun, then Adam, relief washing out of her almost palpably. *I am so glad you are here, sister,* Lassair admitted, after a few explanations had ensued. *I touched the mind of the god-born woman. I found no lies in her. We can trust what she says, but all of her words were founded on what her goddess told her. Her goddess . . . was in much fear, when she touched my mind. She may have been mistaken.*

"If I had been trapped in a prison for two years," Sigrun muttered, "The first thing I would do would be to attempt to *end* my captors. Perhaps the same holds true for this goddess."

She sensed Adam shifting his shoulders, uncomfortably, and watched as Kanmi, as usual, paced the floor as he talked. The short man never stopped moving. And her mouth fell open as she listened to what they all had to say. Livorus' eyes were heavy-lidded as he finally summarized, "So, we have an unknown form of technomancy, either emanating from the towers, to constrain the *entities* inside the Lines, or the entities in the Lines are being used to power the towers. We have spirit-based energy, flooding the ley-grid of Tawantinsuyu, in a geologically unstable area. And we have the Sapa Inca, unlike Emperor Achcauhtli in Nahautl, five years ago, apparently right in the thick of it. A good reason to call on me for diplomatic inveigling, I suppose." Livorus rubbed at his chin, consideringly. "Matrugena, Dr. Sasaki . . . would you say that the region is in imminent danger of geologic activity if they were to have . . . what is that charming phrase so often used by Judean nuclear engineers?"

"A melt-down," Adam supplied, grimly.

"Yes, that." Livorus flicked his fingers. "Would such an event threaten other nations in the region?"

Trennus and Minori traded glances. "Judging from the amount of energy in the grid? I can only compare it to someone flooding the aqueducts in Rome," Trennus said, tersely. "Or ground, oversaturated with rainwater."

"Or my aquifer analogy," Minori put in quietly.

"Precisely. All that energy will need somewhere to *go*, sir. And until a few weeks ago, I would never have thought that you could *add* power to a ley-line. It's never been tried, to my knowledge, before."

Minori looked up now. "As to your other question . . . yes, *dominus.*" Her tone was respectful. "If an energy charge outside of Tenochtitlan could cause the Burgundoi earthquake of 1950, then we could see earthquakes resonating from here up to Tenochtitlan, easily. Into Quecha. Tsunamis in the Pacifica are certainly a possibility."

Livorus looked out the window at the gray skies. "Then that is how I will begin my approach to the Sapa Inca," he said, wearily. "I would *hope* that the ruler of thirty-six million people would have slightly more concern for their well-being, and the well-being of his neighbors, but people can be somewhat short-sighted at times." He looked around. "And the only indication that we have, thus far, as to motivation is that he has attempted to make changes to the social structures of his empire?"

He wished to make his land bloom, Lassair volunteered, unexpectedly.

"Yes," Kanmi muttered. "I spent a good part of last night going through his old speeches in newspaper accounts. He wasn't just talking about jobs and the economy. He wanted a *rebirth.*" Eshmunazar put his hands behind his back and frowned, measuring the room with his strides.

"He wanted national pride. He wanted his people to compete with other nations in natural philosophy, technology, and the arts. He wanted to change the social structure, and move away from *suka kollus* farming."

"Bloom," Sigrun muttered, and looked at Lassair. "Fertility."

The ruby eyes locked glances with her own. *Yes,* Lassair confirmed, and to Sigrun's surprise, a white hind appeared in the room.

"Saraid," Trennus murmured, his voice surprised, but glad. The forest-spirit rarely manifested unasked. "Can you add something to our considerations?"

Yes, I believe so, Saraid said quietly, in all their minds. *I did not dare manifest at the Lines, but I can tell you about the land there. It is a desert now, but . . . once, it was a forest. I could feel the ghosts of the ancient roots in the dust. I could feel the stone axes bite into their long-dead trunks. I could smell the tang of ash in the air, as they were burned to make way for new growth. After the trees . . . maize. Blood in the ground, to make the crops grow. And then . . . nothing. Death and dust and silence.*

"The king is the land," Trennus muttered under his breath. 'The land is the king."

Sigrun understood what he meant, immediately. Both of their people had a tradition of this, though the Gauls emphasized the belief more strongly. For so long as the king was healthy and virile, the land would bloom. If the king, tied to his own sacred earth, failed in vigor, so would the land. Which was why even kings had been offered as sacrifices, in the ancient past. To give their lives to renew the land. "Sayri Cusi isn't married," she reminded Trennus, knowing that what they were saying was probably bypassing the others completely. "I don't think they go in for the Great Marriage to the land here. I know that Quechan nobles used to offer blood sacrifices, sometimes even cutting into their own penises, to try to invigorate the fertility of the land, but it's not quite the same."

He shook his head. "No. But if he thinks the land isn't fertile enough . . . eh. It's a chain of thought that snapped in the wrong place. Nevermind."

Sigrun pinched thumb and forefinger at the bridge of her nose. "So, perhaps sacrifices to make everything bloom once more. Land. People. Nation." She held up her hands. "Maybe the king, too." That, with a glance at Trennus.

"But that brings us to the most troubling part," he returned, his lips pulling down. "They threatened to make a sacrifice of Mamaquilla. That's not really possible. Truthfully, even to *kill* a spirit, you need another spirit." He grimaced. "Unless you're Akhenaten, or one of the godslayers and the *namtar*-demons."

"There were giants that walked the earth in those days," Adam said, quietly.

"Yes. Days best left far behind us."

Sigrun shook her head at Trennus. "I am surprised you didn't think of this," she told him, ruefully. "But perhaps you are too close to the problem. Another god would have no problem killing another god, any more than a spirit would have problems killing another spirit." She sighed, feeling a chill pervade her, to the marrow of her bones. "Which suggests that they have at least one *entity* complicit in some manner in all of this. Whatever *this* is."

The room went very quiet. Kanmi raised a hand. "I think I might like to offer my resignation at this point," he said, dryly. "I hear Australia is *lovely* this time of year. It sounds a peaceful place, where only the wildlife is out to kill you in various horrible ways."

Minori raised a finger. "I'm just not seeing how any of this can lead to, well, fertility," she said, sounding a little helpless. "We're talking about raw energy being dumped into the ground. I could electrify a cow pasture, and it wouldn't do more than make the cows jumpy. Magic needs *intention* in order to function."

Kanmi's head swiveled, and a grin lit up his face, surprising Sigrun. "Well, now *that* is a conversation I would like to have," he admitted.

"Later," Livorus murmured, waving them off. "There is undoubtedly a shaping hand behind all of this. Whose . . . well . . . there's no knowing at the moment."

They were also introduced to Cocohuay that afternoon, and Sigrun felt no more deception from the woman than Lassair did. The woman's luminous eyes met Sigrun's own with no hint of guilt or shame, but her stare was piercing . . . and then, the Tawantinsuyan woman said, in tones of heartfelt sympathy, "Oh, you poor thing. What god put his hand on you, to curse you so? Is this revenge upon *your* god, through you? They can be so . . ." The old woman sighed, and looked as vexed as if she'd found paint spread through a new wool rug, ". . . childish, at times."

Sigrun stared at her blankly, a prickle of unease running down her spine in an electrical sizzle. Adam told her that when she was agitated, she put off enough static electricity to make the hairs on the backs of his arms stand up. It was why, though he'd gotten her a lovely battery-powered watch for Yule two years ago, it had died inside of a month, and he'd had to replace it with an old-fashioned gear-run watch that she needed to wind every night. She wore it on her wrist now, and it even had a cover for the watch face, like a traditional pocket watch; she'd put their wedding picture on the inside. At the moment, Sigrun knew she was radiating enough electricity to operate a small appliance, just by the way Adam pulled his hand away from her, and the light snapping sound that followed the movement. "I do not understand your meaning," Sigrun told Cocohuay, formally. "What curse?"

"It's a shadow over you. It shifts. Hard to see. Not surprised you missed it. Your eyes aren't meant to see things like this. You are a warrior. From a war-like god. My lady is the moon and the sea and the birth of all young things. She takes sailors to their graves, but she gives back life." Cocohuay shook her head. "No life in you, young one. Not while the shadow stays."

Sigrun shuddered. "A . . . conversation for another time, I think," she suggested, firmly, not knowing what in Hel's frozen realm the woman even meant. "We need to understand what your lady wishes done about the Lines."

Cocohuay gave her a dubious glance, but acceded, just putting a hand gently to Sigrun's face. "You change your mind? I will help you, child. If I can."

By the end of the ensuing conversation, Livorus had agreed to allow Trennus and Kanmi to accompany Cocohuay back to the Lines the next day. To see if they could gain access to the tower at the center, and see what kinds of technology were contained therein. "If you find anything at all, to include human remains, contact me *immediately*. I will need to know this in order to deal with the Sapa Inca. In fact, if you *fail* to find anything? Contact me, as well."

"I wish to go with them," Minori protested. "I can be of help with the technical aspects."

Livorus shook his head, his expression grim. "I would send both you and Lassair, my dear. However, the last time Matrugena's lady went to the Lines, the locals are under the impression that she *defaced* them." Livorus' tone became astringent. "I strongly doubt that they will permit her to return. Matrugena alone, bearing my aegis? Will still have problems dealing with the guards, priests, engineers, and officials on site."

It was not my intention to cause difficulties, Lassair said, her full lips turning down.

"I realize that, my dear," Livorus told her, calmly. "But with that in mind, you cannot stay here alone. Not if there is any possibility that they might make an attempt to capture you. You must be guarded, and thus, two of my lictors will stay here, as will Dr. Sasaki. Who *also* requires guarding." He looked up at the ceiling. "The two of you may even guard one another."

Sigrun suppressed a smile. Trennus looked twitchy at the thought of leaving Lassair alone. And Kanmi didn't look much happier, to her surprise. "The notion is not entirely bereft of sense," Sigrun told them.

"Thank you for that rousing endorsement, my dear," Livorus put in, raising his eyebrows at her.

Sigrun returned the glance, and went on. "Minori is a capable sorcerer. Lassair is hardly defenseless."

I feel defenseless in this form, sister.

Sigrun shook her head. Lassair was probably at least as well equipped to defend herself as Minori was. Possibly more so. The spirit had largely manifested healing properties and transformative abilities before, but Sigrun had been watching Lassair carefully for years now. She suspected that Lassair was capable of far more, under pressure. There was *power* lurking behind that merry façade, and it was a power that Sigrun didn't want to try to match.

"Is there anything else?" Livorus asked. "Ah, yes. Eshmunazar. Did you make contact with this technomage who reached out to you? Micos Cornelius?"

Kanmi grimaced. "Mostly seemed like a waste of time, though he seems to be one of Sayri Cusi's top advisors."

"And is a legend in his own mind," Trennus put in, sourly. "I think he mentioned at least three times that he sees the emperor more often than his father the governor does."

Kanmi's lips quirked a bit. "He couldn't stop looking at Lassair. Minori might as well not have been in the same room. That, and he talked our ears off about crop yields and returning fertility to the land." He shrugged. "I'd put him at a three out of ten on the 'people who should be watched for extremist tendencies,' except for the fact that his wife's terminally ill. That can be a terrible lever to use on people."

"Isn't that interesting," Livorus said, looking off into the distance. "Thank you all. That gives me a starting point or three for my initial conversations with the ruler of this land."

The next day, Maius twenty-first, Adam and Sigrun saw Kanmi and Trennus to the ornithopters pad in the gray light of dawn, and watched them take off, heading back to Nazca. Their own meeting with the Sapa Inca wasn't until afternoon, so they ensured that the Nahautl and Hellene lictors who'd be keeping an eye on Lassair and Minori were briefed in on the man who'd been seen conducting surveillance on the group. Arkadios Sanna was a Hellene, and a competent traditional sorcerer, focusing on fire incantations, and Chimali Matlal was a former Eagle Warrior. Sigrun had seen him spar with Adam a few times, and the contests had actually been surprisingly evenly matched; the Nahautl man gave up a few inches to Adam in height, but made up for it in speed and raw ferocity, and like most other Nahautl special forces, his skin was dense with protective charms and tattoos. "Keep them safe," Adam told the two men. "They're both capable of defending themselves, but they're not lictors. They're not Praetorians."

"Matrugena shouldn't have brought his wife along," Sanna muttered. "Made him vulnerable."

Adam gave the Hellene a dark look. "Funny," he commented, dryly. "Just about five years ago, we all owed our lives to her being there for us. Several times over. Keep in mind that she's a spirit, not just a pretty face."

Sigrun, for her part, had just leaned against the doorframe, and met Sanna's eyes as the Hellene man looked around in exasperation. And *smiled* at him, knowing it didn't enter her eyes. *You want to say that my being here weakens Adam? Go ahead and make that assertion.*

His eyes dropped first, and Sigrun said her farewells to the human and the spirit, Lassair surprising her with a kiss to the cheek. *Be careful. The longer I am in this land, the more uneasy I become.*

You are not the only one of whom that might be said. Sigrun raised her eyebrows, nodded to Minori, and got out the door.

The emperor had sent a motorcar for them, and Sigrun looked out the windows as they drove, noting that alpaca were still used to carry goods around the city, and that, for the most part, people still walked this city. Some pulled wagons themselves, or used horses, and there were a few trucks here and there for truly heavy loads. *The Sapa Inca's social reforms seem to be slow to percolate through,* Sigrun thought, dryly. She approved of greater freedoms for everyone, so long as it could be attained in such a way that no one suffered during the reform period. Unfortunately, historically, that was never actually the case.

The palace of the emperors, Sacsayhuamán, was enormous, built on three terraces of carefully shaped megalithic stone. "Three tiers," Sigrun murmured to Adam. "Like the *ushnu* that Trennus mentioned. I wonder if that's common here."

"Would it make a difference?"

"Their kings were always the representative of the sun-god on earth. Their homes were . . . sacred sites. This palace *is* a temple, in a sense." Sigrun groped for the words. "And the royal family are supposed to be priests, or at least . . . intercessors for the sun god. Inti."

They were ushered through the first two tiers, to the innermost layer of the fortress, which was luxurious on a scale that Sigrun equated with the palace of the Imperator in Rome . . . though the décor was different, naturally. The floors were flagstone. Traditional local stone reliefs, pictures of gods, ancestors, battles, treaties, were all carved directly into the megalithic walls, and then painted vibrantly. The waiting room into which they and Livorus were escorted was sumptuously decorated, with mahogany wood worked into local-style furniture. Low tables, set with exquisite local pottery. Rich carpets, imported from Persia and Qin, lay alongside local rugs woven from alpaca wool, all shrouding a cold stone floor, and softening their footsteps. There were sandalwood screens scattered here and there, blocking their views of doors, and Sigrun twitched a little. She disliked having her eye-lines closed off like this.

The entire palace was lit by ley-powered lamps, all the chandeliers apparently made of real gold and silver, and attars and perfumes had been left to warm in bowls supported by tiny tripods over candle flames, scenting the air . . . but again, even these knickknacks were crafted of precious metals. Sigrun looked around uneasily, noticing that Adam was rubbing gently at his nose, as if trying not to sneeze. *What does this room say about the person meeting us?* Sigrun thought, trying to categorize it. *Someone educated in Rome, a part of the melting pot that is modern society. But also, incredibly wealthy. The palace of the Imperator is designed to awe with its grandeur, to convey the power and might and culture of Rome, with its vaulted ceilings and pillars. But for all the beautiful furniture, it's an austere place. Caesarion and most of the emperors since the Latter Decadent Period have tried to hearken back to the Empire's roots in the Republic, and made the virtues of that era public ones once more. This palace is . . . nothing like the one in Rome. It's divided against itself. Judea holds onto tradition and balances modern convenience with it, comfortably. This . . . tries to be everything at once. Traditional and local, modern and cosmopolitan. There's no order here, no central thread that connects it all. It's as if the palace itself has a split personality.*

The wait was a tedious one. "Shouldn't the regional governor be here by now?" Adam asked, after a while.

Livorus nodded, once, over his dispatch case. He was, as usual, making use of the dead time. "When I made contact with his office this morning, Cornelius *pater* could not, apparently, come to the telephone for a mere propraetor." Irony filled his tones. "His *clerk*, however, seemed uneasy, and asserted that the governor had been ill. There was also a suggestion that the governor could not intrude himself on the emperor without being first invited to the palace."

Sigrun raised her eyebrows. This was not generally the way in which governors and the rulers of subject nations interacted. Tawantinsuyu was something of an exception; they had allied themselves with Rome, willingly, and had a few more privileges than other subject nations, as a result . . . but the governor should have been able to gain entrance to the palace on a *whim*.

She paced, glancing out the room's window, pausing at the doors periodically to listen past them, as time ticked by, once more. Close to a half an hour later, Livorus glanced over at her, and murmured, suddenly, "The problem with dealing with kings and emperors, I have found, over the years, is that they all believe themselves to be gods. Admittedly, quite a few of them *are* god-born. But even the ones who are not, almost invariably come to believe that they are above all others. That is why every one of them should have a man positioned at their elbow, all day, every day, whispering to them, *Remember, you must die. Remember!*"

"As legates do, when they're awarded their triumphal marches into Rome, sir?"

"Precisely so, my dear."

The door at the far end of the room swung open, as if someone had awaited these words, as a cue, and the Sapa Inca, Sayri Cusi, entered the room. Sigrun's eyes widened fractionally. The emperor wore an incredibly fine robe of undyed vicuña wool, heavily embroidered with silver thread. He also wore a heavy golden crown, which had pieces that dangled down beside his cheekbones, and which drew attention to the fact that he had been, like many Tawantinsuyan nobles, subjected to head-binding at birth. Unlike the commoners of his kingdom, his skull had been elongated into a cone-like protrusion that she found herself staring at . . . and then hastily pulled her eyes back where they belonged, as a series of guards filtered into the room behind the man with the dark eyes and sallow skin.

"A fascinating concept," he said, suddenly, as if he'd been taking part in a conversation with Livorus all this time. "The skeleton at the feast. How very Roman." He paused, and his eyes flicked from side to side, narrowed and he shouted, flecks of spittle flying from his mouth, *"This is not Rome!"*

Sigrun stiffened, and glanced around. She had access to the sky, thanks to the window, and she had never actually heard *anyone* speak to the propraetor like this. Even Persian diplomats, furious, and their country in the middle of a war with Rome, had spoken in courteous enough tones. They were, after all, professionals. *He's either unbalanced, or pretending to be so*, she thought, and glanced at the guards behind the emperor, who were now fanning out around him. All of them had double-barreled derringers in their hands, openly. *We are in a wondrous good position here. He actually wishes to start negotiations with the propraetor of Rome under the gun, as it were.*

This was unheard of, in diplomatic circles. One did not overtly threaten a diplomat. It put all of your own country's diplomats in peril. And considering that Tawantinsuyu was a subject nation of the Roman Empire . . . this was lunacy.

Five of them. Sigrun stepped, carefully, closer to Livorus, feeling Adam do the same, though he kept a step or two further away. She'd be able to throw herself atop Livorus and take any bullets; Adam needed to keep their shots *separated*. As she moved, Livorus, who hadn't shifted from where he was standing, met the Sapa Inca's eyes steadily. "Ah, but I must respectfully disagree with you, your majesty," he replied, his calmness contrasting with the man's incomprehensible fury. "Tawantinsuyu is a subject kingdom of Rome, by treaty. You have regional autonomy, it is true, and you are a valued ally. But it must also be noted that as propraetor, and with my lictors appointed as diplomats, wherever we happen to stand, is Roman soil." Livorus smiled, faintly. "Come now. I meant no offense by my off-hand comment to my lictor. Let us speak as men do."

The emperor seemed to compose himself, his expression going still by degrees. He tilted his head to the side, as if listening to an inner voice, and his brown eyes went blank. Sigrun had seen that look before. She'd seen it in Sophia's face. Her stomach twisted. *He's mad. But what kind of madness is it? It can't be the voice of prophecy. I have heard that voice too often not to know it.* Sigrun felt the weight of the .45 caliber gun tucked into the small of her back, but her spear was, as a *ceremonial* weapon, already in her hand. She knew she couldn't *use* either of them, but faced with a twitchingly erratic man, both weapons' weights were a comfort.

After a moment, in a calmer voice, the emperor told Livorus, "You may be seated in our presence." He took a seat on a throne-like chair, and, after a moment, Livorus sank to a backless bench, his head tilted slightly, evaluating everything around him. The emperor looked down for a moment, as if studying the floor, and then raised his eyes. "What may we of the land of the four quarters do for Rome, our trusted and valued ally?" All business, suddenly, all trace of erratic behavior gone. Sigrun reminded herself that the emperor had been trained in sorcery and summoning. One could not be a dunce and master those disciplines.

Livorus glanced around the chamber, and said, mildly, "Should we not wait for the presence of the regional governor? While you are, of course, supreme in your realm, I am sure that the governor remains one of your trusted advisors." A quiet, careful bid to get another stabilizing voice in the chamber. Surely, the local governor had a handle on the emperor.

Sayri Cusi flipped two fingers at Livorus, disregarding the words. "The *governor* that has been foisted on us by Rome provides little that is of worth to us. His son, Micos, however, is one of our trusted advisors." His eyes drifted from side to side for a moment. "He understands our true goals. His father is narrow of vision, and we have no use for him." His eyes refocused on Livorus. "We asked you for your purpose here."

A heartbeat's worth of silence, as Livorus shifted gears. "Rome asks that you set our emperor's mind at ease regarding some of your public works projects," he replied, smoothly. "Rome is concerned for the potential hazard they might pose to your people, and to your neighboring nations." This was one of the tactics Livorus had previously decided to use. Couching the situation as a public health hazard, rather than conspiracy, treason, or rebellion.

Sigrun watched the Sapa Inca's eyes drift to the right. "Our public works projects have drawn the attention of Rome?" he murmured, his face lighting up from within. "That our ideas may have the potential to light the whole world, we already knew, but for them to have already captured Rome's attention . . . it is far more than we had thought we would receive for our efforts." His smile widened, and in spite of herself, Sigrun wanted to respond to that smile with one of her own. The corners of her lips twitched, but then her truthsense slapped her, *hard*. He'd looked to the left before he'd half-screamed at Livorus, he'd looked down and right for the *trusted ally* comment, and he'd looked up and right before this oddly breathless speech. Not once had he looked straight ahead for the entirety of a sentence. And his speech pattern . . . it had retained the royal plural, but now there was a *simper* to it that simply hadn't been there before. Almost that of a coquettish young girl. *Does he have some manner of a split personality? Or is he possessed?* It could happen, she knew, even to a skilled summoner. And Sayri Cusi was, unlike many of his line, not a god-born. *Did he make a very bad bargain with a spirit?*

Livorus cleared his throat. Sigrun glanced at him, and then over at Adam, who shook his head infinitesimally. After a moment, Livorus answered, his voice rougher than it normally was, "Be that as it may, we have substantial concerns as to the methods you are employing to saturate the ley-lines in the Nazca valley with additional energy. We are concerned about the origin of this excess energy, safety factors, and what you intend to do with this excess."

The emperor blinked, rapidly, and his tone remained almost coy as he replied, "Surely, what we intend to do with it, so long as it does not transmit outside our borders, is our own business, and not that of Rome? Surely, our regional autonomy gives us license to do as we will, within our domain?" Sweet reason. Honeyed tones. Sigrun felt it hit her mind like a wave wrapped in velvet, and dimly recognized it. *This is what Lassair is capable of doing, but she does it with nothing but her good nature and her presence. This is why every man and half the women on any given street look up when she laughs. This is not a sorcerer's power, nor a summoner's.*

The words sounded almost dragged out of Livorus now, like gravel from a pit. "You have autonomy . . . yes. But I am reliably informed . . . that the energy levels . . . could transmit . . . waves in the earth. Earthquakes in other regions . . . are possible . . . as a result."

Sigrun stole another glance at the two men beside her, and saw sweat beading Livorus' face. Adam looked strained, but then again, he and Sigrun had spent at least a night every week with Trennus and Lassair for the past five years. As the spirit's power had grown, so had her charm, so saying *no* to her whims had become more difficult over time . . . but they'd also had time to learn to resist her. Not that Lassair usually asked much, besides those annoyingly loverly kisses on the lips.

"Oh, no," the Sapa Inca assured them now, sweetly. "Whoever told you so, was in error. Our experiments are perfectly safe."

Sigrun felt Livorus sway, as if hit, beside her, and put a hand on his shoulder. "Untrue," she said, simply. Her voice sounded like the croak of a crow in the room after all that honeyed sweetness. It wasn't diplomatic of her, but then again, she was no diplomat, no matter what words on a piece of paper said. Since she was speaking out of turn *anyway*, and Livorus seemed to be fighting a battle to find his tongue, Sigrun glanced down for permission, got a dazed nod, and continued, "The propraetor would also like to ask you a few questions about the methods by which you've been adding power to the grid. Specifically, have spirits been bargained with, and their power directed into the ley-lines?"

She'd been careful not to use the word *sacrifice*. Livorus had been specific. That wasn't a term to put on the table until they heard back from Kanmi and Trennus. Nevertheless, the Sapa Inca's face twisted into a mask of fury. "Interloper," he hissed at Sigrun. The word confused her, but then he went on, "This is not your place. These are not your skies. You have no right to call *us* to account, not you, and not your pale and sickly northern gods. Hold your tongue, else we shall have it ripped from your skull." No coquetry now — just raw rage, and a sense of power.

Sigrun stiffened. She could feel Adam take a half step forward, and her mind raced. She didn't want to offend — further! — the ruler of a subject nation, but . . . . She cleared her throat and replied, mildly, as if the rage hadn't been a slap in her face, "I am a duly appointed diplomatic envoy in the service of Rome, your Majesty. We have letters—"

He cut her off, hissing, "Your letters are meaningless to us. Be *silent*, and let your betters speak."

"In the event of the propraetor's indisposition," Adam managed, his voice harsh, "we are required to speak for him, and for Rome." She could hear the anger in his voice, tightly controlled, but present, as he took another wary half-step forward. Separating the lines of fire from the bodyguards around the Sapa Inca.

"We care not for your *right* to speak, or your requirement to do so. We will speak only with the propraetor of Rome." The Sapa Inca's eyes were suddenly bright, and he smiled, as Livorus clearly struggled to clear his mind of the fog under which he labored.

Sigrun grimaced. Adam was getting out of her range, her ability to protect him. Thought her most vital job was taking bullets for *Livorus,* she also had to keep the conversation going until Livorus had recovered himself enough to speak . . . and she thought she could see a pattern here. Though patterns were hard to be certain of, with the mad. "If you seek to provoke me, your Majesty," she interposed, calmly, "know that I do not duel those who are not god-born. It represents an unfair advantage on my part." The words were polite, but held a slap in them. They suggested that she rejected his categorization of himself as her better. He might be ruler of a nation, he might be a powerful sorcerer and summoner . . . but he wasn't god-born.

The emperor's eyes, which had been locked onto Adam, snapped back towards her now, as she stood more or less in front of Livorus. He half-rose from his chair, and Livorus, clearly reacting out of instinct, rose as well. "Unfair *advantage*? You and your squabbling, childish northern gods are no match for us. We are eternal. We are the union of opposites. We bring renewal to our lands."

Union of opposites? Gods. The catchphrase was used in mysticism, frequently for the ultimate power of generativity to be found in the combination of male and female essences, light and dark, physical and spiritual. In eastern terms, yin and yang. In western terms, Gaius and Uranus, Cupid and Psyche, and any number of other holy unions. For a single person to claim it, in a single body, suggested that someone sought, like Aphroditus, hermaphroditism, and the crossing of boundaries . . . or something else. *Tren was close. The king is the land, the land is the king. He wants rebirth and generativity in the land, and in himself, but he wants to be both halves, rather than sharing the power with anyone, or anything else. He wants to encompass it all, inside himself. Like Cronus eating his children.*

All that flashed through her mind in an instant, but the Sapa Inca raised a hand and blue-white light exploded from his fingertips, hitting her, and the thunderclap of displaced air resounded in the tiny confines of the room, tearing at her ears. Adam, Livorus, and the other bodyguards all raised their hands, trying to protect ears and eyes, and Sigrun actually staggered backwards, mostly from the force of the displaced air . . . and then shook herself a little, feeling the hairs on the back of her neck rise, but nothing more. Lightning was her old friend and boon companion. Livorus, reflexively, reached out a hand to catch her elbow, and she barely jerked her arm away in time. "No! Don't touch me right now, *dominus.*" Sigrun reached up and touched the metal point of her spear, and heard the loud *pop* as all the electricity still coursing through her body found a path with less resistance, and *arced* to it in a blue-white spark.

Livorus, now on his feet, and clearly back in control of his wits, glared at the Sapa Inca. "I asked you to meet with me, and speak as men do, and in our very first meeting, you have attempted to beguile an envoy of Rome with enchantments woven around your words." There was leashed fury in Livorus' eyes, and his mouth was pinched tight. "And now you resort to unprovoked violence against another envoy of Rome, appointed by the sacred hand of Caesarion himself." He shook his head, and Sigrun could see the Sapa Inca's bodyguards shifting uneasily. "You are a spoiled child, not a leader of men." He stepped forwards, and Sigrun shifted, carefully, trying to match his movements. "It has been a long time since a propraetor or other envoy of the Empire has been forced to do this," he went on, grimly, and untucked the *fasces* he carried in his belt. It really was nothing more than a completely unmagical bundle of sticks. Plain, commonplace branches, peeled and smoothed and stained brown by the passage of time and many hands. A red leather cord wrapped around it, and an axe, iron blade facing out, was in the middle of the bundle. As such, the whole thing was about three feet in length; he could have used it as a cane, had he so wished. And it would have made a very poor weapon, indeed. All it really held, was its symbolism.

Sayri Cusi's eyes darted from side to side, expressions flickering over his face so quickly, Sigrun couldn't read them all. He opened his mouth to speak, but no words emerged. It was as if he couldn't control his own tongue.

"Allow me to be painfully blunt, your Majesty," Livorus said, after a moment's pause, waiting for the man's response. "You clearly *wish* conflict with Rome, and think that because we are already engaged in hostilities with Persia and the Mongol Khanate, that we would shrink from chastising you and your domain, if there is need. Let it be known that we would not hesitate for an instant." Livorus inhaled, and Sigrun edged forwards again, trying to keep her body between him and the Sapa Inca—and the gun-wielding bodyguards. Livorus was clearly angry, and in a very personal way. The propraetor had just had his mind clouded by magic, and he clearly did not appreciate it. "We have reason to believe that your 'public works' project carries on in a similar vein to the experiments conducted in Nahautl five years ago. We are attempting to ascertain if human sacrifice to your gods has been re-instituted, and that you are attempting to use the power of these gods, pushing it, for whatever reason, into the ley-grid. Rome requires that you cease and desist in all such efforts, immediately, and present those involved for inquiry into the matter. If all is aboveboard, you will be permitted to continue, but with public oversight. If your efforts involve human sacrifice? Then all the perpetrators will be brought to justice. Be they ever so high."

The *fasces* still in hand, Livorus brushed Sigrun out of the way, and began to draw a circle around the feet of the Sapa Inca. Sigrun remembered, vividly, history lessons that spoke of a Roman envoy doing just this around the feet of Antiochus IV, when the Persian emperor had invaded Egypt. And had told the man to decide between leaving Egypt and war with Rome, before stepping over the line drawn at his feet. Livorus clearly meant nothing more by his gesture than this, but before Livorus could complete the invisible circle around the emperor's feet, Sayri Cusi clenched a fist and lifted it up, almost as if offering Livorus a decidedly rude gesture.

Sigrun leaped forwards, Adam moving at the same moment, as the flagstones underfoot erupted, as if the earth itself had just punched upwards with a mighty fist. Livorus went flying. Sigrun landed across the propraetor's body, taking fragments of rock and debris that flew everywhere across her back and shoulders, even as she felt Adam shoulder his way in between her and their protectee, and the mad emperor. "I think we have your answer," Adam said, grimly. "Caetia, get the propraetor to the door."

"We have not dismissed you," Sayri Cusi growled. "We are the hand of Inti on earth. You will treat us with the respect due to a god."

"I'm Judean. I don't bow to other people's gods." Adam's tone was clipped. "Sig. Door. Now."

"Guards? Shoot the Judean if the other two move." Sayri Cusi's voice was suddenly richly amused.

Sigrun, just in the process of getting up from having thrown herself over Livorus, froze in place as she heard the sound of various derringers being cocked. She'd have done the same if it had been Tren or Kanmi or anyone else being threatened. She turned her head just enough to verify that the five bodyguards now had a bead on Adam. She took a look at the angles, and swore, internally. She could get to one, maybe two of the guards, in a rush of speed, but the others were all on the far side of Adam, and no matter how fast she moved, their fingers on the triggers would be faster. He'd fall, riddled with bullets, and she'd have left Livorus to do it. She could *heal* their wounds, if Adam and Livorus were injured . . . but she'd need to take out all five bodyguards without them dealing any mortal wounds. And a head of state who was a powerful sorcerer, as well. *All right. Violence isn't supposed to be our first option in most cases, anyway.* Sigrun glanced at Livorus, and asked, quietly, "Sir?"

"We're not going anywhere, for the moment," Livorus said, his tone suddenly preternaturally calm. Almost soothing. "However, I would like to return to my feet. Would that be acceptable to your Majesty?" *He's in damage control mode now. Soothing. Giving the man the respect he believes is due to him. Gods. Livorus probably made a tactical error giving the madman an ultimatum, but what else was he supposed to do after we'd just been attacked?* Sigrun's head whirled.

"You will stay on the ground for the moment. We are minded to take you to our palace at Machu Picchu for a time, Propraetor. You will *enjoy* our hospitality there. But your lictors . . . yes. We will take both of them to our facility at Coropuna. They will see the glory of what we are creating here in our land. If the god-born woman gets out of line, the man dies. If the man attempts to escape, the woman dies. But they will see what we do here . . . and you, propraetor, and Rome, will be satisfied with this." A canny little smile. Offering them what they wanted to hear, and the little eye-flick to the right conveyed volumes, as his manner became, once more, coquettish. Sigrun thought, *Lie. We all die, any way this goes.* Again, she glanced around. The urge to attack now, and sell her life as dearly as possible, was powerful, but if she did so, Adam and Livorus would both likely die before she could save them. *The best we can do is play along, for the moment, and look for a better opportunity to escape.* Sigrun flicked a glance at Livorus as she slowly pulled back from the propraetor. She couldn't even pull lightning into the room. Not and hit six targets, *without* hitting Livorus and Adam, and the gods only knew what lightning would even do to Sayri Cusi. *Gods. I'm seriously considering attacking a head of state. Even if our lives are in danger, do I have the right to start a war?*

Livorus' eyes held bleak awareness. He'd clearly come to the same conclusions. But he mustered a smile, and told them, as calmly as if he were seated at his desk in his study in Rome, and not partially pinned to the floor, with weapons trained on him and his lictors, "Of course, you two must go. Observe. Analyze. Report back to me. And, given the opportunity, you must, of course, do what you both do best."

Tacit permission. Livorus *knew* what they did best. She was, when everything was reduced down to its base elements, a weapon. So was

Adam, though Adam was capable of much more.

Sigrun watched out of the corner of her eye as her spear was scooped up from the floor by one of the bodyguards, and Adam and she were both frisked, and relieved of their guns and knives. Their hands were shackled behind their backs, and she could almost *feel* the anger radiating off of Adam now in waves. She let herself lean against him for a second, as bags were crammed over their heads. Unspoken reassurance. *We're getting out of this, Adam. I don't know how, yet, but we will. They're smart enough to realize I can't hit what I can't see.* But the manacles? So long as she could get her hands in front of her—easy enough to step through, so long as no guards happened to be watching—she should be able to free herself, and then him, assuming they were kept together. Then again, if she were their captors, she wouldn't keep them in the same room. And nothing so far about their captors had yet said *unintelligent*. Mad? Certainly. But the emperor wasn't stupid.

At the hotel on the other side of Cuzco, Lassair and Minori were, once again, cooped up in the same room together. Minori was rather surprised to realize that the room actually felt *more* crowded with Trennus and Kanmi gone, rather than less; Lassair's presence was powerful, and when the two men were there, her *attention* tended to be split between them all, or, at least, more focused on Trennus. As it was, Minori was trying to concentrate on reading the files Kanmi had left for her to examine, but finding it hard to focus with little coils of energy twining all through the room. Lassair, for her part, studied the plants in the patio area outside the room Minori and Kanmi had been sharing. Minori thought she could see the buds on the plants starting to swell and grow under the spirit's concentrated attention.

Did you like it? Lassair asked, suddenly.

Minori blinked, and looked up from the files that she was patently not reading. "Excuse me?" she asked. Plainly, she'd missed something.

When Emberstone kissed you, outside the hotel. Did you like it?

Minori flushed. "We have spirits and, ah, *entities* potentially being bound and being used to pump power into the ley-grid. We might have seismic disturbances that run the length of Caesaria Australis. We might have a massive conspiracy that could threaten the lives of all of us." She looked up, swallowed, and met the spirit's ruby eyes. "And you ask me this?"

It is, as they say, a hobby. The mating rituals of humans interest me.

Minori *choked*. Lassair waved a hand at her, smiling cheerfully. *Mostly because, properly done, by people in proper resonance, they seem to do the impossible within the bounds of this universe: they seem to* create *energy. I realize that this is an illusion, but I do sometimes wonder if the exchange of energies between two humans creates enough of a nexus to open tiny fissures to the Veil. A little more energy in the universe, a little localized loss of entropy. Love does seem to be a potent force. I like it.*

Minori's eyes were wide. Hearing emotional states and *physics* put into the same sentence, and particularly *those* emotions? Added to which was their personal application to herself? She didn't know whether to tell Lassair that the spirit's grasp on the laws of natural philosophy was . . . tenuous, at best . . . or laugh, blush, and splutter. She opted for the latter three, more or less at the same time.

Lassair smiled, and crossed the room, and suddenly, the spirit was directly in front of Minori. Her current physical form was easily Sigrun's height, the better to match her human lover's frame, and she'd clearly taken her proportions from the slender curves of the Venus de Milo. Small, high breasts, and an athletic, healthy body, rounded hips, all outlined by a tight wool tunic. She had altered the cosmetic appearance of the body several times over the course of the past weeks, but had stayed in this body, specifically, the entire time, something that was evidently unusual for the spirit. There had even been an entire conversation last night on Lassair's ability to disguise herself. "Make yourself horse-faced and flat-chested if you need to disguise yourself and run," Sigrun had suggested, arching her eyebrows. "No one will look for that, if they're all looking for the single most striking-looking woman in the area."

I could. Technically, I could take hermaphroditic form, and diminish the breasts to minimum. That would keep the uterus and the baby intact, but I'm unsure what the additional hormones in the blood would do to the development of the child. It would probably be safe for a short duration, however.

Everyone in the room had stared at her. Kanmi had cleared his throat. "You can make yourself into both genders at once?"

Yes. Actually, I can make my form male, as well, but that would leave the child with no place to go. Lassair's tone had been bland.

"Do you do this regularly?" Kanmi asked, his eyebrows rising.

I prefer female form when I take a human shape. It's the most comfortable for me, and the one Flamesower enjoys the most. But hermaphrodite form has some benefits as well. Eliminating waste while standing up is certainly more efficient.

Kanmi's eyebrows had gone up, and he'd looked directly at Trennus, who was flushing. "You know, for once in my life, I think I'm not going to ask any more questions."

"Thank you," Adam had answered, shifting his shoulders uncomfortably "This conversation is rapidly degenerating."

Trennus had looked up at the ceiling. "Lassair? Please fix this."

I am a spirit. Functionally, we are genderless. Organic life in your world generally takes two genders. Simple, on the face of it. What confuses me, however, is that human spirits can resonate with each other perfectly, but the bodies also need to be in resonance. It is a complicated system. But one I enjoy studying, in all its combinations.

Kanmi had laughed out loud. "That was an absolutely perfect politician's answer, Lassair. You said everything and nothing at the same time. You must be taking lessons from Livorus."

I endeavor not to give offense, and make no apologies for it. Lassair had smiled merrily.

"And we already know that you can change species on a whim. Phoenix, tiger, kitten, human. And they all seem to be beautiful, no matter what." Kanmi's grin had widened.

"I thought you said 'no more questions,'" Adam put in.

"Work with me, ben Maor, work with me."

Yes? I enjoy making the forms aesthetically pleasing. Lassair's tone was amused.

"So you could make yourself the most desirable sheep in existence, if you so chose."

. . . yes. I could.

"Gods, Kanmi, you had to say it, didn't you?" Trennus shook his head. "You're as bad as my family."

"No, no. I didn't say you were shagging a sheep. I said that Lassair was broad-minded enough and capable of making it an *option*." Kanmi's tone had been virtuous. "I am *complimenting* her."

You are not. You are amusing yourself at our expense.

"It's all right, Lassair, he's just jealous," Trennus said, long-sufferingly.

"Baaaaa."

The conversation had broken apart into laughter at about that moment.

Now, however, as Lassair touched her cheek, Minori stopped laughing. She also stopped breathing. *I can change my physical form to something that disturbs you less. Something more masculine?*

"Don't . . . don't do that, on my account." Minori swallowed again.

So, answer my question. Did you like it when Emberstone kissed you?

Minori's entire world had become the flame-like ruby eyes. "I don't know what you mean."

Lassair leaned forward and kissed her, full on the lips. Minori stood rigid for a moment, shocked, and then melted under the spirit's touch. *I think you understand,* Lassair told her, pulling back. *Did it feel like that? Safe and not-safe at all, at the same time?*

Minori nodded, numbly. This was all bringing back terrible recollections for her. Most of the experiences hadn't seemed bad at the time, but everything that had resulted from them *had* been, and perspective was everything. Lassair brushed the hair back from Minori's face, and told her, gently, *Emberstone and you both have bad memories. You should make new ones together.*

She started to shake her head in confused denial. "He can't stand me."

The role he is bound to play, that of one who seeks resonance with you? He fights the role because he desires that resonance, but does not think he should. The role is everything he wishes he could have, but knows that it is a role. An illusion. A lie. And Emberstone hates lies, though he employs them freely. Do you understand?

"Not at all." Minori swallowed. Lassair was still standing much too close. Just like Asuka had done, years ago, in another life.

And you? You have been burned by the fire, not once, but twice, and because you desire so much, you bind yourself away from it all. It does not have to be this way. Unbind yourself. Lassair looked apt to continue, but then the spirit's head jerked up. *Someone comes? Oh. Those bound to protect us for a time see two serving men with the maids. But I only see one spirit. How odd.*

Minori's mind cleared, rapidly. "Mouse form," she said, and pointed at the nightstand. That had been a stroke of brilliance on Kanmi's part. Lassair's body flickered, contracted, and then a little golden-furred mouse scurried away under the nightstand. Minori pulled out her derringer, made sure her enchanted bullets were in place, and dropped down behind the sofa, facing the room's door, pulling up a defensive incantation. The air around her would steal energy from any incoming projectiles, and disperse it outwards, as heat. The room, in a firefight, might ramp up by over twenty degrees ambient, but it beat getting *shot.*

Voices, in the hallway. The harsh tones of the Nahuatl lictor, telling someone, *No, no housekeeping today. No, no towels. No sheets. No, there's no problem with the heat. Be off with you.* "Lassair?" Minori whispered.

I am trying to tell him — oh!

That was timed with a muffled exclamation from the hall and a thud. Minori swore internally, and aimed, carefully, for the door, two competing courses of action outlining themselves in her head. *I should put Lassair in my pocket and run out the patio door. I should do that. Staying and fighting is stupid. Wait. Wasn't there supposed to be a lictor covering the back — ?*

The door in front of Minori opened with a crash as two men entered. One of them held a long tube in his hands, and she didn't need any more than that. She had only two shots, but she'd also enchanted the bullets for accuracy. She could make them count.

The first man fell, shot in the chest, and the second put the blowpipe to his lips and fired it. The dart caught and tangled in her shields, dropping to the ground at her feet. Minori shifted her aim and fired, but the second intruder was already moving. She only clipped his arm. Then he was on her, trying to grapple with her, and Minori dropped the gun, caught his incoming hand, stepped into his charge, around, and under, snapping his hand down and pulling back at the same time, like a whip, throwing him to the floor. Untrained people never rolled. They generally plowed, face-first, into the floor, as this man did. *I can't believe that worked,* was her single numb thought, as she reached inwards for power, freezing the air in front of her into a shard of solid matter with a phrase. Two hundred and ten degrees below zero, it was already out-gassing along the edges, and she needed to do something with the excess heat she'd pulled from it, but she held that in a ball just above her right hand, as she brought the frozen air-knife down into the man's chest in a finishing blow, as hard as she could, with her mind.

Blood sprayed up, splattering her cheek, and for in instant, Minori was frozen with horror. She'd never killed before, and she'd just done it twice inside of half a minute. She stumbled backwards, away from the body . . . and found hands grabbing her from behind. She tried to grab the hands, turn her head to avoid the choke, step back to get her hips free . . . and felt cold steel against her throat. Pressure and an edge, and she froze in place, frantically trying to get an incantation formulated in her mind. It would turn the air around her into thousands of tiny, sharp needles of solid matter, just like the knife she'd made a moment ago, and would hurl them, like arrows, at everyone around her . . . but she couldn't release that spell without at least a word or a gesture, and either one would result in her throat being sliced open. "One word," the person with the knife at her throat whispered. Woman's voice. Quechan accent to the Latin. "One wrong move, and you die. We know you're a sorcerer." The knife pressed a little tighter, and Minori could feel movement behind her. Found her hands taken roughly behind her. Cold steel of manacles, the click of metal closing around her wrists.

The door to the patio slid open, and Minori looked up, hoping that it would be the Hellene lictor . . . and saw a familiar face. The Tawantinsuyan man who'd been following them, periodically, whom she'd seen at the conference in Lutetia, now moved into the room, dragging the limp body of Arkadios Sanna behind him, by the ankles. He kicked the lictor's gun across the floor, and closed the door. Minori stiffened. She could see blood leaking out of the Hellene lictor's mouth, eyes, nose, and ears. *What did he do to him?* she thought, in horror.

Lassair, tucked under the nightstand, in rodent form, seethed. Old memories called to her. Whispered that she should be able to burn these interlopers to *ashes*. The old memories spoke of becoming flame once more, lambent and pure, and raging through the room in a fiery blaze. But these recollections could not stand in the face of new priorities. *If I dissolve the body and become flame, can I make the child flame with me? Can I carry it with me? If I re-materialize, what do I do with it? Do I . . . make a new one? I don't know what to do. I need to save Truthsayer. I need to save myself. What do I do?* The others in the room were almost impossible to understand with spirit eyes, though mouse-eyes detected them without difficulties. Her Veil senses, however, showed them . . . *wavering*. Each of them carried a spirit of some sort with them, bound to an amulet, perhaps. That spirit overlapped their body, as she did, when she shielded Trennus from flame or cold, or as Saraid did, when she shielded him against physical harm. Lassair's whiskers twitched. They all smelled *bad* to mouse-nose. Like blood and ozone.

"Call your spirit," the man ordered, getting closer to Minori, his hands up in a casting position. "Just one word. Her Name."

Minori shook her head, slightly . . . and then gave a choked cry as the man hooked his fingers and twisted them in the air. Lassair could *feel* what he was doing. He was *moving* Minori's entrails, as if he'd reached into her guts and seized a handful. *Say my other name!* Lassair said, urgently. *Say it!*

"A-asha," Minori mumbled, and Lassair spun herself into human form, knocking over the nightstand as she did so. The various humans all turned towards her, and Lassair looked at her hands. *There's a way to do this. There's a way to be flame and flesh at once. I know there is.*

She didn't have time to decipher the memories—if they were even *memories*. They didn't feel like who she was. Who she was, *now*, anyway. The woman with the knife pressed to Minori's throat tightened her grip. Lassair could see strength in those hands; the woman had worked, and worked hard, her whole life. Perhaps she even *was* a maid. No way to tell, with the mind locked away behind the spirit's shield . . . and she couldn't *reach* the spirit. It was terrified, and would not speak with her, bargain with her. Anything. Just a low green glow that reeked of fear to spirit senses. "Asha?" the man said now, his tone skeptical. "You will come with us. You will permit yourself to be bound, or your friend here will die."

Lassair smiled, and put all her charm into it, but it was *hard*. She realized that she *hated* this particular human, and in the main, she liked humans. But this one reminded her of the one Trennus had unNamed. This one would use force to gain what he wanted. *It's not really necessary to bind me,* she murmured, gliding forwards. *I'll come along peacefully. We can get to know each other better, you and I, if we each bargain from . . . a position of trust.* She peeked out from under her body's lashes.

She could watch the body react. Hormone surge, flushing through him, starting at the fork of the legs. But the mind, protected by his bound spirit, was able to shake off the suggestion, at least this time. "No," he told her, his voice harsh, and pointed out into the hall at the metal cart. No towels. No blankets. But the inside of the doors in that would normally house all such things . . . were covered in words of powers. Lines and tracings. Lassair shuddered at the very sight of it. *Trennus!* she cried out, sending the words down along the bond that connected his soul to her. *Trennus! Flamesower! We are bound, we are captive, and I do not know where we are being taken! Come to us! Come to us now!*

Chapter XVIII: Xenocrysts

Any student of history understands that wars are very rarely actually fought for religion or ideology. These are most often the excuses used to clothe the poor, naked <u>casus belli</u>, and dress it like a strumpet togged out in a noblewoman's garb. One can, however, almost always detect the rouge and stale perfume beneath the borrowed finery. Wars are most often fought for resources, and, secondarily, to check perceived or actual aggression from neighboring states. The history of war, and, perforce, that of humanity itself, is closely tied to geology, geography, and mineralogy.

On establishing <u>colonia</u> cities in the new world, Rome at first thought that Caesaria Aquilonis was a poor colony site — a hardship land, best suited for the barbaric Gauls and Goth. Several of the first colonial sites suffered from starvation in the early days. A few disappeared entirely, leaving no survivors for the next ships to find, but only a mass of graves, and a few forlorn words chipped in Gothic runes or Latin letters on the walls of a building. From 500 AC until 1190 AC, the Gauls and Goths stretched out slowly across the continent. The reader must imagine an era in which there were no railroads. They moved and advanced along rivers and seacoasts, much as their ancestors had moved through northern Europa. They met the local tribes, and either made peace or made war, resulting in the patchwork of small allied and neutral kingdoms that dots the landscape of Caesaria Aquilonis to this day.

And then, in 1190 AC, Hakon Hallstein, wading across a stream near what is today Burgundoi, noticed a particularly shiny yellow rock, and picked it up. It was soft enough to scrape with a thumbnail, and when he brought it to market with him the next time he came to town, a local smith knew <u>precisely</u> what it was: gold. Hallstein invented a completely spurious location for his find, and went about purchasing the land around the creek he'd been wading across when he found the nugget of gold. The Hallstein Goldrush ensued, and hundreds of Goths, Gauls, Hellenes, Romans, and even a handful of people from Nippon and Qin moved to the western coast of Caesaria Aquilonis and began panning and digging for gold. Turf wars broke out, the legions were mobilized to maintain order, and the tiny hamlet around the port of Burgundoi became, overnight, a boomtown. Miners were <u>rich</u>, and wealth begot wealth. They needed more facilities, a larger port, more hotels, more baths, more everything . . . and they had the money to build it. A great deal of that gold found its way into Rome's coffers, and it funded the newborn navy of the Empire — largely built by Gothic and Gallic shipwrights, admittedly — and allowed Rome to control the seas. (For general reference, the city of Cuzco, far to the south in Caesaria Australis, began to be settled in or around 1190, as well.)

It wasn't for another one hundred and sixty years that a similar lode of mineral riches was uncovered, but in 1350, silver was discovered in enormous quantities in the mountains of Nivalis, east of Burgundoi. The mining infrastructure already existed, and had for generations; the miners themselves simply decamped to the forested, snow-covered mountains, and began to dig. However, the Kolr Lode, as it became known, for the prospector who discovered it, was positioned deep inside the mountains, and was by no means as readily accessible as the gold fields of Burgundoi had been. As such, there were battles between rival miners, and the legions once more had to be mobilized. Yet the technical challenges that needed to be overcome in order to access the ore were towering, and required miners to work together, as never before. Gunpowder charges were imported from Judea to facilitate the digging. New support systems had to be devised to hold the access tunnels. Entire new systems of pumps had to be built to remove scalding hot water from the depths of the mines. Earth and water elementals were summoned, at great personal cost, to dig and remove what water the pumps couldn't reach, and a few golems were used in areas of the mines too hot for humans to bear.

And in the end, the empire was, once more, enriched, but for Rome to receive this wealth, it had to be transported, either by wagon, across the continent, or by sea, across the Pacifica, around the southern tip of India, and through the Gulf of Persia. Piracy was rampant, and the Roman fleet, fought valiantly against thieves and bandits on the waves for centuries. The area around the island of Hawai'i, in particular, is known as the Graveyard of Ships, for the many pirate and Roman vessels that lie beneath its waves.

When the locomotive was invented in 1548, and tracks were laid, connecting the whole of Caesaria Aquilonis, Novo Gaul and Nova Germania and all the other subject kingdoms, undoubtedly a great sigh of relief was breathed. But no sooner had a means of moving the goods from one end of the continent to the other been put in place, then another immense trove of mineral wealth was uncovered, this time in Africa.

The small trading colonia of Cyrenus had been founded in 1501 AC at the southern tip of Africa by traders who thought that they might be able to compete profitably with the established trade routes and their expensive portage across Judea. The colony was a backwater, primarily concerned with resupplying ships, and little more, until 1565, when one of the local tribesmen traded a shiny pebble for a half a solidus. The pebble traded hands a half-dozen times before winding up in Rome, where it was identified as a diamond. The mad dash began as people of a dozen nationalities descended on the region. Pitched battles between the outsiders broke out over who had claim to the land, though in truth, none of the interlopers did. The locals were nonplussed. They attached no particular value to the shiny rocks, but the few who abandoned their herds to dig were paid the same amount as any European for the diamonds that they found.

This discovery of what appears to be an ancient volcanic shaft, in which diamonds were compressed and welled up, over time, in the earth, is the single richest field of diamonds currently known of on Earth. Diamonds found in the volcanic rock are generally xenocrysts, which is to say, foreign minerals that have intruded into an otherwise homogenous mineral mass. One might well term the miners who pursue them by the same name.

— Abdeshmun Shafat, Blood, Gold, and Diamonds: Mankind's Relentless Quest for Resources, pp. 28-9. University of Carthage Press, 1958.

<u>Maius 21, 1960 AC</u>

Trennus and Kanmi had arrived at Nazca around noon, after a long damned flight from Cuzco. "You're shaking less than you used to," Kanmi congratulated Trennus as they disembarked.

"I think I'm getting used to it," Trennus muttered. "Fourth or fifth flight in a matter of weeks." He felt oddly naked and more than a little out of sorts. Flying wasn't the only thing he'd grown accustomed to; he was used to having Lassair in close mental or physical proximity. He understood that distance didn't actually matter much to the soul-bond between them, but it still felt vaguely attenuated. *Psychological. You probably don't need Lassair to hold your hand crossing the street, either.*

You promised Stormborn — and me! — that you'd be careful doing that. We both need you. Rich amusement in the spirit's slightly distant voice, and Trennus had snorted and relaxed at the reminder of his joke in Judea, after he'd bound the *pazuzu.* If he died, the damned statue in which he'd embedded it would shatter, wherever it was on the ocean floor today. He had an obligation to Sigrun to make sure his life was as long as possible. Not to mention, to Lassair.

I'm always careful, he returned. The internal conversations took eyeblinks, as he and Kanmi found their way to the location from which he and Lassair had taken a bus to Nazca, last time. *Just missing you.*

Saraid is with you. A light, blithe assurance.

Yes, and I am uneasy, the quiet sylvan spirit put in, as Trennus trudged up the steps of the bus and found a seat. *You gave me blood, Flamesower, to allow me to protect you better this day. I hope I will not have to do so, though I will make good the bargain.*

Trennus smiled faintly. *I know you will.* Saraid had been with him when he'd rescued Lassair. She'd seemed quietly fascinated by the soul-bond, but had told him, emphatically, *Such is not necessary between you and me. I am not weak.* And she had yet to say a single word about the physical relationship that Lassair had initiated with him.

"Communing?" Kanmi asked, a little sharply, as he took a seat beside Trennus on the bus.

Trennus blinked. Talking with the spirits didn't distract him; he could remain perfectly aware of his surroundings, watch for attacks and ambushes and anything else. But he found it hard to carry on two conversations at once. He wasn't a spirit. Time was finite and linear for him. "Yes. Sorry. Didn't realize it was obvious."

"You go silent, and tend to smile." Kanmi looked out the window at the barren plains around them, dotted with scrubby brush here and there. "Tell me. Is seeing spirits innate, or trained?"

"I think anyone *could* be a summoner, if they're trained."

"But *seeing* them, unmanifested. I can't do it. I've tried. You can tell me to defocus my eyes all day, nothing happens."

Trennus coughed into his hand. "I think it's . . . well, it could be innate. But you have to understand, the first time I saw S . . . the white hind, I was six years old. My father and brothers had taken me hunting with them, and they didn't believe me. They couldn't see her."

I have watched over you for a long time. Saraid's tone was equitable. *You could see me. That interested me. And I had a sense of things to come. A sense of time and power and connections. Of opportunities to be pursued. You are a nexus. Or will be one.*

Trennus blinked. It was the longest speech he'd ever heard from the gentle spirit on the topic, and he filed it for later consideration, before admitting to Kanmi, "For the longest time, I thought I'd just imagined her. I could always see the house-spirits, though again, my brothers didn't believe me." He paused. "The local ley-mage—Senecita Tancorix—took me as her apprentice when I was thirteen. She never told me why, but now I tend to suspect my parents told her about my seeing spirits. And when I was eighteen, a rogue summoner was on the run. Tried to hide from the authorities in the Caledonian Forest."

"The one from Blood Pact, or whatever that group was called?" Kanmi's memory was good.

"That's the one." Trennus grimaced. "Senecita, my father, my brothers . . . everyone took to the woods, the hills, the crags. We *know* them, as no outsider can. Still took two weeks. He was using his spirits to help hide him. Senecita went off ahead at the end, and found him. Challenged him to a formal wizard's duel."

Kanmi snorted. "No one does that anymore. That was charmingly old-fashioned of her. Not to mention, forgive me, somewhat stupid."

Trennus shook his head. How to convey that the chase itself had been *thrilling*? Like the best game ever invented, running through the snow in the forest, hip-deep in places, chilling to the bone, but *knowing* that something out there was dangerous, and in need of being put down. He and his brothers had laughed about it at night, but his father, Senecita, and the grim-faced Praetorians had been quiet at the campfire. All too aware, Trennus knew now, of the risks. Of *course* Senecita had been aware of the boyish bragging going. Of the fact that Vindiorix, ten years Trennus' elder, had lightly told him that he should have stayed home with his books, by the fire, for all the use he'd be. *I'm a ley-mage,* Trennus had objected, angrily. *I don't see you telling Senecita to stay by the fire. Perhaps you're scared of her? A little woman you could pick up with one hand, Vindiorix? Then again, you'd be right to fear her. She could snap you in half.*

Vin had punched him in the shoulder. *Hark, he barks and shows his teeth. It's a fine sheepdog you'll make, little brother. But you're not a hunter of wolves and bear. You don't have the stomach for blood.*

How to convey that Riacus, next-oldest, had chuckled and bragged he'd bring the man down with an arrow through the eye, *and that will teach lowlanders to come running through our forest, eh?*

Of course she didn't want me, or anyone else, to do something stupid out of false pride or slighted ego. Trennus' mouth formed a hard line. "She put her life on the line to protect others, Esh. Even if it was mainly from our own stupidity and arrogance."

"I have a hard time putting *arrogant* in the same sentence as your name, Matru." Kanmi's tone was dry. "For a noble-born, you're remarkably self-effacing."

"Everyone is stupid and arrogant at eighteen. I wasn't immune." Trennus winced. He hadn't bragged, but he'd definitely envisioned success. Being the one to bring in the summoner's head. He just hadn't expected success to come with the kind of price it had. "She had old-fashioned honor in a world that has no time for such, anymore. She was a good teacher."

"What happened?"

"As I said, she'd gone off ahead. I . . . climbed to the top of a crag to get a better view." Boots slipping on ice and snow-covered rocks. Breath coming in white clouds, looking down into the tangle of the forest. Vertical lines of tree trunks, crazed, mazed, horizontal lines of limbs in black, against a white backdrop. And then he'd caught sight of movement, and pulled his bow over his shoulder . . . and held his breath in awe. Spirits spinning in the air around the summoner, dazzling, beautiful, terrible, all at once. Senecita trying to crush the summoner with a fist made of earth.

And then one of the spirits pulled itself into a *tree*, used it as a golem-like body . . .and had picked Senecita up and broken her spine, like breaking a piece of kindling over a man's knee. "It was the first time I'd ever seen someone killed," Trennus admitted. Even at that distance, it had been shocking. The numb, dazed look on his mentor's old, lined face as the tree had dropped her. "The white hind appeared right next to me. She told me she hated this man, these spirits, in *her* woods. And said she'd help me if I shot him. She'd make sure the arrow got through the spirits."

Saraid had been as good as her word, shifting to stag form, and racing forward. Tossing this creature or that out of the way with massive antlers, even as Trennus had lined up the shot with his bow. Allowed for wind. Quietly prayed not to clip a tree branch along the way. He'd fired, and the summoner, distracted by the spirit of the Caledonian Forest in front of him, hadn't felt it coming till the arrow found his heart. Trennus had slipped and slid his way down the rocks. Run through the snow to Senecita's side . . . but it was too late. He hadn't dared touch the body. It seemed so . . . small. Not really *her*, with all her force of personality. He'd crouched beside her for a long moment, remembering the first time he'd successfully tapped a ley-line, with her help. The way she'd occasionally thrown a bucket at his head when he'd been particularly dense with his lessons. And then he'd stepped over and looked down at the summoner. Saraid had whispered, *Take his book of Names. His grimoire. It holds things that I do not trust with anyone but you.*

"What if someone asks me what happened to it?" His voice had been dull, and he hadn't been able to register the importance of her words.

Say his spirits made off with it, as they fled. I will take it for you, for the moment, that you may honestly say that you do not have it.

He'd looked up then. "Why do you trust *me* with this? Why not one of the *gardia*? One of the Praetorians chasing the man?" He'd barely been able to choke out the words, and the clearing in the woods, snow muffling his voice, had been appalling quiet.

Because I know you. I know your heart. I have watched you for a long time. My Name is Saraid. Call on me, when you need me.

He'd called on the patient spirit often during his four interminable years in Londonium. His pronounced Pictish accent in Gallic had gotten him his fair share of hazing. He'd never mentioned to his classmates that he was a king's son. It didn't really matter. Picts didn't go in for primogeniture. Kingship had to be earned. It could fall to any child in the line, or even to a brother or an uncle of the sitting king — or, these days, it could go to a sister or an aunt. There were literally more than a dozen people in line ahead of Trennus, and he genuinely didn't care.

So, he'd had Saraid's mark tattooed across his back, sealing himself to her, as she was bound to him. He'd studied the forbidden rituals in the book she'd kept safe for him, and committed them to memory. But she hadn't prompted him to use them in Gaul, on the summoner who'd been forcing Lassair. Trennus had made that choice of his own free will. *Senecita would probably have considered it reprehensible. Then again, considering what the man was doing? Maybe Senecita would have approved. It's a little hard to ask her, now, though.*

Kanmi's voice roused him from the memories. "I take it the arrow got through?"

"Yes. It did." Trennus kept all emotion out of his voice. Killing was a . . . private thing. He didn't like doing it, but when it was necessary, he'd gotten appallingly good at it.

"Good." Kanmi's tone matched his. Empty. "We're coming up on the Lines. Hopefully we'll meet interesting people while we're here today."

Trying to shake off their persistent escorts, in light of Lassair's having *desecrated* the Lines last time they'd been there, was annoyingly difficult. Finally, however, they managed to walk off on their own, and that was when Cocohuay appeared, as if summoned, herself. "Finally," the god-born woman muttered, dusting off her clothes. "I have been hiding in the underbrush like a chinchilla. I may have *ticks*." She scratched at her hair—freshly dyed and darkened, and grimaced. "I have tried to disguise myself. Do I look like a tourist?" She gestured down at her clothing. No more alpaca wool and elaborate beadwork. Instead, she was evidently trying to pass for Nahuatl, with a white, thin shirt and a colorful skirt. And smoked lenses, to hide her piercing eyes.

"You look *cold*," Kanmi told her, bluntly. "Gods know, I am. But with luck, people won't look twice at you, and we can say we blundered into you when you got lost from your tour group."

"I will try not to speak. Some of the guards here have seen me before. Many times." Cocohuay sounded apprehensive. "I do not know if I am to be detained on sight, or not, but it is best not to take the chance, yes?"

Smart woman, Trennus thought. She reminded him of Senecita, and the thought brought with it a pang. No-nonsense, straightforward, a little gruff. *Sigrun might seem like both of them in forty years or so . . . assuming a valkyrie ever really ages.*

They trudged across the hard-packed ground that felt as forgiving as any poured-stone road underfoot, feeling the dryness in the air suck at their mouths. "Tower first," Kanmi said, tightly. "A few of the Lines along the way."

Most of the actual animal figures, such as the Condor, to their left, were interlaced with long, straight lines that connected them, one to another, tracing the conduits of the ley-lines in the earth. It was a maze, and they had no choice but to walk *on* some of the Lines to cross them.

Trennus could feel a flush of power every time he did. "Verify," Cocohuay told him, sharply. "Is there a being trapped in the Condor?"

Trennus nodded. He could *see* the interlocking web of power that streamed up, like a vortex, from the Lines. "Yes, but I can't sense power or intent." They looped north, letting Trennus re-verify that the Spider figure was occupied, and, hesitantly, they walked along the rectangular outline between the Spider and the Flower. This one made Trennus suck in his breath. "This one, I can *feel* what's inside," he muttered, a little dazed. "There's a sense of water, but . . . gentle. This is a beneficent spirit, I think. Trapped like one of the damned *alu* was crammed into a bottle."

"Then *release* it," Cocohuay told him, instantly. "You know this to be unjust."

I tend to agree, Saraid said, quietly.

From Lassair, at the moment, nothing. His usual chorus was missing a vital voice. This agitated him, but Kanmi caught his elbow and kept him moving. "Research," Kanmi told him, curtly. "Then we need to get back to Livorus and the others with more information."

Back to the south now, past the Lizard figure—occupied. Past the Tree. Emphatically occupied. Cocohuay's luminous eyes never seemed to leave Trennus' face, and in spite of the light chill in the air, the Pict was sweating. Finally, they made it down to the tower, which was positioned near the road, and between the Tree and a figure meant to look like Hands. The tower itself was comparatively modest, about sixty feet tall, and narrow. It had evidently originally been an observation point, built here sixty or seventy years ago, to allow people to get a good view of the Lines in all direction. Now, however? There were guards by the entrance, and a few up on the observation deck, armed with muskets. Trennus could feel energy resonating from the structure, and had to close his eyes for an instant. It was positioned directly over one of the intersecting ley-lines. "They've drilled down and laid copper directly to the ley-line's position."

Kanmi dropped to his haunches and put his hands on the ground, and *something* moved past Trennus as he did; a rush of power, and a sense of weight. One of Kanmi's targeted gravitic waves, being sent into the ground ahead of them. "Huh. They drilled right through the foundation, feels like," Kanmi said, thoughtfully. "Normally that would weaken the structure, but I expect they thought it was worth the risk. Goes . . . yes. A solid forty feet down, right into the bedrock." He stood back up, brushing his hands to remove the khaki dust from them. "I think it's time to throw our Praetorian weight around and get a tour, don't you?"

"They might let me in," Cocohuay murmured, "but my disguise is not good for up close. More for at a distance."

Trennus grimaced. "If you distract the guards," he told Kanmi, "make a big Praetorian *fasces* of yourself—"

Kanmi's grin split his face. "That's become such a *useful* word for us . . . ."

" —I can probably *make* us a door around the back."

"The guards up on the observation platform are going to notice us, and that's probably not optimal for stealth." Kanmi grimaced.

At that moment, something in Trennus' chest tugged, *hard.* *Trennus! Lassair's voice cried out. Trennus! Flamesower! We are bound, we are captive, and I do not know where we are being taken! Come to us! Come to us now!*

Trennus dropped to his knees, wind knocked out of him. The stones of the desert pavement dug into the bare skin left uncovered between boots and kilt. It didn't matter. He wasn't *there.* He was five hundred miles away, in Cuzco, ducking down, pulling himself into a ball inside a . . . cart? A push-trolley such as those used by housekeeping? One with symbols and signs etched into the metal on the inside. Binding symbols. *No, Lassair, don't —*

They have a knife to Truthsayer's throat. They are taking us away. I do not know where —

There were cracks in the symbols, between the door and the metal that held the hinge. Marred spots in the binding. *You can free yourself. Leave.*

I cannot. If I do, Truthsayer will die. If I de-manifest, I might lose the child. A child I did not think we could have, Trennus. No. I will not take that chance, not while there is still a choice. Best they think me utterly helpless, for the moment. And this way, I can still reach you, for a time. Lassair's voice held a frozen sort of calm, over the top of raging fires of anger that were threatening to break free. *Feel where we go, dear one. Feel me. I am here. You are here. We are one.*

Trennus opened his eyes, staring to the south, dazed. "Who?" he said, out loud. "Show me a face. Give me a Name." Rage started to build. This was a different sort of feeling than it had been a few years ago, when he'd first found Lassair. There was *panic* in it this time, not just anger and outrage. This was his life. This was his *family,* incipient though it was. *I'll kill them. I'll unName them.*

Kanmi had a hand on his shoulder. "What's going on?"

"Someone's taken Asha and Minori." Trennus' voice was dazed.

"What?" Kanmi's voice was a rasp.

"They're prisoners." Flicker of vision through Lassair's eyes. Two lictors, on the ground, one bleeding from eyes, ears, nose, and mouth. *Just like the professor in Lutetia,* Trennus thought, numbly. "Chimali Matlal is down, not sure if he's alive or not. Arkadios Sanna . . . probably dead. Massive hemorrhage, looks like, from the brain."

"Fucking Baal, torn asunder and scattered to the waves. Where? When? *Who?*" Kanmi was exerting surprising pressure on Trennus' shoulder, as if trying to pull the answer out of him by hand-strength alone.

Two female faces, both Tawantinsuyan, one with a knife to Minori's throat. A male face, familiar. "Morrigan's mercy, it's the man Minori recognized from the conference. Two women with him, one with a knife to Min's throat . . . two men I don't recognize, dead on the floor . . . Lassair says *Minori* took them out." Trennus' surprise was distant, and he felt Kanmi's hand tighten further on his shoulder.

"Well, now, isn't that something?" Kanmi said, quietly. "They're going to be all right, Matrugena."

Trennus shook his head, blindly. "They're in transit. I can't tell where they're going. But they're still . . . in Cuzco, I think." The vision dipped and swayed. "They have L . . . Asha confined. Think they're getting into a vehicle now." He raised his head and stared at Cocohuay, not really seeing her. "Can your lady do anything?"

Cocohuay shook her head, looking lost. "I do not know. My lady loses power, the further she is from the sea, but gains in power when the moon is full . . . and when it is visible in the sky." She gestured up at the noonday sun.

"In other words, in Cuzco, in broad daylight, don't ask for much," Kanmi interpreted, grimly. "Matru. *Tren.*" The Carthaginian dropped to a crouch beside the Pict in the dirt. "Ask Asha this. How did they sneak up on them?"

Masks. Masks of spirit and blood. Trennus was hardly aware that he was relaying the words even as Lassair spoke them, his voice taking on her inflections. He could feel cold steel all around him, trapping him, confining him, and all he knew was that he needed to get to her, and *now*.

"All right." Kanmi's tone became harsher. "We need to get to a phone line. And, chances are, the closest one is in that tower. We now have a bona fide reason to get in there. We need to contact Livorus and the rest of the team. They're closer to the problem than we are. They can get to Minori and Asha faster than we can. So first, tell Asha to yell at Caetia."

I cannot reach Stormborn, Lassair reported, her tone frantic, and Trennus found himself mouthing the words with her. *She is outside of my range, and I am not soul-bound or blood-bonded to her.*

"Fine. Screw it. Phone it is. Cocohuay? Mistress, if you would stay out here, and try to look as much like a tourist as you can? We'd be obliged. Come on, Trennus. On your feet. You're fully linked with her right now, aren't you?"

Trennus nodded, his eyes still fixed on the darkness all around him, the tight confines of the cart. "I need you to drop it down to regular levels. I know she's scared right now. Scared for herself, scared for Minori, scared for everything. I know you want to be there for her. But right now, I need you *here*, not five hundred miles away."

The bracing good sense in Kanmi's voice got Trennus' attention. He sent Lassair a mental caress, and pulled his attention back into his own body. And as he did, the distance that had been keeping the rage at bay shattered, and he rose to his full height. "I'm going to kill them," he said, quietly. It wasn't a snarl, or a growl or anything like that. It was a plain, calm, empty declaration.

"Yes. You will. And whatever you leave of them, I'm going to turn into *confetti* fit for a coronation parade." Kanmi's dark eyes glittered. "But now? We get in touch with the team."

That was more easily said than done. Kanmi's polite smile and badge didn't get them past the door into the tower. He stole a look to his left, at the vacant, empty look in Trennus' eyes, and shook his head at the guards outside the door. "Look. We're Praetorian Guard, and we need to check in with our superiors. Just let us use the phone line, and we'll be out of your hair."

"This area is strictly off-limits—"

Kanmi sighed. "I did try to warn you," he said, folding his arms across his chest. Trennus was a very damned powerful ley-mage. On a *bad* day, he could squeeze energy out of the faintest resonances from miles away. He was currently very angry, and standing atop the richest field of ley-energy any of them had ever seen.

The stone of the walls of the tower itself *melted* around the door, glowing red hot and extruding like rapidly caramelizing sugar, reaching out in whorls and loops of red-hot lava for the guards. They caught the movement out of the corners of their eyes, turned to look, yelped, and ducked out of the way as the stone sloughed itself like a snake's skin. Then the wave of rock crashed to the earth, splattering to the ground in a spray of melted slag. It splattered the guards, whose clothing caught fire, and who screamed and threw themselves to the ground, fruitlessly trying to put out the liquid heat that seared their flesh. Kanmi flicked a hand at the spray, catching and freezing it, repelling it like a handful of gravel thrown by the wind. Then Trennus caught Kanmi's arm, and hauled him a step or two back, as the door, which now no longer had walls to support it, teetered, wobbled . . . and then fell inward.

Kanmi looked up at his friend as they walked over the warmed steel of the door. "Would have been more impressive if we hadn't scuttled out of the way." He didn't actually feel like joking. Trennus in a murderous rage was like watching a big, friendly dog remember that it had wolf in its ancestry. His own rage was a black and bitter thing, comforting in its familiarity. It was what kept him company in the long watches of the night.

Just inside the door, various guards frantically reached for their guns. "Stand down," Kanmi told them, calmly. "All we need is to use the phone. Maybe the lavatory while we're at it."

Half a dozen muskets rose and aimed, and Kanmi exhaled and snapped out the command word to a pre-prepared spell, freezing the air not in front of himself and Trennus, but in a semicircle around the edges of the room, blocking the guards with frozen nitrogen an inch thick. He pulled the heat in, and used it to power the second spell, which he began to incant on the heels of the first. Concentrated the heat, condensed it to a blade, and sent it whipping around the outside of the icy enclosure. He was breaking one of the cardinal rules of both weapons use and sorcery: never aim at what you can't see. But he was letting the enemy see the heat blade as it came, though it was so hot it was damned near invisible. He fueled it with his rage, and did not actually care at the moment, if it worked as intended, and sawed off the muzzles of the muskets, or if it sliced through flesh instead. From some of the muffled cries, he thought a few of the slower learners might have lost some fingers. Then he nodded to Trennus. "Your turn."

Tren's head came up, and he slapped at the icewall with force from under the ground, shattering it, and slabs of dry ice toppled backwards to lean against the far walls, effectively entombing the guards. *Sucks to be them today,* Kanmi thought, distantly, and walked forwards to the front desk. He and Trennus had practiced this as a breaching technique that would, optimally, leave very few dead. And the glorious thing about this set-up was, the guards could only risk moving the ice if they were willing to lose a few layers of skin . . . or had thick leather gloves.

Kanmi lifted the phone, and dialed the number of their hotel from memory. The front desk *should* be able to put him in touch with Livorus. At worst, he could tell them to have the local *gardia* and the tiny contingent of local Praetorians—all members of the secondary, non-lictor division concerned with counterfeit coinage, as best Kanmi remembered—call him back.

Every day at this time, Kanmi knew, there was a woman at the front desk. He'd noticed it in particular because the Tawantinsuyan woman had chattered freely with both Minori and Lassair, asking them about their homelands, and Lassair hadn't known what to say. It had also been intriguing, because the woman hadn't seemed to notice that Lassair's lips never moved during their conversations. Too blinded by the spirit's beauty, perhaps.

But it was a man's voice on the other end of the line that answered. Kanmi's eyes narrowed. It might be *nothing*, or it could be something. *"Ave,"* he said. "This is Grigorius Zabat, *Athens Daily News.* Would it be possible for me to speak with Propraetor Livorus? My paper would like to interview him for a story on the Chaldean offensive."

Grigorius Zabat was one of their prepared codes on the team. All press queries were supposed to be directed first to the lictors, and from the lictors to Livorus. Claiming to be Grigorius was a way of asking anyone currently on duty, *This is us. Is it safe to talk?*

"I'm sorry, Master . . . Zabat? . . . Give me a moment and I'll patch you through to one of the lictors."

Kanmi relaxed, slightly. Ben Maor, Caetia, and Livorus had to be back from the palace by now. Had to have found the four men on the floor of the otherwise empty room. He could hear footsteps running down the stairwell behind him, and, covering the mouthpiece with one hand, asked, "You want to get that?"

"Not a problem." Trennus' reply was flat, and he pulled stone from the walls again, this time shaping the molten mass across the steel inner door. Kanmi muttered a quick incantation, stealing the heat, and poured it into one of the batteries in one of his pockets. There was pounding on the other side of the door now, but the guards on that side weren't going anywhere, any time soon. A muffled musket shot, and Kanmi rolled his eyes and kept the mouthpiece covered until all the ammunition on the other side was spent.

"Ave," a new voice said, and Kanmi's spine prickled. "This is Agent ben Maor speaking."

Cold settled over Kanmi. Even a *gardia* member would have been told to put Grigorius through to a real lictor. And this person was assuming Adam's name—something ben Maor would never permit. So he put a smile on his face to ensure that there'd be one in his voice, and replied, "Oh, Agent ben Maor! The head of the propraetor's security detail.

I've wanted to interview *you* since that incident in Judea. This is Grigorius Zabat. Could you tell me and my paper just a *little* about that dreadful night at the convention center?"

"I'm sorry, no." Kanmi was listening, intently, for accent and intonation. Quechan inflections to the Latin, but only faint. "I'd be happy to pass along your request for an interview to the propraetor."

"When might he be available?"

"I really couldn't say. He might not be for some time."

"Can you tell me how his meeting with the Emperor of Tawantinsuyu went this afternoon?"

"How did you know about that?"

"It was on the propraetor's public schedule, Agent." Kanmi said it innocently. It *hadn't* been, of course, but the more he got this man to talk, the more he *might* let slip.

A pause. "It went very well. The propraetor has agreed to further talks over the next several days. He and the emperor are closeted in the palace here in Cuzco." Another pause. "You're not calling on an international line." Sudden hostility. "You're not a reporter—"

Kanmi hung up. The black rage was now a seething mass in the middle of his skull, pushing out all thought. "Tren?"

"Our people aren't at the hotel?"

"I'd put money on it that our people aren't even in Cuzco. I'd bet my sons' *college fund* that they're prisoners."

"I don't bet against you when our luck is this bad."

Cocohuay now moved into the building as Kanmi and Trennus began hauling people out from under the dry ice, and binding them with whatever was available. Telephone cords. Power cables. In a couple of cases, Trennus bent pieces of metal with ley-energy and looped them around the guards' hands, embedding the ends in the walls. Then they peeled the stone back from the door Trennus had entombed, and took down the next set of guards, including a commander. Cocohuay was patient throughout this, and even healed most of the guards' wounds. "You must see what is in the center of this place," she told them, urgently. "You must feel it."

"I must find out what has been done with our people," Kanmi told her, sharply. "That just became our priority."

"I think," the god-born woman told him, regarding him with her huge, moon-like eyes, "that everything here connects in some fashion."

Kanmi rose from securing one last prisoner, and pulled her into a side room. "You're damned right. It does." His voice was a harsh whisper. "The Sapa Inca started this whole 'public works' project. There are *entities* trapped here. These lines connect to the towers. Similar things up north in Nahautl. Our people go missing when we investigate, and *right* when we send them to talk to the Sapa Inca. At the moment? I'm going to find out which of the towers is the main one, and find someone here who can call in and confirm where the *fuck* our people are, and I'm going to make him do it." The black morass was threatening to gape wider in his mind, and he clamped down on it, hard. "Once we have that confirmation? *Then* we'll figure out what to do about it."

———————————

Minori Sasaki regained consciousness slowly. She remembered, dimly, a cloth that smelled of camphor and other chemicals being pressed to her face after the man and the women had forced her into a truck at the back of the hotel, near the garbage collection area. The world had wavered for an instant, and gone black.

Now, she wasn't sure where she was. It was dark, and she was no longer moving. Tightness across her cheeks, and something stuffed in her mouth. A gag, to prevent her from incanting, though all she really needed was a word or a gesture for focus.

She was lying on her back, on a hard, cold, flat surface, and her arms were stretched above her. Her hands were on fire with a prickling sensation—precursor to total numbness, probably, and there was resistance, tightness, around the wrists. Manacles, apparently. Her feet, when she moved them slightly, encountered similar resistance, and she could hear a clink and clatter. *Chains. Metal.*

She could feel something across her face—rough fabric. *That explains the darkness.* They'd put a hood over her face, to prevent her seeing targets for her sorcery. While it was true that not being able to see made casting *much* more difficult, it didn't make it impossible. She couldn't see the insides of a lock, but she could *pick* one with her abilities just fine.

She moved slightly, trying to get some sort of bearings. Her head was blocked in place by something. Padded bricks, for all she knew. She couldn't turn her head at all. The mild sensory deprivation, being left here alone, was probably intended to heighten her terror. *Lassair?* She cast the thought out, hoping she might hear the spirit's voice.

I can barely hear you. Lassair's voice was apprehensive. *They have me bound in a circle. I . . . think that I can perceive Stormborn and Steelsoul here, but they are . . . distant.*

Minori swallowed. That didn't bode well at all. *So much for being rescued.*

Flamesower and Emberstone will come for us.

Yes, Minori thought, trying to keep the thought quiet. *But will it be in time?* She moved her fingers, trying to work blood back into them.

Click of a door opening. Minori stopped moving, went limp, to simulate unconsciousness. *Tap, tap, tap* of hard-soled shoes approaching on a stone-tiled floor. Fluid rush of air as someone's body came close enough to eddy and ripple it across her body. And then the hood was jerked off her head, and Minori had to squint her eyes against the brilliant lights bearing down at her from above. Inescapable, even through her lids, red and blinding. "Ah. Good. You're awake, Dr. Sasaki." A calm voice, speaking Latin. "I'm Dr. Huallpa. Like most people in this region, I only have the one name, I'm afraid. My doctorate is in medicine. I studied that, and sorcery, right here in Tawantinsuyu. University of Cuzco." A cool hand touched her cheek, and Minori recoiled, or tried to do so. "I have been told that I must work on my bedside manner. To explain to the patient precisely what the treatment will entail, before it begins."

She couldn't *see* him. There was a shadow to her right, but the lights overhead, the ley-powered, were blinding. The cool, calm, rational voice went on. "You see, you have information, Dr. Sasaki. You are going to provide it to us. To that end, I will be employing both my sorcery and my medical knowledge. You'll recall the way I twisted your bowels when we first met?" He might have been asking her to recall a particularly fine tea party. "That's a simple matter for me. Every internal organ is held in place by ligaments. Fibers. Tendons. I can move them inside the body cavity. I can rearrange them. I can stop your heart, and start it again, as many times as I feel necessary in order to gain the truth. The human body is my canvas, and you . . . you are about to be made my *art*."

Minori stopped breathing. She recognized what he was doing. Facelessness, to prompt terror. The bright lights, inescapable, to create a feeling of pain and helplessness and loss of control. All of this was calculated. Inexorable. She blinked away tears from the bright lights, and arched her eyebrows, trying to look imploring. It wasn't hard. She was genuinely terrified.

"Ah, so you want me to remove the gag? And you *won't* immediately attempt to cast something?"

She shook her head, as best she could. "But no," her captor told her, calmly. "You see, I don't entirely trust you. I'll want you *quite* unable to focus on casting spells before I release your gag. So, first thing's first, Dr. Sasaki. I found your research on ley-grid activity and seismic activity quite compelling. I note that the Praetorians also seemed to take an interest in this. Let us begin with what you know about the Source Initiative and its membership in Nahautl."

Something *twisted* in Minori's stomach. Something *moved*, and while she couldn't look down to see her innards writhing, she could *feel* it, and it took everything she had not to scream. She bit down on the gag and a strangled sound emerged from her throat, anyway. She couldn't move. She couldn't escape.

Give the pain to me, Lassair urged, but the spirit's voice was distant. A shadow, ephemeral at best. *Minori, please, give the pain to me. I'll make it better. I'll take it all away.*

No . . . no . . . if you do that, they'll know . . . you aren't fully bound . . . or he'll do worse . . . . And there was worse that could be done, Minori knew. Tears rolled down her cheeks, as the questions continued, but she had no way to answer them. The point wasn't even *to* answer. The point was to show how completely Huallpa controlled her existence. He did, in fact, stop her heart for half a minute, just to let her experience the crushing terror of her mind slowing. Fading. Twisting away . . . and then the jolt of pain as her heart spasmed back to life again. After that, every so often, he'd loosen the gag for a moment.

And then he finally removed her gag, moved in close, and whispered, "You can make it all stop, Minori." Her first name. Intimacy. Not the distancing *Dr. Sasaki*. "What's the spirit's Name?"

Minori had no idea how much time had passed, but could feel

Lassair, grieving for her, reaching out, taking the pain away, somehow. Taking it into herself. Whispering heart-felt reassurances that Emberstone and Flamesower would come for them. Minori knew that Trennus would move the world to get to Lassair's side. If she were rescued as a side-benefit of that, so much the better.

But what buoyed her, what she reached deep down into her core for, was something that her captor couldn't touch. Couldn't understand. She was the daughter of a samurai. She was steel, but she was air and water, too. She would not break. She would flow away from the blow directed at her, and not be cut, but would cut, in turn. "Her Name," Minori whispered, "is Asha."

Lassair had remained fully conscious the entire trip. She wasn't sure where on the planet she was, but from the minds around her, she was fairly sure they'd come to a mountain to the south, a temple complex on the dormant volcano Coropuna. She'd tried to relay that information to Trennus . . . but *something* had cut her off. Something that dimmed even the soul-bond between the two of them. She could still feel him, vaguely, but it was like a limb that had fallen asleep, there but not there.

She'd been aware of a truck ride, an ornithopter trip, and then another, briefer truck ride. Then the trolley had been propelled along a rocky road, and into a structure, inside of which she could feel . . . a presence. A powerful one, but diminished. Drained. As Tlaloc had been. Sizzling energies all through the air. Spirit senses showed her a vortex of browns and blues. Rock-like center, stability . . . but being drawn out from a binding area, and then sucked down, into the earth. Like a stone held at the heart of a djinn. Pinpricks of light all around her, then muffled even further as the trolley came to a halt. Lassair swallowed. She remembered *this* feeling. It was a binding circle. A hand opened the trolley's metal doors, and Lassair slowly crawled out, every limb aching from the long, cramped trip. Her feet were numb. Her neck was stiff. *Bodies complain so much*, she thought, and looked around with her physical eyes now.

A massive open room, three stories tall. Humming equipment, like the machines Trennus called Tholberg coils, lining every wall. But there were other devices, too. Huge, enclosed cylinders that held heat inside of them, under pressure. *Those are like the small cylinders of stored energy that Emberstone carries with him. But far larger. This looks . . . very much like the Pyramid of the Sun.* Insulated copper wires ran from the machines, along grooves in the floor, to prevent them from being moved, to the center of the room. And the center of the room had a simple, lined figure etched in the poured-stone floor . . . a triangle, surrounding a huddled male figure. Unmoving. The lines were all two inches wide, and filled with gold, at least a half inch thick. Lassair's eyes didn't widen; wealth was a fairly meaningless concept to her. What she did sense was what the gold *did*.

A flash of memory. Visiting a temple in Rome with Trennus, and looking at the opulent effigies of Jupiter and Mars. Real ivory, centuries old, carefully cut, unrolled, and shaped with heat and steam over metal frames. Gold adornments, gold hair, silver and bronze weapons. Bronze effigies of the gods in all the niches at the Colosseum. Trennus chuckling and telling her, *It's not just that copper, bronze, and gold were easy to cast, though they were. When it comes right down to it, people could have stuck with stone statues for making images of the gods and spirits. Stone's just as solid as metal for containing a bad spirit's essence. And it's not just that the statue itself is an offering, though that's a factor, too. They were giving something up. Sacrifice.*

Gold is not very useful in the Veil. Truthfully, it's not very useful <u>here</u>. Her tone had been breezy.

Ah, but that's where you're wrong. Copper and gold are highly ductile. They conduct electricity and ley-power very, very well. And the ancients had the belief that their gods were . . . well, resident in the statues in the shrines. That's why this king or that one would make a raid and 'steal the gods.' Partially to break people's morale, but also to steal their power-source. Trennus had wrapped his arm lightly around her waist as they'd continued on down one of Rome's bustling streets, looking at all the white buildings gleaming in the sun, listening to street vendors hawk their wares. *The statues were a conduit for the gods' power, because they're so ductile. But because they're metal, just like stone . . . .*

. . . the gods were bound to them.

Maybe. I think so. At least <u>part</u> of them. Think about how many current religions ban graven images. Judeans are forbidden to depict their god. Atenists can only use a symbol, the sun disk, and nothing more.

If I'd been bound to a statue for a few millennia, I wouldn't want to be bound anymore, either, Lassair had noted, shuddering.

And consider how many religions forbid the worshipper to invoke the god's true Name.

Well, there's a reason for that. Someone says my Name, I'm more or less obliged to <u>listen</u>. Lassair shrugged. *If I had twelve million people all saying my Name all day, I'd go deaf or insane. Or I'd start <u>ignoring</u> them.*

Trennus had shouted with laughter, and Lassair had smiled, too. But the conversation had brought back flickers of memory more distant yet, and she'd fought to catch them, like minnows in her fingertips . . . only to lose them once more.

Here and now, however, she looked at the binding symbol on the ground, the gold used to form it, and her lips curved down as she regarded the huge figure in the center. Threefold vision. She could see him at the apex of his power, eight feet tall, bounding over rocks and escarpments with the agility of a goat. Standing on the peaks, with snow up to his waist, a mask over his face, and arms raised to the heavens with the pure joy of being in this world. And she could see him now. Body withered. Drawn in on itself. Unmoving, as if he were already dead. But behind him, beyond him . . . power. He was the rock at the center of the vortex. Thousands of tiny, hair-fine lines connected him to other spirits, but these were gray and dull right now, like cobwebs. And his power was being drained.

Lassair looked down. *Is this my fate?*

At her feet, a binding circle, etched into the poured-stone floor. *Not flagstones. They're more careful here about breaks in the symbols.*

Footsteps behind her, as the people who'd taken her captive retreated with the trolley. Lassair sent out a cautious, questing thought, and it mostly rebounded from the binding circle around her. Her connection to Trennus was little more than a whisper now, and it took several moments of intense effort just to find Minori's mind; the woman was still unconscious. And the huddled mass of bones and energy in the center of the triangle was wholly unresponsive to her quiet greeting, as well.

Footsteps again, echoing back from the stone walls, audible even over the hum of the machines. Lassair spun, nervous, and watched as the man who'd captured them headed through a door into a separate room. All she caught were faint intimations of his intentions, but his spirit, gray though it was, now held shadows over it, that shifted and writhed . . . and every last one of those shadows was a human form. Twisted, distorted, almost beyond recognition, and all those shadows seethed with malice and anticipation. Lassair choked on her own bile. She hadn't seen *that* before. He wasn't wearing a spirit-mask now.

More footsteps. Lassair turned again, feeling exposed and vulnerable, and stared as another human male advanced towards her, smiling a little. Giddy anticipation in him, as he pushed a woman in a wheelchair. The woman's body was . . . ill. Lassair could see it, from the inside. Nerve pathways that should have been shot through with fire, were, instead, decaying. Turned to ashen cobwebs, like the strings that bound the god in the triangle figure to the rest of the world. The nerves, which should have bound her spirit and mind to her body, were dying. Outwardly, she had silvering dark hair and eyes, a face that had once been long, a little rectangular, but fine-boned. Beautiful. But now the flesh sagged on the bones, the head slumped on the neck at an awkward angle, and the hands, just as fine-boned, were useless claws, folded in her lap.

It was sometimes hard to recognize humans just by their flesh, but Lassair *recognized* the man, all at once.. He was the mage who had invited Emberstone and the rest of them to dinner at his estate a few days ago . . . but he'd worn a mask of a lock of his wife's hair and had had at least one spirit-mask, at the time. She tilted her head to the side, and said nothing.

"I apologize," the man said, immediately, his eyes avid as he stared at Lassair, "for the method of your conveyance here, spirit. Asha, wasn't it? I recognized what you were the moment I saw you. Fire-feathers in your hair, fire in your eyes. Not just a mere god-born. A little goddess, out and wandering the world. I *had* to take the chance. I had to bring you to where she was." He nodded down at the woman, who slumped, as unresponsive in her chair as the massive god was in binding circle. "I couldn't bring her to you." He ran a hand over the woman's hair. Lassair could see the woman's eyes lift, though her slumped head couldn't move.

You could have _asked_, Lassair told him, trying to keep her tone calm, which was hard. Spirit senses now focusing on Truthsayer's terrified mind, and the first pangs of *agony* emanating from her. Human eyes focusing on the pair before her. *Instead, you compelled. Why?*

The man — she couldn't remember the word sounds by which he was called, but they didn't matter; they weren't his Name — gestured down at the woman. "My wife. Paredes' disease. She's only forty, you understand? And she's had it for *ten years*."

Lassair could read the raw emotion in him. Pain, and memories. Memories of better times. Laughter and love. The first tremors in his wife's hands. The loss of control. Having to feed her. Having to bathe her. And always, cursedly, *awareness* in her eyes. The spirit was still in there, alive, bound to a body doomed to slow death. The man looked up, staring again at Lassair. "I brought her here. Chullpa, the high priest of Supay, offered to help. He can't heal. But he can hold death at bay." His hands opened and closed on the handles of the chair. "None of the gods, none of the god-born, none of the doctors besides Huallpa would help. We thought . . . I thought . . . that being around so much *energy* would heal her." Tears in his eyes, just for a moment. "Like taking the waters for gout. The energies were supposed to revive the land. Why not take just a *little* for her?"

I don't understand. All of this is really to make the land bloom? Lassair couldn't fathom it. Yes, a spirit with enough power could make plants grow, encourage rain to fall, but it required . . . motivation. Emotion. Willpower. Another spasm of pain from Truthsayer, and Lassair reached out. Tried to cradle the human's spirit with her own.

"Yes," the man replied, speaking quickly now. Excited, agitated, angry, all at once. "The emperor will direct it, when there's enough. He will be the conduit. He'll focus the power, direct it, and the land will be reborn through him." He shook his head. "But he *won't* heal her. I've spent the last eight years working like a slave for him. Building his towers. Building the *future* of this land. And not *one drop* of power, to save Pitahaya." He touched his wife's hair again, and Lassair could see a tear trickle down the woman's slack face.

I am very sorry, Lassair said, and she meant it. She had been bound, horribly enough, within a *truly* dead and rotting body, forced to send fire along its nerves and make it move, like a puppet, for another's pleasure. Taking phoenix form for the first time had been terrifying and exciting. She'd taken a shape that was still mostly fire, so that it didn't feel like *flesh*, like water and clay congealed into something cold and flaccid around her. But phoenix-form hadn't been quite enough. Trennus needed her, and she needed him. His emotions, his desires, his needs, had shaped her . . . and she suspected, that on some levels, she was shaping him, too. But she couldn't imagine any fate worse than being trapped within a dying shell, and *knowing* it. *But what has that to do with me and my friends?*

"Friends?" The man's bark of laughter was sharp. "*Friends*? You're a spirit. You . . . oh, gods, that's *funny*. There's only binding and being bound with you. Friendship . . . love . . . you might know the words, but you don't understand them. You're not capable of them." He rubbed at his face. "Nevermind. That's not important. I know what you *are*. You bring the flowers to life in the dead of winter, just by being around them. You're *life*. You can heal her."

Lassair blinked, and then winced as she could feel the agony coming from Truthsayer, and hear the woman's muffled scream. *I . . . do not know if I can. This disease comes from within her. The life-essence is warped; she has carried the seed of her own death with her since she was born. The best I could do would be to . . . remove some of the damage the disease has wrought.*

"Then *do* it!" the man demanded, taking a step forward, his eyes ablaze.

Lassair swallowed. This wasn't a bargain. There was no exchange of energies. And it wasn't a free sharing, a gift returned and returned and returned, as it was between her and Trennus. She'd been *compelled* before. But she could also read the desperate hope in the man's heart, and the faint flickers of it in the woman, who had longed for death as a release from pain for years now. *I can only heal from within someone's body,* she told him, quietly, as Truthsayer screamed once more in her mind and her muffled voice crept out from behind the closed door in the wake of that silver-sharp sensation. *I cannot do that, without de-manifesting this body.*

"You mean, you'll have to possess her?"

That is correct, but I cannot do it. Lassair actually wrung her hands, conflicted. The gentler parts of her pitied the woman, and wanted to help her. But the parts of her that had been *compelled* before raged up in refusal, hissing *no, no, not again, never again, my spark will not be put out because another demands it, I am not a thing, I am not a tool, I am not a toy, I am not a resource to be drunk down and exhausted.* And, too, Truthsayer's agony in her mind.

The man couldn't hear her inmost thoughts, of course. He took another impetuous step forward, pushing the wheelchair closer to the binding circle. "Do it. Release that body — I'm sure whoever's it used to be will be grateful to get their mind back — and enter my wife's. Heal her."

Lassair's head snapped up in affront. *I do not possess this body,* she replied, a little more sharply than she'd intended. *This is my own creation. I am not a thief. I do not steal the bodies of others.*

"Drop your meat on the floor, if that's what it takes. Heal her. She doesn't have much time."

Another white-hot spasm of agony from Truthsayer. Lassair couldn't *think.* Too many competing demands. Too much, from too many directions at once. She cast around desperately, and finally settled on the truth. If this man truly understood love, if he truly understood generativity . . . he'd understand this. *I am with child,* she told him, silently. Not, as she'd intended at first to say, *this body is with child.* The words simply formed themselves, and she put a hand, apprehensively, to her belly. *Please. I cannot disperse the body. If I leave it, the body will dissipate, and the child may go with it. But I swear, when the child is born, I will heal your wife. You have my word. Please. Stop hurting Truthsayer. Release me. I will heal her . . . but not today.*

And not, a voice whispered at the back of Lassair's mind, *because you've demanded it of me. But because she does not deserve to die in this way.*

The man's head came up, and there was a strange, wild expression there that Lassair didn't recognize. For a moment, he looked alien, his eyes no more than wet, gelatinous orbs, his face a rubbery mask that his spirit wore. "You're *pregnant*?" he demanded, fury uncoiling from him like a dark lash. "*You*? We couldn't even *have* a child, because of Pitahaya's condition, and you, who aren't even *human*, are going to have one?"

The woman tried, valiantly, to raise her head. Tried to grunt out words, but her husband was clearly past hearing her. A muscle twitched in his cheek. "She doesn't *have* nine months, spirit. She has less than six weeks."

I am sorry —

"No, you're not!" It was a shout that bounced back off the walls, which coincided with another scream from Truthsayer and the continued slack indifference of the god bound in the center of the chamber. "All I've had from the gods is *silence*. All I've had from the emperor I've served is *indifference*. The gods will pay for their silence, their indifference to all of us. The emperor . . . .I can't do anything to him. But you? I can hold you to account." His eyes glittered. "Your so-called friend will continue to have Huallpa's *attentions* until you give in, or she gives us your Name. Either way, you *will* be healing my wife today."

Lassair closed her eyes on a fresh wave of Truthsayer's agony, and tried, again, to take the pain away. Made it her own. Suffered with her new friend, for her new friend. Absorbed it into her light, and burned it out. But she could do nothing about the actual damage being done. And now Lassair was caught. She had to weigh the tiny, incipient life within her against Truthsayer's pain. Against, perhaps, Truthsayer's life. On the one hand, it was hardly more than a ball of cells, though it represented so much more to her. It was a symbol of her bond with Trennus. Something they'd *created* together, when she didn't even know she *could* create. And on the other hand . . . was it selfish of her, to weigh that against the human woman's suffering?

Her will wavered. The stubborn refusal almost banked. Almost bowed. She didn't want to be the cause of Truthsayer's pain. *She does not know my Name,* Lassair whispered, but it was a lie.

She reached out. Touched the human's mind. *They say they'll stop tormenting you if I heal this man's wife. But if I do that, I think that I will lose the child.* Infinite tenderness in her tone, as she again leached the pain away. Gave the woman a moment of peace. *I will heal his wife. You should not be in such torment for my sake.*

No! Truthsayer's words were almost incoherent, but the sense of them was clear to Lassair. *They will go on! They will go on and on and on, because this one enjoys suffering, because they would know all our secrets, the only way out is through, I will allow this to pass through me and over me and it will not touch me —*

I will end this —

NO! They will cometheywillcometheywillcome. I am the daughter of a samurai and I willnotbreakIwillnotbowIwillnotyield. Neither will you!

Lassair recoiled from Truthsayer's mind, stunned by the force there, and opened her eyes. The human's spirit was formidable, and bolstered her own. *No,* she told the man, feeling nothing but pity for his wife, and sudden, renewed anger at *him*. He was the cause of Truthsayer's pain, not Lassair's refusal. *He* was the reason for it all. *I will not.*

The man's eyes narrowed. "No? So much for your love for your friend. But there's another way I can compel you. I can relieve you of your *excuse*, spirit." He wasn't thinking clearly. Lassair could see the rushes of adrenaline and stress cortisol moving through his body and brain, inhibiting higher brain functions. She knew that the body did a lot of humans' thinking for them. That the body and the spirit were connected in such fundamental ways, that they needed time to be able to separate the physical from the mental. Of course, for her, time was an endless plane that curved forever, in every direction. She had time. Humans . . . didn't.

She could feel his decision before he made it, and flinched, pulling her hands up, uselessly, to defend herself. He incanted, rapidly, and it was a *relief* when his first attack on her was fire. Fire was a *friend*. It sheeted over her skin, warming her, soothing her, curled up and puddled at her feet. Not hot enough to melt rock. And poured-stone never burned. It took temperatures akin to those at the heart of the earth to melt poured-stone. It had to become lava in order to melt. The fire even left her clothing untouched; she *made* her clothing, every day. Willed it into existence, as part of herself. Deprived of sustenance, the fire died, and Lassair felt colder for its absence. *I'm afraid*, she told him, quietly, *that you cannot harm me in that way.*

"No? Then if not fire, spirit . . . we'll try force." He incanted, even as his wife twitched and tried to mumble something that sounded like *no*.

What felt like a cannon ball rammed into Lassair's stomach, and she was thrown backwards—not out of the circle, but slammed against the invisible wall of force that was intimately bound to the symbols on the ground. It wasn't just marks that held a spirit, but a summoner's *will*. Lassair clutched her stomach, and reached inside. Verified that while there was bruising, everything, including the tiny spark that dwelled within, was safe. And then she raised her head, her red eyes glowing like coals. *I will end you. You will die in fire.*

They'd kept a bag over Sigrun's head the entire flight. This hadn't surprised her. They assumed she needed her eyes to target her god-born powers, and for the most part, they were right. She could, at any time, call lightning to her *own* body. It wouldn't damage her, but it would surely hurt anyone in contact with her. But she needed to be under an open sky for that . . . and while being shackled to a seat in an ornithopter was definitely 'under an open sky,' she did not think that slamming the vehicle with lightning was the best idea. She might survive the crash, though she wouldn't put long odds on it. Adam, however, certainly would not.

Livorus was still probably in the palace in Machu Picchu. Though he could have been kept in Cuzco, too. The Sapa Inca seemed to change his mind a dozen times an hour, as far as she could tell. Over the course of the flight, he screamed at a servant, gave an order to have the servant flayed alive for having spilled a drink on him when the ornithopter caught an updraft, and subsequently forgave the man. At least, that's what she was catching, when they occasionally slipped into Latin. The Quecha language had no cognates in any of the languages she did speak, so listening for more than tone was something of a lost cause.

She was all too aware of the fact that someone had a gun on Adam. There was probably one pointed at her, too, but that worried her less. *Then again, that's what they're counting on. They're using him to compel my obedience. Him and Livorus.*

The ornithopter came in for a landing; the bird-like vehicles didn't always require runways, but could take off and land like a helicopter, in many cases. Sigrun raised her head as their captors shoved her, ungently, out the door of the vehicle. Cool air slapped at her skin. Hint of snow and thin air. Just from the feel of it, she knew they were a solid 13,000 feet above sea level. *Lassair and Minori will realize that we haven't come back to the hotel,* Sigrun thought. *They'll call Kanmi and Trennus. We'll have backup.*

She stumbled on the rocky path, and fell into Adam's arm, only to be jerked back upright. And that was when Lassair's frightened mind seined through her own. *Stormborn! Stormborn, you are here!*

Lassair's voice was muffled, and Sigrun stumbled again, this time in shock. *Lassair? You're here?*

I am bound. The spirit's voice seethed with frustration and anger. *I am in a place of machines and metal, a tall place, I am bound, Truthsayer is being tormented, and I could not sense you or Steelsoul until this moment. Something blocks my sight, something beyond the binding that encircles me.*

Sigrun tried not to stumble again. *So . . . Kanmi and Trennus most likely won't know we're gone. Gods. We're going to have to get ourselves out of this. And get Lassair and Minori, as well.*

It was a long hike, blindfolded, easily a couple of miles. Finally, the dirt track underfoot became stone. Sound of doors opening ahead, and closing behind them. The wind's breath stilled around them. Then they were propelled through various rooms and halls, until the rattle of iron bars was audible, and, hands still shackled behind her, Sigrun was shoved into a cell, and rough hands removed her hood. Her head came up, and she could see, as they pulled the barred door in front of her shut, that they'd put Adam in a cell across from her own. *They want me to watch when they threaten or beat him,* Sigrun decided, meeting Adam's eyes from across the way. He looked disheveled, but remarkably calm. For all that his hands, too, were locked behind his back, he stood with his back straight, eyes studying their captors and surroundings. "This does not," Sigrun said in Latin, "seem like quite the tour of the facilities that the Sapa Inca promised."

The guards didn't laugh. Most of them didn't speak Latin, but one of those who did raised his head and met Sigrun's eyes, just for an instant. Regret there, but also fear. Fear that if he didn't do *precisely* as he was told, he'd be flayed alive, or some other torture inflicted on him, by people equally terrified of the same ruler. And this ruler's power did not stem merely from his control over other humans. He'd been trained as a sorcerer and a summoner . . . and he had powers that seemed to be divine in origin, as well. *But he's not a god-born. And he's not the avatar of a god, the way*

Xicohtencatl became Tlaloc's, right at the end. His body was dead, so Tlaloc assumed him, wore him as a spirit wears a corpse to become a <u>ghul</u>, or a manufactured body to become a golem. Sigrun's few discussions with representatives of the Odinhall had garnered her one fragment of information in the intervening years. If a god used the living body of a human as a vessel, instead of manifesting their own form, they could derive power from taking the mind of the body and devouring it—a form of sacrifice. A kindly god—or one secure in its power—could allow the mind of the human to continue to exist, though it would be subsumed to the power of the god.

They were left with only two guards, for the moment. Sigrun switched languages, into her heavily-accented Hebrew. *"Asha and Minori are here."*

"I know. Asha touched my mind." Adam's tone was grim. *"Can you break us out of here?"*

"Yes. I can break the manacle chain. I doubt the bars on these cages are more than wrought iron. But I don't think I can do it before they can shoot you." She inclined her head towards the guards, who were already looking at them in deep suspicion, and raising their muskets, pointing the weapons at Adam. *"Now? Or wait?"*

Adam grimaced. *"We're not going to get far unarmed."*

"Nonsense. I see at least two weapons in the guards' hands."

"True. Be ready to heal me, Sig. I don't want to slow you down."

"You never do."

But before she could move, a distant door opened, and she could hear footsteps coming towards them. Could see, just around the left wall of her cell, that the guards had both stiffened to attention. Sigrun exhaled and stood. She wouldn't meet any captor on her knees.

Her eyes widened as a figure in a colorful red and blue robe, heavily embroidered with gold threat, moved around the edge of the cell block. The man was at least eight feet in height, and twisting horns protruded from his forehead, like a gazelle's. His skin was brick-red, with symbols that looked like eyes, worked in white paint, all over his face and bare arms, while his own eyes were black, from lid to lid, and glossy, like polished onyx. White fangs curved against his lower lip, which protruded with a marked underbite. In his hand, he carried a heavy club, made from solid obsidian. And the *sense* from him . . . cold crept over Sigrun's skin, though she could walk barefoot through snow without noticing. But this chill was like oil, and left a crawling sensation in its wake. Sigrun turned and looked directly at Adam. She could see the rigidity in her husband's body, the tautness in his muscles. He knew *precisely* what they were looking at, just as she did: a god who had taken a mortal form.

The *aura* around him was overpowering. It spoke of dissolution and despair in the voices of a thousand whispering ghosts. It spoke of bodies rotting in the earth, and the end to which all mortal things came. It spoke of finding death on one's knees. Of giving in. Surrendering to the inevitable. It even hinted, teased, that only through death, could new life begin. *But not yours.*

The guards had fallen to their knees, and put their heads on the floor, abasing themselves. Other prisoners, in the cells around them dropped as well. Protecting their eyes from the glory of the god, perhaps. Sigrun fought the insinuating whispers that pressed in on her mind. Heard Adam groan across the narrow corridor, as he sagged for a moment, then pulled himself upright again.

How interesting.

The avatar's lips did not move. The voice was a dusty rasp in Sigrun's mind, like sand sifting out from the ceiling of a cave as stone shifted against stone. ***A child of one of the northern gods? You have power young one. More than you imagine. Your sacrifice will be a fitting one. Your strength will be added to mine.***

"*Fikkest thu.*" Sigrun's voice was thin, but even. She rarely resorted to profanity, but this certainly seemed an appropriate moment to start. She could see the muscles in Adam's arms straining as he tested the strength of his own manacles. Could see that his eyes had narrowed, the look of murderous intent there clear. Part of her, the part subject to the despair that surrounded the figure, wanted to tell him, *Don't. Don't bother. There's nothing we can do. There's nothing you can do. He's a god.* But that part of her, she realized, distantly, could be overcome. That voice needed to be reminded that Adam was, for all that he was a mortal . . . a godslayer. They'd fought a god before, and *survived.*

This god wasn't Tlaloc. He wasn't constrained to a binding that she could see, and his power wasn't being drained, visibly, by machines and wires. Sigrun swallowed, and forced her mind to calmness, even as the red-and-white creature turned his head to study Adam for a moment, and actually sniffed at the man for a moment. ***This one has the reek of destiny on him. But no power in his blood. We shall save him for consecrating the ground at the final point on the circle. Make your peace. We will begin the ceremony soon, for you, child of the northern gods.***

Sigrun lifted her head. "Kill me, and they will come for you," she said. Her voice was barely audible, a thread of sound, but grew in strength as she spoke her defiance. "Are you so strong, that you would defy my gods?"

They will not make war for one foolish child who has entered another's territory unbidden. And soon, they will not dare come at all. The fanged mouth smiled, and he turned and walked away once more, leaving dizzying clouds of despair in his wake.

Sigrun *shook.* That yawning pit of despair, of the certainty of mortality, loomed before her. No matter what Sophia had always claimed about her accursed visions, this was where she and Adam were going to die. Even the forlorn hope that her gods might avenge her was foolish. They wouldn't make war, disobey the Pax Romana, just for her. She and Adam were on their own. *Idiot. We are always on our own. The gods reward right action, but every child knows that we are expected to stand on our own two feet. That is why we do not kneel before our gods. We must do for ourselves. Make our own choices. No fate.*

"Sig?" Adam's voice was a harsh whisper. "*Come on, neshama. Stay with me. Focus."*

Her eyes snapped open. *"We need an exit strategy,"* she said, simply, as the guards, very much alerted now, walked up and down the halls of the cells. *"But even if we get out of the cells . . . he'll <u>track</u> us."*

"One thing at a time," Adam told her, his dark eyes on the guards. *"Be distracting, <u>mami</u>."*

"You mean, I should be rude?" A brief quirk of humor, as she began to regain her mental equilibrium. No, this god wasn't Tlaloc. But he also wasn't *Tyr*. That much, too, was true. In spite of the overwhelming aura that he possessed . . . he didn't have Tyr's *presence*.

"Yes, Sig. Be very, very rude." Adam's lips quirked up.

Sigrun called her power to her. Let light well out of her rune-marks, head down, as if meditating, and let the blinding white light grow and spread. The other prisoners in the cells began to shout in alarm, covered their eyes once more, and backed away from the bars. And the guards, equally alarmed, moved towards her, pointing their muskets, shouting orders at her in their native language, as they squinted into the brilliance. *A good thing I have so many scars*, Sigrun thought, distantly. *Else I could not make so bright a light.*

Behind the guards, Adam had slipped his own feet over his manacles' chain . . . and now moved, fast, sliding his bound hands between the bars of the door, snapping the chain around the throat of the closest guard. Yanking the man back into the bars and strangling him. The musket went off with a cacophonous bang, and the ball slammed into the wall of Sigrun's cell, sending stone chips into her skin. The second guard, stunned, whipped his head back and forth, indecisive for an instant, and then turned away to raise his gun at Adam . . . who kept the body of the other guard between him and the second, even as the man kicked and fought, his face turning purple from loss of air. The free guard spun back, trying to aim at Sigrun . . . who had already brought her hands to her feet and stepped directly on the chain of the manacles. She might not be able to snap the chain behind her with the power of her arms alone—the leverage points weren't quite right, even for a bear-warrior—but with her leg and arm strength together? More than adequate. She tried to call her spear to her. It was blood-bound to her, and she was used to it coming at her call. It took her a disgruntled moment to realize she wasn't in a line of sight of the weapon, followed by a brief instant in which she thought, *Wait, didn't it come directly to my hand in Judea in spite of walls . . . ?* No time for the thoughts, however, With an irritated shake of her head, Sigrun reached for the bars of her cell door, and pulled, just as the man fired on her.

She twitched aside, somehow, the bullet only skimming along her left shoulder. Blood welled, but she knew that it would heal. Wrought iron in her hands, cold and brittle, for a metal. She hauled back on it, and it snapped in half at the center of the door. Sigrun evaluated the piece of metal in her hand for an instant, even as the guard began to back away, shouting for help . . . and threw it, like a javelin. Her makeshift spear went through the man's throat, and he fell to the ground, clutching at the improvised weapon. Sigrun realized, at that moment, that this had been the man who'd made eye-contact with her, before, when she'd commented that this wasn't a tour. She knew that in his heart, he was guilty of nothing more than a little moral cowardice and human frailty. He'd followed orders, rather than die, and maybe see his family die, too. *Hardly worth a man's life.* But she for damned sure wasn't going to give hers for him. His death; her choice. But she could at least meet his eyes as the light left them. Silent apology.

Then she wrestled with the door, pulling the bars apart, and wiggled though the space she'd created, even as Adam let the deadweight of his own guard drop to the floor. Sigrun allowed the light in her flesh fade, as she dropped to her knees and found key at the belt of one of the dead guards. Fumbled them into the door of Adam's cell, and finally got it open, before finding a smaller key for their respective manacles. Then she turned and tossed the keys to one of the other prisoners in the cells, who caught the ring with a dumbfounded expression on his face, as if he could not quite believe in the possibility of hope. People began to stream out of the cells, dazed, confused, and unsure of what to do with freedom. Reprieve.

"Where are we going?" Adam asked, picking up one of the muskets with distaste, and loading it with the supplies at the guard's belt. Powder, shot . . . no ramrod, so he just tapped the butt against the floor. Quick, expert motions. "What I wouldn't give for my *own* weapons," he added in a terse mutter as he loaded the second, and handed it to her, even as she yanked another piece of wrought iron free. It wouldn't make a good spear. It wouldn't even make a good staff, to be honest. But it was a *weapon.*

"I do not know. Asha . . ." Sigrun paused, looked around vaguely for a moment, and then pointed. "Her presence came from *that* direction. I think."

"As good a way to go as any," Adam agreed, and grabbed a knife from the waist of one of the dead guards. "Let's *go.* Let me go ahead. I can manage a little more stealth than you can."

Sigrun darted a glance at him. "I thought, after the *alu*-demons, that you weren't going to complain about my light anymore."

"I'm not complaining. I'm *observing.*" Adam caught her hand and kissed the back. "We might be up against a mad emperor, his cronies, and a god, Sig. But we're fighting in pretty good company." He wasn't disregarding the enormity. Far from it. "We're going to get through the night. We're going to get out of here. And we're going to do that, and get Minori and Lassair back, too."

Assurance in his voice. Sigrun squeezed his fingers, and accepted the morale boost for what it was. Adam was a damned fine leader. He could make the impossible seem doable, with just a few words, and his personal guarantee that he'd be right there beside you. To the end.

Just as they headed for the door, two more guards, alerted by the noises, entered the prison area, and the other prisoners all *tackled* them, wrestling their muskets away before they could be fired. In the confusion, Adam and Sigrun left . . . and realized that they were inside a massive stone structure. Halls and doorways everywhere. Ley-lamps hung on the walls from brackets once intended for torches. Hide rugs on the floor, in place of more luxurious, woven carpets. "Sky," Sigrun muttered. "I need the sky, Adam. I can *fly* us to Lassair, if we can just get out of this building without being caught."

"Sky is what you want, sky is what you get. This way. I think." Adam's eyes were devoid of expression now, and he moved ahead of her into every room. Killing guards from behind, snapping necks, slashing throats. Sigrun followed behind him, noisy musket unfired in her hands. Behind them, turmoil. Alarms, as guards ran towards the prison, only to have Adam and Sigrun emerge from doorways and put them down. The escaping prisoners were a wonderful distraction, but Sigrun wanted to give those people as much of a real chance at freedom as she could.

And then, solely by chance, they actually found a door that led outside.

It was night past that door, a testament to how long the flight from Cuzco, and the fight to get out of the building had been. Black sky, bereft of stars; a thick pall of cloud-cover, marked solely by a lighter patch, through which the full moon tried to peer. Behind them, light and pandemonium. Bells ringing, voices shouting, as the whole facility looked *inwards* towards the prison that they'd just left. No trees outside, but downhill of them, dozens—no, hundreds of lights. A small city, a maze of huddled stone buildings.

"Need cover," Adam said, tersely as they moved out of the arch of the doorway, into the darkness. Light snow on the ground, crunching under their feet.

"Someplace to hide while we figure out our next move," Sigrun agreed, her breath forming in a white cloud ahead of her. "There." She pointed up the face of the mountain, to the next ridge, and the building there. Lassair's presence came from more or less their left, but was distant. This building was . . . perhaps north of them. Hard to tell, without stars for a reference.

Adam stared at the building. Three-tiered, each tier far longer than it was wide. "Sig?"

"Yes?"

"That's an *ushnu*. A libation and offerings place."

"Yes. But usually not a sacrifice place, if Tren was right." Sigrun swallowed. "This should be the last place they'll look. And less risky than the town. And then we decide on a course of action that . . . takes us to our people." *I hope.*

Adam paused. "Sig? Asha has no problem seeing us a mile away, most days. How do we know that that *entity* isn't watching us? Toying with us?"

Sigrun closed her eyes for a moment. She wished he hadn't said that. "We don't."

Adam exhaled. "Yes . . . I was afraid you'd say that. All right. Let's move, then."

Trennus and Kanmi had had a busy afternoon. Once they'd secured all of their prisoners, Trennus had watched, his mind dull and incurious at first, as Kanmi questioned them. He didn't trust himself to be the one asking the questions. That being said, after the first two, he wasn't sure if Kanmi were fully in control of himself, either. The technomancer had worked his way up through the ranks of the tower guards, starting with no more than a couple of broken fingers to get the various guards to point out their supervisor. And with the supervisor, Kanmi was far less gentle. There was no enjoyment in Kanmi's face. Just grim purpose and black anger, as he asked the tower supervisor, "Did you have orders to kill us, or take us captive?"

"Standing orders were . . . to capture anyone who tried to get into the tower . . . ."

"Where would prisoners have been taken? Which of the towers connected to this one is the main complex?" Kanmi was biting off the words. He had the man by the throat, had him pinned to the wall with loops of metal over wrists and ankles.

"Don't . . . don't know . . . ."

Trennus didn't need Sigrun's truthsense to know that one was a lie. Just then, Lassair's frantic voice reached him, and he swayed. "A mountain! Esh, she says they're on a mountain. She can feel the dormant fires underneath it . . . volcano. She says the name is—" The words, which had been tumbling out of his mouth, stopped, as Trennus blinked, rapidly. He could still *feel* Lassair. Dimly. But he couldn't *hear* her at all.

"Well?" Kanmi asked, impatiently.

"I can't *hear* her. She's been cut off somehow. Maybe sealed in a jar for all I know." Trennus' hands began to shake again, and a growl of frustration escaped him. "I can feel her. She's . . . southeast of here. I could follow that line like a hound, Esh, but we have to *go*."

"And get there how? On foot? Commandeer a bus? When we get there, what are the defenses?" Kanmi rapped out. "What's waiting for us? How many men? Matru, *think*." The dark eyes glittered. "What's the name of that volcano that had a tower on it? Corona-something?"

"Coropuna," Trennus replied, automatically. He'd spent hours analyzing the geology of the area, the ley-grid, everything, since arriving.

Cocohuay, sitting on the desk, watching the proceedings, chimed in, unexpectedly, "There are two temple complexes on Coropuna. Maucallacta and Achaymarca. Achaymarca has two hundred buildings around the temple, and a long trail leading up to the glaciers, to the ancient sacrifice site, where *capacocha* was carried out." This meant, of course, the rite in which children had been sacrificed to the mountain gods, left to the elements, or struck with a stone club. Her lined face was infinitely tired. "A hundred children a year were sacrificed to Supay, the death god, and still he hungered for more. Till Rome came."

Kanmi swore under his breath. "My ancestors did much the same," he admitted, grimly. "So, that would be an ancient place of power. Fits with the usual blood-binding and sacrifice we've seen before." He looked over at Trennus. "But I remember you saying the other name. Mau . . . whatever."

"Maucallacta," Trennus said, emptily. "It's the place that has the *ushnu*. It's considered a place of power, where oracles have dwelled for centuries. The tower's built closer to it, than to the other site. But both are within about five miles of each other. But rugged terrain."

"Thirteen thousand feet up the side of a volcano that is over five hundred miles away," Cocohuay acknowledged, her lids low over her eyes. "We will not be climbing that path easily."

"And we still don't know which location," Kanmi said, that black rage simmering behind his eyes again. Trennus watched him, blankly, as the Carthaginian turned and looked at the supervisor. "You have one more chance to answer. Which complex would prisoners be taken to? Which one is the main facility associated with this tower system?"

The prisoner shook his head, an expression of terror crossing his face. Kanmi exhaled, and raised his right hand. "You're not giving me much choice here," he said, grimly. "I hope you weren't too fond of your face. You're about to lose it." He incanted, and the air began to *freeze* in a mask over the man's face. Kanmi delicately avoided the nostrils, but even the eyes were entombed under the growing mask of nitrogen ice.

The screams were no less terrible for being muffled. Trennus stared at Kanmi. He'd never seen this side of his friend before, and, at any other time, he might have been disquieted. At the moment? Trennus didn't care what Kanmi did, so long as it got results.

After thirty seconds—enough time to kill a wart on human skin, Kanmi let the mask dissipate into smoke. The man's face was almost dead white underneath; the first and second layers of skin were, quite probably, dead tissue now. Kanmi caught the man's jaw in iron fingers, and said, grimly, "I'm done being gentle. Which facility would prisoners be taken to? What are the defenses like? What can we expect there?"

The man hesitated. Kanmi clenched his fingers. "Answer me, or the next batch of liquid air goes down your windpipe and dry-cleans your lungs."

"Maucallacta! Maucallacta is the main facility! Oh, gods, please, stop him!" The man was imploring Cocohuay, who folded her arms across her chest and looked stern and saddened at the same time, like a disappointed grandmother. "You don't know what they'll do to me!"

"Kill you?" Kanmi said, his voice disinterested.

"Worse! They'll give me to the *supay* and let them dine on my flesh while I live!"

Trennus looked up at that. He knew that the word *supay* meant both the god of death, and a group of demonic spirits that made their home in caves and mines in the region. They were subject to Supay himself, according to lore. He shook his head. "Is the entire area warded? Is the whole area a giant spirit-trap, like the Lines?" His voice sounded flat to his own ears.

"I . . . I don't know. I was only there once. They took me before the high priest of Supay. He's was marked out for the god since birth, they say, and the god has *taken* him. I was . . . sealed to the god." The man's voice was frantic. "They said the god would see through my eyes. Would know if I betrayed them and their secrets."

Kanmi glanced at Trennus, who shrugged. "Did they take blood from you?" Trennus asked, remotely. He didn't actually *care*. The only thing that mattered was getting out of here, and he couldn't do that without Kanmi. He *chafed* at it, but Kanmi was right. They *did* need more information.

"Yes. They used needles in the penis, like the blood sacrifices of old."

A muscle twitched in Kanmi's face. Trennus shrugged again. "He's probably blood-bound. That'll let a spirit keep track of him. A normal spirit couldn't see through his eyes. I don't know about a god, though."

"Either way, we've got confirmation. We need to figure out how to get there. The only one of us who can fly a damned ornithopter is ben Maor, and guess who's not here?" Kanmi grimaced, and turned back to their captive. "This Supay. He's there? Is he bound to anything besides his god-born?"

A frightened, uncomprehending look. "I . . . I don't understand —"

"Answer the question! Does he wander around like he owns the place? Does he fly around in the sky in a gods-be-damned chariot? Is he *free* or is he *bound*?"

Kanmi's voice had become a snarl, and Trennus caught his arm and dragged Eshmunazar away for a moment. "I know why *I'm* angry," Trennus said, and again, it was as if he were watching himself, from a distance. Observing his body go through the motions. "You're supposed to be the calm one right now." And Kanmi had been, in the main. He'd been stable and calm enough to let Trennus ground himself, but it was like children playing on a teeter-totter. One went up, the other went down. "What's the problem?"

A glare, and at first, Kanmi wouldn't answer. After a moment, a tight grimace. "I gave her my *word*, Matrugena. I swore we'd keep her safe. That *I'd* keep her safe. First time I turn my back? Baal's teeth, Trennus. I gave her my word, and I let her down. This is my —" He cut himself off, but Trennus knew what the last word would have been. *Fault*.

No more yours than mine, he thought, but couldn't say the words out loud. He just nodded. "Keep it together. We've got a location."

"Next step, transport. Think any of these guys can fly an ornithopter?"

"Find a volunteer. I have work to do here. And when I'm ready, we're probably going to have to release these men from the tower."

"Release them? What the fuck *for*?" Kanmi's voice was furious. "They're all part of this, Trennus. They might be pawns, but they're all in on it. Let them *hang* here for a day. Let them *rot*."

Trennus had been staring into the mid-distance, at the ley-lines and energies that he alone could see. "Because I don't think the tower's going to be standing when I'm done," he said, grimly. "This tower is the hub of the wheel. It's the stable center around which all else turns. Breaking it won't break the whole wheel. But it'll start destabilizing the whole system. So . . . yes. I'm going to break this tower. I'm going to free every damned one of the spirits in the Lines. Good, bad, ugly, indifferent. I'm going to learn their Names. And the backlash from their confinement being broken is probably going to weaken the containment at the towers."

Kanmi froze. "Wait. I thought that the towers were what was holding what's here in the Lines under control."

Trennus shook his head. "I've had a lot more time to study the energy now, Esh. The towers form a binding circle, and they focus the energies coming from the towers *inwards*, yes. Into the land itself. The power here in Nazca? Points outwards. Imagine a soap bubble. It can only hold its shape so long as inner and outer pressure are about the same, right?"

Kanmi paused, picturing it. "So they trap spirits here. Trap *gods* here, with raw ley energy. Convince powerful ones like Mamaquilla to put themselves into human avatars, or . . . jars . . . ."

"Statues, probably," Trennus replied, distantly. "Would work better if there's a physical resonance between their ideal form and the form of the container."

"Tren, that doesn't *work*. You'd still need more power to *start* with . . . ."

"Yes. Which suggests that at least one god is helping the humans with this. Perhaps this Supay."

Kanmi stared at him. "Well, you've got this all figured out, now don't you?"

He has unraveled a surprising amount of what has been veiled from me. The voice spoke in their minds, like a wash of waves under moonlight, silver on black.

Trennus' head rose, and he stared as Cocohuay walked out of the main room where they'd been questioning the captives . . . but then his eyes shifted to the figure beside her. Nearly eight feet in height, the woman's form was larger than life, and she was built on curves. She wore nothing but a short kilt, unashamed of the beauty of her body . . . and her skin was covered in iridescent peacock-blue scales, like a fish, shimmering with silver highlights. She had long black hair, braided intricately around her scalp, like a crown, and her eyes were identical to Cocohuay's, luminous white irises against black schlera. The feeling of her presence was overwhelming. Cool, as deep as the sea and as remote as the moon. Alien and terrifying, and yet motherly, in a strange way. Cocohuay's lined face was wet with tears as she looked on the face of her goddess, and Mamaquilla spoke in all their minds once more. *I am glad that you will release those bound here, summoner. I might be able to shatter the Lines, but my manner of doing so would cause more destruction to this earth than I can bear to deal. I have searched for my husband-brother Inti, and I can find he who is the sun, as I am the moon, nowhere. He is gone from the sky. His voice is not even a whisper on the wind. All the voices that should be a chorus in my mind are no more than shadows now. If Supay is involved in this, then today, death will die.*

Trennus lowered his head, in respect, but watched out of the corner of his eye as Kanmi's head rose. The Carthaginian cleared his throat, and asked, in a far more subdued manner than usual, but also without any preface, and without honorifics, "If you'll forgive me for asking . . . if you'd appeared an hour ago, couldn't you have just looked into these men's minds and *told* us where to go? Without our having had to rack them for answers?" Kanmi's tone warmed into anger. "You're a goddess. Aren't gods supposed to be omniscient?"

Trennus *winced.* This wasn't outright defiance, but Kanmi definitely bordered on . . . insolence. Then again, he was Carthaginian by birth, and more or less worshipped Carthaginian gods. Quite a bit less than more, really.

The luminous eyes of the sea-goddess regarded Kanmi steadily. *We are powerful within our realms, and powerful among those who give us allegiance and worship. But the man that you questioned was blood-bound to Supay. That binds him as a servant to the death-god. I cannot meddle with the servants of others. I cannot see into their minds . . . often, I cannot even see them at all. The more tightly someone is bound as a servant, the less another god can touch them, in this way.* A scaled hand reached out and rested on the shoulder of the god-born woman beside the goddess. *Cocohuay, my beloved granddaughter, is my bound servant, by blood and by choice. No other god can see into her mind, not truly. They can attempt to command her. Trick her. Harm her. But they cannot read her thoughts, nor easily find her on the surface of the world, unless she stands directly before them. Some god-born are brighter presences than others. Depending on the nature of their powers, and their degree.*

Trennus' eyes widened. It was far more of an answer than he'd anticipated, and it meshed with why Lassair was usually unable to see many Judeans. He'd thought Kanmi would be *slapped* for his presumption. He glanced at Kanmi, who regarded him, wide-eyed. "Do you think Caetia realizes that?" Kanmi asked, dryly. "Baal's teeth. Ben Maor should be damned near invisible as well. He goes to temple a lot more often than I do."

It requires being the bound servant, the goddess corrected, sternly. *Consecrating oneself to a god.*

Trennus raised his head. "If that's the case . . . then why can Asha . . . the spirit I'm soul-bound to . . . see their spirits?"

For that you are bound to them, they love her, and she loves them. The goddess' tone was calm. *And not every servant of a god or goddess has bound themselves utterly to his or her service. Some give lip-service only.* She turned and looked at Trennus, expectantly. *I cannot, for example, see deeply into your mind. You serve another. You are bound to her, heart and soul.* She glanced at Kanmi. *You? You are not. You are open.*

" . . . and suddenly, I feel a need to get religion," Kanmi said, dryly.

No. You do not. That impulse does not exist in you. You would stand alone. You would stand apart. It is in your nature.

Kanmi *twitched.* Trennus might have laughed, had it been any other day. Instead, he looked around. "Please. Everyone. We need to remove the men from this tower, if I'm to release the entities bound here."

The various men were all Tawantinsuyan by birth. They knew their goddess by sight, and, as she released them, seemed to regard her as their savior and deliverer . . . until she began to chastise them. Angrily. Trennus, already at work inside the tower, wasn't the focus of that godly wrath, but when the floor shifted underfoot, he could feel it with his ley-senses down into the bedrock, and looked up, hastily, and put a hand to the window-frame as the tower rocked like a boat. Outside the window, the Nazca valley *had* no lights. No cities. No *people,* beyond those charged with protecting the Lines.

The whitefire gleam of moonlight suddenly suffused the landscape, turning the men around the goddess into black shadows. In that glow, Trennus could see the land outside actually bulging *up,* rolling and undulating like waves. *Tidal forces,* he thought, numbly, feeling the strain and pressure in the earth below his feet like a bellyache. *She's a moon goddess. She can use the effect of gravity on the ground, as well as on the sea. Let's hope she doesn't set off an earthquake till I'm ready in here.*

Cracks radiated out from the goddess' feet like a spider web in the desert pavement, following the ripple of the earth. The various men dropped to their knees, as the whitefire crawled towards them, along the cracks . . . and then water fountained up along those lines. Trennus *winced.* There was an aquifer, about a mile below the surface here. He could *feel* it. Boiling hot, and dense with salts and minerals, and the goddess had just reached down through the earth and brought it *up.* Some of the men screamed and danced, trying to get away from the scalding water spraying them. Others stood still, clearly terrified, but untouched by her wrath. The dancing, screaming men were suddenly *shoved* down by another wave of gravity, their faces pressed into the boiling pools of watery mud . . . and pushed down, into the ground, still struggling.

The water receded. Some of the men still stood, gasping and shuddering, and Trennus wouldn't be surprised if some of them had wet themselves. On the ground . . . ten perfectly preserved statues of men's bodies. Like something from the original city of Pompeii. An object lesson, clearly illuminated, as the full moon rose above.

The guilty parties have been identified and judged, Trennus thought, numbly. He thought, given the amount of ley-energy in the valley, that he could have done the same thing. But he was also terrified, at the same time, that the subsidence as the water was released on the surface, would make the valley shift before he was ready. It would change his calculations.

He went outside and drew his protective circle carefully, using ley-energy to carve the desert pavement into the protective lines, and infusing them with power, and told Kanmi, "Get in here with me. Just in case."

Kanmi looked at him askance, and noted, dryly, "One of these days, I'm going to make you a technomantic device that can flash-cut those damned things. Save you a lot of time and worry." Then he stepped over the lines, and stood out of Trennus' way as the summoner and ley-mage got to work.

Trennus spread his awareness down into the rock. Found where the shelves of the continents were pressing against each other. This line of magma, upwelling, to the south . . . one of the many volcanoes in the region. This fault line, over here . . . how it could echo and resonate and trigger *that* one, miles away. And, interwoven with his understanding of the land, was his awareness of the ley. There was so *much* trapped energy here, both in potential, in the rocks, and in the lines, that tripping one could trigger the other. Understanding ley, and how one line could make another resonate, was good practice for understanding fault lines. They were all interconnected, a vast system, and touching, even lightly, in one place . . . moved everything else. The ultimate chess and puzzle game, combined, and making one wrong move in a place like this? Could bring down a city a hundred miles away. He didn't think he could level Cuzco or Machu Picchu from here, but Ica? Certainly possible. So he prepared places for the energy to go. Set up paths of least resistance, so that the spirit and divine energy sunk into the ley-lines could discharge safely. It took almost an hour before he was satisfied.

Kanmi had long since taken a seat on the ground, and was evidently doing mental work of his own. Tingle of the sorcerer's will in the air. "I'm ready," Trennus said, his voice distant again.

"You sure about this?" Kanmi asked.

"They have no right to imprison most of these spirits. You imprison the maleficent ones, if you can't *kill* them. You don't bind the good ones. You don't destroy them. Yes. I'm very damned sure." All of Trennus' rage at Lassair being imprisoned was behind his words.

"All right. I've got contingency barriers around us. Hopefully, we won't need them. Go ahead." The sorcerer from Tyre crossed his arms over his chest, and remained prudently seated.

Trennus nodded, and reached down into the earth. And redirected the main ley-line directly into the earth around it, bleeding off energy into his pre-determined paths.

The valley shook underfoot. Sharp, snapping sounds, like gunfire, went off in the distance, as fault-lines cracked open. Ground past each other. A rumbling, undulating flow as a transverse fault, deep underground, began to move against the rest of the flow, and Trennus sweated and poured more energy into the system, directing it, delicately, away from that dangerous transverse. He needed that rock to go *there*.

Seventy feet in front of them, the tower began to dance to the rhythm in the earth. The walls cracked. Shattered. Trennus, his breathing labored now, redirected the ley energies, again and again. Dim awareness that to the north, cracks had formed in the Spider. That the Lizard was pulling *apart*. The Monkey, with its infinitely spiraling tail, shattered. *I'm defacing works of art over a thousand years old, and I do not care,* Trennus thought, grimly. *Because no one has the right to use them for this.*

The tower *fractured* as the ground itself tore asunder. The walls split apart, like the petals of a flower, flinging themselves to the trembling earth, and a rain of debris flew out. Old, shaped stone fragmented and struck Kanmi's shields, which flared into life on impact, stealing the kinetic energy of the rock, and redirecting that power into the shields themselves. A brilliant golden light exploded from the center of the tower itself, rising like a star, and a scream filled the air around them, wordless and joyous and fierce, all at once. Ley-energy, tied to the center of the tower, *rebounded.* Five pre-disposed paths, radiating outwards to five towers, and a shockwave pulsed along each, traveling hundreds of miles in an instant. What they'd do when they *reached* their destination, Trennus didn't know. Any man-made system should have safety protocols. Backups. But the primary systems *might* fail.

Trennus couldn't focus on any of it. At the moment, he *was* the earth. He was part of the ground, and the ground was buckling. Heaving. Twisting. Trying to move more. Further. Half the valley wanted to be two miles further south than it currently was, and the other half wanted to be two miles further east, and he couldn't *let* them take the paths that should, by rights, require millennia to unfold. He dispersed the seismic energy, poured ley into it, and flattened the sine-wave that was the motion in the ground before dropping to his knees, panting. "I think," he told Kanmi, wiping sweat off his face, "that I may . . . just have wrestled with the *earth.*"

"Did you win?" Kanmi asked, looking around, wild-eyed.

". . . not sure. I . . . *think* I accounted for everything. There might be aftershocks for a while. A couple of months. Gods. I . . . " Trennus sagged back now, dizzy. "I'm . . . tired."

The lights, which had lifted into the sky, red, blue, green, yellow, and violet, circled. Swayed. Formed patterns together . . . and then descended, lazily, as Mamaquilla and Cocohuay moved to the edge of the protective circle in which Trennus and Kanmi huddled. Trennus looked up, dazed, registering the lights, and his eyes went wide.

There were *hundreds* of them. Some, no more than amorphous balls of wispy light, like Lassair had been, with shadows that might have been the impression of eyes. Others were far more unambiguous. A stout, dwarf-like man with twisted, monkey-like features and moon-silver eyes threw back his head and laughed like a hyena, giving Trennus chills—he sounded like an *alu*-demon. A small, squat woman, with hair and eyes that were the green-brown of pond-water, and whose footprints were damp, no matter where she walked. Another woman, who, like Diana of Ephesus, had dozens, if not hundreds of breasts, as she danced free of the ground. *Coniraya, Copacati, Mamallpa!* Mamaquilla cried out. Trennus put a shaking hand to his face. These were gods. Lesser gods, certainly, but still orders of magnitude more powerful than ordinary spirits. And the others . . . he could feel them, outside the protective circle. Many were beneficent. A chorus of voices in his mind. Each telling him their story, till he thought he might go mad of it.

. . . they worshipped me, they loved me, they bound me here hundreds of

years ago, and then they forgot my Name and came no more to dance along my Lines . . . I am Ozcollo, the spirit of the great hunting cat, and I owe you a debt . . . call my Name . . . .

. . . they sang my Name and gave me praises when the winds were good and the rains came, and then the land dried up and the crops failed and the people left, and left me here, alone, trapped. They did not take me with them, even in their hearts. They left me imprisoned for so long, and now you are <u>here</u>, and I thank you, human. I am Taruca, the deer, who roams the crags . . . know me, say my Name, and I will requite you for your service . . . .

. . . free, free, free, I danced too close to the Lines, and then they caught me, I thought I would go mad, cut off forever from the Veil. I am Aquana, water-spirit, and I will repay you. Know me! Know my Name!

. . . I would kill the ones who imprisoned me, I would spin webs of fire around them and lay eggs in their bellies that they would birth screaming, but they are all long since in their graves. But why should I not take my vengeance on their descendants —

<u>I forbid this! Begone, Lilka!</u>

On and on and on like this. Trennus fumbled out his grimoire, and, his hands shaking too much to write, burned each Name onto the pages with a whisper of ley-energy. Each time promising the spirits, *I will remember you. I will remember you. You will not be alone. I will remember.*

Trembling with exhaustion, as the last spirits dissolved once more on the wind, Trennus looked up. *Lassair would rejoice, to know so many of her kin have been freed,* he thought. *No. She will rejoice. But we have to get to her.* "We need to *go,*" he said, dully. "We have to get to the others."

<u>Yes. Inti was not among those trapped here. He was not at the hub.</u>

"Who was in the center tower?" Kanmi asked, sounding wary.

<u>Mamallpa . . . goddess of crops and fertility. They wanted me, as a water goddess, in one of the other towers.</u> Rage in that silver-black voice, like waves crashing. **<u>If he is anywhere, and I would have felt his death, for we two are bound . . . he must be where I cannot feel him. This tower to the south, where your others are bound? May hold him. The place is blank to my senses.</u>**

Trennus shook his head. Releasing the spirits was what Lassair would have wanted him to do. Now, all that mattered was getting to her. "How do we get to them?" he asked, his voice barely a whisper. "Esh and I can't fly."

Kanmi helped Trennus to his feet, and out of the protective circle. Outside of its confines, Mamaquilla actually reached out and touched Trennus' forehead with one large, gentle hand, and Trennus felt as if white light flooded through him, arcing from his head to his feet. Almost more than he could bear, and it touched the place in him where his soul tied to Lassair. **<u>Peace, young one. The one whom you serve still lives. And I will take you to her. I will take us all.</u>**

A part of him wanted to protest the word *serve,* but it wasn't important now. A moon-white pool coalesced around their feet, at first as evanescent as a cloud, but as Trennus and Kanmi both shifted uncomfortably, the energy seemed, somehow, to solidify. Became material, though Trennus could *feel* energy in it, still. "Ah . . . what's this?" Kanmi asked, uneasily, as the circle's edges pulled up, encircling all of them, sealing them inside a perfectly white, opaque orb. Kanmi reached out and put a hand to the soft, faintly yielding, glowing surface and asked, again, his eyes going a little wild, "What's this?"

A wonder.

"It is a conveyance," Cocohuay told them both, sitting on the floor, and putting her back against the soft, curving wall. "I have only traveled in this way once. I . . . believe you should sit down."

Trennus did so. Kanmi, clearly panicking a little, joined him. Trennus knew the sorcerer was stretching out every arcane sense, trying to understand what he was seeing.

Force. Raw force, shoving them back and *down*, against the resilient wall of the sphere. The sickening lurch in his belly that Trennus associated with taking off in a plane, and the wobble that meant that air was moving around them, though it was . . . far more distant than it would be in a human vehicle. But he could feel them leaving the *ground*. He could feel the ley-lines receding behind them—fast. Very damned fast. Trennus closed his eyes and prayed, very hard, to any of *his* gods that might be listening, and felt Saraid touch his mind, reassuringly. *You are safe,* she told him, gently. *I am with you. I am always with you.*

A *sway*, a curse from Kanmi, and then a shudder through the whole of the sphere. "What was that?" Trennus asked, shaking.

"I think we just broke the sound barrier," Kanmi said, grimly. "Where's ben Maor when we need him? He'd be *loving* this. We're heading *up* along a parabolic curve."

Trennus froze. "We're going into *space?*"

Only the very highest portion of the atmosphere. This is faster for me, than a straight line, I assure you.

"Do I want to know how high up we are right now?" Trennus asked Kanmi. He was trying very hard not to pay attention to his ley-attunement, which was screaming at him that the ground was very, very far away at the moment.

"No. You don't." Kanmi actually sounded sick as the acceleration pushed them back into the walls. Remarkably, there was almost no trembling. A rocket had to fight friction in the air, which resulted in a lot of shaking. This godly vessel? Had no such problem, it would seem.

They hit the top of the arc, and for a moment, there was *freefall*. Trennus actually drifted in air for a moment . . . and then gravity recaptured them, his back slammed into another softly yielding wall, and then they were sailing *down*, and it was every nightmare he'd ever had about flying, all at once. Entombed in a vessel, hurtling through the sky, falling. Falling forever.

Chapter XIX: Lahar

Once upon a time, there were two woodcutters' children who lived near the Black Forest in southern Germania. Their names were Halvar and Gudrun. Their mother had died when they were young, and when their father married again, it was to the village herbalist. Every day, when their father went into the forest to cut trees for other people's fires, Halvar and Gudrun followed their step-mother under the shade of the branches that blocked out the sky, and helped her look for mosses, herbs, and mushrooms.

The spirits of the Black Wood were capricious in those days, and a dark mood gripped the forest. The trees whispered of a man with an axe made of steel, who cut too deep, and took too much. The spirits whispered in the dreams of the woodcutter, and showed him blood pouring from the trunks of the trees wherever his axe bit deeply. <u>You have taken our sons and our daughters, root of our root. You will give us yours, in return, or the next time you come to the forest, your axe will turn in your hand, and the earth will drink your blood.</u>

Weeping, the woodcutter knew that he had done wrong, and that he had to make recompense in some way. But he did not wish to give up his son and daughter. He did not speak of the dream to his wife, but rather took Halvar and Gudrun into the forest without their step-mother the next morning, with a piece of bread each. He told them that he loved them, and that the spirits would take care of them. And with that lie, he turned and left them alone in the woods.

But Halvar and Gudrun knew the forest well. Halvar had marked their trail with little cairns of stone, and they skipped out of the forest before nightfall. Their father rejoiced to see them; he thought that the spirits had let them go. But the dream came to him again that night. <u>Give us your children, or your axe will turn in your hands, and the earth will drink your blood.</u>

So the next day, the woodcutter took his children into the forest once more. And this time, he walked so fast that Halvar couldn't leave cairns of stone behind, or mark the trunks of the trees with his little knife. And again, he said goodbye, and told them that the spirits would look after them. And then he left, weeping.

The children wept, too, because this time they knew it was not a game. As they wandered through the woods, hand in hand, they noticed that birds followed them. Ravens with the eyes of men. But they knew that ravens were the messengers of Odin, and they were not afraid.

After hours of wandering, they found a tiny house, where there never had been one before, in all their wanderings through the woods. A wonderful smell came from the windows of that house, a smell of pies and cakes and all such good things to eat.

Halvar said, "I'm so hungry. Should we knock at the door? Maybe whoever's inside can tell us how to get home."

Gudrun shook her head. "No one lives in the forest. Whoever this is, must be an exile."

"Or a spirit."

"Or a witch."

Before they could walk away, the door opened, and an old woman emerged.

"Who whispers outside my house?" she demanded. Her eyes were like old gold coins, yellow and a little blind.

The two children remained silent, hiding in the trees. They could feel the forest whispering around them. They watched as the old woman built a pyre of wood in the center of the clearing, near her house. They watched as she wove a little cage made of stout, tough branches. Just the right size for a child. "Come out," she called towards the woods. "Come out, children. I know that you are there."

"You've made a cage," Gudrun called back. "What is it for?"

"Why, to hold a little piglet in, when I go to market."

"You have built a pyre," Halvar called out. "Who has died?"

"Why, no one, child. I built it to welcome summer next week. Come out, little ones, I have food and drink for you."

Halvar and Gudrun were tired and hungry, and the food smelled good from inside her house. They came out of the woods, and the woman gave them honey-cakes and cider, and then, quick as could be, she shut Halvar up in her little cage. "See what a fine piglet I have," she told them, smiling. "When you're fat enough, I will put you in the cage, on the pyre. I will have my blood, as I did in all the days that went before." And she put on her tattered cloak, which Gudrun could see now was made of bark and leaves, and the girl knew that this was the Black Forest, the spirit that dwelled at its heart.

For a week, she made Gudrun her slave, and Halvar, she fattened with wheaten cakes. Then she bade Gudrun light the pyre. Weeping, Gudrun did . . . and as the old woman moved the cage to the pyre, their step-mother emerged from the forest at the edge of the clearing. There were good spirits with her — spirits of the deer and the trees — and on her shoulder, a raven perched. The old woman screamed when she saw them, and their step-mother called to Gudrun, "Push her! Push her into the fire!"

Gudrun, who was right behind the old woman, did. The old, withered body fell into the flames, and burned with a smell of wood-sap. Working together, Gudrun and her step-mother released Halvar from the cage, and the brother and sister fell on each other's necks and wept.

They returned home to their father's cottage, where he begged them for forgiveness; the raven on their step-mother's shoulder flew towards him, and plucked out one of his eyes. Their father wept, but he had learned wisdom, and he had his children back in his arms. And once one has suffered punishment, and justice has been done, then forgiveness can be offered.

— Willahelm and Jacobus Grahn. <u>Stories for Children: One Hundred Traditional Tales,</u> Ambrones Press, 1888 AC.

Maius 21, 1960 AC

A wave of energy pulsed through the earth from far to the north, rippling through segments of the continental plate, following the ley-line connecting Nazca to the complex at Maucallacta. Almost no one along the route that the energy took could feel it for what it was; they only knew that the ground shook, and moved outside. Everyone in this tectonically-active area of the world knew the dangers of earthquakes.

The seismic pressures had attenuated by the time they reached the slumbering giant that was Coropuna, but the spirit-born energy needed somewhere to go, and the ley-line was the closest thing it had to an attuned conduit. The Mountain began to tremble and shake, sending rocks tumbling down cliff-faces, and causing the glacier atop the volcano to crack, a slab of ice a hundred feet thick calving off and sliding down the northern face, effacing the land of the few scrubby trees and bushes that clung there.

In the complex around the Oracle of Maucallacta, people felt the ground quiver, and scrambled away from dinner tables, running for doorways, looking up apprehensively, at the snow-covered peaks above them. Coropuna had slept for centuries, as the glaciers attested . . . but there were dark outflow marks all along the mountain's sides. Testimony of a different sort. A few, looking up at the right moment, pointed and cried out, "*A shooting star!*" Coupled with the earthquake, it didn't look like a good omen.

In the tower on the western side of the complex, Minori's gag had just been pulled back, briefly, for her to respond to one of her tormentor's questions. She could feel the vibrations transmitted up from the floor, into the table to which she was strapped. She couldn't feel ley-power, most days; that's why she carried a multimeter with her to job sites. Whatever this was, however, she *could* feel it as it surged along every copper line in the tower, like a buzzing sensation in her blood. The ley-powered lights over her head flared brilliantly, and *exploded,* and she barely closed her eyes in time as broken glass showered over her and darkness fell. The ground trembled, and Minori cautiously squinted, feeling glass shards shift against her lids as she did so. There was a little ambient illumination in the room, coming from the emergency lights near the door, which had just flicked on. Just enough to see that her captor had staggered at the roll and pitch of the ground, and had turned away from her to see what was going on.

It was a second, maybe two, of distraction on his part. His body was barely a shadow among the brilliant afterimages dancing in her eyes, but now Minori had a location for him. She'd been prepping the framework of the spell in her mind every time he'd let her have even a tiny break from the pain. The framework was simple, almost delicate. It required very little power. All it needed was accuracy, and that was a function of concentration. Difficult, but not impossible. Minori's whole *world* had become that spell. She wove herself into it—dangerous, that, with a killing-spell; you risked killing a part of yourself, or at least taking backlash this way, but she had no other tools besides her mind, her body, and her will. The electricity of her own body generated the initial energy spike, and, unable to move her numb hands, Minori quickly croaked out a single phrase to focus her spell and bring it to life. "*Kuuki wa kekkan wo haire!*" she rasped.

Sorcerers native to Europa who learned spells by rote, ancient ones passed down from times gone by, learned them in Attic Hellene or ancient Chaldean. Sorcerers like Kanmi, who devised their own spells, generally defaulted to their native language for precision and nuance. Minori had trained in Nippon, and thus, she used the elegant, formal form of Nipponese used at the Imperial Court. This wasn't a traditional spell, however. Traditional air spells treated air as *wind*. They whipped it into a gust to carry an enemy over a cliff, raised a storm to wreck a ship, or lifted the caster off the ground in a self-contained vortex. They *might* go so far as to create a dagger of ice from the water ambient in the air. That was the basis of Minori's combat training. But she'd been arguing with Kanmi for a solid month on the perils of relying on the traditional. And traditional would have been too cumbersome and visible and required too much *power* to be useful in this room. This was unconventional casting.

No sooner had she spoken, than her captor spun towards her, slapping one hand to the side of his neck. Minori sank back against her bonds, letting her eyes close. Felt the sting of particles of glass that had seeped past her cracked lids. It didn't matter. At the moment, it didn't even matter if he managed to kill her in the next thirty seconds. It didn't make her victory any less complete.

Prompted by her will, a tiny splinter had formed in the air, the size of a hypodermic needle. Wider bore than a bee's stinger, it had embedded itself in the man's carotid artery. Just long enough for the second half of the spell to take effect, as air was pushed, forcibly, through that tiny tube, and into his blood vessel.

She couldn't see him, but she could hear him stumble. Felt him fall against the table to which she was strapped, trying to steady himself. "You *bitch*. What did you do? I am going to *end* you —"

Minori let her eyes crack open. She was hazy now, drifting just above the pain that completely filled her body. "*Sayonara*," she whispered.

The air bubble, injected into his artery, hit his brain less than thirty seconds after being introduced to his circulatory system. The result was an embolism and a stroke; his entire body stiffened. His hands rose to his head. And then he fell to the ground. She couldn't see him from her angle, but she could feel him jerking and spasming briefly as blood vessels inside the brain exploded, tearing the brain itself apart with the force.

I am the daughter of a samurai. I do not bow. I do not break. I do not give in. Minori began to shiver, convulsively. Shock was setting in; the *doctor* had been carefully treating her for that in between sessions. He apparently knew, very well, how to prolong the lives of his subjects. *I have to get out of here*, Minori thought, but the words were distant inside of her own head. She couldn't open her eyes, for the glass, and she was shackled at hands and feet. *Just . . . need to form the air inside the locks. Press each tumbler, just so. And then turn it. Just like so long ago, in the Palace.* But it was so hard to concentrate now. She didn't have her hatred of the torturer to help her focus. Shock was making everything seem less real. And she was so tired. It would be good just . . . to slip down into the darkness. Where the pain would go away. Every organ in her body had been twisted. Turned. Bruised. Shocked. The connective tissue holding each piece had been pulled like candy floss.

No! Lassair's voice echoed in her mind. *Do not go! I won't let you go!*

Stay!

In the central room of the tower, Lassair had been pinned in the circle, trying, futilely, to protect herself. Binding circles were permeable to a spirit from the outside, in; protective circles reversed this, keeping a spirit *out*. Part of it was the energy and focus of the summoner who'd created it, and some were powerful enough to persist past the death of the summoner. The Nazca Lines, surely, had been created by *generations* of summoners and priests. This circle was powerful enough to keep her contained, at first as if her back were against an invisible wall of glass, as Micos continued to slam her with raw kinetic force. It wasn't fire. It wasn't earth. It was simply energy, clenched around a tiny speck of dust, and slammed into her like a fist, over and over. Lassair slipped to the ground and curled into a ball, knees to her chest, trying to keep her head and vulnerable abdomen safe as another kinetic punch hit her in the ribs. And another. And *another*. She didn't think Micos was rational anymore. Her spirit-mind could absorb that, understand that, while body-mind spasmed with pain and panic. Spirit-mind knew that for the sorcerer, she'd become a symbol of everything that had told him *no* in his quest to save his wife's life. The gods. His emperor. Nature. Natural philosophy. And she, herself.

She tried to reach out, desperately, along the cord of soul that connected her to Trennus, through whatever *shell* covered this place and muffled her ability to hear others. Another buffet, and Lassair curled in more tightly on herself, feeling a rib snap. Tried to pour body-mind into spirit-mind, where the pain couldn't reach. Spirit-mind could feel Stormborn and Steelsoul fighting. Freeing themselves, and a tiny part of her rejoiced, though she could feel their fear, their panic, their need to *hide*. *Come to us, come to us, come to us*, she called, almost incoherently, and *then* the wave of energy hit the building. The tower shook to its foundations. Breakers all over the room popped and flung themselves to their offline positions. Half the Tholberg coils in the room overloaded and began to overheat, throwing out sparks, beginning to melt.

Lassair couldn't reach any of that fire, any of that heat. She was separated from it, like an insect in a bell jar. The floor rocked and swayed, and her captor, distracted for a moment, stared around him as guards ran for the doors, and technicians abandoned an office off to the left, a couple grabbing for fire extinguishers, but the majority of them fleeing the building.

For spirit-mind, time was infinite. For body-mind, time was both too slow and too fast, relatively speaking. Spirit-mind felt the roof overhead begin to crack, weaken, slide. Spirit-mind reacted before body-mind could, rolling the body out of the way as a chunk of mortar and tile plummeted towards her and her captor. Micos had had less warning, just an ugly *crack* from above. He glanced up, and reacted, on instinct, trying to jump out of the way of the falling masonry . . . and hopped ahead, directly into the circle.

Spirit-mind saw him coming. Saw the arc that his trajectory would make. Saw that he might hop out of the circle entirely again. And body-mind saw the causer-of-pain, the one who had threatened the child within and the body's own life, and simply *reacted*, faster than spirit-mind for once. Lassair lashed out a leg, tripping Micos, bringing the man down heavily atop her, just as the mortar and tile landed between them and his helplessly watching wife, confined as she was, in her wheelchair. Her body shrieked at more injuries, but spirit-mind had caught up now, and Lassair realized in a blinding instant that she had her captor, her tormentor, in *reach*. Someone who would have forced her to give up who and what she was, for his own ends. No matter that he'd wanted her to heal someone he loved. He would have forced what should have been a gift, when she was powerless to protect herself.

Never again.

Flames began to lick along her forearms, stood out in her tumbled hair like a corona. Fire couldn't harm her, couldn't consume her. She *was* the phoenix, the living flame, eternally reborn, no matter what body she wore. The spirit reached up and wrapped her arms around the man like a lover, and, as he screamed and recoiled, wrapped her legs around him, too. And let the fire come, raging out of her flesh, as if she were the living heart of a star. For an instant, the inside of the tower was so bright that it looked as if a nuclear reaction had taken place, and a few of the technicians fighting the fires around the Tholberg coils, who had looked up and over, now screamed and clutched at their eyes, blinded. If the god confined in the triangle had looked up with his divine eyes, he would have seen a shadow being consumed by white flame.

As the man's body split and cooked, instantly, to ashes, Lassair could feel a warm, inviting rush of power. Could watch his inner spirit, unbound from its shell of flesh, shocked, pale, evanescent. Waiting. Lassair felt two conflicting desires at that moment. The rage screamed inside of her, *Consume him! Destroy him, as he would have destroyed you!*

The other voice felt *pity*. Wanted to cradle that lost and lonely spirit, so confused now that the only home it had ever known was gone. Wanted to pull it into her heart, and give it peace.

And in the balance point between those two impulses, Lassair refused both. Denied both. She would not take his life-energy, though he surely deserved consumption. And she would not make him part of her eternal core, either, would not bind him into her. He had loved, but he had not loved *her*. He was not part of her.

The wisp of energy wavered. Flickered. And dissipated.

For an instant, Lassair was . . . elsewhere. Time, always relative for her anyway, ceased to matter at all, as memory stirred. *At the heart of a fire, somewhere in the northern lands. Her sisters, dancing in the flames with her . . . yes, she'd had sisters. Latirian, last to come beyond the Veil of the three, and the coldest. She Who Brings the Harvest, She Who Harvests Souls. Inghean, second of the three to leave the Veil, She Who Tends the Crops, She who Watches Over Mothers. And Lassair, She Who Makes the World Blossom, She Who Gives Life. The humans had given the three of them many names, but they knew their true Names, too. Lassair had called her sisters from the Veil, knowing she was diminished without them, knowing that they were three and they were one, and they had come at her call, delighting in this new, strange world, where things* *happened one after the other, and when something ended, it <u>stayed ended.</u> Where change was possible and where death was real. Delicious, the danger. Wondrous, the experiences. The humans knew them and loved them, and they loved their humans, and cared for them. But there were other spirits who shared these humans with them, and some of those spirits wanted more. Wanted more power.*

Fear generated power. Worship generated power. They could <u>take</u> life-energy, if the body-shell was slain, or if the blood was given as a gift. Lassair hadn't cared much about it, either way. All she'd cared about was dancing in the fire, and drifting through this beautiful, alien world. Examining its flowers. Watching the strange creatures that inhabited it. Feeling the rush and surge of passion and love in her humans. Watching, through Inghean, sister-self's eyes, as the new lives the humans planted in each other were birthed . . . and sometimes, with Latirian, watching the women die in blood and in pain, as their bodies could not bring the new life forth. Lost energy. Lost life. And when it ended here, it <u>ended</u> . . . unless someone caught the spirit before it could dissipate. Latirian, because she had a fascination with such things, had tried to take a few of those ragged, evanescent spirits to the Veil . . . .

And that night, Lassair had looked out of the fire's heart, and seen the humans — ones sealed to other spirits, who let the spirits enter their flesh and touch their essences — dragging a large wicker cage to the fire, and had seen that a man was inside of it. A captive, from a recent battle, he was bound to serve Lassair's humans, and that hadn't much concerned her when she'd first seen him and the others taken in that battle. Now, however, the humans stood around him and chanted, as they often did when they were about to offer her and her sisters wine and cakes. Lassair and Inghean and Latirian stopped their eternal dance, as the humans lifted the cage . . . and flung it into the fire.

Lassair had fled, shooting like a star across the heavens, Inghean at her heels. Latirian, because the humans always called on her when there was a death, stayed. Watched. And came away changed, as this world always changed those in it. Colder. Darker. She had learned to hate the humans, at least a little, for what they did to one another.

. . . why could I not remember this before? Where are my sisters now? Lassair thought, still hovering in that timeless moment of memory. They'd fled the humans, and, because the three-who-were-one could not bear to face their humans again, their humans forgot them. Forgot their Names. Forgot to love them, because they no longer loved their humans. Until all three of them were little more than flickers of what they had been, and they, too, began to forget who they were. And then *he* had come, the vile one. He had found their Names on an old piece of stone. Little more than scratchings in a language no one could read anymore, but he'd decoded it . . . and had summoned them. Bound all three of them. And Latirian had been the first used and burned out. It had taken a hundred years, but she, youngest and coldest, had dwindled down into nothing more than a whisper, and Lassair had only just been able to catch her sister-self's Name and the last echo of her being, rather than letting her disperse. And then *he* had begun to use Inghean the same way. Forcing her to prolong his life. Heal him when he was ill. Burning her out, giving her nothing in return that would fuel the fire. And when she was nothing more than a shimmer,

caught within Lassair's own mind, he'd turned last to her, oldest and brightest . . . and he'd used *her* for a hundred years, as well. Until Trennus had come.

She threw back her head and keened for a moment, as all the years of sorrow and aloneness and desperation hit her at once. She had been three and then she'd been one, but now with Trennus, she was two, and if the child was born, she'd be three once more. And all of it, *all* of it, depended on escape. Escape meant life. Captivity meant dissolution. She had only to look at the slumped avatar of the god inside his golden bonds to know that.

Lassair made her body sit up, and, looking down, dusted herself free of the fine ashes that covered her. A quick glance around; only seconds had passed while she was caught in literally millennia of memory. As a spirit fresh from the Veil, a second or a century had had no meaning for her. She'd glanced up from watching a meadow slowly change and shift, to realize that twenty years had passed, and those who had been calling her names had withered and died in the interim. It had surprised her, then, that time bound humans so tightly. She'd learned to pay *attention*. And that seconds really could matter.

Quick blinks, as she assessed with body-eyes and spirit-senses. The technicians . . . all blinded, on their knees, clutching their faces and still screaming. Pitahaya, tears running helplessly down her slack face, sitting limp and unmoving in her wheelchair. Blind now, too, as well as unable to move, and Lassair felt a wrench of pity go through her for the human woman. Even if she'd closed her eyes, she'd been unable to look *away* from what Lassair had done. No evidence in the woman's mind that she'd seen her husband consumed by flame. All the human woman knew was that he'd fallen, light had exploded, and then nothing more. Conviction in her, than she was dead, in fact, and *relief* and bewilderment, by turns . . . and then a surge of *victory* from Truthsayer, and Lassair shouted in jubilation, sharing her friend's triumph . . . and then felt Truthsayer start to slip away. *Do not go! I won't let you go! Stay!*

Lassair clung to Truthsayer's fading consciousness, and glared down at the symbols on the floor that bound her. The heat of her fire couldn't *burn* poured-stone. But there was nothing that couldn't *melt*, given the right temperatures. For an instant, she'd reached those temperatures, in the heat of her rage. But while the floor under her feet was searingly hot at the moment, it hadn't reached plasticity. The earth had stopped trembling underfoot, and the ceiling no longer shook. She could feel guards coming back into the tower now, and wanted to scream in rage. She couldn't take them all, not all at once, not in a human body, fragile and so easily broken, even if she managed to break the circle around her.

And then Trennus' voice in her mind suddenly clear and strong, as it had not been in hours. *Flameheart, Lassair! Where are you?*

Here! In a high place of stone, a tower. How are you so close, so suddenly? She could actually see his essence now, as she could see, distantly, the blue-white spark that was Stormborn, the silver, gleaming blade that was Steelsoul, the dull red glow that was Emberstone, his inner energies limning the dark core of his rage. And with them . . . Lassair cringed and withdrew her senses. A vast *personage*, who felt of night and seawater.

Don't ask. Please, don't ask.

When the earthquake hit, Adam and Sigrun had been heading towards the *ushnu*. Adam had stumbled, Sigrun had caught his arm, and they'd found cover, for a second, behind a piece of carved stone, and waited for the world to stop moving. Lassair's voice, imploring them to come to her and to Minori. Adam tried to send a wave of assurance the spirit's direction that they would, just as soon as they figured out *how*. He could see a streak of white light arcing through the sky, and thought, *shooting star*, but the closest meteor shower on the calendar was the Eta Aquariids, and he'd watched those from the balcony of their home in Judea two weeks ago. *Worry about it if we need to worry about it. Could have been an ornithopter crashing.*

Shouts of alarm, muffled, from the building they'd just left. Adam knew that the guards inside would be in a bind. Stay inside, doing their job, rounding up prisoners and looking for *them*, and risk the roof falling on their heads, or make their way to an exit, and possibly let prisoners escape. Either way, the earthquake was a great distraction. He eyed the *ushnu*, and caught Sigrun's arm as she started to move towards it. Sigrun sank back down, following the line of his finger as he pointed.

He'd caught movement out of the corner of his eye, and now they could both see it, he knew, feeling Sigrun stiffen. Whatever the creature was, a spider-web of molten red cracks pulsed across a roughly humanoid body, alternating between a lava-like glow and near-invisibility in the darkness, a steady cycle that matched the pace of human breathing. It was also, Adam estimated, about twelve feet tall, and it was apparently patrolling around the *ushnu*. It paused at a corner near where they hid, and turned its head, the moonlight revealing dark pits where its eyes might have been. The creature peered in their direction for a long moment, and Adam's nerves screamed at him to be ready for an attack . . . and then it shuffled on, passing around the front of the long, three-tiered stone structure. The creature's skin, this much closer, appeared rocky and pitted in places, and glossy in others, as if it were made of pumice and obsidian.

Once the creature had passed out of sight, Adam whispered, "What was that?"

"A stone elemental of some sort," Sigrun replied, after a brief hesitation. "We're on a mountain. Maybe it's the spirit associated with this place?" Her tone said she didn't entirely believe that.

"That would be almost too easy." Adam gestured at the *ushnu*. "Besides, he was acting like the night watchman. If that's his temple—"

"Yes. I don't think it's his. But that's a heavy guard to have on that place." Sigrun's tone was considering now.

"Recon?"

"Information is a weapon, too, Adam. And we need to work our way . . ." Sigrun looked up; the clouds were letting the moon's face show now, but no stars. "West, I think."

"True. But not everything is a weapon." *Though, explain that to the Romans. I think they'd weaponize their fasces, if they could. Magic symbol, instrument of justice, and their favorite toy.* Adam didn't say that one out loud. No time, no breath.

They hustled over the broken ground, and got up against the short side of the rectangular, stepped structure, and moved along in the dark, crouching low. Adam swore mentally every time his foot slipped on the loose scree around the structure. *It would be nice to be able to see in the dark. JDF R&D is supposedly working on some crazy idea of 'night-vision goggles.' Like something out of a Coemegin Cearmada Battle for Mars science-fiction novel. Doesn't do me a damn bit of good now, and I can't ask Sigrun for light, because then even a blind man would be able to spot us.* Adam continued in the lead, and then the wall under his left hand changed texture, and the ground ahead of them shifted. Became a set of stairs leading down under the *ushnu*. "This thing's supposed to be a solid structure, right?"

"Three platforms, one built atop the other," Sigrun confirmed, softly. "Solid rock."

Adam looked up. They had time before the stone creature would completely circle the building . . . assuming there wasn't a second guard plodding along in exactly that same steady pace. "Underground," he muttered, his palms already sweating. The memory of the *ghul* was still powerful, but it had been replaced by the Pyramid of the Sun in his dreams. Mostly. Sometimes, the cave under the pyramid had *ghul* in it, as well. Looking at the rough-cut steps leading down into the tunnel, the darkness yawned like an eye socket in a skull, or the mouth of a monster.

"Are you well?" Sigrun asked, edging forwards.

"Just need a moment." Adam swallowed, reminded himself forcibly that guards could be returning any moment now, and that all he had to fight a creature made of *rock* were two muskets, a folding knife, and Sig's natural gifts. He slipped over the edge of the stairs, dropping down from the upper edge of the wall to land neatly on the stone below. He ignored the sensation that the walls were closing in on him, and led the way into the tunnel. Faint glimmers of dim light up ahead. Light that came and went, irregularly, dimming to a faint spark now. *If the tunnel runs the length of the structure . . . could be a very good way to move westwards without being seen. On the other hand, this might be where their entity stays when he's not threatening prisoners.* Adam shifted the musket in his hands, and crept forward, feet silent on the stone floor, feeling Sigrun behind him.

There were random pieces of rock and rubble on the stone-lined floor of the tunnel, and dust still hung in the air with a musty scent at which Adam grimaced. Clear evidence that the ancient structure had been rattled by the surge of the earthquake.

The passage widened towards the middle of the structure, becoming a large underground room. The dim glow of the lights rose and then faded again, and there was no cover . . . but Adam also didn't see guards. So they crept onwards, even though he now wondered if this was a waste of time—time that Lassair and Minori might desperately need from them—or, worse yet, if it was a dead end in which they could be trapped.

He held up a fist to stop Sigrun at the end of the passage, and peered into the dimly-lit room, his eyes widening. A few dim, bare bulbs, ley-powered, swayed at the ends of their chains, providing dim light with which to survey the scene. Monumental stonework, just like the walls of the fortress in Cuzco. The ancients had sunk their massive stones down deep, and had carved into the bedrock to do so. Pillars rose up to support the ceiling, and the weight of the *ushnu* itself, and a symbol had been traced on the floor, in what looked to be solid gold. A circle, surrounded by triangles . . . sun with rays. The symbol of Inti, the sun-god, used on the flag of Tawantinsuyu to this day. And in the center of that symbol was a very tall man, wearing nothing but a loincloth, his arms stretched out wide, bound by iron chains to the massive pillars on either side of him. He was emaciated, every rib visible and countable. But in the diffuse glow of the ley-powered lights, his body looked gilded, and reflected light, as if he were made of metal.

Adam's eyes went wide, and his fingers tightened on the musket in his hand. He'd felt that sense of *presence* before. The man's head rose, and his eyes opened, and the source of the periodic light that had come and gone was revealed, as golden fire blazed behind his lids, no orbs visible at all. The light flooded through the room, making it difficult to see the man's face. ***You are not of my children***, a voice spoke in Adam's mind. ***You are subject to others. Why are you here?*** The voice was powerful, but gentle, with a sense of nobility and suffering to it.

Adam swallowed through a dry throat, and hoped, fervently, that the word *godslayer* was not visible in his mind to this creature. Rationally, he knew that the entity was bound. Theologically, he knew that this wasn't *his* god—the creator of the heavens and the earth. This was a spirit. A very powerful spirit, but not *god*, as it were. That being said, he'd fought Tlaloc, his marriage had been conducted by *Tyr*, and he was now face-to-face with a chained being who inspired awe and pity, commingled. Questions were starting to crawl in the theological portion of *his* brain, and they were questions he'd be stupid not to ask at this point, but he'd prefer not to think them. Adam shook his head, rattling his brain back into place. He didn't have time for existential quandaries right now. He could consider this over a glass of Trennus' beloved *uisce beatha* some other time, could debate it with Kanmi and Trennus and Sig. If they survived, that is.

Sigrun had already stepped in, responding to the query. "We were taken prisoner," she told the god, her back straight and her chin raised. A valkyrie did not bow to a foreign god any more than a Judean did. "Both of us have been threatened with sacrifice by a god wearing a mortal form."

A low growl echoed through the chamber, a sound of anger and anguish at once. ***This should not be. We treated with the gods of Rome. We gave up human sacrifice. Told our followers, only animals, else all that we*** *had built together would be destroyed. I gave my oath to the gods of Rome, and was bound to them. Compromise, and peace.* He hung his head, closing his eyes, dimming the chamber once more. *And yet, this is my fault.*

Adam had never thought that *shame* was possible for a deity. Infallible, omnipotent, and omniscient, this one was not. He swallowed again, and asked, quietly, "What do you mean?"

Years ago, my human descendant called for me in the great temple of Cuzco. He was not a god-born, but all the brothers of his line had died, leaving him the only heir. He was an intelligent man, and cared for his people, and he told me that because he had no brothers, and was now first among all nobles, he was the Sapa Inca, my representative. And because he had no brothers, there was also no **Willaq Umu**. *High priest and field marshal, always a brother of the emperor. He asked me to allow him to be his own high priest, and I asked him, "But to whom will you turn for advice? You are mortal. You must expand your perspective with the wisdom of others."* The golden eyes opened. *I suggested Quehuar. One of my god-born, of a line distant to Sayri's. He refused. He told me that he had learned much of summoning and sorcery in Rome, and had many trusted advisors. His intentions seemed pure. He wanted to better his people. He wanted them to grow and thrive, and for the deserts to bloom. And tradition is only . . . a guide. Not a prison.*

Adam glanced around at the prison in which they now found themselves, feeling the irony as well as his own unease. He wasn't sure they had time for this. "But he trapped you here?" he asked, tentatively. "How could he possibly do *that*? How could he hide his heart from you?"

He masked himself. He wove a cloak of spirits around himself, for he feared assassination attempts, he told me, when I asked. It was true. There had been attempts. There was much unrest at his changes to the social order, but I saw no harm in the changes, and much possibility of good. The golden eyes closed again, leaving the room in near-darkness. *He came to my main temple, cloaked by his spirits, and told me that he was rebuilding the oracle here on Coropuna. He asked me to bless it, make it better. And when we walked under this place of offerings, I was trapped. There is power in the earth here, and this is my* symbol. *It . . . contains much belief, among my people. It is a focus for how they see me.* The god's head lowered again. *At first, I could not manifest. I was trapped, a presence without a body. Then they brought Quehuar to me. He could have challenged for rule of these lands, but had chosen not to do so. They bade me take his body, and I refused.* There was pain now in the god's voice. *In some ways, an avatar gives more power than merely manifesting. They become an additional conduit to this realm, empowered by the human's sacrifice of their body. But I was weakened by my captivity. I feared I would snuff out Quehuar's spirit. And an avatar becomes a weakness, if we value the mortal. And I valued Quehuar.*

In other words, if they care *about the human they're possessing, it becomes something that other people can threaten.* Adam shook his head. "So what happened?" he asked, having a bad feeling that he already knew.

After all, the god *was* physically present.

They shattered his head before me, as a blood-sacrifice, and threw his body into this binding place. Now, I ride his body as gently as I can. He is . . . aware . . . within, as I am aware, without. I healed him. They deprive his mortal body of food, so I must sustain him with my power. And in this body, trapped, and forced to sustain him . . . they draw on me with their machines, even more than before. Sustain a link between this and five other temples. They feed me with life energies and sacrifices, and drain it away just as quickly. My brother, Supay, conducts the sacrifices. Inti raised his head, and Adam could see tears of liquid fire run down his face. *I hold him here. I can reach out of this binding place just far enough to keep Supay here. Limit his growing power. But I know that some of the sacrifices have not been human. They have been gods. My sisters. My brothers. My children. Rendered down into raw energy. And to sustain myself, in the hopes of defeating them all . . . I have partaken. Else I would be burned out. Drained wholly, utterly. Unmade.*

Adam shook. The agony in the creature's voice was appalling. Shame. Rage. Humiliation. The vast spirit was being forced to cannibalize its own kind, its own family, in furtherance of whatever scheme the Sapa Inca and, apparently, Supay, had devised. "They're holding you here with ley-power," Sigrun said, quietly. "Power in the earth."

Yes. I can also feel essences not of this earth entwined with it. It is a complex working.

"The spirits trapped at Nazca," Adam muttered. "Their power, siphoned off to bind . . ." there wasn't much way around the word, so he just said it, "gods at each of the towers, and you, here. And your power is being used to contain the other gods, at the other temples?"

Yes. And some is being sunk into the earth itself. I am told that they wish to make the pampas bloom. Inti's voice was weary. *But that would take changing the entirety of the local climate, which would, in turn, change the climate elsewhere. Changing the essence of the soil. If our lands bloom, another land would turn to desert, unless the change is done carefully, and with skill and love.*

"Why not have made the change before now?" Adam asked, before he could stop himself. "Why not give your people a paradise?"

Because it is better for humans to have challenges. You are at your best when faced with adversity. You invent more, think more, dream more, in harsh conditions, than when surrounded with plenty and ease. Inti studied them both for a moment. *And because every father wishes to see his children grow to adulthood.*

It wasn't far from Adam's own feelings on religion. A guide to behavior, and a deity who expected humans to grow. Know right from wrong, but make their own decisions, their own way in the world, without having to ask for help to tie their shoes. His respect grew, unwillingly.

Sigrun inclined her head for a moment. "You remain powerful enough to bind Supay here?"

They are as bound by this system they have created as I am. They could reduce the amount of power they feed me, but then they might not be able to draw enough from me to maintain their machines. So I bind Supay, and they bind me, and I also bind others. Interlocking wheels, crafted by minds made of metal. A picture, suddenly, in Adam's mind, of gears and cogs. All grinding, possibly fruitlessly, towards some greater end. *But I believe they feed Supay, as well. He grows stronger. Harder to bind. And when the Sapa Inca has come before me of late, he, too, has been fed.*

Adam's mind reeled for a moment. "That's *possible?*" he demanded, not even realizing his tone. "He's taken the power of spirits into him?"

A spirit must have been forced into being a conduit, even as I am the conduit, the lens, for their great machine. He was a summoner and a sorcerer, after all, a mortal of great will and learning. He has fragments of gods within him now. They are not whole. They are barely aware. And they fight him for control of his body. I can see changes in him, every time he comes to me now. Perhaps he thinks that if he takes enough pieces into himself, he will achieve . . . equilibrium.

Sigrun's head had come up in horror. "Akhenaten," she blurted. "Akhenaten slew the gods of Egypt, or tried to. He effaced their names. He shattered their statues, when they were bound to them. And he drew their energies into himself, and he had a god as his . . . sponsor. . . Aten empowered him, at least somewhat. . . ."

Just like Sayri Cusi has Supay as his benefactor. "And went *mad*, and then a godslayer showed up to erase him." Adam rubbed at his face. "It's possible that the . . . pieces . . . inside of him could just tear him apart, right?"

Such has been my hope, but it may take years. Decades. I do not think this land has that much time.

"Can we release you?" Adam asked, after a moment. "If we do . . . we might be able to help one another."

"If Supay is the god with the red skin, black eyes, and fangs," Sigrun added, quietly, "he's the one proposing to sacrifice us. I would . . . very much appreciate assistance if he chooses to come for us."

That is he. And this seems a fair bargain.

Oh, please don't say that word. I'm treating with foreign gods. Then again, we've got people trapped here, a mad emperor, and we're separated from our protectee, and everything else.

Inti paused. *I will warn you . . . I have been weakened. I have been bound here for eight years, as best I can tell. It is hard to hear the world outside of these lines. I cannot see the sky. Cannot count the days, or feel the world turning. But it has been . . . a long durance.*

Adam gestured at the chains and the symbol. "All right. How do we release you?" He eyed the chains. "Those . . . hardly seem enough to hold a . . . an entity such as yourself . . . in place."

Sigrun kicked his ankle for the word *entity*. Inti turned his golden eyes towards Adam. *They are a humiliation. Supay placed them on me, himself. As a reminder of his ascendance. If the symbol at my feet is broken, and its connection to the machines and the spells are broken, then iron cannot bind me.*

Adam looked down at the thick gold, which had been poured into graven lines in the floor, grimaced, and set the barrel of his musket against the line. It was a solid two inches wide, and he had no idea how thickly the gold had been laid into the etched line on the floor. Pulling the trigger would definitely be audible; there were no doors between here and the entrance of the tunnel. *They didn't think he'd ever escape. Why put up doors and guards for someone who's so completely bound . . . and who, if he did escape, could simply slaughter the guards?* Adam's lips pulled downwards. "Are we ready to do this?" he muttered. "The instant this line goes down, they're going to know he's loose. Won't the rest of the g . . . entities in the towers . . . be freed the instant you release your hold on them, too?" For an instant, Adam pictured all of the brethren of this creature, flying to this mountaintop, and laying it waste with fire and lightning, and twitched. He really didn't want to be caught in that kind of crossfire. Ever.

I do not know. I know I bind each to each. I know that energy from the earth binds me. It may bind them, as well. The bindings will be weakened. Inti hesitated. *Also . . . I do not know what will happen if I release my bindings, all at once. They have told me, that if I were ever to hesitate, ever to struggle, that the workings are so intricate, that losing one cog will damage the entire machine. It is possible that the land might . . . twist . . . when the energies release.*

"Twist?" Sigrun said, sharply. "Like an earthquake?"

Like the one we just felt, yes. I wish to see my brethren freed. But not at the cost of the lives of our people.

Adam swallowed, and looked up at the ceiling. For an instant, he pictured the art history book Sigrun had purchased, years ago, with its images of the tomb of Nefertiti, and the death of Akhenaten pictured therein. The black beast that had come for the pharaoh's life had been crushed under tons of stone when the palace collapsed on it, leaving nothing but the gleam of yellow eyes in the darkness. *I might be a godslayer, but . . .* "We might have an emperor here intent on re-enacting the life of Akhenaten, but I would really prefer not to see quite the same ending here today."

I will attempt to loose the energies gradually. And I will not permit my rescuers to die in the attempt to save me.

Adam turned. Met Sigrun's gray eyes. And even as his finger tightened, he thought he could hear footsteps behind them. He swore internally, and pulled the trigger, the noise resounding cacophonously from the stone walls around them, stone chips spraying up from the floor at his face. He pulled the musket away, and verified that the gold now had a ball embedded it in, and was twisted and distorted in a circle around it. "Enough?" he asked, urgently.

Inti grimaced, and wrapped his fingers around the chains that bound him. Pulled. Snarled. Adam could see the chains themselves glow red-hot under the entity's *attention* . . . and then they stretched and *snapped,* sending glowing, broken fragments of links across the room. The god stepped forward, almost staggering, and Adam instinctively threw out a hand to steady him. Inti's form was well over eight feet in height . . . but

Adam could feel bone underneath the skin. No fat. Almost no muscle left, either. *If he leaves the body of his descendant now,* he thought, distantly, *the man will die. There's nothing left of him.*

And the instant Inti stepped out of the circle, the ground began to shake once more, dust and small pebbles raining down on them from above. Groaning, creaking noises in the earth. Adam swore, "*Harah!*" There was no exit beyond the way they'd entered. Sigrun handed him her confiscated musket, and lifted, instead, the iron bar she'd liberated as a makeshift spear, even as Inti raised his shaking hands, with manacles still wrapped around the wrists, and put his palms to the ceiling overhead. The trembling continued, but the roof *held,* and Adam was not about to quibble over the origin of that particular miracle.

The footsteps in the corridor had paused, and now hastened, directly for them. *Probably standard procedure to check on Inti here after an earthquake. Or, damn, after a prison break. We're lucky they didn't come in right on our heels.*

Adam hastily cocked the accursed musket, wishing, again for his own weapons, and ducked behind one of the pillars, aiming for the tunnel's open mouth.

Fewer than ten minutes before, the white sphere in which Kanmi, Trennus, Cocohuay, and Mamaquilla herself had leaped up into the sky, only to plummet back down towards the ground again at incredible velocity, had landed on the side of a mountain. Trennus shook for a good ten seconds after landing, trying to regain control of his limbs. "Where in Baal's name are we?" Kanmi asked, his tone more subdued than usual as he glanced at the tall figure of Mamaquilla.

Trennus' ears popped as the glowing walls of the sphere dissolved into mist around them. "Coropuna, I suppose. We're . . ." he closed his eyes and looked at the ley-lines around them. *Oh, gods, what a tangle.* "About five hundred miles southeast of the Nazca Lines. I can see pulses still rippling from there, to here. We're . . . shit." He paused, and swallowed. "This mountain's atop a bulge in the mantle, and it's upwelling."

"You got a line to tap into?" Kanmi's words were terse, clearly trying to ascertain what their assets and liabilities were.

"Yes . . . and no." Trennus' mouth was dry. "There's a nice strong one running northwest/southeast here, right at about the altitude where we're at." He stomped the ground underfoot in illustration.

"And?" Kanmi's impatience was clear.

"And it's in resonance with an intersecting line two miles under our feet, running directly through an upwelling surge from the mantle." Trennus flicked both hands, miming an explosion. "Volcano. Energy. Do the math."

"You're going to be a little subpar, is what I'm hearing?"

"Can't provide earthquakes on command, no." Trennus' voice was distracted, as he cast out his mind, reaching for Lassair. "I can do normal things, however."

Kanmi finished checking over his pistol, and pointed to the one that Trennus, reluctantly, now carried at his waist himself. Adam had *insisted* on firearms training for all of them. Trennus personally preferred a bow with solidly enchanted arrows, but he'd checked out on the Velserk .45, mostly to humor Adam, and to keep the request from becoming an order. He had to admit that it was quite a bit more concealable than a bow. He just *hated* the damned thing. But now he drew it, checked it, and took the safety off with a grim expression.

I still do not hear Inti. Mamaquilla's tone was oddly forlorn.

Trennus raised his head, and called out, *Flameheart! Lassair!*

Her immediate reply lightened his heart, but she was evidently in pain, and Trennus swore under his breath, and pointed to the northeast, up the hill. "That way. Asha's there. Minori's with her. She feels like she's been beaten, and she's worried about Minori—terribly worried." Though his words were steady, his mind had gone distant again, even as Lassair reassured him that she was fine, the baby was fine . . . *my captor is dead, but there are guards moving into the room, looking for him, asking why people have been blinded. The circle that binds me is . . . mostly intact. I think that they may decide to try to shoot me very shortly. There are spirits in the vicinity, incarnate ones. Creatures of fire and earth. I cannot affect them, but they are not in the room with us now. They . . . patrol. Also, I am trying to keep Truthsayer conscious*. Her tone became anguished, and she conveyed images, as well as words. *They have caused her great pain.*

Trennus rode along the wave of information, his stomach turning. "She says Min's been tortured for information," he passed along, tersely, as they jogged along a narrow, twisting path up the mountainside, their only light a tiny, glimmering white ball that Mamaquilla sent out ahead of them. The air tore at Trennus' lungs. They were well over two miles above sea-level, and he wasn't used to it.

Kanmi, following along behind him, tossed back, curtly, "Then I'm going to kill every motherfucking one of them that touched her."

They had a minute, maybe two, in which to prepare. Trennus called to Saraid in his mind. *The guards have guns. Can you protect me from the bullets?*

Of course I can. But I will need to overlap you. Prepare.

Trennus exhaled, and Saraid's evanescent self appeared, as a white stag, and passed through and into him, before his skin tingled. Tightened. He inhaled again, and looked down; a green shimmer, shifting from lighter to darker, like leaves on a wind-tossed tree, encompassed his skin, rendering the tattoos on his forearms dark shadows under a nimbus of paler light. He glanced up, and caught Kanmi staring at him.

"People are going to take one look at the antlers and the glow, and run screaming," the Carthaginian informed him. "She's never been that visible before when she's shielded you."

"Antlers?" Trennus reached up, and felt nothing. "I look like Cernunnos?" The horned god had many names, but generally related to virility, fecundity, and the wilderness.

"I'll get you a mirror later. Just don't be surprised if someone tries to take your head for a trophy."

"I'll try to persuade them otherwise." Trennus' voice was dry. "Are we ready?"

They hit the door of the tower slightly out of breath, but with spells already firmly in their minds . . . though Mamaquilla actually was the one who blinded the guards outside with a flash of white moonfire, and simply wrenched the locked door off its hinges with her bare hands. Trennus had an impression of flashes of muzzle-fire, red-yellow sparks, and *impact*, but Saraid's shield caught the incoming bullets and dissipated their energy. His ribs and sternum might be bruised, but he'd live. He caught a glimpse of Lassair, curled on the floor in a fetal ball, her arms over her head as she tried to make herself less of a target, and a woman inexplicably in a wheelchair positioned outside of her circle. Past her, a huge man, with stone-colored skin sat on the floor, unmoving, and apparently oblivious to the firefight raging over his head.

Trennus' first consideration wasn't actually returning fire immediately. It was securing the hostages. He did fire a couple of rounds, to force the guards, reloading their muskets, to keep their heads down, and then pulled, delicately, at the ambient ley-energy, not tapping the lines directly. Step one, pull up the stone around Lassair into a half-shell, giving her cover . . . which simultaneously destroyed the circle that bound her. *You're free*, he told her, *but stay down till we've dealt with the guards.*

Most of the guards threw down their weapons as Mamaquilla entered the room. Even in the dim red glow of the emergency lights, they obviously knew who she was, and dropped to their knees. One of them, clearly a summoner, panicked and drew a protective circle around his feet . . . causing the goddess to turn and regard him with a baleful white gaze . . . and Kanmi laughed, harshly, and fired his pistol at the man, even as he continued to incant charms to protect himself. Kanmi's aim was true, and the summoner dropped to the ground, his chest a bleeding mass.

Once the room was secure, Trennus moved to Lassair, picking her up from the ground and cradling her tightly, feeling her arms snake around him, in turn. The woman in the wheelchair he glanced at, but disregarded for the moment. "Are you all right?" he asked her. He already knew she was, but he had to hear the words. Had to reassure himself, as he smelled the rose-and-smoke of her hair, felt the warmth of her skin.

Yes. Much better for your presence. Relief. Gratitude. Love. *But . . . Truthsayer. She fades!*

Kanmi was already moving towards the door Lassair indicated. He was dimly aware of the various guards on the floor, bowing before an angry Mamaquilla, and he flashed back, briefly, to the fate of the guards at Nazca, scalded by boiling groundwater and then drowned and encased in mud. He wondered, distantly, if any of these men would live out the day.

He doubted it.

Trennus, behind him, called, "Need help?"

"No." Kanmi replied, tersely. *If anyone is still in there, alive, and able to hide from Lassair? They're fucking _dead_.*

Kanmi kicked open the door, holding his pistol in one hand, and all the accumulated heat he'd pulled from the smoking Tholberg coils and the red-hot stone around Lassair's feet wrapped around his other fist, warping the air, but otherwise invisible. The room beyond was only dimly lit, and he saw, first, a crumpled body on the floor. A table, past it . . . and Minori was strapped to it. Kanmi incanted, softly, for light, and a spark of it appeared overhead, giving him enough illumination to clear the room. Then he holstered his pistol and released the heat back into the ambient air. Made sure the body on the floor was dead before stepping over it, and felt *something* hit his shields as Minori raised a hand. He caught her fingers, saying, quickly, "It's me! It's me, Min, it's just me, shhhh." *Oh, gods.* Seeing her like this, her hands and feet purple from the constricted blood-flow, limp, her lips and eyes puffy and swollen, made his stomach twist, but he couldn't see any actual *wounds.* "Gods, I am so sorry. We promised we'd protect you. I swore I'd take care of you." *And look what these bastards have done to you.*

He started by unshackling her, and tried to help her sit up . . . and was rewarded by a low cry of agony. Kanmi froze and started using his other senses, running his hands along her arms and legs, first, checking for breaks. "Not . . . not there . . ." Minori mumbled. "All . . . internal organs . . . . He moved them. Twisted them."

Oh, fucking Astarte. Kanmi checked her pulse, which was weak, and her skin was clammy. Shock. He lifted her feet, and put his hands on her, wrapping her in warmth with a spell. "You're going to be all right, Min," he told her, simply, keeping his voice calm. "Bastard who did this is dead?"

"Killed him . . . myself." She opened her dark eyes, and managed to focus on him. "Air bubble . . . bloodstream. Embolism. Not . . . traditional."

He registered that with a blink. Understood what it meant. "A crying shame I didn't get here earlier." Kanmi knew his face must have shifted. "Your way took far too little time. I'd have turned his bones to *powder* for this, Min. And I'd have helped you stand up so you could put a foot on his throat while he suffocated to death under his own weight."

". . . you . . . really . . . know what to say . . . to reach . . . a woman's . . . heart."

"Yes, that's me. Smooth-talker." Kanmi didn't stop wrapping warmth around her, like a cocoon. Moving her seemed deeply inadvisable. She had internal bleeding, at the very least. Instead, he turned and called out the door, trying not to sound panicked, "Cocohuay! If you would, please?"

The god-born woman left her goddess, and moved to the smaller side office in which Minori had been tortured. Her luminous eyes widened as she took in the scene. "How can I help?" she asked, immediately, as Kanmi gestured to Minori's prone form.

"You healed the guards at the tower in Nazca," Kanmi said, bluntly. "We need Min here able to move. I won't leave her here like this while we go off looking for the rest of our team. There's no way to secure this place, and I won't risk her and Asha being captured again."

Cocohuay's lined face crinkled. "Those were cauterized wounds and freeze-burns. I can try." She stepped forward, and put a gentle hand on Minori's arm, and murmured something fervent and under her breath in Quecha. Kanmi didn't need to be fluent to understand, *oh, by the gods*. It was all in the tone.

A gentle blue-green radiance spread from her hands, and Minori gasped, wrapping a hand around Kanmi's wrist, clutching him tightly. Kanmi didn't move. Just let her hold on, as every muscle in her body tightened. It wasn't unlike having watched Bastet in childbirth . . . but this seemed far worse. There would be nothing to *show* for all this pain. Finally, Cocohuay exhaled, explosively. "That is all I can manage," the older woman said, sounding tired.

"Thank you," Kanmi told her, simply, and put his free hand to Minori's hair, feeling her body relax a little. "Better?"

"Hurts less." Her voice was still low and raspy. She'd obviously done more than a little screaming, and Kanmi's heart twisted. "Better, yes." She looked at Cocohuay. "Thank you."

"Can you stand?" Kanmi asked her. Part of him wanted to pick her up and carry her out of here, but it was probably important for her to be able to walk out of this room on her own two feet.

"Not . . . not sure."

"Try. Please. If you can stand, you can *walk* out of here. You leave his body in the dirt, and spit on him if you want to in passing, but you don't let him win, even a little bit." Kanmi's tone was fierce. *I didn't know you were this much of a fighter, doctor.* "I won't let you fall, Min, but if you can . . . walk out of here."

Minori groaned and let him help her sit up. Slipped her feet to the floor, where broken glass crunched under her shoes, and staggered. Kanmi wrapped an arm around her waist and pulled her arm over his shoulders. Only three inches separated their heights; this was easy. And so he steadied her as she emerged from the room, and he met Trennus' and Lassair's gaze from the south side of the tower. "Let's get these two ladies to an ornithopter," Kanmi said. "Then we can go after the rest of the team. And anyone else around here in need of rescue." He looked down at Minori. "Though you two pretty much rescued yourselves." He settled her down on one of the nearby workbenches, and found there, much to his surprise, weapons. Minori's small derringer. Ben Maor's two pistols, still in their holsters, ammunition clips, and Caetia's spear. *Must have brought their weapons here to study the spells I put on the bullets and the spear, and what Min put on her own ammo.* Kanmi wasn't aware that he'd shifted to thinking of Dr. Sasaki by her first name, now. He just made sure she was able to sit there, comfortably, as he took possession of his teammates' weapons . . . and handed her her own pistol once more, too.

Mamaquilla had turned away from the human guards, and was now studying the god in the center of the triangular binding at the heart of the tower. *Apu?* she said, softly. *Apu, Lord of the High Places, mountain's king, hear me!*

The creature at the center of the binding didn't move. Didn't look at her. He remained, listless and limp, precisely where he had been.

"Should I free him?" Trennus asked, his voice a little apprehensive. "I don't know what will happen if I do. I had an hour to look through the seismology in Nazca, and this mountain seems a little more active than I like out of a volcano at the moment."

No. Wait. He is unresponsive. Releasing him now . . . we will need time to draw him back from where he has gone. Mamaquilla sounded sorrowful. *He has given in to despair.*

At that moment, the tower and the ground *shook*, violently. "Not me this time!" Trennus shouted. "That's coming from at least two miles down."

Mamaquilla's head snapped up. *Inti!* she cried, her tone joyous, and then horrified. *What has become of you, beloved?*

No audible reply, but the goddess looked somehow stunned. *We must go to him. Now. Your friends are with my brother-husband. And Supay comes for them.*

"Stay here," Trennus told Lassair.

"No!" Kanmi snapped out. "Not secure—"

No, Lassair said, sharply. *I will go with you. I will fight for Stormborn and Steelsoul, as best I can. I will not be separated from you again.*

"I'm coming, too," Minori whispered.

Kanmi turned back, an objection ready on his lips. She was a civilian. She was *hurt*, gods damn it all. Minori met his gaze, and, hands shaking, began to load her derringer. In spite of himself, the words died on his lips.

"I owe these people," she said, softly, but determination clear in her expression. "I owe them vengeance."

Yes . . . you sort of do, don't you? But while he liked her spirit, it was her body he was worried about. On the other hand, they couldn't take the time to evacuate the two of them, and this tower wasn't safe. It took him seconds to make the decision, and he didn't know if it was the right one. But not to choose was *always* the wrong course of action. "You're with me," he told her. "Don't point that gun near any of us. That's going to be your last resort. You're all right to cast spells?"

"Yes." Her eyes narrowed.

"Stick with that. Your aim will be better." He squeezed her shoulder, very gently. "Stay behind me. You've never been in real combat before." *Then again, we're looking to go free a god. Or attack him for doing . . . all of this. Tlaloc was one thing. This . . . .* "We're heading into an almost entirely unknown situation with a lot of variables." Kanmi looked around. "Let's go."

He was carrying ben Maor's and Caetia's weapons for them. He wanted to make damned sure all their teammates were *armed* when he found them. The more so, because he had no idea what was going on, who precisely was involved in all of this. He didn't have all the pieces of the puzzle, he knew it, and it made him twitch. And then the weapons dissolved, the weight of the gun belts over his neck and the weight of the spear on his shoulder simply vanishing. Kanmi stared at his empty hands in consternation, and blurted, "How . . . what?" His own gun remained at his waist, in its holster. He hadn't been disarmed.

Lassair answered, *I believe Inti took them. I felt a power reach for them, and pass them into the Veil. It is faster for spirits to move through the Veil than through ordinary matter. There is no time in the Veil. Physicality doesn't matter as much there, either.*

All right, if that's the case, why didn't Mamaquilla just take us through the Veil to get us here faster? Kanmi demanded in his mind.

There is no time in the Veil. There isn't even dimensionality, as you experience it. Lassair's tone was grim. *I do not know what would happen to a normal human pulled through the Veil. The Odinhall, for example, uses interventions to allow humans to perceive it.*

Kanmi, still jogging, each step jolting through his frame, decided to think about that one later. The implications made his mind reel too much right now.

Under the *ushnu*, Adam and Sigrun had moved to opposite sides of the room, each taking a pillar for cover. Adam, still aiming at the tunnel entrance with his pitiful musket, tried to urge Inti into cover as well, but the emaciated *entity* was still heavily occupied with trying to keep the ceiling stable above their heads. Adam ducked around his pillar and peered out, his eyes widening as he took in the figures approaching.

Two of the rock creatures flanked the Sapa Inca, Sayri Cusi, like bodyguards; the hulking creatures were twice the size of the emperor himself, and the human bodyguards who trailed along behind the creatures looked dwarfed in comparison. And behind them? The vast, red-and-white creature that Inti had called Supay, the god of death. *There has to be a reason Supay's involved. I can't imagine that he's at all interested in watching the nation bloom. Whatever Tren has to say about death and fertility always going together . . . oh, harah. I'm speculating as to the motives of gods.*

Flanking Supay were eight tiny creatures, no more than four feet in height, which also looked to be made from the rock itself. But while whenever the giants moved, their rocky outer carapace split and showed a red-hot core, these smaller creatures were cool and gray, hard to see in the dim light of the lanterns that the human guards carried. Their eyes caught that light, however, with gem-like sheens, though their faces were vaguely rat-like, with pronounced fangs, and their three-fingered hands held long, wicked claws the length of a sloth's. *So, those would be the supay, the spirits that Tren said were subject to their lord, Supay himself. Harah.* "That's . . . a lot of bodies. And here I am, with one bullet," Adam muttered.

Sayri Cusi lifted a hand. "Is this how you repay my hospitality?" he asked, looking at Inti, his head cocked to the side, with that oddly girlish tone in his voice again. "You should not have left the circle, Lord of the Sun and Skies. You will cause great damage to the Land of the Four Quarters. And all out of . . . selfishness? Pride?" The honeyed words had a twisting, manipulative edge to them, and Inti, weakened as he was, swayed under their force. "Return to the circle, my lord. Let us continue to make our land bloom. Let us bring our people out of darkness."

This time, Adam had an inkling of what was going on. *God-fragment. Rather, a goddess-fragment. Probably one who was at least as charming as Lassair on her best days. He's using her power . . . but there might be enough of her left that he's . . . channeling how she might have spoken. But why would he have taken a goddess into him?* Adam again flashed to the book of Egyptian art, in which it had been mentioned that Akhenaten had had himself depicted with both male and female attributes. Beasts and a beard, for example. *The union of opposites, like yin and yang, embodied in one figure, like Aphroditus, but . . . incorrectly done. Aphroditus, for his/her adherents, is the divine figure of boundless creation. All the Sapa Inca's works are . . . fruitless.*

Sigrun, across the way, had surely followed the same trail of thought, and spoke now, her voice as harsh as a raven's call in the wake of all that honey. "In eight years," she said, bluntly, "your pampas have not bloomed. You can take the power of a dozen more gods. You can pour out the lives of a hundred, a thousand more humans on the ground. It won't bloom any more in ten years than it has so far."

Sayri Cusi hissed at her, "Silence, you whey-faced bitch!" as his various guards dropped their lanterns on the floor, and unshouldered their muskets.

Undeterred, Sigrun went on, from the cover of her pillar, "If you bury a live electrical wire in the ground, it does not make the ground bloom. Pouring energy into the earth will not make it fertile. You have power, Sapa Inca. Great power. But you have no idea how to wield it. You are like a man who has been given a fine sword, and tries to kill the ocean with it."

Silence. This time, the word came from the red-and-white, grinning creature in the mouth of the tunnel.

"You cannot silence truth," Sigrun shot back, and Adam could see his wife's face. He knew the tightness of her lips, the tension in her shoulders, and the glimmer of rune-fire under her skin. Sigrun was terrified, but giving words their due. Words always came first. This was probably going to end in their deaths, but she was trying to stall. Trying to give Inti time to recover.

Inti now lowered his hands from the ceiling, where he'd stood all this time like Atlas, holding up the world. The gods glanced at Adam and Sigrun. *I know the truth when I hear it, Sayri Cusi. Your intentions were pure when you first came to me, but they have been corrupted. I will not treat with you. You have given up that right.*

"You cannot treat me with such contempt," the Sapa Inca growled, his voice, for the moment, apparently, his own. "I have more power now than you can imagine, Lord of the Skies. I am a god now, myself. I am your equal. No. I am your *lord.*"

Borrowed raiment does not make you any more than a child crying out "Look at me! Look at me!" A costume demeans the one wearing it. A lie with no substance to it. Like this child of the northern gods . . . I prefer truth.

The Sapa Inca's head rocked back at the god's rebuke. Adam was awed. Inti wasn't using power. He was simply using *words*. Adam shook his head. *This is what a god should be. Altering ideas and perceptions with truth and ideas.*

"No *substance?*" Sayri Cusi hissed, and his hands blazed with blue-white light. Levinbolts streaked out from him, slamming into Inti, who actually took a half a step back, grunting in pain. Sigrun burst out of cover, taking two or three shots from the various bodyguards, and flew directly in front of Inti, taking the rest of the electricity directly to her own body, the pure white of her rune-marks blazing in the darkness. She was a living lightning rod; Adam had seen her accidentally damage a calculator just by *touching* the damned thing.

For his part, Adam took advantage of the distraction she offered, spinning out of cover to fire his single bullet at the emperor of a sovereign nation. *I can't be in any more trouble than I am already . . . .* He saw the shot slam into the emperor's side, and the man took a step back now, his head turning towards Adam . . . . but when he reached down and touched his side, there was no blood there. He laughed now, a dark, rough sound, like rocks grating on one another. "I am the master of earth and sky now, the world above and the world below. I hold the power of life and death within me. I *am* a god, more truly than any of my ancestors. You challenge me, mortal?" Sayri Cusi smiled, a merry, fey little smile, suddenly coquettish again. "Then you can just *die.*"

The pillar behind which Adam had taken cover shattered, and the huge blocks of which it was comprised toppled backwards, as if pushed by an unseen hand. Adam threw himself backwards scrambling away like a crab. Time slowed as adrenaline pounded through his system, and through his panic, he knew he couldn't move away in time. Even if the pillar didn't kill him, the ceiling would collapse on his head . . . .

. . .and Inti reached out a hand and the pillar blocks simply *stopped* in place. The upper blocks hung in mid-air, motionless; the lower blocks, still tipped past the incline of repose, looked like nothing so much as a child's slide. Adam swore again, silently, and scrambled back, still further, feeling the cold, rough stone of the floor against his palms. Comforting sense of reality, with it.

He'd have felt a good deal better, however, if Inti's enormous voice hadn't sounded quite so strained as the god next spoke. *These two are my champions, as are any others who choose to fight on my behalf. I stand against you. I will not permit any more harm to come to my land and my people. I have been trapped, in a snare at least partially of my own making. But no more.* Inti's head turned towards Adam slightly. *You had weapons when you came here. Be armed once more.*

Adam had, reflexively, dropped the useless musket when he'd thrown himself away from the pillar. Now, as he stood, he found the comforting weight of his Velserk pistol in his grip, and ahead of him, he could see that Sigrun had a holster wrapped around her waist once more, and her hands gripped the haft of her spear, where she stood between Sayri and Inti. Adam found another pillar to stand behind, grimly aware that cover could be turned into a weapon against him in this fight. *The odds aren't much better now, but at least I'll die with a weapon in my hands,* he thought, numbly.

Supay bared his fangs, his mouth stretching and distorting that brick-red face with the white eyes painted all over the skin. ***You are unarmed, brother. Today, I will become the new king of the gods.*** He raised the massive obsidian club he bore, and stepped forwards, with slow deliberation, pushing past the Sapa Inca.

Oh, and now I have a motive that even my feeble human brain can grasp. Power. Control. That's an easy one. Adam raised his gun.

Inti lifted one hand, and responded, calmly, ***I am unarmed, brother. But I am not alone. Away with your vaunted darkness. Let there be light.***

Adam turned his face away, closing his eyes as Inti's entire form burst into glory; he didn't dare look into that blaze, any more than into the heart of the sun. It dimmed Sigrun's light into that of the distant stars, and Adam could feel searing heat come out of Inti's form, in waves. There was no darkness, anywhere in the room now; even the shadows behind the pillars were filled with that unearthly glow. ***Will you challenge me, brother? Will you, truly?***

The death-god bared his fangs and leaped forward, swinging that massive club, and to Adam's sick horror, Sigrun threw herself in between, like the champion Inti had named her. She flew forwards, ducking under the overhand swing of the club, and jabbed the point of her spear at Supay's throat. To Adam's surprise, the blow connected; though the god turned his face aside at the last moment, her spear sliced through his cheek, opening a new mouth between the various eyes. Adam had rarely seen Sigrun use her full speed in sparring; she pivoted now, before Supay could react, whirling the spear in her hands, slamming the butt of it against his head, so far above her own. There was little difference between a staff form and a spear form, really, and Sigrun's style was all about *speed.* Not being there when an opponent turned on her. Another swirl of the spear in her hands, and the point was back in place, slashing into Supay's back from above.

The death-god snarled, black blood flowing from his cheek, and spun on her, swinging his sacrificial club in a lateral arc, aiming for the valkyrie's ribs, and Sigrun rolled to the floor, changing levels, and only one of her feet tagged by the vicious strike as a result.

As she tried to regain her footing, Adam raised his gun and fired directly on Supay. He rather hoped Kanmi's handiwork on the bullets would let him have *some* kind of effect on the god; bare bullets hadn't done a damn bit of good with Tlaloc, after all. But he wasn't surprised to hear the sound of a ricochet, either. *Sig isn't particularly mortal,* Adam thought, grimly. *But I am. Guess I'm in charge of keeping the rest of these creatures off her back.* The thought took less than a heartbeat, and then he'd turned and fired, once more, this time on Sayri Cusi.

The Sapa Inca staggered backwards, but there was no blood. Still, the momentary look of panic on the emperor's face did Adam's heart good

. . . and then the two massive creatures made of rock stepped forwards, forming a protective wall between Cusi and Adam, and the human guards, looking panicky, moved forwards — the ones who hadn't been caught trying to reload their weapons, anyway. Musket balls clattered against the closest pillar as Adam ducked behind it.

The huge rock creatures had glowing-coal eyes, which now focused on him as the spirits turned to face him . . . and he knew he'd better make his shots count. All the little demons, gray-skinned and gem-eyed, hissed and moved to their master's defense. They were small and they were quick, and they ran in a wave, right for Sigrun's back.

For Sigrun, there was nothing in her mind but defiance and fear. She *knew* there was no way in which she could defeat Supay. This was not Tlaloc. This was not a weakened god, drained by men and machines. This was a god bloated on blood and sacrifice, like a tick or a leech. She'd gotten in a few lucky hits, but looking up into the god's eyes, she could feel darkness and dissolution radiating out of him. No hope. Nothingness. The destruction of all things. She would die here, and there would be nothing after. No reunion with her gods. No Valhalla. No Adam. No consciousness. She would go out, like a candle, and for nothing, she'd *be* nothing

The despair moved over her in suffocating waves, and Sigrun's hand slipped on her spear. Nothing but nacreous blackness in Supay's eyes, and oddly, in spite of everything . . . it was seductive. No more fighting. No more struggling. No peace, but also, no more war. *No,* Sigrun managed to think. *No. Others rely on me. I do not just fight for myself. I fight for Adam. I fight for Livorus. I fight for my gods and my people.*

The struggle inside her mind had taken less than two heartbeats, and she managed to raise her spear again, as if against the force of three times normal gravity . . . and then Adam shouted, "Sig! Behind you!" and *something* landed on her shoulders, digging in with razory claws, and Supay took advantage of her shock to slam her in the side of the head with his club, slamming her to the ground. Then claws. Claws and hands and teeth, everywhere, and Sigrun fought. She landed on her side and rolled to her back, feeling a body, clinging to her tenaciously, like a monkey. Heard the mad screams and chitters as three more *supay* landed atop her. She fended the first away from her vulnerable eyes, backhanding the creature away, but the one still clinging to her back had dug in with its teeth and now pulled back, ripping and tearing. Sigrun choked down the scream, feeling blood pouring down from the wound, and kicked away a third gem-eyed creature as it darted in, slashing at her belly with its claws. The fourth fell away from her, its face a ruin, as Adam fired a round into its head, and Sigrun's heart, already pounding, increased its pace. That bullet had passed right above her head.

She rolled over, reaching back with her left hand, and tried to drag the monkey-like creature off her back, but she could feel talons digging into her hips from its feet, more talons hooking into her arms for better purchase, and then it was trying to bite at her throat, going for the carotid artery this time. Sigrun jammed stiffened fingers back, gouging at the eyes . . . with no effect, as they were made of the same stone as the rest of the creature's body. Fruitlessly, she tried to call down lightning. She couldn't, of course; the stone roof cut her off from the sky. *This is the Pyramid of the Sun all over again,* Sigrun thought, dimly, and finally hooked her fingers under the line of its moving, biting jaw, and pulled, hard, throwing herself forward at the same time, so that the small creature rolled off her shoulder, and she slammed its head into the ground. Stone against stone; it sprang up, almost unscathed, and came right back at her, Sigrun catching it once more by the throat and holding out at arm's length, even as its stone talons slashed at her left forearm, raking deeply. She called her spear to her hand, and, holding the *supay* off the ground, sank the point into its eye. Past the gem-like surface, the flesh gave way easily enough. "They are flesh beneath the stone!" Sigrun shouted. "But they will not die while in contact with the earth, I think!' With that in mind, she threw her current target to the ground, and the other two latched onto her legs, biting and clawing. She could feel blood pouring down from her shoulder, from the gobbet of flesh the first one had removed, and jabbed at the two currently attached to her legs. They hadn't caught the femoral artery yet, but that was just a matter of time, and she could bleed out from that faster than her body could heal the damage.

While Sigrun was scrambling on the floor with four of the little demons, Supay closed on Inti himself, and the sun-god caught the obsidian club in his golden hands as Supay swung it at him. Adam swore, again, because the instant Supay swung at Inti, the sun-god's blazing light went out, leaving them with nothing more than the glimmer of ley-powered bulbs and dozens of afterimages clouding his vision. He could barely make out the two titanic figures as they wrestled for control of the weapon, and felt worse than useless as he squinted, found a target in one of the little demons, and fired again. He felt the ground under his feet shift, and he leaped out of the way, ducking and rolling, and, as he came back up again, he saw an enormous hand made of stone had just snapped its fingers closed where he had just stood. *Sayri Cusi,* Adam thought. *The emperor's still very much in this fight. Damn it. We need help. We need a _lot_ of help.*

Outside, the others ran in Mamaquilla's wake. The goddess had assumed a form that looked like pale moonlight cutting through fog, and streamed ahead of them through the empty air, racing to the side of her brother and husband, Inti. Kanmi kept a steadying hand under Minori's elbow as they jogged, a litany of curses going through his mind. *This is stupid. She had internal injuries before Cocohuay worked her healing. She's grunting with every step.* "You're going to jostle something loose," Kanmi snapped at Minori. He wasn't angry with her. He was angry with absolutely *everything* else.

"I'm fine," Minori gritted out. "Keep . . . going . . . ."

They rounded the corner of a long, tiered building, which looked like nothing so much as a very fancy cake, to Kanmi's eyes, and followed the ghost-pale form of Mamaquilla as she blurred forwards, and down into a tunnel entrance, a hundred feet or more ahead of them. "Nothing like directions," Kanmi muttered, between pants. He was in damned good shape . . . at sea level. Two miles above it? He had an unaccustomed stitch in his side. At the entrance to the tunnel, he stopped everyone, however. "Cocohuay," Kanmi asked, sharply. "What can you do in combat? Fire arrows of moonlight, falling stars, anything?"

The older woman, who'd brought up the rear, and now stood, panting and wheezing, raised her head. "Nothing like that," she said, shaking her head. "My lady is not a warlike goddess."

Trennus, the dappled green spirit-armor of Saraid swirling around him like leaves in a storm, antlers sprouting from his head and twined with what looked like phosphorescent ivy, turned his head towards her. "What *can* you do?" the Pict asked, frowning. Kanmi choked back any ribald jokes about Trennus wearing horns. Technically, antlers weren't horns, and he liked his teeth where they were. Besides, now *really* wasn't the time.

"In two hundred years in her service, I have driven fish to the nets, kept the waves gentle and mild for sailors, and eased the danger and rigor of childbirth for hundreds of women." Cocohuay sounded irritated. "I can heal, as I did your friend, but I have never held a weapon in my life."

"Wonderful." Kanmi gritted his teeth. "Stay at the *back*. Stay in cover. If you need to touch someone to heal them, wait for one of us to come get you. Gods. This isn't going to be one of the good days."

"Have we had a good day *yet*?" Trennus asked. For an instant, Kanmi thought he could see an ethereal stag's face in front of the Pict's own, and shook his head in reply, bringing his defensive incantations to mind.

They moved down into the tunnel, and Kanmi could see a sun-bright gleam ahead of them in the darkness, and they all began to hustle forward . . . and then it went out, entirely. Mamaquilla's voice, crying out in anguish. ***Inti! Beloved! I am here! I will fight by your side!*** Her fog-like essence was one of the few sources of light as they stumbled forward, and Kanmi gestured for the others to halt as they came to the edge of the tunnel. He could feel Minori pressed up behind him, the chill air of her shields against his back. And as he looked into the battle area, Kanmi couldn't tell friend from foe in the swirling mass of bodies.

Look through my eyes, Lassair urged them all, her voice terrified, but strong, as she hugged the wall behind Trennus. *See as I see.*

Kanmi sucked in his breath as the spirit's perceptions overlaid his own. He already could perceive energies, but he never associated that sense with his eyes; it was more of a pressure against his skin. But now, there was no more darkness, just swirling fields of different types.

At the center of the room, a figure outlined in golden fire that blazed like the sun, circling, moving, grappling, with something. An *absence.* A void. *I'm looking at a black hole,* Kanmi realized, mildly horrified. *Entropy incarnate.* It was only discernable in Lassair's vision by the fact that it blocked out the sight of other beings behind it, and because it drew energy from everything around it, spiderlike strands of power being sucked in from everyone in the room, even from the blazing golden glory that was, surely, Inti the sun-god. Inti himself had golden streamers of light pouring out of him in every direction. Some being pulled into that black pit of entropy that occasionally resolved itself into a vaguely man-like form. Some being pulled out in five or six different directions . . . *towards the binding seals around the other towers,* Lassair whispered to them all, in explanation. *He maintains them, still, for fear of what will happen if all are loosed suddenly.* And some of his power rose upwards, spreading along the ceiling like a golden veil of flame. Holding the ceiling up, preventing it from being pulled down on all these fragile mortal forms.

Kanmi took in the rest of the figures in seconds. Mamaquilla's shimmering white light over a core of blue-green surged forward, trying to reach the sun-god at the center of the room. Massive creatures of flame and earth turned and attacked her, fire blazing out of their hands. Elementals. *Cherufes,* Lassair, specified.

Smaller creatures, also mostly of stone, but linked to the death-god through tendrils of black, wavering smoke . . . *supay.* Humans, gray, dim, terrified. A creature that twisted and distorted, making his head ache to look at . . . a vaguely human outline of gray fog, but inside of it, encysted, were . . . formations of light. Like crystals, intruded into the matrix of a rock formation. One looked like a chunk of gray metal, the second cyst looked to be formed entirely of lightning, and the third cyst was comprised of an orb of golden light, which, blister-like, burst for a moment, coruscating out. Trying to spread, like a disease, rippling over the body, only to hit the other two cysts, and be repulsed. *That one is the lord of this land,* Lassair whispered.

Gods. You don't mean that's the <u>fucking emperor</u>? This isn't going to be a good day at <u>all</u>.

And there, fighting with the damnable little creatures, was a female form comprised of blue-white fire surrounded by veils of fog, and at the very back, ducking out from behind a pillar . . . the shining silver form of a man. "We found our lost goats," Kanmi said, his voice sounding very small in his own ears, and trying for a little bluster. "Let's get them home. "

His own vision returned, briefly, as Mamaquilla flooded the room with her own white light. The goddess threw one of the massive stone creatures away from her with little more than a flick of her hand, but the other snarled and vomited lava directly in her face. It wrapped its arms around her, its entire body going from rock to magma in an instant, and tried to crush the female form it held to the ground. It hit, but Mamaquilla shifted to her moonlight form and danced away, flowing forward, trying to engage with the darkness that was Supay. *<u>We have always been stronger together, Inti, my love! Take of my power, and be renewed.</u>* Love and longing in that beautiful voice, the silvery hiss of waves lapping the shore. The sound Kanmi had loved and feared all his life.

<u>No! If I take of your power, it will flow through the entire great</u>

machine. The entirety will be unbalanced, and you may be as trapped as I am!

No time to watch, to listen to wonders. Kanmi heard Caetia shout, again, that the _supay_ could only be killed once lifted free of their native earth, even as the valkyrie threw one of the creatures into the air, ducking back down again, to allow ben Maor to shoot it, catching it like a bird on the wing. He saw Trennus push Lassair back against the wall, and lift a hand; the earth around their feet carved itself and smoothed itself into the unbroken loops and whorls of a very large protection circle. "Stay in the circle!" Trennus shouted across to Kanmi and Minori. "Should keep the spirits out. Won't help with the humans, though!"

Then Trennus, disregarding his own advice, slipped out into the main room, circling around to the north, trying to get to ben Maor, and give their friend backup, as four more of the damned _supay_ rose up out of the earth, between Adam and Sigrun. The human guards to the north, spinning, realizing that they now had enemies on all sides, and a full-scale conflict between gods in front of them, fired wildly at Trennus, the bullets bouncing off the man's shields. The human guards to the south, and the _supay_ still positioned there, turned towards the mouth of the tunnel, facing Kanmi. And then Kanmi lost his ability to keep track of the entirety of the battlefield, and he rapidly began to incant. Distorting gravity was the single hardest skill Kanmi had ever learned. He couldn't manage more than one creature at a time, and no more than about two hundred pounds of mass at one g. As the rat-like, monkey-like _supay_ skittered towards him, Kanmi thought, _No. Not the ahuizotl and Tlaloc all over again,_ and yanked the closest up into the air, aiming with his pistol and firing. He didn't want to waste the energy or the concentration to use magic both to hold it up, and to kill it.

"Lift," Minori urged behind him, pressing closer. "I'll kill!"

They're about to hit Tren's barrier, Kanmi thought, but lifted the second as the creatures continued to charge, and watched in a kind of delighted awe as Minori took the air in the room, turned a thin slice of it to solid state, and lashed out with it, like a flying sword. Exquisitely controlled, like the reed sword she'd used in demonstrating her kendo skills, the blade of ice froze the rock hide of the creature as it struck. A secondary blade, this one comprised of the raw heat that she'd removed from the air in order to create the ice blade, whirled in the first's wake. Cold and then heat, rapid expansion. Artistry in the incantations, too.

The rock hide shattered, and the heat blade, invisible but deadly, continued right through into the neck, taking off the creature's head. "You didn't _tell_ me you could cast like this!" Kanmi shouted, and then, catching sight of the men beyond the monsters raising their muskets, he incanted, rapidly pulling up a wall of dry ice in front of them, holding it in place with raw will as the two _supay_ closest to them leaped into the air, trying to climb over the wall before he could build it to the ceiling. Bullets from the muskets of the other guards slammed into its surface, spidering cracks all along it. He hadn't been able to build it thick enough before they'd opened their fusillade, and he could see the dark forms of the _supay_, clambering up the wall, shadows outlined by the white glow coming from Mamaquilla herself.

"You didn't *ask*," Minori reminded him, tartly. "You didn't even want to test my skills, because at a certain level, almost every spell can be deadly."

"I take it all back," Kanmi told her, balancing an equation in his mind. "Shield us!"

All the energy he'd pulled out of the air to build his shield wall, he now redirected, in the form of tiny orbs of flame, sending them through the cracked wall, directly at the shadows of the *supay*. The dry ice shattered, parts of it subliming away, and the bullets formed of heat hit the first *supay*, killing it, but missed the second. Kanmi swore as the ice wall fell and shattered at his feet.

As the *supay* leaped, Kanmi ducked reflexively, his instincts telling him that the creature was about to land and bite out his throat . . . but instead, it slammed, face-first, into the invisible wall over Trennus' symbols on the floor, and fell backwards. It looked so surprised and disgruntled that Kanmi let out a bark of laughter, and then spun as a late musket shot clipped his arm, and he threw his arms around Minori, preparing to take them both to the ground. She shoved *back*, however, and he felt the spell she'd been holding release, and looked back over his shoulder as the dozens of fragments of dry ice left behind by his wall collapsing, lifted up into the air as a tiny cyclone spawned. Pressure inside her vortex lowered, and then the spinning dervish of dry ice and savage winds moved for the men and their guns, catching at least one of them and hauling him into the air, screaming. The other men fruitlessly tried to haul their companion to safety, while the *supay* in front of Kanmi gibbered and screamed, clawing at the air, trying to get to them. "I don't do shields very well," Minori shouted over the noise of battle. "I'm much better at offense!"

"And I am perfectly fine with that!" Kanmi called back, and then swore, as one of the giant creatures at the side of what was apparently the emperor of Tawantinsuyu, turned and lumbered directly for Trennus. To his frustration, Trennus, ben Maor, and Caetia were well outside of his effective casting range. "I'm going to have to leave the circle," he shot at Minori. "Stay *in* it. You're hurt. Just keep them off my back!"

Adam currently had the best view of the combat situation, and swore as yet more *supay* appeared between him and Sigrun. He fired on one, trying to incapacitate it, even as three others leaped onto his wife's back. He was out of rounds, and didn't have time to reload; as such, he holstered the gun and moved out of cover, grabbing one of the creatures by the head and neck. They were human-shaped, more or less; they had flesh under a hide that appeared to be made of rock. He thought he could assume that they might have a comparable skeletal system underneath. His hands moved into the right positions, automatically. Right hand lifted the chin and rotated it, with a push, counterclockwise, while the left hand provided the counterbalancing torque. He could *feel* the bones inside the creature's neck rotate and snap, as he more or less unwound the vertebrae. And because it wasn't in contact with the earth, it promptly went limp, and he was able to haul it off of Sigrun's body as she staggered, trying to tear the remaining creatures' clawed hands away from her throat.

Movement, skirmishes all around him. One of the magma-like creatures had just been backhanded away by, startlingly, a blue-green, scaled woman. *Where did she come from, anyway? Her voice held enough power to mark her as an entity* . . . The *supay* flew past Sigrun, taking with it one of its brethren that had been attacking her from the front, before slamming into a pillar near Trennus. Now Trennus had *two* of the damned giants right next to him, and a handful of human guards. Sigrun tore one of her remaining *supay* off her back, shifting the grip on her spear to use the blade like a knife, slitting the damned thing's throat. "Help Tren!" she told Adam, two more *supay* still on her, biting and tearing. "I've got this, *go*."

"Not yet," Adam told her, sharply, and snapped the neck of another *supay*, leaving only one small monster clinging to her, biting away another mouthful of his wife's flesh. Horror in the pit of his stomach. Sigrun didn't even scream. Too much adrenaline to *feel* it, probably. But already the glimmer of light that told him that her body was regenerating. "Help *Inti*. I'm with Tren."

Trennus, for his part, swore as he saw the first creature coming for him, and cut a binding circle into the ground. The massive creature hit him at a full charge, and its body went from cold stone to molten magma in an instant even as it toppled him to the ground. Saraid groaned with the strain in his mind. *I cannot hold the shield for long. Not against so much fire. I am a creature of woods and streams. Fire is my bane.*

Just hold on as long as you can. Trennus hadn't fought something this damned big since the *alu*-demons, and this creature was easily twice the weight of the emaciated hyena-like creatures. The one that had tackled him to the ground shifted to its magma form, and rose up just long enough to drop its weight onto him again. And again. Like a parody of intercourse, or a repeated belly-flop. The only thing keeping him from being pancaked and burned alive at the same time was Saraid's shield. But the creature was stone. And Trennus was *very* good with rock.

He reached down into the ground for ley-energy, and channeled it into the body of the magma-beast, reforming its body for it. Took igneous rock, and applied pressure, twisting, shearing. Compressing. The beast froze in position, as its outer coat went black and cool once more, and Trennus compressed, even harder, scooting out from under it as it wavered in place at the center of the binding circle. He felt its will surge against his, and fought it. Wrestled with it. Gritted his teeth, and solidified the entirety of the elemental's body with ley-power . . . and, hissing between his teeth, forced binding sigils into the stone, like brands. The resulting boulder rocked back and forth, once or twice, and then remained absolutely still. *You're <u>bound</u>. Now stay down.*

And then a *second* black-rock beast slammed into the pillar beside him, and Trennus rolled out of the way as chips of stone went flying across his face. Even as the *cherufe* rebounded and stood, suddenly aware of *him*, standing no more than ten feet away, Trennus was aware of something else. The Sapa Inca had turned, as they'd moved into the room, to stare back at the intruders. And, at the moment, the man stood completely alone, in the center of a dozen skirmishes. But his eyes were locked on *Lassair*, who stood just inside the protective boundary of the circle Trennus had drawn, peering out into the maelstrom of combat, expression uncertain.

And then a fist the size of Trennus' own head, comprised of rock, slammed into his ribs, knocking him back into the wall behind him. Then Adam was there, firing point-blank into the back of the *cherufe's* head, for all the good it would do. Trennus lay there, dazed for a moment, thinking, *A good effort, old friend. But that's not going to kill a creature that doesn't have a brain* . . . . His eyes dropped down. "Center of the abdomen, Adam!" he shouted, dizzily, as the *cherufe* spun on ben Maor. "Where it's all obsidian. *While* it's still stone!" Volcanic glass was brittle. Fragile. A bullet would be useless, however enchanted, once the creature became magma, but while it stayed stone? Aiming for the most fragile portions of its hide would certainly hurt it. Distract it, while Trennus started to bind it.

———

Lassair stared at the fighting, unable to contribute in any meaningful way, horribly frustrated. If she were *sure* that passing into a different form, or into the Veil, wouldn't harm the child, she could shield Trennus herself, instead of leaving it to Saraid. She could fight one of the stone *cherufe*, or turn some of the little *supay* into ash. She could go to Stormborn and heal her as the *supay* gnawed at her flesh and lapped at her blood. She watched as the god-born woman flew straight up into the ceiling, slamming the creature on her back against the rock there, over and over, trying to dislodge it . . . finally succeeding.

A voice whispered to her, suddenly, and her head tilted up, meeting the Sapa Inca's eyes. *You have power, spirit. You know what it is, to make green things grow. To bring life to barren places. You should join with us. Join with me.* The voice wasn't human. It also wasn't *male*. It was distinctly feminine, and vibrated with power . . . only to fade away. To be replaced with another. <u>All your humans will die, if you do not come to me. Your beloved, too, will die. Only by joining with me, can you save them.</u> This voice sizzled like electricity in her mind, and carried with it the scent of rain. And, close behind it, a third voice. **Bow before me, spirit, and be spared. Earn mercy for yourself. For the unborn within you. Surrender. Subsume yourself to my will.**

I . . . no. Lassair was horribly confused, for a moment. She was speaking to three different voices at once. And all of them wanted her. Desired her. Not for her fleshly form, but for her power. She could read desire, in all its forms. Each voice thought of her as the tool by which it would achieve ascendancy over the others. And the voice behind them, the human one, which tried to hold them all together? Wanted her power, too. *She's the final piece. If I have just one more god-fragment within me, reduced to nearly a flat-line state, I'll be able to balance them out. Earth, Sky, Life . . . she's fire . . . no, one more after her. Water. I'll be the whole of creation in one body. I'll be* _perfect_. *I'll be able to control them all.*

No. I will not join with you willingly. You are insane.

Then I will consume you, spirit, as I have consumed a hundred others before you. You are more powerful than the spirits I have eaten to prepare myself to become a god, but I hold the power of three gods within me. Surrender, and be bound. Fight, and die.

I will not be bound by such as you. Lassair held up her hands, and sheathed her entire body in flames. The warmth and comfort of a banked fire, but she was already reaching for the star's fury she'd used once before today. She was, however, not infinite in her resources. She hadn't been able to return to the Veil to bask in the endless energies of that place since having used the attack before. Trennus was a conduit point, but a weak one. She might have to pull on his reserves, and she didn't want to do that. It could damage him.

All the fragmentary consciousnesses within the human man gave voice at once. *Fool*/Whore/**Stupid child**/*And so you die.* A momentary war within, and then the man reached out a hand, and energy sizzled through the air towards her, a blue-white levinbolt that she couldn't defend against. Spirit-senses saw it, in slow motion, the formation of electrons in charged chains flowing towards her. Body-senses were far behind, but spirit-mind took over, throwing the body to the floor, hoping that the lightning would pass her by.

Minori and Kanmi reached out, as one, and pulled that energy towards them. Redirected it back out into the combat area, sizzling it over several of the human guards, who screamed and fell, dropping their weapons. Smell of cooking flesh in the air, making them all gag. Lassair lifted her head from the ground, feeling Trennus' wave of concern. Saw Supay, struggling with Mamaquilla and Inti, finally regain control of his obsidian club. Mamaquilla had been pulling down shafts of silver light from above, needling the death-god, while clawing at his avatar's eyes. Now Supay spun, his sacrificial club in his hands, and struck Mamaquilla in the face with the weapon. The goddess stumbled backwards, jade-green blood pouring down her face, and slid to the ground, limply. Inti roared, a mental wave of fire and rage, and Lassair pulled her arms up over her head on the floor as Inti slammed a fist sheathed in sun-fire into Supay's chest, trying to reach for the death-god's heart. Supay kicked Inti back and stepped forwards, holding the club high. He swung, and Inti managed to catch it on a forearm, and a sharp sensation of pain rippled through the room. What the bodies were doing was one thing, but Lassair could *also* see what the gods were doing on another level. Could see Inti's trapped, bound energies, struggling against Supay's. Supay's draining him. Devouring him. Mamaquilla's energies struggling as raw entropic force *ate* at her avatar.

Behind Lassair, the god-born healer cried out, and *ran* to her goddess, right through the combat zone, even as Stormborn spun, the last of the *supay* finally dispatched, and attacked Supay from behind with her spear, only to have Supay turn and swat the valkyrie into one of the nearby pillars, as if batting at a fly. Trennus and Steelsoul continued to fight with the *cherufe* . . . and then the one to whom others were bound raised his hand again, and this time, Lassair was suddenly sucked down into the ground. Not magma, but mud. *Lahar,* a whisper at the back of her mind said.

Water everywhere, dousing her flames. Trying to pour into her body's nose and throat. Darkness, everywhere. No matter how she struggled, sensation of sinking deeper. Spirit-self didn't need to breathe. She could suspend the body's need for air, but she didn't know what would happen to the child if she did. Only one thought, as she tugged on the cord that bound her to Flamesower. She fought to hold her breath, held her nose closed with one hand to keep the enormous pressure of the wet earth from sliding into her lungs. Suffocation. She had *fire*, she could dry this earth with it, she could turn it to magma and swim up through it, but so . . . much . . . pressure . . . *Trennus! Flamesower!*

Across the room, Trennus could *feel* earth pouring into his own mouth. Could feel himself choking on dirt and mud, being buried alive, as he had, over the years, buried others in combat. It wasn't a recurring nightmare, but he'd definitely woken up sweating, at least once, having dreamed of being buried under an oak tree, the roots growing through his chest. *Lassair! Hold on!* He and Adam had the *cherufe* between them now, the creature having heated itself into magma, and vomited flame in Adam's direction. The Judean had had to spring and roll out of the way, and had just come back to his feet, panting. Trennus didn't have time for an elaborate binding. He pulled on ambient ley, not tapping the line directly, and focused on the superheated form of the *cherufe*. For all that this form was more dangerous, it was also more *vulnerable*. Magma had plasticity. Trennus pulled, bracing his back against the wall, and watched the creature split down the middle, strands of molten rock hanging between its halves like taffy.

Trennus! The thought was frantic now. *Pull me out!*

Trennus reached out through earth and stone with his mind. Found Lassair. Pulled.

Nothing happened. Trennus' eyes went wide, and he set himself, pulling again with all his strength, burrowing through the rock with his mind. Looking for leverage points, fractures in the stone, anything. There was nothing. She was in a womb made of earth, an egg made of stone, and it would not *move*. A hiss from the center of the room, and Trennus looked up in time to see the Sapa Inca, sweating now, throw lightning at him — only to have it redirected by Kanmi, right back at the emperor. "I can't reach her!" Trennus shouted.

He saw Minori take two steps away from Kanmi, and begin trying to chip her way down through the stone. Blasting at it with a drill made of ice, then heat, then ice again. Oscillating heat and cold, trying to weaken the rock, shatter it. Trying to reach Lassair in time. "No!" the emperor hissed, and a hand made of earth reached up for Minori now, and Kanmi reacted, instantly, directing raw heat at Sayri Cusi, enough that it should have crisped his skin. A captive spirit flared to life around the emperor, taking the hit on its essence, dispersing the heat. Cusi himself didn't move. Didn't flinch. Just kept bearing down on Lassair. Trennus could hear it now. *Surrender yourself. Surrender yourself. Give me your Name. Give me your essence.*

None of it mattered. Trennus reached down, touched the ley-line for the power he needed to shatter the stone, and stopped, horrified. The mountain itself was waking up. It had slept for hundreds of years, as the glaciers all along its calderas attested. But in reaction to all the heavy magics being tossed around on its surface . . . it was coming alive. If he pulled on the ley-line directly, it would erupt. And it wouldn't be a gentle, slow thing, like a shield volcano in Hawai'i. It would be cataclysmic. *No,* Trennus thought, frantically. *No, no, no, no . . . Lassair! Don't go! Don't surrender!*

Body-senses were shutting down. Lassair was close to being trapped in a husk of dead and rotting meat. She could escape to the Veil if she left the body behind. She might be able to shatter the prison around her if she turned it to magma, and she *tried* to do precisely that. Fire couldn't hurt her, couldn't touch her. She heated the rock around her, dimly seeing the glow with spirit-eyes, but mortal eyes were failing . . . . *Trennus. Flamesower. He has gods inside him. Like a god-born. When he kills this body . . . I think he might be able to kill* me. *And I can't fight it.*

No. I won't let this happen. I won't. Trennus was watching his life end, or at least, the only parts of it that mattered to him. He drew his silver-edged steel knife, dimly aware that Sigrun had peeled herself off the floor and was going back after Supay. That Cocohuay was kneeling by her goddess' side, healing the shattered avatar, pouring her power into Mamaquilla's body. That Inti and Supay were still fighting, that Kanmi was throwing everything he had at the emperor, and that Adam was firing, uselessly, alternating between Cusi and Supay. *No. You don't get her, you bastard. Lassair! Take the rest of me. I give myself to you. Take the gift, flameheart. Use it.*

No . . . the thought from Lassair was distant, and Trennus ignored it, and the wash of anguish that poured out of Saraid now, almost inchoate. Set his knife just under the xiphoid process, the fragile tip of the sternum, and setting his teeth, made sure of his aim . . . and then jerked his arms back before he lost his nerve.

Blood *bound.* It also *freed. Nothing from nothing. From sacrifice, glory.*

It hurt. Dear gods, it *hurt,* which was why he'd wanted to make sure of his aim. He didn't think he'd have the strength to try again if he *missed* the first time. He could feel his heart spasming on the blade. Cutting itself on the edges, flailing itself apart. But as his life's blood poured out, Trennus wound his Name into the blood, the Name Lassair had given him to know. Poured *himself* out, along the cord of soul that stretched between them. Felt his awareness compress to a thin, two-dimensional line. Sailing into warmth, into fire, held tight for a moment, and then . . . . *elsewhere.*

. . . his mind screamed in primal terror and confusion. Where he was, his senses distorted. He couldn't understand them. He smelled purple fire raining down on what might have been his skin, if he'd <u>had</u> skin. He could hear perfume and clouds and sulfur, a ringing sound, a chime, and a trumpet's blat, respectively. His eyes saw nothingness, but his <u>spirit</u> saw shapes, colors, but the shapes were all without <u>dimension</u>. His mind gibbered back from what made no sense, not in human terms, for this was a space where humanity had no place. The human mind had not evolved to comprehend it.

He saw wonders, and he saw terrors. As his awareness became clearer, Flamesower saw a red deer being stalked by a jade jaguar, through a forest made of crystal. The jaguar leaped and killed the doe, but no sooner had it torn the throat out, than the deer's body vanished, and the beast was off and leaping through the woods, tail flicking behind it. No light, but light everywhere. The forest vanished, and a woman-shaped creature with a dozen arms walked through a black void, holding open a gaping hole cut into her stomach, playing with the entrails within. Where she walked, the blood splattered, and stars — huge, flaming balls of gas and dust — appeared, swelled into giants, and then went nova, only to return to their young, golden, life-giving state again before the nova had finished. Effect without cause. Effect <u>preceding</u> cause. The black void vanished, and a spider-web filled Flamesower's mind. A huge spider, with furry-looking legs, crawled towards him, eight eyes gleaming as it studied him, where he was trapped, mandibles twitching. <u>You do not belong here. You have a Name, but you are not of this place.</u>

    <u>Yes. I have a Name.</u>

<u>Will you give it to me?</u> The mandibles twitched in interest.

<u>It is not mine to give,</u> he hedged. <u>I have given it to another.</u>

<u>Then you do not really have a Name, do you? A Name entirely given, is not your own anymore. You need another one. Of course, you have one. You just do not remember/know it properly.</u> The spider studied him again. <u>You are weak. You are hunted, and you are eaten. You rise again, though. Everyone does. The Game goes on. The Dance continues. You are/will be stronger?</u> The words weren't quite that. They didn't have <u>tense.</u> They combined present and future as the same concept.

    <u>I . . . don't know. Where am I? The Veil?</u>

<u>You are where you are. You are who you are. Strange questions. But yet, you say you have a Name. Though you have surrendered it. That makes you a cousin. You are neither Nameless, nor UnNamed.</u>

    <u>Nameless? UnNamed?</u> Flamesower felt dim stirrings of awareness. He remembered these things. At least, somewhat. <u>What are these things?</u>

<u>This,</u> the spider told him amiably, <u>is the only world that matters. This is home. There are other places. There is a cold place, a place of death, where everything ends, and when it ends, it ends forever.</u>

    <u>I . . . know this place. I come from there, I think.</u>

<u>Oh, how horrible.</u> The spider shuddered, and the whole web shook with him. <u>You're better off here, I assure you. You are/will be stronger. Of course, there are those who think the taste of endings is sweet. They like that which is different. The taste of danger. They are seeking/will seek you.</u>

I don't wish to be sought.

Then you are hiding/should hide. Hard, though, with that which you carry. The spider reached out a massive foreleg and touched something at Flamesower's heart. *You carry your line with you, as I do. Are you spinning your web here?*

Flamesower looked down. Hard to see himself. His form was . . . spindly. Amorphous, compared to the spider's clear, hard, perfect form. Blobs and roils of energy, spreading out, carried by a chiming breeze, all stemming from his . . . heart. Yes. He had one. A glowing core of red-and-white fire . . . and from that heart, a long, thin filament of brown-and-green light, stretching off, endlessly, into the distance. Fire sheathed it, and for a moment, he <u>knew</u> it . . . and then recognition faded.

No. I do not know how to spin webs. Curiosity. You are speaking of Nameless and UnNamed?

A chitter. *Nameless come from the cold place. We call it the Aether, but if those who dwell there have no Names, it seems likely that they have no Name for their home. We cannot go there, cousin. Those from that place are uninterested in us and our doings. They are Order. They are the Law. They are Fate. We sense them, dimly, through the barrier, shadows and lights against a window. The barrier between there and here is stronger than that which divides us from the place of endings. Not that I wish to go there, either. Another shudder. Those who try to enter the Aether, END. Whether it is the place that devours them, or the creatures there, I do not know. But they end without beginning.*

And the UnNamed?

The UnNamed go there, from your place of endings, cousin. When they have had their Names stolen from them. They try to stay here, but we do not let them. They try to tear our Names from us, in fear. And then they go. They become one with the Aether.

Flamesower felt coldness in his glowing heart. Something about the UnNamed. *Do the UnNamed ever come back? Do the Nameless ever go to the place of endings?*

If they do, they do not come through our home. We stay out of their home. They stay out of ours. But your home interests many. The spider tapped again on the long strand that connected Flamesower to . . . something. *You are removing/leaving that behind? It is making you visible/trackable.*

No . . . it's . . . important. . . . Flamesower paused. *Thank you, cousin. It is good to meet you and not be your prey today.*

I have no taste for endings. Go in safety/You are safe.

Flamesower pulled on the cord with his will, and began to speed along it. It seemed to allow him to move much more quickly, though he didn't know where it went. There was no up or down or any other directionality. There was just . . . everywhere. But the only familiar thing was the cord, so he followed it, through crowds and thickets and storms and stars and voids. For years, or centuries, or heartbeats. The words lost meaning.

Less than a second had passed. Lassair felt the remaining portion of Trennus' life-essence course into her along their soul-bond, and wailed

No! But with it, with the blood on the ground, the willing sacrifice of a good man, came power, infusing her. She didn't want it, didn't want to accept it, but not to take it would be to *waste* everything that Trennus was to her. But their bond was as much about giving as it was about taking, and she had, in spirit-mind, all the time in the world to understand that, to comprehend what it meant, and what she could do with it. So as his life-energy came to her, Lassair reached out and tucked part of *herself* into his frail and dying form, where it could grow and kindle into flame, healing the body that his spirit had vacated. At the same time, the spirit tenderly extricated him from her, refusing to consume him, subsume him. She took the energy of the love—and she was dizzyingly aware that the love was a greater power than the blood or the worship ever could have been—and tucked him, still attached to her, into the Veil, as her sister Latirian had tried to do with many mortals, so long ago. *He's strong. Stronger than any of them. And he's bound to me. He shares my awareness. He'll be safe.*

Spirit-mind, infused with power, examined the dying body in the earthen egg, and reached out. Found the energies that were compressing the earth, and with all the power of Tlaloc's legacy and Trennus' sacrifice, shattered them. The egg cracked. The earth above that cyst glowed, red-hot, becoming a pool of magma. Deep in the pool, Lassair coughed once, as she flushed the mud out of the body's lungs. Took a deep breath, feeling the air, relishing it, as she made spirit-and-body *one* for the moment. Infused her fire all through the flesh, and stepped up out of the red-hot pool of liquid rock, her phoenix wings streaming behind her, fire and flesh as one, reborn.

She paused there for a moment, feeling Trennus' faint tug on the end of a very long cord between them, and then leaped directly for the Sapa Inca, with a cry like a hunting bird, feral and keen. Her wings scraped the ceiling as she landed on him, and her hands were full of flame as she tore at the rock-like skin under his royal raiment. *No more!* Lassair told Sayri Cusi, and the insistent fragments of gods encysted within him. *No more!*

———————

Adam had staggered back as the creature of molten rock had been torn apart. Saw Lassair sucked down into the floor, and, not knowing what else to do, had reloaded, and started firing at Supay and the Sapa Inca, his bullets impacting uselessly. *At least I might distract them. I can't do what I did to Tlaloc. If I bring any part of this ceiling down, it comes down on all of us.* His mind churned. As Minori and Kanmi both engaged Sayri Cusi with all their considerable magic—with little more effect, sadly, than his bullets—and as Sigrun once more threw herself at Supay, Adam glanced around, looking for options. Cocohuay had the head of her goddess cradled in her lap, and was trying to staunch the bleeding there. "I can't heal the damage. The wound is too great, and it's a wound to more than just the body."

I . . . know . . . leave me. It is my time. Supay has become too powerful.

"No. Come into me," Cocohuay told Mamaquilla, tears running

down her weathered cheeks. "It's not much of a body. But it's healthy. It's served me well for two hundred years. I give it to you. Freely. Take me."

Adam's eyes widened, and he turned to shoot a look over his shoulder at Tren, wanting to tell his friend, *That's dedication. That's love. That's sacrifice* . . . but before he could form a word, he realized that Trennus was on the floor, a knife buried deep in his heart, his eyes fixed on where Lassair had been. *No,* Adam thought, dumbly. *No, no, there had to have been another way, Trennus, you fool, you idiot* . . . he ran to his friend's body, holstering his gun, and ripped the knife out, throwing it aside. Put two fingers, idiotically, to the side of Trennus' throat. He knew he wouldn't find a heartbeat. There wasn't a heart *left* to beat.

Against all expectations, he felt . . . something. Not a reverberation. Not a heartbeat. Warmth, rising and falling, growing almost searing hot, and then cooling again. Adam pulled his hand away, looking down at the body, and hadn't the slightest idea of what to do. *CPR? Should I pump his chest? Should I give rescue breaths? What in god's name do I do?*

He looked up, feeling a black wave of despair crash over him. He was useless in this fight. He couldn't help Lassair, he couldn't help Sigrun. He couldn't even help Trennus. He lifted his friend's limp hand, sticky with blood, and looked down at him, helplessly, and then assessed the battlefield again. Sigrun was still in the thick of the fight, blood staining her clothes, clotting her hair together in places, rune-marks ablaze as she warily moved in, trying to jab her spear into Supay's side as he lifted his club again and drove it down at Inti. The sun-god's left arm already hung uselessly at his side, though Adam wasn't sure if that meant that bones had been broken, or if the avatar's injury correlated to spiritual damage. Now Inti threw himself out of the way of the devastating strike, aimed for his head. Supay darted in, redirecting the failed swing, and slammed the club into the god's right ribs. Adam could hear the crunch of bone, and winced, knowing that Inti wore the body of one of his god-born, a living, breathing, mostly mortal man. Someone just like Sigrun.

This isn't right, Adam thought, as Inti staggered back, and set Tren's limp hand down on the ground once more. He unholstered his gun, this time with his hand coated in Tren's blood, and fired once more on Supay, as the death-god turned on Sig yet again. The valkyrie managed to block a hasty shot with the club with the haft of her spear, turning to let the energy dissipate past her, so that the impact wouldn't splinter her spear, and Adam caught the look on his wife's face. It was the expression that she always wore when she told him, *I was born to fight lost battles.*

Flickers of awareness. Lassair burst out of the earth, her body made of fire, and with peacock-feather wings made of flame easily fifteen feet in length, unfurling from her shoulders. She screamed and leaped for the Sapa Inca, knocking the man to the ground, her fingers clawing at his face and body. Feral. Primal. *Nature, red in tooth and claw.*

Just past Sigrun and Supay, their faces lit dimly by Inti's dying light, and Sigrun's rune-born glow, Cocohuay pressed her lips to Mamaquilla's ravaged forehead, and a mist began to rise from the goddess' body. Gleaming, pearlescent fog lifted, and breathed itself into the woman's form. The transformation was not gentle. Cocohuay screamed in pain as her body began to ripple and distort. Her spine contorted as her body began to grow, rapidly, and scales unfurled across her skin. Before the transformation was even complete, Mamaquilla lunged back into the fight, again sheeting lines of silvery light across Supay's body. She seemed stronger now, somehow, more agile, as the broken and bleeding body she'd left behind slumped to the ground, as limp as Trennus. Adam edged forward, leaning against one of the pillars for cover, and swung around. Aimed at Supay, but couldn't get a clear shot. Sigrun was moving too damned fast, here, there, her spear flicking. Mamaquilla, in Cocohuay's body, was slashing at Supay with her lines of light. All to no avail. Adam aimed, hesitated, began to pull the trigger . . . .

Wait. Inti had regained his feet and staggered out of the combat area, barely dodging an errant spear-strike from Sigrun. Adam's finger released, and time seemed to slow, all around him, as Inti approached. Sigrun's lightning-fast dodges and strikes became dream-like. The pulses that made up each line of Mamaquilla's moon-born light became evident. *Do not waste your bullets, human.* Inti collapsed at Adam's feet. Left arm shattered. Right arm holding ribs that had been crushed. Golden, fiery blood dripping from mouth and nose. *Not when there is a better target.*

"What . . . what do you mean?" Adam asked, staring around him. Lassair's mouth was bloody; he thought she'd *bitten* Sayri Cusi, like a falcon savaging its prey, but the man was fighting back. Kanmi had pulled Minori back against the far wall, and was shielding both of them now.

Me.

Adam's mouth dropped open. "What? I can't — you're — "

I am at fault. Inti's voice was weary. *I failed to see the trap for what it was. I failed to undo its workings for years. I am bound to it, and remain bound in it, for all that I am free of the circle. It still leeches life and energy from me to bind my brethren. I could drop it, all at once, and perhaps heal myself. Perhaps defeat Supay. But thousands would die in the cities of this land. Supay is counting on it. I can see it in him. Their deaths, his sacrifice. A rush of power with which to claim his ascendancy.* Inti's voice was bleak. *Sacrifice is power. Blood is power. Can I see your friend give his life for his beloved, can I see Cocohuay give herself to my beloved sister-queen, and dare to do less than what a mortal might?*

Adam's mind reeled. "If you die . . . won't all the power backlash *anyway*? Won't it flood the whole machine, and destroy the towers, make the ground shake?" He watched as Sigrun's spear began a slow downward arc.

It is certainly possible. I will not be able to control it. I will be no more. I cannot even guarantee that you and yours will live. But my sacrifice will be more powerful than Supay can understand. I would rather die, knowing that I have taken him with me into unbeing, than allow everyone to continue to fight and die, without hope of victory. Inti regarded him steadily, the sun-bright eyes unbearably difficult to look into. *Will you do this, mortal?*

Time continued to crawl past. Adam swallowed, feeling sweat

trickle down his spine. "I *can't*. There's no possible way in which I could kill you."

You have done so, before, Godslayer.

Oh, harah. There really is a backroom somewhere, where all the gods chitchat. "Tlaloc . . . I collapsed a ceiling on his body . . . he was weakened . . ."

And am I not? Inti stared into his eyes. **But I understand. You believe that your weapon will be unable to kill me. A not insupportable conclusion, given the lack of effect on Supay and my poor Sayri so far.** The god reached out, and touched a finger to the barrel of the gun. The grip turned blisteringly hot in Adam's hand, and when he looked down, he saw that the image of a sun had been etched there. **The tears of the sun,** Inti said, with infinite weariness in his voice, **are now yours to use as you see fit, Godslayer. I could not choose a more worthy mortal with whom to leave this burden.**

Adam shook his head, minutely, and then with growing force. "I wouldn't just be killing you, correct? I'd be killing the god-born who . . . carries you, too?" He cast around in his head for the name. "Quehuar."

The sunblaze of the eyes didn't fade, but the stance altered, slightly. Inti put his good arm against the pillar, leaning there, and when he replied, it was in a human voice. The resolute, stern lips moved. "I am . . . dead already, Godslayer. I would have died months ago, of starvation, if not for my god."

Adam couldn't help but picture, in his mind, the tale of Elijah, condemned to starve in prison, and sustained by bread brought to his cell by ravens, as Quehuar went on, swallowing hard. "We have both been fed by the sacrifices of others. We have been turned into parasites. Cannibals. Murderers, by proxy. Let us make something good out of all of that. Better us, and surety that Supay will be defeated, than so many others, without hope. And we . . . Inti can't kill himself. He'll be loosing his power. Willingly dissolving himself, rather than incarnating again. But we need . . . a push." The man closed his eyes, and when he spoke again, it was Inti's voice once more. **Please.**

"You're surprisingly hard to argue against," Adam admitted, tightly. "Yes. I'll . . . help you." *And god help me for doing so.*

Time began to flow again, and Adam's stomach turned as Inti stood. **I will meet death on my feet,** the sun-god said, quietly. He turned his face away, and called, with so much love in his voice that Adam actually shook from it, **Mamaquilla! Moon to my sun. Sister. Wife. For you. For our land. For our people. Keep them well.**

The goddess had just enough time to look up from where she was trying to tie Supay with her lines of light. Just enough time for the luminous eyes to widen in horror. **Inti! Beloved! No!**

Supay turned, and Adam could see the exact moment of realization in the feral eyes as Adam stepped behind Inti, placed the barrel of the gun against the back of the god's head, and asked, "Are you sure?" His voice was shaking. He'd killed before. But *never* in cold blood. This felt like murder.

I am, and I thank you for this, Godslayer. Do it. Do it NOW.
Adam felt, more than saw, as Supay began to leap for them.
He pulled the trigger.

Chapter XX: Kipuka

The notion of the destruction of the world is inherent to most mythology. As a theme, it derives primarily from an era in which a valley, a river, a few hundred square miles, was the entire world. It is difficult for human beings to have a true appreciation of the scale of the planet on which we dwell. If a flood, a fire, or an eruption affects us, then yes, egocentric little apes that we are, it is the end of the world. Or at least, of our world.

It is important to keep this concept in mind when examining the accounts of ancient disasters, and attempting to verify their historicity. There are, for example, multiple accounts of a great flood in Mesopotamian cultures. The earliest written account is found in the Epic of Gilgamesh, *and the eponymous hero is not even the hero of the flood story. The hero wants eternal life, and thus seeks out Utnapishtim, the man who saved humanity from the flood, and was rewarded with the secret to eternal life for it. When he finds Utnapishtim, the saga describes how the gods of Babylon conspired to punish mankind, but one god, Ea, refused to destroy all of their people. He whispered directions to Utnapishtim through the reed wall of his house, telling him to go to the river. To build a vast boat, like the covered apsu used on the river, and to lie to anyone who asked him why he had moved, and to say only that he had gone to dwell with his lord, Ea.*

The gods flooded the river, and Utnapishtim loaded all of his family and as many living things as he could into his boat, and saved them from the flood. Later variants of the text say, no, it wasn't just a river, but the whole world. (And so it was, to a culture that dwelled beside a river, and saw their lives, livestock, and livelihoods wiped out.) Utnapishtim finally landed his boat upon a mountain-temple – a ziggurat – as the waters receded. There, he made sacrifices and the gods, short-sighted as they seem to have been, turn out to have been starving for sacrifices for the entirety of the flood, as there have been no humans to make them! They descend upon his slaughtered sheep and his libations like flies. And then they squabble amongst themselves, trying to determine who the guilty god was, who permitted Utnapishtim to know of their plan. Ea calls his brethren to task for their short-sightedness, and belatedly, the gods reward Utnapishtim and his wife with eternal life, making them gods, and requiring them to live "where the rivers begin."

Gilgamesh, for his part, never learns the secret to immortality. He's done no deeds great enough to prompt a god to love him. And he fails to speak to a snake. Serpents, as the keepers of wisdom, were widely held to be immortal, and the ancients believed that they sloughed off their years with their skins. All chances at immortality lost, Gilgamesh returns home, disconsolate, and praises the works of mortals, in building cities. In building civilizations, the text tells us, humans achieve a kind of immortality.

This tale is familiar to Judeans under the far more pronounceable name of Noah's Flood. In which the world ends in flood, one man and his family set out in a boat, and finally crash into a holy mountain. Literary plagiarism has a long history, it seems.

We must look at the rivers as the source of the legend. The rivers are where the god-touched Utnapishtim and his wife dwelled. A river boat is what he built. They were sent to live at the source of the waters. And archaeological evidence indicates that many of the cities in and around the Tigris and the Euphrates did suffer flood damage in or around 2700 BC, more or less just before the time in which Gilgamesh is said to have been king. The move from a flood that threatened a city—which was, to its inhabitants, the whole world—to an ocean that covered the entire world after forty days and forty nights of rain, is clear.

The gods of Babylon seem to have been arbitrary, short-sighted, and petty, not to mention careless with the lives of their followers. Then again, their followers were somewhat careless with their gods. After all, the godslayers came first to Babylon and Assyria . . . .

— Akakios Halkias. From The Great Deluge to Ragnarok: The History of the End of the World and Why it Won't Happen in Our Lifetime, pp. 22-24. University of Athens Press, Athens, Hellas, 1946 AC.

Maius 22, 1960 AC

In the early morning hours of Maius 22, the priests in the Inti Kancha, the great temple of the sun in Cuzco, moved in their appointed rounds, lighting fresh oil in ancient lamps and braziers, and polishing the altar, and the various relics gathered on its surface. The outermost walls of the temple had been sheathed in pounded gold foil centuries ago, and still reflected the sun's light blindingly on cloudless days. The interior was no less lavish, and the décor culminated with the sun-mask of Inti, which hung above the priests' heads on the rearmost wall, behind the altar. Eighty pounds of heavy gold, pounded over a metal form into the likeness of a stylized human face, at the center of a circle surrounded by rays of light. The end of each ray held a human hand or the face of a jaguar. The lamps in the temple were all carefully positioned to reflect light back off the grinning mask of the Benevolent Sun, and thus, he perpetually shone down on his priests and any worshippers who might have come to his temple to beg for his guidance and mercy . . . even in the darkest hours of the night.

The worship of Inti was state-mandated, and had been since the first Sapa Inca, the legendary god-born Manco Cupac, who had begun building Cuzco in the 1190s AC. Currently, thirty-six million people worshipped Inti as the principle god among the many gods of Tawantinsuyu. Thirty-six million people greeted every dawn with at least a token nod towards a small sun-mask on a wall in their homes. While Diana and Artemis might be mentioned in the same breath as Mamaquilla, here, Apollo and Helios had no sway. The worship of Inti had been institutionalized for over eight hundred years.

The ground in Cuzco shivered. Those people who were still out drinking *chicha* and imported *pulque* from Nahautl might have felt the first tremors, but most of them were warm, happy, and elevated by the liquor and its fumes. One man fell off a barstool, but his friends attributed it to him not being able to hold his drink.

In Machu Picchu, at the summer palace of the Sapa Incas, Livorus was being kept in relative comfort. He still wore his ceremonial toga; it wasn't as if his captors had brought his luggage from his hotel for him. He'd been permitted to read, and he trusted that the encoded dispatches in his travel case were proving entertaining reading for Tawantinsuyu's intelligence services. The security breach couldn't be helped, so he was disinclined to worry about it at present. So he sat, reading Caesar's *History of the Gallic Wars*, a kerosene lamp at the desk providing just enough illumination for the pages. The light trembled across the page, far more than a flickering flame should, and Livorus raised his head. Studied the oil quivering in the glass base of the lamp, and saw ripples developing there. *I didn't hear artillery or a bomb blast. I don't smell sulfur, so I don't suppose there's a summoner at work. And the region is notably active, in a seismic sense, as Dr. Sasaki has repeatedly pointed out.* Livorus rose, smoothing his clothing, and moved to the door. Tapped on it, and waited for his guards to open it. "I believe we are experiencing earthquakes," Livorus informed them, calmly. "I would like to take a stroll in a garden away from walls and ceilings until they pass."

They gave him sardonic glances. "This is a ploy, yes? You think you can run away from us, in the darkness?"

"You may shackle me, if you wish, but I would greatly prefer not to be indoors for the next hour or so." Livorus kept his tone completely calm.

"These walls are built to withstand earthquakes, Roman. They are all already falling in on themselves. Wedged tightly, so they cannot fall any further than they already are." A slightly condescending smile for the nervous foreigner. "We know our land."

"Yes. I'm sure you do. Still . . . a turn in the night air would surely do no harm?" Livorus offered his hands, just as the second, and much stronger quake hit—and this time, the guards looked down, in surprise, at the floor.

A younger man would have tried to take advantage, instantly. Leaped on them, attacked them in their moment of confusion. Livorus did not. He understood the value of patience. Understood that he did not know the palace's layout, the guard routine, anything. Escape was exceedingly improbable from within the fortress. His best bet lay in getting *outside* the palace . . . and being locked in his room, with guards unresponsive to his requests, ran counter to that goal. "So," he murmured, as the guards regained their footing. "About that garden stroll?"

The guards exchanged glances. "A little night air might do us some good," one of them admitted.

As the ancient stone walls of the summer palace of Machu Picchu began to shake, the newer buildings of Cuzco, Ica, Ayacucho, Sicuani, and other cities in a roughly circular region began to shudder and collapse. The older the architecture, surprisingly, the better it held up, but the skyscrapers whipped back and forth like reeds in a high wind.

Back in Cuzco, the priests of Inti gathered near the altar, gesticulating. Earthquakes were the province of Mamapaca, the dragon goddess of the earth. For the earth to move suggested that the world of men was about to be punished for some misdeed. Oh, everyone *understood* plate tectonics. But it was hard not to think of the bump and jostle of continental plates as something fundamentally connected to the world beyond.

One of the priests happened to be looking up at the exact moment it happened. A third earthquake began, and this one was much, much worse than the first two. He saw the sun-mask of Inti tremble on the wall, and then the massive face, which had hung in the temple for eight hundred years, slipped from the secure fastenings that held it, and fell forty feet, slamming down onto the altar and floor. It had not been made in a single piece, but had been welded together with discreet seams. The soft, heavy gold had required bracing and support behind the face, to help it hold its shape. When the mask hit the ground, it broke apart, into a half-dozen fragments, but the priests, shouting in consternation, hardly had time to notice this, as the ceiling of the temple overhead began to cave in on them.

On the side of the mountain of Coropuna, the *ushnu* erupted upwards, the massive stones thrown like ejecta from a volcanic blast. A pillar of fire reached skywards, and astronauts working on the Libration space station and the L'banah moon base reported seeing an orb of what looked like fiery plasma rise, at high speed, from the planet's surface. The ball of plasma actually hovered in orbit near the space station. It was hundreds of miles away, but the astronauts—rightfully concerned about gravitic disruptions to the delicate orbital placement of the station, not to mention radiation—took video and telemetry of the phenomenon, as best they could.

Only a small section of Earth's night-side itself was affected; this included Tawantinsuyu itself, and a strip of the surface north into the Taino Islands and the eastern seaboard of Caesaria Aquilonis. Residents of Novo Trier, the Iroquois Confederacy, Crann Péitseog, Romaine, and dozens of other cities, were awakened as the night-time sky lit up as if it were noon, as a second sun had been born in the sky. People in Cuzco, already panicking at the earthquakes, and evacuating from their collapsing houses, screamed and pointed skywards. News crews scrambled to get footage that would have been called a clever hoax by residents of other nations, if not for the footage also streaming in, live, from outer space, Novo Gaul, and Nova Germania.

Beneath this newborn star, the tower beside the Coropuna *ushnu* collapsed in on the resigned figure of Apu, the mountain's king. The god, though surely he felt the release of the power that held him there, did not move. He accepted his fate, and allowed himself to disperse, flooding the great machine of wires and spells that connected him to the land with his own energies. The only revenge he could take on those who had drained him was to destroy their works.

In Nazca, the energies from Inti's death and Apu's ripped through the wounded earth, setting off violent aftershocks, and the ley-lines conveyed the spiritual energy of two gods' deaths to the tower outside of Ica, continuing in the near-instantaneous traverse of the circuit.

Clouds gathered overhead, and torrential rain began to fall. Inside the Ica tower, Kon, the god of rain, lifted his silvery head, and regarded the heavens with his gleaming blue eyes. Energies buffeted him, a tide that he could not resist. Could not ignore. The binding surrounding him snapped, but snapped *inwards* under the pressure, and he closed his sky-blue eyes, and released himself to the flood. Outside, the rain began to pool on the hardpan, and localized flooding tore at the earth.

Energy swept around the circle, past Machu Picchu, and, like a tide, struck the tower outside of Cuzco. In it, Urcuchillay, lord of animals, lowered his llama-like head. The bindings collapsed inwards, and the raw tide of energy hit him. Dispersed him. Sent him into the flood with the rest. The tower collapsed, and Cuzco danced once more on its foundations. The ancient fortress of Sacsayhuamán remained standing, but hundreds of other buildings collapsed.

The energy continued around its circuit. The empty tower at Sicuani, where Mamaquilla would have been imprisoned, collapsed under the strain, the last point in the circle, but added nothing more to the total energies being loosed. The town around it was spared the scale of the devastation suffered in places like Ica and Cuzco, and the energies sped along the last line available, returning to the awakening giant that was Coropuna.

Underground, Adam's finger had compressed the trigger. He'd stood behind Inti, knowing that he couldn't look into those sunblaze eyes, no matter how calm and resolute. No recoil in the pistol. For a moment, Adam didn't even think he'd *fired*. Then he saw the golden, bloody mass that was the back of the god's head, and Inti's form sagged forwards, and Adam leaped forward to catch the body, as best he could. Heavy as an eight-foot-tall body should have been, Inti's form was emaciated, and Adam levered him, gently, respectfully, to the ground. *There's no way to be forgiven for this, is there?* he thought, numbly, inconsequentially, looking up again. *Yes, a god, and no, not mine, and yes, he asked me to . . . but murder is murder, isn't it?*

As the body touched the ground, and Supay and Mamaquilla were both still in mid-motion, trying to reach Inti, a pillar of light and fire had exploded up from the body, and Adam barely flung himself out of the way in time. This wasn't the gentle warmth of the sun on a lazy summer's day. He threw his left arm in front of his face, just in time to save his vision, as streams of plasma exploded from Inti, like the prominences of a solar flare, blasting away at the stone overhead, vaporizing tons of rock in an instant. It should have carbonized every living being within that enclosed space, but somehow, the heat directed itself solely up, while Adam could sense waves of . . . something . . . moving through the earth, expressed mainly as vibration. He didn't dare open his eyes. Didn't dare pull his arm away from his face. But in his right hand, the gun remained, cocked and ready, and Adam was listening, intently, for anything that told him that enemies were approaching, even though he knew that it was futile.

Kanmi had had about five seconds of warning as he saw ben Maor, with blinding speed, simply *flicker* behind Inti. Saw the resolute, noble, yet terrified expression on the god's face. Minori blurted out, "He's ending himself! He's sacrificing himself!" and Kanmi had reached down for every reserve of power he had. Pulled it out of batteries, out of his nervous system, the air and rock around them, and rapidly pulled a barrier up in front of them, nearly tripping over his syllables in his haste. And at the same time, he could hear and feel Minori doing the same thing, their power weaving into and around and through each other's, building the wall thicker, pulling particles of stone and dirt and anything else into it, thickening the air and earth into a protective wall in front of them. Kanmi reached out, pulled Minori into his arms, and turned his back on the blaze as the god's self-made pyre went up. His body probably wouldn't stop any serious radiation, but any fire, any heat, any projectiles that weren't stopped by their barrier, would have to go through him first, before reaching Minori. Their barrier *would* stop UV. Some radiation. X-rays, certainly, but probably not gamma. Then again . . . the gods only knew if a dying god gave off *gamma* radiation. Tlaloc hadn't, but Tlaloc hadn't been a sun-god. Recently, anyway. Depending on how one read Nahautl mythology.

Kanmi, unlike Adam, could feel the raw energy being expelled into the air, into the earth, into the *ley-lines*, into the magma lurking below the surface. He'd run estimates of Tlaloc's expended energies, that had set the explosive force as similar to that of four medium-sized power plants running at normal capacity, being released all at once. This was far greater. This felt like the power of a thousand tons of chemical explosive, like dynamite. He could feel it being grounded by the ley-lines, but also by bodies in the room itself, and thanked his stars that there was someplace for the power to go . . . and hoped, deeply and sincerely, that it wasn't being consumed by Supay or Sayri Cusi. And because that energy was being passed along ley-lines, which resonated with one another over vast distances, without time delay . . . Kanmi could feel the energy that had been dispersing coming *back*, like a tidal wave. Only it was stronger now, because that tide had picked up the flotsam and jetsam of the rest of the system, and was bringing it all back to the beginning. Completing a circuit.

Kanmi felt Minori's arms tighten around his waist, and knew she was bracing for the impact, too. "Don't try to absorb it!" he shouted over the sound of combat. "It'll burn you out!" He could feel her nod in response, and they both frantically wove more and more of themselves into their shields, trying to deflect as much of the energy as possible.

Sigrun had looked away as Adam lowered Inti to the floor, but was still blinded for a moment. She could hear Mamaquilla's silent keening as energies pulsed and coursed through the room. Dizzying. She hadn't been as aware of this when Tlaloc had died; she'd been unconscious at the time. This time, she could feel *everything*, and her senses became oddly heightened.

Energy. Movement of bodies around her. The destruction of the *ushnu* overhead let fine drifts of dirt sheet softly down over hair and face. *Open sky* above. The struggle between Lassair and the Sapa Inca as they grappled on the ground. A barrier resonating around Kanmi and Minori. But at first she had no idea where *Adam* was. Or even if he'd survived the blast. Her heart wrenched, but she didn't have time to dwell on it. Supay was still in play. So was the Sapa Inca.

She opened her eyes to see Mamaquilla staggering to her husband's body, pulling Inti into her arms. Dazzling light of a midnight sun overhead, piercing through the clouds that covered the sky. Inti's last gift to his people. It surely wouldn't last long. Adam — *oh, gods, thank you, he's alive!* — pressed up against the wall behind Mamaquilla and Inti. Rumblings in the ground, underfoot, a surge that made her stagger for a moment.

All this in eyeblinks of time, and then she caught a glimpse of Supay charging Mamaquilla, fangs bared, and his club swinging back to attack the peaceful goddess of the moon and sea, as she clutched her husband's body and wailed, silently, ***Inti, no, Inti, no, I cannot do this without you, I cannot, I cannot . . . .***

No time. Sigrun had open sky and a death-god to deal with. At least she could distract him until Mamaquilla had had a chance to mourn her beloved, and regain her composure. Sigrun pulled at the sky above, and lighting came at her call, slamming down into Supay, the impact of the thunder itself a physical force. Supay stopped in his tracks. Turned, slowly, and faced the valkyrie, his black eyes vacant of all expression. As he paused, Sigrun gritted her teeth, and hit him with lightning again, the blue-white bolt hitting him, and the rock under him, as well.

Supay bared his teeth and laughed at her, a sound that tore at her mind. ***Pitiful child of the northern gods, is that the best you can do? Feel my power. And know that when you die, your blood and life will only serve to feed me.*** He lifted a hand, and Sigrun's heart twisted inside of her chest. Clamped down, stuttering. The cardiac tissues burned, and for an instant, Sigrun's vision wavered, and she thought she would pass out of existence, not on her feet, and not of a battle-wound, after all.

The rune-wrought light on her skin dimmed for a moment, and then flared more brightly, as the pain simply passed. Sigrun hissed, "Fikkest thu, cwealuwyrm, inanwyrm. Héodæg, thu forðferest!" *Death-worm. Gut-worm. Today, you perish.*

She managed to slash at Supay's face once more as he charged in, swinging his heavy club once more, pivoting, light-footed, to the right, letting him move past and through where she'd just been, shifting her grip to bring the butt of the spear down at the backs of his knees. She hadn't thought the strike hard enough, but all she needed to do was continue his forward motion, take advantage of what was already there, and then she brought lighting down on him again. Spun her spear in her hands, bringing the point back up, and slashed into Supay's unprotected back on the upswing. Not a deep hit, but it didn't need to be. Not every stroke needed to be a kill-shot. She just needed to wear him down. Keep him at bay until Mamaquilla recovered from her shock. Except . . . Mamaquilla was still prostrate with grief. Still on the ground, cradling Inti's body.

Sigrun was distantly aware as the clouds opened up, and frozen rain and hail started to fall, a heavy, pounding downpour that meant that she needed to watch her footing. Supay spun back towards her, showing her the self-same strike that had been aimed at her ribs earlier in the fight. Time seemed to slow—pure adrenaline—as Sigrun evaluated the angles and the options in fractions of a second. Every time she'd been hit with the club so far, it had carried hurt beyond just flesh and bone. Each strike had felt as if it had sucked away part of her soul with it. Allowing it to hit her again seemed a . . . very bad idea.

This time, however, Sigrun had no ceiling over her head. She threw herself skywards, and the club, heavy, bulky thing that it was, wailed through the air under her feet this time, and Sigrun brought lightning down again, a triple fork of it, directed right at Supay himself. He staggered back, and looked up, taken off-guard, just for an instant, and Sigrun followed her lighting down. She was half a step ahead now, and considering her speed and agility, that was all she needed. Supay was slow by comparison, and the club was lethal, but Sigrun dodged a half a dozen wild swings, while returning her own. Supay was forced to try to catch her where she'd been a moment before, but she was simply no longer there.

She hadn't been pushed this hard in combat since the Odinhall. This was the speed she couldn't use in practice against Adam, Trennus, or Kanmi—it simply wasn't fair to them. And Lassair had no interest in such things, so Sigrun never got to practice using her full range of abilities. To an outside observer, like Adam, who had his gun leveled at Supay, the two combatants were smears of motion. Sigrun's spear blurred in her hands, and she constantly circled her opponent, looking for an advantage. Threw herself into the air, got clipped by the club for her pains, and then dove in to attack again. Lightning flashed, blinding him; thunder roared, staggering him. Every time Adam thought he had a shot, Sigrun was right back in his way again. "Sig!" Adam shouted, watching her step back, rocked by a heavy hit. "Sig, clear out of there! Let me take the shot!"

She barely heard the words. Her concentration was absolute, and this time, as she leaped into the air, she saw the perfect opening as she pulled down lightning, and followed the strike down once more. All the advantages of high ground and the reach of her spear, and the further advantage of Supay's momentary shock at the lighting hit. Instead of her usual fast, lighting-like strikes, she allowed herself a hard, sweeping blow, directed at his neck, at the downwards angle.

For a moment, Sigrun actually thought she'd missed. She hovered there for a moment, staring at Supay, and the death-god stared back at her.

Supay's head lifted, as if he were about to nod, mockingly. His neck arched. Gaped. Black blood began to pour out of the wound, and then his head simply fell back off his neck. But the body didn't fall. It staggered, lifting its club once more, and Sigrun just stared at it for a moment. *What, should I be surprised that a death-god acts like a ghul?* she thought, and pulled her spear back. Slid it home, up under the sternum, and into the heart.

An electrical sensation coursed over her, and for an instant, Sigrun could have sworn she saw blackness pouring out of Supay's body, rising as a mist, and something cold and silvery leaped out with it, aimed like a spear at her own heart. Sigrun jerked back, her own spear still caught in the body, and slapped a hand to her chest, looking for the surely mortal wound, and found . . . nothing. "You missed," Sigrun told the god's broken form, her voice a harsh croak. Whatever it was, it had surely passed through her, without harm. She didn't feel any different at all.

Other than the fact that I just killed a god in single combat. Shouldn't have been possible. Maybe all the ambient energies . . .Hel's frozen heart, he was a death-god. What does that even mean? Her thoughts raced. *Does that mean Trennus is going to live? Does that mean that the Sapa Inca can't die right now?* And on the heels of those thoughts, another: *If I thought I was in trouble last time, when I was just present when a god died . . . .*

Adam stared at Supay's body as it hit the floor. His eyes flicked up, and he called to Sigrun, "You all right?" There was an awful lot of blood on her.

"Fine! Asha—"

"On it." Adam had been trying to keep his attention evenly divided, Sigrun dueling Supay on one side, and Lassair keeping the Sapa Inca down on the ground, on the other. The spirit's mouth was red with blood, where she'd been apparently tearing at Sayri Cusi's throat. The two of them were grappling back and forth now, and Adam felt another rumble from deep underground as he stepped forward, training his gun on Sayri Cusi's back. *I have no idea how powerful this ammunition is. It could go through him and kill Lassair. And then Tren will kill me.* The train of thought halted in a surge of wrenching grief as Adam remembered that Trennus was dead. *Come on, Lassair, hold him so I can shoot him without hitting you.*

The pair on the ground reversed positions again, and Lassair wound up, once more, on top, the blaze of her fires almost too bright to look on. He had no idea how the emperor wasn't screaming in pain. How the man wasn't *dead* yet.

His skin is as rock, and the god-fragments within him sustain him. Lassair didn't have much energy with which to direct the thought at Steelsoul. She could feel Stormborn approaching, leveling her spear, looking for an opening. Could feel a darker, colder edge in her sister than had been there before. *Stay your hand, sister! I will end this!*

The one to whom so many were bound had worn fine clothing at the beginning of the day. It had, in the main, burned away at this point, leaving only the rock-like skin. Lassair wasn't particularly strong or agile, but she'd been watching Trennus and Adam wrestle every day for five years now. That and her inner will had been enough, so far, to keep her ahead of the human, who seemed to be channeling strength up from the very stone. She had managed to get on top again, her legs wrapped around his thighs, her weight back at first, and then had slammed her forehead forwards, into his cheekbone, sinking her weight down. Grinding her head into the sensitive portions of his face, and just bearing down. The rock armor might shield the flesh beneath from impact, it might shield his flesh from her flames, other than where her talons and teeth had managed to pierce, but this position, with her face tucked away, protected her eyes, while she clawed at his with her left hand, and jammed the point of her right elbow into his shoulder. She was, in effect, letting gravity do the work, while increasing skin-contact. Trying to burn through the rock-hide, while the one with the screaming pieces of others trapped inside of him tried to send electricity through her body.

Lassair laughed, and dug her talons into an eye-socket, pulling the lid up and spearing in with the talon on her thumb. *Skyfire will not harm me in this form.* She heard him *scream,* and hooked her thumb back out, taking the eye with it. The eye cavity had been almost instantly cauterized by her strike. No blood. The one who held so many bound fought harder, trying to punch her, dislodge her, and Lassair half-closed her eyes. Let her body, which had been magma-like till this point, become pure flame. Evanescent. His punches went right through her, but she remained manifested. Wholly present. Just another form. *You want me to be inside of you, is what I understand?* Lassair said, very softly. *Oh, you had only to _ask_.*

She poured herself in through the seared eye socket. Distilled herself to raw starfire, and raged through his body, burning him from the inside out. The spirits inside of him wailed in terror and tried to stop her. One of them tried to sheathe her in electricity. Another tried to turn the body wholly to stone. The third begged her, *Sister, mercy, please . . . .*

It almost stayed Lassair's hand. But then spirit-senses looked out of the body and saw Trennus' still form, lying in the corner, and Lassair hissed and wrenched the fragments free of the flesh that bound them. *Return to the Veil, if you can,* Lassair told them, as they began to dissipate. Not enough energy to sustain them, and she wouldn't let them drink from the tremendous ambient flows. *That is the only mercy I offer you today. For the one who bound you? Nothing.*

She pulled herself out of the body, going up like a pillar of flame, before settling back into her winged human female form, before looking down at the charred remains of the one who had presumed to bind so many. She met Steelsoul's eyes, then Stormborn's. Looked past them to Mamaquilla, who still knelt in place, rocking the body of her beloved in her arms. And then, wearily, Lassair stepped over to where Trennus lay. Her power still pulsed in him, keeping his heart alive, pushing a little blood to his brain. Light still shone down from above, from Inti's final gift to his people. Only five minutes had actually passed since Trennus had given himself to her, completely surrendering himself. *Oh, beloved,* Lassair said, kneeling to lift his head, and cradling it in her lap. She could feel the earth shifting below them. Fire building in the mountain. *You dared so much for me. How can I not match you with equal daring?*

Stormborn, after embracing Steelsoul, followed after her. Lassair could feel Truthsayer and Emberstone unbind their protections, and enter the room, their spirits fearful within them. Saraid's presence was a tiny flicker of will. The forest-spirit was only manifesting enough of herself to protect Trennus' body from further harm, the bulk of her attention apparently elsewhere. The hind did not even acknowledge Lassair's presence.

Stormborn crouched down beside Lassair, and put a hand to Trennus' chest. "Worse than the wound Adam took in Judea," she assessed, quietly. "You've kept him alive?"

The spirit lives. The body is . . . preserved. Can you . . . ?

"I can only heal by taking the wound, and this is too grievous. It would cost my own life." Stormborn's voice was choked with tears, and more hail rattled into the ruins, pelting against the floor. "If you can heal it partially, however . . . ."

You can take the rest?

"Yes."

"Sig—" Steelsoul's voice was horrified. "I can't watch you go through that again—"

"I will not let Tren die if I have it in my power to save him," Stormborn returned, her voice resolute. "A death-god *died* here today. Let's put whatever reprieve that grants us, to good use." She swallowed. "If there's any reprieve at all. The emperor died, after all."

There has been a reduction in local entropy, Mamaquilla said, her voice plangent with sorrow. ***You will find it easier to heal your friend and reunite body and spirit. But you must hurry.***

Lassair felt a wave of gratitude pass over her. She closed her eyes, and once more, poured herself into a body. She found the grievous wound in the heart, and knitted the tissues back together. Poured her own life-essence into them. *Flame-heart*, Trennus had always called her, a loving nickname. Now it might well be his own name, as she wrote herself into his tissues, scribed herself into his essence, and then pulled back, exhausted. The work was delicate and exacting, and there was a sense of *pressure* in the earth. *We have to hurry,* Lassair told the others. *Saraid, sister . . . can you help us?*

I will help him. Saraid's voice held reproof and grief, but Lassair didn't understand it. She only cared that the forest-spirit was already pouring her energies into Trennus' body, binding the damaged flesh back together. But Saraid left no marks of herself, no traces.

Then Sigrun reached out and put her hand to Trennus' chest. Rune-born light flared, and then she fell back with a groan, blood beginning to pour from between her breasts. Steelsoul caught her, but Truthsayer and Emberstone both leaped forwards as well, Truthsayer reaching for Stormborn's shoulders, while Emberstone moved to Trennus' side.

. . . *Flamesower had traveled for a long time, always along the length of the cord. It seemed infinitely long, and he had seen much. The spider had been correct. The cord seemed to attract denizens of this place to him. Many wanted to consume him. Some had tried, and he'd learned to flee, quickly. He fought when there was no other option. He'd been surprised at his own strength. So had been those whom he fought. He looked tiny. An amorphous blob, with no true shape, and only a Name burning at his heart. But he wouldn't surrender his Name, and, when he needed to fight, he could reshape himself. He took a dozen forms, whatever seemed best. A stag, a bear, a bird of prey, a snake. He wrestled and he contended. Sometimes, he was devoured, but even then, the cord persisted, and he refused to give up his Name. He would not be bound.*

Saraid. That was the name of the hind that followed him wherever he went. His first ally in this place. She trailed along behind him. Told him when there were traps. Told him which other spirits might make trustworthy allies. Guarded him, guided him. He didn't know how he knew her, but he was indebted to her. Loved her. And realized that when she was present, a second cord — a much finer one, like gossamer — tied him to her, and her to him. <u>*This is as it is meant to be,*</u> *she told him.* <u>*We are bound, we two. We always have been. Because we always will be.*</u>

No weariness, because there was no time. But even though there was no time, there was . . . experience. He was learning. And with knowledge, came power. He wasn't sure what his true form was, anymore. Who he was, other than his Name and the cord, had ceased to matter. Memories of another life, a time in the world where everything ended, were distant. Trifling. Except that there were other Names that he knew. And those were important to him. He wouldn't give up those Names, either, no matter what creature had managed to defeat and consume him. Because he understood that consumption didn't matter. It was a game.

He learned the names of the ones he defeated, however. And his travels went on forever . . . until he felt the cord throb against him. A voice, whispering his Name. <u>*Flamesower. Beloved. Come back to me. Come back to us.*</u>

He was confused, but the voice was familiar. And because he was bound to it, utterly, he had no real choice, but then, he had already/always chosen . . . His last sight was the leaf-dappled eyes of the hind. He thought she looked joyous, but also deeply sorrowful, at the same time.

Trennus opened his eyes. His body felt heavy. Leaden. He could barely move, and felt trapped inside of it, horrible, lumpen thing of clay that it was. His center hurt. No. His *heart* hurt. *That would be because you were the idiot who stabbed himself in it,* he told himself, seeing the faces of his friends above him. For a moment, they didn't look *real*. Nothing more than masks with liquid, gelatinous eyes. Too-solid flesh. Trennus panicked for a moment, and then Lassair slipped her hand into his, and he turned towards her. She looked real. Beautiful. Phoenix wings spreading out from her shoulders in blazing glory, her body all fire. Thrumming along the bond between them. A glowing coal at the back of his mind, which, when he touched it, he realized, *was her.* She was in him. A part of him. And there was this unbalancing sensation, as if he wasn't entirely in *himself,* either. Glorious. Ecstasy-inducing. She slipped into him, and he slipped into her, and they were counterpoised in their minds, slipping into and through one another, over and over again. Trennus blinked, dazed. Refocused on the fire that was her flesh. There was something . . . wrong . . . about that . . .

The child? he asked silently, not trusting his voice.

I made it fire, too, she admitted, casting down her eyes. *I will make it flesh again, when I am. I am . . . not entirely sure what this will do to it. But your gift gave me power. Inti's sacrifice, too —*

"Inti's *what?*" Trennus was appalled. He'd apparently missed a few things while he was, well . . not to put too fine a point on it . . . dead. He hadn't really expected to be alive again. Breath in his lungs felt strange. And he had memories. Horrifyingly clear ones, at least, for the moment, of the Veil. The spider. Of what it felt like to be devoured, over and over again. The alliances he'd made there with the spirits he'd defeated, and whose Names he had learned. How they'd sometimes worked together, to fend off greater Names. And how they'd all scattered and hidden when a Greater Name moved through the area, like a leviathan, heedless of the little fish that spun in its wake, as the water swirled in vortices. And a brief, faint recollection of the hind. The one who'd been with him, every step of the way. *Saraid . . . .*

And then, distraction. Chatter of voices, as Kanmi and Minori both tried to describe what had passed: "Mamaquilla was injured, and Cocohuay gave up her body so that Mamaquilla would have an avatar —"

" — and then Adam *shot* Inti in the back of the head, and I haven't actually figured out why, or even how it *worked* yet."

Lassair provided a blur of images to supplement the words, as Sigrun sat back up, wincing openly as she inspected a wound just under her sternum, and Adam reached out and gripped Tren's shoulder, hard. "Your eyes, Tren," he said, cutting through the chatter. "What happened?"

Trennus raised his hands to his face. "I have no idea what you're talking about," he admitted.

He gave himself to me, Lassair explained, simply. *He is my servant now, body and soul. I am in him, and he is in me, and we will be, forever.*

At that moment, Saraid gently disentangled herself from his body, and faded out, demanifesting. And the loss of her gentle presence suddenly left Trennus bereft, even though his soul and senses sang with Lassair.

Sigrun heaved herself back to her feet, with Adam's aid. "Spirit-touched," the valkyrie muttered.

The ground shook underfoot. Focus returned with it, and Trennus reached down into the earth, and swallowed. "We have to get out of here," he said. "Everything else can wait. Coropuna is about to erupt."

Adam's head swung around. The miniature sun still hung in the sky overhead, sending brilliant, cold light through the clouds that still spat hail and freezing rain down on them. He knew that physicists would be studying any and all video records of the tiny star for years to come. Inti, like every other god, had mostly obeyed the laws of physics. He hadn't turned the world on its axis faster to create sunlight at midnight; he'd created a very small star, instead. And that star was burning out. Adam just hoped that it hadn't perturbed the orbit of the Libration point space station, or, god forbid, the moon itself. He rather thought not, though. Inti had been motivated to save Mamaquilla. And while Mamaquilla wasn't the moon, itself, it was her symbol.

The ground shuddered under his feet. Trennus looked up at them all, and staggered to his feet. "Did you hear me? We have to get out of here—"

Adam nodded to his friend. "I heard you." Trennus' eyes were hard to meet; they burned blue-violet now, like the heart of a flame. He knew he should be deeply disturbed by this; Trennus had given up his soul to Lassair. He'd *died*. Technically, he could be now considered some . . . aberrant form of *ghul*, with Lassair's power possibly providing the motive force for his once-dead body. But Adam couldn't think of Tren like that. "Give me a moment."

He walked carefully across the icy, rubble-strewn floor. Knelt down beside Inti's body, and met Mamaquilla's moon-white, luminous eyes, as the goddess looked up at him. "Forgive me," Adam asked her. "He asked me to do it."

I know, mortal. Her voice was weary, and held all the sorrow in the world in the soughing of the sea. *I do not hold you or yours accountable. All those to whom blame accrued, are now dead.*

Adam swallowed, and unholstered his pistol. Turned it around, and presented it to her, butt-first. In spite of her words, he could clearly picture her taking the gun, and firing it on him. In a way, she'd have the right.

Mamaquilla regarded the weapon with distaste. *No. I cannot take this. Inti was the one to whom soldiers looked in battle. I . . . do not use weapons, beyond a net. And your weapon is strange to me.* She looked down at her husband's fallen form. *He entrusted this weapon to you. He could have made it so that it could only kill him. He did not. He would not have done that, if he did not see a future need, and if he did not trust you. Keep the last-forged weapon of my husband's hands, and know this: it will only fire in your hands, or the hands of one of your line. Inti trusted you. Not all of mankind.*

The ground trembled underfoot once more, and Adam nodded, respectfully. Rose to his feet. Kanmi raised a finger. "We passed a field of ornithopters on our way in," he said. "Between the light show, the *ushnu* going up, and the mountain shaking, the chances that they're still there are slim to none, but that's our best bet."

Adam glanced back over at Mamaquilla, who still sat there, rocking the body of her husband. Another tremor, and Adam looked, uneasily, at the ruined roof overhead. "Tunnel?" he asked.

"No time," Sigrun replied, and wrapped her arms around his waist. The ground dropped out from under him as she raced upwards, arcing out of the ruins. He had enough time to see that the megalithic stones had been melted together along the path of the solar prominence that Inti had deployed. Sigrun set him at the foot of the *ushnu*'s southern face, and then leaped up into the air once more. Adam huddled in on himself as another surge of sleet and hail hit his body, and looked up in time to see Lassair carry Trennus out of the ruins, with Sigrun following her, holding Kanmi . . . and Minori slowly rose through the air in Sigrun's wake, buoyed by a howling vortex of wind that made her look uncannily like a djinn.

Adam glanced at the glacier-covered peaks as another rumble shook the earth. The pristine white snow-and-ice caps reflected the dying light of the tiny sun above as it dimmed. Became ruddier. The red disc was now larger than the tiny pinprick of incandescent light it had been previously, but was still perceptibly smaller than the moon, as seen from Earth. In its light, Adam could see cracks forming in the glacier caps, and turning, he spotted people scurrying in and around the buildings downslope of the *ushnu*, frantically loading belongings into cars and trucks. None of them were looking at the *ushnu*; everyone was far more involved with trying to get *out* of here.

"Looks like the evacuation is underway," Adam noted. Part of him said *Some of these people are innocents. We should help organize the evacuation . . .* and the rest of him said *Not our job. Our job is to get out of here, locate Livorus, and then get him out of Tawantinsuyu.* "Which way to the airfield?" he asked Kanmi, who'd just let go of Sigrun. "If we can, we can bring some of the survivors with us," he said, trying to get his conscience to shut up.

"Right," Kanmi told him, dryly, huddling against a rush of sleet and wind. "We'll just be the foreigners who were taken to the *ushnu* by their emperor and mysteriously survived the explosion when the head of state didn't. Let's not complicate things, ben Maor. Airfield is *that* way." He pointed to the southwest, and downslope. When Adam hesitated, Kanmi gave him an irritated look. "They're evacuating. They have a plan. We can't save them all."

Another rumble, and they all looked up, as a vast piece of one of the glaciers sheared off, and began to plunge down the mountainside to the east of them. "Let's survive, first!" Kanmi shouted over the roar of the distant avalanche. "You can beat yourself up later! I'll provide the damned stick! Go!"

They only had three people capable of flight, and Minori couldn't manage Kanmi's weight, so they *ran* for the airfield, slipping and sliding on the hail and sleet and mud. As they did, Adam's mind continued to churn, but he was focused now, on just one problem: ensuring the survival of his team. People were streaming into the airfield, but while there were six ornithopters present on the field, Adam saw only two pilots. Both of whom were arguing with frantic, frightened people, on the north end of the field. He pointed towards the south end of the field. "Kanmi," Adam said, grimacing as they all crouched in the tall grass near the field. "Can you do something fairly distracting?"

"More distracting than half the mountainside falling?" Kanmi's voice was tart.

"Less distracting than that." Adam looked up at the clouds. "This is going to be really bad flying, if the weather doesn't let up soon."

"Have Caetia here set off a couple of dozen lightning bolts north of our position," Kanmi said, dryly. "I guarantee, people are going to look."

Adam felt foolish, and looked up at the sky. It might be his imagination, but the hail suddenly seemed to be slacking off dramatically. "Ah, Sig?"

"On it," she muttered. "Esh, you must be weary. You are forgoing a perfect opportunity with which to show off your skills."

Kanmi's grin was forced. Adam could read weariness in all their body language now. Sigrun set off the lightning, and they all moved south, while everyone in the field stared north in consternation. Minori unlocked the cabin door of an ornithopter, and they all clambered inside, Adam grabbing a flight manual to start preflight checks. "I don't think the aviation administrators will down-check you for your safety routine," Kanmi muttered. "Just *go*."

"And when we crash because the wings are icy, what then?"

"I'll melt the ice on the wings," Kanmi retorted. "Or Lassair will, or Min will, or Caetia can get out and *push*. Just start us up."

Another prolonged, and deep rumbling that passed through the vehicle's frame, and Adam tossed the manual at the copilot's chair, and started the engine. Spirit-powered or not, the whole vehicle thrummed a little as he did so. "Everyone strap in. Return your tray tables and chairs to their full upright positions, and if you're inclined towards prayer? Now is probably a really good time."

People up the field from them heard the engine switch over, and he could see heads turning. Could see guards with muskets, alarmed that one of their vehicles was being commandeered, dropping down to aim at them, while various people began to run, right across the line of fire, charging for their ornithopter. Adam looked over the various controls, which had labels in Latin and Persian—the vast majority of ornithopters were, after all, Persian-built—and got the ungainly wings to deploy to their liftoff position. Ornithopters didn't require as long of landing strips as fixed wing crafts, because lift-off of an ornithopter relied not on thrusters, and not entirely on building up speed, but on hydraulics in the landing/takeoff struts that functioned like a bird's legs, throwing the vehicle airborne before the first down-stroke of the wings. "Get the wings cleared," Adam said, and turned the ornithopter to send it down the short runway. "And hope for a good updraft before we hit the edge of that cliff there."

That was, of course, the easiest way to get an ornithopter airborne. Start like a glider, and drop from somewhere high. And pray that the wings handled properly, because otherwise you *would* plummet like a rock.

Facing away from the field now, he could no longer see the people running towards them. It let him clear his mind, and he went through all the practiced motions of flight. This craft was larger than the ornithopters he'd flown before, but seemed responsive. They built up speed towards the edge of the cliff, as Kanmi, Minori, and Lassair all worked to de-ice the damned wings. "Getting close," Adam noted, clinically. "Twenty feet. Ten. Deploying wing extensions." He paused. "Brace."

The vehicle lurched sickeningly, and then its wings clawed at the air. Adam felt through the control stick the instant an updraft caught the wings, and they began to soar on it, reducing the need for the vehicle to flap strenuously, at least at first. He angled the nose just so, and they began to ascend, using that sharp wind to their advantage. "We're going to have to circle to gain altitude," he told them.

"Don't worry about altitude right now," Trennus told him, his voice sick. Adam knew that his friend's eyes had to be squeezed shut. "Even if all we do is glide in an angle downwards, we can take off again from a valley somewhere. We need distance, not altitude."

Trennus is correct, Lassair told him. *Do not look back, Steelsoul. Not until we have some fifty miles between us and this place.*

Adam, against most of his flight training, obeyed, and got them moving. A craft this small didn't have an autopilot. He couldn't do what the others were doing, and look out the side windows as he moved them southwest, gaining distance. He needed to bank, eventually, to get them back on a northeast heading, back to Cuzco and Machu Picchu, but as insistent as Tren and Lassair were? He'd be a fool not to listen to a ley-mage and a fire spirit about a *volcano.*

Less than ten minutes later, Adam knew they were a solid twenty miles from the landing field, and banked to head due north. As he did so, he heard a low rumble that transmitted through the frame of the ornithopter, and Lassair whispered, *Brace yourselves.*

"Oh, gods," Trennus said, quietly, but fervently.

Adam swallowed. The main peak of Coropuna, the western face, had exploded, and belatedly, gusts of wind buffeted their ornithopter. He steadied them in the air, staring at what he could now see. The white glacial cap was gone, and a vast plume reached up into the gray light of the pre-dawn sky. "Tephra," Trennus said, tightly. "Ash, debris, ice, water, rocks. Anything that makes it into the air as ejecta. That's what we're seeing right now."

Kanmi's voice then. "A damned good thing we're not flying a fixed-wing craft. The engines and the intakes would be filling up with ash."

"Microscopic fragments of volcanic glass. Yes." Trennus sounded concerned. "Ah, Adam? Esh *is* right, isn't he? The engines aren't . . . ."

"The moving parts don't require a lot of ventilation in ornithopters, because of the power source. Just lubrication for the rotors and pulleys and everything else." Adam was proud that the words were coming out as coherent sentences. "What about the people back there?"

"Depends," Trennus admitted, quietly. "After the initial upwards explosion, there's usually a pyroclastic flow. That can be magma, but the first thing they're going to see, I would think, is lahar."

"And that is . . . ?"

"Water and mud. All those glaciers, Adam. Flash-melted, and coursing down the side of the mountain, tearing the land free. It'll pass down the sides like an avalanche and a flood combined, burying anything in its wake." Trennus sounded somewhat ill. "That'll mix with the ash already on the ground. Harden like cement. The volcano might alternate between tephra and magma for a while, or it might not expel magma at all. Result will still be the same. Everything in the path of the lahar will be entombed. Covered by ash. Or swallowed by magma."

Kanmi admitted, after a moment, "Not that it's something I never wanted to see this close . . . but damn if it isn't beautiful, in a way."

"Kanmi!" Minori's voice was shocked.

"If it weren't for the people in the way, and how close we are to it? Look at it. Look at the way the clouds are forming above us. Look at the way the gases respond to heat and convection. A natural system, chaotic, and ordered at the same time."

". . . I'll admit that there is beauty in the savagery of it, but yes, the *people*, Kanmi . . . ."

Adam took his eyes off the instruments for a moment, and tried to figure out where on that mountainside the *ushnu* had been. He thought he saw the glimmer of ley-powered lights in a cluster, about two-thirds of the way up the mountain. "Do you think," he said, after a moment, "that Mamaquilla will protect her people?" *Inti died to protect them, in a way.*

Sigrun's voice rose through the ensuing silence, the first time his wife had spoken since boarding the plane. "I do not know, Adam," she said, quietly. "She was desolated. She had lost her husband, and they had been together for a very long time. I am sure that part of her would be quite willing to let the world burn. Or at least, that part of it which had contributed to his death." A pause. "I know I would be."

Don't say that, neshama. I know you better than that. You'd keep on fighting. Adam returned his attention to the flight controls.

Lassair's voice now, quietly, *I think she will protect them. In his memory. And will not allow his resting place to be covered over by the mountain's rage.* The spirit's voice was tired as she went on, *She gained much in that place, but she also lost much. She was gravely wounded by Supay. His club drained the life of any it touched, did it not, Stormborn?*

"It felt as if my soul were a oyster being pried from its shell," Sigrun confessed, sounding weary. "I am, however, in better shape than after the fight with Tlaloc. I cannot complain."

Yes. But Mamaquilla was not a warlike goddess. She was badly injured. Her light almost went out, until her granddaughter gave her the use of her body. Lassair's tone became poignant. *It was a sacrifice of more than flesh.*

Adam's head came up, warily. He'd learned far more in one day about all manner of foreign gods than he'd ever expected to in a lifetime. "Inti said that he rode his host's body lightly. And I spoke to the god-born whose body he shared, directly." He checked their course and speed, satisfied that they were travelling at around a hundred and fifteen knots. Still, he didn't dare get on the radio just yet, and he was doing everything right now with a compass and dead-reckoning.

Correct. Gods can manifest their own bodies . . . as I can do. But I believe it is easier for many of them, if they have a compatible host body.

"Speak the words, Lassair," Sigrun said, tiredly. "God-born." She paused. "So what you mean is, because Mamaquilla was so badly injured, Cocohuay needed to give her more than just her body to ensure her goddess survived."

She gave her life and her spirit, and I do not think more than a flicker of her remains. Lassair's voice was a dirge, for a moment. *But what of her remains, I think, would counsel her goddess to protect their people. They have, after all, midwifed many of them into life.*

"There was . . . quite a lot of energy," Kanmi noted, quietly, after several minutes had passed.

Yes. Lassair hesitated. *I think from more than Inti and Supay. I felt much come from . . . without.*

"So . . . Mamaquilla absorbed it all?" Kanmi's tone was distant. Professorial.

I . . . do not think so. But she gained much today, while losing everything she held most dear.

"Kanmi?" Adam said, quietly. "Subject for another time." He knew *precisely* where the sorcerer's mind was headed. The mystery of the missing energy from Tlaloc had taken up a good deal of Kanmi's thought processes for the past five years. Lassair had obviously been a grounding rod for some of it. Possibly Saraid as well. And Adam knew precisely whom Kanmi considered another candidate for absorption. Adam turned his head, trying to catch sight of Sigrun's face in the darkened cabin, and, after an instant, realized that she had fallen asleep.

In an ornithopter, no less. I think I've just had my flying complimented. Either that, or it's testimony to her exhaustion.

"Mmm. As you wish."

The flight back across Tawantinsuyu was long; their ornithopter was a very small model, compared to the commercial air travel models that had taken them here in the first place. Five hours, and Adam only got on the radio halfway through their flight, identifying them merely as a scientific expedition that had been surveying Coropuna's ley and geologic fields when the mountain had erupted. "I've got scientists and engineers aboard," he said, and looked up. It almost wasn't a lie.

"You saw the first eruption? Gods, people are going to want to talk to you when you land."

"I'd like to get clearance for Machu Picchu's main airfield. Can you get me on the right transponder beacon and tower frequency? I imagine there are a lot of relief flights heading out right now—"

"You have been off the grid, haven't you? Not as many flights as you'd think. Coropuna's a pretty remote area, and we've had massive earthquakes in Cuzco. Machu Picchu's actually the best place for you to land right now. The airport at Cuzco's a madhouse right now. Adjust your course, bearing . . . ."

Adam swallowed, hoped to god that Livorus was in Machu Picchu after all, and adjusted his bearing and speed. He could hear Kanmi behind him in the main area, getting Minori to lie down, stretched out across one of the bench seats, chiding her, gently, "Cocohuay may have healed *most* of the damage, but then you spent the afternoon in combat casting conditions, and then we all had to run half a mile to the airfield. Lie back, close your eyes, and let yourself rest for a bit. We'll get you checked out at a hospital as soon as we can."

There's going to be a line, from the sound of it. Adam heard a little more shuffling, as Trennus and Lassair curled into each other, trying to sleep, as well.

The weather away from Coropuna had calmed. No more ice, hail, snow, or freezing rain. Just a few prevailing winds from the west, pushing them towards Machu Picchu, as if nature itself wished to hasten their pace. With the flying itself taking so much less of his attention now, Adam had to resist the gray edges of exhaustion that tugged at his eyelids. Easy enough to distract himself. He had a lot to think about.

First and foremost, he'd just killed a god. Again. *It's not like it's a hobby,* had been his half-joking defense every time Kanmi had called him *godslayer* in private in the past two years. He now carried a weapon he wasn't sure he could get *rid* of, that had proven capable of killing a god — admittedly, a weakened god who'd offered himself up in self-sacrifice — but it was still a weapon capable of deicide. The only way, Adam decided, that he wasn't going to get himself flagged as "too dangerous to be allowed to live" would be to lie his *ass* off about how Inti had died. Or at least, just always leave it as "Inti sacrificed himself for the good of his people" and simply omit his own involvement in that, entirely. Sigrun wouldn't lie. But she might *omit*, for his safety, and her own, at least to Rome and the Praetorians. To the Odinhall . . . Adam stifled a groan. *Maybe that's why Tyr had no objections to the marriage. He was keeping an agent more or less sitting atop the godslayer at all times, with Sig married to me. Of course, Sig is probably in just as much, if not more trouble now, herself. She took out Supay in single combat. Admittedly, there was an ungodly — hah! — amount of energy in the air. Otherwise . . . I don't think a valkyrie could do what she did.*

From the personal ramifications of what would happen when they reported in, in Rome, to the somber realization that they were going to be lucky to get out of Tawantinsuyu alive. An angry mob, could, rightly, tear them apart for having killed their emperor. *How does it feel to be an assassin?* Adam thought, grimly, his hands tightening on the controls. *We'll go down in history as that, if any of this ever gets out. God. No. Worse.* He cleared his throat, slightly, and murmured, "Lassair?"

He didn't want to wake her, if she were asleep, but her mind responded, immediately, *Yes? Do not fear, Steelsoul. My body rests, but I have learned to divide spirit and body better. You will not fall asleep while controlling this vessel.*

"Thanks for that. I was a little worried." Adam marshaled his thoughts. "You said that more energy than just Inti's came back to the *ushnu,* right?"

. . . yes.

"Enough so that perhaps, when the system broke down, each of the *entities* in the other towers . . ." Adam decided to go back to that word. It seemed safer. ". . . dispersed?"

I think it very likely. Lassair's tone was sad. *There were also the remains of three in the one who bound this land.*

"You catch any names?"

Yes. It was difficult, because they were so . . . fragmentary. One had been worshipped by his people under many different names. Three different cultures worshipped him as three different lightning gods, but all were the same creature. Catequil. Apocatequil. Illapa. Lord of Thunder.

"That would explain the lightning." Adam nodded. "Who else?"

Pacha Camac. An earth-god. And Chasca Coyllur. Maiden-goddess of fertility.

"And the others? The ones in the towers?"

Mamaquilla wailed each name in my mind as the seals broke. Apu, lord of mountains. Kon, lord of rain. Urcuchillay, lord of beasts. Mamazara, lady of grain. We freed a few at Nazca, but they were all . . . lesser names. Lassair paused. *I know what you will ask, Steelsoul. And it is true. The only greater god left in Tawantinsuyu is Mamaquilla herself. And yes, I believe she absorbed much of the power of her brother-husband, and the others who died. I am grateful for that. There is no one better suited to protecting and nurturing her people, than she.*

Adam struggled with it. Grappled with it. All the dossiers and guidebooks to Tawantinsuyu had spoken of it as a land comparable in spirituality to India or Tibet. Hundreds of gods. Thousands of shrines. To go from that, overnight, into monotheism . . . a devastating social change, and again, it was, in a sense, *his fault.*

No. It is not. Lassair's tone was emphatic. *All fault accrues to the ones who bound this land, and the people in it.*

Explain that to the people who live here, Adam thought, swallowing. He could envision holy wars raging across the entire western half of Caesaria Australis as a result of all of this.

The smell of blood and steel and sweat, mixed with apple shampoo and the hint of warm skin underneath, was his only warning, before an arm wrapped around his neck from behind, and a light kiss brushed his cheek. "Lassair woke me and told me to distract you from brooding on consequences," Sigrun told him. "Let us leave that to people like Livorus, for the moment."

"Is there anything else we could have done, Sig?"

"The die was cast before we ever came here."

"And now you sound like your sister." Adam felt the ornithopter rock as a buffet of wind caught the wings, and adjusted course. That had actually felt as if the sky had reached out to slap him.

Sigrun slapped his upper arm, without force. "I didn't mean it in terms of fate, Adam. I meant that when we approached Sayri Cusi, he was already fully committed to this course of action. And that once Livorus spoke to him in such a way that he took offense . . . everything that you and I did, proceeded from that point."

It would have made no difference, if you three had not gone to the one who bound so many, Lassair contributed. *I would still have been a target. They would still have attacked, to try to capture me, so that I might heal the man's wife.*

"I thought," Kanmi said, sleepily, from somewhere near the back of the ornithopter, "that we'd be waiting on the debriefing till we retrieved

Livorus."

"I'm wondering how we're even going to do that," Trennus put it, clearly having awoken. "It might not be a good time to show Praetorian badges. Some of the emperor's people knew you'd gone with him to Coropuna, Adam."

"So we go to the Praetorian branch closest by, grab every single officer there, even if it means taking them off disaster relief work —" Adam waved off the chorus of questions that rose at his words, "and get Livorus out of wherever he's been put. Lassair, you can sense him, right?"

From up to two miles away, yes. He has a bright and distinctive mind.

All right, how do you do that, if gods can't see the bound servants of other gods . . . .

Livorus is not bound to any particular god. He underwent initiation rites to Mars when he entered the Legion, and he donates charitably to the temples of Jupiter, Mars, and Apollo, but he only attends services once a year or so, when required by his duties in the Senate. He is not blood-bound or soul-bound. He makes . . . limited sacrifices. Lassair paused. *The ones that I could not see properly at Nazca, were blood-bound to Supay. They had made sacrifices, human or animal, with their own hands. They were consecrated to him. Bound. Sealed. Their minds were blank to me, I think, because they belonged wholly, to Supay.*

Adam blinked, and the ornithopter dipped a little, as they entered a turbulent area. Sigrun scrambled for the co-pilot's seat, and buckled herself in, even as Trennus groaned, audibly. Adam had rarely entered into individual, mind-to-mind conversation with Lassair. So, out of courtesy, he continued, out loud, "Fair enough. That doesn't explain why Inti and Mamaquilla said they had a hard time seeing me. I've never performed blood-sacrifice in my *life.*"

"But Lassair can see you." Trennus put in, and then groaned again as the ornithopter dipped and swayed.

You are a different case, Steelsoul. Your brother? I could barely see him. The same was true of many other people in your land. It was a very quiet place, for me. Few spirits. And thousands of silent minds. Lassair paused. *Your people do not sacrifice blood, it is true. Even animal sacrifice is rare in these days. But you make smaller, daily sacrifices, instead of large sacrifices once or twice a year. And all of you perform those sacrifices, not just a handful of priests. You are all sealed to your god. And because the sacrifices are daily, it increases the number of times you think of him, in terms of worship. It binds you more closely, than a human who makes sacrifice a few times a year, and barely thinks of his or her gods in the interim. Your god is very clever.*

Adam winced. He wasn't sure he was entirely comfortable talking about his faith so analytically. "All right. Then you can see me more clearly, than, say, my brother, because I'm not particularly strict in my observances?" He paused. "Actually . . . is that why Tlaloc —" an apologetic look at the others, for using the name, "didn't seem to pay attention to me?"

In part, perhaps. But you also have a Name, Steelsoul. It rings out in the air around you. I am not sure that even if you performed every sacrifice, daily, with perfect precision, that it would entirely hide you from me. I know that Name.

Other do not know that Name. Also, you hold me in affection. That makes a difference. It opens your mind and spirit to me, in part. Lassair paused. *Stormborn is much the same. Her Name rings out. Declares itself, and what she is.*

"This is all a conspiracy to get me to go to temple and bow in Baal-Hamon's direction more often, isn't it?" Kanmi muttered, and everyone chuckled

You give faith and trust to none. You perform no sacrifices to gods, curry favor with no spirits. You are . . . open to others, yes. And you have a Name, which lights up the air around you.

"And you know what? I'm all right with that." Kanmi's tone was cynical. "I'm not going to start bowing and scraping just to try to cover my ass."

You would not be you if you did so. I would think that you had lost your Name.

This time, Minori's laughter was the loudest of all.

They made it to the airport by seven antemeridian. Adam was grainy-eyed by that point, and exceedingly grateful to have tower directions. On the ground, they were on edge, and Adam had to remind himself not to pull a gun as a handful of reporters surged towards them, begging to know what they'd seen at Coropuna. It took everything he had to respond, politely, "We were in the air, and it was dark by the time the eruption took place —"

"Yes, but did you see the source of the sun rising at midnight, the beam of golden fire that has been reported? Scientists have triangulated it, and say that Coropuna itself was the most likely source."

"Did a ley-facility explode?"

"No." Much to Adam's surprise, that was from *Minori*. She pushed her way forwards, looking haggard, and Kanmi moved right with her, a hand just behind her back, in case she needed support, but not touching her. "I'm one of the scientists with this, ah, expedition. I can say, without room for contradiction, that ley-power was not the cause of Coropuna's eruption. There may have been human factors involved, but ley-energy remains safe to use, so long as people do not make radical alterations to the existing grid."

"And you are . . . ?"

Minori threw Adam a quick, apologetic glance. "Dr. Minori Sasaki."

"Thank you, Dr. Sasaki. We have more questions —"

"No more questions," Adam told them, briskly. "The scientists and engineers have had a very long night, and we would like to find a hotel." *Or, rather, Livorus. Sleep can wait till we've grabbed the local Praetorians, found him, and gotten to a secure location. Oh, and getting Minori checked by a doctor. I'd add Trennus to that list, but . . . well . . . .*

They gathered a group of local Praetorians, as much to bodyguard themselves as Livorus, and went directly to the summer palace of the Sapa Inca. Lassair confirmed from a mile away, that Livorus was present, alive and well, if a little harried. The palace guards were at first reluctant to admit that the propraetor was on site, but Adam pointed out, quietly,

"You're aware that your emperor was at the sacred site on Coropuna during the explosion?"

The various guards all glanced at one another, sidelong, and eventually moved Adam up the chain of command until he was speaking to the highest-ranked personal guard of the Emperor available on site. There were uncomfortable questions about how the propraetor's lictors had escaped the destruction, while the Sapa Inca and most of his bodyguards had yet to check in. Adam, backed by twenty local Praetorians, however, had enough weight to throw around to snap out, finally, "I'm not going to answer one more damned question until you provide to me my protectee, in good health and condition. And if you do not do so in the next five minutes, we are going to start going through the *walls* to get to him."

The royal guards backed down at that point. They had no leadership structure in place; the emperor's chief bodyguards had gone with him to the volcano. They didn't have an emperor. And they were in the unwanted position of holding a propraetor of the Roman Empire *hostage*.

Livorus himself was unharmed, just as Lassair had sensed. "Ah, there you are," he said, on being brought out from wherever he'd been housed, as calmly as if his various lictors had been slightly overdue from a long stroll. "These gentlemen were most accommodating about allowing me outside of the palace during the recent earthquakes. I did make a few observations about how Rome might be amenable to sending relief workers and supplies to an ally of such long standing, were it not for the fact that one of the Empire's representatives was currently being held captive, but alas, no one here was of an appropriate rank to make decisions regarding my status. Until now, apparently." He gave Adam a piercing glance. "Shall we make our way hence?"

"Yes, sir," Adam agreed. Having someone else around to make decisions was a complete relief.

"I look forward to the debriefing." Livorus bowed, very slightly, over Sigrun's hand. "And I am delighted to see you all well and comparatively healthy."

Most of the hotels in Machu Picchu had been shaken by the earthquakes; but they now had running water and a rotating watch of twenty Praetorians. Kanmi, however, took Minori to the local hospital, and used his badge without compunction. "I'm not saying to skip her to the head of the line," he told the nurses. "I'm saying that she had internal injuries, severe ones, earlier in the day. She was given some healing by one of your priestesses, but we need some follow-up care here, to make sure her organs are back in the right places and there's no internal bleeding."

The nurse behind the desk, who looked harried, and had a waiting room filled with bleeding, hurt people, gave him a tired stare. "She walked in here on her own two feet. She can wait with the rest of the non-bleeders."

Kanmi wasn't much in a mood to deal with this. "Listen to the words I am speaking to you," he told the nurse, leaning forward, and lowering his voice. Quietness sometimes got people's attention more quickly than yelling. "She has had internal injuries —"

"So have most of the people in the room. She's had more healing than most of them had —"

"How many of them were tortured by a fucking maniac of a sorcerer for four hours, and how many of them had a random piece of debris fall on them? Now, can we reassess the triage line?" Kanmi glared at the nurse for a long moment, and her mouth opened into an O of pure horror.

Minori reached out and caught his elbow. "It's all right. I'll wait my turn," she told him. "You don't have to stay."

"Where in Astarte's name did you get the idea that I was going anywhere?" Kanmi gave her a look. "That's all we need. Someone hears you're alive, and comes here for try number three."

Minori gave him a look. "You are paranoid, Master Eshmunazar."

It had been *Kanmi* for the past three weeks. He grimaced. "Not paranoid enough, Dr. Sasaki."

Four hours later, Kanmi gave up. He took Minori back to the car, and hustled her back to the hotel. "I don't see why," she protested.

"By the time they finally give you an MRI and determine, yes, there's been internal bleeding, you're going to be in your eighties and have healed on your own, or dead. Let's just have Caetia fix the damage before the internal organs scar up, and before the wounds aren't fresh enough for her to do her thing." Kanmi started the car, annoyed with himself. "I should have asked her before this. I just don't like to bother her, because there's a price-tag attached. I'm sorry."

"I didn't think you knew those words. But you've said them quite often today." Minori's voice was drowsy as he took off through the crowded streets. Everyone in Machu Picchu was out of their houses and on foot, or so it seemed.

"Oh, I'm sorry about a lot of things in my life. And when it's true, I say it. But there isn't a lot of point in apologizing just to apologize." Kanmi slowly made his way through a crosswalk where the pedestrians simply would not clear the way, and tried not to visualize shoving them out of the way with sorcery. "In this case? I'm not sure I or any of the rest of the team can make it up to you, that we weren't there —"

Minori, who'd been leaning her head back against the seat, opened her eyes and looked at him. "Members of the team *were* there, Kanmi. Two men *died* trying to protect me. And Asha." Her dark gaze held his. "I don't think you have to apologize."

"Yes. I do. The men who were there weren't me. They were excellent at what they did, but they weren't me." It sounded arrogant, said out loud, but his voice was empty. He turned off into the newer residential area where their hotel was located. The oldest buildings in the city, with their monumental, inwards-inclined walls, were untouched. The newest buildings, with steel frames and earthquake reinforcing, were in good shape. Anything built between 1500 and 1890 AC, however, seemed to have taken heavy damage.

"So because they weren't you, they were doomed to failure? You're a good sorcerer, Mas . . . Kanmi. So am I. I couldn't get free of all of those sent against us —"

"Yes, but if I'd been there, you and I *probably* could have dealt with them, together." Kanmi sighed and followed the orders of a *gardia* member, out directing traffic around a street filled with fallen building debris. A sidelong glance at Minori, as he finally reached their hotel. "You are an incredible caster, Dr. Sasaki. You can do a few things I absolutely *can't*, and I'd really like to discuss them with you, at your convenience." He found a parking spot in an area clear of debris, and hopped out to open her door for her. Catching her opening the door herself, he chided her, gently, "Until we know for sure that everyone who wanted you dead, is actually dead? You should let me cover you getting in and out of vehicles."

Minori sighed a little, and nodded. As they entered the hotel lobby — catching lungfuls of dust from the walls that had had shed cracked plaster all over the interior, she asked, quietly, "You said there was a price on Caetia's healing? She's going to ask me for my firstborn, then?"

"Ah, no." Kanmi cleared his throat. "She literally takes the wound from you. Whatever the injury is, broken bone, a cut, a bruise . . . it gets transferred to her own body. She heals a good deal faster than the rest of us. But still, it hurts. And it takes energy for her to heal. So I don't like to ask her to do it."

Minori's mouth dropped open, and she started to shake her head in refusal. "Don't," Kanmi told her, trying not to sound harsh or abrupt. "I have no idea if Cocohuay healed you enough to prevent scarring to the internal organs, or if they're permanently damaged. That's all I was hoping the MRI would tell us. On the whole, I'd really prefer for you not to suffer any long-term damage because of *our* fuck-up."

By now, they'd reached the elevator, which had an out-of-order sign on it. Kanmi exhaled. He hadn't actually been *in* the hotel yet, not any longer than to grab his room key, which he now checked, and verified yes, first-floor. *Gods bless Tren and his absurd anxieties, this once*, Kanmi thought. It was easier to think about things like that, than the fact that Tren had been dead today for a solid five minutes. Just put one foot in front of the other for now, and just plod onwards.

Minori didn't know what to make of Sigrun's healing abilities, once Kanmi had tapped for admission to Adam and Sigrun's room. The valkyrie knelt in front of her as she sat on the couch, hands lightly pressed to Minori's shoulders, lit up from within with her god's power. And she could see what it cost the woman, as the light faded, leaving Sigrun looking weary, and her skin ashen. "Cocohuay did her best, but I'm surprised you were able to walk, let alone run, earlier," Sigrun assessed quietly. "In a strange way, though, it's fortunate that the wounds weren't too much healed. I couldn't have helped, otherwise." She paused. "You weren't in pain?"

Minori couldn't deny that she felt *much* better now. Every lingering, residual ache had passed out of her body, followed by a soothing warmth. She stretched hesitantly, and then with more enthusiasm. "I was," she admitted. "But it was much less bad than it had been before the first round of healing magic." She arched her back. "This feels . . . rather like cheating."

"What, you earned your aches and pains?' Sigrun replied, slowly getting back to her feet. "You have shown us the quality of your steel today, Minori. You need not prove anything else."

Adam curled a hand under Sigrun's elbow to steady her, his eyes concerned. "Livorus wants us to get together in his room for a debriefing in a couple of hours," he told Kanmi. "I don't think he wants us to stay and dig in the rubble. We're going to catch the local news . . . assuming any of the far-viewer stations are on the air right now. Might as well see how everything's being covered."

"Should I be in the room for the briefing?" Minori asked, tentatively.

"You were there," Adam said, simply. "Yes, you should be."

Kanmi nodded, and looked over at Minori. "I'll walk you to your room."

"We've got Praetorians on every entrance and exit of this place," Adam noted. "Esh, get some sleep at some point, all right?"

"I'll sleep when we get back to Rome. Or, possibly, when I'm dead. Whichever comes first." Kanmi stepped out into the hall, and then held the door for Minori.

Minori hesitated outside of her room, as the other sorcerer looked around the hallway, alertly. "Would . . . would you like to come inside?" she offered. He stood relatively close to her, not really in her personal space, but she swore she could feel the heat of his skin. A day's worth of beard growth, harsh and dark against his jaw line. Hair rumpled, and clothing, too. Blood splatters here and there, particularly along his sleeves, as if he'd been working like a butcher. *Then again, weren't we all?*

And as she spoke, she saw his eyes snap back to focus on her, clearly startled. She had a fairly good idea of how his mind operated now, and had seen under several layers of granite-like masks he maintained, at all times. The caring father of his two sons . . . that was an identity that he rarely, if ever, let anyone see. The mocking, sharp-tongued, unrepentant gadfly . . . that one was used to keep everyone around him at a nice, safe distance. Where he could see their eyes and their hands. She'd seen him fight now, too, and the *mind* behind those perfectly composed, balanced spells, each one mathematically *pristine* . . . that was remarkable, as was the cold fury with which he faced enemies. Indomitable, really. There was no surrender in him, not even on a subject like the *gods* themselves. *His wife couldn't understand that*, she realized, suddenly. *He may have chosen not to fight on this issue or that, but he never surrendered. He's not capable of it. It must have made him very difficult to live with . . . but it also makes him very much like a samurai.* She could understand that. It worked with established norms in her mind. And coupled with that sudden flow of comprehension, was a rush of warmth. She'd come very close to dying today. She'd killed her captor with her own mind and hands. She and Kanmi had stood side-by-side, fighting the *impossible*. And they'd survived.

A large part of her wanted to celebrate that simple fact. At his startled glance, however, she immediately began to shift back a little. Preparing to recant, to say she hadn't meant it that way, if his reaction was anything other than agreement.

So she was rather surprised, herself, when he leaned down. Cupped her face in his hands, and kissed her. Soft-rough of lips and facial hair against her skin. Neither of them had yet had a chance to bathe properly. She was dismally aware that she smelled of sweat and pain. All of those uncomfortable realizations however, faded rapidly. *He's really a lot better at this than Calgacus was*, she thought, dimly. *Asuka was really good at kissing, but then again, we weren't supposed to . . . .* The old memories stirred, and she tried not to stiffen, but Kanmi was already pulling away, one of the usual masks shifting up and over his face. "I'm sorry. Misread you there. It's just that . . ." He shook his head, clearly irritated, and rubbed a hand over the back of his neck. "You know how it is, when you get the math just right, and everything adds up, and everything works? You . . . add up, Min." He shook his head again. "And you can't stand me. It's all right. Most days, I can't stand myself. Get some rest before the meeting—"

Minori tried to get a word in edgewise, failed, and finally leaned up and kissed him, herself. His body had gone rigid, and it evidently took a moment for him to register that she was serious about the kiss. After realization sank in, however, she found herself boosted up into his arms, the door unlocked, and both of them in the room beyond more rapidly than she could have imagined.

She was honestly surprised by his patience after that initial burst of speed. She was all too aware of her hesitancies and fears; she knew that she wasn't good at this. His whisper of "What do you like?" was met by her head-shake and silence. Rustle of the sheets as he pushed her back against the bed, still kissing. Running his hands along her sides, all the way down, then following another downwards trail with his lips, although she stiffened in reaction as he reached her breasts. "Not something you like?" Surprise in his tone.

"Not . . . not really . . ." How to explain that she'd been fine with it when Asuka had played with her breasts, but that Calgacus had squeezed them like ripe melons, until they *hurt*, and would never leave them alone?

"Hmm. Interesting." He worked his way lower, sliding the pants she'd put on . . . *gods, yesterday morning* . . . out of his way. And then worked her with lips and tongue and fingers, glancing up every now and again to verify that the incantation he was weaving was having its desired effect. And then he added a fine thread of actual magic to the mix, using air itself to brush over her most sensitive places. Creating just a little more friction, a little more pressure. Ebbing and flowing, fast and then slow, in response to the expressions on her face, and her inhalations of pleasure.

Minori clutched at the sheets as he built fire in her, and finally released, like the new star she'd seen in the heavens last night, feeling fluids pulse out of her. But Kanmi wasn't satisfied yet, insistently building her back up again. And again. Her relaxation, however, gave way to surge of anxiety as he groped, a little blindly, in the nightstand. Almost every hotel in lands controlled by the Roman Empire provided complimentary condoms. *Better safe than down with the clap*, was the motto usually printed on the sides of the waxed paper packets, and this hotel was no exception. The delay, however, gave Minori time to worry, and when Kanmi turned back to her, he clearly caught the crease between her eyes and the bitten lower lip. "I might be a little rusty," he said, raising his eyebrows, "but surely it can't be *that* bad."

Minori shook her head, rapidly. So far, he'd given her more pleasure in one night than Calgacus had in six months. She reached out her arms, and smoothed her expression. "I'm not very good at this," she admitted, her voice small. "I'm sorry. I wasn't even sure I liked men until about ten minutes ago."

Kanmi blinked rapidly, absorbing that, and then kissed her again, stealing her words for the moment, and then gently pushed himself into her. Checked on angles, vectors, and velocities. Whispered little jokes about determining trajectory into her ear, making her laugh, and brought her back to the point where the fire overwhelmed her again, before finally finishing, himself.

Stroking her hair out of her face as their bodies cooled, Kanmi finally said, yawning, "There's nothing I really want to do right now more than sleep . . . but if I do, we're going to wake up for the debriefing still stinking."

"You are a master of romance." She raised her eyes to his for a moment.

"I'm renowned for it, far and wide." He arched his eyebrows at her. "I know we don't have a damned thing to change into, since our luggage is down in Cuzco . . . but I could really use a bath. Want to join me? And maybe you might explain a few things, while we're in there?"

He got a shy smile in response, but when they padded into the bathroom, nothing but air came out of the pipes for a minute or two. Kanmi's eyebrows went up as the water guttered out at last, brick-red and cold. He was about to incant to clean it up and warm it, but Minori beat him to it, the sediment congealing into a brick that sat at the corner of the tub, so that they could scoop it out and throw it away. And then she warmed the water, chilling the air around them to do it.

Kanmi hadn't been joking when he said that she added up for him, but right now, the equation had gone back to missing a variable or two. Her reactions to him had damned near been those of a virgin, but she'd mentioned some previous experience. And then her comment about not knowing if she really liked *men* or not . . . when clearly, she did. Or at least, she'd liked what he'd done. "You told me once," he said, idly, as she slipped into the tub, and he followed after, "that you had been bored at the Imperial Court. Why is that?"

The question made her stiffen a little, even though the warm water was soothing, and he had to urge her to lie back against his chest. "The Imperial Court . . . is not like the Imperator of Rome's," Minori began, carefully. "It is not like the Emperor of Tawantinsuyu's, either. The

Emperor in Nippon is cloistered. He is a religious figure. *Kami*-born, he is a figure of respect and veneration, the spiritual heart of our land . . . but he is, by tradition, not the military leader of our people. That responsibility is that of the shogun. The shoguns were meant to be temporary leaders." She chuckled a little. "A thousand years of temporary. But you see, the Emperor's Court is meant to be austere. Formal. Quiet. A place of contemplation and study of the *kami*, of magic, of natural philosophy. It was everything I wanted, but it was also horribly boring, yes. I loved the studying. I hated being cloistered. There were guards and chaperones everywhere. And the Emperor had his Empress and about a dozen bound concubines. All of whom were meant to be upright examples of virtue, just as any concubine bound to a lord should be."

Kanmi's eyebrows rose. "Your culture deals with this *very* differently than mine," he admitted.

"There is no shame in it," she told him, earnestly, turning to look up at him a bit. "My mother is a bound concubine to my father. She and I lived under the same roof with him and his lady wife. She and his wife were most agreeably behaved to one another. Polite. Kind."

"So, the various concubines . . . all the Emperor's age?" Kanmi asked, playing a little with Minori's hair. He rather liked the texture.

"No, not at all. Some were as young as eighteen, when I came to the court at the age of thirteen."

Kanmi looked up at the ceiling. "Rigidly-controlled environment. Young people. Boredom. This cannot end well."

Minori turned back away, and let her hair fall across her face. "It doesn't." She sighed. "I told you that I learned to unlock doors at the palace. I wanted to go outside, into the gardens, without a chaperone. I wanted freedom from the routine. I was caught once or twice, early on, and after that, I learned how to listen for the guards, and stay out of sight. When I was sixteen . . . Asuka, the Emperor's newest concubine . . . five years my elder . . . decided that my ability to unlock doors that were closed would be *useful*." Minori swallowed. This was painful, and not a little humiliating. But the water was warm, and Kanmi's fingers against her scalp were amazingly soothing, and she was about as tired as she ever had been in her life. Most of her defenses were down. "She was beautiful. And she began to bring me little gifts. We didn't need a chaperone, since we were both women, and she had always conducted herself in such perfect conformity to the rules of the palace. Everyone said what a good influence she would be on me. She became my dearest friend . . . and I hadn't had many friends at all, before her." Minori looked down into the water, and exhaled. "It started with little things. Hugs. Kisses. I fell a little in love with her. Everyone was. She was that beautiful—not like Lassair, but . . . it was impossible not to love her."

Kanmi's voice behind her held an odd note. "I've met the type, yes." He scooped warm water up and over her shoulders. "And then what happened?"

Minori shrugged. "She wanted to do more than that. She told me . . ." A slightly watery chuckle. "She told me that it wasn't really sex. That it wasn't anything to be embarrassed about. And it wouldn't compromise my virginity. I could still be given as a wife or concubine, without shame to my father."

She could feel his body stiffen a little. "Minori," he said, quietly, "if it's something you feel a need to hide from people . . . it probably actually *is* sex."

"Yes. I realize that. But at the time, I was sixteen, and it was fun. Exciting. I was old enough to know better, but I didn't care. Well, that's not true. I did care, but by the time I realized how serious what I was doing *was*, I was in over my head." Minori shrugged a little, hating her sixteen-year-old self. Intensely. "And then she told me she wanted me to open a door for her, and I did . . . only to realize she wanted to go there to meet with her *other* lover. Mitsuo. One of the guards." Minori swallowed. "Asuka laughed when I told her that it was wrong, and informed me that if I breathed a word, she'd tell everyone what we'd been doing in her chambers." Her voice was dull. "I was now a means to an end. I never let her touch me again, but I now had a choice. I could do the honorable thing, and reveal everything . . . and probably have to commit suicide to prevent my shame from staining my father . . . or I could remain silent." She bowed her head. "I remained silent. I opened doors, until Mitsuo gave her a set of keys all her own. And then I was in a position in which I could remain apart, silent, and blessedly uninvolved. Technically, I could have blackmailed her in turn, but she had an equal hold on me. I could see no good in fighting, when the result would be mutual destruction."

"Please tell me this bitch got what she deserved," Kanmi said, his voice grim.

"That depends greatly on what your definition of justice is." Minori looked up at him, sidelong, through her hair. "When I was eighteen, she was caught with Mitsuo. Mitsuo was executed. I'm not sure he deserved that. Asuka was sent to be a shrine-maiden. I was pleasantly surprised when she did not mention my early involvement in the affair to anyone at court. But I took the first opportunity to leave that I could. Begged my father to allow me to study in Gaul, under a different name. Away from court, and its intrigues. My father finally agreed. My skills were too masculine, and while I had not brought him any shame, he could see that court life . . . had not agreed with me."

Kanmi rubbed a damp hand over her hair. "All right. That explains a . . . well, a lot. But, Minori . . ." He winced. "I have evidence that you weren't even a *technical* virgin just now."

"Yes. My first year at the University of Lutetia, I went about disqualifying myself from being given as a concubine or wife." Minori huddled in on herself again. "I found an obliging Gaul named Calgacus, and was . . . intimate with him, for about six months."

"And this also ended badly?"

"It wasn't very much fun." Her voice was low. "Most of the time, it hurt, and at the end, I decided I should probably just focus on my studies." She peeked up through her hair. "So . . . here I am." Her voice wavered. "Now you know everything. Including why my name is different here than in Nippon, and why I do not go home."

Kanmi shook his head. It was a lot to absorb. A lot of baggage. Then again, he had more than his fair share, himself. "The Gaul you *disqualified* yourself with . . . gods, what a phrase . . ." He looked up at the ceiling. "I take it he was about your age?"

". . . yes." Minori peered at him. "Why?"

"It's a skill, Min. It takes practice. No one ever got good at sorcery by not practicing, did they?" Kanmi brought his eyes back down from the ceiling. "Young men tend to be very randy, and very bad at sex. I was." He did his best not to wince at the recollections. "Put an inexperienced young man with an inexperienced young woman, and either they break each other in and magically stumble their way into competence, or they wind up needing practical experience with a good tutor, or a lot of exposure to books and cinema."

He caught a rather watery chuckle from her direction, and she mopped at her face with wet hands. "You . . . don't mind? About Asuka?"

"That you're attracted to both genders?" Kanmi snorted. "Lassair has an effect on you, but I think Lassair would have an effect on a *stick.*" He paused, listening to her slightly livelier chuckle. "No, to me, doesn't matter at all. That being said, cheating is cheating. Doesn't matter with which gender." He looked down at her. "Then again, you had a lying bitch use you so she could cheat on you *and* her . . . husband . . . ."

"Lord."

"Semantics, Minori. My point is, you know first-hand why it's a bad idea." He leaned his head back. "Something heavier of a topic than I had imagined for in here." *Then again, I had no idea how __bad__ her background was. Gods. For noble-born, she's been used as much as any commoner, and by people who are supposed to be better than the rest of us.*

She half-turned again, and gave him a very serious look. "Yes. I . . . yes." A little, shamed shrug, and he winced; he hadn't meant to make her look like that. "I was stupid. And I was wrong."

"We're all wrong, sooner or later," Kanmi told her, glumly. "That's the only way we mortals ever learn anything."

"And what have you been wrong about?" she asked, as he pushed her forwards, so he could stand and exit the tub, wrapping a towel around his waist temporarily.

"Put your head back. I'll get the blood and dirt out of your hair, all right?" He leaned against the edge of the tub, and worked with shampoo powder — compliments of the hotel — and very patient fingers, to untangle a dozen knots. "Lots of things, I'm sure. Trouble is, I'm never exactly sure where the mistake actually was." His fingers caught on a knot, and he slowed down and tugged more gently on the hair, separating it carefully. "Take my ex-wife, for example. I have no idea what it was that I did or said that convinced her that I was a bad father, let alone that I was going to take the boys away entirely. I was going to share custody. I'd have let them visit her. I wasn't going to excise them from each other's lives."

"Ouch."

"Sorry." He knew he shouldn't be talking about this, not now, but then again, she *had* asked. Kanmi forced his fingers to relax. "I've been back over it in my mind a hundred times, and I still have no idea where the turning point was. I missed it. I'm never going to know where, precisely, I fucked up." He exhaled through his teeth. "And that's a worse feeling than knowing exactly how you screwed up." Kanmi helped Minori sit back up, and handed her a towel.

"So what do you do, going forwards?" Minori asked him, drying off her hair, first. Kanmi's eyes slipped downwards, and he entertained serious thoughts of trying to pull her back to the bed, but he didn't want to push his luck right now. She might have been keyed up from adrenaline an hour ago, but sooner or later, she was going to remember that he was abrasive, rude, arrogant (not that it wasn't *warranted*, but, still . . .), and further remember that she couldn't stand him.

He realized he hadn't answered her, when she started combing out her hair, studying him patiently with her dark, liquid stare. "Try not to wind up going down exactly the same path," Kanmi supplied, picking up his clothes in the next room, and grimacing at the sweat, dirt, and blood on them, before incanting quietly. All the foreign contaminants leaped off, and fell into a pile of dust on the floor. "Try to find new and exciting ways to fuck up completely." He stepped into his pants, and started lacing the fly, as Minori came back out of the bathroom, and stared at his clean clothing.

"How did you *do* that?" Minori laughed, sounding delighted. "You . . . you have a *laundry spell?*"

"Doctor, how do you think I managed to get myself and two small boys out the door every morning for the past four years? Of *course* I developed a laundry spell. You have any idea how hard it is to find exactly the number of assarii I need for the laundry machines at the *ablutum* down the street?" He paused. "I take it that means you want yours cleaned, too?"

Minori covered her mouth, laughing. Kanmi looked across at her. "Nothing from nothing. What do I get in exchange?"

She walked over, and, rather shyly, raised herself up on tiptoes to kiss him on the lips. Kanmi considered that, kissed her back, saying, "There's your change," and incanted again, ensuring that her clothes, too, were free of stink, blood, and dirt. He shrugged on his shirt, and, back in the bathroom, held up the shampoo box and eyed the soap inside consideringly. "I don't suppose it would be safe to use this on my teeth. Even if I had a toothbrush."

"Ah, no. Not unless you wish for your insides to be very clean as well." She shrugged. "Aside from which, the water is contaminated."

"Water I can fix. Mildly toxic soap is much harder to deal with." He shrugged. "Maybe the gift shop sells toothpowder." He paused. "Assuming the gift shop is open." Kanmi set the shampoo tin aside, and as Minori, dressed now, edged closer and slipped her arms around his waist, looked down in surprise, and then wrapped his arms around her, in return. "I would very much like to see more of you, doctor. If that would be acceptable to you."

"Well, I live and work in Gaul," she said, quietly.

"That presents a possible issue. But I travel somewhat extensively in my job."

She nodded against his chest. "Also," she noted, "what are the chances that Eleutherian Industries is going to let me keep working for them after today?"

Smart lady. "I don't know. On the one hand, you were on-site for a fairly large eruption, and can confirm it wasn't the ley-grid's fault. On the other hand . . . ."

". . . that non-disclosure form Livorus made me sign probably means I can't actually say what happened, until someone else makes it public? Which will rather cast doubts on all of my results and theories, or at least, leave a gaping hole in the middle of them."

"Burn that bridge once you've left it behind you," Kanmi advised. "Let's go see about this meeting, shall we?"

Once they'd all assembled in Livorus' room, Sigrun found a seat next to Adam, and surveyed everyone. So many faces, new and old, who had their places in her heart, now. She felt dizzy. A little disoriented, really, and had been since the mountain. She hadn't wanted to mention it to Adam during the flight; she'd put it down to the swaying motion of the ornithopter's wings, and the fact that it was a smaller model than the large commercial liner they'd used to get here.

That didn't, unfortunately, explain the borderline synesthesia she was experiencing. Or perhaps it was more of a pre-epilepsy symptom. Either way, it disturbed her. She wasn't *used* to having her body disobey her; it was as much a tool as she was, herself. But now, every time she looked at someone, she saw . . . colors. Like a halo, all around their bodies, shifting like the aurora borealis, but each person had a different, distinct shade. Adam gleamed a brilliant silver. Trennus had rich earthen browns and forest greens, overlain by a shimmer of Lassair's yellow-reds . . . and Lassair was a creature entirely comprised of that fire, in spite of the fact that she was firmly in human form right now. And Trennus' colors wrapped around her, as well. *They're a living Ouroborus, Jormungand,* she thought. *No end. No beginning.* Kanmi had smoldering red light around his body, while Minori had a veil of two tones of blue, light blue and dark, enfolded around her like gossamer . . . and to Sigrun's fascination, as she looked at them, Kanmi's light, and Minori's, oscillated at the same rate. *They . . . resonate. Like a ley-line. Or perhaps I'm just losing my mind.*

No, Lassair told her, gently. *Your eyes are simply more open now. You see as I do, sister.*

Sigrun grimaced, hoping that it would pass. Or at least settle down a little. The effect was both giving her a headache and making her sick to her stomach, two states with which she'd had little experience in her life. She didn't catch diseases, and she couldn't *get* drunk, and thus, had never been hung-over. And by and large, motion on waves or in the air didn't unsettle her.

Alone in the room she shared with Adam, with only a brief visit from Kanmi and Minori, the colors had been . . . manageable. And Adam had picked her up in his arms in the sheer exuberance of being *alive*, and had murmured sweet things in her ear, and they'd found their way to the bed. Sigrun usually had to remind herself not to clench her fingers too tightly against Adam's arms. And periodically had to remind him that she could take hard and fast. "You're sure?" he'd asked, looking concerned. "You *did* just take all of Min's internal injuries."

"I don't feel any pain right now." She'd smiled up at him, and slid her arms around his neck, enjoying the silvery bright halo around him. "Adam, the gods made valkyrie with bear-warriors in mind. When I say harder, I do, in truth, *mean* it."

His face had lit up with love and amusement, and he'd taken her at her word.

In the here and now, Adam pointedly sniffed as Kanmi and Minori took their seats. "I don't mean to be intrusive," he said, in a tone that suggested he was about to have a little fun at Eshmunazar's expense, and Sigrun watched Minori's face flicker with alarm and embarrassment, "but . . . ."

"Watch it, ben Maor," Kanmi muttered, clearly expecting Adam to go a certain direction with this conversation.

Adam grinned outright, and went the other direction entirely, "The two of you are *clean*. You didn't happen to get the only room connected to the only unbroken water pipe in the hotel. You cleaned the water up and bathed, and laundered your clothes, too." He looked around. "I think it would be a needed boost to everyone's morale if you provided bathing and cleaning services to everyone else, as well."

Except for me. I am clean. And all that water is a little disturbing. Lassair's admission made everyone around the table start to chuckle. The laughter held a slightly hysterical edge.

Livorus, at the head of the small table in his hotel room, smiled faintly. His aura was different than the others. Darker. Subtler. Not the same steel as Adam, but . . . still metal, of a sort. Pitted and scored with use, like a meteorite fallen to earth. "Also, potable drinking water. All the hotel has, that was previously bottled, is *chicha*."

"The good news is, they haven't manufactured that by chewing the corn and spitting it into a bowl to ferment for five hundred years," Trennus pointed out. "It's all stone-ground these days."

"Still, I will, I believe, pass," Livorus replied, firmly. "Wine is the drink of a civilized man, not some form of beer. Unless it is a choice between that, or dysentery." He gave them all a direct stare. "Potable water, the ability to bathe, and clean clothes would, I think, be in order. At the very least, we will not put a strain on the locals' emergency supplies, in this fashion."

Kanmi waved a hand. "After the meeting, I'd be happy to accommodate."

Minori raised hers, tentatively. "Ah . . . you don't wish us to go and assist with relief efforts? Clean water would be a tremendous help to people in the city."

Sigrun smiled. Minori was a very good person. Beginning, middle, and end of story.

Livorus waved. "I can't order you to do so, Dr. Sasaki. But while I believe it would be an excellent public relations gambit, not to mention the right thing to do, I am rather concerned for everyone's safety at the moment. Our goal is to leave this country on the first flight available, before we can be delayed for any further questioning by local authorities, or become the subject of any riots."

"On the plus side, I don't think there were any survivors from Nazca who'll target us. I believe Mamaquilla took care of the guilty parties." Kanmi's eyes were hooded.

"Yes, but the palace guards are sure to be trying to determine what happened to their emperor," Livorus pointed out. "We are, however, putting the cart ahead of the horse. For the moment? Start at the beginning and relate to me precisely what occurred over the past thirty-six hours. We'll decide the rest from there."

All of them exchanged wary glances. They'd barely begun to sort it out amongst themselves. Trennus began by noting that Lassair had called to him across the miles, letting him know the instant that she and Minori had been taken captive. Lassair stated that she hadn't had the power, as far as she knew, to protect the child she carried, and shift form to something capable of repelling the attackers. Jumbled explanations, that Sigrun could barely keep track of, as her focus faded. The colored lights around people's bodies were distracting, but she registered the fact that the wards on the hotel room doors had been rigged for silent alarm, not for 'lethal force.' The deaths of the Praetorians assigned to guard them. Minori paled. Saw Lassair turned her face aside, leaning against Trennus' shoulder. Trennus, with his eyes like the inmost heart of a flame now. Marked.

Sigrun wavered in her seat and struggled to control her mind, as they all worked through the past day and a half. Explaining decisions made—Kanmi in particular, had struggled with the decision to bring Minori, as a civilian, into an area where a firefight might have been ongoing, but he defended it, simply, as the only course of action open to him. "If I'd taken her and Lassair to the airfield, and stayed there to protect them, that would have left Matrugena alone, trying to find ben Maor and Caetia, with the assistance of . . ." He paused. "What are we calling Mamaquilla and Cocohuay on the official reports? An *entity* and an outside civilian contractor?" He drummed his fingers against the table.

Another nervous, borderline hysterical round of laughter. Livorus rubbed at his eyes. "Call them both outside agents. That should . . . distinguish them from the other *entities* in your report."

"Right. And the Sapa Inca? Head of state? Supreme executive authority?"

"Regional autocrat suffering from delusions of grandeur," Trennus suggested, after a moment.

"Too long," Kanmi shot back. "That'll get red-lined from the report. But I can work with *regional autocrat*."

And then they came to the portion of the discussion that was going to be the hardest to negotiate. Sigrun listened, as Adam tried to finesse the issue. "In the end, the . . . main entity, who had been trapped, asked me for assistance in terminating his existence, in order to create a . . ." He looked at Kanmi and Minori.

"Cascade failure in the entire system," Kanmi supplied. "At least, that's what *resulted*. I can't tell anyone what the entity said. I don't remember any of this conversation actually happening."

"I was unconscious for it." Trennus supplied, with a sidelong shift of his eyes.

"The, ah, entity slowed down my perception of time to relay the message," Adam supplied.

"So, you killed the main entity." Livorus' eyes were hooded. "How precisely did you manage that?"

Adam appeared to be choosing his words with great care, but Sigrun wasn't sure why. "He required some assistance with his suicide, sir. Just as Roman might ask for a friend to be at hand while the blood runs freely, to ensure that there are no errors and no pain." Adam winced. "Not that I am calling myself his friend, in this example," he added, hastily.

"Your point, ben Maor, please?"

"I was, momentarily, a vessel of his power, in a sense. I fired my gun, he released the body he held, and dispersed himself. It was his sacrifice that saved us all, sir. Not any real action of mine." That, at least, had the ring of conviction in it.

"And the enemy combatant entity, and the regional autocrat?" Livorus had been taking notes, the entire conversation.

"That was all on Caetia and Lassair," Kanmi supplied, with an acerbic grin. "No involvement from the rest of us *at all*."

"Can I just remind everyone that I was unconscious?" Trennus repeated.

"Your support touches my heart," Sigrun muttered. She tried to focus through the haze of colors around her. "I was engaged in combat with the enemy entity with the assistance of one of our two . . . civilian support specialists?" She raised her hands. "When the major entity sacrificed himself, I believe that weakened the one with whom I fought sufficiently to allow me to gain a killing blow. That is my only explanation for events."

A very likely one, Lassair agreed, faint amusement in her tone.

"You, my dear, just as much a nuisance as the rest of them," Livorus told Lassair. "We simply cannot list you on these forms as 'spouse of one of my lictors,' or 'intermittently-corporeal bound spirit.'"

"Civilian liaison to the Veil," Kanmi suggested, leaning back in his chair.

"Not helping matters, Eshmunazar." Livorus got back to work with the fountain pen.

"I'm not sure there's any help to be had in this or any other world, *dominus*." The mix of respect and effrontery in the words was pure Kanmi, and Sigrun put her face in her hands and *laughed*.

Livorus shook his head as weary laughter once more swept the room. "And Cornelius?" he prompted Kanmi now. "Any links to the Source Initiative?"

Kanmi's face darkened. "I underestimated him," he said, his voice tightening. "I'm the one who said he rated no more than a three on my damned threat radar."

"He was a good actor," Trennus put in, his face dark. "I knew there was something off about the way he was watching Lassair at dinner, but I didn't imagine *this*."

Kanmi rubbed at his face. "He wasn't on the membership rolls for SI. That doesn't mean that he didn't *know* some of the people in it."

"You tend to meet people at conferences," Minori admitted, quietly.

"Someone will undoubtedly be tasked with going through all of his correspondence," Kanmi replied, and then added, acidly, "Someone who will *not* be me, more than likely."

Another set of chuckles, but this time, more thoughtful ones, as each of them began to grapple with the enormity of what had passed today. For her part, Sigrun was terribly concerned about Trennus. She liked Lassair. But she wasn't sure that being Lassair's bound servant was likely to be healthy for her friend. And of course, there was the whole having *died* part of the problem.

And then there was Minori's torture; technically, some polite priest of Isis or Vesta should be talking to the woman right now, to see how much mental damage had been done. The possible damage to all of them, from having been so close to the deaths of not just one god this time, but several. *It might explain the colors,* Sigrun thought, and then put it out of her mind. She'd be reporting to the Odinhall soon enough.

Livorus broke the silence now, gesturing for Sigrun, who happened to be closest, to turn on the far-viewer. "We have all of one working far-viewer channel. Let us see what the news is, shall we?"

Sigrun reached out, under the table, and took Adam's left hand in her right, rubbing her thumb against his forefinger, where he wore his wedding ring. The far-viewer warmed up, and they could see in the sphere's depths that the massive fortress of Sacsayhuamán was intact. The megalithic architecture of the ancients had once again proven its worth. A news reporter stood before the palace, clutching a large microphone, and explaining to the viewers, *"There was a precursor earthquake, with its epicenter near Nazca, in the late afternoon hours of yesterday, which registered five point two on the Rihtære scale. Then, as an anomaly of unknown origin burned in the sky, lighting up the night as if it were noon, Cuzco was rocked by a succession of further earthquakes. The first, centered at Coropuna, measured eight point two on the Rihtære scale."* Sigrun's mind wandered, and the words became a meaningless buzz of sounds in Latin. She managed to focus as the reporter continued, *"Seismologists say we cannot tell how long aftershocks will go on, but divination experts suggest four to six weeks, assuming there are no further anomalies. The successive earthquakes have left Cuzco, Ica, and several other major cities in the region in ruins."*

The camera panned, to show skyscrapers without windows, their facades ripped off, and the underlying metal scaffold bare. Brick buildings, lying folded in on themselves, unrecognizable, but for a wall here, the outline of a window, there. And that was the *wealthier* districts of the town. The hovels of the slums, to the eastern side of the city . . . which had been comprised of wooden shacks with tin roofs and brick tenements in various states of disrepair . . . had been flattened entirely. Not a single building stood upright.

Trennus' jaw worked as he got a good look at the destruction caused by the earthquakes. Of all of them, Trennus most intimately understood geology, and its effects. For her part, Sigrun swallowed, and put her face in her hands. "And this was the *good* option," Adam muttered, his tone horrified. "Are there estimates on casualties yet?"

Livorus shook his head. "Not as yet, ben Maor. We all know that the first reports will be inflated, then deflated as they find people alive who were merely missing . . . and then will escalate as disease and lack of clean water take their toll." He gave them all a quick, piercing glance. "I've made a call or two to Rome. I've recommended that relief supplies be flown in, immediately. And I've requested that we be evacuated as quickly as possible. For the moment, we're merely taking up rooms and supplies that could be used elsewhere." A quick, grim smile. "I am, however, quite certain that as soon as the governmental situation here manages to coalesce a little we will doubtless have many questions about the Sapa Inca asked of us. I would prefer to make my answers from the comfort of Rome."

Sigrun's stomach churned. She knew she was going to have to pay the reckoning for having killed Supay. Her gods had turned a blind eye, when it came to Tlaloc. And while Supay had been just as involved in this conspiracy, if not more, than Tlaloc had been in the schemes conducted in Nahautl, she knew she'd be making her accounts. But at the moment, she would rather face her gods, than the people of Tawantinsuyu. The gods, given previous events, seemed as if they might be reasonable. The people, however, might well tear them apart.

The news broadcast turned then to footage of the anomaly in space, with footage shot from the Libration point station, which made Adam lean forwards in fascination. With filters on the cameras, the miniature sun had clearly had a spherical shape and even a corona around it . . . until it expanded out, dissipating. "*No damage to either the moon base or the Libration point station. Scientists indicate that it will be months, or even years, before they are able to identify what the object was. Persia has accused Judea of testing a bomb capable of being launched from space to a location on ground. Since this object directly threatened the Space Coalition's own station, and was located directly above Tawantinsuyu, most observers are discounting this accusation for what it is: propaganda. Hellene scientists believe that it may actually have been the exit point of a white hole, which served as a conduit to pull material from our sun to just inside of Earth's orbit. This is, they say, actually a far more troubling possibility than a mere missile.*" The news reporter looked grim. "*If a spell-caster were capable of creating a white hole that could conduct matter from the sun to Earth's orbit, they could transmit that fire to the planet's surface, as well. For the moment, however, the anomaly is being categorized as the act of a god."*

The room was very quiet indeed, for a long moment. "Accurate assessment," Kanmi supplied.

"Our latest story is the footage we've received from the valleys around Coropuna." The sphere shifted to showing them black-and-white footage of Coropuna, in daylight, this time, from the southern side of the mountain. *"The Maucallacta Oracle, including its <u>ushnu</u>, or what remains of it, is directly at the center of your screen,"* the voice told them, obligingly.

The pristine white glacier cap on the western side of the mountain was simply *gone,* though the caps on the eastern peaks of the long ridge were still present, if ash-strewn. A vast plume of smoke still billowed out of the mouth of the volcano, and massive mudslides had scraped away large swathes of the mountainside, scouring it of plants and animals. Trails of hot lava roped down the same paths that the lahar and pyroclastic flows had taken . . . but none of it had touched the small village at the center of the screen. Maucallacta itself was untouched by the flows, although, through the telescopic lens, it was clear that many of the buildings had collapsed around the ruined shrine. *"This type of phenomenon is called a <u>kipuka</u> by the Polynesians, we're told. A place where the lava does not reach."*

There was a pause, and then the news station jerked back to the studio—which had clearly been shaken by the earthquakes as well. Lights hung loosely on the walls, and Sigrun could see wires dangling down from the ceiling, into the frame. The news anchor, a Tawantinsuyan, from the look of him, suddenly appeared harried. *"We've been told that there is an announcement being made at the Temple of the Sun in Cuzco. We have one truck nearby with a working transmitter, and our reporter is making her way through the ruined streets to reach the temple. Please, bear with us . . . ah. Live from Cuzco, Cuxi Palta."*

The news went black for a moment, and then returned, fuzzy, rapidly dialing back into focus. Everyone in the room stiffened as the image sharpened into what was, clearly, the sorrowful visage of Mamaquilla.

"Has . . . any god . . . ever allowed themselves to be caught on film before?" Adam asked, tightly.

"You mean, other than your wedding pictures?" Kanmi asked, his tone uneasy.

"No, I mean . . . live-action." Adam sounded dazed. "God. No possibility of misinterpreting anything she might say, is there . . ."

Mamaquilla, close to eight feet in height, and covered in glossy, dark scales, towered over the human reporter, who came to approximately the goddess' sternum as she followed, at a respectful, awed distance, timidly holding up her microphone and occasionally looking back at the camera as if to ask, *Is this real?*

The goddess was clearly not a statue. She moved, flowing like a wave, up the steps of the Temple of the Sun, holding . . . yes, it was Inti's limp body in her arms. At the top of the steps, framed by the pillars, she turned back, still holding her husband's body, and looked directly at the camera. Her luminous eyes glowed, almost hypnotically, and for a moment, Sigrun swore she could see *color* on the black-and-white image. As if the blue-greens of Mamaquilla's scaled skin filled in, suddenly.

"Don't know how she's going to talk," Kanmi muttered. "She wasn't exactly using her mouth to speak last time . . . ."

"Do you think she can use the radio waves as a carrier for her power?" Minori asked, interestedly. "I mean, that's more or less what they were trying to do with the ley-lines. All she really needs to do is modulate the carrier waves, and, well, she's a sea goddess." The small woman spread her hands. "I assume she understands waves better than the rest of us do."

Kanmi gave Minori a direct look, opened his mouth, as if to reply, and was cut off, as all their heads rocked back.

To all within the reach of my voice, I bid you now, take heed. Mamaquilla's voice was soft, but powerful. It radiated through Sigrun, and she knew, without question, that even people who hadn't turned *on* their far-viewers could probably hear this. Anywhere that the radio waves were carrying right now. This was . . . a living testament. It would be recorded in the film . . . perhaps . . . but it would be more essentially encoded in the minds and hearts of those who listened now. *Your emperor, Sayri Cusi, was Sapa Inca, first among you. He betrayed you. He betrayed the gods. He sought to follow in the footsteps of Akhenaten. He was the cause of all the destruction you see here today. He practiced forbidden magics. Formed an alliance with Supay, to destroy all the gods of this land, and almost succeeded. Inti . . . my beloved Inti . . . gave his life, so that the destruction would be less. Because of his sacrifice, the emperor is dead. Supay is no more. But unfortunately, the emperor was responsible for the deaths of many other gods. Mamazilla. Kon. Urcuchillay. Apu. Hundreds of the small gods were sacrificed to sate his hunger and slake Supay's thirst. Now, I remain, and three of my servants. Coniraya, who was so despised of the gods that a goddess once unmade herself, rather than bear his child. Copacati, lady of the lake waters. And Mamallpa, lady of fertility.*

Sigrun swallowed. She couldn't have imagined that Mamaquilla would do *this*. Gods tended to reveal themselves to only a few devotees at a time. Gave new truths to someone, and sent them forth to give that light to others. Public revelation like this was unprecedented in human history.

Mamaquilla went on now, with a grim note of power in her voice. *It is left to me to heal and nurture this land. I ask that Inti's great temple be rebuilt, and that his tomb be venerated, and that you continue to love and worship my beloved, as the Sacrificed God. In the hopes that, through your love, he might one day be reborn.* She lowered her head, and Sigrun saw two luminous tears course down that dark face, like comets in the night sky. *I command that the name of Quehuar, he who gave his life for Inti, that his god might have comfort in his captivity, be honored, forever. I command that the name of Cocohuay, who gave her life, that I might live, be honored, forever. I command that the name of your Emperor be forgotten, for all time. Let it be effaced from every book, every monument, every relic of his reign. I will permit a god-born of my lineage to rule in*

Tawantinsuyu after this day. But there will be changes, my children.
Many of them.
    And for the rest of my commandments? Let the word go forth that
Tawantinsuyu holds to its bargain with the gods of Rome. No human
sacrifice will be permitted. You will love and honor me, as you will love
and honor Inti, the Sacrificed God. And we will work together to heal our
sore-troubled land.

The news report cut off then. Going to the window of the room, Sigrun could see, outside, that everyone in the streets had stopped where they were, to look up into the sky. "Social disruption," Adam muttered, quietly. "There's no place in this country that's going to be the same after today."

"Yes," Sigrun told him, letting the curtain fall. "That does not, however, mean that it must be *worse* than it was before."

Livorus looked at Sigrun. "You find hope in this, my dear?"

She nodded, feeling her throat tighten. "Yes. Mamaquilla is the moon. The moon . . . is mutable. It waxes. It wanes. It changes." She paused. "She's also the sea. Tides rise. Tides fall. It's always in motion. A sun-god . . . rarely changes. The day passes into night, and night becomes day." Sigrun smiled a little. "The night need not be terrible."

Trennus looked up. "And out of death, new life."

She met his eyes, and nodded.

The meeting disbanded after that. Livorus enjoined them to get a good night's sleep, as their evacuation flight from Rome should be arriving around five antemeridian. "At least, after the *entity's* news broadcast," Livorus said, looking at the ceiling, "no one should, I think, be hunting for our heads. We can be grateful for that. For so long as people pay her words heed, at least."

"Which means we've got about a six weeks' grace period before someone decides it's a massive conspiracy by Rome," Kanmi said, cynically.

Once out of Livorus' room, Adam beckoned the others into his and Sigrun's chamber, and explained, quietly, what Inti had done to his gun. None of them, besides Lassair, who had registered the words between Adam and Inti clearly, had known. Sigrun swallowed in disquiet as she studied the weapon. She could see colors around it. Just as she saw them around the humans in the room. It shimmered, faintly, golden as sunlight. *Something is wrong with me.* But she didn't volunteer a word about the weapon. Or her condition.

Kanmi and Minori were studying the weapon in fascination. "I don't sense much beyond a very light enchantment," Minori said, after a moment. "I'd say it converts the bullets, in the barrel, to . . . another form of matter?"

"If it converts the matter into plasma, it would melt the gun into slag the first time he pulled the trigger. There's got to be more to it than that." Kanmi almost reached for the gun, then put his hands behind his back, as they stared at the Velserk, which currently lay on a towel on a small table in Adam and Sigrun's room. "Maybe a cooling enchantment? I just can't *see* it."

"It's all spirit-energy," Trennus commented, distantly. "I can see it. The metal's practically permeated with it." He looked at Adam, his eyes shining in the dim light of the room. "You're carrying around a modern version of *Caledfwlch.*"

"Caled . . . what?" Adam decided not to bother with the rest of the twisting Gallic syllables.

"*Caledfwlch*. Romans usually make it Caliburn. Easier for them to say, when they're retelling Gallic legends. It's the sword that could cut stone. Given only to the high king, and only in times of great need." Trennus smiled faintly. "It hasn't been seen in over a thousand years."

Adam shook his head, clearly rattled. 'All right, well . . . that's neither here nor there. What do I *do* with it? I can't keep this. Do I . . . sink it to the bottom of a lake, or the sea? You said water buffers things like this." He shifted a little. "Mamaquilla wouldn't take it back."

Kanmi snorted. "If you drop it to the bottom of a lake, ben Maor, it's going to be a bitch getting it back if we need it again."

Trennus looked at the ceiling, clearly amused by something. "Well, the ancient legends do say that Caliburn is kept by a water spirit, a lady of the lake, when it is not needed. If we drop it in the right one, she should lift it forth for the rightful bearer and give it back, Adam."

Adam gave them both a dark look. "I'm failing to see what's so amusing about this."

Lassair interposed, gently, *If Mamaquilla would not take the weapon back, Steelsoul, it is because she knows you have yet more to do with it.*

Trennus' lips quirked. "There's that. And there's the fact that you've just been told you're the modern equivalent of a high king, you've been handed a weapon out of legend, and the first thing you want to do is sink it in the ocean." He shook his head. "Only you, Adam."

Adam grimaced. "All right. I take the point. It's my responsibility. I'll lock it away in a safe, or in a box in my nightstand in Judea, or some damn thing."

Sleep didn't come easily to Sigrun that night. Usually, she could sleep anywhere, any time. A habit honed by being in combat-type situations throughout most of her adult life. On restless nights, now, all she needed was Adam's arm, draped loosely around her, in order to relax and doze. But tonight, when she desperately needed the sleep, in the hope that the pre-epileptic colors would fade from her field of vision, sleep would not come.

At midnight, she realized why, as the phone in the room rang. Somehow, she'd been waiting for this. Dreading this.

Adam sat up in bed, reaching for the phone. "Don't," Sigrun told him, huddling under the sheets.

"What?" He sounded surprised, and the phone rang again.

"Don't answer it."

"Sig, it could be Livorus."

"It's not going to be. It's her." Sigrun's tone was dull.

Adam turned to look down at her in the dim moonlight coming in through the window. "Her?" he asked, blankly, as the phone shrilled again. "Who?"

"Sophia. I've been expecting this."

The phone paused, and then another ring. "Sig, I'm not going to listen to this all night." Adam plucked the phone off the cradle, and said, in Latin, "*Ave?*"

After a moment, he sighed. "Yes, Sophia. That would be the second time. How many more times do I get to do this?"

There was a pause, and then he handed her the phone. "Please deal with your sister," Adam told Sigrun, before getting up and heading to the bathroom, where she could now hear water being poured from the clean pitcher Minori had prepared for them.

Sigrun put the phone to her ear. "What do you want, Sophia?" she asked, wearily.

"*There you are. You were trying to hide from me. Silly thing.*" Sophia half-sang the words. "*What does it feel like, Sigrun, having taught death how to die?*"

"I cannot help but notice that quite a few people died anyway," Sigrun said, staring off into space.

"*The sun died, too, but there was still a dawn,*" Sophia replied. "*What is a god but the symbol of something greater? A concept. A belief. Inti was life, and he died. Supay was death, and now there's new life!*"

Sigrun shifted, and looked out the window at the moon. *Things can change. Spirits have a symbiotic relationship with humans, as Tren has said. We change them. We change ourselves. We saw the biggest change in the gods in modern history today. Not since Akhenaten has so much changed in a faith. In a people. In a land.* "Your fate is broken," Sigrun told her sister, sudden conviction in her tone. "For these people, the world as they knew it has ended. A new one has begun. So much for prophecy, eh?"

"*Oh, not at all, Sigrun. You were always going to do this. You're just taking the inevitable steps along the road. Look around you. The ruined land of the Four Quarters? It's just a microcosm of what's to come. Pompeii will burn once more. So will most of Caesaria Aquilonis. Only Judea will be safe. It is a promised land, after all.*" Sophia giggled. "*Let me tell you more.*" Her voice took on the hated cadence, once more. The voice of prophecy. "*I see twin goddesses. One fire and one ice. One life and one death. One beginnings, and the other endings. They're beautiful, and they're terrible, Sigrun. But they're only two of three. The first is the maiden, who runs through the woods, the second is the mother, who nurtures the fields, and the third is the crone who buries the dead. Oh, how I wish I could see their faces, but all I see are their eyes —*"

"*Stop.*" Sigrun had switched to Cimbric, and she said it with all the force she tried not to use with mortals. "*Stop it right now.*"

"*But Sigrun, this is important! This is about why you're not going to have children until the world ends in fire and frost . . . .*"

"*Stop!*" Sigrun sat up in bed and shouted the word. "*I will hear no more of this! I am done with gods and demons and prophecies and futures. There is only one future I want. I want a mortal life. With Adam. Nothing more. I will hear not one more word of prophecy, Sophia. Not one more word, or I will never* *hear <u>any</u> other pass your lips again."*

There was a long, shocked silence on the other end of the phone, and Sigrun's stomach churned. This was her *sister*. This was her baby sister, nineteen years her junior. Whom she loved almost as much as if Sophia had been her own daughter, but for whom she could do *nothing*. *"Sigrun,"* Sophia said, and suddenly, it was the voice of the frightened ten-year-old again. *"Sigrun, please. I knew you would be angry. And you have no idea how sorry I am. But you're never going to get what you want."*

Sigrun hung up the phone, very carefully. Turned her face into the pillow, and *wept*.

After a short time, Adam came back to bed. Wrapped his arms around her, until the tears passed, and they listened to the sound of sleet slamming into the windows, as clouds covered the moon. And eventually, as the tears faded, and they began to kiss, Sigrun suddenly remembered something. "Adam?"

"Hmm?"

"I left my pills in the hotel in Cuzco. They're under forty tons of rubble by now."

Adam considered that. "Good."

Sigrun pulled back. "What?"

"We wanted children, right? We're probably going to be on administrative leave for a year, thanks to all of this mess. If we're going to do this . . . it's probably the best time we'll ever have to do it. Let's have children, Sigrun."

She looked up at him in the dark. "My sister says I won't have children until the world ends. A pretty way of saying never."

Adam leaned down, and kissed her, fervently. *"Neshama* . . . Sigrun . . . Let me just say this." He paused. "To *gehenna* with prophecy."

Interlude II: Settling Dust

1960-1964 AC

<u>1960-1961 AC</u>

Thirty thousand people died in Tawantinsuyu in the aftermath of the earthquakes, eruptions, and the cholera and dysentery outbreaks that followed the disasters. This was in spite of aid sent from every subject nation in the Empire; the infrastructure was inadequately developed to move supplies to the hundreds of mountain villages affected by the scope of the devastation. The lictors had a hard time considering their mission a *success* . . . but they had the word of Inti and Mamaquilla that it would have been worse if they had not been there. If they had not intervened.

That didn't make it any easier to sleep at night, after watching the news.

Adam's prediction of a full year of administrative leave wasn't entirely accurate. They were, however, given a full six months of it, which consisted of literally hundreds of interviews with various people, from Praetorian Guard Internal Affairs to the diplomatic corps to the high priests of Jupiter, Juno, and Mars, and the Imperator himself. And that was just dealing with Rome. They also had to meet with representatives from Tawantinsuyu repeatedly, in the safety of Rome, and answer questions, at length, about the death of the Sapa Inca. Most of the time, they were able to default to the answer, "As Mamaquilla indicated, the late emperor attempted to destroy the gods of your nation, with the assistance of Supay. Mamaquilla has forbidden his very name to be spoken. Why does it matter how, precisely, he met his end?"

The answer was, of course, that various factions among the Tawantinsuyan nobility wanted someone to *blame*. They wanted a godslayer. They wanted the black-clad figure on Nefertiti's tomb wall, all hooks and barbs. The lictors, as one, stonewalled. They refused to specify who had killed whom, to anyone except for Livorus and the Imperator of Rome. Adam admitted, reluctantly, to Livorus and Caesarion, that he'd pulled the trigger on Inti. Sigrun and Lassair both admitted to their roles, and Caesarion IX, after three days of consideration, informed them that he was choosing not to commit any of this to paper. "In this much, I can protect you and your descendants," he told them, quietly. "The information can and must die with all of us."

Sigrun had found that to be a partial relief, but she was traveling from one meeting to another so often now, she usually didn't know what time zone she was in. She and Adam spent much of that six months of leave in Judea, rebuilding the inside of their house. Adam joked that the concept of having children had lit a fire under him, because he really didn't want to see her holding up drywall for him to hammer in place when she was eight months pregnant. "I know you, Sig, you'll be out wrestling pythons and Nile crocodiles when you're out to here." He gestured with the hammer in front of his own stomach, and then dropped it on a work table.

"Ah . . . Adam?" Sigrun hesitated. "It probably won't be nine months."

He'd turned away to measure the new window they were cutting into the inner wall of the house, facing out into the Roman-style atrium. Now, he turned back, and squinted at her. "What do you mean?"

"Valkyrie, like my great-grandmother, who are chosen? God-touched, not god-born? They come to term in human time." Sigrun took the tape measure out of his other hand, and fiddled with it, extending it out to nine inches, and then halving its length. "I am god-born. And we are meant to fight. We can still fight when we are gravid, but not as we should. Thus, the gods were kind enough to halve our term."

Adam blinked. "I . . . see." He looked around. "So what you're saying is, once we're sure you *are*, it's going to happen fast . . . so I should really start with the nursery?"

"It might be wise." Sigrun had decided to ignore every word Sophia had ever said on the subject. Human beings could not function without hope. She might not be entirely human, but she needed the last denizen of Pandora's box as much as any of them ever could.

"All right. Let's get this window finished, and we'll move on from there." Adam had sounded a little rattled, but had smiled anyway, and she'd brushed a strand of long hair back from his sweating face, and tucked it behind his ear.

Working on the house had actually been the best part of those six months. When they weren't doing that, or flying to Rome for more hearings, Sigrun would often awaken with a dream still burning in her mind. *You will report to the Odinhall at once. Transportation will be provided.*

There were only a handful of entities — the word inevitably made her twitch now, even in her own thoughts — who could instantaneously transport humans and materials from place to place. She suspected that the gods of Rome, who had over a billion worshippers, who at least paid them lip-service, could manage it. The gods of her people, with two hundred and twenty-five million worshippers, between Germania, the northern kingdoms of Europa, Novo Germania, and parts of Raccia, could transport someone like her to either the outside of Valhalla, or to the Odinhall, in a heartbeat. They just had never *done* so before this incident. She hadn't even known it was possible.

She was always aware of being *someplace else* when the Odinhall called her. Of flying in a vast and timeless place, where there were clouds that went on forever . . . but at the same time, the journey always seemed to transpire instantaneously. And her ears inevitably popped when she appeared in the lobby of the Odinhall, halfway around the planet from Jerusalem. She was almost positive that this transit was the effect of an 'interface matrix' similar to the great room near the top of the Odinhall. What little Trennus had said about his own sojourn in the Veil had convinced Sigrun, however, that most mortals would be deeply troubled by going there. They would probably return from it stark raving mad, in fact. *Perhaps that explains Sophia,* she thought, miserably. She and her sister had not spoken in months.

In the Odinhall, the routine was the same, every time. She endured scrutiny from Odin, Thor, Tyr, Freya, Heimdall, and even masked Hel herself. They never explained what they were doing, but it mostly seemed to involve her standing at the center of a perfectly white, empty room, while they paced around her. Their auras were blinding, and Sigrun had squinted a bit the first few times she'd arrived. Freya, a mistress of *seiðr,* or magic, noticed this immediately, and asked what troubled her. Sigrun had described the colored auras, and had seen intrigue rise in the goddess' golden eyes, and the significant look Freya shot Odin. *I will help you learn to control this,* Freya had told her, toying with a necklace around her throat, which reached her waist. Brísingamen, it was called, and it supposedly held half her powers. *Odin gave up an eye to see the mortal world as humans do. You have somehow developed the ability to see as spirits do. Interesting. But, with practice, it will be something that you can control, child.*

Hel, however, seemed almost personally offended by Sigrun. The gaunt goddess, whose frost-white hair and face were covered by a black hood and eye-mask, periodically wiped away tears of blood as she paced around Sigrun, *sniffing* at her, as a wolf might scent its prey. Sigrun had never seen the goddess before, and tried not to show emotion or fear. *You,* Hel finally scoffed. *You slew* **Supay?** *I believe it not.*

And yet, there is no lie in her. My child speaks nothing but the truth before us. Tyr's voice was calm.

I was not overly fond of Supay, Hel allowed, after a moment. *I found him quite distasteful, in fact. However . . .* She sniffed at Sigrun again, and under her mask, she licked her lips. *You smell of carrion, valkyrie. Odin's ravens will follow you as if you were a moveable feast, I think. You reek of death.* In a flash, she smiled, a dreadful expression. *Perhaps I should claim you for my own. I think I would have the right to do so.*

I will grant my daughter the choice of whom she would serve. Tyr's voice held the ring of law. *But all those here will abide by her decision, and I will suffer no attempts to make her recant. So, whom would you serve?*

Sigrun raised her head. "You, my lord," she replied, immediately. "After you, our people and Rome. As I have ever done." And there was nothing but gratitude in her heart for her grandsire's protection.

While she was interrogated by the gods themselves, almost every visit, Sigrun was also periodically taken to a small room, furnished with old oak furniture. Comfortable chairs, a long, polished conference table. Little paper cups of water. On the whole, she'd have preferred to be stared at, sniffed, and weighed by the gods, to the hours she spent in that room.

For in that room, inevitably, Reginleif awaited.

Reginleif Lanvik was a valkyrie, god-born of Loki, and over two hundred years old. She had the frost-white hair that marked most of those born of Loki, whether they were Hel, the Fenris wolf, or a mere valkyrie, and wore it cropped short. Her face was unmarked by her years, and she bore not a single rune-mark on her pale skin. Her eyes were a piercing sky blue, and she had been one of Sigrun's teachers in her four years at the Odinhall, primarily teaching her students how to recognize and avoid magic. How to discern what was illusion, and what was not. "You'll never see through an illusion crafted by Loki," Reginleif had told the class, years ago, smiling. "But mortals inevitably falter. They simply lose track of the details. They don't know when they can allow the mind of the viewer to interpolate their own information into the construct, and where to focus the details. They'll forget one of the senses . . . smell or touch, usually . . . and if you're *aware* enough, you'll know what's reality, and what's falsehood. Let's try it again, shall we? This time, Erikir, do try not to charge directly through the illusion into the gap in the floor, hmm? Bear-warriors do not fly so well, but they fall most excellently."

The sessions with Reginleif nowadays were much less physical, but they were mentally and emotionally exhausting. The tone of them differed each time, but Sigrun had sat in on enough interrogations over the years to know precisely what Reginleif was doing. The first session had been adversarial, at best. Eviscerating, at worst. "Explain to me precisely why you chose not to inform the Odinhall about your mission to Tawantinsuyu in advance." Reginleif folded her hands on the table, and stared Sigrun down.

Sigrun opted, at first, for the rational. "The mission was for Rome, not for the Odinhall."

"And where then, do your loyalties lie? With Rome? Or with your gods?"

"The gods themselves have permitted me to serve Rome—" In sober truth, fifty people were allowed to go about their normal lives, every year, without being levied to serve in the Legion or the Imperial navy, because Sigrun served in their place.

Reginleif cut her off. "Irrelevant. When loyalties come into conflict with one another, you have forgotten that you serve the gods *first*."

Sigrun shook her head mutely, her eyes turned inwards, in self-examination. She didn't think that this was the case.

"Oh? Is this not true, Sigrun Caetia?" Reginleif had settled back in her chair, folding her hands in front of her.

"I serve the gods, our people, and Rome." Sigrun raised her eyes and met Reginleif's. "Those duties rarely, if ever, conflict."

"Then why did you not *immediately* inform the Odinhall of the events transpiring in Tawantinsuyu?" The words were rapped out, coldly.

And why were the gods not actually aware of those events, themselves? Sigrun felt like asking in return, but she didn't quite dare. The truth was, she *knew* why. The gods could not see the bound servants of others. Could not intrude upon each other's people, as a result of their compact with the gods of Rome. Humans weren't allowed to proselytize. Gods weren't allowed to encroach. People had free will and self-determination. Sigrun had come to understand in the past weeks, that the gods were *forced* to work through agents like herself, when they wanted to understand what was going on among the servants of other gods. Her gods relied, more than she'd ever known, on their bear-warriors and valkyrie. They weren't just hands and weapons. They were eyes and ears, as well.

Even knowing that, however, Sigrun had had reasons. "There was nothing, at first, to tell, Reginleif. We didn't know for certain what we were going to encounter there. Dr. Sasaki had seen a pattern of earthquakes, and she had tied that to ley-power—"

Reginleif cut her off. A standard interrogation tactic, not allowing the person being questioned to finish their thoughts. Keeping them off-balance. "But you certainly *suspected* a correlation to divine matters," she rapped out. "It followed the same pattern set in Nahautl five years before. You were *remiss*, Sigrun, in not informing the Odinhall immediately. You were *wrong*." She narrowed her eyes. "What do you have to say for yourself?"

Sigrun didn't reply, at first. "Well?" Reginleif demanded. "Answer me."

"There was a possibility that it could be related to interference in divine matters," Sigrun admitted. "That is why part of our team was sent in advance, to investigate. To find information. Without more information, I was unwilling to contact the Odinhall."

"And when your 'team members' confirmed that there were *gods* involved, why did you not contact the Odinhall immediately?" Reginleif shot back, her blue eyes wintery.

Sigrun's stomach churned. She'd thought about doing so. At length. And in the end, she'd refused to do so. "For the past five years," she said, putting her hands on the table, and looking up at Reginleif, "every question I have had about the Nahautl incident has been ignored, or deferred to you, and you have been unavailable to answer those questions."

"What has that to do with anything?"

"I feared that if I told the Odinhall about our discovery, I would be ordered not to accompany the rest of the team."

"You certainly would not have been permitted! I would have been sent, in exchange—"

This time, it was Sigrun who interrupted. "You might have been sent, Reginleif, but you would not have been accepted. You are not a Praetorian. You are not a lictor. You are not a member of our team."

"And your precious Praetorians have never worked with someone outside their ranks before?" Reginleif's eyes narrowed. "I note that Dr. Sasaki is not a Praetorian or a lictor."

"No. She is not. However, you would have been viewed as an intruder, an attempt by the Odinhall to assert control over a Roman mission, and Propraetor Livorus would have rejected it, immediately. The other members of my team would have rejected you." She swallowed, and focused on her hands.

"Oh, so this was all a masterful attempt on your part to ensure that there would be no political repercussions to the Odinhall." It was an outright sneer.

"I wish I could claim to that much foresight." Sigrun's tone was rueful. "No. It was much simpler than that. If the Odinhall had commanded me to stay away, Rome, in the person of Livorus, would certainly order me to go. And my personal loyalty to my husband and to my friends would compel me to go, in any regard."

"Even before your loyalty to your gods?" Reginleif's tone was scathing now. "You do not know your place! It will be my job to *re-educate* you."

Sigrun winced, and raised her eyes. This was one of her oldest teachers, after all. "I am sorry to disappoint you," she told the older valkyrie, her stomach churning. "I used my best judgment to prevent a conflict of loyalties from occurring—"

"And instead you left us all in the dark." Reginleif's voice was harsh. "I should have been the one to go! *I* should have been there, on that mountainside, not you."

Sigrun didn't know what to make of that. The words could have meant that Reginleif was outraged on her behalf, and that she, older and wiser, should be bearing the burden of the mission in Tawantinsuyu. But Sigrun wasn't sure that that was what the other woman actually meant. "I am sorry—"

"You damned well should be. You substituted your own judgment for that of the gods. You *presumed*, in your arrogance, that you knew better than they. That you should be the one there, on scene, not whom they would have chosen."

Sigrun swallowed. The words were a lash. "We are given free will," she said, looking down at the table, and then up again, her voice barely above a whisper. "We are given choices. That means that we are *expected* to use our judgment, not merely to defer to the will of the gods and fate. Else all we could do is sit like stones—"

"A very pretty tautology, Sigrun." Reginleif actually clapped her hands, slowly. "But the fact remains that you are a disobedient child. And disobedient children must be punished. What *are* we to do with you? Perhaps we should no longer permit you to be a Praetorian. A lictor. Obviously, there are conflicts in loyalty and obedience for you, and the role only seems to foster arrogance and pride in you."

Sigrun took a deep breath, and calmed herself. Reminded herself that this was an interrogation. Every word uttered was calculated to cut her, diamond against diamond. To reveal the flaws in her. "That is certainly possible," she acknowledged. She *had* wanted to be the one sent. She *had* been angry that they'd closed her out of the Nahautl investigations, in spite of the fact that she'd *been there*. Sigrun swallowed through a tight throat. "I maintain that we are not mindless. That we are expected to make decisions. Even mistakes—"

"People with powers like ours cannot be *permitted* to make

mistakes!" Reginleif's voice slammed into Sigrun again.

This time, however, Sigrun went on doggedly, through the interruption. "We are still human, Reginleif. Mistakes will happen—"

"And are you admitting that this was a mistake?" Reginleif suddenly purred. No anger. No annoyance. She just leaned forward, eyes almost feral.

Gods. I walked right into that one. She's very good at this. Sigrun exhaled. "I know not if it was a mistake," she replied, with grim formality. "You are certainly attempting to persuade me that it was. I do not know if your judgment is that of the gods."

"So, then. Again, what to do with you." Reginleif appraised her, openly.

Sigrun lifted her head. "The Odinhall may certainly recall me from my service to Rome," she said, quietly, accepting it with a certain measure of resignation. "Given my marriage to Adam ben Maor, however, it would be difficult for them to forbid me from having further knowledge of the situation."

"And if we were to bid you stay here, in the Odinhall, for the rest of Adam ben Maor's life?" Reginleif raised her eyebrows. "What then?"

Sigrun stared at her. It was nonsensical. "You are suggesting that I should be imprisoned for the term of Adam's life?" She was aware, distantly, that the edges of her vision had gone gray, in an adrenal reaction. "I would never stop trying to escape."

"You would reject the justice of the gods? You would, again, substitute your judgment for theirs?" Still that dangerous, measured purr.

Sigrun laced her hands together to conceal the shaking. "I doubt that the gods would do this, for it is not justice. But if they did? I would *question* them, yes."

Reginleif had sat back in her chair, her eyes sparkling now. "Well now. Isn't that *interesting*? You may go now, Sigrun. But do recall that you're to return here in a week's time for another interview."

Sigrun had walked out of that meeting room with her back straight and her head held high, but she hadn't been able to feel her knees at *all*.

―――――――――

For the first three months, they'd hardly seen the others, other than at hearings. Sigrun was just glad to see that Trennus seemed to be doing all right after his experience in the Veil. She didn't want to think of it as a death and resurrection. It hadn't quite been that, after all. Lassair had kept his body alive, and kept his mind intact. Trennus seemed sane, and he and Lassair had purchased a small house in Britannia, "Just for the summers, since she doesn't really like snow," Trennus had said, looking sheepish. "Winters, we're going to buy that house in Judea you two keep mentioning."

Adam had grinned in response. "What changed your mind?"

"She did. She was very specific about wanting to be closer to our friends. You just have to help us fix it up."

"That's not a problem. We'd be happy to—right, Sig?"

"You feel free to speak for me in this?" Sigrun had said, without rancor.

Adam looked abashed, then grinned, ruefully. "I somewhat assumed, yes."

"Yes, I'll help, too." Sigrun had been sitting next to Lassair in the living room of their Roman apartment, and Lassair, laughingly, had taken Sigrun's hand and put it on her swelling abdomen to feel the baby kick. Lassair was now six months pregnant, and the glow that lit the spirit from the inside out had nothing to do with flame, and much more to do with happiness.

It is good that you will do so. I have not the slightest idea where to begin with any of this.

"Were your parents at least pleased about the baby, Tren?" Sigrun asked him.

"My mother? Ecstatic. My father . . . concerned. At least one of my brothers asked if it was going to come out with sheep's hooves and little ram's horns." Trennus shook his head. "At this point, I think they're trying to bait me, deliberately. So I just smile." He bared his teeth. "For some reason, they seem to have trouble meeting my eyes anymore, so it does make things both easier and harder at the same time."

Sigrun had given Trennus a single concerned glance, but on the whole, if anyone was suited to become spirit-touched, he was. He had enormous self-control and considerable training with his existing powers. And he and Lassair certainly seemed to be happy.

Minori, in the meantime, had been put up, periodically, at a hotel in Rome by the Praetorians, when she had to fly in from Lutetia in northern Gaul to testify. She and Kanmi seemed to be seeing a good deal of each other, but they had also started, very quietly, on a secondary research project. One that *all* of them were working on, in their suddenly all-too-copious spare time. When Sigrun had regained a little more access within the Odinhall, and was permitted to use the facilities there for more than being poked, prodded, interviewed, and *sniffed,* she began working her way through the historical archives, slowly and warily. What she was looking for, she didn't really want to ask a reference librarian, or, gods forbid, Dvalin himself, for assistance in finding. Asking the Master of the Runes "could I please see everything that we have on the godslayers of old?" would only lead to more *interviews,* after all.

And while she was pursuing leads within the Odinhall, on vellum scrolls that were brown and cracking with age, rune marks carved into stone stelae thousands of years old, and images cast on golden *bracteates* amulets, preserving in the peace-gold offered by Rome to some of her ancestors, legends that the gods might remember, but that humans had forgotten, Adam began digging, just as quietly, at the University of Judea. His father's connections in the intelligence community, and rank within the Judean Intelligence Agency got him entrance to the Temple archives, as well. He cast his questions as a rekindled interest in the history of his people, brought on by the recent events in Tawantinsuyu. Hebrew, being a living language, had undergone massive changes in the past two thousand years, so he needed to teach himself to read the archaic form. He wasn't a scholar of Aramaic, either, so he initially had to read those scrolls and scraps of papyrus in translation—always a dubious thing. He was muttering about taking classes in the dead language, however.

Trennus, being a summoner in very good repute with his home university, had contacts all over the world, as did Kanmi and Minori. They all realized that this particular research project might well take up the bulk of their lives. The majority of information commonly available was on Akhenaten and Akhenaten's assassin. The information on the destroyers of Babylon and Akkad was scanty at best, in the west. But Kanmi held a surprisingly good relationship with Lady Erida, to this day. The Chaldean magus was part of a broader effort among the Magi to protect their ancient books and scrolls, which were vulnerable, even within climate-controlled vaults, to strikes from enemy forces. "The Persians don't want to destroy the College of the Magi," Kanmi told them all, one night over dinner at a restaurant. "They do that, and if and when they get Chaldea back under their control, they've lost an important resource. But the fact of the matter is, bombs *miss*. And once you let an efreet go on a rampage, they're not particularly discriminating about which buildings they burn."

"Lady Erida's summer estate is right on the Caspian, right?" Trennus played with a piece of bread before feeding a bite of it to Lassair.

"Yes. She says once the situation there stabilizes a little, we're *all* invited. Apparently, we're her favorite Romans." Kanmi snorted. "I pointed out that not one of us is an actual bona fide Roman. She answered that that makes us the best *kind*."

By November, Lassair and Trennus had moved into Adam and Sigrun's house in Judea, since it was in far more habitable condition than the one they'd purchased next door. Trennus had busied himself with both buildings. Other than the palace of the Roman governor, ley-power was virtually untapped locally, and no one had honored house-spirits in the area in about three thousand years. He bound a half-dozen spirits to small contracts for both homes. These ranged from spirits of the hearth that would work to prevent kitchen fires and would eat and dispose of refuse— he saw no need to throw out leftover food, when a spirit could turn that into perfectly useable energy—to earth spirits that would stand guard, and would emerge from the ground like wolves made of black stone if an intruder passed the door without one of them giving that being permission to enter. He bound other sprites with promises of bread and milk once a week, to look out for termites and other vermin. And he just grinned whenever Adam told him that the neighbors on either side of his parents' house were gossiping about having heard strange noises in the night coming from the two homes. "I don't mean to be unneighborly," Trennus said, "but good. I don't want to scare people off, but I also don't want people necessarily walking in unannounced."

"I don't exactly want people looking through my dresser drawers, either," Adam admitted, turning his head slightly, as they sat in the atrium, cooling off a bit after having finished framing new walls in Tren and Lassair's house. Trennus knew what Adam meant. The Velserk he'd carried in Tawantinsuyu was locked in a box and hidden in Adam's bedside table. "I don't want to keep the world at a distance . . . but no one in or out of the house without one of us being here, for certain."

The constant round of pure activity ensured that Trennus rarely had time to *think*, and that was, for the moment, how he wanted it. If he worked himself into a solidly exhausted state by night, he could sleep, and he wouldn't dream. Or at least, the chances were better that he wouldn't remember them. Every dream he had now, took him back to the Veil. At first, he thought it was just the work of a very active subconscious mind . . . until the morning after a particularly vivid dream, in which he'd wrestled with and bound a spirit there, and had bidden it to speak of what it knew of the godslayers of old. He'd woken up with a page of foolscap beside the bed, with names scribbled there in his own handwriting. The names didn't make sense. They weren't *Names*. Some were common human names, each of which meant something, in its original language . . . once he looked them up, anyway.

Adam, for instance, meant *man* or *clay*, out of Hebrew. Seeing that name written down had given Trennus a start, but all the others were equally . . . names, or words that were parts of modern names. Then there was *Fosa*, meaning *light*, in Hellene. *Lylh*, the Egyptian word for *night* . . . which happened to be very similar to the Hebrew word for the same. *Saras*, part of the Hindu name Sarasvati, was Sanskrit for *water, fluid*, or *lake*. *Azar*, which was an ancient Persian word for fire. *Adamas*, the Hellene term for *invincible*, which had become adamant, or diamond, in other languages. *Vayu*, back into Sanskrit for *wind*. *Gevah*, which was the Hebrew word for *mountain*. And it was the same word that Lassair had long ago told them had belonged to the godslayer that had beaten the *pazuzu*.

Each name wasn't a Name . . . but they each embodied a very simple concept. Generally, an elemental one. As in the earliest forms of sorcery people had understood, on looking at the natural world around them. Dualisms. Air-earth, fire-water, light-dark, and how they could be combined, perhaps. And none of it made sense.

But that was all the spirit in the dream had known, and Trennus had realized, with a surge of nausea, that he was still connected to the Veil. Part of him had never really left it, perhaps.

Lassair held his hair for him as he threw up in the lavatory after that realization. *You are still who you always were,* she told him, comfortingly. *You are just a little more.*

What happens if I lose *in my* sleep? *What kind of information might I give up, to an unfriendly spirit? What if a* god *comes looking for me in the Veil?* All horrifying realizations, strung out like beads on a chain.

I am always with you, Trennus. And I am always here, as well. We are one.

As he walked the Veil in his sleep, he saw the white hind, as he always had, and followed her wherever she led. He hadn't seen Saraid during his waking hours in six months, and he'd found he missed her gentle voice. But when he pressed the hind to return to him, she merely told him, I have never left you, and never will. But you have no need of me, at present. Save here, in the Veil. Where you require a guard and a guide.

His waking life was too full of changes to dwell on such things, however, and made more so in the early morning hours of Februarius 15, 1961, when Lassair rolled over in bed and rubbed his back. *Flamesower?*

Hmm? His drowsy mind took a moment to come back from the Veil to the room they were borrowing in Adam and Sigrun's house.

It is time.

What time?

The baby. It comes now. I will wake Stormborn. Lassair's tone was delighted and nervous at once.

Trennus sat up bolt upright in bed, throwing off the sheets. Even when he'd lived in the coldest, more northern parts of Britannia, he had slept in the nude; most people did, except perhaps those in the tundra regions of northern Europa, Raccia, and Caesaria Aquilonis. He hadn't even registered that he was still naked, however, before he was out the door of their room, and calling down the hall, urgently, "Sigrun!" Framed in the doorway, he turned back towards Lassair. "You're sure you don't want to go to the hospital? The doctors here are very, very good. Best in the world, really, besides maybe Hellas and Nippon."

Given the problems that they had with understanding Stormborn's healing, I have doubts as to how well they will react to me in one of their delivery rooms. Lassair's tone was utterly placid, and then shifted to mischievous. *Flamesower? You may wish to put on a kilt.*

What?

Stormborn is coming down the hall. You may wish to be dressed, unless you wish to impress her.

What — oh. Shit!

Sigrun had arrived in their room about a minute later, as Trennus was still frantically wrapping and buckling. "So, contractions?" Sigrun asked Lassair.

Yes.

"Painful?"

No.

That pattern repeated itself through the day. Lassair had finally agreed to overcome her fear of water enough to deliver in the bathtub, for comfort and ease of cleanup, but while Trennus crouched beside her, offering her his wrists to clutch, as Pictish men were told, from childhood, they ought to do, Lassair laughed and chattered through most of the delivery, pushing as needed.

She was initially concerned about just one thing. *What's wrong with my hands?* she demanded, sharply, holding them out of the water.

Trennus and Sigrun both stared at her for a long moment. "They're a little wrinkled," Trennus said, slowly.

Exactly! Is my body aging rapidly? Am I losing energy because of the birth process?

Sigrun coughed. Trennus began to laugh. "Ah . . . no. That's a perfectly normal part of being in *water*, Lassair," he told her, as Sigrun turned her face away.

Around the fourth hour, he finally believed it. "This . . . really isn't hurting you, is it?"

No. It does not hurt. It started to, at first, and then I adjusted the body's responses. It seems to me that people pursue actions as much for the reward of pleasure as from the fear of pain. The stronger the contraction, the better it feels to push. Lassair's smile was radiant, if a little tired. *However, if something is truly wrong, I will also know.*

Sigrun had been on hand, mostly because she'd sat with birthing mothers in Raccia before, and so that, in case something *did* go wrong, she could take the wound from Lassair, so that Lassair wouldn't have to try to heal her own body while still trying to give birth. She shook her head at the incarnate spirit now. "I do not know if I should chide you for cheating, remind you that birth is an essential human experience and you are missing an integral part of it . . . or *beg* you to do the same for me, when it is my time," the valkyrie said, arching her eyebrows. "I think one, perhaps two more strong pushes will do it, Lassair. I can see the head."

And then Latirian will join us. Lassair's tone was calm.

"Latirian?" Trennus blinked. "That's your sister's name, isn't it?"

I would prefer that name. And, as I have told you from the moment she was a ball of . . . thirty-two or so cells . . . she is a girl. Lassair's smile was infectious, and then she bore down again.

Two minutes later, Trennus held his daughter. She looked impossibly small in his hands, and Trennus' world faded out a little. Noises in the background, as Lassair dealt with the mucky business of the afterbirth by simply changing her body, and stepping out of the bloody water and accepting a towel from Sigrun. *I will agree, the water was not entirely a bad experience,* Lassair admitted, and sat down on the edge of the tub as Sigrun pulled the plug. *Let me hold her? I have waited so long to see her face.*

Trennus handed the baby over, gingerly, and watched as Latirian's eyes opened. The baby was sleepy, a little red . . . had ten toes and ten fingers, and brilliant, carmine-red eyes. The first wisps of fine pillow hair on the little head were as fiery red as her mother's, and as Lassair smiled and cradled the baby to her breast, Saraid finally appeared in the form of a hind, pushing her head through the wall to study the child. *It is very well,* Saraid said, quietly. *This one will run and play in my forests, will she not?*

If you wish her to, yes. Trennus was startled by how relieved he was to see his oldest ally and friend, whose mark rode across his shoulders in blue ink.

I would welcome the sound of her laughter there. The spirit's voice was affectionate, but there was a hint of sorrow there, too, which he did not understand. And then she vanished once more.

Sigrun helped Lassair to the bed, got her neatly dressed in a robe, so that she could receive visitors, when she so chose, cleaned out the bathtub for them, and started for the door. *Do you not wish to hold her?* Lassair called after the valkyrie. *You were here all through the labor. Should you not have some of the reward?*

Trennus watched Sigrun turn, the gray eyes a little disconcerted. She came back over, and perched, on the very edge of the bed that he shared with Lassair, and accepted the infant, who'd just finished a stint at Lassair's breast, and was sleepy and sated as a result. "She definitely favors you both. Lassair's eyes and hair, of course. But there is a good deal of Trennus in the facial features. She will be striking." Sigrun rocked the infant, looking a little uncertain about it, and Trennus thought that this might be the first time that the valkyrie had ever actually *held* a child. Oh, she'd helped with labor and delivery, but actually holding one? She looked almost as frightened of breaking the infant as he felt, himself.

Ah, but she definitely has your nose and cheekbones, Stormborn, Lassair told the valkyrie, calmly, and Trennus tried not to choke.

"Ah . . . what?" Sigrun said, sounding a little confused.

I used some of your life-pattern to shape this body when I created it. I admire your appearance, strength, and certainty, so I wished to replicate it. Unsurprisingly, some of that pattern appears in Latirian's life-essence as well.

About five different expressions rippled across Sigrun's face, each one clear and distinct, and Trennus cautiously took Latirian out of her hands. He was seeing shock, agitation, anger, a little affront, and . . . fear. Quickly masked, but he knew Sigrun pretty well by now. Lassair, thankfully, intervened, taking Sigrun's hand in hers, lightly. *I did not intentionally put some of you into the child. I only patterned myself off of someone I admired. I did not know that I could create a life, much less that your patterns could pass to her.*

Sigrun swallowed. Pushed everything down, visibly. "Poor thing," she told the baby. "At least between Lassair and Trennus, that should cancel out absolutely anything you get from me." She stood, and ran the backs of her fingers against the baby's cheek. "Lassair, if you and Trennus decide to have more children? I would recommend *asking* someone before you use their . . . life-pattern again."

I like my base body perfectly the way it is. I adjust it a little from day to day, manifestation to manifestation. You could think of it as us being . . . sisters, in truth. Or very distant cousins. Lassair paused. *Which we already were, anyway, Stormborn. You know this.*

Sigrun lowered her eyes. Swallowed. "I'll let you three finish getting acquainted," she said, without responding to Lassair's words, and left the room quickly.

It took another two months to finish getting their own house here in habitable enough condition that they could finish moving in; this was made worse by the fact that they were, once more, back in the business of guarding Livorus. That meant that they all once more were based out of Rome, and Livorus was once more, constantly on the move. All of them were used to the peripatetic lifestyle, however, and Lassair insisted on one very important experiment before she went on the road with Trennus. *I have to be able to protect this child,* she said, simply. *And my most certain methods of protection all revolve around flame. Latirian, I know you cannot understand me yet, but if this does not work, I truly do apologize.*

As she cradled the infant in her left arm, Lassair had let just her right hand become flame, and had, very slowly, reached a hand towards the sole of their daughter's right foot. Trennus had watched, eyes wide, and resisting the urge to reach out and snatch Lassair's hand away. Lassair had let her hand hover near the baby's foot for a moment, measuring the reaction to the heat without actually touching the baby. And then she'd rubbed her forefinger along the arch of Latirian's pudgy sole, and the infant pulled away, as from a tickle, stuffed most of a fist inside her mouth, and drooled, but didn't scream. Didn't cry. Didn't react in pain at all.

Trennus examined his daughter's appendage carefully. "No sign of pink. No burns," he said, after a stomach-churning moment of anxiety.

Lassair took it slowly, making sure that Latirian was, in fact, as fire-proof as she seemed. And to both parents' enormous relief, Lassair could actually shift fully into her flame form, and hold the baby totally ensheathed in fire . . . and the most that would happen was that Latirian would go to sleep. "Wish we'd figured this out earlier," Trennus muttered. "If I'd known she had an *off* button like this, it would have made for many fewer sleepless nights."

It had been close to a year since the events on the mountain, and Trennus had, with much help from Lassair and Saraid, begun working to secure his dreams. *Beings with enough willpower can shape the Veil around them,* Lassair had explained, patiently. *You have enormous will. You can construct for yourself a place of safety, where others cannot intrude. You simply must learn to impose your reality upon the Veil.*

It had been enormously difficult, at first. The Veil *fought* him. It was a place where everything happened, and nothing had consequences. It resisted linear reality. It resisted one-thing-after-another. It resisted ordering. It took months, learning to visualize what he wanted to see, and patterning reality around him, but Trennus began to manage it. Night after night, he recreated the Caledonian Forest in the Veil. Saraid's forest. He wasn't entirely sure why, except that this was the place closest to his heart, of any in the world. It was where he'd grown up. Where he'd made the decisions that had led him to where he was now. Where he and Saraid had hunted together for the first time, and where he'd been bound to her, and she to him. She paced the imagined woods with him, a certain proprietary gleam in the hind's eyes, and Trennus spangled the sky with stars and constellations. Not the ones of the real world, but as if they were on a planet somewhere much nearer the galactic core. The stars were thus huge, and the entire sky was filled with them, and there was never really *dark*. Just a dimmer form of light, and the trees of his imagined forest yearned towards the stars.

The more strongly he imagined it, the harder it was for creatures he did not wish to enter, to enter at all. The landscape itself began to resist them. And the various creatures he had befriended, or defeated in amicable combat, and whose Names he had learned, began to people that place that wasn't a place at all. Some of them were transient, there for a night, and then gone, then back, as if they'd never left. Others seemed content to become permanent residents. "I have a kingdom of the mind,"

Trennus told Lassair, one morning. "And here I never once wanted to be a king."

Better in the Veil than on this world, I think.

"I certainly don't have to worry about taxes."

There is that. But they are tithing you energy, are they not, in exchange for protection?

"Ah . . . I don't think so? I think we're just all unified, and there to protect each other."

We shall see, she said, and smiled, a little winsomely, as she patted Latirian on the back, as the infant goggled over her shoulder.

———————————

For Kanmi and Minori, the first year after the destruction in Tawantinsuyu had seen a great number of changes. On getting off the plane in Rome, Kanmi's first sight had been Bodi and Himi, there at the airport with their pedagogue, both tearing loose from the woman's grip and plunging towards him at a dead run. They practically tackled him, and held on as tightly as they could, babbling, "I thought you were hurt, I thought you were dead!".

"We saw the news on the far-viewer—"

"Yes, but I *called*, remember?" Kanmi dropped to his knees, and let his bags slide to the floor, pulling both of his sons to him in a tight embrace. "Don't tell me you forgot about the phone call."

Himi, the older one, pulled back first. "You called. Bodi was in bed, though. He didn't believe me when I said that you were all right." In spite of his brave words, Himi looked worried. He'd clearly understood a good deal more about the disaster than his younger brother had. "Did you see the mountain explode?"

From very close range, yes. Kanmi couldn't say it like that. Not without spooking them worse. "I did, actually. I even took a few pictures. It was dark when the volcano first erupted, but I have a few tricks to let me take night pictures that look like daylight." Casual tone, casual words. Making it less of a big deal. "I had my camera in my work bag, like I always do. Got some pictures of the ornithopter that Agent ben Maor was flying when I took the volcano shots. You'll like that." Admittedly, the pictures had all been taken in an effort to get the details of the destruction down for the intelligence wing of the Praetorians, but his boys would just see smoke, fire, and a good deal of debris. They wouldn't realize just how close the ornithopter had been when Kanmi had started snapping pictures. "And you know what? When the gift shop in the hotel in Machu Picchu opened up, I grabbed a few things for you two," he told them.

Bodi sniffled and turned his face up. "You did?"

"What did you get us?" Himi chimed in, a little more eagerly.

"You'll have to wait till we're home to see. But I got your presents at the same time Agent Caetia over there was picking up a really nice picture of Machu Picchu for her home. Showed the old stone palace, beside the skyscrapers." *Something of a collector's item now,* Kanmi thought, grimacing internally. *Though, a city that old? They'll rebuild.*

He'd glanced over his shoulder at Minori, who had two fresh-faced young Praetorians now flanking her, clasping her wrist, and introducing themselves as her bodyguards while she was in Rome. Making it clear that she had a hotel room to go to, courtesy of the Praetorians, and would for as long as the hearings . . . interviews . . . interrogations . . . whatever you wanted to call them . . . about the Tawantinsuyu incident would go on. Minori's face had cleared of all expression, but Kanmi knew her well enough to read her eyes now. She was terrified. They hadn't been confident in their ability to keep her in a safe house here in Rome four weeks ago, when there had been a nameless, faceless assassin possibly after her for *perhaps* knowing more than she should. That assassin had a face and a name now, and was dead, but only after torturing her for four hours — an incident that had been the direct result of being separated from the rest of them.

Kanmi straightened up, lifting Bodi up so that the boy's legs dangled. "Dr. Sasaki?" he called over, very formally. Very politely. As if they hadn't spent a night in bed together before close to twenty-four interminable hours of cramped quarters in an ornithopter and then a fixed-wing plane across the Sea of Atlas. "It would give me great pleasure if you'd join my family for dinner tonight. And any other night that you might wish to do so."

Minori's look of relief had warmed him, but he knew this was a stepping stone for her, a way to regain her confidence, and a way to remember how to live without paranoia. Although, given her experiences in the past month? She'd never regain that patina of innocence. The blinders that most normal people wore, that let them ignore just how dangerous the world really was, had been ripped off, and could never really be put back on again.

And so, Minori had stayed with him and the boys for the first week in Rome. He offered to take the couch this time, so that she could have his bed, and she'd shyly shaken her head. "Oh, so you actually like the couch?" he asked, raising his eyebrows. The boys were in bed, and they were standing in the living room.

Minori shifted a little. "You . . . I mean . . . you don't wish to . . . ?" Sudden insecurity in her voice, and Kanmi damned himself.

He took her hands in his, and told her, simply, "I don't want to pressure you, or make you feel like you *have* to, just to have a safe place to sleep." Kanmi shrugged. "This apartment is as safe as I can make it, and I've had a lot of time to prepare the place. You, Minori? You can sleep anywhere you wish." He paused. "Besides the boys' bedroom. I think that may confuse them. Also, the kitchen might be uncomfortable."

They still argued, of course. But these were arguments about *work*. About *magic*, the proper use of it, about the merits of traditional spell-casting and modern innovation, how natural philosophy and magic could work together. About physics, and whether or not the universe was expanding, and what the math actually *meant*. Kanmi wasn't sure when he'd last smiled this much. He cooked dinner every night, as he had for four years now, whenever he was home to do so. Made coffee, Nubian-style, which Minori tried, politely, but at which she still wrinkled her nose. Two days later, she brought oolong tea from a Nipponese market, and let them all try it. Her version of a tea ceremony was at *least* as involved as Bastet's coffee preparation had been, and Kanmi was somewhat amused by the mental comparison he'd drawn. It was about the only resemblance between the two women at all.

Himi and Bodi watched them argue over the dinner table, wide-eyed, until one night, Bodi burst into tears, and Kanmi stopped in mid-sentence. "What's the matter?" he asked, sharply.

"I don't want you to argue," the boy said, miserably. "I like Minori. I don't want her to leave."

Minori's mouth had fallen open. Kanmi immediately reached out and tousled Bodi's wavy hair. "We're not fighting," he told his son, calmly. "We're arguing about ideas, but we're not fighting. There's a difference, Bodi. A really big one."

His son's dark eyes were woebegone, and Himi didn't look any more like he believed Kanmi. "All right, I'll tell you what. I won't raise my voice when we're arguing. That way, you'll believe me, right?"

It took a little effort to remember. Kanmi had had to shout over the top of a loud and boisterous family just to be heard from an early age, and had used volume as a method of compensating for his short stature for years. But he was rewarded when the boys started to realize that he and Minori weren't lacing into each other. Began to relax.

But that being said, when it was time for her to go back to Gaul, the boys were heartbroken, and clung onto her at the airport, until she hesitantly, with glances at Kanmi, promised to return.

"Oh, I expect you won't have any choice about that," he told her, cheerfully. "Hearings. Questions. Investigations. It'll be *fun*."

The six months of administrative leave, Kanmi took as something of a blessing in disguise. It let him spend a copious amount of time with his sons, reassuring them that he wasn't about to disappear from their lives. He suspected that when Himi reached adolescence, he was probably going to hear a good deal about how he'd *driven off* their mother, so he wanted to make sure there was a solid foundation of trust between him and his sons before the young adult years. And he made sure to tell them both, that once they reached eighteen, if they wanted to reach out to Bastet again, they could. "Just not until you've reached your majority," he told them, simply. "That was the court's decision, and I think it was the right one. What you do when you're adults, and can make your own choices, will be up to you."

He also used that time to start nosing into the whole *godslayer* issue for ben Maor and Caetia. If he couldn't do research on the energy distribution loads in Tawantinsuyu, the least he could do was historical research. Progress was . . . very slow indeed. Much of the information, such as it was, seemed to be obscured in legend and myth, if not deliberately occluded. Distorted. Destroyed. *Then again, if I were an <u>entity</u>, I wouldn't want to leave directions on how to kill me lying around, either.*

As for Minori, while her employer, Eleutherian Industries,

definitely enjoyed the publicity that her presence in Tawantinsuyu brought them, as well as her steadfast assertion that ley-power itself had had nothing to do with the disasters, her constant absences that year, as she was summoned, again and again to Rome for hearings, wore on their patience. The fact that she had two bodyguards assigned to her in Gaul wore at *her* patience, as well, but at the same time, she was grateful to have them. Her tiny, one-bedroom apartment in Lutetia was at least easy for them to secure, but it really wasn't designed for more than one person at a time—as she discovered anew when Kanmi and his sons came to visit her in the capital of northwest Gaul for about a week. The two boys were noisy and didn't stop talking or moving until they crashed, completely asleep, on her spare *skihibuton* atop the tatami mat, just beside her low eating table in the small living area. She was marginally surprised that Kanmi didn't object to her own cotton mattress on the mat in her bedroom, but he reminded her, rolling his eyes, that he'd slept on a pallet on the floor as a child, and that the only difference was that hers was nicer, and he didn't have to share it with anyone but her. "Most people at home say that our beds have health benefits," Minori told him as she unfolded the pallet one night.

He shrugged. "The only difference between a poor family in Tyre sleeping on the floor and a rich family sleeping on the floor in Hokkaido is that for one family, it was a choice, not a necessity. That, and I suspect you didn't have rats scampering over you in the night, or occasionally wake up with one of them eating a cockroach inches from your face."

Minori had winced, and Kanmi had reached out, and slipped a hand under her elbow. "I'm just saying, I don't think it's the *bedding* that has the health benefits. People on every continent slept on the ground for many years before bed frames were invented. Personally, doesn't matter a bit to me where I sleep, so long as the place is *clean*." He leaned down and kissed her forehead, a little apologetically. "However you're comfortable, Min."

He'd been as good as his word, too. He didn't complain about a stiff back in the morning. Didn't complain that he couldn't get to sleep, either. Just held her close, and usually fell asleep long before she did. When she asked him about that, he snorted. "Just testament to the fact that I spent too much time near the Mongol border, really. You really can learn to sleep through anything. Musket-fire, in particular. This? This is much more pleasant, Min."

The boys, she'd discovered, would eat almost *anything*, no matter how strange. They'd been raised on a mix of Carthaginian, Nubian, and Roman foods. They were thus a little surprised when she served them steamed rice and a little soup for breakfast, but to her pleased surprise, they simply ate it like starving wolves, and got on with the day.

Kanmi and the boys toured the historic places of Lutetia. It was a scenic city, and the Sequana was a beautiful river; she even went with them on one of the boat rides that took tourists all the way out to the Britannic Channel, and the boys fell asleep against them on the long evening ride back, where there was nothing to do but look at the city lights along the banks, and the stars above.

She was astounded, however, at how *empty* the apartment felt when they left. As if most of what made life interesting had departed with them. The bodyguards, who had maintained a quiet vigil at the periphery of her awareness while Kanmi was there, closed back in again.

Around that point in time, she received a letter from her mother, Aika Mori, very delicately chiding her for not having contacted her or her father. *A few words to let us know that you were in good health would not have gone amiss,* Aika wrote. *Additionally, you seem to be in a position of uncomfortably public prominence. Is there anything that the family can do to offer you some protection?*

Minori had rubbed at her face, and had begun a letter in reply, before wincing and doing something she had not done in almost twelve years. She called her mother on the telephone. Her mother had told her, all through her long years at the Imperial Court, that she cherished the finely-written missives Minori sent her, the ability to hold the paper in her hands and know that her daughter had gracefully written the words by hand. Telephone privileges at court had been nonexistent, and Minori had maintained the same behavior in Gaul, partially out of habit, and partially out of . . . embarrassment, really. Shame. She was an exile, she knew it, and she shouldn't be seen or heard.

Thus, it took a moment for Aika to recognize Minori's voice, but once she did, Min was astounded by the relief and joy in her mother's voice. *"Oh, Minori, it is so wonderful to hear your voice! Are you all right? What happened to you in Tawantinsuyu? Do you know how many Roman officials have come to see your father and ask questions about you? They asked him why you'd been trained in withstanding torture. Do you know what hearing that did to your father? To all of us?"* Her mother wasn't letting her get a word in edgewise. This was exceedingly unusual behavior for the exquisitely-mannered Aika.

Minori apologized. And apologized. And apologized. To her frank amazement, her *father* came to the telephone, and spoke with her for several minutes. She wasn't sure if his gruff, reserved tone meant that he was disappointed in her, for her having failed to speak with them first, or some sort of strange pride in her. She apologized to him, as well, and he handed the phone back to her mother. And when Aika demanded, again, *"Why didn't you contact us before now?"* Minori started to answer, *you could have called me* when she realized that this wasn't entirely true. She'd moved several times in Lutetia. She couldn't even remember if she'd given them her most recent phone number. The plain fact was, she hadn't thought that they would care, so long as she didn't shame them.

That was the assumption of the eighteen-year-old, who'd spent five years separated from her family, and had been facing at least four more years of separation, if not more. The assumption had made it easier to bear that separation. She'd told herself, stubbornly and repeatedly, that they didn't care about her, because distancing herself from them mentally, made the distance hurt less.

And it had been a lie. She'd convinced herself of it fairly thoroughly, though. Convinced herself that her mother's beautifully-written, poetically-worded letters were just . . . thought exercises. A noblewoman writing as a noblewoman should. Not the only expression of love she'd *permitted* her mother for . . . at least twelve years.

She wasn't on a secure line, and had to plead that excuse, several times, when her mother asked about the events in Caesaria Australis, but she could understand her mother's curiosity. Minori had *lived* through the events, and some days, still wasn't sure she understood everything that had happened.

"*At least tell me what your plans are?*" Aika finally asked, once she'd wound down a little.

Minori winced. "*I have been attempting to demonstrate to my employer that I am worthy of remaining with them. My managers have been generous to a fault, and I work until seven in the evening, most nights, to make up for the fact that I used all of my vacation to go to Tawantinsuyu. All the hearings I must attend in Rome, however, are wearing at my managers' patience.*"

A pause. Aika had never held a job. She was a noble. This undoubtedly sounded like an exceedingly middle-class concern to her. "*And what will you do about this?*"

"*I have applied for a job at the University of Rome,*" Minori admitted. She hadn't told Kanmi that yet. If she got the job, she'd tell him then, but not before. "*Their school of technomancy is not as good as the University of Edo or the University of Athens, but it would be steady, professional work.*"

A pause. "*That seems a big step, to account for hearings that should only last a few more months.*"

"*It's not just that.*" Minori took a deep breath, and swallowed. Nippon had, because of its status as an island kingdom along several major trade routes, never been an insular culture. Still, intermarriage with foreigners among the nobility was somewhat frowned upon. *Not that we're getting married. Though that may make it look so much worse to my family.* She hesitated a moment longer, and finally said, in a rush, "*I actually would like to move to Rome. I have . . . friends there.*"

"*Oh, do you have a lover there?*" Aika chirped cheerfully.

"*Mother!*" Minori was horrified. Her father could well still be in ear-shot.

"*Minori, you are thirty, and you have never once in any of your letters mentioned any attachments of the heart. I thought I would die without grandchildren. So, tell me . . . do you have a sweetheart or not?*"

In her living room, where she sat on the floor beside her small eating table, Minori slowly crumbled in on herself and put her head on the cold, hard surface. "*Yes, but Mother, please, it might not lead to anything.*"

That didn't help matters *at all*. Aika was far too happy now to be halted in the full career of her imagination. She wasn't even discomposed when Minori haltingly mentioned that Kanmi had children from a previous marriage. "*What of it? Your father has half a dozen children with his lady wife.*" A pause, and a muffled sound of voices in the background. "*Your father wishes me to tell you that if you wish to come home and visit, it would be acceptable to him. He would be willing to meet with this man at that point in time, to see if he is worthy of his daughter.*"

Minori's head, already on the surface of the table, couldn't sink any lower. But she did feel as if gravity had, by some unknown quirk of physics, somehow just tripled.

A week later, she had a letter offering her a solid professorship at the university of Rome, and, holding her breath, called Kanmi to inform him. "You're moving to Rome, eh? Is it to cut down on the commute, or am I a factor in your decision-making process?" Mild irony in the tone.

"A full professorship in technomancy and sorcery looks good on the *curriculum vitae*." Minori kept her tone sweet. "May I . . . ah, prevail upon you to help me find an apartment there?"

There was a long pause on the other end of the line. Kanmi finally replied, "Do you really think we need to do all the dancing around? I've got two kids. I'm not going to be running over to your place, having to call on the pedagogue to stay in while I'm out, racing back across town, and just plain not getting any sleep. Can't do it, Min. If I'm not at my best, someone dies." He paused. "And if you're coming across town all the damned time, then you're just wasting time in traffic, and the fact is, you need sleep, too, especially if you're going to be teaching sorcery, damn it."

Minori swallowed, the phone suddenly heavy in her hand. "What are you saying?"

"I mean this. I might be terrible at saying it, but I'm more than a little fond of you. And we're either in each other's lives, or not. I might have trouble trusting people, Min, but I don't have intimacy issues. None of this separate apartments, separate lives shit. If we're in, we're in. No in-betweens. No separate bedrooms, either. We'd be *together*, not roommates with the option to fuck each other, like the warm and wonderful relationship Livorus has with his wife. Life is too short for the games people play when they're not sure they're with the right person." He paused. "I'm pretty sure about you, Min. You add up." Another pause. "Admittedly, from your perspective, I might be missing a variable or two . . ."

Minori let out the breath she'd been holding. It was so *hard* to do so much of this by phone, or letter. "Numbers are wonderfully comforting things," she said, softly. ""If we input *this* amount of energy into a system, and there's *this* much resistance or friction in the system, then we can expect *that* amount of force or *energy* output. There are always losses. That's the nature of the universe. It's in determining which losses are the *acceptable* ones that is where engineers and sorcerers become artists."

"And this is precisely why I love talking to you." Kanmi's voice warmed.

"The thing is . . . when I'm with you, there don't seem to be any losses. Oh, there's friction in the system—"

"I'm rather fond of the friction, myself—"

Minori choked. It wasn't the words themselves. It was the way he said them. "What I mean," she said, clinging to her dignity, "is that when I'm with you, there aren't any losses. There are just . . . *gains*. And so . . . I really would rather just be with you," she admitted. "I have no objections to the arrangement. And we're both quiet people. We share most of our interests." It was all true, too. It wasn't just that she felt safe with him, though he'd certainly worked hard to make sure she did. It was the overall feeling of wholeness. Of not having to compromise on dozens of issues, because they were simply so eminently comfortable with one another.

"Yes. I see long evenings in the living room, with both of us reading. I don't see either of us inviting over friends and irritating the shit out of each other by talking loudly all night about things that the other one finds inconsequential. Loud drinking parties? We're both pretty high on the list of people who should never, ever get drunk." A pause, and a vocal inflection that sounded like a shrug. "Besides, you've met the people I'm closest to in the world. I work with them."

"And I like them," Minori said, quietly. "They're good people. There are people in the world who are talkers, and there are people who are doers . . . and you're all doers."

Kanmi snorted. "Yes. There's a big difference between the waitress at the corner *taverna*, who's 'only waiting tables until she's discovered as an actress,' and people who've actually worked to make themselves who they want to be." He paused. "So, we're settled then? You're just moving in with us?"

Minori swallowed. "Yes. I think I am."

"Good. The boys have been asking when they get to see you again. They'll probably beat the next rocket to the moon when they hear you're *moving in* with us." Kanmi chuckled. She'd gotten used to the various masks he wore. The inmost man, the person she and his sons got to see, was a surprisingly gentle being, and the towering anger he usually carried with him was primarily composed of raw outrage at the injustices he saw in the world around him.

"Ah, there is one more thing . . . ."

"And that is?"

She braced herself, and stared at the twisting knot-work patterns in wallpaper that her apartment had been furnished with before her arrival. "My, ah, parents. They want to meet you."

Another pause. "I thought you didn't really talk with them."

"I hadn't, besides letters, for years, until last week. They were . . . understandably upset that I hadn't spoken with them, and that, well, apparently Roman agents had been there to ask about . . . resisting torture and things like that." Minori realized she was twisting her finger in the cord of the phone until her skin turned purple. She did not like thinking about the four hours in which she'd been the object of Huallpa's attentions on the mountain. "One thing led to another, and my mother asked why I was looking into moving to Rome . . . ."

"Aha. Caught you in an admission. I *was* a deciding factor in the move." A solid poke, to get her mind off the bad memories.

"Perhaps you were." Minori, in spite of the fact that he couldn't see her, lifted her nose in the air.

Kanmi chuckled. "All right. I have . . . at least another month of this damned administrative leave ahead of me. Let's look at the calendar, see when we're both scheduled for hearings, and . . . go to Hokkaido, I guess. Can I bring the boys? Another country to color in on their map of the world."

Minori blinked, rapidly. "You . . . you don't mind?" Her voice rose a little, nervously.

"No. Figured I might try doing things right this time around. Bastet mostly married me, I think, in retrospect, to make sure she wouldn't have to go home to her family in Nubia. She'd fallen more in love with Hellas, than with me, and didn't want to be stuck as her extended clan's main doctor forever. So I never actually *met* her parents." She could picture him shrugging again. "I would love for you to meet my mother, Min, but I won't subject you to my brothers. Maybe I'll send her money for a plane ticket at some point." He paused. "So, I have to ask . . . ."

"What?" She was simply trying to picture Kanmi in her father's *shoin-zukuri* house, and failing, completely. She couldn't imagine him speaking with her severe, distant father, or her father's wife, or even her mother. Oddly, she *could* picture Bodi and Himi staring around themselves, wide-eyed, and probably getting in trouble running through the gardens.

"Right. You're still technically a noblewoman, Minori." Kanmi's voice was long-suffering. "You're going to have to tell me how I'm supposed to ask your family for permission to marry you, and if this is going to result in me having to fight a duel with your father or anything like that. For the record, I am *not* getting my head cut off for you. He's going to find that his sword has disintegrated in its sheath before he can fully draw it, and that's final."

About five total responses all competed for control of Minori's mouth at once. The one that won out was *"Marry?"*

"Look, I figure if I'm inviting you to live with me, that's sort of part of the equation. And I certainly don't think it'll particularly look good to your parents if I *don't* ask you. It might look disrespectful, in fact. So, is there anything in particular I need to know? Do I need to bribe him?"

"Bribe?" Minori's voice was strangled.

"That's what most dowries seem to be, though technically, that money was usually supposed to be kept for the maintenance of the daughter given in marriage, and her children. Amazing number of noblemen seemed to use that coin for something else, though." Kanmi's voice was dry. "Information, Min, please. What do I need to know?"

Minori got her rattled mind back together again. "Were you going to ask me, first?"

"I asked you to live with me. You said yes. Do I have to fly up there and pry this out of you with a crowbar?"

Roman culture didn't put much of a premium on romance. Most love-stories from the classical period ended in tragedy; a moralist might suggest that an overabundance of passion was a flaw, and that the best way in which to live was to live moderately, in all things. Even in comedies, too much passion made people the butt of jokes. Marriage in the classical period had largely been for purposes of controlling reproduction, and for the economic benefit of the family. People had not married for love; they had married at the directive of their families, for their families' benefit. Rich and poor alike. Gallic and Gothic culture, on the other hand, both very much did stress the importance of romantic love. Cultural syncretism had led, over the centuries, to a balance between the two competing concepts, but the Roman view of romantic love remained, perhaps a little surprisingly, jaundiced. Foreigners, barbarians, could be slaves to passion, but not a proper Roman man.

Minori explained, simply enough, "Feudal Nippon was much the same as Rome. People married for the good of their families. There were . . . go-betweens. Arranged marriages were common. Men would come to work for their wife's family, because labor was in demand, and that was what was . . . valued. He could visit her at night, and she would stay with her family until she was pregnant, or until one of her parents died."

Kanmi cleared his throat. "That's a very long commute just to try to get you pregnant, Min. I assume there's a different way forward nowadays?"

Minori leaned against the wall, chuckling helplessly. "After the shoguns came to power, the system reversed, and women went to work for their husband's families, instead."

"So, no bribes?"

"No, but he will probably wish to ask you many questions. You *are* a foreigner. He doesn't know you, or your rank, or if you are . . . suitable. If they agree, they'll arrange for you to give me an *obi* sash and for me to give you a pair of *hakama* pants. They may even insist that the ceremony be done before we leave. Propitious dates are difficult to find." Min swallowed, tracing a finger over the knot-work on her wallpaper, and wishing that she weren't hundreds of miles away from Kanmi right now. This didn't feel quite real.

"No rank. Probably not suitable. Marrying you, regardless. Assuming, yes, that you want to." A hint of anxiety. "You do, right?"

Minori smiled a little. "Well, I don't know. This is a little sudden, isn't it?"

"Ahh. I see how it is. You're only after me for my body."

"Your mind, Kanmi, your mind."

"Package deal. You don't get one without the other."

So, in Ianuarius of 1961, they'd gone to Hokkaido. It was possibly the worst time of the year to visit, and the entire prefecture was cloaked in snow. Minori was used to this sort of climate, and hadn't been home in twelve years, so she all but hung out the window of the train to stare at beloved hillsides and buildings, her breath clouding the air. Kanmi, Himi, and Bodi, on the other hand, were accustomed to Rome and Tyre's mild winters, and even though they'd brought warm cloaks and were wearing double layers of tunics, the boys shivered. Kanmi, apparently wanting to put a good foot forward, actually had not put on jeans, a tunic, and his usual vest covered in pockets filled with technomancy gear. Instead, he wore a white Carthaginian caftan, under his long winter cloak. "If I'm going to look like a barbarian, I might as well look like *my kind* of barbarian," he'd told Min, grimly, before they'd boarded the train.

Formal greetings, in the snowy courtyard of her father's house. Servants had been out to sweep the snow into heaps, at least. Her mother had gray hair now, much to Minori's shock; she had only ever pictured her mother as the serenely beautiful woman that Aika had been in her thirties. Her father, Tadaoki Ijiun, was every bit as formal and severe as she remembered, and Minori bowed to him, respect and courtesy ingrained and reflexive. When she rose from her bow, however, she was startled to see a softness in his eyes she'd never realized before was there. She'd known he loved her enough to permit her to go to Gaul, but she hadn't realized that he'd *missed* her. *I am learning that I have been a child in my thoughts for at least a decade longer than I should have been,* she realized. *I am seeing my parents for who they are now, instead of who I perceived them to be, when I was young. Gods. I was a fool.*

And again, to her surprise, Tadaoki offered Kanmi a very Roman wrist-clasp. His Latin was rusty, and Kanmi had picked up only a word or two of Nipponese from Minori, though she suspected that might change when they moved in together, so Minori had to serve as an interpreter, at first.

The weeklong visit went far better than Minori had ever thought it would. She had to give Kanmi and the boys credit. Again, they ate anything put in front of them without comment or hesitation. The boys were a little restless during a formal tea ceremony, but a word from their father quelled them. And when her father took Kanmi off for a private conversation the second day, Aika pulled Minori off to the side, an hour or two later. *"You told us he was a sennin,"* she said, smiling. The word could mean either *kami*-touched or sorcerer, in context. A learned user of magic, *or* a god-born. There was less of a division between sorcerers, summoners, and god-born in Nipponese culture than in Roman. *"Your father said that you did not tell us he was also a samurai at heart."*

Minori had long since come to that same conclusion, but still smiled a little. Outwardly, there was little similarity between Kanmi, who was abrasive at best, and the calm, restrained manner that a warrior who practiced bushido would cultivate. Most days, he deliberately flouted manners, though he was clearly on his best behavior here, for her sake. But for her, it was all about the will of the person, the refusal to be defeated.

She did need to poke Kanmi several times before he'd tell her what they'd talked about. "Mostly financial details," Kanmi finally told her. "I told him that your money would stay your money. Anything that you've made from Eleutherian, anything you make at the University . . . that's yours. I'll pay for rent and food, and you'll be on the Praetorian's medical insurance program which is . . . surprisingly good." An acid grin. "It has to be, of course." He shrugged. "He asked about children. I said that that was up to you." He picked up Minori's hand, and kissed her gloved fingers, as they walked in the snow-draped gardens that were tucked between the buildings of her father's estate. Himi and Bodi, bundled up against the cold, bounded through the snow to either side of them, pelting each other with snowballs, and hiding behind exquisitely trimmed trees, possibly to the despair of her father's gardeners. One errantly thrown missile came in on an attack vector for their father's head, and exploded into fragments three feet from his face, without Kanmi looking away from Minori, which just made the boys *laugh*. "I'm open to the idea, if you want one of your own, Min." Kanmi used his free hand to brush snow off his shoulder, and looked up at the sky. "Though I can definitely understand if, with these two already around, if you would prefer *not* to."

She smiled a little, wide-eyed. A year ago, she'd thought that none of this would ever be in the stars for her. "Yes. I want to. But . . . not right away," she told him, after a moment.

"No. Let you get settled in. Make sure you think you've made the right decision, get comfortable at the University of Rome before there are any major changes." Kanmi looked over his shoulder to make sure they were alone—even sending out a gravitic pulse, to ensure no one was nearby—and leaned in to kiss her.

And so, before they returned to Rome, her parents took them to a local shrine. She was painted white from head to toe . . . a sign of virginity that she emphatically hoped the gods would forgive her for wearing, though her mother whispered in her ear, *"Perhaps you should consider this the gods' way of making you a virgin again. A fresh start?"* as she settled the veil atop Minori's hair that would conceal her 'horns of jealousy.'

The kimono she wore was one of her mother's oldest, and was of very high quality, with a train and sleeves so long a shrine maiden had to help her with them. Kanmi had been bundled into a male kimono and black *hakama* pants, and wore with them, an expression of extreme patience.

The Shinto ceremony was not particularly long, and mostly involved the ritual drinking of nine cups of sake, and making an offering of branches before a sacred tree. 'That's it?" Kanmi asked, quietly, as they passed back out of the shrine. Only her father, mother, and the two boys had been present, besides the priest and shrine maidens.

"That's it. We're simple."

"Thank the gods."

The next month, they saw Latirian, when Trennus and Lassair brought the baby up from Judea to Rome for yet another hearing. Minori held the baby cautiously, and a little awkwardly. She'd never actually held one before, in thirty-one years of life, and she wasn't convinced, entirely, that it came naturally to every woman. Lassair laughed at her for that. But then again, motherhood sat exquisitely on Lassair. She was summer and spring at once, mother and maiden, and Minori was, again, simply awed by the fact that this creature had *chosen* human form. Lassair could be *anything*. And she'd chosen this.

Minori was also aware that she was being questioned a good deal more by various Praetorian agents than the others were, but she wasn't entirely sure why. A number of the questions seemed more hypothetical than directed at her experiences in Tawantinsuyu. On the whole, she was grateful for that. She was doing her best not relive the memories, and constantly having to answer questions about the experience wasn't letting her *forget*. That being said? Many of the memories didn't actually bother

her. And some, she didn't *want* to forget. She didn't want to forget the exquisite sorrow of Mamaquilla, the sacrifice of Inti. She didn't want to forget Kanmi's rage. She . . . could live without remembering the fear and the pain. She'd prefer not to dwell on the memory of killing her foes, but that recollection didn't disturb her at all. But she would prefer not to remember the torture, and if she could efface it from her mind, she would.

The *only* fly in the ointment of married life with Kanmi was that yes, his job really did require quite a bit of travel. Sigrun Caetia usually called their lifestyle peripatetic, with a faint smile. That was an understatement. Three out of four weeks a month, the lictors were usually out of Rome. Minori treasured her time with her new husband, and adjusted, slowly, to the fact that she now had two young step-sons. Who, while generally well-behaved, now that she was underfoot all the time, did start to challenge her authority a bit.

In May of 1961, while Kanmi was off in Qin, escorting Livorus on a diplomatic mission, Minori found herself back in Lutetia, at the University's ley-magic and technomancy conference, presenting her first paper on the Tawantinsuyu Incident, as it was being called. She'd been aware that there would be some media scrutiny, and she'd had to have her paper vetted by the various lictors before she was allowed to submit it, to ensure that no classified materials were leaked in it. This was her first conference here, without Professor Camulorix on hand to support her, and she blinked a little, before preparing to enter the conference room. She missed her old mentor, and being back at the conference brought back the memory of his murder powerfully.

She was so wrapped in that memory that she walked into the conference room, looked up, and blinked. Last year, there had been a fairly good attendance. This year? The room was *packed*, and there were people there with cameras. Minori swallowed. *Oh, gods. Kanmi, I think I would prefer that you and Trennus were here to savage my math, than the reporters. You, I know how to answer. Plain facts and numbers make sense to you.*

She went through her presentation, showing how there had been two sets of equipment established in Tawantinsuyu. One standard ley-grid, and, at five or six sites, experimental equipment rigged to take energy from an alternate source—she left that source deliberately vague—and drive that energy through the ley-lines themselves. The differences in the experimental ley-towers' machinery she stressed, went against all occupational and power safety standards. In the end, she concluded, "This was not a failure of ley-power. This was human error. They deviated from known safety standards, used an entire geographical region as an experiment, and paid the price."

"Dr. Eshmunazar!" One of those present—not one of her colleagues, but a reporter, raised a hand. She'd shed her assumed name with no little relief when she'd married Kanmi, and didn't actually care if it made it harder for people to find all of her academic papers in journals. The assumed name hadn't really been hers. It had just been a way of hiding.

Minori ignored the reporter, and gestured to one of the various scientists in the room. "Bjarga Bartos, University of Lipsk," the man introduced himself; it was a city in the eastern part of Germania, in Sachsen, on the border of one of the many smaller Slavic countries that stood between Germania and Raccia. "Dr. Eshmunazar, you have been one of the foremost voices suggesting that ley-power may not be as safe as everyone has previously assumed. Last year, you correlated earthquakes and volcanism with the spread of ley-power grids through previously uncovered regions of Caesaria Aquilonis and Australis. You're here today to tell us precisely the *opposite*?" Skepticism rang in his voice.

Minori couldn't really blame him. "I believe we had a goddess inform the entire world that the earthquakes and volcanic activity in Tawantinsuyu were the result of combat between the gods." Minori grimaced, internally. Mamaquilla hadn't precisely lied. She'd . . . omitted. And Minori, Kanmi, and the rest of the lictors were deeply grateful for the omissions about *them*, so they were doing their best to return the favor by not mentioning the precise means by which the Sapa Inca had tried to become a new Akhenaten.

"I am aware of what the news broadcasts have said," the professor replied, with a dubious glance over his shoulder at the various reporters, whom Minori was ignoring, steadfastly. "Unfortunately, the . . . testament of a goddess is unquantifiable and unverifiable. You noted that the ley-engineers in Tawantinsuyu flooded their ley-lines with alternate power. Like adding too much water to an existing, natural aquifer, I believe was your exact comparison." He leaned back on the bench seat he shared with about a dozen other conference attendees. "What was the source of this power? The *gods*, perhaps?" He essayed a laugh.

Minori took a paper cup filled with water off the podium and sipped, trying to buy herself some time while the rest of the people in the room chuckled, uneasily. "I really can't say what the additional source of power was," she finally said. Which was, technically, true. She couldn't say anything about it. "What I can say is that it was not electrical, and no one has, as yet, found any evidence of nuclear plants, such as those used in Judea, and the power was definitely not ley in origin. That leaves magical methods of energy production to be investigated. The system was obviously radically unstable."

"I simply find it remarkable that you've pulled a nearly one hundred-and-eighty-degree turn since a year ago, Dr. Eshmunazar. You say that it is magical energy that caused the devastation in Tawantinsuyu. You say it was transmitted along the ley-grid. The simplest explanation is that it was, in fact, ley-energy, and that you are engaged in some sort of a cover-up."

Ripples of laughter and murmurs, and Minori was aware of various cameras flashing at her. "Let me see if I have this straight," she said, mildly. "A year ago, I worked *for* a ley-energy company, and expressed concerns about ley-power that could have cost me my job, if Eleutherian Industries hadn't taken the possibility very seriously, and, being an ethical corporation, given me free rein to investigate. A year later, and six months after leaving the company for a faculty position at the

University of Rome, which is unaffiliated with the ley-industry in any way, I present a paper suggesting that ley-power isn't dangerous. And *you* are the person looking for the simplest answer here?" Minori listened to a another rustle of laughter go through the crowd.

The conversation went on in circles from there. Minori was in the uncomfortable position of having information that she couldn't reveal, and having a marked gap in her data that she couldn't defend. She retreated, merely, to the broad-minded position of allowing other people to do the research into what, precisely, the other energy that had flooded the system had been. It was merely her intent, she maintained, to show where information was lacking, and to allow others to do the research. And whenever the various academics and even reporters in the room tried to push her to comment on what she knew, personally, about the energy source used, she maintained that she had not had an opportunity to examine the wreckage of the various *experimental* ley-facilities, or to see them in their working state, but that other people had, and she trusted them when they said that there were nonstandard configurations and components. "Yes, but you are a trained sorcerer and technomancer. Surely, you can provide eyewitness testimony. You surely had a gauge or a meter with you?"

No, actually, my captors rather inconveniently didn't bring my equipment with me. And I was, at the time, rather too busy being tortured, healed, and then fighting for my life to take measurements. Minori shrugged slightly. "If those here assembled would not take the word of a goddess as testimony, since it is unquantifiable and unverifiable," she said, dryly, "why should anyone trust my eyewitness account, based solely on what my senses told me at the time, and based solely on human memory, that most fallible of instruments?"

She got out of the conference feeling oddly mendacious, and not having enjoyed the pure play of ideas nearly as much as she once had. She had too many things she couldn't say. And she wasn't the same person as she had been a year ago. As Kanmi liked to put it, like a soldier in ancient times, she'd been out into the darkness, beyond the lights on the city walls. She knew what was out there, beyond the illusions that civilization wrought for itself in comfort and safety. And she'd come back changed. Marked.

<u>1963 AC</u>

Sophia Caetia continued in her daily round of activities at Delphi, as she had every day since her arrival there in 1947. Every morning, she dreamed about the end of the world.

. . . beautiful cities in flames, the glory of Rome collapsing under the earthquakes and a drift of ash from Vesuvius, the beautiful bridges crisscrossing the lake of Tenochtitlan collapsing as the lake drained into the cracks in the earth, the Pyramids of Nahautl and Egypt, the temples of Hellas falling in on themselves as the earth tears itself asunder. The armies of the desperate, the frightened, and the mad gathering and rolling across Qin. The blood-red light over the eastern sky

of Burgundoi as the supervolcano located at Goldeseasteð, also named Mitsi'adazi, the place of the gold-rock river, begins to erupt. It's close to a thousand miles away, but the ashes rain down like the ghost of snow, catching in Sigrun's hair as she drags herself out of the ruins of the Odinhall. She's a ghastly figure, scarcely recognizable —

— so much blood, it's turned her hair to stiff hanks, and there are gobbets of flesh here and there that the raven, one eye milk, and one eye topaz, picks out of the tangles to eat, as it lands on her shoulder —

— leaning on a spear that isn't her own, face blank, eyes staring, but not seeing her surroundings as the buildings all burn around her and the ashes of a dying world fall on her head and shoulders, wounds healing as they always heal, rune-wrought light barely visible under the caked-on gore, <u>but the wounds of the flesh aren't the worst ones, now are they, sister?</u> —

— mad eyes, clawing fingers, distorted bodies. A man flayed of all skin, but still alive, leaping out of a fallen building, screaming and throwing himself at Sigrun, and the spear whirls in her hands, and he falls, mercifully dead, at her feet. The valkyrie, all light gone from her skin, limps on, out of the broken city, as another creature, and another, came howling for her blood. <u>Blood binds, Sigrun, blood binds in more than one way! Sometimes the blood is just a metaphor. Sometimes a cigar is just a cigar, oh, gods, that's an odd expression . . . what's a cigar, anyway? Huh.</u> —

The dream always ended the same way. *Sigrun finally found the energy to fly instead of walk. Found her way to the black road, which, to Sophia's eyes, looked like the Styx, frozen over, and began to walk along its length. Between steps, the ash stopped falling on her head, and Sigrun turned. Looked back. Met her sister's eyes. <u>Good-bye, Sigrun, last of the valkyrie.</u>*

And she disappeared.

There was always a moment at the end of the dream that Sophia struggled to see *beyond*. Once in a while, she could catch hazy images. It wasn't entirely unlike watching a bad transmission on a far-viewer. A lot of static in the intended image, and . . . ghostly faces, bleeding through, from a different channel. She'd thought that very amusing as a child, watching a children's show, and seeing, behind the puppets on the screen, ephemeral beings, locked in a tight embrace, kissing and undressing behind them. Now, it was merely frustrating.

And every morning, she knew precisely when she was going to wake up, before she woke up. Opening her eyes the second time was always jarring, and the headache always started at that exact moment.

Routine was the only thing that let her get through her days. She got up. She brushed her teeth, always the same way. She ate the same breakfast—yogurt with honey—because that was all she could see herself doing, and if she deviated, even an iota, it meant that something *had changed* and nothing *could* change. She tried, because Sigrun would want her to try, to hold off from using the medication in the mornings. Tried to face reality, the way her strong, sure, beautiful older sister would do. She sat on her divan and listened to the plaints of her morning appointments. All people who wanted to know what their futures held.

Will Tomas marry me?

Is my family going to accept the fact that I'm homosexual?

Is it safe to have children with my husband? We both have a family history of cystic fibrosis . . . .

Should I invest in sorghum or in wheat?

My family says I should train as an accountant, because that's a career that'll support me and my kids, but I really think I'm an <u>artist</u>. Tell me they're wrong, tell me I'm going to be the next Praxiteles . . . .

. . . tell me I'm going to be an actress . . . .

. . . tell me everything's going to be all right . . . tell me I'm going to be rich and famous and never going to have to work . . . tell me I'm going to win the lottery . . . tell me . . . tell me . . . tell me . . . tell me the answer to the riddle of the sphinx, tell me that I'm going to be king of all Asia, tell me how to solve the Gordian Knot . . . and then he cut it with his sword, imagine that . . . .

No one ever came to Delphi expecting bad answers. At most, they looked for confirmation of their fears.

By nine antemeridian every day, Sophia's hand crept into her sash, where she kept, always, one or two pills of the blood of the poppy. A little mescaline. Something that kept her from telling each of them the *truth*. That it didn't matter that Tomas would never marry Cestina, or if Donatus' family accepted the fact that his adolescent romance with his boxing partner had matured into a stable relationship, or that Franzeza and her husband absolutely would not have any children with cystic fibrosis. It didn't matter that the would-be artist had all the talent of a can of peas, and that the best acting the would-be thespian would ever do would be on the director's couch before landing her first role.

She saw it all. Their lives unrolling before her, and every last one of them ended in death. Donatus got off easy; he'd have a heart attack, and die in his lover's strong arms at the age of fifty. Cestina would marry someone else besides the hoped-for Tomas, and she and her entire family would drown in mud when Vesuvius erupted. Franzeza, her husband, and their four children would be crushed to death when their apartment complex collapsed. The actress would be trampled when people fled the theater, as fire broke out in the rafters, her body broken and bleeding under their feet. The would-be sculptor would die in a pauper's house, having eaten his way through every one of his relatives' charity. He'd have syphilis, and a drinking problem, and not one shred of actual talent, but he'd die convinced that someone would, eventually, discover his genius.

By lunch—always the same, phyllo dough triangles wrapped around spinach and cheese, a salad on days on which she could see herself eating one—Sophia had usually already dry-swallowed one or two of her pills. Three, if she could see she would need a little more comforting haze.

After lunch, another round of prophecies, until three postmeridian, when she could stop for the day. Go practice wrestling with the other priestesses, or swim, whatever she knew she would be doing. Take another pill. Meet with a lover. Whoever she saw herself being with that day. She had a hard time remembering the names, to be honest. Male or female, it didn't matter. Anyone who could make her forget, just for a little while, the inevitable.

Of course, she knew it wouldn't work. But she had to go through the motions, anyway. Even though she knew that the pleasure would be transitory at best. Even though she knew she *would* see the face rising from between her legs to smile up at her as a rotting skull . . .

. . . and then she *did see* it as a rotting skull . . . .

. . . and had to turn her face away from whoever it was in her bed in a whirl of confusion, because now she didn't know if she was seeing it ahead or seeing it now or just remembering yesterday. But if it happened to be *now*, then she needed to make sure that they couldn't see it in her face. Not that it mattered. Not that any of it mattered.

Visions that didn't have to do with her clients whirled through her head, sometimes unsummoned, and sometimes summoned by her thinking about someone in particular. Sigrun always inspired the visions. Her beloved older sister had been the only one to believe her when the visions had started. And when Sigrun was *around*, the visions were so much less intense. As if she were a stable rock to which Sophia could cling. Part of it was the fact that Sigrun's was one of the only faces that didn't look like a rotting skull to Sophia. No matter how Sophia squinted at her, Sigrun's eyes never fell in on themselves and decayed. The skin stayed whole. The lips didn't pull back in a rictus grin from the teeth. The others, Sigrun's friends . . . did and didn't. The Archmage would die, but even though his face was a skull, his eyes remained clear and lively and cynical, though not a scrap of flesh was on his face. The Summoner was god-touched, as young and immortal as Sigrun herself. Lassair was Lassair. Truthsayer would age at first, but then she'd age in reverse, and certainly wouldn't die. And the Godslayer . . . he always looked wrong to Sophia. And yet, somehow right, as well. But she knew he'd live. After he gave up his life. Sigrun wouldn't like it, but then, Sigrun didn't want to believe any of it anymore. She was afraid. Sigrun, the last of the valkyrie—or at least, she would be—was afraid.

So Sophia actually rather *liked* thinking about the lictors. Thinking about them brought visions of their lives, and she knew more about them each, probably, than any of them would ever have cared for someone outside of their own minds to know. It was just so hard to know what had happened already, and what hadn't yet, some days.

One moment, she'd be walking to dinner—always the same meal, lamb stew, except for very special occasions, on which she had seen herself having fish—and the next, she'd be in her sister's body, smiling up a little at the Godslayer as he leaned down to kiss her. Walking through her sister's house, in her sister's body, looking down at the lithe, athletic body, and wanting to run her hands down it, just to show Sigrun how beautiful she actually was, but knowing better. This was just a vision. No mirrors in the house, besides a small one that the Godslayer used to shave his face in the mornings, so Sophia couldn't even get little peeks at her sister through Sigrun's own eyes. Not that Sigrun ever looked in mirrors. She wouldn't even look at herself in the window of a shop. *Mother used to cane her when she caught her looking at herself in the mirror. And now, she sees the runes, and all she sees are scars. Pretty scars, but still scars . . . .*

And then flipping through bodies. Visions. Present and future were the same thing. *Minori, the Touchstone, the Truthsayer, telling the Archmage that if they had a little girl, she wanted to name her for Hojo Masako, the wife of the first shogun, Minamoto no Yoritomo. "Why's that?"*

"She's always been a heroine of mine. They actually married for love, you know. She rode with him on his campaigns, and when she was there, he never suffered a defeat."

"This is the same guy whose relationship with one of the young imperial guards started the whole 'the older samurai should have a physical and romantic relationship with his apprentice samurai' thing? In which they swore oaths not to take any other male lovers, and so on?"

Minori raised her eyebrows. "He loved both of them. The same way my father loves both his wife and my mother. It hardly signifies."

"I just think that this lady put up with a lot of shit she probably shouldn't have had to put up with. You really want to pin that on our kid?"

"And what does your name mean again?"

"Gods only know. 'He eats babies,' maybe. I take your point. Masako is really <u>pretty</u> in comparison." A pause. "And if it's a boy?"

It <u>won't be</u>, Sophia thought, and came out of the vision in time to walk back to her room and write a very nice letter of congratulations, sending it off with the evening post. It wasn't until the next morning, when a night's sleep had left her mind and god-born body all too devoid of chemical supplements, that she'd realized that she wasn't sure what day it was currently. She looked at her calendar, and sighed. She'd known a week ago that she was going to send the letter eight months too early, but sometimes, she had the blissful luck of forgetting little details like this. And she knew that when they received the note in a couple of days, the fact that she'd told them that *Masako* was a perfectly beautiful name, and that they shouldn't worry about boy names for forty years would simply annoy them both.

Another swirl of visions, as she swam through the pool in the temple's *frigidarium* in high summer. Cool swirl of the water around her bare limbs, sunlight pouring in through the high windows above her head.

This time, she was in the Godslayer's body, as he and Sigrun held the Summoner and Lassair's new-born twins. A boy and a girl this time, both with coppery hair and this time, their father's flame-blue eyes. Their first-born was now a pudgy toddler of two, and called Sigrun Aunt and Adam Uncle. Sigrun was already testing Latirian's abilities, and helping Lassair come up with a plan for raising a child who was spirit-touched. <u>No, Sigrun, they're god-born. They're all god-born. You and the others just don't want to admit to it yet. Then again, the neighbors in Judea are having enough trouble dealing with a summoner and his spirit-wife living next door, without them having to deal with the fact that the spirit-wife is actually a fertility goddess who takes out her own trash.</u>

Adam's mild concern that he and Sigrun had been trying for a child of their own for three years now, without her ever quickening. A little ache in his heart when he put one of the infants over his shoulder, and wondered when he'd find out what it felt like to hold his <u>own</u> child. Flicker forward, and it was late at night, and rain was pattering lightly against the windows of their bedroom as

Sigrun dozed off beside him. Adam got up and went to his desk. Pulled out a small ledger he was keeping. He'd been taking notes on this topic religiously since Tawantinsuyu, but he knew it had started earlier. He just hadn't made the correlation at first.

Sophia looked at the columns in the ledger in fascination. Really? You're scientific enough to take notes on the fact that every single time you have sex with your wife, it seems to rain, at least a little? Except when you happen to be outside. Of course, it also storms when she gets angry. And Sigrun hasn't noticed yet, herself. Or she has, and just won't admit it. I should tell her . . . no, I don't see myself telling her. She said she wanted a mortal life. And I know I'll respect that until I can't respect it any more.

Shift of scene, as Sophia walked through a grassy meadow, hand-in-hand with a lover whose name didn't matter, and whose fingers kept turning into bones and snapping off, only to turn back into flesh again. She took another pill when her lover wasn't looking, and damned the constitution of the god-born that ensured that one was never enough, and none of them lasted longer than a half-hour anyway. Sophia lay back in the soft grass, and let her lover do what she wanted with her body. Responded when appropriate, and tried not to let her disgust show when she went down on a mouthful of rotting flesh. Tried, very hard, to focus on *now*, and for a shining moment, as her lover came beneath her fingers and tongue, the drugs and pure concentration let her be in *now* and not in *then* and the smells were good, and not putrid, and the skin was pink and soft, not desiccated and rotting.

And then, lying in the meadow, she was away again, this time in the Summoner's body, as he and Lassair made love. Saw all the different configurations that a creature that shapeshifted as freely as breathing was capable of. *You're going to be fairly unshockable in a few years, Trennus, but in a way, you'll never lose that otherworldly innocence. You're not Actaeon, ripped to shreds for 'looking on' the moon goddess, ah, what a silly myth that is. A rare euphemism among our Hellene gods, when Actaeon probably actually tried to seduce the virginal moon goddess. All it is, is a cleaned-up version of Osiris being killed and Isis resurrecting him, or Tammuz being torn apart to bring fertility once more. Only because they didn't mate before Actaeon was torn apart, Artemis doesn't bring fertility. Just sleep with her silver arrows. You, on the other hand, Trennus, are the mate of a fertility goddess, but your sacrifice was gentler. You could have become Endymion, fated to 'sleep forever' but spewing your seed from your dreams into the moon's willing womb so that she could birth children and people the world. But your Lassair is not the moon, not Isis, not Selene, not Artemis, savage and unkind. She is fire.* Sophia felt free, in her visions, to think as she willed, though she knew Apollo, source of her visions, was probably not going to take the words about his sister very kindly. Then again, the vision was Apollo's, and thus, those thoughts might actually be his, and not hers, and thus, she wasn't responsible, was she? *Of course, soon enough, Saraid will remind you that you were bound to her long before Lassair came into your life. And you'll realize how much more she is to you . . . .*

At the moment, they were quibbling, the sacrificed godling and his goddess, about . . . oh, how Sophia wanted to laugh . . . how the children should be educated. Trennus wanted to send them to school, but that would require them to travel less. Britannian schools could handle the spirit-touched, but then again, he'd been educated by pedagogues, himself, at home, as the son of a king. Judean schools, which were stronger in math and natural philosophy, would have difficulty accommodating the children . . . . "They could be picked on," Trennus said, clearly worried. *"Then again, they need to see more people than just you, me, and our friends."*

They'll be fine, *Sophia wanted to tell them.* <u>They're going to have at least seventeen other brothers and sisters before the end comes, anyway, so don't worry too much about teasing.</u>

Somehow, unaccountably, she'd wound up deviating from her routine. Sophia realized it dimly, as she walked along a rocky path and stared around herself, numbly. This was where it was going to happen. She crouched down in the dust and vomited, tasting the bitterness of the pills she'd taken an hour ago. This was where she was going to meet the centaurs. Oh, it wasn't going to be for a very long time, but she also knew she couldn't escape. She couldn't avoid this fate. She couldn't escape the fact that it was going to drive her mad. No. Madder. She already knew she was well past the edge, but she also knew it was only going to get *worse.* Sophia looked around at the cliff-wall. *Sigrun will come for me. She'll be too late. Oh, gods, she's going to tear them to pieces. There will be nothing but death, and then she's going to pick me up, and I won't let her heal me. The healing of the god-born will be enough for me, and these are wounds I won't permit her to take. Not ever. She'll pick me up, and fly off with me, still covered in their blood, and take me to Judea, and I won't be able to* <u>stop</u> *speaking prophecy anymore. It's going to happen. It was always going to happen. Has it already happened?*

Suddenly, frantic, Sophia pulled up her dress, and checked between her thighs. No. No blood. No ravaged flesh. No pain. She was safe . . . for now.

It was hard to know what day it was. There was a hint of a chill in the air as she swam in the frigidarium. Another of her lovers had broken up with her, and she'd just smiled, almost in relief, and told him, kindly, that it was all right. She'd always known they weren't going to be forever. And it was a relief, not to see his rotting skull anymore. She knew she was capable of love. She *knew* it. But she never saw herself falling in love with anyone at all. Which meant that it would never happen. There was no one in any world who would be strong enough not to let her destroy herself.

. . . going to the Odinhall for yet another 'interview' with Reginleif. Sigrun thinking that she's being kept on a very short leash, and that it might take three or four decades before they'll let her off the rope again. <u>Don't worry, sister, in about thirty-six years, there won't be any leashes at all anymore. Or any gods. Or people, for that matter.</u>

Reginleif giving Sigrun a faint smile, near the end of the 'education' session. "You know, you and I are more alike than you know."

"Why is that?" *Politeness in Sigrun's tone, and nothing more. Sigrun thought of Reginleif as one of the best teachers she'd had in the Odinhall. Tough, but always fair. A little condescending, but that was to be expected when someone two hundred years old was teaching a bunch of hormonal eighteen-year-olds.*

"Because you have a mortal husband. So do I." Reginleif lifted the locket she wore at her throat, and opened it, showing two pictures. *One was an old-fashioned daguerreotype, a young man in his twenties. Blond hair, at least it seemed so in the sepia-toned image. A Frisian, possibly. The picture next to it was of an old, old man. "My Joris was born in 1892. I think the same year as your father, Sigrun. He just turned seventy-one. Oh, how I used to love to kiss those lips. Do you know, he has dentures now? Walks with a cane?"* Reginleif's voice turned bitter. *"Time is a thief, Sigrun, as you'll discover with your mortal lover. It's a dishonorable foe who robs people first of dignity, and then of life."*

Sigrun, staring at the pictures. Swallowing hard. Sophia urging, silently, Don't be swayed, sister, don't be swayed. *But of course, Sigrun was. How could she not be?* "It's not something that I look forward to seeing," *she admitted, softly.* "I try to treasure every single moment with my husband. His time is finite. Then again, so could mine be. We can still die, Reginleif. All it takes is one wrong step in combat, and we're gone, too."

"Yes . . . but so long as we are skilled, and lucky, it's not inevitable for us." Reginleif sounded bitter. *"And all for an accident of birth, we cannot stand beside them in time. They cannot stand beside us."*

Not an accident, *Sophia thought, just as Sigrun said,* "Accidents happen. It is what we do about them that matters."

A glint in Reginleif's eye. "Oh yes. Yes, indeed. You see, Sigrun? We aren't so very different after all. What do you think we should do about our . . . circumstances?"

Sigrun blinked. "Personally, I . . . do not plan to outlive Adam." *She swallowed.* "It will depend on the situation, but I will probably put our affairs in order and follow him to whatever afterlife there might be for such as we are." *Unspoken, Sigrun's internal doubts:* if there even is an afterlife. *So strange to hear such things from a* god-born, *but Sigrun had many questions, after the incidents in Nahuatl and Tawantinsuyu. Questions she wasn't about to ask Reginleif, or even admit to having.*

"And if there were a way to extend their lives?"

"Would that not be unjust to the rest of the mortals?" Sigrun plainly thought this was another test.

"Ah, yes. The fine sense of justice inherent to the daughters and sons of Tyr . . . ."

The vision ended there, and, suddenly awake, Sophia started. "Oh . . . oh no," she said, out loud, realizing she was in her room, sitting up in the dark, and feeling a loose arm fall from her shoulders as her bed-partner . . . whatever his name was . . . mumbled a complaint. "It can't be that time already. Oh, gods." She stumbled out of bed, and made her way to her desk. Turned on the light, and stared at the calendar. No. I'm in time. I'm just in time, as I always was going to be.

She picked up the phone, and dialed from memory. She hadn't spoken to Sigrun in two and a half years, and she'd *ached* to do so. But she'd known she wouldn't speak to her sister again, until it was time.

In Judea, Sigrun cursed, and picked up the phone as she woke up. "Waes hael," she snapped out in Cimbric, not bothering with Hebrew or Latin. Anyone who wanted to talk to her at three antemeridian could simply *deal* with the fact that she wasn't going to speak anything but her native tongue until she was properly awake. It didn't help that she and Adam had spent the entire day baby-sitting for Lassair and Trennus. Adam was a natural with children. He'd had two younger siblings, and it obviously made a difference. Sigrun was not.

"*Waes hael, Sigrun.*" For a wonder, Sophia's tone was completely sober.

"*What's wrong?*" Sigrun asked, immediately, her mind clearing in an instant.

"*You need to get on a plane for Cimbri-on-the-Caestus. Now.*"

"*Why?*"

"*Our father is dying.*"

For a stunned instant, Sigrun couldn't think at all. "*But I just spoke with him last week,*" she said, helplessly.

"*I know. He had a cough then. It was viral pneumonia, and he was getting treatment for it. Unfortunately, he picked up a strain of bacterial pneumonia to go with it.*" Sophia's tone was . . . crisp. As if she were reading from a medical report. "*The doctors have him on a lot of antibiotics, but it's not going to work, Sigrun. He's going to go into systemic shock in about twenty-four hours. You need to be there.*"

Sigrun swallowed. "*Thank you,*" she whispered into the phone, and hung up, moving out of bed and hauling on clothes numbly, even as Adam sat up and asked her what was wrong. "It's my father," she told him, simply, and turning on a light, looked around the room aimlessly. She'd packed her bags a thousand times, at least, to go on this mission or that. Suddenly, she had no idea what to put in a suitcase. "Sophia says he's going to die tomorrow. I . . . need to be there."

Adam sat up as if he'd been jabbed with a needle. "She's sure?" He paused. "All right, that's a stupid question. Of course she's sure. Let me call Tren and Lassair and get them to pick up their children. We need to catch a plane."

He helped her pack, took over all the duties of calling the Praetorians, arranging for a leave of absence, and getting the plane tickets sorted out. Sigrun was infinitely grateful. Her mind didn't seem to want to work. Her relationship with her father had been distant for the past thirty-five years, since he'd married Medea. And before that, he'd always been at work. But when he *had* been around, she'd idolized him. He was a *gardia* member, a representative of the law. He had dozens of stories about chasing bank robbers from when he was young, and once he'd been promoted to full detective, he'd sometimes told her stories over dinner about tracking down murderers. Cimbri was a large city, and its trade revolved around the slaughterhouses that processed the bison and cows and pigs of the plains to the south, and redistributed them across the continent. It tended to be, as her father liked to say, a tough beat.

He'd taken her on hunting trips when she was young, though. He'd taught her how to take down a deer with a musket or a bow. He'd taught her how to gut and dress the carcass, and when they'd come home, he'd taught her how to remove the skin, and they'd taken the hides to a local tanner and had them prepared and turned into a little cloak for her. She'd been . . . eight. Perhaps nine. He'd taken her to Germania and Gotaland, when she was fourteen or so. A skiing trip. Medea had been along for it, but had refused to go out in the snow, preferring to sit by the fire in the hotel and drink tea. All the little things came back to Sigrun now, and she sat in the plane, a lump at the back of her throat. Hoping against hope that her sister was *wrong*.

Sophia wasn't.

Twenty-four hours later, Sigrun was in a hospital in Cimbri. A pleasant enough room, with a view of Lake Caestus, shimmering under the setting sun in the distance. She listened to her father's labored breathing as he struggled for air. She held his hand, trying to give him whatever healing she could, but she knew better. A valkyrie always knew. And death was in the room with them. Adam sat beside her, a gentle hand on the back of her neck, and Medea sat on the other side of the room, holding Ivarr's other hand. Sigrun could see in the woman's face that she genuinely grieved. It made Sigrun thaw, at least a little, towards Medea. She'd never really registered that Medea's feelings for Ivarr were real before, and she was ashamed of that realization.

Adam murmured, in quiet Hebrew, *"Should we have brought Lassair? She can heal things that you can't, mami."*

Sigrun shook her head. Her mind had already flitted to Lassair, and retreated back again. *"She's the first to say that she's not good with water in the lungs. Like Kanmi in Jerusalem, years ago. This is . . . too far gone. Perhaps if Sophia had called a week ago . . . I don't know."*

She covered her face with her free hand, even as Medea lifted her head and gave them a reproving look. "It's rude to speak so that others can't understand you," the Hellene woman told them, sharply, and went back to holding Ivarr's hand. Smoothing the long hair back from the pallid face.

Ivarr regained consciousness, once. Long enough to give Sigrun a dazed, uncomprehending look, just as Sophia finally slipped into the room. *"Ragnhildr,"* he murmured, between wheezing breaths. *"Ragnhildr, I've missed you so."*

Sigrun shook her head a little. *"Not Ragnhildr. Sigrun, Fæder."* She glanced up at Sophia, who looked completely focused. Not even a little drunk or drugged. *"And Sophia, too. Your daughters."*

Ivarr smiled a little, but it was an evident effort. *"Sigrun. You look . . . so much . . . like your . . . mother."* No recognition in his eyes as they flicked to Sophia. Only a glimmer, when he glanced at Medea. *"Be brave, little valkyrie. Be strong."*

He closed his eyes again, and, about two hours later, the monitors attached to his chest began to ping in alarm, informing everyone that his laboring heart had surrendered to the inevitable. They didn't need to do so. Sigrun already knew.

Medea remained stone-faced, a single tear trickling down her face.

Sigrun swallowed, hard, and fought down the tears. She would *not* weep in front of her step-mother. She laid her father's hand down on the bed, and stood. "Thank you," she told Sophia. "Thank you for telling me before it happened." She reached out her arms, hesitantly, and Sophia stood, immediately, and returned the embrace, wrapping her arms around Sigrun. It was the first time the sisters had embraced in at least eight years.

"It's been hard to be close to him for a long time," Sophia admitted. "Every time I looked at him, all I could see was this moment."

"Then why," Medea demanded, her voice harsh, "didn't you call and say he was going to be sick? Why didn't you intervene and save your *father's life?'*

Sigrun had never seen that black rage directed at Sophia before. She'd seen it, often enough, directed at her, but never at Medea's own daughter. Sophia just looked at her mother, blankly. "Because I didn't see myself calling. It was his time. He was always going to die this way. Just like you were always going to die of a stroke. It'll be in about twenty years. You'll be in a wheelchair for a while, paralyzed on the left side, and then the second stroke will finish the job in the nursing home." Sophia tipped her head to the side. "And I know that telling you that won't make you feel any better, or change the future at all. Why should I have told *Fæder* the details? It would only have preyed on his mind." Sophia shrugged. "As this will prey on yours."

Medea slapped Sophia across the face, ten feet from the cooling body of her husband. Sigrun moved so fast, even she was surprised, and had Medea up against the wall of the private room, while a couple of white-robed doctors looked in from the hall in dismay. "She is precisely what you made of her," Sigrun said, softly, each word cold. "Never in her life have you struck her, save that you threatened to beat her when the visions began. I told you then, as I tell you now. You will not raise your hand to her when she speaks of what she sees, for she does not lie."

Belatedly realizing that she had her stepmother pinned against the wall, Sigrun released her hold, and controlled her temper. "Medea . . . I know that your grief makes you irrational. And I am sorry for your loss. Sincerely." The words almost choked her to say, but she *had* to acknowledge it. She had to acknowledge that this woman *had* had feelings for her father. That Medea had shared his life for decades. She *had* to respect that.

Medea raised her eyes and stared at Sigrun. "I have no need for your false sympathies. Eternally young. Immortal. And always wearing the face of his dead wife, a constant reminder of what he lost. Take your hypocrisy and get out of my sight, you little whore."

Adam moved forward, suddenly, his body language suddenly angry, as if mass were elective, and he suddenly bulked twice what he normally did. Sigrun put a hand to his arm, even as she turned her face aside sharply, as if slapped. She'd tried. She'd reached out, and whether it was motivated by grief or decades of resentment, she couldn't tell, but Medea had squelched a peace offering given across the body of the man they'd both loved. "As you wish," Sigrun replied, blankly, and gave her father's body one last look. The anger was, at least, keeping the grief at bay, for the moment, though she knew she was going to find her way to their apartment in Rome or their house and Judea and simply *scream*. Let her own four walls be the silent witness to her loss of control. "Sophia . . . I will wait for you outside."

"Oh, no need. I'll come with you." Sophia wiggled her fingers at her furious, grief-stricken mother, and said, calmly, "I'll see you at the funeral, Mother."

Hers or our father's? Sigrun wondered, staring at Sophia blankly. Sophia caught the expression, and said, a little wistfully, "Our father's, silly. I won't be able to go to Mother's. I won't be . . . well."

Sigrun caught Adam's head-shake as they stepped out into the hall, and whole-heartedly agreed with it. Compared to her family, his was *paradise*. Rivkah had a solid job as an oncology nurse, and had married a young Carthaginian engineer, much to her brother Mikayel's displeasure. She spent her weekends with her husband's family in Tyre. Chani, the rebel of the family, had shown a strong aptitude for art, and had actually opted to get her teaching certificate, so that she could do what she loved — painting — while actually earning a paycheck doing it. She'd also just gotten married. There were little irksome moments, mostly revolving around Mikayel's staunch conservatism, but nothing yet like the scene Adam had just been a witness to in the hospital room. "You all right, Sig?" he asked, in the hall, brushing her hair back from her eyes.

Sigrun considered that for a moment, and felt her lower lip quiver. Compressed it. "No," she admitted, as Sophia slipped out behind them, closing the door. Sophia surprised her by wrapping her arms around her again, and leaning into her for a moment. "Sophia? I am so very sorry for everything in there. And I regret, deeply, that you'll have to continue to deal with her. For me . . . other than you . . . I am done with the family." Sigrun swallowed, and put her cheek against her sister's hair. "You are . . . all right?"

"Oh, I'm fine." Sophia said, calmly. "I knew what she was going to say and do before I walked in the room. You know, I actually enjoyed finally getting to say the words to her? I knew she was going to slap any words of sympathy right out of your mouth, sister. I know she's going to ignore our father's request to be cremated, and will put him in some hole in the ground, instead. I know she's going to sell the house, instead of giving it over to you, the way it says in his will, and I know you're not going to contest her on that, because you feel *guilty*. Guilty because she believed that *Fæder* loved you more than he loved her, " Sophia shrugged. "She's going to move back to Hellas, and all my aunts and uncles — the ones you've never met — are going to tell her she should have convinced him to move out of that dreadful northern climate years ago. She's going to wonder where all her brothers and sisters were, when their father sold her into slavery to pay for his business debts. She's going to think that they're all after her money — oh, and some of them will be, relatives are like that, you know — but she'll shut all of them out of her life. And she's going to die alone. The hospital will be overrun with monsters." Sophia shrugged.

"Note that I didn't tell her that. I didn't tell her that it's going to be hard for her to push the chair and flee, with half of her body paralyzed, or that the stroke will be a mercy compared to what they would have done to her." She smiled at Sigrun. "Oh, it's so much better when you're around, Sigrun. It's so much easier to see the *now* when you're here."

Sigrun had let Sophia pull back, so that only her fingers were still on her sister's shoulders. She had absolutely no idea what to say to any of that. Just stared, wordless, at her younger sister. Sophia reached up and patted one of her hands, lightly. "Thank you for believing me," she added. "Of course, I knew you would." She tipped her head back, and Sigrun could see the tears suddenly collecting in her green eyes. "Of course, if you believed me about this, doesn't that mean you believe me about everything?" Her voice was like a child's.

Sigrun flinched. Adam moved up behind her, resting a hand on her shoulder. Communicating without words, that he was *here*. "Sophia," Sigrun said, her voice breaking, ". . . Yes. I believe you when you say that you see what you see. But I don't believe that it's immutable. I don't believe that there's nothing we can do about it."

Sophia sighed. "I knew you'd say that."

Sigrun closed her eyes. "Can we," she asked, carefully, "have one day . . . *one day* . . . in which to mourn for our father? One day in which there is no prophecy? No futures?"

She felt a hand touch her face. "Of course," Sophia said, consolingly. "I did all my mourning years ago, the first time I watched him die. It's different for you. Oh, but I did want to tell you something, before anything else."

Sigrun opened her eyes, and her stomach clenched. "Yes?"

"It's all right," Sophia told her, gently. "I forgive you in advance." At Sigrun's bewildered glance, she said, "The centaurs. You're not going to be in time. And I won't leave, because it's the only thing I see for myself." A single tear coursed down Sophia's cheek. Not for their father, but for . . . both of them? "You won't get there in time, Sigrun. But it's all right. Because you were never going to win."

Once everything fell out precisely how Sophia had said that it would — *damn her* — and Medea moved to Hellas, after selling a house that Sigrun didn't actually feel was her home anymore, and therefore didn't want to contest for ownership of . . . Sigrun was the one who called Sophia, late in 1964. "Sophia? I'm going back to Cimbri. I . . . would like it very much . . . if you came with me."

"I don't see myself going there, Sigrun."

From anyone else, that would be a casual brush-off. From her? Anything but. "I'm going to have our father exhumed. Burned on a proper funeral pyre and sent to the gods the way he wanted to be sent." Sigrun sat at her kitchen table in Judea, staring out the window. Lassair had been going from neighbor to neighbor in the past few years. Helping with little gardening tasks. Trennus and Lassair's house actually had grapevines running up the sides, heavy with fruit in the fall, and beautiful cypress trees. Sigrun's yard, thanks to Lassair, had the only lilacs she'd ever seen blooming in this miserably hot climate, and in the kitchen garden, helped by the little house-spirits, there was a white cherry tree that Sigrun privately went out, late at night and without a ladder, to pluck fruit from the highest branches so that the birds didn't get it all. "Come with me."

There was a pause on the other end of the line. Sophia was actually breathing hard, in short little pants. "I . . . ."

"Come with me. Please." Sigrun swallowed. She hadn't even been able to cry at her father's funeral, not with Medea right there.

". . . he didn't want this . . ." The words were a sad echo of the words Sophia had whispered at the funeral, a year ago, in Cimbri, watching as the casket was settled into a mausoleum wall. *This isn't right. But it's how I saw it.* "I . . . I don't see me *not* doing it . . . . And in the end, it . . . probably doesn't matter if he's in a wall or in ashes, will it?" Tremulous uncertainty. Asking permission of creation.

Sigrun stirred at the table. She hadn't actually thought Sophia would come with her. She'd been resigned to going alone. Adam was stuck in Raccia with Livorus, and Sigrun was taking a week to do this, between assignments. "That sounds . . . good," she said, hesitantly.

And so the two sisters flew to Cimbri. And as they stood by the ritual pyre, watching the flames dance and the smoke rise to the pale gray sky, Sigrun finally was able to weep for her father, and it started to rain, the water from the sky concealing the tears on her face.

Sophia's hands were clenching and unclenching. "I'm glad I came, Sigrun," she said, finally. "But I . . . I can't do this again. I could do this, because it didn't matter. But . . . this . . . was of my own free will."

Sigrun's throat tightened anew, and she put her arms around her sister. *One more try,* she thought. *One more chance to try to save you, little sister.* "Does it matter what you eat for breakfast?" Sigrun asked, as gently as she could. "Does it matter who you sleep with?"

". . . no."

"But you still do what you see yourself doing, anyway."

A pause, and a sigh. "Yes. Always." A little smile as Sophia looked up at her. "You're a servant, and I'm a slave, Sigrun. That's the difference between us. But it's all right. In another life? I'll be free."

Appendix I: Geography

Asia
Korea
Seorabeol — Seoul
Nippon
*Edo — Tokyo
*Hokkaido Island
Qin
Beijing — Capital of Qin
Llasa — Capital of the Tibetan Protectorate of Qin

Europa
Geographical features
*Áhkká — Mountain in far northern Sweden; site of an entrance to Valhalla
Haemodae — Shetland
*Mount Parnassus — Mountain in Hellas. Location of the Corycian Cave.
Orcades — Orkney islands
*Pielinen — Lake in Fennmark
Sequana river — Seine
*Taunus mountains, Greater Feldberg and Smaller Feldberg — Located in Hessen, Germany
Tamesis river — Thames
Britannia
Subprovinces
Cantium, petty kingdom — Kent
Caledonia, petty kingdom — Scotland
Cymru, petty kingdom — Wales
Eboracum, petty kingdom — York
Kernow, petty kingdom — Cornwall
Umbria, petty kingdom — Northumbria
Cities
Dhu Rinn — Durness
Dubrās — Dover
Inbhir Nis — Inverness
Londonium — London
Tarvodubron* ("Bullwater") — Current capital of Caledonia. (Thurso)
Continental Gaul

Named Subprovinces:
>   Aquitania (Southern France)
>   Belgae (Belgium)
>   Tarraconnensis, Lusitania, and Baetica (Iberian Gaul)
>   Isle of the Blessed — Madeira

Cities:
>   Carthaginensis — Cartagena, Spain
>   Lucentum — Alicante, Spain— Seville, Spain
>   *Lutetia Parisiorum — Paris
>   *Toxandria — Campine, Belgium
>   Valentia — Valencia

Germania
>   Agrippinensium — Cologne/Köln
>   *Frankonovurd am Main —Frankfurt

Raccia
>   Kiev — Kiev
>   Novgorod — Novgorod
>   Moskva — Moscow
>   Varangkov — St. Petersburg

Rome/Italia
>   Lilybaeum — Marsala, Sicily
>   *Rome

Other locations in Europa
>   Athens — City in Hellas
>   Argos — City in Hellas, noted for claiming to have the tomb of Prometheus
>   Cimbri — Denmark
>   Delphi — City in Hellas, home of the Oracle
>   *Gotaland — Southern Sweden
>   Jönköping, capital city (Jönköping, Sweden)
>   Mjölby, city on northern border. (Mjölby, Sweden)
>   Ostrogotia (eastern province of Gotaland)
>   Fennmark — Finland
>   Lieksa— City in Fennmark (Lieksa, Finland)
>   Turku — Capital of Fennmark (Turku, Finland)
>   Polania — Poland

Caesaria Aquilonis (North America)
Geographical features
>   Aeturnus Flumenis — Mississippi river
>   Apalachen mountains — Appalachian mountains
>   Bláthach Peninsula — Florida
>   Lake Caestus — Lake Michigan

Lake Erielhonan — Lake Erie
Lake Monache — Mammoth Lakes
Mannahata — Manhattan Island
*Mitsi'adazi (or Goldeseasteð) — Yellowstone, river and region
Muhheakantuck — Hudson River
Nivalis mountains — Sierra Nevada mountains
Ohio Flumenis — Ohio river
Saxetae mountains — Rockies
Tó Ba'áadi river — Rio Grande
Yohhe'met — Yosemite

Novo Germania
Cities and landmarks

*Burgundoi — San Francisco
    Odinhall
    Ceasterhild Brycgian (Citygate Bridge – Golden Gate Bridge)
    Pellicane Island — Alcatraz island
Cimbri-on-the-Caestus — Chicago (Sigrun's birthplace)
Duwamish — Seattle
Frisii – Montreal
Marcomanni – Cincinnati
*Nova Trier — New York
    Statue of Odin and his ravens in Muhheakantuck Harbor
Saxony — Detroit

Novo Gaul
Cities and landmarks

Alba Aesculus — Albuquerque
*Arlesus — New Orleans
Caddo Bluff — Dallas
Clovis — St. Louis
*Crann Péitseog — Atlanta
Croatoan — Roanoke, Virginia
*Divodurum – Houston
*Féir Crompán — Carrizo Springs
*Nimes — Los Angeles
*Ponca — Omaha
Romaine — Richmond, Virginia
*Tongeran – Phoenix
Tidewater — Norfolk, Virginia

Non-affiliated countries of Caesaria Aquilonis
*Chahiksichahik territory
Chinooks
Comanche Alliance
Diné Lands

Iroquois Confederation
Lakota Nation
Hopi Nation
     Oraibi — Major Hopi city
Ute Federation

Nahautl
Cities and regions
    *Fuscus Lapillus — Piedras Negras
    *Tenochtitlan — Mexico City
    *Teotihuacan — Ruins of the same name
    *Tikal, Tikali region — Guatemala

Caribbean region
    Borikén — Puerto Rico
    Coabana — Cuba
    Karankawa — Galveston island (part of Novo Gaul)
    Kùutsmil — Cozumel (part of Nahautl)
    Taino islands — Caribbean islands

<u>Caesaria Australis (South America)</u>
Geographical features
    *Ibirapitanga rainforest— Amazon rainforest
Tawantinsuyu
Cities and landmarks
    *Coropuna — Volcano
    *Cuzco — Cusco
    *Machu Picchu
    *Nazca Lines

<u>Middle East</u>
Cities
    *Borsippa — Location of major Magi academy. (Southwest Iraq)
    Byzantium — Capital of Lydian province (Istanbul, Turkey)
    *Chalus — City in Media, on the Caspian. (Chalus, Iran)
    Damascus — Capital of West Assyria, province of Rome
    Ecbatana — City in Media, southwest of Chalus. (Near Lalejin, Iran)
    Gazaca — City in West Assyria (No current real-world location. Approximately Zanjan, Iran.)
    *Jerusalem — Capital of Judea
    Meggido — Judean city (a place called Armageddon)
Persepolis — Capital of Persia (Real world: ruins south of Estakhr, Iran)
Shiqmona — Port city of Judea (Haifa, Israel)

*Tyre — Carthaginian city, province of Rome (Tyre, Lebanon)

North Africa
Cities and landmarks
>*Alexandria — Capital of Egypt
>Carthage (city) — Carthage, Tunisia
>*Chott el Jerid — Saltwater lake/salt flats, Tunisia
>Hippo Regius — City west of the city of Carthage. (Annaba, Algeria)
>Mauritania — Westernmost subprovince of African Carthage
>Oea — City east of the city of Carthage (Tripoli, Libya)
>Rusicade — City east of Hippo Regius (Skikda, Algeria)
>Tacape — City between Oea and Carthage (Gabes, Tunisia)

Oceans
>The Sea of Atlas — Atlantic
>Pacfica — Pacific
>Erythraean Sea — Arabian Sea
>Imakpik — Bering Strait

Miscellaneous
>Aotearoa — New Zealand
>Rapa Nui Island — Easter Island

Mythological
>Ynys Afallon — Isle of Apples, Avalon

* Indicates a region or city in which narrative events take place. This list is not comprehensive, and is intended to help readers orient themselves, nothing more.

Appendix II: Calendar Terms and Alternate History

Caesarian I, called by history "Caesarian the God-Born," undertook a major reform of the Roman calendar system, which was decidedly out of joint. In antiquity, the year began at the spring equinox, in Martius, and the number of days in the year did not reflect properly Earth's full solar year. This led to seasons and months no longer matching up, over time.

Hence, Caesarion the God-Born and his advisors — and other scientists, over the centuries — made the following changes: All months but three were regularized to thirty days. The calendar year's beginning moved to Ianuarius, instead of Martius.

One month was renamed for Julius Caesar, becoming Iulius. Two days were added to it, for a total of thirty-two. One month was renamed for Caesarion, and two days added to it, as well. One day was added to the end of December, and, once the notion of Earth orbiting the sun came into vogue, every four years, a second day was added to this last month of the year, to account for leap years.

Edda-Earth does not concern itself with multiple calendar formats, though the Nahutl (Aztecs), Maya (Quecha), Judeans, and other civilizations have their own calendars. All dates are presented in Roman format for simplicity.

Months

Ianuarius 30
Februarius 30
Martius 30
Aprilis 30
Maius 30
Iunius 30
Iulius 32
Caesarius 32
September 30
October 30
November 30
December 31, +1 at leap year.

Days of the Week

Multiple languages and gods result in a wide variety of terms for days of the week. Gothic and Roman terms are used throughout the text of the trilogy to provide a feeling of cultural syncretism.

English	Latin	Gothic	Gods/Symbolism
Monday	dies Lunae	Monandæg	Moon
Tuesday	dies Martis	Tiwesdæg	Tyr/Mars (War)
Wednesday	dies Mercurii	Wodensdæg	Odin/Mercury (Wisdom)
Thursday	dies Jovis	Thunresdæg	Jupiter/Thor (Thunder)
Friday	dies Veneris	Frigedæg	Freya/Venus (love/beauty)
Saturday	dies Saturni	Sæternesdæg	Saturn/Cronus (death/wisdom)
Sunday	dies Solis	Sunnandæg	Sun

Ascensio Caesare vs. Anno Domini/Common Era

The Edda calendar takes as its start the year of Julius Caesar's ascent to the throne of Rome. This occurred in 44 Before Common Era (BCE). Thus, all Edda dates are offset by forty-four years from AD/CE dates. For general reference purposes, see the table below:

Real Earth	Edda
100 BCE	55 BAC
45 BCE	1 BAC
44 BCE (year of Caesar's assassination)	1 AC (year of Caesar's ascent)
43 BCE	2 AC
42 BCE	3 AC
41 BCE	4 AC
40 BCE	5 AC
30 BCE	15 AC
20 BCE	25 AC
10 BCE	35 AC
1 AD/CE	45 AC
5 AD/CE	49 AC
1000 AD/CE	1044 AC
1906 AD/CE	1950 AC
1910 AD/CE	1954 AC (story start)
1955 AD/CE	1999 AC (end of trilogy)

Alternate timeline events

In the Edda-Earth reality, the library of Alexandria did not burn at the hands of Caesar's troops. Rome never fell. There were no 'dark ages.' No medieval period. Science continued to progress at a steady pace, and was supplemented by magic. As such, scientists discovered some technologies before Real-Earth did. . . and in some areas, due to the prevalence of magic, technology actually lags that of Real-Earth.

Ancient times

ca. 2226 to 2171 BAC: Reign of Sargon of Akkad. Within 100 years after his death, the godslayers and *namtar*-demons were at work in the world, tearing down the temples and killing gods.

1583-1556 BAC: Range of dates for the Thera eruption and the destruction of the Minoan civilization.

1292 BAC or 1290 BAC: Death of Akhenaten. Imperfect suppression of the cult of Aten

ca. 1146 BAC: Destruction of Homer's Troy.

ca. 1035-963 BAC: Life of Saul; ban of magic in Judea. End of golems.

The Rise of Rome

102 BAC: Fall of Carthage. Carthage conquered by Rome; the city is burned, but the inhabitants are permitted to retain their language and religious beliefs.

4 BAC: Julius Caesar did not accidentally burn the Great Library of Alexandria down when he set fire to his own ships.

1 AC: The Failed Assassination of Julius Caesar. Brutus informs Caesar of the pending attack, and assembles legionnaires to protect Caesar's life. Brutus took one of the assassin's knives through his own back as he and others protect Caesar from the conspirators.

All of the conspirators are tried, found guilty, and executed.

Caesar sets aside his 'adopted' son of Octavius in favor of his natural son by Cleopatra, Caesarion.

15 AC: Ptolemy XV Caesarion Julius Philopator Philometor, Caesarion the God-Born, ascends the throne.

Octavian's Rebellion. Brief. Assassination attempts against Caesarion.

26 AC: Caesarion meets with the Zealots of Judea, and offers them improved self-rule in exchange for loyalty, with the Legions waiting on hand to burn Jerusalem if needed. (Second Temple is never burned. No Diaspora.) Judea becomes a loyal province of the Empire.

<u>55 AC</u>: Caesarion's death. He is followed by his son, Philometrus Julius
   Caesar Albius. Brief period of unrest and rebellion.
<u>114 AC</u>: Colosseum construction begins.
<u>264–324 AC</u>: First hot air balloons developed in Qin for military signaling.
<u>350 AC</u>: **The Edict of Diocletian.**
   Diocletian decrees that all subject/client states have autonomy in
   matters of religion. Proselytizing banned.

Exploration of the World
<u>500 AC</u>: Fleet led by Hrolfr Njordr crosses the Sea of Atlas and lands in
   Newfoundland.
<u>515 AC</u>: Second fleet lands near what is now Novo Trier.
<u>550 AC-675</u> AC: Early Decadent Period.
<u>600 AC</u>: Explorers have canvassed the eastern coast of Caesaria Aquilonis
   as far south as the Bláthach peninsula.
<u>675-750 AC</u>: Reform period.
<u>700-880 AC</u>: <u>Building of Domitanus' Wall</u> in Judea.
<u>880 AC</u>: Kievan Rus attempts to invade Asia Minor. Domitanus' Wall
construction halted, series of armed forts built along northern border,
instead.
<u>1000 AC</u>: Leif Dalgaard circumnavigates the globe.
<u>1100 AC</u>: Sea-trade with Qin and Nippon and India now possible, as well
   as the overland Silk Road.
<u>1150 AC</u>: Gunpowder introduced to the West and dismissed, largely, as a
   novelty item; cannons tended to explode.
<u>1190 AC</u>: Gold discovered near what becomes Burgundoi, making this
   city-state in Nova Germania fabulously wealthy. This gold funds
   the fleets that now began to sweep around the globe.
<u>1190 AC</u>: Cuzco settled by Inca.
<u>1223 AC</u>: Mongols begin invasion of Kievan Rus.
<u>1250 AC</u>: Mongols invade Qin. Romans aware of this as a disruption in
trade.
<u>1264 AC</u>: Mongols attempt to invade Byzantium... and are vigorously
   repelled by the much more technologically advanced and
   organized Romans.
<u>1275 AC</u>: Mongols diverted east into Persian subject kingdoms, and get as
   far south as Judea, where <u>cannons are used for the first time
   effectively</u> from Domitanus' Wall.
<u>1304-08 AC</u>: Plague years.Many merchant ships were lost at sea in this
   four-year span, and a number of port cities suffered from the
   plague, but the result was limited, because so much of trade was
   conducted by sea. . . and many of the ships were simply lost with
   all hands as a result of the virulent plague.

   Total effect on Europa's population: -2 million people, not the -75
   million or -100 million of Real-Earth's Black Plague.
<u>1325 AC</u>: Tenochtitlan built.

<u>1334 AC</u>: Lavish additions made to the Palace of the Imperator in Rome.

<u>1350 AC</u>: Rich silver lodes found in the white-capped Nivalis mountains, east of Burgundoi. Accessing this required massive innovations in mining technology. Gunpowder explosives used.

<u>1360 AC</u>: Founding of the empire of Tawantinsuyu.

<u>1427 AC</u>: Rome meets the new-formed Nahautl Empire, and demands an end to human sacrifices if they're going to be neighbors. Residents of Novo Gaul do not appreciate being captured and dragged off as sacrifices

The Industrial Revolution

<u>1450 AC</u>: Industrial Revolution begins.

<u>1475 AC</u>: First contact between Novo Gaul, Novo Germania, Rome, and Tawantinsuyu.

<u>1500 AC</u>: Discovery of electricity.

<u>1501 AC</u>: Small Roman colony founded at the southern tip of Africa, Cyrenus.

<u>1505 AC</u>: Wan Quan publishes study on the efficacy of inoculating against smallpox by taking the dried scabs, powdering them, and blowing them up a patient's nose with a blowpipe. This variolation method became transmitted by medical texts to the west over the next one hundred years.

<u>1528 AC</u>: Steam engine invented.

<u>1528 AC</u>: Rebellion in Nahautl against Rome.

<u>1531 AC</u>: Hellene physicians discovered the anesthetic properties of diethyl ether.

<u>1548 AC</u>: Locomotives invented and tracks begin to be laid.

<u>1550 AC</u>: Thomas Mauritis determines that ley-power can power an engine just as well as steam or electricity.

<u>1565 AC</u>: Nomadic Bantu tribesmen trade a few shiny rocks to the Romans at the port in Cyrenus. It takes over a year for the shiny rocks to migrate their way to Rome, where they're discovered to be very large diamonds.

<u>1568 AC</u>: Mauritis develops the incandescent bulb as a novelty.

<u>1575 AC</u>: Eadward Gann, in Britannia, used cowpox as a method of inoculating against smallpox. This, combined with the innovations of Wan Quan, begins to change medicine forever.

<u>1576 AC</u>: Diamond mining expedition sets up camp outside of Cyrenus.

<u>1585 AC</u>: Germs and microbes observed with microscopes for the first time. Germ theory developed, Judea.

<u>1590 AC</u>: Telegraph invented by Samuel Maurus, the son of a Roman man and a Judean woman, in Judea. Competing inventors included Agapetus Metaxus, who developed the code system used for telegraphy to this day.

<u>1580-1590</u>: AC Plague years in Tawantinsuyu; inadvertent introduction of smallpox decimates population.

<u>1597 AC</u>: Tawantinsuyu agrees to formal treaty with Rome, becoming a subject state.

<u>1600-1750 AC</u>: Latter Decadent Period
<u>1601 AC</u>: Incandescent bulbs replace oil lamps in parts of Europe.
<u>1607 AC</u>: First *tethered* hot air balloon flight in Rome, performed at the Imperator's palace.
<u>1615 AC</u>: First coal-fired power plants come online in Judea to produce electricity.
<u>1645 AC</u>: First *untethered* hot air balloon flight, again demonstrated in Rome, this time by the Gaulish Locinna brothers. Largely a novelty at first, except in Judea, where balloons were later used to conduct surveillance over the Wall.
<u>1660 AC</u>: Temple of Jupiter rebuilt in Rome after a great fire swept through the city. The emperor of that period, Julian III, had rebuilt the temple, larger and grander than before.
<u>1675 AC</u>: Laudanum distilled, precursor to morphine.
<u>1697 AC</u>: Morphine developed for use in battlefield medicine.
<u>1701 AC</u>: Chloroform and ether used for the first time to allow for first non-agonizing amputations and surgeries during the Invasion of Asia Minor.
<u>1750 AC</u>: Laws giving slaves rights passed in Rome.
<u>1756 AC</u>: Penicillin developed and used in field hospitals during the War of the Caspian Sea (1753-1763; Rome vs. Raccia, Raccia vs. Mongols, Mongols vs. Rome, Mongols vs. Persia, Persia vs. Rome. It was ugly.) Dr. Alexander Argyris the first to really study the mold that had been a folk remedy for generations.
<u>1769 AC</u>: Reginleif Lanvik born.
<u>1771 AC</u>: First successful Caesarian in medical history, in which both mother and baby lived. Conducted in Jerusalem.
<u>1825 AC</u>: First manned plane flight performed just outside Novo Trier, by a pair of brothers by the names of Ursus and Wystan Abered.
<u>1830-1845 AC</u>: Mongols invade Qin.
<u>1850 AC</u>: Radio invented, in Hellas.
<u>1855-1860 AC</u>: Caspian Crisis; Mongolia attempts to annex most of the Caspian Sea, resulting in a four-way battle between Rome, Raccia, Mongolia, and Persia; this was the first major war involving Rome since the War of the Caspian Sea a hundred years before.

Death of Solveig Caetia.
<u>1875 AC</u>: Helicopter invented, Judea. Widest adoption in Raccia and Novo Germania, however.
<u>1890 AC</u>: Brandr Ilfetu born.
<u>1895 AC</u>: Ornithopter invented, Persia.
<u>1900 AC</u>: Far-viewers developed, in Nippon.

Recent History

<u>1905 AC</u>: Antonius Valerius Livorus born, Rome.
<u>1910 AC</u>: Sigrun Caetia born, Cimbri-on-the-Caestus, Nova Germania, Caesaria Aquilonis.
<u>1915 AC</u>: Jet turbine engine developed.
<u>1923 AC</u>: Livorus enters the Legion.
<u>1924 AC</u>: Kanmi born.
<u>1926 AC</u>: Sigrun enters the Odinhall.
<u>1927 AC</u>: Slavery abolished in Nova Germania and Novo Gaul.
<u>1927-1930 AC</u>: Raccia-Mongol Conflict.
<u>1928 AC</u>: Trennus Matrugena born.
<u>1929 AC</u>: First rocket launched into space from Judea, sparking space-race between Hellas, Judea, and Nippon, with Britannia an interested observer.
<u>1929 AC</u>: Adam ben Maor born. Sophia Caetia born.
<u>1930 AC</u>: Sigrun leaves the Odinhall.
<u>1930 AC</u>: Minori Sasaki (Ijiun) born.
<u>1930-54 AC</u>: The Shadow War. Proxy war; Persia and Rome fight through provinces and subject kingdoms like Chaldea, Media, and Judea. Re-ignites every 3-4 years.
<u>1930-1932 AC</u>: Sigrun on Roman-Persian Border, in Asia Minor.
<u>1932-1934 AC</u>: Sigrun on Roman-Mongol border, within spitting range of Raccia.
<u>1933-43 AC</u>: Livorus serves as *aedile* in Rome. Roof over Colosseum built.
<u>1934 AC</u>: Transatlantic cable laid, allowing for overseas telephone calls.
<u>1936-38 AC</u>: Sigrun begins protection work for diplomatic envoys to the independent Nordic countries.
<u>1939 AC</u>: Splitting of the atom in Judea.
<u>1939 AC</u>: Sophia Caetia's first visions.
<u>1939-1948</u>. Sigrun works as an *ælagol* in the New World.
<u>1943 AC</u>: Livorus' unsuccessful run for *quaestor*. Appointed diplomatic envoy to India, instead.
<u>1944 AC</u>: Trennus' mentor killed by a rogue summoner. He goes to University of Londonium thereafter.
<u>1945 AC</u>: First satellites settle into orbit.
<u>1946 AC</u>: Kanmi graduates the University of Athens and gets married. Immediately leaves for Mongol border.
<u>1947 AC</u>: Adam goes to the Persian border.
<u>1948 AC</u>: Caesarion IX crowned. (God-born).
<u>1948 AC</u>: Livorus appointed ambassador to Qin.
<u>1949 AC</u>: The Mongol-Qin Provocations.
<u>1949 AC</u>: Sigrun recruited by Praetorians; appointed to Livorus' detail after the Mongol-Qin incidents.
<u>1950 AC</u>: Kanmi returns home from Roman-Mongol border. Recruited by Praetorians.
<u>1950 AC</u>:. Trennus leaves Londonium for work with the *gardia*.
<u>1951 AC</u>: Adam recruited by the Praetorians.
<u>1953 AC</u>: Adam paired, late in the year, with Sigrun.
<u>1954 AC</u>: Story begins.

Appendix III: Glossary

Languages in Edda have not been locked in time or sealed away in a vacuum chamber. They have lived, breathed, and developed in interrelation to one another.

Gothic

I use Old Norse and Anglo-Saxon terms to give Sigrun's language flavor. Given that the various branches of Germanic have been under heavy influence from Latin for some 2,000 years, it is very likely that her spoken dialect, while it retained the characteristic "we two" pronoun of Anglo-Saxon, *witan*, and the equally characteristic lack of a future tense, would be somewhat closer to Mittelhochdeutsch or Middle English. The Great Vowel Shift never occurred. If you wish to imagine what she'd sound like, grab a copy of Chaucer's *Canterbury Tales* or the work of the *Pearl* poet, and read it out loud to yourself. . . being sure to use the vowel sounds of continental European languages.

For example:

Whan in Aprille the shoures soote,
the droughte of Merche hath perced to the roote. . .

=

W(ahh)n in Ah-pr(ih)l the sh(oo)r-es soat
the drou[ch]t of Merch hath per-ced to the roat. . .

There are almost as many dialects of Germanic and Gallic as there are subprovinces. There are more and less dominant dialects. For example, Sigrun speaks, initially, a dialect of Gallic common to the Bláthach peninsula; it serves her as a bridge to Trennus' Pictish dialect, but it is about as close as, say, modern Dutch and modern German. Other dialects are more distant kin—more equivalent to modern Swedish to Swyzerdutch. This is attributable to how early colonization took place, how isolated individual *colonia* were for hundreds of years, and how little literacy/mass media was available to keep the languages from altering substantially over time.

Latin

Latin is spoken throughout the Empire. It is the universal *lingua franca* of the Western World. It, too, has not been preserved in a time capsule. It has a variety of dialects, but almost every schoolchild is taught "standard received" Latin (think BBC English) and "classical" Latin to ensure that the language doesn't deviate too far from its roots.

Hebrew

Hebrew is a living language, rather than a resurrected one, in Edda. It has picked up thousands of loan-words from Latin, Persian, Egyptian, Carthaginian, and other languages of the Empire. Most students in Judea are taught, again, the classical form of their language, so that they may read their religious writings.

I am not a scholar of this language; therefore, I have used modern equivalents wherever possible.

Nipponese/Japanese

This island nation did not experience any periods of isolation. Their daily language has been highly influenced by Korean, Chinese, and even Raccian and Latin, as they have been a major hub for trade for hundreds of years. The language of the court in Kyoto is precise, formal, and harkens back to a bygone era—an older form of the language, entirely.

Again, I am not a scholar of this language. I have used modern equivalents wherever necessary, and I invite the reader to imagine what the language would sound like, if it had developed differently, due to different historical pressures.

The list of terms offered below is *not* exhaustive, and I have tried, whenever possible, to translate within the text.

Terms

ablutum — Latin, laundromat
Æðeles ides — Gothic, noble lady
æðelinga — Gothic, noble one, feminine ending
æðeling — Gothic, noble one, masculine ending
ælagol — Gothic, law-giver, law-keeper, adjudicator
a thaisce — Gallic, 'my treasure.'
atzmay — Hebrew, Maverick
auhz — Hebrew, Goose
bitahevn — Hebrew, defense. Term used in place of Krav Maga.
cwealuwyrm — Gothic, deathworm
dominus, domina — Latin, lord, lady
ex nihilo nihil fit — Latin, "from nothing, nothing comes."
forðferan, forðferest — Gothic, literally, "to go forth." To perish.
fikken, fikkest thu — Gothic, to fuck; "fuck you" (informal second person)
géa — Gothic, yes. (equivalent to *ja* and *yeah*)
harah — Hebrew, Shit.
héodæg — Gothic, today. (Directly related to modern German *heute*)
hrímþursar — Gothic, rime-giant, frost-giant
hveðungr — An alternate name for Loki, it has also been used as "monster" in Old Norse.

inanwyrm — Gothic, gutworm, parasite
jaso — A joule
kami — Nipponese, spirit or god
leh lehizdayen — "Fuck you." (to a man)
nið, niðing —Gothic, anathema, evil, malice, cowardly, unmanly, accursed.
nitzen – A Newton of force
ollamaliztli — Nahautl ball game
Paredes' disease — Parkinson's
perfututum — Latin, literally, "fucked out."
photogram —coined word that describes a device that plays music encoded in light on crystalline storage discs.
Póg mo thóin — Gallic, "kiss my ass."
rihtære scale — Richter scale
Sangua Foederis — Latin, Blood Pact
seiðr — Gothic, magic
sennin — Nipponese, immortal person, transcendent, mage, spirit, sage, hermit
shtoyut — Hebrew, Bullshit, crap, nonsense
thaum — Unit measuring magical energy, equivalent to wex
Tholberg coil — Tesla coil
Tlatoani — Nahautl, emperor of Nahautl
uisce beatha — Gallic, whiskey
wex — A watt of power.
ya ben shel zona. — Hebrew, "You son of a bitch."

Air travel
Hatasahl Air — Judean airline, chemically-fueled jets.
Hellene Air — Hellene airline, chemically-fueled jets
Alroma — Roman state airline, ley-powered.
Qin Air — Quin state airline, ley-powered.

Motorcar brands
Judean:
> Tsunams and Mehymans. All are electrically-powered.

Nipponese:
> Kusabanas and Takas. Ley or electrical power, depending on market demand.

Hellene:
> Arma, Aloga, and Epibintores. All luxury-brand vehicles, entirely ley-powered.

Weapons
Aphek 5 assault rifle
Velserk (Colt) .45 caliber pistol, which holds 6 rounds when fully loaded.
Vheva (Cobra) 9mm.

Legion organization and ranks

All levy forces, regardless of their province of origin, use Legion ranks.

Legion
1280 men. Commanded by *Legion Legate*, or *legatus*.

Tribuni angusticlavii – Tribune of the soldiers. A soldier who ranks above a centurion, but below the legate. (This is Sigrun's rank, when she serves in the Legion actively.) These are officers, usually career military, and their rank gives them a fair degree of latitude. Many of them handle paperwork, but others are used to cut *through* paperwork, at the discretion of their legate.

Primus pilus centurion — Commanding centurion of the first century, first cohort and the senior-most centurion of the entire legion.

Cohort
4 centuries 320 men each, roughly; 4 cohorts per legion

Pilus prior centurion commands a cohort.

Century
80 men (16 centuries per legion;)

Primi ordines command a century.

Maniple
40 men.

Rank centurion.
Commands a maniple.

Optio
A junior lieutenant, essentially. This was Adam's first rank. An optio commands 20 men, or half a manicple.

Hasta
Lowest enlisted rank.

www.ingramcontent.com/pod-product-compliance
Lightning Source LLC
Chambersburg PA
CBHW070531030726
47505CB00001B/4